LUNARIA REALMS

Omnibus One

Alex Frost

GREYMALKIN

Published by Greymalkin Press
www.greymalkinpress.com

Dev & Line Editing by Proofs by Polly
Copy-editing and Proofreading by Rachel Top Edits
Cover Design by Charlotte Slegers

Ebook ISBN - 978-1-963368-23-9
Paperback ISBN - 978-1-963368-33-8

The Lunaria Realms Series

A House of Fangs & Deceit

A Court of Bones & Sorrow

A Throne of Blood & Vengeance

Note From Author

A gentle reminder that this is a why choose romantasy, which means there are going to be multiple love interests. And our dear, sweet Samara will not be choosing between any of them.

You can still pick a favorite though. I won't tell.

Let's chat real quick about what to expect in this book. This is a fantasy novel that contains adult content and situations. If it was a movie, it would probably be rated "R" for violence, language, and sexual content. If you want to go into this book completely blind and prefer not to read content warnings, you can skip on ahead, my friend.

If there are certain topics that you need to avoid for the sake of your own mental health, or that you simply don't like, please take a look at the list below for some things you will find in this book.

- Explicit consensual sex scenes (there is no dub-con or non-con)
- Blood drinking
- References to parental death
- Cheating but **not** between love interests

Also... quick little note on language. I am a strange, strange person, and I've lived a bit of an odd life. I was born and raised in California, but was mostly raised by my Canadian grandmother and was then unofficially adopted by an Irish family in my late teens. You might be wondering why I'm mentioning this, and the reason is that I have a bit of a magpie approach when it comes to the English language.

Sometimes I like the American English spelling... sometimes I'm really attached to that extra "u" and go for the non-American version. Variety is the spice of life y'all.

Bless the soul of my copy-editor because she just sighs heavily at the start of each manuscript and deals with my eccentricities. So if you're an American and looking at a word and thinking it's not spelt right... it is most likely the non-American version of the word.

LAKE SPIRIS
ALPHA PACK DEN
ORDER OF AVALA TERRITORY
VELESIA
LAKE TUROTH
ORDER OF FERVIS TERRITORY
DRUDON
LAKE ARIDESH
FAE TEMPLE RUINS
FURIE REALM
THE BADLANDS
FURIE STRONGHOLD
TO THE DISTANT

TO NORTHERN WATERS
REALM
ORDER OF NARCHIS TERRITORY
LAKE MALOV
HOUSE CORVINUS
HOUSE TEPES
MOROI REALM
SOVEREIGN HOUSE
HOUSE HARKER
HOUSE SALVATORE
HOUSE LAURENT
LAKE MYALIS
HOUSE DEVEREUX
THE THREE REALMS OF
LUNARIA
SOUTHERN SEAS

A House of Fangs and Deceit

Lunaria Realms Book 1

To Ash, for encouraging me to get my smut on.

Prologue

WE WALKED single file to our deaths. The cool night air seeped through my thin cloak, but I didn't mind.

Being cold was the least of my concerns. Whatever happened on this night, we would not live to see the morning.

Not as humans.

What remained of the village elders walked in front of us. A few more years and I would have been considered one of them.

I was Rosalyn Harker, and my family had been part of this village for generations. Our name passed down through the maternal line. The women of our family were strong. Resilient. Natural-born leaders.

But that was a different future, one that I couldn't even imagine anymore.

A few sobs escaped those trailing behind me, but nobody turned back. There was nothing to return to. We'd fortified the village as best we could over the last few months, but nothing kept the monsters out.

When the elders had first suggested this idea, they were met with harsh denial, then silence, and finally, reluctant agreement.

In the end, we all knew it was clear the future only held death for us now.

So, we might as well do it on our terms.

When we finally reached our destination, the elders formed a small circle around three flat stones, each bearing a carefully carved symbol within its face. The shiny black surface of the stones perfectly reflected the light of the moon.

The elders gestured for me to join them and then instructed everyone else to form circles.

We'd already practiced this, so everyone fell into place quickly, and soon we had six circles expanding from the one I stood in with the elders.

I spared a look over my shoulder and met the even gaze of my daughter.

The barest hint of sorrow flickered deep within my chest. She was almost twenty years old, but she would always be my sweet little girl.

When my sleep wasn't plagued by nightmares, I had dreams of summers spent in flowery fields with her laughing as she raced along, chased by her twin sister, while they plucked purple and blue flowers to wind into crowns later.

She hasn't laughed since the monsters tore apart her sister.

I twisted back around to stare at the carved-up stone at my feet. It would be our death, but it also might be our salvation.

The Fae had vanished, leaving us defenseless against the cruel beasts that prowled these lands. They may not have been the kindest of rulers, but they had kept the worst of the horrors at bay.

Now they were gone, leaving us not only at the mercy of the monsters of old but new ones made of nothing but shadows.

The elders suspected that the Unseelie had done something, performed some spell, perhaps against the Seelie, and lost control of it.

After all, it couldn't be a coincidence that the Unseelie, who could send their shadows off to spy or shape them into vicious guardians, had disappeared without a trace, and now creatures of darkness roamed our lands at night. They'd likely killed all the Seelie in the process of whatever wicked magic they had worked.

The clouds above us parted, revealing the bright, full moon. We'd been waiting for this night for weeks, and there were times when, admittedly, I thought we wouldn't make it.

Six months ago, there had been hundreds of thousands of us living across these lands. Now there were less than ten thousand humans left. Our village had fared better than others. Almost five hundred of us remained of the twelve hundred who had once called this place home.

My mind wandered bleakly to the graveyard not too far from here. My parents were buried there, as well as my grandparents. Generations of Harkers had lived and died here.

I hadn't been able to bury my daughter or my husband. There had been nothing left of them to bury.

The lack of feeling that had become my constant companion since their deaths lifted for a moment, and in its place, I felt unimaginable pain.

I swallowed and begged the numbness to return. For the pain to abate, if only just for now.

I needed it to get through these next few moments.

We all knew what we were giving up with this spell, not only our humanity but our identities as well. Who we were would die tonight.

It had started as a plan for survival.

We couldn't live as humans anymore, not in a world ruled by monsters.

We had to become monsters as well.

The elders believed that we might remember bits of our humanity if we survived long enough. That we could claw it back from the darkness.

But I didn't want it. Fuck humanity.

No, what I wanted was far simpler. I wanted to race away from this village tonight and tear into the beasts that had torn into my daughter. Who had snatched away the man I'd loved since I was sixteen years old.

I wanted to make the monsters afraid.

"It's time," Irina said from where she stood opposite me on the other side of the stones.

I could remember her sitting in our house sipping coffee when I was a little girl. My mother would braid my hair while they discussed potential new hunting grounds. She had a slight curve to her back, and her chestnut hair was mostly grey now, but she still had a will of iron. The Laurent family had been in this village even longer than the Harkers.

The whispers and shuffling died down as the elders started chanting, keeping their words slow and carefully enunciated.

Irina turned towards her right, and the woman standing there bared her neck. Tali, our neighbor. Her dark brown eyes used to be so warm and inviting. Now they were cold and hollow. She was the only surviving member of her family.

Neither hesitated nor flinched as Irina carved a symbol into her neck from a blade made from the same type of stone at the center of our circle. Once Irina was finished, she passed the blade to Tali, who did the same to the man standing at her right.

One by one, the elders marked each other until it was my turn.

I barely felt the blade dig into my neck. When the cool stone knife was placed in my hand, I turned around to face my daughter. My hand hesitated, but Nysa wrapped her fingers around mine and guided the knife to her neck.

Our bloodline was strong. And Nysa was owed vengeance too. I would not deny her this. The sharpened stone cut into her skin. The magic guided my fingers as I etched a crescent moon into the left side of her neck.

Choosing that particular symbol hadn't been a conscious decision on my part.

The elders had convened for weeks to settle on what beasts we would turn into. It was impossible to know which ones would fare best against the monsters of our world, but if too many were chosen, we risked the spell being watered down and failing entirely. In the end, these were the three that were selected. Each bearing different strengths to better our odds of surviving.

The blood trickling down my neck started to burn, but I kept saying the words over and over, only vaguely aware of their meaning.

Across all of Lunaria, what remained of the humans had gathered to conduct the same ritual as we asked the moon to bless us.

A haze filled my mind, and I felt myself unravel. But I welcomed the feeling and begged it to take me faster, only wavering when I felt my daughter's hand slip into mine. I turned towards her and watched as her light sky-blue eyes darkened until they were almost black.

She smiled at me for the first time in ages as the magic took her, the chant never faltering from her lips. I gave her a vicious grin in return as the last of the words rang into the night sky, their meaning revealed.

"We will give our lives for the blood."
"We will yield our fates in the wild."
"We will lose our souls to the fury."

CHAPTER ONE

—

Samara

200 Years Later

"Is that what you're wearing?"

I glanced away from the mirror outside my closet to the bed, where a man with auburn hair and light brown eyes lounged. Demetri's lips twisted in a concerned frown as he gestured towards the dress I'd just put on.

"What's wrong with it?" I turned my attention back to the mirror. The deep royal-blue color complemented my golden-hued brown skin. Twisting around so I could see it from the side and back, I peered over my shoulder at him. "Everything is covered up, and it's not *that* formfitting. Not a hint of cleavage to be seen," I teased.

My husband of three years rolled his eyes. "I think you look perfect, but you know how things are around here."

Boring. That's how things were at House Laurent. *Fucking boring.*

I plastered a pleasant smile onto my face and sauntered over to the bed. Demetri's eyes lit up as he watched me approach, but he didn't bother getting up.

"I'll see what else I can find in the closet," I told him. "I'm meeting with your mother and her council today, so it's probably for the best that I don't *offend* anyone by reminding them that I have curves."

He snorted a laugh as I placed my hand on my chest dramatically. Demetri wasn't nearly as conservative as the others of House Laurent, but he also wasn't the type to push for change.

But it was easy for him to follow the unspoken fashion rules of this place, unlike myself. Unless I donned a shapeless sack, anything I wore would be obscene by their standards. Even then, I'm pretty sure my large chest, wide hips, and luscious ass would still make whatever I wore too scandalous for my husband's House.

"I'm sure you'll find something." Demetri's gaze went a little distant, his mind clearly already moved on from our conversation.

I held in a sigh as he rolled out of bed and gave me a chaste kiss on the lips.

He murmured, "A friend of mine is visiting from one of the other Houses today. I'm going to catch up with them and probably plan a trip to go to their House and a few others this month."

"You're going to leave again?" My hand froze on the dress I'd been about to shove aside. "But you just got back."

"You know how the life of an Heir is," he reminded me, already walking away. A moment later, I heard the door to our suite open and shut.

I knew *exactly* what the life of an Heir was like. I'd grown up as the Heir of House Harker and had only given up that title to marry into House Laurent... where I was supposed to be an Heir alongside Demetri.

Every time I suggested that I should travel with Demetri to other Houses, I was shot down for one reason or another.

For a long time, I'd been determined that I could make this work, that eventually Demetri and, more importantly, his mother, would realize they were wasting my potential.

But now I was starting to wonder if I'd made a serious mistake coming here.

"Are you happy?"

Those three damn words had been bouncing around in my mind since Rynn, one of my best friends, had asked the question during our weekly check-in.

I was the daughter and former Heir of House Harker, and now I was the wife of the Heir of House Laurent. Both Houses were made up of some of the strongest Moroi bloodlines, and I now represented them both.

This marriage arrangement might have been my aunt's suggestion, but I'd not only agreed with her idea, I'd been *excited* about it. The marriage between our two Houses was an important alliance for House Harker. I was happy to serve my House in such a way and had worked hard my entire life to be the perfect wife and partner.

But in the decade I'd spent studying and training for my fated role in life, I never thought to question if it would be something I'd actually enjoy.

In the three years that I'd been married to Demetri and living in House Laurent, I'd never really thought about whether I was happy or not. This was my life, and it was important for me to be successful. My happiness shouldn't matter. It was as simple as that.

Yet that moon-damned question was all I could think about. Fucking Rynn and her pointed questions. She knew I wasn't exactly happy, but had she said that, I would have denied it. By phrasing it as a question, she was forcing me to answer. It was one of her more aggravating tactics of getting me to face the truth.

Cali would never have asked such a thing. No, she just noted every time my eyes were red-rimmed from crying over my loneliness at House Laurent or from the constant slights and barely disguised insults that greeted me almost every day. I'd gotten the distinct feeling over the years that she was very much considering killing Demetri for not protecting me in his own House. I'd had to make her swear to me that she wouldn't harm a hair on his head.

It wasn't out of love for my husband, as we didn't have that kind of relationship. But as Heir of House Laurent, Demetri's death wouldn't exactly go unnoticed. Besides, I could fight my own battles and didn't need Cali sweeping in to save me.

My two best friends were the opposites of each other in so many ways, but they loved me as much as I loved them. Even when they asked questions that sent me down an emotional spiral.

I chucked the dress I'd chosen off and put the new one on, frowning as I looked at myself in the mirror. Demetri's mother would likely hate this one too, but there wasn't much I could do about it.

Hopefully, I'd be able to impress her enough with my trade proposition that she'd overlook my appearance.

Thoughts about the conversation with Rynn and Cali and my time at House Laurent clouded my mind as I absently made my way down the long hallway outside our suite. Servants scurried by with their eyes firmly on the floor.

When I had first come to this place, the opulent decor and meek servants had thrown me off. It was so different from the understated elegance of my own family home and the humble furnishings of Drudonia where I'd studied in my teenage years.

Happiness was something I could seek later.

At least, that's why I told myself these past few mornings when Demetri gave me a dutiful kiss and a charming smile before disappearing for his various House responsibilities.

It was what I repeated throughout the day as I sought out knowledge of what was happening outside these fortified walls.

"Do you need anything, my lady?"

I tore my gaze away from the painting of some distant relative of Demetri's great uncle, perhaps, and looked at the girl before me.

Despite my attempts to befriend the household staff—because as a good friend had taught me, the servants always held the best gossip—they treated me the same as all the Laurent family.

I wasn't used to failing at anything, so I kept at it, hoping I would one day win them over.

The servant girl's blonde hair was neatly tucked away in a braid, and her eyes were firmly fixed on the tips of my toes, her expression submissive, albeit slightly nervous. The latter struck me as odd, something I'd noticed around the premises on occasion.

"I'm fine, Rose. Thank you," I said kindly. Her pretty green eyes peeked at me before hastily looking away. "My mind is just a little adrift this morning. Perhaps I'll swing by the kitchen for a second cup of tea."

"I can bring you some," she said quickly. "Black tea with honey."

"That would be lovely," I lied.

While the tea sounded fantastic, I'd really been wanting to get it myself as I so often did in the morning.

The kitchen was one of the few places the staff relaxed enough to talk, and I'd been hoping to maybe overhear some gossip, but it was probably for the best. I should be preparing for the meeting later today anyway.

"Would you mind bringing it to the study on the third floor?" I asked. "I have some paperwork I'd like to review."

She nodded once and hurried away.

I frowned after her departure. Demetri and Marvina, his mother, had always treated the staff fairly. They may not be kind in their orders, but I'd never seen anything to explain why there was such an undercurrent of fear amongst them.

Shaking my head, I continued on to the study that I had taken over as an office of sorts.

I hadn't been lying about feeling off-kilter today. Rynn's simple question had hit me when I was already in a weird mental state, and I hadn't been able to snap out of it since.

After years of being shoved to the sidelines and playing the role of the smiling bride, I was finally making headway in getting involved in House politics. Demetri's mother ruled House Laurent with an iron fist and was pleased that her son held zero interest in taking over one day. She was less pleased about my interests in ruling, or at least co-ruling.

Though, for the last six months, she had allowed me to sit in on meetings with her advisors. I wasn't entirely sure why she had offered this, but I suspected it was my Aunt Carmilla's doing.

Being that she oversaw House Harker and was close friends with the Sovereigns who ruled over all the Moroi, she wasn't shy about flexing her political power when she needed to. If she had stepped in on my behalf, I was grateful... but also a little annoyed that I'd needed her help, which was probably why she hadn't told me about her interference.

I'd been working on a trade proposal for the last week with some of the

Velesian packs, mostly of the Narchis Order. It wouldn't bring us in any great riches, but it would help the tension that had been growing between the Moroi and Velesians for the last decade.

I just had to present it in the right way. It had taken some time, but I was beginning to learn how to manage Marvina. Now, if only I could figure out the same with my dear husband.

Maybe then I could get a damn orgasm once in a while.

I didn't count the one I gave myself every morning before I rose from bed after Demetri had already gotten up and left.

I laughed softly to myself, earning a few wayward glances from a servant girl as she hurried by. Cali had quickly pointed out my rather lackluster sex life after Rynn had asked about my happiness, which summed up my two besties rather accurately.

We might come from different species and backgrounds, but we each knew each other well. Far better than anyone else could claim.

"Give her a break, Rynn," Cali had said. *"Her husband might be easy on the eyes, but he's clearly as boring in bed as he is in conversation."*

"He really doesn't have a lot going on upstairs." Rynn's voice sparked with the mischief that she hid from everyone but us.

"Not a lot going on downstairs either," I'd drawled wryly, prompting a laugh out of them.

It'd been a bit mean of me, but I knew that they'd never share anything we talked about, so I tended to let my inner catty self out around them.

I needed the break from having to constantly measure out my words and watch my tone every day. Besides, they knew I was joking.

During one of our many chats via shadow magic, Demetri had walked in from the washroom completely naked, unaware that I was talking with Rynn and Cali, and gave them both an eyeful.

Truthfully, there wasn't anything wrong with Demetri. He was a perfect specimen of a Moroi male in every way.

Every way.

Unfortunately, he was rather uninspired in how he used that perfection.

There'd never been any kind of passion between us, but at least we didn't outright hate each other like some of the other married couples I knew.

Maybe once I got Marvina to take me seriously, I could spend more time with Demetri, and we could figure out how to get some spark in our relationship. Give my poor fingers a break.

I breezed into my study, pleased to see that everything was exactly as I left it. Chaotic.

I knew it made the servants nervous to leave the room in such a state, but *I* knew where everything was, and that was all that mattered. Settling into my favorite chair by the window, I picked up the thick tome from where I'd left it on the windowsill and plucked out several papers.

The musky smell from the pages made my nose twitch as I carefully unfolded the map and stretched it out on the low table in front of me.

House Laurent was located on the coast and had the most mines out of any of the Moroi Houses. At least half a dozen deposits of gold, silver, and iron wound their way under the House itself before stretching far out, and the coastline that was less than an hour's walk from where I was sitting was lined with basalt.

It was these metals and minerals that allowed us to safeguard our territories against the monsters that roamed these lands, but there was one crucial resource that House Laurent didn't have. Malachite.

The Velesian packs in Narchis territory had plenty of it, though.

I wasn't able to get the exact numbers, but I was reasonably sure that our stock of malachite was running low. Likely to run out within the next year, in fact.

In the past, House Laurent had gotten the resource from other Moroi Houses, but it made far more sense to go to the Velesians because they had so much of it, and the few Moroi Houses that had it would demand far more in trade.

The wards that were used by the Houses to keep out the wraiths were created with blood magic and various metals like gold or silver, but minerals were required to keep them powered up, and malachite was the best. Other minerals like quartz could be used, but they had to be replaced every few weeks, whereas malachite could be powered up to last for almost a year.

Footsteps sounded from the hallway, and a moment later Rose entered with a steaming cup of tea in one hand and a plate of pastries in the other.

"Thank you," I murmured as she set everything down on the table, taking care not to disturb the map or the teetering stacks of scrolls and books.

"Can I get you anything else, my lady?" She studied the map curiously but didn't ask about it. When she felt my attention on her, she quickly cast her eyes to the floor and hunched in her shoulders.

"I realize that telling someone you can trust them doesn't mean much. Trust is something that can only be earned through actions and time." I reached over and broke a piece off one of the pastries. "But if there is ever something... amiss about how you or any of the staff are treated here, please find a way to let me know, and I will help."

A slight tremble ran through her, and she opened her mouth, only to snap it shut.

"All is well," she said finally before turning to leave the room. As she arrived at the doorway, she slowed and rotated her head slightly, not completely turning towards me. "Thank you for your concern."

Disappointment weighed heavily on me, but she was gone before I could respond. I popped the pastry morsel into my mouth and chewed thoughtfully. Rose seemed like a naturally shy person, so it was hard for me to get a read on her. The servants here were much more reserved and timid than the ones at House Harker, but that didn't necessarily mean anything was wrong.

Maybe I was just looking for something that wasn't there, and they were all intense introverts who wanted to retreat to their rooms and read. Perhaps my being nosy all the time was what set Rose on edge.

A smile tugged at my lips. If only I had Kieran's charm. My childhood friend could talk to anyone and put them at ease.

I sipped my tea for another hour, the floral blend my favorite because it was good even after it had cooled. My argument for why we needed to improve our trading with the Velesians was sound and my proposals perfectly reasonable.

Confidence firmly in place, I rose ten minutes before the meeting was due to start and made my way to the second floor.

There was a large room dedicated to assemblies, but that was mostly used when representatives from other Houses or from the Velesian packs visited. I strode past that room and instead headed to Marvina's study where she ran all the meetings with her advisors. It was easily four times the size of the cozy one I preferred to work in.

Almost everyone was seated when I entered. There were six chairs with thick cushions and tall regal backs spaced out in a half-moon shape, all facing a massive desk with a single chair behind it.

I strode over to the desk with my chin held high and placed my proposal on it.

Hestia and Gaelin, who were the closest to my age and also originally from other Houses, nodded to me in greeting, but the others dismissed me. They took their cues from Marvina, and until she took me seriously, they didn't consider me worth their time.

Rather than take a seat and wait in awkward silence as everyone tried to pretend I didn't exist, I did the same thing I always did—toyed with them.

I aimlessly walked around the room, studying the various paintings on the wall as if I hadn't already looked at them a hundred times. Although, I did pause with genuine interest when I reached the large map that took up almost a quarter of the wall space. It was beautifully painted, displaying not only Moroi territory but also that of the Velesian's and Furies' as well. Every city and stronghold was carefully placed on the map, along with all existing trade routes.

As I studied the map, I felt several of the male advisors' eyes on me as they hungrily took in my flesh, and my lips curled in satisfaction.

House Laurent was different from the House I'd been born into. House Harker was well-respected both because of our age and because my aunt was close friends with the ruling Moroi queen and her consort, known collectively as the Sovereigns. But my birth House still retained a bit of our wild side, and I'd grown up amongst Moroi who dressed with most of their flesh on display.

We thought bodies were things to be worshipped and celebrated. It'd been quite a shock when I'd visited House Laurent for the first time, shortly before I'd married Demetri, and seen everyone wearing conservative clothing that played down their curves rather than enhanced them.

Marvina had arranged for an entirely new wardrobe to be made for me, and it had awaited me in my suite when I'd visited for a second time. The message of how I was expected to dress while in the walls of her House was quite clear. I'd added different pieces to my wardrobe over the years that were slightly more risqué than what most wore here, but nothing too daring.

I hated my new wardrobe, but I tried to be respectful of House Laurent's customs... most of the time.

Everyone in this House pretended to be so uptight, but it wasn't like they didn't have dirty thoughts spiraling around in their minds like the rest of us heathens.

We were Moroi for fuck's sake. We craved sex almost as much as we craved blood.

Absently, I trailed my fingers down my soft belly and then rested my hands on my hips. One corner of my mouth tugged up in a smirk as Gaelin caught the movement and gawked openly before Cazimir cleared his throat and Gaelin quickly looked away.

Cali always teased me that I had a body for sin, and it was a waste for me not to use it to my advantage. I always rolled my eyes when she said it, but I had to admit that it was fun to mess with Marvina's advisors and see how close I could get them to outright drool over me.

It was petty, sure, but things around here could be dreadfully boring, and I had to take my fun where I could get it.

Before I could think of more ways to torture some of the advisors, Marvina swept into the room and took a seat in her chair. With its wide back made of rich dark wood and grooves inlaid with obsidian and silver, I always thought it was more throne than chair.

I calmly took a seat in the remaining empty chair and folded my hands across my lap, then swept my gaze over her while the rest of the council settled further into their seats.

Demetri had taken after her, sharing the same dark auburn hair and beautiful light brown eyes. I didn't know what his father looked like, as he died over a decade ago, and his portrait was oddly absent from all the walls. When I'd asked Demetri about it, he'd just shrugged and said he had no idea. Marvina's skin was a few shades lighter than Demetri's lightly tanned hue, and the sharp features that were charming on my husband always gave off a haughtier expression on Marvina.

I gave her a polite smile when her piercing eyes fell on me before she flicked her fingers towards my proposal. Then she plucked the pages up and skimmed through them, her face unreadable. I forced myself to remain calm and fixed my features into a neutral expression.

My proposal was sound and made both financial and political sense. Rynn was technically supposed to join the Alpha Pack, who belonged to the Order of Avala, but she'd been born into the Order of Narchis, which meant she had experience with both Orders.

Like me, she had been training her entire life to serve in an elevated position, and she'd been an excellent resource to help smooth things out from the Velesian standpoint.

I was confident in my proposal and hopefully, Marvina would finally see me as the asset I was.

"Well, Samara, I have to say that it's fascinating to me that in the three years you've been residing in my House, you never once displayed such an interesting sense of humor," she said in a light, airy voice.

My breath caught in my throat as several of the advisors snickered in their seats. "I'm sorry," I said tightly with a false smile. "I'm afraid I don't understand."

"You want us"—she placed a hand ordained with rings of gold and glittering jewels on her chest—"to trade with the mongrels? What could they possibly want with gold and silver? They spend half their lives in fur."

Anger flashed through me then, vibrant and hot. For a second, I felt my bloodlust rise.

I should have known that Marvina belonged to the group of Moroi who thought they were better than the Velesians. She'd never been so obvious about it in the past, but she'd made little comments here and there. It was one of the reasons why I'd never invited Rynn here, despite her hinting that she would like to come and see me.

We were all Moon Blessed. Our human ancestors had performed a ritual to make themselves better able to survive in a world full of monsters. The Moroi, Velesians, and Furies had just as much in common as we had our differences, but some refused to see it that way.

"While they have no need of gaudy jewelry,"—my eyes flicked to the rings on her finger—"gold and silver are used to lay enchantments on weapons so that they can fight against the wraiths. We need malachite. Everyone wins in this trade." I said straight in my chair, refusing to give up under the weight of her glower.

The advisors who had been snickering at my expense earlier were now completely silent as their eyes darted back and forth between me and Marvina. Tension filled the room as everyone waited to see how Marvina would respond to my refusal to back down.

"House Laurent is one of the oldest Houses in existence," she said coldly. "I agreed to the marriage between you and Demetri because it was in the best interest of our House at the time. I have made sure you remained in these walls because I refuse to allow you to represent us to the other Houses. Not with the way you are and the way you dress. You should have been grateful that I've allowed you to sit in on these meetings but instead, you bring me this ridiculous trade proposal."

I bristled as rage and humiliation warred within me. House Laurent might be one of the oldest Houses, but House Harker *was* the oldest. My ancestors had been the first of the Moroi to claw back their humanity.

As much as I wanted to rub that into Marvina's face, it wouldn't help anything, and it would only cause a problem for my aunt and House Harker. I knew Marvina thought poorly of the Velesians, but I thought she'd been smart enough to at least see the value of this trade.

I had miscalculated badly, and I was furious at myself for such a misstep.

A persistent ache flared in my gums as my bloodlust stirred thanks to my spiraling emotions. I wrestled it back, but it still felt like my blood was burning through my veins.

"My apologies," I said tightly as I rose from my chair, barely managing to keep my emotions off my face. "I will work on a different trade proposal that is more befitting for House Laurent." *You stuck-up, arrogant bitch.*

"That's not necessary. I have my advisors to help me with such endeavors. Your only job here is to make my son happy, and you can't even manage that." She gave me a cutting look. "I suggest you spend your time trying to rectify that situation."

CHAPTER TWO

—

Samara

PAIN SHOT through my gums as my fangs started to extend further. Heat burned behind my eyes, and all I could do was jerk my head in a nod before fleeing the room.

Amused snorts and chuckles followed in my wake as I clenched my fists until my nails bit into flesh and blood dripped from my knuckles. I used the sharp pain to help ground me as my feet carried me through the halls and stairwells until I found myself in the main garden located in the center of the fortress that was House Laurent.

I sucked in a breath as I wiped the blood from my hands onto my dress. The crescent cuts across my palms stung from where my nails had dug in. At least they hadn't shifted into claws and done more damage.

After a few moments of steady breathing, my fangs receded to their normal length of being only slightly longer than the rest of my teeth.

It'd been a while since I'd drunk from Demetri, and I was overdue for some blood. He tended to treat our feeding sessions like an unavoidable duty, if not a nuisance, so I only did it when I had to, which usually led to me putting it off for longer than I should. My bloodlust had come dangerously close to rising in that room, and Marvina likely would have had me chained in the dungeon if that had happened, even though I wouldn't have actually attacked anyone.

Probably not... unless one of them tried to run. I hissed as my fangs once again lengthened at the thought of chasing down prey. Screw it. They could stay out for a bit. They would naturally recede once I calmed down.

Since I was a Harker, it was unlikely I'd completely lose control of my bloodlust and be unable to come back from it.

When that happened to a Moroi, we referred to them as Strigoi. To my knowledge, no one had ever come back after earning that title. All Moroi had to contend with bloodlust, but some were more likely than others to completely lose their grasp on humanity and devolve into beasts driven by nothing but hunger and survival.

Our bloodlust gave us an edge in a world full of monsters. Not only did we grow fangs and claws, but our instincts also went into overdrive.

Truthfully, I found it a little intoxicating, but mostly because I never feared losing myself to it. My bloodline was strong; even our ancestors who originally turned Moroi had retained some of their humanity.

Most of the Houses, including Laurent, could boast the same. The strength of our bloodlines was the foundation for the ruling Moroi Houses.

We had yet to discover why certain bloodlines were so resilient against turning into Strigoi. There were many reasons I was thankful to be born a Harker, but not having to fear losing my humanity every time I got thoroughly and completely pissed off was definitely at the top of the list.

But even without the risk of turning Strigoi, it was still not a good look to lose control of your bloodlust. It was bound to happen, and Carmilla was forgiving about it, but Marvina would no doubt view it as *unbecoming*. She was bothered enough by my appearance and bold demeanor as it was.

I wanted nothing more than to scream at the top of my lungs and kick something. Repeatedly.

But while that would feel fucking glorious, it would also no doubt get back to Marvina, and I refused to give her the satisfaction of knowing just how much she had hurt me.

A few courtiers walked through the garden, glancing at me sideways while whispering furiously amongst themselves.

Great. Marvina and her lackeys were likely already telling everyone about what happened in her study. Now I was a spectacle for all of House Laurent. It wasn't even lunchtime yet, and this was already shaping up to be a spectacularly bad day. On the plus side, it was unlikely things could get worse from being laughed out of Marvina's study.

When yet another group of whispering courtiers passed me, I gritted my teeth and headed for the structure on the other side of the garden.

The three-story building continued the House Laurent trend of being ridiculously opulent. Gold and silver accents bordered the windows and shone brightly in the late morning sunshine. Those materials would have been better served on weapons in the hands of Velesians than on a fucking building.

This was exactly why so many Velesians hated the Moroi. I'd hoped to start mending that rift with the trade agreement I'd put together, but it was clear that wouldn't be happening.

"Your only job here is to make my son happy, and you can't even manage that." Marvina's insult rang through my mind, and I had to shove the bloodlust down again.

Demetri and I might lack passion, but I desperately needed to blow off some steam and get my blood fix.

When he was home, Demetri tended to have a wide-open schedule because he was content to let his mother rule over everything. It was one of the many things he had never understood about me, my desire to want more in life.

But right now, I just wanted to bury my fangs in his neck while he buried himself inside me.

I entered the guesthouse and made a left down the long hallway that led to the main set of guest suites. Demetri had mentioned that some courtiers he was friends with were currently in residence and that he'd be visiting with them today. I was pretty sure Demetri spent most of his time in the guesthouse when he wasn't traveling to other Houses.

Despite being the Heir to House Laurent, he lived his life more like that of a courtier, spending all of his time socializing and none of it ruling.

A low, throaty moan carried down the hallway followed by a deep, masculine laugh, and my pace slowed. I knew that laugh.

A peculiar, numb feeling crept over me as I slipped forward, quiet as a ghost.

The door at the last suite was left ajar, and there were pieces of clothing strewn about as if someone had pulled them off in haste. I froze in the doorway with Demetri's back to me, all of his lovely flesh on display as he pounded into the woman stretched out on the bed. She moaned as he thrusted harder and faster. Her legs were over his shoulders, and I watched as his fingers dug into her thighs, pulling her closer.

Either she was one hell of an actress or Demetri had some skills that he'd just never bothered using on me.

I should be angry about this, I thought as I watched with an odd sort of detachment about his betrayal. I'd been loyal to him and him alone since we'd signed the marriage contract. I should be fucking pissed, and I definitely was. Nestled between the shock and the disjointed numbness was definitely rage, but not just because he was cheating on me. That was almost secondary to the other reason my blood felt like it was boiling.

No. I was pissed because she was enjoying the hell out of getting screwed by my husband, and I'd never *once* found pleasure in it.

Are you happy?

I was goddamn brilliant, my mind was sharp as hell, and I was a fucking asset to any House. I spoke two dead languages, was well-versed in the political machinations of all the Moon Blessed, knew the strengths and weakness of every single Moroi House. The elders I studied under for the years I was at Drudonia had said they'd never had a student with such a sharp mind for political negotiations.

And yet Marvina and everyone here treated me like I was fucking beneath them when I was made to rule a House.

Are. You. Happy?

When I walked into a room, every being looked my way because I was hot as fucking sin. The same people who looked down on me couldn't keep their eyes off of every flash of skin I showed and every rise and dip of my body.

Demetri should have been on his knees crawling to me, *begging* for the privilege of touching me, because I was made to be worshipped.

ARE. YOU. HAPPY?

"No," I spat out.

The woman yelped as Demetri whirled in surprise, grabbing a pillow off the floor to cover himself as he stepped towards me. I laughed. Modesty? Really?

"Fuck. This." I spun on my heel and stalked back down the hall.

"Samara!" Demetri called frantically after me. "Wait!"

I stopped halfway to the exit and spun to face him.

His steps faltered as he quickly buttoned the pants he'd pulled on and brushed his dark auburn hair away from his face.

My eyes ran over his body, taking in his well-muscled chest that was slicked with sweat and the flushed color in his lightly tanned face. He really had put in more effort into fucking whoever the hell that was than he ever had me.

My lips curled, putting my fangs fully on display. Demetri's gaze widened at the sight.

"Let's discuss this," he started, holding out his hands in a placating manner as if he were trying to calm down an unruly horse.

A humorless laugh poured out of me, and whatever he saw in my face made him flinch and take a step back, still holding his hands up, but now it felt more defensive on his part.

"There is nothing to discuss," I said coldly. "My life here is a joke. I should have realized it sooner, but the events of today have made it very clear. I'm fucking *done*."

"What does that mean?" His eyes widened, and he reached for me, but I stepped back.

I needed to get the hell away from him. From Marvina. From this House. There was only one place I could go to regroup and figure all of this out.

"I'm going home."

CHAPTER THREE

—

Samara

"You can't be serious," Demetri said for what felt like the hundredth time. That seemed to be all he was capable of saying at this point, and it was really getting on my nerves.

Exactly how the hell was I supposed to react to walking in on my husband fucking someone else? Our marriage might have been arranged for political purposes, but I'd been loyal to him all these years.

Clearly, I'd been an idiot for thinking he would be the same.

"It's in your best interest to let me leave and cool down," I said evenly as I scoured my room for what to pack.

The numbness had crept back in after my outburst, and I was embracing it wholeheartedly so that I didn't rip out Demetri's throat and enjoy the feeling of his hot blood on my face as he bled out at my feet.

Right. The bloodlust was still there.

I pulled in a deep breath and let the rage settle back a bit, then focused on the task at hand. I needed to get out of here and put some distance between me and my piece of shit husband and his domineering bitch of a mother.

If I left within the next hour, I could easily make it to House Harker before nightfall.

I looked around the room, eyeing all of my things. Most of my possessions here meant little to me and could be easily replaced.

My eyes fell on a stack of scrolls and notebooks that I'd piled haphazardly on top of a dresser. All my notes about things I'd learned about House Laurent while I was here plus several ideas for trade alliances between the Houses and Velesians.

I snatched them up and shoved them into my pack. Otherwise, there was nothing else I cared about here.

My eyes met Demetri's and while I felt hurt and betrayed, I was surprised to find cunning calculation in his eyes. I blinked and whatever I saw was gone, replaced by a chagrined expression that had me briefly doubting what I thought I saw seconds before.

"I'm so sorry, Samara." He closed the distance between us and clasped my hands in his. "It was never my intention for you to walk in on us like that, but I assumed you knew that I had other partners on the side, given the nature of our marriage. Let's talk this out. I'm sure we can come to an understanding."

I stared at him in disbelief. Was he seriously apologizing for *how* I found out about him fucking other people behind my back and not the actual fucking?

He took my silence as an opening and gave me a beautiful yet apologetic smile.

Yep. He really was.

"The only *understanding* I'm capable of coming to in the next five minutes is one that involves your cock flopping around on the floor and you bleeding out at my feet." He blanched and dropped my hands as he quickly staggered away from me. "I'm going back to House Harker where I will consider my future and decide if you will continue to be a part of it or not. I strongly advise you to get out of my sight."

Demetri's mouth gaped open, and I found satisfaction in the fear that shone clearly from his eyes. He snapped his mouth shut and fled without another word.

I snorted. Such a coward.

Once he was gone, I quickly changed out of my gown and into a soft, long-sleeved shirt and a stretchy pair of riding pants that I kept hidden in one of my bottom drawers. Marvina didn't approve of a lady of my stature wearing such attire, and I knew she told the servants to confiscate the clothes whenever they saw them. Speaking of...

I dropped to my knees at the foot of my bed and stretched my hand underneath, grasping around until I finally felt the bundle of fabric I'd tucked up between the boards that supported the mattress.

I withdrew my prize and shook it free as I rose. The matte black cloak fell to the floor, not a single wrinkle in the fabric despite being wadded up into a ball for the past three years. Only the symbol of House Harker, two crossed axes over a crescent moon, adorned the cloak. I ran my fingers over the symbol before throwing the garment over my shoulders and securing it in place.

After one last sweep of the room, I headed towards the kitchen to grab a snack on my way out.

"My lady!" Rose squeaked as I swept into the room. The other two servant girls sitting with her froze, their eyes darting to the exit. They'd have to walk past me to get to it.

"Don't worry yourself, Rose. I'm just grabbing some food for the trip." I plucked a couple of freshly baked rolls from a basket and wrapped them in a cloth napkin. Some shiny red apples caught my attention, and I added them to my pack as well.

"Your trip?" Rose asked in confusion as she watched me pack up the food.

"I'm leaving," I said hesitantly, unsure how much of my personal business I wanted to share. "Things haven't gone the way I'd hoped they would here, and I just need a break to collect my thoughts."

"Surely, you're not planning on going out on your own?" one of the other girls blurted. When I looked at her, she paled and shook her head violently. "Apologies, my lady! I didn't mean to question you! I just—I wasn't—"

She looked at Rose for help as she started to hyperventilate.

"Don't worry yourself, Catrina," I said gently. She blinked at hearing her name come from my lips.

Rose was the one who waited on me the most, but I'd been working on learning the names of all the staff members while I'd been here. Some of them I rarely interacted with though, such as the girl sitting with Rose and Catrina. She might be new, or she worked somewhere in the large fortress I didn't frequent often.

I calmly explained, "The road to House Harker runs along the coast, and there are rarely attacks there. Besides, I'll arrive well before dark."

If it'd been even a couple of hours later, I wouldn't have considered making this ride today despite how desperately I wanted to get out of this House. The world outside the thick walls of our fortresses was a dangerous one during daylight hours, but the dark belonged to the wraiths and other monsters.

I shivered at the thought of being out at night. I'd only experienced it a couple of times in my life, but the memories were forever etched into my mind.

Rose bit her bottom lip as she looked at me, clearly not liking this plan, but also knowing she couldn't stop me.

"Here, take these too." She quickly packed together some dried meat and more fruit, which she handed to me, and I tucked them away in my bag. When she passed me a couple squares of chocolate, my eyebrows crept up in surprise.

It was a delicacy and usually saved for special occasions. I couldn't even remember the last time I'd had some. Maybe my birthday two years ago?

When she noticed my expression, she gave me a sheepish shrug. "Lady Marvina requested some for a meeting last week, but they barely ate half of it, so we stashed it in here."

I smiled as I pulled one square out and placed it in my pack with the rest of the food. "The three of you should enjoy it." Rose tried to refuse, but I grabbed her hand and somewhat forcibly placed the chocolate in her palm. "You deserve it far more than me, and chocolate is one of those things that should be enjoyed whenever you have the chance."

Catrina and the other servant girl shyly smiled at me before breaking off a piece and popping it into their mouths. Then they both let out twin moans of pleasure before staring at each other and bursting into giggles. I huffed a laugh at their antics before I shifted the pack further onto my shoulder.

"I need to get going," I said. "I suspect my dear husband is crying in his mother's lap right now, and I don't want to be around for any further drama."

Rose barked out a laugh, and the other two girls covered their mouths while they tried to hold in their chuckles.

I winked at Rose. "If you ever need help, don't hesitate to reach out. I mean it, Rose."

"Do you think you'll be coming back?" I felt a little guilty at the sadness that touched her eyes, but I didn't want to lie.

"I can't say for sure, but I'd say it's unlikely."

She nodded in understanding. "Safe travels, Lady Samara."

With that, I took my leave and headed towards the stables. I hoped that Rose would reach out to me if she or any of the other staff needed help, but I wasn't holding my breath. If I ended up truly never returning here, I'd have to figure out a way to check in on them.

Thankfully, I didn't encounter anyone else on the way to the stables. I was a little surprised to find them empty but decided to count my blessings. I was perfectly capable of saddling my own horse.

"Hello, my love," I crooned at the dapple grey mare who stuck her head out at my arrival.

Most of the horses were used by the rangers to patrol the surrounding area, but one of my only requests upon arriving at House Laurent was a horse of my own.

Zosa had been a wedding gift to me from Demetri. At the time, I thought it was very sweet, and I gave him a very enthusiastic thank you that night, but now I knew that he'd likely had nothing to do with choosing Zosa. He'd just put in the request to someone else, and they'd done it.

I set my bag by her stall and quickly went about collecting her tack and readying her for the journey. She snorted and nudged me in the shoulder as I led her out of the stall.

"We'll be out of here soon, sweetheart," I murmured.

I tied my bag to the back of the saddle and did a final check to make sure everything was secure.

Zosa thought it was fun to hold her breath and puff up her belly so that the saddle came loose after someone climbed onto her, but I'd grown up riding far trickier mounts, so none of her shenanigans got by me.

The sun shone brightly above us as I led her out of the stables. It was nearing noon, which meant I now had less than seven hours to make it to House Harker. The single guard on duty at the gate leading out of House

Laurent spotted me from his perch, and his eyes widened. I chuckled under my breath as he desperately swung his head back and forth, probably looking for someone of higher rank than him to deal with this.

Usually, when I went out for rides, I had at least two rangers with me, but there was currently not a ranger in sight.

Somehow, I didn't think asking Marvina to spare a couple rangers to escort me the hell out of her House would go over well. But I was more than capable of getting myself home, at least during daylight hours.

"Open the gate, please," I said in a pleasant tone that was still clearly an order.

I'd been perfecting both the tone and facial expression over the years, and I found that it worked very well. When the guard saw no one else in the vicinity who could override me, he nodded in a jerky motion and pulled on the thick chain next to him.

The portcullis rose, and I led Zosa underneath it.

"HALT!" someone commanded from further behind us. I looked over my shoulder to see Demetri running towards me with half a dozen guards and Marvina striding out onto a balcony to overlook the scene playing out before her.

My heartbeat picked up as I rapidly thought through my options.

I could stay to hear them out and then politely decline whatever they offered before leaving. That was probably the more politically advantageous approach and would help reduce the fallout between House Harker and Laurent.

Despite that, my head whipped towards the open road that beckoned to me beyond the gate.

I didn't want to wait.

I didn't want to hear Demetri's false platitudes and Marvina's thinly veiled threats.

I wanted to get the fuck out of here.

Before the guard who'd opened the gate could stop me, I vaulted onto Zosa and spurred her forward. She didn't need any more encouragement as she leapt into a gallop, kicking up dirt in her wake.

I laughed as we raced away from House Laurent, my raven-black hair intertwining with the cloak as they both whipped behind me.

Demetri's scream for me to return echoed through the trees, but I ignored it. I was done with him and his bloody House, and that thought felt just as freeing as the wind on my face.

Excitement coursed through me as I crouched over Zosa and she only ran faster, her mane flying back to brush against my cheeks. After a few miles, I pulled her back into a ground-eating canter and glanced behind me.

No one was following us, but I suspected they would soon. If we stayed on the main road, our only option was to outrun them.

I looked to my right and left as Zosa continued her steady pace. She was in good shape thanks to our frequent rides, but I couldn't ask her to keep this up forever.

The right led to the coastline, and I knew from experience that the ground would turn sandy very quickly, which would be tiring for Zosa. To the left meant more forest-type setting, where the ground was firmer but uneven.

Choices, choices.

"A little further, girl," I whispered over Zosa's neck. "Then we'll take our chances in the forest."

Once I was confident we'd put a decent amount of distance between us and House Laurent, I slowed Zosa and directed her off the trail.

As long as we stayed close to the main road, we'd be fine. After some trial and error, I found a good path that wasn't too far from the main road but also wasn't overgrown so much that it hindered Zosa from continuing her steady jog. My thighs and core burned from maintaining my seat with the bumpier gait, but I promised myself that I would soak in a bath all night and possibly all day tomorrow.

My bloodlust had all but disappeared now. The physical exertion of riding had helped, but it was mostly the distance between me and House Laurent. I should still feed soon because I was overdue, but at least I didn't have to worry about showing up at House Harker's gates with my fangs on display and a wild look in my eyes.

Now that I had successfully escaped and my mind was more settled, my thoughts turned to the future... which for the first time in almost a decade looked drastically different. If not hopeful.

My parents had jointly ruled House Harker until they died, and then my mother's sister, Carmilla, took over because I was too young. She'd adopted me and I was officially named Heir, but as I grew older and became more involved with the runnings of our House, we'd discussed how I could benefit House Harker the most.

Carmilla was a fourth-generation Moroi, and despite being only a few years away from turning a century old, she was showing no signs of slowing down. House Harker was in good hands with her, so we'd turned our attention to other Houses and what they could do for us.

There were a few contenders, but we'd ultimately decided on House Laurent because they controlled a lot of resources and there was already a strain between them and our House.

Really, between them and most of the other Moroi Houses. I wasn't the only one who had a problem with Marvina; her opposition to the Sovereign House was well-known, although nobody exactly knew why. Even in the three years I'd spent at House Laurent, I'd never been able to uncover the reason Marvina hated the Sovereigns so much.

The marriage proposal between our Houses had been initially suggested when I was fourteen and Demetri was sixteen.

After some back-and-forth negotiation, everyone had agreed to the marriage that would take place when I turned twenty-one with the understanding that either House could break the arrangement prior to then with no penalties.

From that moment on, I'd spent my life preparing for my marriage and joining House Laurent. I retained my title as Heir to House Harker, but it was more of a courtesy title until another was chosen. I was supposed to eventually rule House Laurent alongside Demetri. Maybe one of our children would have taken the title of House Harker Heir someday.

But after the events of today, I no longer believed my future was with House Laurent. Even if things could be repaired between me and Demetri, it was clear that Marvina had no intentions of allowing me into a more authoritative role, and apparently, Demetri was more interested in finding new women to sink his cock into than learning how to rule a House.

With my background and education, surely I could be of more use to House Harker than playing a minor, powerless role in House Laurent.

I wasn't entirely sure what the current state of my birth House was. While I'd grown up there, I'd moved to Drudonia when I was sixteen to further my education. Scholars from all three types of Moon Blessed lived in the enormous fortress, and almost every piece of knowledge that we had of our history could be found in the libraries of Drudonia. I'd loved it there. Having so much knowledge at my fingertips had been a dream.

Even before I'd left, I'd spent most of my time studying in preparation for going there.

While my aunt and I regularly traded correspondence, that wasn't the same thing as being immersed in the day-to-day dealings of the House.

I knew that my childhood friend, Kieran, and my childhood archnemesis, Alaric, were still there, and to my disappointment, Vail not only remained at House Harker, but he was now the Marshal, which put him in charge of all the rangers. He was definitely going to be a problem.

Alaric, Vail, and I had grown up together, while Kieran didn't move to House Harker until later.

Alaric and I had always been at odds. His parents had served as advisors to Carmilla and had personally trained their son to replace them one day. He thought I was bold and reckless, whereas I thought he was arrogant and boring. But we were both brilliant and ambitious. Our rivalry had been instantaneous.

The history between Vail and I was completely different. He'd also grown up at House Harker but was three years older than Alaric and me.

His parents had been the previous Marshals, and they trained their son to be the same. As different as the three of us were, the one thing we all had in common was that our destiny was not our own. We each had responsibilities set in motion by our parents, or in my case my aunt, that we couldn't sway from.

There was a time that Vail and I had been friends, but that all changed the night our parents died.

Now Vail hated me with every fiber of his being because he held me responsible for their deaths. Despite the fact that my parents had died alongside them, and my actions had saved his ungrateful life. It was possible that hatred had dulled over the years, but I doubted it.

As a ranger, Vail spent most of his time out in the wilds hunting down monsters that were causing problems along supply lines or specifically attacking some of our outposts. With any luck, I wouldn't have to see him anytime soon. I was looking forward to seeing Kieran again, although we hadn't spoken much since I'd been gone. I even missed Alaric and the nearly constant annoyed expression he wore in my presence.

An hour into me plotting out my theoretical future, I heard hoofbeats beating into the ground back on the main road.

I instantly pulled on the reins, and Zosa obediently stopped. She stayed still as a statue as I held my breath. My heart was beating so loud that I had the irrational fear that they would somehow hear it. The sound of a dozen horses running down the road came toward us and then gradually faded as they raced away.

I waited a few minutes before urging Zosa onward. At some point, the search party would be doubling back, so I'd have to listen out for their approach.

They no doubt knew I was heading back to House Harker; there was nowhere else for me to go, and I'd told Demetri I was going home. But I was pretty confident that the rangers wouldn't ride all the way to House Harker because then they'd have to not only explain that I'd left House Laurent, but also why.

Rangers were excellent at fighting monsters and surviving in the wilds when no one else could. But they did not handle delicate political situations. That was something Demetri or Marvina would try to explain while they attempted to convince me of all the reasons I should come back.

Like hell that would happen.

Currently, I couldn't think of any reason why I'd ever want to go back to that House, but maybe after my temper cooled, I'd change my mind. Or at least think of a solution benefiting both Houses.

Zosa and I continued unhindered on our journey throughout the afternoon, and whenever I heard hoofbeats coming from ahead of me, I halted Zosa where we were still tucked away in the woods away from the main road. I could just barely make out the dark green cloaks bearing the symbol of House Laurent that the riders wore.

Once I could no longer hear them, I maneuvered Zosa back onto the main road so that we could travel faster.

Just as the sun dipped dangerously low on the horizon, I glimpsed three silver-capped towers rising towards the sky in the distance.

The tension I'd been carrying since leaving House Laurent eased, and a long sigh slipped from my lips.

I was home.

CHAPTER FOUR

—

Samara

As I approached the portcullis that was almost identical to the one I had passed through this morning, two guards immediately raised it. Zosa pranced as she walked underneath, apparently feeling the need to show off and make sure everyone appreciated just how beautiful she was.

"Welcome home, Samara." The older of the two guards gave me a warm smile as she took Zosa's reins and stroked the mare's neck.

I slid off the saddle and returned her friendly smile.

"Hello, Denisa. Aren't you supposed to be retired?" I teased. "That's what you claimed you were finally doing when I visited two years ago."

The corners of her eyes crinkled as her smile widened. "I tried the whole retirement thing, but honestly, it was really boring. For a while I helped out in the garden, but the other workers got tired of me killing all the plants, so I volunteered to help train the next generation."

She jerked her head towards the other guard who appeared to be a few years younger than me. He was tall but still in that awkward gangly stage where he hadn't grown into his body yet. My lips twitched in amusement as he tried very hard not to check me out, but his gaze kept dropping down to my chest. I winked at him when I caught him looking, and the tips of his ears burned red.

Denisa chuckled. "This is Jesper. It's only his second day on the job and he already gets to meet our long-lost Heir."

"I wasn't lost, Denisa," I said dryly before holding my hand out to the young guard in training. "Hello, Jesper."

He grasped my hand and shook it a little too eagerly. Color stained his cheeks when he realized what he was doing, and he quickly released my hand before running his own through his hair as he blustered through an apology.

"It's fine," I said with a laugh and then pointed to my bag. "Would you mind getting that for me?"

Thrilled to have something to do, he leapt at the chance and quickly untied my pack from the saddle, all awkwardness from before forgotten.

I turned to Denisa. "Thank you. Would you mind seeing Zosa to the stable? I'd like to check—"

"Sam?" a deep, masculine voice called out from above me. I looked up towards the balcony across the main courtyard, smiling more broadly than I had in three years.

"Hello, Kieran." I laughed as the golden-haired man leapt off the balcony, landing on his feet like the twenty-foot drop was nothing, and raced towards me. He crushed me in a hug and spun me around, sending my black hair flaring around us. "You're making me dizzy," I complained, and he finally set me down after one more twirl.

"You didn't tell me you were coming for a visit!" He looked over my shoulder toward the gate, eyebrows bunching together as he saw no House Laurent rangers behind me. "Where is your escort?"

"Well..." I started, reaching for my bag that one of the guards still held, but Kieran snatched it from him first.

"Where is your escort, Sam?" He narrowed his eyes at me. I'd spent a significant portion of my childhood lusting after those deep brown eyes that were flecked with gold.

Moroi's had multi-colored eyes. We had one dominant color and then another secondary color that weaved through our irises like thin little cracks. Most of the time, the secondary color was only faint, but the lines would widen whenever our bloodlust rose until it completely dominated our eye color. Strong emotions brought on the color change as well.

Kieran's eyes were currently blazing gold.

Rynn and Cali were my best friends, but Kieran and I were just as close, only in a different way. He'd been my first serious crush, and while we'd always just been friends, there was a part of me that had desperately always wanted more.

I wasn't entirely sure he had felt the same back then because he was a notorious flirt and regularly practiced his skills on me.

We'd also always known that I was going to marry Demetri, so there had been a line we didn't want to cross. Leading up to my marriage, I had few regrets. Not being able to explore things with Kieran had definitely been one of them.

Given how quickly my body came to attention at his presence, my crush clearly hadn't faded over the years.

"My trip was unplanned," I said smoothly.

Kieran was usually pretty easygoing, but he could be obnoxiously protective of me sometimes. I needed to keep my explanation short and simple and then distract him with something else.

I continued, "An escort wasn't a possibility, but it was daytime, and you know it's a relatively short trip between House Laurent and here. Besides, I mostly stuck to the main road."

Shit. I shouldn't have said that last bit.

"Mostly?" His nostrils flared as he kept his gaze trained on me.

I raised my chin and tried my best to look down on him, which was a little hard to do because he had several inches on my five-and-a-half-foot frame. "You're not the boss of me, Kieran."

The annoyance slipped off his face as he gave me a charming grin. That same damn grin was what had the ladies in court taking off their panties and throwing them at him. Or just throwing themselves at him in general. It had driven me insane when we were younger.

Thanks to my marriage agreement, Kieran had always been off-limits to me, so I had to stand by while he flirted with every girl who caught his eye.

"You're right. I'm not the boss of you."

He looped his arm through mine and tugged me inside towards the stairs that led to the upper floors of the main house.

"Kieran," I warned, struggling to keep up with his fast pace.

He didn't say anything as he pulled me through the hallways, and I let him because I knew where he was taking me, and it's where I wanted to go anyway.

Although, I would have preferred to walk there at a leisurely pace while I gathered my thoughts instead of being dragged through the House for everyone to see.

"Samara, you're home!" an older Moroi wearing an apron dusted with flour and stains called out in greeting.

"Hi, Leora!" I waved and eyed the empty platter she was holding in her hands. "Are there any more honey cakes left?"

"I'll send some to your suite in a bit!"

Two more servants came around the corner and smoothly slid out of Kieran's way as he continued pulling me along.

"Oh! Hey, Floran! Hi, Nora!" I grinned at both of them. They were a few years older than me and worked in the gardens.

Two years ago, they'd gotten married, and I'd come back for the ceremony. I'd had to lie to Marvina about my reasons for visiting House Harker because she never would have approved of me coming back here for the wedding of low-ranking servants.

"Hey, Sam!" Floran laughed. "I see nothing has changed between you and Kieran."

"He's still very emotional." I patted Kieran's hand where it rested on my forearm. "He needs to find a nice Moroi to settle down with like you did with Nora."

Kieran let out an exasperated breath before he spun around. Suddenly, my world tilted, and I found myself tossed over his shoulder.

"Ow!" I tried to shift, but his arm clamped around my thighs. "Your bony shoulder is digging into me."

"It's not bony." He swatted my butt. "You can chat with everyone later."

I raised my head and waved at the two love-birds. "Come and find me tomorrow! We can valiantly raid the kitchen and then catch up on the garden!"

"Pretty sure Leora will be baking all morning to celebrate you being back!" Nora snickered. "Have fun managing Kieran and your aunt!"

Kieran carried me up to the third floor with only a few more interruptions. I was kind of impressed; I wasn't exactly light, but he wasn't even winded. Growing up, Kieran had always been on the slender side, but it had been three years since I'd seen him last since he'd been away during Floran and Nora's wedding.

My pondering of Kieran's new physical prowess ended when he dropped me back to the ground in front of a familiar study. The large double doors were open, revealing walls lined with books and scrolls, some well-used couches and chairs, and a large desk at the back of the room.

A woman who looked like an older version of me sat behind the desk, the last rays of sun shining through the floor-to-ceiling windows at her back.

My aunt was wholly focused on the scroll in front of her. Out of nowhere, heat built behind my eyes, and I found myself fighting back tears.

How many times had I sat on one of the comfortable couches complaining about some asinine thing Kieran had done? Or how I vehemently disagreed with one of my instructors over marks I'd received on my work?

She would let me ramble on and on, seeming to not be paying attention as she focused on her own work, only to raise her head when I finally stopped talking to smile at me and say, *"That sounds like quite the problem, my dear. So, what are you going to do about it?"*

I blinked my tears away at the memory and the crushing realization of just how much I had missed my home.

Kieran nudged me further into the study before dropping down onto one of the couches and arching an eyebrow at me. I envisioned grabbing one of the throw pillows and smothering him with it when he smirked and settled further into the thick cushions.

Carmilla Harker finally raised her head. Her dark, ivy-green eyes met my deep purple ones, the color of our eyes only distinguishable because of the last rays of the dying sunlight.

At night, our eyes looked black. It was a trait shared by all those of the Harker bloodline.

"Samara?" She blinked in surprise before rising from her chair and rushing towards me. "What are you doing here? Has something happened?"

The familiar sound of her rich, captivating voice was my undoing. Tears flowed down my cheeks as I threw myself into her arms.

"Shhh. Shhh, my dear," she said as she stroked my hair. "It'll be alright."

After a moment, I sucked in a rattling breath and pulled myself together. My cheeks were likely stained red with mortification. I was goddamn twenty-four years old. Way too old to be sobbing on Carmilla's shoulder.

Sensing the shift in my mood, Carmilla tutted. "You'll always be my niece, and you need never hide anything from me. Outside of these doors, present a brave, unbreakable front, but not in here." She settled down on one end of the settee and looked pointedly at the other end.

I immediately sat down, wiping the last of my tears from my face with a sniff.

"If you need another shoulder to cry on, you can always use mine." The grin Kieran gave me was truly wicked, but I saw the concern in his eyes. Apparently, he still felt the need to cover up any true emotions with his ridiculous flirty behavior.

"I will smother you in your sleep." I narrowed my eyes at him, but Kieran merely cocked his head to the side and raised an eyebrow.

"So, you still want to climb into my bed then?"

"Children," Carmilla smoothly cut in, "you can continue whatever this conversation is later. For now, I'd like to hear what has brought you home, Samara."

I stared at my folded hands, suddenly feeling small.

Had I made a foolish decision to return here? Maybe I should have stayed and tried to figure things out with Demetri.

My returning home didn't just impact me; it would put everyone in House Harker in an uncomfortable position. I had signed a contract with House Laurent, and I was now in violation of that. My knuckles turned white as I squeezed my fingers tighter together.

"Hey." Carmilla's soft tone broke through my panic, and she leaned forward to wrap her hands around mine. "While you have quite the temper, you're never one to act without reason. I love you, and I will support you in anything."

Releasing the breath I'd been holding, I loosened the death grip I had on my fingers as Carmilla reclined back in her seat. "I think me marrying into House Laurent was a mistake." I proceeded to recount the past three years to her, trying my best to keep things succinct, focusing on my efforts to prove my worth to Marvina and earn a spot on her council, and trying to be a good wife for Demetri.

Kieran offered colorful commentary throughout my story, mostly at the expense of Demetri, and I was thankful for the distraction, otherwise I probably would have gotten super pissed-off again.

I left out the part about walking in on Demetri cheating on me. Carmilla would need to know that, but I couldn't bring myself to say it in front of Kieran. To admit that I hadn't been enough for Demetri. Rationally, I knew it was foolish of me to think of it that way, but I didn't always think logically when it came to Kieran.

Carmilla maintained a neutral expression through it all, which set my nerves on end, even though I knew this was how she typically reacted in these situations. My aunt was always calm and levelheaded, and it was something I hoped to claim as well someday. My damn temper still got the best of me sometimes.

Silence fell over us once I finished catching them up on the events of this morning and basically the last three years of my life.

Carmilla knew some of it because she and I corresponded regularly, but I hadn't told her everything like I had now, and Kieran hadn't known any of it. We hadn't spoken much since I'd left. I didn't know his reasons, but mine were because it hurt too much. I hadn't fully realized just how deep my feelings were for him until I'd left House Harker.

There hadn't been anything I could do about it, and he hadn't reached out, so I assumed he wasn't as affected by my leaving as I was.

So, I'd just packed up that painful realization and tucked it away. Right next to all the other painful memories.

But as I looked at Kieran's tight expression, I realized maybe there were other reasons he hadn't contacted me. He looked pissed enough to grab a horse and ride all the way to House Laurent just to beat the shit out of Demetri.

It helped settle me a little to know that he was still in my corner, even after all these years apart.

Carmilla finally rose and stepped around her desk, grabbed three crystal glasses and a bottle of dark amber liquor, and then returned to where we were sitting. She poured the brandy generously into each of the glasses before nudging them in our directions.

I plucked mine up and inhaled the earthy aroma. I might be biased, but I maintained that House Harker made the best moon brandy.

My aunt raised her glass in the air, with Kieran and I doing the same before we each slammed back the shot.

Heat burned down my throat and filled my center. I'd missed that feeling. The wine at House Laurent was nice, but sometimes you just needed a goddamn shot of liquor.

"Fuck Demetri," Carmilla said loudly with a determined nod.

My hand flew to my mouth as I choked, and Kieran's mouth dropped open as he stared at my aunt. I could count the number of times I'd heard her swear on one hand, and apparently, Kieran felt the same.

"Fuck that bitch, Marvina," she continued. "And fuck House Laurent. They don't deserve you."

I gawked at her, my mouth gaping in what was probably a very unattractive manner as she poured us each more liquor. This one I sipped as I came to terms with my aunt's proclamation.

"We can work with Alaric to draft the marriage dissolution. It was clearly stated in the contract that you would be offered an advisory position once you had proven yourself capable. I have no doubt that you have done so, and we can provide more than enough evidence of this. If Marvina wants a fight, she'll fucking get one."

I lost it and threw myself across the couch, hugging her fiercely. Carmilla laughed as I spilled liquor everywhere.

"Thank you!" I squeezed her once more before pulling back to look her in the eyes. "I promise you that I will be a strong asset for House Harker and will do whatever I can to support our House in the future."

"I know you will." She patted my cheek lovingly. "Now, you've had a long day. Go get settled. Your room has been kept up while you were gone, and all your belongings are still there. We'll speak more tomorrow."

Kieran trailed after me as I found my way back to my old room, and I only half paid attention to everything he was saying. For the first time in years, I had a future in front of me that I was actually excited about.

"Have you been listening to anything I've said?" he asked when we reached the doors to my suite.

"No," I said honestly. He huffed a laugh and moved to follow me inside, but I blocked his entrance with a pointed look. "Nuh-uh. I'm going to have a nice long soak in my tub and call my besties."

"Or,"—he offered me a heated look—"I can join you in the bath and maybe rub some of the tension from your shoulders?"

I leaned against the doorframe and tilted my head while I gave him a very obvious once-over, noting all the ways he'd changed in the years I'd been gone.

Kieran had never been that tall or big. When he'd first arrived at House Harker, he'd just turned fourteen like me. I'd just gone through a growth spurt and towered over him with my five and a half feet. He'd gradually caught up to me and during my years at Drudonia; every time I came back to the House for a visit, Kier would be just a little taller. I unfortunately never grew any further, so now I was the one always tilting my head back to look up at others.

Even after surpassing me in height, Kieran had been on the slender side back then. That was no longer the case. While I wouldn't describe him as bulky, his lean frame was now corded with muscle. Fuck. Kieran had always been good-looking, but now he was absolutely gorgeous.

"Based on the way you're practically drooling over me," he drawled with a smirk, "I'm assuming the answer is yes to that shoulder rub."

"It's not my shoulders that I'm interested in having rubbed," I said with a shrug, pleased when a spark of surprise lit up his eyes.

Our flirting had always been harmless and mostly one-sided growing up. Kieran was a flirt with everyone, and I'd been promised to Demetri. Part of me had always wanted to flirt back, and sometimes I did, but normally I refrained because it'd felt too dangerous at the time.

Because I *liked* Kieran.

It would have been too easy to cross that line with him, and that would have ended with me nursing a broken heart.

But now, even if I didn't go through with the marriage dissolution... Demetri clearly didn't view our marriage as one based on love and respect. If, and that was a very big if, I decided not to dissolve our marriage and return to House Laurent, our marriage would be one in name only. I wouldn't deny myself pleasures any longer.

However, I would deny them for this night, because now that I had the conversation with my aunt over with, all I could feel was the sense of grime on my skin. I needed to cleanse myself of the trials of the day and fill Rynn and Cali in on everything that had happened.

I reached out and flicked Kieran on the nose. "See you in the morning." Then I shut the door in his face.

"I'm gonna cut off his balls and make him choke on them!" Cali snarled. Her shadowy form was perched on the edge of the bathtub and was practically vibrating with unrestrained rage.

Rynn waved her hand dismissively, causing the shadows that made up her fingers to swirl through the air from where she was leaning against the wall next to the tub. "Demetri has always been worthless. He's hardly worth the effort. I'm more pissed about his mother. Who the fuck does she think she is?"

"The head of House Laurent," I said dryly as I sunk further into the bath.

As the Heir of House Harker, my suite was comprised of a large sitting area, a bedroom, and a rather lavish en suite. Every time I used the tub, I silently thanked the Fae for being such fans of luxury and leaving this all to us.

Granted, that probably hadn't been their intention, but whatever. Finders, keepers.

Cali snorted and flicked her hand. A dark tendril whipped towards the water, solidifying for just a second, and water splashed against my face. I wiped it off with a laugh. If anyone else saw Cali using her magic so casually they would be terrified.

Shadow magic was feared thanks to the wraiths that roamed the nights, but the Furies excelled at wielding it the same way Moroi were skilled with blood magic and the Velesians had some psychic abilities.

Cali, in particular, was quite talented, well on her way to becoming the strongest Furie in existence. That is, if she didn't lose herself in the process.

At least, that was what her family and the Furie elders feared. The Rayne bloodline was notorious for being incredibly powerful... and going insane. Because of that, the family worked hard to control and tamp down the rage that burned within them.

It required a delicate balance on their part because they needed that rage to fuel their magic the same way Moroi required blood and the Velesians relied on a connection to the earth.

They devoted their lives to walking the line of suppressing their rage without making it disappear completely. That meant they avoided anything that might tip them over the edge.

Like love.

While the Moroi and Velesians used marriage for political jockeying, the Furies never married.

Lust and short pairings were acceptable, but nothing long-term. Even children were raised in a communal sense so that they didn't form too strong a connection to their biological parents.

I thought it was a sad way to exist, but I'd also seen the carnage left behind by a Furie who had lost themselves to the pull of their magic. The Furies had taken longer than the Moroi and Velesians to claw back their humanity, and their grasp on it was tenuous. Perhaps that would improve for future generations.

Cali, however, refused to fall in line. She pushed boundaries constantly and probably would have been shunned by her people if not for her power.

They couldn't afford to lose her because when Cali cut loose, she was a one-woman battalion.

Still, lately, I had noticed something off about her. She was still the wild Furie I'd always known and loved, but there was a distance to her now. She was like that with other Furies, but she'd never been like that around us.

I wasn't sure what was going on with her, and neither was Rynn. We'd discussed it and tried to pry it out of Cali, but she had just laughed us off.

I refused to believe that my friend would ever lose herself, and I didn't love that she was keeping secrets from us when we'd always sworn to be open books to each other, but all I could do was lead by example and hope she came clean with us eventually.

"So, what are you going to do now?" Rynn asked.

"Well, I have some time to figure that out." I lifted my hand and watched the soapy water drip through my fingers. "Right now, I'm leaning towards drafting up that marriage dissolution with Alaric and writing off the last three years, but that feels like a waste, considering my upbringing."

I frowned and sank all the way down until the water covered my face before resurfacing.

"The same skills and knowledge that made you an asset to House Laurent will make you one to House Harker as well," Rynn scoffed. "They were foolish to treat you this way and let you go. Hell, I would snatch you up for whatever Pack I go to if I could."

"Whatever Pack?" Cali spun to face Rynn, causing shadows to swirl around her. "Like you don't know where you're going."

Rynn stuck out her tongue. "It's not completely settled yet."

I rolled my eyes, agreeing with Cali. Rynn was destined for the Alpha Pack the same way that I had been destined for House Laurent.

Although, I hoped my friend's fate would work out better than mine. But Cali didn't have a set path ahead of her. She'd been just as well educated as me and Rynn, but there was no marriage laid out for her and no high-ranking position within a Pack arranged.

Cali's only goal in life was to not go insane and kill us all.

"So," Cali said mischievously, "how is Kieran looking these days?"

I flicked some bubbles in her direction, which only made her smirk as she let them pass through her shadow, causing it to flicker briefly. "He's fine," I muttered.

Rynn laughed. "That man is more than fine."

A smile tugged at my lips as I recalled his physique from earlier. "Yeah, fine doesn't quite capture his hotness."

"The question is, what are you going to do about it now that you're back?" Cali asked.

Both she and Rynn arched their eyebrows at me as they waited for my answer.

What *was* I going to do about it? My life had radically changed in a day, and I didn't think I could ever go back to how I'd been living these past three years.

Our world was a dangerous one, and while I hoped to live a long and fulfilling life, there were no guarantees. Why should I deny myself pleasure when the opportunity presented itself?

With my mind made up, I gave them a sinful grin. "I'm going to try a new motto in life."

"Oh?" Rynn tilted her head at me in a way that always reminded me of her wolf's side.

"Yeah," I said slowly. "If I see something I want, I'm going to take it."

CHAPTER FIVE

—

Samara

I WOKE up early the next morning and stared at the intricate design laid out on the ceiling of my bedroom.

All of the Moroi Houses were originally built by the Fae. This fortress must have been built by the Seelie because the mural above me portrayed a bright, sunlit setting of grassy hills.

I loved the painting, but I always thought it was strange because I'd never seen anything like this in Lunaria. Most of the continent was covered by thick forests. The only places the woods retreated were on the coasts and in the badlands, but nowhere were there long stretches of gently rolling hills.

When I was a child, I used to gaze up at my ceiling and wonder why they had chosen to paint this scene.

Had Lunaria changed? Was this what it used to look like once upon a time? Or had the Fae come from somewhere else, and these murals reminded them of a home they had lost?

I never found an answer to my childhood questions. The Fae had loved art, and most of the fortresses that had been repurposed by the Moon Blessed held murals like this in them. Sometimes they were of scenery that made no sense, but other times they were of places that I recognized.

House Laurent had belonged to the Unseelie, and its murals were always of night skies and dark forests. I loved both sides and wished the Fae hadn't hated each other so much. It would be nice to live somewhere where I had both types of murals to peruse.

My thoughts briefly wandered to Demetri and how he was dealing with my departure. I wondered what had been said to explain my sudden disappearance. Marvina had no doubt spun the story to make me look bad. Did I care?

I chewed my lip as I thought about it and decided that I didn't. Neither Demetri nor House Laurent were worth it. I would prove my worth here, at House Harker, and make them regret how their actions had resulted in losing me.

A distinct, slow three-beat knock sounded on my door, and a grin tugged at my lips. I'd been curious as to how long he'd wait before coming to harass me.

I hopped out of bed and threw a robe over the thin shift I'd slept in before going to open the door. Kieran's hand was raised to knock again, but he reached out to pull on my tangled hair instead.

"Sleeping in?" he tutted. "You've become lazy in your old age."

"We're the same age," I grumped, swatting his hand away from my hair as he peered over my shoulder and into my room. "Something I can help you with, Kier?" I shoved him back a step.

"Just trying to see how you were settling in." His lips twitched as he slowly scanned me from head to toe. "Want me to help you pick out your clothes for the day and brush your hair?"

"No." I slapped his hand away again when he went to teasingly pull on another knot. "I'm perfectly capable of getting myself dressed."

"Just trying to be helpful." He shrugged. "Come get breakfast with me?"

"I can't," I said reluctantly. But lazing around with Kieran all day sounded really tempting... "I promised Carmilla I would have breakfast with her this morning."

"Lunch then?" he asked hopefully.

I bit my lip, not really sure what my schedule for the day was going to be or how I'd feel after talking to Carmilla. "Sure, but no promises. I might get caught up in something else."

"The only thing you'll be getting caught up in later is me giving you all the gossip you've been missing out on." He brushed a kiss against my cheek before strolling down the hallway.

I closed the door and leaned against it, holding a hand to my cheek. It'd been three years since I'd seen Kieran. Despite being a courtier who regularly traveled around to the different Houses, he'd never once visited House Laurent, and the few times I'd returned to House Harker, he'd been away. I'd never been sure if he was avoiding me or if his life was simply busy.

I'd assumed that when I returned here, things would be different between us, but instead, we'd slipped right back into our easy friendship that included some light flirting. Okay, maybe heavy flirting.

The sun rose higher into the sky, and golden light filtered in through the windows of my room, reminding me it was time to get on with it.

I tossed on a deep forest-green dress that was made of a stretchy soft fabric, which meant it hugged all of my curves and was incredibly comfortable. After spending a few minutes detangling my hair and tying it up in a bun, I made my way to Carmilla's study.

Several other Moroi passed me on the way, all flashing welcoming smiles. I wasn't sure if they knew the exact circumstances of my return, but it felt so damn nice to be somewhere I was wanted.

"Good morning, dear," Carmilla said warmly as I entered her study. "The tea should be set if you wouldn't mind pouring us some cups."

Shutting the door behind me, I nodded. "Of course."

I noticed several pastries piled up on a plate as I poured our tea, and I quickly snatched the one that had sugary crumbles along the top. I tore off a chunk and popped it onto my mouth, savoring the flavor while I watched Carmilla furiously scribble something onto a scroll.

When I'd arrived yesterday, I'd been in such a weird state that I hadn't looked that closely at my aunt, but now, as my eyes swept over her, I was happy to see that she looked the same as she always did.

At ninety-five years old, Carmilla didn't look a day over forty. We had similar facial features and the same straight black hair, but Carmilla's skin was several shades lighter than mine. I had my father to thank for my darker complexion. Aside from that, I'd taken strongly after my mother's side of the family, which meant Carmilla and I looked a lot alike. An old pang ran through me as I thought of my parents. I'd lost them over a decade ago, but I still missed them fiercely.

Carmilla sat down on the couch beside me and blew a wayward strand of hair out of her face, drawing me from my melancholy.

I chuckled and passed her a teacup. "Rough morning?"

"Yolanthe is supposed to be working on a trade agreement with House Devereux," she sighed. "Unfortunately, in the midst of negotiations, she learned that the nephew of the ruler of House Devereux had a tryst with her sister, and it ended badly. Nothing terrible happened, just young people getting wrapped up in their passion, but Yolanthe still doesn't like the boy, and it's clouding her judgement."

"Who's leading negotiations on their side?" I asked as I blew on my tea to cool it down.

Carmilla's lips twisted into a frown. "Severen. He's the father of the boy who was involved with Yolanthe's sister."

I did a quick rundown of the Devereux family. The current leader of the House was Thessalia, her brother was Severen, and from my understanding, they were close. Thessalia was old, at least a decade older than Carmilla, and Severen was her baby brother. Their parents died when they were young, and Thessalia basically raised him. She'd be protective of his children.

"Why don't I catch up with Yolanthe this week and see where I can be of assistance?" I suggested. "I would love to get her opinion of the trade agreement I've been working on with one of the Velesian packs. She can look that over while I review the trade agreement with Devereux."

Truthfully, I didn't need Yolanthe to look over my trade agreement. I'd already done all the hard work on the offer because I had Rynn as a resource for the Velesian side of things, but I knew enough about Yolanthe to know that she would be more amicable to me stepping in on her negotiations if I asked for help on mine. She could be stubborn, but she wasn't impossible to work with.

"Are you sure?" Carmilla asked with a gentle tone, studying me carefully. "You don't need to jump back into things right away. Why don't you take this week to think about what you want to do?"

"You mean if I want to walk away from the marriage we spent a decade planning for and was supposed to help our relations with House Laurent? The relationship I just completely and utterly ruined?" I'd meant to play it off as a joke, but my voice cracked on the last word.

Who was I to think I could just come back and help with negotiations and establishing solid alliances with other Houses when I hadn't even been able to keep my political marriage going?

My throat tightened, and I gave Carmilla an apologetic look. "I'm sorry."

"Samara," my aunt said firmly as she peered over the rim of her teacup. "You did nothing wrong. We didn't arrange the marriage with Demetri solely for the benefit of House Harker. I honestly thought the two of you would be happy together. If you had told me earlier about what was going on with Marvina and House Laurent, I would have called you back here and ended the marriage immediately."

I swallowed, blinking back tears. Carmilla's faith in me never wavered, and it helped me brush aside my doubts.

"Now, I want you to take this week to think about what you want to do." When I opened my mouth to argue, she raised a hand to silence me. "I'm not going to stop you from talking to Yolanthe if that's what you want to do, but you do *not* have to do it. You have nothing to prove to me or to House Harker. We're all simply happy to have you home."

"Thank you," I said quietly, trying to wrestle my emotions back under control. "Have we received any messages from House Laurent?"

Carmilla stared at me for a beat before answering, "No."

I popped another piece of pastry into my mouth and chewed slowly. Part of me had expected some type of message from Demetri. He wasn't the type to ride back here heroically and apologize for all of his mistakes, but it wasn't that damned hard to scribble a note together and send it on its way. We were close enough that the message could have easily been delivered overnight.

"I'll take your advice and think things over this week," I said. "But unless new information surfaces,"—*or Demetri stops being a useless asshole*—"I think it's likely that I will move to dissolve my marriage. Marvina might be a problem."

"My dear..." Carmilla gave me a sharp smile. "If Marvina comes looking for a fight, I'm more than happy to give her one."

CARMILLA and I chatted for several hours before I took my leave and aimlessly wandered around the grounds of House Harker.

It was nice to catch up with my aunt. We'd spoken while I'd been at House Laurent, and I'd come home a few times to visit, but I'd always felt this underlying pressure to maintain a positive attitude around her. Now that my marriage had gone down in flames, I didn't have to lie about anything.

Despite Carmilla's reassurances though, I was still determined to prove my worth to House Harker and planned on tracking down Yolanthe tomorrow.

A splash of purple caught my attention, and I wandered over to the delicate flowers of the coastal lavender plants that were in full bloom lining the back of the garden. It was late spring, and a few stocks here and there had been harvested. I ran my fingers along one of the long stems, breathing in the relaxing scent. Further inland, lavender blossoms were larger and held a more earthy scent, but I'd always preferred the coastal variety.

"Thought I'd find you here," an amused voice called out.

I glanced over my shoulder to where Kieran leisurely made his way through the garden. He'd changed since this morning and now wore a turquoise doublet that made his golden hair and lightly tanned skin further stand out.

"Aren't you hot in that thing?" I gestured towards his outfit. "It's almost summer and you're wearing, like, three layers of clothing."

He raised an eyebrow to match mine. "Is this your roundabout way of asking me to take my clothes off?"

I rolled my eyes. "If you pass out from heat exhaustion, I'm leaving you here."

"You would never," he retorted with an easy grin. "I've been down in the cellars all morning catching with Caedmon."

"Were you actually talking, or were you sampling all the wine and ale he's been working on?"

"Both, of course." I laughed and shook my head at him as he gave me a wounded look. He added, "I'll have you know I picked up a lot of useful information."

I crossed my arms. "Do tell."

"He recently met with one of the Velesian brewers to arrange a trade of our grapes and their grain. Apparently, another trade deal broke down between the Narchis and Fervis."

"Interesting. What else did you learn?"

Rynn was my main source of gossip on the Velesians, but it was nice to get other information. Plus, Rynn wasn't exactly social whereas Kieran did his best to be in everybody's business.

"You'll have to join me for lunch to learn more." He held an arm out to me, and I looped mine through it without hesitation.

A few Moroi came out to tend the gardens and waved at us as we passed. Like me, Kieran knew everyone by name and asked after them or their family as we walked by. I recognized most of the names, but I filed away the ones I didn't, along with other bits of information.

Kieran was one of the reasons I always made such an effort to learn everyone's names and about their lives, no matter their position in the House.

Not only was it polite, but servants picked up all kinds of information, so it was always useful to be on their good side.

"I had everything brought to your suite. Is that okay?"

"That's fine." I let out a sigh of relief. "Everyone has been really nice to me, but if I get one more sympathetic look or pity hug, I might scream."

Kieran released my arm so that he could pull me in for a side hug. "I promise to give you no sympathetic looks or pity hugs. Only amused looks and sweaty hugs." He leaned over to wipe some of the sweat that had been dripping down from his forehead onto my cheek.

"Ugh!" I shoved him away from me. "I told you that doublet was too warm for this weather!"

He chuckled as his fingers nimbly worked to undo the front buttons while we hiked up the stairs to my room. By the time we got there, the doublet was slung over his shoulder and Kieran had unlaced the top of his shirt, putting a decent amount of his chest on display.

I fought back the blush that was threatening to creep up my neck as I realized we were about to be alone in my room with Kieran looking absolutely indecent.

My emotions were all over the place, and I really didn't need this right now.

Thank the moon Carmilla had insisted I feed from her earlier when she found out it'd been over a month since I'd last fed. It was a little awkward, since at this point, I was used to having sex with my blood, but that probably wouldn't be happening anytime soon, and I had desperately needed a blood meal.

Even with my thirst being sated I was still nervous about being alone with Kieran right now. I could have blamed my wanting of him on the bloodlust, but that would have been a lie. The desire was always there and had been from the first day I'd met him.

My hand hesitated on the doorknob as I tried to come up with an excuse not to go inside. But the decision was taken away from me when Kieran brushed past me to open the door and waltzed into my suite.

Shit.

Steeling my inner turmoil, I walked in after him, because like hell would I run away from my own damn room.

I froze a few paces in as I took in the feast before me. Honey biscuits, several types of fish sliced up into thin pieces, and an assortment of berries and salted nuts.

Kieran's grin faltered when he saw my expression, then he looked over the food he'd set up on the low table in front of my settee before facing me again. "Is it too much?" he asked, concern lacing his words. "It's too much. I'm sorry. I just... I thought..." He ran a hand through his hair. "I'll go get us something else."

"You remembered," I choked out.

His expression softened then. "Of course I remembered, Sam. I'd never forget anything about you."

The memories of us raiding the kitchen and throwing together this exact meal every time one of us had a bad day paraded through my mind.

The last time we'd done it had been when my wedding date was set. At the time, I hadn't been willing to admit I had any reservations about the marriage itself. Instead, I had mentioned how sad I would be about leaving House Harker.

About leaving him.

He remembered. After all these years. He *remembered.*

To my absolute horror, I burst into tears. Body-racking sobs tore out of me.

I was vaguely aware of Kieran as he swooped me up into his arms and placed me down carefully on the chaise lounge near the table of food before leaving quickly.

I didn't blame him. *What the hell was wrong with me?*

Gradually, the sobbing abated. Unfortunately, hiccups were quick to step into their wake.

I mournfully looked at the food that had set me off. My appetite had fled, and all I wanted to do was curl up in my bed and hide under my covers for the rest of the day. I was working on convincing myself to get up and shove the food in my spelled cold box for keeping when the door to my room opened again.

I peeked over the back of the lounge to see Kieran storming back in with a somewhat panicked look on his face.

"What are you—" My words were cut off when he dumped an armful of sweets into my lap.

"That's my entire stash," he said as he knelt in front of me and started holding up various pieces. "A few different types of chocolate. This one is a caramel. These are different types of hard candies."

I took the carefully wrapped candy out of his hand and unwrapped it before popping it into my mouth.

"Strawberry," I whispered as the sweet flavor exploded across my tongue. Infusing fruit flavors into hard candies was a relatively new technique, so even though the ingredients required were more common than the ones for chocolate, few people knew how to do it. "This is easily one of the best things I've ever tasted."

Kieran's bright hazel eyes looked at me as his features softened. "I'm sorry about lunch. I didn't mean to upset you. Whatever you want, I'll get it for you. Just *please* don't cry, Sam."

Carefully, I moved the ridiculous pile of candies from my lap to the table and patted the seat next to me. Kieran carefully joined me while keeping an eye on me like I would break down again at any moment.

"Lunch is perfect," I told him earnestly. "It is absolutely perfect, and you are perfect."

"Your reaction said otherwise," he said wryly.

"My mind is kind of weird right now," I admitted. "Carmilla advised me to take this week off and give myself time to adjust to everything that has happened. I brushed her off, thinking I could just dive back into my life here, but I think she was right, and I need to give myself some time to adjust to... everything."

"It's almost like your aunt knows what she's talking about since she's been alive for almost a century." He gave me a pointed look.

"Shush, you." I bumped my shoulder into his as a smile tugged at my lips. "I'm going to try to give myself a break this week and think carefully about what happened at House Laurent and what I want to do going forward." I gave Kieran a rueful glance. "Chances are pretty good that I'll be randomly bursting into tears all week. I totally get it if you want to avoid me."

Kieran held my gaze for a moment before he shifted until he was sitting on the floor and leaning against the settee. "This isn't my entire stash of candy. I lied before. I can break out more as needed."

I laughed as I joined him on the floor and leaned my head on his shoulder. "I knew you were lying, you greedy asshole. Now, pass me a dark chocolate."

CHAPTER SIX

—

Samara

I TWISTED from side to side as I studied my reflection in the mirror.

Okay, maybe I was dressed a *little* over the top, but after spending a week in comfy clothes and alternating between lounging in my suite or Carmilla's study, I needed to get back to a normal schedule.

This morning when I walked into my closet, I bypassed my loungewear to where my favorite dresses waited for me.

Aside from keeping my suite clean, nobody had moved anything in the years I'd been gone. I didn't know if that was because Carmilla expected me to visit more often, or if she somehow knew that I'd be back here someday.

I may or may not have cried when I saw my clothing hanging exactly where I had left them. My emotions had continued to be all over the place this week, which was why I'd mostly hidden away in my rooms. Kieran brought me lunch every day, along with a new assortment of candies. When I had random meltdowns, he didn't say anything. He just held me through it and then continued on with the conversation like nothing happened.

I absolutely adored him for it.

My random crying bouts were mostly over now, which I was extremely happy about. I was far from being back to my normal self, but I felt ready to tackle my new life.

Absently, I swayed in front of the mirror, flashing bits of skin with each movement. This dress would have been absolutely scandalous in House Laurent, but here, no one would bat an eye at the amount of skin I had on display. It was the golden threads that wound through the fabric in an ornate design that would draw attention and would have made the dress more reasonable for a fancy dinner instead of a normal day.

But as I pulled the long pieces of fabric through my fingers and let them fall back down to my ankles, I knew I wouldn't be changing into anything else.

Today would be the start of my new future, and I wanted to wear this dress while I set things in motion.

Want. Take.

My simple motto rang through my mind, and I smiled. It's not like it would truly be that easy, but I could still embrace this new outlook for a while and see where it got me.

I didn't bother with any makeup and pulled my hair back into a high pony-tail so that it tumbled down my back in a long stream, showing the black outline of the crescent moon shining boldly on the left side of my neck.

It was the symbol that all Moroi were born with, the same as the Velesians and Furies who were born with their own crescent moons. The Velesians bore theirs on the right side of their neck, and the Furies at the base of their necks, with both points facing upwards.

The symbol of House Harker was tattooed on the right side of my neck. Fortunately for me, House Laurent turned up their noses at tattoos, so I didn't have to worry about bearing their mark for the rest of my life. Instead, they bore rings with their sigil stamped onto them. I'd tossed my ring into the drawer where I kept all my miscellaneous jewelry my first night back. I had another tattoo on my bicep that was a mishmash of the three crescent moon symbols.

Cali and Rynn had identical ones on their arms. After spending five years together while we all studied at Drudonia, we rarely saw each other in person anymore, but our bond ran deep, and something so insignificant as distance would never dampen our loyalty to each other.

I bit my lip as I thought back to our conversation last night. Rynn and Cali had been focused on supporting me, but I was still worried about both of them.

Despite Rynn's nonchalant words, I knew she was stressed about serving the Order of Avala. Unlike the Moroi, the Velesians didn't organize around specific bloodlines. The Moroi had seven Houses in our realm, including the Sovereigns, each ruled by a different family. The Velesians only had three Orders: Narchis, Avala, and Fervis. All of their territory was divided up among those three Orders, and leadership changed as new Velesians rose and challenged those above them. It always seemed a little chaotic to me, but it worked well enough for them.

Despite her timid personality, Rynn was brilliant at planning defensive and offensive moves across Lunaria. She knew everything about the monsters that roamed these lands, all their strengths and weaknesses, and when she was in her element, few things rattled her.

She could be staring death in the face and calmly recite all the various points where mortal wounds could be dealt, but she was also terrible at talking to people without sounding like she was talking down to them.

Which, to be fair, she normally was. Not because she was a snob but because Rynn was perfectly aware that she was usually the smartest person in the room, and she didn't understand why people didn't just listen to her. It had been a good source of entertainment for me and Cali over the years.

My frown deepened as I thought about Cali. She was another concern.

I was pretty sure that if something was seriously wrong, Cali would tell us, but I also knew my friend's definition of "seriously wrong" and mine were quite different. Maybe once I got my life figured out, I could plan a trip to visit both of them in person.

Their ability to appear to me in their shadow forms was convenient, but it made it hard to read their facial expressions that way. Plus, I knew that if I pushed Cali on it, she would simply disappear and probably refuse to talk to me for weeks.

I was still lost in my thoughts about Cali and Rynn when I realized I'd walked up to the third floor of the main house, where most of the studies were, but I didn't know which one was Alaric's, and many of the doors were closed.

Carmilla wanted me to work with him on drafting my marriage dissolution, which I personally thought was unnecessary. I was more than capable of writing it myself, but Carmilla had simply smiled at me when I'd voiced that opinion and asked me to work with him as a personal favor to her.

My aunt knew exactly how to manipulate me into doing things her way, and I couldn't even be mad when she did it because it was so annoyingly impressive.

Alaric had still been studying under some of the elders when I'd last lived here and hadn't had his own space yet. I glanced up and down the hallway but wasn't able to find any clues about which way to head.

I supposed I could just go to Carmilla's study and hope she wasn't in the middle of something and ask her.

"I'm assuming you're looking for me," a sardonic voice said from behind me in a tone that made it clear it wasn't a question.

I bit back the insult that tried to leap out of my mouth. While Kieran and I traded barbs with each other in our own weird way of flirting, Alaric and I had never gotten along. I would have been happy to avoid him entirely growing up, but his family had already resided in House Harker instead of one of the outpost towns and, much to my dismay, he became best friends with Kieran.

The two of them were as close as I was to Rynn and Cali, so Alaric and I had to tolerate each other to the best of our abilities once Kieran entered the picture.

It appeared nothing had changed. Great.

I plastered a smile on my face before turning around to face him. "Yes, I was. Carmilla thought it would be best to speak with you about dissolving my marriage agreement."

His always serious light green eyes flittered across my body, lips curling in distaste at my choice of dress.

I sighed inwardly. One of the many reasons Alaric didn't like me was because he thought I was just the spoiled niece of House Harker, flitting about through life without a care in the world. The fact that I had studied my ass off at Drudonia and gone through all kinds of training for my marriage to Demetri meant nothing to him.

Alaric's biggest fault was that once he'd made up his mind about something, nothing could change it. I thought it made him a stubborn ass and had told him as much to his face regularly, which usually caused him to make some sort of cutting remark, and then we'd trade insults until one of us stalked away or Kieran interrupted us.

I liked my dress. If he thought less of me for wearing it, that was his problem.

"Is there something wrong with my outfit?" I asked.

I made a show of looking it over as I tugged on the fabric a little, causing a little more of my cleavage to be on display.

Alaric gave me a flat stare in return, which I returned with a salacious grin. He let out a long-suffering sigh next, which only made me grin wider. He was so easy to mess with.

"Come on." He stepped around me and continued down the hall. "Let's get this over with."

I followed him around the corner and down another long hallway until we entered a door at the very end.

Of course, he would choose a study as far away from others as possible. Aside from Kieran, Alaric preferred to keep his own company as much as possible.

He went directly to his desk and took a seat before gesturing at one of the dark red velvet chairs across from him. I ignored him and walked around slowly, continuing my perusal of his space, partly to annoy him but mostly because I was curious.

Despite Alaric and I disliking each other, we were similar in a lot of ways. We were the same age, both of us had grown up in the shadows of others at House Harker, we both claimed Kieran as a friend, and we were both ambitious and more than willing to be cutthroat when needed. Despite all of that, our ideal workspaces fell under the "different" category and not the "similar" one.

"Are you sure this is your study?" I frowned, glancing around dramatically. "There's nothing in here. Do you just sit at your desk and glare at anyone who dares to enter your domain?"

"You are literally surrounded by floor-to-ceiling bookshelves, all of which are full," he replied evenly. "Now if you'll just—"

"There's nothing on your desk, though." I perched on the corner of his very large, very empty desk and tossed one leg over the other. The movement made the fabric part, leaving most of my right thigh exposed.

A muscle ticked just below Alaric's right eye, and I gave him a lazy smile.

"It's okay." I leaned over and reached out to pet his hand, which was clenched so tightly into a fist that I was surprised there wasn't blood leaking out. The movement gave him a view straight down my dress. "I won't tell anyone that you hide out in here all day just to play pretend advisor."

"Get. Your. Ass. Off. My. Desk," he ground out. "I know what you're doing, and I didn't have time for it when we were kids, and I sure as shit don't have time for it now."

I snickered before sliding off his desk and onto one of the velvet chairs that were every bit as uncomfortable as they looked. While my aunt liked to invite people into her study to discuss things, Alaric made it very clear that people only needed to state their business and get out.

"You make it so easy to push your buttons." I laughed. "Just checking to see if maybe you'd developed a personality over these last few years."

"It's a shame you didn't trade out your personality for one less annoying," he sniped back.

"Looks like that's something you and Marvina agree on," I said dryly.

He snorted, making the sound somehow seem intelligent, and pulled out a stack of papers from a drawer. "I spoke with Carmilla earlier this week and drafted up a dissolution based on the marriage contract between you and Demetri. Even without the recent events, they're in violation of several stipulations. Marvina will likely push back just to avoid looking weak, so I kept it simple for now."

"She will absolutely fight it." I held my hand out, but Alaric just stared at me. Shadows be damned. He was so frustrating.

Keeping my left hand outstretched, I braced my other elbow on the desk and plopped my chin into my palm. If he wanted to be childish, I could play that game too. It's not like I had anywhere else to be.

After a minute, he caved and slapped the papers into my hand, then looked towards the door in clear dismissal.

Nice try.

"Did Carmilla also tell you that I wanted to support House Harker?"

"She might have mentioned it." He leaned back in his chair and gave me an appraising look. "I assumed you'd be assuming the role of the House Harlot."

"That does have a fun ring to it." I let my eyes wander over his face.

Even I had to admit that you'd have to be blind not to find Alaric attractive. His skin was a rich dark brown that seemed to glow against the well-fitted black clothes he always wore.

I'd witnessed more than one courtier openly admire the chiseled jawline, sharp cheekbones, and striking eyes that made up his handsome face. His mouth was wide with lips that I would have dreamed about kissing if they were on literally anyone else.

Those gorgeous lips flattened into a hard line, and one corner of my mouth tugged up into a lopsided grin.

While Kieran knew how gorgeous he was and absolutely loved the attention, Alaric always seemed to be uncomfortable when others checked him out. I was pretty sure that was the reason he always wore nothing but simple black clothes instead of the bright clothing Kieran always donned. Alaric was more than happy to blend into the background and let Kieran attract all the attention.

But those goddamn eyes of his always drew people in. They reminded me of the ocean with their dominant sea-foam green and the turquoise lines that weaved through them.

Truth be told, one of the reasons I loved to annoy him so much was because I loved to see the turquoise color spread, making his already beautiful eyes truly extraordinary. I'd thought about telling him that before but decided that if he knew just how much I adored his eyes, he'd find a way to deny me the pleasure of seeing them in their true glory.

So instead, I always kept my tone teasing. That way I could both annoy him and admire him at the same time.

"With that gorgeous face of yours, I think you'd be better suited to the title of House Harlot," I drawled. "You'd just have to pull that stick out of your ass." Turquoise fractures bled through the light green, and I snickered. So easy to rile. "Look, you know that I'm good at negotiations. The same ones I was working on for House Laurent would work for House Harker. We'll just have to tweak them a little."

"We?" He arched an eyebrow at me.

"I'm not trying to step on your toes or make your life harder," I said quietly. "We had similar instruction, Alaric. You know what I'm capable of. I'm not asking you to be my best friend and dress in matching outfits every day. I'm just asking you to work with me."

I kept silent while he stared at me and thought over my words. His eyes roamed over my dress, and I saw the disapproval in his face, but still, he said nothing. It was just a damn dress and had no bearing on my ability to think. It wasn't any more scandalous than what most of the other Moroi in this House wore.

"You were raised and trained to be a wife. Nothing more. All those years of education were just so you wouldn't make a fool of yourself," he said matter-of-factly. "You were meant to serve House Harker by joining House Laurent and improving our strained relations, and you failed spectacularly."

I stiffened, unable to keep the hurt from flashing across my face. He began pulling out scrolls and papers, setting them in organized little piles on his desk as he barreled on.

"You may have left that House, but they were probably close to throwing you out of it anyway. You still act like a spoiled little brat, Samara."

"Don't hold back." My jaw flexed. "Tell me how you really feel."

"I have no choice but to work with you because Carmilla requested this." He raised his eyes to look at me, his expression cold and full of disdain. "It's a waste of everyone's time and this House's resources, but congrats, you'll get your way. For now. I'm sure you'll fuck it up and even Carmilla will have to admit it was a mistake."

I was practically vibrating with anger and the need to reach across the desk and slam Alaric's head into it repeatedly, but I took a deep breath and swallowed down my rage.

He wanted a reaction out of me, something he could add to the list of why I was unsuited for this task, but I refused to give him that.

"Thank you for drawing up the first draft of the marriage dissolution." I rose from my seat, my head held high. "I'll make the corrections to it this afternoon and run them by you tomorrow morning before we send it off to House Laurent."

"Fine." He waved a hand in casual dismissal.

"Fine," I echoed and left without another word.

I FORCED myself to take calm, measured steps as I left, even though I wanted to stomp out and toss some stuff on the floor for good measure.

But I wouldn't give Alaric the satisfaction of knowing just how much he'd gotten to me.

Fucking prick.

Once I was down the hallway and around the corner, I stopped and leaned against the wall. I'd forgotten just how much Alaric got under my skin when he wanted to.

After a few deep breaths, I was settled enough to acknowledge that I had also behaved badly. I'd started needling him right away and pushing his buttons, which only encouraged him to do the same. It was an old habit that I'd fallen back into instinctively the same way I'd slipped back into my easy friendship with Kieran.

Nevertheless, I was older now, and I needed to do better. I couldn't dictate how Alaric acted, only my own behavior and actions. He might still view me as a spoiled, privileged daughter of House Harker, but I wouldn't make it easy for him.

In fact, I'd make him work for it. A devious smirk slowly spread across my lips. Nothing would annoy Alaric more than me succeeding and proving every insult he'd ever hurled at me wrong.

The game of annoying the hell out of each other would continue. I was just changing the rules.

With a new goal in mind, I continued down the hallway. I needed to find a space to work in.

Technically, my suite was more than big enough and had a large sitting area that I could use as a study, but I always preferred to keep a separate workspace so that my suite could be a place to relax and take a break from the pressures of work.

I walked past the closed doors of Carmilla's study. I couldn't hear any voices from within, so either she was deep in thought over some problem, or she had activated the silencer spell that was standard in all of our studies.

More closed doors lined the halls, and I kept walking.

At least whatever empty space I found would be far away from Alaric.

The hallway eventually ended, and my options were right or left, both of which were dead-ends with only a couple of rooms.

Tentatively, I pivoted left. It seemed unlikely that the room I thought of would be available because despite it being a small space, it had the best view on this floor.

But when I saw that the door was open, my steps quickened. I peeked inside and, to my delight, the study appeared to be unclaimed. It was almost half the size of Alaric's, with a desk on the right side of the room, angled so that you could see both the door and the window.

My feet carried me to the floor-to-ceiling window of their own accord, and I rested my hands against the glass as I looked out.

From this high up, I could see over the thick stone walls that protected all of House Harker to the sandy beach beyond. The tide rolled in gently over the shore, making it glisten as the waves pulled back before pushing inward again.

When we were growing up, this was where Kieran and I would work on our studies or just hang out. Occasionally, Rynn and Cali would come visit me, and we would use this space as well. It had never officially been mine, but looking back, Carmilla must have told everyone to leave it unoccupied so that we could use it.

Glancing around, I noticed that it was very clean, despite not being in use.

I wasn't surprised by the lack of clutter, but why would the staff bother dusting a room that no one was using? Even the rich wood of the desk shone like it had been polished recently.

"Thought you might claim this one."

I smiled over my shoulder at where Kieran was leaning against the door-frame. His loose blond hair fell around his face in soft curls, and his eyes shone with pleased satisfaction.

"Are you the reason this one is still free?" I tossed the marriage dissolution draft onto the desk as I hopped up onto it.

He shrugged. "No one has ever officially claimed it. It's mostly been used by visiting nobles and representatives from other Houses. One of the studies down the hall was free, so I helped the most recent occupant move to that one this morning."

"Thank you," I said honestly as I leaned back onto my palms and studied my new space.

The wall opposite the desk was mostly filled with bookshelves, but there was still some wall area left. Maybe I could get a miniature version of the map from Marvina's office and hang it there.

Thinking back to my encounter with Alaric, I grimaced. "My morning had a bit of a rough start, so this was a pleasant surprise."

Kieran pushed off the doorframe and took a seat in one of the chairs facing the desk. Then he swung his long legs over the arm of the chair so that he was sitting sideways and let his head hang back. It didn't look comfortable at all, but it was such a Kieran move that it tugged another smile out of me.

Kieran was as good at cheering me up as Alaric was at pissing me off. It was a cruel joke of fate that they were best friends.

"You were in Alaric's office for less than fifteen minutes, and you already pissed him off." He smirked. "Impressive."

"He's the one who pissed me off!" I seethed as flickers of the anger I'd felt at Alaric earlier caused my body to tense up again. "Whatever. Glad to see that you're still taking his side."

"Did you do that thing where you flash unnecessary amounts of skin just to make him uncomfortable?" He looked pointedly at the bare thigh I was now showing. When I glowered at him, he just laughed. "I thought so."

"Fine," I admitted, my shoulders slumping a bit. "I've already acknowl-edged to myself that I could have behaved better, and I will do so in the future, but we both know it won't make a difference. He's never going to change his mind about me, and I don't care."

"Hmm," Kieran mused but didn't deny my statement.

"Anyway," I drawled, "I'm going to review the draft that he wrote up for dissolving the marriage between me and Demetri. I promised to bring all the changes to his office tomorrow morning."

I leaned over and started flipping through the paperwork. Despite Alaric claiming to have just pulled together the basics, he appeared to have done a thorough job. I chewed on my bottom lip as guilt began to set in. Carmilla had no doubt ordered him to do this, but he still obviously put a lot of effort into it.

"You really going to go through with it?" Kieran's tone was curious with a touch of something else that I couldn't quite place.

"They'd have to work very hard to change my mind," I said simply, already half-focused on a particularly tricky wording I'd stumbled onto in the third paragraph. "I spent the last three years trying to make not only my marriage work but also demonstrate that I was an asset to House Laurent. They put zero effort in. If anything, they worked against me. I realize that this marriage was arranged to better our relations with that house of vipers, but it just wasn't working."

I blinked several times when I realized I'd just been reading the same sentence over and over again. With a sigh, I dropped the document back onto the desk and focused on Kieran once more. He'd repositioned himself so that he was slouching against the back of the chair with his legs stretched out in front of him, giving the impression of languid ease.

"I wasn't happy." I tried to keep my tone even, but a little of the pain I'd felt leaked through, and Kieran's expression hardened.

"What did he do?" His eyes scoured my face as if he would find the answer he sought there.

Seeing Kieran's protectiveness over me helped ease some of the pain left over from my time at House Laurent. I'd been alone there, but here I had the full support of my aunt. And I had Kieran.

"Nothing I shouldn't have expected." I let out a mirthless laugh. "I knew that our marriage was a political one. There was never anything romantic about it. We didn't exchange love letters, we exchanged updates about our Houses. Updates that were carefully reviewed by others because, despite the impending marriage between our Houses, information is still something that should be tightly controlled."

I could still remember walking to Carmilla's office every morning and handing over my drafts. We'd discuss them over tea and make slight adjustments to make sure we weren't giving House Laurent, Marvina in particular, something that could be used against us later.

Demetri had almost certainly done the same. I snorted at that thought because he probably never wrote them to begin with. That was likely either done by Marvina herself or one of her underlings. Never once in our three years of marriage had I ever seen Demetri do any work other than visiting the Houses to "strengthen relations with House Laurent."

I supposed sleeping with various courtiers was one way to strengthen relations.

"Our marriage wasn't something built on love, but I did think it would be one built on respect and loyalty. And monogamy." Understanding dawned on

Kieran's face then. "I know," I groaned and slapped my hands across my face. "I was an idiot."

"I wouldn't say that." He winced. "You found out that monogamy wasn't part of the deal, I'm guessing?"

The sounds of moaning and a squeaking mattress replayed painfully in my mind.

"Yeah," I said dryly. "Walked in on Demetri showing a hell of a lot more enthusiasm for his mistress of the week than he ever had in our bed."

"Well, fuck him," Kieran scoffed.

"Nah, I don't think I want to do that anymore," I deadpanned.

He chuckled, and I couldn't help but laugh too. The more I laughed, the more emotions poured out of me from the whole situation. Hurt and rejection from Demetri's betrayal. Humiliation from the meeting in Marvina's study. Rage at both of them for, well, everything.

And guilt because despite all that had happened, I was so fucking happy to be home. My laughter gained a maniacal edge until I was laughing so hard, tears streamed down my cheeks.

Kieran waited until I'd wiped the tears from my eyes and rested my hands on my thighs to say anything.

He murmured, "I'm sorry, Sam."

He leaned forward in the chair and placed his hands on top of mine, giving them a gentle squeeze. Heat burned in my eyes as more tears threatened to fall at the simple gesture, but I blinked them back. I hated crying, and I'd been doing a lot of that lately.

Kieran added, "I know that you did everything you could to make it work. No one has ever doubted your dedication to House Harker."

"Tell that to Alaric," I muttered.

"You should cut him some slack," Kieran said carefully. "He's been under a lot of pressure lately."

"He's always under pressure." I shot him an annoyed look. "You don't need to defend him constantly, you know?"

He let his head drop back once more so that he was staring up at the ceiling. "Am I once again going to have to play peacekeeper between you two? Because that shit was getting old before you left."

"Please," I snorted. "You loved any opportunity to be the center of attention. It's why you love being a courtier so much."

The House Kieran was born into was one of the lower-ranking ones. Both of his parents were high-ranking courtiers and had arranged for Kieran to travel to other Houses to better represent their interests. House Harker had been the first House he'd been assigned to, and we didn't want him to leave because everyone here adored him.

Kieran felt the same, and luckily his parents had been thrilled because it would be hard to get a more prestigious House unless he landed in the Sovereign Court.

"You and Alaric have your talents, and I have mine," he said smugly.

"I wasn't aware that being able to schmooze for hours amongst boring nobility counted as a talent."

"We both know that's not true." He gave me a cocky look. "How many times have I had to rescue you before you mouthed off to some nobility creep or fell asleep face-first while listening to the ramblings of an elder?"

The corner of his lips tilted up into that stupid, mischievous grin of his that always sent my thoughts scattering when we were growing up. My eyes trailed down his body, snagging on where his shirt had ridden up, giving me a glimpse of his muscular abs.

Despite spending most of his time behind the safety of our walls, Kieran had always taken training seriously.

I could still remember Rynn and Cali dragging me off to spy on his training when we were younger. He'd been well aware of our antics and always made a show of pulling off his shirt early in his workout to give us a better view. Sometimes he'd even do some ridiculous poses and wink at us before concentrating on training.

It was during those workouts that I couldn't resist flirting back with him, much to Alaric's disapproval, but we'd never gone beyond flirting.

Kieran followed my gaze and instead of pulling his shirt down, he shifted, causing it to ride a little higher.

I swallowed as want and heat spread through me.

My marriage, as I knew it, was over. Even if we hadn't signed the paperwork yet, Demetri had made it quite clear that he didn't view monogamy as a part of our marriage.

I thought back to what I had told Rynn and Cali about my new life motto. *Want something. Take something.*

"So..." I crossed one leg over the other, causing even more skin to show. Kieran's eyes tracked the movement, and the gold threads weaving through his deep brown irises started to blaze even brighter. "Is that clever tongue of yours good for anything other than charming your way out of trouble?"

"Yes." His voice was deep as his heated gaze traveled slowly upward, taking the time to drink in every one of my curves. "It's also quite good at charming me into trouble."

CHAPTER SEVEN

—

Samara

"Is that so?" The corners of my lips curved up as I brazenly took him in.

The golden streaks in his eyes grew wider, and my heart beat a little faster every time more of the brown gave way to gold.

"As much as I enjoyed this game when we were growing up, I'm not sure I can play it now. At least, not with the same rules." His voice was still playful, but there was now an underlying edge to it.

Still, he didn't move, giving me the choice of how far I wanted to take this. I waited for the guilt to hit me. For the logical voice in my head to remind me that I was still technically married, but the voice remained silent, and the guilt never came.

My heart had never been part of my marriage, and my mind knew that it was over. All that was left were the details of ending it.

There was no reason, logical or otherwise, to deny this any longer.

"Same game." Exhilaration rushed through my body as I stood and strode over to the door to close it.

I leaned my back against the solid wood and reached my hand out to the side where the silencing spell was engraved into the wall. My fingers nimbly ran over the glyph to activate it, and then I pushed off the door, my hips swaying as I returned to the desk and perched on it once more.

I leaned back and spread my legs wide instead of crossing them. Kieran went completely still. "New rules," I cooed.

"Fuck." His eyes turned completely gold, and I laughed huskily.

"The only orgasms I've had these past three years are the ones I gave myself."

An ache pulsed from between my thighs as my heart continued its attempt to pound its way out of my chest. I'd had so many wicked dreams of Kieran over the years, but I never once thought they would become a reality.

"That's a shame." His voice took on a rough quality that had me wanting to clench my thighs together.

"Are you going to do something about it?" I arched an eyebrow at him when he continued to sit there. "Or should I see if someone else is available?"

Before the last word was out of my mouth, Kieran leapt from the chair and closed the distance between us. He nudged my knees further apart so he could slip between my legs as he braced his arms on either side of me. My pulse pounded as I held his gaze, acutely aware of the barely-there inch separating us.

"I've been dreaming about what you taste like for longer than I care to admit," he murmured as he ducked his head to kiss my neck.

A breathy sound escaped me at the touch of his warm lips against my skin, and then his hands slipped under my ass. He jerked me forward until I was flush against him. I slid my hands under his shirt, running my fingers over the taut muscles of his stomach, and he groaned against my skin, his fingers digging into me harder.

My fingers trailed up his back until I reached his hair just as I felt his fangs graze my neck. I yanked his head back, heat striking through my core when he let out a growl of irritation.

"No blood for you," I said in a breathy voice. "Not yet."

"Is that one of the rules?" He gave me a sly grin.

I tugged on his hair again. "Yes."

"Any others I should know about?" he asked lazily as one of his hands moved to graze the inside of my thigh. My thoughts scattered at the sensation, and he let out a deep, knowing chuckle. "Any other rules, Sam?"

"I'm sure,"—I gasped as his fingers brushed over my panties—"I'll think of something."

"Mmm," he hummed as he continued to trace slow patterns up and down my thighs. I could practically feel the wetness dripping out from within my core, and in the spirit of embracing my new wanton self, I widened my legs even more. Kieran growled in approval, which only further flamed my desire.

"You want to know what I taste like?" I released my hold on his hair and leaned back onto the desk. "Then find out. If you make it good, I might even let you come back for another taste."

I gave him a challenging look, and he returned it with a salacious grin before dropping to his knees.

He looked at me from between my thighs, and I almost came right then and there. I tried to maintain the haughty expression on my face, but the smirk on his told me he saw through it.

"You'll be coming to *me* after this," he said arrogantly. "And I'll make *you* beg for it."

"Unlikely," I retorted. "You think that I'll—"

I was cut off when he licked a blazing path on the inside of my thigh as he settled my legs over his shoulders and pulled me further towards him. I bit my lip to contain the wanton moan that threatened to escape, determined to hold out for as long as possible because the competitive side of me didn't want to let Kieran know just how quickly he could make me come undone.

Same game. New rules.

We weren't just flirting anymore. Touching, tasting, and fucking were now on the menu, but that didn't mean I was going to let him think that he had me wrapped around his finger. I wouldn't be begging him for anything.

Two fingers slid beneath the fabric of my panties and circled my clit. I cursed as I jerked at the new sensation, but Kieran had a strong hold on my thighs.

He laughed, and I felt the heat of his breath against my skin, which sent shivers up my spine.

"Already so wet for me."

"I was thinking about someone else," I lied. It probably would have been more convincing if my voice hadn't been so breathy.

"Oh?" He leaned back, and his nimble fingers pulled my underwear down and over my legs before he dropped them to the floor. "Tell me about this someone else. I'd *love* to know who my competition is."

He gave me a bemused look, clearly not buying my story at all, and arched an eyebrow as if daring me to lie once more. Before I could piece together another lie, he moved forward and that clever tongue of his slipped into my pussy at the same moment he ran a finger over my clit.

I was so goddamned keyed up that I let out a strangled scream as pleasure ripped through me. So much for playing hard to get. It'd taken him less than a minute to give me a better orgasm than I'd had in years.

I thought he'd pull back to gloat at making me come so quickly, but instead, it only seemed to drive Kieran mad. He devoured me like he was starving and I was the first good meal he'd had in weeks. One hand reached up, slowly trailing over every curve and dip in my body until he reached my breast, squeezing it at the same time as he sucked my clit.

A whimper tore out of me as he pushed me towards the edge again. *Fuck.* My body was still trembling from the last orgasm, yet I could already feel another one building. A fang grazed my clit as he released it, and I arched my back, trying to chase the sensation.

I started to protest when I felt him pull away, but I screamed instead when two fingers plunged into me.

He feverishly yanked the top of my dress down, freeing my breasts, and ran a thumb over one of my hard nipples. I shivered when he did it again.

My eyes closed as pleasure rippled through me with every thrust of his fingers.

"Fuck, Sam," Kieran growled, and I slowly opened my eyes to meet his blazing gold gaze as he took me in, spread out on the desk. "You taste better than I ever dreamed."

"You dreamed of this?" A playful grin spilled across my lips.

He gave me a wolfish one in return. "You gonna tell me you haven't?"

"Never crossed my mind." *Lie, lie, lie.*

"Such a liar you are."

He thrust his fingers inside me and I bucked at the sudden fullness. A mewling sound I'd never once made in my life loosened from my lips as he continued to slowly push his fingers in and out, his other hand toying with my nipple.

"I *have* dreamed about this. About what you would taste like." He drew his fingers out of my dripping pussy before sucking them clean.

There was no doubt in my mind that my eyes were pure violet right now as I watched with complete rapture as Kieran finished cleaning his fingers. A deep chuckle spilled from his lips while he reached down to teasingly graze my clit.

I raised my hips to meet his fingers, but the bastard pulled his hand away and stood up. A needy snarl ripped out of me at being denied what I so desperately wanted. I tried to shove myself up from the desk, but he leaned over and pushed me down with one hand.

"Is there something you want?" he purred, and the hand that wasn't holding me down trailed down between my breasts, past my stomach before stopping so achingly close to where I wanted those fingers again. "I'll make it easy for you."

He bent down and sucked a nipple into his mouth. I gasped at the contact, rapidly losing control over this situation and not giving one single fuck.

"Tell me what you want, Sam." Kieran moved to suck my other nipple, eliciting another whimper from me. "Fingers, tongue, or cock?"

Cock! I screamed internally but kept the word from leaping from my lips.

If Kieran was able to undo me this much with just his tongue and fingers, it would be all over once he fucked me with his cock. I had just enough of my mind left to be terrified of that and what it would mean.

"Tongue," I rasped.

He tutted, "We both know that's not what you want."

I raised my chin and met his heated stare. "Tongue," I repeated, my voice louder this time.

"No," he said with a smirk. "We'll compromise, though. I want to watch you come undone before I lick you clean." Before I could argue, two fingers thrust into me while his thumb pushed down on my clit.

"FUCK!" I screamed.

Another finger joined the other two while Kieran built up to a brutal pace. My hips ground against his hand as filthy words spilled from my lips.

"That's it, baby," Kieran groaned when my pussy tightened around his fingers. "Come for me again. I want you dripping all over my fucking hand."

I cried out as he pushed me over the edge again.

He let me ride his fingers for a few more seconds before his tongue swirled around my clit and I fucking detonated.

Thank fuck I activated the silencing spell because I'm pretty sure my screams would have shaken the entire building, and Carmilla probably didn't want to hear that. Alaric probably didn't either, but fuck him.

I laid there while panting, trying to catch my breath as Kieran slowly drew his tongue over my slick heat, and I shivered at the sensation. Then he drew himself over me and plunged his mouth into mine as he kissed me deeply. The taste of my pleasure on his tongue was fucking hot as hell, and I gasped slightly as he pulled away.

"You're welcome," he said in a satisfactory tone.

The pleased look on his face was enough to get at least some of my brain back on track.

I pushed myself up, and he backed up to give me space. Slowly, as if I didn't have a care in the world, I pulled my dress back up and got myself sorted.

"That was adequate, I suppose." I shrugged.

"Adequate?" He arched an eyebrow at me. "You're sitting in a puddle made of your own pleasure. If you stood up right now, we both know it would be running down your thighs, and that was just a warm-up."

Fuck. Me. There was no way that was just a warm-up.

My fucking clit was still twitching, and he wasn't wrong about where I was sitting. Even now, I could feel my dress sticking to my skin.

I pursed my lips. "Somehow, you're even cockier now than you were in our youth," I said breezily.

"You're just sore because I didn't show exactly how *cocky* I can be." It took a valiant effort on my part not to drop my eyes to his crotch, and based on the way his mouth twitched in amusement, I knew Kieran was perfectly aware of my inner struggle.

"This was a good show on your part. Maybe we should just leave it on a good note." I plastered a bored expression on my face. "I'm sure you would enjoy thrusting wildly over me for a few seconds before spasming and rolling over, but I think I'll pass."

He let out a low laugh and once again leaned over me to whisper in my ear, "We both know that you want my cock buried inside you at the same time my fangs pierce that lovely neck of yours. You'll be screaming my name."

"Whatever you need to tell yourself, Kier." I tapped my finger against his chest. "I think we both know that you'll be the one begging for another taste."

Heat and amusement flitted across his features at the challenge I'd just thrown down. My hand flattened against his chest as he leaned in to give me a quick kiss before turning to leave. Just as he opened the door, he glanced back at me and grinned. "I like this new game."

CHAPTER EIGHT

—

Kieran

I stared at the closed door for a solid minute, convincing myself not to barge back in and toss Sam back onto that damned desk and bury myself inside her.

At the time, I'd meant every word I'd said about making her beg for it, but now as I stood here in the hallway, staring at the closed door with a raging hard-on, I realized just how much of a mistake that was.

Sam *loved* challenges.

If you told her she couldn't do something, not only would she do it, but she'd do it in the most spectacular way possible just to rub your nose in it.

She was a deliciously spiteful thing, and I had always absolutely adored that about her.

Until now.

"Fuck me," I muttered before forcing myself to step away from the door and across the hall to the study I'd claimed as my workspace.

This morning, I'd been very proud of myself for securing the study directly across from me for Sam. I had a feeling she would be drawn to it again, so I'd helped the visiting noble move and then cleaned it up. It hadn't taken long, and the delight on Sam's face had been entirely worth it, but there was no way I could now sit at my desk all day and stare at that closed door.

Or worse, knowing Sam, she would open it at some point and perch her luscious ass on the desk and continue her work just to taunt me.

I spun away from my study and headed towards the stairs, trying to get a hold on myself. I had some appointments later in the morning with some visiting courtiers, but nothing that required much preparation on my part. That meant I had a couple of hours free.

A distraction. That's what I needed. Just something to take my mind off that throaty sound Sam made just before she came that was part moan and part plea. Or the way the violet fractures of her eyes wound their way through the deep purple reminding me of how the night sky was often painted in Unseelie murals.

I sucked in a deep breath when my cock strained against my breeches as I recalled the feeling of her thighs tightening around me while my tongue devoured every inch of her.

Distraction. Right.

Normally, I didn't train until the afternoon, but there were always some off-duty rangers around. Someone who would likely spar with me.

"What are you doing?"

I turned from where I'd stopped in the middle of the hallway and saw Alaric walking out of Carmilla's study. He took in my disheveled appearance, eyes darting down to the bulge in my pants before he gave me an exasperated look.

"Really, Kier?" He shook his head and stepped around me.

I trailed after him, trying in vain to adjust my pants to make myself more comfortable.

This was far from the first time Alaric had caught me in a compromising position. If anything, this was tame compared to the rest. Thankfully, my dick started to calm down by the time we reached his office, and I settled down in one of his chairs.

"It's too early for you to be smelling like pussy in my study," Alaric said in an annoyed tone as he stared forward.

"It's never too early for that," I scoffed as I slid a scrutinizing glance over his face and noticed him clenching and unclenching his jaw.

That was the Alaric equivalent of screaming and punching a wall. He must still be really pissed about his encounter with Samara earlier this morning, which meant I should probably avoid mentioning what I'd just done with her.

Alaric sighed. "Do I even want to know who your dalliance for the week is this time?"

Shit.

I paused, thinking about what I should tell him.

Alaric wasn't just my best friend, he was my first friend. Everyone had an agenda in the House I grew up in, including my parents. They arranged "friends" for me throughout my childhood, making sure I only associated with the children of Moroi who could provide my parents with political connections.

When I got shipped off to House Harker at fourteen years old, I was well-practiced in wearing different masks.

The dutiful son.

The charming young man.

The future heartbreaker.

A different mask for every occasion.

I excelled at determining which one would work best and continued to add more to my collection, but being myself was another matter.

I barely remembered how to do that when I was alone, and I certainly didn't know how to do it around others.

Alaric and Samara were the same age as me and both had grown up in this house and had a bitter rivalry. They fought over literally everything. Including me.

Alaric had been the first one to get past my defenses and see the real me, something he still held over Sam's head, much to my annoyance. The only reason he'd "won" the friend card first was because Sam was my first serious crush and I struggled with how to act around her. I thought that she would like me more if I wore the charming mask all the time.

It was years before I let her start to see through the cracks and get a peek at the real me. Even then, I still held back so much.

Like how devastated I was when she left for Drudonia and how I counted the days until she would come back for various House events. The last thing I wanted was her pity over how fucked-up I really was.

But when she left for Drudonia, it was a rude awakening to the reality of my situation.

My crush had turned into something so much more than that, but I knew Sam and I couldn't be together. She'd agreed to the marriage between her and Demetri when she was fourteen years old, a month before I'd arrived, and from everything I'd observed, she was happy about it.

I knew that Sam had the option to break off the arrangement before they wed when she turned twenty-one, and I'd secretly hoped that she would.

But I'd been too scared to ever say something to her about it.

There were a lot of things I could handle in life, but a rejection from Sam wasn't one of them.

Samara had thrown herself into preparing for the marriage even as she supported Carmilla at House Harker however she could.

I knew she had a crush on me, but she never gave any hints that it was anything more than that. So I kept my true feelings to myself and pretended to only miss her as a friend and nothing more even as it shredded my fucking soul in two.

While I hoped that someday Alaric and Sam would figure out a way to hash out their differences and at least become civil towards each other, it seemed unlikely. Though, with Sam back at House Harker, and our... evolving friendship... my role as peacekeeper between the two of them was about to get a lot more complicated.

Alaric zeroed in on my silence, and he scrutinized me further. His green eyes wholly focused on me as he thought about what could possibly cause me to hesitate.

"Fuck," he ground out, crossing one arm across his stomach while the other rubbed at his face. "Tell me you didn't."

"Are you asking me to lie to you?" I asked in a teasing tone even though I couldn't hold back my wince. Shit. He was going to be so pissed.

The turquoise cracks woven through Alaric's light green eyes spread for a second as his temper flared before retreating. Apparently, he wasn't in the mood to be teased about this. Even when Samara wasn't in his presence, she *still* somehow managed to be one of the few people who could get my friend to lose control.

"Why her?" His voice was even, if a little flatter than usual. The tightness across his face still betrayed him, though. Alaric was beyond pissed about this turn of events.

He would just have to fucking deal with it.

"Don't act so surprised." I shrugged. "You know her and I have always had a complicated friendship. We couldn't do anything about it before, but now she's back, and things are different."

"She's still married to the Heir of another House!" Alaric threw his hands in the air. "You're thinking with your dick and not your head!"

"Please, we both know that marriage is over and was probably a mistake to begin with. Marvina is going to rule House Laurent until her last dying breath, and given that she's fourth generation, we have no idea when that's going to be." I arched an eyebrow, daring him to tell me I was wrong, but he just shook his head and looked away. I smiled victoriously.

The first generation of Moroi, Velesians, and Furies had burned fast and bright. Most hadn't lived more than twenty years after their transformation from being human, but every generation since then lived a little longer.

Those who belonged to the fourth generation were well over eighty years old now but still looked as if they were in their mid-to-late thirties or forties. Their aging had slowed drastically, and we assumed that our generation would be the same. How long we all would live was anyone's guess.

"Besides," I continued, "we both know that prick is probably balls deep in someone who is very much *not* his wife right now."

"It's still a complication that House Harker doesn't need," Alaric argued, refusing to let this go.

"No, it's a complication that *you* don't need right now." I gave him a flat look. "But you're just going to have to deal with it."

"Whatever," he said flippantly. "Just don't start shoving your tongue down her throat in front of me. I don't need more nightmare fuel."

"I'll be sure to protect your delicate sensibilities," I retorted in an equally flippant tone.

Although, with the challenge that Sam had laid down, it would probably be a while before my tongue was anywhere near her. Despite my raging hard-on earlier, I wouldn't be begging for shit. Sam wasn't the only one who loved a challenge.

"Thanks," he said dryly. When he rubbed his face again, I noticed that his expression hadn't loosened. Faint dark circles were present under his eyes too.

Something was deeply troubling him.

"Has there been another attack?" I asked quietly, all thoughts about my new game with Sam forgotten.

Alaric's eyes flashed to the open door, and I got up to close it. It seemed unlikely that anyone would be eavesdropping on us from this floor, but Alaric was clearly worried about this, so I kept my thoughts to myself.

Once the door was shut and I was settled back in my chair, Alaric reached behind him and brushed his fingers against a dark red symbol that had been painted against the wall. All Moroi could perform blood magic, and a silencing spell was one of the first we learned, right after healing.

"Three more outposts have been hit," he admitted. "Two in Velesian territory, but one of them was ours."

I swallowed. "Survivors?"

He shook his head.

"That brings us to eight attacks in the last year." Only a few of them were public knowledge. The outposts that had been small and remote had been kept secret.

Technically, each House was supposed to be responsible for patrolling a section of the Moroi realm. In reality, the Sovereign House and House Harker oversaw everything. The Sovereigns commanded more rangers, but we had Vail. He was cunning and knew the wilds better than anyone. It was the reason he was put in charge of investigating the attacks.

Unfortunately for everyone, despite his skills, we were no closer to knowing what the hell was going on or how we could protect our outposts against future attacks.

Each of the Houses had taken over a Fae fortress to serve as their stronghold. The abandoned fortifications were perfect at first because they could easily house a thousand or more Moroi. The walls were not only thick but seeped with magic that we still didn't fully understand. We only knew that it kept monsters out.

On top of that, we'd added our blood wards to protect us from the wraiths. But even the largest of the fortresses had run out of space decades ago.

The Velesians were in the same situation. The Furies didn't have that problem, but nobody wanted to live with them because most of us still viewed them as potential threats. True, it had been a while since a Furie had lost control, but the last incident had resulted in over a hundred Moroi and Velesian deaths. It had taken half a dozen Furies to bring the culprit down, and only three of them had walked away from that fight.

When Furies lost themselves, they went mad... and that madness leaked to everyone around them until everyone was swimming in a sea of blood and violence.

There was a reason some within the Houses and Velesian Packs called for the extermination of all Furies. They were a brutal weapon to be wielded against the beasts that prowled the night. But that weapon could just as easily be turned on us.

Even if some were willing to take that risk and live closer to them, the Furie realm lacked the resources to support large populations because most of their territory consisted of the badlands.

The solution had been to build outposts throughout the Moroi and Velesian realms to protect trade routes, add more farmlands, and provide housing.

We'd done the best we could to make them secure, but clearly, it wasn't enough. If word spread about how fast the outposts were falling, people would panic, and we couldn't house and feed everyone within the strongholds, not indefinitely.

It was cruel, and I knew it deeply bothered Alaric. The two of us only lived in House strongholds because we were born into noble families, but the Sovereigns had decreed to keep it quiet, and the leadership of the Velesians and Furies agreed. Well, the Furies did. I'd heard that the Velesians were less than pleased about the decision but were going along with it for now.

"Is this the reason why there have been so many closed-door meetings in Carmilla's study?" I asked.

Alaric nodded and unrolled a map across his desk. I rose from the chair and leaned over the desk, watching as he crossed out each of the outposts that had been attacked recently.

"If there is a pattern, I don't see it," I admitted. Not that this was in any way my area of expertise.

As a courtier, I hosted visiting nobles and representatives from other Houses when they came here. Frequently, I traveled to other Houses to help support our alliances with them... or gossip and collect valuable information for Carmilla.

During those visits, I'd stop at outposts along the way, so I was familiar with all the ones on the main routes. But seeing patterns or weaknesses in defenses was far outside my skillset.

"I haven't been able to find one either." Alaric ran a hand over his closely shorn hair before planting both hands back on the desk and staring at the map like he could force it to give him answers. "But we have to figure out something, and soon. The wraiths have found a way to slip through our wards.

We're quietly trying out new ones, but there is no way to know if they will work or not."

I swallowed past the icy dread taking root inside me. The wards around the Houses were considerably more powerful than the ones around the outposts thanks to the leftover Fae magic, so we were likely safe for now. But I had friends who lived in outposts, and all their lives were at risk. Plus, I spent a considerable amount of time traveling outside the safety of House Harker walls and had always considered the outposts secure. That was clearly no longer the case.

"Seems like most of the attacks are in the Velesian realm, with some spilling over in ours." I ran my fingers across the southwestern portion of the map. "Only one in Furie territory?"

"Yes, but that doesn't mean much." Alaric tapped a finger on the only outpost in Furie territory that had been crossed out. "Their outposts are almost all along the coastline. Nothing can survive in badlands, so they've never bothered to build any outposts there. Their outpost that was attacked was next to the Velesian border."

It was debatable whether the Furies had the best or worst territory out of all of us. They suffered the least attacks from wraiths and the other monsters that made Lunaria their home because the badlands served as a buffer between them and the rest of Lunaria. The only way to reach where most of their population lived was to cross the badlands, which meant almost certain death, or go along the coastline, which was heavily guarded.

But they also had the least amount of livable territory, because even the Furies couldn't survive in the badlands. The terrain was too arid to grow any crops, there was no food to hunt, and the harsh landscape made it impossible to establish reliable trade routes.

Sooner or later, they would have to expand into other territories.

That political nightmare would be something people like Alaric and Samara would have to deal with someday.

Not me, though. I excelled at finding secrets and playing host to visiting nobles and courtiers, but tedious negotiation was not in my skillset, and I had no interest in learning.

"Vail is coming," Alaric said casually.

I whipped my head up from the map. "When?"

"Three days. He's currently further north dealing with a pack of howlers. Carmilla wants to talk to him in person before he goes to visit the sites of the recent attacks."

I grimaced. Vail Ferenc was the Marshal of House Harker, which meant he was in charge of all of our rangers.

Both of his parents had been rangers, and Vail had quickly risen through the ranks. No one, not even me, could deny that he was gifted. The man had survived multiple wraith ambushes that would have left anyone else in pieces, not to mention all the fights he'd survived against the other terrors that roamed these lands.

He was vicious with a short temper, which was why Carmilla rarely called him back to the House.

Vail was a monster, but he was our monster.

He also hated Samara with every drop of blood in his veins.

"Well, with any luck, he'll provide his update and then be on his way back to the wilds where he fucking belongs." I crossed my arms stiffly, trying to ignore the knot of tension that was starting to form in my chest.

Alaric gave me a pointed look. "Vail has never wavered in his support of House Harker. He deserves our thanks and respect."

I rolled my eyes. "And he has it. Doesn't mean I have to like the guy or want to be around him."

Alaric shook his head and went back to staring at the map. If I left him to it, he'd stand like this all day.

"Come on." I rolled up the map before he could stop me and held it out of his reach when he tried to snatch it back. "You need to give that crafty mind of yours a break."

"I don't have time—"

"Just a quick break, I promise." I smirked at him and tossed the map onto the desk. "It won't take me long to beat the shit out of you."

His lips pursed together, suppressing a grin, and then he deactivated the silencing spell. "I have to let you win. Your fragile ego wouldn't be able to handle constantly losing to me otherwise."

I slapped him on the back as we sauntered towards the door. "Keep telling yourself that."

CHAPTER NINE

—

Samara

I WOKE WITH A START, my sweat-drenched sheets sticking to my skin. Whatever I'd been dreaming slipped away, just like it had for the last two mornings.

Ever since I learned that Vail was coming here.

Alaric had been the one to tell me, no doubt enjoying seeing how much it rattled me. He was such an ass.

Trembles raced up and down my body as the aftereffects of the nightmare slowly faded. It had been years since I'd had one. They were a frequent visitor to my mind in the years after my parents had been attacked and killed in front of me, but I was nothing if not a pro at compartmentalizing.

Swallowing over the lump in my throat, I shoved that memory into its prison once more and buried it deep inside my soul. Every once in a while, it would slip free for a night of terror, but it hadn't been this bad since I'd been a teenager.

I knew it was only happening now because of Vail.

One of the few good things about living at House Laurent for the past three years was that I never had to see the Marshal of House Harker. I knew when I returned home that I'd have to see him sooner or later, but I'd really been hoping for the latter.

I'd thrown myself into perfecting the marriage dissolution these past few days. Alaric and I still traded barbs, but we managed to work surprisingly well together despite our dislike. We both agreed that the dissolution was as good as it could get for the opening volley.

I was a little surprised that neither Demetri nor Marvina had contacted me in an attempt to smooth things over and convince me to come back to at the very least discuss things there.

They had to know that I would return to House Harker where I had a support system. At House Laurent, I'd been isolated, and they would have held more power in any negotiations. I'd expected Demetri to apologize in some shallow or meaningless way and then argue that our marriage could still work since everything was out in the open now. Marvina, I had expected to simply demand my return at once, but there had only been silence from House Laurent.

I'd mentioned my confusion about this to Alaric and that it made me suspicious, and he agreed that it was odd. Then he said something rude as if he couldn't stand the idea of having a civil conversation with me. Nothing unusual there.

We'd handed over our final draft to Carmilla last night, and she promised to send it first thing in the morning, which meant they'd have it early this afternoon. The strikers were fast fliers, and they'd make the trip to House Laurent in a few hours and then wait for them to send back a response.

I doubted we'd get one today, so I was going to be a nervous wreck for the next twenty-four hours at least. I just wanted this to be done.

Maybe I could do something to break Kieran and get him to beg tonight to distract me. I smirked and stood from my bed.

He'd remained strong since declaring that he'd never beg and that I certainly would. I'd come pretty close to getting him to give in yesterday when I'd left the door to my study open and perched on my desk to "ponder how I wanted to decorate my study."

At least, that was the excuse I'd given to Kieran when he demanded to know what the hell I was doing with my knee bent and leg propped up on the desk, causing most of my thigh to be on display. I'd slowly tapped my fingers against my leg, inching a little higher each time before dropping my hand.

The third time I did it, Kieran let out a groan and started to get up when Alaric had shown up and interrupted.

I'd been disappointed at being denied victory but had been extremely amused at Kieran trying to hide his rock-hard dick from Alaric. Given the annoyed expression on Alaric's face and the death glare he shot me, I was pretty sure Kieran's attempt had failed.

Golden sunlight warmed the hardwood floor as I padded over to the washroom. I felt my senses dull a little more with each step as night gave way to day.

Despite being used to it, I still hated feeling that loss every morning. I understood why some of the Moon Blessed chose to stay awake at night and sleep through the day. All sorts of monsters came out to play in the dark, making it far more dangerous than the day, but we were also at our strongest under the moonlight.

Besides, as long as you remained behind the walls and wards, you were safe no matter the time of day. The rangers were the only ones who spent most of their lives outside the protection of our fortifications, and they often traveled at night.

I ran my fingers across a symbol consisting of a triangle overlaid with three wavy lines on the tiled wall before stepping underneath the hot water that fell like rain from the ceiling. The shadow magic of the Furies might be impressive, but nothing beat the blood magic developed by the Moroi to get the indoor plumbing working again. Access to hot water whenever we wanted was the best magic in the world.

My thoughts drifted back to the rangers as I scrubbed my hair. Vail seemed to prefer the dangerous wilds over the Houses and outposts.

As he climbed the ranks of the rangers, he spent less and less time at House Harker. Since taking over as Marshal, he rarely came back to this House. I knew this because, as much as possible, I tracked his whereabouts. It was important to know where your enemies were, and few people were my enemy more than Vail Ferenc.

A chill ran through me despite the steam rising off my skin, and I shut the water off before wrapping myself in a towel.

Vail might want to kill me, but he was completely loyal to Carmilla and House Harker. He would never act on his desires, but he'd also never save me if I got into trouble. Not again, anyway.

While I was far from excited about Vail being here, I was admittedly interested in what he had to say about the attacks.

I'd glimpsed a map in Alaric's office and pestered him about it until he finally relented and gave me the barest amount of information to placate me. I'd then gone to Carmilla, and she'd filled me in on what was going on with the promise that I wouldn't repeat it to anyone else.

I understood why the Sovereign House wanted to keep the escalation of the attacks quiet. Panic wouldn't help anyone.

Still, I knew what it was like to be out there in the wilds, at the complete mercy of the beasts that prowled the night. The experience of those nights when Vail and I huddled in a cave together, listening to the monsters searching for us outside, had fueled my nightmares for over a decade.

We needed to figure out why the wraith attacks were increasing and also how to better safeguard our outposts. I'd been doing research these past couple of days in addition to working on my marriage dissolution, as well as catching up on general House Harker politics.

The small amount of sleep I got every night was plagued by nightmares, and today it felt like it had all caught up to me.

My fingers played with the cool, silky fabric of the sapphire blue dress I'd pulled out. With its soft, stretchy fit, it was one of my favorites. While the neckline was modest compared to a lot of my other dresses, it still clung to every rise and dip of my body.

A smirk played across my lips as I imagined Kieran's expression when I walked into a room wearing it.

Rich, black fabric snagged my attention, and my gaze flipped back and forth between it and the dress. After some thought, I hung the dress back up and reached for a pair of pants stacked neatly on a shelf.

As much as I adored wearing dresses, I was itching to go for a ride. The weather had been sunny and beautiful the last couple of days, and I'd spent all of it indoors.

Zosa would enjoy the exercise too, and I hadn't been to the beach since I'd returned home.

I pulled on the black pants, which were made of the same breathable, stretchy fabric as the blue dress. They were incredibly comfortable and made my ass look amazing.

Since the dress was still on my mind, I picked a light and airy blouse of the same sapphire-blue shade. It was slightly too large for me, so I tied a knot around my waist. Marvina would have had a conniption if she ever saw me in such casual attire, which only made me enjoy it more.

After towel-drying my hair and combing the knots out, I twisted it into a braid and stepped out of my bedroom into the sitting area of my suite.

I froze at seeing Alaric standing over the table where I'd brought some work back from my study last night. I'd had tea with Yolanthe yesterday afternoon under the pretense of catching up, which wasn't entirely a lie. I'd mentioned my concerns around House Laurent retaliating against me requesting to dissolve the marriage, and that had gotten her all fired up. Yolanthe could be a bit rough around the edges and stubborn about things, but she was incredibly loyal to House Harker.

She reassured me that all would be well and that she'd speak with Carmilla to see if there was anything she could do to help. Which was exactly the opening I needed.

I'd profusely thanked her for her assistance, even though I didn't need it since between Alaric and I we had the situation under control, and asked if I could help her with anything to repay the debt. And then coyly mentioned the negotiation she was working on with House Devereux.

I'd also mentioned that I desperately needed to take my mind off everything, and she would actually be doing me a favor by allowing me to make a few suggestions.

Floran and Nora had stopped by my suite later on to catch me up on all the gossip and had brought along a copy of Yolanthe's current draft to pass on to me. Yolanthe preferred to work in the gardens as much as possible because she enjoyed the fresh air, so Floran and Nora were used to delivering her missives. We'd spent a few hours catching up, and then I'd gotten to work on improving the draft.

"By all means," I huffed as I crossed the room to stand at the opposite side of the table, "let yourself in."

"I already did." Alaric flipped a page over, his eyes already skimming the next one. "This... isn't terrible."

Could I use the early hour and the lack of tea as an excuse to kill one of my aunt's advisors? Surely, she would understand. Tea first thing in the morning was vital to my ability to function. Everyone knew this.

"You worded this cleverly." His fingers trailed down several lines. "Hinting at the falling out between Yolanthe's sister and Severen's son without stating it outright."

Wow. *A compliment.* He must be too distracted in reviewing the document to realize what he'd just done. The corners of my mouth quirked up, and a little of the annoyance I'd been feeling faded away.

"Both Yolanthe and Severen are smart and loyal to their Houses. They know this trade agreement makes sense, but they also love their family." I shrugged. "The negotiations have stalled because they're both pissed off on the behalf of their loved ones, and that needs to be acknowledged and settled so that we can move forward."

Alaric grunted, and I had no idea what to do with that. Seriously. It was too early, and I *needed* tea.

I sighed. "Not that you're not absolutely delightful and the first thing I want to see in the morning,"—Alaric's eyes snapped from the paper he'd been reading through to mine—"but what are you doing here?"

The usual mask of arrogance and disdain slipped back onto Alaric's face.

"Carmilla has asked for your presence." The muscles of his jawline flexed. "For both of our presences, actually."

"Did she say why?" My brows pinched together.

"No." Without another word, he strode towards the door and left it open as he continued down the hallway. Rude.

I sighed. Carmilla would have tea in her office. I just had to not murder Alaric between here and there. A few servants greeted me cheerfully as I followed in Alaric's wake. None of them were the least bit upset or offended by my lack of enthusiasm in returning their greetings.

Everyone, except Alaric apparently, was well aware of how I felt about mornings.

"Ah, good," Carmilla looked up from her desk when Alaric and I entered her study. "Vail has arrived, and I would like both of you to hear what he has to say."

"Of course." Alaric nodded and took a seat on one end of Carmilla's well-worn but cozy settee.

"Tea?" I asked hopefully.

Carmilla rolled her eyes. "Obviously. Take a seat, dear."

I plopped down on the opposite end of the settee from Alaric while Carmilla carried over a tray and set it down on the table before sitting between us. Once the tea had steeped, she poured the dark liquid it into four teacups.

Each House favored different types of teas. Laurent's was lighter and more flowery. Harker used a darker, more robust blend that resulted in a black tea with a bolder flavor. I was loathe to admit it, but I preferred the sweeter tea of Laurent over Harker's.

My aunt was well aware of my love of sweet things which was why she added several spoonfuls of honey into my cup before handing it over to me.

"Thank you." I blew on the steaming brew before taking a sip. The decadent flavors danced along my tongue, and I sighed. Delicious.

Surprise flickered through me when Carmilla put even more honey into the next cup and handed it to Alaric. I stared openly at him, but he stoically ignored me as he sipped his tea. She'd put almost *double* the amount of honey into his drink. Just how much of a sweet tooth was he, and how did I not know that?

Carmilla took a seat in one of the chairs opposite the couch and placed the last teacup down in front of the chair next to her. She took a swig of hers before setting it down on the table as well.

"I sent the paperwork off to House Laurent this morning with my seal of approval," she said kindly. "You and Alaric did an excellent job in getting that together. I think we both know that Marvina will likely not accept, at least not right away, but I do believe that we'll be able to get this resolved quickly."

"Thank you," I said, and I meant it. Carmilla had never wavered in her support of me, and I hoped to be able to repay her one day.

"Of course." She smiled gently at me. "Not only are you a member of House Harker, but you're the only family I have left. Once we have the marriage dissolution finalized, I'll officially reinstate your full status as Heir. As part of that role, I'd like you to serve as one of my advisors."

"Really?" I breathed out, setting my teacup down before I spilled the liquid in my excitement.

Her smile grew wider as she nodded back at me, and exhilaration pumped through my veins. I'd hoped that Carmilla would allow me to help her run the House, but I didn't expect her to do it this quickly or in such a major role.

"I won't let you down, I promise," I swore.

"I know you won't," Carmilla replied warmly. "Marvina was a fool to let you go. You have one of the sharpest minds of your generation, and I'm lucky to have you back."

A quick glance at Alaric told me just how excited he was about this turn of events. He was scowling deep into his teacup, which only made me grin harder.

But the grin faltered slightly when I realized that meant the two of us would likely be working closely together constantly since he was one of Carmilla's other advisors. Shit. My aunt's eyes twinkled with amusement as she saw this dawn on me.

"Given how well you and Alaric worked together this week, I trust the both of you will have no problems working together for the benefit of House Harker?"

Her no-nonsense expression made it clear this was more of a polite command than a question.

"Of course," we both answered at once.

"Excellent." She gave us a beaming smile before continuing, "Vail should be here any moment, and then we can get started."

"I'm here."

I turned towards the doorway where the low, gravelly voice had come from, and my lungs seized as I struggled to breathe.

He was exactly as I remembered, if a little broader. His dark graphite eyes latched onto mine, and I suddenly felt very much like prey. I waited for the silver fractures in his eyes to widen, but his eyes remained dark grey, not a flicker of emotion in them as he lurked in the doorway.

Carmilla spoke, breaking some of the tension between us, even though neither of us took our eyes off the other. "Come sit, Vail."

My lungs wanted to suck in a deep breath as soon as Vail tore his gaze off me, but I forced myself to breathe normally so as to not draw attention to just how much Vail's presence affected me. I could feel Alaric's curious gaze boring into me, but I ignored it.

It wasn't a secret that the Marshal of House Harker despised me. The secret was why, and I wouldn't be telling Alaric that anytime soon.

Even Kieran didn't know. Only Cali and Rynn were aware of the whole story.

And Vail.

My fingers remained steady while I wrapped them around my teacup, using the warmth of it to ground me. I sipped from it slowly and looked through my lashes as Vail sat in the chair next to Carmilla.

I'd never understood how a man so large could move so silently. Both Kieran and Alaric were tall and in good shape, although Alaric was always on the slender side, even more so than Kieran. Vail was several inches over six feet and had a body built for battle. He didn't have Kieran's carefully carved muscles and perfect flat abs. Instead, he had slabs of thick muscle layered over his body, covered in scars from fights that he'd survived, if not won.

I fought to keep my eyes off the jagged lines that ran down the right side of his face and continued down his neck but failed. The memory of hot blood running through my fingers burned through my mind, and I quickly looked away and set the teacup down, its heat no longer comforting.

"Thank you for coming," Carmilla said. "I know you wanted to head directly to the outposts that were attacked, but the Sovereign wants more updates, and I'll be traveling to discuss the attacks and other things later this week. I wanted to speak with you first."

"You're leaving?" I asked, hating how much I sounded like the scared girl I had been all those years ago.

"Not for long," my aunt assured me. "I'm overdue for a trip to the Sovereign House to visit Velika, and with the recent attacks, I can't delay any longer."

Trepidation ran through me at the thought of her being away and essentially leaving Alaric and I in charge, but I nodded anyway. "Of course."

Silver flashed from a ring on Alaric's pinkie finger as a small hidden blade snapped out and he sliced open the back of his hand. The coppery scent of blood filled the air, and all of us went still for a moment as our bloodlust flickered awake. My attention immediately went to my aunt, but as usual, she was completely unfazed.

Over half of her generation had eventually lost themselves to bloodlust and had to be put down. The ones we could catch, anyway. More than a few Strigoi had escaped to the wilds and blended in with the other monsters of the night.

Rationally, I knew that as a Harker, Carmilla was unlikely to ever completely lose herself to bloodlust. But she was the only family I had left, so rational or not, I still worried.

Every Moroi child grew up listening to bedtime stories full of warnings about losing ourselves to bloodlust and becoming Strigoi, but so far, very few of my generation had suffered this fate. Maybe the fifth generation wouldn't have to worry about it at all.

Pressure built along my top jaw as my fangs fought to descend, but I held them back and watched as Alaric let his blood drip over the moonstone orb that rested in a cradle in the center of the table. The deep blue crystal glowed from within as the memory spell woven into it activated.

I was admittedly a little surprised that Carmilla didn't use her blood. The memories captured within the crystal could only be accessed by the Moroi who provided the blood, but they had been working together for a while, so I didn't question it. I had plenty of time to figure out the intricacies of how this group worked together.

"What have you learned recently?" Alaric asked, leaning back against the couch and wrapping a handkerchief around his hand.

Vail's eyes fell on me again, but he didn't question my presence here, instead turning his attention to Alaric, who shifted slightly under the weight of Vail's unnerving gaze.

My lips curled into a small smirk that I did nothing to hide.

It seemed I wasn't the only one who found it uncomfortable to have the attention of the Marshal on them. There was a wild edge to Vail that made everyone nervous. Except Carmilla, who had always been perfectly comfortable around him just as she was with everyone else.

"Not much," Vail said in an even, measured tone. "Wraith activity is increasing, particularly in the northwest area of our territory. I've spoken to the Velesians and Furies. They're also noticing pockets of increased activity in their territories."

"Did the Velesians have anything to share about the last two attacks on their outposts?" Carmilla asked.

"Nothing different from the other attacks," Vail replied, the barest amount of frustration slipping into his words. "Given how the bodies were found, there wasn't a single point of failure in the ward, but rather, the wards failed completely. Those on guard duty fell where they were stationed. No one had a chance to counterattack. The guards fell first, and then the wraiths swept through the outpost, killing everyone while they slept."

Horror flashed through me, but I shoved it aside. It was of no use to those already dead and wouldn't help those still alive, living in our now vulnerable outposts.

"Nothing was taken?" I asked carefully, weighing my words. "In any of the attacks?"

Dark grey eyes focused on me. "No."

"Not even any of the..." My throat bobbed, and I swallowed. "Not even any of the bodies?"

His answer was immediate. "No."

"That's weird, right?" My eyebrows bunched together as I gave Vail a puzzled look, momentarily forgetting how uncomfortable he made me while I thought about the oddness of the attack. "They went through all that trouble to kill everyone in the outposts but then left the bodies behind? Even if they did eat their fill there,"—my stomach churned at the thought—"they should have taken some of the bodies with them to feast on later."

Vail, although clearly reluctant to agree with me on anything, said, "I also thought that was odd."

"Why didn't you mention it then?" Alaric asked sharply.

The steely gaze finally left me to fall on Alaric. "I don't have to explain myself to you."

Tension built in the room, and I wished Kieran was here. He was always good at calming everyone down in situations like this, although even he might be out of his depth with this group.

"Let's just focus on what we know so far." I stared at my teacup without really seeing it as I pieced together what I'd learned over the last few days. "I'm still catching up on all this, but there have now been eight attacks, correct?"

Vail and Alaric nodded once while Carmilla sipped her tea. I recognized the look on her face as the one she always wore while she listened to me work out problems I was stuck on. She was giving me a chance to prove myself in front of Vail and Alaric.

They didn't need to like me, but they did need to respect me if we were going to work together.

"Four in Velesian territory, one in Furie territory, and three here," I said, recalling the map I'd studied in Alaric's study.

"There's no pattern in the attacks," Alaric said. "Trust me, I've stared at that map for hours, trying to see some type of reasoning behind why those particular outposts were attacked."

Vail nodded solemnly. "Agreed. Me and my best scouts have studied the attack locations as well. The assaults appear to be random. The most recent three have all happened in the center of Lunaria. Prior to this, there were two in the far west region of Velesian territory and before that, in the south of our realm. They jump around too much to indicate any sort of pattern."

"It does seem unlikely that there is a pattern." I pursed my lips. "Vail, do you know if Rynn Valatieri has been consulted? She's a Velesian."

"I know who she is," he said, surprising me.

Rynn had been assigned to the Alpha Pack, but she hadn't officially joined them yet. She was still active in Velesian politics, but Rynn preferred to work behind the scenes as much as possible.

He continued, "I don't know if anyone has asked her."

"With your permission,"—I looked at Carmilla—"I would like to bring Rynn into this. She'll be joining the Alpha Pack later this year and will probably be told of all of it then anyway. There's no one better than Rynn at seeing patterns."

"The Velesian pack leaders have studied the attacks. Do you really think some young, unproven Velesian could see something they haven't?" Vail asked as he leaned forward slightly. There was nothing hostile in his tone. If anything, it beheld faint curiosity.

"There's no one better than Rynn at seeing patterns," I emphasized again. "There's a reason she was tapped for the Alpha Pack."

Vail stared at me for another moment before dipping his head in a small nod. Then his attention returned to Carmilla. "I brought a small group with me. We'll leave after this meeting."

"I'd like to join you," Alaric said.

Vail's gaze slid to Alaric, and his mouth tightened, but he didn't argue.

"I'd also like to come," I said firmly.

"No," Vail said instantly, causing me to stiffen at the outright rejection. "I'll already have to babysit him. I can't spare anyone else to watch you too."

I allowed myself a few seconds to appreciate the outrage on Alaric's face.

"I'm not asking you to take me with you all over Lunaria. I'm telling you to take me to the outpost that was attacked less than a three-day ride from here. I haven't seen any of the outposts that were attacked, and neither has Alaric. We need more information if we are to help in solving this problem." I didn't bother holding back my grin. "Besides, Alaric goes for a run every morning. He can just run away if we encounter any danger."

I would cherish the infuriated look Alaric gave me until the day I died. The satisfaction it provided was palpable.

"And you?" Vail gave me a flat look. "What will you do if we are attacked?"

"I'm good with knives," I said coolly.

It wasn't a lie. After my parents had died, I'd had a lot of anger, grief, and frustration to work out. One day I'd been stomping through the training courtyard and had picked up a throwing dagger before hurling it at a target. I hadn't hit the bullseye, but I'd been close and spent the rest of the day practicing.

It wasn't long before I moved on to different types of bows. Something about the blend of concentration that it took for range weapons provided peace for my wounded soul.

"Good with knives?" Vail shook his head with a scoff. "You'll be a hindrance. There is no reason for you to come."

I flushed at the reprimand, but before I could argue, Carmilla cut in.

"I agree with Samara and Alaric." She gave Vail a stern narrowing of her eyes. "There have been eight attacks thus far, and we're no closer to understanding the intentions behind them. There is an outpost between here and the one that was attacked. It's slightly out of the way, but it will give you a secure place to stay on the way there, which will limit your time in the wilds."

"It will slow us down," Vail argued.

It didn't escape my attention that the venom in his tone whenever he spoke to me was absent when speaking with my aunt.

I didn't think it was simply because she was the Head of the House; I believed that he genuinely respected her. My mouth flattened into a hard line. Unfortunately, none of that respect transferred to me.

"Speed doesn't matter as much as information," Carmilla countered.

"Fine," Vail said in a tone that made it very clear he was still against this idea. "But she is to come to training this afternoon so we can determine just how much of a liability she will be."

I bristled at being referred to as a "liability," but Carmilla agreed on my behalf.

"Of course. It's a perfectly reasonable request for you to be aware of everyone's abilities. Alaric will attend as well." She paused until we all nodded in begrudging agreement. "Excellent. I have a few more things I wanted to discuss before I need to prepare for my own trip."

The rest of the meeting went by quickly with Carmilla just asking for clarification on a few things before going over some minor House logistic items that Alaric and I might need to attend to while she was away. She'd be here for another couple days but would likely be leaving a day before we returned.

"How long do you think you'll be gone exactly?" I asked, setting aside the scroll I'd grabbed to take notes on. Technically, it was all recorded, but I'd have to ask Alaric to replay the recording for me, so it was easier to take my own notes.

"A month," Carmilla said slowly. "Perhaps more."

Alaric's apprehensive grimace matched my own. It was rare for the head of any House to be away for that long. I knew that Carmilla and the Sovereigns were close friends, but still...

"Is there anything we should know?" I asked carefully.

She rolled her eyes. "Perhaps the two of you working together is a mistake. You both have a tendency to act like mother hens." When neither Alaric nor I disputed this, she sighed. "You know that Queen Velika and I have always been close. She has some personal things going on that she needs my help with. I'll be assisting her with that, as well as updating her on the attacks."

"Okay," I said skeptically. "But you'll tell us if you need help with anything, right?"

"Of course." She rose and made a shooing motion towards the door. "I need to prepare for the journey to the Sovereign House and my stay there. I'll expect updates about what you find out after you visit the outpost." She gave me a pointed look. "And please inform me soon as you're back so I know you're safe."

"I will," I promised.

My eyes slid to Vail, who had been quiet since agreeing to allow me to travel to the outpost, answering any questions directed his way with the barest amount of words possible.

His wolfish gaze was on me, and I felt a shiver run through my body as I realized exactly what I had gotten myself into.

I would be out in the wilds with Vail and his rangers, with only Alaric to watch my back.

As if he was reading my mind and seeing the realization hit me, Vail did something he'd never done since that fateful night in the forest when we were kids.

He smiled.

CHAPTER TEN

—

Samara

Sweat beaded across my skin as I reached down and clasped my left ankle, feeling the muscles along my back and leg loosen. I had no idea what type of exercises Vail was going to put us through, but stretching beforehand seemed like a good idea.

Alaric was sitting only a few feet away from me, doing his best to ignore my existence, while Kieran hung out with some of the rangers on the other side of the training yard where he had a perfect view of everything.

This courtyard was located in the back half of House Harker and was mostly shaded by trees, yet even in the shade, the heat was damn near stifling. It was still only spring, but apparently the weather today had decided to give us a taste of summer.

I was still wearing the pants I'd put on this morning, but I'd ditched the blouse as soon as I'd got here so I didn't pass out from heat exhaustion, leaving me in only the chest band.

The feeling of sweat pooling in between my breasts where they were smooshed together thanks to the band around them wasn't great, though. The thick straps that held the band up kept slipping down, and Kieran was continuously glancing over at me in hopes I was about to have a serious wardrobe malfunction.

The third time I caught him looking, I mouthed one word back, *BEG*.

The corner of his mouth tipped up into a lopsided grin before he mouthed back, *NEVER*.

I laughed and reached for my discarded blouse to wipe the sweat from my face before promptly dropping it in disgust.

Before coming for my mandatory training session, I'd swung by the stables to apologize to Zosa for having ignored her the past few days and not being able to take her out for a ride today. I promised her that we'd be going out soon to stretch her legs, and she'd thanked me by snorting what seemed like ten gallons of snot all over my blouse, which I'd forgotten about until now.

Thankfully, none of it had gotten in my hair. I still desperately wanted to rinse off, but something told me Vail wouldn't accept horse snot as an excuse to miss this.

If anything, he'd use it as an excuse to leave me behind tomorrow.

Speak of the devil...

Vail strode into the training yard, three rangers following in his wake. My eyebrows rose in surprise as I took them all in.

As the Marshal, all House Harker rangers reported to him, but I knew that he had his own personal unit that went out with him on most missions as well. I had expected his unit to be full of copycat Vails, big and burly with matching beards. Each with a different assortment of scars to prove just how badass they were and matching scowls that they always broke out in unison.

But these rangers couldn't be more different.

The one to Vail's right was a man a few inches shorter than me. He had a stocky build but still appeared small next to Vail.

On Vail's other side was a woman who looked like she should be on the arm of a noble at one of the House courts wearing a fine gown. Instead, she was here, wearing russet-brown leathers that looked like they had seen better days, and she had bits of what I was pretty sure was dried blood in her ashen-blonde hair.

I squinted, trying to get a clearer look. Definitely dried blood. Though, it looked too dark to be Moroi blood, so I didn't worry too much about it.

The rangers often returned with bits of monster blood and pieces on them, so it was a fairly normal sight, but if they came back with Moroi blood on them that wasn't theirs, it meant they'd had to hunt down a Strigoi. The occurrences of Moroi turning Strigoi were becoming rarer, but it still happened, and I was always worried it would one day be someone I knew.

It was one thing when the monsters that roamed the wilds were nameless beasts, but it was quite another when they wore a familiar face.

Vail and his three companions moved with a dangerous air about them as they surveyed those gathered in the courtyard. I was wondering about what type of weapons they used when my gaze fell on the third ranger who trailed behind them.

They were dressed in a way that leaned neither feminine nor masculine. Gender fluidity was common enough among the Moon Blessed, especially the Velesians.

As my gaze traveled over them, I was startled when I took in their face.

Nyx.

It had been at least five years since I'd seen them, but I'd recognize those sky-blue eyes anywhere.

Back then, they had seemed so unsure of themselves. Nyx was several years younger than me, Rynn, and Cali, and when they'd arrived to study at Drudonia, we'd done our best to take them under our wing when it was clear they didn't have any friends.

They'd never really settled in there, despite being very bright and showing an aptitude for House politics, but after years of struggling, they had simply disappeared.

I'd worried at the time and put out inquiries to find out where they'd gone. Cali and Rynn did the same. We learned that Nyx actually came from House Corvinus and was the younger sibling of the Heir. They'd been sent to Drudonia so that they could support their older sister when she eventually took over the rule of the House.

Through the process, House Corvinus confirmed that Nyx was alive and well but wouldn't give us any other information. I'd even asked Carmilla to look into it, but she'd just given me the same line.

Nyx has found a place in the world that suits them. Let them be.

With no other choice, I'd had to drop it, but now, here they were. Alive and well. With Vail.

They held my stare for another moment before dipping their head slightly in acknowledgement. I did the same but made no move to approach. We had been friends once, though I assumed their loyalty now resided with Vail, considering they hadn't reached out to me once since leaving Drudonia.

I was happy that they'd found a role in life that fit them well, but I was more than a little hurt and miffed that they hadn't told me. There was no way they didn't know that I'd been asking around about them.

I tried to subtly study them a little bit more. They seemed very at ease around Vail and the other two rangers. Nyx likely knew at least some of the history between Vail and me, although I doubted the grumpy-ass had told them everything. Maybe Nyx just felt uncomfortable telling me they had joined up with my arch-nemesis, so they'd simply avoided the conversation altogether.

More rangers came around the corner and casually leaned against the walls and buildings that surrounded the courtyard. I didn't know if they came because Vail ordered them to, or because they heard about what was about to go down and wanted a front-row seat.

I pursed my lips into a hard line. Probably the latter.

"Nyx with Alaric," Vail ordered. "Emil with the Heir."

I held my chin high as I moved to stand in front of the male ranger. Surprise flickered through me when I noticed the fine lines around his eyes and the corners of his mouth. His black hair was pulled back into a bun, but there were some grey streaks that I had somehow missed before.

He must be a fourth generation like Carmilla, which meant he could be anywhere from sixty to a hundred years old, maybe even older.

I'd thought all the older rangers had retired to be instructors or hold positions that didn't require them to travel as much.

The ones that had survived this long anyway.

The stunningly beautiful female ranger with the dried monster blood in her hair eyed Kieran, who was still perched on a barrel on the sidelines.

Like me, she'd ditched a layer of clothes and was only wearing a tight pair of pants and a band around her chest. Her well-toned body was wrapped in lightly tanned skin that showcased her ashen-blonde hair quite well. More than a few rangers were subtly checking her out.

Hell. I was checking her out.

"You been practicing, pretty boy?" she asked Kieran with a familiarity that made me suspicious. My gaze pinged back and forth between them as jealousy spiked within me.

Before I could act on my completely irrational wave of jealousy, my feet were swept out from under me, and I crashed hard on my ass.

"Fuck!" I swore and glared up at Emil. "What the hell was that for?"

He smirked at me. "For being distracted in a training session."

"We hadn't even started yet," I grumbled.

He held his hand out and I clasped it, letting him pull me to my feet.

"When you're in the training ring, it's always an active session," he lectured, and I nodded. Despite his sneaky maneuver, his expression was kind.

"So, are we going to spar, or what exactly are we going to do?" I asked, resuming my position opposite Emil.

Alaric and Kieran regularly trained with the rangers, but I never really did. When I was younger, all my time was spent studying and preparing for life at House Laurent. The only combat skills I possessed were with range weapons, and that was something I practiced on my own because I found it relaxing.

Out of the corner of my eye, I spotted Nyx pulling the same sweeper kick on Alaric, who had been distracted by something Kieran had said.

Unlike me, however, Alaric's reaction time was on point, and he leapt over the kick and quickly took a couple of steps back to evaluate the threat.

Show-off. I bit back a scowl.

"We're going to test your instincts," Vail said quietly into my ear.

I'd like to say I handled his sudden appearance at my back well... but I did not. A shriek tore out of me, and I leapt several feet into the air.

When I landed, I whirled around to shove Vail away, but he was already gone. Kieran snickered at me while Alaric just shook his head disapprovingly.

"What?" I snapped. "He fucking snuck up on me like a—"

"Wraith," Vail cut me off from where he now stood facing me several feet away. "Like a wraith or any number of other monsters out there that are just as stealthy. You want to come with us, and for now you have Carmilla's support in this." I narrowed my eyes at his phrasing. Clearly, he was still hoping he could change her mind without me there to argue my case. "I know how all of my rangers will react in any situation, and I even know how Kieran and Alaric will react because they train regularly."

"So, you thought sneaking up behind me and scaring the shit out of me was a good idea?" I asked incredulously, taking a step towards him.

"Yes." He shrugged without a hint of remorse. "Now we know that you're not at all aware of your surroundings and that you scare easily. That scream would have attracted all kinds of things at night."

Kieran shot me a sly grin. "You are a bit of a screa—"

The pretty ranger slammed her elbow into his gut, and he dropped to the ground with a grunt of paint. "Not... nice... Adrienne," he gasped. The ranger—Adrienne, apparently—winked at me and sauntered away from Kieran.

Despite the flash of jealousy I felt earlier, I instantly liked her.

"We need to know how you'll react when you're frightened," Vail continued as if nothing had happened. "How quickly you can get out of the way so that one of us can step in and keep you from being torn to shreds or dragged off into the night."

I shifted uneasily at the predatory look in Vail's eyes.

"If we're attacked," Emil said quietly, "you need to be able to get away and run. I'll show you some basic evasive tactics once we evaluate what you're best suited towards."

"She's best suited towards lounging around and being waited on." Vail's mouth twisted in disgust.

"I have muscles," I scoffed. "Just because I'm not a trained fighter doesn't mean I can't learn enough to get out of the way and run."

"Muscles?" Vail crossed his arms and let his eyes roam over my body, his expression making it clear he wasn't impressed by my soft build.

I mirrored his position and gave him the same flat stare he was giving me. "They're sneaky muscles."

Kieran chuckled while Alaric just sighed in annoyance. "Samara, can't you take this seriously?"

"Don't be such an ass-kisser, Alaric." I rolled my eyes.

Emil took advantage of the situation and tried to knock my feet out from under me again, but this time, I was ready for him. I wouldn't call my jump over his legs smooth, but I stayed on my feet, and that's all that mattered.

"Good." He smiled at me.

"The training ring is always an active session." I returned his smile with one of my own.

Vail glared at me for another moment before waving over Emil and Nyx. The three of them conversed for a few minutes before deciding on a training course for Alaric and myself. After an hour, I was covered in sweat and dirt and sporting more than a few bruises, but at least I knew a few basic maneuvers that might save my life if we were attacked.

I wasn't delusional enough to think that I now actually stood a chance against a wraith or any of the other monsters that roamed the wilds, but maybe I'd managed to stay alive for the few seconds it took Vail or one of the rangers to get to me.

Unfortunately, my tentative confidence in my abilities to stay alive in a monster attack was short-lived.

"Don't know why you're smiling," Vail drawled. "The past hour has only made it clear how much of a liability you are."

None of the rangers voiced a differing opinion, and the grin I'd been wearing slid off my face. Kieran glared fiercely at Vail, but Alaric was looking at me with an *"I told you so"* expression.

I didn't know why he was so cocky. He'd barely done better than me, and the layer of dirt over his clothes proved it.

"We'll be on horseback," I said defensively. "I'm a good rider."

Really, I was an amazing rider. My mother had taken me riding before I could even walk, and riding had always come naturally to me.

"And if we're attacked?" he sneered. "You'll just run away and leave us behind."

"First of all,"—I took a step towards him—"hasn't this entire exercise been about teaching Alaric and I to get out of the way so that all of you can fight? I'm not an idiot, Vail." I threw my hands in the air. "I know that I won't survive a fight, so yes, I will get out of the way if I can so that none of you have to worry about me, but I won't leave you behind."

Silver lines burst through Vail's steel-grey eyes, giving them a ghostly appearance before vanishing.

I took another step towards him. "And I wouldn't just sit there while all of you fought for your lives. I told you before, I'm excellent with a bow, and I'm good with knives too."

"Good with knives," he scoffed and sauntered over to where clean towels were hanging off the wall of a small wooden building.

Some of the rangers laughed and started to walk away. Seething, I snatched the dagger out of Emil's thigh holster, and it flew from my fingers before I could think better of it.

Vail froze as the dagger sank into the wood, directly in between his fingers.

Then, slowly, he turned to look at me.

"I told you," I said evenly. "I'm good with knives."

"You didn't," Rynn said for the third time. Even with her shadowy form, I could still make out the disbelief on her face.

As soon as I'd retreated to my suite to draw a bath, I'd reached out to Rynn and Cali for a call because I needed my besties after my encounter with Vail. Rynn had appeared almost immediately in her shadow form, but Cali hadn't acknowledged my summons at all, not even to say she was busy, which caused a pit of dread in my stomach. It wasn't like Cali to not at least respond in some way.

"Okay, so, maybe antagonizing the man who very much wants to kill me right before I go off with him into the wilds wasn't my best idea." I scrunched my nose up.

"You think?" Rynn's fingers rubbed her temples in frustration.

I grinned ruefully at her. "When my rotting corpse is eventually discovered, I want it to go on record that it was totally worth it for the look of surprise on his face when that dagger slammed between his fingers."

"No dying." Rynn wagged a finger at me.

"Fiiine," I drew out the word dramatically and sunk lower into the tub, the near scalding hot water helping to soothe my abused muscles. "Ignoring my questionable actions this afternoon, what are your thoughts about everything else?"

Shadow Rynn pursed her lips. "I'm annoyed that no one has told me about all of this. Obviously, I knew about some of the attacks, but not all of them."

"They're keeping it hush-hush." I shrugged.

"Yeah, but I'm supposed to be joining the Alpha Pack in less than a year. I'm already privy to all sorts of information in preparation for that." She waved a hand. "Never mind. It doesn't matter. I need a list of all the outposts that have been attacked and the dates it happened."

"I'll send a striker with it to our usual drop-off. Do you need anything else?"

"That's enough to get me started. Ideally, I'd like to visit some of the outposts myself, but that will take time to arrange." She went predatorily still in the way she often did when she was thinking. With her soft-spoken nature, it was sometimes easy to forget that my friend was a lycanthrope and frequently shifted into a dangerous beast.

I waited silently for Rynn to think through whatever had snagged her attention.

If Cali was here, she and I would be trading amused looks right now, both of us used to Rynn's tendency to zone out mid-conversation, but she wasn't here.

A fact that still made me nervous. She usually always answered calls.

"You should reach out to Roth," Rynn said finally. "They're back at Drudonia using the library there to research more about Lunarian history. They might be able to shed some light on how the wraiths are getting past the blood wards."

"Roth?" I tilted my head back as my brows furrowed together. Why was that name so familiar?

It came to me almost instantly. A young Moroi girl, a year younger than us, arriving at Drudonia. We'd been in the grand library when she'd arrived, and I still remembered the expression of awe on her face as she took in the seemingly endless amount of books and scrolls. It'd taken her a solid five minutes to snap out of it before she saw us sitting there and introduced herself.

"I'm Astaroth Devereux." And then, a little hesitantly, she said, *"I prefer Roth."*

The rest of what Rynn had said filtered in, and I noted the use of *they*. It fit them, the same way that Roth better suited them than Astaroth. Although both names were pretty badass.

"How are they doing?" Envy crept into my voice. While I was happy with the direction my life was now headed in, part of me was jealous of Roth being able to dedicate their time to studying our history. What little we knew of it, anyway.

The spell our human ancestors had cast to turn us into monsters cost us so much more than our humanity, it also cost us our past. Entire generations' worth of wisdom that would usually have been passed down through stories, advice, song, and a myriad of other ways was simply gone. Which meant we were completely reliant on what had been written and books were painfully fragile.

We kept lists of past human settlements and noted their current state. The vast majority of them had been burnt to the ground or reduced to rubble after monsters had torn through them. Whatever knowledge they had forever lost to us. While the Fae fortresses still stood, many had been completely stripped of anything valuable, which suggested that at least some of the Fae had made it out alive. Where they had gone, we had no idea.

Any books or documents that we did manage to find were taken to Drudonia. It was the central source of all our history and knowledge now. And Roth had all that at their fingertips.

I hadn't interacted with Roth all that much while at Drudonia. They'd been Rynn's friend more than mine, but I got the impression that they were still figuring a lot of things out. Both about themselves and their place in the world.

House Devereux was a smaller House like the one Kieran was born into, which meant it was full of schemers and Moroi with scrupulous morals. Growing up in it couldn't have been fun.

"I think they're okay…"

When Rynn didn't say anything else, I leaned forward in the tub, my unruly long hair plastered along my shoulders and back. "Are they back at Drudonia because they want to be back there or because shit went down in their House after they went back?"

Roth wasn't in line to take over the House leadership. If I remembered correctly, they were a cousin to the current Moroi ruling House Devereux, but since they were still family, it was expected that they would do whatever the House asked of them. Whether they wanted to or not.

Rynn bit her lip. "I got the impression it was the latter, but you know what Roth is like. They didn't offer any personal information, and I didn't push."

No. Rynn wouldn't push. She never did. It's why Roth had always liked her, but never bothered with me or Cali. We were nosey assholes. It hadn't helped that I'd quickly become attracted to them, and my flirtation might have been a *tad* over the top. I was used to the flirty banter between me and Kieran. Roth had not been impressed with my attempts, and it'd led to a bit of awkwardness between us.

Well, awkwardness on my side. Roth had simply moved on like it'd never happened. Despite never getting particularly close to Roth, I still liked them. And I felt a sort of camaraderie with them because of our time together at Drudonia.

Not many people went there to study. There had only been a dozen of us of similar age the entire time we'd been there. I knew Cali felt the same, and if she thought House Devereux was being cruel to Roth, she would have flown straight to the House and given them a piece of her mind.

I would have been one step behind, rooting her on. I had calmed down over the years and developed a more "political mindset," as Rynn called it, but Cali… Cali still embraced her inner fire and refused all attempts by the world to snuff it out.

No matter how dangerous that was.

"I'll reach out to Roth when I get back. If House Devereux wants to throw them away, I'll snatch them up for House Harker, just like we did with Kieran. A mind like Roth's shouldn't be wasted just because they don't want to play bullshit House politics."

I rose from the tub, and Rynn quickly averted her eyes. How someone who regularly stripped down and shifted into a wolf was shy about nudity, I'd never understand. I wrapped a towel around myself before doing the same to my hair. "Alright, now that we've gotten the talk about the attacks out of the way, I think it's time we discuss Cali."

Rynn's gaze fell on me again, and she nodded, causing tendrils of shadow to drift off her. "Something's wrong."

"And she's not telling us about it." I let out a frustrated sigh.

We told each other everything. Always.

"I think she's afraid," Rynn whispered.

"Of what?" I snapped before catching myself. It wasn't Rynn's fault that I was pissed off at Cali. I sat on the edge of the tub and let my shoulders sag as I took a few deep breaths. "She is fearless. Always has been."

"Our Cali has always been fearless," Rynn agreed, "but we know what all Furies fear."

We will lose our souls to the fury.

So much history had been lost when our ancestors cast the spell to give up their humanity and become monsters instead.

We'd managed to put together bits and pieces of it, along with clawing our humanity back, but there was still so much we didn't know. Like why the Furies had been impacted worse than the rest of us.

The Velesians had been the first to gain back some of their humanity. Even their second generation had been mostly stable, and because of that, they had the greatest numbers of any of us. The Moroi had struggled, with some of our bloodlines having fared better than others. They were the ones who established the Houses and helped the others battle their bloodlust.

But the Furies... so few of them remained compared to the Velesians and Moroi, and the ones that did were always at risk of losing themselves to the never-ending fury within their souls.

Fear clamped its hands around my heart. "Do you think Cali is losing herself?"

"No," Rynn said quickly. "But I think something about her magic is scaring her. She's the most powerful Furie of her generation. Possibly ever."

She raised her hand, displaying the silver band she wore around her wrist. The shadow magic within it was what allowed Rynn to appear as her shadow self. Only Furies had the ability to wield shadow magic themselves or imbue other things with it.

Rynn explained, "It normally takes several Furies working together to craft magic like this, and Cali was able to do it on her own, on basically a whim."

"She was scared about us being apart," I murmured, remembering our last day at Drudonia and Cali clamping that band around Rynn's wrist.

But despite her power, it still hadn't worked for me. Moroi could wield blood magic but not use shadow magic. The Furies wielded shadow magic but couldn't use blood magic. The Velesians could wield neither, but they could use objects that had been spelled with either magic. No one knew why.

"You know how the other Furies are around her," Rynn said sadly. "She can't go to them with her concerns. They'll just spout more useless garbage about how she needs to tone down her emotions and not form strong bonds. Blah, blah, blah."

I snorted. The Furie elders were not pleased about how close the three of us were. More than once, they had told Cali to end our friendship. Fat chance.

"We need to go and see her. In person," I insisted. "She won't be able to brush us off so easily then."

"Agreed."

I unwrapped my hair, letting the towel drop to the floor, and snagged my brush off the counter. "And maybe then you can tell us how you're really feeling about joining the Alpha Pack." I cocked my head knowingly.

Rynn froze. "I've already told you I'm fi—"

"If you say 'you're fine' about it, I'm going to scream." I pointed my brush at her in warning.

"Fine." She grinned at me when I arched an eyebrow at her. But after a few seconds, the grin slid off her face. "I'm getting nervous about it."

"Have they been pressuring you to come?" I asked carefully.

If she said yes, I wasn't sure what I would do, but whatever it was, it would probably be a political nightmare. My aunt had raised me after my parents died, but she was often busy ruling House Harker and supporting the Sovereign House.

Cali and Rynn had equally sad and complicated family histories. We were each other's chosen family. There was no stronger bond than that, as far as I was concerned.

"The opposite, actually." She fidgeted with her hands before catching herself.

While Cali and I didn't care about her nervous tells, we had been working with her on them. Of the three of us, Rynn managed to be both the smartest and the most inept at communicating. Given that she was supposed to join the Alpha Pack and serve as an advisor... that was a problem.

We'd come a long way from those original humans who had turned themselves into monsters, but we were still predators, and showing weakness was never wise.

"I requested some time after we left Drudonia to help my mother. Then I made another request after she passed to get her affairs in order."

"What was their response?" I asked. "The exacting wording."

"*Of course.*" She closed her eyes briefly before letting out a long breath. "Just those two words and nothing else. They haven't followed up since. What if they don't want me?"

"Then they're idiots," I growled. "You can come here and help me at House Harker. I don't care that you're a Velesian." The brush pulled on a tangle in my hair a little too hard, and I winced.

"Thank you, but we both know that won't work." Rynn gave me a sad smile that made my heart ache for my friend.

"I know," I said softly. Moroi needed blood ties. Velesians needed a pack.

Rynn's shoulders sagged, causing shadows to roll off her and twirl in the air.

"We're all doing fantastic, aren't we?" she said with a snort. "The marriage that you were destined for fell apart, the pack I'm promised to doesn't want me, and Cali is keeping secrets from us, which means something really bad is going on in her life."

I rose from where I'd been perched on the tub and stood in front of her with my fist held out. "But we still have each other, so we'll be fine."

"Yeah, we will. I'll keep harassing Cali until she answers so I can fill her in." She tapped her fist against mine. "Do us a favor and don't antagonize the big, bad Moroi Marshal over the next couple of days?"

"No promises," I said wryly.

CHAPTER ELEVEN

—

Samara

Zosa danced restlessly beneath me as we waited for the gate to be opened.

Once again, I'd slept poorly, and it had put me in a foul mood. Fortunately, after giving me one look that was dripping heavily with contempt, Vail had ignored my presence all morning. Fine by me.

We'd have to ride hard and fast to make it to the outpost before dark, which I was fine with because that meant I wouldn't have to talk to anyone on the way.

Alaric had nodded at me once in greeting, and I'd been too stunned at the almost nice gesture to respond in kind. He hadn't noticed, though, clearly too caught up in his own thoughts. As I watched him adjust himself for the third time on the saddle, I wondered how often he had been out riding.

Unlike me, he hadn't gone to Drudonia. His parents had provided his tutorage. I knew he had traveled to other Houses before, but given how uncomfortable he looked on a horse, I'm guessing it wasn't often.

While I debated teasing him about it, Kieran appeared around the corner, mounted on a tall, chestnut gelding.

He would be traveling with us to the outpost and then remaining there so he could catch up with some other courtiers and see if they had any useful information to share. His horse pranced up to us before tossing his head, his pale mane shining brightly in the morning sun.

"Did you seriously find a horse that likes to preen as much as you?" I asked in disbelief.

And may the moon bless us, but Alaric *laughed* at my joke.

"Don't be jealous," Kieran said smoothly. "Green is one of the few colors that doesn't suit you."

I glanced down at the forest-green tunic I was wearing, then back up at

Kieran. He grinned at me, and I started to maneuver Zosa so I could smack him when Carmilla interrupted us.

"Children,"—she gave pointed looks to me, Kieran, and Alaric—"focus."

"Don't know why I got grouped in with them," Alaric complained. "I wasn't even doing anything."

Kieran reached out and gently punched him on the shoulder, causing Alaric's fingers to tighten around the black mane of his mare as he glared at Kieran. *Just how terrible of a rider is he?*

Carmilla walked over to me and rested a hand on my leg as she peered up at me. "Be careful, Samara. I may not have given birth to you, but you are a child of my heart, nonetheless."

"I will, I promise." I rested my hand on top of hers. "We'll be there and back in a matter of days, and hopefully, Alaric and I will be able to find something that will help us figure out why these attacks are escalating and how they're getting past our blood wards."

The portcullis clanged open in front of us, drawing Carmilla's attention. The two rangers from yesterday's training session, along with Nyx, rode out. Vail's enormous, dark bay mare shook her head as he held her back from joining them.

"Bring my niece home, Marshal," she commanded.

Vail clenched his jaw and nodded. "Of course, my liege."

Carmilla squeezed my leg once more before removing her hand. Then Zosa eagerly trotted forward, with Alaric and Kieran following me. I glanced over my shoulder and saw Carmilla speaking quietly with Vail. Whatever she was telling him, he clearly didn't like it based on his stormy expression.

"The three of you will ride in the middle," Nyx said. "Emil and Adrienne will take the lead. Vail and I will bring up the rear."

"How fast will we be going exactly?" Alaric asked nervously.

Nyx gave him an appraising look before apologetically saying, "For most of the journey, we'll be at a brisk jog, but we'll be letting the horses stretch their legs off and on. We need to make it there before dark, and all of our mounts are fit enough to be pushed a bit."

Alaric grimaced. "Great."

Kieran and I shared an amused look before his eyes dropped and snagged on my breasts, which were now bouncing around thanks to Zosa practically jogging in place. I really should have taken her out for a ride sooner. She hated being cooped up.

I cleared my throat, saying, "Have you changed your mind about green not being my color?"

His eyes snapped up, the golden fractures a little more apparent. "Not at all. Just thinking about how much better you'd look in a nice, vibrant blue."

I eyed his blue tunic and arched an eyebrow. "Really? You think blue is my color?"

The look Kieran gave me was positively wicked, causing me to clench my legs in a way entirely unrelated to the horse dancing beneath me. "Only one way to find out."

"Kill me now," Alaric muttered.

Nyx laughed, but the other two rangers remained stoic as Vail joined us. "We'll let the horses stretch their legs for a few miles, then we'll slow the pace a bit."

My shoulders itched at Vail being at my back, but there was nothing to be done about it. Besides, I had no doubt that he would follow Carmilla's command. He was blood-sworn to her and would never disobey a direct order.

It was when we were at the outpost that had been attacked that I'd have to be careful.

He was cunning, and if he saw an opportunity to get rid of me without it being technically his fault, he would seize it.

The rangers in front of us spurred their horses forward, and a delighted laugh poured out of me as I loosened Zosa's reins and she surged into a ground-eating gallop.

I bent over Zosa's withers, urging her to go faster, my heart beating wildly in my chest.

Hooves pounded behind me as the others launched themselves after us, and I half-heartedly wondered if Alaric would be able to stay mounted, but that thought drifted away as the wind tugged at my hair, pulling strands free from my braid.

This would quite possibly be the best part of our trip, and I was going to enjoy the hell out of it.

WE ARRIVED AT FAYBELL, the outpost we'd be staying in for the night, an hour before sunset.

Since we'd made good time, we'd slowed to a walk for the last couple of miles to let the horses cool off before they got settled into the stables.

I slid out of the saddle with a spring in my step, earning a glare from both Alaric and Kieran.

"What?" I demanded.

"We've been riding nonstop all day," Kieran said. "How are you still so"—he waved a hand at me—"spry?"

I shrugged. "What can I say? I've got endurance for days, and I'm all kinds of spry." I gave Kieran a sly grin, earning a heated glance in return.

"I'm not listening to this," Alaric groaned as he handed his horse off to the stable kid and took an awkward step towards the tavern where Vail and the rangers had already disappeared to.

I couldn't help but laugh when Alaric groaned and rubbed at his thighs. "Do you seriously never ride?" I asked.

"Why would I do that?" he snapped as he stopped to glare over his shoulder at me. "I don't see what is so appealing about sitting atop a hysterical, foul-smelling beast."

Kieran patted his mare before she was led away. "All of our horses are extremely well-trained. I don't think any of them qualify as 'hysterical.'"

"Whatever." Alaric limped towards the tavern without another backwards glance at us.

Then Kieran held out an arm to me. "Shall we?"

"What do you think the chances are that they have running water here?" I asked as I looped my arm through his.

"Sorry to dash your dreams so soon, but there is no running water here," he said as we followed after Alaric. "Despite the name, Faybell wasn't built on the backbones of an old Fae town. It was built completely by us. The tavern servants can draw a bath for you, or..."

"Or..." I eyed him as he opened the door to the tavern and we stepped inside.

The large room was filled with Moroi, and the boisterous conversations almost drowned out Kieran as he leaned over to whisper in my ear, "There are natural hot springs in the back corner of the outpost. Those who run this place like me. If I requested to have sole access to them tonight... they'd probably be willing to make sure I had the springs all to myself."

"Is that so?" I whispered back. The idea of slipping into some hot water sounded positively magical right now.

"Mmm," he hummed. "Of course, if I'm to share these hot springs with you... there might need to be some begging on your part."

I slid my eyes towards him as we made our way to the table where Alaric sat. "Maybe I'll just find the person in charge of them and persuade them on my own."

"Don't be hasty," he said quickly. "Just come with me after we get something to eat, and we'll discuss it then."

Alaric eyed both of us. "I don't want to know, do I?"

I opened my mouth to respond, but Kieran beat me to it. "Probably not."

Food magically arrived in front of us moments later, and I gave Alaric a questioning look. He shrugged. "It's not like there are a lot of options on the menu, and I figured you'd be hungry."

"Thanks," I said before tucking into the spread of dried meats, roasted vegetables, and bread.

Faybell was far enough inland that fresh fish wasn't readily available the way it was at the coastal Houses like Harker and Laurent. Crops were easy to grow because none of the beasts that prowled the forest had any interest in them, but livestock was challenging.

A few outposts managed to keep around some goats and the occasional cow and used the milk from them to make cheese. Clearly, this wasn't one of them.

Some of the locals came over to talk to us as we ate. Well, they really came to talk to Kieran, but were nice enough to me and Alaric. I occasionally glanced towards where Vail and his rangers were sitting, curious about what they were talking about.

"You ready?" Kieran asked, drawing my attention away from the rangers.

I slipped my hand into his and rose from the table. Alaric's gaze flicked over us briefly before he went back to his meal.

"For you to beg?" I smirked at him. "Absolutely."

He rolled his eyes and tugged me up the stairs.

"Uhh... I thought you said the hot springs were towards the back of the outpost?" I asked in confusion as Kieran opened a door, revealing a small, tidy room with our packs from the horses stacked on the beds.

"Were you planning on putting on the same dirty clothes afterwards?" He pulled out some clean clothes for himself before digging into one of the other packs. "Or were you just going to walk back here naked? I'd vote for that option, personally."

I snatched the pair of panties he had dangling off his finger, and he smirked at me before quickly folding up a set of clean clothes.

"You're making it more and more tempting to find someone else who can show me these hot springs," I said in a mock growl.

He just grinned as he once again grabbed my hand and pulled me out of the room. I laughed as he practically dragged me to the hot springs, as if they'd disappear or I'd change my mind if we didn't get there fast enough.

"Oh," I breathed out when Kieran tugged me through the door of a simple but well-constructed building.

The wooden walls had been stained on the inside so that it was a deep reddish-brown, and dark grey stones had been stacked against the back wall, giving the room a cozy, natural feel. Fae lanterns provided a gentle blue glow that catapulted the already gorgeous space into something magical. A pool of crystal-clear steaming water awaited us.

I whispered in awe, "This is amazing."

"I know," Kieran said smugly as he placed our clothes on a bench in the corner. "There are other outposts I could visit that would be more convenient to meet people, but none of them have hot springs like this."

He moved to stand in front of me, and we stared at each other. Suddenly, I felt awkward.

Aside from that day in my office, we hadn't been intimate. I'd dreamed about it every night and thought about it when I touched myself, but this was *Kieran*.

My childhood crush who was even more gorgeous now than he was when we were teenagers. I'd been impulsive in my office earlier. It wasn't that I didn't want to move on from Demetri, because both me and my pussy were very much in agreement about moving the fuck on, but my feelings for Kieran were complicated, and I wasn't entirely sure I could handle a casual fling with him.

Yet at the same time, I wasn't ready to walk out of one long-term relationship and directly into another, assuming Kieran would even be interested in pursuing a relationship with me.

Fuck. How did I let things get so complicated so quickly?

I'd been so caught up in our flirting and teasing that I'd let myself fall into this too fast. Just because Kieran found me attractive didn't mean he felt anything beyond that. During our entire friendship, he'd always flirted back with me, and then I'd returned to House Harker and basically presented myself as a challenge.

I bit my bottom lip as I tried to contain my inner freakout. Kieran's exploits in the House courts weren't exactly a secret. Even at House Laurent, I'd heard whispers of his various bed partners.

Was I reading far too much into this when he really just thought of me as another notch on his bedpost?

Kieran started pulling off his shirt, and I stood there frozen in panic. I couldn't just leave without him asking questions, but I wasn't ready to answer them yet either.

Boundaries.

That's what I needed to do. Just set some boundaries to make sure things didn't go too far while I figured out my inner turmoil over this.

"Do you need help?" Kieran teased. "Or were you planning on getting in fully clothed?"

I gave him a breezy, confident smile to cover up the panic that had threatened to seize me moments before. Something flickered in his eyes, but it was gone before I could figure out what it meant.

"Just enjoying the show," I said in a husky voice as I very slowly perused him. His pants were untied and hanging low on his hips, allowing me a very enticing view.

He smirked as he finished pulling his clothes off until he stood there completely nude, and my mouth went dry.

Boundaries, I reminded myself firmly.

"Your turn." He winked at me and strode over to the wall to tap a glyph. Water fell from a cleverly hidden outlet in the ceiling, and he quickly washed himself off before sliding into the hot springs. "The water for rinsing off comes from the same hot springs, so it's warm. Try to get most of the grossness off you before getting in."

He leaned against the side of the pool, putting his perfectly carved chest on full display, and gestured for me to get on with it.

I casually shrugged one shoulder as if a thousand dirty thoughts hadn't just raced through my mind, and then I quickly disrobed. My plan had originally been to do it in a slow, teasing manner, but as soon as I started to unbutton my shirt, a whiff of the day's travels drifted up to my nose, and suddenly I couldn't wait to get the filth and grime off of me.

Kieran chuckled as I very unsexily tore my clothes off and chucked them onto the floor in disgust. But his laughter died off when I turned to face him and brushed my hair back over my shoulder so that I was on full display.

It was my turn to laugh as his eyes flashed gold. True to his word, the water was warm, and I scrubbed a day's worth of travel off me before languidly walking over to the pool.

"I'm ready for you to beg now." I lowered myself into the water, and a moan slipped from my lips.

Fuck. I closed my eyes. *This is heaven.*

"If you make that sound again, I just might," Kieran whispered into my ear.

My eyes snapped open to find him right in front of me with both arms braced on the pool's edge, caging me in.

"Hmm," I hummed as I ran my finger across his chest and down his well-defined abs.

He leaned into my touch, and I kept traveling southward, down past his waist before moving my hand away from the erection that was currently pressed against my leg.

He let out a frustrated groan as I dipped under his arm and moved to the other side of the pool.

"Sorry, I didn't hear any begging," I told Kieran cheekily.

Over towards the wall, several benches of varying heights had been set up so you could sit out of the water if you so desired, and I slowly swam over there.

There was nothing fancy about this building. The town residents had no doubt procured all the wood and stone from the nearby forest. Fae lanterns were easy to come by and took minimum tinkering to get working again.

If it'd been at one of the Houses, it would have tiled obsidian floors and all kinds of flourishes. But you could tell that the locals had taken pride in their work, and they'd built this place to give themselves just a little bit of peace in a dangerous world.

I sat on one of the stone benches that made the water come up to just below my chest. My long black hair was plastered to me, and I let out a contented sigh.

Kieran pushed off against the wall and slowly swam over to me before pulling himself up onto one of the taller benches. The water only covered that one by an inch, which meant he was completely on display.

I fixed my gaze on his face and kept clinging to my bored expression with everything I could. The corners of Kieran's mouth twitched as he watched me valiantly struggle not to look down.

"See anything that *you* want to beg for?" he taunted.

"Nope," I breathed out as I felt myself finally lose the battle to not look south.

My eyes widened as I took him in. I'd felt him pressed against my leg earlier, but he was even bigger than I imagined.

It took great effort not to lick my lips. "Not a single thing."

"Huh." A self-satisfied look appeared on his face as he took in my shocked expression. Then he leaned back against the pool's edge and fisted himself. My thighs snapped together, creating a splash of water. "You sure?"

"Absolutely," I said evenly. Although, my words probably would have had more impact if I wasn't staring at his dick.

With a truly heroic self-control on my part, I raised my eyes to meet his as an idea popped into my mind. My mouth curled into a sultry smile, and I bit my bottom lip, Kieran's gaze immediately snagging on the motion. Slowly, I ran my tongue across my top lip and was rewarded with his eyes turning solid gold.

The hand that had been stroking his cock froze, and I was pretty sure he stopped breathing as I maneuvered between his legs. I placed my hands on the smooth stone on either side of his legs and then leaned forward to lick his chest.

"Fuck," he ground out as his head fell back and he released himself so that he could lean back on both hands. I continued kissing and licking my way down his chest, tilting my head slightly so I could watch the muscles of his jaw flex.

I laughed huskily against his skin but stopped my downward direction before I reached his hard length.

He raised his head and stared down at me with a heat that had me wanting to climb on top of him and ride him until he screamed my name.

"Say it," I purred before licking my lips again.

"Fuck, you are evil," he growled. "And it's really fucking hot."

"Hotter than me running my tongue up your cock?" I tilted my head and sucked on my bottom lip.

"Fine!" he snapped. "Consider this me begging you to put that gorgeous mouth of yours to good use."

Fucking finally.

I held his gaze while I licked him from base to tip before swirling my tongue at the end. He let out a deep groan that sent shivers down my center. I loved hearing that sound from him and wanted to make him do it again and again.

"Shit," Kieran panted as I wrapped a hand around his thick length and sucked him into my mouth. His hips bucked as I took him in further, and he wrapped one hand around my hair.

I licked and sucked, enjoying every sound that spilled out of him. His hands tightened around my hair, but I could feel him keeping himself in check as he kept his thrusts slow and shallow.

That won't do. When he'd gone down on me in my office, I'd completely unraveled. I wanted him to do the same.

Slowly, I drew my mouth back up his cock until I swirled my tongue around his head. More rapid swearing erupted out of Kieran as I wrapped a hand around the base before sliding it up and down. The grip on my hair tightened as my tongue and hand worked in tandem.

A salty taste spread across my tongue, and I felt myself growing wetter as I clenched my thighs together.

"Sam," Kieran ground out.

My lips released his head with a pop, and I looked up at him through my lashes, a devilish smile on my face. This time when I took him in my mouth, I swallowed him all the way down, barely managed to hold back a gag when his cock hit the back of my throat.

Kieran's control snapped.

He pulled back hard on my hair, forcing me to raise my head a few inches before he thrust back into my mouth.

My fingers dug into his thighs as he bucked beneath me. Each rise of his hips was rough and wild, and I fucking loved every second of it. Tears squeezed out of my eyes as he pumped harder and harder into my mouth, and I had to concentrate on not gagging.

His cock swelled and Kieran came hard, roaring my name. I greedily drank every drop of him down as he spilled his hot climax at the back of my throat.

Once I'd wrung every last bit out, I slowly slid him out of my mouth and licked my lips. I would definitely be thinking about this tonight while I got myself off.

I calmly pushed off against the wall and floated back to the side of the pool closest to the doors.

"Where do you think you're going?" Kieran eyed me with a hungry expression.

"It's late." I shrugged, trying very hard to come across like I was in total control of this situation and that I wasn't planning on running back to my room where I could thrust my fingers inside myself and replay this whole encounter in my mind. Repeatedly. "We have a long day ahead of us tomorrow, so I'm going to get some rest."

Kieran let out a deep chuckle. "Do you really think I'm going to let you out of here wanting?" He slid off the bench he'd been sitting on and back into the water.

"I don't know." I swallowed. "Are you?"

I watched him swim towards me at a leisurely pace. My plan had been to walk out of here feeling like I was the one in control, but the closer Kieran got to me, the more I felt my resolve to leave fading.

Kieran reached for me and gently guided me to the edge of the pool. "Sit your ass up there and spread those gorgeous thighs of yours," he ordered.

Heat flashed through me, and I bit back a whimper. I thought about arguing or making him beg for a whole two seconds before I did exactly as he instructed.

I hopped out of the pool so that my back was towards the door before lying down with my legs still dangling in the water. Kieran wrapped his arms around my thighs, pulling me towards him before licking me straight up the center.

"My, my, my..." He let out a hot breath against my pussy. "You got off on me fucking your mouth, didn't you?"

"Hardly," I lied, even as I could feel myself growing wetter at the mere mention of it.

"Really?" He drew out the word before thrusting two fingers inside me.

My back arched, and my thighs clamped around him as need and pleasure built up in tandem. He withdrew his fingers and sucked them clean.

He drawled, "Because you're really fucking wet, love."

Any hope for coming up with a retort died when Kieran ducked his head again and sucked on my clit as he thrust those two fingers back inside, causing the orgasm I'd been racing towards to erupt. Just as a wall-shaking scream tore out of me, the door opened.

Kieran went still between my thighs, but I couldn't move because of the firm grip he had around my legs. A laugh barked out of me when I arched my back and twisted my head to look at the door behind me. Of fucking course.

Alaric stood there frozen as he stared at the both of us with his mouth gaping open.

"You here for dessert, friend?" My gaze snapped to Kieran, who was now resting his chin on my thigh with a cocky grin.

"Kieran!" I snarled and tried to tug myself free, but he just clamped down harder on my legs and laughed.

Alaric stared at us for a beat longer before spinning around and practically running out of the building, slamming the door shut behind him.

"So that's a no on dessert then?!" Kieran called after him.

"I'm going to kill you!" I hissed.

Alaric was going to be pissed about this, and I'd have to hear about it all day tomorrow.

Kieran just let out another chuckle before tugging me closer. "Guess I'll have to work hard to change your mind then."

CHAPTER TWELVE

—

Samara

I FROWNED at the wall surrounding the Millfell outpost and tugged my cloak closer around me despite the warm spring air. Our ride here had been uneventful, but a cloud of tension seemed to descend on everyone and only got worse when we arrived at the fallen outpost. It just looked so... normal.

All of the defenses appeared to be intact. It was a beautiful day, and there were rows of flowers blooming around the gates entering the town.

We should have been listening to the outpost residents bustling around, finishing their chores before night fell. Maybe some children running around playing. Instead, there was only silence. Stark, deafening silence.

My internal dread only increased the lower the sun sank in the sky.

It would be dark soon, and we'd be staying here tonight. I inhaled a deep breath and did my best not to think about it.

I agreed with Vail's decision for us to stay here instead of traveling back to Faybell. Traveling at night was too dangerous, especially with the horses, who would advertise our presence with every step and snort. I needed to make the trip here worth it, which meant I needed to focus and not freak out about spending the night in an outpost that had already been brushed by death.

"The wards look fine." Alaric's words jolted me out of thoughts, and my head snapped away from the wall I'd been staring at to him.

Those were the first words he'd spoken to me all day. Although he wasn't exactly talking to me, more so thinking out loud.

I'd overheard him and Kieran exchanging harsh whispers this morning, but they'd both stopped at my approach. Alaric had stalked away, and Kieran had simply planted a kiss on my lips before telling me to be careful.

I hadn't pushed Alaric to talk, mostly because I'd expected that we'd just argue, and I wouldn't apologize for what was happening between me and Kieran.

My feelings about it were complicated enough without having to deal with Alaric's shit on top of it. Although, I'd realized on the ride here that I actually *did* like working with Alaric. He was an arrogant prick, but he was also incredibly smart and often brought up flaws in my plans or thinking. Our working relationship wasn't perfect, but it was getting better, and I didn't want to lose that, so I decided to seize this opportunity and work with him on the problem at hand.

"Agreed." I crouched down next to the faint, dark red line that ran around the base of the perimeter fence.

Blood wards were some of the simplest spells, but they required a lot of blood to set up. Everyone who had lived in this outpost had donated theirs, and it had failed them.

I wanted to know why.

Alaric rose from where he was crouching and moved further down the fence before repeating the move. I did the same in the opposite direction. Emil went with Alaric, and Nyx followed me, keeping silent watch while I worked.

"There are no weak points, no broken segments," I said when Alaric and I met on the other side of the outpost. "Did you see anything?"

He shook his head. "Either whatever was done to the wards was temporary, or the wraiths have found a way to pass through them."

We were fucked either way. The blood wards had been a game changer for all of us, Velesians and Furies included. My generation had been born into relative safety as long as we stayed behind the wards. The previous generations had lived in a world where the monsters could attack at any moment, and they had.

The only reason our populations were steadily growing was because of the safety the blood wards provided.

I could tell by the deep crease between his brows that Alaric was having similar thoughts. We had to figure out a solution to this before more outposts fell and everyone started to panic.

"Let's look inside. Maybe we can find some clues there," I suggested.

The rangers followed Alaric and I back around the outpost to where Vail and Adrienne waited. I braced myself for whatever caustic comment Vail was going to make about how pointless it was to bring us, but he just looked us over and, upon seeing our frustrated expressions, moved towards the front gates.

Not before I saw the flash of disappointment across his face, though. Vail might hate me and be pissed about being ordered to bring us here, but he wanted to find out just as badly as we did why the blood wards were failing.

The silence as we entered the outpost set my nerves even further on edge. Aside from the lack of people, it looked like your typical outpost village. In front of us, a wide path led to the tavern. On either side were small shops and stalls where vendors could sell their wares.

I trailed my fingers across some sturdy dresses and tunics that were still hanging on one of the stalls, waiting for someone to buy them. Clothing, tools, and other items were displayed in the others.

This outpost was small enough that nobody was worried about theft. They'd probably been a tight-knit community that only saw the occasional visitors. This far off the main road, there wasn't much reason to come here unless you were visiting someone.

I veered off the path I was on and down one of the side streets to where the houses were.

A discarded doll lay on the steps outside of a simple but well-kept cottage, and I went still. It wore a dress that had seen better days. Even from here, I could see where the fabric had been patched.

Had the child dropped it on their way to bed? Or had they woken up during the attack and grabbed it while they ran from the house?

I squeezed my eyes shut. I hoped it was the former, and if not, then that their death had at least been quick.

It felt horrible to wish such a thing, but the alternative was that they spent their final moments in terror before getting ripped apart.

"We burned the bodies," Vail said quietly.

I jumped and slid to the side, turning to face him. He didn't comment on how badly he'd just scared me. Instead, his eyes were staring at the doll, and I didn't think he'd done it on purpose this time. Rangers survived by being able to move silently through the wilds just as much as being able to fight off attacks. It probably took more effort to make noise while he moved.

"Given the lack of smell, I figured that was the case." My words came out even but toneless.

Those who had died wouldn't even have a grave to remember them by. There were two gravestones in a small cemetery just outside House Harker that were supposed to mark my parents' final resting place.

But it was a lie. The graves were empty.

The wraiths and other monsters had ripped their bodies to shreds along with everyone else in that caravan.

Maybe burning the remains was better.

I shook my head slightly, trying to get my mind back on track. "You said the guards were attacked where they stood, but everyone else was killed while sleeping?"

Steel-grey eyes fell on me, and I fought the urge to shudder. "Yes."

I studied the houses that lined this street and then walked back to the main street. Something was bothering me about the buildings.

Vail trailed after me, a terrifying shadow in my wake, as I went to the other side of the village where more houses were packed in. They'd started adding second stories to some of the houses, but they were clearly outgrowing this outpost.

Alaric emerged from one of the houses with Emil. The crease between his brows had only deepened, and his movements were stiff. Some of that was likely from riding for the last two days, but I suspected more of it was a reaction to this place.

A few weeks ago, over two hundred people had lived here. Now, it was a solemn reminder of how quickly we could be wiped away.

"Have you looked in that one?" I pointed towards the cottage that sat at the end of the road.

Its door was closed, and there was no visible damage to the exterior that I could see. Cheerful yellow flowers with long, delicate petals bloomed from boxes beneath the windows.

"Not yet. That's the last one." Alaric studied the house. His usually bright, sharp eyes looked haunted. "It's the last one on this side. We should check it out, just to be thorough."

Vail and Emil took the lead and entered the house first while Alaric and I waited until Emil whistled the all-clear.

I headed inside when Alaric hesitated and quickly took stock of the home. Similar to all the other ones, this one was simple but well-kept. A small, sturdy table was set against one wall with a couple rows of dried herbs hanging above it.

I reached out and gently brushed the lavender. Alaric and Vail explored the other rooms while Emil poked through the small cooking area and the cupboards above it.

"Pantry?" I waved my hand towards the door in the far corner.

Emil glanced over his shoulder. "Yes. I checked it out and didn't see anything, but help yourself."

Leaving the herbs behind, I went to investigate the pantry. I wasn't exactly sure what I was looking for, but I was determined to leave no stone unturned while we were here. Maybe the locals had found something strange in the area and didn't realize what it was or that it was dangerous, so they tossed it somewhere for storage.

Before the thought even finished forming, I dismissed it. I let out a sigh that turned into a bloodcurdling shriek as I opened the door and was knocked off my feet by snarling beast.

"Shit!" In an instant, Emil was there pulling the creature off me.

I scrambled backwards until strong hands grabbed me and yanked me off the floor. Vail thrusted me at Alaric before going to help Emil.

"Strigoi," I rasped. Not that there was any need. We all knew what it was.

Emil grunted as he was slammed back into a wall. The Strigoi slipped from his grasp and darted towards the front door only to be blocked by Vail. The monster that up until recently had been a young Moroi male let out a low hiss and backed away.

Its deep green eyes took each of us in, looking for a weakness as it flexed claws dripping with Emil's blood at its sides.

Given the opportunity, it would run. Strigoi were monsters, but they weren't mindless. They were us at our most lethal level. And like any good predator, they knew when it was better to retreat and find easier prey.

"It must be one of the townsfolk." Alaric's words were barely more than a whisper.

I tilted my head up towards him and saw the haunted look in his eyes was still there, but now it was edged with pain. His family, I realized with horror. Some of Alaric's family had turned Strigoi when we were young. It had been a few years before my parents had been killed.

"Both of you, get out!" Vail growled.

Alaric gave no indication that he'd heard the order and remained frozen in place. I gripped his hand and pulled him after me as I raced towards the door.

Out of the corner of my eye, I saw Vail's silver blade flash followed seconds later by the sound of bodies crashing into the table I'd stood beside earlier.

I didn't look back and just kept running until we were halfway down the street. Nyx and Adrienne appeared seemingly out of nowhere.

"Strigoi!" I yelled, thrusting my hand towards the house we'd just fled from.

"Stay with them!" Adrienne ordered and took off down the street."

"What happened?" Nyx asked, taking a position between us and the house.

"One of the townsfolk must have turned Strigoi during the attack and escaped." I sucked in a deep breath as I tried to calm down. "Maybe it hid here? Or snuck back in?"

Alaric swallowed. "They like to go back to their original homes if they can. Part of them still remembers."

Nyx's eyes flicked back to us and lingered on Alaric for a moment before returning to the end of the street. "That's right. Our blood wards don't keep them out because... well..."

"They're still us," I said quietly. "We may call them something different. But there is no physical or magical difference between us and them."

Humanity. That was the only difference.

None of us spoke after that. An unnerving wail came out of the house before being abruptly cut off. A couple minutes later, the rangers stepped out, blood splattered on their clothes, and Emil had a nasty cut down his right arm.

"It's done," Vail said gruffly. "Do either of you want to inspect that house any further?"

"No," I said softly. "We saw all that we needed to."

"THESE BUILDINGS..." I halted where I'd been walking down the street on the other side of the outpost and spun around in a slow circle. Something about them was different, and it was bothering me. "This was a newer outpost, right?"

"Yes and no," Nyx said hesitantly. They hadn't left my side since the Strigoi attack.

Even after a second thorough search of the outpost, we hadn't found any other creatures, but I was grateful for their comforting presence.

Nyx went on, "It was never a Fae village but rather an old human one. The tavern and a few of the homes were from that settlement. It was the reason this was chosen as an outpost. The old human buildings were in disrepair, but it was easier to fix them up than build everything from scratch."

"Has that been the case with the other outposts?" I asked with a frown, still not sure why I felt the need to pull on this thread, but any information could prove useful.

Plus, as long as I focused on the problem at hand, I could almost forget the mind-numbing terror I'd felt when the Strigoi had pinned me down. I was lucky its claws had sunk into the floorboards above me instead of into my neck and shoulders. Having been so close to death...

Eventually, I had gone back to the house so I could examine the body. When deceased, the Strigoi looked even younger. Maybe sixteen at most. But in the home, I didn't find anything useful.

It didn't feel right, leaving him in his house, but Vail promised they'd bury the body later.

Nyx glanced at Vail before answering, "I'm not sure. The history of the outposts isn't always clear. Some of them were definitely built on top of old human towns, but the early outposts came about before we started keeping records, so we don't know as much about them other than that they're old."

"Hmm," I hummed, still staring at one of the houses that was likely originally built by a human.

"Do you think it matters?" Nyx asked.

"I don't know," I said honestly. "But any information about what could be a connection between the attacked settlements might prove important."

Alaric and I continued walking around the village, wandering in and out of houses. The three rangers trailed us, not getting in our way, but not willing to let us split up into smaller groups either.

When we found ourselves back at the front gate, I looked up at the darkening sky. There was maybe an hour left until sunset.

"I'd like to check the surrounding area."

Vail stared at me for a long moment before opening the gate and beckoning me through. "Emil and Nyx, guard the gate," he commanded. "Adrienne, stay with Alaric. Stay close."

Everyone nodded in agreement, but I hesitated as I looked at the woods beyond the gate. I really didn't want to be alone with Vail, with no witnesses around, especially with the night creeping up on us.

"Well?" The corner of his lips tilted up ever so slightly, as if reading my thoughts. "You coming or not?"

I swallowed and stepped through the gate before Vail shut it behind us, trying to ignore the uneasy sensation of having him at my back.

My heartbeat only picked up though, feeling like it was trying to break out of my chest, and I knew that Vail could hear it. Amongst the Moon Blessed, Morois had the best sense of hearing, and rangers worked hard to hone their senses even further. He knew I was terrified of him, and the sick bastard was probably enjoying it.

The forest here was different from the ones that ran up and down the coast. The trees were shorter and more dense, thick brushes grew between them, covered in sharp thorns, and a few ravens huddled together on the upper branches, watching me with intelligent eyes.

The shadows were already starting to deepen within the woods, but I steeled my spine and continued onward.

I had no idea what I was looking for, but after ten minutes of wandering around, I felt a subtle tug. It felt like when I used blood magic and directed my power towards an object. Only, in this case, it was like my magic was being pulled forward.

Slowly, I followed the feeling as my pulse picked up. Vail moved to my side, and I felt his curious gaze on me, but thankfully he didn't question me as we wandered deeper into the woods. The tug was so faint I was worried that if I spoke, I would lose it. My foot snagged on an upraised root, and I stumbled, but Vail's hand shot out to grip my arm.

I froze as I stared down at my feet, barely noticing Vail's fingers, which were still holding tightly onto me. Then the tugging feeling within my chest faded, leaving the barest trace of satisfaction behind.

The root I had tripped over widened as it got closer to the tree, rising several feet above the ground and creating a small shelter beneath it.

Within that shallow space lay the body of a young Moroi boy.

Vail released my arm and knelt down next to him. Now that I was no longer caught up in the strange pull of my magic, the smell of death hit me. My stomach churned, and I barely managed to hold down the bread and cheese I'd eaten for lunch.

Large chunks of his body were missing. Clearly more than a few somethings had been feasting on him. I watched as Vail methodically examined each of the visible wounds before turning the body over to look at his back. His fingers briefly skimmed down the boy's neck, brushing the hair aside, and I caught a glimpse of a dark red line.

"What's that?" I dropped to my knees and leaned forward.

I'd thought the smell of decomposition couldn't be worse. I was wrong. With a grimace, I pushed back the boy's dark brown hair and looked at the symbol that had been carved into the back of his neck.

Vail shifted closer to me, his thigh pressed against mine as he studied the symbol. "Do you know what it is?"

"No." I cocked my head to the side as I puzzled over the markings for a few more seconds before pulling a folded piece of paper out of my pocket.

Carefully, I unfolded it and placed it flat against the boy's neck, then pinched the corner of the paper between my thumb and index finger where a symbol of two interlocking squares had been drawn in blood.

A tingling sensation nipped at my fingers as the blood magic sparked to life. This particular spell was one of my own creation, and I was rather proud of it. I held the paper in place as faint lines started to appear and soon the symbol on the back of the boy's neck copied over to the paper.

My head cocked to the side as I held it up and studied the lines more. "Something about it is familiar, though... I think."

"How did you know he was here?" Vail asked.

Something in his tone had me moving to create distance between us. It wasn't threatening exactly, but there was a faint accusation to it.

"I didn't." I pushed up so that I was standing and then I shifted further away from the body and Vail. "I just felt... a pull."

"A pull? Towards a dead body with a blood magic symbol carved into it?"

"Don't get pissy just because I found a major fucking clue that you missed!" I snapped.

Silver lines flared to life in Vail's eyes before vanishing, and I took a deep breath, willing myself to calm down as I refolded the paper and tucked it safely back into my pocket.

I said carefully, "Look, I'm more than a little freaked out right now. I'm not exactly used to being around dead bodies. My magic is acting weird, and you fucking scare the shit out of me. Can you just... not right now?"

"Fine, but this conversation isn't over." He glanced back at the body, lips twisting into a grimace. "I'll take you back to the village and then come back for the body. We'll have to examine it further to figure out what he died from. Most of these wounds are from scavengers."

I was grateful he didn't ask me to help him carry the Moroi corpse back. My stomach was still queasy, and if I had to touch the body again, I was fairly certain I would be vomiting up everything I'd eaten today.

We swiftly made it back to the village, where Emil and Adrienne left to help Vail fetch the body.

Alaric, Nyx, and I crowded around a table in the tavern, the paper with the symbol on it stretched out between us. Neither of them had recognized it, but I knew that I had seen it somewhere. But no matter how hard I wracked my brain, I couldn't remember.

CHAPTER THIRTEEN

—

Alaric

EXHAUSTION TUGGED at me as I stretched out on my bedroll the following morning. Nothing had bothered us during the night, but I'd had a hard time sleeping, knowing that the wraiths could get past the blood wards.

Technically, that was true of all our outposts, and probably our fortresses too, but at least in those, I was able to lie to myself about them being safer because of how many rangers patrolled the grounds and the strange Fae magic that still lingered in our perimeter walls.

It had only been the six of us last night, and the encounter with the Strigoi had unsettled me more than I had let on.

Unlike Kieran, Samara, and or even Vail, my bloodline was one of obscurity. My parents had originally been born in an outpost where they eventually fell in love and became the leaders of things when they were older. My mother was incredibly sharp, and nothing ever slipped her memory. She could remember the exact amount of wheat harvested from the previous five seasons in an instant.

And my father absolutely loved to solve problems and was always level-headed. Their strong aptitude had eventually come to Carmilla's attention, and she in turn recruited them to be her advisors.

I was born after that, so House Harker was all I knew. My mother's family died when she was young, but my father still had family in several different outposts, and we'd occasionally go and visit them. Faolan was a cousin who was close to my age, and we'd gotten along well. The only kids my age at House Harker, before Kieran had arrived, were Samara and Vail.

Samara and I had never gotten along, a situation that hadn't much improved, and Vail was almost always gone with his parents or training with the rangers. Even from a young age, he'd been determined to be one of them.

The outpost that Faolan lived in with his parents wasn't the same one my parents had been from. It was a newer one that they were trying to build up and secure. The first few years of a new outpost's existence were always the riskiest. Most of the monsters that prowled the wilds of Lunaria had specific territories, and they didn't like it when something encroached on them.

Faolan's outpost was under frequent attacks, and it caused a lot of stress amongst the townsfolk.

My parents had pleaded with them to move back to the outpost they'd all been born in, which was older and far more secure, but Faolan's parents had been determined to make it work.

It didn't.

We'd arrived for one of our regularly scheduled visits only to find the outpost gate torn open.

Most of the residents were dead, their bodies shredded and partially eaten by whatever beast had broken through the defenses. Those who hadn't died to the monsters coming from the outside had fallen to those within.

Some of the Moroi had given into their bloodlust in an effort to survive. Their attempts to survive were successful... but they couldn't come back from it.

I still vividly remembered standing in the center of the town as my parents wept next to me and seeing Faolan peel away from the shadows of a partially collapsed house. As a Moroi, he'd always been cheerful and boisterous. But as Strigoi, he'd prowled towards us in complete silence, his eyes locked on his prey with an intensity I'd never once seen on his face.

I'd been too terrified to say anything until I saw three more dark forms moving in the house Faolan had emerged from. His parents and younger sister.

A scream tore out of my lungs, but it was too late. Faolan and the other Strigoi in town ripped into us.

We'd only survived because of pure luck. The outpost had built a secure bunker, and its door had been only a few feet away from us. It hadn't saved the residents of the town, but it had saved us. My mother shielded me as best she could while my father shoved us all towards the sanctuary.

Both of them had been severely injured, and I bore a long scar down my back where Faolan's claws had ripped into my flesh.

Eventually, the Strigoi had left to find easier prey, and we'd fled. My parents rarely left the walls of House Harker after that, and I only did so when I absolutely had to. I didn't know if Faolan was still out there somewhere, stalking in the dark forests of Lunaria, or whether he'd fallen to a ranger's blade.

It might make me a coward, but I didn't want to know. I usually preferred to deal in absolute certainties but when it came to my cousin's fate, I found an odd comfort in the ambiguity of it all. He was both alive and dead and until I knew which I preferred, I'd rather not know.

The rangers had handled keeping watch so that Samara and I could sleep. Although, based on the way she tossed and turned, I think she got even less sleep than I did.

Vail made everyone stay in the tavern so that we were all in one location, and we all pulled down mattresses and blankets from the rooms upstairs. Eventually, I'd given up on sleeping and simply stared up at the ceiling, trying to figure out what that symbol could mean. Samara claimed to have recognized it, but I'd never seen anything like it. Granted, I hadn't studied blood magic beyond the basics that everyone knew.

Even though I didn't know what the symbol meant or what it was used for, I did know that it was made with blood magic. We could all feel it, and only Moroi used that kind of magic.

Maybe the boy's parents had used it on him in an attempt to save his life, and it was some protection spell none of us were familiar with.

If that was the case, their efforts had clearly failed.

The coldness that seeped through my bones had nothing to do with the drafty tavern. Maybe the wraiths were getting past the blood wards because a Moroi was *helping* them.

It seemed unthinkable because while the Houses bickered amongst themselves, we'd always known that sticking together was the only way we'd survive. It was the reason the Moroi were arguably the strongest of the Moon Blessed. The Velesians seemed to be getting closer and closer to outright war between their Orders, and the Furies were always on the brink of going insane and slaughtering us all. I'd thought that at least the Moroi had their shit together.

I was still trying to think of reasons why the symbol could have been on the boy that didn't mean a Moroi was betraying us when the sun fully crested over the horizon. It was an odd feeling that I'd mostly grown accustomed to but still didn't like. I could feel some of my strength flee my body. The world became... less.

Colors became less vivid. Scents less acute. At night, everything felt so alive, while during the day it felt like life slumbered.

Fatigue slammed into me, and suddenly going all night with basically no sleep seemed like a really poor choice on my part. A groan slipped out when I thought of the all-day ride ahead of us.

Samara rose from where she'd been curled up in no less than five blankets. She stretched towards the ceiling, arching her back, and the blanket she'd had wrapped around herself fell away. Every thought emptied out of my head, and certain parts of my body became concerningly hard. At some point in the night, she'd pulled her shirt off and had slept only in a tight-fitting camisole.

Every inch of her ridiculous body was on display. I mean, really. Who the fuck had curves like that?

I quickly looked away, but it was too late.

My treacherous mind took advantage of my distracted state, offering up the memories of her with Kieran the other night and the way her lips had parted when she'd moaned as he gripped her thighs and feasted on her.

I wondered what she'd feel like beneath me.

Or better yet, on top of me.

What it would feel like to run my fingers over her soft skin and dig my fingers into those luscious curves.

What it would be like to part those thick fucking thighs and taste—

"Alaric?" Samara sang from where she now stood behind the counter.

My gaze snapped back towards her. Thankfully, she'd put the rest of her clothes back on and was shaking an empty teacup at me.

She arched a brow. "Do you want tea?"

"No, I don't want fucking tea!" I snapped. "I want to get on the fucking road and back to House Harker."

"Somebody's grouchy in the morning." She smirked, and my cock twitched.

Fuck my life.

This was not happening. I did *not* like Samara. This was just the result of me seeing her with Kieran. That was all.

I repeated that thought in my head as I mentally tried to wrestle my stupid body under control and caught the tail end of a conversation among the rangers. They'd bundled up the body of the boy in several blankets and had used blood magic to prevent further decay. We'd be taking him back with us for further examination.

My brain was still sluggish, so it took me a moment to understand what the problem was.

We needed to carry the body back, and we didn't have a spare horse. Shit.

"Alaric can ride with me," Samara said loudly.

"No. Absolutely not!" I couldn't keep the edge of panic out of my voice as Nyx flashed me a knowing grin.

Samara glanced up from where she was hunting through the cupboards for something, and her eyes searched my face, but I forced my features back into my normal, bored expression. I wasn't as good as Kieran at moving between different masks, so I'd perfected this one.

"You're the worst rider of the group," she said evenly. "Someone has to give up their mount for the ride back, and you're the logical choice."

I glared at her, the muscle beneath my right eye twitching because her reasoning was perfectly logical, which only served to piss me off more. "Fine, but I'll ride with someone else."

There was no way I was riding pressed up against her all day. Not happening.

She shook her head. "The rangers shouldn't be hindered by a second rider. If we run into trouble, we need them to protect us."

Vail's expression remained blank, but the other rangers nodded in agreement.

I wondered if Vail thought he would be struck dead if he agreed with Samara on anything. There was something between them; everyone knew that he hated her.

Since I grew up at House Harker, I'd known both of them my entire life. I still remembered the night that the news came in, that their caravan had been attacked and both of their parents had perished. Vail and Samara had been with them, both children at the time.

A search party was sent out to locate them when their bodies weren't recovered with the rest. Three days after the attack, they were both found in a nearby cave. Badly injured, but alive.

They were the only survivors.

Most people assumed that was why he hated her, but I thought there was a little more to it than that.

Vail was asshole, no doubt. But he wouldn't hate Samara the way he did simply because she had survived. She must have done something to earn the kind of hatred that burned in Vail's eyes every time he looked at her. Though, the only one who could answer that question was them.

Samara lined up four teacups on the worn wooden counter before pulling down two more, and then I watched as she poured everyone tea. She added some honey to hers and then more to another cup, which she nudged in my direction before setting the honey jar down next to the others.

I stared at the steam rising off the tea, carrying with it a tangy sweet scent. Rationally, I knew Samara was smart and observant. Her ability to read others and identify any personality traits or quirks that could be of benefit in a negotiation was unmatched. I also knew that she viewed me as an adversary, so it made sense she would study me in this way. And yet I still felt a pleasant warm tingle in my chest as I took in the tea before me.

No. I scolded myself. This is exactly what she wanted and I wouldn't fall prey to her the way Kieran had. Sooner or later, his feelings towards Samara would blow up in his face and I needed to be at my best to pick up the pieces.

All the rangers except Vail took their drinks and thanked Samara. Nyx snatched the remaining tea and thrust it at Vail, not flinching as some of the hot liquid sloshed out over their fingers. He glared at the cup, but Nyx just kept holding it out to him until he begrudgingly took it.

I caved and snatched the teacup that had been nudged towards me and took a sip. *Delicious*. Argh.

I felt Samara's smug gaze on me, and I narrowed my eyes at her. "What?"

"I'm waiting for my thanks." She arched one perfectly sculpted dark eyebrow, and the muscle beneath my eye twitched again.

"You'll keep waiting." I set the cup down with a disinterested expression even as I wanted nothing more than to wrap my fingers around the warm ceramic and savor the perfection of it for the next few minutes.

Samara sniffed and sipped her tea but otherwise kept quiet. Nyx smiled into their drink, and I wanted to smack it out of their hands. They noticed too much, and I didn't like it.

"We'll ready the horses," Adrienne said as she tugged Nyx towards the door.

"Thank you for the tea, Samara!" Nyx shouted, holding their tea up in the air in salute. Vail's annoyed expression was twin to my own.

We finished our drinks in silence before heading outside. I was beyond ready to get the hell out of here and return to the safety of my study at House Harker.

I would declare that a Samara-free zone from now on. Maybe I could make a blood ward specific to keeping her out? Pure genius.

The rangers secured the unmoving body over the back of the horse I'd originally rode on and guided it through the front gates. I followed as everyone else led their horses out, tension ratcheting up with each step.

"I really think I should ride with one of the other rangers," I said. "They have more experience, so they won't be thrown off by a second rider."

Samara snorted. "I'm just as good as them." She easily mounted her mare and flashed me a smug look. "Kieran used to ride with me all the time when we were younger."

Yeah, because he's been in love with you forever and seized any opportunity to get close to you, I thought.

Kieran would say he was in lust, but I knew it was more than that. It was one of the many reasons I could not dare to get on that horse. Samara was annoying, and I wanted nothing to do with her.

And my best friend was in love with her.

I desperately looked towards Nyx for help, but they just gave me that damn lazy grin of theirs. No help there.

The other two rangers had already moved forward, tugging the reins of the horse with the body draped over it behind them. That left only Vail, and there was no chance in hell he'd let me ride with him even if I asked, which I absolutely would not.

Shit.

"Quit being such a baby," Samara said, nudging her mare closer to me. She pulled her foot out of the stirrup and shifted in the saddle. "Mount up behind me."

Fuck.

Nyx snickered, and I gave them a death glare before turning back towards Samara, who was just looking at me expectantly.

I didn't know if she was messing with me on purpose or if she had no idea about my body's obnoxious attraction towards her, but I was officially out of options, so I walked stiffly over towards Samara and shoved my foot into the stirrup. With an extremely ungraceful hop, I shoved myself up and swung my leg over the mare.

"Scoot closer," Samara commanded, reaching back and pulling me forward.

My jaw hardened as I did as instructed. Thankfully, the seat of the saddle curved up in the back, so my dick was nestled up against that instead of Samara's ass. It wasn't comfortable, but I didn't care.

I awkwardly tried to figure out where to put my hands, but apparently, Samara had run out of patience because she grabbed my arms and yanked them forward.

My chest pressed against her back as she wrapped my arms around her waist, and I fought back a flush.

"Hold on." I could hear the grin in her voice. Before I could snap back at her, Samara dug her heels into her horse, and we took off.

I'm not proud of the yelp that came out of me. Thank the moon, Kieran wasn't there to hear it.

A joyous laughter poured out of Samara as she urged her mare faster. The others had also spurred their mounts onward as we raced down the trail.

I squeezed my eyes shut and held onto Samara for dear life, despite everything in me screaming to let go. That this was *Samara*. I shouldn't be touching her at all.

After what seemed like forever, we finally slowed down to a more reasonable pace. Unfortunately, despite how smooth Samara's mare was in her steps, the jog was still bumpy, and I had to continue clutching onto Samara to keep from falling off.

This was going to be an excruciatingly long ride. I desperately needed a distraction. Anything.

Swallowing, I said stiffly, "Any idea where you recognize that symbol from?"

"No." Samara let out a breath of frustration. "But I *know* I've seen it before. Maybe at Drudonia? Their library is massive, and I took advantage of that while I was there. Rynn was in love with that library, so she always wanted to be there."

I could feel Samara's chuckle beneath my hands, and my heart beat a little faster.

She added with a shrug, "Cali, on the other hand, wanted to be outside all the time. She thought the library was stuffy and too confining."

"They are... very different people," I admitted.

Both Rynn and Cali had stayed at House Harker less often the last few years while Samara had been gone, but I was familiar enough with both of them to know that Rynn and Cali were exact opposites. Samara shared qualities with both of them, so it made sense that she was the middle ground between them.

I liked Rynn. She was quiet and soft-spoken, but also incredibly intelligent. Every conversation with her was fascinating.

Cali, however, scared the shit out of me. I couldn't explain why. She'd never done anything to me, had never shown any signs of losing herself to madness like so many Furies, but every time I was around her, my instincts screamed at me to get away.

Something powerful and monstrous lived inside Cali, and I didn't want to be anywhere near her when it eventually broke free.

"I've told them everything about the attacks," Samara said lightly. "Well, I told Rynn who has probably told Cali by now."

"Of course you have." I fought the urge to rub at my face in frustration. There was no way I was letting go of Samara's waist. For safety reasons, of course.

"We all agreed to bring Rynn in on this," she said defensively. "And it's not like Rynn and I could not tell Cali. We tell each other everything."

I didn't bother arguing. Cali might freak me out, but I had no doubts of her loyalty to Rynn and Samara. She wouldn't tell anyone.

"There's someone else I would like to bring into this," Samara continued. "Roth Devereux."

I frowned. The name sounded vaguely familiar.

When I didn't say anything, Samara rushed on. "They were at Drudonia with us, but a year behind. Rynn says that Roth has continued studying the history of blood magic and that they're currently back at Drudonia. I was going to send a message to them when I get back and see if they wanted to come to House Harker, otherwise, I'll go to them."

My brow creased. "I don't know if it's a good idea for us to bring more people into this." The Sovereigns probably wouldn't like it, and I didn't know this Roth person. "The more people who know, the more of a chance there is of this getting out and causing widespread panic."

"If the attacks keep increasing, then there is just as much chance of it getting out anyway," she countered. "The last few attacks have been at outposts that are off the beaten path, but some of the early ones were main outposts. If another large outpost is attacked, people will start asking questions again."

"Alright," I sighed, weighing our options. "But I want to be involved with any conversations you have with Roth."

"Of course," she said cheerfully. "I wouldn't *dream* of keeping you out of the loop." I stared at the back of her head and debated shoving her off the horse, but I would definitely fall with her. Still... almost worth it.

Ahead of us, Adrienne veered off the road and dismounted. We all stopped while she crouched down and studied the ground. I carefully leaned towards the side to get a glimpse of what she was looking at.

Footprints. Many large footprints.

My blood ran cold as I glanced around the tall trees surrounding us. It was daylight, so we should be fine. Most of the nasty creatures that roamed these lands only did so at night.

But still...

"Problem?" Vail asked as his beast-sized horse stopped beside us. Samara subtly nudged her mare a few steps away from him.

"Howlers," Adrienne spat. "Looks like a large pack."

"Shit," Emil and Nyx said at the same time.

Samara's body stiffened beneath me. She recognized the name too. Of course, we would run into one of the rare monsters that preferred to hunt during the day.

Howlers weren't as dangerous as wraiths or many of the other beasts that prowled the night, but they were still nasty to deal with and preferred to travel in packs, using their numbers to overwhelm their prey.

The six of us with our horses would be a very tempting meal for them. An abundance of flesh and blood.

"How old are the tracks?" I asked, fighting to keep my voice steady.

"They're fresh, probably from this morning."

Vail scanned the forest around us as we awaited his command. My heart continued to thump loudly in my chest, and I couldn't help but hold this irrational fear that it would draw the howlers to us like a dinner bell.

While I knew about the wraiths and other monsters, I'd hadn't actually seen all that many of them firsthand. My parents rarely traveled after their encounter with the Strigoi, and I'd only begun traveling again when I took over their post as an advisor.

After this fun adventure, I'd be perfectly happy to not leave House Harker again for at least another decade.

"We'll pick up the pace a little but keep it reasonable. We still have a long way to go, and we need to preserve as much of the horses' strength as we can in case we need to run later," Vail said, solemn grey eyes still on the surrounding forest. "No talking. Stay as quiet as possible. We can't do anything about the horses, but no need to draw further attention to ourselves." Vail eyed Samara then. "Does your hand-eye coordination extend to crossbows?"

"Why, Vail, are you finally acknowledging that I'm good with daggers?" Samara drawled.

I couldn't help but be a little impressed by her brazenness. I knew she was scared of Vail. Anyone with an ounce of common sense knew to be wary of him, but that fear didn't stop her from being her usual cocky self.

When Vail just continued to stare at her, Samara let out an annoyed huff. "Yes, I'm good with crossbows."

Vail grunted and reached behind him, pulling off the second crossbow that was attached to his saddle pack. He nudged his horse closer and handed it over to Samara as she wrapped the reins loosely over the front of the saddle and took it from him. After looking it over carefully, she nodded and clipped it to a ring on the front of her saddle, where it was within easy reach. Then Vail handed over half a dozen bolts, and she slid those into a pouch on the other side before picking up the reins again.

Emil and Adrienne took off at a slightly faster pace. I grimaced as Samara's mare followed after them.

This fast trot proved to be even bumpier than the steady jog had been, and my grip around Samara's waist became even tighter, but she didn't complain.

Apparently, my dick lacked all self-preservation though, because while my heart was still pounding rapidly, and my brain was thinking about all the ways the howlers could attack, my dick's only reaction was to harden at the increased contact. Great. Just perfect.

I needed to get laid when we returned. It'd been... a while. That's all this was. Just my ignored libido demanding attention.

There were bound to be some visiting nobles at the House sometime soon. I preferred to have flings with people who would be leaving at short notice, as I had no desire for a relationship and all the hassle that came with it.

We rode for hours without stopping, my thighs burning, and I knew that every part of my body would be aching tonight, but there would be no breaks today. I sighed with relief when we finally passed a sign displaying the distance to the Faybell outpost. At our current pace, we'd be there in less than an hour. Maybe I'd make use of the hot springs tonight.

Not with Samara, of course. Just on my own. She and Kieran would just have to enjoy each other's bodies somewhere else because I wanted absolutely nothing to do with their ill-fated relationship.

I was still trying to convince myself of that thirty minutes later when the attack happened. It was so fast that I didn't even process what was going on until my body jerked back as Zosa leapt into a full-fledged gallop.

"Hold on!" Samara screamed. Only her reaching back and gripping the front of my tunic kept me from falling off.

I locked my hands around her waist once more and held on for dear life. Zosa's hooves pounded into the dirt, her long strides keeping pace with the rangers in front of us. I looked over my shoulder and saw Nyx and Vail right on our heels, and behind them... Fear clamped me when I spotted howlers tearing down the trail after us.

Excited yips filled the air as they kept pace with us. Their long legs were made for running. They weren't faster than the horses, but they were just fast enough that we were barely increasing the distance between us and them.

Samara shifted the reins to one hand before unsnapping the crossbow from the saddle and carefully loaded a bolt into it. She kept it pointed down as she urged Zosa faster.

The road curved, and I saw the outpost in the distance nestled between the trees. An alarm blared as they caught sight of us.

We just had to make it to the outpost. We were so damn close.

A sleek, furry shape launched itself from the forest edge directly at Emil before I could scream a warning. Not that it would do any good. Everything was happening too fast.

Samara snapped up the crossbow and fired. The bolt pierced the beast's eye, and it jerked its head to the side before falling in a broken heap to the ground, scarcely avoiding a collision with Emil's horse.

Samara loaded another bolt, barely breaking a sweat.

I'd thought her throw the other day at Vail had been pure luck. Apparently not. Maybe I'd be more careful about pissing her off in the future.

The alarm in the outpost continued to wail as the guards raised the gate. We continued onward, not slowing down until we were within the safety of the outpost's stone walls. Then Samara steered Zosa in a wide arc to slow her as the portcullis slammed down behind us.

But not without trouble snaking its way through the gate.

Two howlers had made it inside, but the rest snarled and howled from beyond the walls, a cacophony of darkness within the forest. The rangers within the outpost were quick to dispatch the two interlopers who had made it inside and after a few arrow shots, the howlers outside melted back into the trees.

Our rides were breathing hard and dripping in sweat, and I couldn't help but feel for the beasts.

I slid off Zosa, my lip curling as sweaty horsehair clung to my skin and clothes. My knees threatened to buckle beneath me, but I forced myself to stand straight, refusing to lean against the sweaty mare for support.

Samara leapt off Zosa as if she hadn't been riding all day and nimbly landed on her feet, crossbow still in hand. I held back an eyeroll. Show-off.

The blaring alarms were finally silenced, and after a minute, the windows and doors from the buildings within the outpost started to carefully open as Moroi peered around, ensuring the danger was actually gone before they came out to greet our entourage.

Emil dismounted and walked over to the bodies of the two beasts that had made it inside before being slain. He raised his eyes, which were full of sincerity, and looked at Samara. "Thank you," he said quietly. "That was one hell of a shot."

"Don't mention it." Samara shrugged and handed him the crossbow.

Then Kieran came running and pulled me and Samara into a hug. "You two just had to make a dramatic entrance, didn't you?"

"Yep," Samara retorted, her words slightly muffled because she was pressed into his shoulder. "Didn't want to disappoint you."

"We thought about riding in here all calm-like," I said, "but then we thought, why do that when we could be chased by monsters instead?"

Kieran pulled back slightly so he could peer at me. "Did you just make a joke?"

I scowled and shoved him off me. "I'm going to clean up and get some food."

"The hot springs are real nice," Kieran said slyly, tucking Samara into his side. "The three of us could check them out later."

It was Samara's turn to shove Kieran then. He laughed as she shook her head at him and stalked off, leading Zosa away. Vail and the other rangers followed her with the exception of Emil, who was still next to the bodies of the howlers and toeing one of them with his foot.

His lips curled. "Looks like meat is on the menu tonight."

CHAPTER FOURTEEN

—

Samara

I STARED at the box of my belongings that waited for me in my suite back at House Harker. We'd arrived in the late afternoon, the second leg of the trip home considerably less exciting than the one yesterday. Vail and the rangers had veered off to secure the body, and Alaric had gone along because he wanted to examine it again and had dragged Kieran with him.

My plan had been to rinse off and draft a letter to send to Roth, but halfway to my suite, a servant stopped me to let me know that a letter and package had arrived from House Laurent while I'd been gone.

I'd been alternating between pacing back and forth and staring at the letter I'd tossed onto my bed. Its words had yet to fully sink in.

But at the same time... they felt freeing.

House Laurent accepts the request to dissolve the marriage between Samara Harker and Demetri Laurent. Effective immediately.

I was officially a divorced woman.

The letter had been signed by Marvina. I thought for sure she would make more demands or draw this out just to be petty. I also thought Demetri might send a letter, pleading for another chance to make this work,

But there was nothing from him. Nothing at all to signify our relationship had ever meant anything.

Just the simple letter from Marvina and a signed copy of the marriage dissolution we had originally sent her. The box contained all the clothes I'd brought with me from House Harker, but none of my House Laurent possessions.

The message was clear. *You will get nothing from us, and we want nothing from you.*

I should be relieved that it was over so easily, and I was, but I was also suspicious. It seemed out of character for Marvina to give me anything I wanted. She could have easily made this process more difficult and made demands of House Harker since I was the one requesting to dissolve the marriage.

She could have gotten some very favorable trade deals. Instead, she asked for nothing, like she was as eager to have this all done as I was.

Odd.

My finger grazed the silky grey fabric of the dress I'd worn the first day I'd arrived at House Laurent.

It was one of my more modest dresses, but the look on Marvina's face had told me it wasn't modest enough. I pulled out the other dresses that I'd never worn while there because they were far too scandalous. Slowly, a smile spread across my face. I could wear whatever the hell I wanted now.

I dug through the box some more until I found a dress made of the same silky material as the grey one, but this was a rich, vibrant purple. It was a halter top style, which left the entire back open. The fitted top hugged my breasts before cascading into layers of sheer fabric.

It didn't have any high slits on the side, but the bottom half was just see-through enough to be interesting without revealing everything. It'd been years since I'd worn it.

Kieran would lose his mind when he saw me in it tomorrow.

I grinned wickedly as I gathered up all the dresses to hang them up in my closet. Once that was done, I rinsed off and tossed on a pair of comfy pants and a thin, light-weight top.

I was drying my hair when a slow, three-beat knock sounded on my door.

There was only one person who would knock on my door like that.

I swung it open, revealing Kieran leaning against the doorframe. His eyes roamed up and down, snagging on my breasts where my nipples were probably clearly visible through the thin fabric.

"Really?" I arched an eyebrow at him. "What are you, sixteen?"

He scoffed, "Please, I was much more subtle at sixteen." He breezed into my suite, and I shut the door behind him.

"I'm busy, Kieran," I said, continuing to towel dry my hair. "I need to write some letters updating Carmilla and requesting some assistance from someone at Drudonia."

"Ugh," he groaned before collapsing onto my bed. "You're just like Alaric. It's always work with you two."

"Yes," I said dryly. "Us working hard to prevent more attacks on our outposts must be a real inconvenience for you."

"Thank you for acknowledging that." He rolled over to his side and propped himself up on an elbow. "What's this?" He picked up the letter from

House Laurent, where it still lay on my bed, and read it. Given that there wasn't much to read, it only took him a few seconds. His eyes flicked up to mine, both eyebrows raised. "Is this for real?"

I nodded. "It has Marvina's official seal on it. The signed marriage dissolution is over there." I pointed to the table in my sitting area. "I'm officially no longer married."

He leapt off the bed and gathered me in his arms, spinning me around. "Congratulations on the happiest day of your life!"

An embarrassing giggle bubbled out of me that I hoped no one else ever heard. Rynn and Cali would tease me about it mercilessly, and gods only knew how Alaric would react to it. He'd either ridicule me, or his lips would curl in that tiny, amused smile of his that always commanded my attention. It was rare that I'd see that smile directed at me. Usually Kieran was the recipient, but every once in a while, when the three of us were hanging out, Alaric would forget that he despised me. And I would forget every nasty word said between us as that smile sent my heart racing.

Then I would mentally slap myself and do my best not to ponder why I had such a reaction. Alaric didn't want me in that way, and I would never pursue someone who wasn't interested in my advances.

"Isn't the day you get married supposed to be the happiest day of your life?" I asked when Kieran finally put me down but didn't release me entirely. His hands were still resting on my hips, and I decided that I liked them there.

"Only for suckers."

I snorted. "Such a romantic you are."

"I can be romantic." He gave me a heated look.

"I think you're confusing romantic with horny."

"It's a personal fault of mine." His eyes twinkled for a moment before turning more serious. "Are you happy?" He gestured towards the letter. "With it being over and done?"

And that was why I adored Kieran. Even with us... taking things to the next level, he was still my friend and deeply cared about me.

Of course, that's also what terrified me about him.

Our friendship was rapidly moving toward something else, something foreign, and I didn't know what I wanted, let alone what he wanted. All I knew was that losing him as a friend would be devastating.

"Happy doesn't even begin to explain it," I said honestly. "I had resigned myself to spending the next few months arguing with Marvina and then feeling guilty about whatever demands she made of House Harker that Carmilla would have no doubt accepted. But now I'm free, and it was all pretty easy. Even got some of my favorite dresses back."

"No doubt those dresses will be tormenting me in the future," Kieran mused, but his eyes grew a little distant. "It is weird though, right? That Marvina didn't use this to her advantage?"

I chewed on the inside of my cheek. "I thought so, too."

"Maybe Demetri asked her to sign it?"

I thought about it and then shook my head. "Even if he did, which I doubt, Marvina isn't really the doting mother type. She does what's best for House Laurent. Always. No matter what that means for others."

"And signing that contract so easily was not in the best interest of her House." He frowned at where the letter still lay on my bed. "I'll be visiting House Corvinus soon. I'm friendly with one of the Heir's best friends, and she's friendly with the daughter of one of Marvina's advisors."

"She?" I stiffened before forcing the tension between my shoulders to loosen, and then I casually waved a hand to hopefully cover up my momentarily flash of irrational jealousy. "Which advisor? I've met most of their children, at least the ones that were living at House Laurent. Several of them had children at Drudonia or at other Houses." Realizing I was babbling, I snapped my mouth shut.

Kieran traced a finger down the side of my neck and across my collarbone. "Sam?" he purred as I leaned into his touch without even thinking.

"Mmhmm," I breathed as his finger continued its lazy path back up the side of my neck and down my collarbone once more.

"Are you jealous?"

I quickly reeled back and threw my hands out to the side. "No!"

"You totally are." He grinned and matched my steps as I backpedaled across the room.

The back of my legs bumped into the bed, and Kieran neatly pinned me in so my only option was to try and shove him away or fall back onto the bed. The traitorous part of my mind that was forgetting we were annoyed at him was very excited about the second option.

"Yes, you are," he said in a satisfied tone.

"Fine." I glared at him. "But it doesn't mean anything. It turns out that maybe I'm slightly territorial when it comes to people I care about."

He went completely still, the grin slowly sliding off his face, and I realized my mistake. "You care about me?"

"Of course I do, you idiot." I shoved his chest, but he didn't budge. Damn him. "Although, I'm finding myself caring a little less right now."

A deep laugh rumbled out of his chest as his eyes sparkled. "Liar. You still like me." He grabbed my ass and lifted me up onto the bed.

I scooted back, but he moved forward, placing an arm on either side of me and pinning me against the bed with his chest. Heat pooled between my thighs, and my pulse pounded harder.

"There's no reason to be jealous. I'm not Riah's type."

"Oh?" I said breathlessly. "She doesn't like prissy courtiers?"

"She *adores* prissy courtiers." Kieran ground his hips into mine, and I swallowed back a moan. "Just ones with a nice rack instead of a hard cock." Then he leaned down to nip my bottom lip before rolling off me and snuggling into the bed.

I shot him an annoyed look. "By all means, get comfortable."

"Thanks, I think I will." He winked at me.

My heart started to pound frantically, only this time it was driven by panic and not desire. I was definitely still more than a little turned on, but Kieran being in my bed like this was exactly what I was trying to avoid. It felt like crossing a line that I wasn't ready for.

"Hey," he said softly. When I didn't turn to look at him, he gently guided my face towards his. "What's going through that chaotic mind of yours?"

"I don't know how to do this." I sat up, twisting so I was looking down at him, and then waved a hand between us. "It sounds stupid, I know. You're used to doing this type of stuff, whereas I have no idea what I'm doing."

A devilish grin flashed across his face. "Given how things went at the hot springs, I'd say you know exactly what you're doing."

"I'm serious, Kieran." I scowled at him.

"I know." He reached up to wrap a strand of my hair around his finger. "You're my friend, Sam. Whatever happens between us, wherever this goes, you will *always* be my friend."

Doubt flickered through me. Even if we stopped messing around, I couldn't go back to how things were between us. It'd been hard when we were younger, having him flirt with me and then go after other girls, but I'd dealt with it because I knew what the future had in store for me.

I looked to where the signed marriage dissolution sat on the table, my gaze hardening.

"I know that look," Kieran sighed.

"What look?" My lips thinned into a flat line. Damn Kieran and his ability to read every single emotion on my face.

"The 'Sam is overthinking everything' look." He raised an eyebrow as he studied my face. "It's reaching dangerous levels, too. There is only one thing that can fix this."

Realizing what he meant, I tried to scramble off the bed, but strong arms pulled me back. High-pitched screams tore out of me as Kieran tickled the shit out of my sides. Then he grabbed one of my legs and hauled it up so he could reach my foot.

"Don't you dare!" I shrieked. With valiant effort, I ripped out of his hold and flung myself to the side, then fell completely off the bed.

Kieran's head popped over the side, his golden hair all tousled, and laughed. "You okay down there?"

"I hate you." I crossed my arms, determined to keep my dignity intact despite how ridiculous I looked lying on the floor with half my hair covering my face.

"No, you don't." He leapt off the bed and scooped me up, propping me up on one side of the bed before he walked around my room, gathering some paperwork I'd stacked on a table along with writing supplies.

He carried it all over, setting it on the table next to the bed, then poured me some tea that he also placed on the table.

"What are you doing?"

"You said you have work to do," he said smoothly. "You're going to do it in bed. I'm going to cuddle up next to you and allow you the privilege of watching me sleep."

I choked on a laugh. "How are you so ridiculous?"

He fluffed up some of the pillows next to me before settling onto that side of the mattress.

"I know things are moving fast between us and that it's freaking you out," he said pointedly, and I bit my lip. Of course, Kieran would figure out why I was stressed out. "We'll take it as slow as you want. Whatever you need, I will give you, Sam. Minimum begging required."

I huffed. "Minimum begging?"

He shrugged. "I'm enjoying our game, and you know that you are too."

The herbal scent from the tea drifted over, and I picked up the cup, holding it in both hands over my lap. Despite my emotional turmoil, I didn't regret taking things further with Kieran, even if it probably would have been smarter to wait.

"I am," I said quietly. "Enjoying this new game of ours."

"But..." he prompted, and I flicked his forehead at the knowing look he gave me.

I sighed. "But I don't know that I'm ready to step into another serious relationship just yet. Not that you want that," I rushed on. "I know this is probably just casual fun for you and doesn't mean anything. I'm just trying to get everything out there."

I groaned inwardly at sounding like an idiot. Somehow, I could easily navigate complicated political conversations, but talking to one of my oldest friends about how I felt about him and us had me tripping over my words like some awkward, lovestruck fool.

There was nothing playful in Kieran's expression, and I swallowed at what I saw there. I was used to people looking at me with lust in their eyes, but the way he was looking at me went far beyond that.

"I promised not to freak you out earlier," he said seriously. "I'm going to hold to that promise, but don't mistake me giving you space as a lack of interest on my part, and don't *ever* presume that what happens between us doesn't mean anything."

I swallowed, carefully weighing my next words. "What if I want to... experiment with other people?"

No one but Kieran had caught my eye since I'd been back, but I'd also only been home for a few weeks. Maybe some tall, dark, and handsome prince would come strolling into my life soon. I wanted Kieran, but I wasn't ready to swear off all others just yet.

"Gonna take Alaric for a spin?" Kieran waggled his eyebrows suggestively.

"Don't start," I scolded him. "You know Alaric has always hated me. I'm trying to make things at least civil between us since we'll be working together going forward. You baiting him is not helping."

He laughed and shook his head as if he knew something I didn't. My scowl deepened, and he held up his hands in surrender.

"Okay, okay. I'll stop teasing Alaric... a little bit." I rolled my eyes, knowing that was probably the best I was going to get. Then Kieran gave me a serious look. "I don't expect you to be with me and no one else, you know?"

"Really?" I asked tentatively. "You won't get jealous if I take someone else for a ride?"

"If I do, that's my problem and not yours." He shrugged. "You just got out of a three-year marriage where you remained loyal to that stupid asshole, and before that... I know what type of training you went through to prepare for that marriage."

My cheeks heated at the way he said *training*. "You know?"

"You're not the only one I know who was destined for an arranged marriage," he said flatly.

It was expected that when you married, you'd be able to support and *please* your partner. I wasn't a virgin on my wedding night. Far from it, in fact.

A year before I married Demetri when I was twenty, the lessons began. My instructors were kind, and everything was consensual. I wasn't completely inexperienced thanks to a few casual dalliances at Drudonia, but I'd been excited to learn new things. Turns out my excitement was for naught. The lessons weren't exactly filled with passion or pleasure, and some of them were downright boring. Everything had been so mechanical.

Do this. Put your hand there. Harder. A little less hard. Pick up the pace. Dear moon in the heavens, why would you twist that?!

I snickered, and Kieran gave me a curious look.

"While I wouldn't describe the mandatory marriage training as fun, it could be entertaining sometimes." A mischievous grin played across my lips. "I'd been a little too eager to learn and a little too adventurous for my teachers more often than not."

Kieran tilted his head back and laughed. "Somehow, that doesn't surprise me at all."

The grin stayed plastered on my face as Kieran tucked in beside me and drifted off to sleep with his hand on my thigh while I got some work done. I waited for the panic of what it meant to have Kieran sleeping in my bed, but it never came.

CHAPTER FIFTEEN

—

Samara

I SLIPPED from bed early in the morning, careful to avoid waking Kieran, which wasn't hard because that man slept like the dead. I wasn't sure I could have woken him even if I tried.

Sipping the tea I'd grabbed from the kitchen, I read over the letter for Roth one more time. I'd already packed up my update for Carmilla, which was considerably longer, and some information for Rynn. Both the messages for Carmilla and Rynn were enchanted so that the contents could only be read with a drop of their blood.

Unfortunately, I couldn't do the same for the letter to Roth because it required having prior access to the person's blood in order to spell the paper.

I had stacks of spelled paper for Carmilla, Rynn, Cali, and others for just this reason. This meant I had to keep any specifics out of the letter in case it was intercepted. Plus, I wanted to meet Roth in person before I told them everything. If Rynn thought they were trustworthy, then I was inclined to believe the same. Still... one could never be too careful.

Once I was satisfied with the letter, I folded it up and secured it in an envelope addressed to Roth. My eyes drifted towards Kieran's office and the empty desk. He'd be leaving today for House Corvinus, and I already missed him.

Ugh. I was so pathetic.

I meant what I said about not leaping into another relationship and that I wanted to keep things casual between us, but I also acknowledged that the idea of anyone else touching Kieran had my bloodlust rising. It wasn't fair or rational, but no matter how much I told myself that, I didn't feel any different.

Maybe a few days apart would allow me to get my feelings under control. One could only hope.

With all three envelopes in hand, I headed up to the aviary. The strikers eyed me silently as I entered the tower, their forked tongues sliding out from a small groove in their blunt beaks, tasting the air, and their vertical pupils were thin slits against the sunlight that filtered in.

As a child, I'd been terrified of the strange creatures who hadn't been able to make up their mind whether they were reptiles or birds and instead settled on both.

I'd thought they were tiny monsters, which to be fair they absolutely were, but now I thought they were *cute* tiny monsters.

"Who's the most deadly creature in all the realms?" I cooed at one that had sky-blue and vibrant red scales down its throat marking it as male.

He stretched out his long neck and bumped his head against my hand. The scales were warm from basking in the sun, and he tilted his triangular head to give me better access to his throat.

I grinned. "You're the most vicious and prettiest one! Yes, you are!"

Another two hopped down from their perch and vied for attention. Once I had given everyone scratches, I moved further into the tower to where the current on-duty strikers were. We rotated to give them breaks and also made sure we had some for breeding stock.

While they almost always made it to their destination safely, their life expectancy was only five to seven years.

A brilliant green striker eyed me as I approached, and I pulled a harness made of a soft rope off the wall before carefully strapping it on, making sure that it didn't rub against the wing joints.

Once I was confident that it was fitted well, I slipped the letter into a pouch on the back. The striker hopped obediently onto my arm when I held it out, its long talons flexing against my skin but not breaking it. I carried it outside, scratching the underside of its chin while I did so.

Once we were out of the tower, I thrust my arm outward, and the striker took flight, spreading its leathery wings wide as it caught an updraft and sailed away.

After it faded from sight, I went back inside towards the striker that had been trained for the route to and from Drudonia and repeated the same process. After all the messages were on their way, I spent some time cooing over the baby strikers before heading downstairs. Then I stopped by my room and saw that Kieran was gone, likely to pack for his trip.

Refusing to allow myself to dwell on my feelings around that, I decided to track down Vail and his rangers to see if they had learned anything useful about the body we'd brought back with us.

Several small groups of rangers were training in the courtyard as I skirted around the edges, heading for the small building next to the barracks where extra training supplies were kept.

As I approached, Adrienne grinned at me from where she was guarding the door. No bits of gore decorated her hair today, but she still looked absolutely stunning in her brown leathers. I tossed her one of the spare apples I'd grabbed from the kitchen on the way here.

"Are they inside?" I asked when she bit into the fruit.

Her eyes lit up as the juices ran down her chin.

While we'd been traveling together, I paid attention to all the habits of the rangers. Adrienne absolutely loved fruit.

She'd grown up in the northwestern part of our realm where fresh fruit was scarce and lamented over the stew we'd had at the first outpost that she could go through her entire life without ever tasting another root vegetable.

The fruit-loving ranger nodded and opened the door for me. I smiled in thanks and stepped inside.

The first part of the building was a small room with various weapons neatly stored in racks or hanging on the walls. I headed further in, following the voices that came from the next room.

Vail's head snapped up as I entered a much larger room that was mostly empty save for the three tall tables that were spaced evenly down the center of the room. The first one held the body of the boy I'd found.

Vail, Nyx, and someone else I didn't recognize were crowded around it, all of whom watched as I approached.

"What are you doing here?" Vail asked as he stared at me coldly.

"Someone woke up extra grumpy today," I said cheerfully, breezing into the room as if I wasn't at all affected by the look of death Vail was sending my way.

Point of fact, it had taken every ounce of my willpower to not spin around on my heel and come back later. Nyx could probably answer all my questions, but I was here now and refused to back down just because Vail couldn't let the past go.

Nyx choked on air as they looked back and forth between me and Vail, and the unfamiliar man was staring at me wide-eyed like I was a creature he'd never seen before.

"So, have we learned anything useful?" I parked myself comfortably next to Nyx on one side of the table. Vail was still glowering at me, so I turned my attention to the man at his side. "I'm Samara Harker, and you are?"

"I know who you are," he sputtered and wiped a handkerchief over his face. "I'm... uhh... Vasili. Cormel. Vasili Cormel."

"Pleased to meet you, Vasili Cormel." I beamed at him, which seemed to only increase his panic. "I take it you're here because you can offer some insight as to what happened to this young man?"

"Yes! I mean,"—he looked frantically at Vail, who was clenching his jaw so hard I could see the muscle ticking in his cheek—"I've done advanced studies in anatomy at Drudonia. Moroi, Velesians, even some Furies.

"Although, it's much harder to get my hands on the body of a Furie since there aren't many of them to begin with, and it's kind of a weird subject for me to broach. Asking for dead bodies and all." He winced, squeezing his eyes shut and taking a deep breath. "I received a message yesterday morning requesting my presence here."

My eyes flickered to Vail. He must have sent a message from the outpost.

"I left right away and arrived early this morning," Vasili said hastily. "I was just about to go over my findings now."

"Well,"—I grinned widely at Vail—"looks like I have perfect timing."

When Vail and I just continued to stare at each other, Nyx cleared their throat. "Please continue, Vasili."

His rich brown eyes, flecked with green, darted nervously around as he shifted back and forth on his feet. I couldn't really blame him. Menace practically poured off Vail, who was still staring at me in a way that suggested he was thinking about slowly peeling off my skin.

My grin morphed into a frown. I'd been joking earlier, but he really was acting even more pissed off than usual this morning. "Did something happen?"

Vail blinked, and a mask of indifference slammed down on his face. "Nothing that concerns you," he said stiffly before turning to Vasili. "Proceed."

"Right." Vasili swallowed. "As far as I can tell, all these wounds happened after death. There are at least six distinct types of bite marks, most of which are from scavengers, but this one,"—he pointed to where a large chunk was missing from the calf—"is from a banecat. There are drag marks where the clothing he was wearing rode up, and they're quite severe. Given how far you found him from the outpost, I think he was dragged all the way there."

My eyebrows crept up as his voice gained a newfound confidence as well as a hint of excitement. Apparently, his insecurity vanished as soon as he started talking about dead bodies.

Banecats were enormous felines. Despite their size and impressive fangs, they were mostly scavengers. They liked to eat in peace, so it was the most likely culprit for moving the body to where we had found it.

"Not to be callous," Nyx said, pressing their lips into a flat line, "but why did we find the body at all? The scavengers usually pick everything clean within a couple of days, and he was out there for weeks."

"I can't say for certain," Vasili admitted. "Perhaps it's related to whatever that symbol on his neck does, but I can say that none of the scavengers seemed to take more than a few bites, which is unusual."

"So, they started to eat and then stopped?" I frowned at the body. "Odd."

"Very," Vasili agreed.

"What killed him?" Vail asked.

"The oddness continues, I'm afraid." Vasili pulled out a bowl from a shelf underneath the table, and a deep red mass sat inside it. Some type of organ?

I leaned closer, trying to get a look, but it was far too damaged for me to tell what it had been. It looked like someone had smashed it repeatedly with a hammer.

Vasili explained, "His heart exploded in his chest."

"Fuck," Nyx swore, and I nodded in agreement as I stared at the unidentifiable mass that was apparently a Moroi heart.

"That has to be magic, right?" I asked.

Vasili offered me an apologetic shrug. "I can't tell you what caused it, only that the heart was affected. All his other organs are intact."

"Maybe that's what the symbol on his neck does?" Nyx said but immediately shook their head. "No, that doesn't make sense. There are far easier ways to kill a Moroi, but there has to be some connection."

"We have to find out what that symbol means so we can hopefully figure out what type of spell it's used for," I said, nodding as I took all this in. "Thank you for coming and providing us with this information, Vasili. Please let me or Alaric know if you need anything while you're here. We have plenty of guest suites available."

"Tha–thank you," he stuttered. "I'd like to spend a little more time examining the body."

"Of course." I nodded again in thanks and then followed Vail and Nyx outside.

Before I could think better of it, I touched Vail's arm, and he went still beneath my fingers. Slowly, he turned to face me, eyes flashing in anger before he covered up whatever he was feeling again.

"Are you sure you're okay?" I murmured, keeping my voice low.

Nyx and Adrienne were close enough that they probably heard me, but they continued to converse as if they didn't. I didn't miss the slight stiffening of their shoulders, though.

"How I am," Vail said in a low, dangerous tone, "is none of your concern."

He stalked off without another word, and I watched him go, feeling a mix of anger and worry. He was right. Vail shouldn't be my concern. The man wanted me dead.

Nyx cast me an unreadable expression before following after Vail. Then Adrienne walked over and stood beside me.

"One of our scouting pairs was attacked last night," she said so quietly that I had to strain to hear the words. "Unrelated to the outpost attacks. Horned bears did it. They've expanded their territory farther than we realized. Neither of the scouts survived. Both of them had been trained by Vail."

I watched as she moved off in the direction Vail and Nyx had gone without another word.

My heart ached for them. Anyone who signed up to be a ranger knew it was a dangerous position, but that didn't make it any less painful when we lost one. Vail clearly didn't want my sympathy or condolences, but I was glad he had his own unit to lean on.

Laughter across the courtyard pulled me out of my thoughts. When I looked over, I saw three rangers taking a break from training as they watched a man practicing archery on the targets along the back wall. With their back to me, I couldn't tell who they were, but they were a terrible shot. Only one arrow had hit the target, while dozens of others lay scattered on the ground where they had bounced off of the wall.

The person swore loudly as they missed another shot, and the rangers laughed again, louder this time. The incredibly bad archer turned to glare at them.

Alaric.

I stood there in the center of the courtyard, debating whether I should leave or go and help him.

He probably wouldn't want my help because he was a stubborn asshole. Just as I started to turn around, Alaric's gaze fell on me, and I halted mid-step. He gripped the bow tighter, and his jaw was clenched equally hard. Honestly, I would be surprised if he didn't crack a tooth.

His expression said that I was the last person he wanted to see witness his absolute failure at using a bow. So, of course, I grinned widely at him and swaggered over.

"Is there any reason why you're pelting our poor wall with arrows?" I waved towards the target. "It's okay to hit the target, you know. That's actually why it's there."

"Thanks," he ground out. "I didn't realize that. I'll be sure to hit it going forward. You can leave now."

"I mean... I *could* leave..."

"Samara," he drew my name out, and I realized that I kind of liked the sound of my name on his lips. Alaric's voice was deep and smooth. It was a shame he was such a dick though, otherwise, I'd enjoy listening to him talk more.

I chuckled and held my hand out. Reluctantly, he handed over the bow, and I nudged him to the side with my hip.

"Your feet were too close together. Keep them shoulder-width apart." I adjusted my stance to show him, and then I deliberately angled my front foot slightly. "I like to shoot with an open stance, but I would suggest starting with a neutral stance and keeping your feet perpendicular to where you're aiming to start. Once you practice and get a little more comfortable, you can decide which one you prefer."

I showed him the two different stances. He watched me shift my feet back and forth before giving me a slow, deliberate nod. Then I swiped an arrow out of the half-barrel in front of me and raised the bow, nocking the arrow in one smooth motion.

"Don't grip the bow so tightly. It will throw off your aim." I drew my right arm back. "Keep your elbow slightly raised. You should be using your back muscles to draw. They're stronger than your arm muscles, and you'll need them if you need to hold the position."

"Show me again?" he asked quietly.

I nodded and went through the motion a few more times. "I was too far away to see how you were breathing, but there are a couple of different ways you can go about it. You can hold your breath as soon as you start to draw the bow and then exhale once you've released the arrow.

"Or, and this is the way I prefer, you inhale as you raise the bow, and just as you start to draw, you exhale slowly and evenly. You should be exhaling the entire time."

He frowned at me. "Shouldn't you exhale when you release the string?"

"No." I shook my head. "You're drawing across your chest and if you do that, it's going to mess with your motion and impact your aim. Everything about the draw and release should be smooth."

With a quick, practiced motion, I fired the bow without breaking eye contact with him. Alaric's eyes flicked toward the target, and he let out a sharp exhale.

The rangers who were still watching us from the sidelines let out loud whoops and clapped their hands. I dipped into a dramatic curtsy in their direction while holding the bow out to the side.

"How did you get so good at this?" Alaric murmured. I handed the bow over to him, and he accepted it gingerly.

"Practice. Lots and lots of practice." I grinned. "I've always had good hand-eye coordination. My preference will always be throwing daggers, but bows are more practical. They shoot farther and do more damage. Rynn is an excellent shot, better than me. We had a bit of a competition going while we were at Drudonia."

Alaric grunted. "You? Competitive? Shocking."

"Right?" I took a few steps back and gestured for him to take my spot, so he was aligned with the target. "What *is* shocking is that Cali is an absolutely terrible shot. Her best chance of hitting anything is to just throw the bow, and even then, she'd probably miss."

He let out a low, deep laugh that made my toes curl. Fuck, had I never heard him laugh before?

What the hell was wrong with me? I reminded myself firmly that Alaric and I were adversaries, and I was just helping him out because he had looked so pathetic.

I watched as he took up the neutral stance exactly as I'd shown him and raised the bow.

"Not too tight," I reminded him. He nodded curtly and flexed his fingers before letting them rest on the bow with a much gentler grip. "Good," I said in approval.

He started to raise the bow, and I ducked behind him, gently guiding his elbow. "Elbow up a little higher. Remember, you should be using your back muscles, not your arms. Don't fire yet. Let's practice drawing a couple of times."

I moved around him, correcting his positioning, and made him go through the motions a few times.

"This time, when you draw, brush your knuckles against your jawline and then hold just beneath your earlobe. Having anchor points is important to have a reliable aim. Those are the ones I use, but you might find you like something else."

Alaric was looking at me oddly as he held his stance and posture.

The turquoise fractures in his eyes had widened slightly, and I glanced down, realizing that I was resting my hand on his arm and standing intimately close.

Warmth rushed to my cheeks, and I let him go as I took a step back. I'd gotten so used to touching him over the past ten minutes that I didn't even think about it.

"Right," I said quickly. "Try it now and remember your breathing."

For a few seconds, he just stared at me with the same heated expression he'd held when he caught me and Kieran in the hot springs before turning his attention to the target.

I let out a breath once his attention was off me. Whatever this weird attraction thing was between us was confusing and unwelcome.

Maybe my libido was just trying to make up for lost time and, therefore, wasn't making rational decisions.

Alaric drew back slowly and carefully, just like we had practiced, and then let the arrow fly. It gave a satisfying *thunk* as it sank into the target. A wide smile spread across his face as the rangers cheered and before I could think better of it, I threw my arms around his neck in a hug.

"I knew you could do it!" He froze beneath me, and I panicked, drawing back quickly. "Sorry! Got a little too excited."

Alaric opened his mouth. "I—"

"There you both are!" Kieran said loudly as he strode across the courtyard, leading his favorite gelding behind him. "I'm just about to head out. Adrienne and Emil are going to escort me. I'll be back in a few weeks, but I'll send messages if I find out anything good. Try not to kill each other while I'm gone, eh?"

Alaric and I stared awkwardly at each other before quickly looking away. When he made no move to say anything, I finally cleared my throat. "We'll be fine. Promise."

"Of course you will!" Kieran beamed before pulling us both into a crushing hug. I was plastered against both men and found that I really didn't hate the feeling of it as much as I should.

"Well, then." I detangled myself from Kieran's embrace and backed up a couple of steps. "Safe travels!"

"Yes," Alaric said in an equally desperate tone. "That. Safe travels."

Both of us fled the courtyard in opposite directions, leaving Kieran to see himself out.

CHAPTER SIXTEEN

—

Samara

"Another dead-end," I grumbled.

Wordlessly, Alaric reached to the stack of books to his left, grabbed the dark blue one off the top, and passed it over to me. He didn't even look up from the page he was reading.

I sighed and took the book from him before leaning back in my chair.

We'd settled into a routine over the last three days. First, we met at the training courtyard every morning after breakfast and practiced archery for an hour. Then we headed to the library where we poured over every book, scroll, and scrap of paper that had anything to do with blood magic and Moroi history until dinner.

Usually, Rynn would pop in via shadow form at some point in the afternoon to update how things were going on their end.

Neither of us talked about our awkwardness from that day in the courtyard three days ago. But it felt like something had shifted between us, or was at least starting to.

Sometimes we'd go an entire hour without Alaric sending any thinly veiled hostility or cruel insults my way, which was nice.

The problem was that once he realized we were not only getting along but almost approaching friend status, he'd say something cutting to piss me off. His attitude towards me had always pissed me off... but now it hurt a little.

Every time I got him to smile at one of my asinine jokes or felt his muscles flex beneath my fingers during archery practice, I felt things shift between us a little more. Moons damn it all... I was starting to *like* Alaric. It had to be some type of temporary insanity because of the long hours I was working. Surely, that's all it was. Because there was absolutely no fucking way I was developing a crush on the impossibly arrogant Alaric Lockwood.

I was also attributing how much I missed Kieran to temporary insanity. Although, even I recognized that was a weak argument since it'd been just three days and the feeling was only getting worse.

A rather attractive courtier with teal and gold eyes had tried to strike up a flirty conversation with me the other day, and I had grown bored of him in minutes. Plus, I decided that only Kieran should have golden eyes. I made some excuse about having to leave and immediately went to the library.

So apparently, I wasn't horny for just anybody, which was troublesome.

I'd have to play hard to get when Kieran came back. I couldn't let him know just how much I'd missed him. He'd never let me live it down, and then he'd totally use it to torment me.

And I absolutely could *not* let him know about my growing feelings towards Alaric.

Kieran had already hinted about how much that idea interested him, and he would be impossible if he found out my little secret.

It was unlikely Alaric felt the same way, and it would make things weird—well, weirder—between us if he learned about it. I bit my bottom lip as I tried to focus on the book I was supposed to be reading once more.

After a few minutes, I let out a frustrated breath.

"We're not going to find anything." I tossed the book Alaric had given me onto the table after skimming the first twenty pages. "These books are all saying the same commonly known shit." We needed access to better information.

He shrugged. "Once we get through these, one of us can go to Drudonia," Alaric said in a bored tone. "A trip to the Sovereign House might be in order, too."

"You think they'll have something that they won't have at Drudonia?" I furrowed my brows, trying to think of what the library was like at the Sovereign House.

It'd been years since I'd been there and even then, I'd spent most of my time in the gardens or sitting rooms while Carmilla and Queen Velika caught up. They'd grown up together, and their friendship had only strengthened over the years. Carmilla had once confessed that she felt closer to Velika than she had her own sister, my mother. It'd been on a night after she'd had a few drinks, and she'd felt awful about saying it the next day.

I could remember the Sovereign House library being grand in appearance, but I didn't recall anything particularly impressive about the collection itself.

Drudonia was shared between the Moon Blessed. It was the second generation that was cognizant enough to want to gather knowledge and keep it somewhere safe. So early on, any books, scrolls, and artifacts recovered had been taken there. Now knowledge was a little more spread out as Houses became more independent and the Furies more distant.

"I know they have some Unseelie scrolls there that don't have copies at Drudonia." Alaric flipped another page in the book he was reading. "Who knows what else they might have?"

"Well, it's on the way to Drudonia, so I suppose it makes sense to at least take a look." My lips quirked up into a smile. "Plus, it'd be nice to see Carmilla."

He glanced up from his book. "And why do you get to go and not me?"

I raised an eyebrow. "So eager to get back on a horse?"

He blanched and went back to reading. I snickered. Maybe another round of tea was in order. I needed something to motivate me to get through another book or two before calling it a day.

Before I could get up to make the tea, the door to the library flew open, causing both Alaric and me to jump in our chairs.

"Put them over there!" came a crisp command. The voice belonged to a Moroi with vibrant red hair that was shaved on the sides but was kept just long enough on top to be swept back.

"Damn, Roth." I grinned, rose from my seat, and walked over to stand next to the new arrival. Meanwhile, more House Harker staff entered the library, carrying boxes that they carefully stacked on one of the tables. "I see you're still as bossy as ever."

Sharp hazel eyes looked at me from a face with even sharper cheekbones and a strong jawline. The attraction I'd felt towards them at Drudonia came back full force, but I tamped it down, remembering how throughly they had rebuffed me when we were younger. After everything that had happened with Demetri and House Laurent, I didn't think my ego could handle being stepped on again. Especially by Roth and their often acerbic tongue.

"These books are centuries old, Samara," they said in that typical patronizing tone of theirs that at once felt so familiar. "Usually, I wouldn't have even entertained the idea of moving them from their safe location, but I felt it was necessary to do so."

I snorted. "Glad to see you haven't changed at all."

"On the contrary,"—Roth raised their chin as they surveyed the library, lips twisting in distaste, before finally giving me a chastising look—"I've gotten smarter, which apparently you have as well. Heard you dumped that loser Laurent boy. I honestly lost a lot of respect for you when I learned you were willingly marrying him."

They turned to fully face me while I stood there with my mouth slightly agape.

Roth tilted their head, narrowing their eyes. "Did you even talk to him before agreeing to marry him? You could have had more compelling conversations with a doorknob," they sneered, shaking their head.

Alaric made a choking noise that distinctly sounded like he was coughing to cover up his laugh. My head snapped toward him, and he ducked his face behind his hands.

Just wait. I narrowed my eyes. *Sooner or later, you'll find yourself in Roth's crosshairs too, and I'll be the one laughing then.*

I rubbed my forehead as I recalled the finer aspects of Roth's personality. Mainly that they had zero filter and often felt the need to constantly tell you how dumb you were, and then proceeded to list all the reasons why to be 'helpful' so that you could better yourself and not waste so much time in the future.

Rynn had gotten along with Roth great, but Cali and I had wanted to murder them and hide their body in the library stacks on more than one occasion. We'd even selected a couple of ideal locations that were rarely visited.

"Thank you for your commentary on my failed political marriage, Roth," I said flatly. "Really, it's super appreciated."

They flashed a serpentine smile. "You're welcome."

The choking sound from Alaric grew louder, and I prayed to the moon for patience as the staff carried in the last of the boxes.

"Mind telling me what all of this is?" I gestured towards the table that was now completely covered. "When I asked you to come and help with a research project, I didn't think you'd be moving into House Harker."

"Or stealing the entire library from Drudonia," Alaric muttered as he snagged one of the newly brought in books off the stack and started flipping through it.

"I'm not moving in," Roth snapped before stalking over to Alaric and ripping the book out of his hands.

He reached out to grab another book, and Roth smacked his hand away. Alaric glared at them murderously, but when Roth didn't back down, he crossed his arms and looked away. Ha! Not so fun when Roth has their sights on you, is it, Mr. Know-it-all?

Alaric caught me smirking at him and narrowed his eyes in response.

"I knew the books you'd have here would be a waste of time," Roth said matter-of-factly, and I couldn't help but take mild offense to that.

House Harker's library wasn't as impressive as Drudonia, but it was still one of the best ones amongst the Houses.

Roth failed to notice my frown, which wasn't all that surprising, and barreled on. "All of these books are ones that I have carefully curated for Drudonia, therefore, they did not argue with me when I said I would be borrowing them from a bit."

"Probably because you murdered them all in their sleep," I whispered, eyes wide in mock horror. Alaric caught my eye, and his lips twitched in amusement.

Roth rolled their eyes. My whisper hadn't been all that quiet. "Still think you're funny, I see."

"Yes," I said without a hint of modesty.

"Why are you so confident that we won't find anything in our books?" Alaric asked, his tone more curious than hostile.

Roth sighed impatiently. "Because that symbol you referenced is Unseelie, and all of your books are either about the Seelie Fae or were written by the Seelie Fae about the Unseelie Fae, which makes them incredibly biased." They rested a hand on top of the boxes they'd brought with them. "All of these are about the Unseelie, granted some written by the Seelie, but most are in the Unseelie language."

Alaric and I both perked up with interest.

"All of those books"—Alaric waved his hand at the table piled high with boxes behind Roth—"are about the Unseelie Fae?"

"Yes," Roth said with confidence. "And I know that I've seen that symbol in one of them." They scrunched up their nose at what had to be over a hundred books. "I just don't know which one."

The three of us peered at the table stacked to the brim.

"Looks like we have a lot of reading in our future," I said. My stomach rumbled, and I patted it. "But first, let's get some lunch." When Roth started to protest, I cut them off. "We need to fill you in on everything anyway. I had to keep that letter vague, but that blood symbol I sent you is just one of the many mysteries we're currently attempting to unravel."

They scoffed, "Obviously. I'm guessing it's connected to all the outposts that have been attacked over the past year." Roth looked around the library again. "It's really disappointing that House Harker doesn't have a grander library than this. You should work on that when you eventually take over the House."

I gaped at Roth, and I was pretty sure that Alaric had a similar expression on his face. My mouth struggled to form words, but finally, I managed to string something coherent together.

"You know?" I said in a high-pitched voice as my gaze darted to where the blood symbol on the wall beside the doors was still giving off a faint glow. The tightness between my shoulders eased a fraction when I noticed our silencing spell was still in place, so nobody heard Roth just casually mention the secret that the Sovereigns were determined to keep quiet.

Alaric snapped his mouth shut and regained his composure before giving Roth a hard stare. "How? How do you know this, Roth?"

"Because I'm not an idiot?" They glanced back and forth between us, clearly confused as to why we were surprised by this.

Alaric had that look on his face that said he was one step away from strangling somebody. It was weird to see it directed at someone besides me. I gave myself five seconds to enjoy that before turning my attention back to Roth.

"The Sovereigns are determined to keep the attacks quiet so that the outposts don't panic. We need to know how you learned about the attacks, Roth," I said carefully.

"Well, Drudonia monitors certain shipments between all the outposts and outside of the Moroi realm. Anything that contains the rarer resources is tracked. Partly to make sure nobody steals supplies, but also to study how quickly we go through certain gems and minerals so we can create comparisons." Roth paused and looked at us like we were children. "With me so far?"

"We're not idiots," Alaric growled. "We understand how supply chains work and why it would behoove us to study how our resources are being used so we can anticipate shortages in the future and have potential backup plans in place."

Roth blinked. "Sorry. I sometimes forget that other people aren't entirely useless."

Alaric turned his glare to me as if to say, *You brought them here, therefore, this is your problem.*

I withheld an exasperated sigh. "Okay, and how did all that lead you to uncovering what was going on with the attacks?" I attempted to prod Roth along so that Alaric didn't completely lose his mind. Apparently, someone existed who frustrated him more than me.

Although, seeing as I was responsible for bringing Roth here, I suspected he'd be directing all this new frustration at me. Yay.

"There is an outpost two days from Drudonia that has a vendor who makes these delicious treats. She used some type of flakey pastry and honey." Roth's eyes momentarily glazed over at the memory before they continued. "I know the rangers who usually deliver supplies to that outpost, so I checked in with them before their next expected trip, but they said they'd been reassigned to a different outpost. So then I tried to track down who had been assigned to the outpost, but nobody had. At that point, I thought maybe it was just a mistake, so I reviewed all the schedules and trade routes."

I squeezed my eyes shut. Roth was too curious and too smart for their own good. Fortunately for all of us, they hated talking to people, so they hadn't immediately started gossiping about this.

"After some more discreet checking, I determined that the most logical explanation was that these outposts had been attacked, but since they weren't on the main road like the others, it was fairly easy to keep that secret." Roth tapped a long, slender finger on their bottom lip. "Given that at this point, about half of Moroi population lives in outposts like the ones that have been attacked, and we not only don't have space to relocate everyone to the Houses, but we also depend on these outposts for resources and securing trading routes, it made sense to keep it all quiet so we don't have a massive panic on our hands."

"And that doesn't bother you?" I bit my bottom lip. "Everyone who lives in an outpost right now is in danger, and they don't know it."

Roth just looked at me, eyebrows bunched in confusion. "True, but they don't know that. As I previously said, there isn't space for everyone within the House fortresses. Plus, over forty percent of our crops are grown at outposts now. All the stability that we've gained over the last century would be at threat of collapsing if the outposts are abandoned."

Apparently, I was the only one struggling with the ethicalness of this decision. "I understand all that," I said with a sigh. "It still bothers me, though."

To my surprise, Alaric nodded. "It doesn't quite sit well with me either, but ultimately it's the Sovereigns' decision, so all we can do is try to figure out what's going on and how to stop it."

My stomach rumbled loudly again. "I'll have some tea and lunch brought up. We'll fill you in on all the details while we eat, and then we'll dive in."

The three of us stared at the daunting stack of books and scrolls. Maybe we'd get lucky and find the symbol right away with a detailed explanation of what it did and a map pointing to the bad guys.

I was overdue for a bit of good luck.

CHAPTER SEVENTEEN

—

Samara

THE MOON DID NOT BLESS me with good luck. It did, however, bless Rynn.

The ring I wore on my pinkie had two small, embedded gems, one blue and the other red. The dark silver band vibrated slightly, and the blue gem glowed, alerting me to Rynn wanting to chat.

It was midafternoon and I was sitting in my chair by the window reading through one of the books Roth had brought. They'd had an absolute conniption when I had placed a cup of tea down on the table with the rest of the books, so this was our compromise. I could have one book with me and sip tea while reading it while in this chair, a healthy distance away from all the other reading material.

I wasn't exactly sure what they thought I was going to do. Dump my tea over all the books while laughing manically?

But the argument hadn't been worth it. So I worked from my spot while Alaric and Roth both posted up around the table. They were both faster at skimming the books than I was; I tried to only glance at the pages looking for the symbol, but I kept getting caught up in what the book contained.

I'd read some Unseelie texts while at Drudonia, but not many. Roth had been quite busy with collecting all these books and scrolls. It was impressive what they'd managed to track down over the past few years.

"Rynn is coming," I said, putting down the book I'd been so engrossed in for the last hour.

The ring vibrated again, and I held my finger against the glyph that was engraved on the bottom of the band to let Rynn know we were ready. A few seconds later, shadows swirled in front of me until Rynn's form appeared.

"I think I found something," she said immediately, holding both hands up in earnest.

"Really?" I leaned forward in excitement.

"What did you find?" Alaric asked as both he and Roth quickly rose from their seats and came to stand closer to Rynn's shadow form.

"Sam, remember how you said the outpost you'd visited was built on top of an old human town?" she replied, and I nodded.

I'd only mentioned that detail to Rynn in passing because I'd never seen old human buildings, and it'd stuck with me.

"Well, I did some digging, and while I wasn't able to confirm this for every outpost, at least half of them were built on top of human settlements. And I wasn't able to rule it out for the others. There simply aren't enough records for me to prove it one way or another."

"Why would it matter, though?" I furrowed my brows together, trying to see where Rynn was going with this. "I mean, aren't a lot of the outposts built on top of old human settlements?"

"Yes, but when you look at the outposts that are attacked, it doesn't make any sense," Rynn said quickly and started pacing, leaving trails of shadow in her wake. "The attacks have been all over Lunaria, and there isn't a pattern that I can see, except that the outposts I know for a fact have *not* been built over human settlements haven't been touched."

"Assuming Rynn's theory is correct, and it is the old human outposts that are being targeted," Alaric said, "why are they being attacked now? And why?"

"I didn't see anything specifically targeted at the outpost we visited." I frowned, trying to think back and see if there was something I missed. "The buildings stood out to me, just because of the architectural difference, but they were just old buildings, and there wasn't anything done to them that hadn't been done to the rest of the town."

"The ritual," Roth murmured before stalking over to a box they had tucked underneath the table.

We all watched while Roth yanked out scroll after scroll and tossed them aside. I didn't think it was fair that they freaked out over me placing a cup of tea on the table, a careful distance away from any books, while they haphazardly yanked scrolls out, but Alaric and I had quickly learned over the last three days that it was best to just let Roth be Roth and not comment on any of their eccentric tendencies.

"Here!" They pulled a scroll out and held it up in the air before quickly walking across the room to where they had set up a large board.

Roth picked an empty space on the board and unrolled the scroll. As they did so, the dark red ribbons they kept wrapped around their forearms unraveled and looped around the board and its edges, pinning it in place.

I'd never encountered anyone who used blood magic the way Roth did. All Moroi were capable of blood magic, as our blood held magic, and we could use it for all types of castings. The simplest way was to use glyphs. Each glyph was a basic symbol that served as an instruction.

Heat was represented by a triangle. Water by three wavy lines. When combined, those two glyphs gave us hot water. Such a simple trick, but damn, it practically created pure bliss.

Technically, the glyphs could be anything. We'd originally learned how to do this by studying old Fae spells, but over the years, we'd added our own. New glyphs were documented at Drudonia so that we could keep track of what they all meant and scholars could experiment with crafting more complex spells like improved wards and defenses.

Glyphs for silence and healing were the most common. We'd also learned that some of the old Fae spells could be reawakened with our blood. The wards we had around the Houses and outposts had been based off Fae wards. At first, we'd simply reactivated their wards, but over the years we'd learned to improve them even more.

Before I married Demetri and moved to House Laurent, I'd been a lot more interested in learning new blood magic castings. It didn't quite reach my obsession with training with a bow and throwing daggers, but I spent many nights reading through old books filled with Fae spells until the sun rose. I'd create small but useful castings like the one I used to protect letters I sent via strikers.

The ribbons that Roth kept wrapped around their forearms had been soaked in their blood, and Roth had enchanted them so that they could control them within a twenty-foot radius. Usually, they used them to pin scrolls in place or grab books off shelves that were out of their reach, but I was pretty sure I'd had more than one dirty dream about other things those ribbons could do.

Roth caught me looking at them a couple of times and had only smirked, which caused me to blush like crazy, and Alaric to ask what the hell was wrong with me.

But I was hardly going to explain to Alaric that I was having dirty fantasies about Roth and the ribbons that followed their demands.

Roth had also enchanted a pen that could write while they telepathically dictated to it. For some reason, that one deeply upset Alaric, so he always sat facing away from it, but I was determined to get Roth to show me how they did that. My handwriting had never been great, so maybe an enchanted pen would make it better.

"As part of my interest in the history of blood magic, I've also been collecting as much information as I can about the original ritual our human ancestors did," Roth explained as we all moved closer to look at the scroll they'd stretched out on the board. "The spell was definitely of Fae origin, but I haven't been able to determine if it was Seelie or Unseelie. However, I can say with certainty that the ritual itself was performed in their towns around this symbol."

Roth pointed to a symbol of three interconnecting crescent moons. Two of them faced away from each other, the back of each moon just barely touching, and the third crescent moon cut across the middle of the other two with its points facing up.

Alaric and I both touched the crescent moon marks on the left side of our necks while Rynn absently touched the mark on the right side of her neck. Furies bore the mark with the crescent moon facing upward in the center of their necks. I'd never seen this symbol with all three of our marks intertwined, but I supposed it made sense. We'd all been created during the same ritual.

"What if..." Roth stared harder at the scroll. "What if something was left behind in those human settlements? Something from the ritual?"

Alaric shook his head. "We would have found it."

"Not necessarily." I looked at the glyph on the wall that contained the silencing spell.

The glyph itself had been carved into a piece of wood that easily fit in the palm of my hand. It rested on top of a chunk of obsidian to power it. Something that small could easily be overlooked, especially considering the chaos that descended in the century after the ritual took place.

I added, "Most of those human settlements were abandoned for over two centuries. The Moroi who founded the Houses retreated to the Fae fortresses because they were easier to defend. We didn't expand and start building up the outposts until the third generation and by then, the priority was getting them built as fast as possible to make room for our growing population."

"Between whatever was left behind being exposed to the elements for a couple centuries and it being small," Roth said, following my line of thought, "they might have overlooked it."

I nodded. "We need to go to some outposts that were built on human settlements. Ones that haven't been attacked yet and see what we can find."

"It's going to raise a little suspicion if we do that," Alaric argued.

"We'll say it's for research." I waved a hand at Roth. "We'll bring them with us. Anyone who spends thirty seconds with Roth will just accept our reasoning so they can get away."

"I'm not leaving my books and going outside!" Roth's eyes went wide as they snatched a book up and clutched it to their chest.

The three of us started bickering then, each talking louder and louder to speak over the previous person, before a shrill whistle cut through the air, and we all slammed our hands over our ears.

"Or,"—Rynn lowered her fingers from her mouth calmly—"we can visit some human settlements that haven't been turned into outposts yet, which would actually answer two questions for us."

I glared at my friend while I rubbed at my ears. "It's bad luck to whistle inside."

She rolled her eyes. "First, that's not a thing. Second, maybe the wraiths have been searching for whatever is left of the ritual for a long time and they just first searched the human settlements that were still abandoned."

"So even if we don't find what we're looking for, if there are signs that wraiths have already searched it, we'll at least have confirmation that it's the human settlements in particular that they're interested in." I dropped my hands to my sides, ringing eardrums now forgotten. "Based on that smirk on your face, I'm guessing you've already identified some locations for us to check out?"

"I'm not smirking!" Rynn pressed her lips into a hard, flat line, but the corners kept curling upward as she fought to keep the satisfied grin off her face.

"It's hard to tell with the shadows, but I'm gonna agree with Samara on this one," Alaric said. "You were definitely smirking."

Rynn glanced back and forth between Alaric and me. "Since when do you two agree on anything?"

Alaric stiffened, and now Roth was looking at the two of us curiously. Fantastic.

"Focus, Rynn!" I barked. "Where are the settlements?"

She gave me a pointed look that said she'd very much be bringing up the topic of what was going on between me and Alaric later. At which point, I would tell her that absolutely nothing was going on and it was just my libido going insane.

Kieran needed to get back soon so I could get laid. Once I got that taken care of, I was sure I would be thinking rationally again.

Rynn moved to where Roth had hung a map on the board, which was next to the unraveled scrolls. "I've identified three potential locations. It's hard to find information on old human settlements that haven't already been turned into outposts, but somehow we got lucky because there is one about a two-day run from me, and there's one less than a day's ride from you. There's also one for Cali to check out that is on the outskirts of the badlands. I've already spoken to her and caught her up on everything. She's on her way there now."

I looked at where Rynn had pointed on the map close to House Harker. She was right. It was less than a day's ride and was basically up the coast.

"Are you sure there was a settlement there?" I frowned. "I've ridden up and down the coast, and I don't remember ever seeing something."

She nodded. "Given how close it was to the shore, most of the town has probably been wrecked by storms with no one to repair it. If you were riding past it on the road, you probably wouldn't have noticed the leftover debris."

"Maybe." I chewed my bottom lip, still a little skeptical about missing the skeletal remains of a town, but Rynn was never wrong about these sorts of things. If she said that a human settlement used to be there, then it used to be there.

My eyes slid across the map to the general area of where she'd pointed in the Velesian territory, and alarm shot through me.

I hesitated. "Rynn, the outpost you're planning on going to belongs to the Fervis. Have you cleared it with them?"

She pursed her lips together and didn't answer my question.

I stalked towards her, wishing she was actually here so I could shake some sense into her. "Find another one."

"It's just over the border," she said dismissively. "They won't even know I'm there!"

"Rynn..." I growled in frustration. There wasn't a damn thing I could do to stop her, and she knew it.

"Why is Rynn going there a problem?" Roth asked, their gaze bouncing back and forth between me and Rynn while they tried to work out what was going on.

"Things are a little tense between the Velesian Orders these days," I said tightly.

"Understatement of the year," Alaric grunted.

Rynn glared at him, but he wasn't wrong.

While the Moroi had broken up into different Houses, each led by the strongest of our bloodlines, the Velesians were broken up into three Orders. Narchis, Avala, and Fervis. Each Order consisted of multiple packs.

Originally, each Order had primarily consisted of the same shifters. Narchis had lycanthropes, Avala had ursanthropes, and Fervis had ailuranthropes. The aetanthropes were too few in number to hold their own territory, so they had always been mixed in with all the Orders.

These days, the Orders were a little more diverse, but the dominant type of shifter in each was still what the Order was originally made up of.

Shortly after the queen and her consort rose to power in the Moroi realm, the Alpha Pack rose in the Velesian realm. Unlike the Moroi Sovereigns, however, the Alpha Pack was regularly challenged for authority.

Sure, the Moroi Houses bickered and jockeyed for power, but nobody outright revolted against the Sovereigns.

More than one bloody attack had been waged against the Alpha Pack.

Rynn had been promised to the Alpha Pack, not only because she was completely brilliant, but because she was the daughter of high-ranking members of the Order of Narchis. Just like me, Rynn's life had been given away for political reasons. While joining a pack wasn't the same thing as marriage... it was similar enough.

Only Rynn's situation with the Alpha Pack was in a weird state currently, and she couldn't just cross into Fervis territory without at least checking with them first.

I just needed to get that through her thick fucking head.

"You are not—"

"Oh, sorry! The charge is running out on the shadow spell." Rynn held her hands up helplessly. "Must be time for a new gem."

"Don't you dare!" I screamed and shoved my hand towards her shoulder. It slid through the smoke, and I dropped my clenched fist to my side. "Rynn! I forbid you from—"

She vanished, leaving behind curling shadows in her wake.

I stared at the space she'd been standing in and then at the map before returning my gaze back to where she'd been. A warm, sticky feeling slid along my fingers, and I absently noticed that my nails had hardened into claws and my fangs had jutted further out from my jaw.

Roth was staring at me, appearing mildly alarmed by my bloodlust surfacing. Alaric just held his hands out like he was about to calm down a raging beast, which I suppose was a little accurate.

I threw my head back and screamed, "THAT FUCKING BITCH!"

CHAPTER EIGHTEEN

—

Samara

I WAS STILL PISSED off beyond reason when I rode out of House Harker ten minutes later on Zosa.

Nyx had caught me on my way to the stables, and I'd barely managed to speak rationally for a few minutes and explain that I'd be needing an escort tomorrow. They promised to get something arranged and then slowly backed away from me with wide eyes.

I hadn't even bothered saddling up Zosa. Just grabbed a bridle and headed out. Luckily, I'd worn pants today. Riding bareback in a skirt was awkward and uncomfortable.

The rangers at the gate hadn't been thrilled about letting me out, but when I flashed my fangs, they quickly changed their minds. As a Harker, no one was concerned about me turning into a Strigoi. And sadly, it hadn't been an uncommon occurrence for me to storm out of the gates in a huff during my teenage years, usually because of something Alaric said.

But sometimes this would happen because I'd spot Kieran flirting with some gorgeous courtier and it caused me to feel things I had no right to.

My life hadn't been my own back then.

"Don't go far!" Nyx called out from behind me.

"I'll be at the beach!" I called back over my shoulder. Then I wrapped my hands around Zosa's mane and squeezed my legs.

She leapt into a ground-eating gallop, and I leaned over her shoulders for better balance while I subtly directed her with my knees. We ran straight away from House Harker before veering off to the right and down a narrow path.

But all too soon, I had to slow Zosa down as the path started to dip down and become more narrow.

The trees on either side of us became sparser before falling away altogether and the dirt became sand. Zosa trotted up a rolling hill, and I pulled her to a stop, breathing in the salty air. The beach stretched out before us with impossibly white sand.

Normally, right about now would be when I'd be calming down and getting over whatever was bothering me, but not today. Rynn was deliberately putting herself in danger, and there was fuck all I could do about it.

My eyes shifted, and suddenly everything became a little sharper.

I squeezed them shut, but that just made me more aware of the scents and sounds around me. Zosa's quick breathing from our run. The rumble of the waves crashing into the shore.

My fangs slid a little further out. Damn it.

I slid off Zosa's back and pulled my boots off, digging my toes into the sand before removing the bridle. "Go run around, but don't go too far," I told Zosa. She snorted and bumped her head against my shoulder. "I'm fine, sweet girl." I scratched her forehead and behind her ears before giving her a good shove. "Go!"

She took off like a rocket, kicking up sand all over me.

"Thanks," I grumbled, beginning to walk up the beach towards my favorite spot.

My senses were still all keyed up thanks to the bloodlust. It'd been a while since I'd had it this bad. I'd need to get a handle on it before night came because it would only get worse as my magic increased under the moonlight.

We were a week away from a full moon, so any bloodlust would be intense at night for the next couple of weeks.

I should have asked Carmilla for a drink before she left, but I hadn't been thinking about it, and it'd only been a few weeks since I drank from her last. Now I didn't have anyone to drink from. At least, no one I was comfortable asking.

While feeding from someone wasn't necessarily sexual, it was intimate. Growing up, Moroi children drank from their parents as well as from members of the House they belonged to. The bloodlines that founded the Houses were the most stable of the Moroi. We had been the first to pull away from the bloodlust, and it was almost unheard of for any House bloodline to fully lose themselves to bloodlust and become Strigoi.

When other Moroi drank our blood, it decreased the chances of them being completely overcome with bloodlust, but those feedings weren't required often, so family members were responsible for most of the blood feedings. Then, as we matured, lovers, spouses, or trusted friends usually replaced family. Emotions tended to spiral while feeding, especially when bloodlust was running high.

I went to chew on my bottom lip and felt a sharp stabbing pain as I pierced it with one of my fangs. Sweet, coppery blood filled my mouth, and I practically moaned as the pleasure of the taste quickly overshadowed the pain.

Fuck. I needed to find someone to feed from. I couldn't wait for Carmilla to get back. There was no way I was asking Alaric or Roth. Maybe Nyx? It'd be a little awkward, but they'd probably do it.

A smile tugged at my lips as my mood lightened at watching Zosa frolic in the waves. She was literally the only good thing that came out of my time at House Laurent. I laughed softly as she ran out towards the retreating tide only to spin and haul ass back to the shore when the waves came crashing back in, her tail high up in the air as she pranced around.

"I leave you alone for one week, and you're out here grinning like an idiot with blood running down your chin."

"Kier?" I whirled around, and relief poured through me when I saw Kieran sitting on a blanket, perched on top of a grassy dune that rose above the sand, creating a nice lookout spot. "What are you doing here? I thought you wouldn't be back for a couple more weeks?"

He smirked as I scrambled up to join him and rose from where he'd been sitting. "Carmilla requested my presence at the Sovereign House. Since House Harker was more or less on the way, I decided to come back here for a night before continuing on my journey."

Just as I was about to launch myself into his arms, I forced myself to stop. He smelled achingly good. I swallowed and backed up a step.

"Umm, I actually came out here to be alone for a bit." My eyes locked onto where his throat was pulsing, and I quickly looked at the ground. "Roth is here. You should go to the library so they can fill you in. Alaric is there too."

"Sam," he drawled in a low tone that never failed to set my blood on fire.

My gaze rose from the ground as if pulled in. The way the corners of his lips curled up told me he knew exactly what he was doing by saying my name like that.

He tilted his head. "We both know you need to feed."

"I'll ask Nyx when I get back." I licked my lips and took a step forward before catching myself and forcing my feet to remain rooted. "You should go."

Every part of me wanted to sink my fangs into Kieran. The need was so intense that I was having a hard time thinking about anything else, which was exactly why I shouldn't do it. The bond I was forming with Kieran was too much, and it was happening too fast.

I needed to calm the fuck down, but instead, I took another step closer. Then another, and another, until I found myself directly in front of him.

"And if I want to stay?" Kieran's eyes were ablaze as he stared down at me.

"Things will change between us." My desire to claim him was so strong, this was so far beyond the normal bloodlust I felt. It took every ounce of my willpower, but I forced myself to take a step back. "I'm sorry. You make me want things... and I have no right to ask that of you yet."

He stepped forward, reclaiming the distance I had put between us. "Ask whatever you want of me. It's yours."

"Are you sure?" I rasped. "And think carefully, because we both know I'm a possessive bitch, and I know it's not fair because I'm not ready to commit to you and only you just yet. But if I taste your blood..." I closed my eyes and inhaled his rich and decadent scent before snapping my eyes open once more. "If I taste you, then you are *mine*."

The gold in Kieran's eyes spread, drowning out the hazel as he pressed down on the black gem that adorned his left pinkie finger, causing a blade to pop out. I watched with rapt attention when he dragged the blade down the side of his neck, leaving behind a trail of blood.

My nostrils flared as the scent hit me.

"I have always been yours, Sam."

The last of my control snapped, and I leapt forward.

Kieran caught me as I wrapped myself around him, one arm around my back holding me close while the other cupped my ass. My fangs sank into his neck, and he let out a deep groan and gripped me tighter against him.

He lowered us to the ground, settling on his back with me on top. I drank deep as I ground my hips against his, loving the way he hissed every time I did it. The rich, full taste rushed across my tongue and down my throat, and I wasn't sure if I'd ever felt this alive. Kieran's blood was the most delicious thing I'd ever tasted. It was wickedly divine.

My main source of blood these last few years had been Demetri. I'd tried to make it fun whenever we'd had to feed from each other, but it'd been nothing like this.

"Fuck, Sam," Kieran breathed out.

One hand was still gripping my ass, but the other had slipped beneath my shirt. I continued to drink deep as his hand made a blazing path up.

Just as I pulled my fangs out from his neck, Kieran ran a thumb over my pebbled nipple, and I threw my head back with a moan. My body was tight with need, and I wanted his hands on me more.

Nimble fingers unbuttoned the leather vest I'd been wearing before Kieran pulled it off me. My shirt was next, and Kieran wasted no time once my breasts were free. He pivoted up and sucked a nipple into his mouth. I shuddered and arched my back further.

When he moved to give my other breast the same attention, I pawed at his clothes, untying the various knots. He nipped at my skin before leaning back and pulling his vest and shirt off. I frantically tugged at his pants, but Kieran grabbed the back of my thighs and flipped me onto my back.

My remaining clothes were gone in a flash, and I arched my back when

Kieran buried himself between my thighs and dragged his tongue up my pussy before sucking on my clit.

"Fucking hell, you're good at that," I said through panted breaths.

I licked the remnants of Kieran's blood from my lips as his fingers plunged inside me. There was nothing gentle about his movements as he pumped them hard and fast. My hands clenched the blanket beneath us, tension building in my core.

"Tell me how good I am," Kieran purred before swirling his tongue around my clit.

I whimpered as the pleasure started to become too much. Just as I was about to go over the edge, his tongue vanished, and he pulled his fingers out.

"FUCK!" I screamed and glared at him.

The asshole just laughed and plunged two fingers back in while taking up an irritatingly slow pace.

"Tell me, Sam." His golden eyes bore into mine as he demanded again, "Tell me how much you love me fucking you."

His thumb just barely grazed my clit, and a moan slipped out of me.

"I *like* you fucking me," I ground out and raised my hips to meet the thrust of his fingers, but he just pulled them back out.

"That's not what I asked," he tutted. "But maybe you just need more convincing."

"Yes," I breathed out. "That."

Warm breath brushed my inner thigh as he laughed, followed by lips kissing my skin.

"What are you—fuck!" I screamed as Kieran sank his fangs into my thigh just as he pushed two fingers deep inside my pussy again. The pleasure mixed with the brief flicker of pain immediately brought on the orgasm that Kieran had been teasing out of me for the last few minutes.

Another finger joined the other two as he pushed down with his thumb on my clit, all the while continuing to drink deeply from my thigh. My mind shattered, and I welcomed the bliss as the orgasm rippled through me.

I was only vaguely aware of Kieran withdrawing his fingers and fangs and moving up to rest over me, a satisfied grin fixed on his lips.

"Given that look on your face," he drawled, "I suppose I don't need to ask if you loved that."

I nodded, stretching my body out languidly beneath him. His cock throbbed against me, and I reached down to stroke it.

"Sam," he groaned, thrusting into my hand. When I wrapped my legs around his waist and rested his cock at my entrance, he looked down at me with brilliant gold eyes. "Are you sure?"

In response, I thrust my hips up, and he easily slid inside. We both let out twin moans of satisfaction.

"Thank fuck," he growled.

He slid in and out slowly, letting me adjust to him, before leaning back and raising my legs up over his shoulders.

Something between a moan and a whimper poured out of me as he pushed my legs back down, bringing the top of my thighs closer to my chest and letting him thrust even deeper inside of me.

My pussy clenched around him as Kieran built up a fast and hard pace. His lips crashed against mine, and he fucked me with his tongue as he continued to relentlessly fuck me with his cock. Just as I felt another orgasm building, I gripped his hair and tore him away from my mouth so that I could sink my fangs into his neck again.

He groaned as I greedily drank his blood while he continued to pump inside me, fucking me through the orgasm. My legs eventually loosened as the aftereffects rippled through me.

Kieran was rapidly blowing past all of my best sexual experiences and setting a high bar for future encounters.

"We're not done yet, my love." Kieran pulled back and flipped me onto all fours, pushing down on my back so that my ass was up in the air. Even if I'd been capable of voicing a protest through my pleasure-addled brain, all thoughts scattered as he slammed back into me.

"Fuck, Kieran," I moaned, and he knelt to kiss my back while thrusting deep inside me.

"I fucking love hearing my name on your lips." His hips hammered against me. "Almost as much as I love you coming all over my cock."

Between his filthy words and the punishing rhythm, I was already primed for another orgasm, which I didn't think was possible. After experiencing no orgasms during sex for the last couple of years, having more than one felt greedy and impossible.

The sound of flesh slapping against flesh rang loudly around us as Kieran's pace became frantic. A mewling sound tore out of me that if I'd been rational, I probably would have been embarrassed about making. One of Kieran's hands dropped down to rub against my clit, and that was all it took to send me spiraling.

My scream was echoed seconds later by Kieran as he shuddered inside me. Both of us stayed like that, breathing heavily, scorched by bliss.

After a moment, Kieran pulled me down with him so that we were both on our sides, with me tucked against him. His cock was still buried inside me, as if he couldn't bear any level of separation between us just yet. I felt the same, so I enjoyed the feeling of his body wrapped around mine.

We lay there for some time in comfortable silence before Kieran pulled back, a low groan slipping out of both of us as he pulled his cock out and a rush of fluids followed.

He pulled me around so that I was facing him, and I rested my head on his chest with my body firmly pressed up against his side.

"So," Kieran said, "not that I'm complaining about what just happened at all, but what kicked off your bloodlust?"

"Rynn." My voice was tinged with anger, but at least my bloodlust was well-sated now. "She's putting herself in danger, and there's nothing I can do about it."

"She's a big wolf," Kieran said gently. "She can handle herself."

"I know, I know, but I still worry about her, just as I worry about Cali, even though she can definitely take care of herself."

"You know Cali is kind of terrifying, right?" Kieran's head flopped to the side to look at me, a sheepish grin on his face.

"Never to me or Rynn." I grinned back at him before it slid off my face. "I'm guessing you're aware of Rynn's situation?"

He gave me an apologetic look. "It's been making the rounds of the rumor mill for a while now. People are saying that she is refusing to join the Alpha Pack. Others are saying they are the ones refusing to let her join."

He reached out and slipped his hand into mine, and I nestled further into him. The sex was mind-blowing, but so was this.

Kieran added carefully, "I don't know Rynn all that well, but I don't believe she'd refuse to join the pack, and I see no reason why they wouldn't want her. Rynn is bloody brilliant and has that whole lithe and wild werewolf thing going on. It's super hot."

He grunted when I elbowed him hard, and then he gave me a pouty look which I ignored.

"Don't worry,"—he leaned down and kissed my neck, making me shiver— "I have a thing for a certain curvy-as-fuck Moroi."

"You'd better," I muttered.

He nipped my neck playfully, sending all my thoughts scattering until he looked at me with a self-satisfied smile.

I scowled. "Oh, get over yourself."

Kieran chuckled. "I don't know what's going on between Rynn and the Alpha Pack, and you don't have to tell me. But there are a lot of rumors flying around about the growing tension between the three Velesian Orders and a general discontent against the Alpha Pack and how they're handling things... and Rynn's name has come up."

"Rynn and the Alpha Pack are kind of a hot mess," I admitted. "I can't go into details without checking with her first, but to answer your original question of why I was so pissed off earlier... Rynn is going to sneak onto Fervis territory to investigate an old human settlement."

Kieran jackknifed into a sitting position, jostling me to the side before his hands clamped down on my arms.

"You can't let her do that!" His eyes were wide with panic. "The last couple of attacks have been in Fervis land. They didn't even want to let the Alphas in to look at the scenes. Apparently, they've upped all patrols on their border."

"Shit!" I hissed and echoed Kieran's abrupt movement to a sitting position. "There's no way Rynn didn't know that when she announced her ridiculous plan!"

"The Fervis are still pissed that the Narchis chose to ally with Avala instead of them. Rynn wasn't the only one from Narchis chosen to join one of the Avala packs, but she was the most prominent because she's going to the moons damned Alphas!"

"I know! Why do you think I lost my shit earlier?!" I choked on the words. Now that my bloodlust had calmed down, panic was starting to override the rage.

Strong arms pulled me into a hug, and I wrapped myself around Kieran with tears streaming down my face. I hated crying, but whenever I was feeling any sort of overwhelming emotion, tears were inevitable. Especially if I couldn't scream at anything.

Kieran knew it bothered me, so he didn't comment, just silently wiped them away while holding me tightly against him.

"Are you sure you can't talk her out of it?" he asked softly.

I shook my head against his chest, not trusting myself to speak just yet.

Kieran sighed. "Rynn is stealthy and good at remaining unseen. Remember when we used to play hide-and-seek as kids? None of us could ever find her."

I sniffled. "Carmilla was so upset that one time Rynn stayed outside in the woods all night when we couldn't find her. She insisted that we put a time limit on the game after that."

Kieran maneuvered me until I was sitting in his lap and tucked me against his chest again. "I'm not any more thrilled than you are about Rynn going into Fervis territory, but we'll just have to trust that she knows what she's doing and that she'll be okay."

"And if she's not?" I whispered.

"Then we'll unleash Cali on them."

I craned my head to look at him but found his expression unreadable, which was a little unsettling. "Honestly, I can't tell if you're joking or not."

"Kidding." He kissed me softly on the corners of my mouth. "Mostly."

CHAPTER NINETEEN

—

Samara

THE FOLLOWING MORNING, Alaric stood with Kieran and I just inside the gate while we waited for the rangers who would be escorting us to arrive.

Alaric kept switching from giving Zosa the side eye to trying not to gawk at the matching bite marks on my neck and Kieran's. After the beach, we'd moved back to my suite and hadn't left for hours. Taking our time in exploring every inch of each other's bodies.

"If you keep glaring at Zosa like that, I'm going to let her sneeze all over you," I warned.

Zosa's ears perked forward, and Alaric took a step back, disgust tugging the corners of his lips down.

"Don't be too hard on him, love," Kieran said breezily. "He's probably just wondering how you taste." His fingers brushed across my neck, and I fought the blush that was creeping up my cheeks. Alaric fixed a glare on his best friend, but Kieran just grinned wickedly at him. "The answer, my friend, is exquisite."

"Kieran!" I stomped my foot down, and he yelped before giving me a wounded look while rubbing his foot. "It's too early for your bullshit."

He shot me a pouty look, and I rolled my eyes. I was proud of myself for being civil to Alaric all week and ignoring the growing attraction I was feeling towards him.

Alaric might have sent me some heated looks, but those all happened in the spur of the moment. He probably would have reacted that way to anybody. He clearly did not want *me* in that way, and I didn't want to ruin our working relationship, especially since we were just starting to work so well together.

I don't know why Kieran had decided to tease Alaric so much about me, but I was determined to put a stop to it. Before I could apologize to Alaric for

169

Kieran's obnoxious behavior, the rangers came around the corner leading three horses.

Surprise flickered through me when I saw that Nyx wasn't among those present. It was Vail and two other rangers I recognized from the training yard. Raoul and Aerin. They'd been part of the group that had laughed at Alaric that first day he'd been practicing with the bow.

Despite their behavior that day, they'd actually stepped in to help give Alaric advice in the days that followed when they saw he was determined to learn how to shoot. He nodded at them in greeting before he gave me an uneasy look, which I returned. I'd assumed that Nyx would be coming with me today since Emil and Adrienne weren't available. While Raoul and Aerin were nice enough, and probably trustworthy since they reported to Vail, I wasn't sure if it was a good idea for them to escort me today. They would no doubt have questions about why the Heir of House Harker was traipsing around in an old human settlement.

"Raoul and Aerin will be escorting you to the Sovereign House, Kieran," Vail said, causing my brows to furrow.

Who was going to escort me then? I stood on my tiptoes, trying to see if Nyx or someone else was coming behind Vail.

He finished, "I'll be escorting Samara for her trip today."

I froze, my eyes darting to Vail before I slowly lowered myself back onto my heels just as Kieran slid closer to me and eyed the marshal.

His gaze narrowed. "Surely, you're needed here? Isn't there someone else who can escort Samara?"

Cold, grey eyes locked onto Kieran. "Are you saying that I am inadequate to keep the Heir safe in broad daylight?"

"I'm sure Kieran meant no offense," Alaric said smoothly. "We simply wouldn't want to monopolize your time with such a trivial errand."

I gave Alaric a thankful nod, appreciating that he was standing up for me despite Kieran being an ass earlier. While it was unlikely that Vail would try anything today, I was still stressed out about Rynn, and the idea of being stuck with him all day was less than appealing. At least I didn't have to worry about my bloodlust rising so soon after drinking from Kieran yesterday and giving Vail an excuse to get rid of me once and for all.

Vail studied Alaric before looking at Kieran, then he let out a disgusted sound and curled his lip up at me. "Well, it didn't take you long to sink your claws into them. Or I suppose, in this case, spread your legs."

"Shut the fuck up, Vail," Kieran growled and took a step forward.

I slapped my hand across his chest, and he halted immediately. Vail pointedly looked at my hand on his chest and gave Kieran a lazy smile. I felt a growl rumble out of Kieran's chest and swiftly moved to stand between them.

"Enough! Who I fuck"—my eyes flicked briefly over to Alaric's—"or don't fuck, is none of your damn business, Vail, and stop acting like it's irrational for my friends to be concerned about my well-being just because you don't have anyone in your life who gives a shit about you."

The rangers standing near Vail stiffened and shot me murderous looks, but I ignored them.

I spun and placed my hands on either side of Kieran's face, forcing him to take his attention off Vail and set it on me. His hazel eyes were bright in the morning sun, and I gave myself a second to appreciate them before brushing a kiss against his lips.

"I'll be fine," I murmured. "We're only riding a few hours from here. We'll be back well before sundown. Vail is an asshole, but he won't do anything."

The asshole in question muttered something behind me, but I couldn't make out the words, which was probably for the best. I was trying hard to be the bigger person here, mostly to keep Kieran from doing something stupid, but if Vail called me a whore again, I was likely to punch the marshal myself— and then run away as quickly as possible.

"Alright." He tenderly kissed me back, resting his forehead against mine. "Let me know what you find?"

"Of course." I nodded and stepped away from him, immediately missing his body heat in the brisk morning air. "Make sure Roth eats today, will you?" I asked Alaric and clarified when he just arched an eyebrow at me. "They tend to get caught up in their research and forget to do silly things like eat or drink. That's why I've been bringing food up to the library all week and risking their wrath at the books being damaged."

He cringed a little. Roth hated the idea of food, or worse drinks, being brought into the library, but it was significantly easier to bring the food to Roth than it was to get them out of the library and bring them to the food.

"Fine, but you owe me one," Alaric agreed.

I immediately thought of ways I could return the favor and had to slam the door down on all those thoughts. Apparently, even though Kieran had quite satisfied me last night, I was still doomed to have dirty thoughts about Alaric.

Given the way the gold fractures in Kieran's eyes were glowing brightly and that the corners of his lips had tipped up ever so slightly, I figured he'd caught my blush before I had crushed it and had a very good idea of every dirty thought that had just gone through my head.

Damn it. Now he was going to be even worse at teasing Alaric about me.

"Let's go." I quickly mounted Zosa, and the rangers and Kieran did the same as the gate was raised in front of us.

Kieran steered his horse next to mine and leaned over to kiss me, and when he pulled back, he whispered, "Don't have too much fun while I'm away." Then his eyes slid to Alaric and back to me. "But do have a little fun."

The blush I'd just barely managed to force into retreat came flaring back to life. "I hate you," I muttered and urged Zosa forward, leaving Vail to catch up, Kieran's laugh chasing me the whole way out.

Three hours later, Vail pulled up his horse, and I slowed Zosa down to a walk. We'd rode the entire way here in complete silence.

If I hadn't been so stressed out about Rynn, I would have enjoyed the ride. It was a beautiful sunny day, and the road we took was along the coast, so I was able to view the ocean for most of it.

I only had a general idea of where the human outpost was based on the map, but Vail seemed to know exactly where he was going which, for some reason, I found really annoying. Maybe it was because he seemed overly confident about everything, and I'd never seen him be wrong about anything.

For once, I wanted him to be wrong. *It's probably for the best that he's right in this instance though*, I thought begrudgingly.

The quicker we found and searched the human settlement, the sooner we could get back to House Harker and its fortified walls. Away from the monsters lurking in the woods, awaiting their next meal.

Vail dismounted and looped his horse's reins over the saddle, and I did the same, giving Zosa a good pat before joining Vail. Both were well-trained enough to not go far unless we were attacked, in which case it was better to give the horses at least a chance to run for their lives and possibly serve as a distraction. Hopefully, with it still being daylight, we wouldn't have to worry about that.

"I can see why I never noticed it before." My eyes scanned the area, spotting a few pieces of well-weathered wood and some crumbling brickwork. "There really isn't much left."

Vail grunted and began walking around, studying the ground as he moved while I surveyed the area a little more.

The human village had been built very close to the beach. We were on higher ground, but the beginning of the shoreline was directly below us. Based on where the seaweed had piled up, there was less than a quarter mile between the edge of the town and where the water came in at high tide.

Because of how high up the village had been, they would have been fine... until there was a storm.

I wondered what had driven them to build a town here. It didn't seem safe. Then again, the world hadn't been a safe place for humans even when the Fae were still around to keep the monsters under control.

The coastlines had always been safer than living in the forests because the monsters preferred the coverage provided by the trees and thick ground cover. There were more prey options in the forest, as well.

We might be a favorite food source for the monsters, but we were hardly the only one.

My foot slipped on some loose rocks, and I stumbled forward towards the edge. I waved my arms as I tried to backpedal but only succeeded in tripping over another loose rock. Just as I was about to pitch forward, Vail grabbed my arm and yanked me back.

The movement sent me spinning around, and I fell right into his broad chest. "Thanks," I breathed out, placing my hands on his shoulders to steady myself.

"Despite your low opinion of me, you are House Harker's Heir, and therefore, I am bound to keep you safe," he said coldly before stepping away and putting several feet of space between us. "I'm simply not under the spell of that cunt of yours like those two peacocks."

I bit back the retort that tried to burst free. Almost tumbling over the cliff had left me unsettled, and being saved by Vail only to have him throw his cruel vitriol at me had my emotions all over the place, but I absolutely *refused* to let him know he'd hurt me.

I shoved away the anger and lingering fear and planted a sultry smirk on my face while batting my eyelashes at him.

"Well, my cunt doesn't have any interest in you, so that works out for both of us." I tapped a finger against my bottom lip and fixed my features into a thoughtful expression. "I can see how Kieran would qualify as a peacock. Alaric, not so much."

Vail stared at me, uncertainty flashing across his face. He probably thought I'd be mad about his rude comment, but it didn't really bother me all that much.

I enjoyed sex and wasn't going to feel bad about that. Marvina constantly belittling me and dismissing my intelligence had pissed me off far more than any crude insult about my sex life. It was Vail's unwarranted hatred towards me that hurt. But I'd never let him know that.

His mouth flattened into a hard line, annoyance etched in his features at me brushing off his cutting remarks so easily.

I laughed even as a flicker of pain sliced across my heart and set about searching the area, this time further from the edge. "You'll have to work harder to get under my skin, Vail. Also, I'm not sleeping with Alaric."

"Yeah, I give that a week," he said with a slight edge to his voice. "We have two hours to search, and then we need to head back to make sure we make it before night falls."

A shiver ran through me at the idea of being caught out in the wilds at night with Vail. I couldn't help but remember that night when we'd both lost our parents and this animosity between us had started. Before then, we'd been friends in a way. He was three years older than me and was often busy training with rangers or traveling outside House Harker with his parents. But we'd always gotten along, and I'd often sought out his company when possible.

Whenever my parents traveled outside of House Harker, it was Vail's parents who always escorted them. When Vail was old enough, he started going as well because his parents thought it would be a good experience for him. My parents often brought me along too, which I never could understand because I was too young to gain anything from their political conversations, but they rarely left me alone in House Harker.

Most of the time that Vail and I spent together was on those trips. We were usually the only two children, and despite our age difference, we got along really well.

I'd loved picking Vail's brain about what it was like to train to be a ranger and asked him about what types of monsters he'd seen. He was more than happy to show off his knowledge and keep me entertained. Every time we'd stop to rest, he'd show me different animal tracks or point out plants that were edible. Some of my best childhood memories were those trips, solely because of Vail.

I studied his face. With the jagged scars running down the right side across his eye and his long beard, he looked so much older than me when only three years separated us.

I remembered what he was like when we were kids. Even then he carried so much responsibility on his shoulders, determined to live up to the expectations placed on him by his parents who had been the previous marshals of House Harker. It was hard to reconcile the boy I remembered with the man standing before me.

"Will you ever stop hating me?" The words slipped out before I could think better of it.

Vail flinched. It happened so fast that I almost missed it, and part of me still doubted that I'd even seen it to begin with.

"I could have saved them," he said, turning away from me. "Your selfishness cost me my parents."

"Bullshit," I hissed.

"Excuse me?" He whirled to face me, the silver fractures in his eyes widening, making him look more than a little terrifying, but I didn't back down.

"I understand why you felt that way when we were kids." I closed the distance between us until only inches separated my chest from his. "But you are a grown-ass adult now! Our caravan was attacked by over a dozen wraiths! And only the moon knows what else!

"Your parents ordered you to protect me because they wanted you to get away! They knew that they wouldn't be walking away that night, but they wanted to give you a chance!"

"I COULD HAVE SAVED THEM!" Vail roared in my face.

"No! You couldn't have!" I yelled back, leaning forward even more until my chest bumped into his and I had to tilt my head back further to continue holding his pissed-off gaze. "If your well-trained and experienced parents couldn't fight their way out of that night, there was no way in hell their thirteen-year-old kid was going to make a difference. You need someone to blame for that night, and you chose me because I'm a convenient target, but my parents died too, you asshole!" I shoved him with every ounce of strength I had and still only managed to push him back a step.

Vail's nostrils flared, and his eyes turned solid silver, giving them a ghostly appearance. My eyes flicked briefly to his hands, which were clenching and unclenching at his sides like he was imagining wrapping them around my throat.

The small voice that I'm pretty sure was my survival instinct was screaming in one corner of my mind to back away with my hands held up and try to look as small and harmless as possible, but the voice that was full of rage was louder and it was telling me to hold my fucking ground. So I did.

"I guess we'll never know," Vail said in an eerily calm tone. "Because you took that choice from me when you knocked me out."

He stared at me for another moment before taking a step back and walking to the other side of the settlement, where he started angrily sifting through the remains. The tension bled out of me, and I felt so tired all of a sudden. I don't know why I bothered trying to fix things between me and Vail. He was the only one besides me who had survived that night, and I just wanted to have someone to talk to about it.

I wanted to know if he had nightmares. If he still heard the screams and terrified commands of our parents telling us to run and protect each other.

I looked down at my palm and the jagged scar that ran across it. At some point in the attack, I'd cut it deeply, and then when Vail said he was going back to help his parents after we'd gotten away, I'd panicked. I'd screamed at him to stay, not wanting to lose him too. He'd frozen for a moment at my command, but I didn't think he would actually stay, so I'd grabbed a chunk of branch off the ground and hit him with every ounce of my ten-year-old strength.

Normally, it probably would have just annoyed him, but he already had a bunch of wounds at that point and had dropped like a stone.

When he woke hours later, his eyes burned with hatred at what I'd done. He'd looked at me the same ever since. I let out a long breath, trying to expel the last of my anger with it. Vail would have to deal with his issues towards me at some point because I was back at House Harker, and I wasn't going anywhere.

Not wanting to push Vail anymore, I stayed away from him for the next hour while I searched through what was left of the human settlement. A dull pain throbbed within my chest from a wound that had never healed.

My parents had been my entire world. They'd both ruled House Harker and that had kept them incredibly busy. But they'd always made time for me, always making sure that at least one of them was always there to tuck me in at night. It was my father who had instilled my love of riding. And my mother a love of reading.

When they died, it shattered me. I didn't know how to handle the grief and I'd wanted to be strong for Carmilla and everyone else at House Harker. So I had gathered all the jagged pieces and shoved them into a box that I then tucked away into the farthest depths of my soul.

And Vail had just reached in to grab that box and rattle it.

I was debating if I could shove him over the cliff and down onto the beach below when the glint of steel caught my eye. All of the buildings had long since been wiped away but their foundations remained.

Dropping to my knees, I pushed away bits of dried grass and dirt, revealing a locked cellar door. The metal lock remained strong, as did the thick bars stretching between the doorframe like a grate. Some slabs of wood were bolted to the bars, but most of the boards had decayed, allowing me to see a little bit of the room beneath the door.

"I think I found something," I called out.

Vail ambled over and eyed the door, then motioned for me to stand back.

Taking the hint, I moved a few steps away as he stomped down on the door. The wood cracked and buckled immediately, leaving behind only the metal bars. Then he pulled on the frame, but it didn't budge.

"This was probably the safe hideout for the village," he said. "We've encountered them before. They have steel beams that run across the ceiling, and that's what the doorframe is attached to. Some of the outposts have managed to melt away the locks and repurpose them, but I didn't bring anything with me to get through it. We'll have to come back to search it."

My nose scrunched up as I stared at the door. Coming back tomorrow wasn't the end of the world, but patience wasn't my strong suit, and I wanted to know now. We were already here, and I'd be annoyed if we came all the way back tomorrow only to find out that it was empty.

Once again dropping down to my knees, I skimmed my fingers over the joint where one of the steel bars running across the door was connected to the frame. "I think this one is loose? If you kick it a couple of times, it might snap free."

I looked up at Vail just as he shook his head. "Still not enough space for me to get through."

"It will be for me though," I pointed out.

Emotionless eyes looked at me, scrutinizing my body before catching on my full breasts.

I smirked at him and put my hands flat on my breasts and pushed them down. "They're squishy, Vail. I'm pretty sure I can squeeze through, and if I can't, we'll come back tomorrow."

"Fine," he said flatly, still clearly not believing I'd be able to manage this.

To be honest, I wasn't sure I'd be able to squeeze through the bars, either. I was far from dainty, but unlike Vail, who was all slabs of hard muscle, I was soft and there was some give to my body.

It might take some wiggling on my part, but there was a decent chance I could get in. Getting out might be more difficult, but I'd deal with that later.

Hopefully, Vail wouldn't just leave me here. Hmm... maybe this *wasn't* a good idea.

A few stomps and a loud clang later, the bar snapped away, leaving a gap in the door. I knelt down and did my best to peer into the space below, but it was hard to see anything from this angle. But there were no sounds, so I decided to call that good enough.

I maneuvered so that I was sitting across the door with my feet dangling down. Shit, this was really narrow.

"You'll have to hold my arms and lower me down." I scooted forward as far as I could until it would only take a tilt of my hips to have me sliding down and held my arms straight up.

Vail let out a long sigh and then moved so that he was standing directly in front of me with his legs in a wide stance across the door.

If I tilted my head up, I'd basically be staring directly at his crotch.

I did not tilt my head up.

Strong hands grasped my wrists and once I was sure he had a secure grip, I let myself slide forward and wiggled my hips through the gap. Then I sucked in my stomach as much as I could while he lowered me through.

My breasts did indeed get a little stuck, and it was uncomfortable for a few seconds, but then I was past the bars.

Vail held on for a few more seconds before letting me drop to the ground.

"Yes!" I called out in victory while I brushed off my clothes. It wasn't the most pleasant experience, but I made it through and proved Vail wrong, so... worth it.

"We don't have all day," Vail said gruffly. "Take a look around and see if you can find anything. Then we'll have to get you out of there and head back."

"You can just admit I was right about being able to fit through, you know?"

He didn't bother answering, but I suspected he was wearing an annoyed expression and was probably debating the merits of leaving me here for the night. I didn't think he actually would leave me entirely, but I wouldn't put it past him to post up in one of the trees for the night and keep watch while I bunkered down here, cold and terrified.

I moved further into the underground bunker and then stopped until my eyes adjusted to the dark.

It was a big, open space. I was a little surprised that the ground above hadn't caved in, but there were steel beams running across the ceiling. Maybe the townsfolk had strengthened them with magic.

Back then, the Fae had been somewhat willing to share their magic with the humans to help keep them safe. Roth might be interested in visiting this place in the future to figure out how they'd managed to build this underground area. I walked around, scanning the space, trying to find anything of interest.

At first glance, it appeared to be empty, and my hopes sank at finding something useful. I forced myself to slow down and looked over the area again steadily, focusing on different areas. Nothing stood out on the ceiling or walls besides the impressive support structure they'd built, but something caught my attention in the center of the room.

I walked over and studied the ground, finding it was the same dirt flooring as the rest of the room, but parts of the floor were darker here.

My breath caught in my throat as I knelt down and swept dirt away from a jet-black piece of stone.

"Holy shit," I breathed out.

It looked like obsidian, but there were threads of gold running through it, and in the center of it was a crescent moon outlined in blood-red. I dug with my fingers until I could lift up the flat piece of obsidian-like stone. It was oddly heavy in my hands despite its relatively small size and fit neatly inside my two hands cupped together.

"I found something!" I raced back over to Vail and carefully handed it over to him.

I had to stand on my tippy-toes, and he had to get on his stomach and reach down to get it. In the back of my mind, I realized that this meant getting out of here was not going to be fun, but I was way too excited about finding something to care all that much.

"It still contains magic," Vail murmured where he knelt over the grate. "I can feel it."

"This must have been part of the ritual," I said. "Roth and Rynn were right in their speculation!"

"We still don't know if this is why the wraiths are targeting the outposts," Vail retorted flatly.

I rolled my eyes. He was such a downer.

"Let me see if I can find more." I hurried back over to where I'd found the first piece and started moving the dirt around.

Soon, I discovered two more segments, each with a lunar symbol on them. We now had three parts of this strange obsidian stone that corresponded to our three species.

This had to be something. I didn't know what yet, but I was excited to get this back to Roth so we could start figuring it out.

After spending another ten minutes looking around, I was satisfied that there wasn't anything else here to find, so I went back over to the opening where Vail waited patiently above. Apparently, me finding something was enough to buy a little bit of goodwill from him.

"I think that's it," I said, peering up with a frown at the door.

There must have been stairs or a ladder down here at one point, but now there was nothing to help me close the distance.

It'd been a stretch to just pass the pieces I'd found back to Vail. How the hell were we going to do this?

As I was trying to figure this out, Vail moved so that he was squatting over the opening, bent over so that one hand was braced on the other side, and reached down with his other hand. Even with him crouching as low as he could, it was still a good two feet between me and that hand.

"You'll have to jump," he said.

"Sure, no problem," I said wryly. "Are you sure you can hold my weight with one hand?"

In my head, I pictured myself performing a magnificent leap and latching onto his hand, only for him to slam forward into the metal grate and knock himself out, leaving me trapped down here and him bleeding up top with a head wound. I really hated my overly active imagination sometimes.

"I'll be fine. Concern yourself with making the jump," he said gruffly.

"Okay, but if this goes poorly, it's not my fault," I grumbled and then backed up a few paces before running forward and jumping up... and missing by at least half a foot.

"Samara, you're a damn Moroi. This jump should be nothing," Vail said in an annoyed tone. "You should be training more."

"If it was nighttime, I could make this jump no problem," I said, moving back further this time to give myself even more of a running start.

"You shouldn't be dependent on the extra power you get during the night," he said disapprovingly.

"I'm not one of your rangers, Vail," I reminded him.

"Thank the moon for that," he muttered.

I scowled up at him. "Ready?"

"Waiting on you."

Argh.

I eyed his dangling hand and took off at a run. This time, I waited until the last possible second and then pushed up off the ground with every ounce of strength I could muster.

My fingers brushed against his wrist, and his large hand locked onto my right forearm. After awkwardly swinging for another moment, and feeling like my arm was going to get wrenched out of its socket, I managed to grab onto his arm with my left hand.

Once Vail was confident my grip was secure, he started pulling me up. Holy shit, he was strong. He pulled me up like I weighed nothing at all. It was a little uncomfortable wiggling through the small opening, but we managed to get me out a lot easier than I thought.

"Thanks," I mumbled, taking a step back as soon as my feet were on the ground.

Vail clearly didn't like touching me or having me around, so the least I could do was not press him on it. Unless, of course, I lost my temper. Then rational thinking went right out the window.

Vail didn't acknowledge my thanks and instead swiped the three obsidian pieces off the ground and headed over to the horses where he secured them in the saddlebags. I sighed and walked over to Zosa, who butted me gently with her head, and then I prepared myself for another silent ride back.

I hoped Rynn's excursion had gone as smoothly as ours. Even if she didn't find anything, I didn't care as long as she made it back safely.

Without waiting for Vail, I spurred Zosa forward and headed home, to where hopefully Roth could provide us with some answers once they looked over what we had found.

CHAPTER TWENTY

—

Alaric

"IF YOU TAP that thing one more time, I'm going to stab you with it," Roth said in a voice so calm that it took me a moment to register their threat.

I dropped the pencil that I'd been methodically drumming against the table, and it rolled before coming to a rest against a stack of scrolls.

"Sorry," I grunted. "Just a little keyed up today."

Roth glared at me for another second before returning their focus to the book in front of them.

The book had the symbol we'd been looking for, and they were working on translating the text now, but it took time. I was eager to look at it, but Roth was likely faster at translating than me, so I let them have it. Plus, I wasn't ashamed to admit that Roth terrified me a little.

I couldn't exactly explain why. Physically, they were no threat to me, but Roth was just so intense about everything. Plus, they used blood magic with ease more than any other person I'd ever met.

Sure, it was mostly to help them navigate around the library and be more productive with their research, but those ribbons they had wrapped around their forearms could easily be used to restrain someone.

And I was pretty sure their enchanted quill could at the very least gouge out some eyes.

"Is it Samara who has you worried or Kieran?" they asked, not taking their eyes off the page they were reading.

The familiar thread of tension that formed every time Kieran left tugged a little. But now it felt like that thread was split in two, and I was trying very hard not to think about who was at the end of the second one.

"I'm always concerned about Kieran when he leaves House Harker," I admitted. "But he travels fairly often to visit the other Houses and occasionally the Velesians. It doesn't mean I don't worry about him, but he's traveling on well-known roads and stopping at outposts along the way."

The Sovereign House was probably the safest place to be in all of Lunaria. Aside from the impressive blood wards, they had the highest number of rangers out of the Houses. Kieran would be fine... once he made it there.

Absently, I picked the pencil up and started to tap it before a growl rumbled out of Roth and I hastily put it down again. I glanced at the nearest window.

The sun hadn't even started to set yet. There was plenty of time for Samara and Vail to make it back safely.

"And Samara?" Roth prompted.

I stared at the pencil, unsure how to answer that question. Samara confused the hell out of me, and I didn't like it. It was why I always sniped at her in a desperate attempt to maintain some distance between us.

"Samara is the Heir of House Harker," I hedged. "Her safety will always be of concern to me."

That got Roth to raise their head and arch an eyebrow at me. "You are so full of shit."

I bit the inside of my cheek as I forced my expression to remain neutral. I really was. To make matters worse, Kieran had definitely picked up on my increasingly conflicted feelings about Samara.

I thought he would be jealous or upset about it. Instead, he seemed *intrigued* by the idea of me being with Samara.

I'd heard his comment to Samara when he was leaving about her having a little fun while he was gone. I'd also caught her blushing like crazy when she looked at me.

Samara had always been funny like that. She was obnoxiously bold with her flirting, wasn't the least bit shy when it came to sex, and had become even more so since returning to House Harker. Yet relatively tame words or suggestions could get her to blush from head to toe.

I wondered what she'd been thinking about when she looked at me and blushed earlier. The bite marks on her and Kieran's neck had thrown me off, although it made sense. They both trusted each other, and anyone who had eyes knew that they'd been more than a little in love with each other growing up, and with Samara no longer married, there was no reason for them not to be together.

Though, Kieran seemed to think that Samara wanted me too... and that we could *share*.

Fuck. I shifted in my seat as my cock hardened, glad that the table blocked Roth's view. Was I seriously considering sharing Samara with Kieran? How would that even work?

The Velesians usually had multiple partners in a relationship, but the

Moroi were always just a couple. There was also the complication of Samara being the House Harker Heir. Carmilla loved her niece and wouldn't push for another marriage anytime soon, but it would still be expected of her to marry another high-ranking House member someday.

Neither Kieran nor I qualified as high-ranking. What would Kieran do if he were forced to give her up again?

Shit. What would I do?

This was exactly why it would be foolish for me to get involved with Samara as anything beyond friends. There was no happy ending here, and if I went down this path with Samara, I wasn't entirely sure I'd be able to let her walk away.

The rational choice was to be friends and nothing more so that I could support Kieran when my friend's heart was shattered at losing her.

I could do that. I just needed to ignore the throbbing hard cock in my pants.

Something smacked me in the forehead, and I blinked at the balled-up piece of paper before realizing Roth was staring at me expectantly.

"What?"

They sighed and shook their head. "I asked you *twice* what the deal was with Samara and Vail?"

"Oh." I pursed my lips.

The history between those two was a bit of a mystery to everyone, and I really didn't like sharing other people's business. Definitely not those I considered my friends.

I didn't know what was going to happen between me and Samara, but I did know that at the very least, things had changed between us enough that I no longer thought of her as an adversary.

Samara trusted Roth, and if Roth asked around, they could uncover at least some information about what had happened that night.

They might as well hear it from me.

"Samara was traveling with her parents to Velesian territory when she was ten years old for some type of diplomatic meeting. Vail's parents were the previous marshals of House Harker and were in charge of escorting them.

"They brought the best rangers under their command with them, and also brought Vail, who was thirteen at the time," I explained. "A storm hit that day and slowed their travel down significantly. They didn't make it to the outpost before nightfall and were attacked by wraiths."

"Her nightmares," Roth murmured. When I looked at them questioningly, they just shook their head and waved for me to carry on.

I swallowed. "Only Samara and Vail truly know what happened next because they were the only ones who survived." I could still remember what they both looked like that day when the rangers had brought them home.

Samara had been so broken, her eyes red and puffy from crying, and there was such a defeated look to her. Vail had been silent, his rage practically scorching the air around him. He'd learned how to harness that anger over the years, but it still burned.

I added, "Both of them were questioned about the attack after they were found, and I've read the reports. Samara didn't see much, but Vail claimed that there were over a dozen wraiths that attacked the caravan, along with several other monsters."

"Is it normal for that many wraiths to attack at once? And with other monsters?" Roth asked, suspicion brewing in their eyes.

"No." I shook my head. That part of the story had always bothered me too. "That information concerned everyone, and many claimed that Vail simply misremembered what happened. He was only a young boy, and he'd been traumatized. His parents and Samara's were mauled in front of him, along with the rest of the rangers."

"No wonder he is the way he is." Roth's eyebrows stretched to their hairline, their words marred with sympathy.

"Vail says his parents told him to take care of Samara. He grabbed her and ran. A wraith followed them and attacked. Vail managed to kill it, but not before it severely injured him. That's... that's how he got his scars." I let out a breath. "They made it to a small cave where they stayed hidden until rangers found them three days later when a search party was sent out to look for the missing caravan."

"Okay," Roth drawled. "They both share a fucked-up childhood trauma. Doesn't explain why Vail always stares at Samara like he's thinking about slitting her throat and chucking her body off a cliff."

I thought over their words, recalling all the times Vail looked at Samara. "That really is the look he gives her, isn't it?"

"Yes." Roth nodded. "I cycled through quite a few options before settling on that one."

"No one knows why Vail hates Samara the way he does, besides the two of them." I suspected Samara had told Rynn and Cali, but they'd take that secret to their graves.

"Hmm," Roth hummed out loud. "I get why you're worried about the two of them being out in the wilds with no one else around them. I'll still kill the shit out of you if you tap that fucking pencil again, though."

"Noted," I said dryly. "How is the translation coming?"

Roth flipped through several pages of notes before answering me. "Almost done. Still trying to make sense of it. Whoever wrote this used obnoxiously flowery language and a lot of vague allegories, but... I have a theory, and it's not good."

"Really? Because I really expected good news to explain how the wraiths have been getting past our blood wards," I responded flippantly.

If Samara or Kieran were here, they would have called me on my bullshit, and I found myself missing the banter we would have exchanged when Roth just dismissed me entirely and went back to reading.

"Sorry." I leaned back and pinched the bridge of my nose. "I haven't found anything useful, and it's frustrating, so I'm acting like an ass." Serious, hazel eyes just stared at me, and my lips twitched as I put my hand back down onto the table. "More of an ass than usual," I amended.

Roth nodded in what I assumed was acceptance. It was hard to tell because their face seemed to be perpetually locked in this bored expression with just a hint of haughtiness.

Okay. Maybe more than a hint.

"The symbol that was carved into that boy's neck means '*draw unto.*'" I took the book that Roth passed over to me and looked at the symbol on the opened page.

"The boy was drawing magic into himself?" I asked with a frown. "Have we been wrong in thinking that he was a victim? Was he trying to work some type of spell and it backfired?"

"It confused me at first too," Roth admitted. "But the more I read, the more it became clear that this symbol is often used in spells of transference." They paused for a moment before asking. "What do *you* think wraiths are?"

I shrugged, caught off-guard by the question. "The Unseelie always fucked around with shadow magic. The theory that they created the wraiths and then lost control seems plausible enough. The Seelie were pushing back against them, and they didn't want to lose, so the Unseelie tried to make their own shadow monsters stronger and fucked it up for everyone."

Whatever had happened to the Fae happened fast because we'd never found any written records of what went down.

There were some writings in the years before about a growing divide between the Unseelie and Seelie, but that was it. There were no mentions of wraiths in any of the writings we'd located, which implied the wraiths were something new that came about when whatever shit went down with the Fae occurred.

"I don't think that's what happened," Roth said slowly. "Not exactly. I do think that the Unseelie are responsible, though."

"What are you saying, Roth?" I asked, really not liking where this was going.

"Isn't it strange that all the Fae disappeared when the wraiths appeared?"

"I know where you're going with this." I shook my head. "The wraiths are different than the Fae. I've read the texts about the Unseelie and how they used their shadows to spy. Their shadows were an extension of them, but they weren't separate beings, and the Fae themselves didn't turn into shadows."

"We were humans and became monsters," Roth pushed. "I think the Unseelie tried to make it so they could turn themselves into shadows and became trapped in that form. The first humans that turned themselves into the Moon Blessed lost their humanity. What if the Unseelie lost themselves too? And they're just now starting to come back to themselves?"

The crease between my brows only deepened. "And you think that's why their attack strategies have changed from going after whoever they could find to being more concentrated on the outposts?"

Chills ran down my spine. Wraiths were always the worst of the monsters to roam these lands, but they'd still been beasts. The idea that they could be intelligent and capable of using magic... no, that didn't make sense.

I shook my head. "Wraiths are nothing but shadows," I replied, unable to accept this. "They can only become corporeal for a few seconds at a time." Enough to slash open a throat or disembowel a body.

"That's where the symbol comes in," Roth said. "I think it's being used to draw the twisted magic within the wraiths into whoever bears the mark."

"Draw unto," I murmured.

But why? What would be the reason for doing such a thing? I stopped breathing for a few seconds when I connected the dots.

Slowly, I said, "If your theory about the wraiths is correct, and they're actually Unseelie trapped in their shadow forms... then they'd likely want their original forms back. They'd want to undo their magic."

Roth shrugged. "Or at least fix it enough that they can easily move between forms, which was likely their primary goal when they worked whatever spell they'd crafted."

"This is all still speculation. Absolutely *terrifying* speculation," I added. "But still speculation. We don't have enough proof to take this to Carmilla yet, let alone the queen and her consort."

"I know," Roth said begrudgingly. "But I *also* know that I'm right about this. We just have to keep researching and fill in the gaps."

"Maybe Samara and Vail will find something that will help." Assuming they didn't murder each other.

But I instantly dismissed the thought. Samara never returned Vail's hatred. She went back and forth between acting like she couldn't care less about him to being annoyed by his very existence, but there was never any hatred on her end.

If anything, I thought it was the opposite. Samara cared about Vail, and his hatred hurt her.

"Dɪᴅ ʏ'ᴀʟʟ ᴍɪss ᴍᴇ?" Samara asked as she pushed the double doors wide open, a triumphant grin spread across her face.

"You found something," I said hopefully.

If the trip had been a bust, she likely would have stalked back in here with a pissed-off expression. Samara could control her emotions when necessary—usually, anyway—but it cost her.

Outside of delicate conversations and negotiations, she wore her emotions plainly for all to see.

"Whatever you found better not be covered in grime the way you are," Roth snarled. "And your ass better not take one step further in my library until you've cleaned up."

Samara shot Roth a playful look before dramatically raising one foot in the air and taking a step forward. One of the dark ribbons that Roth wore around their forearm shot forward like a whip and slapped Samara across the thigh before drawing back and preparing to strike again.

I laughed as Samara yelped and jumped back... straight into Vail, who had just crossed the threshold.

She bounced off his chest and stumbled forward, but he instinctively grabbed her around the waist to steady her before dropping his hands as if he'd been burned, a hard expression on his face.

I thought I'd seen something else there, but whatever it had been was gone before I could tell what it was.

The amused expression that had been on Samara's face from Roth's ribbons instantly fell, and I found myself hating Vail for it.

I shook my head, trying to focus on what mattered. "What did you find?"

Vail held out a leather satchel, and I rose to take it from him. The instant I did, I felt the pull of magic. As if in a trance, I untied the bag and lifted out a smooth stone the size of my palm with an etching of the lunar moon.

The same symbol that marked the left side of my neck.

"There are two other stones inside," Samara said from where she still stood at the entrance to the library. "They bear the markings of the Velesians and the Furies."

I stared down in wonder at the stone before walking over to the table where Roth waited and set it down in front of them. They immediately snatched it off the table and clutched it in their hands with their eyes closed, no doubt trying to understand the potent magic dripping off of it.

I reached into the bag and pulled out another stone, admiring the glossy black exterior.

If these were used for the ritual the humans had performed to make us all Moon Blessed—and I didn't know what else it could be—then they were centuries old. Yet the stones still gleamed brightly, and the lunar symbol remained a vibrant red, as if the blood had just been painted on it. My brows furrowed.

"How have we never found these before?" Roth said, eyes still closed in concentration.

"The first and second generations were concerned with surviving," Vail said with a shrug. "The Velesians might have regained their humanity before the rest of us, but they've always felt the pull of the wild in their souls. Most of their time was spent hunting down monsters in their territory and carving out a safe place to live."

"Maybe the wraiths have been hunting for these ritual stones longer than we thought," Samara mused. "There have to be countless human settlements that have been abandoned for one reason or another. We only started really building the outpost towns in the last few decades, and when possible, we use old Fae towns."

"Leaving all the ritual stones at the human towns ripe for the taking," I finished with a thoughtful nod.

"We just need to figure out why the wraiths would be interested in these stones to begin with," Samara said, fatigue touching her features. I could only imagine how exhausting the trip had been.

"Why don't you go and get cleaned up, and then Roth and I can tell you what we found?" I suggested.

"That sounds nice," she said, flashing me a relieved smile.

I fought to keep from showing what that smile did to me as I nodded curtly. "I'll have some food brought up as well."

"Thank you, Alaric," Samara said before shooting an amused glance at Roth, who was still doing their weird communion with the ritual stone. "Make sure to set up the food away from the books, lest our dear Roth get upset over their books being in danger."

"If you keep up that sass," Roth replied casually, "I'll show you just what my blood ribbons can do."

"Promises, promises," Samara sang as she exited the library.

My lips quirked up into a smile that froze in place when I caught Vail's glare. I didn't see Vail all that often since he was gone for months at a time, but we'd always had a good working relationship. Though, I suspected that might change with Samara being back and my working closely with her.

I added it to the list of reasons why Samara was a complication in my life and why things had been far simpler at House Harker before her return.

CHAPTER TWENTY-ONE

—

Samara

I STRETCHED my arms up and arched my back as I tried to loosen my body after hours of sitting in the hard wooden chair. The nice cushy lounger by the window was calling to me, but after staying up until almost sunrise pouring over books after getting home yesterday, I suspected I would fall asleep for a late afternoon nap if I settled in that chair.

Just because Moroi could operate on very little sleep didn't mean I enjoyed only getting a few hours of it.

Alaric was attending to some House Harker business today. We'd discussed it this morning over tea, and we'd both agreed that since he had more knowledge and experience with the current day-to-day workings of the House, it made sense for him to handle it and me to continue helping Roth.

It bothered me a little, though. I wanted to be able to help run the House in every aspect, and I felt like I was failing by not being able to do everything.

I knew it was foolish of me to think like that, but I couldn't help it. After failing so spectacularly at House Laurent, I wanted to prove to Carmilla that I was worthy of being her Heir and remaining at House Harker.

I sighed, desperately craving more tea and a cushier seat, but all the books had been laid out on the table and Roth kept snatching them randomly while mumbling to themself. When I'd attempted to take one book that they hadn't looked at once all morning, I'd received a look that froze me in place and made me immediately drop back down in my seat.

Just as I was about to take a break and go chug an entire pot of tea in the kitchen, away from Roth's judging eyes, the blue gem on my ring glowed.

Rynn. Relief flowed out of me, and the tension I'd been carrying since she'd announced her insane plan finally eased. I held my finger over the glyph on the

189

ring and spun to face the center of the room. A second later, her shadowy form appeared.

"Rynn!" I bolted upright, startling Roth, who hadn't even noticed Rynn appear. "Are you okay?"

"I'm fine," she said in a clipped tone. "I told you I would be fine. The trip was a bust. I didn't find anything."

I eyed her carefully. It was hard to tell, given that she was nothing more than a shadow, but her shoulders seemed hunched inward. I glanced down at her hands and saw that her fingers were constantly curling in and out, like they did when she was fighting off a shift.

Something had happened, and she was lying to me about it. First Cali, now Rynn. My temper flared.

"Rynn—" I started, but she cut me off with a wave of her hand.

"I can't talk right now. I just wanted to let you know that I was okay and that I hadn't found anything. We'll catch up soon, I promise."

With that, she vanished from sight, and anger and concern warred within me.

This behavior was something that I'd expect from Cali, but not from Rynn. What the hell had happened to rattle her so much? And why was she hiding it from me?

I sucked in a breath, ignoring the stab of pain in my chest.

"Are you going to detonate again?" Roth asked in a bored tone. "Because I could do without the screaming you did last time."

"No." I forced myself to exhale before calmly returning to my chair. "I'm still pissed off, but at least I know she's safe. Last time, I flipped out because I was both pissed off and scared out of my mind that my friend was going to land herself in serious trouble."

Roth nodded. "Understandable. Still, I appreciate you not losing your shit in my library this time."

"*Your* library?" I smirked at them.

"Any library I'm in is my library."

"Of course it is." I rolled my eyes. "Do you want tea or anything? I'm going to take a break and head to the kitchen."

They waved me off, and I headed downstairs.

After drinking what was probably an unhealthy amount of tea and devouring at least half a dozen honey rolls, I headed back up to the library with a much clearer head.

I'd figure out sometime in the next month to get my two besties here in person. They'd find it a lot more challenging to lie to my face, and if they tried it, I'd just tackle them to the ground and beat it out of them.

Well, I'd do that to Rynn. Cali could kick my ass, so I'd have to figure out a different approach.

Roth was leaning over the table when I walked in, a fierce scowl in place and a few stray hairs broken away from where the rest had been swept back, falling around their face. The deep red was such a striking contrast to Roth's pale skin. They really were striking, even when they did have such a murderous look on their face.

I barely managed to hold in my laugh because I did not want that look redirected at me.

Instead of taking a seat, I stepped around the table to peer over their shoulder. *"Bâm m ḅàchà qe qâ dam,"* I read the phrase out loud. "The flowers remind us of home."

Roth went rigid before slowly twisting around and gazing up at me. "What did you just say?"

I looked at them in confusion. "I was just reading the phrase you were pointing at?" I had no idea why I phrased it like a question, but I didn't understand why Roth was looking at me the way they were. Like I was interesting. Roth never looked at anything or anyone like that. Well, other than books.

They narrowed their eyes. "You said the Unseelie part, and then you said the translation. Did you already know it?"

"No?" I said slowly, still so confused.

"Then how did you know what it meant?" they pushed, leaning further into my space. I swallowed as the green in their hazel eyes started to spread.

"Because I can read and speak Unseelie?" Why the hell was I saying everything like it was a question?

"Since when?" they asked with something in their tone I couldn't quite figure out.

"Since I was a kid." I moved to stand next to Roth, leaning back against the table. "My mom used to always read me bedtime stories in Unseelie. Whenever we were alone, we'd usually speak in Unseelie, too. She thought it was a fun game. I can read and speak both of them, although I'm a little better with Seelie." I frowned at Roth. "I don't understand why you're so surprised by this. We've been reading through all these books for days, so you had to know what I was doing. And you haven't had any problem reading the Unseelie texts."

They shook their head. "I'm not fluent. I'd been stuck on that damn phrase you just read for over an hour. I've had to use translators for the past few days, which is why it's taking forever. You always spent so much time on one book, I thought you were just slow at translating."

My cheeks flamed red. "I would get distracted sometimes and read the books cover to cover. It's not my fault!" I said quickly, flinging my hands up in defense. "You dropped a bunch of Unseelie books that I'd never read before in front of me. I tried to just scan them, looking to see if they had any relevant information, but sometimes they'd be really interesting, and I'd get drawn in!"

"I can't believe you never told me you could read or speak Unseelie!" they yelled back.

"I used to read Unseelie poetry next to you in the library at Drudonia! I'd even say the poems out loud sometimes as I read along! How could you never notice?"

"Well, I never paid you any attention back then because I thought you were just a pretty face! I didn't know you actually had a brain!"

"Rude." I crossed my arms and glared at them before repeating Roth's words in my head. My expression softened before I asked tentatively, "You think I have a pretty face?"

Roth looked at me like I was an idiot.

"I'm not blind, Samara." They tilted their head to the side, causing the light to glint off the dangly earring they always wore. "Can you still recite the poetry from memory?"

"Yes." I gave Roth a curious look as they rose from their chair and moved to stand in front of me, their thighs brushing against mine. "I picked up some new ones this week," I offered.

"Tell me."

"Kov bâm reb qâ qa." The words rolled off my tongue and Roth's hazel eyes darkened, making the dark umber-orange fractures of their eyes stand out like fire in the night.

"Say it again," they breathed out.

"Kov bâm reb qâ qa," I repeated, not taking my eyes off Roth as heat spread through me.

The dark red ribbons on Roth's forearms slowly unwound, and I watched as they brushed against me with fascination, remembering what it felt like in my dreams when they'd touched me.

While I was distracted, Roth seized the opportunity to shove me down onto the table, the ribbons barely managing to push the books to the side.

"Careful with the books!" I cried out as one slipped off the table, only to be caught by one of Roth's blood ribbons.

My concern quickly faded as one of the ribbons brushed the side of my face before sliding down to graze the top of my breasts, and I let out a surprised exhale. Wherever the ribbons touched me, I could feel the warm, lingering traces of blood magic.

And I desperately wanted to feel more.

"Don't worry about the books," Roth said smoothly as they ran a hand down my thigh, causing my flesh to shudder with anticipation. "Just worry about reciting that poetry."

"What exactly are you going to be doing while I do that?" I asked, arching an eyebrow at them in challenge.

The ribbons snapped to wrap around my arms and pulled them to the side, pinning me down on the table. More slipped around my thighs and pulled them apart as Roth bunched up my dress. Excited, breathy pants slipped from my lips as elation filled me. This was already so much better than my dreams.

"I'm going to play with myself while eating out this lovely cunt of yours." They spoke in such a matter-of-fact way that it took my mind a second to process what they'd said.

"Fucking hell, Roth." My thighs quivered as I felt myself get even wetter.

When Roth paused upon lifting my dress, I raised my head to meet their gaze. "Are you good, Samara?" they asked.

"Yeah, Roth," I breathed out. "I'm good, about to be really fucking good."

"Your flirting at Drudonia would have gone a lot better if you'd revealed this talent of yours back then instead of using all those ridiculous pickup lines." They smirked and then tossed my dress up before tugging at my panties. A silver knife flashed, and I felt them pull the fabric away. "Let's hear that poetry, Heir."

"Kov—" A cry tore out of me, cutting me off as Roth brazenly licked straight up my pussy before sucking on my clit. There was such a demand in their movement that I came within seconds. Then they teased my clit while I trembled beneath them before pulling away.

"I can just as easily use these ribbons for punishment," Roth warned as the end of one ribbon rose and snapped against my thigh.

I swore at the stinging sensation and pulled at the ribbons pinning my arms to the table, but then Roth ran one finger across my dripping center before circling my clit again.

My swears turned into whimpers as pleasure quickly overtook the pain.

"Be a good girl," they said soothingly.

Fuck me. I was never going to look at Roth or those damned ribbons the same way again. I licked my lips and started again. *"Kov bâm reb qâ qa."*

Roth's tongue slipped into my pussy, and their finger continued to play with my clit. My thighs strained, causing the ribbons to dig into my skin, and my pulse quickened at the pressure.

I'd never really played with being restrained, only dreamed about it. The real version was turning out to be quite fun.

"Bâm beduv challs bà dov," I breathed out, fumbling over some of the words as Roth slipped two fingers inside of me, dragging them in and out. The wet sounds of my pleasure accentuated my words. Roth moaned against my core, and I wondered if they were fucking themselves as well. The thought made me burn even hotter.

A whimper slipped from me when they pulled their fingers out and tauntingly traced them around my inner thighs.

I raised my hips as much as I could, but the ribbons only tightened and pulled my thighs further apart. Another ribbon ran across my throat, squeezing it for a few seconds, and I gasped when it released me before I pushed out the next verse.

"Hom àlche d ḅà medm," I moaned out the last word as Roth thrust their fingers back inside me and bit down on my swollen clit.

Their movements became harder and faster, and I knew they were building towards their own orgasm.

"Hom bab' mùl—" A scream tore from my throat as one of Roth's fangs pierced me and they sucked hard. I'd never been bitten down there before, but the pain and pleasure wrapping together was one of the best things I'd ever experienced in my life.

The orgasm ripped through me, and I felt Roth scream out theirs at the same time.

My body strained against the ribbons as delicious trembles ran through my muscles. Then Roth moved until they were perched on the desk next to me, gazing down at me with blazing eyes.

"The last line, Heir," they demanded as they lazily swirled one finger around my poor, oversensitive clit while their other hand was still buried between their own legs.

"Hom bab' mùl ḅà ḅâm gàtdi," I said in a husky tone.

"Good girl," they murmured and pulled their hand from their thighs to trace my lips. I opened my mouth and Roth slipped their fingers in as I greedily sucked them clean, enjoying the taste of their pleasure on my tongue.

It was at that exact moment that the library doors burst open. The silencing spell had been in place, but we'd never bothered locking the doors because nobody ever came in here except for us... and Alaric. Whoops.

"I think I have an ide—"

Alaric froze as he took in the sight of me sprawled out across the table full of books, Roth's ribbons still holding me in place and their fingers still in my mouth and between my legs.

"Damn it, Sam!" Alaric yelled. "Why can't you ever lock the fucking door?!"

CHAPTER TWENTY-TWO

—

Samara

ALARIC AVOIDED the library for two whole days. When he did eventually return, he very dramatically knocked before entering.

I briefly pondered letting out some fake moans to mess with him but decided against it, only because we truly needed the help.

Now that Roth knew I could read Unseelie, they snapped at me whenever it became clear I was caught up in what I was reading and forced me to scan the text instead. We'd gotten through all the books on the table and were now going through the ones that we'd pulled out as potentially helpful again.

Roth's previous lamenting about the flowery language used in the texts was spot on. I often had to read passages over and over again, not because I didn't know what the words meant, but because I had no idea if what I was reading was actually poetry or if they were just wrapping up the potentially horrifying usage of a spell in pretty words. It was exhausting.

On the plus side, I'd found more poetry books, and Roth had been very enthusiastic to show me their appreciation.

Those fucking ribbons of theirs were really useful for getting into some fun positions. I'd even distracted them this morning with my fingers and, based on the breathy moans as I finger-fucked their pussy, I'd done a good job.

It was my first time playing with a pussy that wasn't mine, and I'd been a little nervous that I wouldn't do it right.

I knew what made mine happy, but I had no idea what Roth liked. Given Roth's to-the-point attitude about everything though, I assumed they would have been quick to give me commands if I was doing it wrong.

I bit my bottom lip as a smile blossomed across my cheeks. Kieran had told me that he wanted me to have fun and explore what made me happy, and Roth made me happy.

They were absolutely not a cuddler, though.

When I'd asked in my best flirty coy voice if they wanted to come to my room last night, they'd just looked at me puzzled and said, "Why? You can fuck me here well enough."

I missed Kieran. He'd cuddle the shit out of me.

"Why do you have that stupid look on your face?" Alaric snapped.

"Not everyone is determined to be as pissy all the time as you," I snapped back, and then, because I was a goddamn adult, I stuck my tongue out at him.

The corners of Roth's mouth tilted up the tiniest amount, which for them was like a full-blown smile.

I'd decided that we were keeping Roth, even after all this was over. Which, hopefully, it would be soon. I was fairly confident that if I just kept bringing in new books and read Unseelie poetry out loud while they devoured my pussy, they'd be content to stay here.

Maybe I could convince Carmilla to build a bigger library with a dedicated poetry section...

The red gem on my ring glowed brightly, pulling me out of my lust-filled mind. Cali. Finally. The old human settlement she'd gone to inspect had been much more remote than either of the ones Rynn and I had visited.

A mix of concern and annoyance flickered through me as I held a finger over the ring's glyph.

I hadn't heard anything from Rynn since she'd dropped in a couple of days ago. It was unlikely, but maybe Cali would have some idea as to what was going on with our furry friend.

I blinked when Cali appeared in the library. She was still made of nothing but shadows, but there was more detail visible than usual. Normally, her wings were wispy shadows behind her, but now they were fully visible. Even the strands of her hair were more defined.

"Did you improve the shadow projection spell?" I rose and stepped closer as my eyes continued to scan her and pick out more details. "This is incredible..."

"Hi, Cali! It's so nice to see you! I'm glad you made it to the middle of nowhere in the freaking badlands okay!" Cali said in a deep voice with an exaggerated, husky tone that I assumed was supposed to be me. I narrowed my eyes at her as she continued. "Why, thank so much for asking about my welfare and greeting me so nicely, Sam!"

Roth sighed. "So, Cali hasn't changed at all then?"

I snickered as Cali leaned to the side to peer around me at where Roth was still seated at the table. They'd never hated each other the way Alaric and I had, but it was hard to find people who were more polar opposites than Cali and Roth.

"Oh." Cali's wings deflated a little. "Hi, Roth."

I rolled my eyes "Hi. I'm glad you're okay. Sorry for not saying that right away, but your fancy new shadows threw me off."

Cali shrugged, and I marveled at how well I could see the movement right down to the muscles flexing in her arms. "Just been practicing and fine-tuning a bit is all."

My brows started to furrow, but I forced them to smooth out. There was something Cali wasn't saying.

I didn't know if it was because Roth was here or because she wasn't ready to talk about it yet. All I knew was that even though this seemed harmless, it would be yet another thing that made Cali terrifying to everyone else. Especially to the other Furies.

"Did you find anything useful?" I asked, trying to focus on the problem at hand. Cali could explain her upgraded shadow form when we were alone, and damn it, she *would* explain it to me.

"Not at the human settlement. There was very little left of it, and with how exposed it was to the elements, it's hard to say if the wraiths had been there and picked it over or not." She glanced over her shoulder, eyes focusing on something I couldn't see before turning back to me. "But I found something else. While I was flying back, I passed an old temple that had been built into the side of a mesa. I've seen it before and explored it a little when I was a kid. Pretty sure it was built by the Unseelie."

"You know of an Unseelie temple?" Roth suddenly came to life like a monster smelling blood in the night. "And you didn't tell anyone?!"

"It's in the badlands." Cali rolled her eyes. "If I told someone, they would have made me lead an expedition there, and I checked it out. There's nothing there. Or... at least... I didn't think there was anything there..."

Roth looked like they were contemplating how one would go about murdering a shadow, so I quickly asked, "Did you see something there this time?"

Cali dipped her head slowly in a deep nod. "There are wraiths there, but not like any wraiths I've ever seen before. They're more solid and they look..." She paused, again looking over her shoulder. "Sam, they looked like Fae. At least like the sketches I've seen of them in books."

"Holy shit," I breathed out as my eyes snapped to Roth. "You were right."

"Right about what?" Cali said quietly but urgently.

"Cali," I said slowly. "Where are you right now?"

"On top of the mesa."

"Get the fuck away from there!" I snarled. "We don't know what they're capable of! You can't be there by yourself!"

"They can't fly," she said dismissively before tilting her head. "I don't think they can, anyway. The wraiths only glide. Could the Fae fly?"

"I'm going to slap the shit out of you next time I see you," I growled. What the fuck was with all my friends taking unnecessary risks all of a sudden?

Seeing that I was genuinely freaked out and pissed off, Cali reached out and placed her hand on my arm, and I felt it. She yanked her hand away, but it was too late.

"What the fuck?" I whispered in shock.

Cali's shadow form could never physically interact with anything or anyone, but I'd felt her hand on me just now. It'd only been for a second... just like how wraiths could only become corporeal for a few seconds at a time.

"Something's happening to me," Cali said quietly. "It's been happening for a while, but being around these wraiths... or Fae... whatever they are... my magic is changing."

"How?" I asked, trying to stay calm and not have the proper freak-out like I wanted to. "How is it changing? Are you..."

Losing yourself? I couldn't say the words out loud. As if saying it would make it real.

Cali moved closer to me, her hands hovering over mine. "I'm not losing myself," she promised. "Like I promised you and Rynn all those years ago. You both hold my heart, and I will never leave you."

My throat was too tight for me to say anything, so I jerked my head in a nod.

"Whatever is happening to me, we can sort that out later," she said calmly. "Right now, I think we need to figure out what the hell these wraiths are up to and why they look the way they do."

"How many are there?" Alaric asked, coming to stand beside me. "Does it look like they're just passing through?"

"Three of them," she said. "And I think they live here. I kept an eye on them all night. They spent most of it in the front part of the temple, but I couldn't get close enough to hear them."

"They were speaking?" Alaric exclaimed, and I shared his surprise. The wraiths didn't really speak, they only let out strange whispering sounds and occasional shrieks.

Cali nodded. "I couldn't tell what language, but given that they look Fae, I'm assuming it was Unseelie or Seelie." Her gaze flicked back and forth between the three of us. "None of you seem that surprised that they're Fae. I was sure as fuck surprised."

I looked at the map that we'd hung up and did some mental calculations before clearing my throat and turning my attention to Roth and Alaric. "Fill Cali in on what we found. I'm going to find Vail."

Alaric's upper lip curled in distaste. "There's another horse ride in my future, isn't there?"

"You can stay here if you want," I tossed over my shoulder as I headed for the hallway. "But I'm going to that temple and getting some damn answers."

———

AN HOUR LATER, we were riding hard on our way to Cali. She promised to let me know right away if the wraiths went on the move.

The temple wasn't far from the border between Furie and Moroi territory. Unfortunately, we basically had to ride all the way across our land to get there. We had no idea whether the wraiths truly lived at the temple or if they would be leaving soon, so time was of the essence, which was also why we wouldn't be stopping except to change horses at some of the outposts.

Zosa hadn't been happy about me leaving her behind, but I wasn't going to leave her behind at an outpost, even if I could pick her up on the way back. I also selfishly didn't want to risk her life.

We'd be traveling through the night, and the horses were primary targets for most of the monsters that prowled the forests.

I squinted against the setting sun that was currently blinding me. There was less than an hour until sunset. It'd be dipping behind the trees soon enough, and then I'd at least be able to see better.

The black gelding I was riding skittered to the side, and Alaric's grip around my waist tightened.

My brows furrowed. "You okay back there?"

I urged the gelding to move a little faster but didn't let him break out of the canter he currently maintained. He wouldn't last long at a full gallop, and we still had a ways to go before we could swap out for fresh horses.

Hopefully, my next one wouldn't be so skittish, because things were only going to get hairier as night fell.

"I don't understand why I couldn't have my own horse," Alaric griped even as he started to lean to the left and I had to reach back and shove him upright.

"Kieran would be really mad at me if I let you get hurt," I said over my shoulder. "And we both know you would get hurt if you had your own horse. We should rotate riding into our archery practice."

"*Our* archery practice? You're the one who crashed my training. You don't get to dictate what I do."

I resisted the urge to shove my elbow back and knock him off the horse. He wouldn't be that seriously injured from falling off, but it would slow us down, and he'd no doubt tell Kieran... who wouldn't be happy with me.

I silently regretted not convincing Alaric to stay behind and watch over the House while I was gone, but he'd been adamant that he'd taken care of all urgent matters and that everything else could wait until we were back.

If I'd known he was going to be this pissy on the ride, I would have found a way to leave him behind and just deal with his anger when we got back.

Vail pulled his horse back to a trot, and I did the same, maneuvering the gelding until we were riding side by side as Nyx joined us.

"Something wrong?" I asked, keeping my voice low. Not that it really mattered with how loud the horses were.

"No," Vail said, "but we have another twenty miles to go before we reach the next outpost, which means we'll be in the dark for the last portion of that. I want to reserve as much of the horses' energy as possible so that if we have to run later, they won't falter."

"Right," I said, barely managing to keep the tremor out of my voice.

If we rode round the clock with minimal resting, we should be able to reach Cali in three days, but that meant two nights out in the forest. We'd hopefully reach the temple on the afternoon of the third day, so we'd have at least daylight to our advantage then.

"It'll be fine, Samara," Nyx reassured me. "Vail and I have spent plenty of time out at night. The horses can outrun almost anything."

"*Almost* anything?" Alaric asked.

With his chest plastered against my back, I could practically feel him vibrating with tension. I shot Nyx a look. They damn well knew they could have phrased that better.

They gave me an unrepentant look and urged their mount forward. "I'm going to scout up ahead while we still have some daylight left."

"We'll be fine, Alaric," I said with a confidence I didn't entirely feel. "Vail knows what he's doing."

This seemed to relax Alaric enough that he no longer had a death grip around my stomach. Small victories.

I didn't miss Vail stiffening slightly at my words, as if he was surprised that I had such confidence in him, but despite our problems, I didn't doubt Vail's skills at all. He'd spent most of his life traveling these lands, and he was still alive to tell the tale.

"What do you think Kieran is doing?" I asked, trying to keep Alaric's mind off the ever-darkening sky.

"Don't you mean *who* he's doing?"

His words struck a sharp blow just as he intended, and I clenched my jaw against the pain. I'd forgotten with all the camaraderie we'd built up over the last couple of weeks that no one was as capable of wounding me with his words as Alaric.

He had the advantage of knowing me well enough to strike at my weak points, and Kieran was very much my weak point.

I concentrated on the feeling of the horse moving beneath me and the reins made of braided rope in my hands, and gradually, the pain ebbed.

The doubt remained, though. Was it selfish of me to want both Roth and Kieran but not want to share them with anyone else? I hadn't even broached the topic with Roth, but I was fairly confident that, unless someone else walked into that library sprouting Unseelie poetry, I had them to myself for now.

But Kieran was... well... he was gorgeous and well-liked by everyone. I knew that he had lovers in basically every House across Moroi territory. Moons damn him. He probably had lovers in Furie and Velesian territory, too.

He said he only wanted me, but what if he changed his mind while he was away? Would he really turn down an invitation to someone else's bed?

I continued to stew in my self-doubt as we traveled on in silence, only vaguely aware of the rising tension between Vail and Alaric.

"I'm sorry," Alaric blurted out. "That was a cruel thing to say."

"It's fine," I said stiffly, still too absorbed in my own fucked-up head to say anything else.

"Alaric was being a dick," Vail said sharply. "Everyone knows how Kieran feels about you. That boy is stupidly loyal. Even to those who don't deserve it." I inwardly flinched but before I could respond, Vail kicked his horse into a canter, leaving us behind.

"Are you sure you're okay with traveling with him at night?" Alaric asked quietly. "I realize that you and I have our problems, but I'm pretty sure that Vail would be happy to see you dead."

I stared after Vail's retreating form, mulling over Alaric's words. "At least I know where I stand with him so I can watch for his knife in the dark."

CHAPTER TWENTY-THREE

—

Samara

"Easy, boy," I quietly soothed the dark bay gelding as he danced nervously beneath me.

He'd been fine when we'd left the outpost hours ago after swapping out our mounts, but something had been unsettling him for the last few miles. Vail's and Nyx's mounts were also tense, but they were both large draft horses who weren't as inclined to panic.

Still, the horses were clearly sensing something we weren't. When I voiced my concerns to Nyx, they didn't seem all that worried.

"All kinds of beasties prowl the forests at night," they said simply. "Most of them aren't a threat to us, but they would happily snack on the horses if they could. As long as we don't leave the horses unattended, the less dangerous predators will leave them alone to find easier prey elsewhere."

"Unfortunately, the horses tend to draw in the more lethal monsters," Vail said. "They've learned that horses usually have riders." He eyed my gelding when it snorted loudly again. "I'd been hoping we'd procure quieter horses for this portion of the ride."

"Is there another outpost we can go to and switch to a quieter mount?" Alaric asked.

He'd been holding on so tightly around my waist that I was pretty sure I'd have bruises tomorrow. I couldn't bring myself to say anything though because I knew he was just nervous about our situation... plus, I kind of liked having his grip on me like that.

Vail shook his head. "Not without going far out of our way. There's not much in this area; all of our strongholds are either further north or along the coast. No reason to have outposts where nobody travels, and it's too dangerous to grow crops."

"Why don't we pick up the pace for a bit?" I suggested. "This boy is wasting energy prancing around. Might as well let him run."

Alaric let out a low groan but didn't disagree.

"We'll let them canter for the next few miles and then pull back," Vail said as he scanned the woods around us. "Make sure to keep them under control. We can't afford for anyone's mount to get spooked and take off from the group. I'll lead. Nyx will take the rear." His eyes fell on me then. "Stay between us, Samara."

"Will do." I looked over my shoulder. "Ready?"

Alaric adjusted his grip, and I winced as his fingers dug into my hips. "Yes."

Vail's dapple grey mare broke into a canter, and I loosened the reins enough for my gelding to follow after them. He tugged at the reins and tried to break out into a gallop, but I firmly held him back.

The echoes of Nyx's horse came behind us, and my heart started to race as we continued our fast pace down the trail. The horses had been loud before, but now every time their hooves struck the ground, it sounded like thunder to my ears.

The miles flew by, and gradually my tension eased. It didn't completely disappear—that wouldn't happen until we were safely behind some well-fortified walls—but my heart no longer beat like it was trying to break out of my chest.

Alaric maintained his death grip around me, though. Clearly, he wasn't feeling any less stressed out.

Ahead of us, Vail pulled up his mount, and I halted mine next to him as I looked at what had caused him to stop. Several large trees had fallen across the road, their trunks far too wide for the horses to jump over. We'd have to go around.

Vail hopped off of his horse and handed his reins over to Nyx before going to investigate the trees. My eyes scoured the surrounding forest, and I could see more than a few creatures prowling around in the trees, but most of them were small and harmless. At least to us.

The trees here grew tall and thick, their gnarled roots running along the surface, making the ground uneven. Several large flowers bloomed from where they perched atop their thorn covered stems. A sweet, enticing nectar dripped from their wide, brightly colored petals. I watched as a small furry beast with thick hindquarters and long arms that ended in three curved talons leapt to a branch that stretched over a flower with bright orange petals. A black tongue unfurled from its mouth and swiped at the nectar.

A thick green vine with red-tipped barbs slid up behind the small creature. It sensed the danger at the last possible second and leapt away as the vine struck the branch where it had been sitting. An angry chitter erupted from the trees as it took off to find an easier meal.

Good luck, little fella. Everything in this forest wants to eat you. Including the pretty flowers.

I refocused on the blocked road that Vail was still studying. Something wasn't right about this. The positioning of the trees seemed almost intentional. I forced myself to remain calm even as I wanted to spin my mount around and run in the opposite direction.

"These trees weren't here when we passed this way a month ago," Vail said from where he was crouching at the base of the trunk. "Something chewed through the base at just the right angle to ensure they fell onto the road."

"Kùsu?" Nyx guessed. "We saw signs of them last time, and they're clever fuckers."

Vail grunted in agreement as he rose and walked back to us. He took the reins from Nyx and led his horse over to the side. "We'll have to dismount to lead the horses around. The ground is too rough to ride them through it."

"If this is a trap, shouldn't we turn back?" I asked. "I want to get to Cali as soon as possible, but this seems risky."

"They likely set traps like this throughout their territory," Vail said. "The cut in the tree isn't that fresh, at least a week old. Chances are pretty good that they moved on to a different part of the road to set another trap."

I chewed my bottom lip as Nyx and Alaric dismounted, then slid out of the saddle myself. My thighs and butt ached from riding so hard for the last day. I'd probably be barely capable of walking by the time we finally made it to our destination if we kept up this pace.

The three of us followed after Vail and led our horses through the forest. Nyx took up their post behind us once more.

With our keen night vision, it wasn't too difficult to pick out the best path. I understood why Vail had insisted we lead the horses through on foot. There were several spots that easily could have resulted in broken legs and would have been hard to see from the saddle. Even with our careful pace, the horses still stumbled a few times.

The trees and roots were the densest by the road, so we had to venture deep into the forest to work our way around. It would have been nerve-wracking during the day, but at night, with all of our senses and instincts keyed up... it was an odd mix of exhilarating and terrifying.

The faint heartbeats of dozens of small animals reached my ears, and I knew that if I looked, I would see all kinds of creatures in the night.

Our sense of smell wasn't as good as the Velesians unless blood was spilt. We could sense blood from miles away at night. I felt the call of the night, just as all Moroi, Velesians, and Furies did. Our ancestors had remade themselves beneath the moonlit night sky, and that was where we truly belonged.

Unfortunately, while we were all monsters, we were far from the biggest and baddest, and those apex predators claimed the night as well.

Everyone in our party froze when a loud pop sounded from beneath Vail's horse, causing it to shy to the side a few steps before he got it under control.

"What was that?" I asked, keeping my voice as low as possible.

Vail maneuvered around his horse and picked up its right hoof. I squinted, trying to make out what he pulled off of it.

All I could gather was that whatever it had been was a mossy-green color with bright orange speckles. When he started scanning the forest floor close to where his horse had walked, I handed the reins to Alaric and wordlessly moved a little closer to look as well.

"There," I whispered and pointed towards a large, bulbous mushroom that had the same green and orange pattern from whatever Vail had pulled off of his horse's hoof.

"Shit. Poppers," Vail said gravely. "Clever fucks."

"Damn it, I told you," Nyx cursed. "Their traps have been getting more elaborate. They probably chose that section of the road to block off because they knew these things grew here."

"There are more ahead of us," I said. Now that I knew what to look for, I could see the brightly colored mushrooms all over the ground ahead of us. There was no way we could avoid them. "Do we need to turn around?"

We waited as Vail stared at the path before us, thinking through all the options. I returned to my mount, who was growing increasingly more restless, and took the reins from Alaric. Horses were very sensitive to our own moods, so I did my best to repress my panic as I soothed him. We were deep in the woods, in the territory of the kùsu, and I very much suspected we had just rung the dinner bell.

"There is a river ahead, less than five miles away," Vail said. "We get to the road as fast as we can, mount up, and run like hell. The kùsu can't swim."

"Alaric, get on," I commanded quickly. "I'll guide the horse, but it will be too slow for us both to mount up once we reach the road. I'll either sit behind you or ride with one of the others."

He stared at me for a moment, clearly not liking this idea, but finally jerked his head in agreement when neither Vail nor Nyx countered my command. I helped him get into the saddle and handed him the reins.

"Grip tightly with your legs. Grab onto the mane if you have to, but *don't* drop the reins," I instructed. "You fall, you die."

Alaric swallowed but did as ordered. I didn't tell him that I wasn't loving this either.

Alaric wasn't a strong rider, and the horse was nervous as hell, but it would run fast and follow whichever horse was in front of it. All Alaric had to do was hang on. Hopefully, I'd be able to mount behind him, but I was pretty sure our horse was on the verge of bolting, so I wasn't willing to bet on it.

I untied the crossbow from the saddle and strapped it to my back. Then I checked to make sure the dagger at my thigh was secure. The chances of either being useful against a kùsu were slim, but I still felt better being armed.

"Everyone ready?" Vail asked, making eye contact with each of us.

We all nodded before Vail pulled his horse forward, and then we picked up the pace as we weaved our way through the forest back towards the road.

It wasn't long before another loud pop sounded, then another. I kept my hands on the reins of Alaric's horse as it began to shy off the path, refusing to let it and Alaric out of my sight. Vail broke out into a jog, and I did the same, pulling the stupid panicking horse along with me.

Just as the road came into sight again, my foot snagged on a piece of root, and I stumbled. The horse yanked its head up, and the reins slipped through my fingers as I fell.

"Sam!" Alaric called out in alarm.

"I'm fine!" I reached back to pull my foot free from the two roots it slipped between. "Go!"

Even if he wanted to stop, Alaric's horse had decided it was done with all of this bullshit and surged forward towards the road. Alaric yelped as he held on, and I prayed the damn horse didn't break a leg in the remaining distance it needed to clear.

My ears picked up the sound of something very large crashing through the underbrush towards us, and terror-fueled adrenaline flooded my system as I frantically tried to pull myself loose.

With one final yank, my foot finally slipped free just as Nyx grabbed me and hoisted me up. We raced towards the road, but I was too late to stop Alaric's horse from leaping into a full-on gallop and sprinting away from us.

"Go!" I screamed at Nyx. "Make sure they reach the river!"

They nodded and smoothly leapt onto their mount and tore off after them. I took one step towards where Vail waited before stumbling back as a massive black form scuttled onto the road between me and him.

Mindless words and whimpers poured out of me at the sight.

I'd seen drawings of kùsu, but that was nothing compared to seeing the enormous insectoid creature in person.

Its body had to be over fifteen feet long, and there were so many fucking legs. There was a reason we named them after the Unseelie word for *death*. If I survived this, I had no doubt this would be the star of my nightmares for years to come.

The kùsu turned in my direction and raised the upper part of its body until it towered over me.

Large black eyes looked at me above foot-long pinchers that could easily snap my body in half. Even if I could reach the crossbow on my back, it would be useless. The bolts would never penetrate the hard carapace that covered its entire body including its underside.

The best I could do would be to shoot out its eyes, but it would be on me too fast. Plus, they could sense vibrations, so even without its eyes it would still hunt me down.

Vail's horse snorted and danced beneath him as his steely grey eyes met mine.

I let out a sharp exhale at the death I saw in them. This was the exact scenario I'd always feared. He didn't have to kill me. All he had to do was not save me.

No one was here to witness it, and the kùsu would probably chase after him and the others once it was done with me. Alaric and Nyx would be witnesses to the fact that we'd wandered into the monster's territory.

"Don't," I pleaded. The reins tightened as Vail pulled the mare back. Away from me. "Please" I tried again, terror overriding my pride about begging Vail for anything.

Despite knowing that he'd craved my death since the night our parents died, I was a little surprised at the sharp pain that echoed through my chest. Part of me always wanted to believe that he wouldn't do it. That he'd be able to get past what I had done that night to save his life.

Something faltered in his cold expression, but I didn't have time to figure out what that meant before the kùsu dove towards me with its pinchers wide open. Instead of running to the side, I lunged forward and tucked myself into a roll.

During the day, I would have been too slow to pull such a move, but beneath the full moon, with my magic running at full speed, I was fast as hell. The kùsu passed over me, its pinchers slamming into the earth where I'd been standing a second ago. I was on my feet and running before it even realized where I'd gone.

Its large body still blocked the path to Vail, and I didn't trust him anyway. So I ran towards the opposite side of the road from the forest we'd traipsed through, where a ridge bordered the road. My feet slid out from under me as I frantically made my way up the slope.

The kùsu let out a high-pitched scream behind me, and I pushed myself to run faster.

"Sam!" Vail shouted.

I ignored him. For all I knew, he could be calling after me to distract me.

The sound of a hundred legs racing over the ground came from behind me. The damn thing was closing the distance between us.

I needed to slow it down. I scanned the area as I kept running as fast as I could. Several trees had fallen up ahead and landed on top of each other. That would have to do.

My muscles burned as I pushed my body to its limit. I could hear the kùsu as it chittered in excitement at closing in on its prey. I dove forward into the fallen tangle of trees, hissing as rocks and branches cut into my skin. The tangy smell of blood filled the air, and I felt a warm line of it running down my arm where a deep gash had been torn open.

I didn't allow myself to stop as I scrambled deeper into the pile of downed tree trunks.

The kùsu crashed in after me, its long body jostling the trees loose and causing them to collapse on top of it. I barely made it out the other side and was scrambling away on my butt as I watched it struggle to get free.

Pinchers snapped closed, barely six inches away from my foot, and I yelped. Everything hurt as I climbed to my feet and ran. I was bleeding from at least a dozen cuts now, some of them quite deep, and a mind-numbing pain struck me every time my left foot hit the ground.

I'd done something to that knee in my mad dash through those logs, and it really wasn't happy about having any weight on it.

I shoved the pain aside as best I could and kept running. The forest sprawled out to my right, but there was nowhere for me to run in there. The kùsu would be faster than me over the uneven footing, and who knew what other monsters were prowling about?

Vail had said there was a river up ahead. I just had to hope I could reach it from this ridge or find somewhere to slide back down to the road.

A loud crash came from behind me as the kùsu finally broke free of the fallen logs.

Because luck never seemed to be on my side, as the ridge abruptly ended.

I skidded to a halt and looked down. It wasn't that far of a drop, maybe twenty feet. I'd never jumped from anywhere this high before, but theoretically, I was pretty sure I would be fine.

A quick glance over my shoulder told me I didn't have much time to debate this. The kùsu would be on me in less than thirty seconds.

I studied the incline. It was steep, but there might be enough of an angle to it that I could run down it? I'd have to either jump far enough to clear the steep slope entirely and risk breaking something on landing, or run down it and just hope I didn't stumble.

The kùsu let out another ear-piercing shriek... and was answered by a second one.

"Are you fucking kidding me?" I looked on in horror as a second kùsu burst out of the woods just ahead of the other one.

"Samara!"

I looked down to the ground beneath me and found Vail there with a foreign expression on his face. Panic.

"Vail!" Surprise slammed into me. He came back for me after all.

You're only in this mess because he left you, the warning whispered in my mind.

I shook my head. It didn't matter. He was here now, and survival came first. Carefully, I inched closer to the ledge while he maneuvered his large horse as close to the ridge as he could.

"Jump!"

With the monsters bearing down on me, I didn't hesitate. I stepped off the ledge and skidded down the incline in a controlled fall, trying to stay on my butt as much as possible.

More jagged cuts tore through my flesh from the sharp rocks and debris, and I hissed in pain but focused only on my descent. As the distance shrank between us, Vail stretched his arm out. I leapt off the incline, grabbing his arm and letting him pull me the rest of the way. I landed hard behind him, the saddle digging into me, and wrapped my arms around his waist.

He urged his mount forward, and the horse clearly needed no further encouragement to get the hell out of here.

The horse leapt forward, and my grip around Vail tightened. I looked over my shoulder just in time to see the long, dark shape of the kùsu skitter down the side of the ridge. Their legs were moving so fast that they were a blur as they tore off down the road after us.

Shit. I'd really been hoping they would decide the chase wasn't worth it once they saw the horse, but the idea of a larger meal seemed to only excite them more.

We were keeping our distance from them, but Vail's mount wasn't built to maintain this type of speed for long. I could already hear his breathing become more labored.

If we didn't get to the river soon, Vail deciding to not be an asshole and come back for me wouldn't matter, and that really pissed me off because I wanted to survive this so I could beat the shit out of him myself.

"They're gaining on us!" I warned Vail.

"It's not much further!"

With every passing second, fear clamped onto me as the distance between us and the kùsu shrank.

We weren't going to make it.

"Hold on!" Vail clamped one large hand over where both of mine were clasped together.

I felt our horse slow its mad dash and it hesitated before the excited twin shrieks of the kùsu closing in on their prey made it leap forward. My stomach flipped as we plummeted through the air, the wind whipping at my face before freezing-cold water surrounded us.

Letting go of Vail, I kicked with my legs and broke the surface, only to dive back under as one of the kùsu came barreling over the cliff, unable to stop in time. I swam away towards the opposite side of the river as fast as I could. When I couldn't hold my breath any longer, I surfaced again.

Vail had managed to get his horse to land and was currently swimming back for me. The kùsu had apparently latched onto the side of the cliff and was desperately trying to pull itself out of the water.

I snapped my head back towards where Vail had left his horse, and relief coursed through me when I saw Alaric and Nyx. They were both soaking wet and shivering, but unharmed.

Vail reached for me, but I slapped his hand away and swam to where the others waited. Alaric ran towards me and helped me out of the water. Now that I wasn't running for my life, the pain from my knee and the cuts covering my body became agonizing.

I gritted my teeth and leaned on him. My teeth immediately started chattering, which somehow made the pain even worse.

"What happened?" Alaric asked as he set me down carefully on the shore, the sand a welcome relief.

"Vail is a piece of shit is what happened!" I spat. "He left me to die."

Nyx shifted uncomfortably as they looked back and forth between me and a glowering Vail. We'd rekindled our friendship, but they'd served Vail, and I knew they looked up to him. The rangers of House Harker would always be loyal to Vail, not me. I'd have to remember that.

"I did no such thing," Vail said coldly. "I was figuring out how to get to you when you stupidly ran off."

"Bullshit!" I hissed.

Alaric held me back when I tried to struggle to my feet, which was probably for the best, because I'm pretty sure I would have fallen flat on my face.

"Figures you'd be ungrateful for me saving your life," he sneered. "Maybe I should have let you die after you ran off like that." We glared at each other for a moment before Vail stalked off, tossing over his shoulder, "I'm going to check on the horses. We'll rest here for an hour, then continue on our way."

Nyx trailed after Vail, and my lip curled in a silent snarl. Fucking Vail. I didn't care what he claimed. I saw the look in his eyes when that kùsu got between us. He was absolutely going to leave me to die.

But he did come back for me. Why?

The pain in my knee ached, drawing my attention away from his retreating form. I'd have to dwell on Vail's odd decision later.

"What do you need?" Alaric knelt next to me, genuine concern in his eyes.

"Nothing at the moment." I winced as I dipped my fingers into the large cut on my arm and then drew a symbol on my knee with the blood.

I chanted the words for a simple healing spell and fought the urge to scratch my knee as the torn tendons and skin pieced themselves back together. This spell might be a life-saving one at times, but I still hated how itchy it made me feel.

Alaric kept a close watch on me as I slowly healed my injuries. Ideally, I could use a top-off of blood after this, but I wasn't going to ask Alaric for that, and I wasn't willing to ask Vail or Nyx either.

"What do you want to do about Vail?" he asked.

"Nothing for now. We still need him." I pursed my lips. "I'll just have to be extra careful to not be in a situation like that again. Vail may not come back next time."

CHAPTER TWENTY-FOUR

—

Vail

I COULD FEEL Nyx's eyes on me as we approached the boundary of Moroi and Furie territory.

They hadn't brought up Samara's accusation at all over the last two days. Not even when we stopped to rest for a few hours at an outpost. Technically, we could all go a week without sleep, but even getting a few hours would help keep us more focused. It was worth the loss of time.

Plus, I needed to set my head straight.

I'd been waiting for an opportunity like that with the kùsu for over a decade.

The few times my sleep wasn't plagued by nightmares, it was filled with wonderful dreams of watching Samara get torn apart by monsters. She'd stopped me from saving my parents. I didn't care what she thought. I *knew* I could have saved them. I should have let her fucking die.

But that look on her face when the kùsu got between us? The moment she knew that I was going to walk away and leave her there?

I'd expected anger, but that wasn't what I saw.

Instead, Samara was hurt by the betrayal.

Despite everything between us and her knowing that I would seize an opportunity like that, part of her still trusted me.

It was that look that had me racing along the ridge, trying to find a way to get to her. I'd left her to die, only to save her minutes later.

That small amount of trust she still had in me was gone now, and I knew I'd never get it back. I told myself that it didn't matter. That next time I got an opportunity like that, I'd take it and leave her to fucking rot.

The more I repeated it in my head, the closer I came to believing it.

I hated the way Nyx looked at me now. They were still loyal, I knew that, but they liked Samara, and I knew they'd looked up to me since joining the rangers. They were a couple years younger than Samara and the youngest of the rangers that made up my usual crew.

Nyx was like a younger sibling to all of us, and like a younger sibling, they put all of us up on high pedestals. And now they had to reconcile the fact that I'd pulled some shady shit, and I felt bad for putting them in that position.

I'd really fucked this up. As soon as we figured out what was going on with these wraiths, I'd head north for a bit. Maybe get permission from the Velesians to run around in their territory. Tensions were high between them and the majority of the Moroi, but I'd always gotten along with most of them fine. Probably because I spent my time in their territory hunting down monsters and never looked down my nose at them the way many of the other Moroi did.

"What's the plan, Marshal?" Nyx asked tightly.

My jaw hardened until my teeth hurt from clenching them together. I couldn't even remember the last time Nyx had referred to me by my title. Only the rangers who didn't normally work with me did that.

This was Samara's fault. She fucked up everything in my life.

"Cali reached out to me while we were staying at the outpost," Samara said from behind us. "She's going to meet us up ahead. She can guide us the rest of the way to the temple."

I heard her mount pick up its pace until it was on the other side of Nyx. This one was calmer than the frantic one she'd been riding the night we were attacked, but it was solid white and painfully stood out, even here where the forest had given way to scrub lands. I was surprised the damn thing hadn't been eaten the first time someone had taken it for a ride outside of the outpost.

"That information would have been nice to know before now, Heir," I growled.

Samara gave me a cool look. "It wouldn't have mattered before. If we started to veer off course, I would have said something, *Marshal*."

"Did she have any updates about the wraiths?" Nyx asked stiffly before I could say anything else.

"You're leaning to the left again," Samara murmured to Alaric. He really was a terrible rider, and after his horse had run away with him the other night, he was even more nervous around them. Samara helped him center his weight again before focusing on Nyx once more. "The wraiths are still in the temple. They haven't left."

"Is she sure they're still there?" Nyx frowned.

"Yeah," she said uncomfortably. "She can feel them."

My eyebrows crept up. "How far inside the temple are they?"

Samara didn't look at me when she answered, but I saw the strain running through her body. Something about Cali's abilities bothered her. "I'm not sure," she said evenly.

Furies were the most sensitive to wraiths and shadow magic, but they usually had to be fairly close to feel them. Cali had been perched on top of a mesa, and the temple was far below. They should have been too far out of her range to sense.

Unease ran through me. I didn't like Samara, but I respected both of her friends. Rynn was smart as hell and would be a huge asset to the Alpha Pack if they could ever figure their shit out, and Cali was an incredible warrior who had saved some of my rangers' asses on more than one occasion.

Most Furies eventually gave into the rage they all carried inside of them and had to be put down, and killing a Furie who had lost themself was no easy feat.

The current generation seemed to be doing the best. They had strict rules in place to keep themselves level.

But Cali had never followed the rules.

She'd seemed fine every time I met her, but now that I thought about it... when was the last time I'd seen her in person? The idea of fighting any Furie made me nervous.

For one, they were our allies. Fighting one of them was similar to fighting a Moroi who had given into bloodlust and become a Strigoi. You weren't fighting some random monster, you were fighting one of your own, and that was not something I ever enjoyed. The last time I'd had to take down a rogue Furie, I'd brought twenty rangers with me and less than half of us walked away from that encounter.

Cali was the most powerful Furie in existence, possibly ever. Between that and the wild cards that were Samara and Rynn, it would be better for everyone if she stayed sane.

A shadow passed over us, causing the horses to skitter to the side. A few seconds later, Cali landed in front of us with silent wings.

In a heartbeat, Samara threw her leg over her horse's neck and practically leapt out of the saddle, leaving poor Alaric to slide forward while frantically grabbing the reins. The Furie grunted as Samara threw herself at her and wrapped her in a tight hug.

"Fuck you for making me worry so much," Samara grumbled into Cali's shoulder, where she was still tightly nestled.

The Furie's leathery black wings stretched around Samara as if they could shield her from the world.

"Missed you too, bestie," Cali murmured.

As Samara untangled herself, the Furie turned her glowing golden eyes on me, and I tensed at the death I saw in them. I guess that answered the question of whether or not Samara had told Cali about what had happened that night.

I gave her a lazy grin as if to say, *"Gonna do something about it?"*

Cali stared at me for a second, and I forced myself to remain calm and not reach for the sword strapped across my back. Not that it would do me a lot of good against Calpyso fucking Rayne.

The Furie was a few inches taller than Samara and had considerably more muscle, but she was still a fraction of my size. But size didn't matter against someone who could wield shadow magic, was wickedly fast with a blade, and could shred your mind if she really cut loose.

Seconds ticked by before the Furie slowly blinked and the burning light in her eyes dimmed a little.

That told me two things. Cali wasn't that far gone if she could rein in her fury so easily, and I would definitely have to watch my back around her from now on. Samara, Rynn, and Cali were as different as three people could be, but the one thing they all shared in common, besides their love for each other, was coldhearted pragmatism.

Death would come for me on silent wings someday, but not while I was still needed. For now.

"Whatever the wraiths are doing, they've moved much further into the temple," Cali said, tossing the long braid of her hair back over her shoulder. The red color was so dark it looked black at night; only in the day could you make out its true deep red tones. "You should be fine to take the horses and leave them out front without alerting them to our presence."

I looked up at the sun arcing across the sky. We still had at least four hours of daylight left, and there weren't nearly as many creatures that called the badlands home the way they did the forests.

"Alright," I agreed. "Lead the way."

After one more pointed glare at me, Cali shot up into the sky. The horses startled at the sudden movement, but luckily—if not surprisingly—Alaric managed to keep his under control until Samara could reach him.

"You want to ride up front this time?" she asked.

He shook his head quickly. "I'd rather you drive."

"Funny." She shot him a teasing smile. "Kieran says the same thing."

"I somehow doubt that," Alaric retorted dryly, the corners of his lips twitching as if he was fighting off a smile.

My mouth twisted in distaste. "Enough messing around," I said sharply. "Let's go."

Alaric awkwardly shifted back so that Samara could mount. As soon as she was in the saddle, I nudged the horse forward, and she broke out into a steady canter. Cali was slightly ahead of us so that we could easily keep her in sight as we made our way across the badlands. After a couple of miles, she veered off the road, and we had to slow our horses as we traversed the deeper sand.

I wiped the sweat from my brow with a grimace. If I never had to come back to the badlands again, it would be too soon. Between the oppressive heat and being out in the open, I hated everything about it. Luckily, we rarely had to come out this way because most of the badlands were in Furie territory, and there was little out here.

It was probably why the wraiths were able to settle in at the temple for so long without being noticed. We were lucky Cali had spotted them.

I'd have to speak with her or one of the Furie elders later about setting up some type of regular scouting party here. I didn't like the idea of wraiths being able to operate underneath our noses like this.

Cali led us a few more miles in, and I had to squint against the sun reflecting off the white sand. It wasn't long before I spotted the enormous mesa rising out of the ground. I'd never been to this one before, but there were dozens of mesas like this throughout the badlands. They also felt strange to me, like they weren't entirely natural.

"Think that's it?" Nyx asked. They'd draped their extra long-sleeve shirt over the back of their head to keep the sun off their neck and shoulders.

"Must be," I remarked. "The mesas are always spread out, so there won't be another one for at least twenty miles."

"Stay away from that prickly-looking tree up ahead," Samara warned.

"Why?" Nyx asked as they guided their lanky chestnut mare a safe distance away from said tree.

I did the same as I eyed it. It was small, only around six feet, but instead of bark, it was covered in short spines that curved downwards. Three short, stocky branches protruded near the top of the trunk, each ending in a bright red, bulbous flower. More thorns surrounded the base of the flower, but these had vivid orange tips.

"Most of the thorns are just to keep animals from climbing up it," Samara explained, "but the ones near the flower with the orange tips? Those ones can shoot out when it feels threatened."

Nyx gave the tree a wary look and then nodded at Samara. "Thanks for the tip."

I wondered if she would have said anything had Nyx not been riding next to me. Probably not.

"How much time have you spent out here?" Alaric looked at Samara curiously. "As far as I know, even the rangers avoid this place."

"We do," I agreed. "There are enough threats in the forests in Moroi and Velesian territory to keep us busy."

Samara casually shrugged a shoulder. "Rynn, Cali, and I have actually spent a lot of time not too far from this exact spot, just a little further north. It wasn't far from Drudonia, and it gave us a place to be away from prying eyes... and high expectations while we studied there."

I remained facing forward even as my eyes slid to the side to glance at Samara. She was riding tall in the saddle, her shoulders relaxed and a serene expression on her face.

It was a lie.

Samara told everyone that she'd agreed to the marriage with House Laurent, and she'd worn that same expression whenever her aunt or best friends had asked about it. Her response had always been the same: *"I am happy to support House Harker in any way that I can."*

As she got older and more confident, she would crack jokes about how attractive Demetri was and that it wasn't actually a hardship at all. But I remembered coming across a young girl, crying over the graves of her parents and whispering words she'd never utter to a living soul.

"I don't want to marry him. I want to be more."

She hadn't seen me that day, and I'd never once mentioned that I knew her secret.

Not that it mattered anymore. She'd probably sabotaged her marriage in such a way that she knew her aunt would side with her. Samara was nothing if not a long-term strategist.

My lips curled and I slid my eyes back to the temple, which was drawing closer.

She's such a pretty little liar.

"So do you know about the trees from experience?" Nyx asked.

Samara let out a delicate laugh. "You could say that. The three of us used to dare each other to race up the tree and tap the flower and avoid getting a bunch of thorns in the ass."

"That doesn't surprise me in the least." Alaric snorted. "This also explains why you came home that one time and refused to sit down. Carmilla had put on a welcome home dinner for you, and you stood the whole time."

"I remember that," Samara replied with a cringe. "I got cocky and tried to tap two flowers in a row and got an ass full of thorns for my arrogance."

Nyx cackled and even I couldn't keep the barest of smiles off my lips. That was the true danger of Samara. In moments like this, I could almost forget how much I hated her.

CHAPTER TWENTY-FIVE

—

Samara

I POINTED out a few more plants and animals as we made our way towards the mesa where the temple was located. While the badlands weren't my favorite place, there was something about this place that I loved. In moderation, that is. I loved this place in moderation.

Sweat dripped down the back of my neck, and I swiped some of my hair that was stuck to the side of my face away. The sun here was unrelenting. It didn't help that Alaric was plastered to my back, so I had his body heat to deal with as well, but if I asked him to move back a little, he would no doubt lose his balance and fall off. Cali swerved a little more to the west, leading us to the side of the mesa.

"Oh," I breathed out, my eyes widening as I took in the sight. "I've never seen one like this before."

Up close, I could see the veins of amethyst and serpentine running up the side of the mesa walls. The purple and green minerals created mesmerizing patterns against the nearly white stone. I waited for Alaric to dismount and then I did the same before stepping closer to the stone and tracing my fingers along a spiral of eye-catching crystal.

"Maybe this is why they selected this mesa to build a temple," Alaric mused from next to me.

"Perhaps." I tilted my head back so that I could see more of the patterns. "I've seen some of the other mesas and while they're pretty and often have minerals running up them, they're more rugged. This looks too flat and shiny to be totally natural."

"Wait till you see the temple entrance," Cali said as she landed quietly behind us. "The Fae must have used a ridiculous amount of magic to build all of this."

"Why, though?" I asked. "And why here, of all places?"

"Hopefully, we'll find more answers inside," Cali said. "The entrance is around the corner."

We secured our horses using some metal spikes that we shoved into the earth and looped their reins around, and then I fastened the crossbow to the saddle once more. It would be too slow against wraiths, and my aim was just as good if not better with the dagger strapped to my thigh.

Although, if I threw it, I'd be giving up my only weapon.

I frowned. Once we made it back home, I should ask Roth more about the blood magic they used for their ribbons. A dagger that responded to my mental commands could be handy...

"No talking once we're inside," Vail said once the horses were secure. It was still hard to look at him without my bloodlust rising.

The fucker had left me for dead, and now he was acting like nothing happened. I schooled my features into a bland expression while he went through some basic hand signals with us. As long as I focused on the task at hand, I could handle being in Vail's company without attempting to rip his throat out.

Probably. If I stayed *very* focused.

"Remember, our goal is to figure out what the wraiths are up to," Vail said firmly. "We should avoid confronting them if we can. Even if we outnumber them, wraiths are nasty in a fight."

"And if they don't detect us, we can continue to monitor them and gather information," I added.

Something told me we weren't going to get lucky and just walk in on the wraiths carefully explaining all the details of their evil plan. The longer we could watch them without detection, the more information we could potentially gather.

Cali took point since she was the best among us at detecting wraiths, and Vail followed after her. Alaric and I were next, with Nyx once again taking up the rear.

I exhaled sharply when we turned the corner and I saw the front of the temple. Cali wasn't kidding. It was one of the most beautiful things I'd ever seen. The lower half of the white stone had been cut away, creating an overhang that functioned as a roof for the open space below. A dozen pillars sprung down from the ceiling and spiraled towards the earth.

My fingers quietly ran across one. It was smooth and cool beneath my touch. Lines of jade wound around this one, almost as if they had been coaxed toward the surface. There were no signs of any tools being used to create these, making me wonder if they were all done by magic.

Roth would love this place if I could ever convince them to leave the library and traipse into the badlands.

A few yards behind the columns stood an enormous arched entrance. The sun hung low enough in the sky that it hit the other side of the mesa, leaving this side in shadow.

Trepidation ran through my blood as we took in the darkness that awaited us inside.

We'd be able to see just fine in the dark, but we were entering an unknown space where there was likely only one exit, and at least three wraiths waited for us inside.

As much as it annoyed me to do so, I looked to Vail for what to do next. If anyone could get us in and out of here alive, it was him.

Silently, he moved forward, and we all fell into step behind him. Once we'd cleared the entrance and taken a few steps into the dark room, he stopped, allowing our eyes time to adjust. A vast open space greeted us, full of more spiraling columns and tables and chairs carved out of the same stone.

Despite how beautiful everything was, the wonder that I felt outside failed to overcome me now. The wraiths were all I could think about. Our sharp night vision would help us navigate, but it couldn't see the wraiths hiding in the shadows. Only Cali would be able to sense them, though most wraiths had encountered Furies before, and they could sometimes trick their senses.

Cautiously, we continued through the room until we reached another doorway. Then Vail raised a fist in the air, the signal for us to stop, and we all immediately halted. Another signal came, this one to wait, before he jerked his head towards Cali, and the two of them proceeded into the next room.

I remained completely still but studied the area while we waited, trusting Nyx to keep an eye on things. There wasn't much to the room, aside from the doorway where Vail and Cali had disappeared through, but I did spot a set of stairs in each corner opposite the entrance.

Curiosity flickered through me, wondering where they led, but I forced myself to stay put.

After what felt like hours but was probably only a few minutes, Vail and Cali returned, both wearing troubled expressions.

I tapped Vail's shoulder, and once his attention was on me, I pointed out both of the stairwells.

He looked at Cali, and some sort of silent conversation happened between them before she shrugged. Vail gave her a pointed look, and she returned a sharp smile.

My eyes bounced back and forth between them, not really having any idea what was going on but taking away some enjoyment at my friend getting under Vail's skin.

Finally, Vail made a decision and gestured for us to follow him as he moved towards the stairs, which, as it turned out, led to balconies running along each side of the room he and Cali had explored. The walls were lined with empty shelves and narrow, arched bridges periodically stretched across the room to connect the balconies.

What had this place been used for? I carefully looked around the walls and the ceiling for clues.

The first room we'd entered had been pitch-black, but this one was dimly lit. Thick lines of what appeared to be gold ran up the walls and across the ceiling, giving off a faint warm light.

I looked around but I didn't see any other lanterns hanging anywhere. Maybe the golden light used to be brighter? Or perhaps there had been lanterns at one point?

I couldn't tell if this had been built by the Seelie or Unseelie, which I thought was a little strange. The fortresses they'd left behind had very distinct styles based on who built them. But here, there were no distinguishing features anywhere. Everything from the shelves to the bridges had been carved out of the plain white stone of the mesa as if it were all one gigantic piece.

Even in the dim lighting, it was magnificent.

Faint voices came from up ahead, and all of us froze. I tried to make out what they were saying, but they were talking too low, and we were too far away. Vail made us move away from the railing so that we hugged the shelves along the wall as we crept forward.

Vail, Nyx, and Cali all remained calm, but I could hear Alaric's and my heart beating loudly. I did my best to soothe myself, trusting the instincts of Cali and the rangers.

As we closed the distance between us and whoever was speaking, it became clear they were using one of the Fae languages. But their voices were too low and raspy for me to understand any of it or tell if it was Seelie or Unseelie.

When it sounded like we were directly above them, Vail halted, and we all stood still with our backs to the wall. He slowly stepped forward until he could see over the railing and then glanced over his shoulder, motioning us forward. I held my breath as I moved towards the railing and peered down.

My heart threatened to leap up in my throat at what I saw. Normally, wraiths were amorphous shadows. They could contort themselves into various shapes and for a split second take corporeal form. In that small window of time, they would rake their claws down our sides or tear out our throats with long, curved fangs.

Fighting them was almost impossible because you couldn't injure them when they were shadows. Only for that split second they were solid.

The wraiths below were nothing like the ones I'd seen before. Even though Cali had told us that these were corporeal, or close to it, I still hadn't really believed it until now. Three figures stood facing each other, deep in conversation. Dark shadows dripped off their forms and contorted their features, but they were unmistakably Fae.

We were right. The Unseelie *had* fucked up and cursed themselves into shadow monsters. But how? And what were they doing here now? Were they waiting for someone?

A tap on my shoulder got my attention, and I turned to face Vail. He gestured for me to get down, and I noticed that everyone else was crouching. I quickly glanced back at the wraiths below. If I knelt down, I'd still be able to hear them, but I wouldn't be able to see them. Though, if they looked up, it was possible they'd see me.

Reluctantly, I silently sank to my knees with my feet flexed on their toes beneath me. It wasn't super comfortable, but it meant I'd be able to spring to my feet in a hurry.

Time ticked onward, and the wraiths continued with their conversation. No matter how hard I strained, I couldn't make out what they were saying. My damn ears felt like they were bleeding from the effort, but the raspy voices were just low enough to be out of my range.

Alaric shifted beside me, nervously looking back towards the stairwell. I desperately wanted to know what he made of all this, but we couldn't risk speaking. I shared his concern, though. We were running out of time. Sunset couldn't be too far off, and we couldn't chance being here at night.

Cali shifted, drawing my attention. Her black wings were wrapped around her shoulders like a cloak, and shadows began to swirl around her. Vail's hand snapped forward to grab her, but he was too slow. On liquid joints, Cali slipped through the darkness until she was perched on the railing in a shadowy corner. The only reason I could even make out her form was because I knew she was there.

She blended into the shadows perfectly as if she was a wraith herself.

Looking at her scared the shit out of me. Not because I was scared of her, but because I was scared *for* her.

Whatever was happening to Cali, I knew frightened her too, because she was watching the wraiths below with a quiet intensity, like they held all the answers she sought.

Which they likely did. They held all our answers, and we couldn't understand a moons-damned word they were saying. While we'd been listening to them the past hour in vain, I realized what was bothering me about their words.

They seemed to be twisted somehow and reminded me of the sounds they made when in their pure shadow forms.

What the fuck are you saying? I thought in frustration. We'd risked our lives coming in here, and aside from seeing with our own eyes what Cali had already told us, we'd gotten no new information.

Suddenly, the wraiths stopped talking. I couldn't see anything from my vantage point, and Vail cut a glare at me which clearly stated to not move. As much as I wanted to see what was going on and further piss off Vail, I didn't move an inch. My preference was to not die, and that was more pressing than anything else.

"Apologies for the delay," a strong, masculine voice announced in our common tongue.

It felt like my heart froze for a moment before painfully starting to beat again. I knew that voice, but it couldn't be him. There was no fucking way someone that important would be meeting with the wraiths.

Vail and Alaric seemed rooted in place before they both swung their heads to look at me and I saw the shock in their eyes. They recognized the voice, too.

The footsteps slowed, and we all very quietly moved forward enough so that we could confirm with our eyes what our ears had already told us. That the son of the Moroi Sovereign had betrayed us all.

CHAPTER TWENTY-SIX

—

Samara

Prince Draven Nacht looked exactly as I remembered him. Sinfully gorgeous. Which, considering how many attractive Moroi I had surrounding me these days, was saying something. But Draven always held a presence about him. Even the dark, loose-fitting clothes he wore tonight did nothing to diminish his tall, muscular build. His black hair with its unusual silver streaks was contained in a tight braid that fell midway down his back.

My fingers tightened around the railing from where I now peered down as Draven closed the distance between him and the wraiths with languid strides. He was even wearing the same easy, confident grin that he always had when he greeted me, as if meeting wraiths in a forgotten Fae temple was just another day in the life of a Moroi prince.

Because of how close my aunt was to the Sovereigns, I'd grown up knowing Prince Draven my entire life.

While I didn't know him as well as I knew those I'd grown up with in House Harker, I never would have suspected him as the Moroi working with the wraiths. He'd always reminded me of Kieran and seemed content to spend his life socializing and being a flirt.

The wraiths' whispery language filled the room, and the charming grin slid off his face.

"You know I can't understand you when you speak like that," he snapped.

I held my breath as the three wraiths stopped talking and stepped back. A fourth wraith, one we hadn't even known about stepped further into the room and I had to swallow the gasp that tried to escape.

While the other three had form, they still seemed to be at least partly made of shadow. This one only had a few wisps of shadow swirling around him.

Everything about him was bright and golden, completely at odds with the

224

shadows trailing in his wake. The wraiths bowed their heads as he walked past them. I committed everything about his appearance to memory. Deep, golden-blond hair. Bronze skin. Tall and powerful build. From my viewpoint, I could only see his face in profile, but he seemed to have strong masculine features and tapered ears.

Definitely Fae, which wasn't surprising since we already knew the other three wraiths were as well. I assumed Unseelie, given what we knew so far.

"Careful, Princeling," the Fae said in a dangerous, low tone. "The shadows pull to us still, and they are not yet strong enough to speak without the shadows intertwining with their words."

"My apologies, Erendriel," Prince Draven said stiffly, the confident mask he wore slipping slightly. "The ride here was long and arduous."

The Fae, Erendriel apparently, studied Prince Draven the way a predator would study passing prey and debate whether they were hungry enough to go for a hunt.

"Of course. The forests are treacherous these days," he said with a sly smile.

Prince Draven's shoulders loosened just a fraction. These two clearly knew each other, but Draven was definitely wary of whoever this Fae was.

Not that I blamed him. I was terrified of him, and he didn't even know I was here. The only things we knew about the Fae were what we had been able to piece together in the books and scrolls that we found, along with what we were able to reverse engineer from the spell castings they'd left behind.

I was intimately familiar with what wraiths could do, though. A shiver ran through me. Did Erendriel possess his Fae magic or wraith magic? With our shitty luck, he had both now.

"Did you bring me what I asked for?"

"Yes," Draven said before quickly adding, "Mostly."

The golden Fae stared at him with a cold, expressionless look, and the Moroi prince swallowed.

"I brought you a dozen Moroi. They think they're guarding the caravan a short distance away. It was all I could bring without raising suspicion among the rangers."

I glanced at Vail and saw nothing but cold fury as he stared at Draven. Technically, Vail had sworn his oath to House Harker, but all the rangers supported the Sovereign House with undying loyalty. I couldn't imagine what he was feeling at this betrayal. Despite our differences, I felt sorry for him. He had placed his faith in the wrong person.

The question was, did the queen and her consort know what their son was up to?

I needed to warn Carmilla as soon as possible. There was no way she was involved in this. My mother had been the only family she'd had left, and the wraiths had killed her.

No matter her friendship with the queen, Carmilla would never agree to helping the wraiths.

"That is not enough."

Shadows rippled from the three Fae, contorting their appearance and making them more wraith-like.

I leaned forward slightly to get a better view. Earlier, the golden Fae said that the shadows still pulled at them. So whatever they were doing to regain their Fae forms wasn't permanent, and these three definitely had a more tenuous grasp on it.

"I can get you more," Draven promised, keeping a close eye on the three Fae. "But we can't keep this up forever. There are only so many Moroi we can sacrifice before we begin to lose power. The Velesians are already sniffing around, and there are some amongst the Moroi who are taking notice as well."

"You assured me that you could handle it. Perhaps I chose my allies poorly." The Fae's expression remained one of icy arrogance but there was no mistaking the threat interlaced with his words.

"It will be handled," Draven said in a clipped tone. "The Alpha Pack is a problem, but soon they'll be too busy dealing with infighting amongst the Velesian packs to do anything else, and I already have plans in motion for the Moroi who are asking questions."

"Good." A chilling smile spread across Erendriel's face. "Let's go see what you brought me."

"They're camped a few miles from here near the border," Prince Draven said. "The guards wearing red sashes are mine. You can take the others."

Rage seethed out of me, and I could practically feel Vail's anger rippling off of him. Alaric and Nyx both wore matching disgusted expressions. I thought of the boy I'd found outside that outpost and wondered if he'd been someone who the wraiths had found themselves, or whether Prince Draven had handed him over like cattle.

We'd suspected that a Moroi was helping the wraiths, but this was so far beyond what I'd thought was happening. How could Prince Draven turn on his own people like this?

Erendriel turned to face the other three then. "Prepare the ritual. We'll use half to finish your transformations and then bring the rest north."

They whispered their agreements and slipped away.

"How is your supply of the ritual stones?" Prince Draven asked as they headed towards the exit. "We might need to come up with a different strategy for the outpost attacks. Questions are starting to be asked. I was thinking we..."

His words became too faint to hear, and I twisted on my feet as I started to head after them before Vail clasped a firm hand over my arm. I jerked away at his touch, and he gave me a flat look before pointing three fingers at Cali and then gesturing them towards where the prince and Erendriel had gone.

Shadows rippled around her as she shot forward on silent wings after them. My lips twisted into a hard line as I watched her fly away. Rationally, I knew she would be fine, but I didn't like the idea of my best friend going after a Fae with unknown magic.

Once she was gone from my sight, I turned my attention back to Vail, who was gesturing firmly at Nyx while pointing at me and Alaric.

They kept firmly shaking their head at him while their fingers flew through different movements. I only knew the very basic signs that the rangers used, but I suspected that Vail was telling Nyx to get us out of here while he went after the wraiths.

Fuck. That.

The prince said the guards were miles away. This was our chance to see what type of ritual the wraiths were doing to turn themselves back into Fae. While Vail was arguing with Nyx, I slipped towards the rail and leapt over it. A jolt shot through me when my feet hit the floor, but not a sound echoed across the room.

A low growl came from above before Vail swallowed it, and a tiny smirk played across my lips. *Suck on that, Marshal.*

Seconds later, Vail and Nyx joined me, both landing quietly as well. We looked up at Alaric, who peered down at us with a frown. I waved for him to come down, and he glared at me before leaping over the rail into a flip and landing in a kneeling position with one hand raised behind his back.

I rolled my eyes at the showy move even as a part of me found it kind of hot. What other tricks did Alaric have up his sleeve?

Vail headed towards the back of the room, and I shook the dirty thoughts out of my head while I focused on the task at hand. We needed to learn what we could about the ritual and then get out before Erendriel returned.

Another archway appeared along the back wall, this one smaller and more simple in design than the previous ones. Carefully, we crept underneath it and down the hallway as I tried to ignore the growing tension between my shoulder blades. There was no sign of the wraiths anywhere.

It was possible they'd just traveled further into the temple and we couldn't hear them, but I couldn't shake the bad feeling that sunk further into my mind with every step.

The hallway abruptly ended, and Vail stopped. I couldn't see anything past his bulky frame, and when Alaric halted just behind me, I leaned against him slightly, needing something to ground me. As if he felt the same way, he rested one steady hand on my shoulder and the other on my hip. I couldn't pinpoint the exact moment it happened, but somewhere along this journey, our relationship had shifted from rivals and reluctant peers to friends.

I looked over my shoulder as Alaric met my gaze, and I saw trust in his eyes... and maybe something more.

A sound from somewhere ahead of us drew our attention away from each other, and we both leaned to the side, trying to peer around Vail.

From what I could see, there was a small square room. Unlike the previous rooms, however, this one didn't have any columns or seating, but I smelled the stench of blood. Moroi blood. A lot of it.

We need to leave, I thought frantically, but as I reached for Vail's shoulder, Alaric slammed into me, and we tumbled into the room. Two wraiths dropped from where they'd been hovering on the ceiling, and the third hurled Nyx into the wall.

Their body crunched and fell into a still heap as a scream tore out of my throat, and a chilling sound came from the wraiths as they backed us into a corner. Laughter.

We were so fucked.

BEFORE I COULD REACT, Vail pulled his sword free and slashed across the abdomen of the wraith closest to us. I didn't know if was because Vail was so fast or because the wraiths were closer to their Fae form, but his blade bit into flesh. The wraith shrieked as blood and intestine leaked from its stomach.

Bile rose in my throat, but I swallowed it down as I continued backing up towards where Nyx had fallen, Alaric urgently following in my steps.

The wraith Vail had wounded collapsed to the floor and twitched a few times before going still. The remaining two focused cold, black eyes on him. One snapped into shadow and disappeared while the other took a swipe at Vail with elongated claws. He leaned back, narrowly avoiding the strike, and went on the offensive.

I drew the blade from my thigh and stood guard over Nyx, trying to figure out where the other wraith had disappeared to.

I didn't know why they both hadn't turned into shadows. The one fighting Vail was holding its own, but all of their tactical advantage came from being incorporeal most of the time, which it seemed to be refusing to do.

"Grab Nyx," I commanded Alaric. "We need to get out of here."

Alaric didn't question me as he quickly but carefully picked Nyx up off the floor. The ranger didn't so much as stir, but I could still hear their heart beating. They still stood a chance. But there was nothing we could do for them in here; we needed to get the hell out.

Shadows streamed from the ceiling and slammed into Vail, who flew backward and through the hallway before crashing into the other room. Alaric and I darted after him but just as we reached the fallen ranger, he leapt to his feet and started back towards the wraiths. I wrapped my fingers around his arm and pulled, stopping him in his tracks.

Vail snarled and shoved me against the wall next to the hallway entrance. His dark grey eyes had turned completely silver, and his fangs were on display. *Hello, bloodlust.*

"Samara!" Alaric screamed.

"GO!" I ordered. Alaric hesitated, clearly torn between getting Nyx to safety and helping me. "He won't hurt me," I said with a confidence I absolutely did not feel, but I needed Alaric to get out of here. "Save Nyx, Alaric! Please!"

He let loose a pissed-off snarl but did as I asked and took off running towards the exit with Nyx gripped tightly in his arms.

Vail's claws dug into my shoulders, and I heard the wraiths whispering excitedly as the scent of my blood filled the air. Hopefully, that meant they would focus on me and not Alaric fleeing with Nyx.

Fuck. On second thought, wraiths being completely focused on me sounded really, really bad.

Vail tilted his head, mesmerized by the blood pooling in the pocket of my collarbone. I had to snap him out of it, and then we needed to hightail our asses out of here to where the sun was still shining outside.

Erendriel didn't seem to be bound by shadows, but hopefully these ones weren't far enough along in their transformation to withstand sunlight.

"Vail," I warned when I felt him adjust his grip.

Before I could do anything, he yanked me against him and ran a rough tongue against my skin.

Of all the times for his bloodlust to rise, of course it had to be now.

Thin tendrils of shadows leaked from the ceiling and brushed against the blood gushing from where Vail still had a brutal hold on me. Whispers swam through my mind, making me shudder until one word floated to the surface.

Delicious.

"FUCK!" I screamed and threw all of my weight to the side. Agony tore through me as Vail's clawed fingers ripped from my flesh.

Blood that had been steadily streaming now gushed from my wounds, and the wraith that Vail had been fighting earlier laughed and took a step into the hallway. The chittering sound of excited whispers filled the space as shadows slid down the wall.

I slipped the dagger free from my thigh sheath and threw it at the wraith, who was still mostly corporeal. It sank into his throat, cutting off his laughter.

I slapped a hand over my wound and then shoved it into Vail's face.

"You want it? Come and get it!" I dropped my hand and whirled around, running as fast as I could, pissed-off snarls and angry whispers screaming in my wake.

I made it halfway through the large cavern of a room where the prince had met with the Fae before a shadowy figure snapped into existence in front of me and swiped for my chest. My feet slid as I tried to stop, but I wasn't fast enough. Pain flared as claws pierced my skin just above my heart before vanishing, and then I crashed to the floor on my already wounded shoulder.

Blood seeped out of my injuries and formed a pool around me as the shadows swirled; both wraiths had fully retreated to their shadow forms now. I could sense their excitement as they circled, occasionally snapping into physical forms to take another strike at me or graze my skin with their razor-sharp talons.

Stand up. I needed to get off the damn floor and run. But when I tried to rise, my body instantly gave out, and I sank back into my own blood. My thoughts grew hazier, but I forced myself to think.

Why aren't they killing me?

More whispers in my ear, and I was starting to get good at picking out words. *Delicious. Power. Mine.*

Something about their whispered language tickled the back of my mind, but I couldn't figure out what it was. Just when I started to realize why it was bothering me, a loud crash punctuated with snarls came from above me.

Vail was still alive then.

A sharp hiss tore out of me when one of the wraiths gripped my wrist and yanked me forward. It could only hold on for a few seconds, so it had to keep repeating the process. The third time it pulled, I screamed as something in my arm tore and my vision darkened.

My eyelids fluttered as I clung to consciousness. I tried to pull myself away, but I'd lost too much blood. *The ritual.* They must be dragging me back for the ritual.

Well, I'd wanted to know what it was they were doing. I guess this was one way to find out.

Something slammed into the floor next to me, causing my eyes to fly open. I stared stupidly at the huge piece of white stone that had shattered the floor before realizing there was sunshine beaming down on it.

It took me several more seconds to realize the wraiths had released me to get away from the light that now bathed my mutilated body.

"Pretty," I slurred, winding my fingers around the golden light. The wraiths shrieked and backed further away, and then Vail appeared over me. "You're pretty too," I said weakly.

Vail cursed, that predatory gleam still in his silver eyes before he bit down hard on his wrist.

"Sam!" he growled into my face.

I blinked, realizing I must have blacked out. I was practically in his lap now, and he was holding his bloody wrist in front of me.

His blood called to me, and my fangs snapped down to tear into his flesh.

Rich, decadent blood spilled down my throat, and I greedily swallowed as much as I could. A moan slipped from my lips as power flooded me and still, I drank more. A deep rumble came from Vail's chest as he held me tightly against him.

Another piece of the ceiling collapsed, landing with a solid thud a few feet from us. The haze that had been encircling my mind lifted as my body recovered from blood loss.

I instantly released Vail and tried to push out of his arms, but he just clamped me to him as he rose to his feet.

"Nice of you to finally get your head back in the game." His voice had an odd raspy quality to it, and he was looking at me with something akin to need.

I was so used to seeing nothing but hate in his eyes when they fell on me that I didn't know how to process this. It must be some leftover feeling from the bloodlust. Which reminded me...

"Oh, I'm sorry that I almost died from getting clawed up by the wraiths *and* you," I growled back.

His lips pursed together in a flat line. Maybe he was hoping I wouldn't have remembered that part. I frowned. There was something else I was forgetting. Something after I ran away from Vail. I racked my brain, trying to remember, but the last few minutes were such a blur.

A dark shape flashed by our haven of light, followed soon by another. The second one got a little too close to the light, and it let out an ear-splitting shriek before diving back into the shadows.

My eyes roved around the room, but I didn't see the third one anywhere. Maybe it was still recovering from the wound Vail had given it.

"Can you run?" Vail asked quietly.

"Only one way to find out."

He stared at me, and I could tell he was debating trying to carry me out. At least, I hoped he was thinking that and not chucking me off into the shadows and getting himself out while the wraiths were distracted.

But given that he'd just given me blood and probably saved my life, I was inclined to believe that he wanted to save us both.

Which confused the hell out of me given his previous actions, but I wasn't going to question it now.

At least I wasn't dead.

"I'm fine," I murmured. "Set me down quickly and then we make a break for it, okay?"

Vail looked at me with silver and dark grey eyes that reminded me of a storm cloud. When he made no move to set me down, I pushed against him until he finally relented and set me on my feet. I wobbled for a second, but with Vail's blood coursing through me, I wasn't in pain at all. If anything, I felt fucking amazing.

I quickly took stock of my injuries and found that the worst of them had already healed. Vail also looked no worse for wear despite the fights he'd been in with the wraiths and whatever the hell he had done to break down part of the ceiling.

Before I could think better of it, I slipped my hand into his and gave him a questioning look.

Fathomless eyes looked at our hands clasped together before slowly trailing up to my face. He stared at me for a long moment before slowly nodding.

When the wraiths circling us passed by, leaving a wide-open path to the front room, we both bolted forward. Despite the boost of Vail's blood, it only took him a few seconds to outpace me. His fingers clamped down harder around my hand as he pulled me with him.

A scream ripped out of me as I stumbled when one of the wraiths swiped its claws down my back, but Vail only tightened his grip and refused to let me fall.

Finally, we passed the archway that led to the front room, and I could see the sunlit exit ahead of us. Without warning, a wall of shadows slammed into existence between us and it, and Vail yanked me to the side. We raced between the columns, weaving in and out as the wraiths kept trying to slow our progress.

They were clearly trying to keep us alive because they kept going for our legs and arms in an attempt to maim, probably so they could drag us back for that moons-damned ritual.

But their tactics changed when we got closer to the exit and they saw us slipping from their grasp.

I barked out a warning when I saw one of them snap towards Vail, talons solidifying at the last second to rip out his throat. He swerved to the side and swiped at the arm with his dagger. Shadows dripped to the floor like blood as the wraith shrieked in pain.

Alaric appeared in the archway but stayed within the light as he watched in horror as we did our best to outrun our deaths.

The wounds down my back felt like liquid fire, but I was too hopped up on adrenaline to let it slow me down. Anticipation coursed through me as the exit drew nearer, and I could practically feel the sunlight on my skin as we closed the distance between us and salvation.

Vail made it through the exit first, and just as I passed Alaric and felt the sun hit my skin, something wrapped around my throat and ripped me out of Vail's grasp.

"Samara!" Alaric screamed and grabbed my arm with both hands.

Vail reached back for me, but a slash of shadow shot out and knocked him back, far past the columns that decorated the outside of the temple.

The pressure around my throat vanished, only to immediately be replaced by another as the wraiths worked together to pull me back into the darkness. I felt claws pierce my skin where Alaric was holding on, pulling on me with all his strength.

The wraiths were relentless and for a second, I thought I was going to know what it felt like to have my arm torn off.

Vail's pissed-off expression filled my view as he raced back towards us with his dagger raised. The wraiths doubled their efforts to claim me as both theirs and an agonized scream erupted from my throat when my shoulder dislocated.

The cold realization that Vail was going to be too slow slammed into me.

"Don't let go," I pleaded as I stared directly into Alaric's panicked but determined eyes.

"I won't!" Alaric swore, even as his grip on me started to slip.

An outraged roar shook me to my core, and suddenly Cali was there. She reached into the darkness behind me and yanked one of the wraiths out into the daylight.

Its screams were like nothing I'd ever heard as the sun slowly began to burn its existence away. Without another wraith to alternate grabbing me, Alaric was able to pull me free as soon as the wraith still in the shadows lost its grip on its corporeal form.

I crashed into Alaric and we both tumbled, with me landing on top of him and letting out a hiss of pain at jostling my shoulder.

We both turned our heads to where the wraith was still writhing and screaming in agony as it was burned. Every time it tried to run towards the safety of the temple, Cali would coat her hand with her own shadow magic and pull it back.

After one final shriek, the shadow dissolved into nothing.

Cali let out a pained grunt, exhausted. I immediately rushed over to her, shoving aside Vail, who was also going to check on the Furie.

"Are you okay?" I asked frantically, using my one good arm to check her for injuries.

"Fine," she said through clenched teeth. "It's hard to use my shadow magic against the wraiths, and whatever magic they're using on themselves to become Fae again makes it worse."

"Where is the prince and the other Fae?" Alaric asked, scanning the area around us as if he expected them to appear at any moment.

Which, given our shitty luck lately, seemed like a distinct possibility.

"That Fae prick threw up some kind of barrier when they reached the rangers that the prince brought with them," Cali said with a grimace. "I couldn't get through it, so I came back here to see if you needed help."

Vail sighed. "We need to deal with the remaining wraith. Even if he didn't catch our names, he'll be able to describe us, and the prince will figure it out."

Fear washed over me. Both at the idea of walking back into that temple and at the prince learning that we knew about whatever deal he had going on with the wraiths. Cali patted my knee before rising to her feet, a soothing gesture.

"I'll go with you," Cali told Vail. "You two stay here and watch over Nyx."

I wanted to protest as I watched the two of them walk back into the shadowed temple, but Vail was right. We couldn't let the prince learn that we were aware of his betrayal, and with Cali by his side, they should be able to take on the remaining wraith.

Unable to stop myself, I let out a hoarse giggle. Sharp pain barked from my shoulder at the movement and I hissed, clutching my arm tighter. I half stumbled over to a pillar, its top half broken off and lying in large chunks around us. A wheezing sound somewhere between a pained gasp and laugh bubbled out of me, each one hurt but I couldn't seem to make myself stop.

Ugh. This was going to hurt. I should have asked Cali to help me before she flew off. After lining up as best I could, I slammed my shoulder against the hard stone, popping it back into place.

The fiery agony was rapidly replaced by blessed cool relief. I leaned against the broken pillar and let myself slide to the floor as more hysterical laughter erupted out of me

"Samara?" Alaric shot me a concerned look. "Exactly how hard did you hit your head while struggling to get free?"

It took a few attempts, but finally I got out, "Vail saved my life again. He's going to be so pissed when he has time to think about it later."

CHAPTER TWENTY-SEVEN

—

Samara

Alaric groaned as he sat down at the table we'd claimed at the tavern of the outpost we'd been holed up in for the last few days.

Hybell was one of the older outposts that was close to both the Furie and Velesian borders. There were closer outposts to where we'd been in the Furie realm, but we all agreed that we wanted to put as much distance between us and the temple as possible.

Hybell wasn't on any of the trade routes, so the locals were used to keeping to themselves. Our arrival three nights ago had surprised them, but it was when Cali landed behind us, wreathed in shadows, that they'd all screamed and ran to hide in their homes while the few rangers in town called out the alarm. Not that any of us could really blame them.

I'd shot Cali a look, but she'd merely shrugged and let the shadows dissipate.

I didn't know if she'd simply forgotten to pull her shadows away before landing or if she was still shaken up from the fight with the wraiths. Knowing Cali, it could go either way, and she'd never admit to which one.

I didn't like the way Vail was looking at her these days, like he was trying to find weak spots to use when Cali inevitably lost her way.

Every time I caught him studying her, I stepped in between them. I'd cut out his fucking heart before I let him go after my friend.

"How are you still sore?" Nyx eyed Alaric in disbelief.

"Because he's too stubborn to drink from anyone," I muttered, earning me a glare from Alaric. "It's true! Everyone else topped off. I don't know why you're being so ridiculous about it."

We'd all taken turns feeding Nyx on our way to the outpost. It'd taken them hours to regain consciousness enough to be coherent after the hit they'd taken. If I closed my eyes, I could still remember the sound of their bones snapping as they collided with the wall.

Alaric had managed to control his mount enough to ride back even at our fast pace, which allowed me to carry Nyx in front of me as we raced to Hybell.

Thanks to the amount of blood we pumped into them at every break, they looked almost as good as new. I'd also forced Vail to drink from my wrist when I realized he still had broken ribs from the hit he'd taken towards the end of our fight with the wraiths.

It'd been awkward as hell, but he couldn't drink from Nyx in their condition, and neither Cali nor Alaric offered.

But Alaric's stubborn-ass had refused to drink from any of us. He hadn't been injured much in the fighting, but clearly, it'd been a while since he'd partaken in any blood because the days of travel to and from the temple had taken a lot out of him.

"I'm fine," Alaric grumbled as he reached for one of the rolls at the center of the table and stuffed it with a few slices of cheese. "Everyone good to head back today?"

Vail grunted, which I took as a yes. He'd been extra moody all morning. Maybe he was just realizing that he'd missed an opportunity to get rid of me once and for all. Instead, he'd ripped open a hole in a stone ceiling to save my life.

"Cali left this morning," I said, twisting the ring around my finger. "She's going to check on Rynn."

Rynn hadn't reached out for the last few days, which was unlike her. She knew we were going to the temple and should have been harassing me for an update. Instead, there was nothing but silence from her.

"I'm sure she's fine," Nyx said.

"Of course." I gave them a smile that I knew didn't reach my eyes.

"Let's eat and get going," Vail finally said. "We should be able to reach one of the outposts halfway back to House Harker by nightfall if we keep a decent pace."

Alaric grimaced but didn't argue. We were all more than ready to be home and safe.

Two days later, relief swept through me as the gate of House Harker was opened in front of us. Rangers called out greetings as we passed under them and hurried over to take our mounts from us.

It had taken us a little longer than we thought because of some howler activity on the way back. Thankfully, we hadn't run into them, but we'd taken shelter at an outpost earlier than we'd anticipated after leaving Hybell.

"I'm going to help get the horses sorted and then collapse into bed," Nyx announced. "Don't bother me for the next twenty-four hours unless it's an emergency."

The corner of Vail's lips twitched in the closest thing to a smile I'd seen on his face in the last week. But his expression was hard again when his eyes fell on me. We both stared at each other with thinly veiled hostility. Vail confused the hell out of me, but despite him saving my life at the temple, I still didn't come close to trusting him.

I didn't know why he'd done it, and I was pretty sure he didn't know why either. He'd already left me to die once, and I had no doubt that he'd do it again.

But even if I could convince Carmilla to get rid of Vail, it would leave House Harker in a weak position, and we couldn't afford that right now. Vail was an excellent marshal, and all the rangers looked up to him. If we kicked him out of the House, a large number of them would probably leave with him.

We needed Vail. So I'd just have to make sure to watch my back around him.

"Samara?" Kieran called out.

I looked up at the stairs that led to the main house to see Kieran waiting on the landing for me.

My lips broke out into a grin, and I took a step towards him, about to run up the stairs and throw myself into his arms before I noted the strained look on his face and halted.

"What is it, Kier?" I asked as my eyes searched his face, trying to find the answer as to what had upset him.

I got my answer a second later when Prince Draven strolled through the doorway and out into the afternoon sun to stand by Kieran's side.

I felt Alaric stiffen at my side, and out of the corner of my eye I saw Vail go predatory still as he took in the enemy who had so easily waltzed into our home. Thoughts rapidly shot through my mind as to why the prince would be here.

We'd killed all the remaining wraiths. There was no one to tell the prince that we knew he was the one betraying us.

It was possible that there was one hiding in the shadows that we missed, but if he knew what had happened, why not attack us on the way back when we were isolated from the rest of House Harker? Maybe he wanted to find out if we had told anyone else? Or maybe he was here for something completely unrelated, and this was just an unnerving coincidence?

"Prince Draven," I said smoothly and resumed my walk up the stairs to greet him. "Apologies for our greeting. We've been traveling for the past few days to check in on some outposts and reassure them that they're safe. I'm afraid we're all a little tired, and your presence here took us by surprise."

"No need to apologize, Samara." A charming smile spread across his handsome face.

His long hair was loose and fell in waves over his shoulder. In the darkness of the temple, the silver streaks in his inky black hair had almost blended in.

But out here in the sunlight, they gleamed brightly. Intense blue eyes that always reminded me of the color of lapis lazuli stones found along the riverbanks in the Velesian realm sparked with interest as they ran down my body.

He remarked with a knowing look, "Looks like you've had quite the ride."

A muscle in Kieran's jaw ticked before he smoothed out his expression. "The prince is here on official business," he said. "Carmilla asked me to escort him personally since she'll be at the Sovereign House for the foreseeable future."

"Is she okay?" I asked quickly, trying to keep the panic off my face. Did the prince target my aunt as a way to keep me compliant?

"She's fine." Draven gave Kieran a chastising look. "My mother just has a lot on her plate right now, and your aunt is helping her work through it." He offered me a sheepish smile. "Both me and my father have tried to help, but Carmilla is way more qualified."

I laughed politely, fighting back the cringe of how fake it sounded to my ears. "She's a force to be reckoned with, for sure."

Unease coursed through my body as I fought to keep my breathing even. Draven's polite, interested gaze never wavered as I frantically attempted to calm myself enough to speak rationally, causing the moment to stretch.

I cleared my throat, attempting to break the uncomfortable silence. "What brings you to House Harker, Prince Draven?"

It was Kieran who cut in, his frustration and anger slipping through his calm mask. "He's here to court you, Samara. Carmilla and Queen Velika think it's time for House Harker and the Sovereign House to be joined, and as the Heir of House Harker, it's been proposed that you should marry Prince Draven."

I snapped my jaw shut and gave the prince a bewildered look that I didn't have to fake at all as he offered me a salacious smile in return.

Well. Shit.

A Court of Bones and Sorrow

Lunaria Realms Book 2

To my absolutely rockstar editing and beta team: PollyAné, Rachel, Lisa, and Fiona.

Y'all are amazing.

CHAPTER ONE

—

Samara

THE GORGEOUS PRINCE with enchanting blue eyes wanted to marry me, but I wanted to stab him in the heart and set his corpse on fire.

He was the reason our people were dying.

The wards that had protected our outposts for over a century were failing and the wraiths were getting in, and he was the fucking reason. My memory helpfully served up the image of a discarded doll from the last outpost that had been slaughtered by the shadowy monsters. That child had died, and Prince Draven was the Moroi who had let the monsters in.

Fury burned through my veins as I desperately struggled to keep it off my face. It'd been three days since we'd learned the truth at an abandoned temple in the badlands. The wraiths were actually the Unseelie Fae. Somehow, they'd pushed their shadow magic too far and turned themselves into monsters. We'd killed three of them when the prince had left with their leader, Erendriel.

Now Prince Draven was here, standing on the wide stone stairs that led to the inside of House Harker. *My home.* I kept my gaze on him, but from my peripheral vision, I didn't see any guards with him, and the only people I'd seen since we'd walked through the gates had been ours. We'd covered our tracks well at the temple. Was his being here a coincidence?

"This wasn't exactly the response I was looking for," the prince drawled, the smile never slipping from his face even as something else flitted through his eyes. His hair fell in a straight, black curtain to his waist, the silver streaks glittering in the bright sunlight.

"Apologies, my prince." I forced the words out as I bent my knees, giving a slight bow, hoping he mistook my rapidly beating heart for excitement about him being here. Though it was possible he knew exactly what we'd been up to and was just toying with us. "I'm beyond delighted by this news; it simply caught me off guard is all. Given how things went with my first marriage"—I lowered my eyes and clutched my hands together in front of me in what I hoped was a convincing show of uncertainty—"I just never expected another offer to come my way, and certainly not one like this."

Warm fingers titled my chin up, and I barely restrained myself from slapping the proprietary touch away. Something in my expression must have given that away because Prince Draven smoothly pulled his hand back.

"I've always thought Demetri was an over-entitled fool, and the fact that he did something to drive you away only confirms that." Prince Draven's expression was charming, but there was an edge to his voice. "Would you think poorly of me if I told you I was secretly delighted when I heard the two of you were ending things? And that I might have a chance with you?"

His smile morphed into a sheepish but unrepentant grin.

Die.

Instead of voicing how I really felt, I forced the corners of my lips to curl into a sultry smirk. One that always made men think of wicked things. Out of the corner of my eye, I saw Kieran's jaw harden, but he remained a few steps behind Prince Draven. He hadn't been with us at the temple in the badlands and had no idea the prince was the traitor we'd been looking for. I hoped he knew everything I was doing right now was an act and that I wasn't actually falling for the prince's charming bullshit.

Alaric hadn't said a word but remained a steady, calming presence as he stepped from my side to be one step above me, as if to put himself between me and Prince Draven. I couldn't see Vail without turning around, but I assumed he was still somewhere behind me. Probably glowering and very obviously plotting murder.

They would all die if I failed to play this right. We didn't know what Prince Draven knew. We'd killed all the wraiths who had seen our faces . . . hopefully. But it was clear the wraiths had been using that temple regularly, which meant Erendriel had surely returned there at some point. It wasn't like he wouldn't have noticed that the three wraiths he'd left behind were no longer there.

Prince Draven's showing up here now couldn't have been a coincidence. Maybe he didn't know who had been in that temple, only suspected someone from House Harker. Maybe he did know it was us but wanted to find out what we knew and who else we had told, but two could play this game. We had questions, so many moonsdamned questions, and he had the answers.

I might not be much of a fighter, but when it came to politics and deceptive words, there was no one better than me. This was a game I knew how to play.

"My prince," I purred, "you're too kind."

"There's no need for titles, Samara." He gave me a smile that was pure sin and took another step, forcing Alaric to back up until he stood by my side. "We've known each other our entire lives—Draven is fine."

It didn't escape my attention that he could have gone to my other side instead of stepping into Alaric's space. I wasn't the only one who knew how this game worked. Draven not only survived, he flourished in the Moroi courts. I needed to be careful. He held an arm out for me, but I shook my head and waved a hand at my clothes. "I don't want to get dirt and grime all over you."

There was a very real chance that if I had to hold his arm like he wanted, I'd lose my temper and sink my claws into his flesh. That would kind of ruin the whole flirting thing.

"They're only clothes." He shrugged and kept his arm extended. "I'm more than willing to pay the price of a little dirt on me if it means you'll be by my side."

I forced myself to let out a breathy laugh and slipped my arm around his, fighting against the revulsion at the contact, and allowed him to lead us up the stairs towards the main entrance. A dull ache was already settling into my cheeks from how hard I'd been smiling. As we walked past Kieran, I brushed my free hand against his, our fingers curling together for the briefest second. Then I glanced over my shoulder at Alaric as Draven led me inside, and I found him staring at the back of the prince's head with a look of absolute hatred.

The staff and courtiers of House Harker scattered as we strolled down the hallway, Kieran's and Alaric's footsteps trailing behind us, but I couldn't tell if Vail had followed or not. I was a little surprised none of the higher-ranking nobility were here, trying to capture a moment with Prince Draven.

"I've already spoken to many of the advisors and officials," he said with a thick note of satisfaction.

"Oh?" I tilted my head towards him and arched an eyebrow.

A wry, mischievous smile played across his lips. "You were wondering why a hundred Moroi aren't lining these walls, trying to beg a favor of me so they might have a better chance of getting my mother to agree to whatever they are scheming."

"Was I?"

"You were," he said confidently.

A laugh slipped from my lips, and this time, it wasn't forced. I'd forgotten this, how easily Draven could make me laugh. Growing up, we'd spent a lot of time together because I'd visited the Sovereign House regularly. Not as much as I'd spent with Alaric, Kieran, or even Vail, but in the moments when Draven had let go of the charming prince act . . . he'd become someone real. Someone I'd liked.

And that was dangerous. I shored up my mental defenses, my smile becoming sharp like a blade.

"Kieran and I got here early this morning, so I passed the hours by pacifying them to ensure I could have your full attention. I might have implied that I would be willing to speak with them further if they left us alone this afternoon." He leaned closer to me as he spoke, and I just barely heard a growl slip from Kieran . . . and Alaric. If Draven heard them, he ignored it as he tugged me down a hallway that led to a balcony overlooking the beach.

It was one of the best views from the main house, and I was a little surprised he remembered it. He'd only been to House Harker a handful of times to my knowledge. Although I hadn't seen him much over the past couple of years—maybe he'd visited more often while I'd been living in House Laurent.

When Alaric and Kieran moved to follow us out onto the balcony, Draven turned and took a step towards them while raising his hand. "Would you mind giving us a moment alone?"

They both looked at me, and I could see the word "no" in their eyes, but further in the hallway, I saw Vail slip into one of the side rooms we used for storage. I didn't exactly love the idea of relying on Vail to come and save me if the prince tried anything, but it wasn't like we could deny the request without an explanation.

"It's fine," I told Kieran before nodding at Alaric. "Go and get cleaned up, and then we can catch up over dinner. Maybe find that book I need in the library. Kieran can probably help."

Alaric's bright eyes held mine, a completely unreadable expression on his face. "Of course." Then he spun around and stalked back down the hallway. I hoped he understood my unspoken request to fill Roth and Kieran in on what we'd learned. Kieran's jaw flexed as he looked between me and Draven before following Alaric out. Something was going on with him. He didn't know what we knew about Draven, so I didn't understand why he was so apprehensive about leaving me alone with him.

I'd make him tell me later after I thoroughly made it clear I had no interest in a marriage to the prince. Kieran was mine and I was his. Nobody would be getting between the two of us. Well . . . I wouldn't mind Roth between the two of us, but I was pretty sure they were more likely to pin *us* down with those rather useful blood ribbons of theirs. A shiver ran down my spine as I remembered what it had felt like to have the hard wood of the library table pressed against my back while Roth kneeled between my legs and lashed me with their tongue.

"Samara? You alright?" Humor sparked in the prince's blue eyes, as if he knew what I'd just been thinking about. "You look a bit . . . flushed . . ."

"I'm just glad to be home is all." I walked over to the corner of the balcony wall and leaned against it, letting my elbows rest on the sun-warmed stones. Draven hopped up onto the wall and took a seat with his back to the beach so he could fully face me. Then he lazily planted a hand on the stones and leaned on it, radiating an easygoing confidence.

If he knew we'd been the ones at the temple, he was truly skilled at hiding it. Granted, he wasn't acting like someone who was responsible for the deaths of hundreds of Moroi either.

"So," he started, "I'm guessing you have questions?"

Why are you doing this? Why betray your own people? I thought bitterly. "You've never wanted to marry," I said lightly instead. "I believe your exact words when I told you I was marrying Demetri were, *'That's unfortunate. Hopefully I have better luck at avoiding such a fate.'*"

He winced. "To be fair, I do really dislike Demetri. Always thought he was a pompous ass."

"That literally describes over half of the Moroi court." I frowned. "Probably closer to three-quarters at House Laurent. As the Heir of that House, I suppose he never really had a chance."

"I suppose that's accurate," he replied with a chuckle. "It's rather amazing when you think about it. A century ago, we were barely managing to survive, hiding behind the thick walls of the Houses. Now, we've outgrown the Fae fortresses, have dozens of thriving outposts, and we've reached the point where some of us have nothing better to do than float about the courts of the Houses and gossip while making deals with each other behind closed doors."

"It's the same in the Velesian realm," I admitted. "Although they're less about the secretive deals and more about the violently overthrowing each other."

"They're shifters." He shrugged. "Their animal nature is an intrinsic part of them."

"If you're about to go into a spiel about how much better we are than the Velesians because of their *animal nature*, I will shove you off this balcony." Despite my words, I smiled brightly at him. "Fair warning."

"Ah." He let out a raspy chuckle. "I see you've heard Marvina Laurent rant about those *filthy mongrels up north*."

"Unfortunately."

"Alas, you will have to find another reason to push me off this balcony, because I didn't mean any disrespect by that." He leaned further back, resting on both hands this time before tilting his head back. For a few seconds, I let myself admire the early afternoon sunlight reflecting off the silver strands set against his inky black hair. I'd never met anyone who had hair like his, and more than once over the years, I'd had to fight the urge to run my fingers through it.

When I drew my attention away from his hair, I found Draven smirking at me. If his hair was different, his eyes were truly unique. All Moroi had two-toned eyes, a dominant color and a secondary color that expanded whenever our emotions were heightened. Usually, those two colors were similar shades. Bright blue and green. Brown and gold. Odd colors popped up here and there, particularly with the bloodlines that ruled the Houses.

The Nacht bloodline, Draven's bloodline, all bore the same eyes, which were a deep blue, like the color of the sky just after the sun dipped below the horizon, and dark red threads ran through the blue. I'd only seen Draven truly pissed off once, and his eyes had turned almost solid bloodred, only the thinnest lines of blue had still been visible. It had been years, but the memory had stuck with me.

"Just think of how often you can stare at my hair if you marry me." He winked.

"Please." I snorted. "We both know you love being the center of attention."

I turned so I was fully facing the beach. If I hadn't seen Draven at the temple speaking with the wraiths with my own eyes, I wouldn't have believed it. Right now, he was acting so . . . normal, but he'd definitely been there. I frowned. Was it possible to control someone with blood magic?

No. I was just trying to come up with excuses because I didn't want him to be the bad guy. It was terrible enough to know a Moroi was betraying us. I didn't want it to be someone I had a history with. Someone I liked.

Brick by brick, I erected a wall around my feelings. I needed to look at this rationally and be open to any possible explanations. Including that Draven had fooled me all these years and wasn't the charming and often kind male I thought he was.

Draven slid off the wall and turned so he was leaning on the railing next to me before bumping my shoulder with his. "Something troubling you, Sam?"

I frowned up at him. "I don't think you've ever called me that."

"It's how Kieran always referred to you." He shrugged, but there was a forced casualness to it. "Given that we're considering marriage, I thought I'd try out nicknames."

My stomach tightened. I let my gaze fall back to the white, sandy beach stretching out beneath us and the impossibly blue waves rolling in and out.

"Nothing is troubling me," I lied smoothly. "I was just thinking about how much I missed this view during my marriage to Demetri. House Laurent is on the coast, but their fortress is set back further from the water. More than once, I longed to be able to hear the tides while falling asleep."

"The Sovereign House is far inland," Draven pointed out.

"Then you'll have to work quite hard to convince me to marry you and move there," I said in a breezy tone, not taking my eyes off the water even as I was acutely aware of just how close he was standing.

"Kieran can tell you just how persuasive I can be." I went still at his words before slowly turning to face him. Draven cocked his head and studied my expression. "You didn't know about us? Given how close the two of you were growing up"—he gave me a knowing smile—"and how close the two of you are *now*, I assumed he told you."

I smiled wide enough to show my fangs. "First you remind me that the Sovereign House is nowhere near my beloved ocean, and now you try to drive a wedge between me and the man I love with my entire soul. You used to be far more *charming*, prince."

Draven stared at me for a long moment, and the deep red threads that ran through his lapis blue eyes widened slightly like dark rivers of blood. I cocked my head to match his movement from earlier, and for a moment, his eyes flashed almost entirely red before he let out a deep, rumbling laugh.

"There you are." He chuckled. "With all the false politeness and flirting you greeted me with, I was worried the Samara I knew had been lost to the bullshit of Moroi House politics. I knew when I got you alone out here, the real you would bleed through."

"You're the prince," I said flatly. "You are the walking embodiment of *Moroi House politics.*"

"I am what I have to be." He nodded in acknowledgement. My brows furrowed before I caught the movement and smoothed it out. What had he meant by that?

"You didn't answer my question from earlier. About marriage," I clarified.

"Technically, you never asked a question." He shrugged a broad shoulder.

"Don't play coy with me, Drav."

He smiled at hearing the nickname I'd given him long ago. "I never wanted to marry because I'm surrounded by people all day who are only married for political gains. The Houses are all cutthroat with each other, fighting over resources and always trying to get one over on someone else. Even knowing everyone enters into these marriages willingly"—his lips twisted down—"it wasn't a future I ever wanted. So I made sure to make myself useful to the queen in other ways."

This wasn't the first time I'd heard Draven refer to his mother as "the queen." When we were having private conversations, he'd almost always refer to her as "Velika" or just "the queen." Only when he was addressing her in front of others did he call her Mother.

I'd always wondered why but had never asked because it'd felt too intrusive, and because I hadn't wanted to ruin the times when Draven had shed the charming prince persona around me.

But everything was different now, and I couldn't afford to let Draven keep any secrets.

"You mean your mother."

"Sometimes she's my mother." His frown tipped up into a smile, but I knew it was false. "Sometimes she's the Queen of Monsters."

"And was it the mother or the queen who suggested the marriage between us?" I asked carefully.

"You could do worse." He glanced at me with an amused expression. "I *am* a prince. Most people are impressed by that."

"I'm not most people."

"No," he said slowly, "you most certainly are not."

We both turned back towards the ocean and watched the tide roll in and out in companionable silence for a few minutes. I didn't know what to say or think. All I knew was I needed to find the others so we could strategize.

"If you don't mind, I'm going to go get cleaned up now and then rest for a bit." I pushed off the balcony wall and took a step back as Draven turned around to face me, leaning his back against the stones.

"Will Kieran be *resting* with you?"

"Careful." My gaze turned flinty as I told him my next lie. "I'll consider this marriage, but I will not tolerate you coming between me and Kieran or harming him in any way."

For a second, Draven's expression faltered, and something akin to sadness flashed across his face before he slipped on his charming and carefree mask once more.

"Understood."

"Good." I nodded. "I'll see you for supper then."

"Wonderful." He smiled, but it didn't reach his eyes. And I couldn't help but wonder how often he lied with his easy grins. "Enjoy your *rest*."

CHAPTER TWO

—

Samara

I'D BARELY MADE it to the hallway when Vail appeared at my side like a wraith. He didn't touch me or speak a word, just walked by my side as I made my way to the library, where I had no doubt the others were gathered. Since we'd made it out of the temple, Vail had been careful to keep some distance between us. This was the closest we'd been in the last three days.

A phantom pain flared along my shoulders where he'd clawed through my skin while I'd been lost in my bloodlust. Without meaning to, my gaze drifted to his neck and the throbbing pulse it contained. He'd saved my life by allowing me to feed from him, and I still remembered how his blood tasted.

Wild. Dark. Intoxicating.

My fangs slid a little further out of my gums. Normally, I kept them tucked away, hidden from sight unless I was feeding. It was considered a sign of weakness if you allowed your fangs to be out at all times. The Moroi were monsters but tried very hard to pretend we weren't.

I was getting tired of pretending.

A few people slowed and tried to catch my eye as I walked at a brisk pace down hallways and up multiple sets of winding stairwells, but whatever they saw in my face caused them to snap their mouths shut and quickly walk away. Vail's menacing presence by my side likely had something to do with it as well. Whatever they wanted, I'd need to deal with later, since discussing the Prince Draven situation with the others was my top priority.

The dark wood doors of the library were closed as we approached, and no sound came from inside, which meant they had the silencing spell activated. I opened one of the doors and slipped in, Vail following and closing the door behind us before leaning against it with his arms crossed.

Roth and Alaric were seated at a table, books and scrolls stretched out in front of them. Roth's hazel eyes lifted from the page for a moment as they looked me over, then they returned to reading. "Don't come near my books until you've bathed."

"I would never, Roth," I said aghast while holding a hand to my chest.

Their gaze lifted once more, the burnt orange lines that wound their way through the hazel darkening into a smolder. "Good girl." Once again, their eyes lowered to the page, but based on the way their lips curled slightly, I knew they'd heard my heart skip a beat.

My eyes slid to Alaric, who was staring at me with an indecipherable look and a clenched jaw that usually meant he was pissed. The list of things he could be upset about was long, and I had no doubt he held me responsible for most of them, but he'd just have to stew in his shitty mood for a little longer. I only had one priority right now.

Kieran was paused mid-step from where he had likely been pacing back and forth—and probably driving Roth insane—in front of the table. His blond hair was tousled as he stood there, like he'd been roughly running his hands through it. I hated the uncertainty in his eyes, waiting for me to say something.

So I closed the distance between us and cupped his face in my hands. "I don't care. About any of it. You are mine, Kier." Then I kissed him. He just stood there for a second, frozen in place before gripping me to him. His tongue slipped between my lips and grazed over a fang, causing sweet, coppery blood to light up my taste buds.

Just as he swallowed my groan, someone cleared their throat, and we reluctantly pulled apart but didn't completely release each other. Instead, I let Kieran spin me around so my back rested against his chest as he wrapped his arms around me. Then I inhaled his scent and enjoyed the last lingering drops of his blood.

Vail's eyes glittered at me from across the room, his gaze locked onto my mouth and the fangs hidden behind my lips. His throat bobbed once before he looked away.

"What did the prince say to you?" Alaric asked, drawing my attention away from Vail. "Do you think he knows it was us in the temple?"

"Unclear. I don't think so, but I acknowledge the timing of his arrival is suspicious. He could be in the same boat as us. Maybe he only knows that something happened to the wraiths and a Moroi is responsible. Or maybe he knows it was us but doesn't know that we know he is the traitor." I blew out a heavy breath, a headache already forming at all the possibilities. "This whole marriage proposal could be a cover for him to spend time here, figuring out what we know and who we might have told." Kieran's arms tightened around my waist, and I pressed further against him.

"You already married one fool," Roth drawled, not taking their eyes off the page, "I'd prefer you didn't repeat that mistake."

From Roth, that was practically a declaration of love with chocolates.

Alaric glanced at them for a long moment before shaking his head and returning his attention to me. "Did you tell him no?"

"Not exactly," I hedged. "We need to figure out what he knows and why he's really here. If I flat-out reject the proposal, he's not going to just go away. We'd be forcing his hand to take more drastic measures, assuming he knows it was us at the temple. I'll play along for now to buy us time to figure out our next move."

The muscle below Alaric's left eye ticked as he looked over my shoulder to Kieran. "And you're fine with that? Letting her *play* with the prince?"

Kieran stiffened, and the chains I'd been keeping around my temper broke. "First, nobody *lets* me do anything." I pointed a finger at him in warning. "Stay the fuck out of my relationship with Kieran. Second, you're more than welcome to walk your pretty ass down the hallway and bat your eyelashes at the prince. You'd make a beautiful consort," I crooned mockingly.

The turquoise coloring of Alaric's eyes bled into a seafoam green until they were practically glowing like blue fire. It made his already gorgeous eyes absolutely breathtaking. I smirked at him, and his fingers clenched around the book he'd been reading.

"You break my books, I break you," Roth snapped. Alaric dropped the book and leaned back in the chair, crossing his arms over his chest.

"Have your lover's spat later," Vail growled.

I gave him a cool look before slipping out of Kieran's embrace and slumping into a chair at the head of the table next to Alaric, Kieran sitting on my other side.

"Draven was a little cagey about it, but he implied it was his mother's idea for him to marry me."

Kieran nodded. "Carmilla was the one who told me about the proposed union between you and Draven. She said it was the queen's suggestion but that she thought it was a good idea and that you might be open to it."

I mulled that over. My aunt and I had discussed my future quite a bit since I'd returned to House Harker. In all our conversations, I'd made it clear I wanted to stay here and fully step into my role as Heir. I hadn't exactly said I didn't want to marry again, but I'd thought she'd understood I wasn't looking for that. Especially since the ink had barely dried on my divorce papers to Demetri. "And Draven?"

It was odd she would have agreed to such a thing without checking with me first. I needed to find a way to talk to her without the queen knowing.

Kieran's eyes darkened. "He does whatever his mother tells him to." The muscles along my jaw ached as I clenched my teeth. Whatever had happened between him and Draven had hurt him deeply. I didn't feel any jealousy towards what they'd had, only rage at someone hurting Kier. He deserved better, and I'd make Draven pay for putting that wounded look on his face.

"That was the impression I got in my conversation with him." I pursed my lips. "What if Queen Velika not only knows what her son is up to, but she's ordering him to do it?"

Vail scoffed. "You believe the Sovereign House has betrayed all of the Moroi and allied with the wraiths? After everything they've done to protect our people?"

I narrowed my eyes at Vail. His blind loyalty was almost as annoying as his dismissive attitude towards me. "That's exactly what I'm saying."

Vail started, "There has to be some other explanation—" but Kieran cut him off.

"I promise you there is nothing Draven does without the queen's knowledge." He swallowed and stared at the table. "Trust me. I know him better than any of you. If she told him to walk in here and slit all of our throats, he'd do it without hesitation."

"Why though?" Alaric frowned. "Velika is ruthless—she has to be to keep all of the Moroi Houses in line, but why would she agree to help the wraiths? What could they have offered her?"

"We need to find out," I said darkly. "Carmilla is at the Sovereign House, and Draven said she'd be there for a while."

Aggression poured off Vail, I could feel it even from where he stood across the room. "You think they're holding her against her will?"

Of course the idea that the Sovereign House was harming Carmilla would get him to immediately cast aside his devotion to them. There was no one Vail was more loyal to than my aunt.

"I don't know." My frustration with Vail left me, and dread replaced it. "Carmilla and Velika have always been close."

"Carmilla is *not* involved in this," Vail growled.

"Calm yourself. I trust my aunt more than I trust you," I snapped, and Vail's lip curled. "Carmilla would never sacrifice our people for a promise of power, certainly not from the monsters who have been hunting us for centuries, but Velika is her closest friend and she trusts her. If the queen asked her to stay in the Sovereign House as a personal favor, my aunt wouldn't closely examine the reason."

"Which means we have to be very careful," Alaric said. "Carmilla could pay the price if we make the wrong move."

Vail glanced at Kieran. "When did you and the prince leave the Sovereign House?"

"We both left five days ago but split up. He said he had something to take care of . . ." Kieran looked away, his jaw hardening. "He met me last night at the Faybell outpost, and we left first thing this morning. Only arrived here a few hours before all of you."

"So he went to the temple after splitting up with Kieran. We saw him there and left while he was busy serving up our people on a silver platter to that wraith prick." I frowned as I did the math in my head and then looked at Vail. "How did he make it there so fast? Granted, we stopped to rest a couple of times, but we still made good time, and we didn't pass Faybell until this morning."

We'd taken the quickest route to get home, but that still meant we'd had to travel north from the temple, then ride east all the way to the coast before traveling south down to House Harker. There were no roads that ran through the forests in the center of the Moroi realm. It was too dangerous.

Vail grimaced. "He must have cut through the forest. The roads are safer, but they take you out of the way. Through the wilds from the temple to Faybell is almost a direct shot, but he couldn't have ridden a horse through that. It would have been too loud and likely would have broken a leg at anything faster than a trot."

I thought back to Draven perching on the ledge, soaking in the sunshine. It was hard to picture him racing through the woods at night on foot. Then again, I never would have imagined him cutting deals with the wraiths either. Apparently, the prince was just full of surprises.

"All of you will keep working on what the wraiths—the Unseelie Fae," I corrected myself, "are up to. It seems like they want to return to their original forms and need those black stones to do it." I thought about the shiny, obsidian stone stashed safely in Roth's quarters. Our human ancestors had used the stones in the ritual to turn themselves into monsters. Into us. What made the stones so special, we had no idea—but the wraiths had been ransacking our outposts looking for them, so clearly, they were important. "We need to know more about whatever ritual they're doing and what they might have offered the Sovereign House to make them betray us all."

"And what will you be doing?" Alaric asked, even though the prick already knew what my answer would be. He just wanted me to say it out loud.

"I will be flirting with and distracting Draven." I waved a hand dismissively. "Keeping his attention off all of you and also trying to figure out more of his role in all of this."

Alaric looked at Kieran, and some unspoken conversation passed between them. Then Kieran's mouth flattened into a hard line as he glared at his best friend, who only returned the expression with a hard stare.

Yeah, I wasn't touching whatever was going on there. I had enough of my own drama to deal with.

"If our suspicions are right and the Sovereign House is really working with the wraiths, then we can't trust any of the other Houses." I rubbed my face tiredly. "Some of them will almost certainly be in on it too."

"I think we can pretty much count on it with House Corvinus," Kieran said bitterly. "They'd do anything to stay on Velika's good side."

"Tepes and Salvatore are wild cards," Alaric noted. "They could go either way, which means, for now, we definitely can't trust them."

"True. Although I doubt Salvatore would agree to ally with wraiths," I said. "Last I spoke with Dominique, she was still feeling overwhelmed at the loss of her parents and sister and also the pressures of stepping in to rule the House." The stoically beautiful, young Moroi was only twenty-five years old, one year older than me. Her elder sister had been the Heir, so Dominique had never planned on leading. Based on all the interactions I'd had with her, she hadn't been upset by that. She had loved her sister and had been happy to play a supporting role, even planned her life around it.

Then her parents and sister had been killed on a trip to visit House Tepes along with ten rangers and almost twenty other members of House Salvatore. Outside of the recent outpost attacks, it had been the deadliest wraith ambush in almost a century.

"For all we know"—a dark look passed over Kieran's face as he spoke— "Dominique arranged that attack to seize power. Maybe she's been playing everyone all this time."

I wanted to disagree, but if someone had told me two weeks ago that the Moroi Queen was plotting with our enemies, I would have laughed in their face. Nothing and no one could be trusted anymore.

"As much as it pains me to say," I said with great annoyance. "I don't think House Laurent would ally with the Sovereign House. Marvina has always hated Velika and would try to undermine the Sovereign House at any opportunity. She always did it on the sly so it wasn't super obvious, but I don't think she was faking the hostility."

To say my ex-mother-in-law and I didn't get along was an understatement. During my three-year marriage to her son, she'd bounced back and forth between indifference and hostility towards me. My leaving House Laurent and dissolving my marriage with Demetri had almost as much to do with that as it did finding Demetri in bed with someone else.

It still felt odd that merely months ago, I'd been living at House Laurent in a loveless marriage and growing more and more frustrated with my daily life. Given our current problems, my life wasn't exactly perfect now, but I was happy.

And I'd kill anyone who tried to take that away from me, even the Moroi Queen.

"What about House Devereux?" Alaric asked.

Roth let out a humorless laugh. "Trust me, they're not allied with the Sovereign House, but they won't help us either."

As a member of the Devereux line and someone who grew up in the House, Roth likely knew better than all of us. But of course Alaric wasn't willing to let it go.

"But you must know somethi—" he started.

Roth slammed their book shut and rose from the table. "I think I'm onto something with the black stones, but I need quiet to focus on it. I'll be in my quarters."

They gathered a stack of books before stalking towards the door, and I practically jumped up from my chair to dart across the room, cutting them off. Roth paused when I rested my fingers on their forearm.

"Please be careful. We all need to watch ourselves while Draven is here. Your room is far from all of ours, and there are no other living quarters around it." Roth had taken over a small room just down the hall from the library. Most of the rooms in this wing were used for storage or as guest quarters for lower-ranking members of other Houses while they were visiting. Roth liked it because it was close to the library and quiet, but it also meant they were isolated from the rest of us.

A dark red ribbon unwound from their forearm and gently brushed some of my hair back over my shoulder. "I'll be fine, Samara," Roth said in a low, even tone. "He probably has no idea who I am or what I'm doing here. I'll keep to my room and the library as much as possible and hopefully just avoid the prince altogether."

Then the ribbon wrapped around a thick section of my hair before giving it a sharp tug. "You can come check on me later though, if you're worried."

"I'll think about it," I murmured as Roth stepped around me and headed for the door. The ribbon trailed down my backside before wrapping back around their forearm as they stepped out of the library. Once the door closed, I glanced at Vail, who had stepped aside to let Roth leave. "Could you possibly get one of your rangers to keep an eye on Roth in an unobtrusive manner? They'll get cranky if they know the guard is there."

Vail's lips quirked up into the faintest hint of a smile.

"They'll get *crankier* if they know the guard is there," I amended.

"I'll take care of it."

"What now?" Kieran asked.

I plucked at the dark green fabric of my tunic and scrunched my nose. "Now we get cleaned up and pretend to go about our day as we normally would, which to be fair, with Carmilla gone, there are some House responsibilities Alaric and I need to deal with. Then we'll attend dinner tonight with the prince, where we'll find out just how good of a liar he is."

"Want me to grab you some food and meet you in your study?" Kieran offered as he rose before walking over to join me.

"Yes, please." I smiled at him, and Alaric grumbled something under his breath that I chose to ignore. Kieran shot his best friend a sharp look before planting a quick kiss on my lips and slipping out the door.

"I told him starting things with you was a bad idea." Alaric reached for a book across the table and began flipping through its pages. "Neither of you are lovestruck teenagers anymore. You're the Harker Heir, and he's just a courtier."

"Kier isn't *just* anything," I hissed.

Alaric continued like I hadn't spoken. "Sooner or later, you'll have to marry again." He raised his eyes from the book and speared me with a cruel glare. "Although I suppose for your next marriage, you'll clarify beforehand if your spouse is expected to be loyal to you or if fucking courtiers is on the table. Wouldn't want a repeat of Demetri, now would we?"

Something in me snapped. Between the tension of conversing with Draven earlier, the stress of the last few days, and the revelation that the queen we'd all sworn loyalty to had betrayed us, I was fucking done. The slim throwing dagger I kept strapped to my thigh was in my fingers within a second, and the next, I was hurtling it through the air at Alaric's face.

He slid out of the way, but not quite fast enough as a thin line of blood opened up on his cheek. Slowly, he raised his hand and touched his face, his fingers bloody as he pulled it away.

Then I spun on my heel and stalked towards the door, glancing up at Vail as I jerked it open. "Do you have something to add?"

A feral light glinted in his eyes. "Nice throw."

CHAPTER THREE

—

Alaric

I STARED at the bright red streak across my fingers. Samara threw a *knife* at me. At my fucking face. Sure, it wouldn't have killed me, only decapitation or massive trauma could take down a Moroi, but it would have fucking hurt. And if she'd taken out an eye, it would have taken me days to regrow it.

She'd never endanger your eyes, a voice in my head whispered. *She enjoys them too much.*

My cock stirred as I remembered the number of times I'd caught Samara admiring my eyes. Usually, I hated being stared at. I was well aware that many people found me attractive, but while Kieran thrived on that sort of attention, I loathed it. Yet when Samara looked at me like that . . . it definitely wasn't loathing I was feeling.

"Fuck it all," I muttered under my breath before wiping the remaining blood off my cheek, the cut already healed, since it had been little more more than a scratch. A glint of silver drew my eye, and I grabbed the dagger from where it had embedded itself in a bookcase, just barely missing a book. I smiled. If Roth ever found out about this, they'd make sure to punish Samara in a way the brat *didn't* enjoy.

I couldn't wait to let this little detail slip in the future and watch that play out.

Vail tracked me with that stony gaze of his as I stalked towards the door, dagger in hand, aching to hunt Samara down and finish our conversation because I was far from fucking done. I'd warned Kieran that this would happen. Now his heart was going to get broken because of Samara's fucking games.

It wasn't like I expected her to actually marry the prince, but Kieran would have to watch her flirt and lead him on for the next few days. Maybe even weeks or months. Who the fuck knew how long it would take us to untangle this nightmare?

And while, this time, the end result wouldn't be marriage, I knew it eventually would be, because the Heirs of Houses didn't marry lowly courtiers.

Just before I reached the doors, Vail slid into my path, blocking my exit. I was in excellent shape, but I was built on the leaner side, and the amount of running I did only emphasized that. Vail was nearly six and a half feet tall and covered in slabs of muscle. The cloak he wore over his brown leathers only made him appear larger.

I halted, eying him warily. The Marshal of House Harker had always been an enigma to me. On one hand, he was one of the most disciplined people I knew. All of the rangers who answered to him did so with respect and something close to veneration, but there was a wildness to Vail, as if his bloodlust was always simmering beneath the surface, just waiting to be let out.

I still remembered what it felt like to be hunted by a Strigoi, a Moroi who had lost all traces of their humanity. When a Strigoi looked at you, it was from cold, predatory eyes. Vail's gaze always felt the same to me.

"Is there a problem?" I asked cooly, forcing myself not to take a step back and add more distance between us, even as my fingers tightened around the dagger.

Vail's stare never dropped from my face, but his lips curled as if he was acknowledging I had the blade and found it amusing that I thought it would make any difference in a fight between us.

"I don't understand you." He cocked his head, and the pieces of bone braided into his hair and beard slid against each other like little reminders of death. "Usually, I kill things I don't understand."

"That's because you're firmly in the brawn category and less in the brain one." My fingers tightened around the dagger's handle, even as I kept a bored look on my face.

"Hmm," he hummed. "You have feelings for Samara. I'm pretty sure you're in love with her, and that scares the shit out of you, so you strike out to hurt her. You did it before when you hinted that Kieran would cheat on her, and you did it a few minutes ago by bringing up Demetri and throwing that in her face." He leaned forward, crowding my space, and I stiffened but held my ground. "I might not be as well-educated as you, but my instincts are never wrong."

"I don't have the time to tell you how wrong you are, nor would I be interested in wasting the time if I did have it." I held his unflinching gaze. "What I don't understand is why you would even bring this up now."

"Because the prince has information we need. As much as it pains me to say this, Samara's plan has merit." Vail shifted back with a grimace. "You need to be the coldhearted bastard I know you're perfectly capable of being and keep your mouth shut around Draven. Samara has enough to handle without dealing with your emotional bullshit."

"I'm sorry"—I narrowed my eyes at him—"haven't you tried to kill her *twice* in the past month?"

"My bloodlust got a little out of hand in the temple," he said flatly. "But I'm the reason she got out."

"So you don't deny *deliberately* leaving her behind when the kùsu attacked us on the road?" He didn't say anything, and I snorted. "That's what I thought. Maybe you should worry more about your own *emotional bullshit* when it comes to Samara and less about mine."

Vail eyed me for several long seconds before standing aside, and I left without another word.

Fifteen minutes later, I barged into Samara's suite. My temper had only increased on my walk over as several advisors had stopped me to fill me in on various issues that had arisen while I'd been gone. With Carmilla at the Sovereign House, Samara and I were responsible for running things. While most of the more senior advisors were capable and smart, handpicked by Carmilla over the years for their hard work and dedication, some serious problems had occurred while we'd been gone and needed to be dealt with soon. As if we didn't have enough fucking problems.

The large seating area that made up most of her living space was empty. Well . . . empty might be the wrong word. My lip curled as I took in the chaos of the room. There were stacks of books everywhere. On the low table in front of the settee. On the floor. I picked up one that had been haphazardly placed on the back of the lounge chair and flipped through it.

It was written in the Fae language, so I couldn't read it, but I was pretty sure it was the Unseelie dialect and poetry, based on how the lines were arranged. Was this what Samara did in her free time? Read poetry in a dead language?

"Careful, Alaric." Samara breezed into the room with nothing but a towel wrapped around her. "If you keep frowning like that, your face might get stuck, and think of how sad all the lovely, young courtiers would feel if they were robbed of your beauty."

I gritted my teeth. I knew exactly who she was talking about. There was a group of courtiers who regularly visited from Kieran's old House—Corvinus —mostly comprised of young, female Moroi who were on the hunt for a good marriage. There was nothing impressive about my bloodline, but my parents had served Carmilla as her top advisors, as I now did. Between this and my appearance, several courtiers from that group had set their eyes on me.

"Sounds like that would be to my benefit, so I think I'll keep the sneer, if it's all the same to you." I tossed the book back down and crossed my arms.

"Suit yourself." She shrugged and started pawing through the piles of clothes that, like the books, were scattered everywhere. Samara frowned as she tossed aside dress after dress before finally holding up a rich mulberry-purple one triumphantly.

"If you just put your clothes away like a normal person, you wouldn't have to go on a scavenger hunt for the ones you want," I said dryly.

Samara just rolled her eyes and walked back towards the wide-open double doors that led to her bedroom and bathing chamber. My eyes instantly fell to her ass and the way it shifted beneath the thin fabric. Why did that towel have to be so short?

"I'm sorry, why are you here? Generally, when someone throws a knife at your face, that's a sign that maybe they don't want to be in your company."

"I'm here because I wasn't finished with our conversation when you pulled that stunt," I ground out and looked away from that treacherous towel. "Thanks for that, by the way."

"Don't be an asshole and you won't get knives to the face," she said in a breezy tone as I followed her into the bedroom. A large bed with a midnight black headboard and deep red covers took up most of the space. My mind instantly went to Samara in those sheets. I suspected she slept naked or in some type of extremely indecent nightgown. "Alaric?"

I blinked slowly, dragging my gaze away from the bed to where Samara was standing next to it, holding the dress in one hand and dangling undergarments from the other. Suddenly, the only thing I could hear was the rapid pounding of my heart, then twin flashes of pain erupted from my gums as my fangs extended. Throughout it all, my expression remained stoic and slightly annoyed. I wasn't as good at rotating through different masks as Kieran, but I was excellent at this one.

Samara arched one perfect, dark eyebrow. Okay, maybe I was less than perfect at maintaining this mask. Why did she have to continue to be the absolute worst?

"What?" I bit out.

She let out a husky laugh, and the way my dick reacted, one would have thought she'd reached her hand into my pants and stroked it. Fuck. That thought was not helping.

"You just gonna stand there and scowl while I get dressed?" She twirled the black undergarments around her finger. "Because that's not normally the reaction people have when I'm about to get naked in front of them."

"Who exactly are you getting naked in front of?" The sharp words came out before I could stop them.

"Currently?" She tilted her head back and looked up at the ceiling, like she had to think hard about the answer.

"Samara," I growled.

"Alaric," she mockingly growled back as her gaze fell to me again. Maybe Vail would kill her and solve all my problems? When I continued to glower at her, she sighed. "Only Kier and Roth. Despite what you think of me, I do actually care quite a great deal about the two of them, and the three of us have discussed the dynamics of our relationships. Not that our business is any of your concern."

"Kieran is my best friend, and your involvement with him will not end well," I argued, even as I ignored the relief I felt that she wasn't seeing anyone else.

Her lips curled into that flirty grin that I couldn't decide if I adored or hated. "I promise you that I've given Kier more than one *happy* ending."

Argh.

"I'm being serious, Samara." My fingers tightened into fists at my sides. "If you would just think rationally about this—"

"Stop." Black streaks darkened her purple eyes until they were depthless voids. I shifted uneasily. It hadn't escaped my notice that she hadn't put her fangs away since we'd left the temple, and her eyes had been shifting between the colors more than usual. These were all signs that pointed to a Moroi's bloodlust being dangerously close to the surface.

As a Harker, Samara had better control over hers than most of us. It was unlikely she'd ever fully lose control and become a Strigoi. Growing up, she would regularly slip in and out of her bloodlust as if it had been nothing. Even though she hadn't put her fangs away the last few days, she hadn't been acting any differently. Just the same old, frustrating Samara who had always slipped under my skin like no other.

But despite that fact, seeing her like this made me tense. My cousin had turned Strigoi, and I still had nightmares about it.

She squeezed her eyes shut and inhaled several deep breaths. When they opened a few seconds later, they were back to their startling purple that always reminded me of the night sky. They were perfectly stunning, just like the rest of her. Not that I'd ever tell her that. Samara's ego was big enough on its own. Plus, that would be admitting to the attraction I felt towards her every day.

And that would absolutely not be happening.

"I'm done with this conversation," she announced. "And I'll be getting dressed now. Leave."

"We're not done with this conversation, and you can get dressed in there." I pointed to the bathing chambers.

"It's my room, and I'll get dressed wherever the fuck I want." She raised her chin in challenge.

"Not leaving." I crossed my arms. Knowing Samara, she would deliberately take an hour to get dressed just to avoid having this conversation. She'd already stormed away from me once, I wasn't letting her get away again.

Something wicked danced in her eyes, then she tossed the clothes onto the bed and whipped the towel off before I could object.

Fuck. I kept my eyes locked on hers. For three seconds. Three *excruciatingly* long seconds.

My gaze dropped, and I was pretty sure my heart stopped with it. I'd seen Samara naked before, but it'd been steamy and she'd been lying down at the edge of the pool . . . with Kieran's head between her legs. There had been a lot to process, and I'd stormed out before either of them had noticed just how hard my cock had grown at the sight of them.

Well, Kieran had spotted that fun fact. Samara might be oblivious to my frustrating interest in her, but he wasn't, and he absolutely loved to push me about it, because I was apparently surrounded by assholes.

I should have looked away, or better yet, I should have fucking left the room. Instead, I stood there and drank in every delicious inch of her. Samara was nothing but enticing curves. She had the most glorious chest to ever exist resting above the soft curve of her stomach and thick thighs that would feel amazing wrapped around my head. I couldn't see her ass from this angle, but I knew it would be plump, round, and something that would beg me to grip it. Hard.

"Have you looked your fill?" she drawled. "Because I really need to get dressed so I can get some work done."

I snapped my eyes back up, my jaw tightening at the amusement I saw written all over her face. She was the one who'd been naked in front of me, and yet I was the one blushing like crazy.

"I hate you," I said flatly before turning around and stalking towards the door, Samara's deep laugh following me out.

"Good talk, Alaric!"

CHAPTER FOUR

—

Kieran

I SURVEYED the plate resting on the worn, wooden, raised table at the center of the main kitchen. Leora—the Moroi in charge of the kitchen staff at House Harker and the best baker in existence—was shooting amused glances at me while she was baking some honey biscuits. They were a common snack, since they required few ingredients to make and honey was one thing we had in abundance. Almost all of our sweets were honey-something. Luckily for me, I loved honey and never got tired of it. Samara was the same, which was why half the plate was made up of freshly baked biscuits.

"Are you waiting for them to speak some words of wisdom to you?" Leora mused. "I admit, I am rather talented, but even my skills have limits."

"Perhaps I'm debating if I want to bring them to Samara or if I simply want to hoard these all to myself?" I grinned at the older Moroi woman who had been a staple at House Harker for as long as I could remember.

She rolled her eyes and plucked two more biscuits off the tray before placing them on the plate. "There." She made a shooing motion. "Now out with you so I can get back to work. You're distracting me."

"Leora, my wondrous beauty." I gave her my best smile that usually resulted in panties being thrown in my direction. "You know I would marry you in a heartbeat if you would only ask."

"You're just as ridiculous now as you were when you first arrived." She picked up the plate and thrust it into my hands, her light brown eyes glittering with mirth. "And if Calus hears you talking like that, he'll wallop you good."

I laughed and kissed her cheek. "We can't have that. Tell him I'll stop by later this week. It's been a while since we chatted."

Grabbing the food, I beat a hasty retreat. I knew from experience that Leora would go from teasing and laughing to prying into my personal life if I stayed any longer. Her husband, Calus, was the same way. The two of them were fourth-generation Moroi, like Carmilla, and were considerably older than the mid-fifties they appeared to be. We'd celebrated Calus' 130th birthday over the winter, and Leora was only a few years behind him.

When I'd first come to House Harker as a jaded fourteen-year-old, they had instantly taken me under their wings. Everything was so different here than House Corvinus. My parents were high-ranking advisors there, and they'd viewed me and my siblings as nothing more than pawns in their scheming. Growing up, I'd learned quickly to control every single facial expression and measure every word carefully.

It was common for Houses to trade courtiers amongst themselves. Usually the children of people like my parents or the lower-ranking family members of whatever bloodline ruled the House. Everyone knew these courtiers were loyal to their birth Houses, and yet the practice continued, because there was always the chance you could sway their allegiance and then get information about the inner workings of the House they'd come from.

Our survival depended on the Moroi Houses working together, both for a solid defense against the wraiths and other monsters, and for resources like the gems that powered our wards. Every House controlled at least one unique resource, and the negotiations between them were ongoing and tedious. Samara loved dealing with all that bullshit. Alaric liked it too.

But that wasn't where my skills lay. I was excellent at getting people to like me, and when people liked you . . . they talked to you. Carmilla had never asked me to spy on other Houses or collect information for her benefit. The first few years here, I'd been practically holding my breath, waiting for her to make the request, the demand.

It had never come.

And that was why my loyalty would always be to this House. Carmilla wanted her people to be happy, and so did Samara. Both of them could be cunning and underhanded at times when it came to dealing with the other Houses—there was simply no surviving in this world without a little bit of that —but Carmilla knew the names of every single person who worked in this House, down to the lowliest maid. Samara worshiped her aunt and was the same.

House Harker was home to me.

I smiled at some of the servants as they walked by, heads bent as they whispered to each other and giggled, but then my pleasant mood vanished as I heard Draven's name. I'd been trying very hard not to think about him for the last twenty minutes. Not exactly a long-term plan, given his reason for being here and what Samara and the others had discovered about him, but not thinking about Prince Draven had been my go-to strategy for almost a year now.

As if summoned by the brief slip of my thoughts, the dark-haired prince appeared at my side and snatched a biscuit off the plate.

"There you are." He broke a piece off the sweet pastry and popped it into his mouth, then his eyes closed as he savored the flavor, and I couldn't stop my gaze from lingering on his strong jawline, remembering the number of times I had run my tongue across it before grazing his neck with my fangs. I'd never drank from him, nor him from me—that'd been one of the few lines we hadn't crossed in our time together.

I snapped my gaze up and clenched my jaw when his eyes opened and he caught me looking at him. "These aren't for you." Then I quickened my pace down the hallway, smiling tightly at others who passed us as they tried to subtly check out the prince before looking at me curiously. I knew what they were thinking. Why was the Moroi Prince talking to a simple courtier who held no sway in this House, especially when he'd been dismissive of the higher-ranking advisors all morning?

I gritted my teeth. As much as I loved collecting gossip, I didn't like to be the source of it.

"So touchy." He chuckled darkly. "At least you're speaking to me now. It was quite impressive how you managed to avoid me while you were at the Sovereign House and then not speak to me on the entire ride here . . . I recall you being a bit more vocal in our interactions, especially that one time—"

A growl ripped from my throat as I grabbed Draven by the arm and dragged him into an empty meeting room. Then I shoved him away from me and slammed the door behind us, dropping the plate onto the table, resisting the urge to throw it at him. He smirked at me like he knew exactly what I was thinking.

"It's been fun, but I'm bored now," I said coldly, repeating the words he'd said to me. "Also, watch how you speak to me in the future, courtier."

The smirk slid off his face as he tossed the half-eaten biscuit onto the table before letting out a bone-weary sigh. "I had to say that, Kier. The wrong people were noticing how much time I was spending with you, and it was getting dangerous for the both of us."

I flinched inwardly at hearing him call me that. Until Draven, only Sam had ever called me Kier. Hearing the nickname from his lips again caused all the confusing emotions to swirl up inside until I ruthlessly shoved them back down.

"I'm assuming by 'the wrong people,' you mean the queen?" I asked flatly. The muscles along his jawline flexed, but he said nothing. I snorted and shook my head. Queen Velika was a puzzle to me. On the surface, she appeared to be a fair and just ruler who loved her son, although she was occasionally frustrated by his disinterest in helping her rule. But during my time with Draven, I knew there was more to her, something darker.

There was nothing specific I could point to, nothing I'd witnessed with my own eyes, but Draven was a different person around her. It was subtle, but no one was better than me at reading body language. He obeyed her no matter what, but it wasn't out of love. If I didn't know better, I'd say he was frightened of her. And every once in a while, I'd catch her looking at him in a way that reminded me of a predator circling wounded prey.

It was why I had probably been the least surprised when Samara had theorized it was actually Queen Velika who was allied with the wraiths and Draven was doing her bidding. What I'd never understood, though, was why she had such a hold over her son.

Draven's dark eyes met mine. "What have you told Samara?"

"Nothing yet." I waved a hand at the plate I'd set aside. "But I'll be telling her *everything* soon enough."

"She was always the one you wanted." He shrugged a shoulder casually, as if our time together had meant nothing to him. "So I can't say I'm surprised."

"Fuck you, Draven," I snarled. "You weren't a fucking backup plan to me. I fucking—" The words died in my throat, and I took a deep breath. "My feelings towards you were genuine and unique to what we shared. I never hid what I felt about Samara from you. I'm perfectly capable of loving two people at once."

He sucked in a breath, and for a moment, I swore his heart stopped beating.

"You shouldn't have ever loved me." The bloodred threads in his eyes expanded as he pondered me like I was a creature he couldn't understand. "I told you *not* to love me."

"That's not how fucking feelings work, Drav!" I shoved my hands against his chest, and he staggered back a step. "If you hurt Sam, I swear to the gods, I'll kill you."

"I don't *want* to hurt her," he bit out.

"But you will if you're ordered to," I scoffed bitterly.

"Please, Kier," he pleaded. Usually, Draven soaked up attention with his tall frame and broad build, but now, he hunched his shoulders, and there was a desperation to his expression I'd never seen before. I barely managed to stop myself from wrapping my arms around him and telling him that we'd figure it out. That he just had to tell us what the fuck was going on. But I held it all back because, despite the churning feelings burning inside my chest, Draven couldn't be trusted.

"You don't understand what's at stake," he rasped. "Samara is trapped in this, but you don't have to be. Go visit your friends in the Velesian realm. Just leave the Moroi realm."

The urge to hug him instantly turned into a desire to strangle him. Did he seriously think I would leave Samara behind to face all of this on her own?

I picked the plate up off the table. "I don't abandon those I love. Maybe that's something you should consider in the future."

His expression shuttered, but he didn't say anything as I opened the door and left, something inside my soul cracking when he didn't stop me.

SAMARA WAS ALREADY SEATED behind her desk in the cozy little study she'd reclaimed as her own upon returning to House Harker. There were larger rooms available in the wing where Carmilla's spacious study was located—as the Heir, Samara could have kicked out any of the advisors and set up in one of those—but she'd always loved this space the most.

Before she'd left for Drudonia, she'd study here for hours. I'd always keep her company while she buried herself in books, scrolls, maps, whatever she could get her hands on. Even Alaric had joined us sometimes, although that had always devolved into the two of them taking verbal—and sometimes physical—swipes at each other. I let out an amused breath. Nothing had changed there.

Dark purple eyes lifted from the page they'd been reading and latched onto the plate. "Freshly baked honey biscuits?" she asked hopefully.

"Leora just made them." I smirked and walked over to the small seating area I'd crammed into the space. The outer wall was mostly windows, and the other three were lined with shelves. Samara hadn't been keen on adding more furniture to the already small space, but I'd insisted. Her desk and two chairs were on one half of the room, and I'd brought in two more chairs— with far comfier cushions—and tucked them away in the corner next to a window.

I placed the plate onto the table in between them and sank into one of the chairs. "If you want one, you're going to have to come over here though." Her brows furrowed as she frowned at all the papers scattered across her desk. "I promise whatever you're working on will still be there after you've taken a break and eaten something."

She let out an exaggerated sigh but rose to join me. I smiled to myself. Samara was always worried about Roth getting caught up in whatever they were working on and forgetting to eat or otherwise care for themself, but she was the same way. My lovely Samara had a bad habit of putting everyone's needs before her own.

Luckily, she had me, and I had no problem putting her needs before everyone else's.

"This is heaven," she groaned around a mouthful of biscuit, her hair still damp and clinging to the deep purple dress she wore. The color almost perfectly matched her eyes and made her golden brown skin practically glow. I was imagining peeling it off her later when she asked the question I'd been dreading. "So what's the deal with you and Draven?"

A cool dread solidified in the pit of my stomach as I rose to close the door and activate the silencing spell. Samara drew her legs up beneath her and settled further back into her chair as I took a seat again, her expression patient and supportive.

"It was hard when you left for House Laurent," I started. "It's not like I didn't know you'd be marrying Demetri, but when we were growing up, that was always something distant in the future. Even when you went to study at Drudonia, you'd still come back often, but when you left . . ." I swallowed. "It felt like someone had ripped out a piece of my soul, and I didn't know how to fix that."

Her eyes darkened, and her voice was rough as she spoke. "I'm so sorry, Kier."

I shrugged and forced my lips to curve into a small smile. "It's not your fault. Like I said, it's not like I didn't know what was coming."

"Still, I shouldn't have gone through with that marriage." She twisted her hands in her lap as she stared at them with an unseeing gaze. "I was so obsessed with doing what I thought was the right thing for House Harker. After my parents—" Her voice caught on the last word, and my heart clenched.

She never spoke about her parents, and I never pushed her about it. Everyone knew how the previous rulers of House Harker had died. They'd been gone for years before I'd come to live here, and whenever their names were mentioned around Samara, I could practically watch the emotion drain from her face. Everyone seemed to think she had handled the loss of her parents well and had rallied to support House Harker. They praised her as if she were the perfect example of everything a House Heir should be.

I didn't understand how no one could see how, over a decade later, Samara was still devastated by the death of her parents. Her grief was a never-ending well that she did her best to keep covered. I didn't know how to help with that because I'd never lost anyone I'd cared about as deeply as Samara did her parents. The only person I'd ever loved was her.

And Draven.

"I probably should have brought us a bottle of wine in addition to the biscuits." I blew out a deep breath, and Samara chuckled wryly.

"Yeah . . . or maybe some shots of whatever liquor Leora has hidden away in the bottom cupboard of the storage room." Her lips trembled for a second before she caught it and pursed them together. "After my parents died, I felt like I had to do everything perfectly. Everyone was counting on me to uphold their legacy. The alliance with House Laurent was my way of furthering House Harker's power." She shook her head ruefully. "And it was a complete failure."

"Not your fault," I said sharply. "Demetri is a piece of shit, and that House never deserved you. I should have told you back then how much I loved you and begged you to stay."

I'd been too scared that she would acknowledge that she felt the same . . . and then go on to marry Demetri anyway. Because that was what had been expected of her, and she never would have let her House—or more importantly, her aunt—down.

Samara raised her gaze from her hands to look at me and gave me a soft, genuine smile. "I'm sad we wasted so many years." Then her eyes became hard and possessive. "You're mine, Kier, and I'll never leave you again."

"You have no idea how much I want to fuck you right now," I growled as my cock thickened at her words and the truth I felt behind them.

"You can." She winked. "*After* you tell me about Draven."

I sighed and slouched in the chair. "Being at House Harker was hard after you left. So I started traveling even more than normal. Checking in with the outposts, visiting some of the other Houses and also the Sovereign House. During one of those visits, the queen was throwing one of those ridiculous masquerades she loves."

"They're such a waste of resources." Samara's mouth twisted in distaste. "I've brought it up to Carmilla before, hoping that maybe because she's Velika's friend, she could get the queen to tone them down or at least do them less often, but apparently, Velika feels very strongly that it's important we build up and maintain a Moroi culture."

"A culture that only the elite can take part in," I pointed out, and Samara scrunched her nose as she made a noise of agreement. "I was leaning against the wall, watching all those gathered engage in all kinds of wild debauchery, when Draven suddenly appeared next to me. Even with the mask on, I knew it was him."

"He does have a certain . . . presence about him," Samara admitted.

I nodded. "That he does. I didn't know what to do or say to him. We'd been in the same room before, but he'd never directly spoken to me. He just turned to me with a wicked grin and said, 'So, are you having fun collecting all sorts of gossip and potential blackmail material, Kieran?'" I let out a soft chuckle. "I was so fucking surprised not only that he was speaking to me but that he knew my name, that I almost dropped my wineglass."

"He didn't leave my side for the entire party. Other guests would come up and ask him to dance or join them in conversation, and he just politely declined. We spent the entire time pointing out who was fucking who, which House was trying to screw over another one on a trade deal, and any other saucy tidbit we could think of." I chewed on my bottom lip for a moment. "It was the first time I forgot about my longing for you and just . . . enjoyed life."

Samara leaned forward and stretched her arms out so she could clasp my hands in hers. "I'm glad, Kier. Whatever else Draven has done and whatever the future holds, I'm glad he at least gave you that happiness, if only for a night."

"Oh, there were *many* nights he gave me *happiness*." I arched an eyebrow as my lips curved into a satisfied smile. Samara threw her head back and released a throaty laugh as she leaned back in her chair, and something inside me eased at hearing that laugh. I'd been dreading this conversation, not only because talking about it was painful, but I'd been worried Samara wouldn't be comfortable discussing one of my past lovers.

Our relationship still felt so new and fragile that I didn't want to do anything to jeopardize it, but I never should have doubted Sam. She and Alaric were my best friends and had always supported me through anything without judgment.

Okay, well, Alaric could be a judgey bastard, but Sam never was, and eventually, Alaric would get over his opinion of me and Sam being in a relationship. I had a few ideas to help with that and get him to admit what his real problem was . . .

"So what happened?" she asked gently after sitting upright in her chair once more. "Because I could feel the tension between you two earlier."

"For almost a year, I made regular visits to the Sovereign House." I rubbed my face in a vain attempt to make the words come out easier. "Sometimes, he would show up at the outposts I was staying at. I don't know how he did it, but somehow, he'd get into my room without anyone seeing him. We talked. He'd tell me about his life, all the things no one saw, and I talked about mine. What it was like growing up at House Corvinus and moving here. It was nice," I confessed. "Talking to him was just . . . easy. Having someone on the outside of it all to talk to about everything. I think he felt the same."

Samara nodded in understanding. "My relationship with Draven prior to all of this was different than yours, and I wouldn't exactly say we were friends." She paused and thought about it a little more. "No, that's not right—we were definitely friends. We never spoke outside of times when I would visit the Sovereign House or the few times he would come to House Harker, never traded messages via striker or anything like that, but anytime we were in the same place, he would just appear like magic. It didn't matter if we hadn't seen each other in months or even years. The camaraderie was there, and falling into conversation with him always felt so natural."

"You should know . . ." I inhaled a deep breath. "I talked about you with him. About how I felt about you. The way we flirted with each other nonstop growing up. How you marrying Demetri devastated me. He knows all of that." Part of me wondered if that'd been what he'd wanted all along. That everything between us had been a lie and he'd just wanted information on Samara.

But just like I'd been too scared to ask Samara to stay before she'd left for

House Laurent, I hadn't been able to bring myself to confront Draven about it. Instead, I'd just let the humiliating thought fester in the back of my mind.

"I know what you're thinking." Samara narrowed her eyes at me. "That he was just using you for information."

"Your perceptiveness is annoying," I said wryly as guilt nipped at me. I should never have spoken to him.

"I'll repeat what I said earlier," she said, ignoring my comment. "I'm glad you had someone to talk to about all of this, because we both know Alaric would have been a prick about it." Then her eyes darkened, and something predatory looked out. "But if it turns out Draven *was* using you that whole time—which I don't think he was, but I could be wrong—I'll make him fucking regret it."

She would. I had absolutely no doubt about it. "I think we have bigger problems to worry about, but I appreciate the sentiment." My throat tightened around the words.

She sniffed. "You'll *always* be a priority to me, Kier."

I smiled widely at her. "And again, I really want to fuck you right now."

"Of course you do. I'm amazing." She waved a hand towards me, gesturing for me to continue. "How does this story end?"

"We were discreet about our relationship, but I did occasionally speak to him at parties held at the Sovereign House. Six months ago, I walked up to him and greeted him casually . . . too casually, considering he was a prince and I was just . . . me."

Samara's eyes flared in anger as I spoke about myself in such a dismissive manner, but she didn't interrupt, which I was grateful for. I hadn't told anyone about me and Draven, not even Alaric. He would have berated me for being so foolish to get involved with the Moroi Prince in such a way. More importantly, Alaric traveled in different circles than me. As one of Carmilla's personal advisors, there had been a very real chance that he would have been in the same room as Draven one day, seated at the same table, and Alaric had a problem keeping his fucking mouth shut. The last thing I needed was him getting into a verbal sparring match with Draven in front of the queen.

I closed my eyes as I pushed the words out. The ones that had cut a deep wound in my already scarred heart. "He looked at me with this cool, almost bored expression and said, '*It's been fun, but I'm bored now. Also, watch how you speak to me in the future, courtier.*' And then he just walked off to stand by his mother's side. He didn't look at me, but she did." My jaw tightened as I remembered the cruel, arrogant smile that had flashed across her face that night. "She must have learned about our relationship and didn't approve. So Draven ended it. Maybe he already had all the information he wanted . . . I don't know."

Samara stared out the window, her brows slightly creased. I knew that look.

She was cycling through scenarios in her head, analyzing each possibility before moving on to the next. I also knew from experience that it was best to let her sort through her thoughts, so I snagged a biscuit off the plate and ate it slowly, savoring each sweet bite.

"We need to determine what exactly the deal is between Draven and his mother," she said thoughtfully. "Considering what happened between the two of you and the little hints I've seen, I think there is nothing but hate between them, but he clearly serves her. We need to know why."

"Do you want to find this out because it will actually help us, or so that I feel like less of a fool for getting involved with him in the first place?" I tossed the rest of my biscuit back onto the table. "Because I'm an adult, Sam. It pains me that I got played and that I let my feelings go too far. That I thought I might be in—" I yanked that word from my throat before it could slip past my lips and stomped on it. Then I inhaled and let out a deep breath. "Draven and I are in the past. I just wanted you to know because I will never hide anything from you, and because he will no doubt wield my past with him against us."

"He already tried to," she admitted, still staring out the window, half-lost in her thoughts. I bit my lip, toying with the question I wanted to ask.

"If things were different . . ." I cleared my throat. "If you didn't know Draven was mixed up with the wraiths and he came here to ask you to consider marrying him . . . would you?"

Samara's head whipped towards me, and she scowled before unwinding herself from the chair and closing the distance between us. My arms slipped around her as she slid onto my lap, and her fingers trailed up my chest before wrapping around my throat and squeezing lightly. I released a breathy exhale at the feeling of her nails digging into my skin.

"No, I would not consider marrying him," she said evenly, and I believed her. Maybe it made me the biggest fool in the world, but I had no doubt she meant every word. "I do admit that I've always found him attractive and . . . intriguing. Perhaps I would have let him into my bed." Her lips curved into a sinful grin. "*Our* bed. But I would have spoken to you about it first, and if you weren't okay with it, then I wouldn't have taken things any further with him."

Moonsdamn it all, but my cock hardened at the thought of Samara and Draven in bed together. With me. Without me. Either was hot. Even with everything he had done to me and what we knew about him now, my body still reacted to Draven completely of its own accord, the same way it reacted to Samara. The thought of both of them together?

Samara released my neck and let out a husky laugh. "Feeling excited, Kier?"

"You are all kinds of wicked." I shook my head ruefully, even as I smiled at her.

She shifted until her legs were dangling off the side of the chair, and she nuzzled my neck. "Dinner tonight is going to be intense." Warm, full lips brushed against my throat, and I let one of my hands slip down to her thigh, slipping underneath the high slit of her dress. "We should take this opportunity to blow off some steam," she murmured.

"Excellent idea." My fingers drifted upward, and Samara spread her legs a little further apart, causing a deep chuckle to rumble out of me. "Is there somewhere in particular you want my fingers to be?"

She nipped my neck before raising her head and glaring at me. "Don't even think of making me beg. Between Draven and Alaric, I've had more than enough frustration today."

"Oh?" Her breath hitched as my fingers just barely passed over her undergarments. So wet already. I wanted to rip them aside and feel the hot slickness beneath them but couldn't resist teasing her a little. "And what did our dear Alaric do to piss you off this time?"

I let my fingers brush harder against the soaked fabric, and Samara moaned, nestling further into me.

"The same as he always does," she said through panted breaths. "That me and you were a bad idea and that he knew it would end like this. I informed him that nothing had changed and that you were still mine and that he should stay out of our fucking business. I might have thrown a dagger at him to punctuate the point."

"The two of you are ridiculous." I slipped my fingers beneath the fabric, and we both groaned at the dripping heat I found. "I love how wet you get for me," I growled. "Even before I touch you."

"Show me how much." She arched her back, and I leaned down to capture her mouth with mine. Then I slowly pushed two fingers inside her while I continued to circle her clit with my thumb. Samara whimpered, and I smiled against her lips, loving the sounds she made when I was inside her. Maybe I could get some new ones out of her this time . . .

"I have another secret to tell you," I whispered. Alaric would probably punch me for this later, but I knew my friend. His way of handling emotions, particularly confusing ones, was to lash out. I'd given him the time he needed to come to terms with how he really felt about Sam, but he was still stubbornly fighting it. He'd never even admitted to me how much he wanted her. But I'd noticed every heated glance he sent her way when she wasn't looking and the way his heart had practically stopped beating when he'd walked in on us at the hot springs weeks before. Enough was enough.

"What?" Sam panted.

"He's so pissed off all the time"—I thrust my fingers in deep, and her hips bucked in demand—"because he wishes it were *his* fingers doing this to you right now."

Dark eyelashes fluttered as Sam took in my words. "He *hates* me."

"He doesn't." I pumped my fingers in and out, loving the way her pussy clenched around me. "He might wish he did sometimes."

"You can't tell me things like that when you're—" Her words choked off as I pushed down on her clit and she unraveled. "Fuck!"

I let out a dark laugh as she trembled in my lap before pulling my fingers out and licking them clean. "Delicious," I murmured. Sam watched every swipe of my tongue with dark, hungry eyes. "We'll continue this discussion later when you're a little less distracted. Up you go." I maneuvered her body until she was straddling me with her back to my chest. "I might have gotten these chairs with a certain position in mind."

"Of course you did." She laughed in a low, husky tone.

"What can I say?" I teased as I unlaced my pants and pulled my cock free. "Every time I see a piece of furniture, I think about the best way to fuck you on it."

I could feel her thighs quivering as my cock pushed against her entrance, and I felt a desperate need to be buried inside her. Originally, my plan had been to fuck her slow and tease her a bit, but I needed at least the first round to be hard and fast. Just as I was about to thrust all the way in, the door swung open. Shit. I'd forgotten to lock it.

Samara went completely still in my grip as Alaric's pissed off expression fell on the both of us.

CHAPTER FIVE

—

Samara

"WHAT THE FUCK is with you two and not understanding how locks work?" Alaric slammed the door shut, his eyes blazing with anger as his gaze roamed down our bodies . . . and compromising positions.

But there was desire there too.

How had I never noticed that before? I mean, he'd looked at me earlier in my bedroom, but I had been standing there naked, taunting him, and his expression had mostly remained cold and detached. The only thing I'd picked up on was annoyance at my antics. However, that was definitely *not* what I was seeing in his eyes now.

He wanted me. Desperately.

A heady anticipation raced through me. Since returning to House Harker, I'd had more than one lust-filled thought about Alaric, but given that we had to work together and my apparently false assumption that he was in no way attracted to me, I'd done my best to ignore those feelings.

Every time I'd felt Alaric's body pushed against mine when we'd rode together or practiced archery, my core had instantly tightened and my breath had hitched slightly.

My dress was twisted around a bit, but it was still covering all the important bits, and Kieran's hand was wrapped around his cock where he'd been teasing my entrance. I could feel the hot slickness running down my thighs, my anticipation high over him sliding into me. Alaric couldn't see any of this, but given the way I was straddling Kieran, it was pretty obvious what we'd been about to do.

"You're the one who didn't knock," Kieran drawled. "One might think you enjoy walking in on us like this. Now why might that be?"

Alaric's nostrils flared, and the light green of his eyes was completely swallowed by turquoise as his gaze dropped to the apex of my thighs. My legs trembled, and I leaned further back against Kieran, which caused his cock to slide into me a little.

I froze, even as a moan slipped from my lips. Alaric's gaze dropped, as if he could see past my dress to where Kieran's cock was pushing inside me, but he made no move to come closer to us or leave the room.

"All this time," I breathed out, "I thought you hated me, or at best, barely tolerated my existence."

Silence stretched between us for what felt like an eternity. For once, Kieran kept his mouth shut, as if he knew this moment had to play out at its own pace. Alaric's throat bobbed as he swallowed. "I've always tried very hard to hate you."

"And have you succeeded?"

More silence. With a slow, deliberate movement, Alaric reached out and turned the lock on the door with a loud *click*. It felt like every one of my nerves was on fire, and based on how tense Kieran was beneath me, I knew he felt the same. Then Alaric walked over to us and trailed his fingers along my jawline before dipping under my chin to tilt my head back, forcing me to look up at him.

I had to shift a little further back, which caused another inch of Kieran's cock to slide in. Both of us let out a strangled gasp as a close-lipped smile spread across Alaric's face. The bastard knew exactly what he was doing.

"I've been frustrated with you. Annoyed by your antics. Occasionally wanted to strangle you." His bright, oceanic blue eyes darkened as his fingers slid down and gripped my throat just this side of painful. My legs pushed harder against Kieran as I fought to keep myself from climaxing at the contact. I'd had more than one fantasy about Alaric, but I'd had no idea he'd ever felt the same towards me. I was half expecting to wake up from a dream at my desk with paper stuck to my face.

Alaric's smile widened, as if he knew every thought running through my mind. "But I've also wanted nothing more than to kiss you for longer than I care to remember. And ever since I walked in on you and Kieran at the hot springs, I haven't been able to stop thinking about what you taste like."

"What else?" I breathed out.

"I still believe this is a bad idea that will only lead to heartache for all of us."

"You're wrong," I said forcefully and let him see the conviction in my eyes. "I can make this work. *We* can make this work."

"Perhaps." He didn't seem convinced. Alaric might know me well, but I knew him too. He was starting to overthink this and was going to pull away from me. The question was . . . would I let him?

Alaric and I had been at each other's throats for basically our whole lives. It had only gotten worse when Kieran had arrived and we'd started to fight over him as well. Since coming back to House Harker though, I couldn't help but respect him. He was smart and cunning and pushed me to do better—more than anyone else did.

My attraction to Alaric went so far beyond just his body. I wanted him. All of him.

I let my lips quirk up into the arrogant, sinful smile that always set him off. He released my throat and started to step back, but I grabbed his hand and slipped two of his fingers into my mouth at the same time I let myself sink completely onto Kieran's cock.

Kieran swore as I moaned around Alaric's fingers, sucking and licking the digits before releasing them with a throaty laugh as I ground myself further onto Kieran's lap. Alaric's breathing grew ragged as he watched me slowly unlace his pants.

Strong arms pulled me back before tugging my dress down and exposing my chest. "Not yet." Then Kieran's hands gripped each of my full breasts hard as he continued to whisper into my ear. "You're gonna pay for that little maneuver, and he's gonna watch."

Kieran thrust up into me, and I threw my head back against his shoulder as my pussy clamped down around his cock. With my back to his chest and his arms around me, I couldn't do anything to control the pace or angle. All I could do was take it as he rocked into me.

Alaric watched for a few minutes, his eyes glazing over as my tits bounced when Kieran released them to grasp my hips so he could fuck me harder. I never would have thought I would like someone watching, but as Alaric's expression grew hungrier, I realized I loved it. There wasn't a hint of jealousy on his face. Just raw need . . . and excitement.

When Kieran's fingers brushed against my clit before pushing down, it was all I needed to tip me over the edge. I screamed as the climax tore through me before collapsing limply against Kieran.

"You're not done yet," Kieran chided, trailing his fingers up my side to lazily play with my nipples. Every part of my body was so sensitive that I whimpered as he squeezed them gently. "It's time for you to show Alaric just how talented that mouth of yours is, and I'm not done with this perfect pussy yet."

I raised my head from his shoulder, and my mouth went dry as Alaric stroked himself in front of me. "See something you want, Sam?" he asked languidly, his hand gripping the base of his thick length.

All I could do was nod, and Alaric and Kieran chuckled.

"Use your words," Alaric ordered.

I finally ripped my gaze away from his cock, and he raised one haughty eyebrow at me.

"What I want"—I dropped my voice to a low, throaty purr—"is your cock in my mouth and your hands in my hair. I want both of you fucking me hard until I'm not capable of piecing together a coherent thought, and then I want both of you to come inside me so that you're all I can taste for the rest of the day while the proof of how much I belong to Kier is running down my thighs."

"*Fuck,*" both of them swore.

"Is that clear enough for the two of you?" I rolled my hips against Kieran, who was still rock-hard inside me, and he groaned as his hands gripped my breasts again.

"Yeah, Sam." Alaric's molten eyes stared at me before he reached out and gripped my hair. "I think we can do that."

Kieran slid one of his hands down to my hip while the other pushed lightly on my back so that I was forced to pivot forward.

Right onto Alaric's cock.

My lips parted as I took in his hard thick length. The plan that had formed in my mind of teasing him slowly until he begged me to take him evaporated. I should have known that Kieran and Alaric together would be a dangerous combination. One of Alaric's hands was still gripping my hair while the other pushed down my head, forcing me to take every single inch of him.

I gagged, but instead of releasing me, he just pulled my head back before forcing me to take him again. And again. My eyes watered, but I wasn't a quitter, so I sucked him down each time, finding the rhythm in his movements.

Then Kieran's hips shot up, and I moaned as his cock buried inside me even deeper. My hands that had been gripping the chair shifted to Alaric, wrapping around his thighs for balance. I was completely at their mercy in this position, and they both knew it.

"Look at you taking both of our cocks so beautifully," Kieran purred. Another wave of liquid heat raced down my legs as I clenched around Kieran.

Alaric pulled my hair back, drawing my mouth away until his cock slid almost all the way out. My tongue swirled around his broad head, and I was able to tilt my head back just enough to catch the last of the green in his eyes before it gave way to blue. I slid my tongue over the thin slit at the tip of his cock, and Alaric jolted beneath me.

Then his fingers twisted my hair, slamming me back down onto him, fucking my mouth with an almost feral need. Kieran let out a low groan, and the hand that had been on my back moved to curl around my hips. I felt a sharp sting as his nails hardened into claws and bit into my skin. His hips pivoted up, harder and faster each time.

I could feel the pleasure building, the intensity so much, it was almost unbearable. Being between Kieran and Alaric like this felt so *right*, like it was always meant to be this way, and I relished every second of it.

Neither of them held back, and tears streamed down my cheeks as Alaric thrust harshly into my mouth, his breathing ragged. From this position, Kieran was able to bury himself deep, and I moaned every time he hit a particularly sensitive spot, which only drove Alaric wilder.

When Kieran's hand slipped over my clit, I started bucking wildly. Too much. The sensation was too fucking much, but their grips on me only tightened. Neither of their thrusts faltered as they fucked me exactly as I'd told them to, until I was incapable of thinking.

I didn't know how much more I could take as my moans turned into half screams, my thighs trying to clench together only for Kieran to force them apart. A delicious, salty taste started to spread across my tongue as Alaric switched to pulling his cock most of the way out before sliding it back in and hitting the back of my throat.

"Kieran," Alaric growled.

"I know," Kieran ground out.

A whimper slipped from my lips when Alaric pulled me off his cock, and I watched him stroke it in front of me. Kieran switched to excruciatingly slow and deep thrusts, his fingers still teasing my clit.

"Please," I begged. "I'm so close."

Alaric's eyes simmered with need and possessiveness as he looked at me, and Kieran swore as my pussy clenched around him.

"You're gonna drink every last drop," Alaric said. "And then you can come."

"She's our girl." Kieran pushed even deeper inside of me, and my breath hitched. "She'll take everything we give her."

Fuck yes, I would, because I knew exactly what they would give me in return. I held Alaric's gaze as I leaned forward and ran my tongue around his head before sucking it into my mouth and taking him all the way to the hilt.

I pulled one hand away from where I'd been bracing myself on his body and cupped his balls as I worked him up and down. For a few seconds, he let me control the pace and groaned as he took in his pleasure. Then his fingers tightened around my hair once more before he slammed into my mouth. I hollowed out my cheeks, sucking him in with each thrust, and felt his balls tighten in my hand. His cock hit the back of my throat one last time, and he held my head in place as he came hard while I did as I was told and greedily swallowed it all down.

"My turn." Strong arms pulled me back, and Alaric's cock slid out of my mouth. I made sure to lick it on the way, and he trembled at the sensation before staggering back a few steps. I gave him a slightly dazed smirk, satisfied that he was reeling from this as much as I was.

"Kier," I moaned as he palmed both of my full breasts, running his thumb roughly over my nipples as he started to move inside me again.

"Put those hands to use."

It took me a moment to realize Kieran wasn't talking to me. My head had fallen back against his shoulder, and my eyes had closed as pleasure rippled through me. Fingers dipped to where Kieran's cock was sliding in and out of my wet pussy, and I opened my eyes to find Alaric leaning over us, one hand braced on the chair and the other swirling around in the slickness.

"You're dripping all over that chair." His eyes were locked on my pussy, watching his best friend fuck the life out of me. "And you're going to be dripping with Kieran's cum in a second."

Kieran swore and picked up the pace as Alaric's gaze drifted up to watch my face, his fingers moving to circle my clit. Swear words intertwined with moans tumbled from my mouth as Kieran thrust into me over and over again. His hands still squeezed my tits as he groaned, his lips finding my neck and dragging his fangs across it.

Fingers pressed down on my clit, and I exploded. It felt like my mind was unraveling. Then Kieran's fangs sank into my throat, and I came again, feeling him do the same. I was so full of him and so wet already that I could feel it gushing down my thighs.

The fingers that had been playing with my clit suddenly vanished, and I blinked at Alaric, who was now standing several feet away. He'd pulled his pants up and was tucking his cock, which was already hard again, back into them.

"Fuck." He looked at where Kieran was still drinking from my throat, and I saw the moment regret flashed across his face, hurt stabbing me from his reaction. The pleasure I'd been basking in evaporated in an instant. Sensing the change in mood, Kieran pulled his fangs free and looked over my shoulder at Alaric, who just stared at the blood trailing down my neck. His light green eyes flashed solid turquoise before he strode away from us and fled the study.

I sagged in Kieran's embrace, and he sighed before helping me up. His cum mixed with my pleasure slid down my thighs as he pulled his cock free, but that only made me feel worse, because Alaric wasn't here to see it.

"What just happened?" I asked weakly.

Kieran got up and grabbed a towel from a drawer behind his desk and started cleaning me up as I stood there numbly. Then he reclasped my chest band and pulled my dress back up before tucking my hair behind my ear.

"It's my fault," he said softly. "I shouldn't have bitten you in front of him. I got caught up in the moment and forgot about his . . . issues."

"What issues?" My voice sounded numb, even to myself.

"You'll need to ask him." Kieran glanced hesitantly at the door. "I'll just say that Alaric has concerns over his control. For his bloodlust," he clarified when I arched an eyebrow. Alaric was obsessively controlled about everything. Even when his cock had been in my mouth, he'd been in control. "Some of his fears are justified, but some of them, he's just overanalyzing."

"He regretted doing this." I stared at the door, hoping he would come back and explain but knowing he wouldn't. "I don't think he wants to feel the way he does about me."

He regrets me.

"Hey." Kieran tugged me to him and wrapped his arms around me. "It'll be okay. You've just gotten spoiled by how perfect I am that you've forgotten how difficult dealing with other people can be."

I snorted a laugh against his shoulder.

We stood there for a few minutes, and I just enjoyed the feeling of being in his arms and breathing in his scent. Maybe Alaric had been right and that had been a mistake. I had Kieran. We belonged to each other, body and soul, and Roth was mine too. I claimed them as such, and they seemed to enjoy this.

I mean, they hadn't exactly said that, but they hadn't not said it either, and their room was gradually starting to look more homey in that stacks of books kept appearing. So I was pretty confident Roth had decided to stay here and was okay with me keeping them forever.

Then there was the Draven problem . . .

I burrowed further into Kieran's shoulder. "Can we stay here for a while? I just want to hide from the world for another hour."

"Yeah, Sam." He led me over to the small settee that sat across from the chairs and sat down, tugging me with him so I was leaning on his chest. "Whatever you need, I got you."

CHAPTER SIX

—

Samara

"Samara?" a voice called from down the hallway, and I held back a groan. I had really been hoping to make it to my room without anyone bothering me. Kieran had offered to come back to my suite with me, but I'd told him to go after Alaric and calm him the fuck down. Truthfully though, I'd just needed some time to come to terms with everything as well. I didn't regret what we'd done, because being with Alaric and Kieran had felt right, but Alaric had basically fled from that room.

His expression—a mixture of anger, confusion, and regret—had hurt. I was no stranger to the pain caused by Alaric's words, but now I'd just given him a whole new way to hurt me if he decided he didn't want to be with me after all.

I wanted to stand under scalding hot water and let myself sob where no one could see me, because I was the Heir to House Harker. Crying in the halls over a boy was not an option.

Composing my face as best I could, I turned around to face the rapidly approaching footsteps. "Yes, Sofia?"

The fair-haired Moroi came to a halt, the smattering of freckles across the bridge of her nose and cheeks standing out even more at the faint reddening across her pale skin. She gulped a few deep breaths before standing straighter, and I already dreaded whatever words were going to come out of her mouth.

Sofia was Yolanthe's protégé. The sharp-minded advisor had chosen her because the twenty-year-old girl was studious and reliable. Usually nothing rattled Sofia . . . and yet she looked like she'd run up the stairs with haste to find me. Giving up all pretense, she placed a hand on my shoulder and bent over, sucking in breaths.

I'd thought I was bad at running.

282

"Sofia, whatever you needed to tell me wasn't worth you passing out in the hallway," I huffed out with laughter.

Her hand tightened, and she straightened enough to stare at me, wide-eyed. "The House Heirs are here!"

"What?" My amusement instantly evaporated, and I glanced out the nearest window that faced the front of House Harker.

"Well, not all of them," she clarified as my gaze snapped back to her. "Neither Taivan nor Tamsen are here. Taivan isn't that big of a surprise—the Devereux rarely leave their House. Except for Roth of course, but that's . . ." Her hand slipped off my shoulder, and she straightened her dress. "I'm not sure why Tamsen didn't come. It's odd for House Corvinus to not insert themselves into any political situation. Ary and Aniela are in the small reception chamber just off the main tower entrance."

It was suspicious that Tamsen wasn't here, but I'd have to worry about that later because the Heirs of House Tepes and House Salvatore were downstairs.

I swore and headed towards the stairs that would lead down, all while checking my dress on the way to make sure everything was laced up right and running my fingers through my hair. Something told me there was no hiding the fact that I'd just been thoroughly fucked, but I needed to find out why two of the Heirs had shown up unannounced. It almost certainly had to do with Draven's attendance.

"Also," Sofia said hastily as she tried to keep up with me, "you should probably know . . . I mean, just so you know what you're walking into . . ." We rounded the corner, and I ducked into the stairwell, picking up my dress as I hurried down the stairs. "If you want to take a moment and think about this, that's okay. You don't have to see him if you don't want to—"

I whirled on the step, and Sofia yelped as she barely managed to halt before crashing into me. "Don't have to see *who*?"

She swallowed nervously. "Demetri is here too. As the Laurent Heir, the guards at the gate couldn't deny him entry."

"Oh." I slumped against the wall. "Right." It really said something about my current mental state that it hadn't even occurred to me he'd be here despite the fact that he was an Heir.

I hadn't seen or spoken to my ex-husband since I'd stormed out of House Laurent two months ago. The anger had faded, mostly, and any love I'd felt towards him had evaporated over the years of our strained marriage. Now there was just . . . embarrassment? I'd let myself turn into a shadow of who I was at House Laurent, trying to fit their mold of what a perfect Moroi wife should be.

Demetri hadn't even tried to fight for me. House Laurent had signed the papers to dissolve the marriage with zero fuss, which I still found odd. Some part of me had thought Demetri would have apologized for his actions and maybe tried to fix things between us. I most likely would have said no, but it hurt a little that he hadn't bothered. Our three-year marriage really had been a joke.

But more strange was that his mother, Marvina, hadn't used the request to dissolve the marriage to get better trade agreements between our Houses. She had no doubt been happy to see me go, but it wasn't like her to waste such an opportunity. Since I was the one requesting the marriage to end, it would have been House Harker's responsibility to offer any compensation.

"Do you want me to get Yolanthe?" Sofia asked quietly. "We can cover for you if you're not ready to face him yet. No one will judge you for it."

"I would judge me." I gave her a small smile. "Besides, we both know Yolanthe is very calm until she's not, and there's a distinct possibility of her walking into that room and trying to tear Demetri's head off."

Sofia snorted. "True. She can be quite protective of those she cares about. I still have to handle any correspondence with House Devereux because she refuses to speak to Desmond even though her sister has told her she's fine with how things ended between them."

"Nobody holds a grudge like Yolanthe." I shook my head at the memory of listening to the advisor rant about all the things she was going to do to the House Devereux Heir's brother for how he had treated her sister. Most of the threats involved cutting his dick off in rather imaginative ways. For someone who was usually quite prim and proper, Yolanthe had a real mouth on her sometimes.

"I'll be fine." I pushed off from the wall and did my best to channel Carmilla. She was always confident and steadfast no matter the circumstance. I would be the same. "Do you know where Prince Draven is?"

Sofia shook her head. "I haven't seen him since this morning."

Well, that didn't bode well at all.

I drew in an even breath and willed myself to be calm. "Can you track down Alaric and Kieran and let them know what's going on?"

"Of course. Anything you need, Samara." She shot me a mischievous grin. "Even hiding the body of a certain piece of shit Heir."

A sharp bark of laughter leapt from my lips. "Appreciate the thought, but I don't think it'll come to that."

"Kieran might feel differently," Sofia said slyly before darting back up the stairs.

She was right. I had no idea how Kieran would react to Demetri's presence here. On one hand, he was better than me at hiding his true feelings behind all those masks of his, but on the other hand, he was fiercely protective of me. While I was happy to be back at House Harker and finally be with Kieran in the way I'd always wanted . . . Demetri's betrayal had still hurt.

The memory of walking down the hall that day towards the sound of pleasurable moans played in my mind. My fingers curled into fists as I remembered what it had felt like to see Demetri in bed with someone else, displaying so much more passion than he ever had with me, at least in the last year of the marriage.

It was starting to feel like the moon had cursed me. As if I didn't have enough problems just existing in Lunaria and trying to keep my House in order. Now I had to deal with a potential secret alliance between the wraiths and our queen, a wicked but ever so charming prince, and piling onto all of this were a bunch of Heirs who were no doubt here to push their own agendas. And they all may or may not have allied with the Moroi Queen and whatever she had going on with the wraiths.

"Love it," I muttered to myself as I started making my way back down the stairs. "Absolutely love the life as an Heir. I mean, sure, I could be living the simple life at one of the outposts, maybe the one with the hot springs, but who would choose sitting in perfectly heated water every night while you relaxed from the toils of the day over dealing with a bunch of backstabbing, spoiled bitches. I mean, that's not even a choi—fuck!"

"I mean, if you want to fuck, I'm not going to say no." Draven grinned from the step beneath me. I'd almost reached the bottom landing when he'd stepped into the stairwell and cut me off. "Given that I'm basically an Heir, just with a fancier title, do you lump me into the category of 'backstabbing, spoiled bitches?'"

"Yes." I narrowed my eyes at him. "You're basically their leader."

"Harsh." He gave me a wounded look that I didn't believe for one second. "May I escort you into the den of vipers?"

I stared at the arm he offered and raised my chin. "No, thanks. I can walk just fine on my own." Pushing by him, I exited the stairwell and made my way towards the front of the main tower. Everyone I passed shot me relieved smiles. It wasn't that everyone disliked dealing with the Heirs—all of the advisors had met with them at one time or another—but they'd come here without any warning, and with the Moroi Prince here, also unannounced, everyone knew a political game was underfoot, and none of them wanted to deal with it.

Sadly, that was my job since Carmilla wasn't here. Even if she were here, I would still be involved, but at least I would have been able to let her run the show and just provide support instead.

Draven drew even with me, an amused smile playing across his lips. "This is your fault, you know," I hissed under my breath at him, even as I kept a confident expression on my face. As the Harker Heir, it was important that I always presented a solid front, no matter the turmoil I was feeling inside.

"Whatever do you mean, my lovely betrothed?"

"Don't call me that." I ground my teeth. "They're here because *you're* here. It's rare for you to visit the other Houses. At the Sovereign House, they have to contend with your mother, but now, they can get to you directly and whisper whatever they want into your ear, and they no doubt want to know why you came to House Harker so they can use that information in the future."

"Thanks to the friendship between your aunt and my mother, there's already an established relationship between our Houses." He shrugged. "It's not the first time I've visited your home."

We were almost to the room when I stopped and stared at him. "Did you tell anyone why you were coming here?"

"No." Draven cocked his head. "Would you like me to?"

"Absolutely not!" I lowered my voice after taking a deep breath. "Do not mention your ridiculous proposal. If the Heirs learn of it, they'll become determined to hammer through as many trade deals and arrangements as possible because they'll think my House will be directly tied to the Sovereign House. And I do not. Have time. For their bullshit," I enunciated.

Draven just smiled at me, and I threw up my hands in frustration. "Argh! Do not speak," I ordered, knowing it was pointless because the prince would do whatever he wanted. He didn't follow me when I started walking again, but I somehow doubted he was just going to walk away. No doubt he was plotting something I wouldn't like.

I didn't allow myself any hesitation as I strode into the room, feeling three sets of eyes landing on me.

"To what does House Harker owe the pleasure of not one but three Heirs visiting?" I smiled sharply. "Unannounced as it may be."

Ary scoffed, his back to the painting he'd been pretending to admire. The Tepes Heir was a little unkempt from his likely fast ride here. House Tepes was in the northern part of the Moroi realm. His midnight black hair that was shaved on both sides was pulled back into a messy bun, and he was sporting some stubble on his usually clean-shaven face. It was a two-day ride if you hauled ass and rode through the night directly through the wilds instead of sticking to the safer roads. Ary was definitely crazy enough to do that, which meant he'd somehow caught wind of where Draven was heading before the Moroi Prince had arrived.

The same basically applied to the other Heirs. Salvatore was also a two-day ride, although there was a road that went directly from our House to theirs, so it was less treacherous. Laurent was fairly close to us, the ride easily done in a day. If I had to guess, I'd say Demetri had been waiting nearby for the other two Heirs to arrive. He'd probably suspected I would have thrown him out if he'd arrived on his own.

He wasn't wrong.

"Don't be coy, Samara," Ary said in a deep, decadent voice. His light violet eyes shone brightly against his rich brown skin. The Tepes bloodline was the only one that shared purple eyes with the Harkers. Although ours were so dark, they looked almost black in dim lighting. Ary's were light and reminded me of lavender blossoms.

The rough-natured Heir would have probably found the comparison amusing. I'd always thought he was more suited to be a ranger than an Heir with his wild personality. He was built more like Alaric, tall and lean rather than broad and bulky like Vail. When we'd been growing up, his relatively small frame had led other Moroi to underestimate the Tepes Heir and challenge him to fights.

Ary had walked away unscathed from every one. Usually while whistling a jaunty tune. If there were anyone better than me with knives, it was Ary. He was fast and lethal in a fight—and loved every second of it. Despite his ruthless nature, he had a sharp mind, and I couldn't afford to forget that.

"Okay." I bared my fangs at him. "What the fuck are you all doing here?"

"There she is." Aniela laughed.

Out of everyone here, the beautiful, red-haired Salvatore Heir was the one I was most wary of. I was fairly confident House Salvatore was not allied with Queen Velika and the wraiths, but I knew almost nothing about Aniela. While I'd been growing up, Selene—Aniela's cousin and Dominique's sister—had been the Heir, then Dominique's parents and sister had died, and she'd risen to be the ruler of House Salvatore. She didn't have any children of her own yet, so she'd named her cousin, Aniela, as Heir.

"I've got a lot on my mind right now, Aniela." I walked to the center of the room and took a seat in one of the high-backed chairs. "So how about we cut the bullshit and you all tell me why you're here? Then I can tell you that you wasted your time so you can leave and I can get on with my day."

It wasn't Aniela who answered. Instead, it was the Heir I'd been avoiding looking at since I'd entered the room.

"We're here because Prince Draven is," Demetri said smoothly, taking a seat directly across from me. He looked good, much to my annoyance, the sunlight beaming into the room lighting up the golden highlights of his chestnut brown hair. My former husband had always had a sensual elegance about him. It had appealed to me, but now, I just found it rather tedious.

"I admit," he continued, "that when I heard the news, I thought the prince was coming to court you, and yet here you sit"—his hazel eyes traveled possessively down my body—"reeking of two other males. Rather interesting, considering how harshly you judged me, wife."

"Not your wife anymore, Demetri," I said in a bored tone while I held his accusing stare. "And the difference is that I'm not being unfaithful to anyone. I do this thing called being *honest*." Aniela snorted, and I amended. "In my personal relationships anyway. I think I've had my fill of marriage for a while."

"So you deny it then?" Demetri's reproachful, hazel eyes remained focused on me. "That the prince is here to ask for your hand?"

"Oh, I'm definitely here to marry Samara."

I squeezed my eyes shut and counted to ten in my head, hoping it would help.

It did not.

Draven strolled the rest of the way into the room and perched on the arm of my chair, leaning possessively into me. I glared up at him, but he just shot me a flirty grin.

"Prince Draven," Aniela purred, leaning forward enough to put her ample chest on display. "I had no idea you were interested in marriage."

"I'm interested in Samara," Draven said evenly.

Silence reigned while I fumed. Both because Draven just had to open his big mouth . . . and because I was pissed off at myself for the flash of jealousy I'd felt at Aniela flirting with him.

Aniela immediately turned her attention to me, not the least bit concerned about Draven's mild rebuff of her, which told me she had no real interest in him that way. Now she and Ary were both staring at me like I was a juicy piece of meat. Meanwhile, Demetri was staring daggers at Draven.

This was exactly what I didn't want. I'd been hoping to make it clear to all of them that there was nothing between me and Draven, and whatever they'd thought they'd come here for had been pointless. Now it'd be harder for me to get them to leave. As much as I wanted to, I couldn't just kick them out. Being blunt or rude was fine, all of the Heirs played our games with each other, but actually throwing them out would have political consequences. Every House controlled unique resources, and I couldn't afford to alienate any of them.

Plus some of them could be potential allies against the Sovereign House, assuming they weren't allied with them already.

Footsteps echoed down the hall, and we all turned towards the doorway to watch Kieran and Alaric burst into the room.

"Greetings, everyone!" Kieran cheered, holding up a bottle of wine. "What did we miss?"

CHAPTER SEVEN

—

Samara

I FIXED my features into a bemused, somewhat haughty expression as I entered the small dining hall several hours later. When it had become clear earlier that the Heirs wouldn't be leaving any time soon, I'd excused myself and left Kieran and Alaric to deal with them while I'd arranged rooms for them to stay in.

Really, as the Heir, that wasn't my responsibility—I should have asked Kieran to do that since he was a courtier of House Harker—but if I hadn't left that room, I likely would have stabbed either Demetri or Draven.

Or both.

Once the rooms were ready, I'd returned and directed everyone to where they would be staying and threw out a time for when dinner would start. I was sure they'd been conspiring with each other after I'd left them to it, or maybe chatting with whatever spies they had in my House, but I was tired, and there wasn't anything I could do about it at the moment.

Since then, I'd spent the remainder of the afternoon and early evening diving into all the paperwork that had piled up on my desk, enjoying the solitude and losing myself to the management of the House. Kieran had dropped off tea for me at one point but left me alone otherwise. I suspected he'd been busy speaking with Alaric, who had done his best to avoid looking at me.

I raised my eyebrow at Draven as I walked across the room. As the Moroi Prince, he should have chosen one of the seats at the head of the table, but instead, he'd chosen to sit to the right of it, with Alaric and Kieran sitting opposite. I'd invited Vail, but I wasn't surprised to see he wasn't here. He might have come if it had been just us and Draven, but once he'd learned the other Heirs would be joining us as well, he'd likely opted to stay away.

If only I had that option. I had no doubt this dinner was going to be a mixture of frustrating and awkward.

"Sorry, I'm late." I took a seat at the head of the table. "I got caught up in some reports from the Riverfell outpost and lost track of time." It wasn't a lie. House Harker had almost half a dozen outposts that fell under our responsibility to protect, and I took that seriously.

"It's fine. As you can see, the other Heirs are following the standard protocol of arriving at least ten minutes late to any social event," Draven said smoothly. "This just gave me and your friends an opportunity to chat."

"Oh?" I reached for a glass of wine. "Discuss anything interesting?"

"Just the standard topics that arise when running a House." He cocked his head, his eyes never leaving mine. "Did you get up to anything interesting this afternoon? Was your *rest* sufficient before the Heirs arrived?"

Both Kieran and Alaric snapped their gazes to the prince, but he just smiled.

"Would it kill you two to be less obvious?" I muttered.

Draven chuckled. "It seems when it comes to you, Kieran struggles to be subtle." His eyes flitted briefly to Alaric. "And it appears he has similar issues. The three of you should be aware of that. It's a weakness just waiting to be exploited, and you must know the other Heirs will jump at the chance."

The muscles hardened along Alaric's jawline as he swung to look back at me. I didn't need to have the ability to read minds, because I knew his thought was, *See? I told you this was a bad idea.*

"How kind of you to warn us. We'll make a note to practice our acting in the future." I turned to face Draven and held my wine glass up in salute. "After we *rest* of course. Very. Thoroughly. Rest."

"You're always a delight to play with." Draven grinned. "I can't wait to marry you."

"She's no—" Kieran started, but I cut him off with a glare, and his mouth clicked shut.

"As I said earlier, I'm considering your proposal, but you're going to have to convince me. Something you're not doing a very good job of at the moment."

"I'd let you keep them." Draven shrugged. His casual expression was betrayed by the way he carefully glanced at Kieran, who was currently looking at me. "Whatever makes you happy."

Kieran stiffened, as if he knew who those words were really directed at. Just as I opened my mouth to tell Draven where he could shove his offer, the other Heirs flowed into the room and took their seats at the table. Only Demetri slowed at seeing Draven sitting next to me instead of at one of the head seats. His eyes hardened as he sat next to Alaric. The other two Heirs sat across from him, with Aniella next to Draven and Ary next to her.

"Did you see the report from the Riverfell outpost, Ary?" I asked. Even though the outpost was in Harker territory, I knew the Tepes Heir liked to keep track of all monster attacks in the Moroi realm. A door swung open before he could answer, several members of the staff carrying in plates, setting them in front of us, and then leaving without a word. Though a dark-haired young girl caught my eye on the way out, arching an eyebrow before scurrying after the others.

I hid my grin. Olena. She absolutely loved to gossip and had probably been delighted to be working tonight. I'd need to find her tomorrow morning and see if there were any interesting rumors circulating about the prince's or Heirs' visits here.

"Fish." Draven sighed happily. "You coastal houses have it so lucky."

Alaric frowned at the slap of white fish meat on his plate. "You get sick of it after a while."

"No, you don't," Kieran and I said at the same time. Then we grinned at each other as Alaric rolled his eyes.

"I agree with Draven." Aniella shoved in a mouthful and closed her eyes as she thoughtfully chewed. "We never get fish so far inland. It's all root vegetables or questionable meat I choose not to think about. Maybe some fresh fruit in the summer months."

"To answer your previous question, Samara," Ary said, "I did see the report. I'm not sure if you've had a chance to review the history of that particular outpost, but—"

"They had similar incidents last year," I interrupted, "which means this problem isn't going to just go away."

Ary grunted and dug into his food with significantly less gusto than the rest of us. Clearly, he was also not a fan of fish. Draven sent me a questioning look.

"Spine-backed boars," I explained. "There aren't as many here as in the Velesians' realm, but they do occasionally make their way this far south. Riverfell is almost dead center in Moroi territory, and there are a lot of animal migration trails that go directly through it from the north."

"I know where it is," Draven said lightly. My fork stopped halfway to my mouth for a split second before I continued the motion, fighting to keep my expression neutral as I chewed on the fish. It tasted like ashes on my tongue now. As the prince of the Sovereign House, it was expected that he knew all the outpost locations and some basic information about them, but Draven had always come across as more of a pretty figurehead. Did he know the location of this one because the wraiths were planning on attacking it?

My stomach churned. I'd need to find Vail after this and tell him to increase the rangers stationed there just in case. We could use the boar problem as a cover.

"The boars showed up late in the growing season last year." My voice came out smooth, not betraying even a hint of the panic blooming inside my chest. "The hope was that it was a fluke. Sometimes they venture a little further south than usual, but they always go back."

"The herd has almost tripled in size from what I've been told. That's a lot of meat," Ary mused and grinned at Alaric. "Think of all the *not* fish you could be eating."

"We need to take care of the herd for multiple reasons," Alaric replied. "They've almost annihilated half the crops of that outpost, which is one of our best-producing ones. Plus, where there is prey, there will be predators."

"Still, Ary raises a good point." I swirled my wineglass. "If we can slaughter a good portion of the herd, it'll make up for some of the lost crops." I'd looked at the numbers. We couldn't afford to lose any type of food resource. Most of our food these days came from the outposts, and we'd already lost almost a dozen of them to the wraiths. We'd be okay this year, but if the trend continued, things would get bad. Fast.

"Have any of you ever hunted spine-backed boars?" Draven glanced at each of us curiously. Alaric and Kieran shook their heads, but I just smiled.

"Seriously, Sam?" Kieran complained. "And you didn't bring me?"

"You're too pretty for hunts," I teased.

"She's right," Draven agreed, and Kieran's smile slid off his face. Something flashed across Draven's face, but it was gone before I could figure out what it had been. "I would love to hear this tale, Samara."

I took a sip of wine and felt Alaric's heavy gaze on me. When I met his eyes, he looked quickly at Kieran and Draven before focusing on me again. Ah. So he'd picked up on the weird tension between them. Usually, Alaric was . . . not great at reading people. It was why the two of us worked so well together on House responsibilities. He had a sharp mind and was better versed in the current state of things since I'd been away at House Laurent for years, but he often failed to take into account how people's emotions could impact their motivations and therefore influence trade negotiations.

Kieran was his friend, and while Alaric and I had our problems, he was a loyal and good friend to Kieran. I gave him the smallest shake of my head, and he looked away. It wasn't my story to tell, but I would try to convince Kieran to explain things to Alaric so Draven couldn't blindside him with the information the same way he'd done to me. I also suspected Alaric's reaction to Draven hurting his friend might be . . . explosive.

"Ary actually knows this story since he was there too," I said.

He laughed and raised his pint of ale. "True, but why don't you tell it and I'll help fill in the details? You were always a better storyteller than me." He winked at me, and suddenly Draven, Kieran, and Alaric were hyper-focused on the Tepes Heir. He just laughed under his breath and drank half of his honey ale in one gulp in response.

"I was visiting my friend, Rynn—"

"Of course you were," Kieran groaned, giving me a pointed look. Even Alaric cracked a grin, his death glare dropping away from Ary. "Any trouble you get up to always begins and ends with Rynn."

"That's not true," I said defensively. "Sometimes it's Cali's fault."

"Yeah, but I would never say that." Kieran's eyebrows shot up. "Calypso scares the shit out of everyone except you and Rynn."

"Calypso scares the shit out of everyone," Aniela agreed around a mouthful of fish. She'd almost cleared her plate, and I waved at the servant hovering inside the room to bring her a second helping.

"You're friends with Calypso Rayne?" Draven cocked his head at me.

"She's my best friend." I raised my chin and dared him to say anything about her. It'd been years since a Furie had lost themselves and turned on us all, but everyone remained wary of them and was more than happy they preferred to stay within their borders of the badlands.

Except Cali. She traveled all over Lunaria and practically flaunted her shadow magic.

My friend was from the most powerful of all the Furie bloodlines and the one most known for going insane, which would not be happening. I refused to lose her, and Rynn felt the same. If Cali ever lost herself to the rage she kept chained within her soul, we'd just drag her back with our fangs and claws.

"The Rayne bloodline—" he started to say carefully, but I cut him off with a wave of my hand.

Then I leaned forward on the table, placing both hands flat on the wood surface as I let a little more of my bloodlust out. I had no doubt my eyes had darkened to black pools as my nails grew and hardened until claws dug into the hard wood.

"Sam," Kieran warned, but I ignored him, not taking my eyes off the prince. Draven's eyes had turned almost completely bloodred as the predator in him watched me carefully.

"Calypso fucking Rayne has single-handledly turned the tide of more than one fight that would have ended in the slaughter of Moroi and Velesians if she hadn't stepped in," I snarled. "She's never asked for anything, and she doesn't say anything as you fucks whisper behind her back while also *begging* her to help. I will not tolerate you or anyone else talking shit about her."

I pointed a clawed finger at him in warning before sinking back into my chair and letting my bloodlust fall away, taking with it my claws and black eyes. I kept the fangs out though and flashed them at Draven before swiping my wineglass off the table and taking a deep drink.

Ary snickered. He was used to me letting my bloodlust loose and often did the same. Aniella was eying me curiously, no doubt noting how easily I could slip in and out of bloodlust. I didn't bother looking at Demetri. He would no doubt be horrified.

The red faded from Draven's eyes as he picked up his own glass. "I was going to say, before you interrupted, that the Rayne bloodline is a powerful ally to have." He raised his glass. "And that your powerful alliances are just another reason why the marriage between us makes so much sense."

"Perhaps you should work harder on convincing me what you would bring to the marriage." I raised my own glass in salute. "Other than your pretty looks."

Someone, I was pretty sure it was Aniella, choked on a laugh.

"Well, at least you acknowledge that I'm pretty." He smiled, and fuck me, it was a very nice smile. Too bad the Moroi it was attached to was responsible for so many innocent deaths. Even if his mother were the mastermind behind all of this, he still went along with it.

"It's hard for me to picture Rynn hunting spine-backed boars," Alaric said, and it took me a minute to realize he was steering us back to the original conversation. "She's so . . ." He furrowed his brows, as if searching for the right word. "She's just Rynn. Soft-spoken and thoughtful Rynn."

I laughed. "That she is, but our dear, sweet Rynn shifts into a nearly five-hundred-pound wolf whose bite will give you nightmares. Have you ever seen her lycanthrope form?"

Alaric shook his head. "I haven't actually been around many Velesians in their shifted forms."

"It's impressive. They're all ridiculously large but can move with absolute silence. As if the wilds favor them over every other creature that wanders the forests." A small, playful grin tugged at my lips. "Rynn, in particular, is very good at sneaking around. When the three of us were at Drudonia, we'd often sneak out at night and play our own version of hide-and-seek in the forests. Two of us would hide, and the third would hunt. It would drive Cali insane because Rynn always won. We could never find her if she didn't want to be found, and she'd always find us unless Cali cheated and took to the air where we couldn't follow."

"The three of you went into the woods at night on your own?" Draven stared at me in disbelief. Apparently, I'd finally managed to surprise him.

"The wilds surrounding Drudonia are heavily patrolled." I shrugged. "It's rare for any of the beasts to get close, and avoiding the rangers only made it more fun." I glanced at Alaric and then Kieran in panic. "Don't tell Vail."

"You're asking us to lie?" Kieran's expression was full of mock horror. "To our beloved Marshal?"

"Feels like we should get something for putting ourselves in such potential peril," Alaric chimed in. "Lying to Vail is a risk. Even a lie of omission. So what would you offer us, Samara?"

My mouth hung open in what I was sure was a very unattractive way, but I couldn't help it. Alaric was joking. With me. About sex. Maybe there was hope for us after all.

Ary and Aniela were watching the exchange with amused expressions, no doubt filing all this information away in case it was useful later, while Demetri's gaze kept bouncing between Kieran and Alaric, like he couldn't decide which one of them he hated more.

"I'll think of something worth your while." I finally recovered and winked at Alaric, and the corners of his lips quirked into the barest of smiles.

Maybe whatever conversation he'd had with Kieran this afternoon had helped him come to terms with us. A little bit of hope filled me.

"Sometimes, Rynn would help me avoid Cali while we played this game of hers, so I was used to being around her when she was in her wolf form. I was visiting her in Narchis territory when a hunt was declared, and she invited me along. Well . . . I invited myself along, but she went with it."

"And you?" Draven looked at Ary. "How did you get involved in this?"

Ary smiled politely. "I like to get a bit of exercise now and then. Since Tepes' lands border Narchis' ones, they occasionally invite me on hunts."

I snorted. Currently, Ary was dressed in a beautiful, deep red tunic with gold threads, and glittering rings lined his fingers. He'd taken the time to shave and clean up before dinner, and now he appeared as nothing more than a handsome and well-kept Heir . . . but I knew he was far more comfortable covered in blood with his claws buried in the gut of a monster.

The Velesians loved to go hunting with Ary. He was insane and feared nothing. I really hoped he wasn't mixed up in this wraith business, because he was not someone I wanted to have as an enemy. If I could sway him to our side though . . . he'd be an excellent ally.

"It was invigorating hunting under the moonlight." I smiled at the memory. "Rynn's birth pack was hunting that night, so it was mostly lycanthropes with a few ailuranthropes mixed in, but the panthers stuck to the trees, and I rarely saw them."

"How did they bring the boars down?" Draven rose and grabbed the wine bottle at the center of the table to refill his glass before walking around to refill mine. He glanced at Alaric, who shook his head, sticking with his honey ale. Kieran pointedly ignored Draven, who eventually sighed and returned to his seat.

"Easiest way is to get them on their backs—their bellies are their weak spot," Ary explained.

"I'm sure that's not hard at all," Draven quipped.

I huffed a laugh. A full-grown boar weighed close to eight hundred pounds. They were named for the nearly foot-long spikes they could raise down their spine, but those spikes actually covered most of their body, shorter below the spine but every bit as sharp. Their legs and belly were vulnerable though, and if you got too close, they would basically throw their body at you, relying on both their weight and spines to inflict damage.

Boars might technically be prey animals who preferred to root around for nuts and berries rather than tear flesh from bone, but they were ill-tempered and highly aggressive. Lunaria was a land of monsters. Some of those monsters just happened to be herbivores.

"The pack would split up," I explained. "Half of them would get the boars into a panic so they would run, then the other half would run at them head-on and slam their bodies against their sides. It takes careful timing, and the angle has to be perfect, but if you hit the boars right, you can flatten the spikes back down against their body to avoid getting impaled and cause them to stumble, ideally falling completely."

"Exposing their undersides," Draven mused. "Clever."

"And what were you doing?" Alaric cocked his head.

"She was being insane." Ary lifted his wine glass to me, and I raised mine back, a wicked grin on my face.

"There is another weak spot you can exploit. The spines that run along their back and neck are longer but less dense than the rest of the ones on their body. If you shoot an arrow at the base of their neck, you can sever the vertebrae and take them down in a second."

Alaric frowned. "You'd have to shoot at the same angle as the spikes, which means you'd need to be both behind and above them."

"There are dried-up riverbeds all over their territory, and they create narrow channels. Rynn convinced a few pack members to chase some of the boars down them. I would run along the edges and leap across to the other side. At the apex of my jump, I'd have the perfect angle. Could bring down three or four each time," I said smugly.

"You're good with a crossbow?" Draven asked.

Alaric and Kieran snorted, but it was Kieran who answered. "Samara isn't *good* with a crossbow. She's excellent. Pretty sure she's a better shot than any of our rangers, Vail included."

"And let's not forget the bloody knives," Alaric muttered, drawing a grin out of me.

"There are no helpful riverbeds down here, so it'll be difficult for me to pull out that trick," I said.

"I could throw you." Ary sent me a heated look. "It's not exactly how I've always wanted to get my hands on you, but I'll take what I can get. Perhaps offer to rub down your muscles after the hunt . . ."

"You should stick to hunting, Ary." Aniela laughed. "Your flirtations continue to be awful."

"They worked on you." He arched a thick, dark brow at her.

My eyes widened as I looked at the two Heirs who I'd always thought hated each other. "Did you know that?" I gave Kieran a wide-eyed stare.

He shrugged. "Old news. Happened two years ago, not long after Aniela was named Heir." He looked at the beautiful Moroi female who wore a simple, emerald green dress that did wonders for her red hair. "Summer equinox, if I remember correctly. You'd just been dumped by that cute blond boy you'd been seeing all spring."

Aniela glared at him. "He wasn't *cute*, he was *hot*, and I wasn't dumped. We mutually agreed to end things."

"Of course." Kieran smiled, which only pissed Aniela off more.

"So," I cut in and waved my hand between Aniela and Ary, "hate fuck then?"

They looked at each other for a long moment before nodding and saying, "Hate fuck."

Everyone at the table laughed, and some of the tension dispelled. I didn't think anyone else caught how Ary's gaze lingered on Aniela for several seconds after she'd already looked away.

I thought about asking some probing questions to start feeling out where everyone might stand on the wraith situation, but it would be easier if I could talk to them one-on-one. Before I could think of anything to say, Demetri leaned forward and caught my eye.

"Perhaps we should try it?" he suggested.

"Try what?" I arched an eyebrow.

"Hate fucking." He smiled. "It might do wonders to repair our relationship."

Ary looked at Aniela. "Okay, compared to him, you have to admit that I'm charming as fuck."

I took a sip of wine, keeping my expression relaxed even as I fumed internally at Demetri's words. The audacity of that male. Beside me, Draven, Kieran, and Alaric had all gone completely still. I needed to play this down before they did something foolish. As the Moroi Prince, Draven could do whatever he wanted, but if Alaric or Kieran did anything against the Heir of another House, there would be consequences.

"The only relationship we have is the one that exists between all Heirs," I drawled. "There is nothing beyond that, and despite what antics some might engage in"—I glanced pointedly at Aniela and Ary—"I have no interest in hate fucking any of the Heirs." I slid my hand across the table, and Kieran immediately grabbed it, intertwining our fingers. "As you pointed out earlier, I'm already getting quite thoroughly fucked. There is no reason for me to slum it anymore."

"You're fucking a courtier who was a throwaway from House Corvinus and an advisor who came from *nothing*." Demetri sneered. "The Lockwoods are outpost trash who have no business living in a House, let alone advising one."

My fingers curled around the knife next to my plate, but Draven's hand found mine before I could do anything with it, and Kieran's fingers tightened around my other hand so all I could do was glower at my ex-husband and envision slicing his throat open. It wasn't enough. I opened my mouth to tell him off, but Alaric beat me to it.

"House Laurent is going to run out of malachite by the end of the year," Alaric said calmly. "Which means you'll have to rely on other crystals to power your wards, ones that won't last nearly as long. Since you foolishly didn't pursue Samara's proposal of trading with the Velesians—who have malachite in abundance—you have no reliable way of getting more." He took another sip of wine. "She sent that proposal to the Order of Narchis as soon as she returned here, by the way. So House Harker now has one of the best trade deals for malachite in all of the Moroi realm."

"I'd love to speak with you about that tomorrow," Aniela cut in. "I believe House Salvatore can offer favorable terms in exchange for some malachite."

"Of course." Alaric nodded at her. "We can speak after breakfast."

Demetri's hate-filled gaze tore from Alaric to land on Aniela, but she just sent him a polite smile in return. I found myself liking the Salvatore Heir more and more.

"Your House"—Alaric returned his cool, even gaze to Demetri—"thinks of itself as better than everyone else. You forget the reality of our situation, perhaps because you live far enough down the southern coast that you rarely have to fight off any monster attacks. Because we do it for you. The Velesians do it for you as well. As do the Furies. At the end of the day, House Laurent is nothing but a bunch of freeloaders. And when your House falls, and it absolutely will fall, a new line will rise. Perhaps one from an outpost. Most will forget you ever existed. But don't worry." Alaric raised his wineglass in salute. "The Lockwoods will remember you and present you as an example of the terrible fate of mediocrity."

Demetri's face turned bright red, rage simmering in his eyes while Aniela cackled and Ary started to slow clap. Draven and Kieran released me so they could join in on the clapping.

I let out a husky laugh, and Alaric's gaze flicked to mine. "Honestly, Alaric," I purred, "I could fuck you right here."

"I'd watch," Kieran offered.

"Same." Draven sent me a heated look.

Alaric cleared his throat and looked away, focusing on the wineglass in his hand, but I saw the corners of his mouth curl upward.

"This was definitely worth the frantic ride here." Aniela raised her wineglass to Ary, and he bumped it with his.

"Fuck all of you." Demetri shoved his chair back and rose, sending me one last glare. "You and I aren't done." Then he stormed out, and we all watched him go.

"I'm confused," Aniela said after he left. "From everything I've heard, he didn't put up much of a fight after you left House Laurent. So why is he pursuing you now?"

"No idea." I frowned in the direction Demetri had run off to. "Our marriage has been officially dissolved."

She hummed thoughtfully as she sipped her wine. "Well, he's doing a shitty job of wooing you back, which is good for me because it means one less House for us to compete against for your affections."

"You want my affections too, Aniela?" I asked dryly.

She tilted her head back and let out a musical laugh. Interest flashed across Ary's face before he hid it behind a mask of indifference. There was definitely more than just hate fucking there.

"You're beautiful, Samara, but I don't swing that way. My House needs malachite and a few other things. I believe we can make you a good offer."

"Wonderful," I said truthfully. "Perhaps I can come visit your House soon. It's been a while since I've spoken to Dominique in person."

"She would enjoy that." Aniela smiled. "Our closest neighbor, aside from the Sovereign House, is House Devereux, and they're not exactly chatty."

"I'll speak with your Marshal tomorrow about the boars," Ary wiped his mouth with the back of his hand after taking a long drink of wine. "They almost certainly went through our territory to get to yours, which means they could easily turn back and wreak havoc at one of our outposts. We'll help with the hunt."

"Thank you." I gave him a nod. "I'm sure Vail will appreciate that. We'll split the meat of course."

"Something must have driven the boars out of their territory. They prefer the thicker forests of the Velesian realm," Ary mused and looked at Draven. "Wraith activity is definitely increasing. Does the Sovereign House have any information about that? I'm assuming the increasing attacks on our outposts have been your main priority lately."

"It's all my mother and her consort work on," Draven said evenly. "I know she's seeking Carmilla's wisdom on the matter as well. There hasn't been much I've been able to do to help. I'm not a particularly gifted fighter nor was I ever a good student." He gave me a self-deprecating smile. "Not all of us were considered a prized pupil by the scholars at Drudonia."

"You're definitely gifted at bullshitting," Kieran drawled. Instead of being insulted, Draven just looked happy that Kieran had said something to him.

"Vail and a good amount of House Harker's resources have been focused on solving the issue of the increased attacks on our outposts." I fixed my expression into one of concern, which wasn't exactly hard considering that's how I felt. It was slightly more challenging to keep the suspicion hidden away. "But we haven't learned much, and the attacks only seem to be increasing. Has the Sovereign House learned *anything* useful?"

Draven shrugged. "I'm sure you know more than I do at this point. We'll figure it out eventually."

I set my wineglass down so I wouldn't shatter it in my hand. "Eventually isn't good enough. Entire fucking outposts died." *And you played a hand in that,* I thought but kept that to myself. "We need to stop these attacks now."

The charming mask slid off Draven's face, and something dark and predatory replaced it. "This is Lunaria. People die every day. Often in horrible ways." I opened my mouth to argue, but the red bleeding through his deep blue eyes silenced me. "We might be monsters, Samara, but we're far from the biggest or the baddest. You'd be wise to be selective with who you choose to protect, because you can't save them all."

"And you'd be wise to not tell me what I'm capable of," I said coldly. "Some of us can do things you only dream of."

Draven looked at me for a long moment. That feral, predatory gleam still in his eyes. "That's what you've got wrong, Heir. I know nothing of dreams. The only thing I've ever known are nightmares."

CHAPTER EIGHT

—

Samara

"THERE YOU ARE."

Startled, I jumped slightly where I'd been sitting on the low balcony wall, but a strong hand grasped my arm, steadying me. My heart beat painfully, as it'd practically leapt into my throat as I glanced to the ground far beneath us. I looked over my shoulder and scowled at the prince. "I thought you were trying to court me, not scare me into falling to my death."

His lips twitched, and I had the sneaking suspicion he was trying not to laugh at me. "Sorry. That wasn't my intention. I've been sneaking around for the last hour looking for you, trying to avoid the other Heirs and everyone else who '*just wants a moment of my time.*'"

Slowly, he released his grip on my arm, trailing his fingers down it as if he wanted to prolong the contact before stepping back.

"Fair enough. I was just coming to find you anyway."

Roth wanted to do some research in the library, and Alaric was going to help them while Kieran chatted up the rangers who had traveled with the Heirs to see if he could glean anything useful. I was responsible for distracting Draven and keeping him out of everyone's way.

I spun around on the balcony wall to hop down. Demetri had left early this morning, but Ary and Aniela had stuck around. I'd already met with them both over breakfast and was growing more confident that they were not allied with the Sovereign House and the wraiths. Even if I trusted them though, it didn't mean someone in their House wasn't our enemy. We'd have to tread carefully if we wanted to bring them into the fold, and I wasn't ready to do that just yet.

"It's not every day the Moroi Prince graces us with his presence. You can't blame them for trying to get your support on whatever their latest scheme is."

"They're welcome to schedule time with me in the mornings while you're busy with House business." He extended an elbow to me. "But I'd prefer to spend time alone with you for the rest of the day . . . and night."

I did my best to ignore the flicker of excitement that raced through me. Mentally, I knew Draven could not be trusted. He was clearly working with the wraiths, which made him our enemy, but I'd known him for so long, and he was an attractive bastard, and when he said things like that, my body practically screamed, *Yes, please!* I gave him a bemused grin instead and slipped my arm around his. "You can have me . . . for the day."

"We'll see." His eyes roamed over the scenery. "Quite the view up here."

"It is," I agreed. "My study has a good view of the beach, but nothing beats this." I swept my free hand out towards the vast forest that covered the lands before us. "It's one of my favorite places to come and think, and play with the strikers of course."

A low-pitched trill filled the air, and I made a clicking sound with my tongue, keeping my hand extended. Seconds later, a bright red striker landed on my hand, its long talons wrapping around my fingers, the sharp points pushing against my skin but not breaking it.

"Good boy," I cooed. The creature shook its narrow, elongated head, a forked tongue darting out from its blunt beak. "You'll be flying further around here in no time."

Draven reached out and scratched the striker's back, and it flapped its leathery wings before releasing deep chirps of pleasure. "They're cute little monsters."

"I adore them. This one struggled a bit early on. I had to hand-feed it after it hatched because the others kept bullying it, so he's gotten rather attached to me."

"Something he and I have in common it seems."

I rolled my eyes. "Smooth."

"Thank you." Draven grinned.

"Come on." I tugged him towards the large, open-air structure we'd built to house the strikers. "Let's get him settled, and I'll take you on a tour of House Harker."

He groaned. "Did I not mention how I've been trying to avoid talking to people for the last hour?"

The striker hopped off my hand onto a free perch, and I gave him one more scratch behind the head before heading towards the stairs, dragging Draven with me. "Don't worry about it. I have a plan."

"Alright." He gave me a sly look. "But for every person who stops us, you have to spend an hour with me after dinner."

"Deal," I said confidently.

The winding stairwell was too narrow for us to walk side by side, so I slipped my arm free from his as we made our way down. It didn't take long for voices to reach us. This was one of the busier towers and where most of the advisors and courtiers spent their time during the day.

"Given the amount of people we're about to run into, I think you'll be spending all night with me, Samara." The way he said my name was indecent, and it sent a shiver down my spine, but I could play this game too.

I stopped and whirled around. Draven froze as I placed my hand on his chest, a coy smile twisting my lips. His eyes were locked on mine as I raised my other hand to my lips and used my fang to slice the tip of my index finger. A few drops of blood swelled, and Draven's nostrils flared. Without looking, I stretched my bloody finger to the wall, the dormant magic of the glyph engraved on one of the stones calling to me. As soon as my blood touched it, a portion of the wall simply disappeared, revealing a hidden stairwell.

Surprise flickered in his eyes, and I let out a husky laugh before licking the remaining blood off my finger. The red threads in Draven's eyes widened at the sight, and I was pretty sure he had stopped breathing. I licked my lips and leaned forward, one hand still on his chest. "Looks like you won't be getting that night with me after all, Draven."

"Fuck," he muttered as I slipped into the darkness. As soon as he crossed the threshold, I pushed on another glyph, and the wall reappeared, plunging us into absolute darkness. Our night vision was excellent, better than the Velesians or Furies, but even we needed some light to see by, and there was none here. "No Fae lanterns?" Draven asked.

"No." I shook my head, even though I knew he couldn't see it, and reached for his hand. My fingers bumped into his arm, and I slid them down until our hands were clasped. The contact was both intimate and innocent at the same time, and I was suddenly acutely aware of how warm his hand felt in mine. How right it felt. "They don't work anymore, and I never bothered to fix them, but I know the way. Trust me."

His fingers tightened around mine. "Lead the way, Heir."

I started carefully walking down the steps. Draven followed, not slipping once despite not being able to see anything or having my familiarity with the hidden stairs.

"How did you find this?" he asked after a few minutes.

Silence filled the air as I thought about how to answer. What truths to reveal and which to hide. Finally, I decided it was easier to go with the truth when possible—fewer lies to keep track of.

"After my parents died, I started to spend more time visiting the strikers. It became my safe place, especially since I wasn't old enough to leave the House grounds on my own. A week after"—the words caught in my throat—"their death, I was coming down, and I heard Carmilla talking to Alaric's parents. They were discussing the future of the House and their concerns about how I was handling things. I didn't want to face them, so I spun to run back up the stairs and tripped. It was pure luck that I noticed the glyph on the wall."

"I'm sorry," he said roughly. "I don't think I ever told you that, but I'm so sorry about how your parents died. They were always kind to me."

For the first time since we'd entered the darkened stairwell, I felt off-balance and had to concentrate on where my feet fell, despite having walked down these steps dozens of times before. I rarely spoke about my parents. The wound left behind by their deaths hadn't healed, it'd just festered in my soul over the years. I didn't know what to make of Draven's words. There was a raw edge to them that felt genuine.

But my parents had been killed by wraiths, and now Draven was working with them. Was that why he felt so guilty over this? He was only a couple of years older than me, which meant he'd been a teenager when they'd died, so I doubted he'd been working with them then. The urge to turn around and shake him until he told me what the fuck was going on was overwhelming, but I shoved that feeling down.

I had another hundred steps to get my emotions under control. Too much was riding on this for me to stumble now. The others were doing their part, I needed to seize this opportunity to carefully question Draven.

"Thank you," I said tightly. "My parents were excellent rulers of House Harker. I only hope to live up to their legacy someday." Clearing my throat, I redirected the conversation. "Speaking of living up to legacies . . . it's been a while since I visited the Sovereign House. How are things between you and your mother these days?"

His fingers loosened around mine, and for a moment, I thought he would release my hand. But then they tightened once more. "Same as always. She's delighted about our engagement—*sorry*—potential engagement." He'd slipped back into his charming prince mode.

We continued our trek down, and I listened while Draven recounted some of the events that had transpired over the past couple of years at the Sovereign House. About how he was bored and had very little to do these days.

I listened to him lie to me for one hundred and eight steps.

———

OUR FOOTSTEPS ECHOED across the large, empty room we'd entered after leaving the hidden stairwell. Dinner was still hours away, and I needed to come up with something to do with Draven during that time so the others could continue their work unhindered.

Maybe we could go for a ride or something. Although, if Vail found out I'd left House Harker alone with the prince, he'd probably strangle me.

"What is this place?" Draven asked as he glanced around curiously.

"We're right beneath the main tower." I pointed to an iron and wood door across the room. "That leads to the kitchen. We're not sure what the Fae originally built this room for. When they abandoned this place, they took almost everything with them except the furniture. We use it for storage now."

"Hmm." Instead of heading towards the door that led upstairs, he started aimlessly wandering around, studying the walls. "Seems weird they went through the effort of building a secret stairwell only to have it lead to the kitchen pantry, right?"

There was more than one secret passage that led to this room. After stumbling across the one in the upper stairwell when I was a kid, I'd made it my mission to find others. I'd found six in this tower alone, plus another dozen short ones that linked the hidden staircase together. There were more in the other buildings and towers that made up House Harker as well. I didn't understand why they'd done it. There was nothing special about this room, but the Fae had spent an awful lot of time planning a way for anyone to secretly get to this place.

I wouldn't be telling Draven any of that though. I probably shouldn't have even shown him the room we were in. It'd been careless of me, and I couldn't afford to be like that around him. The prince was not my friend, despite our history and how I felt about him. He was our enemy, and he'd hurt Kieran.

I should have pushed him down those fucking stairs. The sensation of his hand in mine and how right it had felt came rushing back. The way his voice had sounded so sorrowful when he'd said he was sorry for the loss of my parents. I ruthlessly grabbed the feeling and shoved it into the same box where I stored my grief for my parents' deaths.

"They built everything out of stone despite wood being far more abundant and easy to move. Paintings of places that don't exist around here adorn the ceiling of every bedroom, and the vast majority of books we've found written by Fae hands . . . is *poetry*," I said in a bored tone as I walked towards where Draven was standing and staring at the dark grey stones of the wall. "Not where they came from, how they ended up here, or why there was such hatred between the Seelie and Unseelie. And then they vanished practically overnight, never to be heard from again."

"Your point?" Draven didn't so much as look at me as his eyes continued scanning the stone surface. Was he looking for something? I started skimming the walls to see if there was something here I had missed this whole time.

"My *point* is that they did a bunch of shady shit." Nothing stood out on the smooth stone surface, but I kept searching. "The secret passages are just another thing on that long list."

"Passages?"

Shit. I hadn't meant to say that.

I felt his gaze on me and turned away from the wall I'd been studying to meet his stare. He cocked his head, causing his long hair to fall over his shoulder in a shimmering curtain. "There's more than one?"

"I hate you."

He chuckled. "I think that's the first truthful thing you've said to me all day."

"Exaggeration," I muttered and turned back to the wall, heaving a sigh of frustration. There wasn't anything here. "Let's get out of here. I need some fresh air."

"Wait." Draven's hand shot out, and his fingers wrapped around my wrist when I turned towards the exit. "Have you ever noticed this glyph before?"

All the thoughts in my mind scattered at the sudden contact. I didn't even look at the wall where Draven was pointing with his other hand. Instead, all my focus was on where his fingers were wrapped around me. Draven stilled, and we stood there for a long moment. Then he gently stroked his thumb over my pulse, and my heart sped up.

Moonsdamn it all. I needed to get ahold of myself.

"Let me take a look." I pulled my arm free and took a step closer to the wall. My heart continued to race, but now it was because I was looking at a Fae glyph that had been created in a way I'd never seen before.

I traced the barely visible glyph. It wasn't all that surprising that nobody had ever noticed it. The glyph was a simple one, just a circle with a straight line running vertically through it, but normally, when glyphs were etched into stone, the lines were a lighter color and they caused a slight dip in the surface.

My finger skimmed over the glyph. The surface remained the same, there was no dip, and parts of the glyph were lighter, while other sections were darker. It was as if the Fae had moved around the natural minerals within the stone to create the glyph. I'd had no idea they could do that.

"How did you even find this?" My brows furrowed. Unless you were looking for it, your eyes would slip over it as just a natural discoloration. I mean, I was looking directly at it, and even now, it was easy to dismiss as nothing.

"Just lucky." Draven shrugged when I glanced at him. "Seemed odd for the stairwell to lead down here, and after you showed me that glyph upstairs, I was on the lookout for another one."

Plausible, but absolute horseshit. He'd been searching the walls as soon as we'd set foot in this room and I'd told him where it was located. He'd known this glyph would be here. Maybe not in this exact spot, but somewhere in this room. I was very curious about how he'd known about it. I was even more interested in why he wanted *me* to know about it.

"Do you know what it means?" Draven asked over my shoulder.

"Safe," I whispered. "It means safe."

I sucked in a breath as a deliciously wicked scent filled the air when Draven moved close enough for his chest to rest against my back. He reached towards the stone with bloody fingertips.

"Are you out of your mind?" I slapped his hand away before he could make contact with the glyph and spun around to smack him on the chest. "We have no idea what that spell was actually used for!"

"You said it means safe." He grinned at me, and I wanted to strangle him . . . and kiss him. Argh.

"Forgive me for not trusting the fucking Fae's definition of safe!" I shoved him away from me and the wall. Distance. That was the key to dealing with Draven—keeping a good amount of space between us so I could keep my unruly thoughts under control.

Unfortunately, Draven was not on board with this unspoken plan because he immediately stepped further into my space, reclaiming the distance I'd put between us. I stepped away until my back was against the wall, and a wolfish grin stretched across his lips as he boxed me in, placing one arm on either side of me. I had to tilt my head back to look at him, my heart thumping wildly as he leaned down to whisper in my ear. "Come on, Heir. It's fun to be dangerous sometimes."

The rational part of my brain was drowned out by the heat dancing across my skin as his lips trailed down my neck. Fangs grazed my pulse, and I didn't know what I would do if he tried to bite me. I knew what I should do. I should push him away again. Fuck, I should be doing that right fucking now.

Draven chuckled darkly against my skin. "You overthink things, Sam."

He raised his left hand and slammed it against the wall directly over my shoulder before I could stop him. The bastard had been distracting me. As soon as his blood made contact with the glyph, magic sparked, and the floor fell out from beneath us.

CHAPTER NINE

—

Draven

I FUCKED UP.

Plummeting into darkness wasn't what I had expected to happen when I'd activated the glyph. I'd known to look for it because we had an identical room in the Sovereign House with the exact same glyph. Though when I'd activated that one, it'd been like being gently picked up and placed in a different room before getting a nice pat on the head.

This had felt like the floor cracking under us and a giant reaching up and jerking our bodies down. I was pretty sure my organs were no longer in the right positions, and I was fighting the urge to hurl my guts up.

On the plus side, Samara was clinging to me tenaciously. Her arms were wrapped around me, and she tucked her head against my chest. If she'd had time to think about it, she never would have done it, but in a moment of panic, she thought I was safe. Someone she could trust to see her through this.

I wasn't.

That fact hurt far more than the way she practically flung herself away from me when we stopped moving, hissing a bunch of words in dead languages that I had no doubt were promises of doing very nasty things to certain parts of my body. I let her get it out while I looked around, getting our bearings. Grateful the nausea had vanished almost instantly after the magic had finished transporting us.

It was foolish of me to turn my back on Samara when she was pissed. I knew from past experience that she had a fiery temper.

"Fuck!" I rubbed the back of my head, where something hard and blunt had just slammed into it. I turned at the pinging sound of something metal bouncing off the floor and I bent down to swipe up the dagger. Given that Sam had just thrown a blade at my head, and I didn't know if she'd meant for the

308

sharp end to hit me, I should've probably been pissed off at her. Instead, I wanted to pass the weapon back to her so she could hold it at my throat while I fucked her against the wall.

Something told me she wouldn't like that though, or more accurately, she wouldn't be willing to admit how much she would like that. I hadn't missed all the conflicting expressions on her face over the past hour. Samara wanted me, and she hated herself for it.

Couldn't exactly fault her for that. I hated myself a little too.

Samara stalked over to me and held her hand out demandingly as black threads wound through her purple eyes. Okay, she was a little more than pissed.

She grabbed the dagger from me and thrust it back into a sheath that was hidden up her sleeve. "Next time you disobey me," she growled, "it'll be the dagger end that goes through your thick fucking skull!"

Guess that answered the question of if she'd intended to hit me with the handle. Apparently, she hadn't been bragging at the dinner table when she'd spoken about how good she was with projectile weapons.

Fuck, Samara got hotter by the minute.

Before I could stop myself, I reached out and ran my fingers down the thick braid that snaked over her shoulder, then trailed my fingers along the top of her chest.

"I can think of some better ways for you to punish me for my disobedi- ence." For a split second, desire lit up Samara's eyes before she ruthlessly stamped it out. It was reckless of me to tease her like this, but I couldn't help it. I'd felt the same about Kieran, and he'd almost died because of it. Not that he had the faintest idea. His hatred of me hurt, but all I cared about was that he was alive.

Samara and her friends had only scratched the surface of how completely fucked Lunaria was. My mother had always been a power-hungry bitch, but now she had strong allies who could make all her dark and twisted dreams come true. Sooner or later, she'd decide I wasn't worth keeping around, and my life would be over. So I might as well flirt with Samara while I could. Thanks to her status as the Harker Heir, even my mother would hesitate to go after her. Kieran hadn't been so lucky.

"What is this place?" Samara stepped away from me as she peered around the dimly lit room. A few Fae lanterns had lit up, but they must have been running out of magic because their blue flames were nothing more than small flickers. I strode over to one of them and sliced the back of my hand, dipped my fingertips into the blood, and then brushed them against the flame symbol at the base of the silver lantern. The flames immediately burned brighter and chased more of the darkness away.

I went to the next lantern and repeated the process, the glyph greedily absorbing the magic in my blood. Samara strode to the wall opposite me and did the same on the lanterns on that side. It didn't take long to light up the enormous room.

"These walls are made out of the same stone as the rest of House Harker," Samara mused as she ran her hand along the dark grey stonework. Then she slowly walked back to the center of the room, her steps echoing across the empty space. "What the fuck is this?"

"There's a door." I pointed to what was likely the one and only exit. So far, the layout of the place was the same as the one I'd explored before. "Maybe we'll find some answers through there."

Samara pursed her lips as she glared at the door like it had personally offended her. I bit back my laugh, not wanting to have another dagger thrown in my direction. On one hand, she was still pissed off over how all of this had played out—Samara liked to be in control and do things in a logical manner—but I also knew she had a bit of a wild streak and was obsessed with learning more about the Fae.

Despite her rant a few minutes ago about the Fae and their shady history, Samara would latch onto any opportunity to figure out more of the history of Lunaria, which meant diving into all the strange things the Fae had left behind, and this whole situation definitely qualified as weird, shady Fae shit.

I was a little disappointed this room was empty just like the one beneath the Sovereign House. Not because I'd expected to find anything that could help me, since my fate was already sealed, but because it would have made Samara happy to find some new piece of history.

"Let's go look," she said with a sigh, but she walked quickly, excitement practically dripping off her. I let myself smile now that her back was to me and I wasn't at risk of sharp, flying objects. She swung the door open and stopped with a sharp intake of breath.

I quickly closed the distance between us, my arm slinking around her waist, ready to pull her back from any potential threat. Another room stretched out before us, significantly larger than the one we'd just been in. The Fae lanterns in this one hadn't weakened, the entire area brightly lit, and neat rows of beds took up most of the space. Unlike the more elaborate beds that had been left behind in the fortresses, these ones were of a simple but functional make. Each one had a bottom and top mattress and blankets and pillows still tucked into place.

I released her so she could explore. This was indeed exactly like the room under the Sovereign House. And just like that one, this one only provided more questions instead of answers, it seemed.

"It's a shelter . . ." Samara walked slowly between the rows, eyes skimming over the room. "Did they never use it? Or did they retreat here and then leave?" I kept my mouth shut since I didn't have an answer and it was clear she was mostly talking to herself at this point.

She stopped by one of the beds and plucked at a blanket, raising it a few inches before letting it drop, a frown stretching across her beautiful face. "Something frightened the Fae enough that they built secret passages leading to a room that held some type of magical doorway to a bunker." Her eyes raised to the ceiling. "I think we're underground, directly below the fortress. If they planned for all this, they must have assumed that the fortress, despite all its wards, could be compromised. They wouldn't trap themselves down here." She looked away from the ceiling and started scanning the rest of the room. "There must be an exit somewhere that leads off the grounds."

"What do you think happened to the Fae?" I asked as we resumed our walk around the unused beds. The stillness of the room bothered me. It was like we were walking through a graveyard that had never actually been used.

Samara glanced over her shoulder at me. "I think the theory about the Unseelie losing control of their shadow magic is the most likely. It would explain the wraiths. From the books we've managed to find, everything indicates the arrival of the wraiths coincided with the disappearance of the Fae. It seems highly unlikely that there isn't a connection between the shadow monsters and the Unseelie. We know they hated the Seelie. We just don't know why."

She turned away and hurried down the row, something drawing her attention. I clenched my hands at my sides as I watched her go, a dull ache forming at the base of my skull. The promise of pain was a reminder of the geas. My mother had a lot of control over me, but even she couldn't compel me not to speak of her secrets.

Erendriel could.

Which meant I couldn't scream at Samara that she was wrong. Even just thinking about doing so was ratcheting up the pain. I paused by one of the beds and pretended to look at something as I leaned against it and pulled in several deep breaths. It'd taken me a while to figure out how to calm my thoughts and empty my mind, but it was the only way I managed to hold onto my sanity. Something that greatly disappointed my mother when she'd tried so hard to break me.

I didn't know why she hated me so much, but there were many things I'd never understood about her. In the end, it didn't matter. I was a weapon for her to wield until she no longer deemed me useful, and that day was coming soon.

All I cared about now was figuring out a way to keep Samara and Kieran safe. There was no saving Lunaria, but perhaps they could be protected. Not if they kept going down this path though. I knew Samara had been at that temple. When I'd returned with Erendriel and smelled her blood at the entrance, I'd felt the same terror I had the night my mother had looked at Kieran and smiled.

Erendriel had raged as we scoured the area, but there had been no sign of the wraiths we'd left behind. To my relief, Samara had already been gone, but it'd been difficult to maintain a steady heartbeat as the scent of her blood had hit me. I'd smelled the blood of at least three others as well, but I hadn't recognized who it belonged to. Erendriel had stared at the bloodsoaked ground, but the Fae didn't have a particularly sensitive sense of smell. He couldn't even tell it was Moroi blood, let alone who it belonged to.

Lying to Erendriel was tricky. I wasn't sure if all Fae could detect a lie or if he could only tell when I lied because of the geas he'd placed on me. Fortunately for me, I'd grown up in the Moroi courts and was quite skilled in misleading words and partial truths. When he'd demanded to know who the blood belonged to, I'd purposely knelt by a puddle of blood that did not belong to Samara. So I had been truthful when I'd claimed not to know who had been there.

My gambit had only bought Samara and her friends a little bit of time. The proposed marriage between Samara and me was real. Currently, my mother thought the Harker Heir could be controlled. If Samara would just agree to marry me, then the queen would be satisfied for a while. It would provide me an opportunity to figure out how to keep her and Kieran safe long-term and make it easier for me to keep track of them, because where Samara went, Kieran would surely follow.

I couldn't let them go back to that temple or stumble into any other areas where the wraiths frequented. They had no idea just how much the world was falling apart around them, and I couldn't let them walk into it blindly, but I couldn't tell them either.

If my mother found out just how much Samara knew . . . she'd make sure Samara met an unfortunate end, likely at the hands of wraiths. She'd also make sure anyone Samara might have told would be killed off as well. The Moroi Queen did not like loose ends.

Carmilla was the wild card in all this. The best I could tell, she was truly just friends with my mother and wasn't caught up in the plot with Erendriel and the wraiths, but I'd been wrong before about people and paid dearly for it. The only two people in the world I trusted were Samara and Kieran, and they both thought I was the villain in all this.

Which I supposed I was. An unwilling one, but a villain all the same.

I started to turn in the direction Samara had headed when the light from the Fae lanterns glinted off something nestled in the blankets of one of the beds. It appeared something had been left behind after all. I strode over to the bed and pulled back the blanket. A perfect glass sphere sat there, a swirl of dark blue and purple with thick white markings that reminded me of clouds cutting through the color.

A Fae memory ball.

Excitement coursed through me, and I picked it up, concentrating on the magic within. But the hope I'd been feeling faded. Empty. Someone had brought it here but had never stashed a memory in it. Looked like whoever had used this safe room before would continue to remain a mystery to us.

I glanced to where Samara was standing at the other end of the room, facing the wall, and hurried after her. There might be another one of those weird portal spells here, and I didn't want to risk her activating it without me.

"Find something?" I asked when I neared her.

"A book. Poetry." She held up a slim, leather-bound book, not taking her eyes off the wall. "And another glyph. I don't know this one."

My arm brushed against hers as I leaned in closer, but she was so engrossed by her discovery that she didn't seem to notice. Unlike the glyph in the other room, this one was carved into the stone and easier to spot. It was a triangle with three horizontal lines slashed through it.

"Never seen one like this before." A mischievous smile curled on my lips as I reached out to touch it.

"Damn it, Drav!" She gripped my wrist and tugged my hand away. "Quit touching shit you don't understand!"

As soon as Samara realized she was still holding me, she released her fingers almost reluctantly. My grin transformed into a self-satisfied smile. She *liked* touching me. Despite everything she knew—or thought she knew— about me, Samara wanted me. I needed to use that to my advantage if I was going to convince her to marry me.

"Where did you find the book?"

"Over there." She pointed towards an empty bookcase tucked into the corner. "I didn't find anything else. Either they never actually used this space, or they cleared everything out when they . . . left."

"Trade you." I tossed her the memory ball, and she snatched it out of the air with one hand. I saw the exact moment disappointment hit her when she realized it contained no memories.

I tugged the book out of her other hand and started flipping through the pages. "Unseelie," I noted, which made sense because, based on the style of murals I'd seen on some of the walls and ceilings here, this had been an Unseelie stronghold. "Didn't know you were a fan of poetry."

Samara's cheeks darkened, and she hastily took the book back, clutching it to her chest. "I'm intrigued by anything they left behind. You know that. Plus . . . I have a friend who . . . umm . . ." Samara stammered, and I cocked my head at her as she continued to struggle. "They like it when I read Fae poetry to them, and this book has a bunch of poems I've never read before."

I had absolutely no idea what was making Samara blush like crazy, but it was highly amusing.

"Here." She handed me back the memory ball. "You found it, so it's yours."

I took the Fae artifact from her and pondered it for a moment. Perhaps it was reckless of me, but if things went bad—which I strongly suspected they would—I wanted her to have at least one good memory of me. Kieran too. Maybe someday, they could view me as someone other than the villain.

"What are you doing?" Samara asked, tension flooding her voice as I sliced open my thumb on my fang and swiped the blood over the glass orb.

My blood vanished, and I felt the tug on my mind as a copy of the memory I'd chosen slipped into the orb.

"Here." I held the glass sphere out to her. "A memory just for you. Might I suggest listening to it at night . . . when you're alone in bed."

Her gaze narrowed on me, and I let my lips curl into a sinful smile. I was rewarded by her cheeks flushing before she scowled. "It'll make a beautiful paperweight."

I laughed before waving a hand at the rest of the room. "Do you want to look around more?" Not that there was much to see. I was curious about what the glyph on the wall did, probably an escape route of some kind, but I could return later and explore.

"No." Samara shook her head, dark eyes darting back to the glyph. She knew something about it. Something she didn't want to share with me. Turning her attention away from the wall, she gave me a brilliant smile that caused my heart to skip a beat. The way her eyes laughed at me, I knew that had been her intention. Samara never had any problem wielding her beauty to knock others off their game. "This place is depressing. Let's go walk on the beach for a bit. I want to feel the sun on my skin."

"Anything for you, Sam." I let my voice drop low so it was more of a raspy purr than anything, and Samara's smile slipped for a fraction of a second, her breath hitching before she rolled her eyes at me and took my arm as I extended it to her. "Hopefully the glyph that got us down here can also get us back up to that room."

That was how the one beneath the Sovereign House worked, so I assumed this one did as well, despite it's magic being a little fucked up. Samara just hummed her agreement as we walked back down the aisle, arm in arm, neither of us speaking.

CHAPTER TEN

—

Samara

"FUCK!" Kieran yelled as I buried my fangs into his neck. His thrusts became harsher, and my thighs trembled while I matched his pace as I straddled him on the couch in my suite. One hand was tightly wound up in my hair, and the other gripped my ass so hard, I knew I'd have bruises. A delicious heat was building in my core as his breathing grew ragged, and I knew we were close.

He'd already made me come several times with his fingers and tongue, but I just couldn't get enough of him. I pulled away from his neck, blood dripping down my chin, and arched my back. Kieran released my hair, both hands moving to grip my hips as he pounded into me. Then he leaned forward, kissing and licking my breast before sucking a nipple into his mouth.

I let myself lean back as far as I could, trusting Kieran to not let me fall, and reached one hand down, brushing over my already sensitive clit as a breathy moan slipped from my lips.

"That's it, gorgeous," Kieran growled. "Play with that clit for me while I fuck this amazing pussy of yours." His words had me practically coming as my fingers swirled through my hot slickness and pushed down on my clit.

"Harder, Kier!" I screamed.

He let go of my breast and leaned back against the cushions, his grip punishing as he did as I commanded, the new angle allowing him to reach even deeper. I couldn't stop the scream that erupted out of me as I came hard all over his cock, and Kieran bellowed as he came with me.

With trembling muscles, I leaned forward and slumped against his chest. "First part of the plan, done," I panted.

Kieran laughed as his arms wrapped around me. "I don't know. Maybe we should go again just so everyone knows for sure where we are and what we're doing."

"That's what you said an hour ago," I mumbled into his chest. "Besides, I'm running out of dirty things to scream."

He tightened his arms around me. "Just please be careful, Sam."

I raised my head enough to meet his gaze. "I will, I promise. It's probably nothing anyway, but I know I saw that glyph in the caves by the beach. I think it's just an escape route, but the Fae might have left something there, and we need to find it before Draven does." I pursed my lips. "He suspected I was holding something back earlier about the symbol. I know he did."

"He's always been annoyingly observant," Kieran said tightly.

"You okay?" I asked, searching his face for the answer. "I know it's got to be difficult being around him again, and I'm sorry I have to spend so much time with him."

"It's okay," Kieran assured me. "Is it fucked up that I'm kind of glad he's here? I should hate him. After everything that's happened between me and him, and us knowing what we do about him and the wraiths . . . plus him trying to marry you for probably bullshit reasons. But . . ." He trailed off.

I kissed him gently. "You missed him."

"This is all kinds of fucked." He blew out a breath. "I'm still *inside* you and I'm thinking about *him*."

"Lucky for you, my ego is unshakable." I bit down on his bottom lip hard enough to draw blood, and he groaned. "I'm equally fucked, because I was thinking about him too, and Alaric."

The glass ball containing a memory from Draven was currently sitting on the table in front of my settee, nestled amidst books and paperwork. I hadn't scrounged up the courage to see what he'd transferred to it and didn't know if I'd ever be able to.

"We are *fantastic* at complicated relationships." Kieran brushed my hair back over my shoulder, gold streaking through his brown eyes. "I love you, Sam. Whatever happens with the others, you have me forever."

"I love you too, Kier." I snuggled back down against his chest and breathed in his scent. Kieran always reminded me of dawn on a spring day. If I closed my eyes, I could almost picture the dewdrops hanging off the tulips that bloomed early in our garden. "We'll figure the rest of it out."

"The rest being the evil prince who we both have the hots for, the Marshal who may or may not kill you, and my asshole best friend who is absolutely in love with you and refusing to admit it?"

"Yes. That." I let out a husky laugh. "I'm reasonably sure Vail isn't going to kill me. At this point, he's had two chances, and both times, he's ended up saving me instead."

"After trying to kill you," Kieran pointed out.

"I mean, he didn't try that hard." Reluctantly, I raised myself off Kieran, both of us groaning as he slid out of me. "If Vail truly wanted me dead, then I'd be dead."

"Was that meant to be comforting?" He gave me a flat look. "Because given that you're about to go traipsing around in a cave with him, I'm gonna let you know it's not."

I cleaned myself off with a towel before pulling on some clothes. Not much point in rinsing off, considering where I was headed. "Alaric will be there too." I quickly braided my hair and then wrapped it up in a bun.

Kieran walked over to where I was standing by the window, concern stamped all over his face. "Don't say anything to piss off Alaric. He might shove you into the water, and then you'll come back smelling like seaweed."

"No promises. I exist to piss that man off."

"That is definitely what Alaric believes."

We both snickered as I unlatched the window and swung it open. This was the trickiest part of my plan. I needed to climb down the wall to the courtyard and then quickly make my way out of House Harker. Draven had said he was retiring to his room after dinner, but I doubted that. Ary and Aniela were also still here, and I wouldn't put it past them to do a little sleuthing before they left tomorrow morning. Luckily, this window opened up to one of the smaller courtyards near the outer wall. There was a secret tunnel on this side that we could use to get outside the walls so we didn't have to go through the main gate.

I just needed to climb down without drawing attention. Or falling.

The cool night breeze danced across my skin as I peered down. My living quarters were towards the top of the tower, and it was a long way to the ground, but it wasn't fear racing through me right now. Exhilaration lit up my skin as I breathed in the crisp air and admired the cloudless and starry night.

We might currently live our lives by day, but it was night that made us feel truly alive. Even tonight, when the moon was barely a sliver in the sky.

Moroi. Velesian. Furie. We were all Moon Blessed.

I sat on the windowsill and swung my legs until they dangled over the edge, Kieran's lips quirking as he watched me.

"You're kind of insane. You know that, right?"

"It's one of the many reasons you love me." With a sharp inhale, I let my bloodlust rise. It was easy to control during the day, but beneath the moonlit sky, it surged forward, and I had to claw it back so I could stay focused.

Kieran's brown eyes studied me, noting the change in my eye color and how my nails had lengthened into claws. There were other small changes, ones I couldn't see but could feel, like the killing instincts that slumbered beneath my skin coming out to play.

Not the least bit afraid, Kieran leaned down and claimed my mouth with his, gold sparks dancing in his eyes when he pulled back. "I want to feel those claws running down my back later as I bury my cock inside you again."

"Have I ever told you that you're excellent at providing motivation?" I smirked before twisting off the window and letting myself fall, my clawed fingertips instantly finding purchase between the bricks. I tilted my head back as much as I could to meet Kieran's stare from where he was leaning out the window and shaking his head at me. "You better be naked when I get back."

He laughed quietly and continued to watch as I hugged the wall and quickly scaled down towards the ground. It'd been a while since I'd done this, but I used to all the time when I'd been a kid. My parents hadn't liked me roaming around at night, but I loved walking on the beach under a full moon, so I'd sneak out without them knowing.

Or try to.

More often than not, my mother would be waiting for me at the bottom of the tower, fighting back an amused grin while she tried to lecture me about the dangers of climbing down a tower wall. Then she'd take me on a moonlit ride.

Of course, back then, my chest had been considerably smaller. I should have wrapped my breasts tighter. Aside from being cumbersome and making it difficult to cling to the wall, they weren't exactly comfortable. As soon as my feet hit the ground, I gently placed my hands over my breasts while I silently apologized to them.

"What are you doing?" Alaric hissed in a low voice from where he was standing with Vail in the shadows.

"Apologizing to my tits for dragging them against the bricks for the last two minutes," I snapped back as quietly as I could, the two of us glaring at each other.

"I'd say fuck and get it over with, but you already did that," Vail grumbled. "We doing this or what?" He didn't wait for an answer, just strode off down the narrow passage that stretched between the main tower and two of the smaller ones.

Alaric started to follow after him, but my hand shot out, and I gripped his arm, letting my claws sink into his flesh. Not a flicker of pain appeared on his face as he took in my predatory black eyes. I knew he didn't like it when I let my bloodlust ride high like this because it reminded him of the cousin who had turned Strigoi when they had been kids. While I understood why he felt this way, I didn't agree with it. Our bloodlust made us stronger, and it could be controlled. Even Moroi who didn't belong to the House bloodlines could do so with careful practice. Alaric was deliberately inhibiting himself by denying his true nature.

"How does he know about us?" Alaric was hardly the type to kiss and tell, and he certainly wouldn't where I was concerned.

"There is no *us*," he growled and yanked his arm out of my grip. His rejection stung, but I refused to let him see that. Alaric clenched his jaw and looked away when I merely arched an eyebrow. "I ran into him after I left your study. He could smell you on me."

"Great." I blew out a breath. "Now he's going to be even more of an asshole." I let my claws shrink back into nails but didn't bother trying to pull my bloodlust back any more than that. This close to the House, it was unlikely there would be any nasty beasties, but it was still nighttime in Lunaria, so one could never be too careful.

Alaric huffed out a laugh. "Can we go now?"

"Lead the way." I gestured dramatically down the alleyway, and Alaric just rolled his eyes before stalking away. Vail had accused me of sleeping with both Kieran and Alaric before, and now he knew it was true. I didn't fully understand Vail's problem with me, but for someone who claimed to hate me, he acted awfully jealous of my lovers.

The Marshal of House Harker was waiting for us at the end of the passage. The sides of his head were freshly shaved, and he'd pulled his shoulder-length, brown hair back into a bun. He'd trimmed his beard back quite a bit and ditched the bones that he often braided into it. Only Vail could still look half-feral despite the cleaned-up appearance.

The silver streaks in his dark grey eyes glinted at my approach. He'd been avoiding me the last couple of days, Alaric having to track him down and inform him of this plan. While Alaric was unnerved by my eyes full of bloodlust, Vail's reaction was the slight flaring of his nostrils and a hard look at my neck. The silver in his eyes expanded before he turned away and flattened his hand on the outer wall, activating the glyph on it. A section large enough for us to pass through vanished from the thick stonework, and the three of us quickly slid through. Within seconds, the hole vanished, and the wall was once again solid.

It was a shame the Fae were gone, because their magic was truly extraordinary.

Not gone, I reminded myself. The wraiths were Unseelie, and now they were using that extraordinary magic of theirs to reclaim what they'd lost. At the cost of our lives.

"LET ME SCOUT IT OUT FIRST," Vail said from where we stood at the mouth of the cave. The entrance was enormous, towering far above us. Water rushed in, surging around the jagged rocks that broke the surface here and there. It was low tide, which would make things a little easier for us. Vail hesitated before glancing at me. "You remember the path we used on the right side?"

"Yes." I nodded. "My memory is a little foggy about where I saw that glyph, but I think it's behind the large, flat rock."

"Alright. Listen for my call, and then follow in after me." He slipped away into the darkness, the moonlight reflecting off the large sword strapped to his back. We'd never encountered any monsters when we'd explored the cave system as kids. Given its location on the beach and the tide rolling in and out, it wasn't particularly appealing to the beasts that roamed the woods.

"I forget sometimes . . . that you and Vail were friends," Alaric said quietly.

"Yeah." A bone-weary sigh slipped past my lips. "He was my first friend, really. You always hated me, and Kieran didn't show up until we were teenagers."

"I never hated you, Samara."

"Really?" My gaze cut to his, and I saw desperation and need in his eyes before he quickly turned away. Frustration filled me. Maybe it would be me pushing him into the seawater, but if I didn't ask him, I knew I'd regret it. "What do you feel for me, Alaric?"

Big surprise, he didn't answer. I rolled my eyes, lacking the patience to deal with Alaric's bullshit right now, and returned my attention to the cave. Occasionally, I'd feel his attention on me and thought he might say something, but he never did. After a few minutes, Vail's sharp whistle cut through the air.

"Let's go." I headed towards the right side, watching my step as we moved from the sandy shore to the slick, algae-covered rocks. "Step where I step. This path was challenging a decade ago, and it's probably gotten worse. I really don't want to go for a swim tonight to save your ass if you fall in."

"You just don't want to get your hair covered in seawater," he sniped back.

I looked over my shoulder at the hair he kept closely cropped to his head. "You don't know what it's like to care for long hair. There's a bunch of algae and seaweed in the cave. I'd probably just cut my hair off rather than deal with the grossness of it."

"No," he said quickly.

"No?" I stopped and turned more to face him.

Alaric stared at me for a long moment, his lips pressed tightly together like he was debating something huge before finally saying, "I like your hair."

"You mean you liked having your hand fisted in it while I sucked your co—"

"Samara!" he growled. I laughed and resumed walking towards the path. He made it too easy.

Silvery beams of moonlight lit up the cavern, courtesy of the random holes in the ceiling. Vail and I used to stare at them and try to figure out what had caused them. Something about them didn't seem natural, but we'd never been able to figure out what.

Bioluminescent algae shimmered in the water as the waves rolled in. There wasn't much of it this time of year, but in late summer, the entire shoreline practically glowed an impossibly bright blue. Right now, it was more like little gems sparkling in the dark.

After telling Alaric to be cautious, of course *I* was the one to slip on a loose rock while admiring the water. A strong arm wrapped around my midsection before he tugged me back against his warm chest.

"Careful," Alaric whispered in my ear. Then he flexed his fingers, his thumb brushing the underside of my breast before he stepped back.

I immediately mourned the loss of heat, even as I wanted to growl at him for being so indecisive. He wanted me, that was certain, but one minute he was determined to deny that feeling, and the next he was running his hands over my body.

Once again, I debated pushing him into the water. It'd serve him right.

With a frustrated exhale, I continued forward, being extra aware of where I was stepping. It didn't take long for Vail to come into view. The cavern basically went straight back before the rest of the tunnel plunged under the water. There wasn't actually that much to explore, it was just precarious to do so because the few rocks that rose above the water level were always damp and slippery. During high tide, it was impossible to get to the back without getting wet.

Vail waited for us on a large, circular, flat rock. It was the only part of the cavern that was never submerged. Just as I was about to jump from our path to join him, something below caught my attention, and I stopped to peer into the depths. The water directly in front of the rock Vail was standing on was cast in shadow, and it was difficult to see anything.

"Samara?" Alaric asked from behind me.

"I thought I saw something," I murmured, my eyes still scouring the water but finding nothing. "Maybe it was just some seaweed."

"Scared, Heir?" Vail taunted, and I glared at him before launching myself across the open water to the large rock, Alaric landing gracefully behind me a second later.

I brushed past Vail and headed towards the back of the rock but couldn't resist looking up to the sky above us. This section of the cavern had the most damage to the ceiling. When we'd been kids, I would beg Vail to sneak out with me to come here at night. We'd lie on our backs and stare up at the stars while the waves crashed around the rocks beneath us. Vail would point out all the constellations to me, and I'd hang on his every word.

Then our parents had died, and everything had changed. I'd only come back here once after the night the wraiths had attacked and changed both our worlds forever. Part of me wanted to ask Vail if this was his first time returning to this cave since then, but I couldn't bring myself to utter the words.

"I remember it being somewhere back here. Be careful around the edges,

Alaric," I said over my shoulder. "This rock doesn't extend entirely to the wall, so it's possible to fall through the crack."

The three of us started searching the cave wall for any sign of the glyph, but because of the constant moisture, algae grew in patches on the rocky surface, making it challenging to see what was beneath. I started running my fingers across the surface instead of relying only on my eyes. Even when glyphs were completely tapped out of magic, something about them still called to the magic in our blood.

Minutes ticked by, and I started to lose hope when I felt it, the slight tingle across my fingertips when they went over a rough patch of rock. I slid my dagger out of my thigh holster and scraped the algae aside, a triangle with three horizontal lines through it greeting me.

"Found it!" I called out.

Vail and Alaric moved towards me, but I didn't wait. I dragged the blade across the back of my hand and dipped my fingers into the blood that welled. Magic pulsed as I pressed my bloody fingertips against the glyph, a static charge filling the air. I barely felt it across my skin, but two pained grunts sounded from behind me.

"What the fuck was that?" Alaric cursed.

"I don't know," I said, frowning at the glyph. "It didn't hurt me though. I felt it brush across my skin, but that's it."

Before we could debate it more, the rocky surface shimmered and vanished. As soon as I stepped across the threshold, Fae lanterns blazed to life, painting the large room in a warm, soft glow. It wasn't nearly as big as the space I'd explored with Draven earlier, but it was more than the simple tunnel I'd been worried we'd find. The walls were lined with shelves, most empty . . . but not all.

I moved to a section that had several shelves full of books and carefully pulled one from the shelf. Just like in the previous room, no dust covered the leather-bound book. Whatever spell the Fae had used to keep this room clean was still working, along with the lanterns.

Alaric appeared at my side, pulling a different book from the shelf while Vail moved around somewhere behind me, but I couldn't pull my eyes from the page, not believing what I was seeing.

"This wasn't written by the Fae," I whispered.

"What?" Alaric's fingers froze mid-page flip.

I swallowed. "This is my mother's handwriting."

CHAPTER ELEVEN

—

Samara

"Your mother?" Alaric leaned closer to look at the book I held open with trembling hands. "What language is that?"

"Ours." Heat built behind my eyes, and I blinked several times to clear away the gathering tears. "My mother liked to use it for personal things she didn't want anyone else reading. She taught it to me."

Alaric glanced between my book and his. "The handwriting in this one is different. Look." He held the book out to me, and I compared the writing to my mother's. He was right. It was written in the same language, I recognized that, but the handwriting was completely different, and the pages looked older.

I carefully set my mother's book back onto the shelf and took the book from Alaric, flipping to the front. "Rosalyn Harker," I read the name out loud. "This is the journal of my ancestor. Rosalyn and her daughter were part of the original ritual that changed us from human to Moroi."

The Velesians and Furies had been born from the same ritual. We still didn't understand exactly how they'd done it or why there were three distinct branches of magic. All we knew was that the ritual had been connected to the moon, and that was why we considered ourselves Moon Blessed. Aside from that, we'd only been able to find part of the wording for the ritual.

"We will give our lives for the blood."

"We will yield our fates in the wild."

"We will lose our souls to the fury."

I hadn't realized Rosalyn had clawed back enough of her humanity to be able to write. Most of that first generation had been completely lost to their bloodlust. They had basically been Strigoi.

The small amount of writings we'd found from that time period suggested the House bloodlines had been the first to come back to themselves, but I didn't think it'd been to this extent. There were at least three dozen journals here. Did they belong to all the Harkers who had come before me? Why hadn't my mother ever told me about this place?

Metal groaned, and I winced when a particularly high-pitched sound echoed across the chamber.

"Sorry," Vail grunted from where he stood before a dark hallway. "This must be the tunnel that connects this room to the one you found earlier." He disappeared into the darkness, and I set the journal down on the shelf before wandering over to inspect the tunnel myself.

I had to step back when Vail appeared again, almost bumping into me. "It's completely caved in." He shook his head. "Unclear if it was an intentional cave-in or if it just happened on its own, but there's no getting through it now."

"Do you think it's worth clearing out?" I looked around him into the inky darkness. "It would give us an escape tunnel if we ever needed it, but it also means someone would have a way to sneak into House Harker."

"I'll think about it." Vail's stormy grey eyes once again fell to my neck, and I suddenly became aware of just how close I was standing to him. I took a small step back, and the silver bled through his eyes until they were like bright moons.

"You good?" I asked warily. Usually, the rangers were pretty good about wielding their bloodlust as a tool. It was rare for any of them to turn Strigoi, but that didn't mean they didn't occasionally lose control for small amounts of time, like Vail had in the temple. My fingers slid down to rest on the handle of the dagger at my thigh.

Vail's gaze dipped down to the blade, and his lips curled in distaste. "Like I would ever want the taste of your blood in my mouth again." He stalked forward, forcing me to jump out of his way, even as a dull ache rose inside my chest. Apparently, being back in this cave didn't bring back fond memories of our friendship for him the way it did for me.

I tucked away the pain of Vail's words—I really should have been used to it by now—and walked over to where Alaric was studying something on the wall. Vail stopped to stand at Alaric's right, so I stood by his left, needing some space between me and the Marshal.

"Map of Lunaria," I murmured. Though calling it a map was a bit of an exaggeration. Someone had scraped landmarks into the stone wall. I recognized Drudonia at the center and some other landmarks, but it was rudimentary at best. We had far better maps than this.

Vail stepped forward and brushed two fingers against a marking that looked like an *X*. Now that I'd noticed that one, more jumped out at me.

"Someone was looking for something, and they didn't want anyone to know about it." I glanced over my shoulder at the shelves where the journals rested. "I don't think it was the Fae."

"Where is this?" Alaric pointed to what looked like a lake with a circle around it.

The three of us leaned in closer to examine the markings. "If that's Drudonia"—Vail pointed to the blocky buildings that looked like a fortress—"then the only large body of water there is Lake Malov."

I chewed on my bottom lip. "What if there is another secret room like this one around there? Maybe that's what whoever made this map was searching for?" I suspected it had been my mother, but what I didn't understand was why she had been keeping it a secret, and did Carmilla know about this?

"Do we care?" Alaric stepped back and crossed his arms. "While I acknowledge that all of this is fascinating, we have some more pressing concerns."

"Agreed," Vail said. "This feels like a waste of time."

"We don't know that," I argued. "Generations of Harkers kept this place a secret. They wouldn't have done that for nothing." My mother wouldn't have done that for nothing. My throat seized as I thought about her sneaking down here and writing in that journal. Had she been planning on telling me eventually? Maybe this would have been something she passed down to me? Part of the Harker legacy. Unfortunately, death claimed her first. "Let me read through some of the journals. Maybe there is something in them that explains this." I waved at the wall.

"However you want to waste your time isn't my problem." Vail shrugged.

"Helpful as always," I snapped. "Where's the bag you brought?"

He flicked his fingers towards the entryway we'd passed through from the cave, which was once again solid. I stalked over to the leather bag lying on the ground. It wouldn't fit all the journals, but I could bring at least half a dozen back with me. Alaric joined me as I debated which ones to grab.

My mother's were definitely the most recent and the likeliest to have relevant information. My heart clenched at the idea of reading her words and getting a glimpse into what she'd been feeling. I checked through the bottom shelf and figured out where her journals started. There were five of them, which I carefully stuffed into the sack before eying the shelf.

It was unlikely Rosalyn had written anything that would help us, but I couldn't resist knowing. I grabbed the first journal on the shelf and placed it with the others before adjusting the strap of the bag on my shoulder.

"Do you think we should come back later for the rest?" I asked no one in particular.

"They're probably safer here than anywhere else," Alaric said. "No one knows about this place, and if Draven goes back to that room the two of you found and tries to use the passage, he'll find it blocked."

I couldn't argue with that logic, even if I didn't love the idea of leaving the rest of the journals here, but if I asked Vail to have some of his rangers guard this place, that would only draw attention to it. The journals had been here for multiple generations, so unless I came up with a better solution, I'd just have to trust that they'd continue to be safe in this room.

"Let's head back." I gave one last reluctant look at the rest of the journals before activating the glyph on the wall again and slipping back into the cave. Now that I knew where the glyph on this side was located, I felt like it would be obvious to anyone.

As if reading my mind, Vail rapped his knuckles against the damp rock. "This type of algae grows fast. That glyph will be covered again in less than a day."

I nodded. Vail might be an asshole to me, but he knew what he was talking about. The only one who had a reason to visit this cave was Draven, and that was only if he tried to map out where the escape tunnel might lead to. Yet another reason for us to keep an extra close eye on him. I couldn't let him find those journals. It was unlikely he'd be able to understand the language, but he'd almost certainly remove them.

A warning whispered across my skin, my instincts picking up on something while I'd been lost in thought, and I halted halfway to the path that led out of the cave. Vail instantly went still beside me, but Alaric continued walking, oblivious to the danger that had crept in while we'd been examining the hidden room.

"Alaric," I said in a low but commanding tone. He froze where he'd been about to jump across to the rocky path before slowly taking a few steps back.

Clouds must have rolled in recently, because the previously moonlit cave was now shadowed in darkness. Only the flat rock we stood on was still mostly lit up, and even that light was filtering in and out.

Something was moving in the shadows. A lot of somethings.

"Vail?" My fingers wrapped around the dagger as I slid it free. It was the only weapon I had with me. Swords had never been my strong suit—I was much better with ranged weapons but hadn't bothered bringing a crossbow because it wouldn't have been that useful here. Now I was kind of wishing I had. If I threw my dagger, I'd have nothing.

"Not sure," Vail murmured, his silver eyes tracking the movement across the walls. "I think whatever they are, they came from the sea. They're moving . . . strangely."

Great. We'd managed to find a monster even Vail hadn't come across. Alaric made his way back to my side, a wicked, cruel dagger in his hand. Of the three of us, he was the most disadvantaged, because he suppressed his bloodlust so ruthlessly. Aside from our fangs and claws only making an appearance when we let our bloodlust rise, we were also stronger and faster when we leaned into it.

Frustration warred with concern inside me. If Alaric got himself hurt because of his stubbornness, I'd beat the shit out of him later.

The hair rose on the back of my neck, and I sidestepped so my back was to Vail and looked at the wall behind us. "Fuck. It. All." My heart raced as I watched dozens of creatures silently crawl down the rocky surface from where they'd been traveling across the ceiling. They vaguely resembled the occasional starfish I'd find while walking along the shore, which would be fine . . . except for the six eyes arranged in a perfect circle and the eight serpentine tentacles that stretched out.

"Can someone explain why the fucking starfish look like spiders?" Alaric cursed.

"Because Lunaria, that's why. Of course we'd have fucked-up arachnid starfish." I glanced up at the ceiling, which was teeming with hundreds of them. "If these things fall on us, I'm going to scream."

I wasn't kidding. There were a lot of things I could deal with. Spiders were not one of them.

"We make our way to the same path as before," Vail said calmly. "Samara, take the lead. Alaric in the middle. I'll cover you both."

"I should go first." Alaric glared at Vail. "Samara is the Heir of House Harker."

"Samara can handle herself just fine," Vail growled.

"Or maybe you're thinking third time's the charm in getting her killed?" Alaric narrowed his eyes at Vail, who was looking at the leaner-built Moroi like he was debating chucking him into the water as bait while we got away.

"It's fine, Alaric." I placed a hand on his forearm, and he glanced at where we were touching before meeting my gaze, a sharp, close-lipped smile stretching across my face. "I'd rather have you at my back anyway."

Vail stiffened, but before he could say anything, I stepped towards the path, my gaze bouncing between the wall writhing with monsters and the slippery rocks. Now was really *not* the time to fall.

I slid to the side just as the air shifted, and a creature slammed into the rock where I'd been standing a second ago. It landed on its back, giving me a view of the center of its underbelly, where five triangular teeth mashed together in its circular mouth. I barely managed to bite back my shriek. Its nearly two-foot-long tentacles slid across the ground, and it started to flip itself over. As soon as its back was to me and the tentacles were pointed in the opposite direction, I kicked out as hard as I could.

A loud splash sounded from where it had landed, but I could hardly make out the rocks two feet in front of me. The rest of the cavern was nothing but inky blackness. Sure would be nice for the moon to come back right about now.

The sound of hundreds of tentacles sliding across the algae-covered wall echoed around us, and I stepped closer to the edge of the rock. Slender tentacles stretched out from the wall towards me, and three more fell from the ceiling around us. I raised the strap of the bag over my head so that it rested diagonally across my chest before tucking the dagger back into the holster on my thigh.

More monsters fell from the ceiling, and one of them hit my shoulder and bounced off, its tentacles grazing my skin. Alaric hissed behind me as several of the starfish critters began to fall on the other side. I'd be jumping straight into them, but right now, there were only half a dozen on the ground. We needed to go before all of them fell off the ceiling.

I backed up a few steps, bumping into Alaric, then ran towards the edge and leapt across, but something wrapped around my ankle just before my feet hit the other side and yanked me back. My scream was cut off as my upper body slammed into the rocky ledge before I was dragged backwards. Tentacles grabbed me from all sides as I desperately dug in with my clawed fingers, trying to find purchase, but the rock was too hard and slick.

"Vail!" I cried as I went over the edge. Water splashed below as several starfish lost their grip on me and fell. Every muscle in my body screamed as my fingers gripped the edge of the rock. Whatever was wrapped around my ankle pulled harder, and pain raced down my arm as one of the smaller monsters wrapped all of its tentacles around me and flattened its circular mouth full of sharp teeth against my bicep.

My fingers started to slip when another tentacle wrapped around my waist, and I felt something pull on the bag. "VAIL!"

Two sets of hands gripped my arms, Alaric grunting where he was flat on his stomach above me, hands wrapped around my left forearm while Vail held my right arm, bright silver eyes shining with determination. "Don't look down."

A low, trembling, keening sound came from beneath me, and I couldn't help but look. Never in my life had I ever so immensely regretted disobeying a command. A shriek tore from my lungs. "Pull me up! Pull me up!"

"We're trying!" Vail ground out.

The enormous, spidery starfish beneath me pulled harder. It had to be at least twenty feet wide, and its eyes glowed a sickly yellow. I could feel something cutting into my skin where its tentacles had wrapped around me, and pained whimpers slipped from my throat. The rock to my right shook as it slammed another tentacle there, and I saw the flash of small, curved barbs on the underside.

Just when I thought things couldn't get worse, the starfish clinging to the ceiling started to drop even more. Alaric's and Vail's grips slipped, and I dropped another inch. "I don't want to get eaten by a fucking starfish!"

"Don't let go!" Alaric ordered. Several starfish chose that exact moment to fall on his back, and he bellowed, fingers digging into me as he tried to hold on. Vail hissed when one fell on his shoulder and latched onto his flesh.

"I've got her," Vail growled. "Keep these fucking things off us. Otherwise, we're all going to die here!"

"Fuck!" Alaric bellowed, tearing himself away to deal with the monsters ripping into him and Vail. The loss of his grip on my arm sent me swinging, and Vail's claws dug into my arm, skin tearing as I was wrenched into an awkward angle. The tentacle around my right ankle was pulling me to the side, while the one around the bag was pulling straight down.

My body pivoted until I was looking down at the beast once more. Terror drenched me at the small bulges moving across its body, unfurling their tentacles before gliding off into the water. That must have been how they'd all gotten here. This was their mother, and she'd carried them on her back.

Blood ran down my arm from where Vail held onto me. Despite his efforts, his grip had slipped to my wrist, and I knew he couldn't hold on much longer. I gritted my teeth and swung my free hand towards the dagger on my thigh, agony shooting through my back. It felt like I was being torn in two, but I freed the blade from its sheath.

I had one chance. If I missed, I would fall. To fall was to die.

Vail grunted as the creature pulled harder on my ankle. I used the momentum of being twisted to the side to my advantage and focused on the closest of the large, yellow eyes. The weak point. No matter the beast, eyes were something to be protected.

"Get ready, Vail." I panted before flipping the dagger in my hand and hurling it a second later. It whistled through the air, the spinning blade catching the small patches of moonlight and reflecting them back before sinking home, straight into the starfish's eye.

Water churned as the tentacled beast thrashed and the tentacle around my ankle slipped away. Vail heaved me up, but I only made it halfway before the tentacle around the bag tightened and pulled me back down.

"Slip the bag off!" Vail commanded.

"No!" I screamed. We needed the information in these journals, and they had belonged to my mother. I couldn't let this part of her go, not without knowing what it meant.

"Damn it, Sam!" Vail clung to me, desperately trying to pull me up. "It's not worth your life!"

The strap snapped, and I barely managed to grab hold of the leather bag before it fell into the water. The tentacle around it tightened while another one tried to pry the dagger out of its eye.

"So fucking stubborn." Silver flashed inches from my face before a blade sunk into the tentacle gripping the bag. The dark, rubbery appendage flinched but didn't let go. Another dagger. Another twitch. Two more daggers joined the others before the beast finally decided this amount of pain and effort wasn't worth it. Water thrashed below as the starfish pulled back its tentacle and retreated further into the water.

A deep vibration I felt in my bones erupted throughout the cavern as Vail pulled me up and the smaller starfish slid towards the edge of the rock before falling into the water. The starfish still making a meal out of my bicep was ripped off, but in my pained haze, I barely noticed. Rough hands yanked me forward, dragging me as I clutched the bag and my shredded arm to my chest.

My ankle didn't feel like it was in much better shape, and by the time we made it to the sandy beach just outside the cave, I was barely capable of limping. I collapsed, my trembling muscles finally giving out, and I pulled aside what was left of my shredded pants to examine the damage . . . and immediately regretted it.

"Fuck," I hissed as I saw white bone peeking through the ripped flesh. I was lucky I hadn't lost my damn foot, because those barbs ripped entire chunks out. Clenching my jaw, I stretched my hand towards the wound to draw the healing glyph, but large fingers wrapped around mine before pulling them back.

"I'll do it," Vail practically growled at me. Apparently, he was still pissed, which was fine. I was used to Vail being pissed at me.

He reached over his shoulder and rubbed his back where the freaky little starfish had fallen on him. His fingers came back bloody. I winced as he drew the healing glyph on a small patch of mostly undamaged skin. The burning, itchy sensation was immediate, and I let out a low hiss, turning my head away from the bloody disaster that was my lower leg.

Alaric gave me a flat look as he knelt beside me. "You should have let go of that fucking bag," he said coldly. Vail grunted in agreement as he looked over the rest of my leg.

"I—"

"Shut the fuck up, Sam," Alaric snarled, and I snapped my mouth shut. I didn't regret what I'd done, so I wasn't going to argue with him or Vail over it. The two of them could just be pissy together. My leg jerked involuntarily as some of the muscles pieced themselves back together. The healing spell might have been incredibly useful and sometimes lifesaving, but it fucking hurt.

Even worse, as the adrenaline continued to wear off, I could feel the rest of the smaller wounds spread over my body. I held my forearm out in front of me and grimaced at the deep grooves Vail's claws had left behind while he'd been clinging to me.

With more tenderness than I thought him capable of, Alaric grasped my arm and tugged it towards him, resting the back of my hand in his palm as he drew the healing glyph right below my elbow. Technically, once the healing glyph was drawn on a body, it would heal all wounds, but it always started with the closest ones.

My breaths came out in rapid bursts as the two healing glyphs worked in tandem. A distraction. That's what I needed. Vail was still busy examining me for any other major wounds that needed immediate attention, which I was a little surprised he cared about but was not willing to bring it up and get into it with him. Instead, I focused on Alaric, who had settled back into a crouching position after starting the healing on my arm.

Dozens of wounds covered his arms, ranging from shallow to alarming based on how much blood was still dripping out of them. Chunks of his tunic had been torn away, and I could see more bite wounds on his chest.

"Come here," I said firmly. Alaric glared at me for a moment before leaning forward again. I brushed my fingers across some wet blood on my arm and pulled his tunic down, revealing more of his chest. He wasn't nearly as large and muscular as Vail, but Alaric was in excellent shape. Like Kieran, he sparred regularly with the rangers and found it relaxing to go on daily runs.

Personally, I only ran if my life was on the line.

I felt his heavy stare on me as I traced the glyph over his heart. It was the best solution when there were multiple wounds like this and none were life-threatening. Our natural healing was impressive, and we could survive almost any wound as long as our heads remained attached and the blood loss wasn't too severe, but it was nowhere near as fast as the healing glyph and could only fix wounds inflicted by non-magic means.

Alaric winced before leaning back and closing his eyes as the magic coursed through his body, and I frowned when he looked on the verge of passing out. While he had a lot of wounds, none of them looked particularly serious. Our blood was necessary to initiate the glyph, but the magic behind the healing spell basically used the magic within our body, just at an accelerated rate. It was why, in life-threatening situations, an injured Moroi was usually given blood to drink as well.

"Here." I stretched my mostly uninjured arm out to Alaric. Every part of me ached, and I was pretty sure I would pass out any second, but he looked worse than me. "Drink."

Alaric reeled back like I'd struck him and leapt to his feet, swaying slightly before stiffening his back. "Absolutely not."

"Don't be a stubborn ass!" I snapped. "It's just blood, Alaric. You clearly need it."

"I'm fine," he ground out, even as turquoise bled through his green eyes as he stared hungrily at my still extended arm. Realizing what he was doing, he tore his gaze away and spun around, stalking away from me. "Get her back safely, Vail."

"Alaric!" I called after him, but he ignored me and kept walking. It wasn't that long of a trip back to House Harker, just down the beach a quarter mile before cutting up a trail. The chances of him running into anything nasty between here and there were slim . . . but I also hadn't expected to find terrifying, spider-like starfish in that fucking cave.

Arachnistar? Arachstar? Starachi?

As far as I was concerned, since I'd found them, I got to name them. I'd have to think of something good. Hopefully they wouldn't make that cave their new home. Otherwise, getting back into that room would not be fun. Then again, they would make an excellent deterrent for anyone who tried to explore the cave . . .

Vail stood up, apparently satisfied that I had no other wounds that required immediate attention. I struggled to my feet and sucked in a breath as aching muscles barked at me. The skin on my arm and leg was smooth and unblemished, but it still felt like my body had been through a meat grinder. I pursed my lips as I stared at the long stretch of beach before us. This would not be a pleasant walk back. I had no idea how I was going to climb back into my room either.

That was a problem for future Samara. For now, I set out at a slow but steady pace. Vail trailed silently behind me, and it set my teeth on edge not being able to see him but knowing he was there all the same. I made it two minutes before I snapped.

"Can you please just walk beside me?"

He sighed and moved to my side, and I started walking again, fighting the blackness that was starting to encroach on my vision. Just ten more minutes on this beach, another ten-minute hike up a fairly steep hill, then all I had to do was scale up the tower wall that led to my bedroom.

Piece of cake.

"Should have just slept in that room," I muttered, and Vail laughed under his breath. It had a deep, raspy quality to it. He might be a Moroi, but Vail's voice had always reminded me of a wolf shifter with its gravelly edge. "I'm glad we didn't run into those things as kids," I said lightly, checking his expression from the corner of my eye.

Vail liked to pretend our childhood friendship hadn't existed, but for once, he didn't bite my head off. Instead, a rueful smile played across his lips. "That definitely would have put a damper on our stargazing. Plus, your screaming was a lot higher-pitched back then. Would have blown out my eardrums."

"Ass." I shoved his shoulder, but the movement proved too much for my body when everything went dark for a second. The world tilted, and suddenly, my head was leaning against something warm and hard. I blinked several times, trying to bring the world back into focus, but ended up peering into Vail's face.

"Rest, Samara." His gaze flickered down to mine before quickly pulling away. "I've got you."

"Please don't feed me to the monsters," I mumbled before burrowing further against his chest. "You've had three chances to kill me now and failed each time. Is this your way of saying you like me again?"

"Sam?"

"Yes?" I answered sleepily.

"Shut up."

The world went black.

CHAPTER TWELVE

—

Vail

SAMARA'S EYELIDS FLUTTERED RAPIDLY. She'd been dreaming for the last hour, and I had yet to figure out if it was a good or bad dream. Her midnight black hair was fanned out across my bed, and she'd been snuggling into my pillows and blankets since I'd laid her here hours ago.

I'd only hesitated for a moment last night before bringing her back to my room. She'd passed out hard, her body shutting down so it could finish healing. The wound on her leg hadn't smelled right when I'd been examining it. I couldn't say for sure, but I suspected there'd been some type of toxin in the barbs of that fucking gigantic starfish. Luckily the smaller ones had yet to develop those barbs; otherwise, all three of us would have been in serious trouble. As it was, Samara had taken the worst of it.

An echo of the fear I'd felt when she'd been dangling off that rock ledge raced through me, followed quickly by rage at remembering how she'd refused to let go of that fucking bag. Not for the first time, I wished Samara had never returned to House Harker. It'd been easy to hate her when she'd been gone, playing the dutiful wife at House Laurent, but that piece of shit Demetri just had to fuck things up.

My fingers clenched into fists, and I felt my nails harden enough to bite into my skin. I'd thrown the failed marriage in Samara's face when she'd come back. It had been an asshole thing to do, even by my standards, but Samara always took my hatred in stride, which only pissed me off more.

No matter what I did, she never broke.

The blanket slipped down as Samara rolled onto her side, burrowing further into the pillow and letting out a breathy sigh. Satisfaction rolled over me at seeing her in one of my shirts but was quickly replaced by frustration... and confusion. Even if I was starting to acknowledge that I didn't truly hate her, I definitely did not like her. Not like *that*. It was just an instinctual response I'd have to any beautiful woman in my bed wearing my clothing.

Covered in my scent.

Fuck. My nostrils flared, and I stalked over to the window. Unlike Samara, I didn't have a large suite. My living quarters only consisted of a bedroom and a small washroom. Carmilla had repeatedly offered me a place in the main tower that had larger and fancier accommodations, but I preferred to be in the barracks with the rest of the rangers.

Samara's spicy and intoxicating scent intertwined with my own drifted over, and I squeezed my eyes shut. I couldn't fucking escape her.

Moroi were possessive. We might have lax views when it came to sex, but once we claimed a long-term partner, we were ruthless about it. There were exceptions, but polyamorous relationships were far more common amongst the Velesians. It was why I found Samara's relationship with Kieran and Roth so confusing. And I'd always known Alaric had a thing for her too despite his attempts to hide it.

More often than not, I found Alaric Lockwood irritating to deal with, but I still had a begrudging respect for him. He was incredibly smart and used his brains to help House Harker instead of the social ladder climbing many of the higher-ranking officials attempted. And now he and I had something in common: we were both struggling to deal with our shifting emotions when it came to Samara.

The anger I felt towards her was still there. Always burning under my skin. The night all our parents had been attacked—the night they'd died—I'd gotten Samara to safety, and when I'd tried to go back and help my parents, Samara had knocked me out. She claimed she'd done it to save my life, but I knew that was bullshit. She just hadn't wanted to be left alone. It was her life she'd been worried about. No one else's.

In the months and years after that night, I'd never seen Samara cry once. She acted like the death of her parents didn't matter and had obsessed over House politics instead. It didn't take her long to secure an advantageous marriage. She'd gone to Drudonia to study and then flittered off to House Laurent to be yet another pampered Heir.

Carmilla had tried to make excuses for Samara's behavior to me, but more than once, she'd confessed she wasn't comfortable grieving her sister around Samara because of how little her niece seemed to care. While Samara had been away, it'd been easy to believe the worst about her.

It was why I'd left her to die when that kùsu had attacked us weeks ago. When the long, insectoid beast had slid between us, its pinchers snapping in excitement at finding its prey, I'd felt a savage relief. Like Samara had been getting what she was owed for costing me everything.

Then I'd seen the flash of betrayal on her face before she turned and raced away from the monster. Away from me. An almost blind panic had overtaken me as I'd chased after her to fix what I had done, to save her, and I had, barely getting there in time but saving her all the same. She knew what I had done though, and now it lay there like an ugly truth between us.

Now I had to live with this simmering hatred and also the memory of how much she'd once meant to me. Samara had been my only real friend growing up. There'd been nothing romantic there, we'd been far too young for that, but the friendship . . . it'd been real.

As soon as we had set foot in that cavern last night, the memories had come flooding back. Us sneaking out under the always watchful eyes of our parents. Laughing as we ran across the beach. Carefully climbing those rocks until we collapsed onto our backs and watched the stars flickering across the sky.

I hadn't just lost my parents the night the wraiths had attacked our caravan. I'd also lost my best friend.

Now that best friend had grown up into the most beautiful woman I'd ever seen and was sleeping in my bed. *In my fucking shirt.*

Blood dripped from my knuckles, and I forced myself to take a slow, deep breath while I unclenched my fists. I wanted to leave, go into the wilds for a few months, hunt some monsters, and clear my head. However, now that we knew Prince Draven, and likely the Sovereign House, was involved with the wraiths, I couldn't leave. Not that I was particularly useful—subterfuge and subtleness were not in my skill set.

The inability to act was killing me, and there were brief moments when I thought about just slitting the prince's throat and dumping his body in the ocean for the sea monsters to feed on. That wouldn't solve anything though and would only draw the attention of that Fae we saw in the temple, Erendriel, and, of course, the Moroi Queen herself. I might not be good at playing this bullshit political game, but even I knew that would be foolish.

Adding to my frustrations was the fact that Carmilla was at the Sovereign House and, as far as I was concerned, in the hands of our enemies, even if she didn't know it. I also selfishly wished she was here so I could talk to her about Samara. Not my attraction to her—that would be awkward—but to maybe clarify some things.

Carmilla had always made it seem like Samara had been quick to move on from her parent's death and wasn't supportive of her aunt's grief over dealing with the death of her sister and sudden rise to the Head of House Harker. But that just didn't seem right. Samara was deeply loyal to those she cared about. Perhaps Carmilla had simply misinterpreted the actions of her niece back then because she'd been caught up in her own grief.

It had to be something like that. Carmilla had always been a presence in my life growing up, but after my parents had been killed she stepped in to fill the void. She never tried to replace my mother or father—that was impossible. But she became an aunt of sorts. Always there to lend support or just be someone I could talk to. I had risen through the ranks to take on the mantle of Marshal all on my own, but I couldn't deny that knowing I had Carmilla's unwavering support had been a boon.

I didn't have any blood relatives left, so Carmilla was basically my only family. After everything she'd done for me, I couldn't let anything happen to her.

Samara stirred again on the bed, drawing my attention. I scowled at her before silently walking over to my washroom and rinsing the blood from my hands. The wounds had already healed, but I could feel the undercurrent of exhaustion in my bones.

I needed to consume blood. Soon.

Like most adult Moroi, I associated drinking blood with sex, but since I was the Marshal, I wasn't comfortable sleeping with any of the other rangers because of the difference in power. More than a few had made passes at me, but I'd always turned them down. Instead, I had some regular partners in various outposts who were more than happy to let me bury my fangs in their flesh while I fucked them senseless. It was a good arrangement that left everyone happy.

Even some of the Velesians I knew were game, although their blood wasn't as fulfilling as another Moroi's. We might all be Moon Blessed, but the magic between the three groups was different enough that it didn't always play nicely together.

Plus I couldn't leave to visit any of them now. I frowned at my now healed palm. Maybe I could ask Adrienne or Emil, two of my most trusted rangers. Not for the sex part, just a little top up of blood. I couldn't afford to be slower or weaker right now.

Just as I was about to step back into the bedroom, a low, throaty moan slipped from Samara's lips. I froze in the doorway. *You've got to be fucking kidding me.* Was she having a damn dirty dream in my bed? I watched as Samara twisted around in the bed, more of the blankets slipping away. The way she was lying caused my shirt to pull tight around her full breasts, giving me a full view of her erect nipples pushing against the fabric.

Then she let out another breathy noise that went straight to my dick.

I'd faced countless monsters in my life. Wraiths. Howlers. Kùsu. Every single one of those encounters I'd survived because I never hesitated.

Yet I had no fucking clue what to do at this moment.

Should I wake her up? That wouldn't be awkward at all. Her moaning turned into quickened breaths as one of her hands started to slip beneath the covers.

Oh, fuck me.

I rubbed a hand roughly against my beard. Leave. That was the best option, because if Samara ever learned of this, she wouldn't be embarrassed. Instead, she'd tease me about it mercilessly, and my feelings for her were complicated enough as it was. I'd just wait outside until she was . . . finished.

Angry banging sounded on the door before I'd made it halfway across the room. Samara bolted upright in bed, her cheeks flushed, and looked around in confusion. Her dark purple eyes landed on me, and her brows furrowed. She glanced down and plucked at the light tan shirt before looking back at me in question.

More banging came from the door.

"Vail!" Kieran yelled. "What the fuck are you doing?"

Samara leapt from the bed and raced to the door while I stood there like an idiot. She flipped the lock and yanked the door open, grabbed Kieran by the front of his tunic, and pulled him inside. He stumbled a few steps before catching himself while she closed the door and crossed her arms.

"Could you be any louder, Kieran? Or did you forget we're trying *not* to draw the attention of Draven?"

"I didn't know where you were!" he said urgently, barely managing to keep his voice down as he glowered at me. If he expected me to tremble before him, he was dumber than I'd thought. I had at least six inches on him and outweighed him by quite a bit. The bright turquoise and gold outfit he was wearing really didn't help the intimidation factor either.

I gave the pretty peacock a flat stare. *Honestly, what does Samara see in him?*

"Alaric told me what happened and that you were with Vail. He said you were fine and then passed out on the settee," Kieran explained as he gave up on staring me down and looked Samara over instead. His eyes widened when he took in what she was wearing. "Why are you in his shirt?" he demanded.

"Oh, this old thing?" she drawled as she twirled the edges of the shirt that dangled by her mid-thigh, and I looked away as it lifted up. "You'd have to ask him."

Kieran whirled around to face me, and for a second, I thought he might punch me. "Try it." I shrugged. "Could use a good laugh."

He actually took a step forward, but Samara was there in an instant, standing between us with her hands on his chest. "How about we use our words instead of our fists?" Kieran looked like he'd bit into something sour but wrapped his arms around Samara when she twisted so her back was against his chest. I kept my eyes focused on hers, refusing to let them drop to where Kieran's arms were now resting across her stomach. "Care to fill us in on what happened last night? All I remember is walking back on the beach with you, and then . . . you caught me when I fell."

"The barbs in those giant tentacles had some type of venom. Probably something to neutralize prey. You passed out, so I carried you back." I crossed my arms. "It was pretty clear you weren't making that climb back into your room, so I figured the barracks were the best place for you to sleep it off."

"So you just stripped her down when she was unconscious?" Kieran looked at me coldly.

"You're lucky she's here—otherwise, I'd break your jaw for what you're implying." My arms dropped to my sides and my fingers curled as I imagined grabbing him by the neck and slamming his head into the wall. "She was covered in dried blood and her clothes were torn to shreds. As soon as I got her into my room, I retrieved Adrienne. *She* was the one who cleaned Samara up. We used my shirt because it's large and baggy and agreed it would be most comfortable for her to sleep in. I slept on the floor."

Samara's eyes cut to the small space between the bed and wall. "You didn't have to do that," she said softly.

I shifted on my feet. "It's fine. I've slept in worse conditions." Her eyes lingered on me, and the discomfort I'd been feeling only increased. I could deal with Samara when she was annoyed or frustrated at me. I could even tolerate her when she was being obnoxious and flirty, but when she looked at me like she genuinely cared about my well-being . . .

"I've wasted too much time babysitting you," I growled. "Your pretty boy can fetch you other clothes. Close my door when you leave."

Before she could argue, I brushed past the two of them and fled into the hallway, and as soon as the door closed behind me, I let out a deep breath.

"Went that well, huh?" a bright, cheery, feminine voice asked.

"Adrienne," I groaned. "It's too early for your bullshit."

The blonde ranger fell into step beside me. She was tall for a woman, only a couple of inches below six feet, but I still towered over her. As the Marshal, I was in charge of all the rangers who belonged to House Harker, but I also had my own unit who traveled with me regularly. Adrienne had been part of that unit since the beginning, so I knew her well. Everything about her reminded me of sunshine. It should have been annoying, but somehow, it just worked for her.

"The sun has been up for hours," she pointed out. "I got here five minutes ago because I was worried Samara might have murdered you for being a prick."

"And you were going to avenge me?" I slid a glance at her.

"Fuck no." She laughed. "Was gonna help her hide the body."

"Your loyalty could use some work," I grunted.

Adrienne gave me a wide-eyed look. "She's the Heir of House Harker. Who else could I possibly be loyal to?" Thick eyelashes blinked rapidly over her bright blue eyes, where only the faintest lines of gold could be seen.

"I'm gonna tell Emil to pummel you in sparring today."

She grinned wickedly. "Please, I could beat that old man with one arm tied behind my back."

We both knew that was bullshit. Emil was older—he was one of the only fourth-generation Moroi who was still an active ranger. Despite being in his late eighties, he still looked and acted like he was in his forties. Even I had a hard time bringing Emil down. As good as Adrienne was, she was still nowhere near Emil's level.

But he had a soft spot for her, so he always went a little easy on her.

We traded barbs back and forth, and some of the tension eased out of me. A few rangers passed us and waved in greeting, but most were already outside or still sleeping if they'd been on night shift. We reached the stairs at the end of the hall and headed down. The barracks were a long, rectangular building that had four levels above ground and two underneath. We weren't sure what the Fae had used the building for, but the original rooms had been much larger before it had been repurposed for the rangers. Now the rooms were small but comfortable with a mix of singles and doubles. There were a few large enough for six or more, as visiting rangers from other Houses sometimes preferred to bunk together.

"Anything to report?" I asked as we stepped out into the bright, midmorning sun. Emil might be a better fighter, but Adrienne was more skilled at dealing with people, so she served as my right-hand. If she ever needed advice, she'd go to Emil. The arrangement had worked well for us for years.

"One of the units is back from investigating some type of burrowing creature on the badlands border. I think you'll be interested in what they have to say." Something about her tone gave me pause, like she was amused, but if she hadn't said it outright, then there was no convincing her to say it now. I'd just have to speak to the rangers and see what they had to say. "Also . . . Nyx has decided they're fully recovered, and they are currently in the sparring ring."

"It's been a week," I said slowly. "They were healed days ago."

"That wraith broke over a dozen bones in their body, including some of the vertebrae in their spine." She clenched her jaw as her cheeriness faded. We were all protective of Nyx because they were like a younger sibling to us, but neither I nor Emil had any actual siblings. Adrienne had a younger brother who had died when they'd been teenagers. I didn't know the specifics of it, only that it was one of the reasons she'd left her original House and came to Harker. "They should take another week off."

"Adrienne." I stopped and waited until she faced me. "Nyx is fine. They're frustrated that the wraith got the jump on them." The sound of bones snapping echoed through my mind as I remembered Nyx slamming into that wall at the temple. It was Samara who'd made sure Nyx got out. She'd prioritized the young ranger over her own safety. It was a surprising move for the Heir of a House. Foolish even.

Yet it had thawed a little more of my hatred towards her.

"Emil will make sure Nyx takes it easy." I rested a hand on Adrienne's shoulder. "And I'll make sure they don't go out on any missions any time soon."

"No missions without my approval," Adrienne pushed. "And they have to go with you, me, or Emil."

"Okay," I agreed, my lips twitching as I fought back a smile I knew she'd punch me for. "But try to limit your hovering. Nyx's confidence in their abilities is in the shitter, and you being a mother hen isn't going to help with that."

She slapped my hand off her shoulder. "I'm going back to my babysitting duties. Not that Roth ever leaves their room." Adrienne frowned. "Actually, maybe I'll stop in the kitchen and grab them something. They didn't eat any of their dinner last night." My lips curved upwards. "I'm not a mother hen!" Adrienne yelled before stalking off in the direction of the main tower, and I laughed under my breath at her retreating form.

"She's a fiery one."

For the second time this morning, I froze, the prince strolling up to stand beside me. It'd been a long time since someone had been able to sneak up on me. Adrienne and I had stopped in one of the small alleyways that led between the barracks and one of the smaller towers. Sound tended to echo against the stone walls, and yet I hadn't heard a single footstep.

"Draven." I didn't bother making my tone friendly. Adrienne and I had been talking quietly enough before her outburst that I was certain he hadn't overheard anything. She would have seen him if he'd been behind me, which meant he'd been lurking somewhere nearby and waiting for her to leave. "Something I can help you with?"

"Not going to fawn all over me the way everyone else does?" He smirked.

"No." For once, I wished Samara were here. She was clever with her words and would have no problem conversing with the traitor. Meanwhile, I was struggling not to bury my dagger in his gut.

"Man of few words." His blue eyes glinted with amusement. "I find that rather refreshing."

"I'm happy for you." I started walking. "You'll have to find someone else to entertain you though. I've got things to do."

"Is Samara one of them? She stayed in your room last night." Moonsdamn it. I stopped and slowly turned back around. "Although . . ." He tapped a finger against his chin. "She was with Kieran early on in the night, and she didn't leave her room through the door. Only other option was the window." Draven cocked his head and suddenly looked less like the charming, harmless prince and more like a cruel predator. "Does Kieran know she's going behind his back to fuck you?"

There was an edge to his voice I didn't quite understand. It sounded like he was more concerned about Kieran than anyone else. If I denied sleeping with

Samara, he might wonder why else she would have snuck out of her room. Fuck.

"Kieran is aware of our relationship," I ground out. "But given her role as Heir and mine as Marshal, we prefer to keep things quiet." There. A totally believable lie.

"You might be an impressive ranger, but you're a terrible liar." The faint lines of red in Draven's eyes started to thicken as he looked at me like I was a bug he couldn't figure out. "She flaunts her relationship with Kieran, who is a courtier and technically below her station. Rumor is she's involved with some scholar from Drudonia—I'm assuming that's the person who's been holed up in that room you have your lovely, fiery ranger guarding. And clearly, there is something between her and Alaric."

"We're a complicated lot." I eyed him warily. There was something . . . not right about him. I was used to being around Moroi who channeled their blood-lust—that was part of it, but not all.

"That is the truth." He stepped closer to me, more red bleeding into his eyes. "I find it strange that Samara would fall into your bed though. It's not exactly a secret how much you hate the Harker Heir."

In a heartbeat, I closed the distance between us until we were almost touching. Draven didn't back down an inch. We were almost the same height, but he wasn't built as broadly. "You know nothing about me," I said coldly. "And you sure as fuck don't know anything about me and Samara."

I looked at him through silver eyes, my bloodlust rising to meet his as he let out a dark laugh. "You'd be surprised about the things I know." The red faded from his eyes until it was barely visible, and the foolishly charming prince persona slid back into place as he gave me a lopsided grin. "Good chat. We should do this again sometime."

Then he stepped around me and whistled as he walked away, leaving me wondering what the fuck had just happened.

CHAPTER THIRTEEN

—

Samara

THE HALLWAY of the barracks was empty when I slipped out of Vail's room, for which I was thankful. I really didn't want to explain to anyone what I'd been doing there. Adrienne knew the truth, and I knew she wouldn't breathe a word of it. Personally, I didn't really care about who people speculated I was sleeping with, but I knew it would piss off Vail. Despite his opinion of me, I didn't actually strive to find new ways to make him despise me more. Thank fuck Ary and Aniela had left, because the Heirs would have had a field day with this.

It'd taken some persuasion on my part, but I'd convinced Kieran to go check on Alaric and preferably get him to feed. I knew Alaric wouldn't listen to me, but maybe he'd listen to his best friend. I also knew Draven would likely be lurking somewhere in the main tower, and I wasn't ready to face him just yet. My mind was still racing from what we'd discovered last night, and my body was tired from healing. I couldn't afford to be off in any capacity around Draven.

Although, I could afford to spend an hour throwing some daggers in the rangers' training area while I thought through some options. Plus, I could check on Nyx, which I hadn't done since we'd returned. They'd still been healing from the wraith attack on our trek back from the badlands, but Adrienne had assured me they were doing okay.

Warm and floral spring air greeted me as I exited the barracks. Summer would officially be here in a few weeks, and the days were already getting hot. I pulled my hair up into a bun as I walked and turned to duck through one of the small alleyways that led to the training grounds before pulling up short.

"Vail?" I took a few unsure steps towards him. He was standing in the middle of the alleyway with his back to me, but I knew he must have heard me approach. Stealthy, I was not.

"The prince knows you were in my room," he said quietly when I reached his side.

"Fuck," I cursed.

"My thoughts exactly." He turned his head to gaze down at me, and I saw frustration in them. "He believes we're sleeping with each other. I didn't correct him. Figured it was better to have him think that than start asking questions about why else you may have been there."

"Okay, not ideal, but I can work with this." I chewed on the inside of my lip as I absently stared off to the side. Vail clearly wasn't happy, considering the tension radiating off him, but this could be to our advantage. I'd reaffirm that Vail and I were sleeping together next time I spoke with Draven. On the plus side, if Vail and I had to look into anything, we could use this fake relationship as a cover.

Vail remained silent as I thought through all of this. His eyes were mostly silver, so something had triggered his bloodlust, but I didn't think it was solely because of this turn of events. "Did something else happen?" I scanned his face, looking for clues but discovering nothing besides the frustration and general anger I seemed to always find in his eyes. "You seem a little intense. Even more so than usual."

The silver receded until only thin tendrils of it wound amidst the dark grey. "There is something off about the prince. I don't know what . . . but he is more than he seems."

"I know," I said quietly. "Even though I've known Draven for most of my life, this past week has made me realize that I actually know and understand very little about him. The prince is full of secrets."

"You sure we shouldn't kill him?"

I honestly couldn't tell if he was joking or not. Knowing Vail . . . not joking.

"Not right now." If I was looking at this from a purely logical standpoint, Draven being dead could solve some problems. Even thinking that caused something inside my chest to tighten, but if the Moroi Prince truly was the villain in all of this . . . could I really put the future of our people at risk because Kieran and I had feelings for him?

No, I couldn't. It would break something inside me, but if Draven truly was choosing to harm other Moroi of his own accord . . . then I'd bury a dagger in his heart myself.

Draven's words from our dinner earlier in the week floated through my mind. *The only thing I've ever known are nightmares.* There was more to this than I was seeing. "Until we understand his role in all this . . . we don't harm the prince."

Vail studied me for a long moment. "You like him."

"It's complicated." Sensing an argument, I started to walk away. It may have been late in the morning, but I hadn't had any tea yet, so Vail would just have to wait to tear into me.

My escape was short-lived though because Vail gripped my arm and moved me back roughly. I hissed as he shoved me up against the wall, boxing me in with his large body.

"Do I need to remind you that he brought guards with him that night at the temple? That he offered them up to that Fae bastard like they were nothing?" Vail kept his voice low, but it vibrated with rage. "Or of the Moroi, including *children*, who have been slaughtered in the outposts by wraiths?"

"My memory is just fine," I said icily.

Vail leaned in closer until his face was only inches from mine. "Then think with something besides your greedy fucking cunt for once."

"Fuck. You." I shoved my hands against his chest, letting my nails lengthen and harden until they were claws that sliced through his leather and into his flesh. "I am beyond sick of your shit, Vail. You hate me. Then you don't hate me. Then you're back to hating me again. Make up your damn mind! Also you don't have a problem with any of your rangers sleeping around, and you have a fuck buddy in almost every outpost. So why exactly are you so concerned about *my fucking cunt*?" I let my last few words turn into more of a throaty purr at the end, solely because I knew it would slip under his skin and enrage him even more.

In a blink, Vail ripped my hands away from his chest and pinned them above my head. The position forced his body to press against mine, and I could barely shift my head back enough to glare up at him. The scent of his blood filled the air, and if my fingers were within reach, I would have licked the blood off them. I'd been delirious at the temple, but I still remembered how delicious his blood had been.

I could be pissed off at him and want his blood at the same time. Nothing messed up about that at all.

"Keep it up, Samara"—Vail's eyes dropped to the throbbing pulse on my neck—"and I'll dump your body and the prince's in that fucking cave for the monsters to dine on."

Despite the harsh words, it wasn't hostility I saw in Vail's eyes. It wasn't just hunger for blood either—although that was definitely there. It was desire. Hot burning desire.

Holy fuck.

"Vail." I smirked at him when his gaze snapped to my mouth and the way my lips had curved. "If you want a taste, all you have to do is ask. Although, if someone walks by and catches us, the rumor about you fucking the Harker Heir will spread like wildfire, which I suppose will help our cover story."

A sharp exhale flew out of my lungs as Vail shoved himself off me and back-tracked until he was several feet away. I casually raised my fingers to my lips and licked the blood off, then I let out a deep chuckle when silver flared in his eyes before they hardened. "Honestly, Vail, you make it too easy."

He took a step towards me, fingers curling into fists before spinning and stalking down the alleyway. Even when he was pissed, he moved quietly. I waited until he was gone before sagging against the wall. "Well, that was a little terrifying," I muttered.

I knew it was a bad idea to antagonize Vail. Although, I was mostly sure he wouldn't actually kill me. He'd had his chance to get rid of me several times at this point and hadn't seized it, or had seized it and then changed his mind in the case of the kùsu attack. He could be such a fucking prick sometimes, and like Alaric, his barbed insults always hit home.

It hurt. I should have been used to it after all these years of being at the receiving end of his vitriol, but I just couldn't bring myself to hate Vail the way he hated me most of the time.

The scent of his blood was still in the air, and I couldn't stop myself from inhaling deeply. He seemed to want another taste of me as badly as I wanted his delicious blood splashing across my tongue again.

I started to walk out of the alleyway, thinking more about the desire I'd seen burning in his eyes. When had that started? There was no way he'd ever act on it, but still—I halted abruptly. Did I... *want* him to act on it? I thought about how it had felt when he'd had me pinned against the wall and a heat unfurled from my center.

No. I shook my head and kept walking. Why was I doing this to myself? I already had Kieran and Roth... and sort of Alaric, if he ever figured his bullshit out.

I was still contemplating this turn of events when I entered the main training courtyard minutes later. There was a narrow passage on the other side with a dead end that was often used for target practice. It was perfect for what I had in mind, I just needed to grab some daggers first.

Emil waved at me from where he was speaking with a group of rangers, and I returned the gesture. Vail might be an asshole, but I liked his rangers. The heavy, wooden door of the weapons storage building creaked open, and I took two steps inside before being engulfed in a crushing grip.

"SAMARA!" a voice boomed. I would have clapped my hands over my ears, but my arms were pinned to my sides.

"Hey, Rokai," I squeaked as the impossibly large ranger crushed me against his chest in a jubilant hug. "Too. Tight."

"Oh!" My feet thumped to the ground, and large hands gripped my shoulders until I was steady. "I was just really excited to see you." Rokai's light brown eyes practically sparkled with joy against his pale skin. "I was just telling Vail about what you did for us!"

Well, shit. I tore my gaze away from Rokai's cheerful round face and found Vail's glittering hard stare on me. Definitely still pissed. I was hoping to give him at least a few hours to cool off before tracking him down again. Unfortunately for me, one of the many plans I was working on would require Vail's help, which meant I would need to catch him in a good mood at some point.

This was definitely not that point.

"I'm glad to see you made it back okay, Rokai." I reached up to pat his shoulder. Rokai was the only Moroi I'd ever met who was larger than Vail. Everyone regularly joked that he must be half-Velesian, but that couldn't be true because he was far too happy. "Maybe we can catch up later? I was actually just hoping to grab some dag— oh!"

Rokai tugged me over to where several other rangers were standing with Vail, and I nodded at each of them in greeting. They all smiled at me, and a few murmured their thanks, although not as aggressively as Rokai, who had me clamped to his side in a one-armed hug.

Vail was currently eying that arm like he wanted to rip it off. A couple of rangers noticed where Vail's attention was, but Rokai continued to chatter on, completely oblivious. "We were investigating reports of some burrowing creatures in the badlands just south of Drudonia, and we fell into a collapsed tunnel. Luckily, the beasties were somewhat shy. They looked like giant grubs." Rokai shuddered. "We killed one of them and the rest backed off, but we couldn't get out."

I snuck another look at Vail. He'd stopped glowering at Rokai's arm like it was offending him and was instead looking at the ranger with a blank expression. I didn't know if that was better or worse.

"It was pure dumb luck that I spotted Samara's striker flying above us, and it came when I called."

"He came because you spoiled the shit out of him every time you stopped by House Laurent," I said pointedly, trying to give Rokai a stern look and failing completely.

"I won't apologize for giving that cute little bastard extra scraps."

Vail's patience finally snapped. "Explain," he barked.

Rokai stood a little straighter, finally sensing Vail's dark mood, and swallowed. "I was on escort duty for most of the last few years and regularly stopped at House Laurent." He glanced at me, unsure, and I nodded encouragingly. "They're . . . uhhh . . . a little unfriendly there, so I never stayed long, but Samara and I would always catch up. We usually went up to where the strikers were housed because nobody ever hung out there."

The poor big softie of a ranger seemed to be wilting under Vail's hostile gaze, so I jumped in. "My striker had been returning from delivering a message to Cali. There are large, flying predators in that section of the badlands, so the strikers usually fly close to the ground so they can duck and cover if they need to. Rokai got the attention of the striker, used his blood to draw their location on the back of the scroll Cali sent me, and I sent some rangers to investigate."

"And saved our asses." Rokai beamed. "We might have had to eat one of those worms if we were in there much longer, and I don't think I would have recovered from that."

"Personally, I would have chosen to starve," another ranger chimed in.

"Well, I'm glad no one had to make the decision between starving or eating an overgrown worm for dinner." I wiggled out from under Rokai's arm and patted him on the cheek. "Good to see you as always. Tell your mother I said hello and that we should have tea soon."

"Of course." He grinned playfully. "And I'll be sure to pay the strikers a visit and give them all treats."

"Obviously." I gave him a wry smile before skirting past the rangers towards the small room in the back, where I knew there were always throwing daggers. The rangers continued the conversation about the new monsters they'd discovered, but I felt Vail's gaze burning a hole in my back the entire way. He was probably pissed off at me for interfering with House Harker business when I'd been at House Laurent, but what was I supposed to have done? Ignored Rokai's plea for help? Sent a message to House Harker and hoped they sent a rescue party in time?

I was fairly confident that no matter what action I had taken, Vail would have found fault with it. Whatever. He could stew in his pissy attitude as much as he wanted. I grabbed half a dozen daggers and headed outside towards the alleyway, which was thankfully empty.

The training courtyard was situated towards the back of the walled fortress of House Harker. The end of the alleyway was the outer wall, and two of the smaller towers made up the side walls. For targets, the rangers had cut down a large tree and sliced the trunk, hanging the circular chunks of wood on the wall. A few of the more creative rangers had used their artistic abilities to paint monsters on them. Once the wood was too chewed up for the blades to stick in, they were swapped out.

I flipped a dagger a few times in my right hand, getting a feel for it before throwing it at the center target. A loud *thunk* sounded as it landed dead center. I sunk into a pattern, aiming for different sections of the targets, trying to be as precise as possible. Daggers weren't entirely practical weapons. The damage they inflicted was too small and rarely fatal for the monsters roaming Lunaria, but sometimes there were specific areas of a body that could be exploited. Even if it didn't result in a fatal wound, it might injure the beast enough for someone else to take it down. Eyes were always a good target. The other problem with daggers was once I threw them, I no longer had a weapon, which I had been reminded of in the cave incident.

I retrieved all the daggers for a third time and set them on a workbench near the front of the alleyway. Then I had a thought: Roth could control their ribbons with blood magic—maybe I could do something similar with a dagger? I thought through a few of the glyphs that might work and then sliced open a shallow cut on my forearm and used my finger to paint one on the hilt of the blade. If I figured out something that worked, I could carve the glyph into the handle to make it more permanent.

After surveying my work one last time, I stepped to the center of the alley and hurled the dagger at the target. The blade dug into the wood, and I took a deep breath, trying to center my focus. No one had been around to teach us how to use our magic, so we'd had to figure it out on our own. Magic worked differently between the Moroi, Velesians, and Furies, but the one thing it all had in common was that intentions mattered.

Moroi couldn't just carve a glyph into something and expect it to work. We had to imbue that glyph with our intent; otherwise, it was just a scratching on a wall. The purpose of the glyphs was to help us channel our intention and keep it there. It was a tricky thing to learn, which was why simple spells were the easiest. I used to tinker around with different glyphs when I'd been at Drudonia, but it'd been a long time since I'd tried to create something new.

Holding my hand out to the side, I tugged on the link I'd formed with the dagger, and an invisible force ripped the blade from the wood before it spun in the air. I had a brief, exhilarated moment of triumph before a sharp pain sliced into my hand.

"AHH! FUCK!" I gripped my wrist with my other hand and clenched my jaw at the pain. The spell had definitely worked, because the dagger had returned to me. Unfortunately, it had returned point-first, and the dagger was now buried hilt-deep into my palm, the bloody blade sticking out the back of my hand.

"Brilliant move," Vail said from where he was leaning against the wall at the alleyway opening. I had no idea how long he'd been standing there, and embarrassment flooded me. He'd once made fun of me when I'd bragged about being good with knives, and here I was, injuring myself with my own moonsdamned dagger.

"Shut up," I growled.

He sighed, walked over, and gripped the handle. Dark grey eyes met mine before I jerked my head in a nod, and I hissed when he quickly but smoothly pulled the blade free. Clearly, I needed to adjust the spell a little bit. Warm blood leaked from my hand as I held my palm out and used my fingers to draw the healing glyph on it.

"Thanks," I mumbled to Vail.

He grunted and studied the glyph I'd drawn on the dagger. "I'm impressed you were able to get it to return to you on the first try."

"I used a similar spell at Drudonia." Trying to ignore the pain radiating from my hand as the wound stitched itself back together, I moved towards the remaining knives on the workbench. "I used that spell to close the window in my room because I always forgot to shut it at night and then didn't want to get out of bed because it was cold. The tricky part of that one was it had to pull the window panels shut without breaking the glass." I winced at both the memory and a particularly painful spot of my hand being healed. Tendons always sucked for some reason. "Might have taken a couple of tries. Rynn and Cali helped me fix the window before anyone noticed."

"Nothing about that surprises me." The amusement I heard in his voice made me look over my shoulder at him. He was still focused on the knife, but I could just make out the ghost of a smile dancing across his lips. "You hate the cold."

I pressed my lips back together before returning my attention to the daggers. Vail was officially more confusing than Alaric.

After some consideration, I tried a few different modifications of the glyph on three of the daggers. This time when I recalled them to me, I was a little more careful. One of the glyphs didn't work at all, another made the dagger only wobble enough to fall out of the target, and the third did come flying back at me, but it was still coming blade-first.

The aim was off, and instead of going towards my palm, it headed straight for my face. I yelped and barely managed to duck out of its way as Vail snatched the blade out of the air without comment.

"Damn it. I really thought that last one would work." I stomped back over to the workbench and scowled at the remaining daggers. Maybe I needed to use a completely different type of glyph. I was using a modification of one that meant summon.

Warmth brushed against my arm as Vail moved to stand next to me. He set the first dagger down, my blood still coating the blade. "What if you use the same spell, but add something to the blade for 'away?'"

"I've never tried to use two glyphs in unison like that." I chewed on my lip as I looked at the original dagger. "In theory, I think it would work."

"Worst case"—Vail swiped the dagger up once more and passed it to me—"you get a repeat performance of getting a blade through the palm."

"Hilarious." I grabbed the edge of Vail's tunic and used it to clean the blade. Then I grabbed another dagger and etched a glyph onto the tip of the original one so it wouldn't get rubbed off when it sank into the wood. I pinched my fingers together where I'd wiped my blood on Vail's tunic and then smeared it over the glyph, letting it absorb the magic.

Flipping the dagger in my hand and focusing my intent, I flung it towards the targets. As soon as it hit the center of one, I called it back to me. The worn handle smacked into my hand seconds later, and my fingers closed around it, a wide grin on my face.

I'd forgotten how good it felt to figure out a new spell, and this would be even more useful than closing a window on a cold night.

"It worked!" I threw the dagger at the targets again but called it back midair, the handle slapping against my palm. I could already feel the magic in the glyph getting depleted. Roth periodically soaked their ribbons in blood to charge up the spell. I'd need to embed a gemstone in the daggers to keep it charged up, but I'd at least figured out the hard part.

I looked to Vail to find him staring at me, that same faint smile on his lips. It slid away as soon as he saw my attention on him though. "Thank you for helping my rangers. You didn't need to, but you did anyway."

Ah, so that was why he was here—and being nice to me.

"My loyalty has always been to House Harker. That didn't change when I married into House Laurent. It will never change." I flipped the dagger a few times in my hand. "Don't ever forget that."

Vail stared at me for a few seconds before giving me a nod. "I won't."

CHAPTER FOURTEEN

—

Samara

THE WORN, brown, leather satchel I'd been carrying around all morning sat next to my curled-up legs. It seemed so innocuous, but the journals resting inside it were anything but harmless. My mother had a whole other part of her life that I knew nothing about. Granted, I'd been young when she'd died, but not *that* young. Was what she wrote in those journals so bad or dangerous that she hadn't wanted to share it with me? Had my father known?

I'd probably find at least some of those answers in them . . . if I could bring myself to pick one up and start reading. Five more minutes. I'd give myself five more minutes to enjoy this tranquility before I dove into my mother's secrets.

Two minutes into my respite, I let out a sigh and raised my head from where it'd been leaning against the tree. Someone was coming—their footsteps were light, but I still heard them. Like most of the Fae fortresses, House Harker was made up of multiple towers with courtyards and gardens interspersed between them. There wasn't space for any serious agriculture, so most of our gardens only had flowers, herbs, and a few easy-growing fruits and vegetables.

I'd chosen to sit in this particular one because it was the least popular of all the gardens. It was nestled in a space behind the main tower and received very little direct sunlight, so it was mostly neglected.

Lavender grew freely and was doing its best to take over the small patch of dirt, though one lone tree sat in the center. We had no idea what type of tree it was, but there was one at every Fae fortress, so everyone just referred to them as the Fae trees.

They bore fruit every year just before summer ended. The palish pink fruit was hard and bitter with bright purple seeds at its center. Aside from tasting horrible, they were highly toxic. One bite, and you'd be hating your life for at least two days. They didn't kill us, but the pain was unimaginable. Or so I'd been told. We discarded the fruit once it fell from the trees to prevent any mishaps.

Maybe the Fae had a different reaction to the toxin. They must have had some reason for growing the trees.

"Oh." Nyx rounded the corner and halted when they saw me. "Sorry, Samara. I'm not used to anyone else being here."

My brows rose. I'd observed Nyx around all the other rangers since I'd moved back to House Harker. Everyone liked them, and they seemed to enjoy the company of others. It was surprising to me that they'd seek out a quiet place like this.

"It's been a little challenging for me to find solitude the past few days." I patted the ground next to me. "Come join me. I wouldn't mind getting out of my own head for a bit."

Nyx grinned and sauntered over towards me. I'd been worried about them since we'd returned, but with everything going on, I hadn't been able to check on them myself. Nyx was a few years younger than me, and I'd known them briefly at Drudonia before they'd disappeared and become a ranger instead of pursuing the scholarly path. I hadn't seen them again until they'd shown up on Vail's personal squad of rangers.

It'd been a little awkward at first because we'd been sort of friends before they'd vanished. Everyone knew things between me and Vail were a little tense, so I hadn't blamed them for being unsure of how to act around me while also remaining loyal to Vail, but it hadn't taken us long to fall back into a friendship of sorts.

My eyes traveled over every inch of their body as they walked across the garden, looking for any hints of lingering damage from the fight at the temple. They'd clearly been working out before heading over here because their light brown shirt was soaked in sweat and loose-fitting black pants were covered in dirt. To my relief, they appeared completely fine now.

"You and Adrienne are ridiculous." Nyx rolled their eyes before dropping down next to me. Then they stretched their long legs out and leaned back on their hands. "Usually I'd be very excited about having the attention of two beautiful women on me. Except I know for a fact neither of you look at me that way and you're just convinced I'm going to collapse at any moment. As if my ego didn't take a big enough hit being sidelined so quickly by those fucking wraiths."

"Sorry." I winced. "To be fair, this is the first time I've seen you in person since we got back. Everyone told me you were fine, but I just needed to see it for myself."

"I promise I'm okay." They shot me an easy grin. "Only thing that's still bruised is my pride."

"None of us did particularly well in that fight."

"Yeah, but I've been working hard to prove myself to Vail." Nyx let their head fall back, and their eyes stared up at the sky that reflected back the exact same shade of blue. "He took a chance on not only letting me join the rangers but also taking me on to serve in his own unit."

I picked up a broken twig and started twirling it between my fingers. "Why did you?" I asked. "Leave House Corvinus to join House Harker? As a ranger no less?"

Nyx's older sister, Tamsen, was the Heir to House Corvinus. She was the reason Nyx had been at Drudonia in the first place. They'd been training to be an advisor to support her and House Corvinus as a whole. I'd always wondered why they'd left. When I'd inquired about their disappearance to House Corvinus, I'd received a letter from Tamsen herself telling me to leave it be and that Nyx was happy.

When Nyx didn't answer right away, I worried I'd stepped too far. Normally, I would have had more tact in asking such questions, but the journals sitting between me and Nyx were messing with my head and making me sloppy. I'd need to get it together before I conversed with Draven again.

"You don't have to answer." I dropped the twig and glanced at Nyx, who was still staring at the sky. "Carmilla approved of you joining our House, and Vail obviously accepted you into the rangers. I meant no offense by the question, I was just . . . curious."

"It's fine." They sighed. "I kind of owe you anyway for how I handled leaving Drudonia and ignoring all your attempts to contact me afterwards."

"That was kind of an asshole move," I agreed.

Nyx laughed and shifted until they were lying down and then let their head flop to the side to face me. "I'm guessing you went through the standard training all Heirs and other high-ranking Moroi go through when arranged marriages are in their future?"

"Yep. Although starting my sex education at twenty was a little late," I said wryly. "Pretty sure I showed the instructors some things that made them blush."

"Somehow that doesn't surprise me."

I did some quick calculations in my head. Nyx was several years younger than me, twenty to my twenty-four. They'd arrived at Drudonia a little over midway through my time there, so I'd been, what? Eighteen?

Only the Moroi engaged in this practice of "marriage training," and it was only for high-ranking arranged marriages, typically those of House bloodlines. The tradition had started with the fourth generation and continued as our inner House politics only grew more complicated. Some of the early arranged marriages had failed, and this had been the solution for correcting that.

The training wasn't *just* about sex and making your future spouse happy in the bedroom. More tailored instruction was created for each person based on the potential Houses they might be married into and the customs within them, but the sex aspect of it was what most people got hung up on. Cali and Rynn had been horrified when I'd first told them about it, but when I'd made it clear I was fine with it, we'd used it as a source of entertainment. Every time I came back from a session, they'd ask for all the details and how many times I'd embarrassed my instructor.

Well, Cali did. Rynn was mostly still mortified by the whole thing but couldn't stop asking follow-up questions.

"How old were you when the training started?" I asked carefully, dreading their answer. As far as I knew, most Moroi didn't start the sexual aspects of the training until they were at least eighteen. I'd been on the later side at twenty, but that wasn't uncommon.

"Seventeen." When Nyx saw my dark expression, they gave me a close-lipped smile. "Tamsen fought with our parents about it—they wanted me to start at sixteen. Seventeen was the compromise."

"You should have told us." I scowled. Rynn and Cali had taken Nyx under their wings too and wouldn't have been happy about this.

"So the three of you could cause a political nightmare by going up against my parents?" Nyx shook their head ruefully. "The only thing that would have accomplished was further fracturing the alliances between the Moroi Houses and making things even more tense between the Moon Blessed."

"We would have figured something out," I said tightly. Since I was an Heir, it was my business to know the history, strengths, and weaknesses of all the other Houses. Kieran was also from House Corvinus, and while he rarely spoke about what it was like growing up there, I knew it hadn't been enjoyable. They were a smaller House that was obsessed with moving up the ranks, and they viewed their children as pawns.

To some extent, all of the Houses were like this, but I'd had a choice in my future. Carmilla never would have forced me to marry Demetri or any of the other Heirs. If I'd told her I didn't want to go through the standard training prior to a marriage, she would have accepted that. I'd assumed other Houses were the same. Clearly, House Corvinus was not.

"Tamsen would have paid the price if there had been any interference," Nyx said. "It didn't take long for our parents to figure out that the best way to control us was to threaten the other."

I'd met Tamsen several times. We weren't friends, but I respected her. Even more so now that I knew she'd at least tried to protect Nyx. She hadn't come with the Heirs to see Prince Draven, and it was likely House Corvinus was working with Velika. But that didn't necessarily mean Tamsen was in on it. She was Heir, but her parents still ruled the House. It was also possible they were forcing her cooperation by promising to harm Nyx if she disobeyed their orders.

Nyx and Tamsen's parents were fourth-generation like Carmilla, which meant they were in their eighties, but that meant nothing anymore. Carmilla was ninety-five years old but had looked like she was in her mid-forties for as long as I could remember. The Moroi were still evolving with each generation, and none of us knew how long we would live anymore.

If Tamsen was to rule anytime soon, her parents would have to meet an untimely end . . .

"Samara." Nyx rapped their knuckles against my leg.

"Hmm?" I blinked down at them.

"Stop plotting the death of my parents."

My hand flew to my chest, and I widened my eyes. "I would *never*."

Nyx chuckled. "You absolutely would, and don't think it hasn't crossed Tamsen's mind too. To say we're not close to our parents is a bit of an under-statement." Nyx folded their hands behind their head and rested back on them to gaze up at the sky again. "There were a lot of reasons I wasn't happy at House Corvinus. My parents raised me as a boy and then expected me to fulfill my duties as a Corvinus male, but that never suited me. I didn't really under-stand why as I was growing up. Then I met Roth at Drudonia, and I realized maybe the reason I felt like I was always crawling out of my own skin was because I was trying to be something I wasn't."

"Never met any chirlìn Velesians growing up?" I asked curiously, using the Fae word for those who didn't fall in the categories of male or female. Techni-cally, the word chirlìn meant either all of something or none of something. Either way, it seemed fitting, and the Velesians had been using it for some time. It was slowly catching on around the Moroi and Furies as well.

"Are you kidding?" Nyx's brows rose. "My parents can't go five minutes without talking shit about shifters. Rynn was the first Velesian I met."

"House Corvinus is even more fucked than I realized." I hesitated before asking, "Did you go through with the training?"

"No. I tried for the sake of my sister, but I couldn't do it." Nyx rubbed their face. "I didn't have any experience before the training. I mean, I hadn't . . . There hadn't been anyone I'd . . . done things with." They caught my eyebrows creeping towards my forehead and laughed. "I know that's crazy, considering most Moroi start humping everything in sight as soon as they hit sixteen if not earlier, but I've never really felt inclined to stick my cock into everything that moves. Add to the fact that physically, I'd matured quickly and looked like this" —Nyx gestured at their handsome, masculine face and broad shoulders—"so everyone treated me like I was a typical male, which only added to internal confusion and ensured my sex drive was nonexistent."

I winced. What a shitty experience. My first time hadn't been amazing, but it'd been my choice, and it'd been with a courtier who was just as inexperi-enced. We'd stumbled through it together with clumsy fingers and panted breaths. Nyx had been quiet at Drudonia, but I'd had no idea they'd been dealing with all this.

"My instructors took things slow, but I panicked two weeks into the training, just as things started to get serious. I grabbed a horse and ran, not even caring which direction I was going as long as it was away from everything." They snorted, a wry grin playing across their lips. "Ran straight into Vail fighting off a pack of howlers. Helped him out, and the rest is history."

"You do seem happier now," I said. "It was the main reason I didn't tear your head off when I saw you for the first time with Vail. I was pissed off at how you just disappeared on us like that, but none of that matters if you're happy."

"Ah. I was wondering why I didn't get the typical *Samara Chewing Out.*"

I shoved my knee out to the side so it dug into their hip. "Don't worry, it's still coming. I'm just letting it stew a little bit more."

"Thank you." Nyx's eyes flicked to mine. "For being my friend then and for being my friend now."

"Always." I wrinkled my nose. "Still think you had poor taste in choosing your ranger unit though."

"We've all decided to not touch what's going on between you and Vail with a ten-foot pole." They shot me a pointed look.

"Can I take that option too?" I dropped my head back against the tree.

"Sadly, I don't think you can." Nyx nudged the leather satchel between us. "Did you steal some books from Roth? Because I'll protect you from a lot of things, but there is zero chance of me getting between you and them if books are involved."

My lips quirked. "I'd never ask you to do such a thing. Besides . . . I kind of like Roth's idea of punishment."

A light flush streaked across Nyx's cheeks, and they squeezed their eyes shut. "I really need to get laid soon." We both laughed, and after a moment, they peeked one eye open at me. "Is Cali . . . involved with anyone?"

"Nyx Corvinus, do you have a crush on Calypso Rayne?" I gaped down at them, and their blush deepened as they quickly squeezed their eyes shut with a wince. "Oh my gods, you do!"

"I swear to the moon and all that she gives us, if you tell Cali, I will bury your corpse beneath this Fae tree."

The threat would have landed better if Nyx hadn't covered their face with their hands and half-mumbled the words.

"Wow." I cackled. "To answer your question, Cali isn't involved with anyone." I thought about it a little more. "Not seriously anyway. You know how Furies are. No serious relationships and all that."

Nyx made a noise of agreement and tucked their hands behind their head. "Do you mind if I nap here? I'm feeling a little tired, and if I go back to the barracks, Adrienne will somehow find out, and it'll only make her worry about me more."

"Sure." I eyed the leather satchel. "I have some reading I was going to do."

"Perfect."

I waited until Nyx's breathing evened out, and then I pulled out my mother's most recent journal. With trembling fingers, I cracked the spine open and started reading the secrets of the dead.

WE'RE CLOSE. I feel it with every fiber of my being.

Kasem is worried, and I don't blame him. The last two sites we searched were completely empty, yet it felt like we were being watched the entire time. Lunaria has never been safe, but the wraiths are acting strangely now. They're less feral than they were before. That should be a good thing, except I can feel them lurking in the shadows, waiting. For what, I don't know, but every time we leave the safe walls of House Harker, I feel death following in our wake.

But we can't stop now. We must find it before Velika does. Otherwise, our fates will be far worse than a grisly death.

I wish we had allies, but I don't know who we can trust aside from Inés and Edric. It feels wrong to lie to Carmilla. Despite all our disagreements, she's my sister and I love her, but our mother entrusted me with this legacy. I'd always intended to tell Carmilla eventually. About the journals. The crown. All of it. But then she became friends with Velika. I can't risk it. No matter how much it pains me, our people must come first.

We're leaving to visit one of the Velesian packs tomorrow. I didn't want to stop our search, but Kasem insisted, saying it's been too long since we've visited any of the Velesians, and he's concerned about the rising tensions between our people and theirs. I only agreed to his request because the next site I want to explore is somewhere around Lake Molov, and we'll need permission from the Narchis Order to go there.

Samara is coming with us, as is Inés and Edric's son, Vail. Part of me wants to keep Samara forever tucked away in House Harker behind the wards, but Kasem is right. She's the Harker Heir and needs to see more of Lunaria. I'm sure it'll be fine. We're taking a main road, and Inés and Edric are the fiercest warriors I've ever met—aside from Kasem of course. It'll be fine. Plus, it will give me some time to spend with Sam. My daughter is a wonder, and she's going to change the world one day. I just know it.

I'm going to try to sneak back into bed without waking Kasem. It never works, but it's fun trying, and I enjoy what he does when he catches me. Maybe when all this is over, we can give Samara a younger sibling. Because we will survive this. I won't accept anything else.

. . .

Heat pooled behind my eyes, and I slammed the book shut. She hadn't survived. This was the last entry of the journal. Three days after this, she'd been killed by wraiths along with my father and Vail's parents. Nyx's light snores filled the air, and I concentrated on their rhythmic breathing as I bottled up everything I was feeling and shoved it down.

I couldn't afford to lose it now. The wraiths were the lost Fae, the Sovereigns were betraying all of the Moroi and working with them, and there was a wicked prince in my home, courting me for marriage. I didn't have the luxury of losing my shit right now.

After a few minutes of steady breathing, I reviewed the facts. My parents had known Velika had been plotting something, though nothing indicated they'd known she was working with the wraiths. Carmilla didn't know about the journals or what my parents had been searching for because my mother had been concerned about how close Carmilla was with Velika.

And finally . . . they'd never made it to Lake Molov.

I'd already been planning on going there. I just needed to talk to Vail and Rynn about it to get them on board. What I hadn't been sure of was if I should prioritize it or not. I had my answer now. Whatever my parents had been searching for had to have been important, and Velika had wanted it too. I needed to go to Lake Molov. Perhaps, Velika had already gone there . . . but maybe she hadn't. Or maybe she'd gone but hadn't been able to find what was hidden there. In either case, I felt I owed it to my parents to finish what they'd started.

The small journal felt heavy in my hands. I'd deliberately started with the last entry because the more recent ones were more likely to have information relevant to our current situation. Maybe some of the earlier entries would mention what exactly my mother had been hunting for.

Fortifying my nerves, I opened the book again and started scanning the pages. I didn't let myself linger on any of the sweet moments she mentioned between herself and my father, and I entirely skipped over the one where she talked about my eighth birthday and how she'd worked with Leora all morning to make me the perfect cake because she wanted to have a hand in it too instead of just passing it off to someone else.

Most of the entries covered their failed search attempts and some mentions of increased wraith or other monster activity. Then I found it, and it was like a snake had reared from the page and sunk its fangs into me.

I had an odd encounter with Velika today. Something about her has always bothered me—I have never been able to describe what it is, and the few times I've mentioned it to Carmilla, she's waved me off as being paranoid, which, to be fair, I am. There is a sickness running through the Moroi. Everyone judges the Furies, but it's not like they choose to lose their minds and slaughter all around them. The Moroi are consciously choosing to harm each other in nefarious ways.

The Moroi Queen is one of those nefarious souls.

She hides it well—the rest of the Moroi practically worship her like she's one of the old gods the Fae prayed to—but this time when we met, she wore a crown. Velika's so vain, it was perfectly within character for her. Especially since she's determined to bring back the old ways of how we believe Fae courts worked. It's foolish. We're barely surviving in this fucked-up land and she wants to hold balls and wear fancy dresses.

But when Velika wears jewelry, it is always dripping in gems. This crown had been so simple. Just a simple silver band with delicate carvings. Parts of it had even appeared broken. Still, something about it had bothered me. I could feel the magic in it, which was odd because I saw no glyphs and it held no gems that would have stored magic.

I couldn't resist asking Velika about it, but I stumbled over the words. Carmilla is so much better at wordplay than me. I'm sure I tipped my hand about my suspicions. Velika just laughed it off as something she had made recently and acted like she didn't particularly care for it, but I didn't miss the way her fingers caressed the silver.

The Moroi Queen has a Fae artifact. I am sure of it.

There must be more out there, and we need to find them before she does.

"Fuck," I breathed out. What if Velika had collected more Fae artifacts since my parents had died? Or maybe she was still searching for them and that was why she had allied with the wraiths? Were they helping her find them in exchange for Velika assisting them in reclaiming their true Fae forms? Once again, I felt like the few answers I got only led to more questions.

I glanced down at a still sleeping Nyx. My parents had given their lives to stop Velika's mad quest for power.

My daughter is a wonder, and she's going to change the world one day.

I would not let them down.

CHAPTER FIFTEEN

—

Samara

"This is magical, Leora," I groaned around a mouthful of tart berry deliciousness. After spending a couple of hours beneath the Fae tree, pillaging the journals for any other bit of information, I'd been in desperate need of a break and something sweet. "I think you're one of the gods in those old Fae stories. That's the only rational explanation."

Leora huffed a laugh and waved off my compliment. I'd missed both her and her delicious baked goods while I'd been at House Laurent. The Moroi who ran the kitchen staff there weren't nearly as friendly nor as talented.

"Agreed," Nora said from where she sat across from me at the small table tucked into the corner of the kitchen. She worked in the gardens with her husband and had been taking a break when I'd stumbled into the kitchen, following the scent of freshly baked goodies. The young, pretty Moroi eyed the plate filled with the spring berry pastries. "I think I need one more to get the taste of that tea out of my mouth."

I nudged the plate towards her. "You definitely do." I flashed her a look of sympathy as her lip curled at the now empty teacup resting next to the pastries. The spelled brew prevented pregnancy. It lasted until we had our cycle, and then it had to be taken again. Apparently, our human ancestors had gone through their cycle every month. When we'd become Moroi, that had changed to every four months, and our bleeding only lasted for two or three days.

Unfortunately, those two or three days were absolute agony. I had no idea if the monthly cycle of the humans had been as bad as ours was. If it had been . . . then the humans who had gone through it had been tougher than we gave them credit for.

The tea was an old Fae spell that for some reason worked for us too. It tasted absolutely vile, like milk that had gone sour, and it coated your tongue and throat, the taste lingering long after. Nora had slammed the tea back in several gulps and then powered through three pastries. I didn't blame her at all. My cycle was due in the next few weeks, and I was very much not looking forward to it.

"So you and Floran aren't going to try for a little one now that you're an old married couple?" I teased Nora, and she blushed faintly. While our cycle was painful, the week that followed was also . . . intense. It was jokingly referred to as the mating frenzy. Couples tended to hide away for days at a time, and single Moroi would often find someone, or several someones, to shack up with. The tea would prevent pregnancy but did nothing to lessen our lust-addled minds.

"No plans for any young ones yet." Nora smiled, and the blush deepened across her cheeks. I was about to tease her again when her smile faded and a crease formed in her brows. She picked at the corner of her pastry as her eyes flicked to mine hesitantly. "We've heard the rumors about the outposts . . . about some of them falling to wraiths. I know Lunaria is never technically safe, but it feels a little more volatile right now. We both agreed now isn't a good time to bring a child into it."

Shit. It had only been a matter of time before rumors started spreading about outposts being wiped out by wraiths, but since most of the ones that had been targeted were more remote, I'd really been hoping we'd have at least another couple of months before it became common knowledge.

"I can't say I disagree with your assessment," I said quietly. Leora continued humming to herself as she alternated between kneading dough and checking the bread baking in the brick oven. I knew she could hear every word we said, but I also knew she would keep it to herself. Leora was happy to gossip about harmless things, but she'd never repeat anything serious, especially if it came from me. "Would you mind sharing how you heard about the attacks? The Sovereign House has been trying to keep it quiet."

Nora paled at the mention of the Sovereign House. "I haven't told anyone," she said quickly and then winced. "Other than mentioning it to you just now."

"It's fine," I assured her. "Personally, I have mixed feelings about keeping this information from the remaining outposts, but I can't go against the Sovereign House. So I'm trying to solve the issue as quickly as possible, but if people start to panic . . ."

"I don't think many people know." Nora twisted the end of her long, blonde braid in her fingers. "Floran's older brother is a tracker. He was training to be a ranger, but it didn't work out. There was a girl he was sweet on at one of the outposts that was . . ." She swallowed. "He went to check on her one day and found the outpost empty and some rangers investigating. They didn't give him the specifics, but wraiths were mentioned. I don't think he's told anyone else, and I'll make sure he doesn't." Nora's breathing quickened, and I reached out and laid my hand over hers.

"It's okay, Nora. It'd be a good idea to let him know that, simply so he doesn't run afoul of the Sovereign House, but neither of you did anything wrong."

"Okay." She smiled weakly.

"We'll figure this out, I promise." I removed my hand from hers and tapped the rim of the empty teacup. "And then you can skip drinking this tea for a little while. If that's what the two of you want of course."

She laughed. "Floran wants to have six kids. I thought we could start with one and see how it goes."

"You always were the wiser one," I said, drawing a laugh out of Leora as she plopped a plate of muffins down in front of us.

"I knew I'd find you here as soon as I caught wind of the freshly baked deliciousness." Kieran breezed into the kitchen and kissed Leora on the cheek and then Nora before pulling up a chair beside me and grabbing one of the berry muffins. Alaric followed a second later and nodded at Leora and Nora but opted to stand awkwardly a few feet away from us. "A certain cranky scholar would like to see you. They're in the library."

My eyes darted to Nora, who grinned and grabbed a muffin as she rose. "I'll leave the three of you to your scheming."

Alaric watched her go before sliding into her seat, then his eyes briefly flicked to mine before falling back to a spot on the table midway between us. I glanced at Kieran, who just shook his head and rolled his eyes. So he hadn't had any luck convincing Alaric to drink either. Wonderful. Alaric was cranky and difficult on a good day. I somehow doubted he'd be more pleasant when he was running low on magic and refusing to do anything about it.

Argh.

"Where's Draven?" I asked quietly.

"He's with Yolanthe," Alaric answered, still not looking at me. "I met with him earlier. He's probably going to look for you as soon as he's done. Something seemed to be bothering him earlier—he was distracted, which is unlike him."

Probably because he thought I was sleeping with Vail. Another lie I'd have to maintain. Speaking of . . . might as well get that out of the way.

"He's just being pissy because I spent last night with Vail." Something slammed into the wood counter behind us, and I looked over to find Leora gawking at me, her discarded rolling pin halfway across the surface. "Apparently, the prince doesn't like the idea of sharing with the Marshal."

"That makes two of us," Kieran muttered, drawing my attention away from Leora's surprised face. Alaric was staring at me intently, his full mouth flattened into a hard line, but he didn't voice any objections.

It annoyed me that he didn't, and then it bothered me further that I cared what he thought.

"It's not real," I said quietly as Leora took a few steps closer to us, abandoning her dough as she sent me a questioning look. "But Draven needs to believe it for now."

Leora studied me for a long moment. "Are you sure about this, dear?"

Reluctantly, I nodded. Leora could help spread the rumor, giving more legitimacy to the claim. I didn't like that it would be yet another complication between Vail and me. He wouldn't like it either and would take out his frustrations on me, but it's not like that would be anything new.

Pushing Vail out of my mind for now, I refocused on our immediate problem.

"We need to distract Draven." I thrummed my fingers against the table. "Whatever Roth has discovered shouldn't be heard by him, and I have something I want to discuss as well."

I twirled the ring on my pinkie, the two embedded gems shining bright against the dark silver band. Rynn, Cali, and I were long overdue for a chat anyway, and I wanted to make sure they were caught up on all the latest developments. Plus . . . Rynn was an important part of what I was planning, as was Vail.

Neither of them were going to like it. In fact, nobody was going to like it, but I was confident I could convince them to go along with it. Mostly.

"Maybe we should wait until late tonight?" Alaric suggested.

"No." I shook my head. "Draven is clearly keeping an eye on my nighttime habits. We're lucky he didn't follow us to the cave, but going forward, he'll likely be monitoring my whereabouts more closely." Kieran didn't say anything, which I thought was odd. I studied his expression as he slowly nibbled on the muffin. He seemed relaxed; there were no lines of tension, and the corners of his mouth were quirked upward slightly. Even his eyes were bright.

It was a lie. I knew that mask. It was the one he slipped on when he knew he'd have to do something he didn't want to. Usually, I saw it when he made the rare journey home to visit his parents.

"Kier?"

His eyes flicked to mine, and he sighed before putting down the half-eaten muffin. "I'll distract him."

"No," I said immediately. "You don't have to do that."

"Well, I'm not planning on doing *that*." His lips twitched into a wry grin. "You know there are other ways to distract people, right?"

I pursed my lips stubbornly. "You don't have to do this—whatever this is— if you don't want to. We can find another way."

"This makes the most sense." He shrugged with a casualness that made me want to scream. I knew this plan bothered him, and I hated that he was trying to hide it. "You don't need me for whatever conversation you all want to have."

"I always need you."

Kieran's eyes softened. "While I have many skills, we all know the three of you are far smarter than I am. My skills are suited towards being a decoy, and if I ask Draven to go for a ride with me, he'll go."

"I bet he will," I grumbled, still not liking this one bit. It wasn't that I was jealous of anything that might happen between them, but Draven was a complication, and while I suspected there was more going on than we were seeing, he was technically the enemy right now. One who had betrayed our people.

He'd hurt Kieran before as well. I loved Kier with all my soul but he was also the most kindhearted person I'd ever met. It was difficult for him to trust people, but once he did, he did so absolutely. Draven had broken that trust and his heart. Kieran would forgive him for it though, whether the prince deserved it or not. I just didn't want to see him hurt again.

"Will one of you please tell me what is going on?" Alaric finally asked, raising his gaze from the table to glance back and forth between me and Kieran.

"I'll explain later." Kieran grimaced before rising and grabbing one of the folded-up towels Leora kept stacked throughout the kitchen, then he stuck a few muffins in it. "How much longer do you think he'll be meeting with Yolanthe?" he asked Alaric.

"They've been talking for almost an hour already, but you know Yolanthe, she'll go on forever. Could be thirty minutes, could be another hour." Alaric stared at his friend for a long moment. "Are you okay?"

"You know me." Kieran shrugged. "I'm always okay."

Alaric narrowed his eyes. He knew just as well as I did that Kieran had a tendency to suppress his feelings around us, like we would think less of him if he presented anything but a strong, confident front.

"I need to get some things from my room." Kieran leaned down to kiss me on the cheek before straightening and looking at Alaric. "I'm guessing they're meeting in Yolanthe's study?"

Alaric nodded, still studying his friend, trying to figure out what was going on that he was missing. Kieran ignored his best friend's gaze and headed towards the back stairwell, his bundle of muffins in tow, and left without another word. I wasn't any happier about this than Alaric, but I had to trust that Kieran knew what he was doing.

"Let's give him some time to get Draven out of here. We can meet in two hours." I snatched up Kieran's discarded muffin and tore off a chunk full of berries. Mmm . . . so tart and yummy. The spring berries didn't last long. They flowered, grew, and ripened over a two-week period, and that was it until the next year, but they were the first fruit of the season to grow and always marked that spring was in full swing. Hence the name. "Any chance you can find Vail and bring him with you to the library for the meeting?"

Alaric frowned. "Why can't you do it?"

"Because Vail isn't in the best of moods and will probably say no just because it's me asking." I let out a bone-weary sigh. "Given that we want the rumor of Vail and me sleeping together to spread, him rejecting a simple request from me in public would be less than ideal."

I shoved the rest of the muffin into my mouth and closed my eyes while I savored the flavor.

"Fine," Alaric ground out. "But I don't appreciate being blindsided by this plan. You're playing it up like it's all pretend, but I haven't missed the heated looks Vail has sent you since returning from the temple, and I know there is something else going on with Kieran that the two of you are keeping from me. I'm tired of being kept in the dark."

"Oh?" I cracked an eye open from my pastry-derived bliss. "Care to enlighten me as to why you're refusing to drink blood then?"

"I'm not refusing."

Pastry bliss officially over.

I leaned across the table and extended my arm to him, my wrist facing up. "Then have a drink." Turquoise flashed across Alaric's light green eyes so fast, I barely caught it. When he made no move to take my offer, I withdrew and crossed my arms. "Kieran will tell you when he's ready. I'm not telling you his secrets, just as I wouldn't tell him yours."

"Fair enough." Muscles flexed along his jawline. "And Vail?"

"Honestly . . . I don't understand what's going on between me and Vail. He might actually be more confusing and frustrating than you at this point." Alaric snorted, and I gave him a tired smile. "It'll just be easier if you ask him. Trust me."

"Alright." Alaric stood and straightened his midnight blue tunic. "We'll meet you in the library in a bit."

I nodded, my thoughts already drifting to my plans and what Roth might have discovered. It took me a minute to realize Alaric was still standing there and looking . . . nervous. I couldn't remember the last time I'd seen Alaric look nervous. In fact, I wasn't sure if I ever had. "Is there something else?"

"If . . ." He trailed off and swallowed. "If the offer of your . . . blood . . . is still on the table later . . ." Alaric released the buttons he'd been fidgeting with and met my eyes. "I'll take you up on it."

I blinked. "Really?"

"Yes," he rushed on. "But it has to be somewhere private."

"Damn," I drawled. "There go my plans of straddling you in the hallway of the main tower entrance."

"Samara," he said warningly, and I grinned as some of the tension eased from his face.

"Whatever you need, Alaric," I said before he could change his mind. "We can do it after the meeting if you'd like."

He hesitated for a moment before jerking his head in agreement. "Alright."

I watched as he practically fled from the kitchen, and then I rose and wandered over to Leora, who had returned to the large workstation and was rolling out dough in perfect rectangles. She shot me an amused glance before passing me a bowl of raspberry jelly. "Spread this in a thin layer while I roll out the next one."

"Sure." I set to work, spreading the thick, dark purple filling across the dough. Leora had been in charge of the kitchens of House Harker for longer than I'd been alive, and I always enjoyed coming in here. Not just to sneak treats but because there was something relaxing about helping her cook and bake things. Sometimes I'd be here for hours and we'd barely talk. I knew others did the same. There was just something calming about being in Leora's kitchen.

"Any advice?" I asked after I'd moved on to the third rectangle of dough.

Leora smiled as she started rolling up the first piece and then sliced it into thick discs. "You really did go out of your way to get yourself a complicated assortment of lovers."

I huffed a laugh. "Exactly how many lovers do you think I have? Because last I checked, it was *actually* only two." I thought about Alaric joining me and Kieran in my study. "Two and a half."

The older Moroi slid me a sly glance. "Trust me, it's a solid three. He just hasn't realized it yet."

"We'll see." I scraped out the last of the filling, put the bowl aside, and started rolling up the dough. I could never get it as perfectly even as Leora, but it'd still taste fine.

"Alaric will come around." Leora paused, and I felt her concerned gaze on me, so I glanced up from my less than perfect rolled out dough. "It's the Marshal and the prince who worry me."

"Leora—" I started, but she waved her hand in the air, cutting me off.

"I know you can take care of yourself." She patted me on the cheek. "But you always worry about everyone else, Samara. Many of us care deeply for you, my darling girl. So we'll worry about you too."

She went back to rolling her dough, and I did the same. When I finished, we moved on to the next round. "I can't help but notice that wasn't advice," I pointed out.

Leora laughed. "That's because I don't have any, and I was hoping you wouldn't notice. I think you're fucked in more ways than one."

"Thanks." I shook my head ruefully because she was probably right.

My damp hair soaked into my robe as I contemplated all the things we needed to discuss at the upcoming meeting. I'd returned to my suite to rinse off because I'd somehow managed to get flour all over me and raspberry jelly in my hair.

I glanced at the large, upright clock that rested between my book cases. Thirty minutes to go. Draven's meeting would be wrapping up soon, and Kieran was waiting to intercept him and get him out of our way for a while. I still wasn't thrilled about that plan, but if Kieran said he could handle it, then I trusted him.

A few scenarios of just how Kieran could keep the prince distracted flashed through my mind. Great. Now I was anxious and horny.

Then again, they would probably just ride around the property. Kieran was really pissed off at Draven. As much as he wanted him, I wasn't sure if he'd be willing to let anything happen between them. Once again, concern for Kier bloomed in my chest. I didn't want him to get hurt, and Draven had already caused him such pain.

"What the fuck are you up to, Drav?" I muttered.

We knew he was working with the wraiths—whether he was only doing so because he was being forced was still something we had to figure out. But that didn't explain why he'd treated Kieran the way he had. I'd known Drav for most of my life, and while he could occasionally be short with people and was excellent at delivering well-crafted insults, I'd never known him to be cruel.

And what he'd done to Kieran had absolutely been cruel. Once again, I wondered if I was letting my attraction to him and our past friendship blind me to the truth.

My gaze fell on the memory ball still resting on the table in my sitting area. What memory had he planted in it? I glanced at the clock . . . I did still have time. And I could always pull out if it was taking too long.

Before I could second guess myself, I strode over to the table and picked up the glass sphere before plopping down on the settee. I leaned back and rested the ball in one palm with the other lying across the top. Memory balls like this one weren't exactly common, but all the Houses had at least a few in their possession. None of them contained Fae memories, but they were useful for recording meetings and other information.

Typically, we locked those memories to our blood so no one else could access them. But I could feel Draven's memory floating inside this one, trying to tug me under. He'd deliberately left it unlocked so I could access it without him.

I closed my eyes and let myself be pulled into it.

"When I said I wanted to escape the party for a while and you said you knew

just the place, this wasn't what I was expecting." I held a warning finger up at the chestnut stallion, who laid his ears back in the stall on the left. The horse snorted like he wasn't the least bit impressed before trying to bite me.

No. Not me. Draven. I was seeing this memory from Draven's point of view. Well, this was a bit disorientating. Normally, when we used memory balls, we just recorded our voices. But Draven had included so much more than that. I could make out some of his thoughts—although many were muddled and I couldn't understand them. But I could get a sense of what he was feeling.

Longing and confliction. Some contentment. He enjoyed my company. But also . . . fear.

Why had he chosen this memory? And why was he afraid?

I tuned back in, letting myself fall back into the echo of Draven's psyche.

"Quit antagonizing him." Samara held up a warning finger in the same way I had just done to the stallion. When I snapped my teeth at her, she laughed and spun away, sending her dark hair flying. That moonsdamned laugh stole my breath. Hearing it was like coming home after being lost in a storm for weeks.

She'd be married to that asshole from House Laurent in a few weeks. Truthfully, I didn't actually know much about him. Only that Samara was too good for him. But it's not like I could marry her. Samara had no idea how I truly felt about her and Demetri . . . Demetri was the safer option.

"I'm just saying"—I followed after where Samara had moved deeper into the stables—"we could have swiped a bottle of wine and been up on the roof right now."

"We can do that after," she tossed over her shoulder. "I wanted to see them first."

"Them?"

Samara stopped in front of a stall and leaned over the door. "Them," she said in a soft voice.

I stepped up beside her, letting my arm graze hers briefly before resting it on the door. A black mare eyed us warily but didn't move from where she was standing over two identical dark bay foals. Both were passed out and sprawled across the straw bedding.

"One of the servants told me about them earlier," Samara whispered, her dark purple eyes full of wonder. "It's a miracle they survived."

"They look very small. Ranger mounts have to be strong and robust. The weak don't survive." A hint of bitterness crept into my voice, and I winced. Samara loved horses—I should let her have this moment of happiness instead of bringing my dreariness into it.

"So they'll be quick and resilient," Samara shot back. "There's more than one way to survive in Lunaria. Don't count them out yet."

I smiled. "You're right of course."

She slid me a cocky glance. "I know."

We both backed away from the door to let the foals sleep in peace. Samara went to each stall, giving every horse a scratch behind the ears—even the ornery chestnut stallion, who was more than willing to let Samara pet him while giving me the evil eye.

"Would you like one of the foals?" I blurted out.

Samara looked over her shoulder at me, dark eyebrows raised. "I would never separate them. And even if you gave me both, it'll be years before they're old enough to ride." A hint of sadness crept into her expression. "I'll be in need of a mount sooner than that. Mine passed away last year from old age. He had a good, long life, but I miss him. I've been using temporary ones, but I'll need to figure out a more regular solution when I move to House Laurent." Something flickered across her face—too fast for me to catch what it had been—then she shrugged. "I'm sure they'll have something there that will work."

"What would your dream horse be?" I asked, unable to stop myself.

She turned around to face me, leaning her back against the stall door. The chestnut stallion nudged her shoulder, and she absently stroked his cheek. "Dark like the storm clouds. With a loyal spirit and a fiery temper." She grinned. "And fast enough to outrun death itself."

"That's a tall order." I smiled back at her.

"You said dream horse." She leaned over and kissed the stallion on the nose. "I suppose we should get back to the party. My aunt is probably wondering where I slipped off to."

"Of course." We walked out of the stables, but I halted after a couple of steps. "Actually, I need to check in with the rangers about something. I'll see you back at the party."

"Okay . . ." Samara eyed me suspiciously. I couldn't say I blamed her, it was rare that I did anything that looked like work around her. Usually, we would just split a bottle of wine or two and talk about random things. Well, I'd ask Samara about her life and then redirect the conversation anytime she asked something about mine.

With a wave, Samara set off towards the main tower of the Sovereign House, where the party was no doubt still in full swing. I waited until she was out of sight before doubling back to the small building behind the stables and rapping my knuckles against the door.

An older-looking Moroi male swung the door open. His light grey hair hung loose around his shoulders. "My prince!" His bushy eyebrows shot up. "I, uhh—" he brushed some crumbs off his shirt, and his posture went ramrod straight. "My apologies. I was just having dinner and wasn't expecting company—definitely not you. Not that you're not welcome her—"

"My apologies for interrupting your meal, Stablemaster." I held my hands up in an apologetic gesture. "I was hoping to intrude on you for just a few minutes and ask for a favor."

"Oh?" A puzzled crease formed between his eyes. "I mean, of course!" He held the door open and waved me inside. "Whatever you need."

I stepped into his simple but clean home, his interrupted meal still on the table. "I'm looking for a particular horse, and I was wondering if you could reach out to the stablemasters of the other Houses to see what they have available—and arrange for me to go see them. I'll need to inspect all the options myself."

"Sure." He nodded slowly. "What type of horse are you looking for?"

I gave him a small smile. "One made of dreams."

The memory faded, and I was vaguely aware of the glass sphere slipping out of my hands to land with a thud on the carpet before rolling away.

Zosa. My hot-tempered and beloved grey mare. Demetri had given her to me as a wedding present, but I'd always suspected he hadn't been the one to find her. That he had just told the House Laurent Stablemaster to find me a horse, and they had done as commanded.

I'd forgotten all about that conversation in the stables with Draven. The weeks leading up to my marriage had been a blur, and then I'd been busy fighting to make space for myself at House Laurent. Not to mention missing Kieran terribly.

One of the few things that had kept me sane had been riding Zosa on the beach. Draven had given me the horse of my dreams. And until now, he'd never said one word about it.

I stared at the Fae memory ball as it slowly rolled across the floor before coming to a stop against the clock. That memory hadn't been at all what I'd expected, and I didn't understand why he had chosen it. Part of me wanted to track down wherever he was with Kieran and demand answers—but another part of me was scared of what he might say.

Because I was absolutely falling in love with Draven . . . but I still didn't trust him.

CHAPTER SIXTEEN

—

Kieran

In general, I prided myself on having nothing but good ideas. Convincing Alaric to stop working for a few hours so we could spar instead? Good idea. Telling Leora she should practice her new pastry ideas and I would sample each one? Great idea. That time I convinced Samara to sneak some honey from the kitchen so I could drizzle it all over her body and lick it off?

Fucking. *Fantastic*. Idea.

Telling the others I could distract Draven for a few hours by taking him out for a ride? Bad idea. Like, epically terrible idea.

The look of surprise on Draven's face when he'd walked out of Yolanthe's study and I'd immediately asked him to come for a ride with me had almost made it worth it. But now we were alone in the woods surrounding House Harker, and the reality of my situation came crashing down on me.

I blamed Samara and Alaric for not doing a better job of talking me out of this. They were the smart ones, and it was their responsibility to point out the stupidity of my ideas. Both of them would be getting an earful when I got back.

"Something the matter?" Draven slowed his enormous black stallion until it was riding next to Zosa. I barely managed to rein her in when the grey mare snaked her head out and tried to take a chunk out of the other horse's neck. She snorted and danced angrily beneath me. I don't know what had possessed me to take Sam's horse out. The stable boy had paled when I'd led her from the stall, but when I'd told him I had Samara's permission, he just jerked his head in a nod and practically ran away, muttering something about me having to saddle the ornery mare myself.

"Everything's fine," I said tightly, steering Zosa a little further away from

Draven. Distance. That was what I needed. Just a little space between the two of us.

Once I had Zosa under control—or at least out of biting range—I glanced back at Draven. He was staring at the grey mare with a strange expression I couldn't read. "If you're thinking about saying something nasty about my mount, you should know this is Samara's mare and she doesn't take kindly to anyone talking shit about her horse."

Draven smiled faintly. "I wouldn't dream of it. Just surprised you're riding such a magnificently vicious creature instead of a flashy, even-tempered mount." His smile grew wider. "Maybe something with a chestnut coat that glistens like polished copper in sunlight."

Damn it. My normal mount—Aelix—*was* a chestnut mare.

The fact that he knew me so well was frustrating. She loved to prance around with her flaxen-colored tail raised as if she knew perfectly well how glorious she was.

Zosa was a storm cloud who absolutely loved Samara and barely tolerated anyone else, but today, I'd needed her strength over Aelix's beauty, so I'd bribed her with an extra ration of grain in hopes she wouldn't throw me.

I felt Draven's heavy stare on me when I didn't answer. In my head, I'd convinced myself this would be easier. Just a nice little ride around the woods full of monsters. No big deal. I gripped the reins tighter, and Zosa tossed her head in annoyance.

"Come on," Draven said suddenly and spurred his horse forward before I could argue. Zosa didn't need any encouragement from me and immediately raced after them, nearly unseating me in the process. Gods, no wonder Samara loved her. This mare was lightning made flesh.

When we pulled even with Draven, I had to tug Zosa back so she didn't take the lead, since I didn't know where Draven wanted to go. I didn't even know why I was following him in the first place. This ride had been my idea—I was the one who was supposed to be leading him around. Plus, I was far more familiar with the area than he was, but this always happened when I was with him. It had felt nice to let someone else take charge, and I'd trusted Draven back then. I didn't trust him now.

Then why are you following him so blindly? The irritating thought surfaced in my mind, and I gritted my teeth, determined not to think about the answer.

After ten minutes, Draven gradually slowed his mount to a walk, and I did the same. It took me a second to recognize where we were, and I'd never felt so much excitement and dread at the same moment. How the fuck did he even know about this place?

We ducked under some branches, and I noted some bright sapphire gems dangling from the trees. Faint magic pulsed from them, a little dimmer than the last time I had been here. They'd need to be replaced within the next two months. This type of ward wasn't as powerful as the ones we used to protect the outposts, but most of the monsters crawling around this area of the forest were harmless to us because the rangers kept all the serious threats away. Once in a while, a pack of howlers would wander this way, but the sapphire-powered ward was enough to keep them out.

A twisted, green vine with bloodred leaves wound around a tree, trembling as we passed it, and I eyed it warily. In a few months, it would grow delicate, white blossoms that had some beneficial medicinal uses. Unfortunately, the leaves were coated in a fine powder that would not only make one break out in a rash, but they'd make one's skin itch for weeks. Not just a minor itch either. It was a deep, burning feeling, like something was crawling beneath one's skin. Anyone who was afflicted had to be tied down to keep them from tearing their own flesh off.

Lunaria, a land of nightmarish monsters, where even the plants wanted to kill you.

What in the fuck had the Fae done to be banished here? Or had they come here voluntarily? And why had they brought humans with them? Most of the time, I left the wondering of our history to people like Roth and Samara. Like Alaric, I was more of a forward-thinking person, and knowing those answers was unlikely to help with our immediate concerns of surviving, but sometimes, even I couldn't help but wonder what had happened five hundred years ago to set all this in motion.

The underbrush started to thin out and the tree line abruptly ended, revealing the reason for the ward, a crystal-clear pool of water in the middle of the clearing. Draven dismounted and loosely tied his mount's reins around a tree. I did the same, although I put a healthy amount of space between them since Zosa didn't look like she would tolerate any of the stallion's bullshit.

"How'd you even know about this place?" I didn't bother keeping the suspicion out of my voice. This little oasis was a hidden gem of House Harker that we didn't tell outsiders about. The water wasn't hot like the springs I'd taken Samara to in that outpost, but it wasn't exactly cold either. An underground stream fed the pool, and wherever that water came from, it was hot. Warm currents lazily circled around the pool, which helped with the overall temperature. On top of that, the bottom was made of black stones that soaked up the heat of the sun. There weren't any stones like that around here naturally, so it was assumed that some enterprising humans or Fae had taken advantage of the fairly shallow and crystal clear water to help increase the temperature a little bit.

"Samara mentioned it years ago." Draven shrugged. "We passed the markers for it a while back, and I wanted to see it for myself."

I frowned. Samara had never come here with me when we'd been growing up and had given me the impression she didn't like this place. I never understood why, because Sam *loved* water. If there was an inch of it, especially if it was warm water, she would crawl into it. She knew this place existed, but I didn't know why she would have talked to Draven about it.

Seeing my confusion, Draven smiled faintly. "Samara and I used to confide all sorts of things to each other. This place was in one of her confessions. You used to bring a lot of girls here when the two of you were growing up before she left for Drudonia. It hurt her greatly."

"Oh." I squeezed my eyes shut as regret at unintentionally causing Samara pain curled in my gut. "We couldn't be together back then—she was promised to Demetri, and even then, despite our young age, we knew nothing between us would ever be casual. I brought any dalliances I had here because I didn't want to rub Samara's face in them."

"She knew you were trying to protect her feelings," Draven assured me. "That's why she never mentioned it to you and told me instead."

Before I could ask him what his confession in return had been, Draven pulled his shirt over his head, and any words I'd been about to speak died in my throat. Fuck, I'd forgotten he was built like that. He might look like a spoiled prince with his well-tailored clothes and easygoing smile, but his body told a different story. I hadn't even known it was possible to have abs that well-defined.

"You're drooling, Kier."

My eyes darted up to his, and I snapped my mouth shut. "Am not."

He laughed and unlatched the coiled whip with bloodred, serrated edges from his belt before setting it next to the edge of the pool. I'd asked him once why he didn't carry a sword, as that seemed like a more practical and effective weapon. He'd simply said he didn't like them, but I hadn't missed the flash of pain and fear across his face when he'd answered.

The only other time I'd seen something close to fear on his face was when he'd pleaded with me to leave the Moroi realm days ago. Samara was convinced there was something else to Draven we weren't seeing. That he wasn't the villain all the evidence suggested he was. I wanted to believe her, but Sam's past with Draven was different than mine. She hadn't had her heart ripped out by him.

The heated desire that had been winding through my body at seeing Draven strip instantly cooled at the reminder. He hadn't just ended things between us. I was an adult, and while it would have hurt, I would have dealt with it, but he'd humiliated me and used his knowledge of my past and my private thoughts I'd shared with him to hurt me. I so rarely trusted people, and he'd known that.

His words had been calculated and cruel.

"It's been fun, but I'm bored now. Also, watch how you speak to me in the future, courtier."

Rationally, I knew this lended more support to Samara's idea that Draven was being controlled somehow by his mother, or at least wasn't the complete villain she'd initially thought. He'd even claimed that he'd said those things to protect me. None of that erased the pain though.

I glanced at Zosa, wanting to jump onto her and ride out of here, but I'd promised Samara I'd keep Draven occupied for a few hours. She'd understand if I bailed, but Roth wouldn't have called a meeting if it hadn't been important. They needed time to talk and plan, and I would give them that time.

Angrily, I tore off my clothing, not even bothering to fold it, just dumping it all in a pile before stomping over to the pool and striding in. Pleasantly cool water greeted me as I swam out to the center where it was deepest and I couldn't reach the bottom. I treaded water while facing away from Draven, only turning around when I heard him enter the pool. The last thing I needed was to see him fully naked.

Every inch of that man was perfection, and I still remembered what it felt like to have his cock moving inside me. My resolve at keeping my hands to myself and maintaining distance would likely crumble if I saw all of him. I'd never really understood the appeal of hate fucking before, but that glimpse of his muscled chest earlier had definitely made me reevaluate my stance on that.

"You're thinking about hate fucking me, aren't you?" Draven drifted in front of me, a smirk stamped on his lips and his striking black-and-silver hair floating around him in the water.

"No," I said lightly. "I was thinking about drowning you, but then your ugly corpse would mess up my favorite swimming hole."

"Please." He smiled. "We both know my corpse would be gorgeous."

I laughed before I could stop myself, and his smile widened.

Then something flickered across his face faster than I could catch it before his smile faded and he swallowed. "I know you have every reason to distrust me. To hate me."

"I do." I watched him warily as we treaded water around each other.

"You need to know that—" He cut off his words as he winced sharply, as if he'd been struck by something.

"Drav?" Concerned filled me as I swam closer to him, sweeping some of his hair away from where it had been plastered to his face.

Bottomless blue eyes watched me with such sadness that I wanted to shake the truth out of him. The anger, the hurt, the fear, all of it fell away in an instant as I stared at him in this moment.

"Everything about me is a lie, Kier," he said desperately. "Half the words out of my mouth are lies. My past, present, and future are all lies crafted by *her*, but this"—he placed his hand over my heart—"this was always real."

Then he yanked me to him, and our mouths crashed against each other. I didn't even try to fight it; I just tangled my fingers in his hair and clutched him to me, our legs kicking in the water to keep us afloat. Draven parted his lips, and my tongue delved in. Fuck, I'd missed the way he tasted.

There'd always been something wild about Draven, different from other Moroi. He reminded me of the woods on a dark night. Dark and powerful and a little terrifying.

He groaned into my mouth when I pulled his hair a little rougher, then I felt his hard cock against my stomach, and when his hand slipped under the water to grip mine, my legs faltered and I almost slipped under. He chuckled and directed me over to the edge of the pool where several flat rocks rested in the water.

I intended to flip us so Draven was sitting on the stairs because I wanted to feel him come apart on my tongue, but just as my fingers gripped his hard length, stroking it once, he growled, "I want you first."

"You don't get everything you want, princeling." I snorted and tried to shove him up onto the stones, but the bastard twisted out of my grip and lifted me out of the water. Before I could slide back down, he jerked my legs apart and slid my cock into his mouth.

No teasing. No playful licking. He just swallowed me whole.

"FUCK!" I screamed as my dick hit the back of his throat and his fingers dug into my thighs. How had I forgotten Drav had zero gag reflex? I raised my head so I could watch him draw back. This time, he did swirl his tongue around my head before licking off the bit of precum that'd already formed.

His wet hair hung around him, the silver more of a dark grey now, looking every inch the wicked prince that he was, and it made my cock twitch in his grip.

"I love it when you look at me like that," he purred.

"Like what?" I said in a strained tone as he sucked the tip of my cock back into his mouth and released it with a *pop*.

"Like you *see* me." Thin red lines raced through his deep blue eyes. "And want me anyway."

He didn't wait for me to respond, and I moaned as he took me all the way into his mouth again. My fingers twisted around that gorgeous hair, and I bucked my hips as I shoved his head down. His grip tightened on my thighs as he spurred me on, loving the brutal pace I was setting for him.

I watched his head bob up and down on my cock, and when his teeth lightly grazed my skin, I saw stars for a moment as my balls started to tighten.

"Fuck, Drav," I ground out. "I'm close."

My words only encouraged him as he hollowed out his cheeks until it felt like I was halfway down his throat. Then one of his hands left my thigh and cupped my balls a second later, fingers rubbing against them exactly the way I liked.

I threw my head back as I thrust up into Draven's perfect mouth and came down his throat. He sucked down every last drop before sliding up and down my cock a few more times as I continued to tremble in his grasp.

"Moonsdamn it all." I panted and let my head fall back as he finally released me. "This was not what I'd planned when I asked you to come for a ride."

"Oh?" I could practically hear the smirk in his voice as he climbed up my body until he was above me and staring into my eyes. "And what type of *ride* were you hoping for?"

I raised my head and kissed him, enjoying tasting myself on his lips. "I don't regret this . . . but it doesn't change anything either, does it?"

Sadness crept back into Draven's face. For whatever reason, he wouldn't or couldn't tell us what was going on and why he was working with the wraiths and helping them attack Moroi outposts. Regardless, he was working with our enemy, which made him our enemy.

"No," he said in defeat. "It doesn't change anything. You and Samara might have my heart, but the Sovereign owns my soul."

CHAPTER SEVENTEEN

—

Samara

As I slipped through the double doors of the library, I was still reeling from what I'd seen in Draven's memory. But I tucked that away for later once I saw the scene before me. Roth was the only one there, and they were pacing.

Roth did *not* pace.

They sat perfectly still with a book in their hand, absorbing all the knowledge it contained before moving on to the next one. In fact, Roth would regularly yell at us for so much as breathing too loud while they were reading.

"Roth." I closed the distance between us until I stood in front of them. Roth stopped, orange fractures winding through their hazel eyes like fire. Usually, Roth's dark red hair was tidily swept back and they kept the sides closely shaved. Today, it just sort of flopped over to one side. I brushed my fingers beneath it, feeling the overgrown sides. "You're due for a shave," I mused.

I wasn't sure if it was possible to have more polar opposites than Kieran and Roth. While I'd known them both for a long time, it was easier to slip into a relationship with Kieran. He was cuddly and usually open with his emotions. Roth and I had known each other at Drudonia, but this romantic aspect of our relationship was new, and I was still learning how to navigate it. Roth did *not* cuddle. They also didn't tell me how they were feeling or whisper sweet nothings.

But they looked at me like I was a treasure when I recited Fae poetry, and they asked me my opinions on translations or history. Roth desired my mind as much as my body, maybe even more so, and I loved being consumed by them.

"Where are the others?" Roth rasped.

"They'll be here soon," I soothed before leading them over to a chair. They thunked down into it and wrapped the soft, dark blue shawl I'd gotten them a little tighter around their tunic. Roth was somehow always cold. They'd mumbled a thanks when I'd given it to them but had proceeded to wear it every single day since.

I brushed my fingers against the two embedded gems on the dark silver ring I wore on my pinky, letting Cali and Rynn know we needed to talk. If they weren't available now, I'd have to fill them in later, but Rynn was vital to my plan, so it'd make this a lot easier if she could join now.

"What are those?" Roth eyed the leather satchel I'd set on the table, the flap open and revealing the journals inside.

"Journals written by my mother." I pulled one of the books out and passed it to them. "There are more. We found them last night in a secret room in a cave down by the beach, all written by Harkers."

"What language is this?" They carefully flipped through the pages.

"I don't know," I said softly. "But my mother taught it to me. She said her mother taught it to her."

"I've never encountered it in any other writings." Roth frowned. "But some of these words . . . they're familiar. We use them in our common tongue."

Before we could dive further into the odd linguistics of the Lunarian language, the library doors swept open, and Vail, followed by Alaric, stalked in. I glanced back and forth between them. Alaric's expression was flat, and his fingers were curled at his sides like he was imagining strangling someone. Thin lines of silver raced through Vail's eyes as menace practically poured off him.

Okay. Clearly they were pissed at each other. What exactly had Alaric said to get Vail to come here?

I decided it was not my problem because they were both here and I was used to dealing with them in pissy moods anyway. I pressed down on the gems on my ring again to get Rynn's and Cali's attention.

"What?" Cali snarled, her shadowy form appearing suddenly in the middle of the library. Alaric jumped, and even Vail looked a little unnerved. All Furies had shadow magic, which put everyone on edge because it made them very wraith-like. The more talented ones could appear in shadow form like Cali, but unlike her, others' forms were less defined and it was hard for them to hold any type of shape.

Cali appeared before us exactly as she looked in real life, only made of shadows instead of flesh.

Darkness billowed outward as she spread her wings wide, causing the individual strands of her hair to flutter around. There was another secret about Cali that only Rynn and I knew. She could also turn her shadows solid for small snatches of time, something that no other Furie could do . . . but all wraiths could.

"I wouldn't have annoyed you if this wasn't important," I told her. "Are you okay?"

Cali's lips hardened into a flat line. "I'm fine. Don't worry about it."

As if that were possible. "Okay," I said instead. "We'll give Rynn a few minutes, and if she can't make it, we'll ge—"

Shadows swirled next to Cali, and Rynn's lean frame appeared a second later. Her shadowy form was a little less well-defined than Cali's since she was using a spell Cali had crafted specifically for her. But I could still make out her expression enough to see Rynn was worried.

That in itself wasn't unusual, because Rynn constantly worried about everything, but she was also in the thick of some complicated Velesian politics that she was trying to shield from me. This also meant my request was going to make her life even more difficult, but I didn't see any way around it.

"Good, we're all here." I grimaced and leaned my butt against the table where Roth was sitting, the others standing around in front of me. "We have a lot to go over. First, Rynn, Cali, let me catch you up on our special guest here at House Harker."

Ten minutes later, I'd told both of them everything about Prince Draven. How he'd been waiting for us when we'd gotten back from the temple, the suspicious marriage proposal, and every conversation we'd had with him since he'd been here. I left out his relationship with Kieran because I didn't feel right discussing that without Kier here, but sooner or later, that would have to be brought up as well. As much as I wanted to leave Kieran's personal life out of this, his history with Draven was relevant.

"Why the fuck didn't you tell us sooner?" Cali exploded. The shadows responded to her tension and skittered across the room.

Rynn's head turned sharply. "Calm down, Cali," she ordered. The pissed-off Furie whipped around to glare at her, but Rynn didn't back down. Dominance radiated from her as if she was in her considerably larger and more lethal lycanthrope form instead of her current lithe human skin. "Find your center, take a few deep breaths, and settle down."

"Fuck you and your peaceful Velesian bullshit," Cali grumbled, but I could see her shoulders dropping a little as she concentrated on her breathing. The Velesians were the only ones of the Moon Blessed who actually transformed into predators, yet in many ways, they remained the most human of all of us.

While Cali reined herself in, Rynn looked at me. "I agree with your assessment that there is more to Draven than it appears. I've only met him twice, but both times, his soul was . . ." Rynn cocked her head in a purely lupine gesture. "He was unsettled."

I nodded in understanding. Most of the Moroi discounted the Velesians because they had little magic of their own. But they could shift into their beast forms and were in tune with the environment to a sometimes eerie degree. A Velesian might be able to sense if the growing season would be poor and the crops wouldn't be bountiful, or sense predators nearby, but they couldn't give you any concrete facts. Only feelings.

The Velesians trusted their instincts, while the Moroi scorned them for it.

They also occasionally had visions, but because of the increasing tensions between our people, they were less inclined to share those visions with us. It was one of the many ways the divide between the Moon Blessed was hurting us all.

"Roth has some things to share," I explained. "And then I have more to tell you all, in addition to what I think our next step should be."

"You mean your scheme," Cali muttered, but she appeared less feral, so I let it slide.

"I've discovered two things." Roth swept a hand through their hair. "Those black stones the humans used for the ritual aren't originally from Lunaria. The Fae did something to either bring them here or summoned creatures who could create them."

They flipped open a book, pulled out a folded piece of paper, and started reading.

Once they were doom
Now they are salvation
At great sacrifice we called
They answered with death
From fire and chaos
A glittering dark was born
Stones lead to home
Where vengeance calls

"I bet that sounded a lot prettier in the original Fae," I grumbled.

"Not all of us are fluent in those languages." Alaric slid me an amused look before focusing on Roth. "If the Fae went through some 'great sacrifice' to get those stones created, then they must be important to them."

"We already knew that." Vail shrugged, unimpressed. "It's clear that's what they're looking for in the outposts they're raiding."

"True," Roth acknowledged with a dip of their head. "This is merely confirmation that there is something important about those stones, and also, more can't be made, at least not easily. I wasn't able to find anything else about what the Fae did to acquire them in the first place, but whatever it was isn't something that can be easily repeated."

"It's in our best interest then to make sure they don't get their hands on any more than they already have." I looked at Rynn. "You were the one who noticed they were raiding old human towns. Can you work with Roth to come up with a list of all known settlements, and we'll try to get to them before the wraiths do?"

"We'll have to do it quietly," Vail said. "If they realize what we're doing, they'll increase their attacks."

I nodded. "We'll get the list to you and trust your judgment on that."

"There probably aren't many settlements in the badlands, but I can take care of any of those," Cali said. "And if there are any in the Northern Ridge, I can take those as well."

Rynn frowned. "That's Avala territory. The Alpha Pack won't like you poking around there."

"It's amazing how much I simply don't care." Cali's wings stretched out further before snapping inward. "Besides, they won't even know I'm there."

Rynn didn't look convinced but didn't argue, instead, she just shot me a concerned glance. I gave her a barely perceptible nod in return. Cali was always a little wild, but she wasn't usually this antagonistic, definitely not towards us. There was zero chance of us getting her to tell us what was wrong with other people around though. We'd have to corner her about it later.

"What else did you find out, Roth?" I asked. The information they'd shared so far was useful, but I didn't think it was what had them so worked up.

"The other day, when you were reading an Unseelie poem, some of it reminded me of something I'd seen before"—their eyes darted to me, orange fractures flashing across the light brown for a second—"but then you distracted me and I forgot."

"I'm so sorry I gave you mind-melting orgasms," I deadpanned.

Roth ignored me, raising a book with a dark red covering and gold foiling off the desk. A Fae poetry book. Human books were always bound with simple leather. Roth flipped through the pages and then turned the book around so it faced us. On one page was the illustration of a crown. It looked like two bands that had been joined together, and a short poem was written in Unseelie on the opposing page.

"Most of the poem is so vague that it's hard to follow, but I think the Fae brought this crown with them from wherever they came from," Roth explained. "It's described as follows, '*A crown of two parts. Glittering gold and frosted silver. One half to see a soul. Another half to bind it.*'"

"Well, that's not good." Rynn sighed.

The others started talking about what this could mean, but I was trying to control my growing panic as I remembered my mother's words from the journal.

"This crown had been so simple. Just a simple silver band with delicate carvings. Parts of it had even appeared broken."

"Samara?"

I snapped out of my spiraling dread to meet Alaric's steady gaze. "I think Velika has the crown. Half of it anyway."

"What?" Roth paled even further. "What makes you think that?"

"That was the part I was going to tell all of you." I waved a hand at my bag and the journals it contained. "I read through some of my mother's journals. She talks about Velika wearing a simple silver crown with odd magic. My mother suspected it was a Fae artifact, and she was searching these lands to find more before Velika did."

"Did she mention anything specific about the crown?" Rynn asked. "Or about Erendriel or the wraiths being Fae? About Velika's alliance with them?"

"No." I shook my head. "Every hidden Fae hideout she and my father found was empty. She mentioned the wraiths acting strangely, but I don't think she knew they were the Fae, and she made no mention of an alliance between them and Velika. I think she only had strong suspicions about the Sovereign House but no actual proof."

"We need to tell Carmilla," Vail said firmly.

I pursed my lips, trying to think of how to phrase this so Vail wouldn't tear my head off. He was fiercely loyal to my aunt, and so was I, but unlike Vail, I could separate my own personal feelings from the situation at hand. "We need to make sure Carmilla is safe," I said carefully. "But we can't tell her any of this yet. First, she's at the Sovereign House, and we can't risk alerting Velika to what we know. If Velika's half of the crown gives her the ability to bind a soul to her, then there is a chance Carmilla is compromised."

The very idea of my aunt's will being taken away from her made me sick. But Carmilla trusted me to keep House Harker safe, which meant I had to consider the possibility that Velika would use her as a weapon against us.

"No." That one word so full of fury echoed in the space between me and Vail as he took a step closer to me. Cali immediately slid between us, and I had no doubt that if Vail continued towards me, she'd solidify enough to tear out his throat. He bared his teeth at her and his eyes bled silver.

She gave him a wicked grin in return, and I could practically see her eyes daring him to do something about it.

"Enough!" I snapped and slid around Cali to stand in front of Vail. I was reasonably sure Vail wouldn't attack me . . . and I couldn't let him know Cali had the ability to become corporeal. I knew Vail already considered her a potential threat based on the calculating way he watched her, looking for weaknesses. He had treated Cali with respect on account of how many times she had saved rangers, but if she ever changed from potential threat to actual threat . . . I had no doubt Vail would do his best to destroy her.

Or try to, at least. My money was on my friend, but I'd rather avoid that fight altogether, which meant keeping him away from Cali so she didn't do something stupid and give herself away. Seriously, what was she thinking antagonizing him like this?

A low growl rumbled from Cali's chest, and the hairs on the back of my neck rose, but I didn't turn around to look at her. No matter how strange she was acting right now, I had to believe she would never harm me. I would keep my friend sane through sheer force of my own will if I had to.

"There is nothing I won't do to protect Carmilla." I met Vail's unrelenting, predatory stare. "She is my aunt and the only family I have left, but if we storm the Sovereign House and tear her out of it, Velika will retaliate, and we have no idea what that crown can actually do. If she's already bound Carmilla to her, we don't know how to break it. We need answers, and we have to find them before showing our hand."

"And where exactly do you propose we find these answers?" Vail crossed his arms and took a few steps back.

Tension still wound through him, but the silver faded until it was only a sliver against the dark grey. Better. I let out a breath and moved to stand next to Cali, who was still staring at Vail like she was imagining carving him apart with her talons.

"My parents were planning on searching another Fae site before they were killed." Grief briefly rose to the surface before I ruthlessly suppressed it once more, keeping my voice even, if a little flat. "That trip they took to Velesian territory wasn't just to try to repair relations between them and the Moroi. My mother wanted to get permission to search around Lake Malov."

"Shit," Rynn spat. "That's going to be a problem."

"I know." I gave her an apologetic look. "But we have to go there. The wraiths have avoided that area too, so there is a real chance that if something is there, they haven't found it either."

Rynn frowned but didn't disagree.

"What's so special about Lake Malov?" Roth's piercing stare locked on Rynn. "I've heard the rumors—it's not just the wraiths that avoid it, other monsters do too. In some ways, it's the safest place in all of Lunaria. Yet the Narchis Order steers clear of it and forbids anyone from going there. I've searched through every text and book I could find, but nothing explains why."

"We don't know exactly." Rynn shifted back and forth on her feet. "Velesians may not have blood or shadow magic, but we feel things. The land whispers to us, and we've learned to always listen to what it tells us."

"And what does the land around Lake Malov tell you?" Alaric asked.

"To stay the fuck away." Rynn shook her head, appearing to be genuinely rattled at even discussing the lake.

"We can't." I sighed. "Maybe the other half of the crown is there and that's what's causing the discontent? My mother said she could feel the magic from Velika's half of the crown and that it felt wrong."

Rynn rubbed her face, causing the shadows to lose their form slightly. "There is a gathering of the packs in one week. All the Orders will be there, and my pack is hosting it in Fervis territory. Lake Malov is only an hour from us. That will be our best opportunity to slip past the patrols unnoticed, but we'll have to be quick."

"All the Orders?" I raised an eyebrow. The Velesians were broken up into three Orders: the Narchis, the Fervis, and the Avala. The Alpha Pack was of the Avala Order and was the one Rynn was to join to further the alliance between them and her birth Order, Narchis.

The Fervis Order was the most volatile of the three, and anytime all of the Orders met up, it was almost guaranteed to result in bloodshed, which meant it would definitely be the perfect opportunity for us to explore.

"All of them," Rynn confirmed, moving restlessly again and causing tendrils of shadows to swirl around her. "Cade made it very clear they're all expected to come."

Ah. That was why she was so uncomfortable. Cade was the leader of the Alpha Pack and the one who had negotiated for Rynn to join their pack. He was also the one Rynn corresponded with the most—and most of those conversations were fraught with tension.

"Alright, that's our best opportunity then," I said evenly. "We'll have to figure out the exact timing, but once we do, whoever goes can meet Rynn and Cali near Lake Malov."

Everyone nodded in reluctant agreement except Cali. "I can't go there," she said in a low, haunted voice and wrapped her wings around her body, shadows dripping off them. With mournful eyes she met my stare. "Something in that place . . . calls to me. All Furies feel it, but I seem to feel it more than any other. If I go there, I will lose myself."

Even from her shadowy form, I could see the genuine fear in her eyes. I knew then that whatever was going on with my friend, she was aware of it, and it terrified her.

Fuck it.

Without giving a shit what the others thought, I moved towards Cali and wrapped my arms around her shadowy form. I could sense her wavering for a moment before the shadows became solid and my friend hugged me back.

Alaric sucked in a breath, but Vail and Roth kept quiet.

"Whatever is going on with you, Cal, we have your back," I whispered. "We'll survive this, and then we'll figure out how to help you."

"Our ties are eternal." Rynn moved closer, her hand hovering around Cali as if she wished she could join in on the hug.

Cali shuddered beneath me, and for a second, darkness spread throughout the room before being sucked back into her. I felt it the moment she became nothing but shadows again, the dark wisps tickling my skin as they pulled away.

"Me, Vail, and Rynn will go," I declared.

"No." Alaric shook his head. "I'll go with you, and you know Kieran will want to come too."

Roth was looking at all of us, a torn expression on their face. They'd spent the majority of their life behind the wards of Houses or Drudonia. Roth wasn't a fighter by any stretch of the imagination, but even they didn't seem keen on me going out into the wilds with only Vail at my side until we met up with Rynn.

"You have to stay, Alaric," I said softly. "House Harker needs someone to run things while both Carmilla and I are away. And I won't risk Kieran."

"That's not your decision to make." Alaric's eyes flashed a brilliant turquoise before fading back to light green.

"She's the Heir," Vail growled. "It *is* her right."

"You would say that," Alaric snapped and stepped towards Vail. "Maybe the third time will be the charm and you'll actually claim her life on your next attempt."

The Marshal of House Harker straightened as he met Alaric's accusatory stare, and then he looked at me, his expression the same as when I'd told him to never doubt my devotion to House Harker. I hadn't been able to decipher it then, but now I could see the emotions brimming in his eyes. Respect. Yearning. Confliction.

Once again, I was confused by Vail's reactions. Even worse . . . my feelings for him were getting confounding as well. Waking up surrounded by his scent this morning had been nice, really nice, and that was an absolutely insane feeling to have about someone who'd tried to kill me recently.

I didn't think he would try to kill me again, but I hadn't thought that the previous times either. The situation in the temple wasn't entirely his fault—it was his bloodlust that had been driving him. Even if I wasn't sure I was safe around him, he was the only option I had to get me through the wilds quickly to Lake Malov.

Vail watched me steadily, and I got the impression he understood every conflicted thought that had just raced through my mind.

"I pledge on the grave of my parents that I will protect Samara with my life." I inhaled sharply as a muscle in Alaric's cheek twitched. He knew the Marshal was speaking the truth, but he still didn't like it.

"It'll be okay, Alaric." I laid a hand on his forearm. "We have to do this, and you know it makes sense for the three of us to go. Vail can get me there safely, and Rynn is the most familiar with the area."

He tore his gaze away from Vail to look at Rynn. "Do you? Know the area, I mean?"

"Yes." Rynn nodded confidently. "It's not a pleasant region to be around, but I wandered there often when I was a child. It was one of the few places I could be alone." She worried her bottom lip. "Lately, I've found myself going back there for the same reason."

This time, it was Cali who looked at me with concern. The three of us all had our issues. Cali struggled with her rage and magic, I struggled balancing being the resilient Heir of House Harker while also processing the grief of losing the two most important people in the world to me, and our sweet Rynn, she struggled with being used as a political pawn her entire life and never knowing who she could truly trust amongst her own people. I had no doubt her parents cared for her in their own ways, but that hadn't stopped them from agreeing to send her away to join the Alpha Pack when she'd come of age.

"What about the prince?" Alaric grimaced. "We won't be able to cover your absence for so long."

"We have at least a few days to figure that out," I said. "We'll just need to keep him occupied for a few hours after we leave so we can create some distance. Maybe mention that more of the spine-backed boars have been spotted and I wanted to investigate myself. Let him know he's welcome to stay here and wait for my return."

Alaric snorted. "That'll go over well."

"It doesn't matter." I shrugged. "Vail and I will keep off the main roads and won't stay at any of the outposts. He won't be able to track us."

"I'll review the list of old human settlements. There may be some close enough that I can investigate them before we have to leave. I need to update Emil as well so he can help with the searches." Vail strode towards the door to leave but stopped when I called out to him.

"Vail, if you find any, tell me. I want to see them for myself." The hand at his side bunched into a fist at the command in my voice, but he turned his head slightly and jerked it in a short nod before leaving.

"I'll find out more about the meeting so I can determine the best time for us to do this, as well as the patrols in the area. They'll no doubt be increased with all the Orders gathering in one place." Rynn waved goodbye and vanished.

Cali stared at the space she'd been standing in before swiveling her head towards me in a movement that felt distinctly predatory. "Be careful."

In a blink, she was gone, a few shadows swirling in the air before dissipating.

"Do we need to worry about Cali?" Alaric asked in a calm, measured tone.

"She's fine," I said with a confidence I didn't entirely feel.

Alaric looked at me for a long moment, and I could see the doubt in his eyes, but he didn't voice his concerns. "I'll be in my study whenever you're ready," he finally said before he too left.

It took me a moment to remember he'd agreed to feed from me. I was a little surprised that not only had he not changed his mind but that he'd reminded me.

"I'll do some research on Furies while you're away," Roth said quietly. "We understand them the least out of all the Moon Blessed, but I have a few scrolls that detail cases of Furies losing themselves. Perhaps I'll find something useful."

They wouldn't. Rynn and I had poured through every scroll, book, and scrap of information we could find over the years. Nobody knew why the Furies were so volatile, but I appreciated the sentiment all the same.

"Stay with me tonight?" I swallowed, feeling a little unsure of my request. Roth's eyes flicked up from the book they'd already started reading, and they arched an eyebrow. "If you grab whatever books you want and head to my suite now, the prince won't see. He's out with Kieran. I'll tell Kier he has to sleep in his room tonight."

I wasn't exactly sure where Roth stood in regards to Kieran. They obviously had no problem with me being in a relationship with him, but as far as I knew, Roth wasn't attracted to Kieran. Even if all we did was sleep, I didn't know if they would be comfortable sharing a bed with him as well.

One corner of Roth's mouth quirked up into the barest hint of a smile. "You will return to your room after dinner," they ordered, and a thrill ran up my spine. "I will have you until midnight, then the pretty one and the grumpy one can come. You'll be passed out by then because I plan on being quite thorough, but they can at least sleep next to you. Want me to take these back with me?"

It took my mind a second to focus on the leather satchel Roth was holding up, the one that contained the Harker journals.

"Yes." I cleared my throat. "Thank you."

Roth swung the bag over their shoulder and flicked their left arm towards the table, the bloodred ribbons they kept wrapped around their forearms unwinding and maneuvering around the stack of books until they were in a neat little bundle. Then Roth winked at me before sauntering towards the door with their ribbons tugging the bundle of books behind them. "See you in a few hours."

CHAPTER EIGHTEEN

—

Samara

MY STEPS WERE quick as I made my way to Alaric's study from mine. His was also on the third floor of the main tower but on the complete opposite side. I'd wanted to go there directly from the library, but instead, I'd forced myself to go to my own study and get some work done. Then I'd met with Yolanthe and a few other advisors.

I hadn't told anyone I'd be gone for a few days soon because I couldn't risk Draven getting tipped off, but I made sure to deal with any issues that needed my attention. And there had been many. Surviving in Lunaria wasn't easy, even when there weren't nefarious plots threatening to damn us all. The wards that protected our Houses and outposts were powered by gems, which we seemed to always be running low on. And then those fucking boars had wiped out more crops. We'd be fine unless something went wrong with the summer crops. If that happened, the upcoming winter would be a lean one.

"Couldn't the Fae have picked a nicer place to drag us all?" I muttered, although I doubted they had come here voluntarily, which begged the question, who was powerful enough to force the Fae to do anything?

I was still musing this over when I reached Alaric's study. The door was open a crack, so I pushed it and stepped inside. Alaric's eyes rose from the letter he was reading, watching as I closed the door behind me and flipped the lock. Then I brushed the glyph on the wall, activating the silencing spell before walking towards his desk. I wasn't sure exactly what was going to happen in the next few minutes, but I was pretty sure we wouldn't want anyone to overhear or interrupt us.

"You came." He leaned back in his chair, a tightness around the corners of his eyes.

"I told you I'd let you feed from me." I moved behind the desk and sat on

390

it, scooting over until I was sitting directly in front of him. As usual, Alaric's desk was perfectly organized, and I was careful not to knock over the stacks of letters and scrolls. "Did you think I would change my mind?"

Alaric's gaze fell to where the high slit of my dress revealed a large amount of skin. Then he swallowed as impossible blue lines flashed across his light green eyes. I could feel the bloodlust rising within him as he wrestled it, and my heart raced a little faster as I leaned back on the desk, the movement causing even more of my thigh to be on display.

I still remembered quite vividly how he had tasted in my mouth. I wanted to feel his fangs in my neck as he buried his cock inside me. He'd been so demanding before, and I wanted him to give in to that urge again, but something told me that if I pushed him on this, he'd pull away. So I forced myself to wait.

"My family has a history of turning Strigoi." The heart hammering inside my chest froze, and Alaric looked at me with an almost mournful expression. "It wasn't just my cousin, Faolan, who turned."

"Who else?" I asked softly, even as my mind was racing, trying to remember anything else about Alaric's family. Aside from his parents coming from one of our outposts, I couldn't think of anything useful.

He looked away, staring at a spot on his desk. "Maternal grandmother—she turned after my grandfather was killed by wraiths—and both grandparents on the paternal side. Best I can tell, over half on my father's side have turned Strigoi, and my mother's side isn't that much better. It's one of the reasons my parents were so relieved to be offered high-ranking positions here."

Because they could regularly drink from Carmilla. Partaking in the blood of any of the House families significantly reduced one's chances of becoming Strigoi. So much so that drinking from the House bloodlines had been the norm for a while, but now there were too many Moroi for that to be feasible. Parents would bring their young children to whichever House they belonged to shortly after they were born so the child could be given House blood, but that was it.

My generation had been the most stable so far, only a few instances of Moroi losing themselves completely in bloodlust and becoming Strigoi, but it did happen. I suspected, with the increased wraith attacks, it had happened more in the past few months and we just didn't know yet. When facing certain death, some Moroi would relinquish their hold on humanity in an attempt to survive. Who knew how many more Strigoi were prowling the wilds after all the outpost attacks?

I mentally added that to the long list of problems we were facing and refocused on the one in front of me. Alaric's cousin, Faolan, had turned, and I knew he'd been there to witness it. It wasn't all that surprising that he'd been scarred by that.

"You won't become Strigoi." It was both a command and a promise. I leaned forward and tipped Alaric's face up with my fingertips. "You are *mine*."

His green eyes turned solid turquoise, and he released a low growl that had me clenching my thighs together.

"I can feel it every time my bloodlust rises, the all-consuming hunger. It's only a matter of time." His eyes fell to the pulse on my neck before he forced himself to look away and stare blankly at the wall. "There is a courtier who I have an arrangement with. She visits every couple of months, and I feed from her then. I only drink a little, and we do it at midday, when the sun is the strongest over the moon."

Because the moon called to our bloodlust. All of our senses were heightened at night, but letting our bloodlust rise under the light of the moon was intoxicating.

The rangers often hunted at night because of it. They'd point themselves in the directions of the monsters and let themselves go, reclaiming their humanity in the morning. They spent years practicing that ability though, always keeping the smallest hold on themselves so they weren't lost forever.

"I almost lost it last time she came." Alaric rubbed his mouth like he could still taste the blood on it. Some part of me raged at the idea of him feeding from someone else, but I bit back the growl that crept up my throat. There was a time and place for territorial bullshit, and this wasn't it.

"When's the last time you fed?" I asked softly.

"Almost four months ago."

Fuck. Our bodies needed food, but our magic needed blood. Most Moroi drank once a month, more often if they'd used a lot of magic for spellcasting or healing. Alaric's control over his bloodlust had to be ironclad if he was still holding it together.

But even he had a breaking point.

"You're only hurting yourself. Harker blood will help you."

"I don't want to hurt you," he rasped as he turned his gaze away from the wall and back to me.

"You won't." I let my bloodlust rise until I knew my eyes were black. "Trust me, I can hold my own."

Alaric went still as he took me in. "What . . ." Then his eyes dropped to my fangs peeking through my parted lips. "What does it feel like to you? You almost never put it away anymore, not entirely."

I thought about it. "Everything is just . . . more. The scents in the air. The colors in the flowers." Slowly, I reached out and trailed my fingers along his jawline, my heart skipping as he turned his head slightly to inhale my scent better. "Your skin beneath my touch."

A few beats passed between us before he looked at me with bottomless eyes. "And the hunger?"

"There," I admitted. "Always there, but it's like an impatient friend I've learned to live with and occasionally throw a bone to." Something shuddered in his expression, prompting me to ask, "What does it feel like for you?"

"Mindless and cruel," he said without hesitation. "Whatever it is that prowls beneath my skin . . . it isn't me. It feels like it wants to devour everything I am until nothing remains but itself. The monster."

I understood that I was part of the small group of Moroi who were exceptions to the rule. Something about us was different, our bloodlust integrated more with who we were, but Vail and the other rangers weren't like me, and they could harness their bloodlust just fine. It was possible for any Moroi.

Alaric was letting his fear override everything else, and that was making things so much worse. There was no separating a Moroi from their bloodlust. It was something that had to be accepted. Alaric was trying to deny an intrinsic part of himself, and it was going to be the death of him someday.

Panic wrapped around my heart and squeezed when a little green came back into Alaric's eyes, and I could tell he was pulling away. If things had been different, I would have let him. I understood now why he was so paranoid and obsessed with control. His perfectly organized office. The clothing that was never out of place. Why he was so annoyed at me every time I got him to lose his temper.

Alaric lived every day terrified he was going to lose control of his bloodlust. Given his family history, his concerns were valid, but starving himself wasn't going to help—he had to know that. His fear was winning over his logic. I was leaving tomorrow, and he was still weak from the monster attack in the cave. He needed to feed, and I refused to leave this office until he was sated.

With slow, deliberate movements, I slid off the desk until I was straddling his lap. Alaric went completely still, his hands hovering around me but not touching.

"Samara," he warned.

"You're not healing the way you should be because you've waited too long to drink," I said calmly. "I'm worried about you, and that means I'll be distracted when Vail and I leave tomorrow. Do you really want me wandering around the woods with this weighing heavily on me instead of fully concentrating on my surroundings?"

He narrowed his eyes. "You won't convince me with logic."

I smiled, completely undeterred.

"There are two ways we can do this." My hair fell in a dark curtain as I pulled it aside and bared my neck to him. "You can drink from me and *only* drink, or"—I rolled my hips, feeling his hard erection, and he groaned—"you drink and fuck me at the same time. The choice is yours, but you have to drink, Alaric."

Blue and green warred in his eyes like waves crashing against each other. Then his lips parted, revealing sharp fangs, but he still didn't move.

"I don't believe you'll hurt me." He shivered as I trailed a finger along his jawline. "But I am capable of defending myself and will do so if I have to."

"Promise me." Alaric reached around me and pulled a drawer open before a silver blade appeared between us. "Promise you'll use this if things get out of hand."

I took the dagger, wrapping my fingers around the handle. His eyes bore into mine, and I knew he would not relent on this. If this was what it took to make him willingly drink from me, then I'd do it, even if my stomach rolled at the idea of hurting him.

My grip tightened. "I promise."

Alaric studied me for a long moment before wrapping one hand around the back of my neck. He was giving me time to change my mind, which was kind of sweet, but I was officially out of patience.

I let my hand holding the dagger fall loosely to my side but slid the other one behind Alaric's head and yanked him towards my neck. His chest vibrated with a deep growl, and the possessiveness in it had my toes curling.

Fingers dug into the ridge of my hip as his hand on the back of my neck squeezed harder. A throaty moan slipped from my lips as I ground against him. If he didn't bite or fuck me soon, I was going to burst. Lips brushed against my neck, the touch delicate compared to the punishing grip of his hands. Then he kissed my neck again before I felt the sharp sting of his fangs sinking into my flesh.

"Yes," I breathed out as the brief moment of pain gave way to pure pleasure.

Alaric drank deeply but still pulled away too soon, and warm blood slid down my neck as I looked into bright turquoise eyes. Quick, shallow pants escaped through his lips, and I could feel how taut his body was beneath mine. He needed more.

I licked my bottom lip, and his eyes snagged on the movement. "You're still hungry," I purred, "so we're not done here." I sucked in my bottom lip and bit down, piercing it with my own fang. Blood dribbled down my chin, and Alaric was there in an instant, his mouth crashing against mine.

The knife almost slipped from my grasp when he suddenly rose out of the chair, taking me with him, but I kept my hold on it. I'd promised him I'd watch out for myself, and while I didn't believe I'd need to, it was important to him. He didn't trust himself yet to not lose control, and that knife was his safe word.

Alaric sucked on my bottom lip before kissing me deeply as he sat me down on the edge of his desk, my legs spread wide on either side of him. Fingers wrapped around my hair to wrench my head back, and I writhed in Alaric's grip when he struck at my neck, leaning me further back on the desk. The neat stack of papers went flying, and I barely managed to slam my hand down on a pile of books to keep them from crashing to the floor too.

Fingers slipped between my thighs and roughly tugged my undergarments to the side before plunging into my slick center, and Alaric gave an approving growl at how wet I was for him. A strangled moan escaped me as he slowly pulled his fingers out, rubbing them over my clit before thrusting them back in. The climax was instant and brutal. I barely managed to keep from slamming my head back onto the desk as my body clamped down around his fingers, the books tumbling to the floor.

Alaric's fangs slipped from my neck as he raised his head and eyed the mess we were making of his desk. He glanced at my hand that was still awkwardly holding the dagger to the side because I really didn't want to accidentally stab myself or him. My mind was still reeling from the orgasm, so I was only faintly aware of him plucking the dagger from my grip before he slammed it into the desk. The blade sunk a few inches into the wood, still upright and within my reach.

I extended my hand to grab Alaric's tunic, wanting to see more of him, but apparently he had the same idea because he ripped the front of my dress in half. I moaned as his mouth found my nipple and sucked hard, his hand gripping my other breast, then I arched my hips up, trying to grind against him. I wanted to feel his hard cock in my hands, but I wasn't in a position to reach it.

Alaric laughed against my skin as he twirled his tongue around my sensitive nipple. "You're very needy," he said roughly before sucking my nipple back into his mouth. "I want to taste you everywhere."

"Fuck!" I cried out when his fangs sank into the swell of my breast, causing me to buck upward. I slipped my hands under the back of his tunic and felt the hard, corded muscles of his back flexing beneath my touch.

Then the hand that had been playing with my breast trailed down my stomach, fingers dipping and rising over every one of my curves until they disappeared between my thighs once more. I felt his nails harden into claws that he slid lightly across my skin before tearing my undergarments away.

Sliding his fangs free, he hovered above me, hunger still shining in his bright turquoise eyes. There wasn't a hint of green to be seen, his bloodlust riding high. The sound of more fabric being torn rang throughout the room, and then I felt his cock nudge at my entrance. Alaric went predatorily still as he took me in, splayed out beneath him, and hesitation flickered in his eyes.

I stretched my hand up and cupped his cheek. "You're still you, Alaric. This is part of who you are, and I want all of it."

My words were his undoing, and a scream tore out of my throat as he slammed into me. There was no easing into it. No going slow. Alaric's fingers dug into my hips as he fucked me hard and fast, and the tension that had been building between my thighs erupted. Alaric didn't slow down a bit, just fucked me through it as I saw stars. I gripped my bouncing tits to keep them in place, and when I saw Alaric's eyes burn with desire, I squeezed them a little harder.

This time, his eyes glazed over, and I let out a husky laugh. One hand left my hip to rub my clit, and my pleasure-laden laughter turned into a strangled scream as his damn fingers played with the already overstimulated bundle of nerves.

"So fucking wet," Alaric growled. "I could smell how turned on you were when Kieran was fucking your cunt and I was thrusting my cock in and out of that perfect fucking mouth." Strong hands gripped my legs, raising them up until the tops of my thighs brushed my stomach. "You enjoyed taking every inch of our cocks, didn't you?"

Fuck. My pussy clenched around him as he continued to hammer into me. I never would have guessed Alaric would be a dirty talker, but I was fucking here for it.

He thrust into me hard one more time, and the desk slid a few inches. My eyes stared into his, and I saw the same desperate need reflected in them. A possessive growl rippled up his throat as he lowered my legs and took a step back, his cock sliding out of me. I let out a whimpered cry at the loss but then yelped when Alaric flipped me over so I was bent over the desk.

"Option two," he breathed into my ear, his chest against my back. I felt him rubbing the head of his thick cock against my slick folds. "You said I could feed from you, or feed from you *and* fuck you at the same time. *Option fucking two, Sam.*"

"Fuck yes," I pleaded in a tone that I'd probably be embarrassed about later, but holy fuck, I hadn't expected Alaric to be like this. I'd expected him to be amazing but in a calm and thorough kind of way, not whispering dirty words into my ear while roughly using my body however he wanted.

His chest rumbled against me as he let out another deep laugh, and I couldn't resist grinding my ass against him. In a second, his body vanished from where he'd been pinning me down, and then a loud slap sounded. I let out a sharp exhale when he slapped my ass again.

Hard.

Wet heat spread down my inner thighs, and Alaric swirled his cock in it as his fingers rubbed the spot on my ass he'd slapped. "You like to play rough, don't you?" I clenched my thighs together, and he chuckled darkly. "When you get back, Kieran and I are sharing you again, and this"—he slapped my ass again—"is *mine.*"

"Sure," I breathed out, my entire body trembling in anticipation. "Just fuck me now please."

"I think that's the first time you've ever said please to me in your life." He nudged my legs further apart so I was even more bared to him and leaned over me again. I moaned as his fingers slipped over my clit before he pushed them slowly inside me. "Grab the desk," he ordered roughly.

Alaric withdrew his fingers, and I grabbed the edge of the desk. Then he kissed my neck over the place he'd bitten me when we'd started all this. The broad head of his cock pushed through my slickness, and he buried himself inside me at the same moment his fangs sank into my flesh.

My fingers dug into the wood as Alaric pounded me into the desk, his grip on my hair almost punishing as he wrenched my head back further and drank deeply. One of his hands seized my left leg and lifted it until my knee was on the desk.

"Oh fuck!" I screamed as the adjusted position allowed him even deeper access, the intensity of it all sending me spiraling as waves of pleasure slammed into me. Alaric's grip on my hair tightened for a second before he ripped his fangs free from my neck and bellowed as he followed me over the edge.

Neither of us moved for a few minutes. Alaric just released my hair and pressed his head to the back of my neck while we panted and trembled as the remnants of our orgasms passed.

Finally, Alaric straightened, and we both groaned as his cock slid free. I winced a little as I stood, feeling tender . . . everywhere. I had an indent on my thigh where it'd been pinned against the desk, my head and neck were sore from the hair pulling, and my poor pussy had taken a beating.

Alaric looked at me carefully, as if he was noting all of this and feeling a little unsure about what we'd just done.

"I loved every second of that, so wipe that look off your face." I grinned at him. "Didn't know you had it in you, Alaric. Want to bet we can break the desk next time?"

"You're a menace." He shook his head even as a smile crept across his lips. "We're using your study next time. It's always a disaster zone anyway."

"Rude." I looked around the floor surrounding his desk that was now covered with paperwork, scrolls, and everything else that had been neatly stacked. "Better idea—we use Kier's study."

Alaric laughed. "Look at that. You and I are capable of negotiating and agreeing on something."

"Keep fucking me like that and I think you'll find I'm a lot more agreeable." I sent him a sly look.

"I think I can do that," he murmured and pulled the dagger free from the desk. Then he studied it for a long moment before raising his gaze to me. "This comes out every time, just in case."

"Okay," I agreed softly, even though I didn't believe we'd ever need it. "Whatever you need, Alaric. Just don't pull away from me if you get scared, because I'm all in on this and I can't watch you walk away again."

He tossed the knife back onto the desk and wrapped his arms around me. "Never again, Sam. I promise. You are all I need."

CHAPTER NINETEEN

—

Roth

I BLEW out a frustrated breath and slammed the book closed. Another dead end. So far, I had a long list of problems and very few solutions, and that list was only growing.

Solving problems was my thing. I enjoyed it and was good at it, but usually the problems I was trying to solve were things I could look at from an abstract viewpoint. If I couldn't solve them, I would be annoyed, but I'd just move on to something else and forget about them in a few days.

It was harder to do that though when my lover, who was a fucking Heir, was counting on me. I didn't want to let her down.

I glanced around the suite and the absolute chaos it contained. For someone who always appeared so well put together, Samara's rooms were a bit of a shock. I'd only been here a handful of times because she almost always came to my room. I had a tendency to lose track of time, and Samara often felt compelled to hunt me down and make sure I was eating and sleeping enough.

At first, it had annoyed me, but after ensuring I ate or drank something, Samara would flop onto my bed and pick up a book. No other demands. No questions. She'd simply wanted to make sure I was okay and, once she'd done that, purely enjoy my company.

Nobody in my life had ever given a shit about me this way, and I didn't exactly know what to do about that, or the fact that I'd been at House Harker for such a short time and already couldn't imagine my life anywhere else with anyone else.

I scowled at the book in my hand for daring to not have the answers before tossing it onto the table in front of me. When it slid across the surface and stopped just before some books that Samara had placed haphazardly into a tall, teetering stack, I winced. I didn't quite understand how it hadn't fallen over yet, but I was worried that if I so much as breathed in its direction, it would collapse. So I'd left it alone and hoped it continued to defy its destiny.

I'd barely gotten into a book again when the door opened and Samara strolled in looking a little . . . disheveled.

The scent of blood, sweat, and lingering lust filled the air.

"You and Alaric are still working things out, I see." I raised an eyebrow at her, and Samara just smirked before heading towards the washroom, stripping as she went.

"I think we've worked past all the hard bits."

"I bet," I said dryly, lips curling up slightly. It was good to see Samara happy, given everything that was going on.

She paused halfway across the room and whirled around in nothing but her panties, giving me a concerned look. "Are you . . . okay about me being with Alaric? I know you're fine with Kieran, but I just realized I never specifically talked to you about Alaric." The smile that had been plastered across her face fell, and her brows bunched in concern. "Fuck, I'm sorry, Roth. Things kind of happened fast between me and Alaric. I wasn't expecting it to be honest, but that's no excuse. I should have talked to you about this sooner and—"

"Samara," I cut her off, a bemused look on my face. It wasn't often that I saw the supremely confident Heir of House Harker looking unsure about anything. "As long as he treats you well and makes you happy, I have no problem with any of it."

"Okay." She chewed her bottom lip. "You're absolutely sure?"

I rolled my eyes before standing from the settee and walking over to her to kiss her lightly on the lips. "Babe." I kissed her again. "It's fine. I appreciate you taking my feelings into account." Another kiss. "But it is impossible for me to take you and this conversation seriously when you're standing there basically naked and chewing on your lip like that."

"Oh!" Samara looked down at herself like she'd just remembered she was in nothing but panties. Then she gave me a sheepish grin as color darkened her cheeks. "I . . . ummm . . . usually start stripping as soon as I'm back in my rooms. Given the option, I prefer to just lounge around naked or maybe in an oversized shirt if it's cold."

"I'm going to be in your rooms a lot more now." The left corner of my mouth tilted up. I'd never just . . . hung out with Samara in her rooms before. Usually we were tearing each other's clothes off or I was tying her down with my ribbons. This was new territory for me, and I fought to keep from running my hand through my hair as I tried to figure out what I was supposed to do.

"Okay," she said again, this time, a little mischievous spark lighting up her dark purple eyes. "You called me *babe*."

Some of the tension bled out of me. She was so adorable sometimes.

"Sure did. Now go rinse off." Then I leaned forward to whisper into her ear, "*Babe.*"

She grinned and sauntered off to the washroom, swinging her hips with a ridiculous exaggeration. I watched every second of it before retreating to the settee and diving into the books once more. A stupid smile stretched across my face, but I didn't care because there wasn't anyone here to see it.

Ten minutes later, a thoroughly clean Samara sat down next to me, towel drying her wet hair as she scanned the books I'd brought with me. Despite the messy state of her room, I had no doubt Samara knew exactly where everything was and easily identified my items.

Her eyes lingered on the neat stack of clothing sitting on one of the chairs. I'd brought not only clothes for tonight, but extra clothes to keep here for whenever I stayed over. She didn't comment on the clothing, but I didn't miss the pleased expression that flashed across her face.

Samara liked me being in her rooms. This wasn't a passing fancy for her, and it sure as shit wasn't for me. She had brought up Alaric and apologized for that misstep, even though I truly didn't care since it had been clear to anyone with eyes that those two were headed in that direction, so it was time for me to come clean too.

"I got kicked out of Drudonia," I blurted out. *Smooth, Roth. Couldn't have come up with a better way to phrase that?*

Once again, the happy expression vanished from her face, and I squeezed my eyes shut with a wince. Why was I so terrible at talking like a normal person?

Oh, right, because I'd barely spoken to anyone for the first ten years of my life.

"What I meant to say—" The words died on my lips when I opened my eyes and met Samara's solid black ones.

A tightly contained fury rolled off her in waves, and she flexed her now claw-tipped fingers. "Was this your House's doing? Their way of forcing you to go back to them?"

"What?" I asked in shock. "No, they don't care—"

"Because I will tear House Devereux apart brick by brick," Samara snarled. "You are *mine.*"

"I am." My hands gently wrapped around hers, and I raised her right hand to sit over my heart, not flinching as her claws pierced my thin shirt to sink lightly into the flesh below. "House Devereux doesn't want me either." I tried and failed to keep my tone light. "So it's good that you're a fan of my tongue and reading comprehension because otherwise, things would not be looking too good for me right now."

Samara took in a deep breath, and I felt her claws slide free before she pulled her hand away and winced at her bloody fingertips. "Sorry." She sighed.

"I haven't bothered to tuck the bloodlust completely away since getting back. With Draven here, I'd rather keep it close." Purple bled back into her eyes as the black threads receded until they were just thin, dark jagged lines, a reminder of the monster always lurking under the surface.

"The fangs haven't escaped my notice." I gave her a reassuring grin that I wasn't frightened of her. Every Moroi treated their bloodlust differently. Some viewed it a weapon to wield. Others would only let it out when they were feeding or fucking. Usually both.

But Samara let her bloodlust out frequently, and there was barely a difference in her personality. This was the first time I'd seen a flash of anything else, and even then, I hadn't been the least bit scared. If anything, I'd wanted to shove her down on the settee and let those claws rip off my pants while I sat on her face.

I squeezed my thighs together as a pleasant heat started to build. Definitely an idea for later.

When she saw I wasn't the least bit disturbed by her outburst, Samara licked my blood from her fingers and then moved to rest her head on my lap. I stared at her wide-eyed for a moment before settling back against the cushions and running my fingers through her still-damp hair.

"Why did Drudonia kick you out? You're brilliant," Samara said. "They were lucky to have someone like you there."

"This may shock you, but I'm not exactly good with other people." I shrugged. Honestly, I didn't know how Samara and Kieran did it. They were both so good at navigating social niceties. Most people were dumb and not worth my time.

She pursed her lips into a hard, flat line. "You're just direct is all."

I snorted. "Well, my *directness* managed to piss off every scholar at Drudonia over the last few years. They couldn't actually kick me out because, despite my estrangement from my House, I *am* still a Devereux, but when I told them I was coming here, they made it very clear that they would prefer I remain here."

Samara didn't say anything for a long moment, and I concentrated on getting some tangles out of her hair.

"Roth," she said slowly, "have you been obsessing over finding answers because you're worried that if you don't, I'll kick you out?"

My fingers froze on a tangle, and I slid my gaze to Samara's. One perfectly sculpted eyebrow was raised as she gave me an exasperated look.

"To borrow some of your directness, don't be an idiot. I adore you, Roth. If all you ever do is sit in my room with me and play with my hair while I read, I'm fine with that. You do not have to earn a place here. You already have it." She snuggled further into my lap, and suddenly, I felt heat building behind my eyes.

No. Absolutely not. I would not cry.

As if sensing my internal struggle, Samara closed her eyes and gave me a few minutes to get a hold of myself. I finished getting the tangle out and moved on to another, the heat behind my eyes gradually lessening.

"I won't ever push you about your family," Samara said, still keeping her eyes closed, "but do you think we need to worry about them allying with Velika? Taivan is one of the only Heirs who didn't come here earlier this week, not that House Devereux is particularly social."

Understatement of the year. While most of the Houses were constantly jockeying for better positions, especially in proving their worth to the Sovereign House, Devereux was happy to remain in the shadows. We were on the southern coast, the border of the badlands to our west and the ocean lapping at our doors to the south. Most of the other Houses were situated on or near the main roads for travel. There was no reason to travel to our territory unless you wanted to visit us.

And House Devereux was not welcoming to outsiders.

"That House is loyal to itself and only itself," I said evenly. "Thessalia and the rest of the Devereux, my parents included, are reclusive, paranoid, and obsessed with enforcing their borders."

"You talk about them as if you aren't a part of their House," she noted.

"I was the youngest of three, and my parents really didn't know what to do with someone who would rather pick up a book than a sword."

So they did nothing. I couldn't stop the bitter thought from surfacing. I wasn't entirely sure they had even noticed when I'd left for Drudonia and never returned.

"Rynn thought you might have stayed at Drudonia after you finished your studies because your Hou—" Samara quickly corrected herself, "because House Devereux was pushing you to do something you didn't want, like a marriage or stepping into a higher-ranking position."

"What?" I frowned. "No, they barely acknowledged me when I briefly returned to collect the rest of my things. Taivan forced me to pack some daggers and other things to bring back to Drudonia, but we barely exchanged a few words. He's the oldest of us, and I think he just feels obligated to act like a protective brother."

"Brother . . ." Samara's eyes flew open, and she gawked at me. "Taivan is your brother!"

"Yes." I stared down at her in confusion. "I thought you knew that."

"So Severen and Celestina are your parents?"

"And Taivan and Desmond, my older brothers." I cocked my head at her wide-eyed expression. "Did you really not know who I was?"

"I mean, I knew you were a Devereux, but you never spoke about your family, and they never mentioned you." She winced. "Everyone has always assumed you were a distant cousin or something, not that your father was the brother of the current ruler of House Devereux."

"Like I said"—I shrugged nonchalantly—"they never really paid attention to me, so I'm not surprised I was never mentioned."

"I'm sorry, Roth." Her expression softened. "That couldn't have been easy growing up."

"It was lonely and frustrating," I admitted. "But it could have been worse. They were never intentionally cruel, and no one has demanded that I return. Though if you're hoping I can help improve relations between House Harker and House Devereux, I don't think I'll be of much help."

"That's fine," Samara said. "I'm leaving House Devereux as a bit of a wild card in all this but leaning towards them not being allied with Velika. Though they likely won't help us against her either."

"I think that is a correct assessment to take for now. If . . ." I swallowed. "If you'd like me to reach out to my parents to arrange a meeting, I can do so."

"Thank you." Samara reached for one of my hands and pulled it away from her hair so she could kiss my palm. "I don't think that's necessary right now, but we'll see what the future brings. But I will never ask you to do anything you're uncomfortable with."

She released my hand and eyed the pen that was resting next to some notes I'd been taking. "Can you show me how you enchanted your pen? I'd like to do the same. It'll help with translating the Harker journals."

I leaned over her and picked up the pen, turning it so Samara could see the tiny glyph carved into the wood and the small sapphire gem embedded into the pen just above the glyph. "It's a combination of 'recite' and 'write.' You can use this one. Just feed it some of your blood, and when you push your intention into it, keep in mind the language you're dictating. The casting itself is simple —the harder part is keeping track of your thoughts and only pushing out the ones you want written down."

"Got it." She took the pen from me, lifting her head out of my lap, and sat on the edge of the settee as she reached into her bag and pulled out a journal. I closed my eyes as she snagged a book off the top of the leaning stack I'd been eying earlier, but when no crash sounded, I cracked one eye open to make sure it still stood.

Samara chuckled as she flipped open the book she had grabbed to reveal a blank page. "You know, Alaric has that same exact expression on his face more often than not when he's in here."

"I can only imagine," I said dryly. Alaric loved order while Samara apparently loved chaos. Their relationship was going to be interesting, especially with Kieran involved, because he enjoyed causing trouble.

Where I fit in, I wasn't exactly sure yet, but I was finding myself more and more curious to figure that out.

"Which journal are you starting with?" I asked, opening both eyes and squinting at the book.

"Rosalyn Harker's," Samara said. "I've already scanned through most of my mother's journals." Her voice tightened for a moment before she steadied herself. "Any important information we need to know, I've compiled into notes, but I'm not ready to dictate it word by word just yet. I need some . . . space. So I thought I would start at the beginning."

I didn't know how to comfort her. Samara had rarely spoken about her parents when we'd been at Drudonia. I didn't talk about my parents because we weren't close and our relationship was one of distance and frustration, but Samara didn't speak of her parents even though she had loved them with her entire heart, and I had no doubt they had felt the same. I had no idea what that type of love was like.

Or how to comfort someone who had lost it.

What would Kieran do?

I raised my hand and patted her on the back. Awkwardly. How did he do this in a non-awkward manner? Was that even possible?

"What are you doing?" Samara looked over her shoulder at me, her fingers resting on the page she'd opened.

"You were sad," I said helplessly. "I was making you feel better."

I patted her on the back again.

She smiled, and I let out a breath. *Look at me. I did it.*

"Thank you." Samara leaned back to kiss me on the cheek before returning to the journal.

"What does that say?" I peered over her shoulder. Not only was it written in a language I wasn't familiar with, but the words were mangled, sometimes crushed together. Other times, they were spread far apart, but I was fairly certain it was the same two words written over and over again.

Samara raised a finger to her mouth and dragged it over a fang, then let the drop of blood that welled fall onto the glyph etched into my pen. It immediately absorbed the blood, and she released the pen so it hovered over the blank page of the other book as she wrestled with her thoughts.

"This is the first page. There are no dates on any of the pages, so I have no idea how long Rosalyn was lost in her early days as a Moroi before she regained enough of her humanity to write, but the first half of this journal is just these two words written over and over again."

After a few seconds, the pen slowly started to move, and two words in the common tongue appeared on the page.

I hunger.

CHAPTER TWENTY

—

Samara

"You seem troubled."

I tried not to jump from where I was sitting on a grassy overlook just above the beach as Draven appeared at my side, seemingly out of nowhere. If it weren't for the fact that it was still daylight, I would have sworn it was shadow magic.

"Next time you sneak up on me, I'm stabbing you." I shot him an irritated look.

He just grinned. "Don't tease me with a good time."

"You're ridiculous." I shook my head even as my lips twitched in amusement.

"What's bothering the lovely Heir of House Harker today?" he asked lightly.

You, I thought. Trying to reconcile the prince who always managed to make me smile with the traitor who was responsible for killing our people was mentally exhausting. Constantly having to stop myself from falling back into our easy friendship and accidentally saying the wrong thing. Giving away everything we knew about him, his mother, and the wraiths.

Or at least what we thought we knew, because it all felt like jagged pieces that didn't exactly fit together.

Kieran was struggling even more than me. He'd confessed what had happened between him and Draven immediately when we'd met up before dinner last night. He'd been avoiding the prince ever since. Based on how Alaric had been outright glaring at Draven every time he was in a room with him now, I suspected Kieran had also told him what had transpired between them in the Sovereign House.

Everyone in House Harker knew something was going on, and there was an underlying tension now in every room I walked into.

On top of that, I'd stayed up late last night translating the first journal Rosalyn Harker had written. Reading as she'd gotten pieces of her humanity back had been heartbreaking. The hunger gave way to grief as she remembered the husband and daughter she had lost.

There were some entries where it alternated between begging the moon and cursing it for giving her back the humanity she'd apparently been only too happy to lose. Most of the first generation of humans who had changed to Moroi had become Strigoi immediately and remained that way for years. Some of them had never regained their humanity. Only the Harkers and a handful of others—most of which made up the current House bloodlines—had changed back to Moroi within a matter of months.

The fact that any of them had eventually recovered enough of their humanity to become Moroi again was impressive. As far as I knew, only the original ones had ever pulled that off. Nowadays if someone became Strigoi— they stayed that way.

For reasons I didn't fully understand, Rosalyn had been pissed off about that. She had tried repeatedly to lose her humanity by completely giving in to her bloodlust and ripping into monsters every night, but by the morning, her bloodlust had always faded.

After a few meetings this morning, I'd been desperate to get out of House Harker, if only for an hour. I couldn't afford to falter now, but I'd needed an hour to settle my mind away from everything that was threatening to tear it apart.

But it's not like I could tell Draven any of that. I thought briefly about asking him why he'd found Zosa for me. And why he'd felt compelled to share the memory.

The questions were on the tip of my tongue, but I bit them back. Whatever his answer might be . . . I knew it wouldn't be something I could handle right now. Not on top of everything else.

"I'm fine, Prince," I said instead.

He raised a dark eyebrow. "You should improve your lying skills, Heir."

I held his gaze. "We can't all be as good as you."

Draven stiffened for just a second before leaning back on his hands and tilting his face up towards the sun. He'd left his hair loose today, and it fell in a dark wave down his back, the silver streaks glistening in the sun.

I wanted to run my fingers through it almost as much as I wanted to trace his jawline and those entirely too kissable full lips.

Instead, I turned away and watched the waves gently roll in and out. It was good swimming weather. Unfortunately, as inviting as the bright turquoise water looked, monsters swam beneath those waves.

A shudder ran through me as I remembered the cave encounter with those damn spider-like starfish. We were trapped on a small continent full of monsters by an ocean that was full of them as well.

Fucking Lunaria.

Draven didn't try to get me to talk again, just sat there like the hot, evil prince he was and soaked in the sunshine. Just when I was about to get up and return to reality, a flash of vibrant green caught my attention.

Raising a hand to shield my eyes against the sun, I watched as an emerald green striker circled above us. I held my arm to the side, and it immediately dove down to perch on it. I barely winced as its claws flexed in and out of my flesh, leaving behind little droplets of blood.

Draven shifted and leaned forward to eye the striker, his nostrils flaring slightly as the scent of my blood filled the air.

"Whose?" he asked.

Some strikers didn't belong to one person in particular, those ones were trained to simply travel to one particular location and back again, but most of us had at least a few strikers that we trained ourselves. It took more work, but we could teach them to deliver messages to specific people and not just locations.

I thought about lying about who this one belonged to, but the red tips on this striker's tail were easily recognizable, and if Draven asked around, someone would tell him.

"Ary's," I said and gave the creature a scratch under her chin. She nipped at me with her blunt beak but didn't break the skin, just a warning. Ary's favorite striker was such an ornery thing.

I plucked the message from the pocket on the back of her harness, and she immediately took off to fly back home. My eyes skimmed Ary's neat handwriting, and I worked hard to keep my expression blank.

"Problems?" Draven asked. I was holding the letter at an angle so he couldn't read it.

"No." I folded up the paper and slipped it into my pocket. "He was just thanking me for hosting him here earlier this week and inviting me to visit him at House Tepes," I lied through my teeth.

"Interesting," he drawled. "Ary doesn't usually bother with such polite words and invitations."

"Perhaps he just finds me a delight to be around." I rose to my feet and brushed some dried grass and dirt from my deep purple dress, the letter burning a hole in my pocket. I needed to find Vail. Immediately.

"No doubt," Draven murmured as he plucked a pink wildflower and rolled to his feet until he was standing right in front of me. My breath hitched as he pulled my long braid over my shoulder and wound the stem of the wildflower into it. "Everything about you is delightful. That's why I'm going to marry you." He winked before tugging on the end of my braid and leaning in to kiss me on the cheek.

"Still not marrying you," I said a little too breathlessly to be convincing. Damn it. Damn him. I cleared my throat. "I have some meetings to attend to. See you for dinner tonight, Prince?"

"Of course." He smiled. "Wouldn't miss it."

IT TOOK me a while to find Vail because he wasn't in any of the training yards. Emil had been the one to tell me Vail was inspecting some tracks that had been found in the woods nearby. Less than five minutes later, I had Zosa saddled up and was racing out of House Harker to find him, Emil's bay gelding hot on my heels.

Zosa nimbly leapt over fallen trees as we turned down one of the lesser-used trails that had never been cleared away after some of the winter storms. It didn't take long for me to spot the bright chestnut mare tied to a tree.

I jumped off Zosa and looped her reins around the saddle, loose enough that she could nibble on grass but wouldn't get tangled up in them, trusting her not to go far, then set off to where Vail was.

Emil was at my side a second later, sending me a curious look. When he kept staring, I glanced at him. "What?"

"I didn't tell you where Vail was," he said slowly. "Only that he was in the forests outside the House, but you seemed to know exactly where to go . . ."

I stopped dead in my tracks. He was right. I'd been so caught up on getting to Vail that I hadn't thought about it, but I'd been growing more and more desperate as I'd searched the House for him. Then Emil had told me he was in the woods and . . . I rested a hand against my chest.

A pull. I'd felt a pull and had just naturally followed it. This had happened before when we'd found the body outside one of the outposts that had been attacked, but I'd assumed that had been because of the blood magic involved and I was just more sensitive to that kind of thing because I'd experimented with it so much over the years.

I rubbed my chest as the pull intensified the more I focused on it. This . . . wasn't normal. I'd never read about anything like this in all my time at Drudonia.

"Okaaay." I drew out the word and dropped my hand from my chest. "We're going to add this to the 'Weird Shit We Need to Figure Out Once We're Not in Danger of Dying' list."

It probably said a lot about my life that strange, unexplainable magic happening in my own freaking body was far down on the list of mysteries I needed to solve. But here we were.

Emil grunted, and we started walking again. He let me take the lead since, apparently, I could magically find Vail now. "Kind of a long name, but I suppose it's accurate." His gaze cut my way again before focusing on the woods around us. "You gonna tell Vail?"

"Depends," I said lightly. "You gonna rat me out if I don't?"

Emil sighed. "I'm getting too old for this. Maybe I should listen to Adrienne and retire."

"Probably." I snorted.

"I'll leave it up to you to tell him," he said. "Unless something changes and I think it becomes important for him to know."

"Fair enough."

"So . . . are you going to tell him?"

"Tell me what?"

I jumped two feet into the air when Vail slid out from between two trees. His dark brown hair was pulled back into a bun, but pieces of it had slipped free and were plastered to his sweat-slicked skin. The light beige shirt he wore clung to his body, and for a second, my eyes snagged where he'd unlaced the top, giving me a good view of his chest.

The man was built like a mountain but could still move as quietly as a wraith. It was seriously hot, and his blood was positively divine.

No. Bad, Samara, I mentally chastised myself. No more complicated lovers. Absolutely not.

Emil snickered. "Apparently you'll need to practice a little more with your newfound talent."

Vail shot me a questioning look, but I shook my head. Given all the mixed messages he'd been sending me lately, I had no idea how he'd react to learning I could apparently *feel* him.

Probably not well.

There were bigger things to worry about. Besides, it was possible this was just a strange side effect of how much we'd been exchanging blood lately. I'd never heard of such a thing happening, but our magic did change slightly with each generation. Maybe this would start occurring more with other fifth-generation Moroi who had lovers they regularly exchanged blood with.

Not that Vail was my lover. My eyes drifted to his chest again. Damn it.

"We've got a problem," I said. Vail's enticing body and the issue of our new magic connection faded to the back of my mind as the urgency of what had sent me racing out here resurfaced. "Ary sent me a letter. He encountered a wraith last night just north of Lake Myalis."

"There's a human settlement there that we haven't investigated yet." Vail's expression hardened. "What happened with the wraith?"

"Ary managed to kill it, but he said it was definitely searching for something before he did." I glanced through the trees to the west and then up at the midday sun. "If we leave right now, we could get to that settlement not long after sunset."

"More wraiths will likely head there tonight to continue the search and possibly avenge their fallen friend if they know," Emil pointed out. "Dealing with one wraith is nasty enough, but if they come in numbers, you're walking into a death trap."

I remembered the three wraiths we battled in the temple and swallowed past the lump in my throat. "Like I said, if we leave now, we can get there just after night falls, do a quick search, and get out before they arrive."

Emil's brows creased, clearly not liking this idea, then he looked to Vail for the final decision.

"We search fast," Vail finally said. "Even if we haven't found anything, when I say we leave, *we leave*." He looked at me with an expression that brokered no argument.

I nodded in agreement. "We leave. I won't argue. I just want the chance to search while we have it."

Because more wraiths would definitely go to that settlement, and if there was still a piece of that strange obsidian stone there, we couldn't not take the chance of them getting it before we did.

"Did Ary provide the exact coordinates for where he saw the wraith?" Vail asked. "I want to make sure we're heading to the right place."

"Yes." I reached into my pocket to pull out the letter, and my blood went cold. Empty.

"Lose something, love?"

For the third time in an hour, I jumped.

By the time I'd landed back on my feet and whirled to look up into the tree behind me, Emil and Vail had already moved to stand beside me, swords drawn.

Draven continued to read the letter—*my letter*—from where he sat on a branch ten feet above us, one leg dangling casually off the side.

How the fuck had he gotten up there without any of us sensing him? And how had he gotten here ahead of us without anyone detecting him? It was one thing for him to slip past me, but Emil and Vail? I added this to the list of things that didn't make sense about the Moroi Prince.

I glanced at Vail's face. Based on how hard he was clenching his jaw and the way the scar that ran diagonally across his face was pulled tight, he definitely hadn't known the prince was there until he'd said something.

"Drav," I half growled.

His bright blue eyes finally looked away from the letter to arch an eyebrow at me. "Oh, we're back to Drav now?" He slid off the branch and dropped to the ground, landing lightly on the balls of his feet before strolling over to me. "I like it when I get to be Drav and not Prince."

"Will you like it when I strangle you?" I snatched the letter out of his hand.

"Probably." He grinned and then looked back and forth between the swords Vail and Emil still held. They weren't angling them towards the prince, but they'd only lowered them a couple of inches. "Are we having a sword measuring contest? I haven't lost one of those yet."

Vail took a step towards Draven, and red flashed through the prince's eyes in challenge. Emil stepped away from me to give himself more space to work.

"We don't have time for this." I stepped between Vail and Draven with my hands held up as Emil paused to watch how this played out. Then I turned to fully face Draven. "Talk. Now."

"I'm coming with you."

CHAPTER TWENTY-ONE

—

Samara

IN WHAT FELT like the first time in ages, the moon smiled upon us. We'd gotten lucky. I slipped the three pieces of smooth, black stone into my pack before securing it on my back.

"Let's find the others and get out of here."

Emil nodded while Ary just scrutinized me from where he waited a few feet away.

The Tepes Heir had found us less than a mile from the remains of the human settlement. He'd claimed to be checking to see if the wraiths had returned while his rangers investigated a nearby monster nest, but I had little doubt he'd been waiting for us.

If he'd truly thought the wraiths would have made an appearance again, he would have kept his rangers with him. Ary was a cocky bastard, but even he wasn't crazy enough to tackle wraiths on his own. No. Ary suspected something was going on and that I was involved somehow. He could have easily sent that letter to House Salvatore or Laurent, both of whom were just as close as House Harker.

He'd sent it to me as a test. I needed to figure out what to tell him, and I needed to do it soon. We needed more allies, but I couldn't afford to trust the wrong person.

Ary wasn't the only addition to our search party. Nyx had found us while we'd been saddling our horses at House Harker and had insisted on coming. Vail had grumbled something about having to inform Adrienne, and then we'd set off.

Currently, Nyx and Vail were keeping an eye on the area around the old settlement in case the wraiths or some other beasts came prowling. I'd told Draven to stay with the horses because they were a tasty snack to most things

413

that went bump in the night. To my surprise—and suspicion—he'd agreed. Unfortunately, none of us could tell the Tepes Heir what to do, so when our group had split up, he'd trailed after me and Emil.

"Shiny," a deep voice purred. "I like shiny things."

A golden-haired man nimbly leapt down from a tree that had grown out of the wreckage of collapsed building. He rose to his full height—which was easily over six feet—and cocked his head, his cat-like green eyes catching the moonlight, which caused a sheen to roll across them.

Emil had his swords free in a moment and pointed at the newcomer. His jaw hardened, probably in annoyance at not detecting the Velesian but it's not like I could blame him. Velesians had an uncanny knack at being undetectable in the woods. They were even more adept at sneaking up on others than Vail or Draven.

While Emil and I might have been caught off guard, it did not escape my attention that Ary didn't appear to be least bit surprised to see the handsome Velesian, who was currently smirking at all of us.

"Bastian," I said evenly. "What brings a member of the Alpha Pack to Moroi territory?"

"Just helping out our neighbors on a little friendly hunt" He grinned and two dimples formed in his cheeks, escalating him from handsome to charming... and a little wicked. "After all, the monsters don't really care about the borders between Moroi and Velesian lands."

My gaze cut to Ary. "Funny how you never mentioned the Alpha Pack being here in your letter."

He shrugged. "Like Bastian said—just a spur-of-the-moment hunt is all."

Spur-of-the-moment hunt my ass. The Alpha Pack usually stayed in the far north of the Velesian realm. While Ary was definitely on more friendly terms with the Velesians than many of the Moroi—thanks to his lands bordering theirs and the fact that he did love to go hunting with them—it wasn't like Bastian would have just happened to be in the area.

According to Rynn, the big meeting being hosted by her pack in Fervis territory near Lake Malov wasn't happening for another week. She would have mentioned if she'd heard of any of the Alpha Pack members coming sooner than that. Which meant they hadn't told her . . .

Bastian let out a low, raspy laugh. "So suspicious, Samara. I can practically hear you sussing out all the reasons for me being here in that pretty head of yours."

"Really?" I drawled. "Then you know the loudest thought in my head right now is me lamenting over the fact that I have to deal with you instead of Cade."

Cade was the leader of the Alpha Pack and the one I preferred to deal with. He was direct and to the point. It was refreshing, albeit a little frustrating at times because once he set his mind on something, it was difficult to steer him away from it.

Bastian was his second-in-command . I didn't know if it was his feline nature—he was an ailuranthrope, a panther shifter—that made him so aggravating to deal with or just his own personal nature.

But the fact that Bastian was here meant two things: there was something going on in the Velesian realm to draw the Alpha Pack south, and Ary was suspicious enough about other Moroi and what was going on in our own realm that he'd chosen to bring the Velesians in on it.

He must have had a better relationship with the Alpha Pack than I'd been aware of for Bastian to join him on this adventure. None of that mattered for the problem at hand though, and I could have punched Ary for complicating things so much.

The amused grin on the other Moroi's face told me he knew exactly how I was feeling and found my pain entertaining.

I couldn't tell Bastian—and therefore the Alpha Pack—about the stones or what was going on. Not yet at least. The Moroi Houses were all about keeping their secrets. Half of our trade deals were sweetened by offering an exchange of information. But the Velesians prided themselves on being more open about things.

If I brought the Alpha Pack in on this, they would feel compelled to tell the rest of Velesian packs. We already knew there were Moroi working with Erendriel, so there was no reason not to suspect some of the Velesians were as well.

And even if I could convince them to not tell the rest of the packs, that would present a problem down the line. Because sooner or later, it would get out that the Alpha Pack had known about Erendriel, Queen Velika, the truth about the wraiths . . . and hadn't told anyone.

Tensions between the Velesians were rising, and that could very well be the final blow that caused a war to erupt amongst the packs.

Rynn was promised to the Alpha Pack. She would be in the middle of it. I would sooner bring the wrath of the Alpha Pack down on me than put my friend in jeopardy.

"You'll have to admire my pretty face another time, Bastian," I said smoothly. "This is Moroi business."

The easy-going grin slid off his beautiful face. "You sure that's how you want to play this? You want me to return to Cade and tell him I saw you skulking around this old human settlement—where wraith activity has been spotted—and that you collected something from it?"

Tension bled between all of us, but I kept my expression even. "That's exactly what I'm saying."

Bastian shook his head. "You're making a mistake, Samara. Thought you were smarter than this."

Doing my best with the shitty options presented to me, furball.

"Duly noted." I flicked my gaze towards the forest behind us. "Time to leave."

He looked at me for a long moment before shrugging and turning around to stride towards the trees. "I'll give Rynn your regards," he tossed over his shoulder.

Before I could curse him, Bastian shed his clothing, shifted into a sleek black panther form, and took off through the trees.

That hadn't been a physical threat towards Rynn—he would never harm her, nor would any of the Alpha Pack. For all intents and purposes, they were good people. Well, as good as anyone could be in Lunaria. But that didn't mean they weren't cunning and devious at times.

Bastian's dig had been a reminder that they had a claim on Rynn.

I'd have to tell her about this encounter when we made it back and hope I hadn't just made her life infinitely harder.

"Interesting way of handling delicate political situations." Ary started walking towards me. "Not sure that's how I—oww!!! Motherfucker!"

He clutched his nose and backed away as blood flowed down the lower half of his face.

"I'll do more than break your nose if you ever ambush me like that again," I growled.

Vail chose that moment to stalk through the few buildings that still stood, Nyx right behind him. The two of them joined our group, and Vail's grey eyes took in Ary before glancing at Emil, who I'd shoved aside to punch the Tepes Heir.

"Ary here thought it would be a good idea to invite Bastian to visit this settlement." A wry smile played across the older Moroi's lips. "Samara was giving him feedback on that."

"Interesting," Nyx said. "I don't recall Drudonia teaching us that providing feedback involved our fists, but I did skip out on my lessons early."

"What did you tell the Alpha Pack?" Vail asked the Tepes Heir harshly.

Ary used the back of his hand to wipe more blood away before directing a hard stare at Vail and then me. "Wasn't much I could tell them, was there? You lot haven't told me anything. All I know is that there is something weird going on with the wraiths and you all know more about it than you're sharing. We all need allies. With the way things are going with the other Houses, I personally think the Alpha Pack is looking like a better choice every day."

We all glared at each other for a long moment before I sighed and stomped over to Ary, who eyed me warily. "You're not wrong." I gripped his nose before jerking it into place. "Come with us back to the outpost, and we'll tell you what we can there. We've already stayed here too long. The wraiths will be back."

The five of us headed in the direction of our mounts.

"Where's your horse?" Vail asked.

"Had to give it to one of my rangers," Ary replied. "I wasn't lying about them dealing with a monster nest. A pack of howlers grew too large, attacked us yesterday, killed two of our horses, and seriously injured a couple of us."

"You can have Samara's mount. She'll ride with me."

My head whipped towards Vail. "Oh, I will, will I?"

"Yes." He bared his teeth.

"Gods, you didn't bring Zosa did you?" Ary interrupted.

I tore my gaze away from Vail. "No, I wasn't sure how much we'd be riding at night and I didn't want to risk her."

Relief flickered through Ary's face. Apparently, the idea of riding my hot-tempered mare was more intimidating than traveling in the wilds of Lunaria at night.

As the horses came into view, concern flared in my chest. Draven wasn't there.

"Where's the prince?" Nyx asked.

Moons fucking damn it all. I slid one of my throwing daggers free from my thigh sheath as I searched the trees around us but saw no signs of Draven anywhere. Was this the moment he betrayed us?

My heart said Draven would never hurt me, but my brain offered up a myriad of ways that he could. I shifted on my feet as the forest around us took on a more ominous tone.

Ary's light violet eyes shone brightly even in the dark. He glanced at all of us before asking, "Are we going to search for him or . . ."

"You're welcome to look," Vail replied, "but we're getting the fuck out of here."

I balked when Vail and the rangers moved in the direction of the horses. What if Draven had gone to investigate something and had been attacked? What if he wasn't betraying us but was actually out in the woods injured?

"Samara," Vail growled, "you promised you would leave when I told you to."

"I know, but—"

"Don't make me force you to leave him."

My fingers tightened around the blade as I focused on taking steady breaths. I couldn't fight Vail. He'd just laugh at my attempt and throw me over his shoulder. Plus, I didn't want to argue with him. I had promised to follow his orders, and I knew he was right, but . . . I anxiously scanned the woods again for Draven but saw nothing.

"Alright," I said weakly and stepped forward only to be shoved back by Emil.

Three wraiths materialized around us, one between me and the others and two on either side of Vail. They'd clearly determined him to be the biggest threat, because neither of them wasted any time in their attack.

I screamed as their shadows stretched into towering, beastly forms, resembling nothing that had ever walked this land and only existed in nightmares. At least, that's where they belonged. The two wraiths struck out at Vail, letting the foot-long talons that tipped their monstrous hands materialize for a brief second.

Nyx moved faster than I could track and struck at the wraith on the left. Their gold and silver blade sliced through the wraith's wrist, and it screamed as the magic within the sword burned through its momentarily corporeal flesh.

I didn't see if Vail had managed to block the attack from the other wraith because the one in front of me snapped into the shadowy form of a serpent and lunged forward.

Another scream ripped from my throat as I slashed at the wraith, but my blade passed harmlessly through its shadow before hot, fiery pain tore through my shoulder as the wraith bit down.

Even through the pain, I still managed to stab at its eyes with my dagger, but my strike had been too slow, and the wraith was already nothing more than shadows again.

"Samara!" Nyx screamed from where they were still battling one of the other wraiths. Emil had joined them, and Ary was helping Vail.

Which meant I was on my own.

Twin rivers of blood coursed their way down my shoulder. I blocked out the pain before carefully gauging how much mobility I had, finding I could still move it easily. For the second time tonight, I'd gotten lucky. The snake's fangs had only punctured me, which meant, while it was painful, it was still a relatively minor wound.

The wraith shrank down into an amorphous form before becoming something more humanoid, the shape sharpening enough for me to make out delicate features . . . and tapered ears.

Fae.

A masculine chuckle filled the air as he raised his hand to his lips. The blood on my shoulder felt hotter as I watched him draw his fingers away and study them before looking at me. Then he cocked his head and smiled.

"Din tros." The words slithered into my ear, and the breath I'd just taken froze in my throat.

The words were mangled and corrupted by shadows, but I'd understood them well enough. He'd just called me *forgotten queen* in Seelie.

The wraiths weren't the Unseelie. They were the Seelie.

More whispered words flowed from the wraith's mouth faster than I could process, then his form stretched upward until he was once again a serpent, this time with a crown of horns extending from behind his head.

My dagger felt so small in my hand as I prepared myself to dive to the side and avoid those jaws that were considerably larger than the first time he'd bitten me.

The wraith struck impossibly fast, and I barely managed to leap aside. The dagger left my fingers a second before his tail slammed into me and sent me hurtling through the air, further into the forest and away from everyone else.

An eerie shriek filled the night air, and I felt a brief moment of satisfaction at knowing my aim had been true before I slammed into a tree.

Something crunched in my back, but I forced myself to my feet and held my hand up. A pulse of magic and a second later, my dagger flew through the air to my waiting palm. Blood so dark that it was almost black coated the blade.

Shadows wound through the trees and snapped back into the giant snake, the eye I'd ruptured already good as new. This time, I had nowhere to go. The underbrush on either side of the tree was too thick. I held my dagger up defiantly as the wraith opened its mouth, displaying long fangs dripping with shadows.

"Spitka e chof." The whispered words wrapped around me. *Come with me.*

"Not a fucking chance," I snarled as pain wracked my body. Only pure rage and adrenaline kept me standing.

A high-pitched wail back towards the others announced the death of a wraith. One down, two to go. I just had to survive a little longer.

Just as I readied myself to try to dive forward to run past the wraith, a dark form fell from the trees to land at my side.

"Where the fuck have you been, Draven?" I snapped.

"These weren't the only wraiths," he said tightly. It was then I noticed he was covered in blood, some the dark purplish-red of the wraiths, but most of it was definitely his.

"Mikin," the wraith hissed.

Draven dove towards it, but the snake burst into a shapeless shadow before quickly disappearing into the trees. "FUCK!" he shouted and whirled to slam a fist into the trunk behind me.

I jumped, and he froze before slowly lowering his hand to his side and unclenching his fingers. The rage that had been on face a second before vanished, and now he just looked exhausted.

"Come on." He grabbed my hand and tugged me towards the others. "He'll be back with more help."

Thoughts raced through my mind as we ran back to Vail and the rest of our party. I'd read that word before—*mikin*—but the translation was escaping me. Then it hit me, and I almost stumbled.

Traitor.

AN HOUR LATER, the six of us were behind the relative safety of an outpost's wards and gathered around a table in the far corner of the tavern. Well, Vail was in a room upstairs, passed out in a healing sleep. He'd managed to kill the third wraith, but not before the damn thing had nearly disemboweled him.

Draven had thrown a fit when I'd slashed open my wrist and practically shoved it against Vail's mouth while tracing the healing glyph in the blood that coated his stomach. I hadn't even hesitated. Despite all the complications between us, all the pain and confusing animosity, Vail had been hurt, and all I'd cared about was making him better.

Even with the strength of my blood coursing through his veins, Vail had barely managed to stay conscious on the ride here. As soon as his head had hit the pillow, he'd passed out. Nyx and Emil had assured me he was fine and would be ready to leave by the time the sun rose.

We all sipped our honey ale as the local residents eyed us curiously. It wasn't unusual for the House Heirs to visit outposts, but it definitely wasn't a common occurrence for the Moroi Prince to stay at one.

The charming mask Draven usually wore as his public persona was nowhere to be seen, and the grim expression on his face was doing an excellent job of keeping everyone away. Only the barkeep had approached us, and that was only to drop off some food and ale.

Ary took a long drink before setting his glass down and sliding a small, wooden square with the glyph for silence to the center of the table. He sliced his index finger open on his fang and let the blood drop onto the glyph.

"This glyph doesn't store much magic. We've got ten minutes." His gaze locked on mine. "Tell me what the fuck is going on, Samara."

Out of my peripheral vision, I saw Nyx and Emil stiffen, but it was Draven who spoke. "You don't give her orders, Tepes," he said in a quiet voice that promised all kinds of violence.

Ary didn't back down, and I saw a flicker of pain in his eyes. "My best friend's husband was in one of the outposts that fell to wraiths. The three of us grew up together. Nicholai was like a brother to me. These attacks aren't random. The wraith last night was searching for something." He leaned forward from where he sat directly across from me. "Something *you* found tonight."

I couldn't tell him everything, not with Draven here, but Ary wouldn't let this go. I had to give him at least some information, and then we could tell him everything later when it was safe to do so.

"You're right," I said, choosing my words carefully but quickly. "They're searching old human settlements for relics of the spell the humans used to turn themselves into the Moon Blessed. All the outposts that have been attacked have been ones built on those old towns and villages."

The muscles along Ary's jaw flexed. "Do you know how they're getting past the blood wards?"

"No." I forced myself to not look at Draven.

"Like passing through a waterfall," Draven said suddenly.

"What are you talking about?" Ary shot Draven a confused look.

"A curtain of water falling, drenching anyone who passes under." The odd cadence to Draven's tone had me looking to him, only to find him staring blankly at the table. "But if someone was to hold an outstretched arm through the water, another could pass underneath it to avoid the deluge."

Ary, Emil, and Nyx stared at him. The rangers didn't bother to hide the suspicion on their faces, but whatever Ary was thinking was behind a mask of cold indifference.

"That actually makes sense," I said slowly. "We're used to passing through the wards, so we don't feel it anymore, but there is a thin veil of magic rising from where we root them in the earth. Draven is suggesting"—my gaze darted to him to find him staring intently at me, as if urging me to continue my line of thinking—"that the wraiths aren't breaking the ward nor temporarily disabling it. They're finding a way to block the upward flow of magic in one specific place and slipping through."

"They can't interact with the wards at all," Emil pointed out.

"A Moroi could," Ary said, his voice hardening in understanding. "You think a Moroi is helping the wraiths. That's why you're being so secretive about all of this."

"Yes, but we don't know why someone would help them." I kept my tone even, but I didn't look away from Draven either. It had to be him. He was responsible for letting the monsters in. "Why would a Moroi turn on their own people? There were *children* in those outposts. Who could do something like that?"

The tension in the air increased until I could practically feel it on my skin. I didn't say anything else, just silently begged Draven to tell me I had this all wrong. That he wasn't responsible for the slaughter of thousands of innocent Moroi.

"A monster," he finally said, still never taking his eyes off me. "A well-trained monster."

I let my fangs slide a little further out of my gums. "Even a monster can refuse."

"Maybe they did." He flinched as if a phantom pain had raised up his back.

Hope and dread warred in my soul. If he had willingly helped the wraiths kill our people, I would never be able to forgive him for it, but if he'd refused . . . what had it cost him?

"How many times did the monster say no?" I asked quietly.

Draven opened his mouth to speak only to snap it shut with a hiss before he rubbed his temples. Ary's expression remained locked down, but Nyx and Emil continued to eye him warily. I just waited. Finally, he dropped his hand away, his eyes dark and bleak. "Who knows what monsters say or do? Does it matter? They're still monsters at the end of the day."

"Drav . . ." I trailed off, unsure what to say.

"I'm tired." He rose from the table. "I'm going to rest for a bit." Then he stepped away before pausing and turning his head slightly so I could just make out his profile. "I've never really liked waterfalls. Refused to go through them nine times. Turns out your body can still be used to block the water even if your soul is unwilling."

A sharp pain struck my chest as he walked away without another word. *A well-trained monster.* Maybe he wasn't so much well-trained as he was beaten down.

"What in the moonsdamned fuck have the lot of you been up to?" Ary stared after Draven, a hint of frustration leaking into his expression.

I pursed my lips together. We'd have to trust others eventually, and Ary had already seen too much tonight.

"Emil and Nyx will fill you in." I looked at both of the rangers. "Tell him everything. I'm going to check on Vail."

Nyx shifted uncomfortably. "You're sure?"

"Yes." I smiled at Ary. "If you betray us, I'll make you beg for death, and even then, I won't give it."

An actual smile blossomed on the Tepes Heir's face. "Honestly, threats like that are the only reason I both like and trust you."

"You're seriously fucked up."

He smiled wider. "It's more fun that way."

"We have two rooms, Samara," Emil said. "You should go rest in the other one after you check on Vail. If you're okay with it, Nyx can sleep on the floor in your room. The rest of us can stay with Vail. I don't think he'll wake, but in case he does, somebody should be there."

"I'll stay with him." The words rushed out before I could think better of it. Nyx arched an eyebrow, and Ary laughed under his breath. "Fuck you both," I muttered.

"Is that an actual offer?" Ary cocked his head and then let out a sharp exhale when Nyx elbowed him in the gut.

"No," I said wryly. "I'll see you all in the morning."

I walked away from the table. If Ary had anything else to say, I couldn't hear it thanks to the silencing spell still surrounding the table. After a few conversations with the locals to assure them that everything was fine, I made my way upstairs and slipped into the room where Vail was sleeping. I made it two feet from the door before I froze at the form sitting in the chair in the corner.

"Figured you'd sleep in the other room," I said to Draven before continuing to the bed to check on Vail. He was still fast asleep and barely stirred when I lifted the sheet to peek at his chest. An angry, pink scar snaked its way down his body, but considering he'd been holding in his intestines a couple of hours ago, this was nothing. He probably wouldn't even have a scar in the morning.

I brushed some loose strands of hair away from his face before tracing the jagged scar that ran across his right eyebrow down his cheek. He'd gotten it protecting me from the wraiths the night our parents had been killed. I'd been too panicked to heal it properly, and by the time we'd been rescued days later, it had been too late to do anything about the scar.

I could bury the emotions from that night deep inside myself, but Vail was reminded every time he looked in a mirror.

"I knew you'd come here," Draven said. "You're rather protective of those you love."

My fingers went still over Vail's skin. "I don't love him."

"Whatever you need to tell yourself, *tros.*"

"I'm not a queen," I snapped. "We going to talk about that wraith calling you a traitor?"

Draven sighed. "Nothing has changed. There is still so much I can't tell you, and you still shouldn't trust me even though I can swear to you that I'm doing everything I can to keep you and Kieran safe."

"I believe you . . . but I don't know what to do with that," I said honestly.

"Two years ago, you came to the Sovereign House." Draven paused like he was remembering it. "After a rather stuffy dinner, Demetri fucked off with some of the courtiers, and you and I went up to the rooftop to stargaze."

"I remember." We hadn't done anything except stretch out on a blanket and talk, but it'd been nice. By that point, my marriage had become so rigid, it hadn't even felt strange to me that Demetri had decided to spend the night catching up with some courtiers rather than with me. I hadn't seen Kieran in over a year, and the only chats I'd had with Rynn and Cali were via shadow magic.

Lonely. I'd been so fucking lonely.

"What if, for the rest of the night, we just pretend we're back on that rooftop?" Draven asked. "I think we've both earned a few hours of peace."

"And you won't tell me anything else, right?" When he didn't answer, I sighed. Fuck it. I was tired, and I had already intended to stay in this room.

I stalked around the bed to where Draven was lounging in the oversized cushioned chair and eyed it. There was plenty of space for two people if he'd just move over.

When I opened my mouth to tell him that, his hand snapped out and grabbed my arm, pulling me forward. I yelped as I tumbled into the chair, but he smoothly maneuvered my body until I was lying snuggly across his lap.

I should have jumped off and shoved him aside to make room. That was definitely what I *should* have done. Instead, I instantly relaxed against his body like he was home and I'd been away for too long.

Then the asshole ruined it by tugging the corner of my shirt down off my shoulder so he could inspect where the wraith had bitten me. "For the tenth time, it's fine," I hissed as I slapped his hand away and pulled my shirt back up. He'd been fussy about it all night, even after I'd cleaned up the blood and changed into a clean shirt. "Puncture wounds always heal fast."

Draven just nodded numbly, still staring at my shoulder. The wraith that had attacked me had gotten away, no doubt to report back to Erendriel. I had no idea if that meant Velika would be informed as well. She and Erendriel were clearly allies, but that didn't mean they shared knowledge freely. Draven probably knew more specifics about how their relationship worked, but it was clear he wasn't going to tell me, or maybe *couldn't* tell me was more accurate.

I thought back to that peaceful night we'd shared under the stars and let my eyes drift closed. My body was tapped out thanks to the amount of blood I'd let Vail drink. Ary had offered to let me drink from him, but Draven's growl had practically made the walls vibrate, so I'd turned him down to keep a fight from breaking out.

"Do you need to drink?" Draven asked quietly.

My eyes flew open, and I blinked up at him. "Are you reading my mind? Is that a thing you do?"

He chuckled darkly. "You just snuggled your face into my neck and inhaled deeply. Pretty sure you licked me."

"I absolutely did not." I thought about it and the fact that I was tucked in against his neck. "Okay, I did smell you, but there was no licking." I grinned at him. "Trust me, you would know if I licked you."

He groaned, and I felt something very hard pressing into my backside. Then Draven's light purple eyes fell on Vail, sleeping only a few feet from us, before he squinted down at me. "How quiet can you be?"

"According to Kieran, I'm a bit of a screamer."

"Not helping, Sam." He leaned his head back against the chair and took a deep breath.

So I leaned forward and gently kissed the side of his neck before slipping off his lap. Instantly, he shot forward and grabbed my wrist. "Where are you going?"

"Bed." I gestured to the large mattress Vail was sprawled on. "It's not like I haven't shared a bed with him before, and I'm not going to be able to sleep in that chair."

"Wasn't really planning on sleeping," Draven muttered before ushering me forward so he could stand as well.

When he followed me over to the bed and stood there expectantly, I crawled into it and arched an eyebrow at him. "Something you need?"

"For you to move over."

"What?" I dropped my gaze to a sleeping Vail before looking back at Draven. Did he really mean to sleep with me when I was in bed with Vail? The chair wasn't big enough to sleep in, but I'd assumed he'd just sleep on the floor.

Draven leaned down until his lips were almost touching mine, and my breath caught in my throat at the intensity in his eyes. "Fucking you tonight isn't an option, because when I do, I want you to be able to scream until the walls shake." Then he kissed the corners of my mouth as I trembled slightly. "You should know that Kieran and I are a bit . . . competitive. If he makes you scream, I'll make you scream louder. If I make you come"—his hand slid down my body until he cupped me between the thighs—"then Kieran will make you come harder."

I clamped my legs around his hand as heat pooled between them. "Now who's not helping?" I growled.

His mouth crashed against mine as his fingers rubbed against the seam of my pants, creating a friction I'd been desperately craving.

Just as suddenly as he kissed me, he broke it off and shoved me further across the bed before sliding in behind me. Then his arm wrapped around my waist to tug me back against his chest. "I can't fuck you tonight, but I can ensure that you dream of me," he whispered into my ear, "while sleeping in a bed with *him*."

"Jealous?" I rasped, glancing at Vail to find him still asleep, but there was a crease between his brows now.

"He's not good for you," Draven said smoothly as his grip on me tightened.

"And you are?"

"No." The arm around me pulled back a little. "I suppose I'm not."

A gap formed between my back and his chest, and fear shot through me at him leaving. My hand clamped down on his arm, and Draven went still. "Stay."

Time stretched as the word hung between us. Finally, Draven settled back down beside me, and the knot that had been forming inside my chest loosened. He let out a long, shuddering breath and nestled his face into the back of my neck.

We lay like that until we both fell asleep. At some point in the night, I woke to find that Vail had rolled over and I was plastered against his chest, his arm wrapped around me. Draven was still tight against my back, his arm draped along my hip.

Nestled between two people who could very well be the death of me, I should have felt at least a hint of alarm. Instead, I just drifted off to sleep and dreamed of starry skies.

CHAPTER TWENTY-TWO

—

Roth

"You're absolutely certain he called you the forgotten queen?" I asked again from where I was sitting in one of the comfy chairs in Samara's living room. Alaric had claimed the chair across from me while Samara and Kieran were sprawled out on the settee.

Well, Kieran was sprawled out. Samara was hunched over the low table, translating the last of Rosalyn's journals.

"Yes, Roth," Samara said tiredly. She'd only returned an hour ago and had announced that there would be no group dinner this evening since everyone was tired from the journey.

I kept glancing at the door to her bedroom, expecting them to knock any second, but apparently, both the prince and Vail had made themselves scarce as soon as they'd stepped foot inside House Harker.

Alaric, Kieran, and I had gathered in her rooms, and she'd told us everything that had happened—although the details of them staying the night at the outpost had been a little sparse. I didn't think Samara was intentionally hiding anything from us. If anything, she seemed a little . . . confused?

I'd have to talk to Kieran about it when I could get him alone. Alaric wasn't much better than me at reading people, but Kieran seemed to always know what was going on in Samara's head.

Was it bad that Alaric and I were likely going to have to depend on Kieran for relationship advice? I frowned and then shook my head. Kieran was pretty and had a praise kink. He'd appreciate being told he was useful, which meant he wouldn't give me too much shit about having no idea how relationships worked.

"He definitely called me that," Samara confirmed without looking up from the page. "And he wanted me to come with him."

"In Seelie?" Alaric asked. "You're absolutely sure he spoke in Seelie and not Unseelie?"

Samara finally looked up from the journal to arch a dark eyebrow at Alaric. "I realize you think I'm nothing more than a pretty face with air between my ears, but between all of us, I *am* the person most adept at Fae languages. So yes, I'm sure it was Seelie."

"I said that one time." Alaric rolled his eyes. "And it was almost a decade ago."

Samara sniffed. "It was on my sixteenth birthday, you ass. Ruined the whole party."

The smallest smile graced Alaric's lips as he looked at Samara with a heated intensity. "If I promise to make it up to you, will you let it go?"

I caught Kieran's eye, and he just grinned before we went back to listening to this unfolding drama like the juicy entertainment it was.

"Yes." Samara tilted her head as she continued to study Alaric. "I remember every nasty thing you've said to me though, just so you know."

A sliver of turquoise slid through Alaric's light green eyes. "Guess I'll be on my knees a lot in the future then."

"Fuck." Kieran slammed a book shut. "The two of you are making it really difficult to concentrate, which really isn't fair, considering I got yelled at for suggesting we relax before diving into work."

"Relax?" Samara laughed. "I believe your exact words were, 'Everyone, take your clothes off. I got a jar of honey and some ideas.'"

"I still have the honey." Kieran smirked at her.

"I'm with Kieran on this," I said, gently setting the book I'd been scanning onto the table before leaning back in my seat.

"You want the honey?" Alaric asked in confusion.

"No, I don't want the honey." I paused and thought about it before amending, "I don't want the honey *tonight*."

"I think what Roth is trying to say is that we actually do need to concentrate tonight," Samara said dryly. "Vail and I are leaving just before sunrise, and Draven has some meetings in the morning, so hopefully it will be at least a few hours before he realizes we're gone."

A weariness flashed across her face before she buried it. My beautiful forgotten queen was excellent at tucking away her emotions, which was a little concerning.

"We assumed the wraiths were the Unseelie Fae," Samara continued, her eyes dropping back down to the journal she'd been translating. "I don't know what it means that they're actually the Seelie, or how they got shadow magic. We don't even really know what the Seelie's original magic was because all the texts are kind of vague about it."

"The Seelie spent most of their time lamenting about how arrogant and devious the Unseelie were," I said. "Most of the writings we've found have been Seelie, so we're most familiar with their point of view. They rarely talked about themselves. And what we do have from the Unseelie is . . . not all that informative."

"Because it's all useless poetry," Alaric griped.

"I wouldn't say it's entirely useless." Samara's lips curved into a grin, and I felt mine doing the same.

"It is strange how little we have from the Unseelie," I mused. "Most of the Unseelie fortresses were entirely stripped of books and scrolls. Literally all that was left was poetry and a few other random texts."

"Maybe Vail and I will finally find some answers up north," Samara said. "Instead of just more questions."

"We'll keep researching while you're gone," I assured her. "Learning the wraiths are actually the Seelie is confusing . . . but at least we're no longer going down the wrong path."

Samara rubbed her face, and I could see the exhaustion of the last couple of days weighing heavily on her.

"I don't know what the queen comment meant," she admitted. "The House bloodlines are clearly different from most of the Moroi, but I've never come across anything to suggest the Harker line is more unique than the Tepes, Corvinus, or any of the others. The only queen we've ever had is Velika, and that was a self-appointed title."

"Maybe it's somehow connected to the crown?" Kieran suggested. "Seems like a strange coincidence for the wraith to refer to you as a queen while we're also searching for the other half of a Fae crown."

"Maybe," Samara said, but she didn't sound convinced. "I'm going to switch to translating my mother's journals. I think the odds are better of us finding something useful in them."

"I'll get us some snacks," Kieran offered. "Seems like it's going to be a long night."

"So you're who Samara has been keeping away from me."

I froze in my seat as Prince Draven appeared between the bookstacks at the back of the library. How had he gotten in here without me knowing? My heart was racing at finding myself in such sudden close proximity to the Moroi Prince. I willed myself to rise casually from my chair, turning my head just enough so I could glance at the double doors. Still closed. I definitely would have heard them open. There were a couple of windows in the back, but I always kept them locked . . .

"Apologies, I'm not sure what you mean," I said tightly before adding, "my prince."

A small, knowing smile played across his lips as he strolled down the line of bookcases on the wall, his finger trailing across the shelves. I glanced at the clock on the wall and cursed inwardly. It was late afternoon. Alaric was supposed to have kept Draven busy in meetings all day, and then Kieran was going to make an excuse for why Samara wasn't at dinner. The hope was that we could delay Draven from knowing Samara had left until tomorrow.

I'd missed working in the library, so I had snuck in here this morning, even though I'd promised Samara I would stay in her suite while she was gone. My plan had been to only be here for a few hours and return to her rooms for lunch, but I'd lost track of time while researching.

And now I was trapped in a room alone with Draven, exactly what Samara had been trying to avoid.

Fuck. Me.

He turned away from the bookshelves and sauntered over to me, his hands in his pockets. He was like the dark mirror of Kieran with his perfectly combed hair and well-put-together outfit, but while Kieran had an easygoing charm, Draven had an intensity to him that had the hairs on the back of my neck rising.

Black and silver hair fell over his shoulder as he cocked his head and studied me. Then his eyes drifted over my features, lingering on my red hair and hazel eyes.

"You're a Devereux." Not a surprise he figured out my bloodline. Most of the House bloodlines had very distinctive appearances. Everyone in my family had pale skin, deep red hair, hazel eyes, and sharp features. If we were in a room together, there was no mistaking the fact that we were all related, whether I liked it or not. "Astaroth?" he guessed.

"Roth," I said stiffly, trying to hide my surprise. Maybe he knew my name because I was the only Devereux ever to go to Drudonia. "I go by Roth."

He smiled. "Pleasure to meet you, Roth. Do you prefer to be referred to as *them* as well?"

I blinked, not having expected the consideration, but nodded.

Draven shrugged. "I might have to kill you after this conversation, but there is no reason not to be polite about your preferences."

Once again, my eyes darted to the doors, and I took a tiny step towards them.

"You won't make it." Draven gestured towards the table I'd been sitting at when he'd arrived. "How about we have a chat?"

His tone was still light, but his eyes were hard as he walked over to the table and pulled two chairs free so they were facing each other. Fear clamped down on my heart. Draven knew Samara was gone, and he'd decided I was the weak link in finding out where she'd run off to. Stiffly, I walked over to the chair, resolution building with each step. He would get *nothing* from me.

My ribbons shifted slightly on my forearms. I just needed to bide my time. All I needed was a few seconds to make it out the door and down the stairwell. Draven had been careful to keep up the persona of the charming prince around others—he wouldn't pursue me in front of witnesses.

I hoped.

Draven folded his large frame into the chair opposite me. I looked him over quickly but didn't spot any weapons on him aside from a coiled whip at his hip. Seemed like an odd choice for a prince. It wasn't like he couldn't afford a flashy sword.

"How exactly did a Devereux find themselves in House Harker?" He tilted his head thoughtfully. "Your House isn't exactly known for playing nice with others."

"I met Samara at Drudonia, and she asked if I'd be interested in doing an extended stay here for the summer. The beaches are much nicer here than further south."

Draven glanced pointedly at my white skin that was so pale, it looked like I'd burn immediately if I stepped outside, which was accurate. More importantly, I would get freckles if I spent too much time in the sun, and I refused to have more freckles than the few I already had.

"Was Samara trying to keep you away from me because you're researching something for her?" Bloodred lines slowly bled into the deep blue of his eyes. "Or because I can still smell her on you?"

I barely restrained myself from brushing my fingers against my neck where Samara had fed from me this morning after Kieran and Alaric had left. At some point, we'd both ended up in the washroom together, but considering what we did afterwards, it wasn't surprising I still smelled like her.

Fuck it.

"Jealous that my tongue was deep in Samara's cunt while she sat on my face this morning?"

"Yes," he said matter-of-factly.

"She's not going to marry you." I raised my chin. "And I'm not going to tell you shit."

Red churned in his eyes like rivers of blood, the blue a distant memory. What unsettled me more was how calm he appeared. His bloodlust was running high, but he was lounging in the chair like he didn't have a care in the world. The only other person I'd seen who could control their bloodlust that well was Samara.

"I could make you tell me." A cruel smile stretched across his mouth. "Believe me when I say I'm quite good at getting people to spill their secrets."

My ribbons shifted along my forearms, the outer layer loosening a little more. "You don't frighten me."

His smile widened. "Lies. We both know I can hear your heart beating faster every second you're in my presence. Where has Samara gone? I know she's no longer within these walls, and I know that temperamental Marshal is with her."

"Maybe she just wanted to get away from you after being forced to see your hideous face every day for the past couple of weeks?" Almost ready. Strike. Run. Find Kieran and Alaric. Whatever game the prince had been playing this week was over.

"Alright." Draven raised a hand, flicking his fingers out to reveal nails that had hardened into sharp, black claws. "Let's see if you reconsider after I peel the skin from your bones. I think I'll start with the face."

Faster than lightning, my ribbons shot forward, aiming for his eyes. I bolted up but stumbled back when his whip leapt from his hip of its own accord to slap my ribbons aside. My hesitation cost me, because when I spun to take off towards the door, something yanked my feet out from under me, causing me to slam face-first into the floor, and I screamed when a snapping sound came from my wrist as I tried to break my fall.

Draven let out a disapproving sound, and I blinked through my tears just as his brown leather boots filled my vision. Then he nudged me over until I was lying on my back, my arm clutched against my chest as I stared up at him. The dark brown leather whip hovered in the air, coiled around my blood ribbons.

"Impressive." He toyed with the end of a ribbon before grabbing them and balling them up in his fist. "Not the best choice for a weapon though. A whip is much better."

I bit back another scream, trembles racking my body as his whip lunged forward and its bloodred, pointed tip stopped less than an inch away from my eye.

"Tell me where she is," Draven purred.

"No." I clenched my jaw, pushing back the pain, and then met the prince's stare again. "Eat shit and die."

Something like respect flashed across his face before his eyes darted to the door. "You just had to scream, didn't you?" I let out a relieved breath as he summoned the whip away from my face.

The doors slammed open, revealing Alaric, Kieran, and Nyx—Adrienne and Emil behind them. The last two had been babysitting me the past week, and I could tell by their expressions that they were annoyed at me.

That was fair. I was annoyed at myself too.

They'd both had things they'd wanted to take care of and had told me to stay in Samara's room. I'd promised to do so, and I'd meant it at the time . . .

but then I had remembered some books I wanted to reference in the library and had figured it wouldn't hurt to sneak out for an hour.

Alaric's eyes were flat and hard, and the rangers were looking at the prince like they were imagining ripping out his spine, but Kieran . . . he looked disappointed.

I laughed, wincing as the movement jostled my wrist. "You and the dark prince, eh? Didn't know you had it in you, pretty boy."

Kieran paled as all eyes fell on him.

"It's"—he swallowed hard—"complicated."

"Everything about you lot is complicated," Adrienne growled. "I still think we should kill him."

"Think you can?" Draven looked at her curiously, not the least bit concerned about being significantly outnumbered.

"Drav," Kieran said tiredly. To my surprise, the prince backed off. Emil and Alaric helped me to my feet while Adrienne and Nyx continued to glare at the prince.

We all watched warily as Draven paced back and forth, his whip gliding down to coil on his hip again. My ribbons were still bunched up in his hand, the ends of them dragging on the floor.

"FUCK!" Draven picked up a chair and slammed it onto the ground. It shattered into several pieces, and he threw what remained in his hand at the table before spinning around to face us. "Tell me where she is. *Now*."

The rangers stepped forward, swords in hand. There was so much tension in the room, I could feel my bloodlust rising.

Alaric was a rigid wall at my back, but Kieran moved until he was standing in front of Draven and cupped the prince's cheek with his hand. "Tell us why, Drav. I love you . . . but I can't trust you."

"Well, shit," I muttered. "I just thought they were fuckin'."

"My mother wants Samara," Draven admitted reluctantly. "She's run out of patience. I received a letter from her this morning telling me to bring the Heir to her."

"Why?" Kieran stiffened.

"I've been buying time, telling her Samara was considering the proposal." Draven stepped away from Kieran and resumed pacing while running a hand roughly through his hair. "She'll know Samara has left and she'll send her guards after her. And Erendriel—" Draven cut himself off as pain flashed across his face. He spoke the next few words carefully, like he was testing how much he could say. "The wraiths will be after her too. You have to tell me where she went, Kier."

"We'll go and get her," Nyx said.

Draven shook his head. "The woods will be crawling with wraiths soon, if they're not already. You'll be cut down before you ever reach her. It has to be me."

"Why do you stand a chance?" Emil asked.

The prince smiled. "I'm more than just a pretty face."

"My ribbons," I spat and held out my uninjured hand.

Draven glanced at me and then down at my ribbons still in his hand. Then he loosened his fingers, and my ribbons shot towards me before I pushed them back with a thought. Kieran yelled as one ribbon wrapped around the prince's neck and the other wrapped around the whip that instantly lunged up to defend the prince before wrapping it around a chair.

Magic flooded the room as the prince rose several feet into the air, his claws tearing into my ribbons, but I just coiled more length around his neck.

"Roth!" Kieran screamed. "Let him down!"

"Still think my ribbons are useless as weapons?" I snarled and flung my good hand out to the side. The prince crashed into an empty bookcase before collapsing to the floor. Then I called both ribbons back to me, and they swiftly wrapped around my forearms, looking a little worse for wear.

Draven slowly got to his feet, rubbing his neck with one hand while reaching the other for his whip, which instantly leapt to his hand. Kieran slid between me and him, a worried look on his face. The rangers raised their swords a little higher, and to my surprise, Alaric moved to stand in front of me too.

"Relax," Draven said smoothly, tucking his whip back to his side. "I'm not going to kill them. Samara would be pissed. She clearly likes the Devereux *outcast*."

My ribbons rustled on my forearms, and Alaric gave me a censuring look over his shoulder. I gave him a cool one in return, and his lips twitched in response.

I stepped around Alaric and moved towards Draven. "Tell us why we should tell you," I demanded. "We know you're hiding things from us, and while Samara and Kieran believe there's something redeemable in you, I remain unconvinced."

"Same," Alaric said as all three rangers muttered their agreement.

Draven regarded me for a long moment before stretching a hand to me, palm up. "May I?" His eyes lowered to my injured arm that was still pressed against my body. Slowly, I extended it until my wrist rested in his palm.

He held my gaze as he raised his other hand to his mouth and sliced open the tip of his finger. I watched as he drew the glyph for healing on my skin, surprised by how light his touch was. Then a sharp exhale rushed out of my lips when I felt the magic from his blood sink into my flesh.

"What are you?" I breathed out.

"Something that shouldn't exist," he said tightly. "My secrets are my own, but trust me when I say I am uniquely suited to fight against wraiths."

I pulled my arm away from him and tentatively flexed my wrist. It was a little stiff, but other than that, it was completely healed. There was something off about his magic though. I'd felt the magic of other Moroi before. Draven's was different. It was . . . more.

Powerful. Chaotic. Wicked.

"Swear it," I said. "Swear on your soul that you will protect Samara from whatever is coming."

Alaric started to object, but I held my hand up, cutting him off. I wouldn't shed any tears if Draven met an untimely end, but I suspected Samara would, and I didn't want her to be sad, because I felt . . . things about her. I scowled at Draven, and he smiled at me in understanding.

Ugh.

"I'm not a good person," he said evenly. "There are reasons I am the way I am and I've done the things I've done, but none of them truly excuse anything." His eyes, which were still more red than blue, held my own without wavering. "But I promise you with every piece of my broken soul that I only want to protect Samara from what is to come. I will do whatever I have to, to protect those I love."

I glanced at Kieran, who was staring at Draven like he wanted to wrap the dark prince in his arms and whisk him away from everyone. Adrienne had been right earlier. We were a complicated bunch.

"Lake Malov," I said. Alaric swore behind me, but I ignored him. "There is something important there, and if you care about Samara as much as I think you do, you'll let her and Vail find it. Keep the wraiths off their backs until then."

Draven's lips pursed together but he nodded. "I can do that."

"I'll come with you," Kieran said.

"No." The prince shook his head sharply. Hurt spread across Kieran's face, and Draven's expression softened slightly. "If you're there, my attention will be split between protecting you and protecting Samara."

Kieran's mouth flattened into a hard line, but he didn't argue.

"This is insane," Alaric cut in. "We can't trust him to protect Samara."

"Is it any crazier than trusting Vail to keep her safe?" Nyx asked softly. "He's almost killed her twice."

My head snapped around so quickly, it hurt. "What the fuck are you talking about?"'

They blinked. "You didn't know? Vail left Samara to be monster food for the kúsu, and things got a little out of hand at the temple."

"He attacked her," Alaric growled.

"But he also saved her," Kieran said. "Both times."

Nyx rubbed their forehead. "Does it count as saving if he was the danger in the first place?"

I should have kept her tied up in bed. Samara would have been pissed about it, but at least she would have been safe.

"Go," I told Draven. "Protect her."

The prince traded glances with Kieran before striding towards the door, the rangers hesitating for a moment before stepping aside to let him pass.

"Prince?" Draven paused mid-step and looked over his shoulder at me. "I don't give a fuck what you are or what type of magic you have. If you betray Samara . . ." Alaric and Kieran moved to stand next to me as I let my own bloodlust rise, knowing it would turn my eyes into a fiery orange. "If you hurt her, we will make you suffer in ways you can't even dream of."

The Moroi Prince smiled. "Good."

CHAPTER TWENTY-THREE

—

Samara

"SORRY, GIRL." I patted Zosa's nose, and the grey mare tossed her head in irritation. "You'll be safe here, and I'll be back in a few days."

"I'll take good care of her," the stablehand promised, and I smiled thankfully at the young girl. Her parents were in charge of this outpost, and I knew they were all good people. I hated leaving Zosa behind, but Vail and I agreed that we had to go on foot from here.

The sun was setting, and we were in the last outpost in Moroi territory. We'd traveled straight up the coastline and made it here in less than two days, pushing the horses as hard as we could. The Velesian border was only two miles away and would be the more dangerous part of our trip. It'd be slower on foot, but we were traveling at night, and the horses would have attracted too much attention.

"Thanks, Nisha." I stroked Zosa's neck one last time before striding towards the front gates, where Vail was waiting for me. Shortly after we'd arrived, a striker with dark blue scales tinged with purple had landed on his shoulder. It wasn't one I'd recognized, but we had over a hundred strikers on active duty, so it wasn't like I knew all of them. It probably belonged to a ranger who was often in the field. Some of them traveled with their strikers, and the flying reptiles only left them to deliver messages.

Vail's brow had creased as he'd read the message, but when I'd asked about it, he'd just said it was a ranger thing he needed to take care of and instructed me to get the horses sorted and meet him at the gate.

The rangers posted at this outpost were standing next to him with frustrated expressions. They hadn't been happy to learn that their Marshal would be traveling into Velesian territory at night, and they'd been even more upset when Vail had refused to let any of them come with us.

"Let's go," he said as soon as I reached them.

My heart beat a little faster as the rangers opened the gate for us, and I followed Vail out of the relative safety of the outpost and its ward. The wraiths had figured out a way past the outpost wards, which weren't as strong as those that protected the Houses, but the outposts were still far safer than the wilds.

Especially the thick forests of Velesian territory.

"We'll stay on the road until we're closer to the border," Vail said quietly. "Then we'll have to move into the forests to avoid the patrols."

I nodded. Thanks to a glyph that would hide our scent and Rynn detailing where the patrol routes were, the odds were in our favor of slipping past the Velesians. I didn't love sneaking into their territory like this, especially after my latest encounter with Bastian. If we were caught, he would almost certainly get word about it, and he'd be only too delighted to take advantage of our situation.

But we didn't have time to get permission to search the area around Lake Malov either. So we'd just have to make sure we didn't get caught and avoided the Alpha Pack at all costs.

"Okay." I looked up at the last rays of sunlight streaking across the sky. "How long will it take us to reach the rendezvous spot?"

"Two days, unless we have to veer significantly off course."

I slid a glance towards Vail. We'd barely spoken since leaving House Harker. Granted, we'd been racing up the coastline so there hadn't really been any good opportunities to speak, but now we'd be traveling on foot and then hiding out together in what would no doubt be a small space.

As if reading my thoughts, he turned his head to look at me. "We'll need to be quiet. This isn't far from where I think the spine-backed boars were driven into the Moroi realm, which means something is creeping around these woods that we really don't want to mess with. The Velesians patrol this area less than the land west of the lake, so it'll be easier for us to slip past their patrols but also increases our chances of running into something nasty."

The fear that had been building inside me since we left the outpost surged forward. The last time I'd been out in the wilds at night, we'd been attacked by küsu and Vail had left me for dead. My gaze fell on the darkening shadows of the woods surrounding us. As bad as the küsu were, there were worse things roaming Lunaria than overgrown insects.

"I'll keep you safe," Vail said softly, his eyes on the forest around us. It was probably foolish of me, but I trusted him. When he extended a hand, I slipped mine into his without hesitation before we stepped off the main road into the midst of the trees. "We'll be at the border in ten minutes. Do not speak unless absolutely necessary. Our scents might be hidden, but the Velesians will easily pick up our voices."

I squeezed his hand in understanding, and we crept forward at a steady pace. The trees grew taller and wider as we moved until they blocked the sky. Vines writhed as if they were snakes, and some of the flowers bloomed as night fell, releasing sweet scents into the air to lure in unsuspecting prey. I felt the moment the sun fully set, giving way to night.

Strength flooded my limbs, and it was like a damper had been lifted from my senses. I could smell the creatures stalking the trees above us and hear leaves crunching to my left where something was slinking through the forest under-growth. The night came alive around us, and despite my fear of what we might encounter, I couldn't help but love it a little.

We were children of the moon, and the night belonged to us as much as to the other monsters.

Knowing I might need every advantage tonight, I allowed my bloodlust to rise as well. Vail looked back at me over his shoulder, my hand still clasped in his, and his silver eyes practically glowed in the darkness. Looked like we were both embracing our inner monsters tonight.

Hours passed as I followed Vail's footsteps, stepping where he stepped and stopping when he stopped. A few times, he squeezed my hand in warning and would then look pointedly in one direction. I'd focus until I saw whatever it was he was pointing out.

A monstrous-looking flower devouring the canine corpse of a howler, some type of tree-dwelling mammal with four arms and hooked claws, and my personal favorite, a baby küsu. I'd almost screamed when I'd spotted the nearly six-foot-long beast curving its body around the trunk of a tree, its shiny, black scales reflecting the small amount of moonlight that peeked through the tree canopy when the wind caused the branches to sway, and it's too many legs propelling it forward as it climbed further up the tree.

Thanks for the nightmares, little buddy.

Vail stopped so suddenly, I ran into him, the hand that wasn't in his instinctively going up to steady myself, feeling the hard muscles of his lower back flexing underneath the leather vest. I immediately started scanning our surroundings while my ears strained to pick something up, but I saw nothing and only heard the insects chirping away in the night.

No. Wait. There. Dark shapes were slinking down the trees around us.

"What are they?" I asked tightly, wanting to know what we were up against. Whatever these creatures were, they clearly knew we were here, so our silence was pointless.

"*Beduv kodgeg.*" Vail released my hand to free his sword. "Moon devils."

Shivers ran down my spine, but I forced myself to remain calm before sliding my throwing daggers out from my thigh sheaths.

The branches above us creaked, and more moonlight danced across the trees, giving me a better look at the creatures. I'd never had the pleasure of seeing moon devils in the flesh before, only sketches from people who had survived encounters with them. They were one of the more reclusive predators in Lunaria, and what they lacked in size, they more than made up for in intelligence.

I had to admit, they had a certain beauty to them. Short black fur coated their sturdy, feline bodies, and silver dapples in the shape of crescent moons decorated their fur. My heart hammered inside my chest when one of them got halfway down a tree and unhinged its jaws to what seemed like an impossible degree, showcasing the six-inch fangs that jutted out on either side of its mouth.

"Do not get bit, Samara," Vail breathed out. "They will snap through bone like it's nothing, and if you can't run, we die."

We die, because Vail wouldn't leave me behind this time. He'd die protecting me.

I tightened my grip on the blades. "Plan?"

More devils climbed headfirst down the trees, and some remained crouched on the trunks while others slunk across the ground and began circling us. Low, throaty clicks echoed throughout the night air, and in the dark, several short barks rang in response, the clicking sounds growing more excited.

The panic I'd been feeling increased until my breaths were nothing but quick pants. There were too many. We were going to die here. They'd snap through our bones and tear the flesh from our bodies as they devoured us. There would be nothing left.

I would die here. In this forest. Far from friends and family. Vail would die with me. Part of me felt guilty at being glad I wouldn't die alone.

But I didn't want to die. Not here. I didn't want—

A steady hand closed around my forearm, cutting off my thoughts. "It's their magic," Vail said softly. "They can increase whatever emotion you're feeling. It's easier for them to take down panicked prey. We need to run before the rest of their pride gets here."

I concentrated on Vail's hand on me, then slowly felt for the foreign magic pushing itself into my mind and shoved it back. The chittering increased, an angrier edge to it now, and several sharp bellows boomed. We were running out of time.

"When I say go, you run towards the tree directly in front of us with the blue vine growing up it. Run past it and don't stop until you reach a dried-up creek bed, then turn west. There's a cave we can seek refuge in. I can find it if we make it to that creek bed." Vail pulled his hand away and shifted lightly on the balls of his feet, holding the sword loosely at his side. "If any of them get in front of us, throw your daggers at them. Don't worry about fatal wounds. We just need to keep them off us. I'll guard our backs."

"How far?" Sweat ran down the sides of my face despite the brisk night air.

"Five miles."

Fuck. Me.

"Don't be a whiny little Heir now, Sam." Vail shoved me forward before yelling, "RUN!"

I took off, darting under a low branch and past the tree Vail had pointed out. Sharp cries echoed around the forest as the devils immediately gave chase. Two shadows peeled off the trees ahead, one darting directly into our path. My daggers were soaring through the air a second later. One sunk into the flank of a devil, and it howled before leaping back into the trees. The other missed by a hair but still caused the feline monster to retreat.

The daggers flew back into my outstretched palms, and I immediately threw them again. More angry screams. The muscles in my thighs burned, but between embracing my bloodlust and it being nighttime, I was nowhere near my limit. Behind me, I heard Vail cut away anything that got too close to us.

For a few minutes, I thought we actually might make it, then my foot caught on a tree root and I stumbled. The moon devils seized the opportunity, and their magic flooded me again.

I stumbled once more and barely managed to right myself as sheer panic gripped me.

"If you can't run, we die."

Another raised root snagged my foot, but this time, I didn't recover fast enough. My shoulder hit the ground first, and I flipped over, barely managing to avoid stabbing myself with my own blades.

"Samara!" Vail bellowed.

The devils were there instantly. One snapped at my leg, and only Vail yanking me back kept me from losing a foot. Then he practically threw me forward, causing me to stagger a few steps before I spun around as he released a pain-filled snarl.

Blood poured from his thigh, but the devil was writhing on the ground where Vail had pinned it with his sword. Another leapt for his back, aiming for his exposed neck, but my dagger sank into its throat instead. The dead weight still carried forward, and Vail grunted when the fifty-pound creature slammed into his back, almost taking him off his feet.

All around us, devils released sharp sounds—an eerie mix between a cough and bark—between those clicking sounds they clearly used to communicate. Blood filled the air, both ours and theirs, and I could feel their magic trying to seep into my mind again.

"FUCK OFF!" I screamed as the dagger slid free from the throat of the one I'd killed and landed back in my hand. We needed to move. Now. "Come on, Vail." I shoved one dagger back into my thigh sheath and grabbed his hand that wasn't holding the sword. "Time to go."

He took a step forward and faltered, blood soaking his entire right leg. I didn't think they'd broken any bones, but the devil had clearly torn through a lot of flesh. I could feel the excitement of the beasts around us as they slunk through the shadows. They'd temporarily backed off after we'd killed two of their own, but it was only a matter of time before they had another opportunity to strike.

"Go," Vail ordered, his face pale. "I'll only slow you down."

"Who's being whiny now, *Marshal*?" I snarled in his face. "We're a team, Vail. You go down, I go down."

Fury lit up his silver eyes, and I let my bloodlust fully off the chain, knowing my eyes were nothing but solid black pools.

"If we die, know that I'm going to beat the shit out of you in whatever afterlife awaits us," he promised.

"Deal." I moved to his injured side and gripped his arm. It meant I could only throw with one hand but I couldn't risk him falling again. "Let's get the fuck out of here."

We ran, not nearly as fast as before, but we kept going. Anytime Vail stumbled, I used every ounce of my strength to keep him on his feet. Between his sword and my dagger, we kept the devils from biting us with their bone-crushing jaws. Unfortunately, they changed tactics and started swiping at our legs with their claws.

Panic and fear still nipped at the edges of my mind. Some of it was definitely mine, but I could feel their influence as well. Up ahead, I could see a break in the trees. *Please let that be the dry creek bed,* I sent up a prayer to the moon. We just needed to reach the damn cave.

Moon devils raced across the branches, chittering back and forth rapidly. They knew we were close to getting free of the forest, and they didn't want to lose the advantage of the trees. I swallowed a scream as one of them deeply dug its claws into my calf, yet I somehow managed to stay upright. Vail grunted when I almost went down, more weight going on his injured leg, but I surged up and kept us both running.

The distraction cost me though when two devils flew from the trees on either side of us. My dagger found one while Vail barely managed to knock the other with his sword. Neither of us saw the third one flying directly towards my side, its jaw stretched open wide to sink its fangs into my ribs.

A sound like thunder cracked through the dark forest, and the devil that had been flying through the air at me jerked and veered off course. Another thunderous boom sounded from behind us, and as one, the devils released a high-pitched, undulating wail before falling back. Whether they were converging on whatever was attacking them or just retreating, I didn't know and didn't care.

"Vail!" I shouted. "Creek bed! Where do we go?"

We crashed to a halt, both of us breathing hard as Vail whipped his head around, taking in our surroundings. "West. Half mile." He grimaced and tentatively pulled away from my support, testing his leg. "Let's go before they come back or something else is attracted to the blood."

For a moment, I stood there, bathed in moonlight, and looked back into the dark forest where I could hear the devils hunting whatever had saved us.

"Thanks, beastie," I whispered, "and good hunting."

TWENTY MINUTES LATER, Vail and I collapsed onto the floor of a small underground cave. The only reason it'd taken us so long to find it was because the sky had opened up and dumped what felt like a lake's worth of water on us. Visibility had been so poor that we'd walked past the cave and had to backtrack, the entrance barely noticeable.

I winced as I dipped my fingers into the bleeding wound on my calf before drawing the glyph for seal in the dirt and on each side of the narrow cave mouth. This spell wasn't particularly powerful—wraiths could have breezed on by it and it would shatter if it was physically hit too many times—but it would prevent anything from hearing or scenting us, and we'd been careful not to let any blood drip from our wounds close to the cave. I waited until I felt the magic lock into place before heading back towards Vail.

"I don't know how the Velesians deal with these sudden showers all the time." I shivered and tugged my cold, wet tunic away from my skin with a grimace. "There's no way these are going to dry in here."

"The sun will rise in a few hours." Vail set his sword next to where he was sitting on the floor, examining his leg. He'd pulled a small Fae lantern from his pack along with a canteen of water and some dried meat. "We'll use that time to heal and rest and then try to cover as much ground as possible during the day, but we'll likely still need to travel at least a few hours at night if we're to reach Rynn on time."

I nodded and sat on the cool, hard floor, trying very hard not to think about the last time I'd been alone with Vail in a cave while I drew healing glyphs around my various wounds. It'd been easy to block that memory before because I'd been so focused on finding safety, but now we were here . . . and exactly like that night, we'd barely survived a monster attack and were covered in blood. At least this time, thanks to the rain, most of the blood had been washed away.

Of course that meant I was freezing, but I was still glad we didn't have to spend the rest of the night covered in sticky blood with no way of rinsing off. One of these days, when I wasn't busy just trying to survive or unravel nefarious plots, I'd figure out a glyph that could instantly clean and dry clothes.

Vail passed me a piece of dried meat.

"Thanks," I murmured before popping it into my mouth. Rabbit. My lips twisted in distaste, but I choked it down.

"Sorry." The corner of Vail's eyes crinkled in the barest hint of amusement as he handed me several more pieces. "Tried to find venison, but meat supplies are running low so rabbit was the only option."

I blinked, a little surprised he remembered my food preferences and my strong dislike for the gaminess of rabbit.

"It's fine," I said and scarfed down the rest of the gamey bits while sneaking glances at him, trying to gauge if the memory of that night was haunting him the way it was me.

At least once a month, I still woke up in cold sweats, remembering how terrified I'd been as the wind had howled outside that cave and we'd heard the shrieks of the wraiths as they'd searched the forests for us, not to mention the trauma of seeing my parents cut down before my eyes. As a child, I'd thought they'd been invincible. My mother had been so confident that nothing had ever rattled her, and my father had been a skilled fighter from a family of rangers.

The wraiths had gone for them immediately, bypassing other easier prey. I hadn't understood it then, but I did now. They'd known my parents had been searching for the other half of the soul crown. I wondered if Queen Velika had ordered the attack or if Erendriel had taken the initiative.

Vail and his parents had simply been at the wrong place at the wrong time. Maybe he was right to hate me a little. My family was the reason his were dead, and I'd stopped him from trying to save them.

"I was wrong."

"What?" I blinked and raised my gaze from where I'd been staring blankly at the floor to meet Vail's solemn expression.

"No one knows you better than me," he said evenly. "Not Kieran. Not Rynn or Cali. Me." He laid a hand over his chest. "You were my best friend long before you were any of theirs. I know every single one of your tells, and I know you better than I know myself."

"That was then. This is now." I shook my head, not knowing how to deal with this conversation. Being trapped with him in a fucking cave again was too much. Especially while hashing out our old pain. "You don't know me at all anymore."

"Oh yeah?" he challenged. "Tell me you're not thinking about the night our parents died. That you're not thinking your parents are responsible for roping my parents into protecting them? And that you're not feeling guilty about stopping me from running out of that cave like a fucking fool." He pulled his hand away from his chest and waved it in my direction, inviting me to argue as he bit out his next words. "Tell me, Samara. I fucking dare you."

I held his steely gaze, refusing to look away, but what the fuck could I say to that? He was right. It pissed me off that he was able to crack open my mind and see all my thoughts so easily.

He let out a humorless laugh. "Exactly."

"Your parents were only there that night because they were protecting mine," I said hotly. "And I did take away your choice, Vail. You were my friend, my only fucking friend, and I didn't want you to die too, but it wasn't my fucking choice to make, was it?" I choked off the last word before rubbing my face. If I could avoid caves for a while, that would be great. Clearly nothing good came of them.

"I was wrong," Vail repeated. "If you hadn't knocked me out and prevented me from running out of that cave, I would have died that night, and you would have too, because we both know you would have followed me out into the night."

He was right. I would have followed Vail anywhere back then. Fuck, I would follow him anywhere now, despite all the animosity between us. Apparently I was a fool too.

"You don't get to rewrite history, Samara." The kindness in his voice finally made me look at him again. It wasn't just the echoes of grief I saw reflected in his eyes. There was acceptance too. "My parents loved yours. It wasn't just a case of the Marshals being devoted to the rulers of a House. They were friends, and they died trying to protect each other, and us. The last thing my father told me to do was protect you."

"The last thing mine told me to do was protect you," I whispered and then shot him a contrite smile. "Sorry I had to hit you over the head with a rock to do it."

He shrugged. "Sorry I almost let a kùsu eat you a few weeks ago."

I laughed sharply. "That was a real asshole move. I'm going to have nightmares for the rest of my life about that overgrown centipede chasing me."

"I really am sorry." He winced. "I was just so angry at you. For so fucking long. I let it warp everything about us."

"Why, Vail?" I searched his face, trying to find the answer I'd been seeking for the last decade. "Why did you hate me so much? We both lost our parents that night, but you turned on me so quickly." I couldn't keep the soft desperation out of my voice.

"It's complicated." Vail's mouth hardened into a flat line, and he looked away from me.

Fuck that. He didn't get to get off this easily.

"You tried to feed me to an overgrown insect." I narrowed my eyes. "Explain it."

Vail's gaze snapped to mine, and I saw a hint of the accusing anger that I was used to in them. "You never mourned them. I was falling apart, and you carried on like nothing had happened."

"Carmilla told me I had to be strong." I swallowed, remembering the exact conversation with her and how distraught she'd been. "That I was the Heir of House Harker and that everyone was counting on me. I wasn't allowed to fall apart." He frowned like something about that didn't make sense, but I barreled on. "My entire life ended in one night, Vail, and when I finally snapped and snuck out of my room to find my best friend and tell him I was fucking breaking, he shoved me into the dirt and said he wished I'd died that night too."

"I'm sorry," he rasped. "I didn't know. I thought . . . Fuck, I don't know what I thought." Vail's brows bunched together before he slowly said, "Carmilla said that you got frustrated with her when she grieved about losing her sister around you."

"What?" I jerked back like I'd been struck. "Carmilla was concerned I was breaking down and that it would harm my future as the Harker Heir. Everything I did was to prove to her—and the House—that I was worthy of my parents' legacy, but even then, I never said anything cruel about her grieving."

Vail's brows bunched together. "It doesn't make sense," he murmured more to himself than to me. "Maybe I'm not remembering it right."

"Damn fucking right, you're not," I said through clenched teeth. There was no way Carmilla would have said such a thing. He must have been so caught up in his hatred that he'd seen or heard something that hadn't been there.

He shook his head as if clearing his thoughts before those grey eyes focused on me. "All I knew was that I was hurting and you seemed . . . fine."

"Fine?" I repeated, my voice cracking. "I was falling apart and had no one to talk to. There wasn't anyone our age back then aside from Alaric, and we didn't exactly get along."

"You get along now," Vail muttered, and I didn't miss the hint of jealousy in his tone, which snapped me out of the heartache I was feeling and sent me straight into pissed-off territory. He was the one who had ended our friendship. He was the fucking one who had been flipping back and forth between hot and cold since I'd returned. One second damning me and the next saving me.

"After you decided I was no longer worthy of your friendship, I had no one, Vail!" My hands slammed against his chest as I gripped the front of his shirt. I didn't know if I wanted to shove him away from me or pull him closer. "It wasn't until Kieran came to live at House Harker that I had another friend, and things between us were always complicated. By the time I went to Drudonia and became close friends with Rynn and Cali—" The words got stuck in my throat as I struggled to get my emotions back in check. "The lie became the truth. Everyone believed I was fine, and I'd gotten really good at hiding the pain. Seemed easier to just go on like that."

Vail placed his large, warm hands over mine, and I stared at them for a long moment before raising my eyes to meet his, which were full of understanding, like he finally saw me, and something inside me settled. Then his lips curled into a lopsided smile. "We're both equally fucked."

"I suppose," I admitted and shivered as the dampness of my clothes sank into my bones.

"Truce?" Vail offered and squeezed my hands.

"You were the only one declaring war," I felt the need to point out.

"Please," Vail scoffed. "You used to prance around in those skimpy outfits every time you were back visiting from Drudonia."

I stared at him wide-eyed. "What are you talking about?"

Vail leaned forward, silver flickering in his eyes. "You know exactly what I'm talking about," he said in a deep voice that had my toes curling. "Every summer, you would come back for a few weeks, usually dragging Rynn and Cali with you, and the three of you would generate chaos around House Harker as you ran around basically naked."

"Oh." I tilted my head and thought about it. We'd started doing that when the three of us were eighteen. Three years before I was supposed to marry Demetri. I'd been going through a bit of a wild phase, and Cali and Rynn had only been too happy to participate. "Honestly, I was just trying to make Kieran jealous. It never worked because usually he had his tongue down the throat of some other girl."

"It definitely worked." Vail chuckled, and my heart skipped a beat. "As soon as you left, we'd all have to deal with Kieran's mood swings for months afterwards. Honestly, I'm surprised Alaric didn't drown him in the ocean. Or himself. I caught him staring after you more than once."

My lips curved into a victorious grin. "Good to know."

"You're ridiculous." Vail shook his head, a faint smile on his lips.

"Did you?" I asked.

"Did I what?" He quirked an eyebrow, and I raised mine in return.

"Ever get jealous?"

Vail looked at me for a long moment and then shrugged. "Of course. Rynn is pretty hot."

"Cade will kick your ass." I glared at him, ignoring the flare of jealousy I sensed and the fact that I actually had no idea how the leader of the Alpha Pack felt about Rynn.

"Unlikely." Vail bared his fangs at me even as light danced in his eyes. "I'm faster than that old bear."

"He's only a couple of decades older than us." I laughed.

Vail gave me an unimpressed look before releasing my hands and stretching out on the cave floor. I didn't think everything was completely fixed between us, but I felt . . . lighter? The painful history was still there, but for the first time, I thought that maybe Vail and I had a chance at something new.

What that *new* thing was I had no idea. Friends? More than friends?

Before I could ponder that more, an involuntary shiver ran through my limbs. This cave wasn't exactly warm, and I was standing there in cold, wet clothes that were clinging uncomfortably to my skin.

Sighing quietly, I started pulling them off. There was no way I was going to be able to fall asleep in them.

"What are you doing?" Vail asked in a rough tone as he stared at me with silver winding its way through his eyes.

"I'm not sleeping in wet clothes. At least this way, they'll hopefully be only damp in the morning." My fingers felt along the wall until I found some creases that I could tuck the edges of my tunic and pants into so they could hang. I left the thin shirt I wore under my tunic on along with my underwear, but I did turn my back to Vail and reach under my shirt to unlace the band I wore around my breasts.

A moan of relief slipped from my lips before I shoved the band into another crevice.

I heard Vail rise behind me, and when I glanced over my shoulder, my mouth went dry as he pulled off his wet vest and tunic. He had his back to me, and it had never occurred to me until this moment that well-defined back muscles were hot as hell. Even though scars littered his lightly tanned skin, my fingers itched to trail over each one and to feel his corded muscles beneath my touch. The healing glyphs hadn't been enough to fix the damage he'd taken over the years.

You're only feeling this way because you almost died an hour ago, I told myself, but when I'd returned to House Harker, I'd embraced a new motto.

Want something? Take something.

Vail could absolutely not be one of those things though... right? Alaric might be complicated, but I had no doubt he desired me. More than that, we had something that could work if we were both willing to try. Despite this heartfelt conversation with Vail, I didn't entirely know what he wanted, and more importantly, I didn't think he did either. Until he made that decision clear, I wouldn't allow him to break my heart more than he already had every time he'd spat on our friendship.

"How's your leg?"

I frowned as Vail tugged his pants off and then realized that by staring at his thigh, I was dangerously close to staring at something else that was hidden only by the thin fabric of his underwear.

Nope. Not going there. I jerked my gaze away and took a seat on the cavern floor again.

"It will be sore tomorrow, but I should be able to move okay." Either he hadn't noticed me almost staring at his dick, or he was choosing not to comment on it. I couldn't decide if I was disappointed by that.

"Do you . . . ah . . . need to drink?" My gaze hesitantly flicked to his as he took a seat across from me.

We both knew I wasn't talking about water.

"No," he said in a guarded tone, but his eyes still darted to my neck as silver flickered in them. "You should save your strength."

"I fed deeply from Roth and Kieran this morning." My eyes fell to his exposed thigh. The six-inch wound was mostly healed across the top, but the skin was still red and puffy. "If you're not at one hundred percent tomorrow, you'll slow us down," I pointed out.

Vail's even stare told me he wasn't swayed by my logic. I shook my head, but it was his choice, and if he said he was fine, then I'd drop it.

I stretched out across the hard dirt floor of the cave. It was a far cry from my soft bed at House Harker or even the lumpy but relatively comfortable one I'd slept in at the outpost on our way to the Velesian realm. Between our surroundings and Vail though, I couldn't help thinking again about those nights we'd hidden in the cave after the wraiths had attacked our caravan.

My already cold body shivered at the memory. I was mentally and physically exhausted from the encounter with the devils and our heartfelt conversation, but we had to keep going in a few hours, which meant I needed to rest. Unfortunately, it was very difficult to force my mind to let me sleep.

The dampness of the cave only burrowed further into my skin, and I began to shiver. I turned onto my side, hoping that less contact with the cold earth would help.

It did not. Neither did my long, wet hair.

I sighed, about to give up on getting any sleep, when a large arm wrapped around my waist and tugged me back against a broad chest.

"Your teeth were chattering," Vail said tightly as every part of me went absolutely still. "It was annoying. Body heat will help."

"Right," I half squeaked. Every part of Vail was pressed up against my back. He'd slid his other arm underneath my head and even threw a leg over mine. *Body heat. This was just about survival.* I was feeling warmer already. My teeth had stopped clacking against each other, and the shivering was mostly gone too.

I snuggled a little further into Vail's arms, and he seemed to stop breathing for a moment. Then the arm around my waist tightened slightly, and I felt his beard tickle the back of my neck. I tried to remind myself of all the reasons getting involved with Vail was a bad idea, but for every bad memory, there was a good one.

"Why is this so confusing?" I whispered.

"Because I should hate you." His breath danced across my skin. "But I can't. And you shouldn't trust me, but you do."

His hand slipped underneath my shirt and made lazy circles over my belly. Each circular motion drifted a little higher until his thumb brushed the underside of my breast. I gasped and pressed a little harder into him, his hard length pressing against my ass, only the thin fabric of our remaining clothing separating us.

"You were right earlier," he said in a soft voice. "I should drink."

Any attempts at being rational and maybe offering him my wrist instead of my neck fled as his teeth grazed my skin, not breaking it, just waiting for me to say yes.

Fuck it. I'd be rational in the morning.

"Drink," I commanded, and a shiver that had nothing to do with the cold ran through me when one hand cupped my breast while the other wrapped around my throat and squeezed lightly. "Fuck, Vail," I groaned and raised my hand so I could bury it in his hair, holding him tighter against me. My thighs clenched together, and an aching need started to build as he roughly rolled a thumb over my pebbled nipple.

The hand on my neck slid up, guiding my face to the side so he could get better access to my throat. Then teeth nipped at me before his beard rubbed roughly against my skin. My breathing quickened as he hungrily kissed my neck, still playing with my nipple, and raised his head enough to whisper in my ear, "Are you wet for me, Heir?"

"Find out for yourself, Marshal," I said huskily.

"I know you are." His hand moved to play with my other nipple, rolling it between his fingers and making me squirm against him. "I can smell it. Your cunt was dripping as soon as I touched you."

"Fuck, why are you all such dirty talkers?" I whimpered.

Vail tore his hand from my breast and shoved it between my legs, pushing my underwear to the side while using his leg to spread mine wider. "Don't"— he shoved two fingers inside me with zero warning, and I let out a strangled moan as he gripped me to him while harshly pumping his fingers in and out— "talk about the others when I'm inside you."

"You weren't," I panted, "inside me yet."

The hand around my chin pulled it further to the side before Vail struck, his fangs piercing my neck just as another finger joined the others that were fucking me hard. The sharp pain mixed with the building pleasure was too much, and I came all over his hand.

He pulled it free to flick my overly sensitive clit before rubbing it with two of his fingers that were slick from my arousal. I jerked in his grasp, but his arm tightened around me, keeping me flush against his body.

"Vail," I half whimpered and half moaned as he continued to tease me. His fangs slid out, and he laughed against my neck before sliding one of his legs between mine to rotate us until he was beneath me, my back still flat against his

449

chest. The leg that was between mine leaned to the outside, making my legs spread even more.

"Next time we do this," he rumbled into my ear, "it'll be in front of a mirror. That way, we can watch me fuck you. Watch as my fingers disappear"—he thrust three fingers inside me, stretching me out, and I moaned from the fullness—"into this perfect, tight little pussy of yours."

Shivers coursed through me as he continued to pump his fingers in and out, his thumb occasionally brushing over the sensitive bundle of nerves, causing my hips to buck. Vail increased his pace until my entire body was trembling.

As if he could sense how close I was, his fangs grazed my neck again before slowly sinking in. He didn't drink, just bit down hard, as if he was pinning me in place, claiming me.

That was all it took to push me over the edge. My pussy clenched around his fingers as the orgasm rolled through me, and I screamed his name again before sagging against him in a boneless heap.

My eyes had shut at some point, but I heard him licking his fingers after he withdrew them. Then he shifted us until we were both on our sides once more. I could feel his erection pressed against me, but when I reached around to slip my hand into his undershorts, he stopped me and guided it back to rest on my hip.

"You need rest," he said roughly. "And if my cock gets inside you . . . I won't be able to stop for hours."

The reality of what we'd just done crashed into me. I was lying on a cave floor with the man who had once been my dearest friend, then became one of my worst enemies, and now . . . I didn't know where we stood or how much I could truly trust him.

CHAPTER TWENTY-FOUR

—

Samara

I'D EXPECTED things to be awkward between us in the morning, but they weren't. We didn't talk about what had happened, but things had definitely shifted between us.

Kieran would probably have mixed feelings about this new development. He was easygoing about a lot of things, but not when it came to people who had hurt me, and almost nobody had hurt me more than Vail. Considering I felt the same about him and Draven, I couldn't really fault him for that. I had no idea how Roth and Alaric would react to Vail potentially entering our . . . thing.

My lips quirked into a wry grin. I didn't know how the Velesians so easily navigated these multi-threaded relationships. Well, most Velesians. Poor Rynn was more lost than I was when it came to this type of thing.

"What are you thinking about?" Vail stretched out a hand to help me over a fallen log.

"Nothing." I slipped my hand into his and gave him a sunny smile. He narrowed his eyes but didn't call me out on my bullshit. It felt strange for him not to launch back a scathing remark. A girl could get used to this.

"If we're to make it to the southern tip of Lake Malov by tomorrow morning, we need to travel a little further tonight." We both looked up at the rapidly setting sun. "Rynn mentioned a cabin about twenty miles from here. It's warded, which means we'll have a safe place to stay tonight, and it'll put us only a few miles from where we're supposed to meet her."

I chewed on my bottom lip. "Do you think we'll run into the moon devils again?"

"No." He shook his head. "We should be out of their territory by now, and they're likely still recovering from whatever tore into them last night."

"What do you think that was?" I asked. While I was glad whatever it was had shown up when it had, that didn't mean I wasn't worried about there being a bigger and badder monster lurking out there—one that could be tracking us now.

Vail didn't answer right away, and I didn't push him as he pondered it. We wound our way through the trees that only grew thicker the further we pressed into Velesian land. The type of fauna changed as well. Along the coast, the trees were spread out a little more, and the other plants . . . well . . . they were devious. Particularly in the Moroi realm further south, everything was deceptively beautiful. The better to lure in unsuspecting prey so it could devour them.

The plant life of the Velesian realm hid nothing about its intentions though. We passed several trees that were weeping what looked like blood, and large, purple flowers stood upright from the ground—their six-foot-tall petals closed tight as something bulged in the center of them—likely digesting whatever they had caught last night with the black, thorny tentacles that slithered around their base.

Not for the first time, I was glad the Moroi had ended up where they had. The Velesian realm was twice the size of ours, but I was pretty sure my ass would have been eaten a long time ago if I lived here.

"Most of my concentration last night was spent on staying upright and not passing out." Vail finally spoke. "I heard several loud cracks, which makes me think that whatever attacked the devils was large. Maybe attacked from above and broke some branches on the way down?" He shook his head, clearly not buying his own theory, and looked at me. "You didn't see anything?"

"I was a little busy keeping your heavy ass moving." I waved a hand at him. "Do you really need all those muscles?"

A squeal leapt from my throat as Vail grabbed me and picked me up like I weighed nothing at all before pinning me to a tree. He was so much taller than me that my feet were nowhere near the ground, so I wrapped my legs around his waist.

"I think you can benefit quite nicely from my muscles." He grinned, and for a second, it took my breath away to see such a carefree look on his face instead of the usual scowl.

"Maybe you can show me later?" I gave him a heated smirk, and his eyes lit up. "We can see how sturdy the walls of that cabin are."

Something roared in the distance, and a chorus of wolf howls answered it. Both of our heads whipped in the direction the sounds had come from, and Vail slowly set me back onto my feet. "The wolves are probably Velesians," he said. "Most of the sentinels in this area are lycanthropes."

We had rangers, the Velesians had sentinels, and the Furies didn't have a dedicated fighting force. There simply weren't enough of them to justify it. Instead, every single Furie was trained to fight, and they were all lethal.

More howls sounded.

"We need to move. They're headed this way along with whatever they're fighting." He held his hand out, and I slipped mine into his once more. We took off at a steady jog, avoiding the more nefarious-looking fauna as we cut our way through the forest.

Only when the forest started to darken did we stop to rest. Unease rippled through me. I really didn't want to spend another night traveling through the wilds, but I also knew we didn't have a choice.

Vail tugged me to him and kissed me gently. I blinked up at him, still not used to this softer version of him, and part of me worried about how long it would last. Vail's temper was volatile. I was bound to do something that would piss him off again. It had been bad enough when our friendship had ended as kids—I didn't know how I would handle it now that we were more than just friends.

If Alaric were here, he would have lectured me. Kieran would have offered me chocolates to ease my concern while scowling at Vail, and Roth . . . They would tell me I was an idiot for getting involved with Vail and to sit on their face as punishment.

I missed them. All of them. My heart clenched. I'd almost died last night and could die tonight.

"Hey." Vail tipped my chin up until I met his gaze. "We'll get through this and I'll get you back to them."

"How'd you know I was thinking about them?" I rasped.

He smiled and kissed the corners of my mouth. "You're easier to read than you think, especially when you're thinking about the people you care about."

We looked at each other for a long moment, neither of us willing to say anything else on that subject. Finally, Vail pulled his sword free and nodded at the daggers on my thigh. "We made good time today and aren't too far now. The further inland we go, the less familiar I am with the terrain, but I think we have less than five miles until we reach the cabin."

"I'll have to take your word for it because I have no idea where we are right now," I admitted. Vail smiled faintly and tapped the tree closest to us with his sword. I looked at where the tip of his blade rested and saw several markings carved into it. A wolf's head followed by what looked like a lake with an arrow pointing in the direction we were facing. Below that, squiggly lines—waves maybe? That one had an arrow pointing back to where we'd come from.

Now that I knew it was there, it was incredibly helpful, but I never would have spotted it without Vail pointing it out.

"Lead the way." I swallowed past the lump in my throat as the shadows around us darkened and the forest became more sinister. I took in a steady breath as magic flooded me. The sun had fully set. We just had to survive tonight, and then we'd get our answers tomorrow. I refused to even entertain the possibility that this had all been for nothing.

We *would* find answers at Lake Malov, though I was less sure we would *like* those answers.

Unlike the previous night, the woods around us were eerily silent. Nothing moved in the trees above us or in the thick underbrush, there were no howls or barks in the distance, and even the insects had ceased their chirping.

Vail kept scanning our surroundings, because something was clearly out there, and whatever it was, none of the other monsters wanted to mess with it. I concentrated on keeping my breathing steady and my fingers loose around the daggers, ready to throw at a moment's notice.

It felt like we'd barely been walking more than a few minutes when Vail whirled and shoved me. Hard. I flew backwards, my back slamming into a tree before I fell to my knees. One dagger went flying from my hand, but I managed to hold on to the other. I staggered to my feet and froze when Vail's pissed-off snarl rang throughout the night and the scent of his blood hit me a second later.

Five Strigoi stood completely still between me and Vail. Two of them were facing me, and the other three were facing Vail, one of which had blood dripping from long, jagged claws.

My heart clenched, and I wished we'd come across any other type of monster. Anything but Strigoi. I'd even take the more dangerous wraiths over this. I looked over the two who were focused on me, trying my best to keep my emotions in check. One of them had been a woman once. Her blonde hair hung in long, tangled knots down to her waist. Like the rest of them, she was completely naked, and her frame was so gaunt, I could almost count her ribs.

The one next to her was equally thin with dark brown hair. He looked like he'd turned when he'd been younger, eighteen at most.

At some point, they'd been living their lives just like me, trying to survive in this fucked-up world, when something had happened to make them lose their humanity and never find it again. Guilt bit at me. I didn't know when they had turned, but I was a member of a powerful House. We should have done more.

I should have done more.

"I'm sorry," I bit out. The words were meaningless, and they wouldn't understand them anyway, but they were all I could offer.

Both of them looked at me with empty eyes. The hunger was all they felt now.

"Blood," the blonde female rasped.

"Don't run," Vail commanded. He backed away, and the three Strigoi watching him stepped with him, further away from me. "Just stay alive. Whatever you have to do, Sam, fucking do it."

If I ran, they would chase me, and unlike many of the monsters that roamed Lunaria, they would catch me. Even if I embraced my bloodlust to its full potential, it wouldn't be enough. They were nothing *but* bloodlust. It made them stronger and faster than any Moroi. The blade felt so heavy in my hand, but I gripped it tighter, and the male Strigoi caught the movement, his lips curling in a silent snarl, revealing his long fangs.

They can't be brought back, I reminded myself. It still felt like I was killing my own kind, but we didn't have a choice. Either we kill them or they kill us.

And I wouldn't be dying here tonight.

With no warning, the female Strigoi dove forward, trying to slash my throat with her claws. I twisted to the side, barely avoiding her attack. My blade kissed her throat, and blood sprayed, but she didn't even notice.

My instincts screamed at me and I whirled, shoving my dagger forward, sinking it into the chest of the male Strigoi. He snarled inches from my face, and then something slammed into my side, ripping me away from the male Strigoi while also tearing the blade from my hand.

I landed on my back, the female Strigoi on top of me. She lunged forward, her fangs bared, and I shoved her to the side but not far enough—instead of her ripping out my throat, she bit deep into my shoulder. A scream ripped out of me as I tried to push her off me, but the male was there immediately. He wrenched my left arm to the side and then tore into my arm.

Bites from a Strigoi were nothing like the ones from a Moroi. These two were feral in the way they bit, their fangs constantly shifting and piercing my skin over and over as they greedily gulped down my blood. I could hear Vail roaring, trying to fight his way to me.

He wouldn't make it though, not before these two sucked me dry.

The male Strigoi still had my arm pinned down, but the female Strigoi had shifted to get a better angle, so my right arm was no longer pinned beneath her. I felt my own nails harden into claws, and I shoved my hips up as hard as I could. It did nothing to dislodge the male, but the female reared back and screamed into my face.

I shoved two fingers directly into her left eye.

She shrieked, and I fought the urge to clamp my hands over my ears. This time when I shoved her, she moved, crashing into the Strigoi who had been frantically drinking from my arm. The two of them went down in a snarling pile of fangs and tangled limbs.

I scrambled back and twisted, trying to shove myself up, but my arm gave out. Then my vision darkened as pain laced up my entire body. I tried again using only my right arm and managed to get to my feet. I blinked several times, trying to clear my vision, but it barely helped. Blood flowed from the wounds on my shoulder and arm. The Strigoi had really chewed the fuck out of me.

"Daggers," I mumbled. "Need weapons."

Before I took a step, both of the Strigoi were rising, still snapping at each other, but my hopes of them taking each other out vanished. The female Strigoi's left eye was nothing but a bloody socket, but her remaining one was locked on me.

I took a step back and swayed slightly. Shit. How much blood had I lost? Too much. The answer was too fucking much.

A flash of silver caught my attention, and I looked towards Vail's fight with the three Strigoi just in time to see the head of one of them slide off its shoulders. The smell of blood permeated the air, both ours and theirs. Something glinted in the moonlight on the ground to my right.

The dagger I had dropped at the beginning of the attack.

I started to move towards it before realizing how monumentally stupid I was being. Flinging my hands out to my sides, I called the daggers to me. Both of them obediently leapt to my palms, one still stained with the Strigoi's blood.

If we survived this, Vail was going to give me so much shit for creating these fun little blood daggers and forgetting to fucking use them.

The male Strigoi cocked his head in a move that was so different from how Moroi moved, it sent chills down my spine. His nostrils flared wide as he breathed in my scent before he stalked towards me. The female Strigoi was struggling a little with depth perception, and her movements had lost some of their fluidity. She jerked forward, a low snarl vibrating from her throat.

My vision started to waver again, blackness seeping in at the edges.

Don't pass out. Don't pass out. Don't fucking pass out. I chanted the words over and over in my mind, the motto the only thing keeping me standing.

The two Strigoi moved farther apart, forcing me to split my attention.

I spun around slowly, trying to keep them both in my line of sight but they were on opposite sides now, so I couldn't guard against one without turning my back on the other.

Without any warning, the male Strigoi leapt at me, fangs bared and claws aimed at my neck. A snarl at my back told me the female was moving in too, and in that split second, I knew I was going to die. I raised the dagger to meet the male, wanting to at least take him out and give Vail a fighting chance at surviving all of this.

Then a whistling sound raced through the air, followed by two loud cracks. I dove to the side, and the two headless bodies of the Strigoi who'd been attacking me crashed into each other before falling to the ground, their heads spinning through the air before landing a few feet away.

Two long, dark, slender shapes moved on the ground, the last couple of feet of each lined with bloodred, serrated edges. I leapt to my feet from where I'd landed on my ass and stared at the tall figure wrapped in a black cloak.

Bright red eyes peered out from underneath the hood. They looked me over once, eyes glowing brighter at each of the wounds I bore, before he snarled and sprinted to where Vail was still squaring off against one Strigoi.

So this was the beast Draven hid beneath that charming prince exterior.

Another loud crack rang through the air. Then the *thud* of a body hitting the ground.

I looked down at the corpses of the Strigoi who had attacked me and offered them a silent prayer to find peace in whatever afterlife greeted them.

"What the fuck are you doing here?" Vail growled in a low, dangerous voice. Knowing exactly what that tone meant, I raced over and slid between the two males before they decided not enough blood had been spilt tonight.

I had a very logical argument prepared about how we needed to work together to get to safety. Unfortunately, my body realized we'd survived the fight, and the adrenaline started to fade. Blood coated every inch of my clothing, the wound on my shoulder and arm still bleeding profusely, and the darkness that had been trying to claim me for the last ten minutes finally won the battle.

The last thing I remembered before passing out was Draven snatching me before I hit the ground, his eyes still a sea of blood. "Don't worry, love. I'll always catch you."

CHAPTER TWENTY-FIVE

—

Samara

I WOKE UP WITH A START, the memory of hungry, vacant eyes, sharp fangs, and long, jagged claws plaguing my nightmares. Strigoi. We'd been attacked by Strigoi. I'd done my best to fight them off, but they'd overpowered me—fed on me. Vail hadn't been able to get there in time . . . but Draven had.

Draven had found us.

"It's okay. You're safe."

Speak of the devil.

I looked to my right to find Draven leaning casually against a wall. His posture was relaxed and almost bored, the same way he stood when attending the Sovereign House masquerades or all the meetings the Moroi Prince was expected to attend. His leisurely facade was ruined by the ominous, black cloak still wrapped around him, splattered with blood, and the whip coiled at his hip. I stared at it for a long moment. It only looked like one whip, but I was sure I had seen two earlier.

His hood was pulled down, revealing his black-and-silver-streaked hair braided back away from his face. I met his eyes, lapis lazuli blue cracks winding their way through the red. He hadn't released his bloodlust, which meant he was still expecting a fight.

"We're at the cabin." My head snapped to where Vail was standing to my left. I was pretty sure he hadn't been significantly injured during the fight, but I still methodically searched his broad frame, looking for any hints of injury.

"You're okay," I said with a relieved sigh and took his hand. Vail pulled me to my feet before directing me slightly behind him. My relief quickly turned to annoyance, and I stepped forward so I was at his side, Draven only a few feet away from us. "He saved my life, Vail. I'm not saying we have to tell him our deepest, darkest secrets, but I'm confident he's not going to hurt me."

A wicked grin lit up Draven's face. "And what would I have to do to get you to tell me such deep, dark secrets?"

I matched his carnal smile with one of my own. "I'll tell you mine if you tell me yours." He stiffened, and I laughed. "Thought so."

"How did you find us? Tell us," Vail asked. He didn't push me behind him again, but I could feel the tension rolling off him.

"I don't take orders from you," Draven drawled.

"Fine." Vail shrugged. "I wouldn't have believed anything you said anyway, but maybe after I beat the shit out of you, something akin to truth will dribble out of your broken jaw."

"Try it." Draven bared his teeth and I felt . . . something. Did the ground tremble?

I glanced down and saw that the cabin had no floor. It was just four walls and a roof over a fairly flat, dirt surface. Given that we were in Velesian territory, it made sense. They didn't like being apart from the earth, even when inside.

"There it is." Vail narrowed his eyes at the prince. "You have magic. More than just the blood magic of the Moroi." His steel-grey eyes fell to the bare floor. "It's earth magic, isn't it? Is that what you used to sneak up on me in that alley?"

Draven's face went carefully blank. "I don't know what you're talking about. Maybe you're just not as skilled as you think."

"Enough," I snapped. They continued to glower at each other, but they ceased with the threats. Good enough. I glanced at Vail. "How much time do we have?" *Before Rynn shows up and we all go sneaking around a forbidden lake looking for a lost Fae crown.* I left that part out but trusted Vail to understand what I was asking.

"You were passed out for two hours while you healed. I gave you some of my blood to speed it up, but the Strigoi tore through a lot of your flesh and you lost a lot of blood." Vail's voice turned raspy as he admitted how badly I'd been hurt. "We have less than an hour now."

Shit.

My eyes softened as I looked at Draven but I kept my voice strong and steady. "You've been trying to play both sides since you arrived at House Harker. Telling me and Kieran you care about us and only want to protect us but in the same breath saying we can't trust you. We can't continue like this. Either you're with us or you're not. Decide."

"It's not that simple." Pain flickered across his face along with something that looked a lot like fear.

"Make it that simple," I pushed. He had followed us here, and while I was grateful for him saving our lives, I couldn't let my feelings for him risk everything. All that mattered was keeping the other half of the crown out of Velika's grasp. Once we secured it, we'd have to figure out how to rescue Carmilla and get the second half of the crown.

"And if I refuse?"

I swallowed before steeling my nerves. "Then we'll make the choice for you."

"I'll happily carve into the Marshal." Draven pulled a blade from somewhere beneath his cloak, and Vail unsheathed the curved dagger he kept at his hip in response.

"What about me?" I stepped forward and gripped Draven's hand, moving it until the blade was at my throat. Vail let out a rumbling growl at my back, but I ignored him, and thankfully he didn't interfere. For now. "Will you cut through me to get to him?"

Draven paled and yanked the blade away. "I would never hurt you."

"I know," I said quietly. It was probably foolish of me, but I did trust Draven. Even more foolish of me was that I wanted him, and that desire I felt was so much more than just a passing fancy. I liked him.

I liked it when he was being a charming prince, I liked it when he was being a devilish rogue, and . . . I loved it when he was just being Draven. I suspected the latter was a side only Kieran and I got to see.

"Please, Drav," I begged. "Give us a reason to trust you."

Slowly, he reached up to stroke my cheek. "I've tried so hard to figure out a way to keep the two of you safe. I thought the best way to do that was to stay away."

Me and Kieran. I thought about how he always kept a careful distance between us when we were in public and how he had pushed Kieran away so cruelly. I was still pissed off about how he'd handled things with Kieran, but I also believed he must have felt he had no other option.

"I know," I said softly. "Tell me why. What are you keeping us safe from?"

We stared at each other for a long moment, and I could see the conflict he was battling within himself.

"Okay." He rubbed his face with clear reluctance before sliding the dagger back into sheath on his thigh. "I'll tell you what I can, but you have to understand that there are *some* things I *can't* speak of."

I cocked my head at how he emphasized two of the words. Magic of some kind. It had to be. I nodded. "Tell us what you can."

"You already know my mother has half of the soul crown and about her allies."

"Yes," I confirmed. "She has the half to bind a soul and is looking for the other piece to see souls, and she has an alliance with the Seelie Fae, who are the wraiths that plague our lands. They're using some type of spell that requires Moroi blood to regain their original shapes."

He looked at me for a long moment, a slight crease forming along the corners of his deep blue eyes, and then he winced. His hands flew to his head as he let out a sharp hiss.

"There are some things I can't speak of."

Something about what I'd said was related to that. Could he not even think about it without pain? What the fuck type of magic was that?

I reached out a hand and rested it on his forearm as we waited for him to continue, scared if I said anything else, it would only cause him to have more thoughts that would hurt him. I glanced over my shoulder at Vail, who was still studying the prince but had put his dagger away. His expression was unreadable, though if he was swayed by the pain Draven was in, he wasn't showing it.

After a couple of minutes, Draven straightened. I started to pull my hand away, but he rested his hand over it, keeping it trapped on his arm. I let him have it.

"Velika came into possession of the crown—half of it anyway—shortly before I was born. At first, she didn't understand how to use it, but she figured it out. Luckily for all of Lunaria, without both halves, the crown is only capable of half of its potential." I watched as his expression closed off until his feelings were hidden behind an emotionless mask that made dread pool in my gut. "But there are many wicked things she can do with that half . . . things she learned how to do by experimenting on me and those close to me."

"But she's your mother," I half whispered as the dread continued to grow.

Draven gave me a small smile that broke my heart. "She wishes she weren't. There is no one the Moroi Queen despises more than her own son."

"Why?"

He winced painfully. Clearly, this fell under things he couldn't speak of. I squeezed his arm. "It's okay."

"What did she do?" Vail asked. "How does the crown work?"

"I'm not sure how the crown worked for the Fae, but for us, it seems there has to be some connection between who wears the crown and the person they want to bind. Velika is currently limited in only being able to control those whose blood she has taken and who have taken her blood in return. Because I am her son and of her flesh and blood, she has no restrictions in controlling me. I can fight it, but I will always lose.

"My mother had no interest in raising me. I always had caretakers," Draven continued in that monotonous voice, as if he was speaking of what he'd had for breakfast and not the horrors his own mother had inflicted upon him. "For the first five years, I rarely saw her. Then she started showing up to check on me. They were short visits, and she always left disappointed."

It didn't escape my notice that he hadn't mentioned his father once. Most people assumed Velika's consort, Lucian, was Draven's father. The Sovereign House had never confirmed one way or another. I always thought it strange since Draven didn't look like either of them with his strange, black-and-silver hair and vivid blue eyes with their secondary bloodred coloring. Both Velika and Lucian were fair-haired with pale skin.

"One of the people who helped raise me was an older Moroi woman. She was always kind to me. Some of the others were distant, but Selia would read me a story every night." His lips curved into a soft smile. "Pretty sure she made up most of them on the spot, because they didn't always make sense, but it was something I looked forward to every night before falling asleep."

"My parents would tell me stories too," I said. "It was nice. I'm glad you had someone like Selia in your life."

Draven's smile died, and I nearly wept at the loss because I knew I wouldn't like what was to come.

"When I was eight, my mother came for one of her visits. She had this . . . maniacal smile on her face." Draven shuddered beneath me and gripped my hand tighter. "When Selia arrived, my mother said we were going to play a game. . . and handed daggers to me and Selia."

Unease swirled in my gut. It didn't feel right to make Draven relive this. As if sensing my thoughts, Draven looked down at me. "It's okay. You need to know what the crown is capable of."

I nodded reluctantly. He was right, we did need to know, but that didn't stop me from feeling sorrow about what Draven had experienced at the hand of someone who should have done everything she could have to protect him.

"She told Selia to slit my throat," Draven said, the barest hint of sadness leaking into his voice. "She told me my options were to defend myself or allow myself to get slaughtered and that she didn't really care one way or another." A hand cupped my jaw, and I met Draven's stare. "I appreciate how murderous you look right now, Sam, but you cannot ever go after Velika. Promise me."

"I won't," I said evenly.

Draven narrowed his eyes. "You promise you won't go after her? Or you won't promise me anything of the sort?"

When all I did was smile at him, he swore and looked over my shoulder to Vail for support.

I glanced back just in time to see Vail shrug. "Trust me when I say it's impossible to get Samara to agree to anything she doesn't want to do."

I turned back to Draven, not saying anything to counter Vail's words because they were the truth. Velika's days were numbered. I may not be the person who ended her life, but I had no doubt I would play a hand in it all the same. The sooner the better.

Seeing the resolution on my face, Draven sighed and dropped his hand away, admitting defeat, at least for now. I had no doubt he'd do everything in his power to keep me away from Velika, not because he cared about his mother's life, but because he cared about mine.

"What happened?" I finally asked, knowing I wouldn't like the answer but needing to know regardless.

"Selia and I both refused to hurt the other, which was exactly what my mother had wanted. She'd wanted to test just how strong the abilities of the crown were."

"She waited all those years for a bond to form between the two of you," Vail said, stepping closer to me. I stepped back enough so I could see both men. The prince to my right and the Marshal to my left. "Selia likely loved you like her own child at that point. Velika wanted to find out if the soul crown's magic could override that."

"She placed that infernal crown on her head and ordered Selia to kill me, and it was like a switch went off in her mind." Draven squeezed his eyes shut. "The woman who had raised me and read me stories every night plunged a knife into my chest. The only reason I didn't die was because she didn't hit anything vital. I tried to fight her off, and in the process, I stabbed her in the throat. It was enough to get her off me, and I scrambled away, bleeding from my own wound while I watched her bleed out on the floor. Even while dying, she attempted to crawl across the room to get to me. To kill me."

"Drav," I rasped, not knowing what to say. He opened his eyes to look at me, and they were so hollow.

"Velika didn't stop there." Draven's hands clenched into fists at his sides. "A day later, I had a new caretaker. I was so traumatized about what had happened to Selia that I didn't even want to speak to this one. I thought maybe if my mother thought I didn't care about her, then she wouldn't do that again, but I severely underestimated her cruelty."

"You were eight years old," I said softly. "No child should understand that level of cruelty, or any cruelty for that matter."

"I learned very quickly." Draven's expression hardened. "By the time I was ten, I'd lost track of how many people she'd ordered to kill me, and I . . . started defending myself. Towards the end, I would attempt to slit their throats as soon as my mother walked in with that crown. Seemed like the least painful option for all of us."

"You did what you had to in order to survive," I argued. "All of these needless deaths lie at your mother's feet."

Draven shrugged. "Doesn't help with the screams I hear every time I sleep."

"Has she used the crown's magic on you?" I asked. "Is that why you serve her despite everything she's done to you?"

"That's part of the reason." The muscles along his jaw flexed as he clenched his teeth. "I can fight against it, but only for a short amount of time. Less than a minute usually, until the pain becomes too intense."

"Is there any way to block the magic? Or better your odds of fighting it?" Vail asked.

"The crown has to be worn for the actual binding, but after that, you have to obey her, crown or not. The binding does fade and has to be renewed occasionally." Draven's lips twisted into a grimace. "The House bloodlines seem to have a greater resistance to it."

"Why does it work on you then?" Vail voiced my question before I could.

"I'm not entirely sure, but I think it's because she's my mother and her blood is my blood," Draven said. "She hasn't exactly shared her thoughts about how the crown works, but I've been able to piece it together over the years." He swallowed before inhaling deeply. "For a while, she had someone of a House bloodline held captive and she tried to use the crown on them. She was frustrated by the results."

"Who?" I asked sharply. Someone from a House bloodline being killed or going missing would have been a big deal.

"Dominique's father didn't die in that attack," Draven said quietly.

"Oh fuck," I swore before shaking my head. "But they found the bodies!"

Draven looked away. "They found the bodies of her mother and sister . . . and part of her father's leg. Everyone assumed he'd been torn apart trying to keep his wife and daughter alive."

I rubbed my face. How was I going to tell Dominique that while she'd been grieving the loss of most of her family, her father had still been alive? Aniela had been close to him as well. Her own parents had died at a young age, and Dominique's had raised her after that. If they'd known he'd been alive, those two would have done anything to save him.

But they hadn't. So he'd died alone.

"What did *your mother* do to him?" Vail asked.

The muscles along Draven's jawline tensed at the reminder that the monster who was responsible for the death and torture of our own people was his own damn mother. I shot Vail a look that said to tone it down. It wasn't like Draven had a choice in who his parents were.

Vail's grey eyes darted to mine, and a crease formed between them before his lips flattened into a hard line and he returned his attention to the prince.

"She would spend hours working on him every day. Trying to bend his will to her own. Sometimes, she would force me to stand there and watch . . . Other times, she would order me to inflict physical pain on him to see if that would weaken his mind enough for her to seize control." Draven held Vail's heavy stare even as a hollowness entered his eyes. "He fought it with everything he had. Until his mind shattered and all that remained was bloodlust."

"You mean . . ." I stared at Draven in shock. The House bloodlines *did not* become Strigoi.

Draven gave me a pitying look.

"Fuck," I muttered "She can turn us Strigoi."

"What happened after he became Strigoi?" Vail pushed. I glanced back and forth between them, not understanding why Vail was being so hostile about this.

The prince raised his chin, defiance in his gaze as he focused on Vail. "I did what I hope anyone would do for me if I became a mindless killing machine under the complete control of Velika."

"You killed him."

"I saved him," Draven countered.

"Death isn't saving someone." Vail's eyes flashed silver.

Red bled into Draven's eyes, and for a moment, I thought he was going to go for Vail. I eased forward, ready to get between them, when the red vanished and Draven's charming prince mask fell back into place.

"You're right," he drawled. "I should have let Dominique see her father one last time. I'm sure she would have appreciated it right before he tore out her throat."

"Enough," I snapped. Both men looked away from each other. Something was bothering Vail, even more so than usual, but I didn't understand what. Everything that had happened to the former head of House Salvatore was fucked up, but it hadn't been Draven's fault. And Draven was right, killing him had been a mercy.

None of us would want to live on as Strigoi, especially ones that could be used as weapons against our families.

A thought occurred to me. The wraiths might have been behind the attack, but someone would have had to take Dominique's father back to the Sovereign House and help keep him under control.

"Are all the rangers who serve the Sovereign House blood-bound to Velika? Or are they aware of what she's doing and serve her anyway?" I rasped.

Each House had their own rangers whose fealty they claimed. But there was also a loyalty that all rangers had for each other because they spent so much time in the wilds, more so than most Moroi. It was common for units from different Houses to team up together for missions.

It wasn't just Dominique's family that had been killed in that attack. All the rangers traveling with them had perished as well. For the Sovereign rangers to see that carnage and continue to serve Velika . . .

"The Sovereign Marshal and most of the high-ranking rangers know what Velika is up to and support her. I'm sure they're blood-bound to her as well because my mother is not a trusting person. Not after—" Draven winced as his words were cut off. "The crown cannot compel loyalty or emotion. Its effects are temporary although I think how long it lasts varies per person based on how strong-willed they are or how much magic runs through their veins. I suspect that will change if she gets her hands on the other half of the crown."

"So you are not under her control right now?" I asked.

"No." Frustration flared in his eyes. "*Her* control of me is tenuous and really only works if she's physically near."

"Then why haven't you run?" I half shouted. "Just don't go back! We can find the other half of the crown before she does and keep it out of her reach, then we'll figure out a way to take her down. You can be free of her once and for all." Draven remained silent during my outburst, which only increased my anger. "What else, Draven? What else are you hiding?"

He flinched. My beautiful and wicked prince *flinched*.

"You think I haven't run away before? The wraiths can always find me and drag me back, and then I'm punished for my insolence," he said with a grim acceptance that made me want to shake him. "My usefulness is running out. I thought maybe . . ." He looked away from me again and out the window. "She knows you were investigating the wraith outposts and wants you under her control. Since you're a Harker, she won't be able to use the crown on you. I thought that if you agreed to marry me, it would appease her, and between the two of us, we could protect Kieran. It would have bought us a little more time."

"Time for what?"

"To get out of Lunaria."

"There is no getting out of Lunaria, Drav." I shook my head. "The ocean surrounds us on all sides, and we have no means to build a boat that can travel far."

Attempts had been made, but enormous sea monsters dominated the waters off the shores. I didn't even know if it was possible to build a boat that was capable of withstanding their attacks. It didn't matter though since that was far outside of our capabilities. There was also the problem of us not knowing what lay beyond Lunaria. Who knew how long we would have to sail for before we reached land again?

"There is no stopping what's going to befall Lunaria," Draven argued. "You and Kier have to get out."

"What about you?"

"Like I said, the wraiths will always find me, and they won't let me go. I've already accepted that my days are numbered."

"Well, I don't!" I hissed and gripped his face in my hands. "And I'm pretty sure Kieran doesn't either!"

"Personally, I'm fine with it," Vail said calmly.

Draven laughed under his breath as he pulled away from me.

I glared at Vail, but he just gave me a dispassionate look. "He's still our enemy, an unwilling one, but an enemy all the same. He already knows too much. We should kill him now, and if he cares about you as much as he claims, he'd do it himself."

"Absolut—" I started, but Vail cut me off, his calculating eyes falling on Draven.

"The Moroi Queen can command you to answer her, can she not? Which means anything you know, she will know."

"Yes," Draven admitted, his expression shuttered. "I've gotten good at dodging her questions and answering as vaguely as possible. Sometimes there is enough wiggle room to mislead her, but if she suspects I'm hiding something, she'll continue to question me until I give her what she wants, and she definitely knows I'm hiding something when it comes to Samara."

I thought about how Draven had practically raced to House Harker after the temple incident.

"You knew it was us in the badlands," I said slowly. "You haven't returned to the Sovereign House because Velika will question you as soon as you do."

"She's not particularly happy with me at the moment," he said tightly. "I received a letter ordering me to bring you to her."

A low growl rumbled from Vail, but he stayed where he was against the wall. We both knew Draven had had plenty of opportunities to snatch me and return me to the Sovereign House, yet he hadn't.

"I can ignore her written orders, but I cannot go against any commands she gives me in person. If she told me to kill you, I'd fight it with everything inside me, but it wouldn't be enough. Eventually, my mind would snap the way Dominique's father's did. I would become a Strigoi—one who was completely in her control."

My blood ran cold at the thought of Draven becoming a mindless Strigoi. I refused to let that happen.

"I wish you had just told us all this at the start," I said softly. "You know we'll help you."

"That's partly why I didn't tell you. I didn't want you to waste time trying to keep me alive when you should be focusing on yourself and Kieran." He paused, eyes flicking to Vail. "And the others you care about. I might be a lost cause, but they're not."

"You don't get to tell me who I deem worth protecting, Prince," I said steadily, raising my chin a little.

"Apologies, Heir." He didn't look the least bit sorry. "There is also a lot I can't tell you, and I realize all you have is my word on that. I wasn't sure if you would believe me."

"I still don't believe you," Vail's grumbled.

"And I still doubt your loyalty to Samara." Red lines wound their way through Draven's eyes again, clashing against the deep blue as he cocked his head at the other male. "I would have preferred to share her with only Kieran. Alaric and Roth, I will tolerate, but her interest in you is the first time I've truly questioned her judgment."

"Technically, I'm not with either of you yet," I said lightly. "And if you keep up the possessive bullshit, it might stay that way."

Draven's piercing gaze landed on me, and my heart skipped a beat as more red bled into his eyes. "Want to bet I can change your mind, love? Tell me you haven't thought about being between me and Kieran. How much we'd make you scream."

"Too late." I gave him a breezy smile. "He and Alaric already did a good job of that, and Roth has some . . . interesting ideas for when I return. It seems I don't really need any more lovers. I'm more than satisfied as it is."

"That a challenge?" He arched an eyebrow at me, and I arched one back.

"Do you want it to be?"

Draven looked out the window to the lightening sky and then at Vail. "How much time do we have before the next part of your scheme comes into play?"

Silver eyes met red ones. Confliction flashed across Vail's face before he answered. "Thirty minutes."

"That's not nearly enough time." Draven prowled towards me, and suddenly I felt very much like prey. "But I'll make it work."

The whip at his waist uncoiled and wrapped around my wrists before I could react. I exhaled sharply as it yanked my arms above my head and held them there. I looked at where the end of the whip had wound itself around the beams running across the ceiling, then jolted at finding Draven in front of me.

"Not only do we not have time for this . . ." I fought to keep my voice even. "But we were discussing how to keep you safe." My words probably would have been more convincing if they hadn't come out so breathy.

I shivered as he trailed a sharp claw along my collarbone.

"It's Lunaria. Any of us could die at any moment, so we have to seize any opportunity we can, even the inopportune ones." Draven kept his eyes on mine as he tugged at the lacing that ran down the front of my tunic. "Perhaps after I've felt you come on my tongue, I'll be feeling more motivated to stay alive."

I opened my mouth to argue, but Draven captured it with his. There was nothing tender or coaxing about it. This kiss was demanding and possessive. I clicked my teeth shut, refusing to let him in, but his fingers finished unlacing the tunic. A second later, he'd tugged my shirt down, unhooked my chest band, and he circled my nipple with a claw. My lips parted in a gasp, and his tongue darted in.

Any remaining protests I had fled as his kiss seared me.

I kissed him back, my tongue playing with his, and I wished I could wrap my arms around him. Feel his hard muscles beneath my fingertips. He laughed darkly against my lips when I tugged hard on the whip.

"You were right earlier when you called me possessive, but that doesn't mean I don't know how to share." Draven spun me around so my back was to him, and I met Vail's heated stare from where he still stood across the room, watching. Draven kissed my neck before whispering into my ear, "Let's find out just how much the Marshal and I can make you scream."

CHAPTER TWENTY-SIX

—

Draven

THIS HAD BEEN A BAD IDEA, but the rational side of me had fled the minute Samara had taunted me with Kieran and Alaric fucking her together. I'd known she'd been with them in that way ever since she'd walked into the room where the Heirs had been waiting—with Alaric's and Kieran's scents woven around her. More than one night, I'd woken up with a raging hard-on because I'd been dreaming about Samara writhing between me and Kier.

Or Kier taking her while I took him.

My dick hardened further against my pants. Samara thought she could save me, and I loved her even more for it. It helped me make peace with the fact that I likely wouldn't survive the day. If the Moroi Queen got ahold of me, she would yank out every thought from my head before killing me or, worse, turning me into one of her mindless Strigoi hunters.

This might be my only chance to be with Samara, and I wouldn't fucking waste it. It was selfish of me, but I would take this moment, however short it was, and enjoy every second.

I would have preferred to have her all to myself, but if I told Vail to leave, he would have refused. The Marshal was still standing across the room, unmoving, focused entirely on Samara. I almost felt bad for him. Conflict was etched all over his face. Whatever had happened between the two of them was complicated, and he was clearly still hung up about it.

Not my problem. He could stay or he could go. Didn't matter to me.

My only concern was making Samara scream my name until she forgot about every single one of her worries. We would both get our moment of peace before reality crashed back in.

"Drav," she breathed out and pulled harder on the whip binding her arms above her head.

I nipped her neck, and she let out a hiss of pleasure. "Yes?" My hands trailed down her breasts to unlace her pants and tug them down her legs, but annoyance flickered through me when I couldn't get them over her boots. I wished we were already naked in that pool Kieran and I had used, that would have made this much easier.

"You're taking too long," Vail growled.

"You could help." I shot him an annoyed look.

"We shouldn't . . ." Samara's protest trailed off when Vail stalked over to us. For a second, I thought he was going to attempt to cut through my whips, and I readied myself to lash out at him. He would not ruin this for me. Not when he likely had his whole life ahead of him.

One with Samara, if he wanted it.

But instead, he knelt on her other side and yanked one of her boots off before glaring at me and dropping his eyes pointedly to her other booted foot still in my hands. "We have less than thirty minutes, which means this is going to be rough and fast. You're wasting time."

Samara inhaled sharply as I pulled off her remaining boot and helped Vail take off her pants and undergarments until she was standing in only her shirt that I'd pulled down to expose her full breasts. I took a step back to admire her. Some people might have shied away from being mostly naked and bound like this, but Samara just arched an eyebrow at me like she was still in control of this situation.

The fabric was bunched up beneath her breasts, and I wanted nothing more than to bury my face between them. Choices, choices.

"Thirty minutes," Vail reminded me. I glanced at him and saw his gaze was locked on her tits as well.

"Limited time." I glided around her, my eyes drinking in every inch of her glorious curves. Then I gripped her plump, luscious ass that I'd always wanted to bite. "And limited resources."

Vail moved to her front, and his hand disappeared between her thighs, causing her back to hit my chest as she let out a gasp. I laughed and reached around to cup her full, heavy breasts while Vail finger-fucked her. "Are you ready to scream now?"

"N-no." Samara shook her head stubbornly. "Kieran . . . and Alaric . . . did it better."

Then she moaned as I pinched her nipples and chuckled darkly. "Sadly, I don't have any oil with me, and we don't have time to prepare you. Otherwise, I would fuck this glorious ass of yours and watch it bounce while Vail buried himself between your thighs."

"Alaric has already claimed my ass," she panted and looked over her shoulder to give me a cheeky grin.

Samara yelped as my fingers wound around her long braid and sharply yanked her head back. "I don't want to hear his name on your lips again while my hands are on you."

"For once, I agree with the prince," Vail growled, then he did something with his fingers to make Samara let out a strangled moan, and I kissed her exposed neck when her head slammed against my shoulder. It wasn't fair that I only had this short amount of time with her. I wanted so much more.

I licked her neck before letting my fangs graze her skin. Life wasn't fair. I knew that better than anyone, so I would take what was offered.

"Is she wet enough for you to fuck, Vail?" I alternated between kissing and nipping Samara's neck, enjoying the little mewling sounds she was making from our attention.

Vail raised his hand from between her thighs, and his fingers glistened with slickness. "She's fucking dripping."

"Perfect." I looped my hands under her thighs and pulled them up until her feet were off the ground and her legs were spread wide. "Don't hold back."

"Oh fuck," Samara whimpered as she pushed further into me. Between my whip holding her arms and me bracing her body and holding her thighs, she was completely at our mercy.

"You okay, love?" I asked her quietly. Everything I picked up from her body said she was into this, but I needed to hear her say it.

"Yes," she breathed out before turning her head to give me a quick kiss. "I trust you, and him."

I wanted to tell her that I loved her. That I had for years and that she and Kieran mattered more to me than anything else, but it wouldn't be right because I couldn't give her a future. All I could give her was mind-numbing pleasure and a hope that Vail and the others would keep her safe when I couldn't.

As much as I wished I were sharing this moment with Kieran, I had to admit that Vail's intensity was turning me on. He gripped Samara's thighs right below my hands and tugged her closer to him, then she screamed as he impaled her with his cock and started fucking her hard. There was no hesitation and no easing into it to let her adjust to him.

Despite bracing myself for it, I still rocked back as she slammed into me, and I laughed as I held her tightly, loving the way she felt between us. With Vail supporting some of her weight, I slipped my right hand between them and started toying with her clit.

"Oh fuck!" Sam cried out, followed by a torrent of words in the Fae languages and something else I didn't recognize. Then her head fell back against my shoulder, exposing her throat to me, and I didn't hesitate before biting down on the tempting flesh.

Vail growled, clearly not liking me tasting her blood, but I didn't give a shit.

I'd wanted to know what she tasted like for too fucking long, and moonsdamn it all, she was divine.

Her rich, spicy blood splashed across my tongue, and I lost myself in the flavor of it, only vaguely aware of Vail pulling her legs away from me so she could wrap them around him. Samara leaned further into me at more of an angle now, and my free hand drifted back to one of her breasts, squeezing it hard at the same moment I pushed down harder on her clit.

"Fuck," Vail cursed, and I had no doubt Samara's pussy had just clamped down on his cock. His thrusts gained a new, vicious edge, and based on the breathy way she was whimpering his name between moans, I knew she was enjoying every second of it. I didn't fully understand what it was between them, other than knowing it was different and more complicated than what she had with the other three, but whatever existed between Vail and Samara was clearly intense.

The scent of more blood filled the air as Vail roared, slamming into Samara one last time. She trembled against me, chest heaving as waves of pleasure rolled through her body.

"Not done yet, love." I chuckled and wrapped my arms around her waist before pulling her off Vail's dick, forcing him to release his claws from where they'd dug into her thick thighs. He stumbled back with a glazed-over expression, and I commanded my whip to unwind from Samara's wrists. Her legs instantly gave out, but I was prepared and tugged her towards me, settling us both on the ground on top of the blanket she'd been resting on earlier with her straddling me.

I held her above me, lowering her just enough to press the broad head of my cock against her pussy that was drenched with her and Vail's arousal. She let out another one of those breathy moans while I groaned at the wet heat that dripped down my cock. "Ready to scream more, Heir?"

"I doubt," she panted and squeezed her legs on either side of me, "that you can outdo—oh fuck." She gasped as I pulled her down so that she took a few more inches of me.

It took every ounce of my control not to yank her the rest of the way down until my cock was buried deep inside her and covered in her come. Based on how those dark purple eyes were glaring down at me, that's what she wanted to.

But if she was going to be a brat about it, then I'd make her wait for it.

"What was that?" I raised her up until I almost slid out before pivoting my hips up in a shallow thrust.

She tried to sink down on my cock but I held her firmly up and dropped my hips back to the ground. A growl slipped from her lips and I grinned. "Use your words, Sam. What were you saying?"

"I think," Vail said, appearing beside us, his dick already hard again as he gripped Samara's hair, tugging her back so that she had to look up at him, "that she doesn't think you can make her scream more than I did."

"Hmm." I dug my fingers into her hips. "Is that so, Sam?"

Vail loosened his hold enough so that she could look back down at me. Her lips curled in a defiant smile. "I'm feeling pretty satisfied, I don't think I have anymore screams left in me."

"Let's find out." I glanced at Vail. "If she gets too loud, I'm sure you can find some way to occupy her mouth."

"I'll think of something." He stroked his hard length, and Samara licked her lips, but with Vail's grip on her hair, she couldn't take him in her mouth until he wanted her to.

I seized her moment of distraction and pulled her down while slamming my hips upward. Samara's resolve not to scream broke as I bottomed out inside her. My own control snapped at finally feeling her tight pussy around my cock.

Over and over, I thrust up, hard and fast. My fingers dug into her waist, keeping her pinned on top, while I kept the brutal pace. She let out another strangled scream as I pumped in and out of her making her take every inch of me.

"Play with your clit," I ordered, and Sam's fingers immediately snapped down to fuck herself.

More words in all sorts of languages poured from her lips as her eyes rolled back. "Look at me," Vail commanded, and Sam whimpered as she looked up at him. Then he pushed his thick cock against her lips and she obediently opened them.

My balls tightened as I watched him slowly slide in and out of her mouth to let her adjust before tightening his hold on her hair and shoving himself all the way in. Sam gagged as he hit the back of her throat but leaned into him as she eagerly swallowed his cock again and again.

I imagined what it would feel like to have her lips wrapped around my cock like that. To have her choking on me and I let out a low groan as I felt my climax building. Vail continued to fuck her mouth roughly and tears streamed down her face even as she ground her hips against me forcing me to take her even deeper.

Fuck. I squeezed my eyes shut, enjoying the feeling of Samara riding me hard while listening to her slurp down Vail's cock. I wanted this to last longer but even if we weren't running out of time, it was too much. Samara's pussy was too fucking perfect and I had wanted this for too damn long.

My eyes shot open and I took in Samara writhing above me. It was enough to tip me over the edge.

"Scream for us, Heir!" My nails shifted to claws and bit into the flesh just above Vail's marks, heat exploding in her soaking wet cunt as I came hard, filling her with my seed until it gushed out. Vail yanked her off his dick so Samara could scream while he came all over her tits.

There was no force in this world that could have made me look away from her face as she unraveled between us. Vail sank to his knees next to us and pulled Sam to him, claiming her mouth with his. Then, to my surprise, he gently pushed her towards me.

Samara collapsed happily on my chest and kissed me deeply, and I ran my fingers down her back as aftershocks of pleasure made her tremble.

Worth it. Absolutely worth it.

Vail rose—albeit a little shakily—and grabbed three of the clean tunics stacked on a shelf against the wall. The Velesians tended to leave clothes scattered all over the place since they never knew when they'd have to shift. Vail pulled the canteen from his pack and poured a little water over the tunics before passing two to me, keeping one to clean himself off.

"I'm going to check outside." He got dressed and gave Samara a pointed look. "We'll have company soon. Be ready to leave."

Without me, because whatever they were doing, it was better if I wasn't a part of it. My plan to marry Samara and keep her safe that way was no longer viable. My mother was plotting something, and whatever it was, Samara needed to be kept away from her. It killed me to admit it, but at this point, I was putting Samara in more danger with my presence, especially since I'd killed some wraiths.

I had no doubt Erendriel knew of my betrayal by now. If he came for me personally, I was fucked.

"Not one for pillow talk, is he?"

Sam laughed, and I automatically tightened my arms around her. Fuck, I loved that sound, even more than her screams of pleasure.

"This is only the second time Vail and I have done anything," she admitted. "And the first time was last night, or I guess early this morning, and wasn't quite so . . . intense. So I can't really speak to his pillow talk habits yet."

"But you want to?" I asked. "Be able to talk to his pillow talk tendencies?"

She fell silent while she thought about it before raising her head to look at me. I loosened my arms so she could do so, immediately missing the feel of her against me.

"Yes." She tilted her head and kept her expression carefully neutral. "Would that bother you? Knowing I want him and the others? As well as you?"

I reached up and tucked a loose strand of hair behind her ear. Technically, the question was irrelevant since I wouldn't be part of this future Samara was already thinking about, but I answered her honestly anyway, allowing myself the delusion for just a moment longer. "No. There might be days when I want to steal you away from everyone else and keep you to myself, or maybe myself and Kieran." I grinned. "But as long as the others love you as I do, then I'm happy you have them in your life."

Her eyes widened. "Drav, I—"

"You don't have to say it back," I cut her off. "I just wanted you to know."

Truthfully, I didn't think Sam loved me yet. How could she? I'd hidden so much from her, and while we'd always been friendly towards each other, up until recently, I hadn't allowed it to go any further. But if she did feel that way . . . and if she did say it . . .

I wouldn't be able to walk away, and that was too dangerous an option to pursue.

"I'll wait here while the two of you do whatever you came here to do." It was a lie. As soon as Samara left, I was going to run far away from her. A plan had already begun to form in my head. My mother would want me, but Erendriel would be pissed about the wraiths. There was a good chance he'd tell them to chase me rather than pursue Samara. Maybe I could lead them away and buy her a little more time.

The question was where to go. I was good at fighting wraiths one-on-one, but now that they knew I'd turned on them, they'd be more careful. I needed to run, go somewhere they'd have a harder time getting to me. The Furies were my best bet. Something about them made even Erendriel wary.

I hadn't gone to them originally because they probably would have laughed in my face and then thrown me out of their realm, but Cali loved Samara and would do whatever she had to in order to keep her friend safe. She'd protect me.

Or kill me if she determined that was the best way to keep Samara safe. I'd have to be very fast about my explanations.

Samara leaned into my touch as I trailed my fingers down her neck and chest until they rested over her heart, which beat strong and steady beneath my hand. I wished I'd had more time with her and Kieran, but this would have to be enough.

I breathed in her scent, which always reminded me of the spicy night blossoms of the plants that grew along the southern coastline. Reluctantly, she pulled away, and I let her go, watching silently as she cleaned herself up as best she could before getting dressed. There was nowhere for her to rinse off, and I reveled in the knowledge that she would smell like me all day.

And Vail, but I decided to not let that bother me.

Samara quickly rebraided her hair and tucked her throwing daggers into the thigh sheaths. By the time she was done, I'd already gotten dressed, my whip once again coiled at my hip.

"We'll be back soon." She cupped my cheek, and I closed my eyes to enjoy the feeling. "I think we might find something that can help you. Even if we don't, I will find a way to keep you safe. Promise you will wait here? Promise me, Drav?"

I opened my eyes and met hers. They were the perfect color of twilight, and I saw how much she believed her own words. The lie rolled off my lips, even as it felt like someone had stabbed my heart. "I promise."

CHAPTER TWENTY-SEVEN

—

Samara

I LOOKED at the cabin one last time before setting off to find Vail. It was a little surprising he had wandered so far away . . . and that Rynn wasn't here yet. Maybe it had just taken her longer than she'd anticipated to slip away without being noticed. I shook my head as I tried to focus my thoughts. They were still reeling from what had happened between me, Draven, and Vail in the cabin, but I needed to pay attention to the task at hand, and that meant bottling up my jumbled mess of emotions and tucking them away to be dealt with later. There were too many people counting on me.

I would not fail them.

Draven didn't believe I could save him. That was fine. I'd just have to prove him wrong. This wouldn't take longer than a few hours, and then I'd be able to return to him. I'd told him to stay inside to avoid running into any Velesians, who may not be too happy about the Moroi Prince coming unannounced into their realm. Hopefully none of them tried to use the cabin today. He'd assured me they wouldn't be able to pick up his scent from outside, which had only led to questions on my end, but I hadn't bothered voicing them.

He was still hiding things from me, and whatever strange magic he had was definitely one of them. Logically, I knew I shouldn't trust him, but my heart said otherwise.

Just as I started to step over a fallen log, my instincts screamed at me that I was no longer alone.

A broad hand covered my mouth and another clamped around my waist, pulling me against a hard body. Panic seized me, and I struggled for several seconds before recognizing Vail's scent.

"Quiet," he whispered faintly in my ear. "The Velesians are here."

Slowly, he dropped his hands and beckoned me forward, further into the forest and away from the cabin where Draven hid.

"Velesians." As in more than one. Rynn was supposed to have come alone.

Something had gone very wrong.

Vail and I quietly made our way through the woods. I was a little disoriented, but I was pretty sure we were headed back the way we'd come, which meant we were going away from Lake Malov. Not ideal, but what mattered more was staying undetected.

Maybe we could backtrack and then make our way around them to the lake? I also needed to find out what had happened to Rynn. Given her status with the Alpha Pack, I knew she wouldn't have been hurt, but maybe they had detained her somewhere.

Fuck, this was already turning into a political nightmare, and we didn't even know if it was worth it yet.

A low, rumbling growl caused us to stop dead in our tracks before a familiar, sleek, black form dropped from the branches above us, blocking our path ahead. The panther surveyed us with its cunning, green eyes.

Hello, Bastian.

Also. Fuck. Me.

All the Velesians were deadly in their own way. The ailuranthropes—usually just called ailurans or panthers—weren't the biggest. Both ursanthropes —bear shifters—and lycanthropes—wolf shifters—were larger than them, but the ailurans were the fastest, and their feline bodies allowed more flexibility in a fight.

I'd never actually seen Bastian fight, but I had no doubt he would be vicious. And he was no doubt very pissed off at us right now.

Vail shoved me behind him but didn't draw the sword strapped across his back. Instead, his hand hovered near the large dagger on his hip. He understood the situation just as well as I did. We were on Velesian land without permission. If we killed one of them . . . the fragile alliance between our people would shatter.

And it would be all our fault.

"I can explain." I stepped around Vail with my hands held out to my sides and dodged his hand when he tried to make a grab for me. The panther's ears flattened back against his head before releasing a high-pitched snarl, and Vail pulled his dagger free. "Let's just calm down," I said frantically. "This is all just a misunders—"

Bastian let out a startled cry as a large, white wolf plowed into his side. The ailuran went flying, his body slamming into a thick tree trunk with a resounding *crack*. Several green vines immediately shot forward, clearly thinking they had just found their next meal. They wrapped around the unconscious beast as the bark down the center of the trunk started to split apart, revealing a dark, cavernous mouth.

"Damn it, Rynn!" I hissed and lunged forward to cut the panther free. Vail joined me a second later, and between the two of us, we managed to free and drag Bastian a safe distance away from the apparently carnivorous tree. I eyed the other trees suspiciously but couldn't tell if they shared the same food tastes.

Fucking Velesian forests.

Bastian wouldn't be unconscious for long. Velesians healed the slowest out of all the Moon Blessed, but they could still heal from just about anything, and unlike the Moroi, they didn't need spells or blood to do it. We needed to figure out a plan to fix this mess. Fast.

"Change back." I glared at the white wolf, whose back was higher than my waistline. Granted, I wasn't that tall, but Rynn's wolf form was massive. She exhaled sharply before turning away from me, a clear dismissal, and I fought the urge to strangle her.

I'd had everything under control before she'd decided to come barreling in. Mostly under control. Well, I'd possibly had things under control.

It wasn't like we could just leave. Bastian would wake up any minute now, and he would absolutely track us. It was hard enough to avoid the Velesians when they didn't know about our presence. We had zero chance of outrunning Bastian in these woods. Not to mention he would report this to Cade, and then we'd have the might of the Alpha Pack falling down on us.

Rynn's involvement only further complicated things.

"Fuck, I wish Kieran were here," I muttered and rubbed my face. Kier had a real talent for smoothing things over.

"It's good he's not," a deep voice drawled. Vail and I whirled around, Rynn somehow already between us and the enormous man who had managed to sneak up on us.

"We like Kieran," another voice rasped from behind us, forcing us to turn so we could keep both Velesians in our sights. "It'd be a shame to have to kill him along with you."

Rynn had been eying the first man warily, but she full-on growled at the second, aggression radiating off her. He cocked his head in a very wolflike gesture, a bright sheen rolling over his crystal blue eyes.

"Ryker," I said evenly to the man Rynn was snarling at in a way I'd never seen her do to anyone before. Then my gaze slid to the larger man. "Cade."

I didn't know Ryker all that well, but Cade I'd met fairly regularly, since he spoke for all the Velesians. He was quite possibly the only person I'd ever met who towered over Vail. He had to be at least six and a half feet tall, and it wouldn't have surprised me if he had to twist his ridiculously broad frame just to fit through doorways. Usually, his light brown eyes were calm, sometimes even welcoming if he was in a particularly good mood.

Today, they were cold and predatory.

"You shouldn't have come here, Samara," Cade said in a chillingly calm voice. "And you definitely shouldn't have attacked Bastian after that shit you pulled at the human settlement."

Guess that answered the question of whether Bastian had tattled on us to Cade. I never doubted he would, just hoped that maybe he hadn't had time to do it yet.

"We had our reasons." I glanced at the panther and then back at Cade. "You know me, and you know Vail. Trust that we wouldn't do anything to jeopardize our relationship with the Velesians, and definitely not with the Alpha Pack."

"If you wanted our trust, you shouldn't have kicked Bastian out of your lands." He shrugged. "And definitely shouldn't have snuck into ours. Your pretty face and words aren't going to get you out of this one."

"Think carefully about what you say next." Vail slid the long, curved dagger free from his hip.

Cade smiled. "Looks like we might get that fight we've been spoiling for all these years after all." He took a step forward, a blade similar to Vail's appearing in his right hand before a raspy growl sounded from Ryker as tension bled through the air.

"STOP!" Rynn barked, her chest still heaving from shifting to her human form. "They're here at my invitation." She raised her chin high, exuding authority despite standing there naked while surrounded by males who towered over her. "As a member of the Alpha Pack, it is within my right to invite others into our territory. Bastian was interfering, and I was merely putting him in his place."

"Funny." Cade gave Rynn a flat look. "Only a couple of hours ago, you were telling me to take my pack and shove it up my ass."

"You must have misheard on account of your thick skull."

What in the actual fuck had gotten into my mild-tempered friend?

Ryker's growling gained an even more vicious edge, but Rynn paid him no mind, despite her back being to him. The insult was clear, and I raised my brows at the brazenness of my friend. She had definitely been leaving out a lot of information on how things were going with her and the Alpha Pack. We'd be having words about this later once we were alone.

Her mismatched eyes, one golden brown and the other a deep, vivid blue, slid to mine, and she pressed her lips into a hard line. Yeah, she knew I'd be grilling her about this later.

The growling abruptly cut off, and I looked away from Rynn to see Cade staring at Ryker, some unspoken communication passing between them. Ryker's lip curled in distaste before he tugged off his shirt and threw it at Rynn. She snarled, but he was already turning away and shucking off the rest of his clothing. Velesians rarely wore boots, as they preferred to stay in contact with the earth. A second after his clothes hit the ground, an enormous wolf with a grey coat flecked with white burst free from the cage of human skin.

Then he darted into the forest without another glance at any of us as Rynn stared after him with a predatory focus before pulling his shirt on with jerky movements.

"*Rynn.*" Cade sank so much dominance into that one word that Rynn's head snapped towards him, almost of its own accord, and he smiled at the venom in her gaze. "Ryker's going to make sure we're not disturbed, and you are going to explain what the fuck is going on here."

"Is that an order?" she asked cooly, not looking away from the alpha stare she was on the receiving end of.

"Does it need to be?" Cade crossed his arms, making his biceps bulge.

Rynn's upper lip trembled in a snarl as she glared at Cade.

"Okaaay." I drew out the word and grabbed Rynn's arm, tugging her away. "We're gonna need a minute."

"I didn't say you could leave," Cade said in a low, threatening tone.

"And I don't give a shit," I snapped. "I need to speak with my friend. Once I've done that, we'll talk and get this all figured out." Bastian started to stir on the ground, and I glanced at Vail. "Why don't you help Cade check on the overeager pussycat."

"Both of you really try my patience," Cade grumbled and moved towards the ailuran, who had managed to shake his head and was blinking blearily at the world. Vail nodded at me. He'd keep them away from me and Rynn while we talked. Velesian hearing was very sharp, but if we kept our voices low, it'd be fine.

Neither of us said anything as I pulled Rynn through the woods. When I was confident we were a good enough distance away to not be overheard, I stopped. She immediately pulled her arm free and fixed her features into the stubborn look I knew so well. It was the one that said she knew what she was doing, she was absolutely in the right, and the rest of us were idiots for not realizing it.

So I did what I'd done every time she'd gotten into this mood while we'd been at Drudonia. I reached out and flicked her on the nose. Hard.

"Fuck off, Sam!" She rubbed her nose and glared at me.

"What in all the moonsdamned fuck is going on?" I mimicked Cade's stance from earlier and crossed my arms. Unfortunately, my biceps were nowhere near as intimidating as his. "Last I checked, you were worried the Alpha Pack didn't want you anymore because you hadn't been able to go to them right away." Rynn's mother had passed away last year. They'd had a strained relationship, but Rynn had still felt obligated to help her elderly mother in her final days. So she'd delayed leaving her pack to join the Alphas, but she'd *wanted* to go, and now she was looking at them like she wanted to rip their throats out.

Rynn's lips trembled, but it wasn't in a snarl this time. Tears welled in her eyes. "I'm being banished from the Order of Narchis."

"What?" My eyes widened.

She looked away as she tried to collect herself, tugging at Ryker's shirt. He was smaller than the rest of the Alphas, but it still drowned her lean frame, falling to mid-thigh. Tears rolled down her cheeks and dripped onto the shirt before she wiped the rest of them away.

"Remember last month when I went searching in Fervis territory?"

"You mean when I told you not to go there because if you got caught it would cause all kinds of problems?" Rynn raised her chin, still defiant despite the tears falling. "Let me guess." I sighed. "You got caught?"

She nodded miserably. "Aetanthrope scout spotted me. I should have known better, but there aren't many eagle shifters in the Order of Fervis."

I squeezed my eyes shut. Rynn *was* really good at sneaking around, but she got too cocky sometimes.

"What did they do?"

"Refused to release me back to the Narchis. They said I'd been promised to them before my pack changed its mind and made the deal with the Alphas. Claimed they were owed compensation. Cade sent Bastian and Ryker to *fetch* me." Her eyes sparked. "Bastian promised them I would be punished."

I was suddenly quite sure she hadn't slammed him into that tree hard enough. "The banishment is your punishment I take it?"

Rynn blinked away her tears as she fought to compose herself. It was strange seeing her cry. I wanted to hug her, but I knew she would have hated that. So instead, I pretended I couldn't see the wet streaks running down her cheeks or the way her eyes had reddened. Within a few minutes, she was back to her normal, cool and steady expression.

"They announced it this morning to everyone gathered." She looked back towards the trees we'd walked through, to where Cade and the others waited. "I'm to leave with them as soon as the meet is over. The agreement is that I'm forbidden from traveling through Narchis territory unless I'm in the company of one of them."

I took that to mean Cade, Bastian, or Ryker.

"And I can only go through Fervis territory if I get permission first—which they won't give." She looked back at me. "That leaves going through the neutral area of Drudonia my only option for getting to the Moroi realm, and Cade could easily tell the rangers who are posted in that area to not let me pass."

"He wouldn't do that," I said but couldn't hide the hesitation in my voice.

"I won't be able to see you, Sam." Panic flared in her eyes. "I'll be trapped in the fucking Alpha House, cut off from everyone I care about."

A low whine punctuated her words. All her life, all Rynn wanted was to belong to a pack that respected and loved her. The one she'd been born into had cared for her, but only as a political pawn to be traded. The Valatieris were one of the strongest Velesian bloodlines, and her uncle ruled the largest of the Narchis packs. Rynn was basically a shifter princess.

"Hey." I ran a hand through her shoulder-length, chestnut brown hair. "Do you really think they could keep me away from you?" I snorted. "Better question, do you really think they could keep Cali away?"

She huffed out a laugh. "No, but I wouldn't let either of you get into trouble for me."

"Oh, my sweet, sweet wolf." I shook my head at her. "You don't *let* us do anything. If the Alphas are going to treat you this way, then they don't deserve you. We'll get you away from them and give you the chance to find a pack of your own choosing."

"Sam, you ca—"

I flicked her on the nose again, and she let out a low growl.

"Trust me. Now"—I rubbed my hands together—"any ideas on how we get out of this current predicament? We need to get to Lake Malov and search for the crown."

She sighed. "As pissed off as I am at Cade and the other Alphas, I think we should tell them. We kind of have to at this point anyway if we want to search that area, and we might need their help down the road. They are a lot of things, but I don't think there is any chance of them being involved in this. Ryker's family was killed by wraiths, and he was taken in afterwards by Cade and Bastian. They would never ally with someone who was working with the wraiths."

"Let's hope you're right." I smiled brightly at Rynn. "On the plus side, if you're wrong and they are working with Erendriel and Velika, then we can just kill them and solve your little problem."

Rynn shot me a wolfish grin. "Always looking on the bright side."

"THIS IS EXACTLY why everyone hates the Moroi," Bastian said after I'd explained our situation. Most of it anyway—I'd left out anything involving Draven. "The rest of us are just trying to survive in this fucked-up land, and you bastards somehow find the time to discover cursed Fae artifacts and use them to enslave others."

The ailuran had been his human form when Rynn and I had returned, wearing a pair of loose-fitting pants and nothing else. It was too bad the Alphas were such assholes and I had a high probability of killing them in the future, because every single one of them was hot. Even with the feline disgust stamped all over his face, Bastian was gorgeous.

Standing next to Cade, who was more of a ruggedly handsome type, Bastian looked almost pretty. I thought it might be his eyes. Even in this form, his bright, emerald green eyes had vertically slit pupils, and something about that with the chiseled cheekbones and full lips made him captivatingly stunning.

"No need to drool, Samara." He finally noticed me outright staring at him and gave me a sinful grin. "I don't usually fuck Moroi, but I'll slum it in your case."

Vail growled, but I just batted my eyelashes at Bastian. "Actually, I was just thinking Rynn should maybe have a go with you before I slit your throat and feed you to that tree that tried to eat you earlier."

His grin got a little sharper.

"Not helping, Sam." Rynn sighed.

"Sorry, I got bored listening to him prattle on about how the Moroi are so awful and the Velesians are so perfect." I shrugged and then looked at Cade. He was the only one I needed to convince. "My mother believed the other half of the crown might be hidden near Lake Malov. We need to search that area."

"And if we find it?" Cade's fingers brushed the scar that ran from his ear down his jawline, the roughly healed, pale tissue standing out against his light brown skin. "If you think I'm letting you walk out of here with it, you're even more insane than I thought."

"Careful," Vail rumbled.

Cade glanced at Vail curiously, but it was Bastian who spoke. "For someone who got drunk with us on more than one occasion and talked about how you dreamed about killing the Harker Heir, it seems a little strange to find you defending her." His nostrils flared as he inhaled and tilted his head slightly. "Not to mention that we can still smell you all over each other. Pussy was that good, huh?"

Vail took a step forward, but I yanked him back, forcing Rynn to step to the side before I raised a brow at Bastian. "My pussy is, in fact, that good. Dream of me." Rynn laughed under her breath while I blew him a kiss before turning my attention to Cade. "It just so happens I agree about the crown. At this point, I don't know which Moroi are working with the Sovereign House. While I can vouch for myself and those close to me, we're also the ones most at risk of being captured."

"What do you propose?" Cade asked, his expression curious. He always was the most reasonable of the Alphas as long as we didn't push him too far.

"We destroy it," I said. "Something like that shouldn't exist to begin with."

Cade studied me for a long moment, and I fixed my features into a pleasant but neutral expression. Something told me he didn't buy it, but he glanced at

Rynn, and something passed in his eyes that I couldn't quite read. Once again, I wished Kieran were here. He was better than me at picking up subtle cues like this.

"Fine," Cade agreed. "We destroy it. But I want to see it destroyed with my own eyes."

"Wonderful." I dipped my chin in agreement. "Can we head to the lake now?"

"Of course. Follow me." He turned and set off through the woods. I looked over my shoulder in time to catch Bastian reaching out for Rynn's arm but yanking his hand away when she snarled at him. Then he stalked off after Cade and we followed after him.

I kept glancing around the woods for Ryker but didn't see him anywhere. Despite that, I was pretty sure the wolf was following us based on how Rynn's gaze kept drifting deeper into the woods.

We walked in uneasy silence for almost an hour before the forest finally ended and revealed Lake Malov. Even before I saw it, I knew we were close because of how tense all the Velesians got. If they'd been in their animal forms, I had no doubt the hair along their backs would have been raised.

It was interesting to me that I didn't feel anything. Vail didn't seem to either, although I'd ask him later to confirm. Whatever was going on with the lake, only the Velesians could feel it. And the Furies according to Cali.

Even though I didn't feel whatever Cali and the Velesians felt, I still found the lake disturbing. I was used to the turquoise waves that crashed against our beaches or the crystal clear waters of the lakes and rivers scattered throughout Lunaria.

Lake Malov was black. Impenetrable, inky darkness. Not even a ripple ran across the surface. It was like looking at glass.

I bumped my shoulder against Rynn's. "No wonder you always want to come to the Moroi Realm. Our lakes are way more enticing for swimming."

Cade looked over his shoulder. "You enjoy swimming?"

"Yes," Rynn said after a long moment.

"Hope you like swimming in frigid water," Bastian quipped. "Because the closest lake to our home is frozen for most of the year."

Rynn's brows furrowed, but before she could answer, Ryker appeared and rammed his shoulder into her as he walked past, wearing only a pair of loose-fitting pants. "Princess wouldn't lower herself to swimming in our lake."

Vail managed to grab Rynn just as she lunged for the lycanthrope. She twisted in his grasp and snarled in his face, but he just gave her a flat look in response. He'd spent plenty of time around Velesians and was used to their bullshit.

"Where should we start?" I asked, trying to break up the tension. "We could split up?"

"No." Cade shook his head. "We might run into some patrols, and it'll be easier to explain your presence if I'm with you. We'll start at the southern tip. Go up the west side and work our way around."

I nodded, and we continued on.

"Stop," I said softly after we'd been walking for less than five minutes. I could hardly believe it, but for once, luck was on our side. The feeling was so subtle, I'd almost walked right by it. "There's a lookaway spell here."

"What?" Rynn perked up, any resentment she felt towards the Alphas instantly forgotten as her academic mindset kicked in. "Where?"

Vail stepped up to my side as we both studied the edge of the lake. Several boulders rose up from the water, and there were several smaller ones on the shore, but none of them were the source. I walked forward a few feet and stopped, bending down to brush away the small greyish pebbles that made up the shoreline. A shiny, obsidian black stone greeted me, exactly like the ones we'd found at the human settlement. The kind that had been used centuries ago by the humans to turn us all into monsters.

"What does it say?" Rynn asked, crouching on the other side of Vail as we all studied the glyph that had been carved into the stone.

Based on how the ends of the symbol thinned out and twisted off sharply, it was an Unseelie glyph. My heart raced faster. My mother had been right. There was something here, and it had likely been hidden from everyone this whole time.

"Salvation." I swallowed. "It means salvation."

CHAPTER TWENTY-EIGHT

—

Samara

WE ALL WATCHED as I dripped some of my blood onto the glyph, the shallow cut on my arm instantly healing. The glyph carved into the black stone greedily drank in the offering until there was none left on the surface. The strange awareness I'd felt when we'd walked by grew stronger, like a humming in the back of my mind.

"I know this," I muttered. "Why do I know this?"

"Sam?" Rynn glanced up from the glyph to give me a puzzled look.

"It calls to me," I said softly. "I've never felt this way about any place in Lunaria."

"What does it feel like?" Cade asked.

"Belonging." I smiled as the feeling settled into my soul. This place was meant for me. I wondered if my mother would have felt the same way if she had found it. My smile slipped. Why did this place call to me . . . but drive everyone else away?

Before I could ponder that thought more, the dark, placid surface of the lake started to shiver, and we all took a step back as the water parted, revealing a set of stairs leading down.

"Holy shit," Rynn breathed out and took a step closer to study the quietly churning water held back by magic. "I can't believe a spell as complex as this still works after all this time."

"It must have been really important to the Fae to keep it hidden and protected." I frowned. How did Erendriel not know of this place? Or maybe he did know . . . but couldn't reach it? Rynn had said even the wraiths didn't come here. Had the Fae crafted this spell to specifically keep the wraiths away too?

"It doesn't make sense," I said aloud as I tried to figure out this puzzle.

488

"What?" Vail asked, watching me instead of studying the newly revealed hideout.

"Let's consider the order of events. The Unseelie and Seelie existed here together, the Seelie did something to themselves that turned them into wraiths, and during that same time, the Unseelie disappeared." My brows furrowed as I glanced back at the glyph and then to the hidden stairs. "So who crafted this spell to keep this place hidden? It clearly targets the wraiths, so it's not like the Seelie did it."

"Maybe the Unseelie did it before they vanished?" Bastian suggested. "We know there was some animosity between the Unseelie and the Seelie. This could have been one last fuck you to the Seelie."

"If that's the case, then this might be one of the last places the Unseelie were before they vanished." I still felt like there was some big piece we were missing from all of this, but maybe we'd find answers inside.

Rynn glanced over her shoulder at me from where she was standing close to the water and shrugged. "Only one way to find out."

"Do not move, Rynn," Cade ordered, but she ignored him and darted down the stairs. Ryker growled and stalked after her.

"I told you this was going to be a problem," Bastian told Cade, who was glowering at the dark passage where Rynn and Ryker had disappeared. I got the impression not many people disobeyed his orders.

"She'll fall in line," Cade said flatly.

I snorted. "You've had all this time to get to know her and yet you've failed spectacularly."

"Watch yourself, Moroi." For a second, Cade's tone gained a deeper edge, and I had to remind myself that, despite his usually calm demeanor, he could shift into a nearly two-thousand-pound bear at any moment. From a purely rational standpoint, that meant I should avoid pissing him off any further.

But he'd messed with my friend, so fuck that.

In a blink, I let my bloodlust rise and shifted my nails into claws. Cade didn't quite flinch when I suddenly appeared in front of him, but he did stiffen. The Velesians might be stronger than us and quite good at sneaking around, but the Moroi were still faster.

I tapped his chest with my index finger, right where his shirt parted to reveal warm, brown skin dusted with dark hair. Blood welled as my claw pierced his flesh with each tap. "Bite. Me."

Cade's nostrils flared, and Bastian laughed next to us. "Isn't that what Vail is for?" the ailuran drawled. "Or maybe whoever was hiding in that cabin?"

I killed the panic before it had a chance to show on my face and gave Bastian a bored look. "You need to get your senses checked, cat. It was just the two of us there. Or maybe you just don't know what a good fuckin' sounds like since you've never given anyone that kind of pleasure."

Bastian narrowed his eyes, but before he could open his mouth to likely say something smartassed, Cade pushed past us. "Come on. Let's go make sure those two haven't killed each other."

My money was on Rynn in that fight. I took a few steps towards the stairs and paused, biting my lower lip.

"Don't you want to see what's inside?" Vail asked, moving to stand beside me.

"Yes." I swallowed. "But this is what our parents died for. No matter what we find in there, it wasn't worth their lives, Vail."

"No." He slowly raised his arm and slipped it around my shoulders before pulling me against him. Somehow, this tentative hug felt more intimate than anything we'd done so far, including in the cabin. "But I think they'd be happy to know that we made it here. Together."

I sniffled and blinked back tears. "Don't tell me you're getting soft in your old age."

"I'm only three years older than you," he said dryly. When we pulled apart, he slipped his hand into mine. "Ready?"

"Yeah." I sucked in a breath. "Let's do this."

We walked hand in hand down the stairs, darkness quickly engulfing us. I had no problem seeing, but I was surprised they hadn't added Fae lanterns or something to light the way, especially considering how long we walked. A little claustrophobia started to set in when I thought about how far we were beneath the lake and all the water just lying above us . . . ready to crush in the walls.

"Samara?"

I realized my breath had started to quicken, and Vail was giving me a concerned look. "It's fine." I smiled faintly and took in a few steady breaths. "Just discovered yet another thing to be frightened of in Lunaria."

The corners of his mouth twitched before he swept his hand towards the open door in front of us. "We're here."

Light crept out into the hallway we were standing in from the brightly lit chamber.

Please let the crown be here, I thought as we swept into the room and paused. "Well, this feels familiar."

Rynn looked up from where she already had her nose buried in a large book. "It does?"

I nodded while looking at the walls lined with floor-to-ceiling shelves and the work tables in the center of the room. "We found a hidden room in that sea cave near House Harker." My eyes widened as I took in all the shelves *filled* with books. "But it was mostly empty. That's actually where we found the journals I told you about."

"Ah." Her eyes dropped down to the book in front of her. "I've barely scratched the surface of the knowledge in this room, but just from randomly selecting books off the shelves . . . these came from somewhere else. I think the Fae brought them from wherever they came from. Some of them are written in Unseelie and some in Seelie, but others are written in the common tongue."

"Really?" I moved to the table and started flipping through the book she was browsing. "You're right . . ." I turned more of the pages. On one side was a detailed illustration of a beast, and on the other were details about it. Size, location, behavior. It was a bestiary, but none of these creatures roamed Lunaria lands, and the language they were written in was like the one we spoke here but different. It was close enough that I could read it easily but not exactly the same. Maybe our language had descended from this one?

"Stop." Rynn's hand fell on mine when I went to turn the page.

A skeletal creature stared out at us from the page, its eyes far too large for its narrow face. The artist had drawn it with its mouth open, displaying fangs eerily similar to mine, but the rest of its teeth were sharp points as well. Its gangly arms ended in slender fingers, each tipped with a three-inch long claw.

Beneath the drawing was one word. *Vampyre.*

"'The vampyre have mostly been hunted to extinction, but there are still some populations left,'" I read aloud. "'In southern regions, they are often referred to as Moroi or Strigoi. Some locals in that area have managed to tame some of these creatures enough to be guardians of their towns, and they call them Moroi to distinguish them from their more vicious brethren, the Strigoi. Note: this practice has been largely abandoned due to instances of the Moroi turning on their masters.'"

"These are the creatures we're based on." My fingers traced the outline.

"I don't know how," Rynn said, "but I think the humans who crafted the spell to change themselves into the Moon Blessed read this book, or one like it."

Vail started searching the table next to us, and I knew I should be doing the same because we needed to find that damn crown, but I couldn't resist turning a few more pages. The library at Drudonia was quite large, but even they didn't have any books from outside Lunaria. Every bit of knowledge we'd managed to scrape together since the Fae had disappeared were from books and scrolls that had been written *here.*

This book, and potentially all the others in the room, could tell us so much about not only the history of the Fae but *our* history. I wanted more than anything to live in this room for the next year and not leave, but that wasn't an option. So I allowed myself a few more minutes.

"Huh." The section of the book I'd turned to had another page folded over the one containing the drawing. I carefully unfolded it and blinked when I had to unfold it again. "Wow."

Rynn and I stared at the enormous reptilian monster that took up three pages. Leathery wings were tucked against its scaly body, and a triangular head rested on a long neck, a crown of horns rising behind it.

We both tilted our heads as we tried to read the word beneath the sketch. It was one I wasn't familiar with, and I didn't know exactly how it should have been pronounced.

"Drakōn?" I guessed.

"It says here they're commonly referred to as *dragons*." Rynn frowned. "It's kind of weird that it doesn't have as much information about them as the other creatures. I wonder what they do," Rynn murmured.

"Hopefully we never find out. I don't ever want to fight anything that large." Reluctantly, I stepped away from the bestiary and started searching the room. Rynn did the same a few minutes later, choosing the part of the room that put her the furthest away from the Alphas.

For over an hour, we searched every inch of the room. We even carefully pulled the books from the shelves to check behind them. Nothing. No sign of the crown anywhere.

"It's not here," Ryker growled. "This was a waste of time."

"Seriously?" Rynn glowered at him and gestured towards the walls lined with books. "There is more knowledge in this one room than in all of Drudonia. Even if the crown isn't here, this knowledge is priceless."

The lycan scoffed. "It's knowledge of a place we've never been and will never go to. Nothing here is going to help you stay alive in Lunaria, Princess."

"I told you not to call me that," Rynn said in a low, threatening tone. "I'm sick of listening to your bullshit." A sheen rolled over her eyes as the wolf in her rose to the surface. Oh shit. I backed away from the two of them as Vail continued poking through some books and the other two Alphas seemed to be pointedly ignoring the fight that was about to break out.

Ryker stepped into Rynn's space, and I tensed, getting ready to intervene if I had to, since apparently the others weren't going to be of any help. "And what exactly are you going to do about it?" His gaze dropped to his shirt that she was still wearing, and he grinned wolfishly. "You look good in my clothes. *Princess.*"

A snarl ripped out of Rynn's throat before she shoved him. Hard. Clearly Ryker hadn't been expecting her to do that or to be so strong, because he stumbled back and hit the nearest bookcase. An answering growl rumbled from his throat as he pushed off the shelves, causing them to shake again, and then something rattled above us.

"Wait, what is that?" I stepped between the two Velesians who were sizing each other up and looked towards the ceiling. "There." I pointed at it. "There's a gap between the top of the bookcase and the ceiling."

We all peered up at the small crevice. As tall as Cade and Vail were, they still wouldn't be able to reach it. There must have been a step stool or something in here. I turned away to scour the room and then jumped when Rynn let out a high-pitched yip. I spun back around to find her glowering at Cade atop his shoulders, his head between her thighs.

"A little warning next time."

"Sure thing, Princess."

Rynn sighed but reached up and slipped her slender hand between the bookcase and the ceiling. I held my breath as she pursed her lips while searching the tight space. Suddenly, her eyes widened, and she slowly pulled her hand back, revealing a slender, gold crown.

"I'm so happy you shoved that asshole into the bookcase, Rynn." I stared at the glittering Fae artifact with a mixture of relief and awe.

Rynn let out an amused snort and glanced down at Ryker. "I guess violence really is the answer sometimes."

Bastian laughed and bumped his shoulder against Ryker's, who was still staring daggers at Rynn as Cade lowered her to the ground.

All of us gathered around and looked at the simple yet elegantly crafted crown. Despite sitting up on that shelf for probably decades if not centuries, it still gleamed in the light with absolute perfection. Most of it was comprised of three gold bands woven together, and occasionally an ornate gold leaf would flow out from one of them, looking so dainty that I was worried Rynn would accidentally snap it off, but when her fingers carefully swept over one of them, it seemed clear it wasn't so easy to break.

"I can feel the magic," she murmured, flipping the crown around as she studied the inside. "But I don't see any glyphs anywhere, so I have no idea how it works."

"Doesn't matter," I said. "We need to destroy it."

Rynn pursed her lips. "I know but . . ."

I shook my head. Rynn didn't like mysteries. While I could appreciate that from an academic standpoint, even if this half of the crown was the lesser of two evils, it still couldn't be allowed to exist, especially considering the Moroi Queen had the other half, and nothing good would come from them being reunited.

"Sorry, Rynn." I waved at the rest of the room. "You'll just have to settle for the greatest find in probably all of Lunarian history."

She grinned sheepishly. "Fair enough."

"The question is, how do we destroy it?" Vail looked at Cade. "Melt it down?"

"We could try." The large Velesian grimaced. "Something tells me it won't be that easy."

"Even if we are able to melt it . . ." Rynn pondered the crown, running her fingers along the inside. "We don't know exactly how the magic works. Usually there is a glyph, but in this case, I think the entire crown is spelled. I don't know if melting it down would destroy the spell or just change the shape of the crown.”

Vail held his hand out, and Rynn passed the crown to him, then we all watched as he tried to snap it. Muscles bulged along his forearms, but the crown didn't so much as crack. He passed it to Cade, who also had no luck.

“I think melting it will be the only chance we have of breaking it apart,” Vail said. “We could melt it and separate it into a few different pieces while it's in liquid form, then scatter those chunks afterwards.”

“Dump some into the ocean and bury others,” Cade suggested.

“If the spell persists in the gold even after it's melted though, will splitting it apart weaken or destroy it?” I grimaced. “Or will each piece retain the full functionality of the spell?”

“We might have to use the crown to test it.” Rynn sighed. “And then again after we split it up.”

Everyone tensed at the suggestion. Sure, we used the remnants of Fae magic regularly. Our wards were reactivated Fae spells and the glyphs that we used around our fortresses were all repurposed Fae magic, but something about this crown felt different. Everything else we used was for defense or making our lives easier.

The soul crown was made to see into the souls of others and control them. It was made to do *harm*.

“Maybe we can find an answer in here?” I looked around at the wealth of knowledge surrounding us. “In the meantime, we need to keep the crown hidden and safe.”

“We could leave it here?” Bastian suggested. “Nobody else knows about this place, and the spell keeps it secure. Thousands of Velesians have walked past it, and none of them detected the spell the way you did.”

“How did you do that, by the way?” Ryker asked, eying me suspiciously.

“I don't know.” I thought back to how it had felt when the spell had skittered across my skin. “Something about the glyph, the salvation one, called to me. I didn't feel anything else while going through the passage or in here.”

Rynn hummed, and my lips twitched in amusement, knowing I'd just given her another mystery to solve.

“I think you should take it, Rynn,” I said seriously. She jerked slightly as my declaration and looked at me wide-eyed. I held the crown out to her. “This place has remained hidden for a long time, but there is a chance that someone followed us here or will detect our scents above. Velika likely has spies everywhere, and we don't know if the wraiths avoid this area because they don't like it or because they can't come here. Until we know for sure, I'd be more comfortable with you keeping the crown on you at all times.”

“Alright.” She looked at the crown and then down at the shirt she was wearing before walking over to one of the shelves on the wall and grabbing a leather satchel. She carefully emptied the contents and then strode back over to Cade with her hand held out. He passed her the crown and Rynn dropped it into the bag.

Vail averted his eyes as she raised the shirt, flashing her goods at all of us, and wrapped the bands attached to the satchel around her waist. I'd seen Rynn naked more times than I could count, so it didn't bother me in the slightest.

An annoyed sound slipped from Rynn as she tried to hold the shirt up while also tying the bands together.

"Would it kill you to ask for help?" Cade grunted and grabbed the bands, shoving away Rynn's hand as he tied them and stepped away. Rynn stared at him with an unreadable expression as she dropped the shirt and looked down to inspect how it looked.

I glanced at Bastian and Ryker and was surprised to find that, like Vail, they had averted their eyes for this whole thing.

Wow. Rynn and the Alpha Pack were even messier than I'd thought. I couldn't wait to tell Cali all about it.

"Good enough," Rynn said as she finished fussing with the shirt. She was right, it was baggy enough that the satchel beneath it was barely noticeable. "When I get back home, I'll find a better solution—something that will work in both my forms—but I'll keep it on me at all times."

"You can do that while you pack up your things to move to your new home," Bastian said smoothly, his gaze once again on Rynn.

"Fuck you, Bastian," Rynn snarled.

"You would be so lucky."

"I'm not joining your stupid pack!" she screamed. "I'll figure out a way out of this."

"The fact that you're wearing his shirt"—Bastian pointed at Ryker—"says otherwise."

She took a step towards him, a snarl bubbling from her throat, when Ryker slid between them, causing Rynn to bump into his chest and stumble back. The lycan's hands darted out, gripping her around the waist, and his head leaned down closer to her shirt—his shirt, technically.

Ryker's nostrils flared, and his gaze dropped to Rynn's chest before he practically growled in her face. "Why were you crying earlier?"

"Seriously?" she snarled and shoved him away.

I bit my lip, not really knowing what to say to make this situation better. Rynn snatched a few books from the table and stalked towards the door, only to be thwarted when an invisible force seemed to wrap around the books and prevent them from passing the threshold. Rynn's body jerked as she was yanked back, and my brows rose as she tried to pass through again, but it was pretty clear the books were not leaving this space.

The Fae had clearly been determined to not only keep this place hidden but to protect the books inside as well. I was dying to know why, but it would have to wait.

After one more pissed-off snarl, Rynn slammed the books down onto the nearest table, causing me to wince at the harsh treatment of books that were likely centuries old, before storming out.

Apparently the crown could leave but the books couldn't. Interesting. Maybe the books were part of the original spell that kept this place safe, and the crown had come here afterwards?

"I'll go check on her," Vail said.

I watched him go, a little surprised that he cared, but I knew he respected Rynn and had dealt with the Alphas a lot in the past, so maybe he could offer her some words of wisdom.

"Explain the clothing," I said quietly.

Bastian looked like he'd bitten into something sour, and Ryker clamped his mouth shut, suddenly looking very young and unsure.

"When a Velesian joins a new pack, it's customary for them to wear the clothing of the other members . . . once they've accepted it," Cade explained in a somewhat strained tone. "It shows to others that they're happy with their new life . . . and family."

"You're not keeping her if she doesn't want to stay." I met Cade's stare and held it even as his dominance slammed into me and the other two Velesians let out warning growls. "We're in agreement for the crown, and that takes priority, but if Rynn wants to leave your pack, know that I will do everything in my power to help her, and if you hurt her"—I pushed my bloodlust until I was sure my eyes were jet-black—"I will cut out your heart and eat it in front of you."

The dominance exuding from him pushed against me one more time before vanishing like it'd never been there.

"Understood. I have no interest in harming Rynn." Cade nodded calmly before striding towards the door and tossing over his shoulder, "But I have no interest in giving her back either."

CHAPTER TWENTY-NINE

—

Samara

"Where'd they go?" I frowned when we reached the surface again. There was no sign of Vail or Rynn anywhere. Rynn had been really pissed, so she probably just needed some distance between her and the Alphas to calm down. Vail would keep her safe.

Apparently not everyone shared my opinion, because Cade let out a frustrated growl and Ryker looked like he was on the verge of shifting again just as Vail appeared from the trees.

"She's fine," he said. "Just pissed off. I tried to calm her down, but I think she just needs time to cool off. She's on her way home now."

Not her home anymore. I closed my eyes. It was always expected that Rynn would go and live with the Alphas up north, but being exiled from her own fucking Order was an entirely different situation. I still couldn't believe Cade had gone along with that plan.

"Princess needs to learn she doesn't get everything she wants in life," Bastian snarled and took off after her. Ryker shucked off his pants and shifted, and the enormous white wolf followed.

"You'll never find her," Vail called. "These are her woods."

Cade snorted. "We'll always find her. I'll get the others to give her a little space. Just for the trip back. She'll need to be with us tonight as part of the celebration."

The muscles along Vail's jaw flexed, but he didn't argue. I didn't like leaving Rynn here. Unfortunately, I didn't see any other options.

"Come on," I said to Vail. "We better get going."

Draven was probably losing his mind in that cabin, and I wanted to return to him so we could figure out our next move. We had the crown, which meant

Velika wasn't getting it. For the first time in a while, I was starting to feel a little optimistic.

We parted ways with Cade and headed south. I allowed myself to get lost in my thoughts, and I put my trust in Vail to keep us undetected by Velesian patrols and safe from any monsters that roamed during the daylight hours.

We would need help to get the other half of the crown away from Velika. After my conversations with Aniela and Ary, I thought they made sense as our first potential allies to approach, but I wanted to wait until we'd destroyed the crown in our possession. I might have trusted them not to side with the wraiths or anyone working with the wraiths, but that trust didn't extend towards Fae artifacts. They might argue that we should keep the crown or use it in the fight. Every part of my soul told me it needed to be destroyed, and until that was done, I wouldn't be able to trust anyone enough to tell them about it.

Ary and Aniela would probably be pissed, but they wouldn't be able to do anything about it.

We were halfway back to the cabin when several cloaked forms melted out of the trees like they were wraiths themselves. They weren't, but they were something almost as bad. Sovereign House rangers. At least twenty of them, which was far more than Vail and I could fight on our own.

"Greetings, Samara Harker," a tall, dark-haired ranger said, then he nodded at Vail. "Marshal, both of your presences are requested by Queen Velika."

My heart hammered inside my chest. At least Rynn had the crown. Unless they had captured her too? No. She had three of the deadliest Velesians in existence with her, and they would have fought hard enough so she could have escaped. Rynn wasn't a coward by any means, but she knew what was at stake. She wouldn't let the crown fall into enemy hands, and no Moroi would stand a chance at catching her in the forest.

"Any particular reason?" I asked, struggling to keep my voice even. "This all seems a bit much." I gestured towards the rangers surrounding us. All of them had their swords drawn, angled towards the ground, but the threat was clear. I was a little surprised Vail hadn't sensed them closing in on us, but these were likely the best of Velika's rangers.

"It is not my place to question the queen, nor is it yours." His gaze hardened. "Your aunt is currently a guest of the Sovereign House. If you care about her health, you will come with us and not impede the journey in any way. Understood?"

"Yes," I ground out. We should have rescued Carmilla first instead of leaving her as a hostage. I'd been so concerned about getting the crown before Velika that I'd left the last of my family at her mercy.

"Marshal," the ranger addressed Vail, "we will leave you and the Heir with your weapons for now, as we will continue traveling through the night to make it back as quickly as possible. Do not make me regret doing so."

Vail jerked his head in a nod. I could feel the fury rolling off him but didn't think he was capable of speaking at the moment. He wouldn't do anything to risk Carmilla, and neither would I.

I'd trust Vail to keep me safe on the way to the Sovereign House, and I'd be plotting how to keep both of us alive once we got there.

***

Two days later, we arrived at the Sovereign House. Usually, the trip would have taken twice as long, but there had been fresh horses waiting for us at each outpost, and we'd had extra protection at night . . . wraiths.

I hadn't seen them clearly, but as we'd raced along the roads, I'd seen shadows keeping pace with us in the woods, keeping the worst of the monsters away. The only attack we'd suffered had been from some howlers during the day. They'd picked off the ranger at the end of the line and carried his screaming body off into the woods before anyone could intervene.

The other rangers hadn't seemed all that upset. They'd just carried on like nothing had happened. I was pretty sure Velika had used the magic of the crown she possessed to bind them. During the journey, they'd rarely spoken to each other or displayed any sort of emotion. The man in charge had been the only one who had displayed the slightest amount of individuality.

They'd also kept Vail and me apart as much as possible, so we'd barely been able to speak the entire time.

I didn't know what Draven had done when I'd failed to return to the cabin. He'd surely looked for me, but where? Had he tracked down Rynn only to learn that I'd parted ways with her already? Had he returned to House Harker to let Kieran and the others know that something had gone very wrong?

Dread coiled in my gut. Or had he returned to the Sovereign House despite the pain and misery that awaited him there, because he knew that was where I'd likely been taken? I'd promised him I would keep him safe, and I'd failed.

I shoved back the grief and despair that had been building the last couple of days. They would do me no good, and I still had friends and family to protect. The situation wasn't ideal, but the other half of the crown was out of Velika's reach for now. If she suspected I knew where it was, she wouldn't kill me, which meant I had something to barter with. I'd never give up its location, but she didn't know that, so I could string her along while Vail and I figured something out.

Curious stares fell on us as the rangers marched us through the halls of the Sovereign House. This Fae fortress was similar to the other Houses but considerably larger. The main tower alone was the size of all of House Harker. Whispers echoed off the walls as the courtiers and advisors took in our state. Vail and I were both covered with a fine layer of dirt and probably looked a little worse for wear given how hard we'd been traveling the last week.

I hoped the queen choked on my stench.

Two guards stood in front of large double doors that I recognized immediately. They were gilded in silver and had an enormous tree engraved on them. We'd been brought to the throne room.

"Queen Velika wishes to speak to Samara first," one of the guards said at our approach. "The Marshal will wait out here."

"Not a chance," Vail growled. The rangers escorting us tensed, and the guards at the door reached for the swords at their hips.

"It's alright." I slid between Vail and the guards, placing my hands on his chest. He tore his gaze away from the guards to look at me, his eyes dark grey storm clouds with silver dancing amongst them. I stood up on my tiptoes and brushed my lips against his. "I'll be okay."

We may not have had a choice in coming here, but we hadn't been dragged here in chains either. That could mean any number of things. Velika could still be feeling us out to find out exactly how much we knew. In that case, she might pretend like nothing was wrong at all and come up with some cover story for why she'd wanted us brought here so urgently. Or maybe she'd just wanted to rattle me, having me brought to the Sovereign House like this, and now wanted to separate me from Vail while she questioned me about the crown.

As much as I wanted Vail by my side so I could draw strength from his presence, he was absolutely terrible at hiding what he was feeling. She'd see every emotion written on his face, not to mention, he might let something slip in anger if he spoke. Between the two of us, I had a better chance of playing this game with the Moroi Queen.

Assuming she didn't just kill me as soon as I walked in. That would be unfortunate.

Vail's expression softened, and he cupped my face with his left hand. "I'll be right here. Just yell if you need anything. These guards won't stop me from getting to you."

The guards in question shuffled nervously before opening the door for me.

I kissed Vail one more time and then took a deep breath before turning and striding into the throne room with my chin held high. The door clanged shut behind me, and I let my gaze skim over the dozens of courtiers and advisors standing around, talking softly.

The throne room was not particularly large, but it made up for that in opulence. The walls and ceiling were made of white marble with silver running through it all, creating elegant patterns. A deep blue stone made up the floor— so shiny, you could almost see your reflection in it.

What truly made it extraordinary was that everything appeared to be one piece. There were no visible seams anywhere. No imperfections. We struggled to keep the wards operational while the Fae had probably created this gorgeous room in an afternoon with barely a thought. I wondered what they would think of this beautiful space they'd created being used by the descendants of humans. Maybe I could ask Erendriel someday.

The exhaustion and stress must have finally gotten to me because I laughed at the thought.

"Something funny?" a light, breathy voice asked.

A tall, slender, fair-haired Moroi female strode into the room, her light blonde hair falling down her back in a wave of curls and her blue gown flowing around her with each step. She took a seat on the throne made of the same blue stone as the floor that rested on top of a dais. The Moroi Queen always did love to make an entrance.

My breath caught in my throat when I spotted the silver crown that rested on her head.

She can't use it on you, I reminded myself. Without the other half, anyone who belonged to one of the House bloodlines couldn't be controlled by its magic. We could be driven insane until we became Strigoi, but that took time. So that was a tomorrow problem. Right now, I just needed to survive this encounter.

"It's nothing, my queen," I said lightly. "Just silly musings about the Fae. I find myself rather exhausted from the ride here, as you can probably tell from my appearance."

She smiled at me, but it didn't reach her golden brown eyes. I saw very little of Draven echoed in her.

"You *are* looking rather ragged," Lucian said in a bored tone.

I glanced at the consort standing at the bottom of the dais. Despite being with Velika for almost three decades, she had never married him or allowed him to stand by her side. I'd never liked Lucian. He represented the worst side of the courtiers. Someone who thought their elevated status made them better than everyone beneath them . . . and enjoyed reminding them of that.

There were whispers of cruelty that had befallen the staff and lower-ranking courtiers, but I'd never been able to confirm anything for sure. Despite keeping Lucian in his place, Velika clearly favored him, and no one wanted to go against the queen.

Instead of responding to Lucian's comment, I ignored him, and his mouth tightened at the dismissal. Velika's lips twitched in amusement, and tension roiled in my gut. Considering how little I knew about this situation, I had no idea how to play this other than to continue pretending everything was normal. Or as normal as it could be when one was summoned to the Sovereign House by twenty armed guards.

"Why were you in the Velesian realm?" Velika asked. "Seems odd for you to leave your House unattended since Carmilla is here with me."

The reminder that she had my aunt sent a chill down my spine. I'd been subtly looking around the room but hadn't seen Carmilla's face amongst those gathered.

"I'm working on arranging a larger trade of malachite with them, my queen," I answered smoothly. "Several of our outposts have been dealing with increased attacks, and we may need to expand the wards that protect them."

"Interesting." She hummed. "That's not what I heard."

I sunk every ounce of will I had into forcing my heartbeat to remain steady as she raised her hand and flicked her fingers forward. Then my resolve broke when the guards dragged a bloody and beaten Draven into the room.

"No!" I cried and stepped forward, only for strong arms to yank me back against a hard chest.

"Don't make a spectacle of yourself, Samara," Demetri purred into my ear, and I went absolutely still. "Good girl."

Then I twisted free and slashed my claws across his face before he could react.

"Fuck!" he screamed as blood streamed between the fingers he'd pressed against his cheek. Damn it. I'd been hoping to scratch his eyes out. I lunged towards Draven, but two guards rushed in and restrained me. No matter how much I struggled in their grasp, I couldn't break free.

Demetri straightened, his hand falling away from his face to reveal three deep gouges. The bleeding had already slowed when he stalked towards me, eyes burning with fury. My head snapped to the side as he backhanded me hard, and I saw stars for a few seconds.

Then a growl rumbled throughout the room.

"Restrain him!" Velika ordered.

I raised my head despite the blinding pain shooting down the left side of my face to see the guards clamping thick, iron chains onto Draven's wrists and attaching them to the nearby pillars. The chains forced him to stand, and the way his arms were pulling against them, I suspected they were all that was keeping him upright. One of his beautiful eyes was completely swollen shut, his face a mishmash of bruises and cuts, and the dark tunic he wore was nothing but blood-soaked rags at this point.

Nobody in the room moved to help him. They just looked at him with amusement or disgust. Sometimes both.

"What did they do to you?" I whispered in horror before turning my wrathful gaze to Velika. "He's your fucking son!"

She shrugged one dainty shoulder. "Technically, this is your fault."

"Bullshit." I seethed. "You're just a sick, twisted fuck with too much power."

A fist slammed into my jaw, and I heard something crack. The guard who had punched me yanked me back when I leaned over and spat out a mouthful of blood. "Do not speak that way to our queen," he warned.

"No." Lucian grinned at me. "By all means, keep going. This is fun."

"Just don't damage her too much," Demetri said mildly as a servant handed him a wet cloth so he could wipe the drying blood off his face. To my annoyance, the gouges I'd inflicted on him had already healed. "She is to be my wife again after all."

"You're fucking delusional." I stared at him in disbelief.

"The two of you can fight about that later." Velika rose from her throne and stepped down the dais to stand in front of me, Lucian moving to stand behind her like the obedient consort he was. "This"—she gestured at Draven, who looked like he was on the verge of passing out—"is your fault because you allowed him to drink from you. He has too much Harker blood in him right now for me to compel him to answer me."

I deliberately kept my gaze on her face, refusing to look at the crown on her head.

"You can stop pretending." She laughed. "I know you're aware of what this crown is, and more importantly, what it does. Just like I know that you're searching for the other half." She reached forward and twirled a loose strand of my hair around her finger. "And I suspect you've found it."

My face hurt from where I'd been hit, twice, but that didn't stop me from raising my chin and spitting in her face. Her hand froze where it had been playing with my hair before moving it to slowly wipe away the blood-tinged saliva.

She pondered it, looking more curious than angry before glancing at Draven and then back at me. "Figures my son would fall in love with the only other Moroi in existence foolish enough to spit in my face." Then her lips curved into a cruel smile. "Demetri was with the guards who captured him leaving the Velesian realm. He confirmed that my worthless son smelled of you. That he never broke while we ripped his body apart is only a testament to how much he loves you."

Tears streamed down my face before I could stop them as I looked at Draven. His wounds weren't healing—blood still leaked from all of his cuts, and the bruising looked even puffier than it had when he'd been dragged in here. I didn't know if it was because his magic was taxed out or if something else was at work.

Where the fuck was Vail? There was no way he hadn't heard the commotion in here. Had they done something to him? No. There was no way they could have hurt him quietly, and I hadn't heard a fight. Maybe he was just biding his time?

I didn't know what one person could do against all this, but I was desperate for anything at this point.

"Here's what's going to happen, my pet." Velika wiped her hand on my clothing, drawing my attention back to her. "I'm going to bring some of your friends here, starting with that pretty blond courtier, or maybe the advisor with the pretty eyes. By the time they get here, your blood will be out of my son's system." She clapped her hands together excitedly. "And then I'm going to command him to inflict every bit of pain on them that we've done to him over the last two days. Now, for all his shortcomings, the prince is quite hardy, so they probably won't make it the full two days."

"Doubtful they'll make it more than a day," Demetri said, and Lucian laughed with him.

A bloody and broken version of Kieran flashed before my eyes, followed a second later by Alaric. I'd have liked to pretend that I would remain strong, that I wouldn't give over the knowledge of where the crown was, and that I wouldn't put Rynn and the rest of Lunaria in danger, but I would break. Even knowing that we were all damned regardless, I would break eventually.

"Ah." Velika gripped my chin, and I stared hatefully into her beautiful face. "Now you get it. There is no one who can save you from this, so you best cooperate with me, and I'll spare you some pain." Her nails shifted to claws, and I felt them bite into my skin. "But trust me, there will be pain."

Devastation and hopelessness threatened to break the strong front I was trying to present. I had no chance of fighting my way out of this. I was good at plotting, but Velika was better. She'd outmaneuvered me, and there was fuck all I could do about it now. The chains rattled again as Draven stirred enough to pull against them.

"I'm sorry." I looked at him through tear-filled eyes. "I'm so sorry."

Lucian opened his mouth, likely to taunt me again, when the doors to the room slammed open and Carmilla stormed in with Vail following her.

Hope rallied inside me, followed immediately by confusion. I'd assumed Carmilla was being held prisoner and Vail restrained . . . but the rangers who had been guarding the door made no move to stop them. Instead, they followed after Carmilla and Vail at a respectable distance. What the fuck was going on?

"Carmilla." Velika released my chin and shot my aunt an annoyed look when she stopped a short distance away from us, Vail standing just behind her, his eyes on the queen. "I thought we agreed I would handle this? You're too sentimental."

What?

Velika glanced back at me, and I realized I must have said that out loud. She frowned and returned her attention to Carmilla, her eyes drifting to Vail behind her and then to Demetri, who had casually strolled over to stand beside them. "What is the meaning of this?"

"I'm sorry, my friend." Carmilla shook her head ruefully. "I've always stood by you, but I can't any longer. You never should have bargained with the wraiths. I cannot abide by that."

For a moment, Velika stood completely frozen, her mouth parted slightly as she stared at my aunt—her friend. Then she pursed her lips into a hard line. Fury fed by betrayal burned in her eyes as she stalked towards Carmilla. I tugged against the grip of the guards, but they held me firmly in place so all I could do was watch this unfold.

"You treacherous bitch!" Velika's eyes sparked with rage as she stopped a foot away from my aunt. "All these fucking years of me helping you, and this is how you repay me?" She scoffed. "It doesn't matter. All of the Sovereign House is bloodsworn to me. You have no power here, *friend*." She bit out the last word.

I tried to catch Vail's eyes, but he wouldn't look at me. Instead, his gaze was fixed straight ahead . . . on Lucian.

"No." Carmilla shook her head slowly. "Everyone in the Sovereign House is loyal to the crown . . . and the head upon which it rests."

A gurgling sound came from in front of me, and I tore my gaze away from Carmilla to find Velika clutching at the sword protruding through her chest. Blood dribbled out of her lips as she gasped, and Lucian wrapped an arm around her like a lover before twisting the sword more as he yanked her back onto it.

The Moroi Queen's legs gave out, and she collapsed to the floor as blood pooled around her. I stared in stunned silence as Demetri strolled forward and took the sword from Lucian before swinging it down. The sound of metal slamming against the hard marble floor echoed across the room as Velika's head rolled away.

Then Lucian knelt down, picked up the crown, and then walked over to Carmilla before kneeling in front of her and offering it up. "Your crown, my love."

CHAPTER THIRTY

—

Samara

"Thank you, Lucian." Carmilla took the crown from him and settled it onto her head, then her dark eyes fell on the guards still holding me. "Release my niece."

"Yes, my queen," they both replied and immediately stepped back. I staggered and almost fell without the support. Demetri stepped forward to steady me but halted at the look I gave him.

"Carmilla," I croaked. "What the fuck is going on?"

"I'm so sorry, Samara. It was too risky to tell you what I had planned considering the company you've been keeping lately." She glanced pointedly at where Draven was chained up before striding towards the dais. Lucian rose and guided her around Velika's still warm body before standing beside the throne as she took a seat.

Everyone in the room knelt before their new queen, except me and Draven, but he was barely conscious at this point and couldn't have kneeled anyway with the chains holding him up.

"The crown . . ." I started and then stopped, drawing in a deep breath. She must not know what it was truly capable of, because she never would have placed it on her head otherwise. "You have no idea what it can do. We have to dest—"

"It's half of the soul crown." She smiled at me. "This part binds souls, the other half sees them. Without that second half, it's quite time-consuming to instill your will on others. A blood exchange is required, and if their will is strong, they can still fight it, but the two halves together will solve that issue."

Dread filled me. "What are you saying?"

"Don't give me that look, Samara," Carmilla chided. "You understand the

506

threat Erendriel and the wraiths pose. We cannot allow infighting amongst the Moon Blessed to weaken us at a time like this."

"I understand that, but enslaving people against their wills cannot be the answer." I shook my head. This couldn't be right. The Moroi leader I'd looked up to for the last decade . . . the person who had raised me after my parents had died . . . she couldn't possibly be doing this. "Please, Carmilla," I rasped. "Take the crown off."

"I was worried you'd react this way." She sighed and traded glances with Demetri, who stepped closer, causing me to tense. The guards who had released me a minute ago moved to my other side, boxing me in. "I'm sure you'll come around eventually. You always were a smart and ambitious girl."

She didn't have the other half of the crown. I wouldn't tell her, and despite everything, surely Carmilla wouldn't resort to torturing Kieran and Alaric to get it out of me? Uncertainty flickered through me. Exactly how much had I gotten wrong about who Carmilla really was?

Draven's labored breathing drew my attention. His skin was pale and clammy, and an alarming amount of blood soaked his clothes. I needed to get him help and figure out why he wasn't healing, then I'd try to talk some sense into Carmilla.

This was still fixable. I could fix this. I could—

"Vail?" Carmilla called as she held her hand out.

"No," I whispered. Demetri's hand clamped down on my arm, and I was rooted in place as Vail strode towards the throne, not looking at me once, and withdrew the gold half of the soul crown from beneath his cloak.

The same crown Rynn had been in possession of.

"I'll go check on her."

He'd gone after Rynn as soon as she'd been alone and taken the crown from her. She never would have given it to him willingly.

"What did you do, Vail!" I screamed, and he finally looked at me.

"I did as my queen ordered," he said calmly, even as I saw the regret in his eyes.

"Rynn . . . Is she—" My voice broke as tears streamed down my face, and I couldn't bring myself to finish the question.

"She's fine," he assured me. "I just knocked her out and then placed a keep-away spell around her so Cade and the others wouldn't find her right away."

"'Just knocked her out?'" I stared at him. "She was your friend. She trusted you. *I* trusted you."

"What did you expect?" Demetri drawled. "He had to choose one of you. His queen or his latest fuck. Who did you think he would pick?"

"Demetri," Carmilla snapped. "Watch how you speak about my niece or I'll change my mind about our arrangement."

I couldn't even bring myself to care about what that meant. All I could do was stare at the gleaming gold crown in Vail's hand. "Don't," I begged him.

Vail swallowed . . . and then passed the crown to Carmilla.

Something inside me shattered into a thousand pieces, and I couldn't stop the pained sound from slipping from my lips. Demetri's grip on me tightened, and I yelped.

"Don't fucking touch her," Vail growled, and Demetri had enough sense to look a little worried before loosening his hold, but he didn't completely let me go.

"Oh, that's rich." Lucian laughed. "You can stop pretending now, Vail. I mean, honestly, I didn't think you had it in you, but good on you for mixing work and pleasure."

"Fuck you, Lucian," Vail snapped before sending me a pleading look. "It wasn't like that, I swear. What happened in the cave, in the cabin, all of it. It wasn't . . . I wasn't . . ." He struggled to explain, but I just turned away, not able to look at him anymore.

I was such a fucking fool. This whole time, I'd been worried about Draven stabbing me in the back when I should have been looking at the male who'd already betrayed me numerous times and had told me to my face more than once that he hated me.

"Sam, I—" Vail tried again, but I cut him off.

My head snapped back to glare at him, hoping he saw every wrathful promise about how much I would make him pay. "You don't get to call me that." Vail's face fell, but he could go fuck himself.

Then I looked at Demetri's fingers still wrapped around my wrist and raised my gaze to meet my ex-husband's light brown eyes. He stroked his thumb across my skin, and I wanted to hurl. "I told you when you left House Laurent that we could come to an understanding about our marriage, but you didn't listen."

"And I told you," I purred and leaned into him, and Demetri's eyes darkened before his gaze snagged on my lips, "that the only understanding I was capable of coming to was one that involved your cock flopping around on the floor and you bleeding out at my feet."

His eyes widened, and he screamed as I dug my claws into his crotch. I was pretty sure I'd missed and mostly gotten thigh, unfortunately. Then I was slammed into the floor as he flung me away from him. Vail was there in an instant to help me up, but I snarled in his face before rising on my own.

"You fucking whore!" Demetri screamed as he cradled his wounded dick. Apparently I had gotten him after all.

Vail growled, and Carmilla let out a long-suffering sigh like we were children fighting over sweets. A pained laugh rang through the air, and I whirled to Draven. He was conscious again and standing but still looked like shit.

"I hope she tore it off." His laugh turned into a cough, and the chains clinked together as he struggled to breathe.

"We need to get those chains off him." I stepped forward, but Vail wrapped his arms around me, pinning mine to my sides. Unlike Demetri, Vail knew I was perfectly capable of violence and made sure I was completely immobilized. "He had no choice in obeying her!" I struggled in Vail's hold even though I knew it was pointless. "Draven is not our enemy!"

Carmilla rose from the throne, taking Lucian's hand as he guided her down the dais. I still couldn't wrap my head around the fact that Carmilla was involved with Lucian. Based on how he was looking at my aunt like she was one of the ancient gods reborn, this was more than just a political arrangement. He was in love with her. Had he always been? Or was this something new?

Exactly how much had Carmilla been hiding from me? Another stabbing pain shot through my chest. Her betrayal hurt just as much as Vail's. I loved her. She was my only family left. I didn't know if she had suggested Vail get close to me or if it had been his idea, but either way, two people I cared for deeply had conspired against me.

Some dark part of me wondered if Alaric was in on it too. I would bet every piece of the shattered remains of my heart that Kieran and Roth had no idea this was going on. Kieran would never have lied to me, and Roth would have told them to go fuck themselves.

"There is so much you don't understand," Carmilla said sadly as she stopped in front of me. Then she raised her hand to tuck my hair behind my ear like she'd done my entire life, but I jerked my head away from her as much as I could, which wasn't much thanks to Vail's iron grip. Though it was enough to make her lower her hand and take a step back.

"Vail informed me of what you all saw in the temple."

"Of course he did," I ground out, and Vail stiffened behind me. "But Draven had no choice! He had to serve Velika because of that fucking crown!" My eyes flicked up to the united gold and silver crown that now rested atop Carmilla's dark hair. "The one that you're planning on using to enslave our people."

"You're being a bit dramatic, dear." She gave me a small, placating smile. "This crown was made for the Fae and it responds to our magic . . . oddly. I'm not going to just walk around Lunaria and make everyone kneel to me. Logistically, that doesn't make sense, and I have no desire to do so anyway. I will only use it in situations where I have no choice."

"Forgive me for not believing you, Aunt," I said evenly. "It seems I've chosen poorly about who to trust these days."

"Draven is Erendriel's son," she said without any preamble. "He is half Fae."

For a brief moment, shock cut through the rage I was feeling. Draven was half Fae. Erendriel's son . . .

Fuck it. I didn't care. Draven was *mine*.

"If you think . . . I'm loyal"—Draven coughed harder and sucked in a breath. I could hear his lungs rattling from here—"to my piece of shit father, you're even crazier than my mother." He rushed out the last words before doubling over and vomiting blood.

I frantically pulled against Vail. "Let me help him, damn you!"

"It's the iron," Carmilla explained. "The Fae can't stand it. Velika used to cut him up with it, and I'm pretty sure there are still some pieces buried in his chest. She really did hate him," my aunt mused. "I never did understand why."

"Please," I begged. "Just let me help him before it's too late."

"He's not dying," Lucian said dismissively. "Trust me—he's looked way worse than this. Haven't you, boy?"

Speaking seemed to be beyond Draven now, because all he could do was glare at Lucian.

"I understand you care for him," Carmilla said softly, "but we don't know how much control his father has over him. He cannot be trusted, and it's a risk to let him live."

"Please," I pleaded. I couldn't lose Draven. Not only because I'd promised to keep him safe, but because I was pretty sure I was falling in love with him. Something in his soul called to mine, and I couldn't let that go. Plus, he loved Kieran, and my sweet Kier loved him in return. "I'll work with you. Help you. Just please don't kill him."

"Seriously?" Demetri sneered at me. "Fuck this." He stalked towards Draven, who pulled against the chains but had nowhere to go.

"Stop!" I screamed, and for a second, I thought Vail would let me go, but then he tightened his grip again.

"Demetri!" Carmilla barked.

But the House Laurent Heir didn't hesitate as he grabbed a sword from one of the nearby guards and shoved it through Draven's gut.

"He's alive," Carmilla said from where she stood on the other side of the bars. After Demetri had stabbed Draven, I'd absolutely lost it.

I was still a little murky about what had happened. The ground had trembled, I remembered that much. Maybe Draven had tried to rally his Fae magic? At some point, Vail had either let me go or I'd slipped free from his grasp to dash towards Draven.

I brushed my fingers together and looked down at the cold and sticky blood on them. Draven's blood. I had reached him. Freed him. I remembered a spark of magic and then the chains disintegrating like they'd never been there.

But that couldn't have been right . . . I must have somehow unlatched them.

Everything had been so chaotic. Draven had sagged against me, the building had shaken, and then . . . darkness.

I'd woken up in a cell, presumably in the dungeon of the Sovereign House.

"It's admirable that you think I'd take your word about anything at this point," I rasped and moved to a sitting position against the wall. My throat felt like it was on fire.

She tossed a leather waterskin through the bars, and I snatched it up. I sniffed it but didn't detect anything obvious in it. Carmilla let out an annoyed sound when I hesitated for another second before guzzling the water down. It's not like I could refuse to eat and drink forever.

Besides, she had a crown capable of binding souls. Poisoned or spelled water was the least of my worries.

I wondered if my bloodline would protect me against the crown. It hadn't protected Draven, at least not entirely. Would Carmilla use it against me?

Had she used it against Vail? Or was I just desperate to believe he hadn't had a choice in betraying me?

Carmilla laughed under her breath. "I can practically feel you thinking from here, trying to puzzle out what has happened and planning for possible contingencies." Her dark purple eyes, which were identical to my own, danced with amusement in the dim lighting. "You make me proud."

"Funny." I wiped the back of my hand against my mouth. "Your decisions lately have made me sick."

The corners of her mouth tightened. "You're young. It's easy to be idealistic when you haven't been dealing with everyone's bullshit and ridiculous demands for almost a century."

I stared at the roughed-up stone floor of my cell. Moroi politics were frustrating because every House was out for themselves. We were desperately fighting for survival, but instead of cooperating, everyone was plotting how to spin the deal in their favor. It hadn't always been like this. I had no actual proof of that, but I had to believe it because there was no way we would have survived as long as we had if we hadn't worked together before.

The Moroi hadn't always looked down on the Velesians or feared the Furies, the Velesians hadn't always been so distrustful, and the Furies hadn't always been so isolated. The Moon Blessed were falling apart.

I refused to believe that using magic to control them against their wills was the answer though, because what was the fucking point of that? There were monsters . . . and then there were *fucking monsters*. I had to make my aunt see that.

"Perhaps, you're right," I said, making sure to add a clear reluctance to my tone. "But surely you see things from my point of view? I mean, you had the Marshal of our House spy on me, betray me, and you commanded him to use our relationship to—" I inhaled sharply. The pain I felt with each breath wasn't an act.

"I didn't tell him to do that," Carmilla said quickly. "In fact, I specifically warned him off that path. Given your future with Demetri, that didn't seem wise."

"What future?" I asked, ignoring the fear igniting in my gut. "Our marriage is over. You fucking agreed to it!" I slapped my palms against the cell floor.

As the leader of House Harker, her signature had been required on the dissolution paperwork, and she'd signed it without hesitation.

"This isn't an agreement with House Laurent," Carmilla said carefully. "Marvina is . . . a problem, but the Laurent bloodline is important, and Demetri and I have come to an understanding."

"What did you promise him?" I asked sharply.

"Not what you're thinking," Carmilla hissed. "If you truly don't want him, then we'll figure something out, but you have to at least give him a chance—"

"I was married to him for three fucking years!" I shot to my feet and slammed my hands against the bars. Carmilla jerked back. "I only did that because I wanted to make you fucking proud of me!"

"Samara." She gave me a chiding look. "Be reasonab—"

"Fuck you!" I screamed. "I've done everything you've ever asked of me, including marrying that asshole! You don't get to tell me who to love anymore!"

"You're a Harker." Carmilla drew herself up and gave me a steady look. "Love is irrelevant. You had to have known your future didn't involve marrying courtiers or advisors."

I was acutely aware of every beat my heart took, and I felt my bloodlust rising in a protective wave around me as my eyes bled black and my nails hardened into claws.

"My future is my own." I bared my fangs at her, and I could have sworn I felt the cell bars trembling beneath my grip. "And I fucking dare you to try to take that from me."

Carmilla touched the crown on her head. "We'll see."

CHAPTER THIRTY-ONE

—

Vail

Hours before the sun rose, I found myself walking silently down to the prison buried beneath the Sovereign House. For a moment during my trek down the winding stairwell, I stopped at a solid wood door and rested my hand against it.

On the other side was a room that contained three large cells. They were nicer ones than the levels below, but a gilded cage was still a cage.

I could feel the lone prisoner stewing in rage over the betrayal she hadn't seen coming.

It had never been my intention for things to play out this way. I'd thought I could obey Carmilla while protecting Samara from herself. She needed to understand just how much of a danger Draven was to her despite the sweet lies he whispered in the dark.

Yet you were fine with fucking her while he watched, a dark voice whispered in my mind. *And watching him slide his cock into the pussy that was still dripping with your seed.*

I'd fucked up. Badly. I let my fingers glide across the rough wood, wondering how much of her rage was directed at Carmilla and how much at me. Just like I wondered if she could feel this pull between us. I'd noticed it a couple of days ago. It had been so faint, I'd thought I'd been imagining it.

Now it felt like a burning chain around my soul.

My fingers curled against the door, and for a second, I almost opened it, but based on how much anger I could feel through this strange magic that bound us, I suspected she'd only spit in my face if I went to her now.

I forced myself to take a step back and then continued on my way to the lowest part of the prison. A few screams and pleas sounded from the other levels I passed. We'd rounded up anyone who had served Velika and contained

513

them for now. Carmilla promised most of them would be released once we figured out who could be trusted.

It bothered me a little. The rangers, I understood. Many of them had chosen to follow the now dead queen even before she had found the crown and bound them with its magic, but most of those contained in the cells were advisors and courtiers . . . and their families. Surely they weren't such an active threat that they needed to be locked up?

I'd speak to Carmilla about it tomorrow. She had a lot to handle in this tumultuous period of taking over the rule of the Sovereign House. Maybe I could offer to do an initial screening of those imprisoned and promise to assign rangers to keep an eye on those who were released?

An iron door awaited me when I finally reached the bottom. The walls contained large amounts of iron too, enough to make even my skin crawl a little bit. Something about our Moroi blood didn't like iron, but not nearly to the same extent as the Fae.

I pushed the door open, and it swung silently inward. There was only one prisoner on this level. Brushing my fingers against a glyph on the inside wall, I activated the Fae lanterns, and the flames flickered to life, bathing the small room and the cells that lined the walls in a warm glow.

"Come to finish me off?" Draven drawled from where he was stretched out on the ground of the cell at the end of the room. He leapt to his feet with a grace I hadn't thought he was capable of in his current state and stood with his hands clasped behind his back. "You're welcome to open these doors and try it." Solid red eyes that promised death locked onto me. "I dare you."

I kept the surprise off my face as I slowly walked over to his cell. Draven was a predator, and it was never wise to let a predator know they unnerved you.

"You're looking better. Last time I saw you, I was pretty sure we'd be digging your grave within the hour, or you know, chucking your Fae corpse off a cliff."

Casually, I let my eyes drift over him. He hadn't been given a change of clothing, so he was still coated in dried blood, but I could see patches of smooth skin beneath the tattered fabric. Even if he had used healing glyphs on himself, he should have been exhausted from the effort without someone to drink from.

Had someone snuck down here and fed him? No. There were guards loyal to Carmilla posted at the entry door to the stairwell, and that was the only way in here.

"Half Fae," Draven corrected. "But it does come with its benefits."

I tapped the iron bars of his cell. "I bet."

Despite his healthier-looking appearance, he was standing in the center of the cell, as far away from the walls and doors as he could get. Clearly the iron bothered him, but it hadn't blocked his ability to heal. Maybe because he was half Moroi, he wasn't as sensitive to it as most Fae? I'd have to tell Carmilla. We might want to have guards posted in this room as well.

"So"—he cocked his head—"if you're not here to attempt to kill me, why did you bother coming down here? Too scared to chat with the dark-haired beauty who you so thoroughly betrayed?"

I winced before I could kill the movement, and Draven laughed.

"Samara will understand," I snapped. "She just needs to calm down for a few days, and then I'll tell her everything. Carmilla has the best interests of the Moroi at heart."

Draven shook his head. "Oh? Is that why she imprisoned children? I can hear their cries even down here."

"It's temporary," I ground out.

"Ah. So cruelty is fine so long as it's only for a short amount of time. Such a wonderful leader to follow."

"She's a vast improvement over your mother." My fingers curled into fists at my sides. "We dumped her body outside, by the way. Figured the monsters could use a snack."

If my words caused him any pain, Draven hid it well. He raised one of his hands in front of him and studied his nails as he let them shift to claws. "Trust me when I say that nobody was happier than me to see my mother's headless body on the floor." He frowned. "Actually, I wish I had been more with it so I could have truly appreciated the moment."

"And your father?" I closely watched Draven's face, looking for any reaction. "How will you feel when it's his corpse in a pool of blood?"

Draven let out a chilling laugh and sank back to the ground in a cross-legged position. Then he let his hands sink into the floor on either side of him, and I noticed some of the stones had been broken up enough that it was more dirt than anything at this point. His posture relaxed, and some of the red receded in his eyes.

"If I were you, I'd walk back up those stairs to where Samara is locked up and plead for mercy. She loves you and, despite everything, would at least grant you a swift death." My heart clenched at the admission that he knew Samara loved me.

"She'll forgive me." Even I could hear the uncertainty in my words though.

Draven just smiled. "She won't. If you had only betrayed her, perhaps over time she would have, because again, my fierce love is kindhearted, but your actions have put Kieran, Alaric, and Roth in danger. Carmilla isn't a fool. She knows the way to controlling her niece is through those she loves. And that"—he leaned forward slightly—"is not something Samara will forgive."

I looked away from the fallen prince, because he was right. Samara would never forgive me if something happened to those she loved because of all this. It had never occurred to me that Carmilla would use Kieran or Alaric like that.

Maybe Roth because Carmilla wasn't as close to them as the other two, but even then, Roth was clearly an asset.

I also hadn't thought Carmilla would imprison children, so maybe my judgment of character wasn't as good as I'd previously believed.

"None of it really matters though," Draven continued, drawing me out of my dark contemplations. "Because Erendriel will come, and then all of you will wish you'd had the foresight to just slit your own throats rather than deal with his wrath."

"I thought you said your father didn't care about you?" I sneered. Of course he'd been fucking lying.

"Oh, he doesn't." Draven shrugged. "I mean, he probably wants to carve me apart himself, given that I killed several of his best soldiers, but Velika was important to his plans, and her death will set him back. He has a bit of a temper when it comes to that kind of thing."

"We can handle him." I crossed my arms. If anything, it might be easier if he came to us. We could get this over and done with once and for all. "I've fought wraiths before, and Erendriel is just one Fae."

Draven chuckled darkly, and the hairs rose on the back of my neck. "He's not though. Erendriel is the Seelie King.

A Throne of Blood & Vengeance

Lunaria Realms Book 3

To my absolutely rockstar editing and beta team: PollyAné, Rachel, Lisa, and Fiona.

Y'all are amazing.

CHAPTER ONE

—

Alaric

I was always in control. Every word I spoke. Every move I made. Controlled.

Even when I allowed my bloodlust to come out and play, I did it carefully and in situations where I'd mitigated the risks.

Most Moroi viewed the tight control I kept over myself as a disadvantage. We lived in a world of predators, and our bloodlust was what gave us enough of an edge to survive. By letting it rise, we became just that much faster and stronger.

Of course, if we let it out too much, we might never be able to pull it back. Some Moroi were willing to risk that. I was not.

But as I looked around the meadow that I'd turned into a sea of blood, a cruel smile spread across my lips. I'd pit my controlled brand of violence against their bloodlust any day.

My eyes scanned the tall grass, looking for any other threats, but only the broken bodies of howlers—canine-like beasts—littered the ground. With nothing left to vent my rage on, the desolation I'd been feeling all week started to creep back in.

"Bit much, don't you think?" Samara's voice said dryly in the back of my mind. I could practically envision her toeing one of the corpses with a smirk on her face. *"You could have just gotten me flowers."*

But Samara wasn't here. She hadn't been for almost two weeks, and we only had rumors to go on for where she was.

Hence the carnage.

Several shadows moved from a patch of the meadow where the grass had grown over six feet tall, the tips ending in seed pods. *Looks like I missed a few.* Exhilaration replaced the despair as three howlers crept closer.

The howlers didn't make a sound. Even if I hadn't known they were sick, that would have been a clue. Normally, the beasts were loud, letting out excited yips and howls as they closed in on their prey, but these ones—like the ones I'd already killed—were rabid and not acting normal.

I watched them draw closer, fighting the revulsion as I slowly slid my sword back into its sheath and drew the bow from my back. Howlers were always a little freaky looking, having only a passing resemblance to the canines I was familiar with—mostly the lycanthropes. There were a few Fae murals that depicted domesticated dogs that, apparently, they'd kept as pets once upon a time.

"Can you imagine?" Samara's voice once again spoke to me. Maybe I was finally losing it. *"Keeping cute little dogs as pets? Such luxury."* She'd have drawn out that last word in a way that would've made me instantly hard. I still didn't know how she did it. Somehow, she could make any word sound obscene.

Gripping my bow with one hand, I pulled an arrow from the quiver.

The largest of the three split off, and I adjusted my stance as I aimed the tip of the arrow towards it. Two pairs of eyes, one stacked on top of the other, watched me from a long, narrow head. The madness that rotted their minds did the same to their flesh. Its sleek black coat was missing large patches of fur in places, and its ribs were starting to show. Howlers were built with speed in mind—a lean body that cinched and narrowed at the hips sat on long legs. Once they got going, they could almost outrun a horse, their stamina definitely better.

Bits of rotting flesh hung from its teeth as its mouth gaped open. The other fun part about howlers was they could open their jaw almost to a perfect hundred eighty degrees. Their teeth curved backwards, and their favorite way of bringing down large prey was for several of them to latch onto it, slowing it down, while others in the pack did their best to trip the panicked prey. Once the prey was on the ground, the pack wouldn't bother to kill it, they'd just start feasting.

I couldn't fall. Howlers might be low on the food chain, but it was still three against one. A little of my bloodlust rose, and I let some remain while pushing most of it back down. It wasn't enough to actually do anything other than change my eye color, but I found it easier to control if I let a small amount linger.

It would've been smarter to let more of it come to the surface. I was bleeding from at least half a dozen wounds that I hadn't healed yet. Plus, I'd need every inch of speed I could muster up for this fight.

But I couldn't bring myself to trust the bloodlust that hummed in my soul, begging to be set free.

Samara was confident that I would never turn Strigoi, especially if I continued to drink from her regularly. But it'd been weeks since I'd sunk my fangs into her soft flesh and swallowed the sweet elixir that was her blood.

As much as I wanted to share her faith in me, I'd seen my cousin turn Strigoi. The funny boy I'd grown up with was gone, and all that had remained was a monster that'd tried to rip out my throat. And he wasn't the only one in our family who had been lost.

I wouldn't risk it.

Besides, I was looking forward to more physical pain. Anything was better than the sharp, bitter feeling of loss and failure that I felt every waking moment.

I focused on everything Samara had taught me about shooting. Exhale when you draw the string and keep that exhale slow and steady through the release.

The sound of the bow string snapping echoed across the meadow, followed by the thunk of it sinking into the neck of the large howler.

Damn it. Missed. I'd been aiming for its fucking eye, but instead, I'd hit the meaty part of it's neck. So all I'd done was piss it off.

Samara wouldn't have missed.

One of the smaller howler's heads swung away from me and towards the larger one, its nostrils flaring at the scent of fresh blood. Usually, they weren't cannibalistic, but when they were this far gone, they'd go after anything that was potentially food—even each other.

The beast launched itself at its larger packmate and the two of them tumbled across the ground. I tossed the bow aside and pulled my sword free. It didn't take long for the larger beast to overpower the smaller one, gripping it by the neck and shaking vigorously. I heard the telltale snap of a neck, but the beast didn't halt its assault.

My instincts screamed at me to move, and I barely managed to step to the side as the third howler lunged for my throat. I brought my sword down on its neck, severing its spine with one stroke.

Pain lanced up my right leg as the large howler clamped down on my thigh. Flesh tore and bone snapped, forcing a scream from my throat. The howler shook its head back and forth, trying to tear my leg away, and my vision darkened for a second, the bloodlust trying to surge forward.

No.

My back hit the ground, and I dropped my sword. Shoving the pain into the same box I locked my bloodlust in, cool metal met my bloodsoaked fingers as I reached for the dagger holstered on my hip. The howler opened its jaws and bit down again, shattering the bone it'd already broken.

With a guttural yell, I slammed the blade into its eye.

The blow didn't slow the beast down at all; instead, it just started shaking its head again, slamming me into the earth. I gripped its head with my other hand and drew the dagger out.

Stab. *Die.* Stab. *Fucking die already!*

Its jaws finally loosened and the howler collapsed partway on top of me. I shoved it off with a groan and left the dagger buried in its flesh.

I needed to heal the wounds—rationally, I knew this; aside from the pain, I was losing too much blood. Moroi were hard to kill, but I'd been a little reckless in this fight, and I was fairly certain one of my arteries had been hit during that last round.

That explained the lightheadedness and my darkening vision.

"Yep. You're the epitome of control," the imaginary Samara teased. But as amazing as she was, Samara didn't have telepathy.

She wasn't here.

I was definitely losing it, but I couldn't bring myself to care. "I miss you. Please be safe."

My body protested as I forced myself to sit up and draw the glyph for healing on my leg with shaking fingers. I panted through the pain of bone fragments piecing themselves back together along with my torn flesh. Once that was done, I set to fixing the other wounds, and twenty minutes later, my body was healed but my soul was still aching.

The sound of hoofbeats drifted to me, and I turned to watch three rangers approach. I was surprised but glad that it'd taken them this long to get here. A few rangers had seen me leave alone earlier, and I had no doubt they had reported that to their superiors—who, in this case, were the rangers before me.

"Damn it, Alaric." The lead ranger glared at me, her blonde hair shining brightly in the afternoon sunlight. "I told you we would handle this."

I shrugged, picked my sword up off the ground, and swung it into the sheath on my back, ignoring the reproachful look the oldest of the rangers gave me over not cleaning it first. There wasn't a patch of my clothing that wasn't coated in blood—mine or the howlers'—and I hadn't bothered to bring a pack of supplies with me since I wasn't far from House Harker.

"Adrienne. Emil," I said in greeting before glancing at the third ranger, who had dismounted and was surveying my work close up. "Nyx."

The young ranger glanced up at me. "Nice work."

I grunted. Howlers were some of the least dangerous of the monsters that prowled the forests. They were pack hunters and really only posed a problem if the pack got particularly large. Occasionally, some type of madness would infect them. We didn't know what caused it, but if one of them got it, the entire pack would and, worse still, would transfer it to any other pack they came into contact with.

They'd turn highly aggressive and would attack anything, even if they had no chance of winning, leaving a trail of corpses behind them until they eventually starved to death. Rabid howlers didn't eat, only slaughtered. This sick pack had been reported a week ago with a warning that they were slowly moving closer to House Harker territory. I'd been sparring with the rangers when the report had come in.

Emil had specifically told me to stay out of it when he'd caught my interest in the news. But the daily sparring hadn't been cutting it anymore, and I needed an outlet to vent my frustrations on.

For a few moments, I'd managed to forget that my world was on fire. The fight had given me some clarity, and even though I felt the embers burning again, I knew I'd be able to concentrate better for at least a day or two.

Then I'd need to find something to kill again.

Emil gave me an understanding look. Everyone at House Harker was feeling the strain. The Head of the House, the Heir, and the Marshal were all gone. Everyone knew Carmilla was at the Sovereign House, but no one had seen Samara or Vail.

Neither of them, or Carmilla for that matter, had sent any messages to clear up the confusion.

Something was very wrong. We all knew it, and we all had different ways of coping while we tried to figure it out.

Adrienne was staring daggers at me from atop her enormous chestnut stallion. Her way of coping had me grinding my teeth on most days. She was second-in-command with Vail being gone and had a tendency to be overprotective of everyone, like she alone could keep us all safe through sheer force of will.

Before, it had been Nyx who had borne the brunt of Adrienne's obsessive protective inclinations, but that had now been extended to me, Roth, and Kieran.

Roth rolled with it, mostly because it was hard to get them out of the library, so the only thing they fought with Adrienne about was eating regularly. Aside from that, they were able to handle Adrienne's constant hovering.

Kieran and I did not handle it well.

Emil sighed, likely sensing the brewing fight between me and Adrienne. He'd been the one to break up the fight between her and Kieran, though not before Kieran got a split lip and a black eye. Adrienne might have been the protective sort, but she also had a wicked temper—and if she thought knocking us out was the best way for her to achieve her goals, she'd absolutely do it.

"Do you need a ride back?" Emil asked. "We should get out of here. The blood is going to attract all kinds of nasty things."

"Which is why we planned to draw the pack farther from the House," Adrienne growled.

I winced. It had actually been my intention to do just that, but I'd underestimated just how good the creatures' sense of smell was. The howlers had been on me before I could attempt to get them farther away . . . which was no doubt one of the reasons Emil had ordered me to not go after them. Not just for my own safety, but because this was what the rangers did. None of them would have made the mistake I had.

"We can send extra patrols this way." Nyx mounted their bay gelding. "Just to keep an eye on things. I'll make sure it gets done."

"You will not be on those patrols." Adrienne finally stopped glaring at me to give Nyx a sharp look.

"Wouldn't dream of it," Nyx replied smoothly.

I was pretty sure they were lying, and based on how Adrienne narrowed her eyes at the young ranger, she clearly thought the same. Good. Maybe Nyx could draw her ire for a while.

"Ride?" Emil repeated calmly.

I raised my fingers to my lips and whistled. Moments later, a dark grey mare came charging past the tree line at the other end of the meadow, where she'd been munching on grass like she didn't have a care in the world while I'd been fighting for my life. She didn't bother dodging the howler corpses on the ground; if anything, she purposely went out of her way to stomp on them.

"Brave of you." Emil's brows rose. "That horse is evil incarnate."

Zosa slid to a stop in front of me, howler blood smeared across her legs and stomach, and her dark eyes were full of a fire and rage that echoed my own soul.

"We have an understanding." I stroked the mare's nose. "She'll take me where I need to go, and I'll kill anything that stands between me and the woman who owns both our souls."

<hr>

"Still no messages from her or the Sovereign House." My fingers tightened on the stone wall of the balcony just off the aviary where we kept the strikers.

"Told you we wouldn't hear anything." Roth gave me a flat look. "Can I return to the library now, or would you prefer to waste my time further?"

This was exactly why I'd snuck out this morning to hunt down the rabid howlers. I'd needed something to take the edge off so I could deal with Roth.

I'd gotten used to their taciturn personality since Roth had moved to House Harker, but it'd been different ever since Samara—along with Vail and Draven—had vanished. Thanks to Kieran's connections, we were pretty certain they were all at the Sovereign House, but the other information we'd received was confusing . . . and disturbing.

Supposedly, Carmilla had overthrown Queen Velika with the help of Velika's consort, Samara's ex-husband Demetri . . . and Vail. What had happened to

Samara and Draven after that was a little harder to determine. There were rumors that the prince was dead, something that didn't bother me all that much but had sent Kieran spiraling. Nobody had seen Samara recently, but one guard who was loyal to Kieran said she was in the dungeon.

That couldn't be right though. If Carmilla had truly overthrown the Sovereign Queen—something that was hard to come to terms with because we all thought they'd been friends despite Velika's ill intentions—why would she throw her niece into the dungeon? Carmilla had helped raise Samara after her parents had been killed and had always been fiercely protective of her, and Samara was completely loyal to her aunt.

None of this made sense. It had been almost two weeks since Samara and Vail had left on their mission to find the other half of the lost Fae crown that supposedly could override the free will of others. Velika had the other half, and those two had raced off to make sure she didn't get the second piece. Against my better judgment, we'd told Draven where they'd been heading when he'd demanded to know, and he'd gone after them.

I glanced at Kieran, who hadn't even acknowledged us when Roth and I had barged up here. Even now, all his attention was on the letter he was composing.

He loved Samara . . . and Draven. Both of the people who mattered to him more than anyone else—vanished. Samara, I understood. She and Kier had been in love the moment they'd laid eyes on each other. The prince . . . *that* I was still having a hard time wrapping my head around.

I hadn't even known Kieran and the prince had been involved until recently, which was something I was still a little pissed off about. Kieran had been my best friend for well over a decade, and he'd kept something major from me.

Despite Draven's declarations about caring for Samara, I still didn't trust the Moroi Prince. Velika was his mother, and we knew he was working for the wraiths and had helped them slaughter several of our outposts in recent years. Despite that, Kieran loved him, and Roth, of all people, backed Kieran up when he suggested we tell Draven. I was the odd person out, but even I had gone along with it because, despite my feelings about Draven, I did believe there was something between not only him and Kieran but Samara too.

And it wasn't a minor something. Not with the fierce and possessive look he'd had in his eyes that day.

"Apologies, Roth." I spun around and leaned against the stone wall, crossing my arms over my chest. "Do you have something useful to add? By all means, speak up and let us know what you've found in the library that will answer what the fuck is going on right now."

Fiery orange flecks burned in Roth's hazel eyes as their bloodlust rose. They'd barely left the library for the past two weeks, but after I'd returned and cleaned myself off, I'd gone there to find them waging war on the books. Several of them had pages torn out, and Roth was cursing in languages I didn't even recognize. I'd tried to calm them down, but they'd only stormed out, as if the books had betrayed them in failing to provide an answer.

It'd taken some doing, but I'd convinced them to come up here for some fresh air. I'd had no idea if it would help, but I needed Roth to keep it together because I barely was . . . and Kieran definitely wasn't.

Given Roth's current mood, I kept one eye on their forearms, where bloodred ropes were looped. They used to be flat ribbons, but now the fabric was thicker and looked like three pieces braided together, making it more rope-like.

The only place Roth had spent any time besides the library was the target range in the training yard. On particularly bad days, they'd trash a dozen targets. With half a thought, they'd have their ropes unwinding from their arms and shooting towards the wood targets we used for archery, and blood-colored protrusions would jut out seconds before the ropes made contact, slicing through the wood.

Roth had always been a bit grumpy and standoffish, but this viciousness was something new that we were all getting used to.

At the rate Roth and I kept going at each other, I knew my blood would be dripping from those ropes sooner rather than later.

Clearly, Kieran felt a fight between Roth and I was imminent because he looked up from the letters he was rapidly churning out to give both of us an annoyed look. "If the two of you are going to bicker, go somewhere else." His eyes, which had been more gold than brown lately, dropped back to the note he was writing. Normally, Kieran kept himself clean-shaven and his hair neatly styled, but he was sporting a week's worth of stubble, and his blond hair looked like it hadn't been brushed in days.

"Are you reaching out to the same people?" I asked tiredly. "I don't see why they'd tell you anything different than they did two days ago."

"Maybe don't tell me how to interact with people." His words were clipped, and there was an edge to his voice I'd never heard from him before. His eyes dropped back to the letters. "Roth is supposed to be good at research, although that's been an epic fail. I'm good at gathering gossip and cashing in on favors, which is why we have any information at all right now. What the fuck do you do, Alaric? Other than going traipsing off into the woods and leaving all the work to us? Do you even give a shit about getting her back? Or does this make you happy?"

I swallowed back my growl. Thank fuck I'd gone out this morning; otherwise, I definitely would have ripped his head off—best friend or not.

"Sorry," Kieran said tightly without looking up.

Roth and I shared a look. We might constantly fight with each other, but that was mostly because we were too similar in a lot of ways. As pissed off as we'd get, neither of us ever held a grudge—at least not for long. Kieran was the peacekeeper in our group, and neither of us knew how to roll with the changes in his behavior.

Roth and I were good at a lot of things, but emotional comfort was not one of them. I cared about Kieran because he was my best friend, and I thought Roth had grown to like Kieran despite themself. Kier was just so . . . Kier. He was honest, loyal, and always willing to help everyone.

Now he was hurting and neither of us knew what to do because we were trying to keep from spiraling into panic and despair ourselves. Samara would have known what to do. She always did.

I missed her so much, it hurt. Up until recently, we'd been adversaries, but even then, I'd been obsessed with her. Samara had consumed my soul long before I'd ever tasted her lips against mine, and now she was missing and I had no fucking answers as to why or how to help her.

She was counting on me—on us—and we were failing her. I found everything about that unacceptable.

I took a deep breath. Letting myself unravel into despair wouldn't help.

The absence of both Carmilla and Samara hadn't exactly gone unnoticed. There was a quiet tension in House Harker, and the other advisors had been looking to me for answers. I'd been Carmilla's top advisor, and since returning, I hadn't exactly hidden that things between Samara and I had changed.

Everyone was aware of her relationship with Roth and Kieran. I hadn't stood in the center of the courtyard and dramatically declared my feelings, but I hadn't needed to. I spent every waking moment trying to figure out what had happened to Samara. And even though we were biting each other's heads off constantly, Roth, Kieran, and I were often together.

It didn't take a genius to figure out that Samara had claimed another lover —just the gossip mill that was the House Harker court.

I was trying to figure out how to suggest to Kieran that maybe he should try some new contacts without setting him off when the doors to the rooftop burst open.

Adrienne stalked out onto the stone balcony, Emil and Nyx right behind her. A few of the strikers flapped their wings in unease at the sudden intrusion, their brightly colored scales glistening in the sunlight.

"I take it from your grim faces that you don't have any news—good or bad —to share?" Adrienne asked. Like Kieran, Adrienne was usually perpetually full of joy, but recently, the ranger, who was only a decade older than us, looked tired and drained. The other two rangers—Nyx and Emil—didn't look any better.

All of the rangers were feeling a little uneasy about Vail's absence. But Adrienne, Emil, and Nyx were part of Vail's personal squad—more than that, they were friends.

The fact that they hadn't heard anything from him either had only increased everyone's concerns.

"No," Kieran replied without looking up from his letter. "Nothing today. You?"

Adrienne didn't answer, and it was then that I noticed the letter she clenched at her side.

"What did you learn?" It took every ounce of my self-control not to close the distance between us and rip that piece of paper out of her hand. But I knew Adrienne would tell us—we'd been sharing information all week—and she could absolutely kick my ass. So I stayed where I was and forced myself to be patient.

"It's not good." Her expression was pinched, and when she opened her mouth to say more, it was like the words escaped her. Finally, she just held the letter out, and I quickly walked over and grabbed it, eyes skimming the words. There wasn't much written, as if the person had only had a small opportunity to send the message and had hastily slapped it together. I'd expected it to be from Vail, but this wasn't his handwriting.

"Well?" Roth pushed. Even Kieran had stopped writing and was completely focused on me.

I swallowed. "It says Carmilla has been seen walking around the Sovereign House . . . with a crown of silver and gold on her head. Vail is often at her side."

Kieran slammed his palm down on the table he'd dragged up here, sending some of the paper flying and several strikers to take off in the air. Then he rose and stalked to the other side of the balcony.

"Anything about Samara . . . or Draven?" Roth asked.

"No." I shook my head and stared at the short note, as if some further insight would magically appear. Based on all the information we'd been able to piece together, it wasn't a surprise that Carmilla was walking around free. Confusing, absolutely, because I didn't understand why she hadn't reached out to us. Queen Velika being dead had been reported by enough sources that we'd all accepted that as well—shocking as it may have been.

But the crown . . . that was new. We'd been so worried about Velika getting her hands on both pieces that it had never occurred to us that someone else might not only know of its existence but would be vying for it as well. And definitely not Carmilla.

As unbelievable as it seemed, if Kieran's informant was telling the truth, Samara wasn't simply missing—she was imprisoned in the Sovereign House. And Carmilla now possessed the whole crown . . . and Vail wasn't sharing a cell next to Samara.

"Did Vail betray us?" I half whisper the accusation. On one hand, it didn't seem possible . . . but then Vail might not have seen it as betrayal, at least not to House Harker. He was loyal to Carmilla, almost fanatically, and his dislike of Samara wasn't exactly a secret, but it'd seemed like things had been changing between them. Had he deceived all of us? A humorless laugh flowed from me. "We were so concerned about the wicked prince that we didn't see the devil already walking amongst us."

"We don't know that Vail betrayed Samara," Nyx snapped. They were the youngest of the rangers and held Vail up on a pedestal, more so than even Adrienne and Emil. "Maybe Carmilla used the crown on him. We know it can force anyone to obey the person wearing it. He may be just as trapped as Samara, even if there are no visible bars around him."

Roth shook their head. "She still would have had to get the crown, and Vail was with Samara. If they found the other half, it's not that big of a stretch to think he stabbed Samara in the back and gave it to Carmilla."

"Vail must have had his reasons," Emil said evenly, which seemed to soothe Nyx somewhat. I could see the doubt in the older Moroi's eyes though. Despite his words, Emil clearly had some concerns about what Vail was up to.

"So what do we do now?" Adrienne asked. "Keep waiting for more information to trickle in? Or go to the Sovereign House to see for ourselves?"

"If that crown truly does everything we think it's capable of, then our free will could be taken away as soon as we walk through those gates." Emil's dark bushy brows creased in concern. It didn't escape my attention that he hadn't said Carmilla's name. We were all having a hard time coming to terms with the fact that the House Leader we'd served our entire lives—someone we'd thought had been just and fair—would be okay with enslaving her own people like that.

I glanced at the letter again. *Carmilla wears a crown of silver and gold.* If my parents had been here, I'd have asked them—they knew Carmilla well since they'd served her for over a century before semi-retiring—but lately they'd been foregoing the safety of the Harker fortress to spend time helping in the outposts. No amount of pleading on my part about the dangers facing our outposts had convinced them to return. Now, I was a little thankful, because if Carmilla truly was seizing power over the Moroi, it would be the Houses she targeted first.

"Roth," I said slowly, my gaze flicking briefly to Kieran, who had silently joined us again, a storm brewing in his eyes. "Do we have any books or documents that show the interior layout of the Sovereign House?"

"No." Eyes that burned like fire looked at me. "But I know where we can get some."

CHAPTER TWO

—

Samara

"Have you reconsidered your answer yet?" My ex-husband smiled down at me through the bars of my cell, where I was leaning against the back wall. There'd been a time when I would have found that smile appealing. It had a charming, sly quality to it, like he was thinking of something amusing and couldn't wait to share it with you. With his perfectly tousled chestnut hair and stunning hazel eyes, Demetri was quite the looker, and he knew it, but I wasn't a sixteen-year-old girl anymore who could be dazzled by easy grins and pretty eyes.

Actually, even at sixteen, I hadn't been that gullible. Just a little more willing to put aside my happiness for the sake of my House.

That was no longer who I was. At twenty-four, I knew exactly what and who I wanted, and I did want Demetri.

I wanted him bleeding out on the floor at my feet.

"Have you considered shutting the fuck up?" I gave Demetri a smile that showed way too much fang to be considered anything friendly. "Or better yet, slitting your own throat?"

The grin slipped as the muscles along Demetri's jaw tightened. He'd come down here every day to ask if I'd reconsidered his offer of marriage. Because being married to that worthless piece of shit hadn't been bad enough the first time—he actually thought I'd willingly sign up for round two.

I had a feeling he'd love nothing more than to open the door to my cell, step inside, and throttle me for all the insults I'd hurled his way over the past week. That would be a nice change of pace. I wasn't particularly good at hand-to-hand combat—knives and bows were my thing—but with how wrathful I was feeling, I had no doubt I could rip out Demetri's throat faster than he could blink.

Alas, the hulking brute standing directly opposite me on the other side of the dungeon kept Demetri from trying anything devious. Well . . . more devious than going along with having your ex-wife thrown into a prison cell while you tried to strong-arm her into marrying you again.

So far, my aunt—the real reason I was in this fucked-up situation—had kept her word about not forcing me to marry Demetri. Although she'd also made it clear that she thought the marriage would be in the best interest of everyone.

Everyone clearly did not include me.

There had to be a reason. Neither of them were the sentimental type. There was some political gain to me being married to Demetri that I wasn't seeing, and they must have discovered it recently because they'd both allowed my divorce to go through, and that had only been a couple of months ago.

But since I was locked in this fucking cell, I had no way of finding out the reason behind all of this. I needed to get out of here. I had to make sure Kieran, Roth, and Alaric were alright. Plus check in with Cali and Rynn, who were no doubt losing their minds over my lack of communication. Draven was alive—for now—but I refused to leave him behind, so I had to devise a plan that got him out too.

There was another complication to all of this. A ticking clock, so to speak. Cramps tore through my lower abdomen, taking my breath away and sending a fresh bolt of pain every minute. I felt like I was dying.

The hulking brute, Vail—also known as the lying sack of shit—glanced at me with a frown. His grey eyes scrutinized me as if he could sense the pain I was in.

I ignored him and tried to will the cramps away. And the Marshal while I was at it. Tragically, they both remained.

When the humans had cast the spell to turn themselves into Moroi, it'd led to a fucked-up reproductive cycle. Every four months, anyone with a uterus would experience the joy of excruciating pain and bleeding. It only lasted for two or three days, but those days were absolute agony. Once that funness was over, my sex drive would go wild. That part *was* usually fun—almost made up for the three days of suffering—but given my current situation, it was a problem.

I wouldn't be completely out of my mind with lust, but thinking coherently would be difficult. So I was basically looking at almost a week of limited cognitive function. Wonderful. As if my situation weren't fucked enough already.

It wasn't as if the woman that I'd respected, looked up to, and absolutely idolized had betrayed me. And not a little betrayal. A *lied to me and manipulated me for years, tortured and imprisoned the man I loved, and had me thrown in a moonsdamned dungeon* type of betrayal.

I rubbed the empty space on my finger where the ring Cali had gifted me should've been. Demetri had been the one to take it off—gleefully. When we'd been married, I'd regularly used it to communicate with Cali and Rynn. He probably knew how much my two best friends didn't like him and took great joy in making sure I couldn't reach out to them.

Rynn was with the Alpha Pack now. No doubt she wasn't happy about that, but at least she was safe. Those assholes would protect her—whether she wanted that protection or not.

It was Cali I was worried about. All Furies had a bit of a short fuse. Cali was pretty good about controlling her temper—unless Rynn or I were threatened, then all bets were off.

The fact that she wasn't already here raining down blood and fury had me worried. My fingers curled inwards until my claws pressed into my skin just shy of drawing blood. I hated Carmilla for imprisoning me and keeping me from helping my friends put out the fires that seemed to be popping up everywhere.

The only person I hated more than her right now was Vail, because he was the reason I was in this mess. When I wasn't trading barbs with Demetri, I was screaming at him. At least, I had been for the first five days. Lately, I'd switched to ignoring his presence because that seemed to hurt him more, based on how his eyes would bleed silver after a few minutes.

I didn't give the slightest fuck about Vail's feelings right now though. He'd betrayed me—after he'd fucked me.

He could rot in a shallow grave right next to Demetri for all I cared.

Demetri's hazel eyes hardened the longer he looked at me, light green flecks starting to expand into the brown as his temper and bloodlust rose. For a second, another pair of hazel eyes surfaced in my mind. But Roth's eyes were far prettier. Their secondary eye color was more of a burnt orange, like little sparks that would flare in their eyes. Compared to my sharp-tongued love, Demetri was nothing.

Less than nothing.

I'd find a way out of here. Back to all of them. Ideally before my lovers tried something insane like breaking into the Sovereign House.

Yeah, because breaking out is a much saner idea.

Shut up, brain. Nobody asked you.

Fuck. *I might be losing it.*

My stomach churned as the pain of my cramps reached a new level. I was going to hurl up my meager breakfast all over this floor if I didn't lie down soon. A bead of sweat formed at my hairline. It was bad enough that I was sitting while he was here, but standing wasn't an option. I settled for keeping my spine ramrod straight while I sat and didn't let my feral smile falter.

"Fine," Demetri finally said, brushing a hand through his hair as if he weren't monumentally frustrated with me. "I'll take my leave for now." His eyes glinted with a slyness I didn't like one bit. "Perhaps I'll pay the fallen prince a visit and test out my new iron-tipped spear. Maybe I'll get him to scream loud enough that you'll be able to hear him all the way up here."

My mask cracked and then shattered into a thousand pieces. In a second, I was on my feet at the front of the cell, wrapping my fingers around the bars that separated us.

"Touch him, and I'll rip out your spine and beat you to death with it!" I snarled and shook the bars even as they burned my skin. All of the bars in the dungeon had a high level of iron because they'd been built by the Fae. Why the Fae had felt the need to imprison their own kind, I had no idea.

Just like I had no idea why I had a reaction to the iron. It felt revolting against my skin.

"Pretty sure he'd already be dead at that point," Vail said from where he still casually leaned against the wall, sharpening one of his knives. "But I've never really tested Moroi healing abilities in that way. Could be a fun little experiment."

"Nobody fucking asked you," I snapped at Vail before mentally slapping myself. Well, he'd finally gotten me to speak to him.

Demetri gave Vail a cool look. "You were told to stay away. I'll be informing Carmilla of this."

Vail shrugged, eying his dagger for a moment before continuing to sharpen it. "Seems like a poor choice."

"And why is that?"

The Marshal of House Harker finally looked up to meet Demetri's gaze, thick silver cracks weaving through his dark grey eyes. "Because then I'd be forced to rip out your tongue for being a sniveling little tattletale."

Demetri's eyes flashed green for a moment before his cool and collected facade snapped back into place. There was a conniving wickedness to Demetri that I'd never seen in all the years we'd been married. Either it was new or he'd done an excellent job of hiding it. I suspected the latter, which irked me because I hadn't seen through his *lazy but mostly harmless* act for all that time.

"Fine. Stay here as long as you want." A knowing smile spread across his lips. "She'll never forgive you. Samara never loved me, but the way she stares at you when you're not looking"—he sucked in a harsh breath—"that's definitely love. The fallout of it anyway. Did you know, Vail? When you agreed to betray her, did you know she loved you? What about when you parted those deliciously thick thighs and fu—"

Faster than I could track, Vail had his hand wrapped around Demetri's throat as he slammed him against the bars of my cell, causing me to jump back. He flung the other Moroi to the floor and took one step towards him before halting and spinning around to pace to the other side of the dungeon.

Demetri had succeeded in getting both Vail and me to lose our tempers.

Instead of being upset, my ex-husband just let out a hoarse laugh as he rose to his feet, brushing away the dirt from his clothes and swiping his hair back. "You're both so touchy." He straightened the collar of his dark red shirt. "See you tomorrow, Samara. I'll tell the prince you said hello."

"Fucker!" I screamed as the heavy wood door closed behind him. A second later, I was bending over and heaving up my breakfast. Then I straightened and wiped my mouth with the back of my hand. It took me a minute to realize Vail had moved over to my cell and was holding a canteen through the bars. I snatched it from him and rinsed out my mouth, then walked as far away from the vomit as possible.

"He's bluffing," Vail said quietly. "Draven scares the shit out of him. He's only been to that level once, and he ran out the door like wraiths were chasing him."

I didn't say anything. Partly to annoy Vail, but mostly because the pain had reached a new level and it was taking all my concentration to stay upright and conscious. A sharp gasp exploded from my lips, and I decided that if I wanted to stay awake, I needed to sit down.

"What's wrong?" Vail crouched outside my cell. Some of the silver had faded from his eyes, but they were still intense as he examined me, trying to find why I looked like a strong wind would blow me over. "Quit being fucking stubborn, Samara, and tell me what the fuck is wrong with you."

"My cycle is here," I ground out. It wasn't like he wouldn't figure it out once the blood started flowing, which would be any minute now, considering how bad the pain was.

"Shit." His eyes widened. "What can I do?"

"Go back in time to when the humans were crafting the spell to turn us into Moroi and maybe tell them to tweak it a little bit so we don't have to suffer through this bullshit every few months?"

"Samara," he growled.

I rolled my eyes. "Just ask the kitchen staff. They'll have some tea that will help with the pain."

He rose without a word and headed towards the door.

"And Vail?" I waited until he looked over his shoulder at me. "Make sure I get some contraceptive tea in three days."

His expression darkened, but he jerked his head in a tight nod before leaving me alone once more. The timing of my cycle was unfortunate for all kinds of reasons. I needed to be sharp right now, and that was hard to do while I was in constant pain. And what came next wouldn't be much better.

Moroi were the most fertile in the weeks after our cycle. Demetri didn't want to marry me because he loved me; I suspected part of it was injured pride over how easily I had left him, but maybe he wanted an Heir—one that came from my bloodline and his. I wouldn't be marrying Demetri again, and I certainly wouldn't be having a child with him. He was too scared to step in the cell with me, but I still wanted to have the contraceptive tea just in case. It would prevent all pregnancies until my next cycle.

And fuck, I better be out of here before then.

When the door opened half an hour later, I raised my head from where it had been hanging between my knees, expecting to see Vail. Instead, my body went still as I took in another familiar face.

"Hello, dear," my aunt said politely. "I think we're overdue for a chat."

A collision of emotions slammed through me like a whirlwind. Hurt and confusion from the betrayal. Embarrassment and frustration for never having suspected her. And a boiling rage beneath all of that.

"Are we?" I fixed my features into a calm but distant expression. Ideally, I would have casually risen to my feet and stood before my aunt, but there was zero chance of that happening. Blood was seeping through my undergarments, and the cramps had shifted to a dull but constant pain.

I wouldn't be moving anytime soon.

Carmilla's dark green eyes swept over me, but whatever she was thinking was hidden behind her own mask. So much of my own tactics when it came to political conversations were based on what I had learned from her. I'd been a constant shadow in her presence growing up—sitting in on meetings and reading the letters she would send to other Houses—I'd absorbed every bit of knowledge and insight she'd been willing to bestow.

And she knew it.

I had never once doubted my aunt. Instead, I'd taken everything she'd told me at face value, whereas if another had spoken similar words, I would have looked closer. And none of that had been by accident on her part. I'd had plenty of time to reflect on my relationship with my aunt the past week, and I didn't like what I'd seen.

How gullible I'd been.

"Don't give me that look, Samara." Carmilla waved a hand as she moved to stand in front of my cell, keeping just out of my reach. "It's not as if I planned on putting you here." She gestured at the dungeon walls.

"But it was *one* of the plans, wasn't it?" I raised a dark eyebrow at her. "'*If you only have one plan, you've already failed...*'" I impersonated her deep, throaty voice. "You might be a traitorous bitch, but I still remember the lessons."

"I haven't betrayed anyone," she said in a calm, even tone that made me want to scream in her face. For a second, my indifferent expression wavered before I wrestled my emotions back under control. "Velika betrayed us all when she started dealing with the wraiths. When she lay with one of them and bore them a child."

My mask shattered.

"So you blame Draven for the sins of his parents?" My voice vibrated with anger. "Do you know? Do you know what Velika did to him as a child? What that fucking crown is capable of?" I flicked my gaze up to the crown made of silver and gold that rested on my aunt's dark hair.

Something tickled the back of my mind. It felt like standing alone in a forest when a predator was stalking you from the shadows.

Was she trying to use the crown on me?

A painful cramp flared, but I hid it behind the rage I was feeling as I tried to guard my thoughts. Although, based on what Draven had said, the crown didn't work well on the House bloodlines, so I should be somewhat protected.

But then again . . . he'd been basing that on only half of the crown. Now that Carmilla had both pieces, could she control me? Was that why she wore it today?

"You truly are remarkable." Carmilla tilted her head as she studied me. "I know you're frightened right now. Probably about this"—she raised her hand and touched the crown—"but you hide it well. Your temper was always your greatest weakness though. I never could break you of that. Something you inherited from your mother, unfortunately."

"Did you ever care for me?" I held my chin high. "Or have I always been nothing but a political pawn for you to groom? The way you did Vail?"

During the long hours I'd had down here to myself, I'd alternated between plotting different ways out and thinking about my childhood after my parents had died. Vail and I had been friends prior to the death of our parents. He'd been enraged at me for my actions the night they'd died—my decision to stop him from going out in a doomed attempt to save them—but we could have recovered from that given time. We could have worked through our grief together. Instead, it had torn us apart.

And Carmilla had played a role in that. She'd been the stand-in parental figure for both of us. It'd given her the opportunity to whisper just the right words in our ears to create a divide in our friendship. She'd fanned the flames of Vail's anger, while at the same time hammering into me how important it was to be strong and not show any signs of weakness. To be the perfect Heir the way my parents would have wanted.

Vail and I had both been too close to her to see it then, and he was clearly still blind to it, but I saw things clearly now.

She could take her pretty lies and manipulative compliments and choke on them.

"Don't be so melodramatic." A half smirk curled up at the corners of her lips as she dropped her hand from the crown. "I only wanted what was best for you, and look how far the two of you rose! If I'd allowed you to remain friends, you wouldn't have reached down deep to find the motivation necessary to recover from a loss like that."

"Did you play a role in the death of our parents?" I pushed.

"Velika ordered it." She shrugged and absently studied her nails. "My sister had been a thorn in her side for too long. Mariona never told me what precisely she was looking for," Carmilla mused. "As much as my sister loved me, she didn't entirely trust me." Those calculating eyes slid to me. "Your sweet, trusting nature, you inherited from your father."

The coppery taste of blood filled my mouth as I bit down hard to keep a torrent of swear words from tumbling out. Apparently, Carmilla was testing for all the sore spots tonight. The question was . . . why? My aunt didn't have casual conversations. I understood that now better than ever before. She'd come down here for a specific purpose, and all her words were crafted to achieve it.

It also didn't escape my attention that she hadn't answered the question about if she'd played a role in my and Vail's parents' deaths. She'd only said Velika had ordered it, but that left plenty of room for her to still be involved. It made me suspect that she had at the very least known about the order . . . and done nothing to stop it. But I dropped it for now. Let her believe I thought Velika was solely responsible. I might be able to use it later.

I knew how to play the long game too.

"Perhaps we can continue this conversation under better . . . circumstances." She walked forward and brushed her fingers against my cell. "I would have come down here sooner, but I've been busy getting this House in order." Once again, my eyes flicked up to the crown.

A crown of two parts. Glittering gold and frosted silver.
One half to see a soul. Another half to bind it.

Those were the words Roth had found in their research. Velika had only possessed the half that bound souls, which meant she'd had to use blood magic to get the binding to settle—something about the ability to see souls made the bindings work better. There was so much we didn't understand about the crown, but clearly, Carmilla wasn't wasting any time testing it out.

I had to warn House Harker and the other Houses; otherwise, my aunt could stroll through their doors and enslave them all within an afternoon. I couldn't pull a complete about-face and suddenly give in to her demands, but getting out of this cell, even under supervision, would help me gather information and improve my odds of escaping.

"And what exactly are these *better circumstances*?" I drawled, my voice deepening towards the end when the muscles in my lower abdomen painfully clenched again. I once again cursed the poor timing of my cycle.

"A dinner." Carmilla smiled. "In three days, when you're feeling better."

I matched her polite smile. "Wonderful. Can't wait."

It wasn't surprising that Carmilla knew I was on my cycle. I had no open wounds, and she could no doubt smell the blood. Plus, my aunt had known me my entire life, so she knew what it looked like when I was trying to hide my pain. The fact that she knew it had just started was interesting. Had Vail told her? Or had she seen him collecting supplies for me and inferred what was going on from that?

"Demetri will be delighted to see you."

My smile turned sharp. So that's what she wanted. Me to be around Demetri when my cycle had just ended, when I'd be in a lust-filled haze.

"I'll be happy to see him again too." I let my bloodlust rise until I knew my eyes had turned black. "Perhaps I can finish what I started in that throne room."

When I'd done my best to cut his dick off.

Carmilla laughed and touched the crown again. I tensed. Would I know if the crown's magic was working on me? Would I feel my free will slipping away? I didn't feel any different, but the fear that I wouldn't know was almost too much to bear.

That alien presence brushed against my mind again, and I felt the hairs on the back of my neck stand up.

"I have much to attend to over the next couple of days." Carmilla's hands fell from the crown as the corners of her mouth pinched slightly, fighting a frown. "I'll have servants come down for you in two days so you can get cleaned up. Perhaps afterwards, we can see about keeping you somewhere else —under supervision of course—depending on how dinner goes."

Then she launched into a speech about how she truly did care about the Moroi. That she was doing what had to be done for the survival of all, and if I'd just see that, I could be of help to her. It wasn't my aunt's speech I was paying attention to though. It was the other voice drifting through my mind. One that felt ancient and devious.

Hello, my little forgotten one.

CHAPTER THREE

—

Vail

SAMARA WAS in so much pain, she was delirious. I knew this because she was currently curled up on my lap—a place she would never have been if she weren't out of it. It was the second day of her cycle. The first hadn't seemed too bad, although that was most likely due to the fact that she'd chugged the tea I'd brought her like it had been the answer to all her problems before asking for more.

I'd traumatized the kitchen staff with the way I'd barged in there repeatedly throughout the day, demanding more of the tea brewed specifically to dull cramps and help with pain.

When Samara had thanked me after the fourth cup instead of threatening to cut my balls off, I'd known things were about to get bad.

But bad had been an understatement.

Samara had barely moved all day. She'd just curled up in the corner of her cell on the pile of blankets I'd stolen from every vacant bedroom I could find. She'd practically bitten my head off when I'd suggested she ask to be moved to a bedroom just until this was over.

"I'm a prisoner," she'd spat. "Carmilla will want something if I make such a request." Then her eyes had flashed black. "She will get *nothing* from me."

I thought about going behind her back and asking Carmilla directly, but she had to know the state her niece was in. Even if she hadn't been to see Samara herself, Carmilla was the type of leader who always knew everything that was going on under her roof, and given how I'd stormed into the kitchen demanding the tea . . .

If Carmilla wanted to ease her niece's suffering, she could have done it at any time, which meant Samara was right. If she asked for a room and a more comfortable setting, she would have to agree to something.

539

Samara was frustratingly stubborn but not without reason. If the situation were reversed, I would have remained in the cell too.

Which was why I was sitting here with Samara wrapped in several blankets and tucked against my chest. She'd been drifting in and out of sleep, mumbling something about a crown that I couldn't quite make out. My arms tightened around her soft body.

This was the first time she'd allowed me to touch her since everything that had gone down in the throne room. Since I'd chosen Carmilla over her. At least, that was the way Samara viewed it.

I hadn't known this was how things were going to go though. I'd thought that once Carmilla and Samara spoke, everything would be okay. That they'd work it out and everything would go back to how it had been—the two of them working together. I mean, they both wanted the same thing—for the Moroi to survive.

It was Draven's fault. Samara had fucking lost it when that prick, Lucian, had stabbed him through the chest, and now it felt like there was a growing divide. Carmilla and her followers—myself included—on one side. Samara with her lot on the other.

I didn't know what Kieran, Alaric, and Roth had been told, and Carmilla requested that I not inform them of anything for now because she wanted to manage what information got back to House Harker. But the rumors about Velika's downfall and Carmilla's rise had to be spreading throughout the Moroi realm, so I wasn't really sure how well her plan would work.

Nobody was better at collecting rumors than Kieran, and he would have shared whatever he'd discovered with Alaric and Roth. I would've thought they would have been here already, demanding her release. But then . . . they knew about the crown. Surely Carmilla wouldn't use it on them though? Roth was a bit of an unknown, but Carmilla had known Alaric his entire life, and she liked Kieran. Maybe if they were here, they could talk some sense into Samara.

Because she sure as shit wasn't listening to me.

She let out a pained whimper, and I slipped one of my hands beneath the blankets to rub her back. "It's okay, Samara," I said roughly. "I got you."

"Vail," she murmured, turning her face into me to inhale my scent.

I bent my head down to nuzzle her hair. She'd be back to either ignoring me or trying to stab me in a couple of days, so I had to take what I could get. I hoped she'd go for my throat honestly. When she'd looked at me with hate in her eyes after everything that had gone down in the throne room, it'd hurt, but that was nothing compared to when she'd coldly blocked me out.

The violence, I could handle, because at least I knew she was feeling *something* towards me. I'd happily take that over pretending I didn't exist.

Samara had always consumed my soul. Love or hate, it had always been her.

I spent every waking moment thinking about her, and the fact that she could so easily cast me away pissed me off beyond reason. It was exactly why she'd done it. Samara could be a vicious fucking cunt.

And gods, I loved that about her.

My body went still as I heard someone coming down the stairwell. The guards did regular sweeps of the dungeon levels, but they never stepped foot inside this one if I was here.

They never went into the room where Draven's cell was either, just looked through the small window in the door to make sure he was still there. Even imprisoned, the Moroi Prince was feared.

Aside from me, the prince's only visitor was Lucian. I hadn't told Samara that though. While I didn't approve of her devotion to that half-Fae bastard, I wasn't going to tell her that the man who had tortured him for most of his life paid him regular visits. He currently wasn't able to do him any physical harm, but Lucian did enjoy bringing a bottle of wine down to Draven's cell and recounting the many ways he had tormented the fallen prince over the years.

It was fucked up. I didn't understand what Carmilla saw in him. It was on my growing list of things that just didn't add up.

It wasn't Lucian who walked through the door though—it was Demetri.

Another mystery I didn't fucking get. Why was Carmilla working with him? And why was she so keen on Samara marrying him again? She'd never mentioned that to me, and when I'd asked her about it days ago, she'd just brushed me off.

"Is there a reason you're groping my wife?" he asked idly as his sharp hazel eyes scrutinized the blankets covering Samara, as if he was trying to figure out where exactly my hands were.

A warning growl rumbled from me. Samara was half delirious. What type of person would take advantage of her in a situation like this? Even when I'd been moving her around, I'd been careful to keep my hands over her clothes. They were currently resting around her lower back and ribs, but he couldn't see that.

"Ex-wife." I gave him a cold look.

"Not for much longer. She'll be mine again soon." He shrugged and moved closer to the cell. I'd closed it when I'd stepped inside to be with Samara, and despite how much Carmilla wanted Demetri around, she hadn't given him the ability to open Samara's cell. Which told me, at least on some level, she didn't trust the Laurent Heir either.

"She was never yours to begin with." Tension coiled within me. I wanted nothing more than to rip out Demetri's throat. He was a threat to Samara, and despite how much she currently hated me, I *would* protect her. Unfortunately, Carmilla had been quite clear that I wasn't to lay a finger on him again. The little prick had mentioned me losing my temper and slamming him into the wall days ago. "Your marriage to her was nothing but a political move to strengthen the alliance between our Houses. Samara *never* belonged to you."

"And you think she belongs to you now?" Demetri skimmed his fingers across the bars of the cage. "Do you really think you'll get her in the end? After everything you've done to her?" He gave me a knowing glance. "She'll *never* choose you. Not now."

The deep pit that had opened up in my soul when I'd handed over that cursed crown cracked open a little more. Demetri's eyes glinted in the dim lighting of the dungeon, and he smiled at seeing his barbed remark strike true.

Samara hissed and tensed in my arms. Another cramp must have been hitting her. The tea that dulled the pain was also a light sedative, and she'd practically chugged the kettle earlier. Her eyelids fluttered for a second, and she turned her head away from my chest, inhaling deeply. She started to settle back down, but then she abruptly went completely still in my arms.

"Samara's a smart girl. She'll eventually come to realize that marrying me again is in not only her best interest, but that of our Houses—and the Moroi realm as a whole."

I stared at him. Moroi tended to be arrogant, but Demetri was taking it to a whole other level.

Samara started to shift her position, her movements slow enough and hidden by the blanket that I didn't think Demetri noticed as he paced on the other side of the bars.

"You cheated on her," I said flatly. "All you had to do was not be an asshole and she'd still be married to you right now."

Because Samara always did right by the House. I'd doubted her for a long time, but I knew that now. Carmilla wanted what was best too. They just needed more time to come to an agreement, but Demetri would not be part of that agreement. That was a line in the sand I knew Samara wouldn't cross. She might hate me, but she loved Kieran, Alaric, and Roth—and Draven, but I was ignoring that for now. She would never leave them.

And they'd slit Demetri's throat before they ever let him lay a finger on her again. If I didn't do it first.

"That was a misunderstanding." Demetri waved a hand dismissively.

"She walked in on you fucking someone else after she'd been loyal to you that entire time." I bared my fangs at him. Everyone at House Harker had known how much Samara and Kieran had wanted each other, but he'd never pushed and she'd never crossed that line. When Samara gave someone her loyalty, she meant it—whether they deserved it or not.

Suddenly, the dagger on my thigh smoothly slid free from the sheath. I should probably be concerned about Samara having a blade so close to my cock —not to mention a lot of vital organs—but I couldn't bring myself to stop her. Or warn Demetri that he might want to step away from the cell.

"It's not like I expect either of us to be monogamous," Demetri continued. "Although I won't allow her to see that courtier she's so obsessed with or that asshole advisor. There are rumors of another lover my beautiful wife has collected as well—that will have to end too. Anyone on the side must be casual. I'll give her some options to choose fr—"

In a heartbeat, Samara was on her feet and across the cell. She'd timed it perfectly, waiting until Demetri reached the cell wall and had begun to turn away to walk in the other direction. Her arm was through the bars and wrapped around his chest before he even knew what was happening. She pulled him back hard and pressed the dagger she'd stolen from me against his throat.

"Not your wife, asshole," Samara spat, her voice low and dangerous.

"Samara! Don't—" Demetri yelped, and a second later, the scent of his blood filled the air. Not much, but more than just a scratch's worth.

I rose to my feet and strolled over to the cell door. Tremors ran through Samara's body. From pain or rage, I didn't know. Probably both.

She didn't say anything as I leaned against the bars, making no move to help Demetri or get the dagger away from her.

"Do something," he ground out before flinching when Samara dug the blade in a little deeper. Nothing vital had been hit, but she was real close to the artery, and blood was steadily dripping from where she'd broken the skin.

I ignored him and looked at Samara. Her black hair was stuck to the sides of her face thanks to the sweat practically pouring off her. Normally, Samara's rich brown skin had a golden undertone to it, but she looked pale now, and her dark eyes stood out starkly on her face.

She glanced at me, eyes burning with fury.

"I'm not going to stop you," I told her. "Personally, I'm sick of hearing his voice, so his death is very appealing to me."

Demetri started to protest but went still when Samara adjusted the blade so it was resting right over his pulse. One move from her, and his lifeblood would be pouring out. He'd survive—if he got help immediately—which was unlikely, given that we were three floors down and he wouldn't be able to call for the guards with a slit throat.

"There will be consequences if you do this." My voice was calm, not giving a hint as to what outcome I preferred. Mostly because I didn't know. I wanted Demetri dead; every time he opened his mouth and made a claim on Samara, it took all my willpower not to slam his head repeatedly into a wall until it was nothing but a bloody mess.

But I wasn't lying. If Samara killed Demetri, she would be punished.

"I don't care," she half growled at me.

Logically, I knew I should stop her or at least try to talk her down, but it wasn't like she'd listen to me. If anything, my apparent disapproval would spur her on. There was also the fact that I *liked* seeing Samara like this. Most of the time, she floated around in her pretty dresses and perfectly brushed hair, but I remembered the Samara who had thrown a dagger across a courtyard to land between my fingers. The one who had taken out a howler with a crossbow shot most of my rangers wouldn't have been able to manage.

Beneath her beautiful exterior, Samara was a ruthless and cunning predator. It was one of the many things I loved about her.

"Vail will be punished," Demetri said carefully. "He's responsible for you."

Something dark and dangerous flickered in her gaze before she looked away from me. "I don't care," she repeated before digging the blade in a little more. Blood started to drip from the new cut.

She might as well have taken that knife and stabbed me. It certainly felt like she had.

"Draven!" Demetri rasped. "She'll hurt him to hurt you."

Samara froze and slowly turned her head to look at me for confirmation.

"You've made it quite clear how you feel about me." I held her unflinching gaze. "I'll be punished because I allowed it to happen, but Carmilla will have to punish you as well. She wouldn't want to cause you any lasting harm . . . so it makes sense she'd use Draven."

I didn't mention that there were many calling for the prince's public execution within the walls of the Sovereign House. Now that Queen Velika was dead, some of her enemies who had been too scared to speak out while she was alive were targeting her son.

My feelings about Draven were complicated. He was half Fae and his father was the leader of the bloody wraiths. Now that we knew the wraiths were just Seelie Fae fucked-up by shadow magic, it made me even more wary of the Fae in general. It felt like nothing good could come of them, so part of me was inclined to agree that Draven should be . . . eliminated.

But I'd also seen the way he looked at Samara. Oddly, it didn't make me jealous. Just grateful that she had another ruthless bastard in her life who loved her and would do anything to keep her safe.

Moons fucking damn me. How had everything gotten so fucking complicated?

The hand Samara had on Demetri's chest slipped down a little, and she leaned forward until her chest was pressed against the bars, her mouth inches from his ear.

"Next time I have a blade in my hand, I'm going to cut off your fucking head. Remember that. In the meantime"—she pulled the dagger away from his throat, flipping it in her hand and stabbing it down all in one smooth motion—"*crawl*."

Demetri released a strangled scream as Samara buried the dagger in his heart, holding it in place for a few seconds before releasing it and stepping back.

I wasn't the least bit ashamed to say the whole thing made me hard as a rock. Gods, she was such a vicious little cunt.

"Help," Demetri panted as he slid to the ground, his hands holding the blade securely against his chest. If he removed it, he'd probably bleed to death before he made it up the stairs. I glanced at the door and calculated the steps. He might make it. Moroi could recover from quite a bit. It would depend on how fast the guards reacted too.

I gave him a bored look. "You heard what the Heir said. I'd hold that dagger still and get to crawling."

Demetri glared at me. I knew I'd get in trouble for this. Carmilla had . . . concerns . . . about how close I was with Samara, but I couldn't bring myself to give a shit. Samara and I watched as Demetri tried to rise to his feet, only to let out a hiss of pain, and then proceeded to stumble to the door. He opened it and staggered outside to the stairs, where he gave up all pretense and proceeded to crawl up.

The heavy dungeon door slowly swung closed, and as soon as it clicked shut, Samara collapsed. I barely caught her before she hit the ground.

"Don't touch me," she growled. It was kind of a pathetic growl though, so I ignored it and picked her up, cradling her against myself. Then I walked to the same spot on the back wall of her cell where we'd been resting earlier and settled back down. Samara remained stiff in my arms, but she didn't fight to get free. I didn't have any delusions about that being because she liked being close to me. Violent shivers were running through her body, and she kept jerking in my grip and sucking in harsh breaths.

"Do you need more tea?" I asked quietly, even though I really didn't like the thought of leaving her. She'd made a good show of things with Demetri, but it was clear it had taken a lot out of her. I was the only ally she had here—other than Draven, but he was locked in a cell several floors below us.

"Won't help," she ground out.

Wordlessly, I reached out and gathered up the blankets she'd cast aside earlier to toss them over her. Samara shuddered but remained stiff against me. Then I adjusted the blankets until I was satisfied. Demetri would be reaching the guards soon, which meant, in an hour or less, Carmilla would likely be summoning me.

I wanted to enjoy the time I had left before I had to go and explain myself to the person who held my loyalty.

Does she though? a voice whispered in my mind.

"Why, Vail?" Samara's question was so faint, I barely heard it as she finally gave up resisting and sank into me. It was only because of the pain she was in, I knew that, but it still had to mean something, right? That, on at least some level, she trusted me enough to be vulnerable like this.

I knew what she was asking. After everything between us, the things we'd done, why had I betrayed her?

My arms wrapped tighter around her as I rested my head against hers, breathing in her scent. At that moment, all my reasoning about how I thought I'd chosen the best option for all of us didn't seem to matter. So I remained silent. And Samara didn't ask again.

"AH. The enormity of what you've done and just how much you've fucked up has finally hit you," the fallen Moroi Prince said with a cold chuckle. Draven's bright blue eyes were threaded with bloodred cracks. He'd kept his bloodlust at this level all week. Not fully risen, but not completely suppressed either.

It unnerved me a little because he didn't act any differently. I knew, based on how wary others were around me when I let my bloodlust rise, that my behavior changed. It wasn't just that my temper got a little hotter. There was just something *more* to me, like the beast I kept chained down was gazing out into the world and thought everything would look better drowned in blood.

But if it weren't for his eyes and the claws on his fingers, I'd never know Draven's bloodlust was out as much as it was. Samara was the same. Something about them was different from other Moroi.

Draven had been damn near death when he'd been dragged down here, but he'd lain on the ground and bounced back within hours. I suspected it had something to do with his Fae heritage. His father was the Seelie King, after all.

A memory of chains disintegrating to dust flashed through my mind. That day, when everything had gone to hell, Samara had reached for Draven in that throne room, trying to free him. Everything had been so chaotic, but I could have sworn I'd seen the chains disintegrate. Draven had barely been alive—if magic had been used, he hadn't been the source. There was also the fact that she was sensitive to iron, something she'd been trying to hide, but I'd seen the way she'd grimace ever so slightly whenever she made contact with the bars.

Those two things had caused suspicion about Samara's heritage to form in the back of my mind, even if it didn't seem possible. I'd known both of her parents—neither of them had been Fae—but could one of them have been part Fae like Draven? I mean, the prince *looked* like a Moroi. It stood to reason that one or both of Samara's parents could have had Fae blood running through their veins. Most likely her father because if Samara's mother was part Fae, then so was Carmilla. And given the way Carmilla talked about the Fae as a blight that needed to be destroyed, I didn't think she had any Fae blood.

I hadn't spoken my suspicions to anyone. And if anybody else had noticed some of the odd things that had happened around Samara lately, they hadn't mentioned them in front of me.

The question was . . . did Carmilla have similar suspicions? She hadn't been spending much time around her niece since seizing the throne, but she still knew Samara well. Maybe there had been other clues earlier in Samara's life that we'd all missed but she'd seen.

But why not be open about it? Why all the secrecy? My parents had loyally served House Harker and it had never occurred to me to not be the same—until the past couple of weeks.

I'd never questioned Carmilla's tactics before, but now there were children locked in the dungeon. Fucking *children*. I'd brought this up to Carmilla the day they'd been thrown in cells with their families, but she'd reasoned that it was impossible to know where their loyalties stood because Velika could have used the crown on them. We didn't know if Velika's death had voided all the forced blood bonds. Maybe they were loyal to her even in death.

But we did know that the bonds Velika had created would fade with time. So Carmilla had assured me that everyone would have access to food and water while in the dungeons and would be well taken care of.

It still didn't sit right with me.

Nor did watching some of the people—particularly those of high rankings who had important knowledge locked away in their minds—be led out of the dungeon to where Carmilla would meet with them. Behind closed doors. While she wore the crown.

I'd done that. It had been me who had handed over the second half of the crown to her, which meant I'd played a direct role in taking away the free will of Moroi.

Carmilla's reasoning had seemed so sound on paper. The wraiths were chipping away at our protections. Velika—and Draven—had been working with them.

Although Carmilla had left out the fact that Draven hadn't had a choice.

It was possible she hadn't known . . . but even I knew that was me being hopeful and only wanting to see the good in her. Carmilla had been sleeping with Velika's consort, and Lucian hated Draven. He also knew a lot about him. It seemed highly unlikely he hadn't shared some of that knowledge with Carmilla.

I didn't want to believe that Carmilla was manipulating me. Both because I loved her as if she were family and because it meant I was a fool.

A fool who had betrayed the woman who *did* love me. The thought jolted me back to the present and Draven's words. Uneasy dread coiled in my gut.

Did I fuck up? Maybe I should have held onto the crown and tried to have Samara and Carmilla negotiate without either of them possessing it.

"Don't recall asking for your opinion." I chucked a canteen through the bars. While Carmilla made sure food and water were brought to Samara and the other Moroi detained in the dungeon, she'd made no such orders for Draven. As far as I knew, I was the only one bringing him sustenance.

Not that he acted the least bit grateful. He did talk to me during these visits though, which was more than I could say about Samara until recently.

I should have stayed away from her. I knew Carmilla wanted me to. She hadn't specifically forbidden me from seeing Samara, but she had strongly hinted at it. I couldn't stay away though. There was this odd pull inside my chest that I couldn't explain. It was like I was always aware of Samara's existence. Her location—not that she was moving anywhere—her emotions, and just . . . her.

In what was rapidly becoming a habit, I rubbed the spot over my heart where I felt the tightness. It was a weird sensation that I was noticing more and more, but I had no idea what it meant. At first, I thought it was stress, but occasionally, I noticed Samara placing a hand over the exact same place on her chest when I felt it.

There was no point in asking her about it. She'd either lie or spit in my face.

And when she did, that awareness between us ached like a wound that had begun to fester.

It wasn't like Samara and I didn't have a history of hostility and distrust, but even during those tumultuous years, Samara had never ignored me.

She'd never loathed my existence.

"How is she?" Draven asked. His tone was even, but a little more red bled into his eyes.

I rubbed my face. "Her cycle started a few days ago and ended last night. She's due to have dinner with Carmilla, Lucian, and Demetri in an hour."

Understanding dawned on Draven's face, and his eyes turned a deep solid red. "And this is the woman you willingly serve? Samara's blood is still running through your veins. That crown isn't forcing your loyalty."

"You're the son of the Seelie King." I bared my teeth. "Don't lecture me about conflicting loyalties when the blood that runs through *your* veins is the same as the man who's slaughtered thousands of us."

He fell silent for a moment, and I started to leave.

"Velika was never a mother to me." I stopped and turned back to face the prince. "She always hated me. I never understood why . . . and now that she's dead, I suppose I never will, but for a while, I thought Erendriel might actually act like a loving parent. Unlike my mother, he did have my loyalty—for a brief amount of time anyway."

"What happened?"

Draven hadn't talked about Erendriel since telling me who he truly was. Whatever spell had been cast on the Moroi Prince to keep him from talking had clearly been broken. Or maybe he'd been lying about that all along. Samara might have trusted him, but I still didn't.

But do you still trust Carmilla? a voice whispered in the back of my mind. I didn't have an answer.

A humorless smile stretched across Draven's face. "I learned that the Fae King does not love—only uses—and one can either volunteer to be of use . . . or be forced to be."

Guilt and unease rose, but I kept it off my face. Carmilla had made it clear that Draven was the enemy. She claimed she was only keeping him alive to use against his father, but I suspected the real reason was because she saw Draven as a way to control Samara.

It seemed like one way or another, the Moroi Prince had been a pawn for most of his life. His mother had controlled him with her half of the crown, and his father had used Fae magic to bind him. Carmilla condemned Draven because he was half Fae . . . but he hadn't had a choice in any of it. Now, she was going to use that crown to manipulate and bind other Moroi . . . the same way Draven's parents had done to him.

Her intentions might be good, but that didn't make it right . . . did it?

"When I was twelve, Erendriel took me away from Velika," Draven continued. "I lived with the wraiths for a while. Up until that point, he hadn't taken much of an interest in me. I didn't want to be anywhere near Velika, so I did my best to prove my worth."

"What were they like?"

Until recently, we'd thought the wraiths were just strange shadow monsters that plagued our lands. There had been some speculation that they were related to the disappearance of the Fae, but not that the Seelie had turned into the wraiths. It still seemed strange to me because it had been the Unseelie who'd had shadow magic. So how had it been that Seelie were the ones turned into nothing but shadows?

I thought of that hideaway we'd found near the lake in the Velesian territory. So many answers could lie there, or in the journals we'd found in the cave near House Harker. I hadn't mentioned either of those things to Carmilla. It felt like my loyalty was being pulled in multiple directions, and I no longer knew which way was right.

Draven flinched and rubbed his forehead. "There are still some things I cannot speak of." A look of concentration fell over the prince's face, as if he was piecing his thoughts together. "I do not know the specifics of the spell that was cast over my tongue, but I've been able to piece some things together over the years. When something I am forbidden to say becomes open knowledge, it seems to fall out of the scope of the spell."

"Like when Carmilla announced your lineage," I said, following his logic.

"Yes." He nodded. "It's happened for other things too. However, every time a new secret is revealed, it's as if the spell reworks itself and I have to figure out what I can and cannot say again." He paused—another wince of pain—then shook his head. "I cannot say anything more on the matter."

"Convenient," I muttered.

His eyes full of fire snapped to me. "You don't know what it's like to not be in control of your own mind. But don't worry—as soon as the strength of Samara's blood runs out, I have no doubt Carmilla will give you a taste."

It was my turn to flinch as his words struck at exactly what I feared.

"If anything happens to Samara while I'm locked up down here, nothing will stop me from getting to you." Draven leaned forward, something feral swirling in his eyes. "I'll make you suffer in ways you can't even dream of."

"Save your threats for someone else. I won't allow any harm to come to her."

Draven laughed darkly. "You already have."

Again, I flinched.

"Samara won't allow her lust to rule her, no matter how hard her body is pushing it," I swallowed and tried to add some confidence into my voice. "And despite what you think, Carmilla won't allow anyone to take advantage of her that way."

"Your precious Carmilla is trying to force her niece back into a marriage she doesn't want, and she's arranged for this dinner to occur on the night when the lust haze will be hitting Samara the hardest." Draven gave me an almost pitying look. "You really don't see her true intentions, do you?"

"So I'll attend the dinner." I snapped. "You're wrong, but I'll be there anyway to make sure nothing happens."

Samara wouldn't touch that piece of shit, even with the intense desire that hit all Moroi who went through the reproductive cycle. And while my faith in Carmilla was waning, it hadn't faded enough that I believed she'd allow someone to force themselves on Samara.

Still . . . nothing in Lunaria would keep me from that room. I didn't know Lucian well, but from what I'd seen this week, he was a cruel piece of shit, and Demetri was an opportunist prick. Carmilla was likely hoping to wear Samara down, plant a seed of doubt during this dinner that Demetri could jump on while Samara would be using every ounce of her unbending willpower to hold the lust at bay.

She needed a friend in that room. I would be that friend. Even if she wanted nothing more than to bury a dagger in my chest.

"You will keep her safe." The dust seemed to tremble at Draven's feet as he spoke, his words somewhere between an order and a plea.

I held his bloodred gaze that promised death to anyone who harmed Samara and said the only thing I could. "With my life."

CHAPTER FOUR

—

Vail

I STOOD near the doors of the grand dining hall, where Carmilla, Lucian, Demetri, and Samara were having dinner. This space had clearly been built to host at least sixty people back in the day when the Fae had lived here. Most of the murals painted on the walls of the Houses were of pretty landscapes, but occasionally, they'd depict the Fae themselves. Usually dancing in fancy clothing with masks on their faces and crystal glasses in their hands.

It was those paintings that had inspired Velika's ridiculous parties. But even she hadn't been able to justify having food at them because there simply wasn't enough to spare.

Moroi numbers had grown considerably over the last two decades, thanks to the security of the Houses and the wards we'd learned to place around the outposts. But the crops had to be grown outside those wards, and it was a dangerous task, even during the day.

On top of that, all it took was one night for a herd of deer or a pack of boars to bulldoze through an outpost's food supply. The wraiths had also wiped out several high-producing outposts in the last year. We could survive one bad harvest . . . but any more than that, and we would be in serious trouble.

Carmilla had never been one to throw fancy dinners, not even back at House Harker. Some of the other Houses would, the Heads or Heirs enjoying their little pretend world where they could spoil themselves in such a way, as if we still didn't dwell in a land crawling with monsters or weren't two bad growing seasons away from starvation.

But tonight, there was enough food for easily double the people here. It was Lucian's doing. One of the many things I'd learned about him this past week was that he enjoyed the finer things in life and didn't give a shit about anyone but himself. What I didn't know was why the fuck Carmilla was working with him.

Maybe she had needed him to take out Velika, but that didn't explain why she was *still* allied with him, and why she hadn't stopped him from wasting all this food. My lips twisted into a grimace, and my gaze slid down the table to Samara, who had an identical look of disgust on her face. She hid it quickly when Carmilla glanced at her though and instead pasted a beatific smile on her face.

I hated that smile. It was a lie. Her real one was usually close-lipped, the corners of her lips tilted up with a sly but content type of amusement. I hadn't seen that one in a while.

Granted, Samara had been a wreck the past three days. I knew she'd been in considerable pain because she'd voluntarily spoken to me, asking me to bring her more tea. I'd brought everything she'd asked for and then some, as if that would help make everything right between us.

I didn't even know what I wanted to do at this point. There was no undoing that I'd betrayed Samara to be loyal to Carmilla, I couldn't fix that, but with every day that dragged on, it felt more and more obvious that I'd made the wrong choice. If I betrayed Carmilla to ally with Samara, would she even accept my help? Or would that only result in both of them wanting me dead?

Moonsdamn it. How had I fucked everything up so badly?

"You're looking much better today, my love." Demetri smiled at Samara, who was sitting to his left. "If you need help with *anything*, do let me know."

"I have not nor have I ever been your love," Samara replied smoothly as she gave Demetri a cutting look before picking up her glass of wine and taking a delicate sip.

This was one of the smaller tables in the room but was still meant to sit eight people. Carmilla sat at the head of the table with Lucian to her right. She'd had her niece sit at the opposite end of the table, which was considered a seat of respect; if an Heir from another House were visiting Sovereign House, it was where they would have been seated. Considering Carmilla had let her niece suffer in the dungeon for the last few days I was a little surprised. I'd have guessed that Lucian would have sat there, but he seemed perfectly content to be playing the part of Carmilla's consort.

I didn't understand any of this. When Carmilla had told me to bring Samara to dinner, I'd expected armed guards to be standing next to her. Instead, Carmilla had dismissed all of them from the room and had been having—what seemed on the surface to be—a pleasant conversation with her niece.

Their words were like hidden daggers volleyed back and forth. Seemingly polite, but both were bleeding from the double-edged meanings. I was so far out of my depth.

I knew how to track and hunt down any type of monster. There wasn't a weapon I didn't know my way around. But I knew fuck all about politics, and suddenly, I'd found myself swimming it.

Whatever game Carmilla was playing, I didn't understand. Just like I was struggling to comprehend Samara's motivations.

If the lust haze was riding her hard, she wasn't letting an ounce of it show. She looked as cool and composed as ever, which I knew was annoying Demetri, based on how rigid his smile was.

The idiot had probably thought Samara would jump into his lap out of desperation to get herself off. My lips curled up into the barest hint of a smile. He'd been married to Samara for years but obviously didn't know her at all. For all her polished exterior and determination to never fail as the House Harker Heir, Samara ran on fucking spite.

Dark purple eyes flecked with black locked on to me from across the room. Samara had been allowed to clean up earlier today and change into clean clothing. When I'd arrived to escort her from the guest room, I hadn't been ready for the sight. She wore a dress made of a deep purple that clung to every one of her curves; the neckline was low enough to show off her ample cleavage, and two slits ran up the sides of the flowing skirt. Every step flashed an obscene amount of thigh.

Samara was the one at war with her body's biology, yet it had been me suffering on that walk to the dining hall. All I could think about was what it felt like to have my hands on her soft flesh. To hear her scream my name as I thrust into her dripping wet cunt.

I knew she had sensed my arousal because she had taken two deliberate steps farther away from me as we'd walked. It'd hurt, but I couldn't blame her for it.

Now, her gaze dropped to my lips and the barest smile on them before jumping to the pulse in my neck. Black widened in her eyes, and my own heartbeat picked up as I saw the lust in them. The moment only lasted a few seconds before she snapped her gaze away, the darkness fading from her eyes until they were mostly purple again.

"Messages from Mora and Dominique arrived this morning." Carmilla swirled her glass of wine. "Both will be coming next week to meet with us."

"Pray tell, what did you say in the letter to the Heads of House Corvinus and Salvatore?" Samara arched a dark brow at her aunt. "'Queen Velika lost her head, I'm afraid, but no worries, the crown landed on mine. Please join me for a cup of tea?'"

"That was more or less the gist of it." Carmilla mimicked her niece and raised a brow back at her. "Despite what you think of my actions of late, I am trying to do what's best for the Moroi, and I'm being as truthful as possible."

"Leaving out the fact that if they walk into this House, they'll leave without their free will seems to be *a bit* of a big omission." Samara's eyes flicked to the crown resting on Carmilla's head. Faint creases formed between her brows and at the corners of her lips.

"That all depends on them. The crown will tell me what their intentions are. If they willingly kneel, then they will leave with their minds intact." Carmilla shrugged.

"So you'll be a generous tyrant." Samara smiled wide enough to display her fangs. "What a relief."

What would Carmilla do if the other Houses didn't voluntarily kneel and fought back against the crown's control? Velika hadn't been able to control House bloodlines, but she'd only had half of the crown. What if, even united, it wasn't enough?

I might have been daft at House politics, but even I knew there were some who would never willingly kneel. Like House Tepes and House Devereux. Surely she had some sort of plan for that? Aside from House Harker, they were the two most powerful Houses when it came to rangers. We needed their support if we were to stand against the wraiths and whatever Erendriel was plotting.

"Don't be so dramatic, dear," Carmilla gave Samara a chiding look before focusing on Demetri. "Have you heard anything from your mother?"

Everyone continued on with the conversation, and I remained in the background, listening. Apparently, Demetri's mother, Marvina, hadn't replied to any of his messages. Not surprising, since she knew he was here and allied with Carmilla. She was technically in charge of House Laurent . . . and she'd always disliked Carmilla for reasons nobody really understood.

For all appearances, Samara looked engaged and contributed to the talks, often coming up with ways to cleverly insult Demetri, who was growing more and more frustrated as dinner went on. Lucian had refrained from saying anything, just leaned back in his chair sipping his wine and letting the barbed words flow around him.

But Samara's gaze kept slipping to the crown. I glanced at it. It was a strange creation. I could feel the Fae magic radiating off it, but as far as I knew, Carmilla hadn't used it on me. At least, I didn't think she had.

It was more than a little unnerving to think that I wouldn't know if my mind had been tampered with, but the crown didn't work as well on those from House bloodlines—or from people who drank from them—and I'd drunk a lot of Samara's blood recently. I was fairly sure I'd be safe from the crown's magic if Carmilla tried to use it on me, but for how long, I didn't know. Something told me Samara wouldn't be opening up a vein for me anytime soon, so it wasn't like I could refill my immunity.

Not for the first time, I wondered why the Fae had made the crown. Had they used it against their own people? We knew there'd been a divide between the Unseelie and Seelie, maybe things like the crown were part of the reason why.

Samara had dropped all pretenses and was staring at the crown now, her expression one of concentration. Suddenly, she jolted in her seat, and the chair creaked. The conversation stopped, and all eyes fell on her.

"Apologies." She reached for her wineglass again. "In the months since our divorce, I forgot how grating it is to listen to Demetri drone on and on about his mommy issues."

Lucian barked a laugh. "I like her."

Even Carmilla cracked a smile.

Demetri glowered. "If you keep it up, I won't bother hate fucking you later when you're begging for it."

I took a step forward before I caught myself and moved back. Earlier, I'd spoken with Carmilla and claimed I wanted to be here tonight because I was concerned Samara might do something rash.

Carmilla wasn't born yesterday, but she'd acquiesced to my request, though she'd made it clear I was not to interfere with the conversations no matter how heated they got. My fingers curled as I imagined wrapping them around Demetri's neck and snapping it. If he laid one hand on Samara, I'd do it, but when it came to verbal sparring, there was no one better than my dark-haired and clever-tongued beauty.

"Demetri, dear . . ." Samara gave her ex-husband a placating smile. "You're saying your inside thoughts out loud again. Nobody wants to hear about the fantasies you have while getting yourself off."

"That's not what—" Demetri's face burned red, but he was cut off by Lucian, who cocked his head as his eyes glinted at Samara.

"What if he was the last person in Lunaria? Would you hate fuck him then?"

Samara tapped a finger against her bottom lip like she was pondering some great mystery. I chuckled under my breath, earning me a death glare from Demetri. I smiled at him. *Try something, asshole. I fucking dare you.*

He looked away from me and went back to fuming in Samara's direction.

"Depends . . ." she finally said and held her right hand up, wiggling several fingers in the air. "In this scenario, do I still have my fingers?"

"What do your fingers have to do with anything?" Demetri snarled.

"Oh." Lucian laughed and gave Samara a nod of acknowledgment. "I see why you don't want to marry him again. Anyone who doesn't understand why fingers are useful probably has no business fucking anyone."

"I think that's enough for tonight." Carmilla gave Lucian a mildly chiding look before giving Samara a much sterner one. "If you promise to behave and not leave without guards, you may stay in one of the guest quarters."

Any amusement she'd felt at putting Demetri in his place slid off Samara's face. "Either way, I'm a prisoner. I'll stick with the dungeons."

Carmilla eyed her niece, clearly trying to figure out why she had chosen a hard floor over a soft bed, but Carmilla knew the politically savvy side of Samara while I knew the side that was survival first. This was enemy territory to Samara, and the dungeons were less guarded in a lot of ways. Only the door in and out had guards posted. If she stayed in the main house, she'd have no idea where the guards were, and she'd be farther away from Draven.

Samara was plotting something, and I needed to convince her to tell me so she didn't get herself killed.

CHAPTER FIVE

—

Samara

My body felt like it was on fire. I'd never denied my needs like this before. In fact, usually the days after my menstruation were *very* fun. It was a perfectly solid excuse to stay in bed and ignore any responsibilities while getting fucked into oblivion.

When I was at Drudonia, I'd often find another scholar, or several, to keep me entertained. After my marriage to Demetri, I'd been a little more limited. He'd been adequate in bed, not the most creative, but I tended to get a little . . . aggressive . . . when I was like this and made it work.

But now, I'd sooner cut off my arm then let him touch me, even if I had no other options. My fingers were going to be fucking aching by the time this was over.

Vail was a silent presence at my side as we made our way back to the dungeon. It'd been difficult, but I'd managed to mostly concentrate during dinner, and I'd been rewarded with lots of useful information between things both spoken and unspoken.

Carmilla was keeping her coup quiet. She couldn't completely control the flow of information from the Sovereign House—there were almost a thousand Moroi living here on a permanent basis and another thousand rangers who regularly rotated in and out.

But she'd been busy these past couple of weeks, ensuring that the key players were loyal to her and her alone. On my way to dinner, we'd passed several advisors who hadn't batted an eye at me being led through the halls with guards in front and Vail at my side.

The other Houses had no doubt heard rumors, but Carmilla Harker had a reputation as being an honest and respectable House Leader. They would give her the benefit of the doubt.

And their Houses would fall because of it.

Lucian was a bit of a mystery to me. He hadn't spoken enough to suss out his motivation or wants. That worried me. I didn't like having such an unknown adversary.

We passed a hallway that I knew led to some living quarters, and briefly, I regretted not taking Carmilla up on her offer—just so I'd have better access to the rest of the House and therefore a greater chance at escape. But I dismissed that notion a second later. Carmilla would have put guards on me at all times, and I wasn't going anywhere without Draven.

Aside from Vail watching over me directly, the guards were only stationed at the entrance to the dungeons. They did periodic checks of the levels, but there would still be less eyes on me down there. I was sure Draven and I could come up with something—once I made it to him.

That would have to wait another couple of days though because despite my belief that I could work through my stupid horny thoughts, that seemed to be growing more unlikely by the second.

More than once, my gaze had drifted back to Vail during that dinner, and I'd remembered everything he'd done to me in that cave . . . and then the cabin. My thoughts had scattered, and I'd lost track of the conversation.

I couldn't afford to slip up like that during an escape, and based on the way I was feeling, it seemed likely that I'd throw rationality out the window and just jump Draven as soon as I saw him, caring way more about getting his cock inside me than getting the fuck out of here.

My core tightened at the thought, and I knew if I reached beneath my dress, I'd find myself hot and wet.

"Fuck," Vail cursed under his breath and started walking faster.

I had to lengthen my stride to keep up with him, which meant even more of my skin showed with every step. Based on the way Vail's jaw was tightening, I knew he was seeing the flashes of my golden brown skin out of the corner of his eye and it was getting to him.

I should hate him—and I did. He'd betrayed me after everything we'd gone through. After everything we'd done. I'd thought we'd finally gotten past all our bullshit, only to find out it'd all been a lie. My brain and heart were very much on Team Vail Can Eat Dirt and Die.

My traitorous pussy, on the other hand, was very much Team Vail Can Eat Us Out And Then Die.

"Fuck," I muttered and picked up my pace. I needed to get back to my cell and away from Vail, because while Demetri had zero chance of me hate fucking him, I wasn't entirely sure I had the willpower to resist Vail for much longer.

Why did he have to smell so delicious? Like the forest after a thunderstorm. That thread linking me to him practically purred as I breathed in more of his scent, though it felt more faint than it had a few weeks ago. Like it was fraying at the edges.

Good. I hoped it fucking vanished entirely.

Two guards stood on either side of the iron and wood door at the end of the hall. The one on the left nodded at Vail and opened the door. But the one on right openly leered at me. Dark brown eyes with cracks of green running through them darkened as he inhaled sharply, and I knew he was smelling my arousal.

Not for you asshole. I'd fuck a pine cone right now.

"Grigor, if you want to keep your head on your shoulders, I suggest you look the fuck away right now and keep your mouth shut," Vail said in a low, dangerous tone.

The pervy guard—Grigor, apparently—jerked his gaze away from me, but not before sneering first.

Vail waved me forward, and I entered the narrow stairwell that wound down to the dungeon levels, Vail following behind me. Fae lanterns gave off a pale yellow light as we made our descent.

I hadn't ever gone past my cell, so I had no idea how much farther down Draven was, but I *did* know he was on the bottom level, thanks to information I'd gleaned from conversations over the past couple of weeks. There were three levels above me, and considering this was built underground, it didn't seem possible that it went that much farther.

At least that was what I hoped, because I really didn't want to run down hundreds of stairs and then have to turn around and go back up.

Fuck. Stairs.

We walked past the first level, and I heard several conversations filtering through the door, but the words were too muffled to make out. It was the same on the next floor. When we reached the door that led to the room that contained my cell, I almost shoved Vail out of the way to race inside and lock the cell door between us.

I was practically panting, and it had nothing to do with all the steps we'd just walked down. My body was keyed up, and every part of my skin felt hot, and this was only day one. Tomorrow was going to be even more brutal.

Vail opened the door, and I had no choice but to step inside. *Go to the cell,* I told myself. *He'll lock you in, and then you won't have to worry about climbing the delicious mountain of a man standing before you. You won't have to resist moaning as he shoves his enormous cock into your dripping cunt, stretching you out—*

FUCK. My breathing grew more ragged, and I realized I'd stopped moving.

For a second, Vail and I stood there looking at each other with less than a foot separating us. Silver bled across his dark grey eyes, gleaming slightly from the ever-burning flames of the Fae lanterns. Something about Vail always looked a little wild, like he wasn't meant to be contained behind stone walls but out in the forest with the other beasts.

Betrayed. He'd betrayed me. I hated him.

Why was this dance between us always so fucking complicated?

With just the two of us in this small, dark space, his scent enveloped me. He smelled rich and earthy. More than a little wild.

Emotions raced across Vail's face. Guilt. Lust. Conflict. I understood those last two because they applied to how I was feeling at this very moment. Only, while he felt guilt, I felt rage.

But I still wanted him. And it wasn't just because of the lust haze coursing through my blood. Nor was it the odd magic connecting us, which I still didn't understand.

For all his hateful words, Demetri had been right when he'd declared my feelings for Vail and why the Marshal of House Harker had been in a position to hurt me so badly.

I loved him. Body and soul. And that wasn't something I could just turn off, even if that love was now twisted with hate.

"Fuck it," Vail growled.

We both moved at the same time, crashing into each other. Vail's mouth claimed mine as his strong hands gripped my ass and lifted me up. Instinctively, I wrapped my legs around his waist, and my fingers wound into his hair, pulling him harder against me as he backed me against the dungeon door.

His tongue slipped into my mouth, and I ground myself against him. Everything I'd been keeping pent up all day slipped free, and it felt fucking amazing. Even with the fabric of the dress between my back and the hard wood of the door, I could feel the iron within it seeping into my body. It felt wrong, but I was too concerned with Vail's hands on me to give a shit.

We broke our kiss when Vail thrust with his hips, one of his hands drifting from my ass to squeeze my breast. A frustrated growl slipped from him before he tore the fabric, then his hand was on my bare flesh as he roughly ran a thumb over my taut nipple.

"Fuck!" My head snapped forward, and then my fangs were buried in his throat. The richness of his blood coated my tongue as I drank him down.

"*Sam*," he groaned as the hand that was still cupping my ass gripped it tighter.

That nickname on his tongue was like an arrow to the heart.

Between one heartbeat and the next, I pulled my fangs out of his throat, gripped the back of his head, and slammed it forward over my shoulder—straight into the door—with every ounce of strength I could muster.

Vail's hands dropped away, and my feet landed on the floor as he stumbled back, a hand clutching his head while blood leaked through his fingers.

I straightened my dress as best as I could, holding up one side of the torn fabric as I calmly walked towards my cell. Once I was inside, I went all the way to the back wall. He'd have to use his blood to lock me in, but I thought I'd gotten my point across loud and clear.

Lust and tension filled the room as I took a seat on the floor. Vail straightened, pulling his hand away and revealing a nasty cut running diagonally from the center of his forehead to just beside his left eye. I tried not to compare it to the scar that traced a path across that eye—the one he'd gotten the night our parents had been killed. It'd been a severe injury, and we'd been too panicked that night to heal it properly, so it'd left a scar.

Panic flared in Vail's eyes as he took a step towards my cell. "I didn't—I'm sorry. I didn't mean to—"

I cut him off. "What just happened was on me. But it won't happen again."

He stopped in his tracks, his expression twisted into one of pain, and something inside my chest wrenched at seeing that look in his eyes, but I didn't let it stop me. He'd made his fucking choice.

"I have given you so many fucking chances. Even when others told me I was a fool to trust you, I still did, at least to do what was best for House Harker, but what Carmilla's doing"—I pointed a finger up to the House that sat above us—"is wrong. I never would have thought you would stand by someone who planned to strip away the free will of our people. I'm pissed at you for betraying me, for letting things progress as far as they did between us, but that's between you and me, and I damn well know how to separate business and pleasure. But you've fucked over all the Moroi with your actions." I leaned forward and bared my teeth at him. "And that, I will *never* forgive you for."

Vail's hands curled into fists at his sides. "I can make this right."

"No." I stepped away and rested my head against the back wall. My body was still keyed up from almost getting what it wanted with Vail. Denying it hurt, and thinking past the lust and pain was hard, so I focused on breathing. "You can't."

I closed my eyes. A few minutes later, Vail left. It was only then that I let the tears fall.

WHEN THE DOOR opened half an hour later, I kept my eyes shut. My emotions had devolved into a maelstrom of lust and rage, so the idea of looking at Vail's face right now made me want to scream. I didn't want to hear any of his excuses or pleas for forgiveness either. I just wanted to be left alone for the next forty-eight hours so I could ride this out.

I'd tried getting myself off after he'd left, but it hadn't worked. It'd only made me more frustrated, so I stopped trying. Vail could probably smell my efforts in the air, but I didn't care. If he wanted to stay in here and stew in it, that was his problem. I hoped he fucking suffered.

"Got an itch you can't scratch, love?" a deep, melodious voice asked.

"Draven?" My eyes flew open, and I expected to see only Vail, as if I'd imagined that other voice. While Vail was indeed standing there—so was my prince, wearing only a pair of loose-fitting pants with his black and silver hair wet and clinging to his sculpted body as it fell to his waist. "Am I dreaming?"

Suddenly, I was at the cell door, clutching the bars.

Those deep blue eyes threaded with red softened as Draven stepped past Vail to my cell. "Pretty sure you and I would have dreamed up something better than this," he said in that dry tone of his. Fuck, I'd missed that. His brows furrowed together as he looked me over, his gaze lingering on where my skin was in contact with the iron bars, as if he could sense the discomfort it caused me. "Are you alright?"

"Am I alright?" I barked out a laugh. "The last time I saw you, a fucking sword was sticking through your chest! You looked half dead, and they *dragged you away from me*. All I've gotten since have been assurances that you are still alive but nothing more."

"Remember the deal," Vail said roughly as he shoved his way between Draven and me to open my cell. There was no door, just a hidden glyph on some of the bars that was keyed to his blood and a few other individuals'—something I was keeping in the back of my mind while plotting how to get out of here. "One hour until the guards change. You have to be back in your cell before then. Don't give me any shit. I'll have no problem killing you, prince."

A warning growl vibrated up my throat, and Draven chuckled darkly as enough of the bars disappeared for him to step inside, then reappeared within seconds, locking us in together.

"Don't mind him." Draven grinned at me. "He's just remembering the last time he had to warn me about how much time I had with you—only now, he won't be getting an invite to join."

"Are you truly healed?" I asked in a low, tight voice. Normally, my control over my bloodlust was absolute. I could let it rise or fall as needed, and even when I let it fully rise, all it really did was heighten my instincts and give me fangs and claws. It didn't significantly impact my temperament the way it did for many other Moroi. But now, I could feel my bloodlust rising and mixing with my arousal. The feeling was intoxicating. I had just enough rationality left to make sure Draven was actually up for this. If he was hiding any injuries and I made them worse . . .

Warm fingers touched my chin as Draven tilted my head up until I met his eyes. "You can unravel those chains you're keeping on yourself. I can take anything you throw at me." Then he leaned down and nipped my bottom lip, causing a shiver to run up my spine. "But before we get to that, I need you to tell me you want this and it's not just your body's needs clouding your thoughts."

"I've had no problem turning down previous offers." I traced several fingers down his chest before toying with the waistband of his pants, right above where his erection was straining to get free. "Before you walked into my little corner of hell, I had accepted I'd be riding this out all by my lonesome. My fingers weren't much help. Think yours will be better?"

Draven's smile was positively sinful, but I caught the calculation in his eyes and suspected he saw the same in mine. We had to make the most of this time. It might be our only chance to plan our escape together. "Challenge accepted."

In a heartbeat, I was pinned against the wall as Draven gripped my wrists with one hand and held them over my head. His other hand slid down my waist to stop on my thigh—right where the slit of the dress opened.

Then his mouth slanted over mine, and I kissed him hungrily before he broke the kiss, his lips brushing down my jaw until they reached my neck. I tilted my head to give him better access.

"Three floors separate us," he breathed into my ear so quietly, I could barely make out the words before he nipped me. "I'm on the bottom level."

He kissed my jawline, trailing down to my neck. I moaned when his fangs grazed my skin before he bit down hard and drank several deep gulps of my blood.

Vail let out a warning growl from outside the cell, and Draven ripped his fangs out before twisting to snarl back at him. I seized the opportunity to slip one hand free from Draven's grasp and wrap it around the silky strands of his hair, then yanked his head down and to the side so I could bury my fangs in his neck.

It was Draven's turn to moan as I drank from him, enjoying the rich and intoxicating taste of his blood. Reluctantly, I pulled back and kissed his skin before whispering in his ear, "Vail is usually here. Guards check on me every hour, but they don't stay long."

Draven grabbed my hand that was still twisted in his hair and not so gently tugged it back up to where my other hand was still pinned against the wall. He released me for a second to secure both wrists again, and then his free hand dove straight through the slit of my dress he'd been playing with earlier to the aching center between my thighs—where he stopped an inch away from where I wanted him.

The lust I'd barely been holding back shoved every rational thought from my mind. We'd have to share notes about our situation later.

I needed to get fucked. Hard.

"Draven," I said in a low, throaty voice.

"Yes, love?" he asked almost absently as he traced an infuriating circle on my inner thigh.

"If you try to tease me right now, I'll have Vail march your ass back to your own cell." My bloodlust rose with my desire, and I felt my nails shift to claws. Draven's gaze flicked back up to them before dropping back to meet my solid black eyes. "But not before I punish you for your insolence."

"I think I'd like your punishments." He grinned wickedly.

"Drav—fuck!" I screamed, and my eyes rolled into the back of my head as he speared me with two fingers and his thumb teased my clit. My hips rolled in time with each of his thrusts as he roughly fucked me with his fingers.

"Gods, you are wet," he groaned as he curled his fingers inside me. "Although I'm a little annoyed that you're not wearing any panties. I was hoping to rip those off you."

"Apologies, my prince," I panted as I tried to grind down on his hand, but Draven just tightened his grip around my wrists and drew me up another inch, forcing me to stand almost on my tiptoes.

"Not a prince anymore."

"Trust me"—a strangled moan tore from my throat when Draven added a third finger while pushing down on my clit with his thumb—"Kier and I will always consider you our prince."

"Fuck," he growled and ripped his fingers out of me so he could roughly shove down his pants. His cock sprang free at the same moment he released my wrists so he could grip my ass and slam me against the wall—very much like Vail had done earlier. His cock slid in all the way to the hilt, and we both groaned as I stretched around his thick length, then eyes more red than blue met mine. "Take whatever you need, Sam. I'll always be yours. And Kier's."

"Show me," I demanded. "Claim me."

All the blue faded from his eyes as the last of his control snapped.

Draven thrust into me, hard and fast, and my claws tore into his shoulders and back while I held on. The scent of blood filled the air, and he only fucked me harder. Then the orgasm I'd been chasing earlier barreled through me, and I screamed, his pace never slowing. He continued as he snaked a hand between us and started rubbing my clit.

"Oh fuck!" I panted hoarsely.

It was too much. My entire body was trembling while my pussy clenched around his cock and his infernal fingers worked my clit. I pushed on his shoulders in a desperate need to make a little space between us—just to give me a moment so I didn't pass out.

Draven was having none of it. He growled, and then his fangs were in my throat again. Vail let out a string of curses, but I didn't understand a word as another orgasm tore through me. It might be poor timing to be going through lust haze right now, but fucking hell they were fun.

"More," I demanded. "Fuck me more."

Warm blood spilt down my neck as Draven pulled back, kissing me hard. I could taste my blood on his lips . . . and it made me want his again.

One of my hands slipped into his hair, and I pulled his head to the side, striking fast. He groaned as I swallowed mouthfuls of his blood while he slowed his pace to hard, deliberate thrusts, both of his hands gripping my ass to pull me against him.

"You are glorious," he breathed. "And this pussy is *mine*."

Another growl from Vail echoed across the room.

My fangs popped free, and I looked over Draven's shoulder to where Vail stood against the back wall. His eyes glowed silver, and his hands were curled into fists at his sides, like it was taking all of his willpower not to do something about the erection straining against his pants.

Slowly, I trailed my tongue up Draven's neck, licking the blood clean, and Vail's nostrils flared when I smiled at him, fangs on display. His gaze dropped to them, and I knew he was remembering what it felt like for me to sink my teeth into his flesh.

Suddenly, fingers wrapped around my hair and yanked my head back.

"Eyes on me," Draven demanded. "Not in the mood to share you right now—even if all he gets to do is watch me take this perfect pussy over and over again."

I whimpered as Draven drew his hard length almost all the way out before slowly sliding back in. Obscene sounds filled the cell as my arousal gushed down my thighs. Draven kept one hand on my hair, controlling where I looked, while the other cupped my ass. My legs tightened around his waist, our panting breaths interspersed with groans as he continued the torturously slow pace.

"Tell me what you want, baby." His eyes bored into mine. "Because I can think of all kinds of wicked things."

"Like what?" I rasped as he bottomed out again.

Red eyes dropped to my lips. "That gorgeous mouth wrapped around my cock. I want to watch your eyes water as you take all of me. Swallow every drop when I come down your throat." His gaze dropped to my cleavage. "Or maybe I'd pull out and decorate those wonderful tits of yours."

My mouth watered at the thought, and I almost demanded he let go of me so I could drop to my knees.

He frowned. "No. I want to save that for when Kieran is with us."

I pouted, and he chuckled darkly before leaning forward to whisper in my ear, "So I can watch him lick my seed off you."

"Oh fuck." My thighs clenched as a slow, delicious need started to build again.

A breathy laugh tickled my ear before Draven straightened. "Maybe you should show me what it is you want right now."

He thrust into me one more time before withdrawing. I hissed my frustration, and he just laughed again as he dragged me down with him. Draven stretched out on the floor and maneuvered me until I straddled him, facing his legs. One hand gripped the rise of my hip, digging into the soft flesh, and the other wrapped around my hair and yanked my head back.

"Maybe you should take pity on him and tug your dress down a bit," he purred slyly. "I think Vail has at least earned a good show. Although, maybe it's more of a *punishment* to be able to see you"—his thick cock slowly pushed inside me again, and I moaned—"hear you, and not be able to do anything about it."

I looked through the bars of my cell to where Vail was still rigidly standing. His eyes tracked my fingers as they tugged at the front of my dress, pulling it down so that my breasts almost spilt out—but then stopped.

My hand snapped up, and I flashed him an obscene gesture.

"Fuck. You're so mean," Draven groaned as he sank in another inch. "I love it. Now show me how much you want my cock, love."

I closed my eyes, forgetting about Vail. He didn't fucking exist in this moment. All I wanted was to feel Draven moving inside me again. The need to feel his cock stretching me out was all I could think about. I dropped all the way down, and Draven swore, his claws digging into my soft flesh.

Fuck, he felt amazing. This angle was *everything*.

My hips rolled forward, and his grip on my hair tightened, forcing me to arch my back more. I leaned back enough so that my hands could grip his sides. This time, it was *my* claws sinking into flesh.

A husky laugh poured from my lips when he moaned. My prince liked a little pain with his pleasure too.

I ground against him, quickening my pace as I rode him hard, and Draven moved his body to perfectly match my thrusts. Something about this angle made him feel like he was reaching even deeper. I lost myself in the intensity. In him. Everything was too much and yet not enough. Pleasure rippled just out of reach as my body keyed up with the building orgasm.

Almost there.

The world tilted, and I had to quickly pull my claws from Draven's flesh as he pivoted us up until I was on all fours and he was thrusting wildly behind me. His hand was still wrapped in my hair, the other gripping my hip.

"Come for me again." He slammed into me so hard, it almost hurt.

"Make me," I half moaned.

Hot pain flared where Draven's claws tore through the soft flesh of my hip, and I gasped at the perfect blend of pleasure and pain.

Everything became a blur. The sound of flesh slapping against flesh. The feel of Draven pulling me harder against himself as he did his best to go deeper with every thrust. The scent of blood filling the air. Mine and Draven's.

Silver eyes held me captive as strangled cries of pleasure tore from my throat. Draven's breathing grew more ragged, his movements harsher until he finally let out a deep groan. Then heat filled me before spilling down my thighs.

My mind floated, and I barely noticed the sting of Draven pulling his claws from my hips and tugging me upright. A small protest escaped me when he withdrew his cock and some of his seed slid down my legs. Draven growled, and then I felt his fingers reach between my thighs and push it back inside my aching pussy.

I was dimly aware that this was just a side effect of the lust haze and that I had nothing to worry about since I'd drunk the contraceptive tea, which meant I could just enjoy the feeling of being the center of Draven's attention. My eyes drifted shut, and I basked in the pleasure of it all as strong arms pulled me back against a warm chest.

"Mine." Draven nuzzled the side of my neck.

"Yours," I agreed.

I drifted off for a bit but was woken up by a tight exchange between Vail and Draven.

"—proven myself."

Draven let out a harsh laugh. "Is that what this was?"

"I didn't have to bring you here," Vail growled. "I could have—"

"You could have what, Vail?" Draven challenged. "Pretty sure she would have fucked Demetri before you."

Vail's growl gained a sharp edge. "Do not speak his name."

"Oh, so now you get protective?"

"Enough," I snapped, opening my eyes and blinking slightly to shrug off the last of the blissful peace I'd found. I was in Draven's lap with his arms wrapped around my waist and chest while Vail stood on the other side of the cell, blood dripping from his fingers like he was about to open it.

"You want to prove yourself, Vail?" My expression hardened. "Get the fuck out and give us five minutes alone."

"You don't think straight around him." Vail stubbornly clenched his jaw. "He's half Fae, Samara. There's nothing about him that's safe."

I shot him an incredulous look. "You're the reason I'm in this fucking cell, Vail!"

"And it's not like she thinks straight around you either," Draven pointed out. "As far as I'm concerned, you are the greatest threat to Samara, because for some reason, she keeps forgiving you, even when you don't deserve it. If anyone could come back from this epic fuck up, it would be you."

"Unlikely." My annoyed glare slid to Draven. "He doesn't deserve forgiveness."

"What he deserves and what you will do are likely two different things." He shrugged.

The face I'd found so kissable minutes ago, I now wanted to punch. Based on the way he chuckled against my neck as he planted a kiss there, he knew exactly what I was feeling. Gods, I'd forgotten how much of a troublemaker he could be. He and Kieran together would be incredibly aggravating.

And hot.

The lust started to rise again, so I shoved that thought away. My mind was temporarily clear, and I needed to take advantage of that while Draven was here.

"Five minutes, Vail," I said firmly. "You fucking owe me."

"Fine," he ground out. "Not a second more." Vail pointed at Draven. "And you will return to your cell when I get back without any tricks."

"Sure thing, Marshal."

"He will," I promised and twisted enough to give Draven a warning look. A chastised grin quickly appeared on his face, but it was far too mischievous for it to be convincing.

After a few tension-filled seconds, Vail stalked towards the door that led out to the stairwell.

"Vail."

He stopped and looked over his shoulder at me.

I held a hand against the center of my chest, the place where I always felt this strange connection to him. "I'll know if you linger outside that door and try to listen."

A storm rolled through his grey eyes, but he jerked his head in a sharp nod before leaving and shutting the door behind him. I felt his presence move farther away, like the invisible rope between us was thinning. It was the first time I'd acknowledged its existence to him, but I knew he was aware of it. Occasionally, when he'd be down here with me—usually glowering at the floor—he'd idly rub his chest in the exact same spot where I felt it.

I still had no idea what it was or how to break it. It always gave me an idea of where Vail was and what he was feeling, but it also gave him the same information about me.

Draven gripped my waist and lifted me before turning me and resettling me on his lap so towards him. Then he raised his hands to cup my face before brushing his lips against mine. It was a sweet kiss, and for some reason, it made me want to cry. I kissed him back before leaning my head against his chest, listening to his heartbeat like it had all the answers I needed.

"Do you know of any other exits down here?" I asked, keeping my voice low. Draven had grown up in this House. If anyone knew another way out, it would've been him.

"None that I'm aware of, but that doesn't mean there isn't one." His arms wrapped loosely around my waist, and he rested his head on top of mine.

"Prior to our current situation, I haven't spent much time down here. The iron bothers me."

"Because you're half Fae."

"Yes." I could almost hear the question he wanted to ask, but he didn't, so I settled it for both of us.

"And so am I." It felt odd to say that out loud, like I was finally putting away the last of my denial.

"It does seem that way," he said gently. "Maybe not half, but you must have a decent amount of Fae blood for the iron to bother you."

"Has the crown ever spoken to you?"

Draven drew back, and I tilted my head up so I could meet his perplexed gaze. "What do you mean?"

"That crown . . ." I swallowed. "It's spoken to me twice. The first time, it called me 'the forgotten one,' and then, earlier, at dinner, it asked if I was ready to 'take my rightful place.' There was a wraith before . . . he called me *din tros.*"

"Forgotten queen," Draven murmured, concern bleeding into his expression. "Are you sure neither of your parents were Fae?"

"My mother was definitely a Harker." I chewed on my bottom lip. "But I don't actually know much about my dad's past. He was born in an outpost. I know his mother died when he was young, and he never spoke of his father. When I was a kid, I just accepted he was my dad and never questioned why he didn't talk about his past."

"We'll escape this place and then find the answers we need." He leaned down and kissed me before pulling back and resting his forehead against mine. "I will always keep you safe, Samara Harker," he swore, "with my life."

"And I will always keep you safe, Draven Nacht," I promised, "with my life."

Suddenly, heat burned inside my chest. I gasped and stumbled back as my fingers gripped the front of my dress and pulled it away, expecting to see burnt flesh, but my skin was perfectly smooth. I looked up to find Draven staring down at his own bare chest, his hand placed on the same spot I'd felt the burn.

He raised his gaze to meet mine. "I'm guessing you felt that?"

I nodded, a suspicion already forming. "Take a few steps back?"

Draven did as I asked, curiosity brimming in his eyes. I also moved back until we were about as far apart as we could get in the cell.

I felt it—the strange awareness of Draven. It was like a piece of his soul had embedded itself inside me.

Draven stared at me in wonder. "What is this?"

"I have no idea," I said honestly. "But you should know, I have the same thing with—"

The door to the dungeon burst open as Vail stormed in. "What the fuck did you two just do?"

CHAPTER SIX

—

Roth

I GAZED up at the utilitarian fortress before us. Most of the castles left behind by the Fae were architectural wonders that combined beauty and functionality.

The Fae who had built what was now House Devereux had skipped the beauty.

Foreboding, dark grey stone walls stretched towards the sky, while a deep moat curved around the outside of the walls. Its waters were obsidian black, and all kinds of wicked things swam in them. Behind the walls, a singular rectangular structure rose. The windows were hidden by glamour, so it appeared to just be solid walls.

The only break in the uniformity was the occasional turret. But those had none of the whimsical designs like those of House Harker or many of the other Houses. Just more grey stone with no visible windows.

I'd once made a comment to my parents that perhaps the House's appearance wasn't enough and we should hang a sign on the outside that read, "You are not wanted here. Leave or die."

My mother's response had been, "Do you think it will help?"

I hadn't been able to tell if she'd been joking.

Kieran and Alaric stood on either side of me, silently lending their support. We'd all agreed that it would be best if I spoke for the group. It wasn't a position I preferred, but it was my House—my family. Nyx, Adrienne, and Emil were fanned out protectively around us.

My siblings wouldn't be happy about outsider rangers being allowed in, but they'd just have to deal with it. It wasn't like I was happy to be back here after swearing to never return.

"Let's get this over with." I grimaced and strode forward, Alaric and Kieran immediately falling into step with me. It was telling how unlike himself Kieran

570

was at the moment because he had barely asked me about my family and why I'd left in the first place on our way here. He was usually so nosy about everything.

I was pretty sure he was clinging to his rage and channeling that into motivation to get Samara back. Because if he allowed himself to feel the despair and panic that we were all dealing with, he'd fall apart and never put himself back together. I couldn't blame him for that, and personally, I preferred this version of Kieran. I could deal with clipped answers and cutting remarks, but I didn't handle criers well.

Alaric had withdrawn into himself a little more than usual but was otherwise acting the same. If Samara were here, I'm sure she would have picked up on more clues as to how he was truly feeling.

We needed her back. I needed her back.

That was the only reason my steps didn't falter as we moved beyond the tree line and into the view of the two guards posted on this side of the moat. The drawbridge was up, and to lower it, the guards on both this side and inside the fortress had to activate the glyphs.

I had no doubt there were others in the forest who had spotted us miles ago, but it was standard operating procedure for the guards posted in the woods to only observe and not intervene unless necessary. They were meant to be the dagger in your back you never saw coming.

Adrienne and Emil were experienced enough that they probably knew where the rangers were. Nyx was still young and had much to learn. I had no doubt Alaric and Kieran were oblivious.

They were both lucky they were so pretty. Not my cup of tea, but I did have eyes.

The guards watched us approach. Neither of them drew their swords, which made me think they recognized me. Impressive, considering I'd been gone for a long time. I'd left for Drudonia almost eight years ago, and I'd never returned.

It wasn't that I hated my family or that they were unkind to me. I just didn't belong here. Looking at the fortress before me brought back all the memories of growing up as the person out of place. The scholar living amongst warriors.

Paranoid. Violent. Warriors.

The guards scrutinized us from underneath silver visors, their helmets hiding most of their features. Neither of them said anything. Didn't welcome me home or ask what the fuck I was doing in the company of House Harker.

They just waited for me to speak. Argh.

"You know who I am." I raised my chin. "Lower the gate."

"Do we?" The guard on the right cocked their head and looked at the other. "Nothing is jogging my memory. You?"

"Nope. Don't remember a thing," the left guard responded, their pale green eyes mostly focused on the rangers. They sparked with interest as they took in Adrienne. She was quite the looker, but if he didn't drop his gaze soon, she'd have his eyes plucked out of his skull before he could blink.

One of my favorite places to work in House Harker overlooked the training courtyard. I'd seen Adrienne take down just about everyone who challenged her. Only Emil was able to hold his own against the beautiful blonde ranger.

Tension rolled off Kieran, and I didn't miss the way his hand slid to the dagger on his thigh. Based on the way both guards subtly adjusted their stances, I knew they hadn't missed it either. I wasn't a fighter—much to the disappointment of my parents—but I was observant. It was impossible to grow up in House Devereux and not have fighting mechanics and strategies drilled into your head.

It was just, for me, they were all theoretical rather than practical skills. When I'd left here for Drudonia and started going by Roth, it'd had nothing to do with my gender. I'd just needed a way to separate myself from my House. From the legacy of being Astaroth Devereux . . . and just be the scholar Roth for a while.

But I knew who I was now. And I was ready to reclaim the part of me I'd left behind. While I would never be like the fierce warriors behind those walls —I was far from harmless. Something my brothers were well aware of. It was time these guards remembered it too.

"Allow me to properly announce myself."

The guards took a step back and away from each other as the ropes around my forearms unwound. Magic pulsed from me, and the blood magic ropes shot forward. Both guards swung with their swords, trying to cut through the ropes, but the bloodred tendrils snapped out from the ropes and wrapped themselves around the swords, yanking them from the guards' grasps. Before they could take another step, my ropes looped around their necks and pulled them off the ground.

Strangled gasps came from the guards as they clutched at the ropes and tried to stay conscious. Another pulse of magic from me had the ropes lifting them higher off the ground as I stepped closer to the ledge, the drawbridge to my right. The ropes turned the guards so they were facing the House, where I knew we had an audience watching us from the top of the wall, hidden from our sight by glamour.

It was very likely that at least one of my brothers was up there. I bit back a frustrated sigh. Would it have killed them to just let me in?

"I'm Astaroth Devereux," I called out in an even, steady voice. "Open the fucking gate."

———

"Didn't know you had it in you, Roth," Kieran said in a voice that was almost back to his teasing, light tone. His blue eyes were still strained and tired, but I was glad to see a hint of his old self.

"That was a bit dramatic," Alaric said dryly as we walked across the now-lowered bridge. The guards I'd almost choked out walked behind us. As soon as the bridge had lowered, I'd released them from the ropes. They'd dropped the ten feet to the ground and landed easily on their feet. Instead of being angered or frightened, they'd taken off their helmets and grinned at me before activating the glyphs to lower their side of the bridge.

No doubt they'd be bragging about almost being choked out by the lost child of House Devereux later while they got drinks after their shift.

"Personally I'm disappointed you didn't drop them into the moat." Adrienne glanced over to the dark water. "I've always been curious about what's hiding in there."

"Have dinner with me later and maybe I'll tell you," one of the guards offered.

Adrienne looked over her shoulder, a bright, sunny smile on her lips. "Or I could just throw you in now and find out."

"Marry me." The guard gave her puppy dog eyes, and Adrienne rolled her eyes, but I caught the hint of a smile on her lips.

Emil and Nyx both zeroed in on the guard and gave him warning looks before returning their focus to the courtyard we were about to walk into. From the outside, it looked like the House went right up to the exterior wall, but there was actually a small space carved out. Lining that small space was a wrap-around balcony, where guards with crossbows would happily point their weapons at any newcomers.

There was a reason other Houses only came here when it was absolutely necessary. More than one House representative had said or done the wrong thing and ended up shot full of bolts and then dumped into the moat. House Devereux was almost entirely self-sufficient and traded very little with the other Houses, and when they did trade, the negotiations were always fraught with tension.

We stopped in the center of the small courtyard while the two guards who had escorted us moved to stand with the others who had lined up on both sides of us. I glanced up to see another dozen guards on the balcony; at least they didn't have their crossbows out. Everyone was just . . . waiting.

I grimaced. This was going to be pure agony.

Adrienne and Emil moved to flank Alaric, Kieran, and me with Nyx guarding our backs. None of the Harker rangers pulled their weapons—as skilled as they were, we were outnumbered, and escalating wasn't in our best interest. Alaric caught my eye and ever so slightly raised his brow in question. I shook my head and mouthed, *Wait.*

Luckily—or perhaps in my case, unluckily—we didn't have to wait long.

Two huge brutes dropped from the second story balcony, landing easily on their feet. They both had the same pale white skin as me and piercing eyes. Unlike me, they had black hair like our father. The one on the left kept his hair long, almost to his waist, with the sides shaved. His eyes were a copy of mine, hazel with orange streaks. The one on the right had always preferred to keep his hair short, only a dark stubble was present, and deep blue eyes flecked with orange stared at me with an intensity that made me want to shift on my feet.

Instead, I raised my chin and gave them both a look of disdain.

Taivan, the long-haired one, broke first. "*Our favorite sibling has returned!*" His voice boomed across the courtyard.

Alaric and Kieran jumped. Even Emil and the other two Harker rangers were surprised, which was probably why they did nothing to help me as my two older brothers charged and swept me up in a crushing hug.

"Gross!" I shrieked. "You're both sweaty and disgusting!" My feet kicked out from where they dangled several feet off the ground. Why did my brothers have to be so freaking tall?

"We missed you, Rothie Bear," Desmond grumbled in a deep, raspy voice. His throat had been mangled in a fight with some wraiths years ago, and while the scar had mostly faded, his voice had been irrevocably damaged.

"Should we . . ." Alaric trailed off. I couldn't see him or the others, thanks to being trapped between the two mountains who were my brothers, but I imagined he had no idea what to do in this situation. Alaric was an only child —something I was very jealous of at this moment.

"No," all three rangers said at once.

"Taivan. Desmond," a clear voice rang out. "Put down your sibling. You know Roth doesn't like hugs."

My feet hit the ground a second later, and a big meaty hand landed on my shoulder to steady me when I stumbled a bit. "Sorry, little sib," Desmond said, looking slightly chagrined.

"I'm not." Taivan ruffled my hair, and I slapped his hand away with a glower. He just laughed at me, the sound threatening to burst my eardrums. Had he seriously gotten louder? "You haven't visited us once since sneaking off in the night. That means you owe me a backlog of hugs."

"That's not how that works!" I snapped. "And you could have visited me!" A small amount of hurt crept into my voice before I could squash it. Nobody in my family had sent me so much as a message since I'd left. I'd always been the odd one out here. They'd likely all sighed a breath of relief when I'd gone to Drudonia—if they'd noticed at all. I wouldn't have been surprised if my parents hadn't realized I'd left for months.

Suddenly, the happy grins on my brothers' faces slid off, and they looked unsure . . . and sad. "We didn't know if you'd want to see us," Desmond said quietly, his eyes on the ground.

What?

Guilt slammed into me. It had never occurred to me that they had stayed away because they'd thought that was what I'd wanted. I mean, it kind of was what I'd wanted at first, but that was just because I'd desperately needed space. But when they'd never come looking for me, I'd just assumed it had been because they had easily wiped me out of their lives.

The air tightened in my lungs. I didn't—

How did I fix this? What was I supposed to say? Fuck! Suddenly, the breaths I hadn't been able to take started coming faster. Oh my gods, I was going to have a panic attack right fucking here in front of everyone.

"It's so wonderful to meet both of you!" Kieran said cheerfully. "I wish we were here under better circumstances, but I am glad that we got Roth here. They've been kind enough to help us with some urgent research over the last couple of months—something they were undertaking at Drudonia—but they've spoken of you often."

Desmond's gaze snapped up to meet mine again, surprise and happiness brimming in them. "You have?"

I hadn't. Kieran was lying his ass off. Sure, I'd talked about my brothers a little bit to Samara, but that was it.

"Of course." I did my best to smile. Both Taivan and Desmond grinned back at me, and the panic I'd been feeling faded. Tension replaced it as I finally looked past my brothers to the woman who had spoken.

In front of the main doors that led inside stood a tall, broad-shouldered woman with the same blue eyes as Desmond. She looked nothing like me— except the hair. We both had the exact shade of deep crimson red. Beside her stood a man who towered over even my brothers. A little surprise ran through me at seeing a few streaks of grey in his black hair. Eyes identical to mine bored into me.

"Hey, Mom." I sighed. "Hi, Dad."

Unlike my brothers—who had always been on the emotional side—my parents gave me nothing in response. Had they missed me? Did they hate me? Were they thinking about what to grab for lunch? Who the fuck knew.

"Astaroth."

My head snapped to the left, towards the woman striding out of the side entrance. Compared to her brother—my father—Thessalia was so dainty. Her hair was almost completely grey, only a few strands of black remaining, but she walked with strength and confidence. All the rangers dipped their heads out of respect and loyalty.

The Head of House Devereux was beloved by her people. And by me.

"Thessalia." Like the rangers, I also nodded deeply in greeting. My aunt was the reason I had stayed sane growing up as I'd tried to devour books while my parents kept trying to shove a sword into my hand. They'd never understood me, but she had, and I had left her behind along with everyone else.

Hazel eyes with burnt orange streaks just like mine and my father's slid to Alaric and Kieran, who had moved a little closer to stand on either side of me. Thessalia's lips curved up ever so slightly at the sight. "Interesting company you're keeping these days."

"They're my . . ." I floundered, searching for the right word to describe what Kieran and Alaric were to me exactly.

"We are theirs," Alaric cut in. "And Roth is ours."

A smile bloomed across Thessalia's face as she looked at me. "My precious child, you finally found your home."

"I did." My voice cracked as heat built behind my eyes. I took a steadying breath as I looked around at the rangers gathered, my thickheaded brothers, my stoic parents, and finally, the woman who had always seen the truth of me. "And I need your help to save it."

CHAPTER SEVEN

—

Samara

I POPPED the last piece of fruit into my mouth and savored the tartness of the coastal berry—and not being in my cell . . . although Draven had definitely made that more bearable over the last forty-eight hours. Vail had snuck him in several times and then waited outside in the stairwell while we'd fucked like animals.

Once Draven had sated my lust haze, he'd remove his scent from my body with his earth magic. As much as I hated the loss of it, I knew it was necessary.

Vail had come back in once we were done, and then we'd gone through different plans for how to get out of this mess.

It hadn't been my idea to involve Vail.

I still didn't trust him and hadn't wanted to include him in any of our plotting, but to my surprise—and frustration—Draven had disagreed. He'd claimed we'd be more successful including him in our plans. I didn't like it, but even I had to acknowledge that having someone who was able to travel around outside the dungeon and get us information improved our odds.

Especially considering none of our plans were great.

Despite being the House Harker Marshal, it was doubtful that Vail would be able to take me past the perimeter wall without someone questioning it and alerting Carmilla—and there was absolutely no way we could walk Draven out with us.

So sneaking out seemed like the best course of action. We just couldn't figure out how. There was one way in and out of the dungeon. The two guards stationed at the top wouldn't be a problem for us, but the entrance was located smack-dab in the center of the Sovereign House, and this fortress was massive.

While being escorted to this dinner, I'd made notes of how many guards

577

were on duty and where they'd been stationed. By the time my count had reached twenty, it had become clear that we wouldn't be escaping this way.

As skilled as Vail and Draven were at sneaking around, we all agreed it was highly unlikely that we'd make it outside the walls without being seen, and as soon as someone sounded the alarm, we would be vastly outnumbered.

Vail had also been able to provide us with the number of rangers stationed on the perimeter walls. Which I hadn't thanked him for—he was the reason we were in this mess—but I had acknowledged that it was useful information. I still fully intended to punch him repeatedly in the face once we were out of here.

Such anger for a young one.

For a second, I froze, but then I forced myself to relax and strike a casual pose. Luckily, Carmilla was deep in conversation with some of her new advisors. They had previously served Velika, and I wasn't familiar with either of them. I also had no idea if Carmilla had used the crown's magic on them or if they had voluntarily switched loyalties.

I'd tried to converse with the crown the night I'd had dinner with Carmilla, but it'd been silent until it'd slithered into my mind with the light reprimand, *I can hear you perfectly fine, little queen. But silence is what I currently seek.*

I'd never been scolded by an inanimate object before, so that had been a fun new experience. But apparently, it was up for chatting tonight.

As much as I wanted to dive into a bunch of questions, I bit my tongue. Maybe this would go better if I thought of it less as a Fae artifact and more as a person?

I'm essentially a prisoner. My gaze flicked to where it rested on my aunt's dark hair. *Don't I have a right to be angry?*

You do . . . as do I, the sly voice replied. *You are my fate. You are mine.*

I wasn't sure what unnerved me more. That the crown could pluck all the thoughts from my mind, or that it believed I belonged to it.

You do.

Great. I now had a possessive Fae artifact in my life. *Not that I'm disagreeing,* I said carefully as I sipped my tea, *but can you elaborate on why you think our fates are linked?*

You are a descendent of the Seelie King.

What? I choked, and the tea went down wrong, causing me to sputter. The conversation died as all eyes fell on me. I ungracefully set my cup down and grabbed a cloth napkin as I tried to get my coughing under control. "Apologies," I rasped. "Swallowed wrong."

Carmilla looked at me with an unreadable expression. "Are you sure you're okay?"

"Yes." I nodded and tossed the napkin down. "Please continue. I believe you were discussing the Houses' inventories of gems to power the wards?"

She studied me for another moment before turning her attention back to the advisors, who had been staring at me wide-eyed before snapping their attention back to Carmilla. I could only imagine the rumors surrounding me right now. The House Harker Heir locked in the dungeons and trotted out to attend various meals by her aunt, who had deposed the previous Moroi Queen.

You need to work on how you broach topics like that, I thought. *Maybe ease into them a little more.*

A tinge of amusement fluttered across my mind. *I will make a note of that for the next time I need to inform someone of their lost royal heritage.*

Was that sarcasm? Did the Fae seriously make a sentient artifact . . . and give it a dry sense of humor?

The Fae did nothing of the sort. I am this magnificent all on my own.

Well, they definitely passed on their arrogance.

You do realize I can hear all of your thoughts, right? I remember the Seelie royals being smarter.

Can you explain why you believe I'm related to the Seelie King? My stomach churned, and I fought to keep the tea I'd swallowed from coming back up. Draven was the Seelie King's son, and we'd—

Flashbacks of the things we'd been up to the last few days played through my mind. Oh god.

Is there a reason why you just threw a bunch of smutty images at me? the crown asked, sounding puzzled. *You seemed to be enjoying yourself quite thoroughly in them, so I'm not really understanding why you suddenly feel like you're going to spew your tea all over the table.*

I've had—some of the best fucking of my life—*relations with the son of the Seelie King, who you just said I was related to. So, yes. I'm feeling a little freaked out right now.*

Dread coiled in my gut. This couldn't be happening. What were were going to d—

That man is not the son of the Seelie King.

Draven isn't Erendriel's son? How was that possible? Draven seemed so sure . . .

He is.

I inhaled a deep breath, trying to not let the tension strangle me—or drive me to reach across the table and rip the crown off Carmilla's head.

You should actually do that. I'm meant to be sitting on your head. People should be bowing to us.

What the fuck?

One of the advisor's glanced at me. Whoops. Must have whispered that part out loud. I gave her a polite smile and took another sip of tea. She stared at me a long moment before returning her attention back to Carmilla.

Can you please explain what you mean about Draven not being the Seelie

King's son? My smile was so tight on my face, it was causing my jaw to ache. *He is Erendriel's son—and Erendriel is the Seelie King.*

Erendriel is an imposter. Rage flashed through me, and it wasn't mine. *Your paternal grandfather was the true Seelie King. Erendriel betrayed him and has been lying ever since.*

What. In. The. Actual. Fuck.

Did my father know he was the son of the Seelie King? He had to, right? The thoughts fired rapidly in my mind. *At the very least, he had to know he was half Fae. Did my mother know?*

Your thoughts are very loud. And confusing, the crown grumbled. *I only knew your father as a youngling. I do not know if he was aware of his true lineage.*

For a second, it felt like everything in my mind went still. *You met my father?*

Before I was split apart and half of me locked away, yes. He was young. I'm not good with human ages, but all he did was cry. I mostly tuned him out and was happy when he was given to the bloodthirsty woman. Although your grandfather was sad for a long time afterwards.

My grandfather . . . the Seelie King. He'd sent my father away. I wondered if the bloodthirsty woman was Moroi, perhaps my grandmother. My father had never spoken about his parents, and he'd died when I'd barely been a teenager. I'd never had the chance to ask.

And now I never would. The crown might be able to give me a lot of answers, but it had admitted to not knowing my father well. It seemed those secrets had been taken to the grave.

I let the melancholy of a truth I'd never know drift through my mind before fading away. There was no point in dwelling on the secrets of the dead when the living hold just as many.

Who locked you away? I asked. It had to have been referring to the room beneath Lake Malov where we'd found it.

I . . . don't know. When I'm split into two parts, I'm weakened. Whoever did it knew what they were doing because they tore me apart before I knew what was happening. Even though I've been made whole once more, there are large gaps in my memory.

I'm so sorry. That sounds terrible. Sure, the crown was capable of tearing the free will away from people . . . but it was also kind of nice. A nice monster crown.

You cannot leave me behind. This woman . . . she has already made me do terrible things. I'm trying to resist, but I'm technically bound to whoever's head I rest upon, and fighting is exhausting.

The pieces clicked together. *That's why you couldn't talk to me the other day? You were tired?*

Yes.

Guilt nipped at me, but I didn't want to lie. There was no point anyway since the crown could read my mind like an open book.

I have no intention of leaving you in the hands of my aunt for long, but I cannot promise that I will take you with me, I said honestly. *Escaping from here is my priority.*

I am your priority. Its words were tinged with a desperate rage.

Not right now, I told it gently. *There are so many people depending on me. I can't let them down.*

Cold silence reigned through my mind. I must have hurt its feelings. Probably not good to piss off an ancient Fae artifact.

I'm sorry, I tried again. *I have no intention of abandoning you for long, but I will do what I must to get free of this place. Once I'm outside of these walls, I'll be in a better position to plan how to fix all of this.*

More silence.

Before I could make another attempt at soothing the crown—something I hadn't anticipated being on my list of problems to solve—footsteps came from outside the hall. Vail's eyes met mine from across the room. From where he was standing, there was no way he could see who was coming, but he'd likely caught their scent, and he didn't look happy.

A second later, I knew why when a stunning woman with golden blonde hair and tanned skin stepped into the room. At her side was an equally attractive man with light brown hair and chiseled features. I'd had the unpleasant experience of conversing with both of them in the past. They were high-ranking courtiers of House Corvinus. Not advisors exactly but they were close friends of Mora and Darius Corvinus—the Heads of the House.

The two courtiers were also Kieran's parents.

"Davon. Narcisa." My aunt rose and greeted the two newcomers. "We didn't expect you until this afternoon. Please join us."

"I think we have everything we need to get started, Carmilla—I mean, my queen," the fair-haired advisor at the table corrected herself. The other advisor glanced at Carmilla in panic, as if he expected my aunt to lash out.

She just smiled. "Thank you both for meeting with me. If you can have the information to me by tomorrow morning, I would appreciate it."

"O-of course," the woman stammered before both advisors practically ran from the table. Kieran's parents observed everything with amused smiles.

I watched them go and pondered the conversation I'd been trying to keep track of while the crown had infiltrated my mind. My aunt was interested in how many gemstones the Sovereign House possessed, as well as a best guess to what the other Houses had. We relied on those stones to power the wards that kept the wraiths and other nasty beasts out of our Houses and outposts.

Why was she specifically interested in the numbers now though? Most of the Houses tried to keep best estimates of what the others had because it gave them an advantage during trade negotiations, but I didn't know what Carmilla was plotting.

It was too much. Everything was too fucking much. Vail's betrayal. Carmilla's coup. That bloody crown. My heart raced as I tried and failed to calm myself. I was imprisoned by my last surviving family member. Someone I cared about very much was also imprisoned, and any day now, they could decide he was no longer worth the risk of keeping around.

Carmilla could order the death of Draven, and I wouldn't know until it was too late. Cold, icy fear gripped my heart. I could lose him.

I tried to pick up my tea again, but my movements were so jerky that I knocked it over instead. It was a red tea blend, and it soaked into the creamy tablecloth like rusty blood. Before I knew what I was doing, I was on my feet and backing away from the table.

Apparently, this was the moment my mind decided to snap under the pressure of everything that had happened over the past two weeks. Ragged breaths tore from my throat. All I could think about was Draven chained up in the throne room the day we'd been captured.

Demetri stabbing him through the chest.

I could have lost him that day. I could still lose him. Magic so different from my Moroi nature rumbled to life, and—

Breath, young queen, the crown ordered. *All is not lost yet. And you will bring the roof down on our heads if you don't stop—not to mention on your lover in the basement.*

The magic died down instantly, but not before I felt it brush against that strange connection I had recently formed with Draven. For a few seconds, I could have sworn I felt his steady heartbeat down it. I had no idea what this was between us, but I grabbed on to it like a lifeline to calm down.

Kieran's parents glanced at me, eyebrows raised as they made their way to the table, but didn't comment. Carmilla's steady gaze fell on me from where she'd already reclaimed her seat, but before I could come up with some excuse for my outburst, Vail was suddenly there, a solid wall of muscle between me and everyone else.

Grey eyes looked down at me. He didn't say anything, just searched my face, looking for a clue as to what was wrong. I clawed back the maniacal laugh that threatened to spill out. What *wasn't* fucking wrong at this point?

Slowly, Vail raised a hand and placed it over my chest. His palm rested on the swell of my left breast, right where that tug I always felt towards him—and now Draven—always was. Nobody else could see us with his broad body blocking their view.

I raised my own hand and placed it against his chest in the exact same spot. A calm steadiness flowed between us. While I might treasure whatever this connection was between me and Draven, it seemed like such a bad idea with Vail. Our conversation from that night in the cave came floating back. When I'd asked why everything between us was so confusing.

"Because I should hate you, but I can't, and you shouldn't trust me, but you do."

How was it that everything and nothing had changed since then? I drew in a steady breath before tugging my hand away from Vail. His eyes flashed, and I sensed a wave of frustration and annoyance through our bond.

Well, that was new. Previously, I had just been able to feel his general whereabouts.

Great. Now I had direct access to the feelings of a man I couldn't—no, shouldn't—trust again, and he probably had the same to mine.

Gods, somehow things had managed to get more complicated between us.

I looked away from Vail's intense gaze and did what I'd done in the years after my parents' deaths when grief had threatened to overwhelm me. I gathered up all the intense emotions I was feeling, shoved them into a box, and buried it in the depths of my soul. Then I envisioned a stone wall between me and Vail. It felt a little clunky, but after a few seconds, the emotions I was feeling from him faded.

Without looking at Vail again, I reclaimed my seat at the table. After a frustrated growl, Vail returned to his post next to the door.

"Feeling alright, Samara?" Kieran's father asked in an attentive but gentle tone that I knew was a lie. I adored Kieran, but there was no one better than my sweet lover at trading one mask for another. Even I was envious of his ability to hide whatever he was feeling and have a completely different emotion on his face. I was good, but nowhere near his level.

And the man looking at me, brows furrowed and eyes shining with concern, was half the reason Kieran could lie so well. The woman next to him, wearing a similar expression, was the other half.

"I'm fine." I smiled at them both. It didn't reach my eyes, but I couldn't bring myself to care. I wasn't at my best at the moment. Even if I had been, I doubted I'd be able to fool these two with charming grins and fluttering eyelashes. It wasn't worth the effort to try. "It's been a long week."

"I'm sure," Narcisa said demurely and took a delicate bite of her food.

"How is Tamsen doing?" I asked politely. The Corvinus Heir was interesting. Her parents were even worse than Kieran's. Mora and Darius were the reason Nyx—Tamsen's younger sibling—had left Drudonia and become a ranger. It was rare for a member of a House bloodline to leave their birth House for anything other than a politically arranged marriage. To leave a House only to become a ranger for another was unheard of for someone like Nyx.

I wasn't close to Tamsen, but I'd interacted with her enough over the years to know she was the least trustworthy of all the House Heirs—except Demetri, obviously. Like her parents, Tamsen was skilled at hiding her emotions, and every exchange with her was like trying to find and avoid the carefully laid traps in her pretty words.

But Tamsen was also the reason Nyx had been able to get free of the toxic political bullshit of House Corvinus. She loved her younger sibling and had fought for them when it'd mattered—and had likely suffered the consequences.

It didn't mean I trusted her . . . but there was more of a question mark beside her name now, whereas before, I'd had her firmly in the box with the rest of her House.

"Our Heir is doing wonderfully." Narcisa beamed. "She's wrapped up in some negotiations with the *Velesians* right now; otherwise, she would have come herself. I fear that each round of trading we do with them becomes more tedious than the last, but Tamsen always does right by her parents. Mora and Darius are so fortunate to have one child who is loyal to the House and willing to put the work in."

I almost clapped at the performance. She'd managed to put down the Velesians and suggest that trading with them was failing as well as make a dig at both Nyx and Kieran. I had no doubt that she and her husband were well aware of my relationship with their son—the rumors of us finally getting together had been quick to spread, and they were the types of people who knew every rumor before the last word of it was even whispered. While Nyx had been with House Harker for years, their parents still probably considered the whole thing a black mark on their House.

"Strange, I very recently finished a trade with the Velesians and had no problems at all." I widened my eyes and gave first Narcisa then Davon a concerned look. "Is House Corvinus struggling with offering fair trading terms? I know how challenging it can be to run a House. We're fortunate in that House Harker is so well-established that sometimes I take our stability for granted." I let a hint of apology seep into my expression as I placed a hand on my chest. "Please let us know if we can be of assistance. Nobody wants to see House Corvinus fall on hard times."

Narcisa's eyes narrowed the barest fraction, but Davon just gave me a grateful nod. "You're too kind, Samara. I wish you good fortune in your *second* marriage—perhaps aiming lower than a fellow Heir will work out better for you? I do believe House Tepes has lots of second cousins available."

My smile sharpened, but before I could reply, Carmilla cut in. Probably for the best. I was too tired to come up with anything clever and probably would have just thrown the butter knife at Davon's head. It was blunt, but I was confident I could throw it hard enough to pierce his thick skull.

"It's actually very fortunate that you're here." Carmilla touched the crown on her head.

I stiffened. Kieran's parents might be horrible and represent the worst of the Moroi, but I wouldn't sit by and watch their free will be stripped away. "Don't—"

"You will not be the one to pay if you interfere," Carmilla cut me off, her dark gaze flicking downward for a second before meeting my eyes again. Draven. She would punish my prince.

My nails shifted to claws that bit straight through the tablecloth and into the wood, but I kept my mouth shut. If I were a better person, I probably would have fought regardless—even knowing it wouldn't matter. The only ally out of the dungeons I had was Vail, and he was questionable at best. Despite Draven's confidence in him, I didn't trust him not to betray me. Definitely not with Carmilla being here.

The last time Carmilla had ordered Vail to do something and I'd begged him not to, he'd sided with her. I had no doubt he would do so again.

Davon and Narcisa were watching Carmilla and me closely. Their expressions were polite with just a hint of curiosity. It was the mask Kieran wore when he was feeling uneasy about something.

"It seems you two have some things to discuss." Narcisa dabbed her mouth with a cloth napkin before folding it neatly on the table. "We wouldn't want to intrude on family affairs."

"Perhaps we can rest in our room and then catch up later this afternoon?" Davon offered as he began to rise from the table, Narcisa doing the same.

"*Sit and be quiet,*" Carmilla ordered.

Both courtiers promptly dropped back to their chairs, and fear cracked through their calm facades as dread pooled in my gut.

"This isn't necessary," I tried again, hoping she wouldn't punish Draven for me merely pleading my case. "You said you would only use the crown when you had no other choice."

She gave me a placating smile. "My dear, you know how House Corvinus is. They are not to be trusted. Their loyalty is fleeting and always for sale. It's not a matter of if they will betray us, but when." Her gaze flicked to them. "Given the horrible ways they've treated Kieran over the years, I'm surprised you're defending them." Those green eyes met mine once more. "Or do you not love him the way you claim?"

"He wouldn't want this." I shook my head and glanced at Kieran's parents. Narcisa's full lips were flattened into a hard line, and her eyes were wide with terror. Davon was trying to keep his expression neutral, but sweat was beading at his forehead. "Imprison them if you must, but please don't do this."

Carmilla tilted her head as she pondered me. "I thought I raised you to be more ruthless than this. This is the perfect opening to have high-level spies in House Corvinus. I will not pass up this opportunity. Unless you want to find out just how much blood your disgraced lover can lose, I suggest you watch what you say next."

A large hand fell on my shoulder. I didn't have to look up to know it was Vail. Whether he was doing it to keep me from doing anything rash or as a show of support, I had no idea.

Please. This time, it was the crown I begged. *You don't have to do this.*

This is why you cannot abandon me. I must obey the head I sit upon—even if I don't want to. She tried to use me on children the other day. Fighting back against that cost me. I do not have the strength to disobey as I am right now. There was a hint of despair in its tone. *I have broken so many. Do not let yourself be added to the list.*

"Davon and Narcisa Blake," Carmilla's voice rang out, filling the room. "From this day forward, you serve me—and only me."

The fear on Kieran's parents' faces was wiped away in an instant before relaxing into emotionless masks. They looked at Carmilla, their eyes hollow and blank. "Yes, my queen," they intoned.

CHAPTER EIGHT

—

Samara

I AWOKE with a start and rubbed my eyes as I looked around. Carmilla had kept me at her side all day, Kieran's parents trailing behind us like obedient pets as she'd checked in with the rangers and other staff of the household. Most had greeted her happily, while some had been a little more reserved but still polite. I'd tried to see if any of them were under the compulsion of the crown. There had been no obvious evidence, but that didn't mean she hadn't been more subtle about it than she had been with Davon and Narcisa.

Carmilla had ordered Vail away after breakfast, something he very much hadn't been happy about, but he hadn't disobeyed her. I'd been pissy about it at the time, even though I knew it wasn't like he'd actually had a choice. And even if he'd chosen that moment to stand up to her, it likely would have ended with him thrown into the dungeon next to me, which wouldn't have helped us in the long run.

Despite me logically knowing this, I'd still been fuming about it for an hour afterwards until the guard escorting me had been replaced by that prick Grigor. He kept finding reasons to touch me. Never in a super obvious way— even Carmilla wouldn't have allowed that—but his hand would momentarily slip from my lower back to my ass when escorting me through a door. Then there'd been the way his knuckles had accidentally brushed across the side of my breast when he'd been reaching for a cloak off the wall.

He'd only stopped because I'd snapped two of his fingers when Carmilla hadn't been looking, and he'd swallowed his scream of pain. Either because he hadn't wanted to risk me telling my aunt what he'd been doing, or because he hadn't wanted to admit that I'd gotten the better of him.

Asshole was lucky there hadn't been any sharp objects in my reach; otherwise, he would have lost those fingers entirely.

The crown hadn't spoken to me, even when I'd tried to coax it into talking. Occasionally, I'd swear I could feel it slipping into my mind. It didn't feel nefarious, rather I got the feeling that it was just seeking refuge somewhere. It didn't like the way it was being wielded. I couldn't explain exactly how I knew that . . . only that I did. Exactly what type of connection did my family have to the crown?

Lucian had joined us for dinner, but thankfully Demetri was nowhere to be seen. I'd thought about asking where he'd been but I hadn't wanted my aunt to construe that as interest in him. Even if she hadn't taken it that way, it wasn't like I trusted her to answer me honestly.

Lucian had been oddly friendly towards me. Apparently, Velika's ex-consort had decided he liked me. Good for him, but it wouldn't stop me from carving out his heart at the first opportunity. I hadn't forgotten his torturing of Draven over the years or the way he had shoved a sword through my prince's heart.

I had a list of people who needed to die—and Lucian was near the top of that list.

Fuck him and his charming smiles.

I looked around my cell. What had woken me up? Nothing looked out of place, and the Fae lanterns still flickered, casting the room in a warm glow. Vail wasn't anywhere to be seen. Not entirely unusual. He came and went as he pleased. Lately, he'd been sleeping on the floor just outside my cell though.

The hair rose on the back of my neck. Something was here. I was sure of it.

A soft chuckle came from the darkest corner of my cell, and then the shadows moved.

I was on my feet in an instant. On instinct, my hands dropped to my thighs —only, I didn't have any daggers strapped there as usual. I had nothing. Absolutely no weapons to defend myself, and it wasn't like anyone would hear me scream.

Damn it! Of all the fucking times for Vail to take a walk!

Shadows drifted through my cell, shifting around until they formed a vague outline of a person. A person with pointed ears.

I started to step back against the wall but stopped myself and moved forward instead. Being against the wall meant being trapped, I wanted to have room to move if needed. What I'd do with that space against a wraith, I had no idea.

"Din tros." The title slithered between us as the shadowy figure gained more form until I could clearly make out the features of their face. Long hair trailed over their shoulder, whisps of shadow curling at the ends. When the wraith spoke again, his words had a distinct masculine tone, and he used the common tongue instead Seelie. "If I wanted you dead, I would have cut your

throat while you slept." He raised a hand, and the slender fingertips morphed into beast-like claws.

Panic at the fact that he was right caused my already rapidly beating heart to go even faster. The wraiths were nothing but Seelie Fae trapped in shadows, but for a few seconds at a time, they could make those shadows solid.

A lot of damage could be done in that short window.

It's why they were the most dangerous of all the monsters in Lunaria. They could only be killed if they were solid, which meant you had to wait to strike until they were about to kill you. Fighting wraiths was not for the faint of heart.

"Alright." I willed my heart to slow down and straightened my shoulders. "If you're not here to kill me then I assume you're here to talk." Chin held high, I stepped forward until only a couple of feet separated us, putting me easily within their reach. "You clearly know who I am—the granddaughter of the *true* Seelie King—I believe it is only fair that I know who I am speaking with."

Shadows swirled as he cocked his head. It was hard to read his expression because so much was lost to the dark shadowy colors, but I thought he was surprised. Both at my fearless demeanor and how casually I talked about my ancestry and the Seelie monarchy.

Which was good because I was still scared out of my mind and had very little to go on when it came to Seelie politics. All I had were the claims from a freaking sentient crown and the fact that this Fae referred to me as the forgotten queen.

But if he thought I knew more than I did, perhaps he would be freer with what he spoke. Fake it 'til you make it. Kieran had taught me that strategy.

"I am Serill." His voice was even clearer now with an almost musical quality. Normally when the wraiths spoke, it sounded like multiple voices layered over each other. It made it challenging to understand them. I could still hear traces of that, but I had to almost strain to notice it. I didn't know what it meant that he was able to speak so clearly now. Probably nothing good.

"Pleased to meet you, Serill." I extended a hand out between us, concentrating hard on keeping it from shaking. "You may address me as Samara."

He looked at the hand for a moment before his lips curled into a grin. I forced myself to remain calm as he reached out to rest a hand beneath mine, shadowy fingers that I could sense but not feel wrapping around it. Then he bowed, and for a split second, his hand became solid as cool lips kissed the back of my hand.

A shudder threatened to race up my spine, but I squashed it and kept a pleasant smile fixed on my face as he rose.

"Even locked in the dungeons, still a queen of old. Despite everything, the blood ran true it seems." He gave me a sly smile. "More so than with the prince."

I assumed the *despite everything* was a reference to my mother's side of the family, and he got in a dig at Draven too. Nice.

"Perhaps it is the blood of my mother's people that strengthened me beyond what the Fae could ever dream of." I arched a dark brow. "And given the prince's heritage, I see it as a strength rather than a hindrance that he is his own person and not a *shadow* copy of his parents."

The Fae chuckled. "Truly, you are a delight. It has been some time since I've conversed with one as clever as you. It makes me remember the olden days."

It was a trap. He wanted me to ask what he spoke of. To reveal just how ignorant I was of Lunaria's past, and even knowing this, I desperately wanted to ask. Was he referring to the early days when the Fae had come to Lunaria? Or where they had been before? What in all the hells existed beyond the oceans surrounding our small continent?

"Perhaps I can have you over for tea sometime while you reminisce," I said breezily instead. "As you can see, my accommodations are not quite up to par for socializing at the moment."

"Indeed." He walked over to my cell and trailed his fingers across the bars. The shadows slipped through and around them easily. I was a little surprised that the iron in the bars seemed to have no impact on him. Maybe in their wraith forms, iron didn't bother them? I wondered if that meant that the enchanted silver weapons we used against the wraiths would be less effective on them if they fully reclaimed their Fae forms . . . I'd have to mention it to Vail so the rangers could be prepared. No matter how I felt about Carmilla and her plans, I didn't want our people to die fighting the wraiths or the Seelie Fae.

Serill turned to face me, his back to the bars and his hands clasped in front of him. "What if I told you we are not the villains you've painted us as? That we are merely trying to survive like you?"

"I'd ask if your survival required our death," I replied calmly. "Because from where I'm standing, the wraiths have been responsible for more Moroi deaths than all the other beasts of this land combined."

"Your concern is valid." He nodded. "But you must understand that our previous deal was with Queen Velika, and it was her idea to raid the outposts as we did. We needed those obsidian stones, and she wanted some population control. The food supplies of the Moroi are getting dangerously lower every year as your population swells."

Not a lie, but not entirely accurate either. We had to take riskier chances while growing crops, often planting in areas with no wards to protect the fields or the workers, but we were managing. Rangers protected the workers during the day, and they retreated to the outposts before the sun fell.

I didn't know if he was telling the truth about Velika. At the very least, she had known about their slaughter of the outposts while obtaining those stones and had done nothing about it. She was dead. It didn't really matter if it'd been her idea or not.

This felt like someone trying to cast the blame on another who couldn't defend themselves. I wanted to know why and what he'd come to offer me.

"That does sound like something Velika would do," I replied slowly like I wasn't entirely convinced but found it conceivable.

Serill pounced on my indecision. "There is so much we can share with you. Truly, we only want to survive in this land full of cruelty and lies. A false queen has risen to the Moroi throne. We would prefer you to sit on it."

My composure shattered for a moment, and I froze. I knew Carmilla had to be stopped, and while I hoped that would be imprisonment rather than death, I would do whatever I had to for our people. But never at the end of this had I seen myself sitting on a throne.

And absolutely not as the puppet queen of the Fae—because I had no doubt that would be all it was. I may not have known much about the Fae, but everything suggested they were not the type to share power.

"I will not allow our past to cloud my judgment of a potential alliance, but I trust you can understand my hesitancy here." I watched him closely, trying to glean any hint of how he was feeling from his movements and expressions, but the shadows made it so damn hard. "Putting aside the fraught history between our people, there is also the fact that I am the daughter of the Seelie King—and Erendriel is *not* the true king."

It was Serill's turn to go still for a moment; even the shadows rolling off his shoulders seemed to freeze. He recovered quickly and gave me a friendly but slightly condescending smile. "Young one, there is so much you don't know of our people. Of what the Fae have been since being exiled to these shores." His smile gained a shrewd edge. "Has the crown that rests on the false queen's head been whispering in your ear?"

"There are many things whispering in my ear these days," I answered vaguely.

"Such is the price of your lineage," he sympathized.

I didn't buy it. There was something about my bloodline that the Seelie Fae found useful—or feared. Perhaps it was the same reason Carmilla was suddenly interested in me marrying Demetri again. Once again, the urgency to get out of here hit me. I needed access to my mother's journals and to the secret room I'd found with Rynn beneath Lake Malov. One of those things had to have the answers I sought.

"What exactly are you proposing?" I fixed my features into a mixture of concern and wariness. "I would not have my people hurt, and not everyone in this House is responsible for my current predicament. If you mean to break me out by the same methods you used in the outposts, you will only make me your enemy."

"Queen Velika left many gaps in the wards here for us to come and go. I'm sure we can come up with a plan that would have minimal casualties while we retrieved you."

And delivered me straight into the hands of Erendriel.

"And what of Draven?"

"What of him?" Serill asked coldly. "His fate rotting in the dungeons below is better than what he would face outside of them. Forget about the *mikin.*"

Mikin. Traitor.

"I will need time to think on this." I waved a hand at my surroundings. "Something I have an abundance of, currently."

"Very well." Serill bowed his head. "I shall return in three days to discuss this further and offer options for getting you out." His form began to lose its sharpness before spreading into a more disembodied state.

"Serill."

The shadows snapped back into a Fae form, and he arched a brow at me in question.

"If I learn that Erendriel has ordered an attack on any outposts or any Moroi while I am thinking this over, any potential alliances will be dead."

"Of course, my young queen." Serill smiled. "Not a drop of blood shall be spilt . . . for now."

CHAPTER NINE

—

Kieran

"We're getting close," Desmond whispered quietly in that gravelly voice of his. I'd been a little surprised when both of Roth's brothers announced they'd be coming on this rescue mission. It was dangerous and a little insane. Plus, neither of them were close to Samara. Granted, we had explained the crown and our concern that it had fallen into the wrong hands, but still, part of me had expected them to lock Roth somewhere safe in their fortress and chuck the rest of us out.

When Roth's parents had announced that they'd also be going on this mission, I'd said as much. I *might* have phrased it in a poorly worded way that called into question their intentions. Actually, there was no might about it. While I didn't remember exactly what I'd said, Alaric and Roth had both winced at my choice of words, and if those two thought I'd been too blunt, then it must have been something really offensive.

The Devereux clan was an odd one though, and they'd just stared at me with a predatory focus. "You might claim Roth now, but they were ours first." Celestina, Roth's mother, smiled at me in a way that had all my instincts on alert. "Our youngest does not love easily. The fact that they have not only found it but that the person they love has chosen them with equal ferocity is something we will protect at all costs. You will not dissuade us from coming."

At the end of the day, despite my scheming and Alaric's near-constant research, it had been our antisocial and taciturn Roth who'd figured out a path forward to saving the woman we all loved. And hopefully Draven.

I was frustrated with myself over how quickly—and badly—I'd fallen apart. Samara and Draven were gone. Instead of keeping it together and doing everything I could to help them, I'd just . . . spiraled.

Sure, I'd done my best to gather gossip and call in favors, but at the end of the day, I'd had nothing to show for it. I'd promised Samara I'd always be there for her, but when it'd counted, I hadn't been. She'd never been bothered by the fact that I was just a courtier. Not when we'd been friends . . . nor when we'd become something more.

I heard the whispers though. People questioning her judgment or assuming I was just a passing fancy. When she was with me, it was easy to ignore them, but now all the doubts had crowded into my mind along with the frustration and terror that something really bad had happened to her.

And Draven. The prince I loved beyond reason. Who had used my lower status as a courtier to hurt and humiliate me. He'd done it to protect me from his mother's machinations, but that didn't make the wound any less raw. Nor did it help with all the insecurity I was feeling now.

I was so lost in my thoughts that I almost ran into Alaric when he suddenly stopped in front of me. Roth missed the message though.

"Oof!" They collided with me, causing me to bump into Alaric, who turned to glare at us both.

He peered around me. "Are you seriously reading a book right now, Roth?"

I turned, and sure enough, Roth had unwound the ropes on one of their forearms just enough to hold a small jar full of glowing stones. A little makeshift Fae lantern. How adorable. I filed it away to tease Roth about later. Ideally, when I wasn't trapped in an enclosed space with them.

"We don't know for sure how to open the door," they said defensively. "My brothers might be confident they can muscle their way through it, but I'd prefer to have an actual plan besides *smashy smashy*."

"It's a perfectly good plan, Rothie Bear," Desmond called from where he'd stopped at the front of the line. "And might, in fact, be necessary because there's supposed to be a door here according to the map . . . but there isn't."

"Let me see." Roth shoved past me and Alaric, grumbling something about being surrounded by idiots. They studied the wall, and we all did the same. The only sources of light were the few Fae lanterns we'd brought with us and Roth's jar of glowing stones, but our eyesight was more than good enough to see our surroundings, which consisted of compact dirt.

Ceiling, floor, walls . . . all dirt. It was a little unnerving because there weren't any support beams anywhere. Logic said that this tunnel should have caved in years ago—if not immediately—but we'd been walking underground for at least a mile, and there were no signs of any weakness anywhere.

It must have been made by the Seelie Fae and their earth magic. I was surprised that it had remained standing all this time though. Most of the Fae spells had burnt out and we'd had to replenish them with our own magic.

As spectacular as the construction of this tunnel was, our trip was pointless if we had no way of entering the Sovereign House from it.

"Are you sure we're in the area?" I squeezed past Alaric to take the map from Taivan. "Or maybe it was marked incorrectly?"

I frowned at the fading lines and scribbles written in what I was guessing was Unseelie. If not for those hastily written words, I wouldn't even think this was the real thing. House Devereux had managed to successfully keep their treasure trove of Fae artifacts and writings hidden from the rest of the Moroi. While Roth might have been obsessed with Fae poetry, their family treasured something else—details about how all the Houses were constructed, including ways to break into and out of them.

I'd been impressed by it all, but Alaric had scowled so hard, I was surprised his face wasn't permanently stuck like that. He hadn't been pleased to learn that House Harker was included in their "information gathering" and that they knew all of our strengths and weaknesses.

It was thanks to their paranoia though that we had an undetected way into the Sovereign House, so he'd held his tongue. Mostly. Now we just needed to find the damn door.

Alaric reached for the map, but Roth was faster, snatching it from my hands.

"This is definitely the place," they murmured, casting their eyes from the map to the wall and back again. "Some type of illusion spell maybe?" Roth folded the map up and tucked it into the book before shoving both into a bag at their waist. "See if you can feel some type of release or glyph carved into the wall. Don't trust your eyes."

We each took a section of the wall and started searching. I ran my fingers across the cool earth, but nothing stood out. My frustration grew over the next few minutes, and I wasn't alone in that. It hadn't been easy to avoid all the patrols and find the entrance to this tunnel.

If it had all been for nothing—

I choked back the wounded sound that tried to escape, but there was nothing I could do against the anguish rising in my gut, filling my thoughts and my soul with a hopeless despair I didn't know how to fight. Losing either Samara or Draven was unimaginable. Losing them both . . . I would never come back from that.

My search became more desperate. Nails shifted to claws as I tried to tear my way through the dirt. Blood scented the air, and then Alaric was cursing and pulling me away.

Just as I started to push past him and continue my frantic attempt at getting through, the wall trembled. Everyone froze. In an instant, all of Roth's family had their swords out. Taivan grabbed Roth and shoved his younger sibling behind their parents.

The wall exploded, the clumps of dirt hanging in the air for a few seconds before falling to the ground. I had my own sword free, as did Alaric, as we waited for the attack to come.

It never did.

"Forgive me, but this is a rescue mission, is it not? Shouldn't you all be moving a little quicker?" an amused voice asked. Dust still floated in the air, preventing me from seeing the person who spoke, but I recognized the voice.

In an instant, I was past the crumbled wall and in what appeared to be the dungeon—the map had been right after all, for the location at least. Whoever had said there'd been a door there had either been mistaken or had known some trick that we didn't.

None of that mattered though as my fingers closed around the bars that separated a cell from the rest of the room. Vibrant blue eyes threaded with red met mine.

"Hello, lover," Draven purred. "Out for a midnight stroll?"

"You know me," I replied, my voice catching. "A bit of a restless sleeper."

He chuckled and laid his hands over mine around the bars. "I promise to thoroughly tire you out after this."

"I don't need to hear this," Roth growled as they came to a stop beside me. "Iron bars," they mused.

"Can you feel it?" Draven asked, shooting Roth a curious look.

I wasn't sure what he meant by *feel it*, but when I glanced down at his hands over mine, I noticed he was being careful not to touch the bars.

"No." Roth's hazel eyes studied the cell, their brows coming together the longer they looked. "But I've seen this design before. Though the color is different from the metal composition the humans used." They frowned. "And anything the humans built had doors."

"Do we have you to thank for opening that wall?" Celestina jutted a thumb over her shoulder at the wreckage in the tunnel.

"Yes. I did my best to quiet the sound. Given that there aren't any guards flooding this room, I don't believe they heard anything." Draven eyed Celestina before looking around at all those gathered in the room, his gaze finally falling back on Roth, no doubt seeing the familial connection. He grinned when he noticed the new blood ropes around Roth's forearms. "Upgraded your ribbons, eh?"

He winked at them, and to my utter shock, Roth winked back. "The better to strangle you with."

"How'd you know we were there?" Celestina asked, her expression unreadable.

Some of the amusement drained from Draven's face, then he squeezed my fingers, being careful to avoid the bars. "I felt Kier's blood." His eyes didn't leave our fingers, and a tension rolled through him.

"No way you would be able to smell the blood through that wall." Desmond prodded some of the wreckage strewn about on the floor. "Too thick. Not even a Velesian would have been able to smell through it."

"Felt," Severen corrected his son. "He said *felt*, not smelled."

"I knew it!" Roth whispered loudly.

"Care to share with the rest of us?" Alaric said dryly. "Or was this just a gloating moment?"

Roth narrowed their eyes. "Don't be pissy because you've contributed nothing on this rescue. I'm sure Samara will still think you're pretty."

"What is going on?" I cut in, turning enough so I could glare at everyone in the room before looking at Draven again, who was avoiding my eyes. "How did you do that, Drav?"

Finally, he met my gaze, a half-hearted smile on his lips. "You know only you and Sam call me that, right?"

"Yeah," I told him softly. "I know."

Draven's eyes didn't leave mine as he gripped the bars with both hands for several seconds before pulling them away. His lightly tanned skin turned an angry red. It faded quickly, but I saw it.

I stared at his palms for a long moment. "Seelie Fae?" The question came out a little disconnected as my mind whirled. I didn't even know if that was possible because Draven was definitely Moroi . . . at least part Moroi anyway.

"Yes." Draven rubbed his hands against the sides of his pants like he wanted to wipe off the taint of the iron. "Half, courtesy of my asshole father." He opened his mouth to say more but then clamped it shut.

My sword suddenly felt very heavy in my hand. We'd told the Devereux clan the truth about the wraiths before coming here. That they were really the Seelie Fae. Roth hadn't wanted to hide that knowledge from their family, and we'd all agreed that they'd deserved to know the truth.

How would they react to knowing that some of the blood running through Draven's veins was the same as the shadow monsters' who had killed so many of their House? I wouldn't just let them hurt him, but I also knew I wouldn't win against them. And Alaric was foolish enough to stand by my side.

Had we come all this way to die?

"Well, your earth magic has already come in handy tonight," Severen said. "I'm sure it will again before this night is over."

Shock washed over me. "That's it?" I gaped at Roth's father and then at the rest of their family, who seemed to be rolling with this.

Celestina shrugged. "He's with Samara. Roth is with Samara. We're basically in-laws at this point."

"I'm kind of curious about how his earth magic can be used in a fight."

Taivan gave Draven an appraising look. "If the wraiths manage to turn themselves back to their former Seelie Fae forms, then they'll have the same magic. Having someone to spar against will be really useful."

"Always thinking with your bloody sword," Roth grumbled.

"In more ways than one," Taivan agreed.

A tentative smile formed on Draven's lips. "I'll spar with you as much as you like if you get me and Samara out of here."

"Can you not use your magic to escape?" I studied the bars. They were a little thinner than my wrist, but when I tugged on them, there was zero give, and as Roth noted earlier, there was no door. How had they gotten him in there in the first place?

"No." Draven shook his head. "Interestingly, the bars don't block my magic—that's why I was able to tear that wall down when your blood leached into the dirt—but I cannot use my magic on the bars themselves, and there are more hidden in the walls of the cell."

"Must be because you're part Moroi too," Roth speculated. "Two forms of magic interfering with each other to create something new . . ." Their lips pursed together, and I could practically see their thoughts shifting. "Do you know where Samara is? Is she in a similar cell?"

"Three floors up," Draven confirmed. "It's only her presence here that keeps me from doing my best to tear down the entire building. I don't have enough control over my magic to ensure her protection."

"How do they open the cells?" I pushed, even as I looked around the room for a glyph or anything that would hint at how the magic worked.

"Blood." Draven sighed. "Certain blood is keyed to open the cells. I don't know everyone who has access, but Vail definitely does."

"Rumor is that Vail has been following Carmilla around like a loyal puppy," I said tightly. "Did he betray Samara?"

Draven cocked his head, causing his long, black-and-silver hair to shimmer in the dim lighting. "It's complicated."

"It's a yes or no question," Alaric growled, turquoise fractures forming in his seafoam green eyes.

"There is no black and white. There is no good and evil." Draven gave Alaric a patronizing close-lipped smile. "Don't be so boring."

Alaric looked like he was on the verge of leaving Draven here to rot.

"Samara can summon Vail," Draven added. His words only increased the tension in the room.

"Come again?" Severen frowned.

Draven opened his mouth—no doubt to say something lewd—but I cut him off. "How exactly can Samara do this?"

My princely lover gave me an annoyed look that clearly said *spoilsport*. "Just trust me on this. Samara can get Vail to come down here, and then we just have to convince him to let us out of these damn cells so we can all get the hells out of here."

"Three floors up, you said?" Celestina was already moving towards the door.

"Yes." Draven started to pace in his cell. "You shouldn't run into any guards —they're usually stationed at the very top entrance—but if you do, be quiet about how you deal with them."

"Not our first prison break, prince." Celestina jerked the door open. Her husband and sons followed after her as she walked into the hall.

I looked at Roth. "Your family is incredible, and I adore them."

"You're welcome to have them," they grumbled and started towards the door, but not before I caught the smirk on their face.

Alaric looked at me before narrowing his eyes coldly on Draven, and I was a little taken aback by his hostility. It felt personal, but I knew for a fact the two of them had rarely interacted before Draven had shown up at House Harker declaring he'd wanted to marry Samara.

Which . . . granted . . . could have been enough to piss off Alaric.

"Be right back," I promised Draven.

"Go get our girl." He cut a glance at Alaric before smirking at me. "If you have to sacrifice someone, I nominate him."

"Hilarious." Alaric started for the door. "It'll be such a shame if we have to leave you behind. Truly. I'll cry myself to sleep every night—after I make Samara scream my name for hours."

Draven chuckled. "Look at that. He *does* have a personality."

I smiled one last time at Draven before racing up the stairs to the third floor, where the others had already found Samara. Roth had slipped their slender arm through the bars to cup her face.

Dark purple eyes latched on to me. "Kier," she breathed out before taking in Alaric too. Then she frowned. "It was foolish of all of you to come and put yourselves at risk like this. You shouldn't have—oww!" she yelped and glared at Roth. "Did you seriously just pull my hair?"

"Don't say asinine things, and you won't get punished."

"It wasn't *asinine*," Samara muttered while rubbing a spot on her head.

"Draven said you could summon Vail," I said quickly. "We have a way out, but only if we get you both out of these cells."

"Quick would be good," Taivan added. "The prince said the guards are only stationed at the entrance, but I'm assuming they make regular rounds?"

"Yes," Samara answered, a crease forming between her brows as she concentrated. "Next one shouldn't be for almost an hour." She placed a hand over her chest, right over her heart. "I've never actually done this before, so I'm not sure if it will work."

I had no idea what *this* was, but I kept my mouth shut while Samara attempted to contact Vail. What had happened between them? I wasn't friends with Vail by any means, but I'd always respected him. His relationship with Samara was complicated, but recently, it'd seemed like it'd been getting better. Then she and Draven had been imprisoned—and he hadn't.

That reeked of betrayal, and yet Draven and Samara both seemed willing to call on him to help break them out of here. Clearly, we had a lot of catching up to do once we were somewhere safe.

Samara let out a sharp exhale.

"What?" I crowded closer to the bars. "Are you okay?"

"Pretty sure that asshole just gave me the middle finger through our connection." She frowned. "I wonder if there's a way I can slap him."

"Babe," Roth drawled. "Did you hit your head?"

Samara rolled her eyes. "Long story. Short version is that I have some type of empathic connection to Vail—and Draven. We can't hear each other's thoughts or anything, but we're . . . aware of the other."

I looked away from Samara and tried to ignore the spike of jealousy that hit. She'd been mine first. Why didn't *we* have a connection like that?

Warm fingers closed around mine where they were wrapped around the bars, and I raised my gaze to find Samara staring at me like I was the only person who existed.

"I hate that you're here, putting yourself in danger," she said softly. "But I'm so fucking happy to see you, Kier."

"Missed you, Sam." I rubbed my thumb across her fingers. "Sorry we didn't get here sooner."

"I never had any doubt that you'd come." Her bottom lip stuck out in a pout. "I was hoping to get myself out of here sooner. Kind of embarrassing that I needed to be rescued, honestly."

"It really is." I nodded, giving her a serious look.

Her pout turned into a wicked grin that had my heart skipping a beat. She opened her mouth to respond when we heard footsteps somewhere above us in the winding stairwell. There was nowhere for us to hide, so everyone except me moved to stand against the wall where the door was. I remained next to Samara so I could draw the attention of whoever entered, and Taivan nodded at me from where he stood closest to the door, his sword ready to skewer anyone who wasn't Vail.

A second later, the door swung open, but the Marshal of House Harker wisely did not charge blindly into the room. Instead, he waited in the hallway with a dagger in each hand. He didn't relax when he saw me; if anything, he looked more pissed off.

"You idiots chose the worst time to attempt a rescue." His silver gaze slid to the right as if he could see through the wall. "Lower your fucking sword, Taivan, or I'll shove it up your ass."

The Devereux Heir snorted but lowered his sword, although he didn't sheath it. "Well, he's as cheerful as ever."

Vail stormed into the room then. "Carmilla recalled all the Sovereign House rangers, and most arrived this morning. There are five hundred rangers in the keep right now, and Lucian knows you're up to something."

CHAPTER TEN

—

Samara

"AND HOW DOES he know that exactly?" I narrowed my eyes at Vail.

"I didn't tell him," he growled as he stalked his way to my cell, not even acknowledging all the Devereux warriors eying him warily. Taivan and Desmond wore matching wolfish smiles that practically screamed trouble. One look from Roth, though, had those smiles dimming slightly, and they gave their younger sibling a chagrined look.

I had a lot to tell everyone once we were out of here, but I was dying to know what the deal was with Roth and their family and how exactly they had convinced not only their brothers but their freaking parents to come here.

But that would have to wait. We had more immediate problems, like the asshole slashing open the back of his hand and smearing the blood over his fingers.

"Then why does he suspect something?" I crossed my arms while Vail slammed his bloody fingers onto the center bar. Glyphs glowed red across a dozen of the bars before they vanished.

"You fucking yanked on our bond, and I damn near collapsed." Vail didn't step back from the cell, which meant he was still blocking my exit as light silver bled through his dark grey eyes. "I was mid-sentence when it happened, and Lucian—obviously—thought it was strange. I might have cursed your name out loud. He put two and two together. I punched him in the face. Happy?"

My fist shot forward, and Vail stumbled back, blood pouring from his broken nose.

"Ecstatic." I bared my teeth at him before stepping out of my cell.

"Okay, I was skeptical before," Desmond rasped, "but I approve of your choice, little sib. She's a vicious thing."

"Do you really want to do this now?" Vail stepped towards me, but Alaric and Kieran blocked his way. He flashed his fangs at both of them before focusing on me once more. "How about you quit giving me shit so we can get out of here?"

I patted Kieran and Alaric on the shoulders, and they stepped aside to let me through. Alaric grumbled a little about it, but Kieran kissed me on the cheek. My sunshine and my grump. I'd missed them.

"I'm perfectly capable of doing two things at once." I dismissed Vail and started striding towards the door so we could free Draven when Vail grabbed my arm. Everyone tensed, and I heard Kieran and Alaric move, but they stopped at whatever they saw in his face.

Vail's lips curved into a tight smile before he leaned down to whisper in my ear, "Don't think I've forgotten how good you are at doing two things at once."

Heat rushed to my cheeks, and I felt my core tighten as I remembered what it felt like to have him and Draven both moving inside me. Draven's fingers gripping my thighs as I rode him hard while I swallowed Vail's cock, his fingers twisting in my hair, spurring me on.

The tension in the room increased as the scent of lust permeated it. Fuck. I was at the tail end of the lust haze, but his damn words had it rising.

"I hate you." I shoved Vail away from me.

He released his grip on my arm and smiled. "It'd be easier if you did."

Was it possible to hate and love someone at the same time? Based on my complicated feelings towards Vail . . . the answer was yes. That didn't mean I trusted him though. Not when we were still standing in the aftermath of his betrayal, and not when the jagged pieces of my heart were still cutting through my soul.

Something flickered in Vail's silver eyes before they dropped to where my hand lingered on my chest. To where the bond between us was tight like a bowstring . . . feeling like the wrong move could make it snap.

"Come on." Kieran grabbed my hand and tugged me towards the door while Alaric appeared at my other side, and they guided me out of the room and down the stairs. Once Vail was out of my sight, it was like the world came crashing back in as I raced down the steps.

"Took you all long enough," Draven drawled as I burst through the door, the rest of the group right behind me. "Was starting to get worried the Marshal wouldn't come through."

"Drav." I crashed to a halt in front of his cell, and he raised his right hand, letting it hover an inch away from the bars. I did the same with my left, my palm tingling from the close proximity to the iron. "We're going to get you out of here."

"I don't think this is a good idea." Vail crossed his arms a few feet away. "We don't know for sure that we can trust him." I laughed and gave him an incredulous look, but he kept going. "Plus, his asshole father is likely going to come after him. The wraiths will be all over us."

"Who's his father?" Alaric peered at the prince as if he was searching for an answer in his features.

"Nobody," I answered at the same time Vail said, "The Seelie King."

We glared at each other.

"I take it back, Roth." Desmond's low voice rolled across the room. "Maybe you did choose poorly. I mean, she's hot and all, but this seems like a lot of dram—oow! Let go of my damn ear!"

I glanced over my shoulder to see Roth and Desmond swatting at each other like five year olds. The older Devereuxes, whom I'd met a few times over the years, just let out long sighs as they watched the squabble unfold.

Taivan rolled his eyes at his siblings before striding over to us. "What's the holdup? Spring the prince and let's go."

"Yeah, Vail." I crossed my arms and matched Vail's glower. "Open the fucking cell so we can get out of here. Unless you're just stalling so we can get caught. Will Carmilla give you a pat on the head then? Maybe a treat?"

His pissed-off gaze stayed locked on mine as he sliced open the back of his hand again, the cut from opening my cell already healed, and smeared some blood on his fingers before slapping them onto the iron bars. Out of the corner of my eye, I saw the same red glyphs glow before the bars disappeared.

In a heartbeat, Draven's lips were on Kieran's, who let out a surprised sound before kissing the prince back. That finally got me to look away from Vail to smile at them both.

"Roth, you're going to have to draw us a diagram or something later. Your relationship is complicated."

A rope shot through the air and wrapped around my waist, then I was yanked off my feet before being set down in front of Roth, who smirked at me. "The rest of them are still sorting themselves out. They're the complicated ones." Orange lines cracked through the haze like tiny lines of fire. "Me and her? We're golden."

Then their mouth crashed against mine.

I FROWNED at Alaric's back as we made our way through the tunnel. He'd pulled me away from Roth seconds after our kiss had begun—earning himself a lashing from their ropes. Then he'd almost gotten punched by Draven when he'd yanked him away from Kieran and shoved everyone towards the tunnel.

He was right of course. The middle of an escape was not the best time for make-out sessions, and I'd immediately wrestled my lust back under control, earning me a *"good girl"* from Roth that almost had me on my knees in front of them. The way their eyes had turned to pure fire told me they'd sensed just how turned on I'd been in that moment—and they'd be doing something about it later.

Apparently, this tunnel system was quite extensive, and there were some underground rooms towards the end that we could make use of to stay hidden a little longer. Draven had managed to put the wall back together after a few fumbled attempts. We couldn't be sure how it looked from the other side, so he'd carefully caved in parts of the tunnel behind us. Even if Carmilla and her rangers figured out how we'd escaped, they wouldn't be able to follow us this way.

In the past hour, as we'd walked towards our resting place for the night, Alaric had barely spoken to me. Nor had he touched me or even glanced in my direction. I didn't know what was going through that head of his, and it annoyed me.

"Got to hand it to Carmilla," Severen finally said. "I didn't see this coming."

I'd just finished recounting everything to them a few minutes ago. Kieran had to be physically restrained from going after Vail when he'd learned what he'd done. Alaric's jaw had tightened, but he hadn't said anything. While everyone was focused on keeping Kieran under control, Roth's ropes had wrapped around Vail and slammed him into the wall.

Repeatedly.

Kieran and Roth were now at the front of the group, followed by Roth's brothers. Draven and Alaric walked on either side of me with Vail—a little roughed up but mostly fine—behind us. Severen and Celestina brought up the rear.

It should've bothered me that Vail was at my back.

It didn't.

Which only made me pissed off at myself. Between that and my growing frustration with Alaric, I was in a bit of a foul mood.

"None of us saw this coming—obviously," I snapped. "She played us all for fools."

"Are she and Lucian really together?" Kieran asked from the front of the group. "He seemed so devoted to Velika."

"Seems they are." I thought about the little touches they'd given each other throughout dinners. "They're definitely sleeping together, and Carmilla trusts him enough to have him sitting in on most of her meetings. I'm not sure if they've always been a thing or if she seduced him away from Velika."

"Lucian is a treacherous bastard." Draven's hand brushed against mine, and I repeated the move back. "He might even be better than you, Kieran, at reading and manipulating people. I don't know for sure what his angle is with Carmilla, but I doubt it's love. The only person Lucian loves is himself. He'll serve her as long as he believes she's the strongest player in the game, but the second she slips, he'll stab her in the back. Likely for a price."

"Could we use him?" Alaric asked. "Offer him something to betray Carmilla?"

"Lucian dies," I half growled, causing Draven and most of the others to glance at me. My prince was the only one I focused on. "He hurt you. He fucking dies."

Draven's fingers wrapped around my hand before he raised it so he could kiss my knuckles without ever breaking eye contact.

"Agreed," Kieran called out.

"I love it when you two get all murderous over me." Draven sighed.

Alaric let out an annoyed huff on my other side, which I ignored. I'd wait until we were alone to figure out what had made him even grouchier than normal.

"The Demetri bit is odd though," Kieran said. "Why is she so interested in the two of you getting back together? If she knew this was endgame, she could have just encouraged you to go back to him. We both know you would have done it if she'd asked, but instead, she let your divorce go through—supported it, even."

He was right. I had been loyal to Carmilla—up to a point; if she'd asked me to betray Rynn or Cali in some way, I wouldn't have done it. I hadn't been blindly loyal the way Vail had been, but if she'd asked me to sacrifice my happiness for the sake of the House? I would have done it in a heartbeat. I *had* done it when I'd agreed to marry Demetri.

"I don't know," I lied. "She must have her reasons though."

During my recap, I'd left out the part about my heritage. Draven and Vail knew I was part Fae, but they hadn't offered up that information, and I hadn't told anyone yet what the crown had told me. About who my father really was.

Everyone would have questions about it, and I had no answers—only more questions of my own.

I would tell the others about it. Just . . . later. When we were alone and had more time to discuss the implications. It wasn't that I didn't trust Roth's family; at this point, I trusted them more than my own House or any of the others. House Harker loyalties would likely be torn between me and Carmilla. The rest of the Houses . . . I only trusted them to do what was best for themselves.

But I wanted to tell my mates first.

My heart skipped a beat. Mates. The word had just flowed through my thoughts like water, but it felt right. The Fae hadn't used the term husband or wife—only mate. Growing up, I'd read so many poems of fated love. Of two Fae coming together despite all the odds against them.

I wondered if there were any Fae poems out there about multiple mates. My lips curled up in amusement. Maybe the crown would know.

The amusement died at that thought. *You cannot abandon me.*

For all its arrogance and sarcasm, there had been fear and loneliness in those words too.

I'm sorry, I pushed out even though I suspected I was too far away for it to hear me. *I will return for you. You are not forgotten.*

Even if I hadn't felt this odd responsibility towards the crown, we had to get it away from Carmilla. It was a weapon just waiting to be wielded against us. The crown might not have worked on me or anyone who had recently drank my blood, but it'd worked against Kieran's parents just fine. Not only were they powerful, but I suspected they regularly drank from the vein of the Corvinus family. They were close friends with the Heads of the House after all.

When Draven's mother had attempted to use the crown against House bloodlines, it hadn't worked well. At best, she'd been able to drive them insane until they'd become Strigoi, but she'd only had half the crown—Carmilla had united both halves. We didn't know what it was capable of now, and I didn't want to let her test its capabilities on the people I cared about.

There was also the fact that it could help us fill in the gaps of what we knew of Lunaria's history. Even with the crown's spotty memory, it might be able to tell us something new. Between that and the Harker journals I'd discover in the hidden cave, we might finally be able to piece together more of our history. Speaking of . . .

"Roth, where are the journals?" I didn't specify which ones because I knew they'd understand.

"Waiting for us at House Devereux," they tossed over their shoulder. "The ones you had anyway. The rest are where you left them."

In the secret room of the cavern by the sea. The Fae, it seemed, had been quite fond of secret rooms and passages. My brows pinched together as I cast glances around the tunnel. Come to think of it, all the secret rooms we'd discovered so far were underground, or at least covered by layers of rock like the cavern. Why had they been so obsessed with keeping things beneath the surface?

"Good." I let out a long breath, dismissing the eccentricities of the Fae for now. "Have you heard anything from Cali or Rynn?" My right thumb rubbed the spot on my finger where the ring Cali had crafted for me usually rested. I hated not knowing where they were, and I knew they likely weren't handling my sudden absence well.

Silence fell.

Kieran and Roth exchanged a look I couldn't decipher since I could only see their profiles. I glanced at Alaric and the muscle along his jaw flexed.

"Reports indicate that Rynn is with the Alpha Pack in the north, but we haven't been able to confirm that with absolute certainty."

I nodded, having suspected as much. The last time I'd seen Rynn and the Alphas, they hadn't been getting along. In fact, Rynn had been adamant that she wouldn't be going with them despite the fact that she'd been promised to join their pack for over a decade. She'd been delaying it for years, and I felt guilty that I hadn't read more into that. I'd been so preoccupied dealing with my failing marriage and trying to sort out my own life that I hadn't realized how desperate Rynn had been to avoid her fate.

Fuck, I was a shitty friend.

I'd make it up to her by busting her out of the Alpha Pack's stronghold—after we got the crown back and stopped Carmilla. For now, Rynn was in the safest place she could be.

"And Cali?" I asked quietly, dreading the answer.

"Nobody knows." Alaric sighed. "There have been no sightings of her anywhere."

He hesitated, and I could tell there was more.

"Spit it out, Alaric," I demanded, earning me a pissed-off look from him.

You can be pissy all you want, but you're going to fucking tell me. I held his gaze and raised my chin, and that muscle beneath his eye twitched.

"Two Furies stopped by House Harker before we left for Roth's House. They—"

"House Harker *is* Roth's House," I cut him off before giving Taivan a challenging look when he glanced over his shoulder at me. Severen and Celestina might be Roth's parents, but Taivan was their eldest sibling—and the House Devereux Heir. He was the one here who could lay claim to Roth. *"Mine,"* I growled.

Eyes identical to Roth's sparked at the challenge, and he stopped. I and everyone else stopped with him.

"Taivan . . ." Roth warned and started towards me, only to be stopped by Desmond.

The Devereux Heir closed the distance between us. When Alaric and Draven moved to intercept, I slammed a hand against each of their chests and shoved them back. This was between me and Taivan. I didn't need them to fight this battle for me.

"Shouldn't you be a little more appreciative?" Taivan raised a dark brow. "If not for us, your pretty ass would still be sitting in that cell."

"I would have gotten out eventually—you just moved up the timeline."

He gave me a patronizing smile. "Sure."

"You threw Roth away." I bared my teeth at him. "Finders keepers. You try to take them from me, and I'll carve out your fucking heart."

Several breaths passed between us, and the tension of those gathered shot up.

Then Taivan broke it when his smile widened and became something real. "Okay, I *definitely* approve of this." He patted me on the head before looking past me to his parents. "Looks like you finally get to plan that wedding, Pa!"

"Yes!" Desmond pumped a fist in the air. "That means we're off the hook for at least a decade."

Roth sighed, and I caught their eye. *What the fuck?* I mouthed. They just gave me a pitying look and turned to move down the tunnel in the direction we'd been headed.

We all started walking again, and Draven grumbled something under his breath when he had to step aside to make room next to me for Severen. A second later, Alaric did the same when Celestina took his spot.

"How do you feel about a summer wedding?" Severen asked.

Before I could answer, Celestina cut in. "You're good with a little pain, right? Our wedding vows are . . . intense."

"Don't worry," Severen said, again cutting me off from responding. "We have a little more time before we get to a safe place to rest. Plenty of time to hash out a plan to take care of this crown nonsense, kill your aunt, and coordinate a wedding."

"Maybe we should worry about the first two things before getting to the wedding bit," I suggested lightly.

Both of them slowed their pace.

"Are you trying to get out of marrying our youngest?" Celestina's voice was lethally quiet.

"No!" I cast helpless looks at both Draven and Alaric, who looked like they were trying to hold back their laughter.

"Excellent!" Severen slapped me on the back, causing me to stumble forward. "Which do you prefer, wildflowers or . . ."

CHAPTER ELEVEN

—

Samara

We made it to our destination in just under an hour, and true to their word, Roth's parents had alternated between plans for how to retrieve the crown, murder Carmilla, and coordinate an epic wedding. Honestly, it was the wedding part that sounded the most complicated, as both the crown and Carmilla plan were basically "stabby stab."

Roth's family was insane. I now understood why they had fled to Drudonia.

I wasn't entirely on board with killing Carmilla. She absolutely had to be stopped—of that I agreed wholeheartedly—but my plan was to strip her of power and imprison her somewhere where she couldn't cause any harm. Nothing else was going to happen tonight though, so I decided to leave that argument for another time.

Because right now, I was tired. So damn tired. I just wanted to hopefully clean off and crawl into bed . . . with company of course. Suddenly, some of my weariness faded as lust slid into its place.

Yep. Still riding the tail end of the lust haze.

"We've found other places like this," Desmond explained as we all piled into a large, cavernous room. We were still underground—something I still found amazing—and the Fae had clearly planned on occasionally having to stay here because there were a dozen entryways off this main room. Several chairs and tables were organized around the room too, with shelves lining the walls. "All the rooms should have bathing chambers. This is our first time in this particular hideaway, but all the previous ones we found still had working water. No food though."

He pulled a few small containers from his pack and tossed them onto the table, and not a hint of dust rose. Despite not having been used in probably centuries and surrounded by dirt, the place was spotless.

Would I be able to do things like this once I understood my earth magic better? We didn't even understand how the Fae had done half the things they had. The glyphs to heat the water made sense because they were literally just a combination of the glyphs for fire and water. But how had they even gotten the water to run into the bathing chambers in the first place? And the bathing chambers' setup, much like the Fae lanterns, still worked all these centuries later, even though the Fae hadn't been here to maintain them.

Occasionally, we had to use our blood to activate glyphs or replace the gems and stones that stored magic, but the actual infrastructure was still working flawlessly.

"There's a room beneath House Harker that is similar to this." I looked around curiously. "How many of these places have you found?"

"We'll tell you"—Desmond grinned at me—"as a wedding present."

"Even take you on a tour of them," Taivan offered.

I rolled my eyes.

"Ignore them." Roth cut their brothers a scathing look before grabbing my hand and pulling me into one of the rooms.

"Get some rest!" Celestina ordered. "We're going to find the exit from this tunnel system and do some scouting above."

I was still shaking my head at the ridiculousness of Roth's family when I came to a sudden halt just inside the room.

"Wow. Not what I was expecting . . ."

The room beneath House Harker had beds, but they were all single beds with one stacked on top of the other. Clearly, the point had been to jam as many Fae as possible into the space, but this room had only one bed—one huge bed—and a settee with several chairs arranged around it to the side.

Interesting. This was clearly a safe place to retreat, but they hadn't expected to house the masses here. I assumed the other rooms were laid out similarly. Which Fae got to stay here and which were sent to the cramped rooms beneath the Houses?

Kieran and Draven sauntered in, each giving the bed an appreciative smile before disappearing through a door on one side of the room. Probably the washroom Desmond had alluded to. A second later came the sound of running water, confirming my suspicions.

Gods, rinsing all the dirt and grime off would feel amazing right now. Even better if I had Kieran and Draven to help me with that. Heat started to build between my thighs, and Roth's gaze snapped towards me, the bright orange of their eyes flaring.

I took a step towards them until I realized not everyone had followed us into the room.

Alaric and Vail hovered in the doorway.

Dark grey eyes met mine, and for once, Vail held nothing back. Longing. Guilt. Confusion.

That'd always been Vail's story, not knowing how to handle his emotions, and somehow, I was always the one who bore the brunt of it.

I was fucking done.

Moving towards the door, I held out a hand to Alaric. Unlike Vail, his expression was unreadable. Something was bothering him, and I was going to get it out of him because Alaric's days of avoiding talking about things were over. He was mine.

And I'd fucking remind him of that.

A faint smirk played across his lips as if he'd just read my thoughts before he slipped his hand into mine. I tugged him into the room before giving Vail a flat stare . . . and then slammed the door in his face.

Roth let out a deep chuckle. "Good girl."

"What do you need?" Alaric asked in a light, casual tone.

I narrowed my eyes at him. That was all he had to say? Not *I missed you*. Or *I'm so glad you're okay*. Or even better, *I can't wait to be balls-deep inside you*.

Fine. The best way to deal with Alaric when he was in this emotionally distant state was to jar him out of it by being incredibly lewd and demanding—something I just so happened to excel at.

"What I need"—I moved towards him, rolling my hips, and a brief flicker of turquoise flashed across his eyes—"is to get cleaned off and then have all of you compete to see whose name I can scream the loudest." A smirk stretched across my lips. "Lately, I've got to say, Draven's been winning. Just a couple of days ago, he had me pinned against the wall with his cock stretching my puss—"

Alaric's mouth crashed against mine. Everything he'd been holding back came pouring out at once. Desperation. Terror. Rage.

Beneath it all was a demanding, possessive love that refused to bend.

There you are. I kissed him back with equal ferocity.

He broke our kiss and stared into my eyes like he was convincing himself I was really here with him. "I missed you so fucking much."

"Same," I breathed out.

I felt a tremble run through him before his lips were on mine again. His hands slid under my shirt, going straight for my breasts. I moaned as he pinched both of my nipples, my own hands dropping to undo his pants as the lust I'd been fighting for the past few hours rose like a tidal wave.

Something rough moved around my waist, and I frowned against Alaric's lips. He pulled back, and we both looked down at the bloodred ropes wrapped around us.

"Wha—" I squealed as I was yanked away from Alaric, who let out his own bark of alarm.

"Shower first," Roth declared, marching towards the washroom and tugging us with them. Alaric and I stumbled forward towards the steam-filled room.

"Take your foreplay to the bed," Roth ordered. "We'll join you in a few."

I peered around Roth's lithe form and groaned as I took in the delicious sight before me. Draven was kneeling on the ground, Kieran's rock-hard cock pressed against his lips. Something told me Kieran's flush wasn't just from the hot water rushing down on them.

"You heard them." Draven licked a broad stroke up the underside of Kieran's rigid length, causing him to moan, before sucking him all the way into his mouth and then releasing him. "Time to change the scenery." He winked up at Kieran before rising to his feet.

"Are you sure we can't just stand here and watch a little more?" I asked breathily, my gaze locked on the two gorgeous Moroi males who were giving themselves one more rinse beneath the steaming water.

"Oh?" Kieran gave me a cheeky grin. "Didn't know you were a voyeur, Sam. Thought that was Alaric's kink."

"I didn't intentionally walk in on you both," Alaric said dryly.

"Of course not." I gave him a patronizing pat on the cheek that had him narrowing his eyes. I'd probably pay for it later . . . but I was very much looking forward to my punishment.

Draven and Kieran stepped out from underneath the water. I belatedly noted that they'd already rinsed their clothes and had them hanging off hooks on the wall.

Both of them sauntered past me, rippling muscles on display, and kissed me on the cheek.

"See you soon, love," Draven purred in my ear.

Kieran chuckled as they left the room, and I took a step after them without even realizing it. Only Roth's rope around my waist stopped me from following them into the bedroom.

"Dry yourselves off before getting into bed!" Roth commanded.

The only response was a groan that made me think one of them had just taken the other in his mouth. A pressing heat built between my thighs, and I pulled against Roth's rope—only to be yanked beneath the warm spray of water.

I sputtered as water doused my face, but the rope held me in place.

"Alaric," Roth said idly, "I do believe our girl needs some assistance getting out of her clothes—and with a few other things. Help her out, would you?"

The rope around my waist fell away as Alaric joined me under the hot water. Unlike Kieran, he wasn't sporting any scruff, and he'd clearly shaven his head recently. Alaric was always in control—even when he was losing his mind.

I traced my fingers along his sharp jawline, and he leaned into my touch and closed his eyes, savoring the moment. Roth cleared their throat, and Alaric's eyes flew open. We both grinned and started helping each other get our clothes off, holding them under the hot spray before tossing them onto the floor to hang up later.

Much later.

Once we were both naked, I turned to Roth and gave them a questioning look. I didn't exactly know how this was going to work. Alaric had already shared me with Kieran, and Draven and Kier were clearly a thing; those two had already hinted about being very excited about having me between them— something I was fully on board with. I suspected Alaric and Draven would just ignore each other. There was an animosity between them, at least on Alaric's side, that I didn't understand.

But to the best of my knowledge, Roth didn't like men. I didn't want them to be in a situation they were uncomfortable with . . .

Roth gave me a wry smile as they stepped beneath the spray and quickly stripped off their clothes.

"You're overthinking things, babe." They brushed my hair behind my ear as I leaned back against Alaric. "I have no interest in their cocks touching me, but I can't wait to see the way they make you scream." A devilish glint flared in their eyes. "Especially when I'm sitting on your face."

"Fuck," Alaric and I both swore at the same time.

Roth's grin widened, and they glanced at Alaric. "I think we should stall a bit—give Kier a little bit of alone time with his prince."

A deep groan came from the other room, proving Roth's point, and I chuckled. While I was very much looking forward to having them both at the same time, I was also happy they were enjoying each other now.

"It does sound like they need a little more time," Alaric agreed, his hands trailing up to cup my breasts as he kissed my neck. Something thick and hard pressed into my lower back, and I groaned as he ran a thumb over my pebbled nipple.

I started to reach back, suddenly desperate to feel his cock in my hand, when Roth dropped to their knees and shoved their face between my thighs.

"Oh, fuck!" I screamed, my head slamming back into Alaric's shoulder. If it weren't for him holding on to me, I probably would have slipped. He just chuckled against my neck and kicked my legs wider apart to give Roth better access as he alternated between squeezing my breasts and playing with my nipples.

Roth had two modes, I'd learned, when it came to eating me out. They'd either torment me for what felt like hours, edging around my pleasure until they drew an orgasm out of me that shut down my fucking mind. Or they'd devour me like they were starving and I was the feast they'd been promised.

Thank fuck Roth chose the latter this time.

A mewling sound bubbled up my throat as their tongue dove straight into my pussy. Then I felt them drag two fingers across the dripping mess they were creating and use the lubrication to roughly play with my clit. My hips bucked forward as Roth savagely licked and sucked me while their fingers practically demanded I climax for them right then and there.

"Be a good girl and come for us, Heir," Alaric crooned.

Oh. Fuck. Me.

Roth's fingers dug into my plump ass as I detonated, their nimble fingers playing my clit to perfection while they lapped up every bit of my desire.

I practically went limp in Alaric's arms, relying on him to hold me up while I rode out my orgasm. The water shut off a minute later, and Roth disappeared, only to return with a couple of towels. I reached for one, but they slapped my hand away and passed it to Alaric. Between the two of them, I was dried off quickly and my hair was wrung out.

My thoughts were still scattered, my lust haze riding me hard. Roth and Alaric grabbed a hand each and tugged me into the bedroom, where Kieran and Draven waited for us in bed. Kieran was on his back across the middle, his hands twisting the covers as Draven deepthroated him.

A whimper escaped my lips, and Draven paused, gripping Kieran's cock with one hand as he drew his mouth off to look at me. "Like what you see, love?"

All I could do was nod, my eyes glued to where Draven lazily stuck his tongue out and licked the slit, where a bead of precum formed. Kieran groaned, and I took a step towards the bed.

"Are you wet for us, Sam?" Kieran asked, and I finally drew my eyes away from Draven working his cock to find Kieran staring at me with a wicked glint in his eyes. I gave him another nod, and he grinned. "I think I should find out."

Alaric and Roth shoved me forward, and I took a few steps before looking back towards the two of them. "Are you coming?"

They both smiled wide.

"In a bit." Roth smirked. "We want to watch this first."

Lust flared, and my legs wobbled a bit at the thought of them watching me with Draven and Kieran. Alaric let out another dark chuckle. "I think our Heir likes that."

I really, really did. I didn't know when the two of them had become buddies, but I was here for it.

"*Sam*." Kieran's voice, tinged with lust and amusement, drew my attention back to him. "Be a sweetheart and sit on my fucking face."

"Okay," I breathed out in a dazed tone. Between the lust haze, Alaric and

Roth getting me off in the shower, and the show Kieran and Draven were putting on . . . it was difficult to string coherent thoughts together.

Draven chose that moment to wrap his lips around Kieran's cock and take him all the way down with zero hesitation. I stood there, mesmerized by Draven swallowing him whole and the way Kieran arched off the bed, making a sound that was pure sin.

Then a desperate ache building between my thighs had me scurrying to the bed and practically jumping onto it. Draven's head bobbed up and down as I threw a leg over Kieran's chest, straddling him. Through hooded eyes, he looked up at me, biting his lip, as if he was trying to hold back a scream.

"You ready to get *me* off while he gets *you* off, Kier?" I gave him a cocky smile. *Look at me using complete sentences.*

The gold that had been weaving its way through his brown eyes expanded as Kieran gripped my waist and hoisted me onto his face. I offered another silent thanks to the Fae who had decided these beds deserved a headboard as my fingers gripped the dark wood. My knees landed on either side of Kieran's head, and he shifted his grip to my ass.

Like Roth, Kieran didn't waste any time. His lips latched onto my clit and sucked hard.

Wood splintered beneath my grip as I climaxed instantly.

"Gods, the lust haze is a wonderful thing," someone—I was pretty sure it was Roth—said with a laugh.

"How many do you think we can get out of her before she passes out?" Alaric asked.

"At least six more," Draven answered in a deep, raspy voice before the sound of him slurping down Kieran's cock filled the room. My thighs clamped around Kieran's head, which only spurred him to start eating me out more.

I trembled as Kieran's grip remained firm, not giving me an opportunity to pull back as he continued to devour me. He alternated between diving his tongue deep inside my pussy to licking and sucking on my clit while I shamelessly rode his face, chasing another climax.

My only goal at the moment was to batter my brain with enough orgasms so I could pass out afterwards. I was pretty sure that was the only way I'd be able to sleep, and I desperately needed some rest.

So really, I was being responsible and taking care of myself.

"Fuck, Kier," I moaned as he dug his fingers harder into my flesh. Between that and the almost frantic way he was eating me out, I knew he was close to coming.

Then Kieran jerked underneath me and moaned directly into my cunt as he came. I joined him a second later when his tongue did something miraculous that I was pretty sure he could have only repeated by climaxing. We'd have to try this again.

For research.

My thighs were still trembling when Draven grabbed me and lifted me off Kieran's face. My sweet lover just gave me a lazy grin, his face glistening with the aftermath of making me come.

"Let's see how messy we can make this perfect pussy." Draven chuckled darkly as he settled me over Kieran's hips before pushing down on my back. My chest pressed against Kieran's, and his mouth crashed against mine just as Draven slowly slid his thick cock into me.

"Fuck, that's hot," Roth swore. Their voice was deep and husky, and I knew they were playing with themself. I wondered if Alaric was stroking his hard length, but just when I started to break my kiss with Kieran to look, Draven slapped my ass and slid his cock all the way in, filling me up.

I jolted up a little, a low groan slipping from me. Kieran groaned with me before licking my nipple and then closing his lips around it and sucking hard. I gasped, and he laughed against my flesh.

These two were going to be the death of me. And I was one hundred percent fine with that.

Draven slapped my ass again, hard enough to sting, then groaned as my pussy tightened around his cock. "You like that, don't you?" He chuckled.

I was rapidly learning that I liked everything they did to me. Still, what I wanted most right now was for Draven to make good on his words. I glanced over my shoulder and almost came at the sight of him glistening with sweat, his long dark hair hanging around him and both hands gripping my ass hard enough to leave bruises.

"Show me how messy you can make me, prince. I want to feel you dripping down my legs." I turned to look at Alaric, who did indeed have his hand wrapped around his thick length as he watched me with a burning desire. "And then I want Alaric to fill me up too."

"You heard her, Draven." Alaric stroked himself harder.

"Make our girl scream," Roth added from where they were slumped on a chair that gave them a perfect side view of me getting fucked. The towel was across their lap, but I could see their hand moving beneath it.

As much as I wanted all of them to be touching me, I was discovering that I really liked to be watched. Especially with how much Alaric and Roth were clearly enjoying it.

Personally, I was really proud of myself for this self-reflection moment.

Draven apparently didn't need any more encouragement because his hands slid from my ass to grip my hips, and then he pounded roughly into me. Kieran gave me a devilish smile as his hands clamped down right above Draven's and he moved farther down the bed into the perfect position to lick and suck my tits.

All I could do was twist my fingers into the blanket and moan as Draven roughly fucked me. One of Kieran's hands drifted from my hip to play with my clit at the same moment he sank his fangs into the side of my breast.

The climax tore through me, and I screamed, but that didn't slow either of them down. My own pleasure was dripping down my thighs, and the room was filled with the sounds of flesh on flesh and other obscene noises. Pain flashed in my hips as Draven's claws tore through flesh and his thrusts became more frantic.

"Gods, you are perfect," he grunted.

Then I felt him fill me with his seed, enough that some of it started leaking out. Gradually, Draven's thrusts became languid and slow. I suspected he was watching his dick sink into my wet and messy cunt and liking the view, but before I could turn around and look, Kieran pulled me down for a kiss. His tongue plundered my mouth, and I let out a lazy moan as his fingers rubbed my clit, which was still oversensitive from my last orgasm.

"Our turn," Roth announced.

My thoughts were so scrambled that it took me a moment to catch up when Draven pulled my back to his chest, his cock still buried inside me as Kieran slid out from underneath us. Then, in one smooth movement, Draven pulled out, and I found myself on my back, peering up at Alaric.

He grinned as he grabbed my legs and put them over his shoulders, lining up his cock with my entrance. There was something around his neck . . . I blinked. A dark red rope.

Roth's rope.

Alaric sank into me slowly, not the least bit bothered by Draven's cum.

"Oh fuck." I pushed my head back into the mattress, and suddenly Roth was stretched out in the bed next to me. One of their hands wrapped around my throat and squeezed gently before trailing down to play with my breasts.

"Alaric needs to blow off some steam, so he's going to unwind that tight hold he keeps over his bloodlust." Roth pinched one of my nipples and somehow timed it perfectly with Alaric pushing another inch into me. I gasped as my back arched off the bed, only to be yanked back down, courtesy of another one of Roth's ropes that had wrapped around my neck. A second later, two more ropes secured my wrists and tugged my arms above my head. "But he has control issues." Roth smiled broadly as I pulled on the ropes binding my wrists and found zero give. "I *excel* at control."

I whimpered. Alaric was holding my thighs against his chest with my knees over his shoulders. Between his unflinching hold and Roth's ropes, I could only move as much as either of them allowed.

Apparently, Roth liked playing with both of us because the thin, braided rope around Alaric's neck moved like a snake and tightened a little more. Turquoise lines bled into Alaric's eyes as he let more of his bloodlust rise.

I didn't actually believe Alaric lacked control of his bloodlust, but he thought so. We'd talked about it before, and I knew that letting his bloodlust rise for more than a few seconds frightened him. Seeing his cousin turn Strigoi when he'd been younger had left psychological damage that my grumpy lover refused to deal with. Instead, Alaric kept a stranglehold over his bloodlust, which meant it was always trying to break free. It was his denial of who and what he was that likely made it feel so chaotic.

But that was a truth I was more than willing to spend years getting him to see, and clearly Roth was on board with helping in the meantime.

"Still with us, babe?" Roth's hand traveled between my breasts at a frustratingly slow pace towards where I wanted their talented fingers. My clit was practically throbbing with need. Maybe it was greedy to want another orgasm after Draven and Kieran had made me come so many times, but I fucking deserved it.

Knowing Roth would only prolong my torment, I looked up at Alaric with wide eyes and slightly parted lips. The bastard laughed and moved his cock in the wrong fucking direction until his broad head was just barely inside me.

"Well, that's just mean," Kieran mused. "Excellent technique though."

I turned my head to glare at him. "Eat a dick, Kier."

"Oh, I plan to later." He winked at me, and Draven snickered. The two of them were cuddled up together on a small settee against the wall, holding hands as they enjoyed the show.

"You know what I'm in the mood for?" Roth asked slyly, drawing my attention back to them.

"If it's not giving me an orgasm while Alaric fucks me until my brain melts, I don't want to hear it," I deadpanned.

Alaric groaned, and more turquoise flared in his eyes, but he didn't slide his cock so much as an inch farther inside me.

"Poetry." Roth's fingers dipped straight into my dripping cunt, sliding past Alaric's cock and drawing out some slickness, which they smeared over my clit as they roughly played with it.

I let out a strangled scream and tried to pivot my hips up, only for Alaric to clamp down harder on my thighs and prevent the movement.

"Make me a fan of poetry, Sam," Alaric ordered, "and I'll give you what you want."

Roth's fingers pulled away from my clit, and they gave me a pointed look.

"*Pib' bomla fi ker,*" I started, only to scream when Alaric slammed all the way in with no warning. My pussy stretched around him as he pulled all the way out and paused with his cock notched at my entrance.

"You stop"—Roth's fingers lifted away from my trembling clit—"we stop."

"I hate you both," I breathed out.

The fuckers laughed.

"*Qu ìb ofgi gef nalmo.*" Poetry spilt out of me. I was pretty sure I was mixing up some poems, but whatever. My pronunciation was perfect, so Roth could fucking bite me.

Only, it wasn't Roth who bit me—it was Alaric.

Sharp, delicious pain raced through me as Alaric's fangs pierced the inside of my thigh and Roth's rope tightened around my throat, cutting off my air as their fingers pinched my clit. Quite possibly the most intense orgasm of my life rolled through me, and every thought emptied from my mind.

Roth teased my clit as they loosened the rope before I could black out. I tried to shift away from them because it was too much. I just needed a second to recover, but neither of them were having it.

Alaric kept a death grip on my legs as he continued drinking from my thigh, all the while continuing to fuck my pussy hard and fast.

"Don't stop now, Sam." Roth's eyes were ablaze as they locked on mine before thrusting their fingers inside me in perfect time with Alaric's thrusts. Their thumb was playing with my clit and applying just the right amount of pressure.

"*B'ib qu ìb mìr!*"

Alaric's fangs popped out of my thigh only for him to bite the other, drawing another groan out of me. My muscles trembled in anticipation as another climax started to build.

"*Goda sotlem qu fì mobof gef fì lìr,*" I panted as I writhed beneath the two of them. "*Kub qu ìb*—fuck!" The scream tore from me as Roth bit my neck.

I came again, and this time, Alaric came with me, his hips slamming forward as he let out a deep groan, releasing my thigh so he could watch me fall apart with bright blue eyes that had only the faintest speck of green. I felt the gush of heat as he filled my already soaked pussy and it started seeping out.

"Messy," I mumbled with a delirious smile. "I go sleep now."

I didn't even wait for Alaric to pull out or for Roth to release their ropes before I passed the fuck out.

CHAPTER TWELVE

—

Roth

I WAS NOT A CUDDLER.

Which was why Samara was tucked between Draven and Alaric with Kieran resting his head on the prince's bare chest. Samara, the lazy shit, had slept through us carrying her to the washroom to clean her up. We'd all agreed to let her sleep a while since we didn't know when we'd have this opportunity again, but she'd woken up soon after we'd all climbed into bed, that sleepy, blissful smile still on her face.

I was sprawled across the bottom of the bed. These rooms had clearly been designed for the high-ranking Fae because this bed was enormous. It was even bigger than Samara's at House Harker. I was already plotting how we could come back here and steal it, because we'd definitely need a bigger bed so we all had room to sleep.

Maybe I could set up a chaise or something too? I'd liked sleeping in the same room as Samara before she'd been taken. Now I didn't think I'd be able to sleep without knowing she was there.

But I still didn't want to fucking cuddle.

I had to admit that this was nice though. All of us together—except Vail. But since he was my least favorite of the group, I didn't really care. The asshole had betrayed her. One word from me, and I knew my brothers would make him disappear. I wasn't sure if Samara would like that or not. She acted like she hated him, and every word they exchanged was caustic . . . but I saw the way Vail looked at her when he thought no one was watching.

And I saw the way Samara looked at him a second after he turned away.

It was the same look—full of hurt and longing.

I had no idea what the fuck to do about that. I'd have to ask Kieran or

Draven about it later; Alaric was almost as useless as me when it came to navigating emotional clusterfucks.

But that could wait. My family wasn't back yet, so we could enjoy this peace and quiet a little longer before the world came crashing back in. Maybe I could nap . . .

"What is our priority going to be once we reach House Devereux?"

Of course, Alaric ruined the mellow vibe.

Everyone groaned, and I grinned. I decided Alaric did have his uses after all. He was worse than me at reading the room. It was nice not being the only socially awkward one.

I propped myself up, bending my elbow so I could rest my head on my hand and better see everyone. Alaric stared up at the ceiling, his mouth pressed into a hard line. "We have a lot of problems and no workable plans for any of them."

I mourned the nap that could have been.

"What? Killing everyone who opposes us isn't a workable plan?" Draven drawled. "Are your sword skills so lacking?"

"My sword skills are just fine," Alaric ground out.

Draven gave Samara a pitying look. "It's good that you have me and Kieran. We're quite good with our swords—definitely better than *just fine*."

"Stop antagonizing him," Samara chided Draven, her expression serious until her gaze collided with Kieran's, then her resolve crumpled in an instant. She made a sound that was somewhere between a snort and a laugh.

A hand flew to her face to cover it up, and we all stared at her. She did it again.

The irritated look on Alaric's face was quickly forgotten when he looked away from Draven to gaze down on Samara. A small, close-lipped smile graced his lips. Wow. I hadn't even known he was capable of smiling.

"It's not funny," she grumbled, even as her lips quirked up.

"False." The corners of Alaric's eyes crinkled slightly. "It's adorably funny."

I chuckled, as did Kieran and Draven.

"Mad at all of you." Samara sighed before scooting back on the bed until her back rested against the headboard. Then she crossed her legs underneath herself. "Alright, let's hash everything out." She chewed her bottom lip, a slight crease forming between her brows.

I knew that look. That was the *I have a lot of emotionally heavy shit to drop on everyone* look.

Oh, nap, how I miss you.

"Samara." Kieran raised his head off Draven's chest and sat up, mirroring her cross-legged pose. Draven took one look at Samara, released a long-suffering sigh, and maneuvered until he was sitting beside Kieran.

Clearly, they both recognized that expression too.

"What?" Alaric blinked at everyone, confusion etching his features.

"Wow." I stared at Alaric in wonder. "Someone more clueless than me at reading people."

Kieran started laughing so hard, tears streamed down his cheeks. Alaric glared at him, then got distracted when Samara bent over and planted an upside-down kiss on his lips. My eyes flicked to Draven, and I found him admiring Kieran, like that laugh was the best thing he'd ever heard.

I knew Alaric still bore a grudge against the prince because of everything that had transpired between him and Kieran. Specifically how Draven humiliated Kieran at an event and then publicly ended their tryst. Alaric and Kieran had been best friends for a long time, and Alaric apparently wasn't as willing to forgive and forget what Draven had done.

I wasn't sure how he didn't see how much Draven loved Kieran though. It was nauseating, really. Kieran and Samara were the prince's *entire* world. If Alaric didn't figure that out soon, maybe I'd have to clue him in.

I chuckled under my breath. Who would have thought that *I* would ever be in a position to give someone emotional insight?

Gradually, Kieran got his laughter under control, and everyone seemed to settle down—although that crease between her dark brows was back on Samara's face. As if she sensed me studying her, those entrancing purple eyes fell on me, and she gave me a small smile. "How about you break things down for us, Roth? Then I'll add in my . . . information."

I was really curious about what Samara had learned, but she clearly needed to build up to telling us, so I did as she asked.

"We should group the problems together as much as we can to minimize how many plans we need." I held up one finger. "The crown and Carmilla are one. Getting the crown away from Carmilla will help neutralize her as a threat and make her easier to capture."

Everyone nodded in agreement as Samara bit her lip. This had to be tough on her. She was an incredibly rational person . . . but Carmilla was her family. I knew she would do what she had to, but I hoped we'd be able to simply imprison Carmilla and keep her from causing more trouble for Samara's sake.

I continued, a second finger joining the first. "Two. Tangentially related, but we need to determine how unstabilized the Moroi Houses have become. Right now, everyone is waiting for the dust to settle after Queen Velika's death and Carmilla rising to take her place. Nobody knows exactly what happened, and Carmilla is using that to her advantage, but when she is"—I glanced at Samara—"taken out of the running, there is going to be a power vacuum."

"House Tepes and House Devereux won't try to fill the void," Alaric said. "The Devereux are isolationists; they'll try to make it on their own." I made a noise of agreement. My birth House did not give a single shit about ruling the other Houses. "And Tepes already prefers to deal with the Velesians over the

Moroi. This will only cause them to further separate themselves from the other Houses."

"House Salvatore is a bit of a wild card," Kieran added thoughtfully, "but my parents and House Corvinus will absolutely try to seize this opportunity to gain more power."

Samara went absolutely still, and her eyes widened in panic.

"Sam?" Kieran focused on her. "Why did you just tense up? Did something happen with my parents?"

Oh shit. Was that what she'd been keeping from us? No . . . She looked almost blindsided by the mention of Kieran's parents, like she'd forgotten something.

"They're still alive," Samara said quickly.

"More's the pity," Draven drawled, earning a smirk from Kieran, who then kissed his chest. Ugh. They were so grossly affectionate.

"I'm sorry, I should have told you sooner, Kier," Samara apologized. "But with the rescue and seeing you all again, it just slipped my mind and—"

"Sam," Kieran cut her off gently. "It's fine. I'm glad we were able to so thoroughly distract you." He winked at her, and she huffed a laugh, some of the worry fading from her face.

Okay. So sometimes his obnoxious, cutesy mannerisms had their uses. I'd put up with anything if it made Samara happy.

"They arrived at the Sovereign House a couple of days ago," Samara explained.

"Of course they did." Kieran sighed. "Let me guess, they were playing the roles of slightly bewildered but oh so supportive courtiers?"

"Yep," she said with a pop.

"Carmilla saw through their bullshit, used the crown on them, and sent them back to House Corvinus to act as spies?"

"Yep," Samara repeated.

"Something eventually is going to have to be done about House Corvinus," Alaric rubbed his forehead. "All the Houses are devious, but *their* plotting is on another level. They don't give a shit about all Moroi surviving, only their House."

"I know." Samara chewed on her bottom lip. "But that's a future problem. We have to stop Carmilla from brainwashing all the Houses one by one and then starting a potential war with the Velesians."

"That brings us to problem three." I wiggled three fingers in the air. "Moroi and Velesian relations have been growing more strained for years. Only House Tepes and House Harker had decent trade policies in place with them . . ."

"And now, thanks to Vail, House Harker can kiss its good relations goodbye." Samara chewed on her lip, debating if she should say something, then decided to just get it all out there. "And you should all know that I won't leave Rynn with the Alpha Pack if she doesn't want to be there."

"Another prison break." Kieran grinned. "Fun."

"Not fun." Alaric glared at him.

"Definitely fun," Draven agreed, earning himself a glare too.

While the three of them argued, I focused on Samara. She was trying to smile at their antics but kept failing. I knew why. The fourth problem.

Slowly, I held up my pinky finger to join the other three. I didn't say it because I wasn't sure if Samara was willing to broach this topic yet, and if she wanted me to drop it, I would. For now.

But my brave girl held my gaze and didn't shy away.

"Four," she said quietly. "Cali."

Everyone fell silent at the declaration. That Cali was indeed a problem. She was Samara's best friend, and we all knew that there was nothing Sam and Rynn wouldn't do for her, but we also knew the damage Cali could do if she truly lost herself. If that happened, then all our problem-solving wouldn't matter.

Because nothing in Lunaria would survive Cali's wrath.

She hadn't completely lost it yet, but something was definitely going on with her. I'd originally met Cali, Rynn, and Samara at Drudonia. The three of them were close and had tried to befriend me. Rynn had been the most successful since we were similar in nature. Samara had been determined to flirt with me—and had mostly fallen flat on her face because she'd been relying too much on her looks and not flaunting that magnificent mind of hers.

Cali had reminded me of my brothers. She was arrogant and brash. Most of our interactions had ended with one of us storming out of the room before violence could erupt.

Most Furies dedicated their lives to keeping their emotions level. They didn't allow themselves to feel anything. Anger. Happiness. Love. Hate. Of all the Moon Blessed, the Furies were the most volatile. Something about the original spell hadn't worked quite as well for them as it had for the Velesians and Moroi. The last couple of generations had stabilized by walling off all their emotions and largely isolating themselves from the rest of Lunaria.

Except Cali.

Few Furies had ever attended Drudonia—and never for years like Cali did —and Cali felt *everything*.

It had alarmed the shit out of me when I'd first met her, but I'd gradually gotten used to it. Even when her eyes had glowed with rage, Cali had still been in control of herself—of her magic.

But I'd witnessed a couple of interactions with Samara since I'd moved to House Harker. Something was different about Cali now. There was a chaotic edge to her rage that hadn't been there during our time at Drudonia, and I'd caught the way Samara looked at her friend now. It wasn't with exasperation or amusement like it had been years ago. Now, Samara looked at her friend with concern and fear.

Not *of* Cali—*for* her.

"The Furies that came looking for her wouldn't give us any specifics," Alaric said.

"One of them was worried." Kieran frowned. "Furies are so hard to read, but there was just something about him that made me think he was personally concerned about Cali."

"Big guy with dark, golden blond hair shaved on the sides?" Samara asked.

"Yeah." Kieran nodded. "You know him?"

Suddenly, Draven and Alaric were very interested in her answer. I rolled my eyes, not the least bit concerned with Samara's past lovers. She was mine now. Ours. That was all that mattered.

"Malachi." Samara pursed her lips. "He and Cali were involved a few years ago. The elders demanded that they break it off; they felt the two were growing too close. Cali refused . . . but Malachi did as he was ordered."

"Idiot," Kieran muttered.

Alaric gave his friend a stern look. "It may seem harsh, but the methods the elders have put in place are working. Only a handful of Furies have fallen in the last century."

"We can save the debate on the approach the Furie elders have dictated for another day." Samara rubbed her face. "I need to find Cali and see for myself how she's doing . . . and talk to her about Rynn—convince her that slaughtering the Alpha Pack to break Rynn out of their stronghold isn't a good idea."

I winced. I hadn't even thought about that. Here was hoping that wasn't where Cali had disappeared to. The only thing worse than the Velesians going to war against the Moroi was them doing it against the Furies. We'd be caught in the middle with no good option on who to support.

"Once we reach House Devereux, I'll ask Thessalia and Taivan to send rangers to search for her—discreetly," I offered. "Desmond is an excellent tracker; he'll probably choose to lead one of the groups."

"Thank you." Samara gave me a grateful smile.

"Of course." I hesitated slightly before asking, "And what information did you want to share with us? We might as well get everything out there."

Please don't be something really bad, I prayed to the gods, who I was pretty sure were long dead. We already had enough to deal with.

"The crown . . . is sentient." Samara let out a long breath while we all stared at her, wide-eyed. "It spoke to me."

"The crown," I said slowly. "It spoke to you? Like with actual words?"

"That's usually how speaking works," she said dryly.

I scowled at her. "Nothing I've ever read has implied that Fae artifacts could speak."

Samara smirked at me. I refused to acknowledge how adorable she was and frowned harder, which only had her devilish eyes sparking with amusement. I was so going to punish her later.

"Did it ever converse with *you*?" Kieran glanced at Draven, who just shook his head.

"Yeah . . . about that." Samara's gaze fell on Draven. "I think the crown only speaks to the Seelie royal bloodline. Turns out your asshole father is a fake. He's not the true Seelie King—my paternal grandfather was."

"Your grandfather?" Alaric asked at the same time Kieran yelled, "*I'm fucking a princess?!*"

"*We're* fucking a princess," I corrected him and held up a hand, shushing him before he could ramble on. "Samara, please elaborate."

"Unfortunately, I don't have a whole lot more to share," she admitted. "Turns out, the crown is kind of sensitive, and I hurt its feelings. It refused to talk to me after that, and I never got a chance to make up for my rudeness."

"How exactly does one offend a crown?" Draven gave Samara a lopsided grin. "You're such an overachiever."

Samara gave him an obscene gesture that had his grin widening enough to show off his fangs.

"So you're half Fae—or at least close to it." I ignored their antics and studied Samara's face, trying to see how I'd missed that before. Then again, we really didn't know much about what the Fae looked like other than that they had tapered ears—something that neither Samara nor Draven had.

"Your father had to have known what he was . . ." Alaric trailed off before pointing at Draven. "Do you have magic like him?"

"I have a name, you know," Draven drawled.

"Nobody cares," Alaric replied in a bored tone.

"Pretty sure at least two people in this room do." Draven winked at me. "And I'm definitely growing on *Rothie Bear*."

I narrowed my eyes at the prince. "I will carve you apart and have Alaric help me dispose of the remains if you ever call me that again."

"This bonding session is going fabulously, I've got to say." Kieran laughed.

A small grin tugged at the corners of Samara's mouth as her eyes scanned each of us. "So . . . none of you care that I'm at least part Fae?"

"I mean, obviously we all find you hideous now," I told her seriously before jerking my head towards Kieran. "Except him." My gaze slid pointedly to Draven before flicking back to Kieran. "He's clearly into the whole Fae thing."

"Maybe we can use him to suss out any other Fae amongst us," Alaric suggested.

"With his dick?" I tapped a nail against my bottom lip. "Kind of curious if it would work. Would we, like, lead him around on a leash like one of those hounds from the Fae murals?”

Draven and Samara glared at the both of us, but Kieran just chuckled.

“No, babe.” I smirked at Samara. “We don’t give a fuck about the Fae blood running through your veins. Any other surprises for us?”

“I spoke to a wraith while I was imprisoned.” She sighed and leaned her head back against the headboard. “Apparently, with Velika dead, Erendriel is seeking a new alliance and would prefer me over my aunt.”

“Which wraith?” Draven asked sharply. The charming prince was gone, and only a predator remained. One who sensed another encroaching on his territory.

“Serill,” Samara supplied.

“Shit,” Draven swore, concern bleeding into his stare as he looked at Samara. “He’s basically my father’s right hand. I suspected he would be the one leading the hunt after me . . . I don’t like that he’s so interested in you.”

“What exactly did he say?” I asked, already thinking through the implications of facing a fight on two sides—Carmilla and Erendriel.

We listened as Samara recapped the short conversation, and Draven paled when Samara finished with Serill promising to return in three days . . . which, at this point, meant two more nights.

“How easily will he be able to track her?” I asked Draven.

“Unless we’re behind a very strong ward in two days”—he rubbed his forehead—“we should expect a visit from Serill.”

“Okay,” I said slowly. “So we have two days to figure out how to either hide from the wraiths . . . or what to tell Serill to buy us more time when he comes calling.”

“Erendriel isn’t the patient sort,” Draven warned. “And Serill hasn’t risen to where he is by disappointing the Seelie King.”

“Fake Seelie King,” I pointed out.

Draven shrugged. “He’s the one currently sitting on the throne, so he’s the Seelie King now.”

“Do we think there’s a throne?” Kieran perked up. “And do we think we can steal it?”

“Dethrone the diabolical queen, rescue the lonely sentient crown, find out what the fuck is going on with my besties, and figure out how to outmaneuver beings known for being clever.” Light sparked in Samara’s deep purple eyes. “Sounds fun.”

“The real question is, what will we do *next* week?” Kieran moved until he was lying down and tugged Samara to lie beside him. Draven followed suit, settling in next to Kieran and wrapping his body around him, one hand resting on Samara’s collarbone.

“Fix the broken alliances between the Houses and somehow make nice with the Velesians." Alaric rolled his eyes and then moved to Samara's other side.

"That sounds less fun." Kieran pouted.

Samara looked at me, clearly wondering what I was going to do. Oh fuck it. I crawled forward and shoved Alaric over. He rolled his eyes but let me settle between him and Samara as I rested my head on her chest and listened to her heartbeat.

"If any of you ever mention to my brothers that I willingly cuddled, I will skin you alive."

"Awww," Kieran cooed. "We love you too, Roth."

I grumbled more threats even as I tucked my face into Samara's body so none of them could see my smile.

***

"Where are you going?" I asked quietly as I propped myself up a little, being careful not to disturb Samara, who was still sleeping next to me.

Kieran paused halfway through getting up, his hand in Draven's, who was already standing next to the bed in a damp pair of pants and nothing else. We'd all done our best to rinse our clothes off earlier, but for all the niceties the Fae had given this place, it was still a damp, underground cave system. Our clothes would take forever to dry.

"We're going to search this place and see if we can find some clean clothes and maybe some weapons," Kieran whispered before standing.

"Good idea," I replied quietly. "We should be ready to go when my family gets back."

The two of them nodded and left. It was then I realized Alaric was already gone. Likely scouring the rooms for any information left behind by the Fae.

Usually, I would be all over the potential of finding new Fae books or scrolls.

Surprisingly . . . I didn't have any inclination to join him.

I looked at Samara's dark hair fanned around the bed and the warmth of her hand on my hip.

There was nowhere else I wanted to be right now.

Samara's brows furrowed slightly before smoothing out, and I narrowed my eyes at her.

"How long have you been awake?"

"Since Alaric elbowed me in the back when he got up." Dark eyelashes fluttered before dark purple eyes gazed at me full of humor. "The ass was just bitter about being on the outside of the bed. He should have been thankful I didn't shove him off it."

"We're going to have to get a bigger bed wherever we end up." I sighed. I'd have to get used to cuddling too.

It hadn't actually been that bad. It had been kind of nice to be cocooned in warmth.

"Yeah," she replied softly. That crease formed between her brows again and stayed there.

"What are you thinking about in that magnificent mind of yours?" I laid my head back down on the pillow so that our faces were only inches apart.

"Assuming we defeat Carmilla and find some way to do all the other things on our list . . . then what?" There was none of that brash bravado in her expression now. "House Laurent is a problem, obviously. Demetri's a piece of shit, and his mother would love nothing more than to see the demise of all Velesians. Corvinus has never been trustworthy. Your family's House is amazing, but they don't exactly play nicely with others. And while we're generally on good terms with House Tepes and Salvatore, I have no idea how they're going to react to all this. And then there is the Sovereign House . . ."

"What about it?" I frown. "You'll take it over. My House will back it up, and it's likely Tepes will too. The others will fall in line."

"I never planned on being queen, Roth," Samara argued. "My *plan* was to be Heir for at least another few decades until Carmilla stepped down and I rose —as the Head of House Harker, not the bloody queen of the Moroi!"

"You have to admit that The Blood Queen does have a nice ring to it though," I mused.

"Not. Helping." Samara huffed and rolled over until she stared up at the ceiling.

I pushed myself up so I was leaning on my arm and looking down at her. "Are you worried about this because you don't want to be queen . . . or because you do and you're concerned that you'll become as corrupt as the previous two?"

Her eyes darted to mine, and I knew I'd guessed right. I'd never be as astute as Kieran at reading people, but I did know how Samara's mind worked. She held herself to an almost impossible standard and was her own worst critic in many ways.

"First, I don't think for a second that you becoming an evil queen is even a possibility."

"You literally called me The Blood Queen a moment ago! That doesn't sound like a nice title, Roth!"

I snorted. "We're Moroi. There's nothing nice about us, and blood is intrinsic to who we are."

She pursed her lips, and I resisted the urge to lean down and kiss her because I didn't want to get distracted—and I absolutely would if my lips touched any part of her.

"But if you need further assurances," I told her softly, "you have us. Do you think Kieran would ever let you strip away the free will of others after growing up in that horribly manipulative House?"

She didn't even hesitate. "Of course not."

"Do you think Draven would let you lock up crying children in a dungeon after he holds himself responsible for the deaths of so many in the outposts?"

"None of that is his fault!" she snarled, her eyes flashing black. "That was fucking Erendriel's doing."

"It was," I agreed. "But there's the truth—and then there is the guilt he carries. He would never sit by while you harmed innocents."

"I know," she said softly.

"And Alaric cares deeply for the outposts because that is where his family is from," I reminded her, even though I knew I didn't have to.

"His parents are at an outpost now." She bunched her brows together again. "We should warn them in case Carmilla—"

"Already done." I reached up and brushed my thumb across her brow, smoothing out the wrinkles. "Alaric sent them a message before we left House Harker. He kept things vague, but they headed to one of the more remote outposts. They're as safe as they can be."

"Oh." She exhaled and closed her eyes as my thumb traced a path across her brow and then down her jawline. "And what about you?"

"What about me?" I tucked some of her dark locks behind her ear.

Those stunning eyes of hers slowly opened. "Will you keep me from becoming a tyrant?"

"Babe, I don't even let you be a tyrant in the bedroom. What makes you think I'll let you be one on the throne?"

A husky laugh tumbled from her lips, and I smiled. I loved hearing her laugh—especially when I was the one who caused it.

I didn't mention Vail, and neither did she. That just seemed like a way to derail this conversation. Besides, Draven seemed to have some vested interest in helping Vail succeed. I had no idea why, but I was more than willing to let him take the lead on that.

"The crown wants me to claim it," Samara said after her laughter died off.

"Do you want to?" I asked curiously. A sentient Fae artifact definitely fascinated me from an academic standpoint, even if the magic it was capable of horrified me.

She thought about it for a long moment, and I didn't push her, just continued playing with strands of her hair. It was so silky. I didn't think I'd ever grow tired of touching it.

"I do want to," she finally answered. "But not for its power—that, I find abhorrent. It's because I feel in my soul"—she placed a hand on her chest—"that it does belong with me. And it's so lonely."

It was my turn to laugh. "Of course you'd befriend an inanimate object."

"Honestly, it has a good sense of humor." She frowned. "We should come up with a name for it. Feels strange just referring to it as an 'it,' but I don't think it has any concept of gender. Maybe I'll just go with *they* for now and ask the crown if they have a preference . . ."

"We'll figure out something with the crown," I assured her. "Maybe there's a way to change its magic. Or we could just keep it—them—somewhere safe where you could regularly visit them."

She sighed and stared back up at the ceiling. "Another thing to add to the list."

"Hey." I tilted her face towards me, and those concerned eyes met mine. "I swear to you that I will help you figure this out. You are not alone in this." I swallowed. "I love you, Samara Harker."

Her eyes got a little misty. "I love you too, Astaroth Devereux."

I smiled at hearing my full name on her lips—the one I'd been running away from my whole life. I'd been running from the mantle of being part of the Devereux line but never really fitting in anywhere.

I was the lost scholar who'd finally found a home in her.

Samara scooted closer, laying her head on my shoulder and her hand over my heart, where heat suddenly flared—and a bond thrummed to life.

"You're mine, Roth," Samara breathed. "Always and forever."

"And you're mine too, my Blood Queen. Always and forever."

CHAPTER THIRTEEN

—

Samara

"We can't wait any longer." Taivan sighed. "Vail will have to find us."

"Are we sure he hasn't gone back to Carmilla?" Desmond looked to me for an answer.

I didn't have one, because while I didn't think he would have, I clearly couldn't trust myself when it came to Vail. I'd learned that lesson the hard way. There was another way I could tell though, one that made no sense but was real all the same. I concentrated on the thread between us, and it felt thinner now, strained.

Was that because of the physical distance? Or because of . . . everything else between us?

"South," I breathed out. "He's to the south of us."

Taivan mulled it over. "The Sovereign House is north, and most of their search parties haven't reached this far yet. If Vail is south of us, then it's unlikely he's met up with Carmilla or any of her rangers."

"What if he runs into them while making his way back to us?" Absently, I rubbed the spot on my chest where I felt the bond. As soon as I realized what I was doing, I dropped my hand. "Vail's a strong fighter, but he'd be outnumbered."

Not to mention the fact that Carmilla would likely make an example out of him if he were captured. He was a traitorous asshole, but if he was truly on our side, Vail would be useful. Just because I was still hurting over his betrayal didn't mean I'd waste such a valuable resource.

So pragmatic. I could practically hear Carmilla in my mind, and I shoved the thought away.

"Let's go then. We'll stick with the original plan and trust Vail to catch up." I nodded at Taivan. "We're following you."

"This way." He entered the tunnel outside the cavern we'd been resting in and went left. "My parents are waiting topside for us. We'll meet up with the Harker rangers—Adrienne, Emil, and Nyx—in a couple of miles. The storm is going to hit any minute, and we'll travel as far as we can. There are a few safe houses we can use, depending on where we end up."

The tunnel split into two directions, but Taivan sliced his finger open on his fang and tapped a glyph on the wall. The compact dirt shimmered, revealing a door, which Taivan pulled open and stepped through.

I started to move towards it when Kieran placed a hand on my forearm, halting me. Gold wove through his brown eyes, a little of his bloodlust peeking through. Everyone except Alaric was riding their bloodlust to some extent because we needed any advantage we could get.

Traveling on a night like this was insane. All kinds of wicked things prowled the Lunarian wilds after the sun set, and we were far from the top of the food chain, but we'd discussed it when Taivan and Desmond had returned and agreed it would be worth it. The storm would cover our tracks better than we could ever manage. With Carmilla and her rangers likely coming for us, I wanted to delay our reunion until I knew of some way to counteract the crown's magic.

"You good, Sam?" Kieran's lips quirked up into a lopsided grin as he tightened the cloak hanging around my neck. He and Draven had burst into the room after I'd formed the bond with Roth and Draven had felt the echoes of the new bond through his.

They'd both been happy for us, but I hadn't missed the uncertainty in Kieran's eyes. I'd tried to explain that I hadn't intentionally done it—not that I wasn't absolutely thrilled to be bonded with Roth—but I still didn't understand why this was happening. I didn't want Kieran to think I wasn't choosing him.

Kieran had seen right through my hasty explanations and assured me he was fine, but then he'd smiled at me in a way that I knew was false. Draven had frowned at him when he'd done it because he clearly recognized that fake smile too.

Unfortunately, that was when Roth's brothers had arrived, so I hadn't been able to discuss it with Kieran anymore.

We'd barely had time to get dressed in the clothing Kieran and Draven had found and adorn ourselves with weapons, which was why I was wearing a shirt that was a little baggy and pants that were way too tight.

On the plus side, two wicked daggers were now strapped to my thighs, and I'd been able to quickly recreate the blood magic I'd had on my previous ones, so now I could recall these to my hands after I threw them.

I reached up to double-check Kieran's cloak. "Absolutely. Who doesn't love a little midnight stroll?"

"The woods are great this time of year," Draven added, kneeling down to make sure the sheaths for my daggers were buckled to his satisfaction.

"Can't beat the weather either," Alaric said dryly as the crash of rainfall sounded from where Taivan had clearly opened another door.

"Definitely nothing else I'd rather be doing right now," Roth grumbled from beneath *three* cloaks. Apparently, their older brothers were very concerned about the cold. At one point, they'd been eying my cloak, clearly thinking about snagging it to give to their younger sibling, but Roth had snarled in their faces and they'd stomped away.

I might have offered *Rothie Bear* my cloak after that, and they might have threatened something along the lines of *you'll get the edging of your lifetime when this is over.*

Kieran booped me on the nose before darting up after Taivan and Desmond. Roth and Alaric both sighed before following, leaving me alone with Draven, who was still fiddling with the buckles on my thigh.

I chewed on my bottom lip. Vail was a good tracker, but the storm might make it more difficult for him to figure out where we'd gone. I could sense where he was through the bond we shared, but I wasn't sure if he could do it too. Draven and I had done some testing with our bond; he could sense where I was just as I could him, and he was also able to tug on it to summon me.

But Draven and I were both part Fae. What if that impacted whatever this connection was and Vail couldn't do the same? Not to mention the fact that the bond between us was stretched so thin . . .

My eyes dropped down to Draven. No. I couldn't ask that of him, and it was stupid to even think it. Vail had made his decision, and he wasn't my—

"Yes." Draven rose, his dark blue eyes twinkling with amusement. "I'll go find your Marshal."

"He's not my anything." I frowned and quickly scanned Draven. Like me, he'd loaded up on weapons. No whip, but he had two swords strapped to his back and half a dozen daggers hidden on his person. His black-and-silver hair was braided back, disappearing beneath his long black cloak. "And I didn't ask you a question."

"You thought it." He kissed my forehead. "It's okay to worry about him. Love's complicated."

"I'm only worried because Vail could be useful, and if he gets himself caught, we'll lose a valuable asset," I hissed.

Draven just gave me an infuriatingly patient look. "Of course."

I thought about stabbing him, but the way he was grinning at me now suggested he'd like it.

Stupid, hot prince.

Kieran was . . . not pleased about Draven splitting off to retrieve Vail. I didn't blame him; I would have preferred for us all to stay together too. The fact that it was my fault Vail had gone off on his own only added to my guilt. I mean, I had every right to be angry with him, but he had helped us escape. It didn't mean I'd be inviting him back into my bed anytime soon. Still . . . I could have let him down easier instead of slamming the door in his face.

It'd been satisfying but not entirely mature of me.

Draven had promised that he was used to traveling in the woods at night and that he could use his magic to find Vail.

I'd asked if he could feel Vail through the bond, but he'd said no, that he could only sense me. He was confident he'd be able to track Vail down quickly though, and then he could use his connection to me to find wherever we currently were.

I looked around the dark forest, which felt extra ominous tonight. I hoped Draven found him and dragged his ass back soon. It could just be my general anxiety about being in the wilds at night, but I couldn't shake the feeling of dread that had been building since we'd left the tunnels.

We'd been traveling for almost an hour, and it was slow going. Severen and Celestina were in the front, Roth's brothers were guarding our backs, and Adrienne, Emil, and Nyx had met up with us not long ago and were guarding our flanks—Emil to our left, and the other two to my right. It felt good to see the rangers again and to have more backup in case some beastie tried to make a meal out of us.

Several times, one of the rangers or Roth's kin sensed something and held up a hand for us all to stop. The first time, we'd quietly climbed up into the trees as an enormous horned bear lumbered past us.

Even on all fours, it would have towered over us. The two horns that sprung from the top of its head before jutting forward brushed the leaves. It was the first time I'd ever seen one in person, as the bears preferred the mountains in the far north of Lunaria. The Velesians were used to dealing with them, since their realm bordered the mountain range, but the bears had only recently started coming into the Moroi realm.

Fortunately, they were usually easy to avoid and weren't as vicious as many of the other predators. As long as you didn't mess with them.

The second time, Emil had barely been able to give us enough warning as three kùsu had barreled through the trees. Luckily, they had been in hot pursuit of some swamp deer they'd managed to flush out of the brush. My heart had pounded rapidly as Kieran, Alaric, and I held ourselves flat against the trunk of a large tree while the twenty-foot-long insect-like beasts had scuttled past. The sounds of hundreds of legs moving across the forest floor while rain pounded around us would likely give me nightmares for weeks.

If Draven were here, he would have been able to use his earth magic to feel their approach far in advance. I'd tried to use my magic a few times, but I hadn't been able to consistently sense anything, and most of the time, it was a feeling that there was *something* there but nothing more. It still felt odd to even acknowledge that I had magic, considering I couldn't feel it most of the time.

So far, the only time I'd been able to use my earth magic was when I'd been desperate or angry—usually both. I'd just have to hope that I'd be able to rally it if we were in a near-death situation. No pressure.

In the meantime, I was using my senses like the others were doing to detect danger, which was difficult because of the storm doing its best to drown everything out. It was why we'd had so many close calls; we'd only detected the monsters seconds before they would have found us.

A blinding flash struck a tree fifty feet away from us, and the smell of burning wood filled the air while thunder roared across the sky. Summer thunderstorms were common, but this seemed more violent than normal. Or maybe it was because I normally enjoyed watching the storms from the safety of my room in a stone fortress and not traipsing through mud and undergrowth while dodging all the monsters that prowled the night.

Currently, the rain had slowed to a drizzle. Not that long ago, it had been a torrential downpour. We were damn lucky we weren't in an area prone to flash floods.

"Shit," I heard Severen say. His wife let out a torrent of swear words seconds later.

I closed the distance between us to stand next to them as I took in what had caused their reactions.

Oh. Apparently our luck had run out, because a river raged through the forest ahead of us. Given that Severen and Celestina had led us this way, I assumed it wasn't supposed to be here but was a creation of the storm. Maybe a watershed or a small creek that had been overrun by the rain.

"We could swim across it?" I suggested just as several large trees tore through the water, smashing into everything in their path. "Or maybe not."

"We'll have to double back," Celestina called out as the storm decided to kick it up a notch. "The ground gets higher to the east. We should be able to cross there."

I nodded and started to back up but froze when I felt it. The wrongness I'd been feeling all night intensified, like the forest itself was screaming at me to . . .

Run.

Without second-guessing, I lunged forward, darting to a tree with a thick trunk for cover and pulling Alaric and Kieran with me. Then I looked over my shoulder just in time to see Roth duck behind a large, rotting tree log, Taivan and Desmond ushering them to safety. Whether they were following my lead or had also sensed something, I didn't know.

When I peeked around the tree, I saw Severen and Celestina had vanished as well—only a few trembling tree branches gave a hint as to where they had gone. The Harker rangers were also nowhere to be seen.

Three howlers slithered through the trees and stopped to sniff the ground. Horror drenched me, and I had to bite down my tongue to keep from swearing out loud or screaming.

As if sensing my fear, one of howlers swung its head my way, and I quickly pivoted back behind the tree, a tremble racing through me.

It had no eyes because the howler was fucking dead. All it had were empty sockets surrounded by clumps of fur and rotting flesh.

I'd seen a lot of fucked-up shit in Lunaria, but something coming back from the dead? That was a new one.

Alaric and Kieran both looked around the tree only to pull back with shock-laced grimaces. Clearly, they weren't fans of this new type of monster either.

"Samaraaa," a voice rang out. Even through the rain, I recognized it. Demetri.

Everyone went still. Gold flooded Kieran's eyes as his bloodlust rose while Alaric's eyes flashed turquoise but quickly returned to their normal light green as he pulled a long, curved dagger from the sheath at his thigh. Kieran's sword was in his hand a second later.

A smile curved at the corners of my lips, and I saw it reflected on Kieran's and Alaric's faces. Sure, we were deep in a Lunarian forest with three undead beasts hunting us down, but Demetri was here too. I didn't know how, but I assumed he was responsible for our walking-corpse friends. He also likely had some Moroi rangers with him.

None of that mattered though because Demetri was standing less than twenty feet from me. He wouldn't be walking out of this forest alive. I didn't care how many fucked-up nightmares I'd have to kill my way through— Demetri's death was mine to claim. My fingers closed around my daggers and silently pulled them free from the thigh sheaths. It was fitting that his blood would be the first to bless my new blades.

First, we needed to know exactly how many others he'd brought with him. I gave Kieran and Alaric a pointed look and mouthed, *Stay*. Both of them gave me murderous looks in return but didn't try to stop me when I stepped out from behind the tree.

Demetri loved the sound of his own voice. Might as well let him dig his own grave too.

I sauntered forward, twirling my daggers casually in my hands a few times before stopping a few feet from where Demetri stood behind the undead howlers that were just standing there, unmoving. Each one bore a leather collar with embedded sapphires. I'd missed that before on account of being shocked by their existence.

What type of magic could bring something back from the dead? And how had Demetri learned of it?

"Like my new pets?" he drawled from beneath his dark cloak. Most of his face was hidden, but his full mouth was curved into a smirk. "Turns out Velika had quite the treasure trove of Fae artifacts. We have no idea what most of them do, but these ones seemed pretty self-explanatory. The howlers make excellent tracking hounds, even if they smell a bit."

"I give you credit for attempting to find a creature more vile than yourself." I studied the beasts once more. Howlers were canine in shape, but they were taller and leaner than lycanthropes. They were built to run for miles on end. These ones were skeletally thin. In fact—I squinted—yep, I could see their bones in places.

A small amount of pity welled in me as I took in the creatures. Sure, howlers would rip me to shreds in a heartbeat if they could, but they were just predators trying to survive in a land of monsters, and they were pretty low on the hierarchy. It felt wrong for them to be used like this. Life in Lunaria was often cruel and heartless; they deserved to find peace.

My gaze lingered on the collars again. They were faint and hard to see in the dark, but two glyphs were carved into them between the sapphires.

Death. Awaken.

I held back my shudder and turned my attention back to Demetri. "They won't win any beauty contests, but if I had to choose between them and you, it's not even a question. Undead hounds all day. You remain the most vile of the Heirs."

Demetri's smirk blossomed into a smile. "Oh, I'm not an Heir anymore, my pet. You're looking at the new Head of House Laurent."

A dozen rangers stepped out of the dark forest, swords gleaming in the moonlight, to stand in a formation behind Demetri. All of them bore the Laurent crest on their tunics.

This time, I wasn't quite able to hide my disgust, so I just leaned into it and sneered at Demetri. "Killing your own mother might be a new low, even for you, Demetri."

Because there was no way Marvina Laurent had willingly handed over power to her son. That woman had ruled her House with an iron fist. It was all she'd cared about.

Demetri let out a cold laugh. "Come now, Samara. Are you really so upset about it? If you think she treated you badly to your face while we were married, I promise that what she said about you when you weren't in the room was far worse."

Not surprising. In many ways, Marvina represented everything that was wrong with the Moroi. She was arrogant and cruel and believed that the Moroi were inherently better than the Velesians and Furies. If I'd had to place a bet on which Moroi had been most likely to seize control of the Houses while wielding a mind-controlling crown, it would have been her.

I supposed the joke was on me that it was my own aunt who had proven to be the true villain.

I didn't mourn Marvina's death, but the fact that Demetri had murdered his own mother was still all kinds of fucked up.

A branch in the tree—the one I was fairly certain Roth's parents had climbed up—trembled slightly. It was behind Demetri and his rangers, so they didn't see it, and the rain swallowed up the sound of any movement. There were likely more Laurent rangers than just the ones I could see. I needed to buy the others time to take them out—hopefully quietly—so we could deal with these ones. As much as I wanted my revenge against Demetri, I wouldn't claim it at the risk of my friends.

"Your mother was no prize." I shrugged and tapped the flat blade of a dagger against my chin before pointing it at Demetri. "Still surprised you had the backbone to do it yourself. Or did you get one of your dogs to do it?" I glanced at the howlers that still hadn't moved. "And to be clear, I mean the rangers who swore an oath to their House and betrayed it."

"Fucking cunt," one of the rangers swore and took a step forward, his sword hand raising, but halted when Demetri held his arms out to the side.

"Hey, Fletch." I winked at the ranger, who was still glaring at me. "Look at you using naughty words. Did your balls finally drop?" I twirled my daggers in an obnoxiously showy move before pointing one at him. "I can fix that for you."

"Careful, Samara," Demetri warned. "One way or another, you will be my wife again. You can live out the rest of your life in luxury . . . or in a dungeon."

Out of the corner of my eye, I caught more movement in the trees— someone timed their jump down right as thunder roared across the sky. Demetri's rangers shifted uncomfortably as they glanced around the forest. They were used to the forests along the coasts that, while still dangerous, were far less so than the ones farther inland like this one.

I was actually surprised Demetri had convinced them to come at all instead of waiting to track me down during the day. So much about this didn't make sense . . .

"Give me an honest answer, and I'll consider coming with you," I lied. "Why do you want to marry me again? Why go to all this trouble?"

He tilted his head, and his hood slipped a little, letting me see more of his aristocratic face that I'd once found very handsome. When we'd been together, he almost always wore a lazy but charming expression. He'd spent all his time lazing about or entertaining courtiers—or fucking them, as I later learned— but there was a cunning glint to his eyes now that had been absent all those years.

Demetri had fooled everyone—myself included. It annoyed me that I'd missed it.

"My original deal with Carmilla was quite simple. She supports me as the new leader of House Laurent, and my House backs her as the new Sovereign." His mouth twisted like he'd just bitten something sour. "Then she changed it. Said that in addition to supporting her, I needed to father a child with you . . . for her to raise. She never did explain but made it quite clear it was nonnegotiable."

A chill ran through me that had nothing to do with the cold rain. She knew. At some point, Carmilla had figured out I was part Fae . . . and wanted a child of my bloodline.

"Why you?" I asked numbly.

My ex-husband watched me closely, likely looking for a hint about what made me so special.

Just wait a few minutes, and I'll show you.

"Like I said, she wasn't keen on going into the details." He gave me a sly grin. "If I had to guess, it seemed like she wanted to compensate for something in your bloodline. Wanted to make sure that a strong Moroi House bloodline was mixed in. Not all the Houses have male children—only Tepes and Devereux. Neither of those Houses were likely to agree to such a thing, but me?" His smile sharpened. "I've already had you before; I don't mind having you again."

"Pass," I said flatly.

"You don't have a choice, Samara." He snorted. "Technically, Carmilla only wants the child. The marriage was my condition."

"Funny. You didn't seem to care about the first one." My grip tightened around the daggers. The others better have taken out any other enemy rangers lurking around us because my patience was waning.

"Do you have any idea how much shit I had to listen to after you left?" he sneered. "At first, you were the butt of the jokes, considering how many courtiers I fucked right under your nose while you were too busy trying to be the perfect Heir, but then you had to go and start a *relationship* with Kieran. That got people's attention, and I had to listen to the rumors swirl about what was so wrong with me that you ran straight into the arms of a lesser Moroi. Let him stand beside you as if he were an equal."

I used to think, for all his flaws, that Demetri was different from his mother. That he hadn't inherited her bullshit beliefs about some Moroi being lesser than others simply because of the families they were born into, but the look of disgust and scorn on his face was an exact match to the one I'd seen on hers countless times.

Rage simmered inside me, knowing that Kieran had likely heard every word. I knew he worried that his station as a courtier made him not worthy of me. It was something I was more than happy to spend the rest of my life proving false to him.

In the meantime, I'd fucking kill anyone who made him doubt his self-worth.

"I'd offer to make you a list of all the ways you fail to measure up to Kieran, but it's too lengthy, and you're not going to live long enough to read it."

Demetri gave me a patronizing look. "I brought *forty* rangers with me." He gestured at the trees surrounding us. "Right now, the rest of them are killing whoever helped you break out—I'm guessing your pretty courtier and that surly advisor. I've only tolerated your pathetic attempt at stalling because I was hoping they would drag the broken bodies of your lovers out in front of you, but it seems they've abandoned you. No matter. My rangers still have orders to kill them."

Two bloodred ropes slowly slid from the trees above the heads of the rangers standing on either side of Demetri. Thanks to the thick foliage, nobody seemed to notice but me. A feral smile spilt across my lips.

"You want me?" I bared my teeth. "Come and get me."

Demetri narrowed his eyes, but like the coward he was, he didn't take a step forward. "Get her. Make sure she's tied up good for the journey back to House Laurent. I don't want to hear another fucking word out of that mouth."

Four rangers stepped forward with their weapons bared and a swirl of two different colors in their eyes as their bloodlust rose. These ones were clearly excited about the idea of hurting me, a cruelty that had been allowed to fester at House Laurent.

That would fucking end now.

The ropes that had been slithering their way through the branches shot forward and wrapped around the necks of two of the rangers moving to apprehend me before yanking them up into the trees. The other two rangers barely had a second to cry out in alarm before they dropped to their knees, screaming, courtesy of my daggers now protruding from their right eye sockets.

Demetri and the other rangers stood frozen in shock.

That was another difference between them and the House Harker rangers; Vail's people would have never hesitated.

I tugged on the magic connecting me to my daggers, and they ripped free of the rangers' eyes and flew back into my hands. Both rangers let out twin shrieks of pain before scrambling back as two bodies thudded to the ground, their throats slit and bodies disemboweled.

The two rangers with eye wounds were cut down by Alaric and Kieran as they leapt down from above us.

Roth's family melted out of the surrounding forest and cut through the remaining rangers like they were out on a morning stroll. A few Laurent rangers tried to flee once they saw that the Devereux clan was here, but their retreat was thwarted by Nyx, Adrienne, and Emil, who took care of them with ease.

Demetri stood frozen in the center of the chaos as his rangers were slaughtered. The undead hounds didn't react at all to the bloodbath around them either. They just stood perfectly still like statues. I got the sense that my earth magic didn't like their presence.

Things that were dead should stay dead.

I stalked towards Demetri, and whatever he saw in my face seemed to snap him out of it because he held up his hands and started backing up. "Samara, wait! We can negotiate a dea—"

Warm blood sprayed across my rain-soaked face as I slammed one dagger into his throat and the other into his groin. Demetri's hands weakly clawed at one of my wrists, but dark red ropes appeared and brutally pulled them away as he gurgled and I ripped my blades away.

The broken scream he released was music to my ears as he fell to the forest floor. Moroi were tough to kill—it was a blessing and a curse.

I watched as my former husband tried to crawl away from me, a cold satisfaction filling me. Kieran and Alaric appeared at my sides, the rain doing its best to wash the blood off their clothes. I sheathed my daggers and held a hand out, then Kieran placed his sword in my hand, and the two of them kissed me on the cheek before stepping back.

Around me, Roth's brothers were gleefully hacking off heads to ensure all the Laurent rangers wouldn't heal and come after us.

Demetri's fingers moved feebly as he drew a healing glyph on his neck, but he stopped when I closed the distance between us and slammed my foot into his ribs. He let out a strangled scream as he flipped onto his back. Blood soaked his shirt and pants, and his usually tan skin was pale.

"Deal," he rasped. "Make . . . deal."

"Oh Demetri," I purred. "The only thing I want from you is to bleed out at my feet." Then I swung the blade, and his scream abruptly ended as his head rolled off his shoulders. "And I can handle that just fine on my own, asshole."

CHAPTER FOURTEEN

—

Samara

"Thanks, love," I told Kieran when I tossed him back his sword.

"No problem, sweetheart." He flicked the blade to the side to get some of the blood off before resheathing it across his back.

"What should we do about that?" Alaric pointed at the three statue-like howlers as he sauntered over and crouched down to wipe his blade clean on the bottom corner of Demetri's pants.

The three of us slowly approached the howlers, who didn't react to our presence at all.

"That's creepy," Desmond said as he moved closer to Roth.

"Death. Awaken," Roth murmured as they tried to get closer to the hounds, only to be tugged back by their elder brother.

"I think whatever magic was used to bring them back from the dead didn't bring back the essence of what they are," I thought out loud. "Like their instincts, what made them predators, are missing. It feels like my earth magic is repulsed by their very presence. They're just empty vessels that can take commands, and it didn't occur to Demetri to order them to attack us."

"Your husband was an idiot," Taivan rumbled. "What'd you ever see in him anyway?"

"Ex-husband," Kieran and Alaric said at the same time.

"Dead ex-husband." Roth smiled.

I rolled my eyes. "Let's chalk up my failed marriage to the foolish and idealistic views of my younger self." I frowned at the hounds. "We should destroy the collars. If it's a spell that's reanimating them, that should allow their bodies to return to the earth."

We all looked at the creatures.

"So . . . uhh . . . who's going to do it?" Kieran scratched his head.

"Oh for fuck's sake," Roth growled, then the ropes that had returned to their forearms shot out and slipped underneath the collar of the nearest hound before ripping it free and tossing it to me. Within seconds, the howler fell apart into a pile of rotting flesh and bones.

I stepped back with a gag, and the others followed suit. Apparently, we didn't even have to destroy the collar, just remove it. With a grimace, Roth's brothers stepped forward and snapped the collars off the remaining howlers. The beasts didn't even move, just crumbled as soon as the leather broke contact with their bodies.

"Let's get the fuck out of here." I stared at the carnage around us before my gaze lingered on Demetri. His death had been too quick, but I was still glad it'd come at my hands.

I looked up to find Kieran also staring at Demetri's corpse, a troubled look on his face that I didn't like one bit. Demetri might have been dead, but the pain of his words was clearly still lingering in Kieran's mind.

Before I could say anything, the storm kicked up a notch, and the rain became more like buckets of water being dumped on us.

"This way," Severen called from where he and Celestina waited in the forest. I shoved some loose strands of hair away from my face and reached out to grab Kieran's hand, pulling him with me.

Alaric glanced at his friend in concern and fell into step next to me. Roth was already bundled up between their brothers—and grumbling loudly about how they never wanted to be outdoors again.

I'd build them the library of their fucking dreams once this was all said and done.

We'd been walking for no more than five minutes when Severen and Celestina suddenly stopped. Everyone halted with them and looked around. Because of the damn rain, I could barely see twenty feet in front of me and definitely couldn't hear that far. All I could smell was the damn forest and the faint scent of ozone as lightning cracked across the sky.

"Run," Severen breathed out.

We all took off without second-guessing the order. Celestina yelled something harshly and Taivan immediately snapped Roth up and flung them over his shoulder, then peeled from the group, going left with Desmond hot on his heels.

Severen darted to my side. "Samara, take your group and go west. We'll keep going north. All three groups will meet—" He shoved me away, and I crashed into Kieran just as a bolt sank into Severen's shoulder.

Our group ground to a halt in the middle of a clearing, Kieran and Alaric on either side of me and the three rangers just to our right. Lightning flashed, and I inhaled sharply as I saw the dark forms taking shape in front of us, becoming easier to distinguish as they closed the distance.

Carmilla sat atop an enormous black steed, and behind her, in two neat lines, were a dozen rangers also on horseback. Just like with Demetri, I had no doubt there were others in the trees surrounding us.

This wouldn't be like fighting Demetri and his rangers. For one, House Laurent wasn't known for creating strong warriors. Their rangers did the bare minimum to protect their lands.

A wordless whisper brushed against my mind.

Demetri also hadn't had a crown capable of warping minds. That was the true danger. Panic threatened to overwhelm me, but I shoved it down. Severen was letting out pained breaths behind me, and I could hear Celestina ripping fabric to tend to his wound. We already had one injured in our party, and two of our strongest fighters were hopefully getting Roth as far away as possible.

There would be no fighting our way out of this one. Unless . . .

I did my best to ignore Carmilla drawing her mount to a stop ten feet away in front of me, her rangers obediently stopping behind her. I followed the strange connection between me, Draven, and Vail. There. Less than three miles from us.

Still not great odds, but I was fairly confident that the crown's magic wouldn't work on me. In the past, it hadn't worked on anyone who had drunk a lot of my blood, which meant Kieran and Alaric should be protected. Maybe Nyx too, although it'd been well over a week since they'd had some, and they hadn't drank all that much to begin with.

Everyone else was vulnerable. I just needed to buy us time until Vail and Draven arrived. Carmilla had purposely driven us into this clearing because their horses wouldn't help them much in the thick of the forest. If we could cause a big enough distraction and get to the trees, we might be able to make a run for it.

During our standoff with Carmilla, the rain had decreased to a steady but less overwhelming amount.

"I thought I raised you to make better decisions than this, niece." Carmilla's dark green eyes looked almost black, but I could still see the disdain in them.

Stall, I told myself. *Stay calm and keep her talking.*

"And I thought you were honorable and dedicated to your people, aunt," I said coolly. "It seems we're both disappointed."

Carmilla shook her head. "You're too weak to do what it takes for our people to survive. I tried to give you an opportunity, but you've spat on my reasonable requests." Her mount took a step forward. "Surrender. Return with me. You will marry Demetri and give me an Heir. One who will do right by me."

I felt Alaric and Kieran go still at my sides. It was an empty threat because she didn't know Demetri was dead. Still, it hurt to hear it from her lips.

Gods, we'd all been such fools. It still smarted that the woman we'd all respected as the Leader of our House had been the villain all along and not a single one of us had seen it.

That was something I'd have to come to terms with later. For now, we needed to survive—and I wanted more information.

It wasn't hard to let the pain of betrayal show on my face. "What did you just say?" I let my voice crack a little.

"Don't play coy, Samara." Carmilla narrowed her eyes. "You must have some idea of the importance of your bloodline by now."

I swallowed and looked at the ground like I was defeated before saying quietly, "I'm part Fae."

"Yes. Courtesy of your father. Knew there was a reason I never liked him." My aunt shook her head in disgust. "As soon as he came into the picture, my sister stopped listening to me. I should have killed him then. If I had, perhaps things would have played out differently."

She didn't look all that heartbroken about it.

"We both know that's bullshit," I snarled. "Was it even Velika's idea to kill them? Or was it an idea *you* whispered in her ear?" I took a step forward, only for someone to grab me and yank me back against a hard chest. Kieran's scent wrapped around me, but I just stared at my aunt. I thought about that scar running across Vail's face. "You tried to kill *us*." The words were barely more than a whisper.

For a second, something like regret flashed across Carmilla's face, but it was gone faster than the lightning dancing across the sky.

"I told your parents to leave you behind, but as usual, they didn't listen to me." A cold mask settled onto my aunt's face.

"Probably because they suspected you were a traitorous bitch!" I hissed, my hand slipping down to the dagger on my thigh, only to be stopped when Alaric clamped his fingers around my wrist.

Something dark and angry twisted inside my soul, and Carmilla's horse stamped its feet uneasily.

Magic. It was my magic I was feeling. Pity I had no idea how to use it. I took a deep breath. Now wasn't the time to dwell on that. I needed to be stalling, not picking a fight and probably getting someone I loved killed.

I did my best to ignore the earth magic churning inside me and instead sank further into my Moroi side, letting my bloodlust rise that much more. At least this magic I was familiar with. I let my nails shift into claws that bit into my flesh when I clenched my fists, the pain grounding me.

"You condemned Draven for being half Fae, yet you want a grandchild 'tainted' with the same blood?"

"The fallen prince was raised by two egotistical maniacs." Carmilla's mouth tightened. "I will teach the child to overcome their foul Fae blood and to wield their power for the greater good. Then I will pass the crown to them so that they might use it to its full potential."

Realization dawned on me. She knew the crown was fighting her and must have thought it was because she wasn't of the right bloodline. It was partially true, but mostly, the crown thought she was a vindictive bitch and didn't want to obey her.

"We won't let you take her," Kieran said before I could come up with a response.

All three rangers stepped forward, placing themselves between us and Carmilla while Alaric and Kieran shoved me behind themselves, both of them drawing their own swords.

Damn it. This was escalating too quickly. I concentrated on the thread linking me to Draven and Vail. Still miles away. Had they run into trouble too?

Stop, I told myself. *Deal with the problem in front of you before you go asking for more.*

My aunt sighed. "Last chance to come willingly."

For a brief second, I thought about it. I'd escaped once, I could do it again, but I dismissed that idea. Kieran and Alaric wouldn't let me go without a fight, and they would likely not walk away from that. Our best option was to hit them hard and then run. Our chances would've been better if Vail and Draven were here, but it seemed our time was running out.

The river was less than half a mile from us. We just had to make it there and then hope we didn't get crushed by any trees while it swept us away. Once we lost Carmilla and her rangers, we'd have to backtrack to locate Vail and Draven. I had no doubt Roth's brothers could find us.

"Remember, this was your doing." Carmilla shook her head and reached into a bag hanging off the front of her saddle.

I inhaled sharply as she settled the crown of silver and gold onto her head. Lighting cracked in the sky above us, and several horses stamped their feet in alarm.

You shouldn't have left me behind, the crown whispered in my mind.

Please, I begged.

I'm sorry. Its voice was tinged with exhaustion and regret. *There is nothing I can do.*

My aunt's gaze fell on the rangers standing guard in front of us. "Nyx and Emil," she said in a clear, commanding voice. "Step forward and hold."

Both rangers moved forward, leaving Adrienne on her own.

"No!" I cried and lunged for them, but Kieran and Alaric grabbed me. I struggled in their hold as they pulled me back several feet.

"Keep her back," Adrienne ordered over her shoulder. Her eyes met mine for a brief moment, and I saw the sorrow and determination in them.

"Nyx, stay still. Emil . . ." Carmilla's dark gaze fell on the blonde ranger, who stared her down defiantly. "Kill Adrienne."

I fought to get free, but Kieran and Alaric just gripped me tighter and murmured apologies in my ear. In that moment, I hated them, even though I would have done the same in their positions.

Carmilla was using our friends to make a point. Even with everything she had done so far, part of me had still believed there would be a way to convince my aunt to step down or end this in a way that didn't require her death.

That belief was now shattered into a thousand pieces as I watched Emil and Nyx tremble like they were fighting the command with everything they were worth before going predatorily still.

"Strigoi," I whispered in horror as Nyx remained but Emil prowled forward.

All Moroi carried a bloodlust that had the potential to turn us into ruthless predators. For some, like myself, we could turn it on and off easily, and even when it was riding us high, we were still ourselves. For others, they became something else when bloodlust claimed them—but they retained the tiniest thread of control so that they could pull it back.

They were weapons you had to aim and then get out of the way.

But sometimes, Moroi lost themselves completely, all of their humanity drained and stripped away. Nothing but the predator remained, and there was no coming back. They became Strigoi.

Emil's eyes were usually a warm brown fractured by light green. Now, there was no brown to be seen. Only a green so pale, it appeared white every time lightning struck over our heads. And Nyx's sky-blue eyes were now the dark blue of midnight.

There was no hint of my friends to be seen. Not in their eyes nor in their expressions, and definitely not in the eerie way they moved towards Adrienne. Predators focused solely on their prey.

A low snarl tore from Emil towards Nyx, an alpha staking their claim. Nyx ducked their head and went still, their eyes still following Adrienne as she adjusted her stance to face Emil.

"I'm so sorry, my friend." Her words were a quiet echo across the clearing that shattered my heart.

"Carmilla!" I screamed. "Stop this!"

My aunt looked at me with cold resignation and shook her head once before focusing back on the brewing fight. I saw the instant her expression changed to intrigue. This show wasn't only to put me in my place. It was an opportunity for her to test the capabilities of the crown.

Growing up, I'd always respected Carmilla's pragmatism, but now I wished she'd demonstrate more humanity alongside it.

Several of Carmilla's rangers moved to stand closer to us. The message was clear—if we interfered, they'd put us down. I wouldn't be killed, but Kieran and Alaric likely would be. All we could do was watch as Emil slowly circled Adrienne with a cruel detachment.

"She's never beaten him." Heat burned behind my eyes, tears made of despair and fury. I'd seen the rangers spar more than once. Adrienne was good, but even she couldn't take down Emil. Any Moroi would struggle to take on a Strigo, no matter how well trained they were or how much they let their blood-lust rise. Holding on to even the smallest amount of our humanity came at a cost—we were slower and weaker.

Nothing held a Strigoi back.

"Adrienne could have bested Emil years ago," Kieran whispered quietly, his voice strained.

I jerked my gaze towards him. "What?"

"Emil started talking about how old he was getting and how he should retire. He's the last of his generation to still be an active ranger." Kieran swallowed and glanced at me. "He told her the day she could beat him would be the day he'd know it was time to hang up his ranger cloak."

We both turned back to the center of the clearing, where Emil had gone still as a statue while Adrienne watched him. Her preferred weapon—a broadsword—was gripped in her hands and held at shoulder level, its tip pointing towards the storm raging above us.

Emil ignored the sword strapped to his back and the daggers on his thighs. Normally, we could shift our nails into claws, but Strigoi took it one step further. Each of Emil's fingers now ended in black, three-inch-long talons, the inside curve of each was razor sharp. Perfect for ripping out throats.

Tension filled the clearing as neither ranger moved, both waiting for the other to attack first. Lightning flashed over our heads, and in the split second that Adrienne was blinded, Emil shot forward. As if she'd anticipated it, Adrienne stepped into his attack and started a diagonal strike, only to spin away at the last second.

It was like watching a dance that two performers had perfected over decades. Adrienne gracefully spun her sword until it was nothing but a silver blur. Emil's opening attack had been a feint, because he'd also twisted to the side, only now, he found his path blocked by steel. With no hesitation, he blurred to the right and tried to maim her thigh to slow her down enough to get in a killing blow.

Adrienne dodged the attack, her movements like flowing water. They danced around each other in the clearing, punctuated by lightning strikes, as if the storm were dancing with them.

Neither scored a hit. Neither slowed down.

My heart raced with every step they took. It felt wrong to root for Adrienne, but I didn't know what else to do as I watched two people I cared deeply about battle for their lives. Even if one of them was already lost.

Suddenly, Emil struck at Adrienne's neck, and when she stepped back to avoid it, his back was exposed. With only the slightest hesitation, Adrienne's sword cut vertically through the air towards Emil's neck. My heart clenched, but I couldn't make myself look away. Only, her blade found nothing but air as the Strigoi leaned backwards until his back was almost horizontal with the ground and the sword whistled over him.

He straightened and lunged for Adrienne's exposed side. She pulled her sword back to herself, trying to get it between her and those sharp talons.

Too slow.

A scream tore through the night sky, followed seconds later by the tangy scent of blood. Emil dove towards Adrienne again, and she raised her sword. I flinched as another burning flash of lightning forced me to close my eyes. When I opened them, I saw Adrienne staggering back, a pained grimace on her face as blood flowed through her torn leather vest. The thing that used to be Emil raised his hand and licked the blood from his talons.

Then, a low, hungry sound came from Nyx, who had stepped forward, only to be cut off by Emil's warning growl. The Strigoi took a step back, their hungry eyes still locked on a wounded Adrienne.

Adrienne resumed her stance, her feet shoulder-width apart, left foot slightly forward. Once again, she raised her sword so the point was to the sky. Blood ran down it. I frowned. When had she gotten him? The lightning strike? My eyes had only been shut for a second . . .

Emil stalked forward, spurred on by the scent of his prey's blood, but when he darted to the right, clearly intent on capitalizing on her already-wounded side, his steps faltered. Inside, I was screaming as Emil's body carried him forward, the momentum too much to stop even as his right leg buckled beneath him. Then he stumbled straight onto Adrienne's sword.

The blonde ranger choked back a sob as she released the hilt immediately and grabbed each of the Strigoi's wrists, preventing him from swiping those talons through her throat. She'd punctured his heart, but it would take him a few minutes to die.

"I'm so sorry. I'm so sorry," she sobbed over and over again as she lowered her friend to the ground. Emil only snarled in return, fighting to get free, even as his lifeblood poured into the ground beneath him. Slowly, she pulled her sword from his chest and rose to her full height.

I tore my gaze away from them and looked at my aunt as tears streaked down my rain-soaked face.

Her dark, stony gaze found mine, and without hesitation, she gave the next order. "Nyx, kill Adrienne."

"No!" I screamed and renewed my efforts to get free, only for Kieran and Alaric to hold me back.

"We can't, Sam," Kieran said through clenched teeth. "There's nothing we can fucking do."

I knew he was right even if I didn't want to accept it. The only reason I stopped fighting was because the rangers standing nearby took a threatening step forward.

Thunder and lightning cracked and sounded over us before the rainfall became more of a deluge as the sky opened up. I shoved my hair away from my face and looked to where Nyx had been waiting while Adrienne and Emil had fought.

The spot was empty.

Adrienne grunted as she brought up her sword just in time to keep Nyx from clawing out her eyes. She'd also angled her sword so that the flat side made contact with Nyx's forearm, a vicious snarl tearing from Nyx's throat as they darted back before hurling themself at Adrienne again.

There was no deadly elegance to their movements like there had been to Emil's and Adrienne's. Just a feral intensity to rend and claw through flesh. Again and again, they struck at Adrienne, and every time, she deflected Nyx's attacks without doing them harm.

But the defense-only tactic came with a cost, because Adrienne's blood now soaked the ground along with Emil's who, based on his slowly rising chest, was still alive but not long for this world.

"Nyx," I half whimpered, but there was no sign of my friend in those wild, dark eyes. My relationship with Nyx was complicated. I'd known them at Drudonia, then they'd disappeared and only reentered my life when I'd returned to House Harker, but in my time back, I'd picked up on how close they were with Vail and his rangers—especially Adrienne. I knew the older ranger viewed Nyx as a younger sibling.

And Carmilla had to know it too. For all the rage I felt towards her now, my aunt knew her people well. This was a test to see how far the crown could push people against their instincts. If it could turn them against those they loved. Her pitting Adrienne and Emil against each other had been bad enough, but Adrienne and Nyx?

Carmilla was responsible for so many deaths—including those of my parents—and while I hated her for it, those had been tactical and efficient. Carmilla could have just ordered her rangers to cut down anyone here with a crossbow bolt to the heart. This felt cruel for cruelty's sake. Something I hadn't thought her capable of until now.

Despite how much Adrienne was bleeding, it seemed obvious she could win this fight at any moment she chose. Emil had challenged her, forcing her to dig down deep and fight to the best of her abilities, but Nyx's fighting skills had devolved. Maybe because they were younger or because the crown's magic had hit them harder. They were only still standing because Adrienne couldn't bear to strike them down.

Alaric shifted his grip so that his arm was around my waist while Kieran's remained across my shoulders. Alaric had been quiet during all of this, but I could feel the tension and fear radiating off him. What we were watching was his greatest fear—losing himself to bloodlust and becoming Strigoi. He'd witnessed his cousin suffer a similar fate, and it still haunted him to this day.

Kieran had also grown silent. I knew he considered Adrienne a friend. All of us were silently suffering in our own hells as we watched Adrienne try to avoid hers—to kill a friend . . . or die by their hand.

The rangers close to us shifted on their feet as Nyx stumbled back from another of Adrienne's deflecting blows. Then Adrienne shoved the young ranger forward, even as they whirled and snarled at her.

"*Nyx*," my aunt's voice, infused with magic, rang out. "*Finish this.*"

Please, I begged the crown again. *Do something.*

I . . . cannot.

You must! I screamed through our connection and could practically feel it wince. *I will do anything. Just make this stop.*

Little queen, its voice whispered through my mind. *You have no idea the cruelties I've seen. This is one of many. If you do not wish to experience this again, you must reclaim what is yours.*

Whatever words I was about to hopelessly plead died as Nyx leapt towards Adrienne, talons outstretched. Adrienne backed up a few steps, but she was too close to the rangers who had moved to stand guard in front of Carmilla, and they shoved her forward. As if moving on instinct, Adrienne dropped one hand from the hilt of her sword to wrap it around Nyx's throat, catching them midair. Then, with one fluid movement, Adrienne had Nyx pinned to the ground by their throat . . . with her sword buried in their chest.

Her sword pierced Nyx at an angle, so if she pushed down on it, the blade would have shred their heart. The predator in Nyx sensed this and went still, their talon-tipped hands wrapped around Adrienne's hand on the hilt of the sword.

For a second, it felt like everything paused. I didn't hear the storm or feel the rain on my face. The only thing that existed was Adrienne and Nyx.

"I love you. Never forget that." Adrienne's voice didn't waver once, her golden hair draped around her face as she held the sword between herself and Nyx. "I know you will find your way back from this. Do not blame yourself."

With that promise and command voiced into the world, Adrienne pulled her hand away from Nyx's throat and loosened her grip on the sword.

Time unfroze, and I watched in horror as Nyx's talons shot up . . . and ripped out Adrienne's throat.

A fragmented scream of denial poured out of me, and Alaric's and Kieran's grasps didn't slip, but I felt their bodies go rigid next to mine.

Blood flowed from Adrienne's torn flesh directly into Nyx's mouth, and they lapped it up hungrily as I alternated between sobs and strangled screams.

"You could have avoided this, my dear, if you had just come with me when I asked," my aunt called out over the rain that pounded into the ground.

I raised my gaze from where Adrienne had collapsed on top of Nyx and pushed aside the hungry sounds of feeding to meet my aunt's eyes. "Someday, I might have forgiven you for what you did to me, maybe even what was done to Draven under your watch, but I will *never* forgive you for this. And if there are any rangers here tonight whose minds you haven't scrambled, let this be an example of how you repay loyalty."

A few of the rangers shifted uneasily and traded pointed looks with each other while others sneered at me, but most of those lined up directly behind Carmilla didn't react at all. They just continued to stare blankly ahead. Not even reacting to the Strigoi hungrily feasting on the blood of one of their own mere feet from where they sat astride their horses. Or to Emil—one of the most well-respected rangers in the Moroi realm—who had finally gone still.

A cold, hard bitterness settled in my gut. She had used the crown on them despite telling me many times that she would only use the crown's magic when absolutely necessary. Apparently she found it necessary to strip the free will of sixty rangers and force them to serve her.

As much as that disturbed me, there was a silver lining. The half of the crown that Vail had given her had the ability to see a soul. I took that to mean she could see a person's true intentions. If my aunt felt the need to compel loyalty from so many of these rangers . . . she must have seen that they didn't believe in her plan.

I had to figure out a way to break them free of the crown's magic and to get it away from her so she couldn't cause any more harm to our people.

"Do I need to continue the demonstration, or will you—" Carmilla's words were cut off when an agonized howl cut through the night.

My gaze fell back to Nyx, and I inhaled sharply. Kieran and Alaric did the same beside me.

The only occurrences of Strigoi becoming Moroi again had been the first generation of Moroi—the humans who had used magic to become something else. The Moroi, Velesians, and Furies. That first generation was special for each of our groups. For the Moroi, they were the only ones we knew of who had lost their humanity . . . and reclaimed it.

Outside of that generation though, it was a known fact that once a Moroi became a Strigoi, there was no coming back.

Nyx was no longer feeding on Adrienne. Instead, they were cradling her close and rocking her back and forth. I saw their lips moving, but I couldn't hear their words over the rainfall. Nobody moved as Nyx grieved the ranger they had loved like a sister.

"'I'm sorry. Please wake up,'" Kieran murmured, somehow figuring out what Nyx kept repeating.

Oh gods.

"Nyx." My voice broke as I called to them. Slowly, they raised their head to look at me. "Not possible," I breathed out, because Nyx's eyes were no longer the solid deep blue of night. Now, bright blue threads weaved their way through the darkness.

When Moroi let their bloodlust rise, it was like racing along the edge of a cliff. Most made sure to keep a decent amount of space between them and that edge—some, like Alaric, preferred to never go near it. The rangers liked to live dangerously, trusted themselves not to slip while getting as close as possible.

Nyx had gone over that edge. I was sure of it. Now, they were clawing themself back up.

But when another ranger stepped forward, the brightness in their eyes faded, and Nyx released a sharp snarl in warning. Not all the way back . . . but not completely lost to us either.

"Interesting," Carmilla murmured. I tore my gaze from Nyx and glared at my aunt, who was staring at the young ranger in quiet contemplation. "It would be handy to be able to turn humanity on and off like a switch."

Nyx swiveled their head towards my aunt. I couldn't see their expression, but whatever was in it had Carmilla blanching. Carefully, Nyx settled Adrienne onto the ground and rose, black talons once again extending from their fingers.

"Stop," Carmilla ordered, her horse shifting its hooves nervously beneath her. Nyx stopped and held still for a heartbeat . . . then they took another step. "Do not move."

I held my breath as Nyx once again stopped, then took another step after a few seconds passed.

Well, isn't that fascinating? the crown's voice swept through my mind.

"How?" I choked as the word slipped from my lips. I felt Kieran's and Alaric's gazes on me but couldn't look away from where Nyx was fighting to get to Carmilla.

I don't know, the crown finally admitted after hesitating.

Several of the horses snorted in distress and pulled against their reins as the rangers tried to keep them under control. Carmilla glanced at them with a frown before looking around the woods. I did the same, scanning the darkness, looking for any sign of a threat.

For quite possibly the first time in my life, I wished for a monster attack. We needed a diversion, and I had faith in us to use the chaos to our advantage and slip away—with Nyx, because there was no chance I was leaving them behind.

Carmilla's mount reared up, and the unease of the rest of the horses increased. Something had them seriously spooked, I just had no idea what. My aunt looked past me, the corners of her eyes and mouth pinched. "I have no quarrel with House Devereux, but I'll be taking the members of my House. If you choose to fight me, know that we'll hunt down your children."

"You can try, bitch," Celestina snarled.

I glanced quickly over my shoulder and saw her standing in front of her husband, a long, curved sword in her hands and eyes glowing with menace.

She would fight. And she would die.

My eyes went to Emil and Adrienne. No more deaths tonight. I'd escaped Carmilla's grasp once. I could do it again.

I moved my hand behind me, where it would be visible to Roth's parents, and made the signal for *stand down*. All rangers, regardless of which House they owed allegiance, used a system of gestures for communicating when speaking aloud was ill-advised. Technically, none of Roth's family were rangers, but House Devereux was a warrior clan, so I had no doubt they knew the gestures.

"Nyx goes with them." I jerked my head over my shoulder towards Roth. "You've caused them enough pain."

"No. Nyx comes too. I want to—" Carmilla cursed as her horse reared again. As soon as its hooves hit the ground, it shied into the ranger's horse next to it. "Grab Nyx and Samara and let's go," she said through gritted teeth as her mount tried to bolt and she barely kept it in check. All the horses looked on the verge of running. I could hear ours stamping their feet behind us as well.

Something was coming.

Half a dozen rangers stepped towards Nyx and another half a dozen towards us.

"Anyone have any bright ideas on how to get out of this?" Kieran asked tightly as he angled himself slightly in front of me.

"Nothing's coming to mind," Alaric replied in an equally strained voice. Both of them were looking at the rangers approaching us. Something, a vague feeling, had me looking to the sky, which meant I saw what no one else did—the dark streak flying through the air on silent wings made of night and shadow.

The rangers were halfway to us when she slammed into the earth between us, cutting off their approach. Leathery black wings spread out from the Furie's back as shadows spun around her, like the night was thrilled by her presence.

Then, glowing golden eyes met mine as the Furie looked over her shoulder.

"Cali," I breathed out.

CHAPTER FIFTEEN

—

Alaric

For a fraction of a second, relief hit me when Cali landed in front of us. The Furies were few in number compared to the Moroi and the Velesians, but they were ruthless in battle, and there was nobody as skilled—and terrifying—as Calypso Rayne.

But then those mesmerizing golden eyes slid from Samara's tear-streaked face to the chaos erupting around us, and I realized we weren't saved—we were fucked. Because something had driven Cali over the edge, and now she was nothing but wrath made flesh.

"Shit!" Kieran swore from the other side of Samara, clearly coming to the same realization as Cali's predatory gaze zeroed in on the rangers tasked with apprehending us.

Carmilla seized the opportunity to turn tail and run, not that her horse needed much encouragement. Over half the rangers lost their battle with their mounts as the horses took off running after the new Moroi Queen. A few tripped over upraised roots, dumping their riders.

"Stall her!" Carmilla commanded over her shoulder, not showing any concern for the rangers she was leaving behind for what would likely be a gruesome death.

I tried to pull Samara back to shove her behind myself, but the leash Cali held over her own magic finally broke. Shadows exploded across the clearing as an alien presence speared my mind, and time seemed to stop only to jump forward and then freeze again.

It felt like someone had placed a vice around my head and was slowly cranking it tighter, all while a rage that was not mine burned hotter than any fire. At some point, I fell to my knees, and I was faintly aware of ripping my nails as I tore at the ground.

Cali vanished into shadow only to reappear behind the rangers, who were clutching their heads and screaming. Her sword flashed. Heads rolled.

More rangers poured into the clearing, only to fall as Cali's magic ripped their minds to shreds, leaving them as easy pickings for her blade.

I didn't know how House Devereux were fairing, but I hoped they didn't do something foolish like try to attack Cali. Taking down Furies when they lost themselves like this required far greater numbers than anything we had at our disposal. It also required careful planning, the element of surprise . . . and the knowledge that you would have to sacrifice some of your own to land a killing blow.

Kieran was kneeling next to me, his face locked in a pained grimace as blood leaked from his nose and ears. There were only three people still standing in the clearing. Cali. Samara. Nyx.

The Furie's molten gaze fell on Nyx, who still seemed to be wavering between Moroi and Strigoi—their eyes mostly midnight blue, but a few light strands remained. I didn't know what it meant, if they could truly come back from turning Strigoi, if they'd want to after what they'd been forced to do— but none of that mattered if we didn't survive the next few minutes.

"Samara!" I half whispered the warning before groaning as another wave of Cali's magic hit me and that vice squeezed a little tighter. Warm blood dripped from my nose. "Not. Your. Friend."

I loved Samara Harker with every bit of my pragmatic heart, and I understood her well. Her greatest strength—and weakness—was that she was loyal to a fault. She did not give that loyalty lightly, but once she did, there was no taking it back.

Even if the person who held it turned into a monster.

When Furies lost themselves, they didn't become mindless beasts. They remained what they'd always been —apex predators who took out the biggest threats first. And right now, Cali had decided that Nyx was the threat that needed neutralizing.

She took a step towards the broken ranger while Nyx held their ground, a silent snarl on their face, even as the flicker of something else danced in their eyes. Cali's golden stare held nothing but cold detachment. I tried to get up— to do what, I had no idea—but a sharp pain cut through my mind, immediately driving me back to my hands and knees.

In a desperate attempt, I tried to let my bloodlust rise to combat Cali's magic, but I'd kept it too ruthlessly locked down . . . so it did not answer when I called

All I could do was watch helplessly as Samara smoothly moved to stand in front of Cali, putting Nyx at her back. Internally, I screamed at the risk she was putting herself in. Cali was not her friend anymore, and only a fool would let a Strigoi be at their back.

Nyx's muscles tensed for a second, and I knew they were about to launch themself at Samara's exposed neck and back, but then they squeezed their eyes shut and jerked their head, stumbling backwards. When their eyelids fluttered open a second later, more light blue was threaded through the dark. Slowly, Nyx took another step back, as if they were trying to remove themselves as a threat.

"Cali," Samara barked. The pressure on my mind eased slightly. "Enough."

"What are you doing?" I asked tightly. Reasoning with Furies in this state was useless. We needed to figure out how to retreat. Maybe get Cali to chase after Carmilla . . .

Samara ignored me. Of course she did. Gods, I was going to strangle her when this was done.

"All these years," Samara sneered, "everyone has been saying you would fall. *'Calypso Rayne is already half mad and too powerful. Better to put her down now,'*" she mocked as she stepped closer to Cali, who had gone stock-still. "I was the harlot, Rynn the screwup, and you the mad bitch."

The magic bearing down on my mind came back, and I growled as I tried to push against it. Kieran crawled closer to me, and we both grimaced as we looked at each other before focusing once again on the reckless woman who held both our hearts.

Samara's hand shot out to grip the front of Cali's bloodsoaked vest. "We do not yield!" she snarled into her friend's face. "Pull yourself together! Everything is fucked right now, and I can't do this without you."

I hated the way her voice broke on that last word. *So fucking do something about it, asshole,* I chided myself.

Cali's clawed hands gripped Samara's, piercing her flesh, but she didn't attack her friend. To my amazement, Samara was actually getting through to Cali, even though everything I knew about Furies said that should be impossible when they were in this state.

We just needed to give Cali another push.

Shoving aside the pain that still had a grip on my mind, I rose to my feet. Cali's head snapped towards me. "I think I know where Rynn might be," I said quickly but clearly before rushing to get the rest out. "There is much we need to catch you up on, Cali, and Samara is right, we will need your help because you will be able to retrieve Rynn faster than any of us."

I was embellishing a little. Okay, a lot. I suspected I knew where Rynn was because it was the only place that made sense. Assuming I was right about her being in the far northern reaches of the Velesian realm, Cali was our only hope of reaching her because we definitely wouldn't make it there on foot.

Kieran got to his feet next to me but didn't make a move towards Cali. We'd both experienced a Furie's wrath before, but that time had been only the barest splash of it, and that Furie had never been given the chance to come back. She'd been hunted down and exterminated.

Samara would never allow that to happen to Cali though, and against all odds, it did feel like Cali was drawing her rage back. I could still feel it on the outskirts of my mind, but the blood was no longer pouring from my nose, and I was capable of thinking for more than a few seconds at a time.

Which was why I was able to contemplate the way Cali had moved. In addition to the strange mental attacks Furies could invoke, they all had a little bit of shadow magic. That was the true reason they'd always felt apart from the Moroi and Velesians. Their shadow magic was just a little too similar to the wraiths that haunted these lands.

Over the generations, the Furies had learned to lock down their magic. They only wielded their mental attacks as a last result, and most refused to touch their shadow magic altogether.

Except Cali.

She'd always been the exception. Much like Samara was somewhat of an exception amongst the Moroi, as she frequently flaunted her bloodlust. And Rynn had her own eccentricities that set her apart from the rest of the Velesians.

It was almost like fate had drawn the three of them together. Bonded them on some deep level that no one else could touch.

I normally didn't believe in such things, but it was hard to deny it as the most powerful Furie in existence clawed back her magic, looked at her friend, and wept.

I didn't know what to do, so I looked at Kieran.

He looked at me wide-eyed. "This is outside my area of expertise."

Great.

I rubbed the back of my head and turned away from Samara and Cali. Something told me the Furie wouldn't want anyone to see her cry, and I really liked my head being attached to my body.

Kieran moved to huddle next to me. "Go check on Roth," he said quietly. "I'll make sure Nyx is . . . alright."

Nyx was definitely not alright.

I jerked my head in a nod and strode towards the Devereux clan. Other than a few patches of dark red hair, I couldn't even see Roth past all the muscled bodies guarding them.

"Samara has it under control," I told Taivan and Desmond as I approached. They'd put themselves in front of their sibling with Severen and Celestina guarding their children from the sides.

"Does she?" Desmond rasped.

"She does," I said flatly.

The brothers traded a look that said they didn't quite believe that, but then they both let out twin shrieks as Roth grabbed them by the ears and yanked.

"I'm officially out of patience." Roth shoved past their brothers and crashed to a halt in front of me, their eyes a burning orange. "Move, or I'll move you."

"I was actually coming to get you." I gave them a wry smile.

"Oh." Some of the fire banked in their eyes. "Let's go then."

Roth started to walk past me before turning back around to face their family. "Uhh . . . thank you for keeping me alive."

Severen rubbed his face, clearly at a loss for patience when dealing with his youngest child, but a faint smile of amusement teased Celestina's lips. Meanwhile, Roth's brothers both smiled like they'd just been paid the highest of compliments.

That was clearly too much emotion for Roth because they practically fled past me, and I quickly followed after them, not wanting to be left behind to deal with the strange family dynamic that was House Devereux.

We walked across the clearing to where Samara was wiping some of the blood off Cali's face while offering soothing words. I cut a glance to Kieran and found him standing a few feet away from Nyx, who was rooted to the same spot, tension rolling off them, but at least they weren't actively hunting anyone nor had they bolted into the woods, so I'd take that as a win.

Samara's dark gaze cut to us as Roth and I approached, then she dropped her hand to her side and moved her fingers in a way that had to be some type of signal. A ranger signal maybe? Kieran spent a lot of time sparring with the rangers, so he probably would have known what it meant, but I had no idea. I opened my mouth to ask when Roth's fingers briefly closed around my forearm, drawing me to a stop.

Wait and hold, they mouthed.

Surprise flickered through me. It was well-known that every member of House Devereux went through ranger training, but I'd assumed Roth had been exempt from it because they were . . . well . . . they were Roth. If it wasn't a book—or Samara—they didn't give a shit.

Any musings I'd had about Roth and their upbringing evaporated as Samara tucked a strand of hair behind Cali's ear and started asking her questions—ones I was really curious about the answers to.

"How did you know where to find us?" Samara asked her friend gently.

"Whispers." Cali's eyes were wide. "Don't you hear them?"

Roth and I shared a look. Furies were prone to madness. Nobody knew why. The Moroi lost themselves to bloodlust, but the Furies . . . they lost themselves to rage. If our hunger for blood was its own entity, then so was that fury that burned within them.

Only the Velesians had no such hardships.

It was one of the many mysteries I and so many others had pondered over the years.

"I don't hear anything." Samara shook her head, keeping her voice calm and soothing. "These voices . . . they told you to come here?"

Cali's head snapped towards the north. The sudden movement had me reaching for the dagger on my thigh, but I stilled my hand.

"He told me. I've never heard his voice so clearly before." She turned back to face us—Sam, really. I didn't think she was entirely registering our presence at the moment. Her mouth hardened into a flat line as her brows furrowed together. "The lake."

"Lake Malov?" Samara prodded, reaching out to grip her friend's hands.

The Furie looked down at where their bloody fingers were intertwined, then her eyes cleared a little more, the glow dimming. "You were missing," she said slowly. "So was Rynn. The last place I knew you were was Lake Malov."

I cursed under my breath, drawing Samara's attention for a moment and letting me see the fear in her eyes. Fear for her friend, who had said that all Furies avoided the area around Lake Malov because it made them uneasy . . . but that it had always called to her.

Something had been trying to get Cali to go to Lake Malov for a long time —and it just got its wish.

"Can't we just go one fucking day without more fucked-up bullshit raining down on us?" I half growled.

Someone grunted next to me, and I almost jumped out of my skin. Taivan's eyes never strayed from Cali, but the corners of his mouth quirked up into a grin, clearly amused at having scared the shit out of me. I glowered at him. How did someone that large move so quietly?

"This is Lunaria." Taivan gave me a sly look before returning their vigilant gaze to the Furie. "There's never a time when it's not fucked."

I snorted. True enough.

"Do you still hear it—him?" Samara corrected herself, once again focused on her best friend.

Cali tilted her head as if she was listening for something, and we all waited for a few tension-filled seconds until her shoulders sagged in relief. She smiled weakly at Sam. "No. I think I burned myself out. The whispers will be back— he'll be back—but for now, it's quiet."

Lightning flashed across the sky, and thunder rumbled in the distance a few seconds later. The downpour had lightened up, but the rain showed no sign of stopping anytime soon.

As if reading my thoughts, Samara looked up to the sky and then surveyed all of us, her eyes lingering for a moment on the fallen forms of Adrienne and Emil. A hint of grief broke through her calm and determined mask before she hid it.

For years, I thought Samara was self-serving because she'd always seemed so above everyone. Always breezing into a room with a confident swagger that had immediately put me into a foul mood, but now I realized what that had cost her. Samara never allowed anyone—in our House or any other—to see her as anything but unbreakable.

So many times, I'd said something cruel to her just to try to get a reaction. I almost never got one. Instead, she'd say something back that would have me seeing red and usually storming out of the room, but I suspected my words had always cut far deeper than I'd imagined. She was just better at hiding her wounds than I.

Fuck. I'd been such an asshole. To make it worse, Kieran had always seen the truth of Samara, and he had hinted at it over the years. I'd just chosen to not believe him because of the often conflicting feelings I'd had towards the House Heir.

That was all in the past though. I could make up for it now—starting with not making Samara bear all of this alone.

"We need to regroup. Preferably somewhere indoors and behind wards. We can't be that far from House Salvatore." Cautiously, I closed the distance between myself and Samara, keeping part of my attention on Cali. She seemed calmer now, more like her usual self, but I didn't want to risk upsetting her.

The Furie just gave me a tired, wan smile and extended her wings up, curving them forward slightly to provide a little bit of shelter from the rain.

"We don't know where House Salvatore stands with Carmilla's rise to power." Samara chewed on her bottom lip, her eyes distant as she thought it through. "Draven and Vail are south of us. We could rendezvous with them and then continue to Salvatore. Hopefully Carmilla hasn't sunk her claws into them."

Or used the crown's magic. Although we still didn't know if the crown could be wielded against a House bloodline as it could any other Moroi. Nyx might be one of our rangers, but they were technically of the House Corvinus bloodline.

I didn't know if Carmilla had intentionally turned them into a Strigoi or if, even with both halves united, that was still the only way it could work on a House bloodline. She'd definitely been able to control them. I thought about the way Nyx had been fighting towards the end. One rebellious step at a time.

Something about the crown's magic hadn't entirely worked on Nyx.

A howl rose in the night, sounding a few miles away from us. "No matter what, I think we want to head south." I reached out and brushed back the hair that was plastered to Samara's face. "We're lucky we haven't drawn the attention of wraiths or any other nasty creatures." I glanced around before looking back at Samara and suggesting a plan of action. "Find Draven and Vail. Evaluate House Salvatore when we get there. If anything appears suspicious, we don't set foot inside their walls and we continue on to House Devereux."

"Okay." Samara nodded and then glanced at Taivan, who hadn't tried to crowd in under Cali's wings and was just standing in the rain, not looking the least bit bothered by it. "Does that plan work for you?"

"Yes." The Heir of House Devereux nodded. "We've had scouts keeping an extra close eye on House Salvatore since Roth arrived home. Best we can tell, they've had no communication with Carmilla."

"Good enough for me." Samara looked around at the corpses littering the clearing—Cali's work. Again, I saw that hint of sadness in her eyes before she tucked it away. Some of them might have willingly served Carmilla, but not all. "We can't take them with us," Samara said softly.

There were far too many for us to carry, and we needed to move swiftly. It was a miracle that the Lunarian beasts hadn't already come to investigate the tang of blood in the air. The storm might be making us all miserable and cold, but at least it was keeping scents down.

"I'll send my people to come and collect the dead as soon as I can," Taivan offered.

It was nice of him, but we all knew there wouldn't be much left. The beasts that prowled the forests were not ones to waste such a meal.

Suddenly, Nyx snapped out of their almost comatose stance, causing everyone to stiffen. Taivan had a blade in his hand in an instant, but Nyx ignored him along with the rest of us as they walked over to where Adrienne lay and carefully lifted her, cradling the ranger to their chest, as if they could protect her in death.

Not a flicker of emotion appeared on Nyx's face as they looked to where Emil rested. Wordlessly, Cali tucked her wings back and strode over to the other ranger, easily picking him up. Together, Nyx and Cali began walking south.

The rest of us followed, leaving the dead behind.

CHAPTER SIXTEEN

—

Draven

"These howler nests look like they were abandoned weeks ago." I toed a pile of branches, leaves, and other debris collected from the forest.

Vail just grunted. That seemed to be his main form of communication since I'd tracked him down half an hour ago.

I sighed. It hadn't taken me long to find him, but Vail kept coming up with reasons to slow our journey back to the others. "We should keep going. The rest of the group is only a few miles away, and I'd prefer to be at Samara's side."

Usually, I loved being out at night. Thanks to my magic, I could sense the nastier of the monsters and avoid them. There was something thrilling about sharing the forest with them, of being just another monster trying to survive, but that thrill was dimmed tonight because Samara was out here too, and she didn't have a good enough grasp on her earth magic to wield it like I did— something we'd absolutely be working on once we had time.

"Carmilla is no doubt hunting her down." I hesitated before adding, "And my father is going to seek retribution for Velika's death. He might decide to take out his frustration on Samara."

Moonlit silver eyes finally met mine. "Will he not come after you?"

"Eventually." I shrugged. "But he'll want revenge for Velika's death first. There was no love lost between the two of them, but Velika helped him get access to those obsidian stones by figuring out which outposts were built over the human towns. She also shared information with him about the other Moroi Houses."

Thunder rumbled in the clouds above us.

"You really don't care that she's dead, do you?" Vail tilted his head as he studied me.

665

"Actually, I'm quite upset about it. I was really looking forward to killing her myself."

A slight tug pulled on the bond, there and gone in an instant. Based on the way Vail stiffened, I suspected he felt it too.

"Let's go. Samara wants us all together."

"*She* slammed the door in *my* face. So, clearly, she doesn't want us *all* together." He pushed off the tree he'd been leaning against. "I'll keep scouting ahead. You go running back to *her*," he tossed over his shoulder as he stalked farther into the woods.

My temper snapped.

Between one blink and the next, I had Vail pinned against a tree while roots shot out of the ground, winding around his waist and legs. My claw-tipped fingers dug into his throat, and his dagger pressed against mine.

I missed my whip. That would be priority number one once we reached House Devereux. No doubt they had a large weapons stash for me to raid and I could find something that would work.

"Get your hands off me, pretty boy," Vail snarled, "before I cut off your fingers and shove them down your throat."

"You're already on Samara's bad side." I snorted. "My fingers are her second favorite part of my body." My brows bunched together. "Maybe her third, I'm not sure where my tongue lies exactly. I'm good, but I have Kier to compete with, and his tongue skills are—"

Vail shoved me away, his blade drawing a bit of blood in the process, and started slashing at the roots holding his lower body. I sighed. This wasn't my problem to fix, and he *had* betrayed Samara, which was something he hadn't really accepted yet. In his mind, he was trying to be loyal to two people at once, but that wasn't possible when they were so opposed to each other.

I didn't particularly like Vail, but I understood what it was like to give your loyalty to the wrong person and suffer the cost. Vail was starting to understand, but I needed to give him a nudge to ensure he didn't betray Samara again.

Try to anyway. I'd kill him before he ever got another chance, which would break Samara's heart—which was the other reason I was trying to help the stubborn asshole out. I had no doubt that Samara still loved Vail, it was just hidden beneath a mound of hurt and fury.

Half a thought from me had the roots slipping back into the earth. Vail stalked away—in the opposite direction of Samara—so I ripped open the wound in my soul that I'd tried so hard not to think about.

"My father killed my older brother."

Rain started spattering against the thick forest canopy. I focused on that sound, doing my best to block out the resounding crack that always came to mind when I thought about Kalias.

Vail stopped mid-step, not turning around but clearly listening.

"Kalias was my half brother. I think it was hard for the Fae to procreate, and the Seelie turning themselves into shadow monsters probably didn't help," I said evenly, as if I were discussing someone else's family history. The branches above me moved closer together to provide me a little bit of shelter from the rain. They did that sometimes, helped without me having to ask. I patted the rough bark of the tree in thanks. "Erendriel was the first of the wraiths to figure out how to get his Fae form back."

"Who was the mother?" Vail asked, still facing away from me.

"A Velesian." I swallowed. "She died shortly after Kalias was born. We . . . were never able to find out anything about her. Not even her name." *Or if she'd been willing*, I thought darkly.

A twig snapped when Vail finally turned to face me. My magic lashed out, silencing the rest beneath his feet. His gaze dropped to the forest floor and back to me. "That's how you're able to move about so quietly—you use your magic to quiet your footsteps."

I nodded shallowly. "Stumbled across that ability by accident." The sound of bone snapping echoed across my mind, and I flinched. "Kalias was five years older than me. I'd met him a few times growing up, but it wasn't until I was twelve and Erendriel took me to live with him that I really got to spend more time with my brother."

"Did he have magic?"

"No." I closed my eyes briefly. "Pure-blooded Fae come into their magic in their early twenties, but they typically start showing signs of it earlier. Kalias was seventeen when I arrived, and it was becoming clearer with every passing year that he wouldn't have magic."

Something our father derided him about every day.

"But you do," Vail pointed out.

I gave him a smile that didn't reach my eyes. "Yes."

"Does your father know?"

The rain started to fall harder, and Vail took a few steps closer so he could hear me. It took me a moment to decide how to answer him. I was already telling him a story I hadn't told anyone else, so I might as well speak the truth.

"Yes," I finally answered. "But he doesn't know how much."

Something that I couldn't read flickered in Vail's eyes, but he didn't say anything. He was a patient bastard when he wanted to be.

"I started showing signs of having earth magic when I was eleven. Minor things like making flowers bloom early, being able to sense nearby animals. As my powers grew, Velika became more . . . perturbed by me." I blocked out the painful memories full of blood and screaming. "But it was the first time Erendriel ever showed an interest."

Few people truly knew me. I was the charming Moroi Prince to most. To some, I was a villain—but those were mostly people I'd killed or those who had been slaughtered in front of me while I'd been forced to stand by. Only Samara and Kieran truly knew me, and even still, they'd probably be surprised to know just how gullible I'd been all those years ago.

That I'd seen the hand Erendriel had stretched out to me as salvation when it had really just been damnation wrapped up in pretty words.

Nobody lied better than the Fae. I'd learned that lesson too late.

"I'd spent the first twelve years of my life under the thumb of someone who despised me. Erendriel treated me like a person, asked my opinions on things, praised me when I did something right. I'd never experienced such a thing, so I naturally gravitated towards it." A bitter smile stretched across my lips. "I was too young to understand the way he was manipulating me."

A small crease formed between Vail's brows, but he didn't say anything, so I continued.

"Erendriel had no interest in Kalias—he'd already written him off—but I liked having an older brother, and Kalias took me under his wing." The bitterness in my smile faded slightly as I thought about Kalias. *Crack.* The smile vanished. "He knew our father was disappointed in him for not having magic, so he tried to make himself useful in other ways."

"Did he betray the Velesians the way you did the Moroi?"

"I was a child manipulated by a centuries-old Fae and then had the pleasure of having my mind shredded by my psychopath of a mother." I gave him a cold look. "What's your excuse?"

Vail looked away.

"To answer your question, Kalias had no interaction with the Velesians— bad or good." I tried not to think about how many times I'd caught him staring at paw prints in the mud belonging to Lycanthropes or other Velesians. My brother had been caught between two worlds, unable to shift into an animal form but unable to do magic like a Fae.

Erendriel had thought he'd been a failure, but to me he'd just been my brother. We'd both been too caught up in trying to win the praise of our father to realize we hadn't needed it. We'd been enough.

"What is the point of this story?" Vail asked when I fell silent. He still wasn't looking at me, but he was idly rubbing his chest in the spot where I guessed he felt the same tug I did.

"During my time living with the wraiths, I was mostly kept away from everything. Erendriel would occasionally ask me to perform small acts of magic, but he dodged any questions I had about him and the Fae. How they'd become wraiths. What they were trying to do. I never truly learned anything about what was driving Erendriel."

Lightning tore across the sky. *Crack.*

"One day, Erendriel brought me and Kalias to a remote Moroi outpost with a handful of his wraiths." Vail's silver eyes suddenly focused on me again.

"He passed me a knife, told me several Seelie words, and then pointed to the blood ward protecting the outpost. I hesitated. Despite my naivety, I knew wraiths had killed Moroi before. I'd convinced myself that it hadn't been on the orders of Erendriel . . . but it was the dead of night and the Moroi were sleeping peacefully in their homes."

"The attacks on the outposts didn't start until recently. You're talking about almost a decade ago," Vail commented.

"It was a test," I said tightly. "One that I failed."

The branches above us creaked, and I felt the forest reach out to me, trying to heal the old wound. I flinched when one of the branches cracked.

"There is so much I don't understand about the Fae, even after being around Erendriel and his followers for so long, but one thing I do know—they plan everything ten steps ahead." I moved towards a tree and laid my palm against it. The branches settled, but the hollowness inside my chest remained. "He needed to know that when the time came, he could get across the wards, and he didn't want to rely on Velika. She was a tool to be used—not trusted."

"What did you do?" The accusing expression on Vail's face told me what he suspected my answer would be. That I'd betrayed our people. A dark part of me wished I could tell him that's what I'd done, because maybe if I'd made a different decision that night, I would have saved my brother. I sure as shit hadn't saved those outposts—only delayed the inevitable. Because those were the outposts Erendriel had slaughtered years later.

Crack.

"I refused," I rasped. "I loved Erendriel. He has this . . . presence about him, and he was my father. I thought he must have valid reasons for anything he did, even if I found some of them suspicious. He had my loyalty—beyond a shadow of a doubt." The muscles along my jawline tensed. "But I did not have his."

"He threatened Kalias if you didn't do it?" Vail guessed.

A humorless laugh escaped me. "That's the other thing about the Fae. They prefer punishment over ultimatums. He snapped Kalias' neck in front of me and then threw his body to the ground. The wraiths he'd brought with him ripped Kalias to shreds. There was nothing left of my brother to bury. It was like he never existed."

A hollow ache settled in the pit of my stomach. I so rarely let myself dwell on Kalias and his fate. But while the others were pissed off at Vail for betraying Samara—and rightfully so—I understood why he'd done it.

Sometimes it's hard to see the monster beneath the mask of someone you love.

Vail looked at me for a long moment with an unreadable expression. "What happened next?"

"Erendriel and his wraiths left me there. The Moroi who lived in the outpost found me crying in the morning. I was returned to my mother and became a tool for her and Erendriel to use when they needed. Erendriel didn't need me to cast the spell to get past the wards. He only needed to slice me open and hold my bleeding body over them while reciting the spell. The night he brought me and Kalias to that outpost had been a test. Not to see if the spell worked, but to see if I would do as commanded."

"Why tell me this?" Vail's brows furrowed. "I don't understand you, prince."

"Few do. Samara is one of them, and she loves you despite herself." I shrugged. "If you attempt to betray her again, I will carve you apart and scatter your body across the earth." Roots rose from the ground and snapped at Vail's feet, causing him to leap back. "It will be like *you* never existed. This is a warning to better choose who you give your loyalty to."

He glared at me. "Carmilla isn't the same as Erendriel. She thinks she's doing what she has to for all of us. I just need to get her to see reaso—"

"Believe me when I say that Carmilla knows exactly what she is doing. Or have you forgotten about the families—with children—still locked in the dungeons of the Sovereign House?" I cut him off. "Samara has already come to harm once because of your inability to see who Carmilla truly is. I know you love her. Do not fuck up again."

His mulish expression morphed into one of uncertainty. "She'll never forgive me," he murmured. "I've tried to explain, but she—"

"Have you tried saying the words, 'I'm sorry?' That's usually a good starting point."

The tug on my chest became more insistent, and I frowned before looking in the direction it was pulling me. Then I exhaled sharply when the tug became a panicked yank and heard Vail do the same.

We looked at each other, then took off at a dead run.

VAIL KEPT pace with me as we raced through the woods towards Samara. The frantic pulling had dimmed, and emotions slid through me that weren't my own. One of them was so strong, it almost took me to my knees.

Grief.

It was still hard to decipher things from the bond, but I was fairly certain Samara was at least physically alright. It wasn't bodily pain I was feeling from her—only emotional.

Something very bad had happened while I'd been fetching Vail. I had no gods to pray to. Instead, I begged the moon that Kieran wasn't the reason Samara was feeling such despair. If my love had suffered because Vail was too fucking stubborn to face what he'd done . . . the Marshal wouldn't have to worry about his conflicting loyalties or emotions anymore. Despite how much I saw myself reflected in Vail's struggles, I'd fucking kill him if anything had happened to Kieran.

The storm was getting worse, and the rain was coming down in sheets now as thunder roared overhead. The thick forest underbrush was getting soggy, and it made running tiring, but on the plus side, most of the beasts that prowled the night had clearly decided to hunker down at this point and wait it out.

Vail's eyes were almost a solid silver—he'd allowed his bloodlust to rise to give him that extra boost of speed. I'd done the same. We were closing in on Samara and the group now, but they'd changed direction slightly. Still heading south but angling west towards House Salvatore.

It was risky to go there to seek shelter—if that's what Samara and the others intended. Dominique was a bit of a wild card. If I were Carmilla, she would have been one of the first Houses I'd use the crown on and force their subservience. Samara was clever, and she knew her aunt better than I did; this must have occurred to her as well, which meant something bad enough had happened to make it worth the risk.

I ran faster.

Almost there. Just a little farther.

The tree line broke, and a flash of lighting revealed a small group of people on the main road to House Salvatore.

"Samara! Kieran!" I called out as I sprinted towards them, only to halt when a half-mad Furie with glowing golden eyes landed in front of me.

"Cali! No!" I heard Samara scream.

The fact that neither I nor Vail drew our weapons was probably the only reason Cali didn't follow through on her attack. Her bright eyes dimmed as she took us in and realized we weren't a threat. There was something still off about her though. I'd met Cali a few times, and she'd always had this swaggering arrogance about her. There was none of that to be seen right now, and it made my panic increase until I saw Kieran shove his way past the Furie, as if that wasn't courting death.

"You're okay," I breathed out as Kieran wrapped his arms around me.

"'Okay' probably isn't the right word, but I'm not seriously injured."

I didn't like the *not seriously* part of that statement, so I pulled back and quickly started scouring him for wounds, tugging at his clothing where it was ripped so I could see the bare skin beneath it.

"Drav," he said softly, pulling my attention away from my manic inspection to his beautiful brown eyes threaded with gold. "I'm fine. I promise."

I let out a shuddered breath and nodded. "I'm not leaving your or Samara's sides until this is over. Not for any reason."

Kieran kissed me and then breathed across my lips, "Good."

"What happene—"

My question was cut off by a rumbling growl and someone crashing into Vail. Two figures rolled across the rain-soaked ground, and I tugged Kieran out of their path as they traded blows.

"Nyx!" Vail grunted. "What the fuck are you doing?"

Nyx? The young ranger who was part of Vail's ranger unit and was friends with Samara? Why were they attacking Vail?

Samara rushed forward but was cut off by Cali, who dove towards the two brawling Moroi and broke them apart. She grabbed Nyx by the throat and held them back when they tried to lunge for Vail again.

I started when I saw Nyx's eyes—they were a solid midnight blue.

Even when I let my bloodlust rise, I still had faint traces of blue in my eyes. Vail's silver eyes had small dark spots of grey, hinting at his tenuous hold on humanity. Samara was the only Moroi I'd ever encountered whose eyes turned the solid color of their bloodlust while remaining herself.

Nyx was clearly not themself; otherwise, they wouldn't have been attacking Vail this way. Between that and their eye color . . . Nyx had turned Strigoi.

"Calm yourself!" Cali commanded and shook Nyx as if they weighed nothing.

I pushed Kieran behind me as I prepared to defend him, but he just threaded his fingers through mine and moved to stand by my side.

"It's not what you think," Samara said as she appeared at my other side, her expression forlorn.

Roth and their family appeared, quietly creating a half circle around Vail and Cali, who were still struggling to keep Nyx under control. They all wore matching expressions of sadness. Alaric stood on the edges of everyone gathered, frowning as if he didn't know what to do. It took me a moment to realize there were two people missing.

"Where are Adrienne and Emil?" It was hard to see more than ten feet in front of me with the rain, but my magic didn't sense any other Moroi in the immediate vicinity.

For a few seconds, it felt like even the storm paused at my question.

Then Nyx let out an anguished scream and renewed their attack on Vail.

"Get him the fuck out of here," Cali grunted as she tried to hold Nyx back. Even with the rain, the scent of Furie blood filled the air as Nyx's claws tore through her skin.

Samara surged forward and grabbed Vail, pulling him away as Cali finally gave up and shot up into the sky with Nyx clamped against her, flying off into the raging storm.

"What's going on?" I asked Kieran.

Mournful eyes looked at me, but before he could answer, Vail released a pained sound.

I looked over my shoulder just in time to see the Marshal of House Harker fall to his knees in front of two bloodied bodies. My magic only sensed the living, and I got nothing from the two broken forms in front of Vail.

Any hopes I'd had that Adrienne and Emil had gone scouting ahead were dashed. I hadn't known them well, but they'd seemed like good people, and they'd come through for Samara when she'd needed them most. For that alone, I would have been loyal to them for the rest of their days.

But it seemed that their days were no more.

"Carmilla found us," Kieran said quietly. "She used the crown on Emil and Nyx. Ordered them to kill Adrienne. She killed Emil . . . but she couldn't bring herself to do the same to Nyx."

My mind flashed back to Selia—the woman who had raised me when my own mother couldn't be bothered. Velika had ordered her to kill me one day, and in less than a second, the person who I knew for a fact had loved me had attempted to rip out my throat. I knew the power of that fucking crown better than anyone.

But if Nyx had turned Strigoi . . . why hadn't the others put them down?

I had my answer a moment later when Cali and Nyx joined us again. The latter still had dark blue eyes, but now there were the faintest lines of bright blue running through them.

They'd come back. Shock rolled through me. I'd never heard of a Strigoi regaining their humanity. There was still something not right about Nyx though. Their movements had a predatory quality to them that was unique to Strigoi. Something about it just set my instincts on edge.

But they made no move to attack anyone and seemed to be in control of themself. I still not so subtly maneuvered myself to stand between them and Kieran. Samara was far enough away that I was confident I could stop Nyx if they tried to attack her.

The young ranger only had eyes for Vail though, who finally seemed to sense their attention. He raised his head in a daze to look at the not-quite Strigoi.

"She did this," Nyx hissed in a low, otherworldly voice. "The woman you so loyally serve. She ordered their deaths." For a split second, the bright blue vanished from their eyes before appearing again. "I still taste Adrienne's blood in my mouth. I don't think I'll ever stop remembering it."

Kieran's fingers tightened around mine, and we all watched as the strong and resilient Marshal of House Harker looked at his two fallen rangers . . . and broke.

CHAPTER SEVENTEEN

—

Samara

"How are we going to handle this?" Alaric's sharp green eyes looked down at the castle from the ridge we'd stopped to rest on. The storm had finally broken, and the rays of the early morning sun were starting to peek through the clouds.

I studied House Salvatore from where I stood next to Alaric. It was a risk to stop here; they were the closest geographically to the Sovereign House. To my knowledge, Carmilla hadn't come here since acquiring the crown, and I hadn't heard of Dominique, the Head of the House, nor her Heir, Aniela, visiting Carmilla. Vail hadn't either.

It seemed odd that Carmilla wouldn't have immediately used the crown to secure her control of House Salvatore, given how close they were.

She didn't need to do anything about House Harker since everyone there would be loyal to her—at least until they learned the truth of what was going on. Some might still follow Carmilla, but I knew many wouldn't be keen on someone manipulating the minds of other Moroi.

For now, House Harker would be low on her list. She already had plans in place for House Laurent and House Corvinus, and I didn't think she'd bother trying to use the crown against House Devereux. If I were her, I'd gain control of the other Houses and then wipe out Devereux—they were too powerful to be left standing.

That left House Salvatore and House Tepes as the wild cards.

Movement to my left drew my attention. Nyx strode towards the ledge, and my heart thudded, as it seemed like they were just going to keep walking. Before I could move, Cali was there. She didn't touch Nyx, but they slowed at her presence, and both came to a stop an inch from the edge.

Nyx hadn't spoken for hours. Not since their outburst at Vail, who had

674

also been quiet after that. I fought the urge to turn and look at the two freshly dug graves behind us. There wasn't time to bring Adrienne and Emil back to House Harker, so we'd chosen this spot for their final resting place. Draven had used his magic to dig deep into the earth, to ensure no beasts would disturb them, and then coaxed some roots to stretch over the tops of their graves for good measure.

Absently, I rubbed my chest, just over my heart. I grieved the loss of the rangers, but it was nothing to what Vail was feeling right now. His grief was like a poker that had been thrust into flames. I could feel the rage beginning to burn, growing hotter by the hour.

We needed to determine if House Salvatore was compromised and warn them of Carmilla if they weren't, but Nyx couldn't set foot inside that castle. We knew they weren't Strigoi—not completely anyway—but they'd slipped more than once on the way here and tried to attack Vail. If the Salvatore rangers saw Nyx lose it like that, they'd kill the ranger.

Strigoi were always put down.

I didn't know what was going on with Nyx, but I wasn't going to give up on them.

"Celestina," I addressed Roth's mother, who was standing not far behind Nyx and Cali. "Would you and your family be willing to escort Nyx back to your House? And keep them . . . comfortable?" *Don't kill them or allow them to harm others.*

"Of course." She hesitated before looking at Roth as they moved to stand next to me.

"I'm staying with Samara," Roth declared.

"Maybe it would be better if you—" I started, only to have my words cut off as one of Roth's ropes wound around my lower face, covering my mouth.

"Babe, it's in your best interest that you don't finish that sentence." Roth glared at me. "I'm staying."

I nodded in reluctant acceptance. Part of me was happy they were staying, but another part wished Roth were going back to House Devereux, where they'd be surrounded by thick walls and quite possibly the most homicidal bloodline of all the Moroi.

"Take care of our favorite sib," Desmond rumbled as he gave me and then Kieran, Alaric, and Draven a pointed look.

"There will be consequences if you don't," Taivan added. Then the two enormous Moroi swept Roth up into a hug, which resulted in some very creative curses being thrown about before they moved off to wait by the tree line.

Roth shuffled on their feet as Celestina and Severen approached.

"I know we messed up when you were younger," Celestina said softly. "We never meant to make you feel unwanted or like you were less than because you're not interested in the warrior path."

"We thought giving you space was what you wanted." Severen reached out slowly, giving Roth time to pull back, but when they didn't, he laid a hand on their shoulder. "Then we let ourselves get caught up in training your brothers and the rest of the rangers. You seemed happy enough to spend time with Thessalia that we just . . . left you alone."

"But we have always loved you, child." Celestina rested her hand on Roth's other shoulder. "And we're so fucking proud of who you grew up to be."

Roth's eyes got a little glossy. "I love you." Then they glanced at their brothers. "And those big idiots too."

Celestina and Severen smiled at their youngest child, and despite everything that had happened last night and the grief I was feeling, my heart felt a little lighter at seeing Roth and their family repairing what had been broken.

I stepped around Roth to give them another minute with their parents and walked over to Nyx. They were looking over the ridge and didn't acknowledge my presence. Cali and I traded a look.

"Nyx," I said carefully. "You're going to go with the Devereuxes, okay?"

The ranger turned their head to look at me. There was something unnerving about the way they moved now. The Nyx I'd always known had moved with this lightness, like despite all the fucked-up shit in the world, they'd never let it truly get to them. Nyx had been quick to smile and easy to befriend.

Now, the easygoing ranger was nowhere in sight. Even in control of their bloodlust, Nyx moved like a Strigoi. Cold and predatory.

"I'm one of the monsters now." A chilling, dark laugh spilt from their lips. "Shouldn't you just kill me?"

Something deep inside me cracked at the hollowness of their words.

Fuck. This.

My hand snapped out, and I wrapped it around Nyx's neck, letting my nails shift to claws that tore into their skin. They didn't even try to stop me. Just looked at me with dark eyes that *welcomed* death.

I let my own bloodlust rise until I knew my eyes were just as dark as theirs.

"We all have monsters crawling beneath our skin—yours is just no longer hidden." My fingers tightened, and more blood dripped down their neck. "You are my *friend*, Nyx, and I won't let you go."

A small amount of light blue bled back into their eyes like glowing rivers in the dark. "Promise me you'll make her pay."

"I promise," I swore and released my hold on their neck. "Stay alive, Nyx."

They held my gaze for a long moment before giving me a deep nod. Then those new strange eyes of theirs flicked to Cali, who just arched a brow at them.

"A little insanity is good for the soul, my pretty fanged friend."

Nyx's eyes darkened in a way that I didn't think was remotely connected to their new not-quite-Strigoi status, and a familiar, lazy smile stretched across their lips. For a second, it was almost like I was looking at my old friend before Carmilla had broken them. "See you around, my beautiful winged friend."

Cali blinked as Nyx moved like a shadow, sliding between us and striding towards where Roth's family was waiting for them. Nyx nodded in farewell towards Alaric, Kieran, and Draven but didn't spare Vail a single glance.

I rejoined the others, Vail moving a little closer, and Cali followed me. "Alright, let's go see what we're dealing with. Carmilla might be licking her wounds after Cali's dramatic appearance"—the Furie snorted at my words—"but I have no doubt she's already plotting. We shouldn't plan on staying here too long one way or another."

If House Salvatore was compromised, we might have to fight our way out, and even if they weren't, I didn't want to stay so close to the Sovereign House.

"Long enough to get cleaned up though, right?" Kieran frowned down at his tunic, which had once been a light cream but was now stained with blood, mud, and gods knew what else. "And maybe something to eat?"

"I'd also like to snag a whip from their armory," Draven chimed in. "I'm feeling a little inadequate without it, especially since Roth has those fancy ropes and you have your clever knives." He looked jealously at the daggers strapped to my thighs that I'd imbued with blood magic.

"Sure," I drawled. "Anyone else have any requests?"

"I want to check out their library." Roth's eyes lit up. "Might need help stealing some shit."

We all chuckled. It felt weird to be joking around, given . . . everything, but I thought we all recognized that we needed some sort of lightness right now. Only Vail didn't join in.

"I'll wait outside the walls. My presence will set them on edge. If I don't receive an all-clear signal from you within one hour, then I'm walking through that front gate. They're welcome to try to stop me." Cali wrapped her dark wings around her shoulders like a cloak, pulled the hood of her cowl up, hiding her distinctive red hair, and started down the path that led to House Salvatore.

Unease rippled through me. Cali had a massive overprotective streak when it came to me and Rynn. She wasn't wrong that her being with us would draw attention, but I was an *Heir*. Only Aniela or Dominique could deny our entry, and they would have to come out and do it in person.

I watched my friend disappear down the trail. Something told me Cali didn't want to go in there because she didn't trust her control. It felt like someone had wrapped a cold hand around my heart and squeezed. For as long as I could remember, people had been terrified of Cali.

I had never been scared of Calypso Rayne—the most powerful Furie to ever exist—but I was sure as shit scared *for* her.

Kill Carmilla. Stabilize the Moroi Houses. Do . . . something about the wraiths. Try to mend things between the Moroi and Velesians. Figure out what the fuck was going on with Cali.

Gods, I would give Vail's right hand right now just to have an easy-to-fix problem so I could get that little thrill at actually solving something.

I thought about our night in the cave that felt like ages ago but had only been a couple of weeks. Maybe his left hand. If I ever decided to forgive him one day, that right hand was *talented*.

A laugh bubbled up my throat and got stuck. Was this what it was like to lose your mind? Because I was drained in every sense of the word. Emotionally. Mentally. Physically.

The world could get fucked.

Suddenly, I felt the weight of several gazes on me, and I briefly wondered if my manic laugh had actually made it past my lips. Then I realized that everyone except Vail had started to follow Cali but stopped when they realized I wasn't moving.

Because I was having a minor mental breakdown. No big deal.

I caught Draven's attention, knowing Kieran and Alaric would be stubborn about this, and briefly slid my gaze to Vail before giving Draven a heavy look. He pursed his lips but jerked his head in a nod, then proceeded to pull Alaric and Kieran away, but not before they both leveled a death glare at Vail.

The Marshal failed to notice. He just stared down at House Salvatore with a distant look in his eyes.

I stood next to him in weighted silence. I was far from forgiving Vail for what he'd done, but I no longer had any doubts about his loyalty. Carmilla had severely miscalculated by targeting the rangers. Maybe she hadn't realized that, despite Vail helping us escape, he hadn't completely turned against her. He would never side with her now. The rangers—especially those rangers—were Vail's family.

"She dies." He finally turned away from the horizon to look at me with eyes of silver fire. "There will be no deal. No life of imprisonment when this is all done. Carmilla fucking dies."

The fury that had been slowly building in Vail ignited into a bonfire that swallowed his grief and forged it into something new.

I let him see the rage I was feeling before I allowed myself to look at the graves of our fallen friends. Carmilla was someone I'd looked up to for most of my life. In many ways, she was the reason I was who I was. Not to mention that she was my last living blood relative . . . which was her doing, since she'd done nothing when my parents had been murdered. It didn't matter that she hadn't been the one to order their deaths. She could have stopped them.

Nobody had forced Carmilla on this path. She'd chosen to be the villain and played us all for fools.

I turned away from the graves to look at Vail. "Painfully. She dies painfully."

———

The mood inside House Salvatore was tense. I suspected if I were anyone other than an Heir, the guards at the front gate would have turned us away. As it was, they had granted us entry, and we'd been quickly ushered into a guest wing.

Half a dozen rangers stood outside our door, and the message was very clear that we were to wait. I assumed for Dominique or Aniela, but the rangers weren't exactly forthcoming with information.

It didn't feel like a trap though, because the air reeked of fear and uncertainty.

The room we were in did have a bathing chamber, so we all took turns cleaning ourselves up as best we could; although, without fresh clothes to change into, there wasn't much we could do.

"We'll give it another ten minutes," I said quietly. The rangers would no doubt hear anything we said, so we were all being careful with our words. "Then I'll insist on seeing Aniela or Dominique."

Everyone nodded while Roth went back to frowning at the small collection of books in the room, as if they were personally offended at the meager offerings. Kieran was cuddled up on the small settee with Draven, his head resting on the prince's shoulder. I hadn't gotten a chance to speak with him alone since our encounters with Demetri and Carmilla. Demetri's words about him being a courtier had no doubt struck at an old wound. I scowled, wishing I could kill my ex-husband all over again.

I caught Draven's eye, and something passed between us, then he gave me a tight smile before kissing the top of Kieran's head. A soothing sensation passed down the bond, and I assumed it was from him because Vail was currently pacing the room like a trapped animal.

Definitely not soothing.

Alaric walked out of the washroom, and for a solid ten seconds, I stopped thinking about all the ways we were fucked.

He carried a damp shirt, leaving his carved chest and abs on display. Like Kieran, Alaric was built on the leaner side. Unlike his best friend though, Alaric spent a lot of time running and rock climbing—something I'd only recently learned about him.

"You're drooling," he said dryly as he closed the distance between us, the corners of his lips curling up into the smallest of smiles. "And you missed a spot."

He used his thumb to brush at my jawline. I closed my eyes and enjoyed his touch. It still didn't feel real that Alaric Lockwood was being affectionate with me.

"I could really go for some hot springs right now," I mused.

Alaric's thumb went still, and I cracked my eyes open to find him looking at me with such wanton desire that my heart started beating faster.

A soft laugh came from the couch as Kieran stirred in Draven's arms. "I think Alaric would go for the dessert this time."

Roth snorted, which made me suspect Kieran had told them about the time Alaric had walked in on the two of us getting hot and heavy and Kieran had asked Alaric if he was there for "dessert."

"I do love how sweet you taste," Alaric said, never taking his eyes off me as his thumb started stroking my jawline again.

A spear of jealousy slammed into me, and I inhaled sharply before glancing at Vail, who was still pacing the room—now with clenched fists.

Despite how frayed our bond was, his emotions were practically screaming down it.

I opened my mouth to say something to hopefully calm him down a bit just so I could think without getting bombarded by his feelings, when I heard the faint sounds of footsteps from the hall outside our room. Kieran and Draven detangled and smoothly got to their feet. I pushed feelings of gratitude down the bond as Draven nudged Kieran behind himself. It seemed unlikely that we'd be attacked now, given that they'd shown us to a guest room and not a dungeon, but after the past week, I wasn't sure anything would surprise me anymore.

Vail stalked over to stand by my side, something that earned him a warning look from Draven that I also felt echoed down the bond. Argh. It was really confusing to feel emotions that weren't mine. Hopefully I'd get used to it over time.

I glanced at Alaric—who'd thankfully put his shirt back on, because if anyone else drooled over him I'd carve their eyes out—and jerked my head towards Roth. He pursed his lips but did as I requested and went to join them.

If Salvatore did decide to attack us, we were spread out across the room and would force them to divide their attention.

The door slammed open, and a beautiful, very pissed-off redhead stormed into the room. Usually the Salvatore Heir exuded a sultry energy while she glided through life. It was often easy to forget that Aniela was a ruthless predator while she batted her long, dark eyelashes.

That was not the case now.

"What the fuck is going on, Samara?" She crashed to a halt in front of me, green eyes flashing in warning. Only two rangers followed her into the room, but given the reputation of the twin sisters, that was all the backup Aniela needed.

Petra and Brennan bared their teeth while burnt umber eyes shone brightly against their rich brown skin. The dual Marshals of House Salvatore.

"You tell me, Aniela," I responded coolly while I arched an eyebrow. "Things seem a little tense around here, and shoving the Heir of another House into a room like this and locking the door isn't exactly good manners."

Cunning eyes searched mine, and I responded in kind. If Aniela had been mind-fucked by Carmilla, I would think she would act like her normal self-assured self and try to keep us placated while she informed my aunt that we were here.

Granted, she could have sent a striker with a message while we'd been sequestered and was now putting on a show to see how we would react, but I didn't think that was the case. Behind the anger brimming in her eyes was something else. Fear.

Something had happened that had put the usually unshakeable Heir on alert.

"Answer the fucking question," Aniela growled. Thin lines of a green so light, it was practically white wove their way through her green eyes. *Interesting.* I could count on one hand the number of times I'd seen Aniela let her bloodlust rise.

Aniela liked to be underestimated, relying on that pretty face to distract the foolish while she angled a dagger at their backs.

The question was . . . was this just another act? Was there a knife at my back?

"I'll tell you," I said slowly, "but first . . . where is Dominique?"

I had a split second to see Aniela's eyes turn almost a solid white before she threw herself at me. My back crashed against the low table in front of the settee, and I let out a harsh grunt as something sharp jammed its way between my ribs.

The sounds of fighting filled the room, but I was a bit preoccupied with keeping Aniela from stabbing me again. I wrapped one hand around her throat, and the other clung to her wrist when she tried to pull the dagger free.

"You did this!" She let out a strangled hiss as she tried to get my hand off her neck. The blade in my side wasn't great, but we both knew I'd recover from that. She wouldn't recover if I tore her throat out, which was why her claws were digging into my wrist.

"Not. Your. Enemy," I ground out.

"Liar!" she growled and twisted the knife.

I gasped as pain laced up my side. Fuck this. I shoved my hips up to unbalance her, earning myself another flash of pain just as I yanked her down by the throat.

Aniela didn't let go of my wrist, so her entire body dipped forward as I leaned up to slam my forehead into her nose.

Blood erupted as Aniela shrieked and her grip on my wrist slipped before I shoved her off me. A fresh wave of pain tore through me as she pulled the knife with her, but I didn't let it slow me down as I lunged forward and hammered another punch to her face.

"Aniela!" one of the Marshals screamed. I rarely heard them speak, so I couldn't tell them apart by voice.

Everyone in the room seemed to freeze, the sounds of fighting abruptly stopping, but I kept my attention on Aniela, trusting Alaric to keep Roth safe and Kieran, Draven . . . and Vail to keep the others off my back.

The Salvatore Heir panted beneath me, her nearly white eyes feral with rage. I held one of my blood daggers at her throat while my other hand caught her wrist before she could raise her own dagger in defense.

"Do it," she spat. "I don't know what you did to my cousin, but I sure as fuck won't be your lapdog. So fucking kill me already."

I narrowed my eyes. "Dominique is with Carmilla, isn't she?"

Aniela went still, and I knew I had guessed right. That alone wouldn't have set her off like this though. I quickly thought through several possibilities, not letting go of Aniela's wrist or decreasing the pressure of my blade against her skin.

"Let me guess." I held Aniela's gaze. "Dominique did something completely out of character. Maybe issued an order that you know she would never give and one that you don't want to follow?"

"Won't," Aniela whispered. "*Won't* follow."

Slowly, I pulled the dagger away from Aniela's throat. I didn't release my hold on her wrist until I rolled back onto the balls of my feet, then I smoothly rose and took a couple of steps back. A quick glance around the room showed everyone a little bloody, but there didn't appear to be any major injuries.

Petra and Brennan sported bloody lips. They looked damn near identical, but Petra's eyes were a touch darker, which was how I knew it was her giving Vail a look that promised death.

He smiled at her in return.

More rangers had poured into the room while I'd been fighting Aniela. To my annoyance, Alaric and Roth were standing next to Kieran and Draven; the four of them had held off the flood of newcomers. I sent Alaric a cool look for failing to keep Roth out of the fighting, only to yelp when one of Roth's ropes snapped against my ass.

Hard.

Roth arched an eyebrow at me while I rubbed my soft flesh, trying to ease the sting. They smirked at me as the thin ropes slipped through the air to wind back around their forearms.

I slid the dagger back into the sheath on my thigh and gave a pointed look at the others. Kieran and Draven immediately put their weapons away, but

Alaric hesitated for a second before doing the same. Silver eyes glared at me for a long moment before Vail resheathed his sword and threw a dagger back to Petra . . . a little harder than necessary.

Oh, no wonder she was so pissed. Vail had managed to at least partially disarm her.

"So," I drawled as Aniela rose to her feet, "how about we try this again? Maybe start with talking? We can always stab each other later."

CHAPTER EIGHTEEN

—

Samara

THE RANGERS who had burst into the room filed out at some silent command from Aniela. I settled onto the largest of the settees that almost resembled a crescent moon. Kieran sat to my left with Draven on his other side. Alaric narrowly beat Roth to sit next to me and earned himself a sour look that he didn't seem the least bit concerned about.

That left Vail standing awkwardly by himself, since Aniela and her two Marshals had claimed the other settee.

"Vail, would you mind letting *our friend* know that we're alright for now." I gave him a pointed look. Cali might have been acting strange, but I had no doubt that she would keep her word and absolutely slaughter her way through House Salvatore if we didn't let her know we were okay, and it was getting really close to her one-hour mark.

"Brennan, go with him," Aniela ordered. "Just let Cali in."

I arched an eyebrow at the Salvatore Heir, and she rolled her eyes. "You wouldn't be worried about a single Moroi breaking into our keep, and it is well-known that you, Cali, and Rynn are a bit of a package deal."

Something bothered me about that statement, even as I made a noise of agreement. How was she so sure it wasn't Rynn? Sure, Cali was scarier, but as Aniela had said, Rynn was also a known friend of mine, and Velesians were tricky.

Vail started to stiffly walk towards the door behind where I was seated, and I reached up to grab his arm. He halted as my fingers closed around his forearm, dark grey eyes meeting mine as I felt his fingers graze my arm almost tentatively.

I didn't know exactly where I stood with Aniela. I was fairly certain she wasn't under Carmilla's control, but that didn't mean we were on the same side, which meant I had to be careful about the information I offered up.

"Go." I held Vail's unflinching stare. "Come back quickly."

Strong, thick fingers tightened around my forearm as he bent down to whisper in my ear, "I'll set whatever pace I damn well feel like, Heir."

It was like a dozen emotions collided inside me. Lust. Amusement. Rage. Somehow, I managed to keep all of that off my face as I gave him a brief nod and released my grip.

Vail's fingers lingered for another second before they dropped away and he strode towards the door. He didn't look back as he left.

Once again, I found myself confused as fuck about Vail Ferenc.

Argh.

"Tell us where your cousin is, Aniela, and why you reacted to our presence the way you did." I returned my attention to the Salvatore Heir and shoved my confused feelings about Vail aside. "And I'll tell you what we know."

Aniela looked at me for a long moment, and I got the impression she was searching for something in my expression. She didn't find it.

"Two days ago, Dominique was summoned to the Sovereign House by Carmilla." Her mouth tightened before she threw the towel she'd been using to clean the blood off herself onto the floor. If she wanted me to feel bad about that, she'd have to try harder. My side had mostly healed, but it still smarted from where she'd freaking stabbed me. "It's a short flight for our strikers from here to there. Before the sun set that day, we received a message from my cousin."

Petra held a folded letter out to us, and I reached for it, but Alaric grabbed it first. Roth read it over his shoulder, and both of their expressions grew grimmer by the second.

"Dominique has ordered the majority of the Salvatore rangers to set up a perimeter around the edges of House Devereux territory." Alaric raised a brow. "We've also all been declared traitors, and House Salvatore is under orders to capture most of us alive if they see us."

"*Most?*" I eyed Aniela while my hand slid towards the dagger on my right thigh.

Petra started to go for her weapon but stopped when Aniela held up a hand. "How did she sign the letter, Alaric?" she asked, not taking her eyes off me.

"She just put her name," Alaric said. "Dominique."

A smile that didn't reach her eyes touched Aniela's heart-shaped mouth. "My cousin might be Dominique to everyone else, but to family, she's always been Mika."

"She's fighting it," Draven mused.

I leaned forward and twisted slightly to look around Kieran so I could see

Draven better, letting my hand drop away from the dagger on my thigh. "Even with the power boost of the crown being united, it's still not enough to fully control those of House bloodlines." My brows furrowed together. "It's not happy about how it's being used, so maybe it's also leaving loopholes in the minds of those it's wielded against—and Dominique seized it."

"So it's true then." Aniela traded a weighted look with Petra. "Velika had a way to control our minds, and now Carmilla has it."

"You knew about the crown?" I went still as surprise flickered through me. Up until recently, I'd never suspected such a thing existed, let alone that Velika had been wielding it.

"Why do you think we stayed to ourselves so much?" Aniela said dryly. "It was impossible to know who we could trust. Everyone thought it was because Dominique was young and inexperienced—we leaned into that, even if it did make our House appear weaker."

"How?" Roth narrowed their eyes at Aniela. "How did you find out about the crown?"

"We didn't actually know it was a crown," Aniela admitted. "There were little things that alerted Dominique's parents to something not quite right. Sometimes, their minds would feel . . . tired after visiting with Queen Velika. And there were other things—advisors and courtiers visiting the Sovereign House and coming back slightly different. Not like major personality changes, but saying things that were out of character."

"The soul crown is a Fae artifact," I explained. "Velika only had half of it. She was able to bind souls to obey her, but the effects were temporary. My aunt has both pieces. It's considerably more powerful now. House bloodlines still have some protection against it—but clearly, they're not immune, given that Dominique has been compromised."

"You said *they*." Aniela narrowed her eyes. "Are you not including yourself in the House bloodlines?"

I pursed my lips as I thought about what to say. We needed allies to defeat Carmilla, and the more information they had, the better prepared they would be. But I was still coming to terms with the fact that I was half Fae . . . and that the crown was my birthright.

Everything was far more broken between the Houses than I had thought. They wouldn't be happy to learn that the crown that could steal their will and control their minds wanted to be united with me. I had no intention of ruling over everyone, but they would never believe that—I certainly wouldn't trust any of them with that kind of power.

"Your father had Fae blood, didn't he?" Petra's sharp eyes studied my face.

I barely managed to stifle the startled motion at the question. It felt like my heartbeat plunged for a few seconds before beating rapidly.

Petra and her twin sister were the same generation as me but older by several decades. They'd served Dominique's parents before they'd been killed.

Oh, shit. Did Dominique know her father hadn't been killed in that attack? That he'd actually been taken prisoner and Velika had experimented on him with the crown? That she'd been trying to figure out how to use it on House bloodlines?

According to Draven, she'd never truly been successful, but she had broken him down enough that he'd turned Strigoi and had been well and truly mad by that point.

Draven had killed him as a mercy.

I decided to not volunteer that information for now. Nothing could change the past, and it was irrelevant to our current situation. Still, I'd have to monitor for any signs that they knew and make sure Draven hadn't been responsible for the former Salvatore Head's imprisonment and torture.

It would be unfortunate to have to kill Dominique and Aniela—and probably their Marshals—over a pointless attempt at vengeance, but I'd do it. Nobody fucked with what was mine.

And Draven was absolutely *mine*.

I tucked away that thought as something to deal with later—or maybe I'd just take the truth of what happened to the grave—and pondered how to answer the question of my lineage. Maybe it was time for the truth, even if that was an odd sentiment in our culture. If the Moroi Houses were going to survive long-term, we'd need to start trusting each other a little more. With some things anyway.

"My father was half Fae." I left out the royalty part because I wasn't ready to share that just yet; plus, I wanted to have more information. All I had was the claim of a sentient crown. "I only learned this recently." I narrowed my gaze at Petra. "What made you suspect he had Fae blood?"

The corners of her lips tilted up ever so slightly. It was the closest I'd ever seen her come to a true smile and not just a baring of teeth.

"He saved me once. I was traveling alone and had been injured thanks to a run-in with a large howler pack. My blood drew the attention of some kusu, and I thought I was done for." She grimaced. "Damn near lost my leg when one of them got me with their pincers. Before they could finish me off, roots shot out of the ground and tore the kusu apart."

Note to self, definitely prioritize learning magic. I loved my blood daggers, but being able to summon roots out of the ground to, at the very least, hold monsters at bay would come in handy.

"You never told me that." Aniela looked at her Marshal. There wasn't anger or reprisal in her eyes—she looked more curious than anything.

Petra's shoulders rose in what I was pretty sure was the smallest shrug I'd ever seen. "When I asked him about it, he said I was delirious and seeing things." A faint smile stretched across her lips for a second. "I was bleeding heavily from head trauma, and my right leg had been holding on by a few shredded tendons, so I wasn't in any shape to argue, and I never mentioned it because I had no proof. Plus, he saved my life that day, and it seemed in poor form to go spreading rumors about him."

"Fair." Aniela nodded and turned her attention back to me. "So you also have Fae blood, and you think this protects you from the effects of the crown?"

"It is my father's bloodline that protects me, yes," I answered. It was the truth—in a sleight of hand kind of way. It wasn't just that my father was Fae; it was that he belonged to the Seelie royal bloodline that was responsible for the creation of the crown in the first place.

At least according to the smart-ass Fae artifact. The wraith I'd spoken with seemed to back that up. Still . . . it'd be nice to get my hands on some unbiased information to shed light on all of this.

Aniela glanced at the door before her eyes flicked back to me. "How do we break the control Carmilla has over Dominique?"

"It's hard to say," Draven answered. "My mother only had one half of the crown. Typically, she had to renew her hold on someone at least once a month, sometimes sooner if they were particularly strong of will. With both halves of the crown united, I imagine it will last longer."

"We could ask it . . . the crown, I mean," I said in an even tone, like it wasn't crazy to suggest talking to an inanimate object.

"Come again?" Aniela arched an eyebrow.

"Phrasing," Kieran muttered under his breath, earning himself a glare from Alaric.

"The crown is sentient," I explained. "It spoke in my mind while I was being held captive at the Sovereign House."

"You're saying the Fae created a crown capable of stealing someone's will . . . and gave it a mind of its own?" Aniela stared at me wide-eyed. "Are you fucking shitting me right now? How is that even possible?"

"Like with most things that involve the Fae"—I rubbed my forehead—"I have no idea, but it definitely talked to me, and it has quite the personality."

Again, Aniela looked towards the door. This time, I noticed the tension in her shoulders. Was she expecting someone else? Or was she worried about Cali getting here? If it was the latter . . . why?

"Something on your mind, Aniela?" I watched her carefully as she swallowed and met my gaze again.

"I don't know who to trust, Samara," she admitted. "I've always liked you, even when Dominique threw you in with Carmilla—who she was always suspicious of because of your aunt's friendship with Queen Velika—but Ary trusts you."

A hint of softness entered her eyes. There was something between Aniela and Ary—the Heir of House Tepes. He was definitely carrying a torch for her, and up until this moment, I hadn't been sure she'd felt the same.

I didn't say anything, and the others followed my lead. Aniela was hiding something, and whatever it was, she feared Cali learning about it.

The moment of vulnerability in Aniela's expression left and was replaced by grim determination. Then she squared her shoulders as she sat straighter and raised her chin while holding my gaze.

"Rynn is locked up in our dungeon."

Well, fuck.

"We haven't harmed her," Aniela rushed on before wincing. "But she was quite injured when the rangers found her two days ago. She kept attacking us when we tried to see to her wounds, so we put her in a cell as much for our safety as hers. Hostilities seem to be rising against the Velesians. I thought it best to keep her out of sight."

"Two days ago," I murmured and then asked sharply, "Does Dominique know she's here?"

If she did, it seemed likely that Carmilla knew as well, and my aunt would absolutely try to capture Rynn as a way to control me. There was nothing I wouldn't do for Rynn and Cali.

"No," Aniela said softly. "The rangers found her in the badlands. She didn't arrive here until after I got that message from Mika. I haven't sent a response back yet."

"Okay." I nodded and rose to my feet. "Aniela, come with me to fetch Rynn. Everyone else, stay here and keep Cali distracted when she arrives."

"Absolutely not," Petra and Alaric said at the same time before glowering at each other.

"Perhaps one of us should go with you," Kieran suggested.

I shook my head. "Cali is . . . testy right now. It'll make me feel better knowing you're all here to help keep her calm. Besides, Aniela picked a fight with me once and lost—badly."

"You kicked me right in the cunt." Aniela glared at me before rising from the settee.

I rolled my eyes. "You punched my tit. Twice."

"What type of fight was this exactly?" Both of Kieran's brows rose.

"A drunk one," Aniela and I said at once.

"Why don't I go get Rynn," Alaric volunteered.

"No." I made a halting motion when Alaric started to stand. "I haven't spoken to Rynn since we separated at Lake Malov. I need to make sure she doesn't lose her shit when she sees Vail—and more importantly, that she doesn't tell Cali."

"What exactly did Vail do?" Aniela arched a dark red brow at me.

"It doesn't matter," I said tightly, not wanting to go into detail about Vail's betrayal and then have to explain why the fuck he wasn't dead in a ditch somewhere, or at least locked up in a cell. I realized I was absently rubbing my chest just over my heart and dropped my hand.

"Funny," Aniela drawled. "It *sounds* like it matters."

I gave her an obscene gesture that had her barking out a laugh.

"I'll be fine," I promised, making eye contact with Kieran, Draven, and Roth before lingering on Alaric, who was clenching his jaw so hard, I was worried he'd crack a tooth. I bent down and kissed him with the intention of it being a quick, reassuring type of thing, but when he wrapped his hand in my hair and pulled me close, I lost myself until someone cleared their throat.

"Cali's gonna be here any minute." Roth gave me an amused grin. "You can make out with grumpy-pants later." Then they shoved Alaric's face away so they could lean forward and kiss me. This time, it was a quick one because they pulled back and pointedly looked at the door.

"So you've got the wicked prince, the heartthrob courtier, the gorgeous advisor, and the cunning scholar . . ." Aniela asked as we walked to the door. "Bit greedy, aren't you?"

I snorted. "Jealous?"

"Little bit, yeah."

"Uh, how exactly are we supposed to keep Cali occupied, Sam?" Kieran asked just as Aniela and I started to leave.

"I'm sure you'll think of something, Kier," I said confidently. If anyone excelled at small talk, it was Kieran. "But feel free to tell her about Dominique. We won't be long." I glanced at Aniela. "Right?"

I didn't know exactly where the dungeon was in House Salvatore, but if it was like House Harker and the Sovereign House, the entrance would be towards the center of the first floor, which we were on.

"Fifteen minutes at most."

"When we're back, we'll plan our next move—with Rynn."

On that final note, Aniela and I started at a quick pace down the hallway. I still couldn't believe Rynn was *here*. She must have had some reason for leaving the Velesian realm. I sighed. Or not.

Most of the time, Rynn was the most levelheaded of the three of us. Cali and I both had tempers that sometimes got the better of us, but Rynn did have a habit of being reckless when she got frustrated—of not taking into account the bigger picture.

So would she have decided to run away from the Alpha Pack on a whim because of some comment they made that she took great offense to? Yes. Was

Rynn capable of avoiding a realm's worth of Velesians and sneaking into Moroi territory? Also yes.

My friend was a sneaky bitch, and usually I adored that about her, but it felt like we were on a collision course with all-out war between the Moroi and Velesians. So Rynn choosing this moment to hold up her middle finger to the Alpha Pack and seek sanctuary with us wasn't ideal.

That said, if Rynn didn't want to go back to the Alpha Pricks, then they could kiss my luscious ass. She'd been mine first.

The Alpha Pack was a secondary problem though, because if Cali learned that Aniela had locked an injured Rynn in the basement . . . things would get bloody real fast. Cali was overprotective of both of us, but normally, she just glowered threateningly, and that was enough. Something was clearly going on with her though. I had little doubt that she would respond with violence at seeing Rynn imprisoned, and we couldn't afford to have our potential allies killed.

Plus, I liked Aniela and looked forward to teasing her mercilessly about Ary when we weren't dealing with a mad, egomaniac queen, conniving and murderous wraiths, and an impending war with the Velesians.

"I need to go on a holiday," I muttered.

"What's that?" Aniela gave me a side-eyed look as we turned a corner and headed down another hallway towards a door guarded by four guards.

"A holiday," I repeated. "It's something I came across in some Fae writings. Basically, it's like a trip you take, but for fun."

"Where in all the hells did they go in Lunaria for fun?" Aniela scoffed. "The beautiful beaches with tentacled monsters hiding just beneath the surface? Or maybe the badlands with its oppressive heat and enormous spiders that hide beneath the ground to jump out and grab you? Oh! I know!" She waved a hand at the guards, and they obediently opened the door at our approach, giving me a curious look but nothing more as we walked past them. "The lovely northern forests! Where moon devils fuck with your head and send you running into huge carnivorous flowers that will spend days sucking you dry before spitting out your dried corpse."

"Actually, I think they went somewhere else."

Aniela stopped on the narrow stairwell, and I did the same. We both stared at each other for a long moment before we burst out laughing.

"Everything is so fucked!" she sputtered between laughs. "Lunaria is the absolute worst!"

"It truly is." I wiped the tears away from my eyes. "Maybe someday, we'll find out what the Fae did to find themselves here."

"Come on." Aniela started down the stairs again. "She's just one level down."

I followed after her, still laughing under my breath. This place truly was fucked, and it only seemed to get worse as the years dragged on. Clearly, something in the spell our human ancestors had cast to turn themselves into monsters had also ingrained a dark sense of humor in all of us.

Good call on their part. We all would have gone insane ages ago if we couldn't look at the dark, cruel world around us and laugh in its face.

Two more guards waited outside the door on the next floor. Aniela had put way more security on Rynn than Carmilla had on me, which made me wonder if my aunt had underestimated my ability to escape . . . or if she'd needed those rangers somewhere else.

"Aniela." The tall, blond guard on the right nodded deeply towards the Heir he served before giving me a shallow nod. "Harker."

Grief slammed into me hard and fast. His hair was the same golden blonde shade as Adrienne's. They weren't related—Adrienne hadn't had any surviving family—and he looked nothing like her in any other aspect, but my grief for her and Emil was still an open wound. One that I'd hastily slapped a bandage on in the name of survival, but it'd just slipped, leaving my wound bloody and raw.

"Samara?" Aniela gave me a puzzled look, her hand braced on the door she'd just started to open.

I slammed the wrapping back on the wound made of grief and rage and gave her a tight smile. "Let's grab Rynn and get back before Cali loses her shit."

"Calypso Rayne is here?" The ginger-haired guard traded glances with the blond one. "Inside our walls?"

"You Moroi are such pussies," a gravelly voice called out from behind the door. "Now let my friend through before she punches you both in the dick. It's her favorite move."

Both guards looked at me.

"She's not wrong." I shrugged.

To their credit, neither backed away, although they weren't really blocking me anyway. More or less, they were crowding my space and forcing me to walk between them, which I did—before I tapped them both on the dick faster than they could block me.

Both flinched and cursed under their breath as I sauntered into the room where my lycanthrope bestie was confined.

"Well," I drawled, "this is considerably better than where Carmilla had me locked up." Half of the room was walled off with thick bars, but that portion had a rather soft-looking bed, a comfy chair, a bookcase, and I was guessing there was a small washroom behind the curtain.

I could smell Rynn's blood, mostly old and dry, in the air. She must have been seriously wounded if she'd still been bleeding when she'd arrived here.

"About fucking time." Rynn smoothly leapt to her feet from where she'd been lying on the bed. Her usually tanned skin was pale, and there were dark circles under her mismatched eyes, but otherwise, she appeared okay.

She strode out the cell door that Aniela had opened with a languid grace and stopped in front of me, hands braced on her hips. One eye was a bright golden brown and the other a deep vivid blue.

Earth and sky. That's what they always reminded me of.

"You look like shit." She arched a brow at me.

"Not all of us have been living that pampered life . . ." I remembered the nickname the Alpha Pack had given her that drove her insane. *"Princess."*

Her nostrils flared. "Sure you want to play that game?" A sly grin spilt across her lips. "Your *Majesty?*"

CHAPTER NINETEEN

—

Kieran

"Why don't you get freshened up while we wait for Samara to return?" I gestured towards the small washroom and gave Cali a bright, charming smile. It was the one I used when high-ranking Moroi started arguments during House events and I needed to de-escalate the situation. Not flirty exactly, but confident with just a hint of mischievousness.

I'd practiced the smile a lot, and it had never let me down. Samara, Alaric, and even Roth might be great at keeping track of facts and the specifics of a trade negotiation, but nobody was better at reading people and manipulating their emotions than I.

"I'm not some simpering fool courting House favor, Kieran," Cali sneered. "So you can wipe that stupid smile off your ugly face."

Apparently, Cali was immune to my charm.

"Rude." I glared at her. "My face is *stunning*."

"Yes, it is," Draven agreed from where he was sprawled on the settee, watching me and Cali square off. Alaric and Roth were also still seated, and I got the impression that they wished they had wine to sip or food to munch on while they watched me try to handle Cali.

Meanwhile, Vail and the Salvatore Marshals were taking turns glaring at each other and watching Cali like she was a predator someone had thrown into the room and locked the door behind.

Which . . . was kind of accurate. Cali had stalked in with a pissed-off expression a few minutes ago, which had turned murderous when she hadn't seen Samara. A quick reassurance from me that Samara would be back soon and that she'd asked us all to wait for her was the only thing that kept the Furie from rampaging past Vail and Brennan, who had followed after her—hands on their weapons.

Cali had glanced around the room and relaxed slightly at seeing Alaric, Roth, and Draven all seated and looking unworried. She must have come to the conclusion that nothing was wrong—at least that nothing in the last forty minutes had gone wrong—and that Samara would be returning.

That didn't mean she was happy about the situation though, and I was trying to make sure no blood was shed while Samara fetched Rynn—something that was growing more difficult by the minute.

"Whose face do you find prettier, Draven?" Cali's head snapped towards the prince. "Kieran's or Samara's?"

Someone—I was pretty sure it was Roth—let out an exaggerated whistle. I was starting to suspect that they were every bit as much of a shit-stirrer as their older brothers and had just hidden it well all this time.

"That's an impossible question, Furie," Draven drawled. "How fortunate for me that I don't have to choose. Instead, I get to enjoy both of their exquisite faces."

"I'm so going to swallow you whole until I choke later." I gave him a smoldering look and was rewarded by his eyes darkening before I returned my attention to Cali.

"What?" she snapped when I just stared at her and didn't say anything. Given how tightly wound she was, I should probably continue trying to calm her, but technically, Samara had just ordered that I keep her distracted, so . . .

I cocked my head. "So, you and Malachi fucking again?"

Her eyes widened to an almost comical degree. "Excuse me?"

Bullseye. I'd known something had been off when that Furie had come looking for her at House Harker. It hadn't been one particular thing, but a bunch of little tells. The way he'd said Cali's name with a hint of dark possession, how the muscles along his jawline had flexed when we'd said we hadn't seen or heard from her in weeks, and how he'd been somewhat reluctant to leave when the other Furie with him had announced they'd tried their best but needed to return home.

"You know, big bastard, about yay high." I held my hand up way above my head. I wasn't short by any means, a solid six feet, unlike Draven and Vail, who both had several inches on me. My hand was above where even their heads would be. "Dark eyes, messy, shoulder-length black hair, leathery wings. Not ringing any bells?"

"That's the Furie who stopped by House Harker looking for Cali," Alaric said out loud—I assumed for Draven's benefit because Alaric and Roth had been there that day, and I didn't think Alaric gave a single fuck about keeping Vail in the loop.

Draven hummed in response. "Interesting."

"It's not!" Cali scowled at him before crossing her arms and glaring daggers at me. "You're mistaken. Clearly, you're losing your touch for reading situations, Kieran."

"Actually, I wasn't *entirely* sure the two of you were at it again." I grinned. "But I am now."

The Furies didn't do relationships or emotional commitments of any kind. It was a strategy to keep their emotions under control and limit the chances of them losing themselves to that all-consuming rage that always burned within them. Cali wasn't one to follow rules, and she'd been involved with Malachi before, but when the Furie elders had ordered them to cease their relationship, Malachi had obeyed.

I was surprised he'd decided to disobey now, and even more surprised that Cali had taken him back and not slit his throat.

Cali's golden eyes glowed, and I saw Vail stiffen out of the corner of my eye, but I just let my grin widen at the pissed-off Furie. "If he disrespects you again, let us know. We'll make sure his body is never discovered and find you a nice Moroi to fuck."

She snorted, and the glow faded from her eyes. "Thanks for the offer, but I'm pretty sure I'd break a Moroi."

Before I could start naming potential fuck buddies for Cali—ones who probably wouldn't mind being broken by the beautiful Furie—the sound of footsteps came from the hall, and we all looked towards the closed door. A few moments later, it opened, and Samara strode inside with Rynn and Aniela behind her.

"Rynn?" Cali started. "What are you doing here?"

"Enjoying Moroi hospitality," she said dryly, flicking her long brown hair that was in desperate need of a good brush over her shoulder.

Samara coughed politely as Cali's piercing stare bounced back and forth between the three of them. I decided that I didn't want to be standing between Cali and Rynn, so I practically dove for the settee and reclaimed my seat next to Draven.

"Smooth," Alaric muttered on my other side.

"Blow me."

Alaric snorted. "Pretty sure that's pretty boy's job."

"You think I'm pretty?" Draven arched a brow at Alaric.

My best friend scowled, sinking further into the cushions.

Ignoring us, Cali marched across the room. Her path took her directly where I'd been standing, and I had no doubt that, had I still been there, she would have flung me out of her way.

"You're okay?" She crashed to a halt in front of Rynn, her hands quickly and efficiently checking her for injuries.

"I'm fine. Quite fussing!" Rynn slapped Cali's hands away, only for the Furie to key in on a spot of dried blood on her tunic and yank the clothing up, exposing Rynn's ribs. Several claw marks were still healing, and she had dark bruises, but nothing life-threatening. Still, it must have been bad if she hadn't healed completely already.

"What the fuck is this?" Cali demanded.

"I'll get to that!" Rynn snapped and again smacked Cali's hands away. She gave Samara a pleading look. "Will you please tell her I'm okay?!"

Samara tapped a finger against her bottom lip. "Mmmm . . . no. We were both worried about you, so you'll just have to deal with some light fussing."

I laughed under my breath, but not quietly enough because Rynn's wolfish eyes narrowed on me. I killed any hint of amusement on my face and gave her a small, supportive smile instead. She wasn't buying it, but when Cali tugged her tunic up again, she broke our stare off and went back to pulling her clothes out of Cali's grip.

Pissing off Cali meant you had to watch your back for a while. She'd never kill anyone Samara cared about, but she wasn't above stabbing you a few times. Nonlethally, of course.

Personally, I preferred that over Rynn's method of revenge. The lycanthrope had a very creative mind when it came to pranks, as I'd learned years ago when I'd been flirting with a courtier from another House in front of Samara. In my defense, Samara had been talking about Demetri all week after visiting him. He hadn't revealed his assholeness back then, and she'd actually liked him.

So I'd flirted with the pretty courtier, whose name I didn't even remember. Samara had cried, and Rynn had put some type of dye into my hair products that could only be described as puke green.

My options had been letting it grow out or shaving my head. I'd chosen the latter and learned that, while Alaric could pull off a closely shorn haircut quite well, I could not.

I'd been very careful to not piss off Rynn again after that.

"Those are wraith wounds." Cali finally gave up on trying to get a better look at Rynn's side but didn't step back. "What. Happened." She somehow made it more of an order than a question.

Clearly sensing how on edge her friend was, Rynn's shoulders sagged and some of the defiance fled from her face. "It's a long story, so I'm going to give you all the short version because we need to get back as soon as possible."

"Get back where, exactly?" Alaric gave Rynn a questioning look.

Rynn opened her mouth but closed it, glancing at Aniela and then to Samara.

It was a gamble, but we needed more help, and my gut told me to trust Aniela. Apparently, Samara felt the same because she gave her best friend a curt nod.

"Ruined temple," Rynn answered. "In the badlands."

"I know that place . . ." Aniela trailed off with a frown. "What does that have to do with anything?"

"It's where we got our asses kicked by some wraiths and barely survived." My brows furrowed together. "Why exactly would we go back there?"

"Because I couldn't remove the scrolls and books I found, and they have answers we need. Plus, Samara can read Unseelie faster than I can, and I'm pretty sure one of the books talks about the Seelie royal line." She frowned. "Although why the Unseelie were writing about that, I'm not sure . . ."

Everyone stared at the lycan. I sighed and glanced at Samara, who was now sitting on the arm of the settee, leaning against Roth, the two of them smirking. They were used to Rynn's roundabout way of explaining things.

I caught Samara's eye and arched an eyebrow. She arched one back but took my hint to steer her friend back onto the trail. "Rynn," she said evenly, "why don't you start at the beginning? Like how you got from the far northern part of the Velesian realm to the badlands?"

"Oh . . . right." Rynn nodded. "I found another one of those hidden rooms, like the one under Lake Malov, but underneath the Alpha House. I . . . uhh . . . might have locked the Alphas out and then stepped through a mirror that took me to another room, which turned out to be underneath that shitty, abandoned temple."

"Feels like there's a lot to unpack there," Draven said in a completely even tone.

I chuckled while Alaric rubbed his forehead and Vail redirected his glare from Cali to Rynn.

Aniela pondered all of us from where she was settled between Petra and Brennan, her lips quirked up in a barely there smirk.

"Fae mirrors," Roth said slowly and then looked up at Samara. "We've read about them, but it seemed like they were for communication—not travel."

"Maybe the Fae here adapted them?" Samara mused. "I mean, it makes sense, right? Before they turned themselves into wraiths, they would have had to travel through this fucked-up land of monsters too. That'd be a lot easier if they could just step through a mirror in one location and end up on the other side of the continent."

"I'm sorry," Brennan cut in, leaning forward slightly. "Did you just say that the wraiths used to be Fae?"

Samara nodded.

Brennan looked around Aniela and pointed aggressively at Petra. "I fucking *told you* they were Fae! The Unseelie fucked up their shadow magic somehow."

"Actually, it was the Seelie," Samara corrected. "We don't exactly know what happened to the Unseelie, but the Seelie did something to steal their shadows. I'm guessing the Unseelie are dead."

"Can we focus please?" Vail growled.

For the first time since entering the room, Rynn looked at Vail, and a golden sheen rolled over her eyes before she went predatorily still. Samara cleared her throat, and after a second, Rynn relaxed. Slightly.

Something told me it wouldn't be a humiliating but ultimately harmless prank she played on him in the future. Vail had knocked her out and stolen the crown off her unconscious form before absconding with it. Sure, he might have stashed her body behind a magical ward to keep her safe until she'd woken up, but that didn't change the fact that he'd fucking attacked her.

For a second, there was regret in Vail's dark grey eyes before he hid it. "You found another hidden room beneath the Alpha Pack stronghold. Somehow—and I don't give a fuck about the specifics or the historical implications"—he gave Samara and Roth a hard look before focusing on Rynn again—"you used the mirror to travel across Lunaria and ended up in a different hidden room, this time beneath the abandoned temple, yes?"

"Correct." Rynn started pacing, stepping around Cali. "It's, like, triple the size of the one beneath the lake. I think maybe it was some kind of archive—"

"Stop," Vail cut her off again, earning himself a warning growl from Cali, which he ignored. Brave man. Stupid too. Pissing off Cali seemed like a good way to get your dick cut off. "Why did you leave the room, Rynn? What sent you into the badlands instead of back through that mirror and to the safety of the Alpha Pack?"

"Cade can fucking bite me," Rynn snarled. "And Bastian can get fucked! Ryker too!"

Guess that answered the question about if things were getting better between her and the Alpha Pack. I bit back my sigh but didn't miss the look between Cali and Samara. Our priority might be dealing with Carmilla and figuring out what Erendriel and the wraiths were up to, but I had no doubt those two were also plotting how to get Rynn out of her messy situation.

I didn't know the Alpha Pack that well. Most of my interactions had been with Bastian. The panther shifter served as an ambassador of sorts and used to make regular trips to the Moroi realm. He was difficult to read because, like me, he was exceptional at slipping into different masks based on the situation. Sometimes, he was self-deprecating and charming. Other times, he had an edge like he was just itching to spill some blood.

Then there was Cade, the de facto leader of the Alpha Pack. He was calm and steady . . . until he wasn't. I'd once seen him tear the head off a rabid howler like it had been nothing.

Ryker was the youngest and a bit of a hothead.

Technically, there was a fourth member of the pack, but I'd never met them.

Rynn paused her pacing and chewed on her bottom lip. I supposed there were five members of the Alpha Pack now. Even if the fifth one might never go back if her friends had anything to say about it.

"What did you find, Rynn?" I prodded gently. Something had sent her running through the badlands on her own. Rynn could be rash, but even she wouldn't have done that unless she were desperate.

Rynn went back to chewing her lip and looked at Samara. My dark-haired beauty held her gaze for a long moment before giving a deep nod, like she was giving Rynn permission.

"I'm guessing some of you already know this, but Samara's grandfather was the Seelie King—the *true* Seelie King. Erendriel is just a pretender." Aniela and her Marshals gave Samara appraising looks but didn't say anything. "I didn't get through all the documents, but I saw enough to know that I needed to warn you." Rynn smiled at her friend. "You've always acted like a queen. I should have known you actually were one."

"Wasn't acting like a queen when she pulled my hair and kicked me in the crotch," Aniela muttered.

"Anything I do is queenly," Samara replied with a sniff.

I. Adore. Her.

"The wraiths can't get into those hidden rooms," Rynn continued. "Trust me when I say they tried once they realized I was in there, but however they managed to break through the blood wards around our outposts clearly doesn't work for these rooms. More importantly, there are things in the room that I couldn't open either—I think only the Seelie royal line can."

"That's why Erendriel is suddenly interested in you." Draven gave Samara a worried look. "Somehow, he learned the truth of your lineage, and now he's trying to sway you to his side. He'll start with pretty words, and when that doesn't work, he'll use other methods. Find your weaknesses and exploit them until you have no choice but to bend to his will. He can use his magic to—" He flinched and abruptly stopped talking.

Apparently, he'd been about to say something that was still protected by whatever spell Erendriel had put on him. His face contorted in frustration and fury at not being able to share whatever knowledge was locked away in his mind.

I turned and cupped his face in my hands. "You know we're going to kill him, right? For everything he's done to you?"

Draven's deep blue eyes warmed. "You say the sweetest things, love."

"Can we please get back to the room full of secret treasures and away from this gross display of affection?" Roth complained.

Samara snickered and leaned down to kiss their cheek, causing the taciturn librarian to blush slightly.

I opened my mouth to tease them, but Alaric gave me a stern look to knock it off, so I pouted and settled back against Draven instead.

"So you left to find Samara," Vail guessed, "but the wraiths found you first?"

"I bolted as soon as the sun rose, causing the wraiths to scatter." Color stained Rynn's cheeks, and she muttered something.

"What was that?" Cali crossed her arms and stared at her best friend.

"I fell into a spider's trap!" A sheen rolled over Rynn's eyes again. "It was an old one, and some debris had fallen over it, so I missed the signs."

Cali threw her hands up. "This is exactly why I've told the two of you to stay out of the badlands if I'm not there! You should have gone back to the Alpha Pack and sent us a message. You could have gotten yourself killed, Rynn!"

I groaned as Rynn closed the distance between them.

"I'm not some helpless pup!" Rynn growled and stopped a hair's breadth from Cali so they were practically touching, aggression rolling off both of them. Samara was the short one of the trio, while Rynn and Cali were almost the same height, but Cali had at least thirty pounds of muscle on her leaner friend. Not that Rynn cared. If she were in her wolf form, her hackles would have been raised. As it was, her words had more of a gravelly tone to them than usual. "Samara needed to be warned, and I didn't know where you were."

She tried to shove the Furie, but Cali didn't move an inch, which only pissed Rynn off more.

"We protect each other, Cali. It's what we do." Rynn pointed a finger in Cali's face. "So don't you fucking *dare* tell me to retreat with my tail between my legs while you two fight!"

"I'm sure that's not what she meant—" Samara started.

"Oh, shut it!" Rynn and Cali both snarled at her.

Roth and Alaric snickered as Samara sulked and crossed her arms. It was really strange how well the two of them were getting on, but I guess it made sense, since they were both grumpy assholes most of the time. I was glad Alaric's friend circle was expanding. He'd always be my best friend; I wasn't the least bit threatened there. Mostly because I knew Roth's ability to socialize had limits, and they were more than happy to disappear for days at a time in the library.

"Are they always like this?" Petra asked Vail.

"Unfortunately." He sighed.

Suddenly, his hand snapped up, and he caught a dagger an inch before it sunk into his face.

"Seriously?" He glared at Samara, who just turned the hand that had thrown the dagger palm up.

"I'll take that back now."

Vail slid the dagger into an empty sheath on his belt and fastened a leather strap over it so Samara couldn't summon it back. "Finders keepers. You're welcome to try to take it."

I didn't miss the flash of desire cross Samara's face before it was replaced with a rage that rivaled a Furie's. Yeah . . . I wasn't going to touch that mess of a situation. The four of us—Draven, Roth, Alaric, and I—had already agreed to let Samara figure out what to do with Vail, but if he gave even the slightest sign of betraying or hurting her again, we'd kill him.

Or tell Cali, and she'd kill him for us. Dead was dead after all, and my face *was* too pretty to get smashed in by Vail's meaty fists.

Draven seemed confident that Vail wouldn't betray Samara again. I'd been doubtful . . . until his rangers had been killed. Now, there was no chance of him going back to Carmilla. That didn't mean he couldn't still hurt Samara though. She was in love with him—had been for a long time—but I knew her. She was a spiteful thing.

I just didn't want her to hurt herself more in an attempt to punish Vail.

"Why do you think we should go back to the room, Rynn?" Samara asked, dragging her gaze away from Vail. "It's not that I don't want to see it, but maybe it shouldn't be a priority? Unless you think there is something in there that can nullify the crown's magic?"

"I'm not sure," Rynn said slowly, her argument with Cali already forgotten. "But I think there is a better chance of finding it there than anywhere else —except maybe the room under Lake Malov. I don't know how to or even if we can change where the mirrors lead, and some of us definitely don't want to cross into Velesian territory right now." She cut a glance towards Vail.

He winced before killing the motion. Vail had always been on friendly terms with the Velesians, but I suspected that had come to an end. Even if Rynn hadn't told them what Vail had done, they had likely been the ones to find her, and they would have smelled Vail on her. Between that and the missing crown, it would have been obvious what had happened.

Vail's days of running with any of the Velesian packs were over.

"Three days," Draven murmured before looking at Rynn. "You're positive the wraiths couldn't get into the room?"

She nodded. "Absolutely. It sounded like they tore down half the bloody temple in a fit of rage over not being able to get to me."

I caught on to what Draven was driving at and locked stares with Samara. "It doesn't matter if that room has the answers we need for the crown or not. Serill told you he'd be back in three days—that's tonight. We need to get you behind a ward that even the wraiths can't break through."

Because I sure as hell wasn't going to lose her again.

CHAPTER TWENTY

—

Samara

IT WASN'T that I'd forgotten about Serril's promise to return, but on my list of problems to solve, I'd been placing the wraiths below Carmilla. The wraiths had always plagued our lands. Sure, now we knew more about them, but they were still an old threat in my mind—one that was escalating but seemed less urgent than my aunt.

The longer we let Carmilla go unchecked, the more she would use the crown on the Moroi Houses. She was clearly targeting House Salvatore, Corvinus, and Laurent. All she had to do was get the key players, and those Houses would be under her thumb. Then she could concentrate on wiping House Devereux out and likely Tepes as well.

As much as I wanted to go back and secure House Harker, there were plenty of people there who loved Carmilla. It was unlikely that they'd believe me if I told them she was now our enemy. Even if they did accept that she had a crown capable of subverting someone's will, they'd probably still defend Carmilla. Claim she wouldn't abuse her power. I wasn't so naive to think there weren't people within House Harker who wouldn't mind if our House became synonymous with the Sovereign House—as the true rulers of the Moroi realm.

There was a very real possibility that Carmilla would have complete control over all the Moroi Houses within months. After that, she'd likely turn her attention to the Velesians. The packs were in a worse state than the Moroi Houses; it was doubtful they'd be able to mount a unified defense. Plus, Carmilla could use the crown on key players to further sow dissension in the ranks.

The Furies were the wild card, as they'd pulled back so much over the last few decades. Cali was the first and last Furie to ever attend Drudonia for more than a year, and she'd done that in defiance of the elders. Most of the Furies rarely left the badlands.

On the plus side, that hopefully meant they wouldn't help Carmilla with her quest to rule over the Moroi and the Velesians. If it came to it, I'd beg the Furie Elders for support, but I knew it was unlikely they'd agree to get involved. It didn't help that the Fury Elders didn't like me because of my close friendship with Cali. I knew they'd ordered Cali to stay away from me and Rynn after we'd left Drudonia, but she'd refused.

For all their power, the Elders couldn't completely control Cali—and they held me at least partially to blame for that. I couldn't depend on any other Furies coming to our aid, and as powerful as my friend was, she was still only one person.

Carmilla was no doubt plotting a way to deal with her. In the back of my mind, I was trying to think of a way to convince Cali to take Rynn somewhere safe—out of reach of the Alpha Pack. If it worked, they would both be out of harm's reach. I just needed to frame it in a way that didn't sound like I was trying to keep Cali out of the fight for her own safety.

I was kidding myself of course. Both of them would tell me to go fuck myself if I suggested they hole up somewhere and hide.

All of this was exactly why I'd been shoving the wraith problem to the side. I'd already survived one chat with Serril. Surely I could do it again and buy us a little more time.

Draven felt otherwise, and to my annoyance, Kieran had backed him up without hesitation. So had Vail.

I'd suggested that we track down Ary and warn House Tepes instead, then retreat to House Devereux. Only Roth and Alaric had agreed with me on that plan, but when Vail had just shrugged and said he was happy to tie me up and throw me onto the back of a horse to get me to the temple in the badlands, neither of them had argued.

I'd decided I'd be withholding sex from all of them. A minute later, I'd changed my mind because I wasn't going to punish myself for their treachery. They'd just have to get down on their knees and get creative with their begging.

"Still mad?" Kieran tucked some of my hair behind my ear, and I glared up at him. All of us were standing around in one of the side courtyards, waiting for the stablehands to fetch horses for us. Fast ones. We had less than eight hours to make it to the temple before the sun set. It was doable, but we'd have to push the horses hard.

I missed Zosa. My fiery mare would have raced across the badlands like she had wings, but she was safe at House Harker, where I would hopefully be reunited with her when this was over.

"What do you think? You're supposed to always have my back, Kier." I pursed my lips together and tried to ignore how gorgeous he looked because of the late morning sun hitting his golden blond hair just right.

Strong arms wrapped around my waist and pulled me back against a hard chest. A second later, Draven kissed the side of my neck, and I barely managed to swallow down the moan that tried to escape. "Don't be mad, love." He hadn't shaved in a couple of days, and the stubble scraped deliciously against my skin as he nuzzled my neck. "I know Serril. He's a tricky bastard. We need to make sure you're out of his reach so we can plan accordingly."

"But House Devereux—"

"Can't keep you safe. Not from wraiths." Kieran stepped closer until his chest was against mine and I was sandwiched between them. Then he claimed my mouth while Draven alternated between kissing and nipping my neck. Both of them had their hands on my hips and were gripping me hard.

Mad. You're mad at them, I reminded myself. *Furious. Don't let them—*

"Oh!" I exhaled sharply when Draven slipped his hand between me and Kieran to rub the seam of my pants.

"Get a room," Alaric muttered.

Kieran broke our kiss to grin at his best friend. "Why? So you can walk in on us again?"

"Wait, is that your kink, Alaric?" I asked a little breathlessly. "Is *that* why you never knock?"

Alaric gave me an unamused look, even as his lips twitched like he was fighting a laugh.

Fuck. It was impossible to stay mad at them. Even if I still didn't love the idea of going to the temple. It was so isolated there. I felt like I was running away when I should be staying and fighting.

Still, I'd be lying if I said I wasn't curious about what treasures the room might hold, especially in the spaces that were locked. I mean, someone—it had to have been the Fae—had gone to a lot of trouble to set up these hidden locations. What had they found so important that they'd decided it needed an extra layer of protection?

And assuming the Fae were responsible for these hidden treasure troves, why couldn't Erendriel get in? He seemed to have at least mostly reverted back to his original Fae form. He was no longer trapped in shadows like most of the Fae.

I loved me a good mystery. I'd love it even more if Lunaria weren't on the brink of collapse.

"Sam," Kieran said in a singsong voice.

"What?" I blinked and found him smirking at me.

Draven chuckled, his hand that had been rubbing my overeager clit through my pants sliding up to wrap around my waist.

"I forgot that's the trick to making you forget you're mad at us—not kisses

—uncovering Fae mysteries." Kier kissed me on the nose and walked to the rangers, who were leading out horses, then Draven kissed me on the cheek before following him.

I wrinkled my nose and opened my mouth to argue.

"Samara, you're with me," Vail announced.

"What?" My head whipped to Vail as he strode over to a large black horse and took the reins from the stablehand, who gave him a respectful nod.

Vail didn't even turn to look at me as he secured several bags to the front of the saddle. "Salvatore can only spare three horses. They already don't have enough to relocate most of their people to House Devereux." He quickly and efficiently started lifting the horse's hooves and inspecting them. "I'm not riding with anyone else. So either you ride with me, or someone stays behind. Horses can only carry two."

The fucking *audacity* of this man.

"Fine," I said evenly. "Then you can go with Aniela and her rangers to warn Ary."

The majority of House Salvatore was going to seek refuge at House Devereux. Roth had written a note to their family explaining the situation. Just like Draven and I had discovered at House Harker, there was a large underground level beneath Roth's birth House. It would be a little cramped, but they'd be able to fit everyone inside.

Aniela's Marshals hadn't been happy about the Heir's insistence on going to find Ary, but she refused to back down. I understood where she was coming from because I would have done the same in her place. I also knew that Ary could be a stubborn ass at times and it would take Aniela to convince him to relocate—albeit temporarily—to House Devereux.

Technically, Ary was an Heir, but he acted more like a ranger. Similar to House Devereux, House Tepes had never had much patience for Moroi politics. They preferred to be in the wilds. Because of how close they were to the border of the Velesian realm, Ary and his rangers spent a lot of time there as well.

Or at least they had. I wasn't sure how much longer even they would be welcome with the rising tensions across Lunaria.

"Not a chance." He finished checking the horse's hooves and patted the mare's neck before looking at me. "I'm not leaving your side."

I recognized the stubborn look quite well. Even if we did have time to spare —which we didn't—there would be no dissuading him.

"Fine," I ground out. "But I get the reins."

He grunted in reply before turning towards the enormous white wolf that trotted into the courtyard. Rynn gave Vail a silent snarl before butting her head against my thigh and damn near toppling me over.

"You sure you're up for running the whole way?" I guided my hand down her side, fingers slipping through her thick coat, searching for any signs of injury. Shifting helped the Velesians heal faster, and I didn't feel so much as a scab. Even if all her injuries were resolved, the amount of healing she'd had to do in the last two days had been taxing on her system. "Cali could carry you."

I barely managed to pull my hand away when Rynn snapped and let out a warning growl.

Touchy, touchy.

"Quit fussing, Sam," Cali said as she landed silently next to me, a mocking smile on her face.

I squinted at her. "Worried I'm going to take your spot as the resident fussian?"

"That's not a word." She rolled her eyes.

"You're not a word." Was I the perfect representation of maturity at twenty-three?

Yes. Yes, I was.

"I don't even know how to respond to that." Cali rolled her shoulders before glancing at the sun. "Follow my lead once we get to the badlands. I'll do my best to guide you all around the worst of it." She grimaced. "But it's leading up to the trapper's breeding season."

"Wonderful," Alaric muttered. "More fucking arachnids. As if those starfish things a couple of months ago weren't bad enough."

"You good?" I tried and failed to keep from laughing as he awkwardly tried to figure out where to hold on to Kieran on the back of their bay gelding. Kieran gave me a mischievous smirk before nudging the horse to the side, and Alaric immediately wrapped his arms around his friend's waist with a panicked expression.

He really was the worst rider.

Roth didn't look happy, but I suspected that had more to do with them having to hold on to Draven and not so much being on horseback. They didn't really like physical contact with people—except me, which made me feel warm and fuzzy inside.

"We're heading out," Aniela announced from astride a white horse, Brennan mounted behind her. She pulled their horse to a stop a few feet from me, and the mare pranced and snorted in Rynn's direction, clearly not thrilled about being so close to a wolf. "Most of my rangers are escorting the elderly and children on horseback. The rest will help those who are traveling on foot."

I tried not to think about all the ways that could go wrong. On horseback, it was a two-day ride to House Devereux. Less if they rode fast, but that was unlikely considering the people riding. Walking would take a solid week.

There were some outposts they could stay at along the way, but that meant collecting more travelers since they'd have to explain things to the locals. All the outposts between here and House Devereux were under Salvatore's control, and Aniela was confident the residents wouldn't question the order to evacuate.

The sentiment that there was something deeply wrong with the Sovereign House had been brewing for a long time amongst the Salvatore Moroi. The abrupt change of leadership would only further their suspicions.

I hoped we all survived this so that we could work on repairing that distrust. For too long, we've had an every-House-for-themself mentality, and that wasn't great for longtime Moroi survival. It was something Carmilla and I apparently agreed on—we just differed on how to achieve unification.

"My brothers should receive my message by this evening," Roth told Aniela. "If all goes according to plan, they'll meet your people with additional rangers on the road."

"You have my thanks." Aniela nodded deeply. "We'll be unreachable while we travel to House Tepes, but I'll send word once we're there."

"Travel safe, friend," I said sincerely. Their trip was just as dangerous as ours. House Tepes was in the north of the Moroi realm. The safe route was to travel to the Sovereign House, then cut west, but obviously that wasn't an option. So Aniela and her small group of rangers would be cutting straight through the forests in the center of our realm. All sorts of nasty things prowled there.

"You as well." Aniela glanced to where Vail waited for me by the horse, an increasingly impatient look on his face. "And good luck with that."

She waved goodbye and turned her horse to leave. Brennan hadn't acknowledged us once. Super friendly, that one.

It was time for us to get moving, yet I couldn't convince my feet to budge. Everything between Vail and me was so fucked. I was excellent at compartmentalizing, but even I had my limits. Keeping physical contact with Vail to a minimum had helped keep him in the category of *useful tool to be wielded as necessary*.

An eight-hour ride was going to smash that to pieces.

Something Vail damn well knew because the bastard *knew* me.

"Sure you don't want us to kill him?" Cali said casually, not even trying to be quiet. Rynn let out a low growl, her gaze locked on Vail.

He apparently wasn't the least bit concerned about my two best friends plotting his death because the asshole just smiled.

"If anyone kills him, it's going to be me," I muttered. "Let's get on with it." I glanced down at Rynn. "Don't fall into anything this time."

Her head snapped away from Vail, and her growl deepened as a golden sheen rolled over her mismatched eyes, which seemed brighter in this form.

If she thought we would ever let her live that down, she had another thing coming.

Holding on to that amusement, I stalked towards Vail and easily swung up onto the beast of a horse. A second later, he landed behind me, one large arm looping around my waist while the other rested on my thigh.

A shiver ran through me before I could stop it. Something told me this ride was going to feel a lot longer than eight hours.

I'D TRAINED myself to be a very patient person. It didn't come naturally to me, which was why sometimes my temper won out, but in general, I didn't mind the quiet. Most people couldn't handle silence in a conversation or negotiation, so they seeked to fill the void. My willingness to embrace the quiet had won me many a trade deal.

Vail hadn't spoken in five hours.

Five. Fucking. Hours.

His arm remained looped around my abdomen, and his hand had only strayed from my thigh to retrieve the water bottle—of which he'd made sure I'd also taken a drink. Not by asking. Just by holding it up for me.

I'd expected him to use this time to once again explain to me why he'd done what he had. That he'd been being loyal to Carmilla and hadn't realized she was seriously fucked in the head. Or that he'd assumed I'd be able to work things out with her and everything would be fine.

None of this would have been news to me. He'd said it all before when I'd been imprisoned and I'd had no choice but to listen to him explain in great detail why he'd chosen to attack my best friend, steal the crown, and do nothing as Draven was tortured and both he and I were thrown in the dungeons.

Sure, he'd done what he could to help me get through my menstrual cycle, but he was the reason I'd been locked up in the first place.

And he hadn't apologized. The moon fucking forbid that the words, *I fucked up and I'm sorry*, passed through Vail Ferenc's lips.

Argh. Maybe I could shove him off the horse?

Subtly, I shifted in the saddle, trying to determine how solid of a grip he had on me.

"Don't even think about it," he grunted.

"Think about what?" I asked casually, as if we hadn't been riding in tense silence for hours.

"Trying to shove me off the horse. That will only result in both of us going down." His breath tickled my left ear as the hand on my thigh dug in a little harder. "And if you're that eager to have a tussle with me, I'm sure we can figure something out at the temple."

Before Vail, I hadn't thought it had been possible to be confused, enraged, and horny all at once. Honestly? Could have gone my whole life without ever experiencing that.

"You're insufferable," I seethed and gripped the reins with one hand so I could reach back and grab my dagger—the one he'd refused to give back after I'd thrown it at him—off his belt. He didn't try to stop me, but I could feel his amusement as I fumbled a bit before getting it free. I considered stabbing him —not lethally, just a flesh wound—but the bastard would have probably just taken that as encouragement, so I slid it back into the sheath on my thigh and left it there.

Right next to his hand.

"I'm a lot of things these days," he said evenly. His grip on my thigh loosened, and he started lazily tracing loops on it. I liked it. The slow, methodical pace was relaxing. Between that and his broad chest against my back, I felt safe.

Which was ridiculous. The man behind me was anything but safe. He'd proven that over and over again. Sure, he might not go back to Carmilla after what she'd done to his rangers, but I had no doubt Vail would find some other way to fuck me over.

I hated that I still liked his touch. *Craved* it.

It had to be this stupid magic tying us together. Maybe I'd find some answers in the temple as to what this was and how to get rid of it. Then I'd be able to think straight when it came to him.

"Why exactly did you insist on riding with me?" I did my best to ignore his damn fingers and narrowed my eyes at the others, who rode ahead of us, giving Vail and me time to clear the air, apparently. I had no doubt that had been Draven and Kieran's doing because Alaric and Roth occasionally turned around to glare at Vail.

Well, mostly Roth. Alaric tried to a couple of times and almost fell off the saddle. He'd gotten considerably better with a crossbow, but riding was clearly never going to be his thing.

Rynn was scouting ahead—I could just barely make out her furry white ass —and Cali was soaring above us. One advantage of the badlands was that they were flat in every direction. Once in a while, a mesa would rise out of the ground, but it was impossible for anyone to sneak up on us.

Above ground, anyway.

Vail didn't answer my question right away, and just as I was about to push him for a response, I felt the echoes of grief and trepidation inside my chest. Not mine . . . I'd tucked my grief for Adrienne and Emil into a box and shoved it onto its metaphorical shelf with all the others. Close to it was the angst and stress for Nyx.

No. What I was feeling now belonged to Vail.

Whatever this emotional feedback was, it seemed to only happen when we were in close contact, and it wasn't all the time. With Draven and Roth, it was more consistent, but between Vail and me, it felt more strained, like flashes of emotions here and there.

"Carmilla . . ." Vail trailed off, then another feeling shot through our connection, so intense, it made me inhale sharply.

White-hot rage.

"What about her?" I rasped, my hand tightening on the reins, causing the mare to toss her head in annoyance.

"Did she have anything to do with our parents' deaths?" He spoke the words so quietly, I knew the others hadn't heard. Not that it mattered. Most of them had been there when Carmilla had stated what she'd done, and I'd told Roth later.

I'd been planning on telling Vail but had figured it could wait. There was nothing to be done for it now, and he was still grieving his rangers. No purpose in opening up an old wound when there was a fresh new one still seeping blood.

"Yes." I forced myself to relax my grip on the reins as a numbness took hold. It wasn't coming from Vail. This was all me. The problem, I was learning, with compartmentalizing things was that, sooner or later, you had to deal with them.

I'd never dealt with losing my parents. I'd just let my grief fester in that damn box.

Something told me Vail had done something similar. He'd thrown himself into becoming the perfect ranger and then taking up the mantle of Marshal— just like his parents. I'd dedicated myself to being the unfathomable Heir and then to solidifying our alliance with House Laurent by marrying Demetri.

Both of us had looked to Carmilla as that stand-in parental figure. She'd shaped us into weapons she could wield—and had made sure to destroy our childhood friendship so that we'd relied only on her in those early years. Before I went to Drudonia and became close with Cali and Rynn. Before Vail bonded with rangers like Adrienne, Emil, and later Nyx.

Looking back, I realized that she had tried to sabotage my relationship with Cali and Rynn, making little comments here and there, but I'd lived at Drudonia, and that distance between me and Carmilla was probably what had saved me. If I hadn't had my friends and if I hadn't carved out a piece of myself outside of that constant pressure to impress Carmilla, would I have left Demetri?

Or would I have remained at House Laurent in a loveless marriage? Carmilla probably had plans to take out Marvina at some point, and then Demetri and I would have risen to the Heads of House role. Carmilla would have had two Heads under her thumb without even needing a Fae crown.

That was what my parents had died for.

Something wet and hot streaked down my face. I raised my right hand from where it had been resting on the handle of the dagger to brush the tears away, but a large hand caught mine and tucked it against my chest—right over where that connection thrummed.

Vail's other hand rose, and he gently brushed my cheeks, wiping away the tears before wrapping that arm around me too.

He rested the side of his head against mine as I silently sobbed in his arms, finally grieving the loss of my parents after denying it for so long. Vail didn't say anything, just held me as I felt his own grief wind through mine. We'd both lost so much because of Carmilla's obsession with power.

Slowly, something else wrapped around my grief. Something enduring and resilient.

It was love. The unbreakable kind.

At first, it was just coming from Draven, but then Roth's bond intertwined with his. I'd been learning over the last couple of days the subtle distances between how their emotions felt through the bond. Another choked sob broke from my lips when Vail's bond joined. Tentatively, like it wasn't sure it was allowed to be there.

I might have lost my parents—and my aunt to her own greed—but I still had family, and they wouldn't ever let me go.

So I let myself fall apart and finally weep for the parents I'd loved and lost . . . in the arms of a man who had broken my heart.

CHAPTER TWENTY-ONE

—

Vail

"Stop!" Cali ordered a second after the white wolf loping ahead of us skidded to a less than graceful stop.

"What is it?" Samara called out even as she tugged on the reins, drawing our mount to a halt. Draven and Kieran did the same.

I leaned to the side a little more so I could scan the ground but didn't release my hold on Samara. She'd stopped crying half an hour ago, and we'd both been content to ride in silence. Not the tense kind of these past couple of weeks, but a strangely comforting one. I didn't think everything between us was resolved, but for the first time, I had hope that I could actually fix them.

I just needed more time to do that, which meant we needed to make it to that damn temple alive. Cali and Rynn had both sensed something—even if I couldn't see it. I grimaced. If it wasn't on the surface, then it was below.

Trapper spiders.

Most of Lunaria was covered in forests, ranging from tropical to snow-covered; it was impressive how quickly the climate changed between the northern and southern ends of the continent. Then there were the badlands, a unique ecosystem that contrasted sharply with everything else. They were flat and arid—so much so that the ground cracked and faint lines scattered out in every direction, as if the earth itself was begging for rain, which it rarely got, as the storms seemed to always bypass it.

Cali landed in front of us, wisps of red hair plastered to her face where they'd slipped free from her braid. We were lucky it was overcast, but even without the sun beating down on us, the heat was stifling. The horses were sweating but so far seemed okay with our steady jog.

"Spotted a trapper." Cali's mouth twisted in distaste. "Where there's one . . ."

"There's more." I grunted and tightened my grip around Samara's waist. "If it's a colony, their tunnels could extend for miles."

"Or it could be just a few that split off from the group," Draven said, but he sounded doubtful.

It seemed unlikely we'd get that lucky.

"I fucking hate spiders," Alaric muttered.

"Same," Samara echoed. "I had nightmares for a solid week after the cave." A chill seemed to run through her, and she leaned further into my embrace—something I greedily accepted as I inhaled her delicious scent.

I'd never admit it, but even I'd had a nightmare or two after we'd encountered those arachnid-like starfish in the cave outside House Harker. The creatures themselves had been nightmare-inducing, but what really terrified me was remembering Samara dangling off the ledge with a tentacle wrapped around her leg while a monstrous starfish waited beneath to devour her.

Those things had been unexpected. At least trappers I'd unfortunately dealt with before.

There weren't as many predators in the badlands because of the harsh terrain and climate, but the ones that dwelled here were crafty. Trappers were spiders as large as Rynn in her wolf form that lived in tunnels beneath the ground. They'd earned their name because they built pits hidden beneath trapdoors in their tunnels. When they felt the vibrations of something walking by, they leapt out and dragged the unsuspecting prey underneath, where the walls were lined with their sticky webs.

Thanks to all the cracks in the ground, it was difficult to tell where the trapdoors were. To make matters worse, their breeding season was coming up, and they were stocking up on food to feed their young, which meant there were probably twice as many traps as usual and the spiders would be extra aggressive.

Because Lunaria was the gift that kept on giving.

Reluctantly, I let go of Samara and slid off the horse. Cali was clearly stressed, because she didn't even bother giving me one of her death stares when I moved to stand beside her.

"You've been in the badlands more than any of us." I kept my gaze locked on the ground in front of us. "What do you think we should do?"

"Throw your body out there, wait for the trappers to jump out, run real fast," she replied without missing a beat.

I laughed darkly, drawing Rynn's attention from where she was also seeking out the trapdoors. Fangs that were several inches long flashed at me as she snarled before going back to trying to find a path.

Remorse hit me hard. I'd always respected Rynn. She was smart and clever, and while she could be blunt at times—she lacked Samara's ability to speak honeyed words—she'd always spoken the truth. I liked her no-bullshit approach to things.

It wasn't just Samara I'd lost when I'd taken that crown and handed it over to Carmilla. It was Rynn . . . and the Velesians too.

Samara, I hoped to win back, but I wasn't sure if Rynn would ever trust me again—and the Alpha Pack would be out for blood.

"As delicious a snack as Vail is," Samara said as she swaggered to Cali's other side, "I don't think he'll be enough to distract all of them. Not if they have a large colony."

My dick instantly hardened at Samara referring to me as delicious, and I had to subtly adjust my pants.

"Won't know until he tries." Alaric shrugged before half falling, half leaping off the horse he'd been riding with Kieran.

I didn't bother hiding my smirk at his ungraceful dismount.

"Knock it off." Samara gave me and then Alaric a warning look. "Both of you."

"Could you fly us across, Cali?" Kieran asked from behind us, where he and Roth were holding on to the three horses. I looked around, trying to spot where Draven had gone, and tried not to be envious of how quietly he could move. It didn't take long to find him, crouching down with his hand flat against the earth a short distance away from us.

"Possibly," Cali answered Kieran. "It'd be easier if we backtracked and climbed up one of the mesas so I could glide and not waste energy just trying to get off the ground. Even then, I'm not sure if I could carry Draven or the asshole."

I assumed I was the asshole.

Fair.

Samara chewed on her bottom lip. I wanted to reach out and brush my thumb across it to get her to stop, but I wasn't sure if my touch would be welcomed. Despite what had transpired when we'd been riding together, I didn't think we were there yet—and I didn't want to fuck up what progress I'd made. So instead, I had to watch as Alaric brushed *his* thumb across her lip and Samara gave *him* a small smile in return.

Cold, green eyes cut to me as soon as Samara turned her attention to where Rynn was nimbly trotting back to us, then Alaric arched a dark brow at me. Out of all of Samara's lovers, he seemed to be the one who had the biggest problem with me, which I found interesting because he was also the one who had been the cruelest towards her.

Sure, I'd tried to kill Samara a few times, but Alaric had spent his teenage years delivering perfectly crafted insults that cut right through her armor. He'd picked that habit back up as soon as she'd returned to House Harker. One day, they were at each other's throats—the next, he was in her bed.

I didn't get it, which was probably how he felt about me and Samara.

Figuring out how this would all work long-term would be challenging, and I suspected there might be a little bloodshed. Samara clearly wasn't going to choose between us. I just needed to make sure she chose me at all.

Which meant I couldn't punch that arrogant expression off Alaric's face.

Rynn finished making her way to us and shifted back to her human form. I almost rolled my eyes at how Alaric suddenly found the ground so interesting. Clearly, he hadn't spent much time around Velesians because nudity was nothing to them.

Unless mates were involved and someone was being disrespectful, but while the Alpha Pack had claimed Rynn, there was no mate bond between them—and likely wouldn't be, given the way things were going.

"Thoughts?" I kept my gaze on Rynn's eyes. Velesians were comfortable wearing nothing, but leering was still considered rude—or an invitation. Neither was of interest to me. I only had eyes for my dark-haired, curvy beauty, but I hoped to mend some bridges with Rynn, so I waited respectfully for her to answer.

Rynn glanced at me, a cool distance in her gaze, before she sighed. "I suspect this colony goes on for a ways. There are a lot of trapdoors, and from what I could see, they don't decrease in any direction. So we could walk for miles and still be in it."

"We don't have that kind of time." I frowned. It was past midday. We'd traveled a good distance, but we still had a ways to go before reaching the temple. Dealing with trappers was difficult but doable—we just had to avoid those damn doors. If darkness fell and the wraiths came for us though . . . we wouldn't be able to fight them *and* avoid the trappers.

"Can you sense anything?" Kieran called out to Draven.

The former prince shook his head and rose, dusting off his hands as he walked back towards us. "Yes, but it's not all that useful. I'm pretty sure I can feel the tunnel system, but I can't differentiate between what are tunnels and what are traps. My magic only senses the spiders when they move; otherwise, I just kind of have an awareness of them but not an exact location."

He ran a hand through his long hair, causing the silver strands to shimmer as they caught the few rays of sun that peeked through the clouds. I tried not to roll my eyes as both Kieran and Samara practically drooled.

"Well, you're doing better than me." Samara wrinkled her nose. "I can't sense anything."

Draven gave her a small smile. "You only found out you had magic a few weeks ago. It takes practice to draw it out and then manipulate it to your will. Even I struggle with it, and I've been practicing a lot longer than you."

Samara nodded, but I could tell it still bothered her. Samara liked to be the best at everything. She was one of the most competitive people I'd ever met. It was probably driving her insane that she had a well of magic inside her that she had no idea how to wield.

I frowned at the ground, imagining the tunnels running beneath them, before glancing at Draven. "Could you collapse the tunnels?"

"I thought about it," he admitted. "But I doubt I could do it all at once. I'd probably have to pick a spot and then expand. It would give them time to escape to the surface."

"Yeah, let's not do that." Kieran kissed Draven's cheek. "I'd prefer to not be suddenly surrounded by dozens of giant spiders."

"More like hundreds," Rynn commented idly, her mind clearly trying to work through other options.

"In the words of Samara responding to that asshole Demetri's marriage proposal . . ." Kieran grinned at Samara. "Pass."

She snorted. "He really was the worst."

My frown deepened. I was happy he was dead—and that she'd killed him—but I'd kind of been looking forward to twisting his head clean off his shoulders, and I hadn't even gotten to see Samara cut the fucker's head off.

Didn't seem fair after I'd had to listen to him run his mouth for weeks.

"So we leave the horses behind and walk through," Samara said, interrupting my internal griping. "Rynn, Cali, and I all have experience spotting the doors because we visited the badlands often when we were at Drudonia. We can forge a path."

I almost pointed out that Rynn had fallen into a trap on her way to us, but I bit my tongue. In some ways, the active trapdoors were easier to spot because the trappers kept the areas clear, whereas the abandoned ones were covered by dried up plants and other random debris.

Cali glanced up at the sun and grimaced before giving Roth an appraising look. "Without the horses, we'll have to run to make it to the temple before nightfall."

"Your point?" Roth asked flatly. I glanced over my shoulder to find them scowling at Cali and rubbed my hand over my mouth to hide my grin. Cali was only voicing what we were all thinking—Roth's idea of physical activity was getting a book down from the highest shelf in the library.

And they'd created magical freaking ropes to help them with that . . . amongst other things, I suspected, based on how I'd caught Samara blushing sometimes when Roth's ropes shifted on their forearms.

"I can carry them if need be," I offered.

Samara's jaw practically dropped as she stared at me.

"What?" I asked, shuffling a little on my feet.

"Aww, he wants to feel useful," Kieran joked. "Let him put all those muscles to use, Rothie Bear."

Roth and I both glared at the blond courtier, but he just smiled wider.

Then one of Roth's ropes started to unwind from their forearms—likely to choke Kieran—but Samara smoothly cut in.

"Thank you for the offer, Vail." She walked over to Roth and took their hand, gently wrapping the rope back around their forearm while Roth continued staring daggers at Kieran. "Roth, will you be okay running?"

Bright orange lines bled through Roth's hazel eyes as their bloodlust rose. "Don't worry about my stamina, Samara. I can sure as fuck outlast Kieran."

"That sounds like a fun game," Kieran murmured.

"I do like games that are a win-win for me." Samara grinned smugly. "Let's make it to the temple, and then we can play."

My mind ever so helpfully conjured up the memory of Samara tied up in that cabin while Draven and I tried to make her scream.

Fuck.

"You okay there, Marshal?" Cali drawled. Her tone was casual, but she still looked at me like prey she was determined to take down.

I'd have to be careful as we made our way through trapper territory. Something told me that if Cali saw an opportunity to *accidentally* knock me into a trapdoor, she'd take it.

"If we're going to do this, we should get moving," I said gruffly, trying to ignore how uncomfortably tight my pants felt right now and willing my hard-on to go away. "Rynn has the best senses out of all of us. She shifts and takes the lead. Cali can scout from overhead. I'll take the rear guard."

It was so easy to fall back into ranger mode, I hadn't even realized I'd done it until I'd given the orders . . . ones I would have given to Adrienne, Emil, and Nyx in different times.

I wouldn't be doing that again. Two of my rangers were dead, and Nyx . . . I didn't know what Nyx was.

For a second, the grief and rage I felt were almost crippling. Until I ruthlessly shoved them into the depths of my soul, slammed the door shut, and threw away the key. Dwelling on what had happened wouldn't help us now. Carmilla would pay. I'd make sure of it.

"It's a good plan," Draven said, cutting off Cali, who looked pissed off at being told what to do. I hadn't meant to give her orders like that, they'd just slipped out. "I'll do my best to sense the spiders if they go on the move, but I likely won't be able to give much warning if it's them springing a trap."

"Understood." I nodded at him thankfully—something I never thought I would be doing. "Let's see to the horses and then get going."

I strode back to the black mare Samara and I had ridden, took the reins that Kieran wordlessly passed to me, and started untying my bags. Suddenly, Samara was there, holding out her hand.

"I can carry it a—"

"Or you can stop being difficult and let me carry one of them." She curled her fingers quickly several times in a very clear hand-it-over gesture. "Crossbow too. I'm a better shot, and you know it."

I grunted because it was true. Samara was shit with a sword, but she was the best shot I'd ever seen with a bow—or a throwing dagger.

"Aim for dead center between their eyes and fangs. It won't kill them, but it will mess up their sense of direction." I passed her the bag, waited for her to secure it to her back, and then unlatched the crossbow. She greedily took it from my hands and checked it over quickly before accepting the quiver of bolts from me as well.

Once she was satisfied, she swung the crossbow over her shoulder. "We should take their bridles off so they don't get caught on anything."

I nodded and slipped the bridle off the mare, who had stood here patiently this whole time. House Salvatore was known for breeding and training some of the best horses—I suspected it was where Zosa had originally come from. How Samara had managed to get her hands on such an incredible horse, I had no idea. These ones might not be as stunning as Zosa, but I had no doubt they were trained to return home. With no riders slowing them down, they could make it before the sun set.

Roth passed the reins of the chestnut horse they'd ridden with Draven to Samara, who patted the horse's head before slipping off its bridle. A minute later, all three horses were cantering away in the direction of home. A few rangers had volunteered to stay behind at House Salvatore to keep watch, so they'd be able to let the horses in—if they made it.

There were no guarantees in Lunaria. Although I suspected the horses were going to have a better trip than us.

I pulled my sword free and jerked my head towards where Rynn waited for us in her wolf form. "Let's get on with it."

Alaric and Kieran both pulled swords similar to mine free and started walking. They both trained regularly with my rangers and were pretty good. Roth's ropes unwound a little from their forearms and dangled at their sides as they followed after the other two.

A low, husky laugh spilt from Samara's lips as Draven whispered something in her ear before pulling the whip coiled at his side free. I still thought a whip was a stupid weapon, even if the prince did wield it well.

By the time we reached Rynn, Cali had taken to the sky above us, and we fell into a single file line. Draven had sped up to be at the front behind Rynn, with me at the end. Nobody spoke as Rynn found us a path through the traps. First one mile. Then another.

An hour ticked by, and I was still spotting trapdoors. How fucking big was this colony?

I spotted some hoof tracks here and there from the deer who cut through the badlands to avoid all the predators that roamed the forests. The trappers were converging where the prey was.

Lucky us.

More than once, Rynn made us backtrack to find an alternate route. I trusted her judgment, but the fourth time she did it, I couldn't stop myself from glancing up at the sun that was rapidly moving across the sky. We still had at least two hours until sunset, but we were also a solid five miles from the temple, if not more. If we didn't get out of trapper territory soon, we would be in serious trouble.

"Wait," Draven said harshly. Everyone froze. "Something's coming. A lot of somethings."

Cali shot higher into the sky.

"It's a deer herd," she called out. "And unless they alter their course . . . they're going to run straight into us."

"Fuck," I growled. "Can you scare them in a different direction?"

"Doubtful." Cali darted down to hover above the ground a few feet away from us. "There are too many of them. I'd be lucky to get half to switch direction."

"So let's use it to our advantage," Samara said quickly. "The trappers will converge on the deer. We wait until they do, then we run like hell."

"The deer are going to trample anything in their path," I argued. "Or impale it."

A crazy light flared in Samara's eyes, and she grinned at Cali. "Remember that time we got drunk on your twentieth birthday?"

The Furie laughed darkly. "Hard to forget waking up naked in a tree covered in sticky berry juice and wearing your panties as a hat."

"Did you three *ever* study at Drudonia?" Alaric gave Samara an incredulous look.

"Cali definitely didn't," Roth muttered.

"Before the tree, we made a bet over who could hold out the longest against stampeding deer," Samara said smugly. "You lost, Cali, but you split the herd."

"We need to discuss fun ways to celebrate a birthday." Kieran shook his head. "I'll give you a hint . . . it should involve too much wine and sweet treats. Not rampaging, horned monsters."

"Don't tell me how to celebrate my birthdays, pretty boy." Cali shrugged.

Faint vibrations started to rumble through the ground, and we all looked towards where a dust cloud was rising into the sky. The deer were still far enough away that I couldn't make out individuals, but Cali wasn't wrong; the herd was massive.

One-on-one, Lunarian deer weren't dangerous. True, they were large—about the size of an average horse—and the twisted horns that rose from their skulls were as sharp as any dagger, but generally, they avoided conflict. It made them hard to hunt because at the first hint of danger, the entire herd took off. Exactly like they were doing now, with their heads lowered so they could spear or trample anything in their way.

We had the unfortunate luck of being in their path. We'd never outrun them, and if we tried, the trapper spiders would be on us immediately.

I knew what Samara was suggesting. It was absolutely crazy . . . but it could work. Maybe. Like a fifty-fifty chance. Honestly, we had no other options because that fucking herd would be on us in minutes.

"We need to group together and make ourselves as small as possible if we're going to pull this off," I ordered.

Roth grabbed Samara and tugged her close while Draven, Kieran, and Alaric closed ranks around them and I stepped to Samara's back.

"Rynn!" Samara yelled.

The large white wolf shoved her way between all of us, and I flinched when she nipped my leg but shuffled a little to make room for her. Cali moved to stand in front of us, her black, leathery wings tucked in tight, and her deep red hair spilling down her back like liquid fire as the afternoon sun finally broke free of the clouds.

"Might want to prepare yourselves," she warned in a low, dangerous tone. "There's bound to be some spillover with me being so close to you all."

All we could do was wait for the herd to reach us. If this was going to work, the timing needed to be absolutely perfect. Out of the corner of my eye, I saw a few long legs prod out from the earth before quickly sliding back beneath the trapdoors. The vibrations were making the trappers antsy.

"Get ready!" Cali ordered as the deer thundered towards us, blood already staining some of their stark-white horns. I threw my arms around Samara and ducked my head, nestling into her hair, then I breathed in her scent deeply to ground myself as I heard Cali snap her wings open and release a bloodcurdling scream.

Chaotic magic full of unyielding rage brushed against my mind, and the thread connecting me to Samara thrummed between us as if it was anchoring me to her. I held on to it as the deer raced past us—not into us.

Fuck me. It actually worked.

The ground shook as the deer thundered across the badlands. Then the spiders attacked, and terrified shrieks filled the air.

Cali cut her scream off, her magic abruptly vanishing, and I instantly straightened. The bulk of the herd had passed us, but there were still stragglers trying to catch up to the rest.

That wasn't the problem though. Random deer, we could dodge. No, the problem was that the spiders were launching themselves out of their trapdoors. If they caught a deer, they did their best to drag it back into their tunnel. Sometimes they won . . . sometimes they found themselves speared and stomped to death.

The hard white surface of the badlands was quickly being stained with red blood and a dark green ichor.

Amongst all the chaos were the trappers who hadn't caught anything but also hadn't been trampled—they were hunting now.

It was hard to believe something so large could be lurking beneath the surface. Their bulbous abdomens were a deep red, and it was the only part of their bodies that had coarse hairs covering it. The rest of their bodies were a shiny black, including the three-inch curved fangs, which delivered a toxin that would start breaking down tissue almost immediately.

A thick carapace protected the top half of their bodies, and the exoskeleton on their legs was equally strong. The abdomen was the most vulnerable spot, as it was the only soft bit of their bodies. I'd learned from experience though that they could shoot those fucking hairs to burrow under your skin or puncture your eyes.

There was also the small problem that the spiders were taller than my waist, and if they reared up onto their hind legs, they would tower over me.

I loved me a good fight, but I also wasn't an idiot.

"*Run!*" I shoved Samara and the others forward.

Nobody needed any further encouragement as we took off at a dead sprint. Deer snorted as they galloped past us, but an enormous one with horns stained completely red, bits of torn flesh still hanging off them, altered its direction to charge straight for us. Kieran was in front, and he started to veer left, only to jerk back when a spider leapt from a trap.

Draven's whip wrapped around one of the trapper's outstretched legs, bright red spikes shooting out from the whip a second before he yanked the whip down. The spider let out a high-pitched shriek as it crashed to the ground and its injured leg snapped in half.

"Take out the fucking deer!" I yelled.

Another spider leapt from a trap, only for Cali to dive from the skies and shove her blade into the space between its abdomen and upper body. The thing let out an ungodly sound, and Cali screamed as its hairs shot out and pierced her wings.

Alaric and Kieran raised their swords as the enraged deer got closer, only for a white blur to leap from the side. Rynn's jaws closed around the deer's throat as her body continued its forward momentum and swung to the other side, jerking the deer with it. The two men were too close to change course, so they jumped over the deer while the rest of us went around it.

To her credit, Samara didn't slow down, not even as Rynn and Cali continued their respective battles. I felt her worry through our link, but she had absolute faith in her friends to come out on top. More spiders poured from the earth, some finding prey to occupy themselves with, others still looking.

If we stopped, we died.

"Six trappers up ahead!" Draven warned, then glanced over his shoulder to make sure I was with Samara. Unlike the others, he trusted me to keep her safe.

A trapdoor opened to our right, and Alaric shoved Roth left before rolling underneath the spider as it launched itself out. Silver flashed, and dark ichor poured onto the earth as Alaric sliced open the underside of the trapper's abdomen. Without missing a beat, he sprung back to his feet and was running again.

I didn't have much time to be impressed though because the spiders Draven had warned us about darted forward. Rynn and Cali hadn't caught up to us yet, which meant it was the six of us against the six of them. Not the odds I would have preferred.

"Make room!" Samara shouted.

Alaric grabbed Roth's hand and pulled them to the right while Draven and Kieran went left, giving Samara a clear shot at the spiders. Samara slammed to a halt and snapped the crossbow up. In the span of a single breath, two bolts soared through the air. Two spiders jerked and crashed into each other as a bolt sunk into the exact two-inch spot on their heads I'd told Samara about earlier.

She reloaded the crossbow and fired again. Two more spiders went down.

The others raced ahead, even as the two remaining trappers keyed in on them. Samara took out the one on the right, and Draven's whip cracked, taking out two legs of the one on the left.

Samara swung the crossbow onto her back again, but I grabbed her before she could dart after the others.

"Wha—"

Her words were cut off when my mouth crashed against hers in a quick but brutal kiss.

I pulled back and grinned wildly at her. "Nice shooting, my queen. Now it's time to run."

CHAPTER TWENTY-TWO

—

Samara

THE MEMORY of Vail's scorching-hot kiss was all I thought about as we raced across the badlands, chasing the dying light.

"My queen." Vail had called me his queen.

After we'd broken apart, he'd pulled me into a run, and we hadn't spoken since. There hadn't been time because those fucking spiders had cost us. We were lucky that most of us had come out unscathed. Rynn's white coat was now a mix of deep red and dark green ichor, but she only had a few minor wounds. Cali was the worst off. Her wings were still fucked from the hairs the trapper had launched at her. Each one would have to be removed before she could fly again, but we didn't have time to do that now, so she was running with the rest of us.

Everyone had let their bloodlust rise to give them an extra boost of speed and stamina—except Alaric. He was stubbornly keeping his locked down. The fact that he was still keeping pace with us was impressive, but then he did run for fun almost every day because he was a psychopath.

Who ran for fun? Someone who didn't have to deal with thigh chafing, that's who.

I slid Alaric, who was on my right, a dirty look, and he glanced at me with a small grin. If we weren't in such a hurry, I would have tripped the bastard for enjoying this.

Kieran was on my left, and his hand briefly brushed mine for the dozenth time. He'd been doing these light touches frequently since we'd been reunited, like he was reassuring himself I was still there. Roth was sandwiched between Kier and Draven, their eyes burning like two suns as they rode their bloodlust hard.

724

Behind us, I could feel Vail's attention on me, as it had been since he'd dropped behind us to guard our backs.

The faint outline of the temple appeared on the horizon, and I could have wept. I tried to calculate how much farther we had to go but gave up with a huff.

"How far?" I wiped at the sweat dripping down my forehead before it got in my eyes.

"Five miles," Draven replied roughly.

My lungs burned at the answer. The sun was dipping into the horizon ahead of us. Even if we picked up the pace—which I was doubtful we were capable of—we wouldn't make it before nightfall.

Luck, you spiteful bitch, please be on our side for once and do not let the wraiths show up, I begged—to whom or what, I had no idea. We were so damn close to safety.

Shadows started to sneak across the ground as the sun fell beneath the horizon, slowly taking with it the last of its rays. Even if I couldn't see it, I could *feel* day giving way to night. My senses became a little keener. Speed a little faster. We were Moon Blessed. We were made for the night.

Unfortunately, so were the wraiths.

"Almost there," I panted, more for my sake than anything else. The temple loomed before us, and I could make out its towering columns and large open entrance.

Rynn and Cali ran faster, and the rest of us did the same. *Straight through the entrance, past the first room, make a right, down the stairs.* I reminded myself where Rynn said the door to the secret room was.

The last of the light leached from the skies, and the badlands fell into darkness. At some point in our mad dash to the temple, the clouds had rolled back in and blocked the stars. Moonrise was still hours away.

Between one blink and the next, my vision adapted for the night. No sign of wraiths anywhere.

Relief coursed through me. Within minutes, we'd be at the safety of the temple. We only had to make it a little farthe—

Shrieks echoed through the dark, and as one, we all slammed to a halt.

The terror that gripped me was instant, but I breathed through it and let it settle in my bones. I'd long since learned that it was impossible to shove fear entirely aside, but you could use it to make your instincts sharper.

Rynn and Cali sprinted back towards us until we all stood in a circle with our backs to each other. Draven stood to my right and Vail to my left. I didn't bother with the crossbow; instead, I pulled out my blood daggers. Vail pulled a dagger from his thigh and passed it to Roth, who grimaced but accepted it because their ropes would be useless against wraiths.

Shadows emerged from the earth like water from a spring, then slid across the ground and circled us.

"Serril?" I called out. Maybe I could talk our way out of this. Erendriel clearly wanted me for something, and Serril served him. I had no problem lying and agreeing to work with them if it meant we got out of this alive.

One of the shadows crept along the ground and twisted before snapping into the shape of a kùsu. Shadows rolled off the long insect as it skittered forward. One by one, the wraiths chose different beasts to imitate. Some I recognized, some I didn't. All of them had fangs and claws though that could tear us to shreds.

"Not Serril, I'm guessing." If he were here, I suspected he would have taken on that Fae form again and tried to speak with me. I'd only met him the one time, but Serril had come across as someone who would use words to terrify you—not rely on monstrous forms.

My fingers tightened around the handles of my daggers. There was no point in throwing them—only blades with a specific enchantment could hurt the wraiths in their shadow forms, and my daggers didn't have it. Crafting the enchantment was time-consuming and required resources that were hard to come by, which was why only the rangers carried enchanted blades—like Vail's sword.

The rest of us would only be able to harm the wraiths for the split second their shadow forms turned solid—and hope we killed them before they killed us.

The wraiths continued circling around us, forming a perimeter.

"I want to be clear that I'm not complaining," Kieran started, "but why aren't they attacking us?"

"Are you seriously whining about the fact that we're not all monster food right now?" Cali growled.

"I said I *wasn't* complaining, Cali!"

"You were definitely complaining, love," Draven said lightly before sighing. "As to why they're not attacking, it's because these are the lost ones—wraiths that don't even remember being Fae. They're what Strigoi are to Moroi. Mindless monsters that only care about killing."

I pondered the wraiths that were making no move against us. "Like Kieran said when he was complaining—"

"I *wasn't* complaini—"

"They're not trying to kill us," I pointed out.

"Left to their own devices, they're nothing but killing machines, but they can be controlled. Serril uses them like hounds to track and sometimes attack prey." Draven glanced down at me. "He likely ordered them to wait in areas where he thought you might make an appearance and delay you until he arrives. I'm sure some of them fled the moment they detected you to alert their master."

"If that's the case," I said slowly, "then I'm technically the safest one in the group. They won't harm me, but they will follow me."

"No," Vail growled.

I turned away from Draven to look up at Vail and arched an eyebrow. "I'm sorry, did you just tell *your queen* no? You sure did a quick turnabout on that one."

"Feels like we missed something," Alaric muttered.

"Vail probably did something dramatic and asinine," Roth agreed.

"You're not using yourself as bait." Vail glared at me, ignoring the commentary.

"It could work," Cali said from where she stood behind me. "Some of us stay with Samara, the rest get to the safe room and make sure the path is clear."

"As much as I despise agreeing with Vail," Kieran cut in, "I don't like the idea of us splitting up."

"It'll only be for a few minutes," I argued, eying a wraith that had molded its shadows into an enormous feline monster with spikes running down its back. What in the actual fuck was that thing? I had never seen a beast like it in Lunaria. "The temple is right fucking there." I pointed towards the structure. "We'll be right behind you."

What I didn't say was that we were going with my plan one way or another. These wraiths—the lost ones, as Draven had called them—might be under orders to not harm me, but I doubted that extended to everyone else. The way they would occasionally drift a little closer before almost reluctantly going back to circling us didn't escape my notice. We had no idea when Serril would get here; he could be hours away.

And there was every chance he would kill everyone but me when he arrived.

Icy fear crept through my veins at the thought of losing even one of the people with me. My true family. I'd do whatever it took to keep them alive. Even if that meant drawing a bunch of bloodthirsty wraiths after me. The question was, who was I going to involve in this crazy plan?

As much as I would have preferred to do it on my own, even I knew that wasn't a good idea because I very much wanted to make it to the safe room. This wasn't me sacrificing my life—it was me giving those I loved time to get to safety so that I could then join them.

Then we could have *Holy Fuck We're Still Alive* victory sex. I might even let Vail watch.

"I can take two of them out temporarily—maybe three." Draven uncoiled his whip.

I nodded. "Okay, Draven and Vail, with me." If Draven could even temporarily put some of the wraiths down, then I wanted him with me—and I knew it wasn't worth arguing with Vail. "Everyone else, get to the room. Rynn, once everyone is there, come back out and wait by the main entrance so we can follow you, since we'll likely be coming in hot."

"Bullshit!" Cali snapped. "I'm coming with you. Vail can go with the others."

"Like hells—" Vail started, but I cut him off.

"You've been limping for the last two miles and trying to hide it, Cali. It's more than your wings that are injured. Your magic won't work on the wraiths anyway. Draven and Vail are the best suited for fighting them, and you know it."

Vail was the only one who had a weapon that could hurt the wraiths in their shadow state, and Draven had experience fighting them.

Cali's lips pressed into a flat line while her eyes glowed with rage, but she didn't argue any further. She knew I was right.

"We'll make this quick." I leaned forward slightly on the balls of my feet. "The three of us will run away from the temple, just enough for you lot to get inside the entrance, then we'll turn around and sprint back. I'll take point since the wraiths won't kill me."

Hopefully. I was counting on them fearing Erendriel enough to obey his orders and deny the drive every predator had to chase down prey and slaughter it.

The kùsu-shaped wraith got too close to one that looked like a seriously fucked-up bear, and the two shrieked at each other.

"Go!" I spun around and shoved Kieran and Alaric hard. "Now!"

Without waiting to see if they obeyed, I took off in the opposite direction. Curses sounded behind me, but when I chanced a look over my shoulder, I saw everyone racing towards the temple. Two of the wraiths started to chase after them, only to stop and shake their heads violently, causing shadows to swirl through the air before twisting back in my direction. Both released pissed-off screams, then charged after me.

Well, my plan worked. Yay?

Draven's whip cracked, and something snarled to my right. In front of us, shadows writhed on the ground before bursting upward and snapping into the form of an enormous beast with wings.

"Oh, fuck me!" I skidded to a stop, Vail and Draven doing the same next to me. "Is that a dragon? Why is it so big?"

"What the fuck is a dragon?" Vail cursed as we all tilted our heads to look at the towering monster.

"I don't know!" I took a step away. "There was a picture of one in a book!"

The shadow dragon snaked its long neck forward until its head, adorned with spikes, was only a few feet from us. A mix of fear and adrenaline slammed into me as the other wraiths closed in behind us, leaving us nowhere to go.

Then it spoke one word in Unseelie, its voice so broken that it took me a second to understand.

"*Birreb*." Kneel.

"*Mur keb*!" I screamed. Fuck you.

The dragon roared, and the other wraiths let out their own shrieks.

"Pissing them off further probably isn't a wise move, Sam," Draven chided even as amusement coated his words and a crazy smile lit up his face. He flipped his whip so that the length stretched across the ground before gripping the handle with both hands and then pulling them apart.

I blinked as a *second* whip peeled away from the first—made entirely of blood.

"I knew I saw you with two whips before!" The bloodred whip looked almost exactly like the first, aside from the color. I pointed one of my daggers at him. "You're teaching me how you did that."

Because having an endless supply of blood daggers I could throw at people who pissed me off sounded *amazing*.

"Maybe. If you ask me nicely." Draven winked at me. "Get ready to run again, love."

The wraith dragon growled and opened its maw to roar at us again, but Draven's bloodred whip snapped forward, growing impossibly long before cutting directly through the dragon's head. Instead of passing harmlessly through the shadows, as most weapons would, a deep red mist burst out from the whip, and the wraith reared back with a pained scream. Then the dragon shape fell apart, as if the wraith had lost control of its shadows, which were now writhing across the ground like a puddle of darkness.

Draven's whip snapped around to the wraiths behind us, but I didn't wait to see what would happen. I just took off running back towards the temple with Vail and Draven hot on my heels. Several wraiths were convulsing on the ground like puddles of liquid night, just like the dragon shadow had.

Unfortunately, not all of them, because the one that was shaped like a kùsu and the feline sporting spikes down its spine cut off our retreat to the temple.

Once again, I slammed to a halt. Damn it. Less than fifty feet separated us from the temple, where I could see Rynn's white wolf form pacing.

"Can you do the whip thing again?" I looked to my left, where Draven panted, then dropped my gaze to the single whip he was holding and felt my hope extinguish.

"No," he ground out. "I can only get in a few hits with the blood whip before it disintegrates. It doesn't kill the wraiths either, just fucks with their ability to control their shadows."

"For how long?" Vail moved to stand between me and the two wraiths

"Another five minutes at most," Draven answered tightly.

I eyed the two wraiths. "They won't hurt me. What if I—"

"Don't even think about suggesting that you run one way and we go the other," Vail growled. "I went along with your plan the first time. The others are safe. I'm not leaving your fucking side."

I opened my mouth to argue, but Draven cut me off.

"I agree with the Marshal." Any trace of amusement was gone from Draven's tone. "Besides, even if they won't kill you, they'll absolutely hurt you."

"Fine." I gripped my daggers tighter. "Then we stick close together and just edge our way towards the temple."

"Quickly though." Draven glanced over his shoulder at the shrieking wraiths. "Those ones are going to be extra pissed once they're capable of moving again. We need to be behind that ward before then."

They could still follow us inside the temple, but Rynn was there to help, and it wouldn't be far to the safe room. We'd made it all this way. I refused to falter now.

Slowly, we started walking towards the temple entrance. I took the lead, Draven and Vail walking at an angle so their backs were towards mine. The two remaining wraiths paced aggressively around us, clearly wanting to attack but bound by the order to not kill me.

A minute passed, and we were halfway to the entrance. Hope started to flutter inside my chest that we might actually make it.

I should have known better.

The feline wraith pounced forward, its clawed paw swiping out for my legs. I leapt straight up into the air, its paw passing underneath me. Then Rynn barked in warning, but it was too late. The kùsu wraith plowed straight into my side with the top of its head. The cool shadows momentarily turned solid, which sent me hurtling away from the temple—and from Vail and Draven.

"Samara!" Draven screamed. I heard his whip crack before one of the wraiths hissed in pain, but it wasn't the agonizing scream his blood whip had gotten.

Then I hit the ground and rolled, barely avoiding stabbing myself with my dagger before springing upright. Twenty feet now separated me from the others.

Rynn had charged into the fight. She and Draven were squaring off against the feline wraith. Every time it turned solid to attack one of them, the other would counter.

Based on the fresh blood on Rynn's coat and the way Draven's arm was hanging limply at his side, it wasn't going well. We only had a small window to inflict any type of injury on wraiths, and as soon as they turned back to shadows, they healed. Rynn's teeth couldn't do any lasting damage, and Draven's enchanted whip could barely do any better.

The kùsu circled me, its long, dark body cutting off my view. I had no idea where Vail had gone, but he hadn't been with Draven and Rynn.

I gripped my dagger, even though it was basically useless. Then an eerie sound filled the night, and I realized it was the kùsu wraith laughing.

It weaved its long body around me. Without the light of the moon or the stars, it was hard to distinguish it from the dark of night.

"*Din tros,*" it mocked. Forgotten queen.

Fuck this. I darted forward, intending to run straight through its shadows, but it snapped its massive form towards me. The hard body knocked me backwards before vanishing into cool shadows once more. Out of the corner of my eye, I could see the other wraiths starting to gain control of their shadows.

We were running out of time.

I shoved myself up, ignoring the bite of pain in my leg. Something had crunched when I'd landed, but I could still put weight on it, which was all that mattered. The wraith could only turn solid for two or three seconds, tops. I just needed to time it better.

Before I could attempt to race through it again, its shadowy form rippled, and it jerked its head up with a shriek as Vail's sword sliced through its midsection, momentarily parting the shadows, before he rolled through it.

"Vail!" I raced towards him but then had to leap back when the wraith scuttled between us. It lunged forward, its pinchers snapping towards Vail, but unlike mine, Vail's timing was perfect. He sidestepped the attack and plunged his sword into the wraith's eye for the split second it was corporeal.

It screamed and reared back, creating a clear path for me. I raced forward but halted when Vail held up a hand.

"I'm sorry, Sam." There was a note of finality to Vail's tone that sent a chill down my spine. Shimmering eyes of silver bored into my soul. "I've always loved you. Even when I hated you." He laughed darkly. "There is no force in this world that could have ever stopped me from loving you. I'm so sorry I fucked it all up."

"Don't," I growled and took a step towards him only for him to move back. "Whatever it is you're thinking of doing, don't you fucking dare."

He smiled at me, and in that moment, I didn't think there was anything I hated more. "I was wrong about the prince too. I'm happy you have him and the others. They'll keep you safe. Now *run.*"

"Vail!" I shot forward, then jerked myself back as the kùsu-shaped wraith recovered and dove at Vail. Just as the wraith solidified and snapped its pinchers, Vail dove underneath it and shoved his sword through the beast's skull.

For a second, I felt relief at knowing Vail had survived his stupid fucking attack—but then the second wraith pounced. The shadow form of the feline wraith lunged towards Vail with his taloned paws extended. It felt like time froze as the outstretched claws swept towards Vail and turned solid for an instant. That was all it took for blood to spray as three jagged wounds opened across Vail's stomach.

"No!" I screamed.

Vail clamped one hand over his abdomen but stayed on his feet. The two wraiths momentarily forgot about me as they found something to vent their rage on.

Just as I was about to dash after Vail—because there was no way I was obeying his order to run and leave him to die—Draven grabbed me and hauled me back.

"Let me go!" I struggled to break out of his iron grip.

"Close your eyes!" Draven ordered.

"Wha—"

Before I could get the word out, a flash of white bounded past us. Rynn. She had a glowing orb in her mouth as she sprinted towards Vail and the wraiths. She tossed her head back, and the orb flew, arcing upward, impossibly bright. The last thing I saw before one of Draven's hands left my waist to cover my eyes was Rynn shifting to her human form, grabbing the orb out of the air, and throwing it down—directly beneath the wraiths.

Through the cracks of Draven's fingers, I caught the blinding light. If I thought the wraiths had screamed before, it had been nothing compared to now. They were still shrieking when Draven's hand fell from my face, grabbed my hand, and yanked me forward.

"Wait!" I tried to pull free. "Vail—"

"I got him!" Rynn yelled as she half dragged Vail. He was conscious but barely, based on the way he struggled to put one foot in front of the other, a trail of blood leaking behind him.

"We'll fix him inside!" Draven scooped me up in his arms. "We're out of both luck and time!"

The four of us raced towards the temple as the last of the light from the orb faded. Cali and Kieran darted out, helping Rynn carry the now-unconscious Vail the rest of the way. Dark shapes rippled across the ground and walls as the wraiths gave chase through the temple, only to slam into an invisible wall as we darted down the secret stairs and across the ward.

We'd survived.

I sucked in a shaky breath as Draven carefully set me onto my feet.

Rynn glanced at me. "Did that wraith turn into a fucking dragon?"

"What's a dragon?" Cali perked up. "And can I kill it?"

I sighed.

AN HOUR LATER, Vail limped into the room we'd all set up in after leaving him passed out but mostly healed on a bed. This space under the temple was massive. It was far larger than the secret room I'd discovered near House Harker or the one under Lake Malov. It reminded me a little of the tunnel system the Devereux clan had found. There were multiple levels beneath this one with living quarters, and beneath that was another level that had some rooms for storage and—much to Kieran's delight—a cavern full of hot springs.

We'd only explored enough to get our bearings and make sure everything was secure. The wraiths were still prowling the temple above us, but Rynn had been right—they couldn't get in here, which was something they were extremely enraged about, based on the way they had screamed and trashed some of the marble structures. I was a little worried they were going to bring the whole temple down in their temper tantrum, but it was still standing for now.

I'd gone back to the entrance a couple of times, but there was no sign of Serril yet. He'd get here eventually, I had no doubt.

Alaric, Roth, and Rynn were pouring through some texts that had been locked away in a chest. Rynn had also been right about me being able to unlock the more secured items. It was a simple locking glyph, but it'd been keyed to my blood. I'd opened everything I could find, and we were sorting through the items now. Most of them were books and scrolls, but there were also some weapons and other artifacts.

Normally, I would have been positively giddy about finding lost Fae treasures and my nose would have been in those books immediately, but I was too fucking pissed to concentrate.

The source of my ire was currently slumped in a chair at one of the tables where we'd piled up the weapons and artifacts, which Draven and Kieran were going through. Cali was passed out and snoring in one of the rooms downstairs. We were under orders to wake her up when "it was time to kill something."

"Find anything good?" Vail asked in a gravelly tone as he idly scanned the weapons laid out before him. He still looked like shit. His normally tan skin was pale, and he'd had none of his lethal grace when he'd walked across the room.

Draven grunted in response, but Kieran just shook his head with an *oh, you poor idiot* look on his face. Kieran had been watching me stew in my rage for the past hour. He knew exactly how explosive my temper could be because he'd witnessed it more than once. Back then, it had been Alaric pissing me off. Now, Vail decided to take that spot.

"How are you feeling?" I fixed my features into one of concern as I walked towards the table. Draven and Kieran scooted aside so I could stand directly opposite from Vail and lean forward, placing my hands on the smooth wood surface.

Right next to so many wonderfully sharp, pointy items.

"Fine," Vail said slowly. His instincts were likely warning him about danger, but he didn't know what to make of my worried demeanor. "Thank you for saving me, but you shouldn't have. I don't want you to ever risk your life for me, Sam."

My smile gained a sharp edge.

"Did you mean what you said?" I leaned forward a little more. The table wasn't that wide. Vail could easily close the distance and kiss me. Based on the way his gaze dropped to my lips, I knew he was thinking about it. "That you're sorry . . . and that you love me?"

His eyes snapped back to mine. "Every word."

"That's what I thought." I nodded. My fingers closed around the two daggers my hands had been drifting towards. Normally, Vail's reaction time was better than mine, but he was tired and still hurting—and I was really fucking motivated. Faster than he could react, I slammed them through the backs of his hands—pinning them to the table.

"Fuck!" he swore. "What in the fuck, Sam?"

I hammered a punch to his jaw, and pain ricocheted up my arm. Why did he have to have such a strong jawline? That fucking hurt. Worth it though. My arm shot back to punch him again, but then Kieran had his arms around my waist, laughing as he pulled me back.

"How fucking *dare* you apologize, tell me you love me, and then sacrifice yourself!" I screamed and flailed in Kieran's hold, who just laughed harder at my antics. "If you fucking die before I forgive you, I will drag you back from whatever hells exist just so I can kill you myself, Vail Ferenc!"

"I was trying to save your damn life!" Vail bellowed as he jerked his hands upward. They hit the flat handle of the daggers, and the blades pulled free from the table, drawing another pained grunt from him. "You should be thanking me!" Blood poured from his hands as he rose and glared at me from the other side of the table. Good. I hoped it fucking hurt.

"Gods, he's dumb," Roth muttered.

"Impressively so," Alaric agreed.

"Can this lover's spat be taken somewhere else?" Rynn growled. "Some of us are trying to read and find solutions to our many problems."

I stopped fighting Kieran, but he didn't release me—because again, he knew better. Instead, he kept his arms wrapped around my waist and started kissing my neck, which did admittedly feel nice, but I excelled at multitasking, so I was perfectly capable of being turned on by Kieran and enraged at Vail.

"Samara, love," Draven purred as he sauntered over to stand in front of me and Kieran. He gently gripped my chin and forced me to look at him and end my stare off with Vail. Amusement danced in his eyes as he brushed a thumb across my bottom lip. "I spotted some clothes in one of the bedrooms downstairs. Why don't you get cleaned up and rest a bit?"

Beneath the desire that Kieran and Draven were drumming up—and the anger towards Vail—exhaustion was tugging at me. Even if I wanted to help with the research, I suspected I'd have to read everything three times before it sank in. We were safe enough here for now. I could afford an hour or two of sleep to better get my wits about me.

"You all should take breaks too," I said begrudgingly.

"We will," Draven assured me.

I managed to turn my head enough to glance at the others, who were all buried in books. "Make sure Roth and Rynn eat something."

"We're not children," Roth said wryly as they flicked their eyes away from the text they were reading long enough to scowl at me before immediately dropping them again. Rynn didn't even bother looking at me, just made a rude gesture with her fingers as she kept reading.

"We will," Kieran echoed Draven's response, and I could feel him grin against my skin. "You going to behave if I let you go?"

"Yes," I promised.

Kieran chuckled and pulled me tighter against his body while Draven leaned forward to whisper in my ear, "Be a good girl, and we'll reward you later."

"I mean, you could reward me now?" I fluttered my eyelashes at him when he pulled back, but he grinned at me before giving me an all-too-quick kiss.

"Go get some sleep, Sam." Kieran released me and gently pushed me forward.

I made it halfway to the door before my anger cut through the dirty thoughts Kieran and Draven had planted in my mind, and I spun back around to face Vail. "Our discussion isn't over, and I'm still mad at you."

"You being mad at me is nothing new, Sam." Dark grey eyes looked at me in challenge. "How about you do what you're told and go get some sleep . . . my queen." He bared his teeth at me.

"Fuck you!" I spat before stomping towards the door—only because I knew Kieran and Draven wouldn't let me beat the shit out of Vail again.

"Fuck you too!" Vail growled.

I was halfway down the hall when I heard Draven say, "Maybe I need to explain how apologies are supposed to work . . ."

CHAPTER TWENTY-THREE

—

Samara

Hours later, I had to admit that I did feel a lot better. The rage towards Vail and the stupid fucking stunt he'd pulled was still simmering, but I was capable of putting that aside to help search this place for something useful. Roth had pointed out the chest where they'd found that orb of light. There'd only been one, but that didn't mean there weren't more somewhere else. Or maybe one of the texts would mention how it had been made.

If we could figure out how to create more, we'd have an actual weapon we could wield against the wraiths. It was a hell of a lot more effective than the enchantments on the rangers' weapons.

Draven's blood whip worked well against the wraiths, and while we'd been exploring this secret level of the temple, I'd asked him more about it. The good news was that I was fairly confident I could recreate the spell on my daggers, making them even more useful. The bad news was that while the spell itself was simple, it required a lot of blood—Fae blood.

Or at least half-Fae blood. Which meant we were limited based on how much blood Draven or I could spill on any given day. Not ideal.

My eyes slid over the murals painted on the walls. Most of the other places we'd found were utilitarian. The living spaces underneath House Harker were clearly meant to house a large number of people—they had the basics and nothing more. The tunnel system we'd stayed at had been a bit more extravagant, with actual bedrooms instead of just a large space with rows of identical beds.

This space felt like someone had lived here though. Something about the rooms just felt more homey than the other places. The clothes hanging in the closets had that distinct look of having been worn before. I tugged at the thin fabric of the deep purple gown I'd found after washing my clothes and hanging

736

them to dry. Whoever had been here before had had good taste, but they'd clearly been taller and thinner than me. Luckily, the material was stretchy, so it still fit.

The dress even had *pockets*.

And these murals . . . I traced the vibrant petals of the wildflowers painted on the bottom half of the wall.

It was a meadow . . . but not like one I'd ever seen around here. The flowers were too dainty and delicate, and it had a peaceful vibe to it that we simply didn't get here. In Lunaria, even the fucking flowers wanted to eat you.

"Where did you all go?" I murmured aloud, because woven into the beautiful painting was poetry—Unseelie poetry.

The Seelie had turned into the wraiths, but there was no hint of where the Unseelie had gone. It couldn't have been a coincidence that the Unseelie had been known for their shadow magic and the Seelie were now trapped in shadows. Somebody had protected this place to keep the wraiths out . . . or maybe some Unseelie had designed it to keep out their own kind?

The hallway ended in a stairwell, and I started to climb up. Between this place, the Harker journals, and the room beneath Lake Malov, we had to start finding some answers. Although, given that the Alpha Pack was probably tearing the Velesian realm apart looking for Rynn and that we were almost certainly not welcome there, I wasn't sure how we'd get back into that room.

Only my footsteps sounded as I made my way up—the wraiths had gone quiet. I worried my bottom lip and hesitated when I reached the level where everyone was likely still convened. Hopefully some of them were resting.

My gaze flicked up more stairs to a small landing that led to an archway. On the other side were a few more stairs and then the rest of the temple, but that archway was where the ward started. If I went up there, I could at least peek out and see if I could spot any of the wraiths—or maybe even Serril—waiting.

Decision made, I tiptoed up the rest of the stairs and peered out into the darkness. The last time I'd been in this temple had been to investigate wraith activity. That night had ended with us thinking Draven was the enemy and wraiths attacking us. Vail had almost lost himself to bloodlust and attacked me —then saved me. During the process, he'd ripped open a hole in the ceiling.

The moon had risen while I'd been asleep. I looked longingly at the moonbeams rippling across the temple floor, beckoning me to come and lie on the cool surface and gaze up into the night sky.

"Does it call to you?" a deep voice asked from the shadows.

I'd noticed that I wasn't alone only a split second before he'd spoken, but even then, I'd barely managed to stop myself from jumping. Or taking a step back from the archway as the figure stepped into the moonlight and strolled down the stairs to stand on the opposite side.

Not Serril.

Dark golden-blond hair framed a handsome, masculine face. I saw echoes of Draven in it. The strong jawline, chiseled cheekbones, and those eyes—lapis lazuli blue—were the exact same shade as Draven's. Only, these had no red fractures interrupting the blue.

"Hello, Erendriel." I leaned against my side of the archway like I wasn't the least bit surprised that the Seelie King was standing a foot away from me. Here was hoping that the Fae didn't have sensitive hearing; otherwise, he'd hear my heart pounding so hard, it was a miracle my ribs weren't rattling.

The last time I'd seen him, there had been shadows trailing in his wake, but there were none now. He looked every bit as flesh and blood as I.

Suddenly, my heart, which had been beating rapidly a second ago, felt like it froze.

Did that mean he could walk through the ward? Had he figured out how to turn himself completely back to Fae? I smothered the alarm that threatened to choke me. No. He'd clearly been waiting for me. If he could have gotten past the ward, he would have by now.

Either the ward was also designed to keep out Seelie Fae, or Erendriel had enough wraith left in him that he was still forbidden from passing.

Not all traps were the physical kind. He was here because he wanted something from me, and something told me a centuries-old Fae was just as capable of ensnaring me with words as he was with actions.

I should have been frightened by this—and I was a little unnerved—but I couldn't deny the thrill that ran up my spine. I was about to try to outwit the Seelie King. Sure, he was a throne-stealing bastard, but he'd been clever enough to depose the previous one and hold on to power all this time.

Let's fucking play.

He leaned his broad frame against the stone archway, mirroring my pose. "Are we on a first-name basis now, Samara?" The grin he gave me was almost playful. "Usually I demand more respect from my subjects, but I suppose you are basically my daughter-in-law, so allowances can be made." He winked.

"Am I?" I gave him a lazy smile, even though I didn't buy his casual and harmless act for a second.

Those cunning eyes studied me. Erendriel had this ageless quality about him. He appeared to be in his early thirties and could have passed for Draven's older brother, but those eyes . . . there was something ancient about them.

"I didn't know my bastard son had it in him," he mused. "Hiding his magic from me all this time." His gaze dropped to my chest, not in a leering way, but like he could see the connection to Draven. "And one or both of you have enough magic to form a mating bond." A crease formed between his brows. "You have . . . three bonds. With who, I wonder?"

Mating bond. The words bounced around in my mind even as I kept a bemused expression on my face, as if Erendriel hadn't just casually solved a major mystery for me.

The strange connections I had with Draven, Roth, and Vail were mating bonds. Holy shit. In my head, I'd occasionally thought of them as my mates, but in name only. I hadn't thought it was possible that we had a true mating bond like the Fae talked about in their stories.

Draven and I might have been half Fae, but Roth and Vail weren't. Did my Fae nature make up for that? What else could these bonds do? Moon bless us, please let the books downstairs have at least some explanations.

Erendriel laughed softly. "You're good. Many in my court would be jealous of your ability to mask your emotions so well."

"I'd be happy to give them lessons." My smile widened. "For a price, of course."

"I see why Serril was so captivated by you. It's hard to impress him, but he was quite intrigued when he returned. It's why I just had to come tonight to see what all the fuss was about."

The Seelie King tilted his head, causing some of his hair to slide over his shoulder, the silky strands falling to his chest. His dark blue shirt was unbuttoned enough to give me a good view of his extremely well-muscled chest, and the fabric clung to his biceps as he crossed his arms.

It all felt very . . . posed.

"Oh!" I snorted and then covered my mouth as giggles escaped. "Was your plan tonight to seduce me? After acknowledging I had a *mating bond* with your son? Maybe you should let Draven show you how it's done. He does the 'effortlessly gorgeous' thing a lot better."

Erendriel straightened, and the charming facade fell like a mask he'd pulled off.

"It seemed worth a try." He shrugged. "Velika was easy enough to manipulate."

"What do you want, Erendriel?" I deliberately didn't use the word *king* to see if it would annoy him. If it did, he hid it well.

"You by my side. As my queen."

I waited for him to laugh. He did not.

"First, no. As you noted, I already have a few mating bonds—and I'm quite happy with all of them." Okay, maybe not the Vail part of it, but whatever. "And before you ask again, you should know I cut the head off the last man who tried to force me to marry him." I narrowed my eyes. "Secondly, why?"

It had to be my bloodline. He must have only recently learned that my father had been the son of the previous Seelie King. The question was, how? And what precisely did he want me for? To get into places like this?

"Mating bonds can be broken."

Dread hit me, and I knew I'd failed to keep it off my face. I had no intention of breaking my mating bond with Draven and Roth, and as soon as I could figure out how to share it with Kieran and Alaric, I would be doing so.

Vail . . . I had no idea what I was going to do about Vail. I was still feeling kind of stabby towards him.

Luckily, Erendriel was looking over my shoulder to the stairs below, so he missed all the misgivings in my expression. "Whatever you find in here will not give you the answers you seek. This place was built by the Unseelie Princes—and they are liars."

Are. Not were. The Unseelie Fae were still alive. At least Erendriel believed them to be.

"And you'll tell me nothing but the truth, right?" I huffed, slipping back into a mask of haughty indifference to not even hint at what information Erendriel had just given away.

His gaze snapped back to me.

"Join me, and I'll take care of your aunt for you. The crown has no control over my mind, but it will tell you if I'm lying or not." He placed his hands on either side of the archway, leaning forward until only a few inches and the thin boundary of the ward separated us. "Right now, you're a queen in name only. Let me make you one legitimately. Right now, the Moroi and the other Moon Blessed are just children stumbling around in the dark and hoping to not get eaten by the monsters."

I snapped my fangs at him. "We hold our own."

"Barely."

"So light it up for me. Convince me to at least *entertain* the idea of trusting you. Why did you kill my grandfather?" I adjusted my position so that I stood directly in front of him. He was easily a foot and a half taller than me, so I had to tilt my head back. "You were his faithful general, no? If you betrayed him, it wouldn't seem that out of character for you to do the same to me once you get what you want—whatever that is."

He pondered me for a long moment. "I want to go home."

"Home," I repeated and thought about the murals here and in all the Fae fortresses left behind.

"Yes." He flashed his teeth at me. "The one your grandfather cost us because he refused to listen to me and allied himself with those traitorous Unseelie Princes. He's the reason we ended up here in this fucking prison."

Prison. That's why this place was like one of the hells the Fae poetry sometimes alluded to. It was a punishment—for the Fae.

"Why were the humans brought here? Were they part of the rebellion?"

It was Erendriel's turn to scoff. "We were hardly going to grow our own crops or scrub our own floors."

"Of course not." I gave him a flat look.

His gaze hardened. "Don't think your grandfather was some hero to the humans. His father had been a good and strong king; he was the only reason I served Lachlan for as long as I did, but Eirac would have been disgusted to learn his only son made a bargain with the Unseelie and lost everything because of it. I did your family a favor by removing Lachlan from the throne."

"Sure," I said smoothly. "Absolutely nothing about it was self-serving at all, *King* Erendriel."

His mouth tightened. "You have no idea what it was like where we came from. How the Fae were treated. We were fighting for a better world—I still am fighting for a better world."

I really wanted to know more about the world outside Lunaria, but I was sitting on a treasure trove of information. Sure, it might be biased, but so was Erendriel, and he'd already given me quite a bit of information in the last ten minutes.

Amateur.

"And whose neck will you step on for your better world?" I drawled. "Or were you planning on taking all of the Moon Blessed with you?"

A faint sneer that he tried and failed to hide trembled across his lips.

I shook my head with a laugh. "*Chil muréd.*" Get fucked.

The last of Erendriel's control snapped as he slammed his palms against the stone, and even through the ward, I felt the power of his magic ripple forth as the ground shifted slightly beneath my feet.

"You've only survived this long because my attention has been elsewhere." He snarled. "When I leave this place—and I will leave Lunaria—I will take you with me as my queen." His fingers danced across the invisible boundary. "If you ask me nicely, I might even let you bring my ungrateful son and whatever other lovers you want to slum it with. I'm only interested in your bloodline, not your cunt."

I rolled my eyes. Did he think crude insults were going to get a rise out of me? Vail and Alaric had already had that covered for the last *decade*. Maybe I should suggest he take lessons from them too?

"As fun as this chat has been"—I tapped my claws against the stone—"I'm starting to feel a bit bored. What specifically are you proposing? I'm not any more interested in your cock than you are in my cunt. My lovers have been keeping me *very* satisfied, and I'll definitely be adding a few more mate bonds in the future."

"You should be begging to be my queen." Erendriel's mouth twisted in distaste.

"The only thing I beg for is Kieran's co—"

"There are more hidden spaces like this throughout Lunaria," he cut me off, clearly annoyed that I did dirty talk way better than he. "If we form a mating bond, I'm confident it will give me access to them."

"To do what exactly?" I arched a brow. "The knowledge within these walls is useful to me, but you likely know all of it already."

He went still for a moment. "Agree to work with me, and I'll tell you."

"I'll think about it." I blew him a kiss and turned to walk back down the stairs.

"My patience only goes so far, Samara," he warned. "You don't want to find out what happens if I set my sights on you as an enemy."

"Likewise, usurper." I glanced over my shoulder, pulling on my bloodlust hard enough to let my eyes bleed black. "You asked me if the moon calls to me? She does. *We* are her beloved monsters. Lunaria might be the prison you were forced into, but it's the fire that forged us."

"*Qìnol, din tros. Leb are fi fel keb' fapnik.*" Careful, forgotten queen. We are the monsters you fear.

I snapped my fangs at him. "*Keb' are fi kuspa fel. Leb are fi men ones.*" You're the old monsters. We're the new ones.

<hr>

AN ENDLESS STREAM of thoughts swirled through my mind as I made my way down the stairs. I needed to inform everyone that I'd just had a conversation with the fucking Seelie King so we could dissect every word that had been spoken. There was so much to glean from my encounter—both about the history of Lunaria and what he needed us for.

What he needed *me* for.

I stepped out of the stairwell into the hallway of the first under level, only for Alaric to grab me by the waist and pivot my back to the wall.

"Alaric!" I squeaked. "What are you do—"

His mouth crashed against mine, demanding and possessive. I parted my lips, and his tongue slipped inside to taste me, then his hands slid from my waist to my ass, cupping me and hoisting me up. Thanks to the high slits on either side of the dress, I was able to wrap my legs around him easily as my arms wound around his neck.

Alaric ground against me, eliciting a moan. One hand gripped my ass harder, while the other roughly tugged the dress off my shoulders, causing my breasts to spill out because I hadn't found a chest band to wear while mine was drying.

"Seelie King," I panted when Alaric tore his mouth away from mine. "He was here. We spoke."

"I know." His head ducked down, and he sucked on my breast before palming it. "I heard every word that asshole said."

"Need to tell the others." I didn't know what had gotten Alaric so worked up, but he was making it increasingly difficult to stay focused on anything other than getting his pants off. "Alaric—oh, fuck!"

The hand that had been cupping my breast ran down my body until it slid between my thighs. There was no hesitation as he yanked my panties to the side and thrust three fingers into me. My hips bucked forward as Alaric pumped his fingers while his tongue teased my nipple.

All I could do was hold on and ride Alaric's hand as he fucked me. I could feel my climax building when he brushed his thumb over my clit before pushing down on it, making me scream his name as I came apart.

He laughed huskily against my skin, his breath tickling my hard nipple before raising his head to meet my gaze again. A satisfied smile stretched across his full mouth as he slowly played with the hot slickness dripping out of my pussy and down my thighs.

"I'll never get tired of feeling you come." A small amount of turquoise bled into his green eyes. "On my cock. My tongue. My hand." He thrust his fingers back inside my needy cunt, drawing another moan out of me.

"We need to tell—" My half-hearted protest was cut off when Alaric snapped his hips forward and I felt every inch of him through his pants. Suddenly, I desperately wanted something other than his fingers inside me.

"They can wait." Alaric grinned at me, desire and need lighting up his handsome face. The knowledge that nobody but me made him smile like that sent a thrill running down my spine. Mine. That smile was mine—just like he was. "Rynn and Roth are passed out. They literally fell asleep on top of the books, and they didn't didn't stir once as Kieran and I carried them downstairs to the room where Cali is still passed out. Kieran and Draven went off to *talk*." He rolled his eyes.

I let out a breathy laugh. No doubt their conversation was similar to the one Alaric and I were having. "And Vail?"

Alaric let out a wicked chuckle. "Knocked out cold on the floor."

"What happened?" I started, only to moan when he slid his fingers over my clit.

"Rynn happened." His gaze fell to where his fingers pumped in and out of me. "Knocked his ass out less than a minute after you left. It was a good hit. Asshole hasn't stirred once."

Any concerns I had for Vail vanished when Alaric shoved his fingers into me and fucked me roughly. I arched my hips into him, spurring him on, only to whimper when he withdrew them.

"I was on my way to find you when I heard you speaking with Erendriel." Fabric rustled, and then something hard and thick pushed into my core.

We both groaned as Alaric bottomed out and my pussy clenched around him.

"Did you mean what you said?" His eyes searched mine as more flecks of turquoise pierced through the green. I didn't even think he was aware of his bloodlust rising. I wasn't the least bit worried, but I was pleased to see him releasing some of that iron grip he kept on himself.

"About what?" I braced my hands on his shoulders, enough that I was able to rise up a bit before sinking back down onto his cock.

"Fuck," he ground out as he gripped my ass with both of his hands and pulled me harder onto him. I tilted my head back against the wall and enjoyed the thrill of him pounding into me. Alaric was always so in control—I loved being the one to make him lose it.

One of his hands left my ass to twist into my hair and force me to look at him again, the blue in his eyes snaking through the green like rivers.

"You have a mate bond with Draven, Roth, and Vail." Not a question—a statement. His pace changed from hard and fast to slow and torturous just as I was on the verge of climaxing again. I hissed in frustration and tried to lift myself up again, only for Alaric to grab my wrists and hold them above my head, his hips and body pinning me against the wall. "Did you mean what you said about forming a bond with all of us?"

"Yes, but if you don't have me coming in the next ten seconds, I might seriously rethink it," I growled.

Alaric stared at me. "I've been going out of my mind with jealousy over that fucking connection you have with those three assholes."

"Draven's not an asshol—"

"I know what he said to Kieran, so yes, Draven *is* an asshole." Alaric glared. "But I'm willing to make allowances since you two seem to like him."

"How gracious of you."

"And Vail is your problem, but just say the word, and we'll happily kill him for you." He maneuvered his hold until he secured both of my wrists in one hand so his other could go back gripping my ass. "I know I should say something clever and charming to assure you that you're making the right decision in forming the mate bond with me."

A flicker of uncertainty flashed in those beautifully mesmerizing eyes of his. After everything we'd been through, some part of him still thought I wouldn't choose him in the end.

"I don't need you to be charming, Alaric," I said honestly. "I just need you to be mine."

He leaned in until our foreheads touched. "Yours," he breathed across my lips. "Always."

"I love you, Alaric." I brushed my lips against his.

"I love you too, Sam." He kissed me again, this one tender and sweet, and yet it still left us breathless when we broke apart a moment later.

When he looked at me, his eyes were almost solid turquoise. I saw the moment he felt it, the panic that bled into his features as he tried to claw his bloodlust back. His hand dropped from my wrist, and he started to pull out of me to set me down but froze when I cupped his face in my hands.

"You're fine, my love." I kissed the corners of his mouth. "Your bloodlust has been rising this whole time, but nothing bad has happened. You won't turn Strigoi, I promise."

He swallowed. "We can't know for sure. I could hurt you or—"

I cut him off with a kiss before nipping his bottom lip. "You won't. Trust me." I leaned back enough so that I could slide my hand through the opening of his shirt and lay my palm flat over his heart. "Trust us."

A new bond burned and sizzled to life. I couldn't explain how I knew it would happen—only that I did with absolute certainty.

Alaric's eyes widened. "I can *feel* you."

"Show me." I shifted my hips slightly where we were still joined. "Fuck me, Alaric. Make your mate scream."

"As my queen demands." He grinned and stepped back from the wall, taking me with him, his cock still buried inside me. "But we're going down to the hot springs."

CHAPTER TWENTY-FOUR

—

Draven

Kieran followed me down the hallway, away from the room we'd left Rynn and Roth sleeping in. Cali had cracked open one golden eye at us but then drifted back into her healing slumber. Rynn and Samara had been the ones to remove the hairs the trapper spider had shot into her wings, and it hadn't been pretty. The hairs were covered in hundreds of little barbs that did just as much damage coming out as they did going in.

Blood magic didn't work on Furies, just as their shadow magic didn't work directly on us, so we couldn't aid her healing. She'd heal fast though, all Furies did, and sleeping it off would help.

Alaric had murmured something about checking on Samara, who was also still sleeping, but based on the pointed look he gave me, I knew he was giving me and Kieran some alone time.

Out of all of Samara's friends and lovers, he was the one I had the most difficulty reading. He and Roth were both equally standoffish, but Roth would just let things go for the most part. If it wasn't a book or Samara, they didn't seem to have the energy to care about it for long. Except for their family. For all their blustering, it was clear how much Roth loved their unhinged brothers and parents.

But at best, Alaric gave me cool looks. Most of the time though, he just acted like he was on the verge of tearing my throat out. I deliberately ignored his antics because I didn't really give a shit; all I needed was Samara and Kieran, and I had them both—and I'd never let them go again. Also, I was fairly certain I knew why Alaric treated me the way he did.

The grumpy asshole might be shit at choosing his words, but he loved Samara and Kieran was his best friend. He was protective of them both, and I'd hurt Kieran. Badly.

Kier might have already forgiven me for the things I'd said to break things off with him a year ago, but Alaric hadn't. It honestly made me respect him more, and I was thankful Kier had someone like that in his life.

Fortunately for me, I wasn't Vail. I knew how to apologize and right previous wrongs, which is something I'd be proving to Kier—and by extension, Alaric—for the rest of my life.

And that's exactly why I was leading Kier to the room at the very back of this floor, away from everyone else. I wanted to make sure we had privacy for this conversation, and for all the niceties of the living quarters here, I hadn't noticed any silencing glyphs.

Over the past few days, I'd been able to draw enough information out of Roth to get an idea of how things had been while Samara and I had been imprisoned. How Kieran had exhausted every single one of his contacts and grown more distant and snappish as they'd failed to provide anything useful. I knew how Kieran thought. He must have believed he was letting us down because my beloved courtier always felt he had something to prove, like he wasn't worthy of being loved.

For all of his confident swagger, Kieran eyed that gulf between our stations. I was a prince, twice over. Sure, mommy dearest was dead and Erendriel was a usurper, but even a fallen prince was still a prince.

Samara was the Harker Heir and likely soon to be Head of House Harker —maybe more, depending on what happened with the Sovereign House after Carmilla's inevitable demise. Plus the whole minor detail of her being the granddaughter of the former Seelie King.

In Kieran's eyes, he was less than us. Something that prick Demetri had only made worse. Samara had shared some of the hateful things Demetri had said during their final encounter, such as the reason he'd been so obsessed with forcing Samara to marry him again. How—in his words—he'd had no choice.

Samara had practically trembled with fury when she'd repeated what he'd said about Kieran. Demetri had wanted to save face because of the stupid gossip in his court about her falling in love with a courtier. His ego had been bruised, and he'd wanted to punish Samara for it.

It was a shame that Samara had killed him because I would have loved to cut out Demetri's hateful tongue and make him choke on it.

"I know the others are excited about the treasures upstairs, but honestly, these clothes are amazing," Kieran drawled as he explored the armoire against the wall of the room we'd ducked into. He held up a deep blue tunic embroidered with gold stitching. "Whatever Fae built this place had amazing taste. Hopefully they don't ever return to look for their stuff because I'm absolutely stealing all this and taking it back to House Harker."

"No doubt it will look better on you than any Fae." I grinned at him.

Kieran smiled back, but it faltered as he carefully folded the tunic and put it back onto the shelf. "I suppose maybe you and Samara won't be returning to House Harker though." He turned away from me and closed the doors to the armoire. "Everything is so fucked in Lunaria right now. You two might have to stay at the Sovereign House while it all gets fixed. Alaric will be useful in negotiating with the Houses, and Roth has a good mind for determining strategies for harvests and trades. Probably not much use for a courtier though." He snorted. "I don't think lavish balls and lazy mornings trading gossip are going to be in our future any time soon."

"Most likely not," I agreed and closed the distance between us. Kieran went still as I wrapped my arms around him, tugging his back to my chest. "But you know what is in my future?"

"What?" he asked tightly.

"You." I kissed his neck. "Always you, Kier."

Some of the tension eased from him, but not enough, so I spun him around until his back was against the armoire and I leaned my body against his. Kieran was only an inch shorter than me, but he was built a lot leaner.

"So this is why you chose a room so far from the others . . ." His brown eyes lit up, and a playful grin stretched across his mouth while he toyed with the ends of my hair.

It was a lie.

Kieran had as many masks as he did clothes—and he changed them far easier. Before everything had fallen apart between us, I'd adored watching him flit about the stupid parties Velika had been obsessed with throwing to boost her ego.

Between one breath and the next, Kieran would change from a sultry lover to an empathetic shoulder to cry on to a charming and self-deprecating friend.

I loved watching him work a crowd, seeing how he could get so many people to eat out of his hand and spill their secrets without even realizing what they were doing.

I did *not* love when he used one of those masks on me.

"Kier," I purred and ran a hand through his tousled blond hair before letting it trail down the side of his face. "What did I tell you about wearing those false smiles around me?"

Those beautiful brown eyes blinked, and then Kieran gasped when my hand dropped to his throat and tightened. "Drav," he rasped.

My mouth crashed against his, hungry and possessive, then I broke off the kiss almost as quickly as I'd started it, leaving Kieran breathless.

"Let me make this perfectly clear." I loosened my hold on his throat but didn't remove my hand. "I have done terrible things in my life. Things that will haunt my dreams until I take my last breath."

"You didn't have a choi—"

"Sometimes I did," I cut him off. "Most of the time, it's true that either

Erendriel or Velika forced me to do things." A lump formed in my throat as I thought of the outposts Erendriel had been able to break into because of me. I hadn't been willing, but it'd been my blood all the same that had allowed all those Moroi to be slaughtered while they slept. Their screams still echoed in my mind. I swallowed as I pushed out the other truth. "But, sometimes, I just wanted to avoid more pain . . . and I did as I was commanded."

"What happened?" Kieran asked softly, no judgment in his eyes.

Fuck. I didn't deserve him.

"Erendriel spends most of his time in the mountains above the Velesian realm, but the wraiths have different strongholds throughout Lunaria, including this temple for a while. More than one ranger has stumbled across them and seen too much." I dropped my gaze to Kieran's throat, where I had absently started running my thumb over his pulse. That constant reminder that he was alive. I focused on that while I continued, "When Erendriel was gone—which was often—he left Serril in charge. That prick reveled in making me choose between being subjected to whatever fun torture he had recently thought up . . . or ending the life of the ranger."

My spine itched where Serril had broken it in multiple places. For all his pretty words and calm demeanor, there was something seriously fucked up about Serril. I didn't know if he'd always been that way or if centuries of living as a wraith had twisted him. My father was a cruel bastard, but at least he didn't take pleasure in it the way Serril did.

Although he had to have known what his right-hand was like and still left him in charge. I shook my head to clear the dark memories.

Then I lifted my eyes to meet Kier's once more, expecting to see at least a hint of disgust, but there was none.

The corners of his lips curled into a lopsided smile that I knew was his real one. "This is Lunaria, Drav. We endure and survive, but that doesn't mean we come out unscathed. Those rangers were dead the moment they were captured. You can't regret granting them what I'm sure was a kinder death than the wraiths would have given them."

"I don't," I said truthfully. "Am I proud that I chose my life over theirs? No. Would I do it again? Absolutely."

He didn't say anything as I dropped both of my hands to his waist and tilted my head to touch my forehead to his. A second later, his hands rested over mine.

"The only thing in my wretched life that I regret is how much I hurt you that night," I whispered, because in my worst nightmares, I relived the scene of Kieran coming to one of my mother's parties and me breaking his heart in front of everyone. That beautiful smile falling from his face as I loudly announced that I was bored with him. That he should watch how he spoke to me since he was just a courtier.

Fuck. I was just one of many who had thrown Kieran's station in his face.

The nightmares never ended there though. No, the grand finale was always me finding Kieran's broken body somewhere. It was me waking up in panic with a pit in my soul, thinking Kieran was dead—and that I'd never have the chance to make things right between us.

That ended now.

"You are everything to me, Kier. I'm the one who's not worthy of you." I pulled back enough to look him in the eyes, which were glistening with tears. "But I will spend the rest of my life proving how much I fucking love you, if you'll let me."

"You have nothing to prove to me," Kieran said forcefully. When I opened my mouth, he clamped a hand over it. A few tears raced down his cheeks, but he was smiling at me. "And I'm more than happy to spend the rest of my life convincing you that you are worthy of being loved, because I absolutely love you beyond reason."

Then he dropped his hand from my mouth and kissed me.

The taste of him flooded my mouth, and when he bit my bottom lip hard enough to draw blood, I moaned. That sound was apparently his undoing because Kieran shoved me back a few steps and tore my tunic off before roughly yanking my pants down.

Before I knew what was happening, he was on his knees and swallowing my cock.

"Fuck, Kier." I grunted as my hand fell to the back of his head, fingers twisting in his hair. "I was planning on doing this to you."

He looked up at me as his lips slid back up my hard length. His tongue circled my broad head before releasing me completely. "Sorry, love." He gripped my base with his right hand and squeezed, giving me a cheeky grin that had me almost coming all over his damn perfect face. "But I was already intending on doing this, and I'm absolutely not stopping now. So how about you be the charming prince you are and fuck my mouth hard enough that I gag?"

"As you demand." I used my hand to push his head onto my cock at the same moment I thrust my hips forward.

Without breaking eye contact, he took me all the way in, his hand moving to cup my balls while his head bobbed up and down. I hadn't been lying, I'd been intending to throw him onto the bed and lavish him with praise and pleasure.

But if this was what my love wanted, who was I to deny him?

My thrusts became harder and more punishing, and Kieran let out a muffled moan as my cock hit the back of his throat over and over again. I felt myself start to coil and tighten. Gods, he was already going to make me come, like I was some inexperienced youth getting off for the first time.

"Kier," I ground out and yanked him off me. "I'm not ready yet, and your mouth is too fucking perfect."

He rose to his feet, that same playful grin on his face as he forced me to walk backwards until I hit the bed. I sat down, and Kieran shoved me onto my back. I was bigger than him and could have held my own, but I was kind of liking this bossy side of him, so I stretched across the bed, propping myself up on my elbows so I could watch him strip.

I gripped myself and lazily moved my hand up and down my cock while I admired Kieran's lean and hard body. Kieran watched me hungrily as he pulled a small glass vial from his pocket before ditching the rest of his clothes.

"Remember the game we used to play at parties?" Kieran moved to the edge of the bed and gripped my legs, pulling me closer to himself before angling them over his shoulders. Then he tipped the vial, letting some of the clear fluid seep out onto his fingers until they glistened.

"Oh, fuck me," I moaned when his hand slid under my ass and those slick fingers started teasing me.

"That was definitely part of the game." He chuckled darkly. "What was the other part?"

One finger slid in, stretching me out, and I bit back the second groan that tried to slip free. "To be quiet," I breathed. "You used to love fucking me near that damned veranda."

"And your favorite spot was in that alcove right behind where the musicians played." He pushed another finger inside me, and this time, I couldn't stop myself from moaning. "The others are only a few doors down. Trust me when I say that you don't want to be around Cali when her sleep gets disturbed."

"You're kind of wicked, Kier." I stroked myself harder.

"You love it." He grinned down at me and added a third finger.

"I do," I panted. "I really fucking do, but if you don't get your cock inside me in the next ten seconds, I'm going to bend you over this bed and—*fuck*!"

I thrust hard into my own hand as Kieran did exactly what I demanded. His thick length glided into me as he spread my legs a little wider over his shoulders.

"That's not staying quiet, my love." He hammered into me again before stopping, buried balls-deep inside. "Now put that hand of yours to work around that gorgeous cock."

His grip on my thighs tightened as he started fucking me hard and fast. I did as he ordered, sliding my hand up and down my length in rhythm with him. His gaze drank in every ounce of my pleasure, darting from where I bit my lip to try to choke back the moans, to where my hand was fisting my cock, and finally to where he was taking me over and over again.

It was getting harder and harder to stay quiet.

Kieran saw how close I was to losing it because gold bled into his brown eyes as he pushed my legs wider so he could lean down between them. I released my cock and pulled him to me, kissing him hard and then moaning when one of his hands found my rigid length.

He broke our kiss and turned his head, bearing his neck for me. I struck just as a scream threatened to escape my throat. My fangs slid into his soft flesh, and he let out a low moan as his sweet blood filled my mouth. His thrusts became rougher as he fucked me while I drank him down.

Then he groaned his release as my own orgasm tore through me. I slid my fangs free from his neck, and he collapsed next to me. Blood trailed down his neck and my cum coated my stomach and chest, but Kieran didn't give a single shit as he cuddled into my side.

Suddenly, a familiar heat flared inside my chest.

"Is that . . ." Kieran trailed off as he stared at the same spot on his own chest before his brown eyes flecked with gold looked up at me.

"Yes," I breathed out.

Whatever bond I had with Samara, I now had with him too.

***

AN HOUR LATER, we were both clean and in fresh clothes, thanks to the Fae who had left their clothing behind. Kieran straightened the tunic he'd been eying earlier as we started up the stairs. Cali and the others must have really needed their sleep because, somehow, we hadn't woken them when we'd started round two . . . or three.

Samara, however, was no longer in bed. There were no signs of Alaric either.

"So, what do you think?" Kieran glanced at me over his shoulder, his golden blond hair still dark from rinsing off. "Are they actually working upstairs . . . or fucking on one of the tables?"

I started to answer when a faint moan echoed up the stairwell.

We both stopped midstep.

"Neither." I laughed.

Kieran's eyes lit up. "I wonder if Alaric locked the door . . ."

I grinned mischievously. "Let me grab something real quick, and then we'll go find out."

A moment later, we were standing outside the large door that led to the underground hot springs. I'd actually been planning on convincing Samara to come down here later with me and Kieran, but it seemed Alaric had beat us there. Now we'd find out how much the grumpy asshole was up for sharing.

I suspected he'd be swayed when I presented the peace offering I held in my hand.

"Oh, fuck!" Samara screamed from the other side of the door. "Harder!"

Kieran reached out and slowly twisted the doorknob, which turned easily. He chuckled. "All his bitching, and he didn't lock the door either."

He flung the door open and we strode in without any hesitation.

The room—really more of a cavern—was completely open, with various pools of steaming water spilling into the others, courtesy of the mini-waterfalls that connected them all, and Fae lanterns cast the entire space in a soft, warm light.

It was one of the most beautiful sights I'd ever seen in Lunaria, but it paled in comparison to what was currently captivating all my attention—Samara leaning over the edge of one of the pools, her long, black hair hugging her body, and giving us a glorious view of her breasts as they bounced while Alaric fucked her hard from behind.

Her eyes widened when she saw us, and a second later, Alaric spotted us too. He slammed into her one more time and held still, his eyes a mix of turquoise and light green.

Interesting. I'd rarely seen him let his bloodlust out, and even then, it'd only been for brief flashes here and there.

"So that's what it feels like," Alaric said dryly, although his tone had a deep rasp to it now.

Kieran and I both let out dark chuckles. He'd told me about Alaric's proclivity of walking in on Samara getting fucked and the tantrums he'd thrown over it.

Samara moaned when Alaric thrust into her again while wrapping his hand around her dark hair and pulling back, forcing her to push those absolutely perfect tits out farther.

My concerns over Alaric not being keen on company vanished, which was good because my cock was getting uncomfortably tight in my pants.

"Need I remind you both that we are in a life-or-death situation here?" Kieran said sternly, even as he stripped and strode towards the pool.

"All the more reason to get some last-minute orgasms in while we can," Samara snarked before yelping when Alaric smacked her ass.

"She does have a good point, love," I said idly, tossing my own clothes aside.

Samara's bloodlust was out to play, and her eyes were like solid black gemstones as she hungrily looked at Kieran's cock and then mine. She was insatiable—I really loved that about her.

"I always have good point—wait." She went still, and Alaric loosened his hold on her hair but didn't pull out of her. Samara's hand fell to her chest as she looked at Kieran, then me. "I can feel Kier . . . through you."

Kieran blushed. Like honest to the moon *blushed*.

"We have . . ." I smiled softly at Kier. "We have what you and I have." My gaze went to Alaric, and I sensed what I hadn't noticed at first—that I could feel him too. "And apparently what you and him have now."

"Holy fuck!" Kieran beamed at his friend. "You two are . . . whatever this is?"

"Mates," Samara said softly. "It's a Fae mating bond."

The magic that coiled in my soul shuffled almost happily at the declaration.

"How . . ." I swallowed. "How do you know?"

For a second, the stupid happy grin slipped from Samara's face. "I'll tell you later—it can wait—let's celebrate." Alaric's hand trailed down her spine to grip her other hip, and she groaned as he shoved his hips forward. "Get your gorgeous asses in this pool."

"So demanding, Sam," Kieran chided before practically leaping into the water.

"Actually," I drawled as I leisurely closed the distance between me and Samara. "I have an idea."

"Oh?" she breathed out as Alaric slowly pumped in and out of her.

"Mm-hmm." I fell to my knees in front of Samara, just far enough away that her mouth couldn't reach my cock the way I knew she wanted to based on how she licked her lips while she stared at it. "It'll require a little rearranging though."

"Not a fan of that idea," Alaric grunted.

"Oh, you will be." Kieran chuckled as he grabbed a handful of Samara's hair and twisted her head enough so his mouth could claim hers.

"What my *mate* means to say"—happiness bloomed inside my chest at calling Kieran that, and I felt it echoed down our bond—"is that we brought you a present."

Alaric looked towards me as I held out the small vial. For a second, he just stared, but then his lips stretched into a smile that could only be described as sinful.

After one more hard thrust that had Samara moaning into Kieran's mouth, he pulled out.

"What?" Samara growled and started to look over her shoulder, only to exhale sharply as Kieran picked her up and slammed her down onto his cock in one smooth motion. "Oh, fuck," she moaned and wrapped her legs and arms around him.

Kieran kissed her as she continued lifting herself up slightly before slamming down on him while he walked them over to a shallower ledge and perched on the edge. Samara straddled him, continuing to ride his cock as the water splashed around them. The back of the pool slanted slightly, allowing Kieran to lean back and pull Samara forward with him.

"I still think you're an asshole." Alaric took the bottle from me.

"Honestly, same." I shrugged.

"You ever break Kieran's or Samara's hearts again, I'll carve out yours and stick it in a jar to decorate my office," he said casually.

"If I ever do that again, I'll let you." It wasn't a lie. I'd sooner break my chest open and rip out my own heart than hurt them again.

Kieran did something to make Samara let out a half-strangled moan, and both of us looked over at them.

"Alright." Alaric glanced down at the vial in his hand. "Let's go fuck our mate until her voice gives out."

I got to my feet as Alaric strode through the water to where Kieran had sat up enough to suck on one of Samara's breasts while his fingers teased the nipple of the other. Her head was tilted back in pure ecstasy as she continued to bounce up and down on his cock.

Sensing our approach, she glanced over her shoulder to where Alaric now stood behind her before looking up at me. "You look like you have a plan, prince." She smirked.

"I do, my queen." I concentrated until the rocks to the left of where Kieran sat moved to form another ledge that jutted out into the water a couple of feet. Kieran raised his head from Samara's chest, and they both watched me take my place on my newly formed seat next to them.

My fingers closed around my cock as I slid my hand up and down before reaching out and stroking Samara's face. "You're going to take all of me and also both of them. Can you do that for us, love?"

"Yes," she breathed out before groaning as Alaric slid a finger into the tight ring of her ass.

"Such a good girl," Kieran crooned. "You're going to be dripping with all our cum soon."

"Fuck, Kier," Alaric ground out. "Maybe tone it down until I'm inside this perfect ass. I'm so hard, it fucking hurts."

"What are you waiting for?" Samara teased. "You were very adamant about claiming my ass, Alaric, so do it already."

She moaned when Alaric slapped her ass hard, but it was cut off when I gripped her by the chin and forced her head back. "That's enough sass out of you." I ran my thumb roughly over her bottom lip before forcing it into her mouth. "He's making sure you're ready to take his cock, because we're going to fuck you hard until you're a trembling mess . . . and then we're going to do it again. We don't want to break you too early."

Her tongue licked my thumb while she sucked on it, a glazed look in her eyes. "Yes, *my prince.*"

I groaned. How did she make that sound so hot?

Fuck it. I pulled my thumb from her mouth and pushed my cock against her lips, smearing the bead of precum over them.

Kieran leaned forward and licked the side of my shaft while Samara's tongue darted out to swirl around my thick head.

"You two are going to be the death of me," I ground out as Kieran and Samara continued worshipping my cock with their tongues. Part of me was desperate to come right now and cover their faces with my seed. If it'd just been the three of us, I probably would have.

But there was no chance I was letting Alaric outlast me. Luckily, I suspected as soon as he was inside Samara's tight ass, he'd be having control issues too.

I let my head fall back and rested my hand on Samara's head as she and Kieran took turns sucking me off. Only when Samara gasped did I look down at them again. Kieran was watching her face with rapt attention, and he'd momentarily stopped thrusting into her.

"Fuck, Sam," Alaric said in a strained tone as he gripped her hips. "You feel amazing."

Samara panted as Alaric pulled back before pushing in again. My hand slipped up and down my cock, still wet from Sam and Kier playing with it, and it grew even harder as Kieran started moving in time with his best friend.

Strangled sounds slipped from Samara's lips as she writhed between the two of them. Kieran's hands moved to her ass and he spread her wide for Alaric. I was tempted to adjust my position so I could watch Samara take both of them, but then Alaric reached up and wrapped his hand around Samara's long hair, tugging her head back.

"Put that pretty mouth of yours to use." He directed her face towards my lap. "Swallow the prince's cock."

Obediently, Samara opened her mouth, and I didn't hesitate. She let out a choked moan as I slammed my cock all the way in, tears streaming down her cheeks as she gagged but kept going.

"You take all of us so beautifully." Kieran licked some of the tears off Samara's cheeks before tilting his head back. Seeing that blissed out look on his face while Samara took us both was becoming one of my favorite things.

The water started to splash more as Alaric's thrusts became harder, and Kieran groaned as Samara was pushed further onto his cock. Fuck, we were doing round two after this. I wanted Kieran to claim her ass while I sank into her pussy.

I hoped Samara knew she wasn't getting any sleep for at least a couple more hours.

Alaric released his hold on Samara's hair so that he could grip her hip with one hand and reach around to play with her clit with the other. She screamed around my cock, and I grabbed her by the hair, pulling her off.

Words poured from her lips in the common tongue, Seelie, and Unseelie, as Kieran and Alaric continued to fuck her hard. I watched as she climaxed, her black-as-night eyes rolling to the back of her head as neither man paused. If anything, they started thrusting into her harder.

It wasn't long until she was coming again, but this time, Alaric came with her with a loud groan, and Kieran followed a few seconds later. I forced her to look at me again. "Don't swallow, my queen," I ordered.

Samara whimpered but nodded and parted her lips as I slid my cock back into her mouth. I set a punishing pace, and she gagged several times but kept trying to take me further.

"Good girl," Kieran praised. "Relax your throat and take him deeper."

I felt myself tighten when she did as Kieran bade. Just before I came, I pulled my cock almost all of the way out of her mouth, and she parted her lips enough that I could watch my seed spill all over her pink tongue. Only when I'd completely filled her mouth did I fully remove myself and push her towards Kieran.

Neither of them hesitated as they kissed each other. When a small amount of my cum dripped out of Samara's mouth, Kieran broke their kiss so he could lick it off her.

Inside my chest, my two mate bonds thrummed happily as Samara collapsed onto Kieran's chest, letting out a low groan as Alaric pulled out of her.

The moody asshole looked decidedly less grumpy as he settled on the other side of Kieran and Samara. I met his gaze over them, and he gave me the smallest of smiles. "Perhaps you're not the worst after all."

CHAPTER TWENTY-FIVE

—

Samara

"Erendriel was here?" Rynn squeaked. "And you didn't wake us up to tell us that immediately!?"

"Cali was sleeping like the dead!" I pointed at my friend, who was leaning her hip against one of the workshop tables. "And then I got . . . distracted . . ."

"With dick?" Cali arched a brow.

I shrugged. "It happens."

"Tragically, I wouldn't know," she lamented. "My pussy is drier than the badlands these days."

Roth and Alaric laughed from where they stood opposite Cali. It was early afternoon, and we were all gathered in the same room as yesterday. It was the only room on this floor that had places to sit and tables for laying things out. The rest of the rooms contained more books, scrolls, weapons, and other odds and ends.

It would take us years to go through everything and thoroughly catalog, which was something I hoped we'd have time to do. The scholars at Drudonia might literally lose their minds over the knowledge contained here.

Kieran gave Cali an exaggerated look of concern. "I didn't realize things were that dire, Cal. As I said previously, I can find some sturdy, non-drama-causing Moroi to help you with that." He cocked his head while twirling a hand through the air. "Do you have any preferences—"

"Can we please stop talking about dicks and pussies for a second?" A golden sheen rolled over Rynn's eyes, and a snarl undermined her words.

"Speaking of not getting any . . ." Kieran said lightly.

Rynn turned her wolfish glare on him and growled, causing him to grab Roth and thrust them in front of him.

"Seriously?" Roth sighed and elbowed Kieran in the gut.

"Sam, control your—" Rynn turned to me and frowned. "What are we calling them? Paramours? Consorts?"

"Mates." I smiled. "I did indeed have a conversation with the Seelie King last night, and during it, he sensed the connections. They're Fae mate bonds."

Cali arched her eyebrows. "What does that mean, exactly?"

"Oh, I have no idea." I shrugged. "I only read the romantic shit about them growing up, but none of the poems had any actual useful information.

"Of course not." She snorted.

"Mate bonds," Roth murmured as they rubbed the spot on their chest over their heart. "That feels . . . right."

I smiled softly. "It does." My gaze went to the shelves of books lining the walls. "If we come across any books that mention them, let's pull them aside to review later. As much as I want to know more about the bonds, it's not as urgent as everything else."

"Fair." Roth nodded. "I'm definitely curious about what they can do and how they are formed." They glanced at me and then Alaric. "You two have one now, right? I can't feel his emotions, but I think I can feel the new bond between you both."

"Gods, Sam." Cali smirked at me. "Here I am living the celibate life, and you have five freaking mates."

"Four, technically," Kieran said. "Sam and I don't have one yet."

The smirk fell off Cali's face, and she rubbed the back of her neck awkwardly as silence fell. *Sorry,* she mouthed at me.

A pit of guilt settled in my stomach. I would have tried to bond with Kieran last night, but he had just done so with Draven, and I hadn't wanted to take anything away from that. What they had was just as valid and special as what I had with Kier, and I loved that they were happy.

But given that Kieran had hang-ups about thinking he wasn't enough, had I messed up? What if he thought I didn't *want* to form a mate bond with him? If I had hurt him—even unintentionally—I'd never forgive mysel—

"Sam." Kieran stepped forward and cupped my face in his hands before kissing the corners of my mouth. "Stop panicking. My feelings aren't hurt. You had just bonded with Alaric, and I had just done the same with Draven. We don't have to rush this."

"Are you sure?" I closed my eyes and leaned into his touch. "Because in my heart, you're already my mate, Kier. I just wanted to give you and Drav some time to settle into your mating bond before we threw ours on top of it."

"I figured." He smiled, and there was so much joy and love in it that my worries instantly evaporated. "Because I very much want to be your mate—in both the name and magic bond kind of way—but I want us to be able to celebrate it."

Alaric sighed. "You want a party, don't you?"

"Of course I want a party." Kieran sniffed and stepped away from me so he could shove his friend's shoulder. "Samara is obviously saving the best for last. That deserves a celebration." He looked at Roth. "Think your parents will be up for throwing a double wedding or something?"

Roth rubbed their forehead. "They would no doubt be thrilled."

I opened my mouth to tease them when Rynn stalked off to the table of books and started flipping through them.

Shit. I exchanged a look with Cali before we both looked at Rynn in concern.

I hadn't thought about how all this talk of mates would affect her.

Normally, Moroi didn't refer to their spouses or lovers as mates, but the Velesians did. They'd been the only ones to pick up that habit from the Fae. It was a big deal for them, although I didn't know the specifics of what it entailed. They kept it all very hush-hush, and it was one of the few things Rynn never talked about.

I did know that mates were *never* forced in the Velesian realm. Rynn might not have had a choice in joining the Alpha Pack, but she didn't have to choose them as mates. Nor did they have to choose her.

But the chances of her finding a mate outside of her pack was complicated. Technically, she could, but how would she know if they truly wanted her or just wanted a way to join the Alpha Pack, who rarely accepted anyone into their inner circle?

Rynn had been a political pawn her entire life. The only people who had ever chosen her just for being who she was were me and Cali. We might be her best friends for life . . . but we weren't her mates.

A good fuckfest might make Cali happy—at least for a while—but I doubted that would work for Rynn. She wanted something more than that.

My heart ached for my friend. I couldn't fix her problems now—or possibly ever—but I could at least distract her.

"Mate bonds aside, there were a lot of other interesting things I learned from the Seelie King." I walked over to one of the tables and perched my butt on it. The others settled into chairs or leaned against tables while I recounted everything Erendriel had said.

"What is with people wanting to marry you?" Vail muttered.

"Jealous?" I arched a brow at him and already started thinking of a pithy response for when he no doubt lost his temper.

"Marriage is too simple a word for what I want from you," he said in a low, deep tone that had me clenching my thighs together. "If Erendriel tries to take you from me, I will tear him apart limb from limb and offer you his still-beating heart as a gift."

The snarky response I'd had ready to go died on my tongue. For once, I had no idea what to say. The sincerity and intense need I saw on Vail's face was echoed in the bond. He really did mean it.

"Wow, Rynn." Kieran clapped slowly. "You should knock Vail out more often. He finally figured out how to use his words."

Instead of getting angry, the corners of Vail's mouth twitched.

May the moons damn it all. Did he almost *laugh*?

"I definitely plan on punching Vail again," Rynn said absently as she stared unseeingly at a spot on the floor while she processed everything I'd recounted before her gaze snapped to me. "He said the Unseelie Princes *are* liars? Not *were*?"

"Definitely present tense," I confirmed. "No idea where the rest of the Unseelie are or if they're still alive, but their princes are still kicking around somewhere."

"There's something in the mountains," Draven mused. "Erendriel spends most of his time there."

"Maybe the princes are there." I looked at the floor-to-ceiling bookshelves that lined the room. "Or maybe there are more places like this in the mountains that don't have wards in place preventing him entry. I don't think he liked that we were able to get into this room. Either because he wants what's in here for himself, or he thinks there is something here that we'll be able to use against him."

"Probably both." Draven snorted and reached behind himself to swipe a dagger off the table. Then he tossed it to me, and I snatched it out of the air.

"These glyphs . . ." I ran a finger down the silver handle. "They're like the ones the rangers use on their weapons but way more complicated."

Erendriel hadn't been wrong when he'd said we were like children bumping around in the dark. We'd only figured out that we could use the magic in our blood to reactivate the Fae glyphs a century or so ago. From there, we'd been able to derive spells of our own, usually by combining glyphs. It'd taken us a while to figure out that we had to pour our intention into the spells as well as our blood.

It took a lot of trial and error, and we still didn't really understand *how* any of this worked, only that it did. I glanced at the mirror that resided in the corner of the room. Rynn had walked through a blood mirror and traveled almost a thousand miles.

That was a little beyond using glyphs to make water hot.

Alaric rose from where he'd been sitting and walked over to me, then held out his hand, and I passed him the dagger.

"These are Unseelie glyphs," he noted, likely spotting the same small flourishes that distinguished their glyphs from the Seelie's. He pointed at the glyph carved into the actual blade of the dagger. "*Gùlma âmâm.*" Light green eyes flicked up from the blade to me. "Shadow killer. Why would the Unseelie make weapons to use against their own kind?"

"Maybe that's not what it does?" I took the dagger back from him and studied the glyphs more. Several of them on the handle I didn't recognize.

Cali sighed and pushed off the bookshelf she'd been leaning against. She stopped a few feet from me, but a shadow version of herself stepped out of her body and kept going.

Everyone except me, Rynn, and Roth stiffened.

We were used to Cali's abilities. The others had seen her shadow form before—she usually used it to communicate long distances and had even given Rynn a ring that allowed her to do the same—but there was still something about seeing the endless pit of darkness peel itself away from Cali that was unnerving.

It was so wraith-like that I often wondered if our human ancestors' spell had been similar to the one used by the Seelie that resulted in them becoming wraiths.

The shadow version of Cali strode forward while the flesh-and-blood version stood there with an impassive expression. We all watched as a shadowy hand stretched out to touch the tip of the blade.

"Maybe this isn't a good ide—" Alaric started, only to be cut off when Cali's shadows exploded, covering sections of the room in darkness.

I fell from the table I'd been sitting on, my knees slamming to the floor and the dagger clattering a second later. My hands clamped around my ears as if that would help as Cali screamed.

Vaguely, I was aware of everyone else hitting the ground too. Pressure built in my head, and it felt like my mind was being shredded as Cali's magic slammed into it.

"Cal," I panted. "*Stop.*"

My back arched in pain as every single nerve lit up.

A large white wolf leapt over a table and barreled into Cali—the real one. She hit the ground hard, and the screaming abruptly cut off, then the shadows that had been convulsing suddenly vanished.

The wolf very ungracefully flopped to her side next to Cali, and a second later, a trembling Rynn was there with a sheen of sweat over her skin.

In their animal form, Velesians weren't as impacted by a Furie's magic, but they weren't entirely immune either. I dropped my hands from my head and groaned as I got to my feet. We were lucky Cali wasn't at full strength and some part of her hadn't wanted to hurt us. Her magical assault had been painful, but at least she hadn't driven us mad.

"Fuck," I ground out and leaned against the table. "What the hells happened, Cali?"

Around me, everyone else was getting up. Draven helped Kieran over to a chair while Roth and Alaric leaned on each other. I glanced at Vail, half expecting him to have a weapon in his hand and looking at Cali like he was figuring out the best way to take her down; instead, I found him looking at me, his hands hanging by his sides—empty.

There was tension in his posture—he still viewed Cali as a threat—but he trusted me to handle my best friend. Silver eyes bored into mine, and I could almost see the question in them. *You okay?*

I gave him a small but genuine smile and pushed a wave of gratitude down our bond. I knew it worked when the tension running through him relaxed slightly and he nodded once.

A very naked Rynn sat up and glared at Cali, who was still lying on the ground, then she smacked the back of her hand against the Furie's ribs. "I second Sam's question. What in the actual fuck, Cal?"

"Give me a second," Cali groaned as she flinched in response. "That was really unpleasant."

"You don't say," Roth deadpanned.

Kieran snort-laughed and then quickly winced and rubbed his temples.

I pushed off the table and took a few wobbly steps before swiping the dagger up off the ground. "Are there more weapons with these glyphs?"

"Yes." Draven gestured towards a neat pile of daggers on the table. "All of these."

"There might be more in the other rooms," Kieran added from where he was seated next to Draven. "We haven't looked at them all that closely."

"Okay, so we potentially have a weapon that can be wielded against the wraiths." I looked at Cali, who had managed to sit up, but her skin, which usually had a healthy tan to it, looked pale and almost sickly. Part of me was troubled by the fact that someone could use these daggers against her. She'd only pricked her finger with the end of it; what would happen if she were stabbed with one? And would the daggers work on her flesh as well as her shadows?

"Don't worry about me." Cali gave me a knowing look. "Now that I know what those daggers do, I'll make sure I don't ever get stabbed with one. And let's be real, nobody in Lunaria is a match for me." A cocky grin stretched across her lips. It would have been more believable if she didn't look like a butterfly could knock her over.

"Can you summon your shadows now?" Alaric's piercing gaze was locked on Cali. "Did it have any lingering effects on your magic?"

Cali concentrated, and then her eyes widened. "I can't feel them." Panic drenched her words. "My shadows . . ." She held up her hands and stared at them with golden eyes that started to glow.

A pressure started to build at the base of my spine. "Cali," I warned.

The feeling disappeared, and she gave me an apologetic look. "Sorry." She dropped her hands. "I felt a flicker of them for a second. My shadow magic is still there; it's just currently out of reach." She paused for a second, and the glow of her eyes brightened before fading. "It doesn't seem to have impacted my mental magic at all."

"We can't be sure how well they'll work against Erendriel." I walked over to the table with the rest of the weapons and placed the dagger onto it. "I didn't see a trace of shadows on him last night, so he might be fully back to his Seelie form now."

"It's possible," Draven admitted reluctantly. "Although, if anyone could figure out how to retain a bit of shadow magic and also get back his original form, it would be that asshole."

"He'll be back to speak with me," I said confidently. "I'll try to suss out a little more of his magic then. In the meantime, Carmilla is just as much of a threat as Erendriel—maybe more so."

Roth nodded. "War will break out in the Moroi realm. My House will never follow her, and it's unlikely that Tepes or Salvatore will either. She'd likely been counting on quietly taking control, going House by House and using the crown to manipulate key players."

I thought about Kieran's parents and how she'd sent them back to House Corvinus to be her puppets. "Most likely," I agreed. "We're ruining that plan because we know the truth and can gather allies. The crown might be a powerful weapon, but it's not making it easy for her."

Because it wanted to sit on my head. It was odd, but some part of me wanted that too. Not for the crown's abilities, but just because it felt . . . right. Some part of me was drawn to the crown—and wanted it back.

"Sooner or later, Carmilla is going to figure out where we are," Vail spoke up. "There could be a traitor amongst Salvatore, or one of the rangers loyal to her could have seen us on the way here. Even if they didn't track us the whole way, there aren't a lot of places in the badlands to seek refuge."

"True. I wouldn't be surprised if she already knows where we are." My gaze fell on Cali. "She'll figure out a way to get you off the board if she can."

"Let the bitch try." Cali bared her teeth.

I shook my head. "We can't afford to doubt Carmilla. She'll come at the problem from an angle we're not seeing. I don't think we need to worry about her attacking while you're here, but we can't count on that. This place might be secure against Erendriel and the wraiths, but we'll be cornered if Carmilla sends a bunch of rangers in here."

"Rynn," Kieran said slowly. "You said you blocked the Alpha Pack from following you into the secret room underneath their castle . . . how did you do that?"

"A glyph . . ." Rynn chewed her bottom lip as her brows furrowed in concentration. "It all happened so fast, but there were some markings on the wall beside the door. A barrier spell—one I'd never seen before."

There definitely wasn't one by the doorway here because I would have noticed last night during my chat with Erendriel. Odd that the room Rynn had found had one and not this place.

"A spell of that kind could be useful," Draven mused.

An idea bloomed in my head. It was kind of crazy, and I'd need to figure out several key elements for it to work, but it could solve two of our biggest problems in one go.

"Rynn and I will go take a look at that glyph to see if we can replicate it here," I said evenly. "Alaric and Roth, you can continue scouring the books to see if you find anything useful. Draven and Vail, go through the weapons and pull out any that can be used against the wraiths."

"Is splitting up wise?" Alaric hedged.

"We're literally just going to step through that mirror." Rynn pointed to where the Fae artifact stood in the corner. "You all can peep your heads through if you want. The room is a lot smaller on the other side, so there's not enough space for all of us. You'd all just be standing around while Samara and I figure out how that glyph works. Trust me." She wrinkled her nose. "Nobody wants to avoid being caught by the Alpha Pack more than I."

Cali grumbled something under her breath.

"You're not killing them," Rynn huffed at her. "Just because I hate their smug, arrogant faces doesn't mean they're not good for the Velesians in general. Two things can be true at once."

"Whatever." Cali flopped back onto the floor, stretching out her wings and whacking Rynn in the face with one. The Velesian growled down at her, but Cali just pouted up at the ceiling. "You lot never let me kill anything, and it's getting tiresome."

Draven chuckled and started going through a stack of daggers on the table. Alaric and Roth came over and kissed me on the cheek before pulling some books from shelves and settling into chairs.

"And what about me?" Kieran arched a brow.

I grinned at him. "You're coming with us. On the off chance one of the Alpha Pack members is waiting on the other side of the barrier, it's your job to sweet-talk them while we steal their shit."

"Sounds fun." His eyes lit up. "I hope it's Bastian. He's fun to play with."

My grin slid from my face, and I narrowed my eyes at him—and across the room, I heard the sound of weapons clattering against each other. I glanced at Draven to find him glaring at Kieran too.

"Linguistically." Kieran rolled his eyes. "The overgrown pussycat is fun to play with *linguistically*."

"You'll be my favorite Moroi forever if you call Bastian that to his face," Rynn said seriously before springing to her feet and trotting over to the mirror.

Kieran chuffed. "I'm already your favorite Moroi. You just let Samara pretend she is to protect her delicate sensibilities—oww!" He rubbed the back of his head where I'd smacked him. "Rude."

"Come on." I grabbed his arm and started tugging him towards where Rynn was waiting for us, only pausing to grab a few sheets of paper and sharpened pieces of charcoal so I could sketch out the glyph for reference.

I thrust them into the pockets of my dress before coming up short when Vail stomped over, shoving between me and Kieran. "If there is even a *hint* of the barrier being down when you get into that room, you get that nice ass back here immediately. The Alpha Pack isn't going to react reasonably if they see you with Rynn."

"You need to work on your compliments as much as your apologies." I poked him in the chest. "And I don't have a nice ass—I have an *amazing* ass."

"Sam," Vail growled.

"Vail," I mockingly growled back.

My heart quickened when he smiled at me before leaning down to whisper in my ear, "If you don't bring that *amazing* ass back in one piece, I'm going to think of all kinds of ways to punish it." Before I could get out a clever retort, Vail's hand gripped the back of my head, and his lips crashed against mine in a searing kiss. Heat coursed through me as I molded my body into his.

Yes. I was still mad at him.

Yes. I was enjoying the hells out of this kiss.

As Rynn had said before, two things could be true at once.

"Stop getting distracted by dick!" Rynn barked sharply.

Vail and I broke apart, both of us breathing a little heavily.

"Also"—his eyes slid to where Kieran was now waiting with Rynn, a stupid grin on his face—"I want credit for allowing you to go with just the wolf and peacock."

"You don't *allow* me to do anything," I sputtered, but Vail was already stalking back towards the weapons table.

Draven shook his head at him. "You almost had it but fumbled the landing."

"Shut up," Vail growled.

"Let's go." Rynn grabbed me. "Deal with your obnoxiously possessive and bossy mates later. Cade and the others are usually patrolling at this hour, and I'd like to get in and out without them noticing," she snapped before shoving me face-first into the mirror.

"Oh fuck, that was weird." I hopped from one foot to the other as I stared wide-eyed at the mirror. The reflective surface looked solid, but as soon as I made contact, it felt like a cold, viscous liquid slipping over my skin. My mind told me I should be dripping wet right now, but my skin was dry and unblemished.

Aside from the weird sensation, it'd been fine. Nothing like when Draven had tripped the glyph at the bottom of House Harker and my stomach had tried to relocate to my throat as we fell.

"Rynn wasn't kidding." Kieran glanced around the space we had landed in. "I'm not even sure Vail would have fit in here, and Draven's ego definitely wouldn't have."

"I'm going to tell Draven you said that." I peered at the completely packed shelves that I could only see parts of, thanks to the wooden crates full of more books and scrolls stacked precariously in front of them.

"Go for it." Kieran grinned at me. "I like his punishments."

I thought of when Draven had used his whip to tie me up in the cabin.

"Good point. Tell him I talked shit about him too."

Kieran snorted. "This place actually makes Roth's room look neat and tidy." He reached out to the nearest stack of books just as Rynn stepped through the mirror.

"Don't"—the books tumbled over with a loud crash—"touch anything," Rynn finished tensely and looked towards the open doorway that led into another small room.

The three of us held still, waiting to see if the Alpha Pack would barge in. We were close enough to the mirror that we could make it back through and smash the one on the other side . . . probably.

Velesians were fast fuckers.

A little tension bled out of Rynn's shoulders when nothing happened. Either they weren't here or the barrier was still holding.

"Come on." She slipped past me and Kieran—somehow managing not to knock over more books—and headed towards the small room that must have been the entryway. "Let's do what we came here to do and get the fuck out before one of those assholes comes . . ."

She trailed off and came to a slow halt a foot past the arched doorway like prey that suddenly realized it was no longer alone.

Immediately, I dashed towards her with Kieran hot on my heels, books crashing behind us in our haste. I'd been right—this room was just a small entryway that led to the stairwell. Another archway was directly to our right, which hadn't been visible from the other room. Clearly, it used to have a door because the black hinges were still attached to the stone—mostly anyway—but now, they were twisted and half torn out, like someone had wrenched the door free with their bare hands.

My bet was on Cade. The ursanthrope spoke with even words and calming smiles most of the time, but when he lost it, you got to see what a three-thousand-pound, pissed-off bear looked like up close.

It wasn't the leader of the Alphas who was waiting for us though. Nor was it Bastian or Ryker—the latter of whom I was happy not to see because Rynn didn't act rationally around the other lycanthrope. Plus, I didn't want to be around two snappish wolves any more than I wanted to deal with the bear.

Leaning against the wall on the other side of the doorway was a man with deep brown skin so dark, it was as if it had been kissed by midnight. His black hair was cut short, and the neatly trimmed beard somehow called even more attention to his handsome features.

I had five extremely gorgeous lovers, and I was not the least bit interested in another, but even I had to acknowledge that this man was hot.

Like, impossibly so.

I also had no fucking idea who he was.

Though I was pretty sure Rynn did, based on the intensity she was staring him down with. She still hadn't moved from her spot, but I recognized the almost cautious aggression sending trembles up her lithe frame. If she were in wolf form, her hackles would've been raised right now.

The handsome stranger's golden yellow eyes barely glanced at me and Kieran before falling back to her. He said nothing, but I saw the hatred burning in his eyes.

"I was wondering when you were going to bother showing up." Rynn finally spoke in a low, raspy voice. "You smell even worse in person."

Kieran and I traded a weighted look. Velesians were kind of particular about scents—especially their own. Telling one of them they stank was a sure way to get your throat ripped out.

"Rynn, who—"

"Just copy the glyph, Samara," Rynn cut me off. "The barrier is up. He can't get through."

Right. I pulled the papers and charcoal from my pocket and strode towards the doorway. The golden-eyed Velesian didn't move, but his eyes did flick towards me for a second before returning to Rynn.

No vertical slits. So he wasn't a panther shifter. All the ursanthropes I'd met had a much larger build. He could be a lycanthrope, but something about that didn't feel right. If I was correct, then that meant he was an aetanthrope—an eagle shifter.

Kieran followed me as I quickly laid the paper over the glyph and then scratched the charcoal over it until the pattern appeared on the sheet. I handed it to Kieran, and he carefully folded it so it wouldn't smudge before tucking it into his pocket. On another sheet, I made some notes about how the glyph was positioned on the wall and some other finer details that might not have come through in my charcoal imprint.

After handing that paper to him and tucking the charcoal back into my pocket, I studied the glyph for a few minutes. My memory was pretty good, so between that and the papers, I was confident I could recreate this glyph.

The man hadn't broken his silence once. It was kind of unnerving. I was burning to ask Rynn who the fuck he was, but she hadn't offered up that information, and the situation felt volatile enough that I didn't want to push her about it.

When I stepped back from the wall to stand beside Rynn, the man finally deigned to speak. "I'm going to enjoy stripping the flesh from your bones, traitor," he said in a deep melodic voice.

"Try me, Warrick," Rynn sneered.

Warrick. Holy. Shit. The missing member of the Alpha Pack. Or at least, a member who nobody in the Moroi realm had seen in decades. We'd all assumed he was dead and that his death was the reason the Alpha Pack had been less inclined to talk to us recently.

Kieran had clearly been thinking similar thoughts because he gave the Velesian a leering look and drawled, "You're looking pretty good for a dead man."

Warrick's cold, predatory gaze flicked to him. "I don't speak to Moroi whores."

"Technically, you just did," Kieran pointed out and leaned an elbow on my shoulder. "Given your whole vibe, I think you really need to get laid. I know I'm absolutely stunning, but unfortunately for you, I'm off the market, so you'll have to look elsewhere."

Rynn choked on a laugh, finally snapping out of her stare off with Warrick, and slid a glance to Kieran. "You are definitely my favorite."

"I know." Kieran nodded sagely.

Warrick's eyes burned with fury, but before he could say anything else, footsteps echoed down the stairwell, and a moment later, Bastian appeared.

In the dim lighting, his usually vertical pupils had rounded out, and he gave Warrick a brief warning look before turning his attention to us. While Warrick exuded a quiet deadliness, Bastian was all sleek underhandedness.

"Rynn," he said smoothly, "I'm delighted that you've returned to us."

"Oh go fuck yoursel—" Her words were cut off as Kieran clamped a hand over her mouth and pulled her snug against his chest. Both Velesians' eyes narrowed at him holding her.

Shit. *Diplomacy,* I reminded myself. *Don't make things worse.*

"Apologies, Bastian." I stepped in front of Rynn. "She's helping us with a minor issue in the Moroi realm."

Sharp green eyes cut to me. "The minor issue being your aunt overthrowing the Sovereign House, seizing power, and according to a few rumors, being in possession of a Fae crown capable of controlling minds."

"You have to admit, he has a way with words," Kieran chimed in. "It's kind of hot."

I gave Kieran a scathing look over my shoulder before returning my focus to Bastian. "I have things under control." Or, really, I had a vague outline of an absolutely insane plan that had a small chance of working.

The daemon is in the details, as the Fae used to say. I had no idea what a daemon was, but it sounded neat.

"Do you?" Bastian cocked his head at me.

"Yes." I took a step back and heard Kieran drag Rynn towards the other room, where the mirror waited for us. "We have no interest in a war with the Velesians. I *will* handle things in the Moroi realm."

"The traitor stays," Warrick said in a calm tone that I didn't believe for a second.

"No." I gave him a cool look. "Rynn's with me."

Aggression rolled off Warrick, but Bastian stepped in front of him in a move very similar to what I'd done to Rynn.

"What my friend means to say is that Rynn belongs with us," Bastian said in that polite tone of his that I always found a little annoying. "She is a member of the Alpha Pack after all."

"Is she?" I gave him a friendly smile. "Because your *friend* seems to feel otherwise."

A muscle in Bastian's face ticked before he could hide it. I stepped forward until I was less than a foot away from the barrier.

"It will solve a lot of problems if you release Rynn from your pack," I said quietly. "The Alpha Pack clearly doesn't want her." My eyes flicked briefly to where Warrick stood behind the panther shifter. "Just let her go."

Bastian studied me, and for a second, I thought he was going to go for it before he dashed that hope. "That's not possible, I'm afraid."

"Why?" I ground out. "She doesn't want to be here—you all don't want her. This is an easy solution to a delicate situation, and you know it."

"Do you need assistance with Carmilla?" Bastian asked. The change in topic threw me for a loop for a second.

"We're not helping her," Warrick growled.

A brief flicker of irritation rolled over Bastian's eyes. It seemed the Alpha Pack wasn't quite the cohesive unit I'd thought it was. If I wanted to destabilize the Velesian realm, I would have rejoiced in that observation, but despite my desire to free Rynn from them, I did want the Alpha Pack to succeed in holding power. If the Velesian realm fell to chaos, it would spill over into the Moroi realm.

Just as they needed me to hold my people together, I needed them to do the same.

"Like I said," I told Bastian, ignoring Warrick, "I have it handled."

He held my gaze for a long moment before dipping his head in acknowledgment. "Then I look forward to discussing future relations between the Velesians and the Moroi—with the new queen."

It wasn't a cold dread that settled in my gut at the inference of me becoming the Moroi Queen. Only acceptance. Perhaps a little reluctance, but acceptance all the same.

My people would survive. All of the Moon Blessed would. I didn't give a single fuck about the Fae and whoever had banished them here. We would not be casualties of their bullshit.

"And I look forward to discussing our future alliance as well." I nodded at him before turning and walking to the other room, where I heard Kieran and Rynn fiercely whispering to each other.

"Samara," Bastian said just as I was about to pass into the other room. I halted and looked back towards him. "We won't let her go. She is *ours*."

Somewhere in front of me, Rynn let out a deep, rolling growl.

"Rynn belongs to no one but herself," I told him simply. "I will not force her to return."

"Even if it means war?" Bastian asked, and for the first time in our conversation, a hint of defiant rage crept into his tone.

"She is my best friend," I told him simply. "Fucking try to take her from me. I'll burn down your world."

CHAPTER TWENTY-SIX

—

Samara

"Okay . . . that could have gone better," Kieran drawled once we stepped back through the mirror.

"Understatement," Rynn growled.

Cali instantly perked up from where she'd been picking through the weapons table. "Do I get to kill the Alpha Pack?"

The leader part of me wanted to say no because the Alpha Pack was all that was keeping the Velesian realm somewhat stable and Cade *could* be reasoned with. But then I thought about the hate brimming in Warrick's eyes when he'd looked at Rynn, and the monster side of me rejoiced at the idea of Cali melting his fucking mind while carving him apart with her sword.

I didn't understand why he'd been so hostile to my friend, especially since it seemed like that had been the first time they'd met in person. Now, I was even less excited about the idea of Rynn going back there. Before, she hadn't been happy but was at least safe. I wasn't sure if that was true anymore.

Rynn stared at the mirror with a defeated expression. "I love you both, but we all know I have to go back."

"No," I said firmly. "You don't."

She turned away from the mirror and gave me a sad smile. "I heard what you said to Bastian, and I have no doubt that you would burn down their realm, but I won't be responsible for the Moroi and Velesian realms going to war. Both realms are already too precarious as it is. We need to figure out how to stabilize them, which means I have to go back—after I help you here."

I deflated a little. As much as I hated to admit it, she was right.

"Fine, but I want a contract."

"Of course you do." Rynn rolled her eyes.

"Will they even be open to that?" Draven asked. "All my interactions with the Alpha Pack have been pretty hostile."

"They never liked Queen Velika," Vail said, not bothering to look away from the sword he was inspecting. "Bastian thought your mother smelled like—and these are his exact words—sour jealousy and rotting deceit with a hint of rancid insanity."

Draven blinked. "Wow. That's actually quite accurate."

"Guess that explains why he spent more time with the other Houses," Kieran mused. "But if we go back through the mirror and catch Bastian before he leaves, I think he'll be willing to work with us. Rynn technically *is* supposed to be with them." He gave my friend an apologetic look. "But we heard Warrick's threat, so we have valid reasons to be concerned about Rynn's welfare."

"What threat?" Cali asked sharply, her golden eyes glowing slightly.

"We'll handle it," I said quickly before looking at Alaric, who was leaning back in a chair behind a table with five open books scattered in front of him. "Are you up for negotiating with Bastian?"

"Sure." He raised his brows. "You don't want to do it yourself?"

"I don't think I'd be able to keep a cool head," I admitted. "I trust you to do it."

Something in his green eyes softened. I believed in him to keep my best friend safe, which was a bigger deal than me trusting him with my own life in a lot of ways.

"I'll go with you," Kieran said. "Bastian and I have always had good rapport."

"Thank you." Alaric nodded and rose to his feet, going to stand next to Kieran.

"Should I go too?" Rynn asked uncertainly. "It feels weird to make the two of you deal with my fucked-up situation."

"Given how hot some tempers are running, I think it's best if you remain here." Kieran gave her a small, reassuring smile. "We got this, Rynn."

"Roth absconded with an armful of books shortly after you all left—they said Cali was breathing too loud," Alaric said in a dry tone, even as amusement danced in his eyes. Cali snorted as she plucked a dagger from the table and slid it into a holster on her thigh. Alaric continued, "I'm not sure what they've found, but I've been reading your notes about this transformation spell, and I think you're onto something. I found a few more books that go into detail about it and might be useful."

Rynn was hurrying over to the table before he'd even finished his last word.

I walked over to Alaric and Kieran. "Thank you both for doing this."

"Of course, love." Kieran shrugged. "Rynn's family."

Both of them kissed me on the cheek and strode back through the mirror

—which was still strange to watch. I walked over to it and studied the glyphs etched into the dark wood frame. Some of them I recognized, but most I didn't.

My eyes drifted to the right, where something tall was covered with a black cloak. I stepped closer and tugged the cloak off. Another mirror. Interesting.

"There is a second mirror in the room beneath the Alpha House too," Rynn said from across the room. "Different glyphs than the travel mirrors. I messed around with it a bit but couldn't figure out what it did."

"Hmm." I looked the markings over, similar to the other mirror, but I only knew what a handful of them meant. "Mystery for another day, I guess."

"I need to stretch my wings for a bit," Cali announced.

"Are you sure that's a good idea?" I turned away from the mirror. "There could be wraiths lurking in the dark spots of the temple."

She shrugged. "Then I'll get to kill something."

Vail and Draven both chuckled, and I rolled my eyes. "Fine, but be careful, and don't go far."

"Yes, Mom." She gave me a finger salute before sauntering out of the room. Rynn laughed at that one.

"It wasn't that funny," I grumbled as I joined her at the table and grabbed one of the books Alaric had left out.

"Yes, it was." Rynn glanced up with a smirk on her face. "Only you would fuss over quite possibly the most lethal warrior in Lunaria going out for a flight in the middle of the day."

"She's not invulnerable," I pointed out. "Plus, I know Carmilla—she's working on a way to get Cali off the board."

The amusement bled from Rynn's face. "You think she's going to send stealth units?"

Over the last few decades, the Furies had gotten better about controlling their magic. It was rare for one to completely lose it, but it did happen. Sometimes they would deal with the problems themselves, but sometimes they would ask for assistance. That was where the stealth units came in. Some Moroi and Velesians were specifically trained to take down rogue Furies. They used a mix of long-range weapons and other tactics to get close enough to do lethal damage fast before the Furie could shred their minds.

It was easily the most dangerous task in Lunaria, but unfortunately a necessary one. Vail had been trained to take down Furies . . . so had Adrienne and Emil. I doubted Nyx had because usually it was only rangers with a couple of decades of experience who went through the training.

Nyx. Sadness washed over me. They'd been so happy being a ranger and belonging to a unit. Technically, they should have served as an advisor or some other high-ranking role in House Corvinus because they were the youngest child of the Heads of that House. If Nyx had remained in their birth House, they'd probably be safe right now. Not trying to piece together a shredded soul.

But they also likely would have been forced into a political marriage they didn't want.

Not a lot of happily-ever-after stories in Lunaria like there were in some of the Fae stories I'd read. I looked across the room to where Draven and Vail quietly bickered over weapons.

We'd get our fucking happy ending. I'd make sure of it.

"She'll leave that as a last resort." I turned my attention back to Rynn's question. "Carmilla would probably like to permanently take Cali out, but without the Furie Elders officially declaring Cali a danger, Carmilla's hands are a bit tied. I don't particularly like them, but the Furie Elders will retaliate harshly if Carmilla kills one of their own without cause. She can't afford that."

"So she'll come at the problem sideways." Rynn pursed her lips, her eyes going distant in that way that meant she was thinking through the possibilities.

"Yep," I agreed. "Hard to say how she'll do it, but if whatever she thinks up is successful and we're separated from Cali, we'll have to be ready for an attack afterwards."

Rynn hummed her agreement. "She'll punch a hole through our defense and then take advantage."

I had no idea how Carmilla would get Cali to willingly leave us, but I wasn't going to underestimate my aunt. She'd think of something, and as soon as she did, the countdown would start for her finding us—if she didn't already know where we were—and attacking.

A plan was coming together in my head, but I still only had fragments of the pieces I needed. I pulled the paper from my pocket and flattened it out, studying the glyph. It had been designed to keep people out . . . but it could just as easily be used to keep people in.

"Tell me what you've discovered so far about this transformation spell, Rynn . . ."

Six hours later, Rynn and I had a long list of notes with whole passages scratched out, plus additional writing on the side. It was messy and had some gaps we had to fill in, but my insane plan was starting to feel more like a real possibility.

We had two main enemies—Carmilla and Erendriel. The Seelie King was trying to court me to his side; I had no doubt he'd be returning tonight to speak with me. I didn't want an all-out war with Carmilla, even if I did have the Houses of Devereux, Salvatore, and likely Tepes at my back. Probably a good chunk of House Harker too.

But a war amongst the Moroi Houses would be the death of our realm. So many of us would die. Not to mention Carmilla wouldn't need to lift a finger —she'd just need to use the crown to steal the will of some key players.

It would be a bloodbath.

I didn't want more Moroi to die in a desperate attempt to stop Carmilla. Wraiths though? Yeah . . . not going to shed any tears over them.

My plan was actually quite simple. Lure Carmilla to the temple, let Erendriel and his wraiths deal with her, secure the crown, and betray Erendriel.

Honor was for suckers.

I'd lie my ass off to save my people.

The problem—or rather one of the problems—was that you had to word things very carefully with the Fae. Draven had explained as much as he could before his head had damn near exploded from whatever magic was still forcing him to hold his tongue.

A bargain with the Fae had power, so I needed to craft my lie carefully.

If I pulled it off, I'd be able to boast that this gorgeous, twenty-three-year-old ass had outsmarted a centuries-old Fae who had stolen her throne.

If that wasn't motivation, I didn't know what was.

Yes, I ran on spite. No, I was not the least bit apologetic about it.

Kieran and Alaric had come and gone several times as they continued to negotiate Rynn's return to the Alpha Pack. Kieran, bless him, had tried to put in a stipulation that Rynn must be allowed to visit the Moroi realm whenever she wanted. Bastian had pushed back on that, so we'd settled on once-a-month visits with exceptions for emergencies.

Those emergencies were explicitly listed because Alaric lived for the small details.

Vail was exploring the temple to better learn the layout, and Draven had gone to join him after answering as many of our questions as he could. We'd also been looking for a way to break whatever magic was forcing him to hold his tongue, but so far, I hadn't come across any explanations. Granted, we'd only begun to scratch the surface of the knowledge this place stored.

If we survived everything with Carmilla and Erendriel, we might finally be able to learn how everything in Lunaria had come to be.

Cali breezed in at one point, saw Rynn and me conspiring over all the open texts, and promptly turned on her heel and walked back out. She mumbled something about seeing what "that treacherous asshole" was up to.

I assumed she meant Vail and yelled after her to not kill him.

She let out a string of curses, but I was confident that she wouldn't, because if that had truly been her intention, she wouldn't have said anything— and I was *mostly* confident she wouldn't pick a fight with him either. Though they could both stand to burn off some extra energy, so a brawl wouldn't be the worst thing to happen right now.

"This is still a problem." Rynn pointed to one of my notes that had several words boldly circled. *Spell requires permission.*

The transformation spell to turn one thing into another was complicated, and most of it was out of our league, given our basic understanding of magic. But several texts alluded to the spell being far simpler if whoever it was being performed on gave permission.

The soul crown wasn't a person . . . but it wasn't just an object either. I'd conversed with it and had felt its emotions. What if the soul crown wasn't just named that because it could bind the will of others? What if the Fae had actually bestowed a soul into it?

My plan hinged on performing the transformation spell. If the crown could give us permission to turn it into something else, then that would drastically simplify things. Unfortunately, that created a new problem—how could I speak with the crown beforehand to determine if this was possible?

Because if we waited until the plan was in motion, there was a very real chance I'd end up dead.

Not my preferred outcome.

We were also running out of time. While we were relatively safe here in the temple, our allies were not. Once Carmilla had a plan in place to deal with Cali, she'd figure a way to lure me out. I knew she wanted to limit the loss of Moroi lives, but I also knew she could be a ruthless bitch when she wanted to be.

What if she found Alaric's parents? Or used any of my friends from House Harker?

I needed to control the information about where I was, making sure it was leaked at just the right time in just the right way so she wouldn't question it.

"Wait." Rynn suddenly sat up straighter, drawing me out of my ponderings. "'While the Unseelie are adept at spying with their shadows, the Seelie have crafted a way to counterspy,'" she quoted. "'By mindwalking through the minds of sentient but simpleminded creatures, they can easily put themselves in the same rooms as their completely unaware enemies. This is why we have put defensive measures in place . . .'" She trailed off, skimming the page before flipping the book to look at the cover. "I have no idea who wrote this, but it clearly wasn't the Fae. It's like a history of them . . . before they came to Lunaria."

I glanced at the page, a frown forming on my lips. "It's written in Seelie though."

"Maybe it was translated?" We both stared at the book before looking around the room and its floor-to-ceiling shelves. "What in the fuck is this place?" Rynn murmured.

"We'll just have to survive long enough to figure it out." I grabbed the book and started scanning the pages until I found what I was looking for—a glyph. I read the words below it, which were simple enough. Focus and intention were key. I could do this.

"Should we wait until the others get back?" Rynn asked hesitantly.

"No, they'll just distract me." I rose from the table, taking the book with me, and sat on the floor, crossing my legs. Then I set the book slightly to my right and bit my wrist until I tasted blood. "Besides, when I checked on Roth an hour ago, they were close to cracking how that barrier spell works, and we're going to need that."

"Fine," she grumbled. "Just don't get yourself stuck in a mouse or something, okay? I can't be friends with you if you're food."

I rolled my eyes as I dipped my fingers in the blood flowing from my wrist and drew the glyph on the floor. "Noted."

Rynn moved to sit beside me. For all her concern, I could feel the excitement practically rolling off her. This was a new spell, unlike anything we'd ever done before.

Following the instructions from the text, I rested my fingertips on the blood of the outer circle of the glyph that vaguely resembled an eye. Then I closed my eyes and focused on my intention, feeling it wrap around the magic that flowed through my veins before pushing it into the glyph.

Sometimes, when I'm sleeping soundly, I jerk awake with the intense feeling of falling.

This was exactly like that.

When my eyes flew open seconds later, they were not my eyes . . . and I couldn't even close them.

Well, this was weird.

My body wrapped around a vine and continued its upward climb along a stone wall. There was a quick tongue flick, and suddenly, I was processing a bunch of different scents from the air. The blooming flowers, the dust that collected in the cracks of the stones, and the delicious bird perched somewhere above me.

Moons fucking damn me.

I was sharing the mind of a snake. With a careful, gentle nudge, I requested that it turn its head so I could look at myself. A flicker of annoyance brushed against my mind, but then the world tilted and I was looking down at a long, scaled body with an iridescent sheen, rainbows dancing across my scales with every movement.

Well, at least I was a pretty snake.

Umm, sorry about this? I thought loudly. *Promise you'll get that tasty snack of a bird later. I just need to borrow you for a few minutes.*

More annoyance.

Apparently, snakes had a one-track mind when it came to food.

I didn't exactly take over control of the snake's body, it was more like I prodded it into doing what I wanted. We continued climbing up the vine for another few feet and then slid through a window, curling our tail around the bars and dangling into the room.

When I'd formed my intention for the spell, I'd focused on getting as close to the crown as possible. Despite Rynn's joke about me not taking over a mouse . . . I'd totally thought I was going to end up in a mouse. They were everywhere, so it had seemed like a logical assumption.

Rynn had a thing about snakes though, so I'd have to lie to her about this.

I looked through the serpent's eyes at the room we were hanging in. It didn't see colors the way I was used to. The blues and greens felt so much more vivid, and its depth perception was different than mine. Despite the differences, I was able to make everything out just fine.

We were high up in a small space; the ground was almost twenty feet below us and the walls were circular. A turret, maybe? Probably one close to the top of the Sovereign House? Because that's definitely where we were. I'd recognized enough of the landscape when we'd been outside to confirm our whereabouts.

There was nothing else in the room besides the table in the center. It was made of the same stone as the floor and walls, and resting on its smooth surface was the soul crown.

Samara? a familiar voice tentatively asked.

Yes? I had no idea why I'd answered the crown's question with one of my own. If I had hands, I would have been slapping my own face right now.

Why do you feel . . . strange?

Probably because I'm sharing the mind of a snake. It's my first time doing this, so I'm still figuring out the quirks.

The snake started to curve back towards the bars as I felt its interest in the bird renew. Gently, I tugged back.

Stay. Just a little longer, I promised.

A chuckle rumbled through my mind, and the snake's head turned back towards the crown. *Of course this is the beast you would choose.*

It wasn't a choice, actually, I admitted. *This slithery friend just happened to be the creature closest to you.*

No. The crown's amusement danced through my mind. Our mind? I wasn't exactly sure if the snake understood amusement. *Your bloodline has long been associated with slithery friends. The last true Seelie King—your grandfather —was known as The Serpent King before he was banished to Lunaria.*

Oh. It was strange to think of a grandfather in general, let alone one that had been Fae—and the Seelie King at that. There weren't a lot of multigenerational families in Lunaria. I was a fifth generation Moroi, and it wasn't until the fourth generation that the Moroi themselves had stabilized and stopped turning Strigoi every time something looked at them the wrong way.

You came back, the crown whispered.

I told you I would.

I know those . . . rangers, I believe you call them . . . were your friends. You begged me to help, but I . . . There was nothing I could do.

The crown had thought I'd completely abandoned them because of what had happened with Adrienne, Emil, and Nyx, but I'd heard their sorrow that day—felt it. The crown had monstrous magic . . . but they didn't want to be a monster.

Talis, I thought softly.

I . . . I do not know this word.

When I was growing up, my parents were often busy, but we had one tradition. Once a month, we would sneak up onto one of the rooftops at House Harker to watch the stars. I actually knew most of the constellations because a friend taught me, but I never told them that.

For a second, I felt my connection to the snake waver, as if the emotions were too much for it. Vail had been the one to point out and name every star in the night sky. His parents had been just as busy as mine. For a long time, it had just been the two of us. Before life had torn us apart.

But I still listened with rapt attention as my father pointed out his favorite star every time, I continued. The crown didn't say anything but I could feel their presence. *It wasn't the brightest star in the sky. Some nights, it was so dim, you could barely see it. Most of the constellations have Fae names, but this one had been named in the common tongue by the humans who had lived here. Talis. Their word for hope.*

Talis, the crown said slowly, as if tasting the word. *I like it.*

Good. Because I think it would be a good name for you.

Another beat of silence. *I have existed for a long time . . . belonged to your family for generations. Nobody has ever thought to gift me with a name.*

It's a new dawn, Talis. Perhaps it's time we change things.

I then told Talis my plan and what I would be asking of them. What they would have to sacrifice.

Yes, they said immediately once I was done. *But I have one request . . .*

CHAPTER TWENTY-SEVEN

—

Vail

"RYNN, CALM DOWN," I tried again.

"You calm down!" the lycan screamed from where she stood on top of the table.

"Little help?" I growled at Draven, who was leaning against a table on the opposite side of the room with a curious look on his face as he stared at Samara —who was very much still out of it—and the three-foot badlands viper coiled up in her lap.

The serpent had a thick body and a triangular head. Its scales were a mix of white and a light tawny brown that allowed it to blend in well with the badlands' arid surface.

It was also highly venomous. Not enough to kill us, but enough to make us hate our lives for a few hours.

I hadn't attempted to tear the thing out of her lap because it seemed very calm, and I was worried about startling it.

"It doesn't mean her any harm." Draven waved a hand towards Samara and her new scaly friend. "This isn't normal behavior for a viper; they're ambush predators. It was probably coiled up somewhere in the temple and the magic of whatever spell she's working drew it towards her."

"I don't care!" A low, panicked whine underpinned Rynn's words. "Nowhere in that fucking book did it mention *anything* about fucking snakes crawling out of the fucking walls!" The viper raised its head from where it had been resting on Samara's knee and flicked a tongue in Rynn's direction. "Fuck!" she shrieked and backed up farther on the table.

"Rynn, if you scream one more time, I'm going to strangle you." Roth stomped into the room, their deep red hair looking a little messy, like they'd been running their hands through it. "I can hear you all the way downstairs.

What are you going on about—oh." They looked at the badlands viper. "Huh. I guess Sam has an affinity with serpents. Or maybe it's all reptiles. The strikers really like her, and they're more reptile than bird anyway."

"Affinity?" Draven glanced at Roth.

They pointed at the stack of discarded books on a nearby table, the ones that didn't contain information useful for our current problems. "One of those books talks about it. I think it's a Seelie thing, which makes sense, I guess, since their magic is earth-based. Normally, they are drawn to one type of animal, and those animals are also drawn to them. Maybe the more in touch Samara gets with her Fae magic, the more weird shit like this will happen."

"You use Fae magic." I looked at Draven. "This ever happen to you?"

He frowned and started to shake his head, but then his eyes widened. "Weasels. The bold little things often come up to me when I'm camping in the woods. I thought maybe they just smelled my food and wanted to steal it. They've never shown an ounce of fear."

The Moroi Prince was friends with quite possibly the only animals that could be considered adorable in Lunaria.

"If somebody doesn't—" Rynn growled, only to be cut off when Samara let out a long exhale and said, "Well, that was fucking weird."

Her beautiful purple eyes glanced down at her lap, and a perplexed expression spread across her face. "Okay. Not what I was expecting. Umm . . . shoo?"

"How are you so calm about a snake in your lap!" Rynn glared at her best friend.

Samara grinned at Draven. "Too bad Kieran isn't here. He'd have so many jokes."

"Is that a snake in your dress, or are you just happy to see me?" Draven asked with a completely straight face.

"My snake's bigger than yours." Samara impersonated Kieran's smooth voice.

"Sam!" Rynn barked.

"Oh, fine." Samara rolled her eyes and gently lifted the viper off her lap like it couldn't knock her ass out with one bite and wrack her body with seizures for hours until it burned off the venom. "I was just in the mind of a snake— southern tree boa, I think—so my tolerance for strange shit has gone up a bit."

"Really?" Roth perked up. "What was that like? Did you completely take over its body? Or was it more of a shared consciousness thing?"

"The latter. It was kind of grumpy about the whole affair to be honest." Samara held the viper up with one hand, letting its body curl around her forearm. "You're not grumpy though, are you?" she cooed, and then to Rynn's horror—and mine too, if I was being honest—Samara booped the thing on the nose with her finger. "I can *feel* how content you are right now. Who's the cutest little viper there ever was? You are!"

Another boop.

"Samara," Rynn whined pitifully.

"Alright, alright." She smoothly rolled to her feet. "Just let me go set this pretty girl outside. I think she's digesting a meal or something. She just wants to find somewhere warm to curl up and rest."

"Sure. Fine. Whatever." Rynn pointed to the exit. "Just get it out of here!"

Samara practically flounced out of the room, and only when her footsteps faded did Rynn hop down from the table, grumbling something about smothering Samara in her sleep.

"Where's the book that has the exact spell?" Roth asked, looking at the glyph on the floor where Samara had been sitting.

Rynn grabbed it off the table and tossed it to them.

"Careful." Roth snatched the book out of the air and turned to glare at Rynn, eyes flashing orange in warning. "You damage any of these books, and you'll be the one getting smothered in your sleep."

The mirror rippled in the corner, and a second later, Alaric and Kieran stepped into the room before freezing.

"Why do I smell Samara's blood?" Alaric gave me an accusing glare.

"Because Samara decided to use a Fae spell nobody has ever heard of that resulted in her sharing a mind with a snake and talking to a crown that apparently has a soul," I deadpanned.

Roth snorted. "Succinct but accurate."

"Bonus points for an excellent delivery," Draven added.

"Right." Alaric rubbed his forehead with one hand and held out some documents with the other. "Look this over, Rynn. I believe we have everything covered. Kieran and I have both reviewed it twice. All it needs is your signature."

Rynn swallowed before striding towards Alaric and taking the contract from him. "Thanks. Be back in a bit."

Without another word, she left the room. A moment later, the sound of Samara coming down the stairs echoed through the hall outside, followed by soft murmurings between her and Rynn. When Samara joined us again, any hint of amusement was gone from her face. Cali was right behind her with an equally grim expression.

"What happened?" I looked between the two of them.

"I'll get to that." Samara sat on one of the tables, and everyone else took a seat. I remained standing against the wall with my arms crossed, feeling too anxious to sit.

Whatever had happened must have been bad because Cali didn't sneer at me once.

"First, the crown has agreed to go along with the transformation spell. So that will make that portion of the plan easier." Her dire expression softened for a moment. "Also . . . I gave them a name. Talis."

The recognition hit me instantly. Samara's parents had often taken her stargazing, and if my parents had been away—which they often had—they'd invite me to join them. The star named after hope had been her dad's favorite.

"It's a good name," I said softly. "He would approve."

Samara looked at me and saw the understanding in my eyes. "I think so too." She smiled back before swallowing and growing serious once more. "Tell them, Cali."

"A striker just delivered a message from a courtier at House Corvinus." The Furie's gaze flicked to Kieran. "Your friend, actually—Riah."

Kieran blinked in surprise. "Is she okay? What did she say?"

"Tamsen defected from House Corvinus. She left in the middle of the night with Riah and a handful of others; they took shelter at a small outpost close to the Velesian border." Cali's fisted hand shook before she tossed the crumbled-up message onto the table. "Carmilla sent three squads of rangers after them. The people in the outpost refused to grant them entry. They said Carmilla was a false queen."

Samara sat perfectly still, but her eyes had turned a solid black.

"What happened?" I asked when silence reigned.

"The rangers . . ." Cali trailed off, clenching her jaw hard enough that I could see the muscles feathering along her jawline.

"They burned the outpost down," Samara cut in. "With the people inside. Tamsen, Riah, and less than a dozen people made it out alive."

Rangers swore an oath to serve not only their House but all of the Moroi. Either those rangers had disregarded that oath of their own volition . . . or Carmilla had stripped them of their free will and forced them to carry out a heinous act that would likely haunt them forever.

A mixture of disgust and rage rolled through me, and I could feel the same sentiments echoed by everyone in the room.

"We have to stop her," I rasped, drawing Samara's dark gaze. "Whatever it takes."

"We will," she swore.

"Where is Tamsen now?" Draven asked.

"The group split up after escaping," Cali said. "According to Riah, the Corvinus Heir refused to risk any more lives protecting hers. Tamsen traveled with them to another outpost but then ordered Riah and the others to keep their heads down and deny any involvement with her before leaving. She told Riah she was heading towards House Devereux."

"Shit," Roth swore. "I can't express how bad of an idea that is. They won't trust her—not a Corvinus. My family made an exception for Nyx because they turned their back on their House and have proven themself over the years, but

Tamsen is the bloody Heir. There's a solid chance they'll kill her on sight with how high their paranoia probably is right now."

"This all happened several days ago—probably at the same time we were leaving House Salvatore. Riah lucked out and found an outpost where another of Kieran's friends was—one who just happened to have a striker that could track Kieran's scent," Cali continued.

"Jasi, probably," Kieran grunted. "I pulled some strings to get him out of a tight spot with House Tepes a few years back, and he's one of my best informants now. Lives in an outpost on one of the main trade routes—hears all kinds of gossip."

"Which one?" I asked.

"Morningwell."

I started calculating the distance in my head and the possible paths Tamsen could have taken. The Morningwell outpost was southwest of House Corvinus, towards the middle of the realm. The main road went directly east and west from it, but Tamsen likely hadn't taken that. It might have been safer, but the road would be heavily patrolled. If she were desperate enough—and it seemed like she was—the rogue Heir had likely cut straight through the wilds.

Which meant she was either dead . . . or was a couple of days away from House Devereux, maybe a little less if she lucked out and didn't run into any trouble.

Hesitation fluttered through my thoughts, but I realized it wasn't mine; I'd been staring at the floor, unseeing, while contemplating all the possibilities. When I looked up, I found Samara's heavy gaze on me, then that flicker of doubt rolled through me again.

"You might as well tell me what you're thinking." I laid my hand flat against my chest, over my heart. "Because I can already feel it, *mate*."

Her gaze dropped to my hand before returning to my eyes. She didn't deny that we were mates or say something caustic to me, so I considered that a win.

"In order to set the plan in motion, we need to let Carmilla discover where we are." Samara held my stare, even as Cali grumbled something about hating this plan. I didn't blame her. If things went the way we expected, as soon as Carmilla learned our whereabouts, she'd enact her strategy to remove Cali as a player.

And we were going to let her do it—as long as the Furie's life wasn't in danger. Samara's plan would only work if Carmilla believed she was winning.

I would have been pissed too if my friends were going to enact an absolutely insane plan that could fall apart in so many ways and I wouldn't be there to help them.

Cali had been the one to read that message first though, so she knew what was at stake. We couldn't let more innocent people die. This plan might have been crazy, but if we pulled it off, it would also limit the bloodshed.

Samara let her words hang in the air, then opened her mouth to speak before closing it again and looking away from me. Fear echoed down the bond before suddenly being cut off. She was walling off her emotions from me, trying to hide.

I knew what she wanted to ask me. To find Tamsen, if she was still alive, and get her to safety. It wasn't hard to figure out because, of those gathered here, I was best suited for the task. Traveling through the Lunarian wilds was literally my job. Draven could probably do it, but he was needed here, as Erendriel would no doubt show up again, and even with the magic binding his tongue, the prince's knowledge of his father would be useful.

But still, Samara didn't ask. Frustrated rage swirled inside my gut, and based on the way she flinched, I knew she felt it.

She believed I would betray her. Even now, after everything I'd done, Samara didn't trust me to do this.

"Roth," I said evenly. "Write a note to your family asking them to protect Tamsen—even if they throw her ass into the dungeon. As long as they don't lop her head off because she looks at them funny."

"Vail—" Samara took a step towards me.

"It'll likely take me at least four days to find her," I cut her off and stalked towards the table with the Fae weapons. On the off chance I ran into some wraiths, these could be useful. "Maybe up to a week depending on how well she's covering her tracks."

Kieran quietly snuck out of the room. Everyone else remained silent, eyes bouncing back and forth between me and Samara.

"Vail." Samara closed the distance between us until she stood next to me at the table.

I ignored her.

"Carmilla is likely watching House Devereux, so I can't just walk Tamsen up to the front gate—that would be too obvious—but I'll make sure she gets there and then double back a bit." I grabbed a second sword harness and strapped it on before sliding a Fae sword next to my regular one. Then I swapped the daggers on my thighs for Fae ones. "Carmilla will only send out her best rangers looking for us. I'll leave just enough of a trail that they can find it but make it look like I was trying to cover my tracks."

"*Marshal,*" Samara said more firmly.

I wanted to look at her but also knew doing so might weaken my resolve—because I didn't want to leave. But it had to be me. If Tamsen had truly defected, we couldn't leave her to the wolves. Plus, Samara's plan to deal with her aunt would only work if Carmilla didn't know she was walking into a trap.

"Here." Roth held up a folded-up letter. "She probably won't get the best treatment, but they won't kill her."

"Good enough." I walked over and took the letter from them just as Kieran strode back into the room, holding a bag.

"We're getting low on food, but I packed what we could spare and some water. You'll probably have to restock somewhere."

"Once I get out of the badlands, there are ranger stashes I can use."

Kieran nodded as I took the bag from him, then I headed towards the door without a backwards glance.

"Stubborn fucking asshole," I heard Samara growl, but I kept walking. My long strides were eating up the distance as I went up the stairwell and then stalked through the temple. Whatever it took to prove my loyalty to her, I'd do it—even if I was pissed that she didn't even seem willing to give me a chance.

Yes. I'd fucked up. Massively.

But I'd also helped get her out of that dungeon. I'd done everything I could to keep her alive while we'd been on the run. Cali was clearly teetering on losing it, but I hadn't said one damn word about it. And I wasn't bitching about the fact that I'd have to share my mate with four others—part of me was actually relieved by that because it meant there were four other people in this world who would love and protect her as much as I would.

None of it mattered though, because apparently, she still believed I was one breath away from betraying her again.

The heat of the late summer afternoon hit me like a runaway horse as soon as I stepped outside the temple. This was going to be a brutal run across the badlands.

My best bet was straight east to avoid the trapper spiders. Once I made it to the forests, I'd angle south a bit and then—

"Oof!"

A pair of bright purple eyes brimming with fury looked up at me from where Samara had slammed me against the wall of the temple.

"Something you need, my queen?" I asked in a flat, bored tone, doing my best to keep my emotions from rolling down the bond.

"I wasn't done talking to you." Her hands gripped the fabric of my shirt as she crowded my space. It should have been absurd. I had over a foot of height on her and could easily outmuscle her, but some small part of me had enough self-preservation to not try.

Samara liked to fight dirty, and I'd prefer to keep all my bits attached.

"Oh?" I tilted my head in a way that I knew would annoy her. Black flashed across her eyes, and I smiled. "You don't have to say anything. I can feel it, remember?" I tapped the back of her hand that was covering my heart. "If there were anyone else you could have asked to do this, you would have because you don't trust me. I felt it all. Your hesitation. Fear."

"Vail," she ground out.

"Yes, my queen?"

She stood on her tiptoes to get a little closer. "You are a fucking idiot."

I blinked. "What—"

Samara let go of my shirt to yank my head down. Then her mouth claimed mine, and for a second, I stood there rigidly, not completely sure this was happening.

I felt her lips curve into a smile against mine before she whispered, "This is the part where you kiss me back."

"So bossy." I smiled before doing just that, sliding my tongue into her mouth, reveling in the way she tasted.

Then I flipped us around so she was pinned against the wall and broke our kiss. Samara panted before going still as I wrapped my left hand around her throat and planted my right hand against the wall.

"You're so fucking frustrating," I growled.

"Yeah," she rasped. "You're a real fucking peach yourself."

I chuckled and squeezed her throat a little harder, and she let out a low moan that went straight to my dick.

"What do you want from me, Sam?" I brushed my thumb against her rapidly beating pulse, and she arched her back at the touch.

"Everything," she breathed out. "I want everything from you."

"You have it." I leaned my forehead against hers. "You are mine, and I am yours. I will never betray you again, and I will spend the rest of my life making up for it."

"I know," she whispered, and I eased my grip on her throat a little but didn't remove my hand.

"Why?" I closed my eyes as I breathed in her scent. "Why did you hesitate in asking me to do this? I felt your fear."

"Because if you get captured, Carmilla will make an example out of you." Her throat bobbed as she swallowed. "I'm not saying all of our bullshit is resolved, but I want to have the chance to fix it—to fix us. You still piss me off half the time you open your mouth, your bullish attitude is incredibly frustrating, and Draven is right, you suck at apologizing, but none of that changes the fact that I love you beyond reason."

"Fuck." I yanked her to me and kissed her hard, pouring every ounce of what I felt for her into it even as I practically screamed it down our bond. I'd never been good with words the way that Kieran and Draven were, and apparently I was even worse than Alaric and Roth at expressing how I felt. I'd just have to make damn sure she knew from my actions that I fucking loved her beyond reason too.

My tongue slid across one of her fangs, and she groaned as my blood filled her mouth. Then I slid my hand down until I cupped her breast and squeezed. She sucked on my tongue as her soft body pushed into me more. Suddenly, I was very desperate to know how wet she was.

I tore my hand away from her breast and roughly dragged up her dress until I felt bare skin. Then my fingers dove underneath her panties.

It was my turn to groan as I found the hot slickness waiting for me. I slid two fingers through her wetness, and Samara moaned, finally breaking our kiss as she tilted her head back against the wall.

"More," she demanded.

I didn't have it in me to tease her right now or go slow. Instead, I just shoved two fingers as deep into her cunt as they could go and started fucking her roughly with them.

"Is that what you want?" I growled as she writhed on my hand.

"Yes!" She looked at me with solid black eyes before tilting her head. "Drink."

My fangs were buried in her throat a second later as I continued to pump my fingers in and out while I rubbed her clit with my thumb. Her intoxicatingly rich blood filled my mouth, and I swallowed it down as she came undone on my hand.

She tasted even better than I'd remembered, but I didn't want to take too much. I started to pull my fangs out, but she pushed hard against the back of my head and held me in place. "More," she panted. "Drink more."

I bit down harder and added a third finger, fucking her faster and rougher as I drank her down. Her pussy tightened around my fingers as she came again. Only when she was finished and I felt her trembling with ecstasy did I pull away from her neck.

Slowly, I pulled my fingers out as well, and Samara watched as I swiped her blood off my lips before sucking each finger clean.

"Come back to me, Vail," she said through heavy breaths.

"There is nothing that will keep me from you." I laid my hand against her rapidly beating heart; the bond that had felt so frayed now felt so much more solid. "I love you too, Samara."

CHAPTER TWENTY-EIGHT

—

Samara

Erendriel did return that evening, an hour after sunset, but he didn't come alone.

"Serril." I nodded in greeting. "Pleasure to see you again in the flesh." An apologetic smile graced my lips. "Forgive me, I mean shadow."

He chuckled, and wisps of darkness rolled off his shoulders as his shadow form strolled towards me. Like the night I'd first met him, he'd chosen to appear in a Fae form rather than something monstrous. He halted a foot away from the archway, where the boundary between us was.

"Feeling bold this evening, are we?" A hand of inky black shadows stretched towards the invisible wall, and he mimed tapping against it.

"It's easy to be bold when you're young and naive of the world around you," Erendriel said evenly.

"Still . . ." Serril pondered me. "I like her more than Velika. Too much human in that one, not enough Seelie."

The question I'd been about to ask died on my lips. "Velika had Seelie blood too?"

Erendriel snorted dismissively. "Haven't figured it out yet, have you? I would have thought with all the tomes at your disposal that you would have by now." He gave me an appraising look. "Perhaps you're not as clever as I thought."

"Oh, come now." Serril's voice held a mocking quality to it. "Let's not judge her too harshly. She's so young, and the only ones who have been able to teach her are other Moroi. It's the ignorant leading the ignorant. That never bodes well."

"I suppose you have a point." Erendriel remained in the center of the small landing with his hands clasped behind his back. It reminded me of the way the

790

old scholars would stand when they launched into a lecture. The false Seelie King might be my enemy, but I'd be a fool to turn down any knowledge. I'd just have to cross-reference whatever he told me with the books to unravel any lies he might have slipped into the truth.

Serril's hand moved away from the boundary to tap a long finger against his chin. "Have you ever wondered what determined who became Moroi, Velesian, or Furie when your human ancestors cast that original spell?"

Disappointment hit me. I did know, and it wasn't particularly interesting. "They chose their symbols." I pointed to the crescent moon on the left side of my neck. "Everyone chose where to paint the symbol. Left for Moroi, right for Velesian, and the front of the neck for Furies."

"'We will give our lives for the blood. We will yield our fates in the wild. We will lose our souls to the fury,'" Serril recited.

They were the original words spoken for the spellcasting. I was a little surprised he knew them, but then again, the wraiths had been raiding the old human settlements to collect the obsidian stones, which had been used in the original ritual. He'd probably stumbled upon copies of the spell they'd used.

"Your point?" I arched a dark brow.

"Just like you, your ancestors tampered with something they couldn't begin to comprehend." Serril held his hand up again, letting talons form at his fingertips. Then he grinned widely, and I was able to make out large fangs. "The spell was already in motion when they began painting those symbols. They did not choose what symbols to carve into their skin; the magic did."

The disappointment I'd been feeling vanished. In all my readings, I'd never come across that distinction. We'd assumed they'd decided who became Moroi, Velesian, or Furie—likely just divided things up evenly—but if Serril was telling the truth, they hadn't chosen . . .

"How did the magic decide?" I asked slowly.

Apparently, Serril didn't like to just give answers. "I think you know. Only the Furies can use shadow magic, some more than others, like your gifted friend. The Moroi can use Seelie magic. And the Velesians, well, they cannot directly use either type of magic, but if a Moroi were to give them an enchanted bracelet of Seelie magic . . . they could use that. Just as they could use something enchanted with Unseelie magic. The Velesians are magic-neutral."

It was like gears started turning in my mind as I took it all into account. How had I never realized this before? It seemed so damn obvious.

"Some of the humans had Fae blood," I whispered. "The ones with Seelie blood became Moroi, Unseelie became Furies, and the pure humans turned Velesian."

Serril whirled to face Erendriel. "See? So much potential in this one. She just needs a little knowledge, that's all."

I was so blindsided by this revelation that I only had a brief flicker of annoyance at his patronizing tone. Was this what made the House bloodlines different? We had higher amounts of Seelie blood, and that gave us the ability to control our bloodlust better?

If Serril was telling the truth, and my gut told me he was, this pointed us in a whole new direction to explore. But first, we had to survive.

As much as I wanted to pepper Serril with more questions, I needed to keep my focus on the goal of this conversation.

"Thank you for sharing your knowledge with me," I told Serril politely. "It gives me hope for a future alliance between us. Speaking of which . . ." My gaze slid to Erendriel. "What are you offering if I choose to ally with you? And what would you require of me?" I raised my chin. "Marriage is off the table. I will not leave my mates."

I'd been preparing for this conversation since Vail had left. Draven agreed with me that his father would be suspicious if I suddenly became open to discussing marriage after being so adamantly against it before. This had to be played just right.

The Seelie King studied me. "As long as your aunt bears that crown, you cannot defeat her. You need me far more than I need you."

"I've made it this far." I crossed my arms. "I'll figure something out."

"Before or after she burns down another outpost?" Serril drawled as he sauntered back over to stand near the archway. "How many more of your precious people do you think she'll kill before you accept that you're in over your head, my pretty little queen?"

"Not your queen," I said coldly before turning my attention back to Erendriel in a clear dismissal.

Serril chuckled again.

"Still feisty." The corners of Erendriel's mouth turned up in a small, amused smile. "I see why Draven likes you. A little bit of light for his dark thoughts."

"I do miss making the half-blood scream," Serril reminisced wistfully.

Rage burned through me, and I let it show on my face briefly before masking my emotions. It wasn't my words that were going to make this part of the plan successful. It was my body language. Those little tells that Erendriel and Serril were no doubt cataloguing.

Young and inexperienced. Overwhelmed by the world falling apart. Angry at my aunt. These were the things I let them see.

But as Rynn always said, an injured and cornered wolf still had fangs. I just couldn't snarl with mine yet.

"Draven is not to be harmed," I said evenly. "Nor are any of my other mates. This will be a business arrangement between us and nothing more."

"Of course." Erendriel gave me a placating nod. "A mate bond would be preferred, as that would almost certainly grant me access to places like this . . ."

His eyes left mine for a moment to peer at the stairs behind me. Whatever he was thinking, I couldn't read it in his expression. Then his gaze returned to me. "But there are other things we can do. Until then, you will answer my call and be my eyes and ears for the other hidden areas throughout Lunaria."

"How many are there? And where?"

"That is not knowledge you need right now."

If I had to guess, they were in the mountains above the Velesian realm. Draven said Erendriel spent most of his time there. Whatever he was searching for had to be in those mountains.

"Anything else?" I looked over my shoulder and down the stairs quickly.

"Expecting someone?" Serril asked, and my gaze snapped back to him. "Or did you not tell your mates the deal you were seeking to make this evening?"

I stiffened. "I am queen. It's my decision."

Erendriel's smile widened, as if he could already see the cracks of descension forming that he could exploit later. I had no doubt that he still planned to pursue me as queen or at least a mate bond. He wanted to get into those hidden rooms, and he likely suspected that some things might be locked down further to my blood. He wanted access—I was that access.

"And what is it you seek?" Erendriel's gaze lifted to the top of my head. "Perhaps the crown that is yours by right?"

"Yes, actually." I straightened. "I have no intention of using it to bind the wills of my people, but it is an object of power that I will not allow to fall into the hands of another."

"Of course," he answered in that placating way of his that was really starting to irritate me. I kept that off my face though and instead let a hint of insecurity flash through my eyes.

"I don't trust you," I said tightly. "I'm not some foolish young girl for you to manipulate. You're still set on trying to make me your mate, but I will never do that." My inflection wavered a bit towards the end, and I halted my words a little too harshly. I stood up a little straighter, as if I were encouraging myself, and stared straight into Erendriel's ancient eyes. "Help me get back my birthright. As long as the crown sits on my head—as long as I possess it—I will not act against you and will assist you in searching these spaces."

"I find this acceptable."

My heart raced a little faster, and I let more uncertainty settle into my features. "I . . ." I trailed off and glanced behind me again. "I can go fetch something so we can hammer out the contra—"

"No need," Erendriel cut me off. "You are part Fae. Let us bargain like Fae."

"How do we do that?" I shifted slightly on my feet before killing the movement.

Erendriel smiled wider. "Simply step across the boundary. Skin-to-skin contact is necessary."

I swallowed.

"Come now, little queen," Serril mocked. "Don't lose that wonderful bravado now."

I cut him a sharp glance before deliberately stepping forward—over the boundary. My heart was beating so hard for a second that I swore it was all I could hear. Draven had warned me that this was likely what Erendriel would ask for. None of us liked it, but we needed Erendriel's help, and he clearly needed mine.

The risk wasn't that he would kill me; it was that he'd simply take me and try to force me to obey him, but I'd thought about the story Draven had told me a night or two ago—about that test Erendriel had put his son through at the outpost. Erendriel would prefer me to ally with him willingly, even if I were doing so reluctantly, because it would make me easier to manipulate in his eyes.

If I ended up defying him like Draven, then he'd fall back on a different plan. He'd learn more about me in the meantime though, so he'd have plenty of weaknesses to exploit.

I closed the distance between me and Erendriel, who just continued to stare at me like a moon devil watching a rabbit hop closer. The hairs on the back of my neck rose as I sensed Serril move to stand at my back.

Erendriel was even taller than Vail, so I had to tilt my head back to look him in the eye, and I could have sworn I saw shadows swirling in his deep blue eyes for a moment.

He held out his hand. "Let's make a bargain, *kilfid min tros*." Little blood queen.

I slid my hand into his and squeezed.

CHAPTER TWENTY-NINE

—

Samara

Four days later, I was still feeling the rush of my encounter with the Seelie King. It wasn't just that I had bargained with him—it was that I'd outsmarted him.

Or at least, I was fairly confident I had.

When I'd walked down the stairs after he'd left, I'd practically fallen into Draven's arms as the adrenaline had worn off. My wicked prince had cooed praises at me for doing well while whispering promises of all the things he would do to me as soon as he had me alone.

Because in that moment, we had very much not been alone. Everyone had been hiding in the stairwell just out of Erendriel's sight so they could listen in, and Rynn had taken notes.

We all agreed that the words spoken in the bargain would work with our plan. I'd been very careful to only refer to Talis as "the crown" in my wording. Erendriel had added stipulations so that it wasn't simply the crown resting on my head but being in my possession—and that allowing my mates to hold on to it still counted as "in my possession," as they were an extension of me in Fae eyes.

I'd conversed with Talis twice more since then—both times borrowing the body of the same serpent, who seemed to live in the vines growing up the Sovereign House. The viper was grumpy each time, but it was getting easier to control his body. I always thanked him, but I don't think he cared. I'd have to make sure he had a nice supply of mice or something when I made it back to the Sovereign House in person.

Each time I'd woken up, there had been a snake in my lap. Rynn was not happy about that.

I was also beginning to notice that I could sense any snakes in the area. My

Fae magic definitely seemed to be stirring more. And I was fairly certain I could summon the serpents to me if I wanted, like if I just tugged on that thread which connected me to them, they would answer.

In addition to my new scaly friends, I'd also been able to do small things like coax some flowers on a cactus into blooming and stifle my footsteps like Draven so I could move about silently.

It was something I'd been practicing by sneaking up on Rynn and scaring the shit out of her. I'd tried to do the same to Cali, but the bitch had *stabbed* me. When I'd shrieked that it was just me, she'd snorted and said, "I know. Why do you think it's just a flesh wound?" And then she'd pulled the dagger out from between my ribs.

In fairness, she had missed my vital organs and I'd healed within minutes. Still, a bit of an overreaction, in my opinion.

Two days ago, Ary and Aniela had shown up looking beat to shit. Apparently, all of the Moroi realm was crawling with rangers who reported only to Carmilla, and the Heirs hadn't been sure if they'd make it to House Devereux, so they'd opted to come here instead. It was actually a boon for us because part of our plan required blood—a lot of blood.

Once we'd told them what we'd been plotting, the two of them had been more than willing to open up a vein and donate to the cause. They'd given quite a bit and were currently passed out downstairs . . . in the same bed.

Something had clearly happened between the two, but I'd have to get the full story later.

We hadn't heard anything from Vail during all this time, and I was trying very hard not to dwell on that fact. Thanks to our mate bond, I could feel him, but it was definitely fainter the farther he went. Our bond was stronger than it had been—it no longer felt like it was crumbling—but, clearly, distance had an impact.

Roth had found a couple of books that mentioned Fae mate bonds. From what we could tell, the bonds formed in one of two ways. Naturally, which only occurred when the people forming the bond were genuinely in love with each other and declared their devotion, or through spell castings. It seemed the Fae had been fans of arranged political marriages, and mate bonds were used in those cases as well.

I hadn't come across anything about them being possible to break like Erendriel had claimed, but the books hadn't had a ton of information. It didn't matter though, because I was keeping my mates, and I'd kill anyone who tried to take them from me—the Seelie King included.

To keep myself from going insane, I'd started limiting how often I checked the bond between me and Vail. Otherwise, I'd just obsess over it, and I was worried that I might tug on it or send some of my emotions barreling down the bond and distract Vail at the worst possible moment.

My imagination had run wild with Vail fighting against monsters or some of Carmilla's rangers, only to miss a step because I'd practically screamed my growing panic through our mate bond.

So I'd diverted my obsessive mind into fine-tuning the transformation spell and going over the plan with everyone repeatedly.

Which apparently was starting to get on everyone's nerves.

Kieran, of all people, had threatened to find a spell to seal my lips shut if I attempted to run through everything again, which had everyone grunting in agreement. According to Talis, I had perfected the transformation spell. Granted, I was pretty sure they'd been only half listening the last time we'd spoken.

I'd managed to bore an ancient Fae crown. Go me.

Logically, it made sense that Vail hadn't sent any messages of his progress. Strikers were our main form of communication, and they were trained to either follow specific routes or track people down. The temple wasn't on any normal routes, and while every House had strikers trained to find me, Vail couldn't exactly stop by and ask to borrow one.

I knew all of this, yet it did nothing to keep me from freaking out. Vail had been gone for five days now. He'd said it might take longer than that to return, but all I could think about were the worst-case scenarios. We'd also been holed up in this temple for a week now, so everyone's nerves were a little frayed.

Erendriel had promised to return when I needed him and gave me a coin to summon him. I didn't understand how he was moving around so quickly, because he definitely wasn't in the temple during the day, and there wasn't much around here. Draven didn't know how he did it either, only that he could go from one end of the continent to the other in the same day—the same hour, even.

Now that I knew about the mirrors, it didn't seem so impossible, but it wasn't like he was lugging an eight-foot mirror around with him.

There had been no sign of Serril or any other wraiths either, but it was still suspicious that Erendriel hadn't left someone behind to keep an eye on us.

We'd been careful about setting up the rest of our plans—only working on the temple during the day and only after Draven did a thorough pass-through to make sure no wraiths had found a dark corner to lurk in. Everything was coming together—we just needed Vail to come back.

I needed Vail to come back.

"Have we accounted for—"

"*Yes!*" Roth, Alaric, and Rynn all said at once.

I stopped where I'd been pacing in the middle of the room and glared at the three of them. "You don't even know what I was going to say," I accused.

"You no doubt thought of yet another variation of how things could go wrong." Alaric closed the book he'd been reading and selected a new one from the piles in front of him.

"Even though we've already come up with multiple contingency plans at this point." Roth's ropes snapped out to steal the book Alaric had chosen and tossed a different one to him.

"It's impossible to plan for all scenarios—that way lies madness—and we've covered all the major ones," Rynn added, not even looking up from the scroll her eyes were glued to.

"Sure, but what if—"

"For the love of the moon, shut up!" Cali growled from where she'd been resting her eyes on her folded-up arms at the weapons table.

"Why don't you go for a walk?" Kieran offered. "Maybe practice your magic a bit?"

"Don't go far though." Draven glanced up from the sword he'd been admiring. "And please don't bring any more snakes inside. I don't think I can listen to Rynn scream again."

"Oh, don't start," Rynn sneered, finally looking away from the text she'd been absorbed in. "I've been listening to all of you make Samara scream for days now. My ears are bleeding, and I'm honestly worried for my best friend's pussy at this point."

"Yeah, exactly how much pounding can that thing take?" Cali twisted her head so she could stare at me—well, a certain part of me anyway.

"Oh, we haven't just been playing with that perfect little pussy," Kieran said cheerfully. "We've als—"

"I'm going to go for a walk now!" I announced loudly and beat a hasty retreat. Rynn was already in a foul mood, and Kieran reciting the many ways I'd been fucked over the last four days would not make her any more pleasant to be around.

The clock was ticking on our plan, which meant time was also running out before Rynn had to return to the Alpha Pack.

I went up the stairs, passing through the ward, and then turned left to head towards the temple entrance. My eyes flitted about the large, open chamber. This was where we'd been sneakily laying all the glyphs the past few days. The even larger room further in the temple would have been better, but that was also where the entrance to the secret level was, and the ceiling was broken in places. We'd needed a room that was entirely contained, so this had been the only option.

The white marble that made up every inch of the room, from the ceilings to the floors and the columns that spiraled up between them, didn't show even a hint of what we'd spent the last three days doing after Roth had perfected the spell.

Or at least, we were hoping that was what they'd done. We couldn't exactly test it beforehand.

If it failed . . . we'd just have to run fast. Real fucking fast.

Maybe I should check them again . . .

My hand flew to my chest at the same moment I inhaled sharply. Then I was sprinting towards the temple entrance and flinging myself into the arms of the approaching man.

"Vail," I breathed out as I clung to him before inhaling that scent I had missed so much.

"Miss me, Sam?" Vail held me tightly against him.

"Only a little," I lied.

He laughed, burying his face into the crook of my neck. We stayed like that for a long moment, just holding each other. Safe. He was safe . . . and he'd come back to me. The bond thrummed happily between us.

"What's that smell?" I wrinkled my nose after taking another deep breath, then stepped back enough to look him over.

"Well, I have been traveling basically nonstop for the past few days," he said dryly.

"Not that." My gaze fell to the bag he must have dropped when I'd thrown myself at him. The brown canvas was stained dark red in places. Blood. Decay. "Are you carrying body parts?" I looked at him, wide-eyed. "Tell me you didn't kill Tamsen!? That was not the plan, Vail!"

"I didn't kill Tamsen." His silver eyes were alight with amusement. "She is safe in the loving and not at all crazy embrace of House Devereux. I brought you a present."

"A present?" I gave the bag and then him a skeptical look. "You know how Draven tried to explain how apologies work? Maybe you should talk to him about how gifts work. See, rotting body parts aren't really—"

"Grigor's dead."

I blinked. "The sleazy guard from the Sovereign House? The handsy one?"

Vail grinned widely. "He's a little less handsy now."

"You didn't," I said with a choked laugh before glancing back down at the bag. It *was* basically the perfect size for two hands . . .

"I saw the way he kept coming up with reasons to touch you," Vail said in a low, dangerous tone. "He volunteered to be on one of the teams to track Tamsen down. Apparently, he is—was—a good tracker. After I got her to safety, I doubled back and took him out."

"How?" I prodded the bag with my toe.

"Lured a pack of howlers to where he was, cut off his hands, and let the pack tear him apart."

"Let's leave them out here—they smell, and it's the thought that counts." I grabbed Vail's hand and started pulling him into the temple.

"So you like my gift then?"

I glanced over my shoulder. "Oh, yes, but we need to get you cleaned up so I can show you just how much."

Vail's hand slipped from mine, and the next thing I knew, I was being thrown over his shoulder. I laughed as Vail jogged down to the secret levels. He paused at the first level, but when I tried to turn to see why, he just slapped my ass.

"Vail!" I shouted and wiggled to get free. Another slap.

"I take it things went well then?" Draven drawled. I couldn't see him, but I could practically hear the smile in his voice.

"Tamsen is safe. At least two of the rangers picked up my trail. They're keeping their distance, but I doubled back a few times to check on them—they're definitely following me." A hand gripped my ass and squeezed. "Also, I killed that prick of a guard I told you about."

"The handsy one?" Draven asked.

"Less handsy now," I laughed while repeating Vail's words.

Draven chuckled. "Do us a favor and keep her busy for a few hours? Everyone is feeling a little stir-crazy, and our devious little Blood Queen has been rather antsy."

First, Vail and Draven had been chatting about the guard, and now Roth was sharing their nickname for me. I kind of liked that all my mates were getting along. Although I wasn't going to let Draven's comment about my antsiness slide.

"It's rude to talk about me like I'm not here," I said in a mockingly stern tone. "And it's not for you both to decide where I go. As you said, I am your queen, so—" I yelped when Vail raised the hand that had been kneading my ass and slapped it again—hard.

There was no way I wasn't going to have a bruise.

"At least two people should be on lookout from now on." Vail started down the stairs again.

"I'll see to it." Draven blew me a kiss when we passed him. I blew one back because apparently I was sappy as shit now that I had five mates.

Plus, I was about to get railed for several hours. That was an instant good-mood maker right there.

Vail went straight to the room he'd claimed on the second level and put me down. The layout of this one was different from mine. A large bed took up the back left corner, its sheets still askew from when Vail had last been in it, and the opposite corner on the back wall had a little alcove built into it. The Fae had taken the time to create a waterfall mural in it using different types of stones and gems.

They really had put a lot of effort into making these hidden layers feel like a home. Once again, I was curious about who had built it and why they weren't here enjoying the fruits of their labor.

All those thoughts fled the second Vail pulled his shirt over his head before tugging off his pants and boots a second later.

"Strip," he ordered before activating the glyph that had been cleverly worked into the waterfall mural. Water started to fall in a controlled spray of fine droplets from the alcove's ceiling.

I briefly thought about saying no just to be contrary, but then I made the mistake of looking at Vail's thick, hard cock, and my mouth watered.

I could always be bratty later.

Vail smirked, as if he'd seen my momentary inner struggle and was amused by it. Then a groan slipped from his lips when I shucked my dress off, revealing I wasn't wearing any undergarments—Alaric had torn my last pair yesterday. It was my turn to smirk at him.

"See something you like, Marshal?" I sauntered past him to duck under the warm water, letting it plaster my long, black hair to my breasts and over my soft belly.

Vail's gaze darkened. "I see something I want to devour."

Fuck. Me.

"Clean first." I curled a finger, and he joined me under the water. "You're covered in dirt, blood, and only the moon knows what else."

Vail stood there quietly while I took my time getting him clean, running my fingers across his broad chest before tangling them in his hair. The more I touched him, the more his dark grey eyes shifted to silver until that was all I could see. His patience finally snapped when I reached down and dragged my fingers up the bottom of his hard length.

One second, I was debating dropping to my knees and teasing him a little more, and the next, I was six feet off the ground with my back against the cool wall and my legs over Vail's shoulders.

"Oh, fuck!" I screamed. There was no teasing. No light little licks. Vail just gripped my ass with his hands and buried his entire face in my pussy. Instantly, my thighs clamped around his head, but he didn't seem to mind. If anything, it only spurred him on.

Arching my back as much as I could and trusting him not to let me fall, I let myself slip into bliss while Vail devoured my cunt. His tongue speared my core, and I ground against his mouth. I didn't even attempt to be quiet as I moaned with every lick and thrust of his tongue, and when he switched to sucking on my clit, I came so hard, I was surprised I didn't pass out.

Hot breath tickled my inner thigh as Vail pulled back. "You still with me, Sam?"

"Mm-hmm," I breathed out as tremors ran through my body.

"I promised Draven I'd keep you distracted for hours. Don't tell me I've already worn you out?"

"Not even close." I leaned my head forward from where it had been resting against the wall and almost groaned when I saw Vail grinning, the evidence of my arousal glistening in his short beard. "That was just a bit of stress relief."

"Oh?" Vail's hands slid up to my lower back, holding me in place as he stepped out of the alcove, taking me with him. I squeaked at my precarious position, which just made him laugh as he carried us towards the bed. "And what were you so worried about?"

I scowled down at him. "You were gone for five days, Vail! Any number of things could have gone wrong, and it's all I could think about."

"Funny. You said you only missed me a little bit." He carefully lowered me to the bed as if I weighed nothing. I should have probably cared about the fact that we were both still wet and soaking the bed, but my eyes were glued to Vail's impressive chest and abs.

Which I would argue were more important from a priority standpoint.

"Okay, maybe I missed you a moderate amount."

Vail's silver gaze bored down on me, the back of my legs still resting loosely against his body. "A moderate amount?" He grinned and jerked my legs so that my butt was closer to the edge of the bed. I inhaled sharply when I felt his cock notch against my entrance. Vail chuckled and leaned down, pushing my legs so that the tops of my thighs were almost touching my breasts. "Is that your final answer?"

I bit my lip and acted like I was thinking about it before nodding. "Yep. Definitely a middling amou—" A scream tore from my throat as Vail buried his cock balls-deep inside me.

"I felt you," he growled. "Every fucking day. You missed me. Desperately. Like your soul had been fractured." Vail pulled his hips away, only to thrust roughly back inside me again, drawing out another moan as my pussy stretched around his hard length. "I felt it too. It was fucking torture to be away from you that long."

"Show me," I breathed out. "Show me how much you missed me, Vail."

"Fuck," Vail ground out, then slammed into me one more time before pulling out. I hissed my disapproval at his cock no longer being inside me, and the bastard just chuckled as he flipped me over until I was on my hands and knees. With one smooth motion, he gripped my hips and thrust back into me.

I screamed and clenched the silky fabric of the bedspread as I did my best to push back against Vail's brutal pace. "Fuck me harder! I want to feel every inch of you."

I felt the second his nails shifted to claws and tore through my flesh. My pussy clenched at the mixture of pain and pleasure, and Vail groaned in response. "You are so fucking perfect." He pounded harder against me until all

I could hear was the sound of flesh slapping flesh. "You like me stretching out your tight little pussy, don't you? "

"I do," I panted. "Fill me up, Vail. I want to feel you dripping between my thighs . . . and then I want you to fuck me again."

"Gods, I love that filthy mouth of yours." One hand ripped away from my thigh to push down on my back until my forehead was against the bed. Then both hands were on me again as Vail rutted roughly into me. "You're going to take every inch of me in this perfect fucking pussy until you can't take anymore, and then I'm going to come down your throat before fucking this glorious ass. You're going to be feeling me for days. Is that what you want, Sam?"

"Yes!" I let out a half-strangled scream.

After that, all I could do was moan as Vail pounded into me until he let out a low groan. He gave me a couple of minutes to recover before flipping me over and spearing me with his fingers. Then I whimpered when he pulled them free and admired how soaked they were before he swirled them around my clit. "Tell me again how much you missed me, *mate*."

"Make me," I said a little breathlessly before giving him a wicked grin, "mate."

CHAPTER THIRTY

—

Samara

I WAS DREAMING about the hot springs and being worshipped by all of my mates. Kier was doing amazing things to my clit with that tongue of his while Draven thrust his fingers into my aching cunt. Vail was fucking my ass, and Alaric and Roth were teasing my breasts.

It was a glorious dream . . . which was completely destroyed by someone pounding on the door.

"Fuck off," Vail rumbled when I started to jerk upright, only to be stopped by his arm tightening around my stomach and chest. My back was to his chest and I could feel his erection pressed against the curve of my ass.

All kinds of ideas popped into my head. I hadn't meant to fall asleep, but Vail had been very . . . demanding. Between the mind-blowing sex and lack of sleep the last few days, I'd passed out shortly after he'd made me come for at least the dozenth time in three hours.

Vail's bossiness might have driven me insane most of the time, but damn did I like it when he was ordering me to come all over his cock while bruising my thighs with his grip.

The knocking increased.

"The Furies are here," Rynn growled from the other side of the door. "They've come for Cali."

All sexy thoughts instantly vanished.

"Shit." I scrambled out of bed and grabbed my dress off the floor, only to remember Vail had shredded it.

"Here." Vail tossed me his shirt, and I tugged it on. It fell to mid-thigh. Good enough.

I yanked the door open and practically collided with Rynn, who was gripping both sides of the doorframe like she needed something to ground her. "How'd they get here so fast?"

We'd suspected Carmilla would put her plans to remove Cali from the picture in motion as soon as she figured out where we were, but we'd assumed it would be tomorrow at the earliest. The Furie stronghold was on the southwestern coast of Lunaria. Even if Carmilla had sent a striker to them right away, they wouldn't have received the message until this evening.

Rynn dropped her arms, grabbed my hand, and tugged me towards the stairs. "I have no idea, but if we don't calm Cali down, she's going to kill him, and then our best-laid plans are going to be absolutely fucked."

"Who?" I ran a little faster to keep up with Rynn's long stride. "Fuck, it's Malachi, isn't it?"

"Of course it is," Rynn answered tightly. "We should have killed that fucker years ago. I told you he was nothing but trouble."

"You said the same thing about Vail," I pointed out.

"Yeah, and I stand by that," she hissed over her shoulder.

"Exactly how long are you going to be mad at me for, Rynn?" Vail asked from where he kept pace behind us.

Rynn slammed to a halt, and I bounced off her, only to be caught by Vail, who steadied me on my feet. My friend turned to glare at Vail, who was only wearing a pair of pants that he hadn't even bothered to button up all the way. "You knocked me out and stole the crown, which I had basically promised Samara I would keep safe."

"Fair enough," Vail replied evenly. "I regret my actions that day, and while Samara and I have already worked out our differences—" I snorted, and he corrected himself. "I am in the process of apologizing to the love of my life and will do so with many, many orgasms. But since I can't offer that to you, I will offer you my sword. Whatever you need from me in the future, it's yours. Want me to kill the Alpha Pack? I'll figure it out. Want to wipe out the pack that essentially sold you to them? Also done. Whatever you want, Rynn. I'll make right by you."

I bit my tongue, not wanting to get between my best friend and my mate— even if I was literally standing between them at the moment—but I did make sure the gratitude I was feeling made its way down the bond. Vail and I might have had our issues, but they were just that—ours. Rynn had trusted him, and he had betrayed that trust. I couldn't fix that between them, but I loved him for recognizing he'd fucked up and attempting to fix it.

"Alright," Rynn said slowly, her mismatched eyes staring at Vail. "I'll hold you to that."

He nodded deeply, but any further conversation was thwarted by angry shouting coming from somewhere above us. The three of us took off running again and quickly made it up the stairwell and through the temple until we were outside in the hot afternoon sun.

Roth, Alaric, Kieran, and Draven stood just in front of the temple columns, watching the two Furies face off. Alaric and Draven observed with tight expressions, whereas Roth and Kieran were looking at Cali in concern.

I didn't blame them. Outside of us, if Cali had a weak spot, it was Malachi.

Rynn was right. We should have killed the prick and spared Cali a world of heartache. The only thing that had stopped me from pursuing such a path was the fact that I very much suspected my wild and untamed best friend was in love with the bastard.

Even though that love might get her killed one day.

Cali had never admitted to such a thing, and I was pretty sure Rynn just thought of him as someone Cali had a passing fancy for, but I remembered what Cali had been like after Malachi had ended things. She'd been so . . . broken.

That kind of pain was only caused by love. I would know.

Rynn skidded to a stop ten feet from the temple, and Vail and I stopped with her. A short distance away, Cali squared off against a dark-gold-haired Furie, who was a few inches taller than Vail and just as bulky.

My mind had trouble accepting that someone as large as Malachi could move as nimbly as he did. But when Cali thrust her sword at his gut, he easily twisted around the blow, his dark, leathery wings tucked in tight against his back.

Cali matched his movements, her dark red hair lit up by the sun, making it flow around her like living flames. Her golden brown eyes came alive in the way they always did when she was fighting. If Cali was fire incarnate, Malachi was the darkness that wanted to swallow her whole.

"Is that all you got?" Cali sneered, backing up a step with her sword raised, blood dripping from it.

"Don't make me hurt you, Rayne." Malachi's black eyes were bottomless pits as he stared at her, not even bothering to acknowledge the rest of us. My eyes were normally a deep purple and only turned black when my bloodlust rose, but Malachi's eyes were always a solid black.

If Cali was the most powerful Furie, he was a close second. I'd always suspected that was at least part of the reason the Elders had forbidden them from being together. On their own, Cali and Malachi were terrifying. But together? They would be unstoppable.

And the Furie Elders didn't like anything they couldn't control.

"What do you want, Mal?" Cali's sword might have been stained with the other Furie's blood, but she'd taken plenty of hits too. Based on the careful way she was standing with more of her weight on her left foot, I suspected the prick had injured her right knee.

Cali had been attacked by wraiths years ago. She'd survived—obviously—but it'd been closer than any of us liked to think about. Her right leg in particular had been badly mangled, and no amount of healing had seemed to fix her knee. It was her weak spot in a fight.

That type of knowledge wasn't something most knew. Malachi clearly did—and he'd used it against her.

Rage at his callousness had my nails shifting to claws. I wouldn't fuck up our plan . . . I'd just make him hurt a little. My Fae magic stirred, and I tried to focus on the ground beneath the asshole's feet.

A crack formed in the dry, compact dirt of the badlands. I pushed a little more—

"No!" Cali snarled, but not at Malachi—at me.

I lost my focus, and the magic slipped from me.

Fuck. We'd all agreed that it was best to keep my abilities and Draven's as much of a secret as possible. House Devereux wouldn't tell anyone, and I'd have to decide if and when I wanted to tell the other Houses once Carmilla was dealt with, but with how tense things were with the Velesians and how unreliable the Furies were, it was better to keep them in the dark on this.

We'd need all the advantages we could get in case we really did go to war one day.

That was fine. I still had my daggers.

Malachi seized Cali's moment of distraction to lunge forward, his sword aiming for Cali's thigh, right above her weak knee.

He was fast—I was faster.

The Furie roared as my blood daggers bit into his flesh. He sensed them just in time to turn so the one I'd aimed for his throat hit his shoulder instead. And the one that had been flying towards his groin sank two inches to the left.

Pity.

His black eyes focused on me. I tugged on the magic within the daggers, and both of them tore free from his body and flew back towards me. I licked the blood off the blades. Not as tasty as my mates', but Furie blood did pack one hell of a punch. It practically sizzled across my tongue.

I pointed one of my now-clean blades at him. "Don't fuck with my friend, Malachi."

"What are you going to do about it, Moroi trash?" he growled. "You seriously think you can take me on with your two little knives?"

"Of course not, silly." I bared my fangs at him. "I'm the distraction."

Four-hundred pounds of pissed-off lycanthrope slammed into the Furie. To his credit, Malachi didn't panic. He just let them fall before twisting at the last second, forcing Rynn to either jump off his back or risk getting pinned beneath him—she bailed.

In an instant, Malachi was on his feet, but I was already sliding behind him.

"How do you like my two little knives now?" I pushed the one at his throat in enough to draw a little blood while tapping the other one over his groin that I'd sadly missed earlier. Hard to miss at this distance though, which was something he seemed to understand because the Furie had gone perfectly still.

Cali walked over to us, her expression tight and a slight limp to her step. I dug my blades in a little deeper—both of them. Malachi didn't seem to care. I couldn't see his face from where I stood, but I could tell that all of his attention was on my friend.

"You ever call my friend trash again"—her hand snapped out to grip his chin—"and I'll rip out your tongue. Now, once again, why are you here?"

"Aiofe is in the pit." He kept his voice even, but I could have sworn I heard a hint of despair in it. Who was Aiofe? His new lover? I swear to fuck, if he came to beg Cali to help him rescue his new love, I'd slit his throat. Plan be damned.

Cali released her hold on him and took a step back, as if she needed the space between them. "Why is your little sister in that godsforsaken place?"

"Because of you and your refusal to obey." Malachi twisted his head slightly towards me, not even caring about the blood dribbling down his neck. "Either slit my throat or get the fuck away from me."

"I vote to slit his throat!" Kieran called out.

"Same!" Alaric and Roth chimed in.

I glanced at Cali, and she shook her head. Reluctantly, I pulled my blades away—making sure to open up some nice cuts on the way out—and stepped back. As if by magic, Draven and Vail appeared on either side of me.

Malachi instantly spun to face me, his expression filled with rage and a dagger in his hand.

"I wouldn't," Vail warned.

"Oh please do," Draven purred. "I've always wanted to taste Furie blood."

"Here." I held up one of my daggers, and Draven leaned forward, his tongue darting out to lick the flat side.

"Mmm." He took another swipe. "Tasty."

Malachi's mouth twisted in disgust, and he took another step towards us, only to stop when Rynn growled behind him.

"Focus, Mal," Cali ordered, "or I'll let my friends tear you apart, and I promise, I won't shed a single tear over it."

Something flickered in those glittering black eyes of his, there and gone in an instant. Regret, I thought. Maybe guilt.

Whatever it was, I didn't care. Malachi had hurt my friend deeply, and he seemed intent on continuing to do so. I had to let the events of today play out, but sooner or later, I was going to bury my blades in his flesh again, and next time, he wouldn't be walking away.

Malachi slid his dagger back into the sheath on his thigh and turned to face Cali.

"The Furie Elders have decreed that they will not be involved in the petty squabbles of the Moroi," he said evenly.

I snorted. Apparently the slaughter of our previous Sovereign and the brutal rise of another was just a *petty squabble.*

Malachi ignored me and kept going. "All Furies have been ordered to return. You've been ignoring their commands for weeks, so they told me to handle you. Aiofe is my incentive to be successful."

"I don't know why they bothered." Cali shrugged. "We both know you would have done it anyway. Always the good little soldier."

The muscles in Malachi's jaw flexed. "Some of us have people we care about—who care about us. We don't get to just flutter about Lunaria doing whatever the hells we want."

"Listen here, you piece of shit—" I took a step towards him.

"I'll go," Cali cut me off. Her tone was harsh, but her look at me was pointed. This had always been the plan. We just had to make it believable in case Carmilla had someone watching. If Cali went without a fight, it would be suspicious. "Let me just get my thi—"

"Now," Malachi interrupted. "We leave now. Aiofe's already been in the pit for two weeks. I've been flying around looking for you this whole time and just happened to stumble across some of the new queen's rangers this morning, who told me where *that one* had been spotted." He pointed at Vail before glancing at me. "Your own people were quick to sell you out to a Furie, by the way."

"Yeah, we're a treacherous lot," I deadpanned.

Malachi narrowed his eyes.

"Let's get this over with." Cali sighed before stomping over to me. "I'll be back as soon as I can. Don't do anything stupid while I'm gone, okay?"

"I don't like this," I said with a tightness that I wasn't faking.

"I know." Cali gave me a sad smile. "But sometimes we just have to deal with the hand we're dealt. I'll see you soon, I promise." Then she took a step back and launched herself into the sky. Black wings snapped open, and she waved a hand at Rynn and the others before flying off.

"She can't keep doing this," Malachi said, a dangerous edge to his voice, his eyes tracking Cali's movements before turning to me. "Her friendship with you is causing her more harm than you can possibly imagine. Stop being selfish and let her go."

I took a step forward, away from Vail and Draven, and let the Furie see the predator in my eyes—ones that were now as black as his. "You were wrong earlier when you implied she didn't have anyone she cared about—or who cared about her." Rynn moved to stand next to me, her lips pulled back in a silent snarl. "She has us—she always will."

"Let's hope that's enough," he said so quietly, I almost thought I misheard him before he leapt into the sky.

———

"Have you summoned him?" Draven asked, his gaze locked on the silver coin I was flipping back and forth across the top of my knuckles. It was a habit I'd picked up from my father. I still remembered him teaching me how to do it. He'd even made me a smaller coin so that it was easier for my child-sized hands.

I'd stopped doing it the day he'd died.

As soon as Cali had been gone from sight, I'd retrieved the coin from the lower levels of the temple. I'd been sitting in the large room in the main entrance—the unwarded part—playing with the coin in the same way my father had once done.

I wondered what he would have said about my plan. About who his daughter had grown up to be.

The coin stopped, balanced on my middle knuckle. For all the secrets he and my mother had kept, I had no doubt that they'd loved me. In keeping my grief locked away, I'd also prevented myself from remembering all the good times. Maybe it was time to change that. Accept the past once and for all so I could truly focus on the future.

I rolled the coin towards my thumb and flicked it up before snatching it out of the air. "No. But I'm about to." Then I rose from where I'd been sitting on one of the long benches and closed the distance between me and Draven, who was leaning against one of the pillars. "You don't need to stay," I said softly. "You can join the others downstairs."

Everyone except Rynn and Vail had retreated back to the first underground level. We had everything in place for our plan, but keeping busy seemed to help everyone deal with the anxiety of what we were about to do. Plus, the knowledge contained in those secret rooms was truly astounding. We'd learned more in the last week than we had in our entire lives. Hells, we'd probably learned more than all of the Moroi had in our collective existence.

Things that could change life in Lunaria as we knew it. Assuming we all survived what came next. If Carmilla was in charge of the information, I didn't have faith in her to let others know.

Knowledge was power, and my aunt had already demonstrated just how far she was willing to go to claim it.

"You're going to kill your aunt," Draven said wryly as he tucked a strand of loose hair behind my ear. "Least I can do is have a face-to-face with dear old dad."

"Someday we'll figure out a way to kill him too," I promised. "He doesn't get to live after everything he's done to you."

"Agreed." Vail strolled into the temple, sweat plastering his hair to the sides of his face. It was a blistering hot day in the badlands, and even in the shade, it was warm and stuffy. "Rynn's scouting a little farther out, but so far, we haven't seen any signs of Carmilla. I doubt she would risk traveling at night, so we likely won't see her until at least tomorrow."

I nodded. Now that Cali was gone, my aunt would come for me. It was unlikely she knew I'd been speaking with Erendriel and had wraiths backing me up, but I agreed with Vail. All kinds of nasty things roamed Lunaria at night, so Carmilla would likely launch her attack during daylight.

"Alright." I held the coin up between two fingers. "Time to get this over with." Erendriel had told me all I'd have to do was think about him and push a small amount of magic into the coin. I wasn't sure if that would be enough or if I'd need my blood to make it work, but I figured I'd try without it first.

For a few seconds, nothing happened, then the coin started to pulse with a soft glow.

"Guess that means it worked?" We all looked around, as if the Seelie King was just going to pop into existence.

He did not.

"Come on." Draven grabbed my hand. "I have a hunch."

I tucked the coin into the pocket of the dress I'd changed into and held my hand out to Vail. He intertwined his fingers with mine, and the three of us headed farther into the temple.

"My father has kept most of his abilities a mystery. Some I know but can't talk about." He winced. So far, in all our readings, we hadn't come across anything to explain how Erendriel had spelled Draven to be unable to tell us things, but I was still hopeful we'd find something. "How he travels around Lunaria is something I don't understand, but I've noticed on a few occasions that if he does it during the day, he always comes from somewhere dark."

"You think he needs shadows to do it," Vail guessed.

"I think so."

Draven stopped, and I did the same, Vail halting next to me. We were in the back of the temple now. Only two rooms were left, and both had a narrow hall that led to them. The last time I'd been in one of those rooms, wraiths had attacked Nyx and hurt them badly. I also hadn't been faring particularly well.

"Let's wait out here." I squeezed their hands. "I'd rather not be in a tight space with Erendriel, even if he is our ally."

"That's a shame," a deep voice called out from the dark passageway, "because I'd very much enjoy being in a tight space with you."

Erendriel strolled out of the hall on the left before stopping a few feet away from us. His hands were tucked into the pockets of his black pants, and the dark tunic he wore was practically molded to his upper body. Apparently, he was still hoping to tempt me into marrying him.

"You'll just have to dream about it." I shrugged. "I'm a happily mated woman—four times over." *Soon to be five once Kieran gets his party.*

Erendriel gave Vail a dismissive glance before looking at his son. "You managed to hide just how strong your magic was from me all this time and get yourself mated to a rising power. I suppose you're not a total disappointment after all, unlike your brother."

Draven's fingers tightened around mine, but he remained silent.

The Seelie King chuckled. "She won't be able to keep you safe from me forever, boy."

"And the deal you have with our queen won't protect you forever either," Vail drawled.

"How about we all play nice so everyone walks away with what they want?" I cut in and gave Erendriel a polite smile, ignoring the way being so close to him without the safety of the ward had my instincts screaming at me to run. Very fast. "It's time to set our plan into motion. Carmilla will be coming for me, very likely tomorrow."

"Of course." Erendriel gave me a deep nod. "Once night falls, I will summon the wraiths here as we discussed." He offered me his hand, and after hesitating for only a moment, I took it and allowed him to tug me away from Vail and Draven, both of whom growled.

Erendriel ignored them as he guided me back towards the front room, one of his hands resting on my lower back. "Now, have you been practicing closing the door as I instructed? I'd love to see what progress you have made with your magic. There is so much I could teach you if you'd only let me . . ."

CHAPTER THIRTY-ONE

—

Samara

"SHE'S ALMOST HERE."

Irritation simmered beneath the mask of apprehension I'd fixed my features into. I'd been switching back and forth between that and one of shaky confidence. Erendriel had barely left my side since arriving yesterday, and while part of me enjoyed the thrill of outsmarting the Seelie King, I was more than a little exhausted from wearing all these different masks.

Honestly, I didn't know how Kieran did it. I hadn't been able to roll my eyes *once* in over twelve hours.

The only reprieve I'd gotten had been when night had fallen and he'd summoned the wraiths to him. For hours, they had poured into the temple. It had been an eerie experience, to say the least. My entire life, wraiths had been something to fear—and they still were—but now, I was relying on them. I tried not to think about the fact that some of these wraiths could have been the same ones that had killed my parents.

Nothing good would come from dwelling on that, and if all went according to plan, we'd only be allies for a little while longer.

To my disappointment, Serril hadn't been amongst the wraiths to answer Erendriel's call. I would have loved to have him caught up in all of this, but for whatever reason, Erendriel had not summoned him. And I didn't want to risk raising suspicion by asking about him. He would almost certainly be a problem when the dust settled, but not much we could do about that now. As my mother used to say, *"No point in asking tomorrow for its problems when you still had to deal with today's bullshit."*

"Just remember what you promised, Erendriel." I glanced to my right, where the Seelie King stood next to me, gazing out into the badlands. "The rangers are not to be harmed."

He gave me a patronizing smile. "Of course, my young queen."

I started to clench my jaw but killed the motion immediately, instead keeping my mask of apprehension and fear on. For just a little while longer, I needed to play the role of eager but inexperienced queen. It was a tightrope to walk, and part of me was thankful that it was coming to an end, but another part dreaded my showdown with Carmilla.

She had to be stopped, I knew this, but it didn't mean I could just turn off my feelings for her. I knew Vail was struggling as well. We had both loved Carmilla as a stand-in parent. Her betrayal had left deep wounds in us both. At least now we had each other to lean on. Another person to talk to who understood exactly what the other felt.

Currently, Vail stood with Draven inside the temple, and everyone else waited in the first underground level until Carmilla was secured.

"Can you feel them approaching?" He gave me a curious look.

We'd been practicing for most of the time he'd been here. By which I meant I'd made pathetic attempts at using my Seelie earth magic and he'd played the role of patient teacher. I'd been mostly honest about my magic capabilities since I already had to balance so many other lies. Plus, I was never one to waste resources, and while I didn't trust everything Erendriel said, that didn't mean he wasn't a fountain of knowledge. One just had to wade through his bullshit.

Although, the scholars at Drudonia had never laid a hand on my lower back while giving instructions or found reasons to brush against my skin.

Vail and Draven hadn't been fans of that but also hadn't interfered—trusting me to handle the situation. They'd just glowered from where they'd been leaning against the wall, watching us.

I wasn't blind—Erendriel was truly stunning, but he was also an arrogant asshole.

I already had plenty of those and wasn't in the market for another.

Plus he didn't understand the concept of no. Sooner or later, he'd meet the same fate as Demetri and that prick guard Vail had so kindly taken care of.

Maybe we could host a celebration once a year in their honor? Like a mock funeral of sorts. *Here lie a bunch of handsy fuckers who got what they had coming. Rest in pieces, assholes.*

"Samara?" Erendriel arched a dark golden brow at me.

"Apologies. It's been a long day." I gave him a tired smile and hoped that covered up the amused one I'd been sporting a second ago. "I can feel . . . something." I looked away from him out into the badlands, and a crease formed between my brows as I concentrated. "But I can't tell what it is exactly. Either it's large or there are lots of somethings, and I get the sense that it's moving this way, but it's more a feeling than anything else."

There was also the fact that I already knew Carmilla and her rangers were out there, courtesy of Rynn's scouting, so my magic had something to go on. I wasn't sure, if I'd had no knowledge of the situation, I would have been able to sense her.

"You're actually doing quite well for someone who is so new to their magic," he said encouragingly. "You'll get better with time and practice, and of course I can teach you to speed things up a bit."

A shriek came from deep within the temple.

"It seems your wraiths need to learn what it means to be quiet." I glanced back towards the only room that was dark enough for the wraiths to gather during daylight.

"They do have a tendency to get excited," he explained. "This temple is where we conducted most of the rituals to make them whole again. The ones who are still shadows are clamoring for the chance to be what they once were."

"There will be no more rituals," I reiterated firmly. "No more spilling of Moroi blood for your wraiths."

"Hold up your end of the bargain, my young queen, and we won't need to. Once we find the Unseelie Princes, their blood will be the answer to everything I seek."

I very much wanted to find these Unseelie Princes, but I sure as shit wouldn't be giving their location to Erendriel. Maybe they wouldn't be assholes like him. I almost snorted. Of course they would be. I was rapidly coming to the realization that all Fae were assholes.

Maybe they were dead and we were all chasing ghosts. That would certainly be annoying. Although, as much as I wanted to find these princes, part of me wondered if it was for the good of Lunaria that they stayed lost.

More loud wailing came from the back of the temple, and a hint of annoyance flickered across Erendriel's face. "I will see to my people," he conceded and gave me a nod. "Make sure you get that door closed so that they can move around easier. They cannot walk in the light as I do and there are only so many shadows for them to hide in."

"Of course." I nodded back, keeping my tone respectful. He smiled at me before striding into the temple. I watched him go, keeping a close eye on his posture to see if he suspected any hint of deception, but I saw nothing.

As soon as he left, Vail and Draven appeared at my side. I sighed contentedly as I breathed in their scents.

"Everyone ready?" I asked quietly.

Draven leaned in to kiss my neck before whispering in my ear, "Of course, my love. Although Rynn is extra grouchy today. Damn near took my hand off."

"You did call her a bad dog," Vail pointed out.

"She growled at Kier," Draven said coolly.

"Don't antagonize Rynn. You know why she's on edge." I leaned against him while holding a hand out to Vail, who took it, intertwining his fingers with mine. "Our guests are doing well?"

"Woke up an hour ago." Draven wrapped an arm around my waist and tucked me further into his side. "They still look like death but will probably come up for the fun part."

"Good." I watched as shapes started to appear on the horizon. "It's just a waiting game now."

We fell silent as Carmilla and her rangers drew closer. Rynn had to keep her distance while scouting, but we knew Carmilla had at least a hundred rangers with her. Maybe closer to two hundred. She clearly wasn't fucking around this time.

When Carmilla was less than a quarter mile away, I stepped back. "Let's get into position."

The three of us retreated back inside the temple, which was as silent as a tomb. Erendriel had gotten the wraiths under control. Good. The last thing we needed was to tip Carmilla off. I tried not to think about all the moving pieces of this plan and how many ways it could fail.

If I stumbled now, it wasn't just my life on the line—it was the lives of all of all those I loved.

I would not falter.

We walked towards the archway that led further into the temple but stopped just short of it. On either side of us, pillars of white stone spiraled from the ceiling to the floor. Only the spirals and a few tables with benches made of the same stone decorated this room.

Standing in the center of the archway was a pedestal that Draven and I had dragged over from a small room in the back. Erendriel had barely glanced at the large shallow bowl full of blood that was resting on it. I'd explained this morning that it was part of the ceremony I would invoke to challenge Carmilla. He'd made some backhanded compliment about me cleverly using the *ridiculous* Moroi customs to my advantage. Clearly, in his eyes, I was more Fae than Moroi.

Draven and Vail moved to stand on either side of the pedestal, facing the temple entrance, while I stood directly in front of it. A few minutes later, I heard the telltale sound of hooves pounding into the hard surface of the badlands.

I took a deep breath and let it out.

"We've got your back, Sam," Vail said solemnly, and I felt Draven's agreement through our mating bond.

Not a flicker of doubt crossed my mind. Vail was every bit mine as I was his, and Draven had been mine for longer than I'd known.

"And I've got yours." I smiled over my shoulder at each of them.

Our attention snapped forward as Carmilla and the rangers flooded the temple.

"So this is where you've been hiding." My aunt walked confidently towards me as the rangers lined the walls. She'd traded her typical refined dress for black pants and a deep purple tunic that matched her eyes perfectly. The soul crown rested on her head, making her look every inch the queen she was—or would be for a few more minutes anyway.

Doing okay, Talis? I asked.

I'll be doing better once you get me off this psychopath's head. Kind of worried that you're related to her, if I'm being honest.

Soon, my friend, I promised. *Soon.*

Only half of the rangers here are bound, by the way. The others have enthusiastically followed her.

That's unfortunate, but we'll deal with that later. I'd made a promise to Vail about how the rangers that came today would be treated, and I wouldn't be breaking that.

"I felt it had a certain amount of charm." I waved a hand flippantly through the air. "Could do with a bit more color though. All this white stone feels a bit ostentatious."

"How fortunate for you that you'll be returning to your cell soon." She smiled.

"No." I shook my head and moved to the side so she could see the bowl behind me. "I don't think I will."

I saw the moment my aunt realized what I intended. "The Claiming?" she scoffed. "My dear, there hasn't been a Claiming in over a century."

"Not since the Tepes bloodline overtook House Stoker," I agreed.

It was a bit of a throwback tradition. The Houses had been stable for some time now, but that hadn't always been the case. Sometimes, a Moroi bloodline had emerged to challenge one of the existing Houses, and that was where the Claiming came in.

A fight to the death between two Moroi. No weapons. No submissions. You fought until one was dead.

Few attempted it, because if they failed, not only would they die but their entire line would be wiped out by the House they challenged. And once a Claiming was invoked, it had to be answered.

Of course, usually it was invoked in a public manner so that if the challenged House didn't answer, they would look weak to the other Houses. One never wanted to be perceived as *weak* in Lunaria.

Carmilla studied the bowl for a long moment before shrugging. "Cute attempt, niece, but I have no interest in fighting you."

"Scared?" I bared my fangs at her.

She laughed. "We both know hand-to-hand combat was never one of your strengths, and the Claiming is just that. Tooth and claw only." A smile stretched across her lips, one that didn't meet her eyes. "I regularly trained with your mother when she was still alive . . . and bested her on more than one occasion, I might add. You cannot beat me, and I'd prefer to take you alive."

"You cannot reject the Claiming once it's been extended," Draven drawled.

Carmilla's temper snapped. "I can do whatever I damn well please, and I think our first order of business when we return to the Sovereign House will be to hold a public execution for the bastard prince." Then her dark gaze slid to Vail. "And for the traitor."

"How fortunate for us," I echoed her previous words, "that you won't be leaving this temple alive."

Her eyes flicked back to me before she waved a hand towards us. "Bind them, then search the rest of this place for anyone else." My aunt stared at me for a long moment. "If the wolf is here, kill it. My niece could use a reminder on obedience."

As one, the rangers stepped forward from the walls, splitting into groups, with some angling towards me and others towards Vail and Draven.

"Last chance," I warned, even as I started to summon my earth magic. "Honor the Claiming, Carmilla Harker."

At the temple entrance, the two large, flat stones on either side of it started to silently move inward.

"It's an outdated ritual," my aunt hissed.

I pushed, and the stone pieces clicked together, cutting off the only way in or out of the temple—and the sunlight that had been beaming in.

Darkness fell, only for the Fae lanterns to flicker to life, their soft blue flames casting an eerie light across the room.

"On that, we agree." Erendriel strolled past Vail and Draven to stand at my side. "A fight to the death without weapons or magic?" He shook his head in disgust. "Honestly, I don't know how you all have survived this long."

Carmilla stared at the Seelie King in horror before glaring at me. "What have you done?"

"What I had to," I said calmly.

Before my aunt could open her mouth again, wraiths streamed into the room, and the rangers immediately backed up. True to Erendriel's word, the wraiths didn't attack. Instead of taking a specific shape, they all joined together until a ring of writhing shadows wrapped around the space with the rangers on the outside and the five of us on the inside.

The only break was in front of the pedestal, allowing a path to it. Now that this part of the plan had been enacted, the others joined us. Kieran, Roth, and Alaric walked up to stand behind the pedestal while Rynn, Ary, and Aniela stood behind them and a little off to the right.

A few rangers tried to step forward, only for the wraiths to turn solid for just long enough to shove them back. One overzealous ranger tried to run through, only to be flung into the wall—hard. A crack formed as he slid down, but he was still moving, and a fellow ranger was already drawing a healing glyph on him.

"So, now what? You're just going to have the Seelie King do your bidding?" Carmilla sneered. "The Moroi will *never* follow you."

"To be fair, they're not exactly willingly following you either." My eyes flicked pointedly to the crown. "The wraiths are only here to ensure you play fair." I looked away from my aunt to address the rangers standing on the outskirts of the room. "You will not be harmed. You are only here to bear witness to the Claiming."

"We'll never follow Fae trash," a ranger called out. "You're not even a true Moroi."

"Technically, we all have Fae blood running in our veins." I smiled in the direction of the ranger who'd spoken. "Surprise. It's true that I have a little more than most, but make no mistake, we're all part Fae. Also"—I pointed at my aunt—"she's wearing a Fae crown, and you seem inclined to follow her. Assuming you're not one of the ones who had their will stripped away."

Several faces tightened at that before wincing in pain.

Roughly half of the rangers here were under the crown's compulsion, but the others had voluntarily come. If I truly wanted to unite all the Moroi, I needed them to respect me.

If I couldn't have their respect, I would take their fear. Despite what Erendriel thought of me, I wasn't some naive upstart. My goal was to be a good leader for all of the Moroi, but that didn't mean I'd allow people to walk over me.

The Claiming was my way of proving myself worthy . . . and performing a little trickery. It was Carmilla who had constantly lectured me to work smarter, not harder. That the best strategy was one which could accomplish multiple goals at once. I needed a demonstration, and we needed to buy time for the transformation spell to work its literal magic.

My aunt hadn't been lying about being my mother's regular sparring partner. Carmilla might have spent most of her time behind a desk these days, but that didn't change the fact that she was a lethal fighter. This was going to hurt.

"Your life has turned out to be a waste." Carmilla shook her head. "I suppose it's only fitting that your death should be too." She walked over to the pedestal, giving everyone a cool look before lingering on Roth. "You won't be alive to see it, but know that I'm going to wipe your family and their House out of existence."

Roth held her stare, orange lines bleeding through their hazel eyes like living flames. "You won't be alive to hear it, but know that my family will get a good laugh when I tell them about your ridiculous claim."

My loves and I smiled at Roth's declaration.

For the first time since striding into the temple, a flicker of doubt showed on Carmilla's face before she squashed it. With a dismissive sniff, she turned away from Roth to focus on the three beings standing behind my mates and slightly off to the side.

"Surprised the Alpha Pack has let you off the chain for so long, Rynn," she drawled. "You never did know your place."

Rynn growled, and her hackles rose. Talis had claimed being in her animal form would protect Rynn from the crown's magic; the last thing we needed was my aunt taking away Rynn's free will and using the Velesian as a weapon. Flanking her on either side were Ary and Aniela, both still looking a little pale, but thanks to taking a long drink from me earlier, they had a little more color in their cheeks, and more importantly, they were protected from the crown.

Them showing up hadn't been part of my original plan, but we were lucky they had. It had taken a lot of blood to pull this off, and having two additional Moroi had helped considerably. It was probably the only reason my mates were standing and not unconscious downstairs.

Erendriel eyed the two Heirs from where he was still standing next to me, several feet in front of the pedestal. They'd spent most of their time sequestered in the hidden levels below and hadn't emerged once since I'd summoned Erendriel. I could have come up with some reason for their presence, but it'd been simpler to just keep them out of his sight. We hadn't wanted to give him even the slightest hint of underhandedness, and the more lies one told, the harder it became to keep them all straight.

The only reason they were above ground now was because I wanted them to bear witness to the Claiming so they could attest to what happened here today.

When the Seelie King's gaze fell on me, I explained quietly, "It is tradition as part of the Claiming for other Houses to be present. Apologies. I should have introduced you sooner."

"Any other change of plans you care to share?"

I gave him a close-lipped smile. "Everything else is according to plan. No other changes."

He stared at me for a long moment, those ancient eyes searching for a hint of deception. "Shall we begin? You and I have things to do." Without another word, he walked to the front of the temple to stand with his back towards the mass of darkness that were his wraiths before clasping his hands behind his back.

I suspected that if he truly thought I was going to lose, he would intervene. After all, he didn't actually give a shit about the Moroi or my leadership of them. All Erendriel wanted was a way to get into all these secret rooms—and he needed me alive for that.

Turning away from the Seelie King, I moved to stand on the other side of the pedestal, facing Carmilla. "I, Samara Harker, Heir of House Harker and beloved daughter of Kasem and Mariona, issue a challenge of the Claiming. For not only House Harker, but also for the soul crown and the Sovereign House."

Carmilla reached up and removed the crown from her head. Part of the tradition was to place something of significance from the party being challenged into the blood of the challenger. I'd had several plans in place if she'd tried to use something other than the crown, but since she hadn't been prepared for this, she likely had nothing else on her that would work, and she knew it.

"I, Carmilla Harker, the reigning Moroi Queen and Head of both the Sovereign House and House Harker, answer the Claiming." Slowly, she lowered the crown into the bowl of blood that was just deep enough to cover the Fae artifact.

You okay, Talis?

The blood is cold. You could have at least warmed it.

Duly noted that you prefer warm blood baths. Let me know when it's done.

Of course, young queen.

Unlike with Erendriel, there was no hint of mockery with that title. More like a term of endearment from an old friend.

I dipped my fingers into the bowl and pulled them out to smear streaks down my cheeks. Carmilla did the same before returning to the center of the room. I glanced at each of the people I loved more than anything. They remained lined up a few feet behind the pedestal, all wearing matching tight expressions.

They knew what was about to happen and that they could not intervene. We needed time for the transformation spell to work on Talis, and that time would be bought with my pain.

Despite their tense faces, I felt nothing but love, strength, and confidence down the bonds. My mates were concerned for me and not looking forward to what was coming, but their faith in me was absolute.

I love you all. I pushed the sentiment down the bonds, knowing they wouldn't hear the exact words but would feel what was behind them. Kieran met my stare, and even though we didn't have that bond yet, we didn't need it to know what each other felt. He was already my mate in my heart, and once we survived this, he'd be it in my soul too.

Then I squared my shoulders and moved to the center of the room. Without looking, I knew Erendriel watched me closely. His gaze felt like a heated brand, but it was the dark-haired woman with eyes that matched my own who took all of my attention.

I watched as Carmilla let her bloodlust rise until her purple irises turned a solid black, then her lips parted enough to display her fangs, and her usually well-trimmed nails shifted to sharp claws. The blood dripping from her cheeks was meant to show that, even with her bloodlust riding high, she was still in control of herself and not lost to our baser need to consume.

My own bloodlust had been simmering just beneath the surface, and with half a thought, I let it out all the way. I felt the instant my muscles strengthened, my body became that much faster, and the sweet coppery tang of the blood rolling down my face became even more intense.

Around us, the wraiths kept up their endless circling, ensuring Carmilla's rangers couldn't interfere. Silence fell across the temple. The only thing I could hear was the solid beat of her heart—and the split second it quickened.

I leaned back just as Carmilla's razor-sharp nails grazed my throat, a small bead of blood forming along the shallow cut. There was no time to dwell on how close I'd just come to having my jugular ruptured, because Carmilla followed it up with a vicious punch to my solar plexus.

"This is going to be over faster than I thought." She bared her fangs at me before licking my blood off her claws. "It was a deliberate choice on my part, you know."

I twisted to the side as she struck at my ribs, only to let out a hiss of pain when she sliced through the top of my hip.

"What was?" I ground out, stepping back to create more space between us.

"Nudging you to not worry too much about learning how to fight or defend yourself."

She lunged to my right, and I spun away, only to scream as she slammed her fist hard against my side, cracking several ribs. I took several sharp inhales, one hand wrapped around my midsection as I tried to breathe through the pain.

"You were easy to manipulate," she continued. "Although I was a little worried about your obsessions with the bow and then the throwing daggers, but those won't save you now."

Carmilla stalked towards me. Fortifying myself, I tried to push aside the fiery pain along my ribs and held my ground as she launched another assault. I managed to block her first punch and turn my hip enough to take her follow-up kick on the side of my leg instead of on the wound she'd been aiming for, but I raised my arm a second too slow for her third hit.

I turned my head in just enough time to take the punch on my jaw instead of my nose and stumbled back several feet.

"Pathetic," Carmilla sneered.

We fought across the temple floor—me desperately trying to keep space between us, and her closing that distance to land hit after hit. Sometimes, I managed to block or at least deflect them, but not often. Ten minutes later, I could tell she was getting bored of playing with me—because she *was absolutely* toying with me.

Which was exactly what I'd been hoping for.

Tell me it's almost done, Talis? Even in my head, my voice had a pained edge to it. Carmilla had landed a solid kick to my ribs a minute ago, and I was pretty sure a bone shard was poking into my lung right now.

Almost, their voice strained. *One. More. Minute.*

Thank fuck.

"Is this the queen some of you would choose to follow, given the choice?" Carmilla looked around at the rangers as she pointed a bloody claw at me. "You may not like how I rule, but at least I'm strong enough to do it. She is nothing." Cruel eyes turned back to me. "This ends now."

I hastily stepped back like I was trying to flee, and Carmilla's eyes lit up, a predator closing in on its prey. Just like with her opening move, she struck for my throat.

This time though, I didn't dampen my speed like I had been doing this entire fight.

My feet slid to the side, and my right hand shot out to grab her wrist, using her own forward momentum against her. She'd been so committed to the move and overconfident that she hadn't been prepared for me to twist her arm back until it was fully extended with her elbow pointing upward.

It was Carmilla's turn to scream as I slammed my own elbow down on the back of her arm, forcing the joint to bend the wrong way.

I leapt back as she twisted and struck at my face, trying to blind me.

"You're right," I panted, doing my best to keep my weight off my injured leg. "I didn't spend much time learning to fight growing up or at Drudonia, but I did spend some time traveling with rangers these past few months. Nyx taught me that move. You remember them, right? The ranger who devoted themself to House Harker? The one whose mind you *shredded*?"

Growls sounded from some of the rangers lining the walls. These ones might belong to the Sovereign House, but it was common for rangers to feel just as much loyalty to each other as to whichever House they served.

Carmilla glared at me, her left arm dangling uselessly at her side. She couldn't heal it until it was pushed back into place—and I'd be on her the second she tried it.

I wasn't foolish enough to think she was defeated yet. Wounded predators could still kill. And buying time had cost me. Warm blood coated my leg; another minute, and it'd give out completely.

Something that didn't get past my aunt, because that was the leg she targeted with a forward kick.

Knowing there was no way to avoid it without falling, I bellowed as her foot connected with my thigh and bone cracked. I went down hard, but I took her with me.

My fingers wrapped around her calf, and I didn't let go when she tried to yank her leg free. Then I sank my claws deeper until I felt bone. Carmilla shrieked as she slammed to the ground a second after me. With a pained grunt, I flung myself on top of her. Agony ricocheted down my left side, and I had to practically drag my leg with me, but I made it.

Carmilla went completely still as my left hand closed around her throat. I was straddling her, with both of her arms pinned beneath my knees. If she bucked up with her hips, she had a solid chance of dislodging me, but not before I ripped out her throat.

I had her. We both knew it.

It's done, Talis whispered through my mind.

"It was Emil who taught me that sometimes you have to take the pain to win the fight." I pushed my claws into the soft flesh of her throat a little more. "And it was Adrienne—someone so bold and fearless that we both know her bloodline could have founded a House—who told me that if you ever get the chance"—my right arm snapped back before plunging down—"go for the heart."

The Head of House Harker and the reigning Moroi Queen gasped as I shoved my hand through her chest. Then Carmilla's eyes locked onto mine, and I watched the light go out in them as I tore out her still-beating heart.

CHAPTER THIRTY-TWO

—

Samara

I STARED at the heart in my grasp. It beat a few more times before going still. Carmilla's blood was warm on my hand, and I was trying not to dwell on that. The time to process would come later—there was still a Seelie King to betray.

Through the mate bonds, I conveyed that I needed some assistance. In an instant, Vail and Draven were there, helping me to my feet. Roth knelt in front of me, and I felt them draw a healing glyph over my thigh and then over my ribs while Alaric offered me his wrist. My fangs sank into his flesh, and I drank deeply as my body burned with healing magic.

Once I was confident that I could stand without my leg collapsing under me, I walked towards the pedestal, my mates falling into step behind me. There was one last thing to do before enacting the final part of the plan. Making good on the promise I'd made to Vail.

I briefly made eye contact with Erendriel and he gave me a shallow nod. Through some wordless command, the wraiths pulled back until they were flat against the walls, coating the white marble in shadows.

"Rangers of the Sovereign House, your new queen requests that you wait outside while I finish my business here." I casually tossed my aunt's heart onto the floor like it was nothing as I summoned my earth magic and pulled the doors of the temple open just enough for them to slip out and only allowing only a sliver of sunlight in.

For a few tense seconds, none of them moved. Then a tall ranger with ashen blond hair made eye contact with me for a long moment before giving me a shallow bow. "You heard our queen. Move out!"

Relief flickered through me. If they hadn't listened, I would've had to ask Erendriel to use his wraiths to force them out, and that would have increased the chance of some of the rangers being hurt or killed. I moved to stand behind the pedestal, the bowl resting right in front of me. Silently, my lovers moved to join me until we created a half circle around it. Ary, Aniela, and Rynn didn't move from their spot behind us.

When the last of the rangers walked out, I closed the doors, and the wraiths flowed down from the walls to gather around Erendriel.

"Well . . ." Erendriel kicked my aunt's heart across the floor, and I tried not to wince at the wet, plopping sound it made when it landed. "Your aunt is dead. You have your crown. It's time to honor what you promised, young queen."

This time, I did allow myself to roll my eyes.

"About that . . ." I drawled, letting my fingers slip into the bowl of blood. Behind me, I knew Aniela and Ary were now kneeling, activating the glyphs we'd painstakingly carved around the perimeter of the room. Most of them were hidden, thanks to Draven and me using our earth magic to bury them slightly beneath the surface, but they were all connected.

"A Fae bargain cannot be broken without dire consequences." Erendriel continued strolling towards us. The wraiths fell in behind him. Some took Fae forms, others chose the shapes of monsters. "You can act like a Moroi all you want, but enough Fae blood is running through your veins that the magic will tear you apart."

"Oh I know." I grinned wickedly. "We found quite a few books on bargains that were *most* helpful. One thing they pointed out over and over again was how carefully words had to be chosen—to prevent loopholes."

"There are no *loopholes* in our bargain," Erendriel growled. "I am six hundred years old. You've barely seen two decades. Did you seriously think you could outsmart me?"

"You think of me as a Fae tainted with Moroi blood." I raised my chin a little higher. "But you have it backwards. I am a Moroi . . . tainted with Fae blood." My grin widened. "And you are nothing but an arrogant old king who should have remained in the shadows."

"Enough of this." Erendriel snapped as he strode closer to where we were gathered at the pedestal—only to slam into an invisible wall.

"Oops," Kieran deadpanned.

Draven chuckled. "What's the matter, Father? Feeling a little trapped?"

Erendriel's eyes widened as he looked down at his feet. The stone floor split apart, revealing a thin channel of blood flowing beneath it.

"It flows around the entire room," I told him. "We had a run-in with some trapper spiders recently, and it got me thinking about all the dangerous things that can lurk right under our feet without us even knowing."

"And you walked straight into our trap." Draven strolled up to the barrier so he could look his father directly in the eyes. "Kalias and I used to think you were untouchable. That there was no one stronger or smarter." My vicious prince grinned. "But from where I'm standing, you seem rather *disappointing*."

"I'm going to break every bone in your body and then give you to Serril to play with." Erendriel's cruel gaze slid to me. "After you watch that whore die a slow, agonizing death as the magic tears her apart for breaking the fucking bargain."

"I haven't broken a thing." I shrugged. To my left, Roth, Vail, and Alaric slid their hands into the bowl. Kieran and Draven returned to stand to my right and did the same.

"You were very thorough in your wording for the bargain, and as someone who has reviewed a lot of contracts, I respect that. But I thought the Fae were known for being clever with their words—that's what all the books say. And you, my friend"—I let my voice drip with condescension—"were far from clever."

"Don't be too harsh on him, Sam," Alaric drawled. "You heard him. He's seen six centuries come and go. Maybe he's just not as sharp as he used to be."

Roth smirked. "That would explain why he never once caught on to the fact that you very specifically referred to the Fae artifact as *the crown*—and only the crown—in the bargain."

"I did, didn't I?" I chuckled. "Look at that . . . a loophole."

Erendriel slammed a fist against the barrier, and the boom echoed across the room, but it held fast. The wraiths scattered in streaks of darkness as they tried to find a way out.

My fingers moved through the cold blood until they touched something solid and considerably smaller than a crown. I felt the ripples in the liquid as my mates continued their own searching.

Erendriel glared at me furiously from the other side of the invisible barrier —the one we'd created based on the spell that had been used here and in the secret room beneath the Alpha House. It hadn't been hard to figure out how it worked . . . and then to adjust it so it could keep something *in* instead of *out*.

"No more queens. No more kings." My voice boomed across the temple, and I slipped the band onto my finger. "No more crowns."

Magic sparked within the bowl, and I felt the echo of it through the mating bond. As one, we all raised our left hands, blood dripping to reveal the rings we all wore on our index fingers—the one that had a direct line to our hearts.

Each ring was made of three woven bands. Gold, silver, and a deep ruby red.

Home. Talis hummed happily.

I bared my fangs at the Seelie King. "Welcome to the dawn of the Blood Sovereign."

827

"When do you think he'll stop ranting?" Aniela stared up at the ceiling from where we were all gathered on the first hidden level.

"Probably not for at least a few more hours." Draven snorted.

"A silencing spell might be necessary." I wrinkled my nose, drawing a chuckle out of Kieran.

Vail and Ary were outside, speaking with the rangers. Thanks to Erendriel and the wraiths being trapped in the front room, the only way in or out was to climb out of the hole in the ceiling in the large room directly above us. Neither Draven nor I were confident enough in our earth magic to attempt to make a hole in the wall and risk structural damage to the temple.

I had no idea what would happen to our spell if the temple collapsed around it. Sooner or later, Erendriel would find a way out. We'd been confident —mostly—that the barrier spell would work, but there were definitely nuances to it that we hadn't had time to fully grasp. I had no doubt Erendriel, or maybe Serril, would find a way to exploit those and get out.

And then I'd have a very pissed-off and powerful Fae coming after me. My eyes flicked to the table full of weapons. How fortunate that we found ourselves in possession of weapons that could harm them. Maybe even kill them.

"So, what's the plan now?" Aniela asked. "Now that you all have those fancy rings?"

I am quite fancy, Talis said excitedly.

Roth frowned. "This is going to take some getting used to."

"What is?" Aniela glanced at them in confusion.

"Talis—that's the name of the crown—now the rings," I corrected myself, "can speak in our heads."

Aniela's green eyes darted between our bands. "While I'm envious of being able to see people's true intentions, not sure I'd be willing to sign up for an ancient Fae artifact to live in my head. No offense, Talis."

Tell her none taken. Not everyone can handle how amazing I am.

Kieran laughed. Something told me he and Talis were going to get along very well.

"They're not offended," I assured Aniela. "And Talis has been through a lot. It's the least we could do."

In truth, we'd discussed it for quite some time. What it would mean for our lives to be forever bound to the rings. Talis had sacrificed the part of their magic that allowed them to control the will of others, but they could still read a soul and reveal the truth of a person. In exchange for their cooperation, they'd asked to never be alone again.

Vail and Alaric hadn't been thrilled about it. I'd been surprised Roth was fine with it, but then I'd realized it was because they now had an ancient artifact they could constantly ask questions. Talis might have been locked away for a long time, but there was still so much they could tell us.

"We need to go to House Devereux first. We won't stay there long, but I need to check on Tamsen . . . and Nyx. Then we'll travel to the Sovereign House to assess things there."

I tried not to look at the silver box that held Carmilla's heart. When Erendriel had kicked it, the organ had landed on the other side of the barrier. I didn't know exactly what had possessed me to pick it up and put it into the box. Nobody had said anything while I'd done it, and it'd been sitting on the table since we'd come down here.

I directed my attention to Aniela. "You should go to the Sovereign House ahead of us to meet Dominique. According to Talis, all the bindings ended during the transformation spell, so her mind is her own once more."

"Alright." Aniela nodded. "When you get to House Devereux, please let my people know they can return home." She swiveled from where she was sitting on the table to fully face Roth, who was seated at the end. "And thank you, Roth—and your family—for taking them in. We are in your debt."

"What kind of debt exactl—" Roth winced, and I got the distinct impression that Alaric had just kicked them under the table. They gave Aniela a curt nod before grumbling, "There is no debt between us. Happy to help and all that."

The discussion moved to what we would do about House Harker—something I didn't have an answer for yet and wasn't in the mood to discuss with my aunt's corpse still lying above us.

I left them to discuss the options for that while I went in search of Rynn.

I let my feet carry me to where I suspected she'd gone—down the stairs to the bottom level. Sure enough, when I walked into the cavern of hot springs, Rynn sat on the ledge of one of the pools, her back to me, legs dangling in the water.

"There isn't anything like this near the Alpha House," she said. "Nothing I've found anyway. Just lakes of ice-cold water."

"Might be nice in the summer." I sat down next to her, hiking my dress up to my thighs so I could slip my legs into the warm water too. "You hate the heat."

We sat there for a few minutes while sadness rolled off Rynn. It was a quiet, defeated kind that made me furious.

"Tell me you don't want to go back," I said when I couldn't take it anymore. "Just say the fucking word, Rynn."

She leaned her head on my shoulder. "I love you, Sam. That's why I'm going back. You would go to war for me—you are absolutely that crazy—and Cali would too. But we have all of our people to think about. You need to get the Moroi Houses in order, and I need to accept my fate with the Alpha Pack.

Cade is tolerable most of the time. I can do some good there, I know it. I just need to not let the others get under my skin."

I thought about it. "What if we just kill one or two of them? Maybe the mouthy wolf and Warrick? Have I told you how much I don't like him?"

"You might have mentioned it a few times," she said wryly. "No killing anyone . . . for now. Just sit with me for a bit longer?"

I wrapped an arm around her shoulders. "As long as you want."

CHAPTER THIRTY-THREE

—

Samara

"Welcome back, child," the Head of House Devereux greeted Roth before nodding to the rest of us as we strode through the main gate of Roth's birth House three days later. Thessalia's long, deep red hair had been pulled back into a tight bun, and her shirt clung to her sweat-soaked skin. The guard who had escorted us inside took the sword from her when she held it out to him, and she murmured her thanks.

Gods, had she been voluntarily sparring in this weather? I was wearing one of Vail's shirts over a pair of pants that were also too big for me. Both were soaked from my own sweat because the sun was doing its best to burn everything out of existence today and we'd been walking all morning. On the surface, Thessalia might appear as fierce as the rest of the Devereax clan but clearly she was just as unhinged about training as the rest of them.

The only thing that could make me run in heat like this was a swarm of trappers. And I had no plans of repeating that experience. Ever.

Fuck. Spiders.

"I'm twenty-two years old," Roth grumbled as their aunt messed with their short hair that was the same shade of red.

"You can be a hundred and twenty-two, my dear." Thessalia smiled as she dropped her hand. "You'll still be that scrawny whelp hiding under my desk to avoid practicing your sword skills with your brothers."

"Speaking of . . ." Roth glanced around the small entry courtyard. "Where are the banes of my existence?"

"You can admit that you missed them, you know," their aunt said wryly.

Roth scowled.

Thessalia's bright hazel eyes danced with amusement. "Your parents are currently in the back courtyard, planning your wedding. I believe your

831

brothers are being their helpful selves and encouraging them to make it a big one. Probably in hopes that it will further take off the pressure of them settling down with someone"—she looked at me and then all my mates—"or several someones."

A torrent of curse words in multiple languages flowed from Roth's lips before they gave me a hasty kiss on the cheek. "I need to go wrangle my parents and probably choke my brothers." Their ropes started to unwind from their forearms. "You going to be okay, babe?"

"Yes." I laughed. "Go."

Roth practically sprinted out of the courtyard. They must have been seriously freaked out if they voluntarily ran without something chasing them. It made me wonder if I should be more concerned about what exactly a Devereux-style wedding entailed . . .

"I'm gonna see how Rothie Bear's parents feel about doing a double celebration." Kieran planted a kiss on my cheek before chasing after Roth.

My wicked prince chuckled as he watched his mate—and my soon-to-be mate—go and stepped closer to me.

"Drav . . ." I rose onto my tiptoes so I could kiss him on the cheek. "Please go and make sure Kier doesn't get carried away and that Roth doesn't have a heart attack."

"I will do my best, my love." His dark brows furrowed. "But honestly, Roth's parents frighten me, so if they push for something, I'm not inclined to push back."

"Wise boy." Thessalia nodded.

Draven smiled at her before dipping his head in a respectful nod and casually strolling down the path Roth and Kieran had taken. Alaric sidled up to my left and Vail to my right.

Roth's aunt stared after Draven in bemusement. "It's good that he didn't take after either of his parents. Would have been a shame to kill one that pretty."

"I mean—"

Alaric grunted when I elbowed him in the gut and gave him a warning stare.

Be nice, I mouthed. He rolled his eyes.

"Why don't the rest of you come inside so we can discuss the future of things?" Thessalia offered. "You're welcome to get cleaned up first while I have some refreshments brought to my study."

"That is honestly the best thing I've heard all day." I picked at my sweat-soaked shirt in distaste. "I desperately need to get out of these clothes."

Alaric and Vail both cleared their throats.

"And into fresh ones," I amended. "Work first. Play later."

"We've prepared a guest suite for you in the same wing as Roth's room—

not that they've used it in years. Your suite has an attached washroom." Thessalia's gaze slid to Alaric and then Vail. "And a silencing glyph for your . . . playtime."

"We thank House Devereux for its hospitality." I grinned. "I'll have to spread the word about how accommodating you are."

"Please don't." Thessalia laughed. "Come on, I'll show you the way."

"If you don't need me, I'd like to go check in with the rangers here," Vail said. "I'll catch up later."

"That's fine."

Vail gave me a quick kiss before striding off down a different path from the one the other three had taken.

I glanced at Alaric. "Looks like it's just you and me then."

His lips quirked up into a small smile. "I do so enjoy when I get you all to myself."

An hour later, some servants kindly directed us to Thessalia's study. Alaric had been very . . . attentive about helping me get clean in the washroom. Then he'd undone all his hard work by shoving me to my knees when I'd sassed him and fucking my mouth roughly until he'd come all over my face and chest.

He hadn't even let me rinse off. Just carried me to bed and devoured my pussy until I'd begged him to fuck me, which he had.

After cleaning up for the third time, we'd successfully made it out of the room.

"Ah, there you are. I was beginning to worry you'd gotten lost." Thessalia's eyes twinkled, and she rose from her desk to take a seat at one of the four chairs casually set up to face each other in the corner of her study. The room was large, and weapons adorned most of the wall space. I suspected the enormous window behind her desk overlooked the sparring courtyard, based on the faint sounds of yelling and metal striking metal.

On the table between all the chairs was an assortment of bread, cheese, and fruit, along with several glasses of water and ale.

"Alaric was *very* dirty," I said with a completely straight face, even as I tried not to drool over the cheese. "It took a lot of work to get him all squeaky clean again."

"I'm sure." Thessalia grinned.

Alaric sighed and moved towards one of the chairs, pinching my side as he went.

I laughed under my breath and followed. We both chose a chair opposite Thessalia, and she watched as we tore into the food for a few minutes.

"Better?" She arched an eyebrow.

"Mm-hmm," I answered around a mouthful of cheese.

She nodded. "A good fuck and some food will do that for you."

Alaric choked on the bread he'd just swallowed, and Thessalia chuckled before sipping her ale.

Once I finished eating and had picked up my own glass of ale, I proceeded to tell her everything that had transpired since we'd parted ways. Alaric occasionally added more detail, but twenty minutes later, we had it all out there.

"I'm sorry you had to kill your own family," Thessalia said solemnly. "That can't have been easy for you, even knowing that it had to be done, but I do think you handled it tremendously well. We'll need to keep an eye on the rangers who willingly followed her of course, but I doubt they will make a move against you anytime soon."

"Thank you." A flicker of grief at Carmilla's death hit me. It felt strange to mourn her, considering all she'd done. Perhaps it was more accurate to think I was mourning the idea of who I'd thought she'd been. Either way, it was something I'd have to work through. I wouldn't be bottling up my grief and negative emotions any longer.

"We're going to do an assessment of the rangers and advisors of the Sovereign House when we return." Alaric hesitated for a moment, glancing at me and only continuing when I gave him a nod. "We don't want people to feel as though they are being punished, because that will only create further friction. After spending many hours discussing this on the journey here, we think it best to keep the ones most likely to stir up animosity at the Sovereign House, where we can monitor them. The rest, we'd like to send to other Houses— Tepes and Salvatore have already agreed to take some. House Harker can take some as well, and we were hoping House Devereux would be amiable to accept some new rangers too."

Thessalia looked at both of us thoughtfully. "To what purpose?"

Some of the tension that had formed in my shoulders while Alaric had been explaining faded. That wasn't an outright no.

"When the Moroi Houses originally rose, they were united with one purpose—to protect our people. Over the decades, that mantra changed. It was no longer *protect all Moroi* but only those who belonged to one's House."

"Perhaps the Houses were all united once, but that time has long since passed." Thessalia shook her head. "There is no going back."

"No," I agreed. "Nor should we try. The past is there for us to learn from it—not repeat it. Part of what allowed Velika and then Carmilla to seize power the way they did is that none of us could trust each other. I want there to be more collaboration between our Houses. I want us to heal what is broken. And that means giving some of the people who willingly followed Velika or my aunt a chance. Some of them might always be thorns in my side, but others could change their tune when they interact with other Houses more— when they start thinking of Moroi as one united front instead of seven fractures."

I sat back in my chair and waited. If she didn't agree, I wouldn't give up. Just rethink my strategy about how to get her onboard.

"I admit that my immediate inclination is to say no." Thessalia snorted. "But I also acknowledge that I—and my House—are part of the problem here. We've isolated ourselves quite thoroughly, and while that has worked quite well for us, some of the younger generation are getting a bit antsy."

"It's getting hard to find new bedmates when it feels like you're related to half the people here." A blond-haired man with a charming grin and bright green eyes chuckled as he practically sauntered into the room.

"Zander, what have I told you about eavesdropping?" Thessalia scolded the Moroi, who appeared to be about my age, as he dropped into the remaining empty chair.

His eyes widened a little as he gave her an innocent smile. "To not be so obvious about it, but I would never deign to lie to you, my liege."

She rubbed her forehead. "This pain in the ass is the son of my most trusted advisor."

"Pleased to meet you." I grinned at him. "Eavesdropping on a Devereux is a bold move."

"To be fair, I only do it on Thessalia because she adores me."

Roth's aunt snorted again before dropping her hand to her lap. "And because the one time he tried it on Severen, he found himself tied up tighter than a hog over a spit and hanging from a tree."

"Took me hours to cut myself free." Zander laughed. "Had to dislocate my shoulder and everything."

Alaric stared at him for a long moment before turning to me. "Clearly it's not just the Devereux line that is insane—it's everyone in this House."

"I think you just need to spend a little more quality time with them." I smiled sweetly, and Alaric narrowed his eyes. "How about the three of you discuss this a little further?"

"And where will you be while I'm talking to the heathens?"

"Why do we get the rude one?" Zander muttered. "That blond fella looked much more easygoing."

I patted Alaric on the cheek. "You'll be fine. Just flutter those pretty eyelashes at them and—owww!" I yanked my hand back and sucked on my bleeding finger.

Alaric licked the blood off his lips, turquoise flaring in his eyes . . . and staying. "Go do what you need to, but you're going to get punished for that sass later."

"Can't wait." I winked.

"I can't believe this is what Astaroth is marrying into." Zander stared at the two of us wide-eyed before gleefully smiling. "This wedding is going to be amazing."

Fifteen minutes later, I found myself in a dungeon very similar to the one I'd been locked in beneath the Sovereign House. Thessalia had summoned a guard to escort me, who was now waiting outside the door to give me the illusion of privacy. He hadn't spoken much on our walk here, but he'd borne a wary expression when we'd stopped on this level, which told me that Nyx hadn't magically gotten better after the crown's magic had changed. It had been a small hope that was now extinguished.

"Is Carmilla dead?"

I looked at the woman in the cell on the right; she'd definitely seen better days. Normally, Tamsen's hair was a shiny curtain of dark russet brown that hung to her waist. Now, it was a dull nest of tangles. Even from where I stood, I could smell the dry blood on her clothing.

"Yes," I answered, continuing to study her profile. "Did they not offer you a chance to clean up?"

"House Devereux isn't exactly known for their hospitality," she said tonelessly. "Frankly, I'm impressed they let me see to my needs twice a day instead of just giving me a bucket, and I'm even more surprised they didn't just kill me." Finally, those sky-blue eyes that were the same as their sibling's looked at me. "I take it I have you to thank for that? Given it was your Marshal who saved me and brought me here?"

I walked a little closer to the cell and rested my hand on the bars. The iron bit at me, and I dropped my hand. "I happen to be marrying into the family, so to speak. It comes with perks."

"So you killed your aunt and you're marrying into the most formidable of the Houses from a fighting standpoint." She looked away from me. "Should I also assume that you're here to order my death, considering my House is far from trustworthy?"

I pondered her. Tamsen was . . . tricky. She was loyal to Nyx—of that I had no doubt—but House Corvinus was a problem.

"Why did you run? All this time, you've played the game with your asshole parents. Played the role of dutiful Heir."

Tamsen let out a joyless laugh. "I stayed because I foolishly thought I could just wait it out. That when my parents died, I could fix things. That they could come home." Her voice broke as she spoke.

For the first time since walking into the room, I allowed myself to look at the person huddled in the dark back corner of the cell next to Tamsen's. Nyx was sitting with their knees bent, arms loosely resting on them, while black eyes threaded with blue stared at me.

They didn't say a word.

"My parents quietly issued an order that if Nyx were spotted, they were to be brought back to House Corvinus by any means necessary."

My gaze snapped back to Tamsen. "Why?"

She let out a chilling laugh. "To get to you. They know of your friendship with my younger sibling—and that Carmilla was looking for you. Nyx was the bait for the trap they planned to set."

"So you ran to find Nyx." It wasn't a question.

Tamsen's face twisted in rage and heartache. "You were supposed to keep them safe. I got them out of our wretched House to keep them safe."

Guilt hit me. I didn't think it would ever stop, but I also knew it wasn't rational. While Tamsen *had* done everything she could have to keep Nyx safe, so had I. And so had Adrienne.

My throat tightened.

I was trying not to lock away my emotions the way I had when my parents had died, but that didn't mean I could fall apart here. That wouldn't help Nyx, and I needed Tamsen to get herself together.

"This is Lunaria. Safety is fleeting," I said softly before unlocking her cell. "You're now the Head of House Corvinus. It's on you to make it so Nyx can come home someday. If that's what they want."

Tamsen blinked. "Just like that? What about my parents?"

"According to the reports Thessalia has received, they're gone," I growled. "So is Lucian."

There were likely others we'd find missing as well. People who saw the way the wind was blowing and decided they didn't want to stick around for it. We only had so many resources. Decisions would have to be made about who to hunt down and who to forget about.

I wouldn't be forgetting about Lucian anytime soon though.

Outside came the sound of footsteps and then quiet murmurs before the guard who had escorted me walked in, carrying a familiar silver box.

Tamsen cautiously left her cell, as if she was still expecting a trap, and eyed the box as I took it from the guard, who left without another word. I turned towards Nyx's cell and almost jumped. Tamsen swore harshly when she did the same.

Nyx now stood at the front, just behind the bars, a little more blue in their black eyes.

"I made it hurt," I told them as I stepped closer. "Not enough, but she didn't go quietly."

"Is that a good idea?" Tamsen asked in a strained tone when I unlocked Nyx's cell. "They're not . . . Nyx isn't themself."

I stayed perfectly still as Nyx stepped forward until they stood directly in front of me. "Nyx is my friend, and I'm not going to give my friend a gift through the bars of a cell."

Nyx watched as I opened the lid. I hadn't realized it until later, but some type of preservation spell was laid into the silver. Carmilla's heart rested within it, just as fresh as the day I'd torn it from her chest. The blue vanished from Nyx's eyes until they were nothing but pools of darkness.

But they made no move to hurt me or their sister. Nyx stared at the heart for several seconds, and then, faster than I could track, they snatched it up and tore into it. My heart raced as they swallowed down the chunks while growling faintly.

Do not run, Talis warned. *Their soul teeters on the edge of the abyss.*

Soon, all traces of the heart were gone, and Nyx closed their eyes and tilted their head back, blood and gore smeared all over their face. I could hear Tamsen's heart pounding as rapidly as my own, but like me, she stayed perfectly still. Waiting.

Finally, after what felt like an eternity, Nyx's head dipped down, and they opened their eyes once more. Obsidian eyes with rivers of blue looked at me, and my friend gave me a bloody smile. "You always did bring me the best gifts."

EPILOGUE

—

Samara

"We're not talking about it." Rynn gave my hair a vicious tug and I yelped, then she glared at me through the mirror resting on the wall in front of me. Four months had passed, and we were back at House Devereux for the wedding and mating bond ceremony.

I hadn't anticipated the amount of jitters that would flutter through me all morning. I mean, Roth and I were already mated, and I was eager to form the bond with Kieran. It had been incredibly challenging to hold back from doing it the past few months, but he had been adamant about wanting the whole ceremony thing.

Plus, Roth's parents had been ecstatic over the idea. Apparently, the only thing that excited them more than wholesale slaughter was a wedding. Or in this case, a wedding followed by a mating bond ceremony. We'd all arrived yesterday and collapsed into the large bed of the guest suite that had been set up for us. It wasn't easy to step away from our responsibilities, but we'd been working around the clock until the moment we'd left.

Surprisingly, I'd all slept until late morning. Although when I woke, Roth and Kieran were already gone, so I had a late breakfast with Vail, Draven, and Alaric. After that, I'd been ushered into this small room.

I'd cackled when I'd walked in to see the weapons on one side and the dress hanging on the other. Clearly, this was just an extra weapons storage space that they had temporarily converted into my dressing room. It was close to where the main event was being held—which, in true Devereux fashion, was the sparring ring.

In their defense, it was the biggest open space within the walls, and many buildings overlooked it.

I'd expected some of the Devereux staff to come help me get ready, but to my surprise, it had been Rynn, Cali, and Nyx who'd walked in. My eyes had misted a little at the latter. Nyx was no longer confined to a dungeon cell, but they still kept their distance from most of the Moroi and really only interacted with me and my mates.

Except Vail. They no longer attacked him on sight, but Nyx had made it clear they had no interest in seeing him. It hurt Vail, but none of us knew how to mend that bridge other than to allow Nyx their space.

We'd set up a small cottage just outside the Sovereign House for them. The ward around it made it safe, but it still worried me that they were out there on their own most of the time.

Several rangers had volunteered to keep an eye on Nyx's new home, not because they were wary of them but because, like me, they were concerned for them. Many of the rangers liked Nyx and wanted to keep them safe. Knowing that helped my stress quite a bit.

I'd invited Nyx to come today, but they'd given me a noncommittal response, so I'd assumed they weren't coming. And while I'd hoped Rynn and Cali would make it, communication with them had been sparse since we'd all parted ways, and they hadn't been able to fully commit either.

"Don't make her cry again," Cali snapped. "Her face will get wrecked." She waved at my eye makeup from where she was perched on several boxes containing crossbows next to me.

Like Rynn, she also refused to talk about her situation. They'd both declared that today was all about me and only happy thoughts were allowed.

Any time I deviated from that, I got my hair pulled or my arm pinched.

I sank into the chair and scowled.

Smack!

"What the fuck, Rynn?" I rubbed the back of my head.

"No frowning!" she barked before staring at the messy braid situation. I'd say it was her fault for smacking me, but honestly, I think that might have improved it. "We might need to find someone to help."

"Or you could just let me do it." I started unraveling some of the braids, which were more knots than anything at this point. Fancy hairstyles were beyond me, but simple and elegant, I could do.

Nyx sighed before pushing off the wall where they'd been leaning since arriving. They hadn't spoken much, but their posture had been relaxed, so I figured they were okay.

"Move," they rasped and hip-checked Rynn out of the way before detangling my hair and sectioning parts of it off. Rynn happily went to sit by Cali, and the two of them started to idly chat about the events today. Mostly placing bets on how long it would take before some of the guests got caught fucking. Or a fight broke out. Or a fight that led to fucking started.

It was . . . nice.

Everything had been mostly nonstop for the past few months. I'd spent most of my time at the Sovereign House, although I had made a quick trip to House Harker just to make sure everything had been in order there. To my delight, our advisors had stepped up and kept everything going without a hitch. They'd quietly admitted to me that they had been uncomfortable with the path Carmilla had chosen.

Nobody was rejoicing in her death; it was more of a bitter acceptance that I'd done what had been necessary and that they were grateful for it. Long-term, I still didn't know what would become of House Harker, but it wasn't something I had to solve right this second.

Which was good because we had a long list of other problems.

Both the Head and Heir of House Laurent were dead, and no suitable candidates had risen to take over yet. With no other choice, Alaric had reluctantly volunteered to step in as a temporary leader—something he absolutely loathed because he had to talk to people on a regular basis. It also meant he had to spend time away from me, but things at House Laurent were improving, and he was confident he'd be able to leave things in the hands of the advisors soon—those we'd borrowed from House Harker and House Salvatore, because I knew all of the Laurent advisors and didn't trust a single one of them. Something Talis backed me up on. They weren't outright evil, so I wanted to give them a chance, but I wouldn't be heartbroken if Vail or Draven made good on their threats involving the advisors having an accident while traveling between Houses.

If the advisors were too stupid to realize insulting me in front of my protective mates wasn't good for their long-term health prospects, then they probably weren't cut out for being a House advisor in the first place.

As much as I wanted all the Houses to play nice with each other, there was no magic fix for that. We were going through a lot of growing pains, but I was hopeful.

Roth had been coordinating with the scholars at Drudonia in cataloging and documenting all the information contained in the secret rooms beneath the temple. We'd discovered that, much like the room beneath Lake Malov, nothing there could be removed, so the scholars had to travel to the temple.

It wasn't that far of a journey, but the problem was we still had a very pissed off Seelie King and almost a hundred wraiths trapped in the temple. Rangers were always posted there, all carrying the weapons we'd discovered that worked against wraiths. We'd also set up more barrier wards to create more safe zones within the temple. I knew it was only a matter of time before Erendriel and his wraiths got free; the wards we'd put in place were merely to ensure our rangers weren't killed when it happened.

I had contingency plans for my contingency plans. The only time I'd stopped working was when my menstrual cycle had come last month.

All of my mates had dropped what they'd been doing to make sure I'd been as comfortable as I could have been. We'd all done the same for Roth weeks prior when they'd had their cycle.

I'd allowed Roth to keep working in bed, but they'd flat out refused to let me so much as *read* correspondence. I found it extremely unfair, but everyone had sided with Roth and outvoted me.

My anger had lasted all the way until my heat had kicked in. Then I hadn't left my bed for five days . . . but for much more fun reasons.

I'd cut back on my work a little bit after that. Nothing terrible had happened during those eight days, so it was clear I could give myself a little more time off. I had five mates to enjoy, after all.

My brows furrowed. Had I sent that letter to Tamsen replying to some of her ideas for improving travel between the outposts? She'd raised some really good points, and I wanted to implement some of them soon. We co—

"Stop thinking about work, Sam," Nyx growled before stepping back and returning to their spot on the wall.

"Damn," I admired myself in the mirror. "You do good work, Nyx."

Out of the corner of my eye, I saw them shrug. "I used to always do Tamsen's when we were growing up. She's even worse at doing hair than Rynn."

"Hey!" Rynn crossed her arms. "I'm not that bad."

"Yes, you are," Cali and I said at the same time.

Nyx had braided the top half of my hair into multiple braids that twisted into a bun with several loops draping down. The rest of my hair was pinned back away from my face before it fell in a dark wave down my back.

"Thank you." I turned in my chair to beam at them. "It's perfect."

Their expression softened for a moment. "You're welcome, Sam."

"We better get going." Cali hopped off the box. "Celestina was very specific about where we had to stand and when." She grinned at me. "Your future mother-in-law is terrifying in the best kind of way."

"I know," I gave her a dreamy smile.

Rynn laughed, jumping to her feet and walking out the door. Cali followed her, only to pause and glance at Nyx. They caught her look and shook their head. "It's probably best I stay here." The blue lines running through their black eyes flashed in and out of existence. "The hunger . . . it becomes more difficult to control around a lot of people."

"It's fine, Nyx," I told them softly. "I appreciate you coming at all."

Cali stomped forward and grabbed Nyx's arm, ignoring their hiss, and dragged them towards the door. "Don't worry, I'll keep you in line."

"Cali," I warned as fear raked its claws across my heart. Cali liked to push things—and Nyx wouldn't respond well to that.

"It's been months, Sam," she called over her shoulder. "Quit babying them.

I mean, who hasn't lost their mind here or there?" A deranged laugh spilt from her lips.

When Nyx glanced back at me before Cali pulled them through the door, I gave them an encouraging look, and they just rolled their eyes. That little hint of the old Nyx settled my concerns. Cali and Rynn would be with them, and I had no doubt Celestina had thought of Nyx's well-being for this. She'd probably set them up with a good view but slightly apart from the rest of the guests.

I turned back to the mirror. The deep purple dress was made of a smooth, clingy fabric that hugged every single one of my curves. It was perfect, and I couldn't wait for my mates to see how spectacular my ass looked in it.

All I had to do was wait for someone to come fetch me. I bit my bottom lip as a happy grin split my face.

Today, I was marrying Roth and finally forging the bond with Kieran, and the rest of my mates would be here to celebrate. I'd asked if they wanted to do something—like take part in their own ceremony—but Vail and Alaric had made it very clear that they didn't want to be, in their words, a public spectacle. And Draven had said he was content with the role he had secured—whatever that meant.

I took a deep breath and let it out. For today, no problems existed. There was no correspondence I needed to read. No deals to negotiate. No advisors to scrutinize.

Today was just for me and my mates.

My fingers ran across the silky fabric of the dress. It might not have had pockets, but this dress was to die for.

"I'm going to need it to go on record that I didn't step into this room and lock the door behind me."

I whirled to find Draven leaning against the doorframe, his gaze slowly drinking in every inch of me.

"So you like the dress then?" I arched a dark brow.

"I love the dress." He pushed off the doorframe and stalked towards me. "Don't get too attached though. We both know Vail is going to be tearing it off you later."

"Not you?" I smirked.

His fingers toyed with the thick straps that supported the corset-style top half. "Personally, I'd love to see it pooled around your feet while I bent you over the bed so you could suck Kieran down your throat while I feasted on your delicious little pussy."

"Fuck." I clenched my thighs together.

Draven spun me around until I faced the mirror again. Then his hands slid down over the tight bodice, giving my breasts a hard squeeze before continuing to glide over my hips. "Not even a hint of a panty line," he commented before his fingers found the high slit over my right thigh.

"We don't have time," I argued half-heartedly.

"My love, do you really think I didn't plan for this?" he purred as he kissed the side of my neck. "We have exactly enough time for me to fuck you hard and fast . . . and for you to walk down that aisle with my seed dripping down your legs."

His fingers grazed my clit, and I moaned. "Roth will be pissed," I said through panted breaths as he sunk two fingers straight into my aching core.

"Already cleared it with them." Draven grunted and kicked my feet apart as he pumped his fingers in and out. With his other hand, he pushed lightly on my back. "Hands on the wall."

I did as he said, planting my palms on the smooth wood on either side of the mirror. Draven took his hand out from between my thighs, and I watched in the reflection as he flipped my dress up over my ass.

"Don't mess up my hair."

"Wouldn't dream of it," he promised as he unbuttoned his pants and then slammed his cock into me. I let out a strangled scream as he bottomed out before pulling back and doing just as he'd promised—fucking me hard and fast.

I watched my tits bounce in the mirror as the sound of flesh slapping against flesh filled the small room. Draven's fingers sank harder into the soft curve of my hips, but he was careful not to pierce it and risk getting blood on my dress.

I felt the mixture of our combined pleasure dribbling down my leg just as he let out a deep groan. Our eyes connected in the mirror, and Draven smiled at me. "You are fucking perfect. Now let's go get you married and bonded."

Less than two minutes later, we exited the room. Draven hadn't been kidding about me wearing him down the aisle. He'd made sure my dress was okay but hadn't let me clean up further. With every step, I felt more of him slip out.

We turned the corner and almost ran into a familiar russet-haired Moroi.

"There you are!" Zander grabbed my wrist and tugged me along. "You're late."

I glared over my shoulder at Draven. "Told you."

He shrugged unrepentantly. "Worth it."

Zander led us through a few narrow alleyways until we reached the edge of the large courtyard where the sparring area was—or had been. I gasped as I looked at the once dirt-filled ground that was now covered with soft green grass. Flowers of purple, yellow, and white rose on delicate stocks, lining a path for us.

"Do you like it?" Draven asked.

I tore my gaze away from the beautiful garden my charming prince had created just for me and drank in his appearance. My eyes stayed locked on his. "I love it."

"I love it too." He smiled.

"Yes, you're both gorgeous and sickeningly in love." Zander let go of my wrist and gently nudged me towards Draven. "Save the fireworks for the main event, yeah?"

Draven extended his arm, and I looped mine around his before we approached the large crowd, all wearing happy and wistful expressions. Above us, petals of soft yellow and purple rained down from those spectating in the buildings.

The crowd parted at our approach, and more petals were tossed onto the soft grass as we made our way forward.

They're so happy, Talis said. *I don't remember the last time I was around this many people and they were all so excited and joyous.*

Just wait until they get a few bottles of wine in them, Draven joked. *Then you can add delightfully drunk and rambunctious.*

Amusement danced across my mind before Talis pulled back. We were still figuring out how their magic had changed. Talis had sacrificed the ability to control souls but could still see them in their own way. They relayed what they saw to us, making us walking lie detectors. But we'd also discovered that, while Talis was actively in our minds, we could hear each other's thoughts.

Which was sometimes handy . . . and other times not so much. Because Vail was still Vail, and nobody—myself included—wanted to listen to his grumpy thoughts all the time.

Plus, Kieran had told me I looked beautiful one morning when in fact he was thinking the shade of my dress was hideous and that I'd done my hair strangely.

Talis was getting better about limiting what thoughts we heard. They were also never pushy through our connection, seeming perfectly content to just soak it all in most of the time.

The crowd finally parted, and I got to see the rest of my mates as well as Roth's family. Vail and Alaric were dressed similarly to Draven in fitted black pants and dark burgundy shirts. Vail had even pulled his hair back into a bun and trimmed his beard, which had become rather unruly lately. Roth's brothers were on either side of them. Both still wore fighting leathers, but the ones they had on today were perfectly clean and a shiny black—not a hint of brain matter or blood in sight. Taivan's hair had been braided neatly back, and Desmond's head was freshly cut.

Standing several feet in front of them were Severen and Celestina. They wore matching beaming smiles. I briefly spotted Cali, Rynn, and Nyx standing off to my right, but it was Roth who commanded all my attention.

I was only vaguely aware of Draven kissing me on the cheek before going to stand between Alaric and Vail.

I practically floated forward, closing the distance between me and Roth. "You look stunning."

Most of the time, Roth wore baggy clothing, which was often smeared with ink. Today, they wore formfitting black pants and a matching button-up shirt, plus a vest that perfectly complemented the purple of my dress.

"Don't get used to it." They grinned wryly.

"Tease." I tried to pout but was smiling too hard for it to work, and based on the snort Rynn let out, my face had contorted into something ridiculous.

"Thank you all so much for joining us today to celebrate the union of our youngest, Astaroth Devereux, to Samara Harker," Celestina announced loudly.

Instantly, my eyes started to tear up, and I had to blink them back. Moons damn it all, why was I such an easy crier? We'd barely even started, for fuck's sake.

"It is the hope of every parent that their child will find someone who loves and respects them. Who makes them happy." Celestina smiled at me and Roth. "I needed only to spend a few minutes with the two of you to know how much you love each other."

A few tears fought their way free and raced down my cheek. *It's okay. You're okay. It's okay.* I chanted over and over in my head. *Your makeup is still fine. You're definitely not leaving blurry black tracks down your cheeks right now.*

Umm . . . is it normal to think to yourself like this?

Not now, Talis!

Roth's lips twitched, as if they could hear every one of my thoughts.

Celestina turned to Roth. "Do you, my sweet and brilliant child, swear to love, protect, and honor Samara Harker for the rest of your days?"

Orange fractures lit up against Roth's hazel eyes. "I do."

"And do you, Samara Harker"—Celestina's intense gaze fell onto me—"swear to cut down any enemy who comes for your beloved, dote on them like the treasure they are, and above all else, love and cherish them for the rest of your life?"

"I do," I croaked as tears streamed down my face, not giving a single shit about my makeup any longer. How could I when Roth was looking at me like I was their entire world?

"Then we welcome you, Samara Harker, into our family as you welcome Roth into yours." Severus stepped forward to join his wife, a long, thin dagger in his hand. "Two souls and two Houses, united to stand strong through the good times and the bad, because there can be no happiness without pain."

Roth raised their hand, palm facing me, a wicked grin on their face. I sniffed and blinked quickly to try to clear my vision before doing the same, connecting my palm with theirs. As we intertwined our fingers, the tears started to dry up as adrenaline kicked in. Roth's parents had explained the ceremony in great detail because, in their words, "We wouldn't want a repeat of Roth's cousin's wedding."

They'd offered no further explanation, and when I'd asked Roth about it, they'd just smiled and strolled away.

While I might not know what had happened there, I knew exactly what was coming next. I kept my eyes locked on Roth's while, in my peripheral vision, I saw Celestina take the knife from her husband and smile at both of us . . . before slamming it through the back of my hand and straight out Roth's.

I'd been prepared for it, so I swallowed my grunt of pain as Roth let out a low, deep chuckle. Fucking House Devereux and their insane wedding nuptials. The crowd cheered as Roth gripped the back of my head with their hand that didn't have a fucking dagger sticking through it and claimed my mouth with their own. They swallowed my hiss as their mother pulled the knife free.

Roth kissed me, demanding but still somehow sweet, and a few more tears leaked from the corners of my eyes. They pulled back enough to laugh breathily. "Such an easy crier."

"I had a dagger shoved through my fucking hand," I whispered adamantly.

"That's not why you're crying, and you know it."

"True," I huffed and kissed them gently again. We leaned our foreheads against each other as Roth's parents wrapped our hands. The knife was enchanted so that it would leave a scar.

"You did so good, babe," Roth praised, and my core instantly tightened. They let out that raspy laugh again that I absolutely adored and leaned forward to whisper in my ear, "And good girls get rewarded."

I whimpered, and they just smirked at me as they took my now-bandaged hand and gently kissed the back of it before cockily strolling over to my other mates, who happily murmured their congratulations.

"And now, for the second part of today's ceremonies." Severen gestured towards the crowd, and I followed his gaze. Once more, everyone parted, allowing Kieran to pass through.

His golden blond hair gleamed in the sunlight, and unlike the rest of my mates, who'd chosen dark clothing, Kieran wore a crisp white shirt with dark blue pants. He was perfect. And he was mine.

He was also riding my fucking horse.

Zosa pranced as she made her way down the aisle. Some valiant soul had woven white flowers into her silvery mane.

"Brave bastard," Vail muttered.

Light brown eyes that I'd been in love with since the moment I'd seen them laughed at me as Kieran drew Zosa to a stop. He slid off the mare and kissed her on the nose before moving to stand in front of me. Draven gracefully stepped forward to grab Zosa's reins and lead her over to stand with him and the others.

"You are absolutely ridiculous, Kier." I grinned at him.

"I know." He winked.

"I can't believe Zosa let you ride her." Or that she hadn't taken a bite out of Draven.

"This might be hard for you to accept Samara." Kieran gave me a serious look. "But your horse is kind of an attention whore. It's why I get along with her so well."

"Rude." I glanced at Zosa, who just so happened to be standing in a way that made the sunlight capture her dapple grey coat perfectly.

Okay. Maybe he had a point.

"Was this suitably dramatic for you?" I asked, turning back to Kieran.

"Honestly, even if it wasn't, I don't think I could wait another day." He smiled at Celestina and Severen. "Everything is absolutely perfect though. Thank you again for allowing us to do this."

"You're family now too, Kieran Blake." Celestina smiled back at him, and Severen looped his arm around his wife's waist, an identical happy expression on his face.

Kieran looked back at me, his eyes narrowed slightly, and he took a deep breath, then his gaze dipped to the apex of my thighs. "I see Draven did a good job of escorting you," he said slyly, hazel eyes twinkling with amusement.

I kept my face perfectly straight. "He was very gentlemanly about the whole thing. Didn't even mess up my hair at all."

Kieran laughed loudly, and my heart clenched with pure joy. I would never get tired of hearing the beautiful sound.

"I love you so much, Kier."

His laughter faded away before his face morphed into a look of pure adoration. "I love you too, Sam."

"Will you do me the honor of allowing me to forge a mating bond between us? To forever bind our souls?" I placed my hand over his heart but held back my magic as I waited for his answer.

Kieran laid his hand on top of mine. "My soul already belongs to you. It has since the moment I met you."

Tears once again flowed as I did what I'd wanted to do for so long. I stopped denying my magic and let it flow into him, joining us. The mating bond lit up like a bonfire, and his emotions poured into me. So intense, I almost fell to my knees. Only Kieran wrapping his arms around me and kissing me kept me upright.

The crowd erupted once more, and I was vaguely aware of more petals raining down on us. Then Kieran swept me off my feet and carried me back through the cheering crowd. The rest of my mates followed after us as barrels of ale and wine were rolled out.

Roth's brothers stood in front of Zosa, as if they were negotiating with the mare to not bite them.

Good luck.

"Our honored guests are going to change into more comfortable clothing," Celestina announced. "Let us drink and be merry while we wait for their return."

"In an hour!" Severen shouted.

"Ah, give them at least two hours! There's six of 'em!" someone shouted.

"Okay, two hours," Severen amended. "But no more!"

"So three hours then?" Roth called back. Loud laughter broke out and covered whatever Severen's response was.

Kieran trotted us up the stairs and into the main building. Within minutes, we were in our guest suite. A bottle of wine and some snacks had been left for us on the table. And *two* pitchers of water.

I giggled at the thoughtful arrangement and then squealed as Kieran tossed me onto the enormous bed. I'd barely landed before soft, bloodred ropes wrapped around my wrists and pulled my arms over my head, then I felt similar ones wrap around my ankles and tug my legs apart. Roth must have stashed them under the bed earlier in preparation for this.

"Something funny, wife?" Roth stood at the foot of the bed, unbuttoning their vest and tossing it aside.

"Someone is clearly worried about us getting dehydrated." My laugh turned husky when Roth's ropes pulled my legs apart even wider.

"It's a valid concern." Draven strolled over and gathered the fabric of my dress before sweeping it to the side, baring my glistening pussy to Roth.

"Already so messy," they tutted. "That simply won't do." Roth glanced over their shoulder to Kieran. "Clean her up for me, would you?"

"Of course, Roth." Kieran grinned wickedly as he tugged off his shirt and sauntered towards the bed. Anticipation raced through me as he crawled onto it, stopping to lick every inch of my inner thighs before sweeping his tongue straight up my dripping slit.

"Fuck!" My back bowed off the bed, and someone chuckled to my right. I turn my head to find Alaric there, already stripped of his clothes, his magnificent cock in his hand. A whimper slipped from my lips as Kieran continued to suck and lick every bit of Draven's cum out of me while my mouth watered at the thought of tasting Alaric.

"Something you want, Sam?" Alaric stroked himself again, and a bead of precum formed at his tip.

I licked my lips before smirking up at him. "See something *you* want?"

"Somehow, you get brattier when you're tied up." He let out a dark chuckle that had my toes curling. "There is zero chance of your hair making it through this unscathed, just so you know."

"It had a good run," I panted, my thighs desperate to clench around Kieran's head but unable to, thanks to Roth's ropes. Alaric climbed onto the bed and knelt next to me, then he gripped the back of my head, twisting it further towards him, and slowly fed me every inch of his hard length.

Someone tugged at the straps of my dress before I felt cool metal slide between my skin and the fabric. I growled around Alaric's cock as my dress was cut away. I really liked that dress, damn it.

Draven laughed. "Told you Vail would be destroying it."

"She has another one," Vail rumbled before making me jump when he ripped the bodice. Alaric grunted as I sucked harder on his cock and pushed my head farther down until my eyes watered.

For several minutes, Kieran continued to eat me out, taking Roth's command to heart as his tongue dove deep to get out any last traces of Draven. Vail leaned over the bed and played with my breasts. First with his hands and then his tongue.

"Don't let her come yet," Roth growled. "I get the first one."

I whimpered around Alaric's thick length because I was so damn close to coming. Vail laughed, his hot breath dancing across my taut nipple.

Kieran must have sensed how close I was because he pulled back after one final lick. "All yours, Roth."

The bed dipped as they switched places, and then Alaric pulled me off his cock. Turquoise lines bled through his green eyes as he smiled. "As much as I love you screaming around my cock, I think we want to hear just how loud Roth can make you come."

I opened my mouth to say something sassy, but what came out was a scream instead because Roth immediately went for my swollen clit. I'd thought for sure that they would tease me a little first, but they swirled their tongue around the sensitive bundle of flesh as their lips closed around it. Vail sucked on my breast, and I felt his fangs graze me just before he bit down—and Roth did the same.

"Oh, fuck!" I arched off the bed as the climax hit me hard and fast. Vail continued to drink harder from one breast while his hand roughly squeezed the other. Roth drank from my clit and slid two fingers into my cunt, pumping them in time with every one of their swallows.

My eyes rolled to the back of my head as I rode the pleasure Roth continued to draw from me. When I sagged into the mattress minutes later, Roth licked me one more time before resting their head on my thigh. I lifted myself up enough to look at them and trembled a little at seeing the signs of my pleasure smeared all over their face.

"As much as I would love to keep you all to myself for a bit"—they grinned at me—"I did promise to share."

The ropes around my wrists and ankles unwound, and then Vail lifted me up and flipped me over so I was on my hands and knees with my head pointed towards the side of the bed. "I was planning on filling your cunt until it was overflowing." He cut away the rest of my dress and tossed the scraps of fabric onto the floor. "But when I saw your gorgeous ass in that dress, a new plan formed."

I groaned as his slick and lubricated fingers slid between my cheeks and he started playing with my tight hole. "And what," I breathed out, "is everyone else going to be doing?"

Draven and Kieran appeared in front of me, both naked and with their cocks at the ready. "We're going to test your gag reflex while Vail plays with you," Kieran replied, bumping the broad head of his cock against my lips. My tongue darted out to lick the bead of precum off his tip, enjoying the harsh inhale I got from him.

"And then we're going to ruin the excellent job Kier did of cleaning up your pussy by filling you up again with all of our cum," Draven finished.

Yes, please.

"I find this plan acceptable," I tried to say evenly, only to moan towards the end when Vail slipped a finger into my ass.

Kieran seized the opportunity and thrust his cock through my lips, making me gag when he hit the back of my throat.

"Relax your throat, love," Draven ordered.

Tears streamed down my cheeks, but I did as he said. Mostly. Sometimes I still gagged when Kier went especially deep. After a particularly hard thrust, he pulled back and bent down to brush a kiss against my lips. "Good girl."

Then it was Draven's cock in my mouth as Vail added a second finger. "Someone play with her clit," Vail ordered.

I couldn't see if it was Alaric or Roth, but somebody dragged their fingers through my pussy and then swirled them teasingly around my clit. A strangled sound leaked from my lips as Draven continued to roughly fuck my mouth.

Alaric let out a dark chuckle. "You love taking all of us, don't you?" Fingers pinched my clit, and I choked on a scream as Draven shoved his cock deeper.

"Fuck," Draven groaned deeply before spilling his seed down my throat.

As soon as he finished and pulled out, Vail withdrew his fingers and lifted me by the hips. He maneuvered us until he was sitting on the bed with his legs dangling off the end and me kneeling next to him.

I hungrily looked at his cock and started to lean towards it, only for Alaric to grab me by the waist and tug me towards him. His mouth slammed against mine, and I kissed him deeply as he raised me up until I was straddling Vail's legs. I felt Vail lean forward more, his chest brushing against my back. Alaric sucked on my bottom lip as he lowered me down slowly, and I felt Vail's cock at my ass.

Alaric swallowed my moan as Vail tugged me down, fully seating himself inside me. Then Roth's ropes wrapped around my thighs and pulled them wide as I leaned back against Vail's chest, breaking my kiss with Alaric.

"Fuck, I'll never get tired of this view." Alaric admired me before notching his cock at my entrance.

His bright eyes, a mix of turquoise and green, were locked on mine as he slowly slid himself into me. Vail groaned deeply as I was pushed further onto him. Once Alaric was all the way in, Vail started to lift his hips, and it was my turn to moan as they both found their rhythm.

My gaze went to Roth, who leaned against the bedpost, watching me get thoroughly fucked. "Strip," I ordered a little breathlessly. "I want to feel your cunt on my fingers."

"Oh, and you think you give the orders around here?" They arched a brow, and the ropes around my thighs tightened.

I gave them a sultry smile. "You said I did *good* earlier and that I'd be rewarded."

They smirked at me. "That I did."

Roth proceeded to slowly strip off their clothing and crawled onto the bed next to me, then knelt as some of their ropes wound their way across the top of the bed's canopy frame before dangling down directly above them.

They reached up and gripped the rope with both hands. "*Ik dov kov fùshuv sarbà.*" Fuck me into oblivion, Heir.

"*Qà hom gaha rùdmàb.*" As my love desires.

My fingers parted their slick heat, and Roth ground down on my hand as my thumb started to circle their clit.

Kieran let out a low groan that instantly had my eyes snapping to where he and Draven stood at the end of the bed, each of them stroking their cocks as they watched me play with Roth.

Kieran caught me staring and laughed. "Two cocks already buried inside you and you still want more. So fucking greedy."

"That party is going to rage all afternoon and into the night. We have to go out there for at least a little bit."

I gasped when Alaric hit a particularly good spot. He grinned and did it again, scattering my thoughts for a moment.

"And I want"—another breathy moan—"everyone"—Vail's hips jerked sharply up, and I let out a strangled scream before finishing—"to smell all of you on me. To know I am yours."

"And we are yours," Alaric grunted as he fucked me harder and faster. Roth's ropes pulled my thighs even wider as Alaric poured himself into me.

After a few more thrusts, he stepped back, and Kieran immediately took his spot, slamming into me and causing some of Alaric's seed to gush out.

"Fuck," Vail ground out, and I felt his nails shift to claws before digging into my skin. "Little warning would have been nice."

"You're the one who wanted that spot." Kieran grinned over my head at Vail. "This is going to be rough and brutal because I have been fucking aching to fuck this pussy all morning—and that only got worse when I smelled Draven's cum dripping down her thighs earlier."

My pussy clenched around his cock, and Kieran swore as he did exactly what he'd warned. He hammered into me over and over again, driving Vail's thick length farther into my ass. Draven reached around Kieran to rub my clit, and I practically combusted.

Kieran fucked me through the orgasm as Vail jerked his hips up harder, and wet heat coated my fingers as I curled them in Roth's tight cunt before rubbing them roughly across their clit. They screamed and writhed over my hand as their own orgasm ripped through them.

Somewhere in my haze, Kieran let out a deep groan as he found his own climax. My mind was still scattered as he slid out and Draven sank into my pussy, making an obscene sound as he pushed through both Alaric's and Kieran's releases.

"I love fucking you when you're messy like this," Draven admitted as he slowly pumped in and out, causing more warm liquid to trail down my thighs.

"We can't have that." Kieran reached around and pushed it back into my aching cunt—right beside Draven's dick.

"Fuck," Draven groaned and started fucking me a little faster as Kieran continued to slide his fingers in. "Next time, you're fucking this sweet little pussy with me, Kier."

I whimpered at the idea of the two of them stretching me out at the same time, while also loving that we still had so many new things to try—and a lifetime to find more.

Kieran bent lower and started kissing the inside of my thigh. To my surprise, Alaric did the same on my other thigh—and he also shoved his fingers into my pussy. Draven's eyes turned almost a solid bloodred as his thrusts became more frantic.

Despite just coming a few minutes ago, I could feel another one building. When Alaric and Kieran bit down and started drinking from my thighs, I let out something between a moan and scream at the intensity of all of it. Roth's ropes tightened further on my legs as they leaned over to sink their fangs into the top of my right breast.

I threw my head back hard against Vail's chest, loving that I was getting throughly fucked and bitten by all of my mates. Tremors still raced through my body, the echoes of that last mindfuck of an orgasm. A litany of curses fell from Draven's lips as he came, and Vail bellowed his own release a moment later.

Roth released my breast and gently moved my hand from between their thighs so they could plop down on the bed next to me. Alaric kissed my thigh one more time before moving to lie down on my left while Kieran and Draven shared a passionate kiss, my blood dripping down Kier's chin.

The ropes binding my legs loosened and fell to the bed, and I practically melted on top of Vail, who was still buried in my ass. Draven pulled out so that he and Kieran could collapse at the foot of the bed, but they reached across my thighs to hold hands, letting them rest on top of me.

A deep sigh of contentment flowed from my lips, not only because of the afterglow of so many orgasms, but at being here with my mates and just enjoying the moment.

There were still so many things I wanted to do—secrets to uncover and problems to solve—but I wouldn't be doing any of it alone.

"You better not be thinking about work," Alaric grumbled.

"We clearly have to fuck it out of her more." Vail sighed.

"Definitely a tragic burden we all must share," Kieran chimed in.

"I hate all of you." I smiled.

"Today is for us to celebrate." Draven kissed the top of my thigh. "Tomorrow, we'll go back to being the Blood Sovereign."

I settled further into the embrace of my mates. "I can live with that."

Want to know what Kieran
was thinking on that beach?

Signup for the Alex Frost newsletter at <u>alexfrostauthor.com</u> to read some of the emotional and spicy scenes from an alternative character's point of view!

Need more fantasy romance in your life?

Lingering Fates Series

A spicy queer romantasy series of interconnected standalones featuring fated mates... who are very much not happy about it. Perfect for fans of stabby morally grey characters, forced proximity, banter and all the found family vibes.

Learn more here - *htttps://greymalkinpress.com/pages/maddoxgrey-lingeringfates*

Lost Legacies

A fast-paced fantasy romance featuring a morally grey FMC with a slow burn romance, banter, and all the found family vibes. Perfect for elder millennials who grew up watching Buffy and Supernatural.

Learn more here - https://greymalkinpress.com/pages/maddoxgrey-lostlegacies

Author's Note

Thank you so much for reading the first trilogy of Lunaria Realms! I started my publishing journey several years ago with my urban fantasy romance series Lost Legacies that I write under Maddox Grey. The thing about being an author is sometimes new ideas just slam into your head and won't let you go.

Lunaria Realms was one of those ideas. The idea of starting another pen name and series was pretty intimating but my friends were pretty consistent in their encouragement. Most of this "encouragement" was in the form of daily text messages that read, "Hey! You write that smut yet?", followed by a rather creative string of emojis.

If you enjoyed reading this book, it would be incredibly appreciated if you could leave an honest review on Goodreads or whichever platform you prefer. Reviews are super important for authors and we really appreciate it when y'all take the time to leave one! Plus it helps other readers find us :)

Also, Rynn's trilogy will be starting in 2026! Followed by Cali's in 2028!

About the Author

Alex Frost is... actually Maddox Grey. Dun dun duuuuun!

Okay probably not that dramatic of a reveal since it isn't exactly a closely guarded secret. The pen name Alex Frost was created to publish the spicier fantasy series that fall under the "Why Choose" genre.

Why Alex Frost? Because Maddox is a freaking nerd. After being trained by local baristas to respond to the name "Alex" instead of Maddox, it seemed like the perfect pen name. Half of it anyway.

Since Maddox already shares their last name with Jean Grey of the X-Men, it seemed fitting to borrow Emma Frost's last name for their other persona. If you know, you know. (insert smirking face)

To get regular email updates about new releases and other announcements, be sure to sign up for the newsletter on alexfrostauthor.com

facebook.com/alexfrost.author

instagram.com/alexfrost.author

tiktok.com/@greymalkinpress